CLASSIC TALES OF SCIENCE FICTION & FANTASY

CONTENTS

INTRODUCTION

A Genre for the Times

Every semester, when discussing the history of pop culture, I tell my students to pay attention to the people with three names, who are sometimes known only by their initials: H. G. Wells, Edgar Rice Burroughs, Robert Louis Stevenson, Arthur Conan Doyle, H. P. Lovecraft, Charlotte Perkins Gilman, and the like. The literary giants of the late nineteenth and early twentieth centuries are taken more seriously. They garner more critical acclaim and are more often read in schools; but the writers of adventure stories from this period have had a far greater effect on our culture, even now, than Edith Wharton, William Makepeace Thackeray, or Mark Twain.

The stories in this book represent classic tales of science fiction and fantasy. By "fantasy" we do not mean "high fantasy" like that of J. R. R. Tolkien, or sword-and-sorcery stories like those of Robert E. Howard. We mean stories of the fantastical, the horrific, and the supernatural. In many of these stories, science and the supernatural are linked.

The Victorian age was one of the most forward-thinking periods in history (in some ways, more forward-thinking than our own). The development of steamships and railroads; photography; and advances in chemistry, electricity, and weaponry all came about between 1837 and 1901, during the reign of Queen Victoria of England. Scientific inquiry opened up new ways to look at both the past and the future. It makes sense that with the prominence of science on the culture of Europe, there would quickly follow science fiction.

Science is frightening. It tears down nearly every old belief and notion (a major theme in H. G. Wells's works). Anything that can't be verified by scientific inquiry is cast aside. Our place in the universe—believed for so long to be at the center of creation—becomes insignificant under the lens of science. This causes cultural tension, the feeling that things are changing too rapidly, the feeling that perhaps we are not created in God's image after all—that perhaps there is no God (or, as Professor Challenger says of his conversation with the Brazilian priest in *The Lost World:* "He proved a very argumentative fellow, who took it absurdly amiss that I should point out to him the corrosive effect which modern science must have upon his beliefs"). All of these stories reflect the tension created by the pursuit of scientific discovery—the hope that we will find the cure to all that afflicts mankind versus the fear of what we might discover or unleash.

This book begins in the Victorian era, in 1858, and extends well past it, all the way to 1928, and these tensions are evident. Two things stand out. The first is how these works not only use science to tell the story, but also use the story to teach us about science: microscopy, paleontology, immunology, geology, archaeology: all are explained (if sometimes not accurately) in detail as part of the tale. The second is the number of authors here who were also social activists—Bellamy, Wells, London, and Gilman—and who used science fiction to describe either their perfect utopia, or else the downfall of industrial capitalism.

Fitz James O'Brien, "The Diamond Lens" (1858)

Fitz James O'Brien was born Michael O'Brien in 1828, in County Cork, Ireland, and was raised in Limerick. He emigrated first to London, where he published some stories and edited a journal. It is believed that at some point he served in the British Army. In 1852 he emigrated to America, first to Washington, D.C., and then New York City. Upon arriving in New York, he devoted himself entirely to writing. He was a successful essayist, playwright, and poet, but his great importance is as a short-story writer. He sold to numerous publications, including *Harper's*, the *New York Times*, and *Vanity Fair*. He was a prominent member of the famous bohemian circle that met regularly at Pffaf's Beer Cellar, the center of New York's literary scene.

In 1862, eager to see action in the Civil War, O'Brien obtained a commission as a lieutenant on the staff of General Frederick Lander, commander of the Union forces in western Virginia. He distinguished himself in the Battle of Bloomery Gap, but was wounded a few days later. He was given a company of thirty-five cavalry and sent to rustle a hundred head of cattle from the enemy, but they were set upon by 150 Confederates under a Colonel Ashley. Instead of fleeing with his smaller force, O'Brien led a charge. According to eyewitnesses, the charge was so fierce that the Confederates believed there must be a reserve nearby, and fell back. O'Brien and Ashley ended up facing off at twenty paces; they fired three shots each. Ashley's second shot passed through O'Brien's shoulder, shattering his scapula, while O'Brien's third shot killed his opponent. O'Brien managed to rally his troops to fight on until another officer saw how badly wounded he was and relieved him to seek a surgeon. He died of tetanus six weeks later in Cumberland, Maryland. His body was taken to Brooklyn, and he was buried with military honors in Greenwood Cemetery.

Although nearly forgotten today, O'Brien is one of the most significant figures in the history of nineteenth-century American literature. His mixture of science and the fantastic anticipated the development of science fiction, fantasy, and horror. He wrote the first story that could be called a "robot rebellion," the first "invisible man" story, and even some of the earliest gothic erotica.

"The Diamond Lens" is a fabulous story. It was a favorite of H. P. Lovecraft (making it a fitting start to this collection). It has the qualities of good horror writing as well as science fiction, and would work well as an episode of *The Twilight Zone.* The murderous protagonist Linley is an early version of the "mad scientist." It is a well-established science—microscopy—that leads the protagonist to his madness. He is already a megalomaniac before he begins his experiment, but he builds a microscope more powerful than any other in the world, and what he sees deep inside a drop of water drives him truly insane. "I had penetrated beyond the grosser particles of aqueous matter, beyond the realms of infusoria and protozoa, down to the original gaseous globule, into whose luminous interior I was gazing as into an almost boundless dome filled with a supernatural radiance."

Jules Verne, *A Journey to the Center of the Earth* (1864)

It's not for nothing that Jules Verne is considered (along with H. G. Wells) the father of science fiction. He is primarily interested—particularly in this story—in science, and in using fiction as a teaching tool. He was born in Nantes, France, in 1828. His father, Pierre, was a successful lawyer, and expected his eldest son to take over his practice one day. Dutifully, Verne went to law school in Paris, and graduated with his license to practice in 1851. By then, however, his literary career had begun. His first success came in the theater. He wrote a play with his new friend Alexandre Dumas, fils (the son of Alexandre Dumas, author of *The Three Musketeers*), which was produced at the Théâtre Historique. In 1862 Verne submitted his manuscript for a serialized novel called *A Voyage in a Balloon* to Victor Hugo's publisher, Pierre-Jules Hetzel.

Hetzel had been planning to launch a magazine called *Magasin d'Éducation et de Récréation*, which would instruct people on geography and science by entertaining them with fiction. In Verne, Hetzel found a perfect author for his project, and signed him to a long-term contract that required Verne to deliver three manuscripts a year. Hetzel's major project was a series of "Fantastic Voyage" novels that would teach readers science through stories about travel. In keeping with this theme, Verne wrote his most famous novels: *A Journey to the Center of the Earth*, *From the Earth to the Moon*, *Twenty Thousand Leagues Under the Sea*, and *Around the World in Eighty Days.*

Verne's work was originally dismissed as children's fiction, not serious literature. It gained critical acceptance in the United States before it did in France. Even now, French scholars and critics are reluctant to label his work as "science fiction," as genre fiction is still not considered literary in France.

A Journey to the Center of the Earth is, at heart, a travelogue. Verne carefully describes a journey that starts on the surface of the globe, penetrates it, and returns. Of character there is a great deal, and a great deal that is interesting; but of plot there is very little other than travel. The point of the book is to describe what the travelers see. Verne is enamored of lengthy descriptions and lists. That's his idea of exposition. Not surprisingly, his characters ramble: but this allows him to cram the book full of scientific facts and theories. One of his most clever devices is that the first half of the book is a travelogue of an alien land, but one that is real and accessible: Iceland. As it moves to a travelogue of the subterranean world, the transition is seamless.

The best writing in this book comes in the form of the relationship between the narrator, Axel, and his uncle, the brilliant and eccentric Professor Liedenbrock. As with so many great sidekicks—Agent Scully, Dr. Watson, Colonel Pickering—Axel is the skeptical counterpart to the unstable genius of his companion—the voice of incredulity and awe who brings an awareness of the sublime to balance out the hyperrational savant. Because, like Dr. Watson, Axel provides the narrative voice, he is also the voice of the reader, expressing the reader's doubts and the reader's fascination. Their arguments about scientific theory, their explanations to each other about their surroundings, form the scientific core of the book. They are also funny—especially Axel—and extremely entertaining.

It is, in the end, a book about spelunking—the greatest spelunking adventure imaginable.

Edward Bellamy, *Looking Backward: 2000–1887* (1888)

Born in Massachusetts in 1850, Edward Bellamy was to become one of the most influential political figures in American socialism. His biography reads like that of many other authors of his day. Like Verne, he first studied law. Like Robert Louis Stevenson, he developed a sickness, tuberculosis, that prompted him to move to the tropics. Like Mark Twain, he spent time as a journalist in Hawaii. Most important, like H. G. Wells, he became an ardent and influential socialist thinker. Until the publication of *Looking Backward*, Bellamy was a literary toiler, putting out fairly unremarkable work. *Looking Backward* was to make him one of the most popular writers in the world.

Looking Backward: 2000–1887 is a condemnation of nineteenth-century industrial society and an expectation of a coming socialist utopia. Julian West is a traveler from 1887. In the nineteenth century, West was a scion of a wealthy Boston family, blissfully unaware of the horrors that keep his family's wealth in place. Placed in a state of suspended animation, West awakens in the year 2000 to find that the world is now a socialist society. All private property has been nationalized. Crime is treated as a disease, not an evil. Everyone gets a free college education, works in a career designed to serve the good of everyone, and retires at the age of forty-five. The book uses a common conceit. It is written as an explanation to people at the beginning of the twenty-first century of what life was like at the end of the nineteenth but, in order not to bore readers too much, it is structured as a romance, telling the story of how West is put to sleep, awakens, and falls in love with the great-granddaughter of his now long-dead fiancée.

Looking Backward was an incredibly popular and influential book. In its time, it was surpassed in sales only by *Uncle Tom's Cabin* and *Ben-Hur*. It sparked a number of social clubs dedicated to seeing its principles to fruition, and inspired several utopian socialist communities. But reading it today is odd. It is an incredibly hopeful tale, but looking back today and seeing that its anticipated utopia never came to pass—but in places where it was tried, terrible atrocities occurred—is rather disheartening.

H. G. Wells, *The War of the Worlds* (1897)

Although remembered today as the other "father of science fiction," during his lifetime Wells was known as a political theorist, and rivaled George Bernard Shaw as the most well-known literary figure in the world. His *Outline of History* was the standard history text in the English-speaking world for decades, and is one of the most widely read history books of all time. Wells is said to have been the inspiration for the idea of the atomic bomb. He helped write the charter of the League of Nations. A committed socialist in favor of a one-world government dominated by intellectual elites, Wells often used his fiction to either anticipate what such a government would look like, or to demonstrate why he thought such a government was necessary. Wells's scientists, whether mad or benign, are always superior to everyone around them, and Wells has little tolerance for the uneducated masses, at least in his fiction. Nonetheless, he was a staunch critic of the Soviet Union, and when he traveled there and wrote about it, he stressed what an utter failure the experiment was turning out to be. Wells was rather embarrassed by the five "scientific romances" for which he is now known. He wanted his more serious work to make an impact—though even in the 1930s with the postapocalyptic *The Shape of Things to Come*, he returned to science fiction to speculate about the future of humanity.

He was born in 1866 in Bromley, County Kent, England. His parents were shopkeepers, but the shop was never successful, and they were always poor. In 1874 a broken leg confined Wells to bed for several months. He began to read voraciously, and from this time came his love of books and his desire to be a writer. He was sent away to school but, after suffering a broken thigh, his father could no longer afford to pay his expenses. Wells's mother was forced to go back to working as a chambermaid, and he was apprenticed to a draper, which he hated, and later to a chemist, which he didn't like much more. He spent his free time in the library reading Plato and Sir Thomas More. Eventually in 1883, he found a position as a pupil/teacher at Midhurst Grammar School, and the next year he won a scholarship to the Normal School of Science to study biology. It was here that he founded the *Science School Journal*, which published his short story "The Chronic Argonauts," the first version of what was to become *The Time Machine*. He also joined the debating society and started his long advocacy for socialism. He sold several short stories between 1888 and 1894, and then, in 1895 he sold *The Time Machine* as a serialized novel for 100 pounds.

Wells was an incredibly prolific writer, penning fifty-two novels and hundreds of short stories, essays, articles, and works on nonfiction, all of which, in one way or another, reflected his thinking of socialism, pacifism, and sexual liberty and equality.

Thanks to Orson Welles and Steven Spielberg, *The War of the Worlds* is among the best-known science fiction novels of all time. It is also one of the most creative and original stories ever written. Never before had anyone considered the possibilities of an invasion from outer space. Never before had someone suggested that humans might not be the strongest and smartest species in the universe. To the Victorians, having conquered most of the world and proven that they themselves were the pinnacle of evolution, the idea that an alien species might come along and treat them as they had treated the native inhabitants of Australia or South Africa was, quite frankly, revolutionary. In *The War of the Worlds*, Wells accurately predicts the possibilities of tank warfare, air warfare, and chemical warfare. It is a gripping story of near defeat and the breakdown of society. Even today, after thousands of alien invasion stories have been produced, Wells's tale about an unforgiving and incomprehensible war is powerful and scary. The sections about the retreat from London, especially the chapter titled "Thunder Child," are among the best things ever written about the plight of war refugees. The description of the ram steamer, plowing ahead at full steam toward the Martian tripods, is one of the most exciting passages ever written in the English language.

Edgar Rice Burroughs, *A Princess of Mars* (1912)

Without Edgar Rice Burroughs there may very well have been no Star Wars. There are essentially two great styles in science fiction: the philosophical science fiction descended from H. G. Wells, and the pure adventure science fiction descended from Edgar Rice Burroughs's John Carter books. When he was writing the screenplays for Star Wars, it was to John Carter that George Lucas turned for inspiration. The desert planet, the hero's extraordinary abilities, the strange beasts and aliens, the evil cult, the speeders, and the sword fights all find their antecedents in John Carter's Barsoom.

Burroughs was born in Chicago in 1875 and grew up in nearby Oak Park. His father, George Tyler Burroughs, was a Civil War major and successful businessman who had made a fortune as a whiskey distiller in Chicago. The younger Burroughs's desire was to be a soldier as well. He attended military school and took (and failed) the entrance exam for West Point. He eventually served an enlistment in the 7th Cavalry, but was medically discharged in 1897. He married his childhood sweetheart, worked briefly at his father's firm, but then left and began years of struggle at low-wage jobs. He was working as a pencil sharpener when, after reading some pulp fiction magazines, he declared that he could write better stories—and if people got paid for writing this rotten stuff, then he could certainly get in on the action.

To Burroughs, writing was a business and nothing more. He did not see himself as being at the forefront of a great literary movement, nor did he see science fiction as an opportunity to ruminate on the human condition, nor as a means to promote his visions of a pacifist-socialist utopia (he was anything but). To Burroughs, it was all about money. Nonetheless, Burroughs—far more than Wells or Verne—launched the entire space adventure tradition.

Tarzan was even more influential from a business standpoint, in that it laid the groundwork for the merchandising that made Lucas and Disney so wealthy. Seeing the incredible popularity of the ape man, Burroughs wanted to exploit him in every medium that he could—books, comic strips, film, toys, etc. Others advised against it, but Burroughs went ahead and created a multiplatform business that became the formula for Disney's and, later, Lucas's success.

But it was the popularizing of science fiction as pure adventure, putting it in the same category as pirate stories, westerns, and chivalric romances, where Burroughs made his biggest impact. Astronomers, writers, filmmakers, and astronauts have all listed the John Carter stories as the inspiration for their careers. Ray Bradbury, author of *The Martian Chronicles* and *Fahrenheit 451*, called Burroughs the most influential writer in history.

John Carter, a former Confederate captain prospecting for gold in Arizona, hides from some Apaches inside a sacred cave and falls asleep. When he wakes up, he has been transported to Mars, a strange desert planet the locals call Barsoom. He is captured by a warlike race called the Tharks, giant green monsters with four arms and huge tusks. They take him as a slave, but because of the lighter gravity and atmosphere on Mars, Carter has immense strength compared to the Tharks, and can leap 150 feet. Thanks to a nursemaid named Sola and his Martian guard dog Woola, Carter learns their language and customs, and becomes a member of the tribe and a great warrior. When the Tharks capture Dejah Thoris, the beautiful humanoid princess of Helium, he comes to her aid, and he and the Tharks join a war between two cities of the Red (humanoid) Martians.

A Princess of Mars is perhaps the most exciting story in this collection. Although we now know what the surface of Mars is like—that it is uninhabited and that the atmosphere won't support human life—none of that was known in Burroughs's time, and his vision of Mars (or Barsoom) is based on the speculations of nineteenth-century astronomers, who proposed that Mars was a dying planet. Unlike the celestial invaders of *The War of the Worlds*, Burroughs's fantastic creations have recognizable emotions and motivations. They have passion, and they share their passions with the hero. Considering that Burroughs once dreamed of being a soldier, it is not surprising that the primary plot device in *A Princess of Mars* is violence. It is filled with epic battles and heroic combats. Enemies must be defeated, the princess rescued, and Mars saved. Only the greatest warrior—a Confederate captain from Virginia—is heroic enough to get it done.

Arthur Conan Doyle, *The Lost World* (1912)

The creator of the most popular and well-known character in English fiction (with the possible exception of Hamlet) was every bit as fascinating as his literary creations. Sir Arthur Conan Doyle was born in 1859 in Edinburgh, Scotland. He studied medicine at the University of Edinburgh, were he worked under Joseph Bell, who was the inspiration for Sherlock Holmes. He was a professional athlete, one of the first people to introduce skiing to a mass audience, and a first-rate rugby player and cricketer. Like Dr. Watson, he was a military doctor, serving in (and writing about) the Boer War. He worked for a while as a harpooner and ship's doctor on a whaler, and then opened an optometry practice. His practice was never a success, and to support himself, he published short stories and serialized novels, the most successful of which were about his unique new detective, Sherlock Holmes. Even without Holmes,

Doyle would have been an important writer. He created a number of good medieval romances (which were his favorite of his own books—he detested Holmes) and also another character, equally as interesting and as fascinating as Holmes: Professor Challenger. At the time of his death in 1930, Doyle was considered the most popular English writer since Shakespeare.

When reading *The Lost World* after *A Journey to the Center of the Earth*, one is struck by how similar they are. They have the same setup. Both tales revolve around an eccentric genius driven to prove his theories. They are both exploration stories. In both of them, a long-lost land where dinosaurs have survived to the present day is found. As with geology and geography in *A Journey to the Center of the Earth*, the book goes out of its way to accurately describe elements of zoology, anthropology, and paleontology (sometimes erroneously but within the accepted science of the times). Most striking of all, both stories are narrated by an incredulous younger man who accompanies the older professor on the prompting of a woman, one with whom he is passionately in love, and to whom he must prove himself worthy. They represent the chivalric romance rewritten for the scientific age.

Unfortunately, a product of its imperialist times, *The Lost World* is also savagely racist and colonialist. The black porter Zambo—and even his name—represents the worst of racial stereotypes. The natives—grinning, fawning, or scheming—are portrayed just as badly. When it comes to the prehistoric ape men encountered on the plateau, things really go off the rails. Slavery and genocide are the natural and justifiable ends of conflict between superior and inferior people; or as the character Sir John says, "For my part I have a score to settle with these monkey-folk, and if it ends by wiping them off the face of the earth, I don't see that the earth need fret about it."

Nonetheless, *The Lost World* is a great adventure, and in some ways is superior to *A Journey to the Center of the Earth*. It has a plot. It has twists and turns and excitement beyond simply seeing something odd or experiencing a natural phenomenon that might kill you. Its characters are deeper and have more relatable motivations. Most of all, it has Professor Challenger, one of the iconic characters of science fiction. The structure of *The Lost World* is much better as well. Each chapter is written as a dispatch. The first paragraph always foreshadows the climax. It reads much like letters from the front would read: "A terrible thing happened today," followed by a chapter-long telling of the tale. It's an excellent structure because, like the Sherlock Holmes novels (and most of the novels in this volume), *The Lost World* was serialized, so each chapter had to be a self-contained story, but one that ends with anticipation of what is to come. Doyle was a master of the form, and managed to pack tons of action into just a few pages, always keeping readers on the edges of their seats.

Jack London, *The Scarlet Plague* (1915)

Jack London was a particular type of writer and a particular type of success. Most of his stories were built around a violent masculinity. His style was harsh and uncompromising, anticipating the naturalism of Hemingway and Steinbeck. His best-known short story, "To Build a Fire," is about the senseless demise of a tenderfoot in the Yukon as witnessed by his dog. It is still one of the best stories about death ever written.

London was born John Griffith Chaney in 1876, in San Francisco. His mother, Flora Wellman, was descended from one of the early Massachusetts Bay Colony families. His father was probably an astrologer named William Chaney. Disavowed by Chaney, and with his mother deranged, London was raised by a former slave named Virginia Prentiss. In his youth London was a factory worker, an oyster pirate, a boxer, a longshoreman, a prospector, a war correspondent, and a hobo. Although he traveled the world, he always returned to the Bay Area as his home. He lived to only forty years of age. He suffered from numerous diseases and chronic pain, he took morphine, and was an alcoholic. He died at his ranch north of San Francisco of a drug overdose, which many at the time believed was a suicide.

London is one of the most successful fiction writers of all time. Like most of the authors in this volume, he sold his stories through magazines, and he became fabulously wealthy as a result. Nonetheless, like Wells and Bellamy, he was a socialist, and most of his stories are from a socialist point of view. His is a more militant, aggressive socialism. If Bellamy and Wells were intellectuals who got their socialism from books, London got his from the docks. He viewed socialism from the vantage of a factory worker and deckhand, and saw work as a cruel trap. Writing was his salvation.

London wrote several science fiction stories, of which *The Scarlet Plague* is the best.

In the story, an old man wanders a forest trail with his grandson. They encounter a grizzly bear that threatens them but leaves them alone. The old man laments that once, there were no bears here. They are on Geary Boulevard, near the end of the streetcar line (now bent and twisted), within sight of what was once the Cliff House, in the ruins of the city that is still, somehow, called San Francisco (interestingly, that area is the site of the only protected ruins in San Francisco today). They come to a meadow on the edge of a beach, where they join the man's other two grandchildren (probably the site of the old windmill in Golden Gate Park). There the grandchildren beg him to tell them, once again, the story of the Scarlet Death. It is the story of the end of the world, brought about by a terrible plague, as viewed by the only surviving faculty member from the University of California at Berkeley—an English professor, now bent with age and wearing only a goatskin. His grandsons tease and torment him, but he teaches as though at his lectern.

London's story of the postapocalyptic Bay Area makes an interesting counterpoint to *Looking Backward*. Both are told as a reflection. Both describe the end of industrialized society from a socialist point of view—but where Bellamy's world evolved peacefully into a socialist utopia, London's took another path. The society described by the old man to his three grandsons, one they cannot comprehend, was an oligarchy. By the twenty-first century, the world is ruled by a cartel of industrialists. All workers are now slaves and are horribly abused. The wealthy are so far above them that one lady would not even accept her own dropped parasol from the hand of one of her servants, and had the man fired for offering it to her. When the Scarlet Death hits in 2013, society breaks down almost instantly, and the workers rebel against their former masters. In the end, only one person out of every million survived. Humanity has devolved into a few scattered tribes of hunter-gatherers. The long-lost world described by the old man—of money, learning, leisure, germs, airships, gunpowder, and above all social stratification—is totally incomprehensible to his savage grandchildren. It's a powerful read from a great storyteller.

Charlotte Perkins Gilman, *Herland* (1915)

Charlotte Perkins Gilman was born in Hartford, Connecticut, in 1860. Her father, the well-known librarian and editor Frederic Beecher Perkins, abandoned Charlotte and her mother Mary when Charlotte was an infant, and she was raised by her famous aunts Catharine Beecher, Isabella Beecher Hooker, and Harriet Beecher Stowe.

Gilman was one of the most important feminists of the early twentieth century, and her life and death was a series of progressive ideas in action. She married the artist Charles Walter Stetson in 1884, and left him in 1888. They were eventually divorced, an almost unheard-of thing at the time. Even more unusual was that she allowed their daughter Katharine to live from time to time with Stetson and his second wife, with whom she remained friends, because she believed they had a right to one another's love. Later, she married her first cousin Houghton Gilman. She was active in many feminist organizations and causes, and her writings reflect her ideals of women's rights and social justice. A longtime advocate of euthanasia for the terminally ill, she committed suicide while suffering from breast cancer.

With a journey up a mysterious river, the refusal to reveal the site's location, the anthropological commentary, and the natives who tell rumors of a land of terrible women, *Herland* is a clever mirror of *The Lost World.* Three men who could best be described as charming, cocky, and decidedly masculine go off in search of a mythical "land of terrible women," where no sensible man dares to go. They are masculine in the same way as the intrepid explorers of *The Lost World*, except their masculinity is comical, and leaves them entirely unprepared for the world and the women they encounter. Locked into their stereotypes of women, and sure of their own sense of superiority, they expect to find either a group of petty, gossiping shrews or else a regimented colony of nuns. They are sure there will be no invention or progress. What they discover instead is perfection: a beautiful, well-ordered world, lovely buildings, fine landscaping, and women so calm and self-assured they seem alien to the three men. This all-female utopia has no war, no poverty, no want of any kind. Removed from the aggression and subjugation of men, the women have created a peaceful, prosperous, and cooperative world.

And a funny one. The comic potential of a world turned upside down, of confident men completely unprepared for the presence of competent women, never lets the reader down. After the utopia of *Looking Backward*, the dystopia of *The Scarlet Plague*, and the chivalric heroism of *The Lost World*, *Herland* is a marvelous, witty commentary on the forms that science fiction takes when written by, for, and about men.

Philip Francis Nowlan, *Armageddon 2419 A.D.* (1928)

The defining element of Philip Francis Nowlan's life is how unremarkable it was. Born in Philadelphia in 1888, he attended the University of Pennsylvania and joined the Delta Epsilon fraternity. After graduation, he went into the insurance business, taking a job at Wagner and Taylor Insurance Agents. He married Theresa Junker, and together they had ten children. One remarkable thing in this history was that, while in college, he was a member of the Mask and Wig Society, the University of Pennsylvania's theatrical club. He performed in several of their productions, including *Herr Lohengrin: An Opera Bluff in Two Acts*, and took on the role of Wendy Darling in *A Travesty of Mr. J. M. Barrie's Fantastic Play: "Peter Pan."* He also wrote quite a bit. He penned skits for the Mask and Wig Society, and wrote articles on business and advertising. These obviously served him well when he left the insurance business to become the financial editor of the *Philadelphia Ledger*. Then, in 1928, he changed science fiction forever.

If *A Princess of Mars* was the first step in the creation of the space opera, then *Armageddon 2419 A.D.* was the second. Nowlan's first attempt at a science fiction novel turned out to be a book that would influence popular culture for decades, and act as a transition between science fiction's formative era, when styles and themes were being experimented with, and its later period as an established genre and pop-culture phenomenon.

Nowlan doesn't focus too much on character development, and his plot is straightforward and formulaic. He is enamored of lists and facts, and in this way it reads like Verne, dispassionately explaining the things the hero encounters and the science (or pseudo-science) behind them, rather than concentrating on action as in the exciting adventures penned by Doyle and Burroughs. As with Doyle, there's a casual racism to this story that is disturbing to modern readers, but it is less prominent.

Nowlan uses the same device as Bellamy: The hero, a World War I veteran and successful businessman named Anthony Rogers, falls asleep in 1927 and wakes up far into the future, in this case 492 years. After a series of wars, the world has been conquered by the Han dynasty of Mongolia, who control amazing science and technology. Americans are living in scattered forest gangs, which he compares to the feudal society that surrounded Norman lords. They have passed through the stages of devolution that London wrote about in *The Scarlet Plague*, from scattered individuals, to loose groups of hunter-gatherers, to cohesive tribes. They have developed a kind of socialism, in that there is no private property wealth, but they have a fierce devotion to individual liberty and personal possessions. The Han have no need of either forests or labor, so they mostly leave the Americans alone. The Americans have been waiting for centuries to band together and throw the Han out of America. Rogers becomes the leader and hero they have been waiting for.

Nowlan's creation was so popular it dominated science fiction for decades—on radio, in serials, on television, with toys, and especially in comic strips. He was praised by real astronauts, parodied by Daffy Duck, and entered the popular lexicon as a synonym for amazing gadgetry. Nowlan, like Burroughs, was a businessman first, and exploited the popularity of his hero in every medium he could. It was not until the comic strips that Anthony Rogers became known by his now-famous nickname, Buck.

H. P. Lovecraft, *The Dunwich Horror* (1928)

When I was seventeen, I took an overnight trip on a bus. A friend of mine had given me a collection of short stories by H. P. Lovecraft, and I brought it along to read on the way. The first story in the collection was "The Haunter of the Dark." It was a tale of an evil god who inhabited a dark crystal and could only be kept at bay by light. When the power goes out in the town, the evil is let loose. It was the spookiest thing I'd ever read. When I'd finished I tried to nap, but couldn't—I was scared. I looked out the window at the streetlights, the headlights of passing cars, and the lights from distant towns, wanting them all to stop rushing by and shine right on me. Unable to sleep, I did the absolute worst thing I could have done: I turned on my reading light and read the next story in the book.

H. P. Lovecraft was born 1890 in Providence, Rhode Island. He was sickly and seldom went to school, but was a voracious reader. When Lovecraft was three, his father was committed to a psychiatric hospital, where he stayed for the rest of his life. Lovecraft himself struggled with mental illness and parasomnia as an adult, and became a recluse. Most of his socialization came through reading and corresponding. After a critical letter he wrote was published in *Argosy* in 1913, Lovecraft was invited to join the United Amateur Press Association (UAPA), a group that produced and distributed amateur magazines and fostered communication among amateur writers and readers. Lovecraft began publishing poetry and short stories through the UAPA and started what grew to be a voluminous correspondence with many aspiring writers, including Robert Bloch and Robert E. Howard. When he was thirty-three years old, Lovecraft married Sonia Greene, a haberdasher seven years older than he was, and moved to Brooklyn. When her business collapsed due to a bank failure, Lovecraft tried to support her, but his writing did not earn enough money. His attempts to work regular jobs only proved that he was unemployable. Eventually, Sonia had to move to Ohio for a job, and Lovecraft, after living miserably alone in Brooklyn, returned to Providence. It was here that he concentrated on horror stories based on an idea he had developed in the UAPA, his "Cthulhu Mythos." These included *The Strange Case of Charles Dexter Ward*, *At the Mountains of Madness*, *The Shadow Over Innsmouth*, and *The Dunwich Horror*. The Cthulhu stories are truly unique. The central idea is that, thousands of years ago, two cosmic armies, interdimensional beings so powerful that on Earth they would be gods, struggled for control of the universe. Those loyal to the god Cthulhu, a giant with a humanoid body, bat wings, and an octopus-like head, lie in a state of eternal sleep at various places on Earth while their monstrous servants try to awaken them. The central theme of the stories—and what makes them so horrifying—is the complete irrelevance of humans. The gods don't give people a second thought, and when humans come into contact with the gods, they are invariably driven insane.

Not surprising for a fictional universe created essentially in a serial magazine, Lovecraft encouraged other authors to write stories about his characters, so the Cthulhu Mythos grew vast during Lovecraft's lifetime, and continues to this day. "The Haunter of the Dark" was actually a sequel to a story by Robert Bloch called "The Shambler from the Stars," and long after Lovecraft's death, Bloch wrote a sequel called "The Shadow from the Steeple." Dozens of authors, including Neil Gaiman, August Derleth, Terry Pratchett, and Stephen King, have written Cthulhu stories. The heavy metal bands GWAR and Metallica have recorded songs about Cthulhu. It appears in several games, including Call of Cthulhu and Dungeons and Dragons. Robert E. Howard's Conan the Barbarian stories are actually part of the Cthulhu Mythos.

Lovecraft created one of the great franchises in pop culture today, but he was never able to earn a living from his writing. In fact, some of his most popular stories emerged only after his death; he never even tried to sell them. At the end of his life he suffered from stomach cancer, which left him malnourished. He died in Providence in 1937. Every year, Lovecraft fans gather to celebrate the anniversaries of his birth and his death. He is celebrated by philosophers, critics, scholars, gamers, fans, and goths—a weird, postmodern intersection of highbrow literary concerns and lowbrow pulp fiction, of serious philosophical inquiry with graphic horror.

The word that best describes the writing of H. P. Lovecraft is "heavy." "Dense" might also be accurate, if not for its connotations synonymous with "dull" or "stupid." It is heavy in the sense that it is thick—thick with imagery and mystery and terror. It is the mystery that pervades. Some of it is so odd that the mystery isn't really ever revealed because it can't be described. Lovecraft acknowledges halfway through the book that it is a weak device (he calls it "trite") to say that a thing is indescribable. If a thing can't be described, then the author is being lazy—except in Lovecraft's case, he does make an effort to describe it. Those efforts, however, fall short, because the human mind cannot truly perceive anything beyond three dimensions, and if Lovecraft is fascinated with any science, it is extradimensional geometry. It can't be comprehended, so it can't be described, and so the thing's indescribability is its distinguishing feature.

There are other ways in which *The Dunwich Horror* is thick: it is thick with ideas, with descriptions, and especially with atmosphere. Taking place in one of those creepy New England backwaters about which Stephen King also writes, peopled with inbred yokels and crawling with demons both real and imagined, the story builds an atmosphere that is oppressive and addictive. It is probably the most readable of Lovecraft's stories, and also the most vivid. The albino mother, her hell-spawn son, the ugly villagers, even the ghostly whip-poor-wills, which have an odd spiritual role to play, are so real that they will haunt your nightmares for days after reading the story.

A Lasting Influence

Star Wars, *Star Trek*, the works of Arthur C. Clarke and Philip K. Dick, the Avengers, the Fantastic Four, the X-Men, fan conventions, Superman, the *Apollo* moon landing: all of these things owe their inspiration to the stories in this book. Whether looking toward the future, speculating about technology, or contemplating the vastness of outer space, science fiction examines humanity's relationship with change. It frightens but it also inspires. The authors whose works are featured in this book take the question "What if?" and milk it for every possibility. What if women ruled the world? What if dinosaurs still existed? What if disease wiped out most of humanity? What if aliens from Mars attacked us? In doing so, these writers created an industry—one of the most popular genres in both film and literature, and one that continues to carry us into the future. Science fiction is not about what is, but about what might be. It speculates about what we may yet discover, the horrors we might unleash, the heights to which we might climb. Good science fiction is also immensely entertaining. All of the stories in this volume fit that description. Above all else, they are really fun to read.

Michael A. Cramer, PhD
Brooklyn, New York
March 8, 2016

THE DIAMOND LENS

Fitz James O'Brien

I

From a very early period of my life the entire bent of my inclinations had been toward microscopic investigations. When I was not more than ten years old, a distant relative of our family, hoping to astonish my inexperience, constructed a simple microscope for me by drilling in a disk of copper a small hole in which a drop of pure water was sustained by capillary attraction. This very primitive apparatus, magnifying some fifty diameters, presented, it is true, only indistinct and imperfect forms, but still sufficiently wonderful to work up my imagination to a preternatural state of excitement.

Seeing me so interested in this rude instrument, my cousin explained to me all that he knew about the principles of the microscope, related to me a few of the wonders which had been accomplished through its agency, and ended by promising to send me one regularly constructed, immediately on his return to the city. I counted the days, the hours, the minutes that intervened between that promise and his departure.

Meantime, I was not idle. Every transparent substance that bore the remotest resemblance to a lens I eagerly seized upon, and employed in vain attempts to realize that instrument, the theory of whose construction I as yet only vaguely comprehended. All panes of glass containing those oblate spheroidal knots familiarly known as "bull's-eyes" were ruthlessly destroyed in the hope of obtaining lenses of marvelous power. I even went so far as to extract the crystalline humor from the eyes of fishes and animals, and endeavored to press it into the microscopic service. I plead guilty to having stolen the glasses from my Aunt Agatha's spectacles, with a dim idea of grinding them into lenses of wondrous magnifying properties—in which attempt it is scarcely necessary to say that I totally failed.

At last the promised instrument came. It was of that order known as Field's simple microscope, and had cost perhaps about fifteen dollars. As far as educational purposes went, a better apparatus could not have been selected. Accompanying it was a small treatise on the microscope—its history, uses, and discoveries. I comprehended then for the first time the "Arabian Nights' Entertainments." The dull veil of ordinary existence that hung across the world seemed suddenly to roll away, and to lay bare a land of enchantments. I felt toward my companions as the seer might feel toward the ordinary masses of men. I held conversations with nature in a tongue which they could not understand. I was in daily communication with living wonders, such as they never imagined in their wildest visions. I penetrated beyond the external portal of things, and roamed through the sanctuaries. Where they beheld only a drop of rain slowly rolling down the window-glass, I saw a universe of beings animated with all the passions common to physical life, and convulsing their minute sphere with struggles as fierce and protracted as those of men. In the common spots of mould, which my mother, good housekeeper that she was, fiercely scooped away from her jam-pots, there abode for me, under the name of mildew, enchanted gardens, filled with dells and avenues of the densest foliage and most astonishing verdure, while from the fantastic boughs of these microscopic forests hung strange fruits glittering with green and silver and gold.

It was no scientific thirst that at this time filled my mind. It was the pure enjoyment of a poet to whom a world of wonders has been disclosed. I talked of my solitary pleasures to none. Alone with my microscope, I dimmed my sight, day after day and night after night, poring over the marvels which it unfolded to me. I was like one who, having discovered the ancient Eden still existing in all its primitive glory, should resolve to enjoy it in solitude, and never betray to mortal the secret of its locality. The rod of my life was bent at this moment. I destined myself to be a microscopist.

Of course, like every novice, I fancied myself a discoverer. I was ignorant at the time of the thousands of acute intellects engaged in the same pursuit as myself, and with the advantage of instruments a thousand times more powerful than mine. The names of Leeuwenhoek, Williamson, Spencer, Ehrenberg, Schultz, Dujardin, Schact, and Schleiden were then entirely unknown to me, or if known, I was ignorant of their patient and wonderful researches. In every fresh specimen of cryptogamia which I placed beneath my instrument I believed that I discovered wonders of which the world was as yet ignorant. I remember well the thrill of delight and admiration that shot through me the first time that I discovered the common wheel animalcule (*Rotifera vulgaris*) expanding and contracting its flexible spokes and seemingly rotating through the water. Alas! As I grew older, and obtained some works treating of my favourite study, I found that I was only on the threshold of a science to the investigation of which some of the greatest men of the age were devoting their lives and intellects.

As I grew up, my parents, who saw but little likelihood of anything practical resulting from the examination of bits of moss and drops of water through a brass tube and a piece of glass, were anxious that I should choose a profession. It was their desire that I should enter the counting-house of my uncle, Ethan Blake, a prosperous merchant, who carried on business in New York. This suggestion I decisively combated. I had no taste for trade; I should only make a failure; in short, I refused to become a merchant.

But it was necessary for me to select some pursuit. My parents were staid New England people, who insisted on the necessity of labour, and therefore, although, thanks to the bequest of my poor Aunt Agatha, I should, on coming of age, inherit a small fortune sufficient to place me above want, it was decided that, instead of waiting for this, I should act the nobler part, and employ the intervening years in rendering myself independent.

After much cogitation, I complied with the wishes of my family, and selected a profession. I determined to study medicine at the New York Academy. This disposition of my future suited me. A removal from my relatives would enable me to dispose of my time as I pleased without fear of detection. As long as I paid my Academy fees, I might shirk attending the lectures if I chose; and, as I never had the remotest intention of standing an examination, there was no danger of my being "plucked." Besides, a metropolis was the place for me. There I could obtain excellent instruments, the newest publications, intimacy with men of pursuits kindred with my own—in short, all things necessary to ensure a profitable devotion of my life to my beloved science. I had an abundance of money, few desires that were not bounded by my illuminating mirror on one side and my object-glass on the other; what, therefore, was to prevent my becoming an illustrious investigator of the veiled worlds? It was with the most buoyant hope that I left my New England home and established myself in New York.

II

My first step, of course, was to find suitable apartments. These I obtained, after a couple of days' search, in Fourth Avenue; a very pretty second floor, unfurnished, containing sitting-room, bedroom, and a smaller apartment which I intended to fit up as a laboratory. I furnished my lodgings simply, but rather elegantly, and then devoted all my energies to the adornment of the temple of my worship. I visited Pike, the celebrated optician, and passed in review his splendid collection of microscopes—Field's Compound, Hingham's, Spencer's, Nachet's Binocular (that founded on the principles of the stereoscope), and at length fixed upon that form known as Spencer's Trunnion Microscope, as combining the greatest number of improvements with an almost perfect freedom from tremor. Along with this I purchased every possible accessory—draw-tubes, micrometers, a *camera lucida*, lever-stage, achromatic condensers, white cloud illuminators, prisms, parabolic condensers, polarizing apparatus, forceps, aquatic boxes, fishing-tubes, with a host of other articles, all of which would have been useful in the hands of an experienced microscopist, but, as I afterward discovered, were not of the slightest present value to me. It takes years of practice to know how to use a complicated microscope. The optician looked suspiciously at me as I made these wholesale purchases. He evidently was uncertain whether to set me down as some scientific celebrity or a madman. I think he was inclined to the latter belief. I suppose I was mad. Every great genius is mad upon the subject in which he is greatest. The unsuccessful madman is disgraced and called a lunatic.

Mad or not, I set myself to work with a zeal which few scientific students have ever equaled. I had everything to learn relative to the delicate study upon which I had embarked—a study involving the most earnest patience, the most rigid analytic powers, the steadiest hand, the most untiring eye, the most refined and subtle manipulation.

For a long time half my apparatus lay inactively on the shelves of my laboratory, which was now most amply furnished with every possible contrivance for facilitating my investigations. The fact was that I did not know how to use some of my scientific implements—never having been taught microscopies—and those whose use I understood theoretically were of little avail until by practice I could attain the necessary delicacy of handling. Still, such was the fury of my ambition, such the untiring perseverance of my experiments, that, difficult of credit as it may be, in the course of one year I became theoretically and practically an accomplished microscopist.

During this period of my labors, in which I submitted specimens of every substance that came under my observation to the action of my lenses, I became a discoverer—in a small way, it is true, for I was very young, but still a discoverer. It was I who destroyed Ehrenberg's theory that the *Volvox globator* was an animal, and proved that his "monads" with stomachs and eyes were merely phases of the formation of a vegetable cell, and were, when they reached their mature state, incapable of the act of conjugation, or any true generative act, without which no organism rising to any stage of life higher than vegetable can be said to be complete. It was I who resolved the singular problem of rotation in the cells and hairs of plants into ciliary attraction, in spite of the assertions of Wenham and others that my explanation was the result of an optical illusion.

But notwithstanding these discoveries, laboriously and painfully made as they were, I felt horribly dissatisfied. At every step I found myself stopped by the imperfections of my instruments. Like all active microscopists, I gave my imagination full play. Indeed, it is a common complaint against many such that they supply the defects of their instruments with the creations of their brains. I imagined depths beyond depths in nature which the limited power of my lenses prohibited me from exploring. I lay awake at night constructing imaginary microscopes of immeasurable power, with which I seemed to pierce through all the envelopes of matter down to its original atom. How I cursed those imperfect mediums which necessity through ignorance compelled me to use! How I longed to discover the secret of some perfect lens, whose magnifying power should be limited only by the resolvability of the object, and which at the same time should be free from spherical and chromatic aberrations—in short, from all the obstacles over which the poor microscopist finds himself continually stumbling! I felt convinced that the simple microscope, composed of a single lens of such vast yet perfect power, was possible of construction. To attempt to bring the compound microscope up to such a pitch would have been commencing at the wrong end; this latter being simply a partially successful endeavor to remedy those very defects of the simplest instrument which, if conquered, would leave nothing to be desired.

It was in this mood of mind that I became a constructive microscopist. After another year passed in this new pursuit, experimenting on every imaginable substance—glass, gems, flints, crystals, artificial crystals formed of the alloy of various vitreous materials—in short, having constructed as many varieties of lenses as Argus had eyes—I found myself precisely where I started, with nothing gained save an extensive knowledge of glass-making. I was almost dead with despair. My parents were surprised at my apparent want of progress in my medical studies (I had not attended one lecture since my arrival in the city), and the expenses of my mad pursuit had been so great as to embarrass me very seriously.

I was in this frame of mind one day, experimenting in my laboratory on a small diamond—that stone, from its great refracting power, having always occupied my attention more than any other—when a young Frenchman who lived on the floor above me, and who was in the habit of occasionally visiting me, entered the room.

I think that Jules Simon was a Jew. He had many traits of the Hebrew character: a love of jewelry, of dress, and of good living. There was something mysterious about him. He always had something to sell, and yet went into excellent society. When I say sell, I should perhaps have said peddle; for his operations were generally confined to the disposal of single articles—a picture, for instance, or a rare carving in ivory, or a pair of duelling-pistols, or the dress of a Mexican *caballero*. When I was first furnishing my rooms, he paid me a visit, which ended in my purchasing an antique silver lamp, which he assured me was a Cellini—it was handsome enough even for that—and some other knick-knacks for my sitting-room. Why Simon should pursue this petty trade I never could imagine. He apparently had plenty of money, and had the *entrée* of the best houses in the city—taking care, however, I suppose, to drive no bargains within the enchanted circle of the Upper Ten. I came at length to the conclusion that this peddling was but a mask to cover some greater object, and even went so far as to believe my young acquaintance to be implicated in the slave-trade. That, however, was none of my affair.

On the present occasion, Simon entered my room in a state of considerable excitement.

"Ah! *Mon ami!*" he cried, before I could even offer him the ordinary salutation, "It has occurred to me to be the witness of the most astonishing things in the world. I promenade myself to the house of Madame ——. How does the little animal—*le renard*—name himself in the Latin?"

"Vulpes," I answered.

"Ah! Yes—Vulpes. I promenade myself to the house of Madame Vulpes."

"The spirit medium?"

"Yes, the great medium. Great heavens! What a woman! I write on a slip of paper many of questions concerning affairs of the most secret—affairs that conceal themselves in the abysses of my heart the most profound; and behold, by example, what occurs? This devil of a woman makes me replies the most truthful to all of them. She talks to me of things that I do not love to talk of to myself. What am I to think? I am fixed to the earth!"

"Am I to understand you, M. Simon, that this Mrs. Vulpes replied to questions secretly written by you, which questions related to events known only to yourself?"

"Ah! More than that, more than that," he answered, with an air of some alarm. "She related to me things—but," he added after a pause, and suddenly changing his manner, "why occupy ourselves with these follies? It was all the biology, without doubt. It goes without saying that it has not my credence. But why are we here, *mon ami?* It has occurred to me to discover the most beautiful thing as you can imagine—a vase with green lizards on it, composed by the great Bernard Palissy. It is in my apartment; let us mount. I go to show it to you."

I followed Simon mechanically; but my thoughts were far from Palissy and his enameled ware, although I, like him, was seeking in the dark a great discovery. This casual mention of the spiritualist, Madame Vulpes, set me on a new track. What if this spiritualism should be really a great fact? What if, through communication with more subtle organisms than my own, I could reach at a single bound the goal which perhaps a life, of agonizing mental toil would never enable me to attain?

While purchasing the Palissy vase from my friend Simon, I was mentally arranging a visit to Madame Vulpes.

III

Two evenings after this, thanks to an arrangement by letter and the promise of an ample fee, I found Madame Vulpes awaiting me at her residence alone. She was a coarse-featured woman, with keen and rather cruel dark eyes, and an exceedingly sensual expression about her mouth and under jaw. She received me in perfect silence, in an apartment on the ground floor, very sparsely furnished. In the centre of the room, close to where Mrs. Vulpes sat, there was a common round mahogany table. If I had come for the purpose of sweeping her chimney, the woman could not have looked more indifferent to my appearance. There was no attempt to inspire the visitor with awe. Everything bore a simple and practical aspect. This intercourse with the spiritual world was evidently as familiar an occupation with Mrs. Vulpes as eating her dinner or riding in an omnibus.

"You come for a communication, Mr. Linley?" said the medium, in a dry, businesslike tone of voice.

"By appointment—yes."

"What sort of communication do you want—a written one?"

"Yes, I wish for a written one."

"From any particular spirit?"

"Yes."

"Have you ever known this spirit on this earth?"

"Never. He died long before I was born. I wish merely to obtain from him some information which he ought to be able to give better than any other."

"Will you seat yourself at the table, Mr. Linley," said the medium, "and place your hands upon it?"

I obeyed, Mrs. Vulpes being seated opposite to me, with her hands also on the table. We remained thus for about a minute and a half, when a violent succession of raps came on the table, on the back of my chair, on the floor immediately under my feet, and even on the window-panes. Mrs. Vulpes smiled composedly.

"They are very strong tonight," she remarked. "You are fortunate." She then continued, "Will the spirits communicate with this gentleman?"

Vigorous affirmative.

"Will the particular spirit he desires to speak with communicate?"

A very confused rapping followed this question.

"I know what they mean," said Mrs. Vulpes, addressing herself to me; "they wish you to write down the name of the particular spirit that you desire to converse with. Is that so?" she added, speaking to her invisible guests.

That it was so was evident from the numerous affirmatory responses.

While this was going on, I tore a slip from my pocket-book and scribbled a name under the table.

"Will this spirit communicate in writing with this gentleman?" asked the medium once more.

After a moment's pause, her hand seemed to be seized with a violent tremor, shaking so forcibly that the table vibrated. She said that a spirit had seized her hand and would write. I handed her some sheets of paper that were on the table and a pencil. The latter she held loosely in her hand, which presently began to move over the paper with a singular and seemingly involuntary motion. After a few moments had elapsed, she handed me the paper, on which I found written, in a large, uncultivated hand, the words, "He is not here, but has been sent for." A pause of a minute or so ensued, during which Mrs. Vulpes remained perfectly silent, but the raps continued at regular intervals. When the short period I mention had elapsed, the hand of the medium was again seized with its convulsive tremor, and she wrote, under this strange influence, a few words on the paper, which she handed to me. They were as follows:

"I am here. Question me.

"Leeuwenhoek."

I was astounded. The name was identical with that I had written beneath the table, and carefully kept concealed. Neither was it at all probable that an uncultivated woman like Mrs. Vulpes should know even the name of the great father of microscopies. It may have been biology; but this theory was soon doomed to be destroyed. I wrote on my slip—still concealing it from Mrs. Vulpes—a series of questions which, to avoid tediousness, I shall place with the responses, in the order in which they occurred:

I.—Can the microscope be brought to perfection?

Spirit.—Yes.

I.—Am I destined to accomplish this great task?

Spirit.—You are.

I.—I wish to know how to proceed to attain this end. For the love which you bear to science, help me!

Spirit.—A diamond of one hundred and forty carats, submitted to electro-magnetic currents for a long period, will experience a rearrangement of its atoms *inter se* and from that stone you will form the universal lens.

I.—Will great discoveries result from the use of such a lens?

Spirit.—So great that all that has gone before is as nothing.

I.—But the refractive power of the diamond is so immense that the image will be formed within the lens. How is that difficulty to be surmounted?

Spirit.—Pierce the lens through its axis, and the difficulty is obviated. The image will be formed in the pierced space, which will itself serve as a tube to look through. Now I am called. Good-night.

I cannot at all describe the effect that these extraordinary communications had upon me. I felt completely bewildered. No biological theory could account for the discovery of the lens. The medium might, by means of biological rapport with my mind, have gone so far as to read my questions and reply to them coherently. But biology could not enable her to discover that magnetic currents would so alter the crystals of the diamond as to remedy its previous defects and admit of its being polished into a perfect lens. Some such theory may have passed through my head, it is true; but if so, I had forgotten it. In my excited condition of mind there was no course left but to become a convert, and it was in a state of the most painful nervous exaltation that I left the medium's house that evening. She accompanied me to the door, hoping that I was satisfied. The raps followed us as we went through the hall, sounding on the balusters, the flooring, and even the lintels of the door. I hastily expressed my satisfaction, and escaped hurriedly into the cool night air. I walked home with but one thought possessing me—how to obtain a diamond of the immense size required. My entire means multiplied a hundred times over would have been inadequate to its purchase. Besides, such stones are rare, and become historical. I could find such only in the regalia of Eastern or European monarchs.

IV

There was a light in Simon's room as I entered my house. A vague impulse urged me to visit him. As I opened the door of his sitting-room unannounced, he was bending, with his back toward me, over a Carcel lamp, apparently engaged in minutely examining some object which he held in his hands. As I entered, he started suddenly, thrust his hand into his breast pocket, and turned to me with a face crimson with confusion.

"What!" I cried, "poring over the miniature of some fair lady? Well, don't blush so much; I won't ask to see it."

Simon laughed awkwardly enough, but made none of the negative protestations usual on such occasions. He asked me to take a seat.

"Simon," said I, "I have just come from Madame Vulpes."

This time Simon turned as white as a sheet, and seemed stupefied, as if a sudden electric shock had smitten him. He babbled some incoherent words, and went hastily to a small closet where he usually kept his liquors. Although astonished at his emotion, I was too preoccupied with my own idea to pay much attention to anything else.

"You say truly when you call Madame Vulpes a devil of a woman," I continued. "Simon, she told me wonderful things tonight, or rather was the means of telling me wonderful things. Ah! If I could only get a diamond that weighed one hundred and forty carats!"

Scarcely had the sigh with which I uttered this desire died upon my lips when Simon, with the aspect of a wild beast, glared at me savagely, and, rushing to the mantelpiece, where some foreign weapons hung on the wall, caught up a Malay creese, and brandished it furiously before him.

"No!" he cried in French, into which he always broke when excited. "No! You shall not have it! You are perfidious! You have consulted with that demon, and desire my treasure! But I will die first! Me, I am brave! You cannot make me fear!"

All this, uttered in a loud voice, trembling with excitement, astounded me. I saw at a glance that I had accidentally trodden upon the edges of Simon's secret, whatever it was. It was necessary to reassure him.

"My dear Simon," I said, "I am entirely at a loss to know what you mean. I went to Madame Vulpes to consult with her on a scientific problem, to the solution of which I discovered that a diamond of the size I just mentioned was necessary. You were never alluded to during the evening, nor, so far as I was concerned, even thought of. What can be the meaning of this outburst? If you happen to have a set of valuable diamonds in your possession, you need fear nothing from me. The diamond which I require you could not possess; or, if you did possess it, you would not be living here."

Something in my tone must have completely reassured him, for his expression immediately changed to a sort of constrained merriment, combined however, with a certain suspicious attention to my movements. He laughed, and said that I must bear with him; that he was at certain moments subject to a species of vertigo, which betrayed itself in incoherent speeches, and that the attacks passed off as rapidly as they came.

He put his weapon aside while making this explanation, and endeavored, with some success, to assume a more cheerful air.

All this did not impose on me in the least. I was too much accustomed to analytical labors to be baffled by so flimsy a veil. I determined to probe the mystery to the bottom.

"Simon," I said gayly, "let us forget all this over a bottle of Burgundy. I have a case of Lausseure's Clos Vougeot downstairs, fragrant with the odors and ruddy with the sunlight of the Côte d'Or. Let us have up a couple of bottles. What say you?"

"With all my heart," answered Simon smilingly.

I produced the wine and we seated ourselves to drink. It was of a famous vintage, that of 1848, a year when war and wine throve together, and its pure but powerful juice seemed to impart renewed vitality to the system. By the time we had half finished the second bottle, Simon's head, which I knew was a weak one, had begun to yield, while I remained calm as ever, only that every draught seemed to send a flush of vigor through my limbs. Simon's utterance became more and more indistinct. He took to singing French *chansons* of a not very moral tendency. I rose suddenly from the table just at the conclusion of one of those incoherent verses, and, fixing my eyes on him with a quiet smile, said, "Simon, I have deceived you. I learned your secret this evening. You may as well be frank with me. Mrs. Vulpes—or rather, one of her spirits—told me all."

He started with horror. His intoxication seemed for the moment to fade away, and he made a movement toward the weapon that he had a short time before laid down, I stopped him with my hand.

"Monster!" he cried passionately, "I am ruined! What shall I do? You shall never have it! I swear by my mother!"

"I don't want it," I said; "rest secure, but be frank with me. Tell me all about it."

The drunkenness began to return. He protested with maudlin earnestness that I was entirely mistaken—that I was intoxicated; then asked me to swear eternal secrecy, and promised to disclose the mystery to me. I pledged myself, of course, to all. With an uneasy look in his eyes, and hands unsteady with drink and nervousness, he drew a small case from his breast and opened it. Heavens! How the mild lamplight was shivered into a thousand prismatic arrows as it fell upon a vast rose-diamond that glittered in the case! I was no judge of diamonds, but I saw at a glance that this was a gem of rare size and purity. I looked at Simon with wonder and—must I confess it?—with envy. How could he have obtained this treasure? In reply to my questions, I could just gather from his drunken statements (of which, I fancy, half the incoherence was affected) that he had been superintending a gang of slaves engaged in diamond-washing in Brazil; that he had seen one of them secrete a diamond, but, instead of informing his employers, had quietly watched the negro until he saw him bury his treasure; that he had dug it up and fled with it, but that as yet he was afraid to attempt to dispose of it publicly—so valuable a gem being almost certain to attract too much attention to its owner's antecedents—and he had not been able to discover any of those obscure channels by which such matters are conveyed away safely. He added that, in accordance with oriental practice, he had named his diamond with the fanciful title of "The Eye of Morning."

While Simon was relating this to me, I regarded the great diamond attentively. Never had I beheld anything so beautiful. All the glories of light ever imagined or described seemed to pulsate in its crystalline chambers. Its weight, as I learned from Simon, was exactly one hundred and forty carats. Here was an amazing coincidence. The hand of destiny seemed in it. On the very evening when the spirit of Leeuwenhoek communicates to me the great secret of the microscope, the priceless means which he directs me to employ start up within my easy reach! I determined, with the most perfect deliberation, to possess myself of Simon's diamond.

I sat opposite to him while he nodded over his glass, and calmly revolved the whole affair. I did not for an instant contemplate so foolish an act as a common theft, which would of course be discovered, or at least necessitate flight and concealment, all of which must interfere with my scientific plans. There was but one step to be taken—to kill Simon. After all, what was the life of a little peddling Jew in comparison with the interests of science? Human beings are taken every day from the condemned prisons to be experimented on by surgeons. This man, Simon, was by his own confession a criminal, a robber, and I believed on my soul a murderer. He deserved death quite as much as any felon condemned by the laws: why should I not, like government, contrive that his punishment should contribute to the progress of human knowledge?

The means for accomplishing everything I desired lay within my reach. There stood upon the mantelpiece a bottle half full of French laudanum. Simon was so occupied with his diamond, which I had just restored to him, that it was an affair of no difficulty to drug his glass. In a quarter of an hour he was in a profound sleep.

I now opened his waistcoat, took the diamond from the inner pocket in which he had placed it, and removed him to the bed, on which I laid him so that his feet hung down over the edge. I had possessed myself of the Malay creese, which I held in my right hand, while with the other I discovered as accurately as I could by pulsation the exact locality of the heart. It was essential that all the aspects of his death should lead to the surmise of self-murder. I calculated the exact angle at which it was probable that the weapon, if leveled by Simon's own hand, would enter his breast; then with one powerful blow I thrust it up to the hilt in the very spot which I desired to penetrate. A convulsive thrill ran through Simon's limbs. I heard a smothered sound issue from his throat, precisely like the bursting of a large air-bubble sent up by a diver when it reaches the surface of the water; he turned half round on his side, and, as if to assist my plans more effectually, his right hand, moved by some mere spasmodic impulse, clasped the handle of the creese, which it remained holding with extraordinary muscular tenacity. Beyond this there was no apparent struggle. The laudanum, I presume, paralyzed the usual nervous action. He must have died instantly.

There was yet something to be done. To make it certain that all suspicion of the act should be diverted from any inhabitant of the house to Simon himself, it was necessary that the door should be found in the morning *locked on the inside.* How to do this, and afterward escape myself? Not by the window; that was a physical impossibility. Besides, I was determined that the windows also should be found bolted. The solution was simple enough. I descended softly to my own room for a peculiar instrument which I had used for holding small slippery substances, such as minute spheres of glass, etc. This instrument was nothing more than a long, slender hand-vise, with a very powerful grip and a considerable leverage, which last was accidentally owing to the shape of the handle. Nothing was simpler than, when the key was in the lock, to seize the end of its stem in this vise, through the keyhole, from the outside, and so lock the door. Previously, however, to doing this, I burned a number of papers on Simon's hearth. Suicides almost always burn papers before they destroy themselves. I also emptied some more laudanum into Simon's glass—having first removed from it all traces of wine—cleaned the other wine-glass, and brought the bottles away with me. If traces of two persons drinking had been found in the room, the question naturally would have arisen, Who was the second? Besides, the wine-bottles might have been identified as belonging to me. The laudanum I poured out to account for its presence in his stomach, in case of a *post-mortem* examination. The theory naturally would be that he first intended to poison himself, but, after swallowing a little of the drug, was either disgusted with its taste, or changed his mind from other motives, and chose the dagger. These arrangements made, I walked out, leaving the gas burning, locked the door with my vise, and went to bed.

Simon's death was not discovered until nearly three in the afternoon. The servant, astonished at seeing the gas burning—the light streaming on the dark landing from under the door—peeped through the keyhole and saw Simon on the bed.

She gave the alarm. The door was burst open, and the neighborhood was in a fever of excitement.

Every one in the house was arrested, myself included. There was an inquest; but no clue to his death beyond that of suicide could be obtained. Curiously enough, he had made several speeches to his friends the preceding week that seemed to point to self-destruction. One gentleman swore that Simon had said in his presence that "he was tired of life." His landlord affirmed that Simon, when paying him his last month's rent, remarked that "he should not pay him rent much longer." All the other evidence corresponded—the door locked inside, the position of the corpse, the burned papers. As I anticipated, no one knew of the possession of the diamond by Simon, so that no motive was suggested for his murder. The jury, after a prolonged examination, brought in the usual verdict, and the neighborhood once more settled down to its accustomed quiet.

V

The three months succeeding Simon's catastrophe I devoted night and day to my diamond lens. I had constructed a vast galvanic battery, composed of nearly two thousand pairs of plates: a higher power I dared not use, lest the diamond should be calcined. By means of this enormous engine I was enabled to send a powerful current of electricity continually through my great diamond, which it seemed to me gained in lustre every day. At the expiration of a month I commenced the grinding and polishing of the lens, a work of intense toil and exquisite delicacy. The great density of the stone, and the care required to be taken with the curvatures of the surfaces of the lens, rendered the labor the severest and most harassing that I had yet undergone.

At last the eventful moment came; the lens was completed. I stood trembling on the threshold of new worlds. I had the realization of Alexander's famous wish before me. The lens lay on the table, ready to be placed upon its platform. My hand fairly shook as I enveloped a drop of water with a thin coating of oil of turpentine, preparatory to its examination, a process necessary in order to prevent the rapid evaporation of the water. I now placed the drop on a thin slip of glass under the lens, and throwing upon it, by the combined aid of a prism and a mirror, a powerful stream of light, I approached my eye to the minute hole drilled through the axis of the lens. For an instant I saw nothing save what seemed to be an illuminated chaos, a vast, luminous abyss. A pure white light, cloudless and serene, and seemingly limitless as space itself, was my first impression. Gently, and with the greatest care, I depressed the lens a few hairbreadths. The wondrous illumination still continued, but as the lens approached the object a scene of indescribable beauty was unfolded to my view.

I seemed to gaze upon a vast space, the limits of which extended far beyond my vision. An atmosphere of magical luminousness permeated the entire field of view. I was amazed to see no trace of animalculous life. Not a living thing, apparently, inhabited that dazzling expanse. I comprehended instantly that, by the wondrous power of my lens, I had penetrated beyond the grosser particles of aqueous matter, beyond the realms of infusoria and protozoa, down to the original gaseous globule, into whose luminous interior I was gazing as into an almost boundless dome filled with a supernatural radiance.

It was, however, no brilliant void into which I looked. On every side I beheld beautiful inorganic forms, of unknown texture, and colored with the most enchanting hues. These forms presented the appearance of what might be called, for want of a more specific definition, foliated clouds of the highest rarity—that is, they undulated and broke into vegetable formations, and were tinged with splendors compared with which the gilding of our autumn woodlands is as dross compared with gold. Far away into the illimitable distance stretched long avenues of these gaseous forests, dimly transparent, and painted with prismatic hues of unimaginable brilliancy. The pendent branches waved along the fluid glades until every vista seemed to break through half-lucent ranks of many-coloured drooping silken pennons. What seemed to be either fruits or flowers, pied with a thousand hues, lustrous and ever-varying, bubbled from the crowns of this fairy foliage. No hills, no lakes, no rivers, no forms animate or inanimate, were to be seen, save those vast auroral copses that floated serenely in the luminous stillness, with leaves and fruits and flowers gleaming with unknown fires, unrealizable by mere imagination.

How strange, I thought, that this sphere should be thus condemned to solitude! I had hoped, at least, to discover some new form of animal life, perhaps of a lower class than any with which we are at present acquainted, but still some living organism. I found my newly discovered world, if I may so speak, a beautiful chromatic desert.

While I was speculating on the singular arrangements of the internal economy of Nature, with which she so frequently splinters into atoms our most compact theories, I thought I beheld a form moving slowly through the glades of one of the prismatic forests. I looked more attentively, and found that I was not mistaken. Words cannot depict the anxiety with which I awaited the nearer approach of this mysterious object. Was it merely some inanimate substance, held in suspense in the attenuated atmosphere of the globule, or was it an animal endowed with vitality and motion? It approached, flitting behind the gauzy, colored veils of cloud-foliage, for seconds dimly revealed, then vanishing. At last the violet pennons that trailed nearest to me vibrated; they were gently pushed aside, and the form floated out into the broad light.

It was a female human shape. When I say human, I mean it possessed the outlines of humanity; but there the analogy ends. Its adorable beauty lifted it illimitable heights beyond the loveliest daughter of Adam.

I cannot, I dare not, attempt to inventory the charms of this divine revelation of perfect beauty. Those eyes of mystic violet, dewy and serene, evade my words. Her long, lustrous hair following her glorious head in a golden wake, like the track sown in heaven by a falling star, seems to quench my most burning phrases with its splendors. If all the bees of Hybla nestled upon my lips, they would still sing but hoarsely the wondrous harmonies of outline that enclosed her form.

She swept out from between the rainbow-curtains of the cloud-trees into the broad sea of light that lay beyond. Her motions were those of some graceful naiad, cleaving, by a mere effort of her will, the clear, unruffled waters that fill the chambers of the sea. She floated forth with the serene grace of a frail bubble ascending through the still atmosphere of a June day. The perfect roundness of her limbs formed suave and enchanting curves. It was like listening to the most spiritual symphony of Beethoven the divine, to watch the harmonious flow of lines. This, indeed was a pleasure cheaply purchased at any price. What cared I if I had waded to the portal of this wonder through another's blood. I would have given my own to enjoy one such moment of intoxication and delight.

Breathless with gazing on this lovely wonder, and forgetful for an instant of everything save her presence, I withdrew my eye from the microscope eagerly. Alas! As my gaze fell on the thin slide that lay beneath my instrument, the bright light from mirror and from prism sparkled on a colorless drop of water! There, in that tiny bead of dew, this beautiful being was forever imprisoned. The planet Neptune was not more distant from me than she. I hastened once more to apply my eye to the microscope.

Animula (let me now call her by that dear name which I subsequently bestowed on her) had changed her position. She had again approached the wondrous forest, and was gazing earnestly upward. Presently one of the trees—as I must call them—unfolded a long ciliary process, with which it seized one of the gleaming fruits that glittered on its summit, and, sweeping slowly down, held it within reach of Animula. The sylph took it in her delicate hand and began to eat. My attention was so entirely absorbed by her that I could not apply myself to the task of determining whether this singular plant was or was not instinct with volition.

I watched her, as she made her repast, with the most profound attention. The suppleness of her motions sent a thrill of delight through my frame; my heart beat madly as she turned her beautiful eyes in the direction of the spot in which I stood. What would I not have given to have had the power to precipitate myself into that luminous ocean and float with her through those grooves of purple and gold! While I was thus breathlessly following her every movement, she suddenly started, seemed to listen for a moment, and then cleaving the brilliant ether in which she was floating, like a flash of light, pierced through the opaline forest and disappeared.

Instantly a series of the most singular sensations attacked me. It seemed as if I had suddenly gone blind. The luminous sphere was still before me, but my daylight had vanished. What caused this sudden disappearance? Had she a lover or a husband? Yes, that was the solution! Some signal from a happy fellow-being had vibrated through the avenues of the forest, and she had obeyed the summons.

The agony of my sensations, as I arrived at this conclusion, startled me. I tried to reject the conviction that my reason forced upon me. I battled against the fatal conclusion—but in vain. It was so. I had no escape from it. I loved an animalcule!

It is true that, thanks to the marvellous power of my microscope, she appeared of human proportions. Instead of presenting the revolting aspect of the coarser creatures, that live and struggle and die, in the more easily resolvable portions of the water-drop, she was fair and delicate and of surpassing beauty. But of what account was all that? Every time that my eye was withdrawn from the instrument it fell on a miserable drop of water, within which, I must be content to know, dwelt all that could make my life lovely.

Could she but see me once! Could I for one moment pierce the mystical walls that so inexorably rose to separate us, and whisper all that filled my soul, I might consent to be satisfied for the rest of my life with the knowledge of her remote sympathy. It would be something to have established even the faintest personal link to bind us together—to know that at times, when roaming through these enchanted glades, she might think of the wonderful stranger who had broken the monotony of her life with his presence and left a gentle memory in her heart!

But it could not be. No invention of which human intellect was capable could break down the barriers that nature had erected. I might feast my soul upon her wondrous beauty, yet she must always remain ignorant of the adoring eyes that day and night gazed upon her, and, even when closed, beheld her in dreams. With a bitter cry of anguish I fled from the room, and flinging myself on my bed, sobbed myself to sleep like a child.

VI

I arose the next morning almost at daybreak, and rushed to my microscope, I trembled as I sought the luminous world in miniature that contained my all. Animula was there. I had left the gas-lamp, surrounded by its moderators, burning when I went to bed the night before. I found the sylph bathing, as it were, with an expression of pleasure animating her features, in the brilliant light which surrounded her. She tossed her lustrous golden hair over her shoulders with innocent coquetry. She lay at full length in the transparent medium, in which she supported herself with ease, and gamboled with the enchanting grace that the nymph Salmacis might have exhibited when she sought to conquer the modest Hermaphroditus. I tried an experiment to satisfy myself if her powers of reflection were developed. I lessened the lamplight considerably. By the dim light that remained, I could see an expression of pain flit across her face. She looked upward suddenly, and her brows contracted. I flooded the stage of the microscope again with a full stream of light, and her whole expression changed. She sprang forward like some some substance deprived of all weight. Her eyes sparkled and her lips moved. Ah! If science had only the means of conducting and reduplicating sounds, as it does rays of light, what carols of happiness would then have entranced my ears! What jubilant hymns to Adonais would have thrilled the illumined air!

I now comprehended how it was that the Count de Gabalis peopled his mystic world with sylphs—beautiful beings whose breath of life was lambent fire, and who sported forever in regions of purest ether and purest light. The Rosicrucian had anticipated the wonder that I had practically realised.

How long this worship of my strange divinity went on thus I scarcely know. I lost all note of time. All day from early dawn, and far into the night, I was to be found peering through that wonderful lens. I saw no one, went nowhere, and scarce allowed myself sufficient time for my meals. My whole life was absorbed in contemplation as rapt as that of any of the Romish saints. Every hour that I gazed upon the divine form strengthened my passion—a passion that was always overshadowed by the maddening conviction that, although I could gaze on her at will, she never, never could behold me!

At length I grew so pale and emaciated, from want of rest and continual brooding over my insane love and its cruel conditions, that I determined to make some effort to wean myself from it. "Come," I said, "this is at best but a fantasy. Your imagination has bestowed on Animula charms which in reality she does not possess. Seclusion from female society has produced this morbid condition of mind. Compare her with the beautiful women of your own world, and this false enchantment will vanish."

I looked over the newspapers by chance. There I beheld the advertisement of a celebrated *danseuse* who appeared nightly at Niblo's. The Signorina Caradolce had the reputation of being the most beautiful as well as the most graceful woman in the world. I instantly dressed and went to the theatre.

The curtain drew up. The usual semicircle of fairies in white muslin were standing on the right toe around the enameled flower-bank of green canvas, on which the belated prince was sleeping. Suddenly a flute is heard. The fairies start. The trees open, the fairies all stand on the left toe, and the queen enters. It was the Signorina. She bounded forward amid thunders of applause, and, lighting on one foot, remained poised in the air. Heavens! Was this the great enchantress that had drawn monarchs at her chariot-wheels? Those heavy, muscular limbs, those thick ankles, those cavernous eyes, that stereotyped smile, those crudely painted cheeks! Where were the vermeil blooms, the liquid, expressive eyes, the harmonious limbs of Animula?

The Signorina danced. What gross, discordant movements! The play of her limbs was all false and artificial. Her bounds were painful athletic efforts; her poses were angular and distressed the eye. I could bear it no longer; with an exclamation of disgust that drew every eye upon me, I rose from my seat in the very middle of the Signorina's *pas-de-fascination* and abruptly quitted the house.

I hastened home to feast my eyes once more on the lovely form of my sylph. I felt that henceforth to combat this passion would be impossible. I applied my eyes to the lens. Animula was there—but what could have happened? Some terrible change seemed to have taken place during my absence. Some secret grief seemed to cloud the lovely features of her I gazed upon. Her face had grown thin and haggard; her limbs trailed heavily; the wondrous luster of her golden hair had faded. She was ill—ill, and I could not assist her! I believe at that moment I would have forfeited all claims to my human birthright if I could only have been dwarfed to the size of an animalcule, and permitted to console her from whom fate had forever divided me.

I racked my brain for the solution of this mystery. What was it that afflicted the sylph? She seemed to suffer intense pain. Her features contracted, and she even writhed, as if with some internal agony. The wondrous forests appeared also to have lost half their beauty. Their hues were dim and in some places faded away altogether. I watched Animula for hours with a breaking heart, and she seemed absolutely to wither away under my very eye. Suddenly I remembered that I had not looked at the water-drop for several days. In fact, I hated to see it; for it reminded me of the natural barrier between Animula and myself. I hurriedly looked down on the stage of the microscope. The slide was still there—but, great heavens, the water drop had vanished! The awful truth burst upon me; it had evaporated, until it had become so minute as to be invisible to the naked eye; I had been gazing on its last atom, the one that contained Animula—and she was dying!

I rushed again to the front of the lens and looked through. Alas! The last agony had seized her. The rainbow-hued forests had all melted away, and Animula lay struggling feebly in what seemed to be a spot of dim light. Ah! The sight was horrible: the limbs once so round and lovely shriveling up into nothings; the eyes—those eyes that shone like heaven—being quenched into black dust; the lustrous golden hair now lank and discolored. The last throe came. I beheld that final struggle of the blackening form—and I fainted.

When I awoke out of a trance of many hours, I found myself lying amid the wreck of my instrument, myself as shattered in mind and body as it. I crawled feebly to my bed, from which I did not rise for many months.

They say now that I am mad; but they are mistaken. I am poor, for I have neither the heart nor the will to work; all my money is spent, and I live on charity. Young men's associations that love a joke invite me to lecture on optics before them, for which they pay me, and laugh at me while I lecture. "Linley, the mad microscopist," is the name I go by. I suppose that I talk incoherently while I lecture. Who could talk sense when his brain is haunted by such ghastly memories, while ever and anon among the shapes of death I behold the radiant form of my lost Animula!

A JOURNEY TO THE CENTER OF THE EARTH

Jules Verne

I.

THE PROFESSOR AND HIS FAMILY

On the 24th of May, 1863, my uncle, Professor Liedenbrock, rushed into his little house, No. 19 Königstrasse, one of the oldest streets in the oldest portion of the city of Hamburg.

Martha must have concluded that she was very much behindhand, for the dinner had only just been put into the oven.

"Well, now," said I to myself, "if that most impatient of men is hungry, what a disturbance he will make!"

"M. Liedenbrock so soon!" cried poor Martha in great alarm, half opening the dining-room door.

"Yes, Martha; but very likely the dinner is not half cooked, for it is not two yet. Saint Michael's clock has only just struck half-past one."

"Then why has the master come home so soon?"

"Perhaps he will tell us that himself."

"Here he is, Monsieur Axel; I will run and hide myself while you argue with him."

And Martha retreated in safety into her own dominions.

I was left alone. But how was it possible for a man of my undecided turn of mind to argue successfully with so irascible a person as the professor? With this persuasion I was hurrying away to my own little retreat upstairs, when the street door creaked upon its hinges; heavy feet made the whole flight of stairs to shake; and the master of the house, passing rapidly through the dining room, threw himself in haste into his own sanctum.

But on his rapid way he had found time to fling his hazel stick into a corner, his rough broadbrim upon the table, and these few emphatic words at his nephew:

"Axel, follow me!"

I had scarcely had time to move when the professor was again shouting after me:

"What! Not come yet?"

And I rushed into my redoubtable master's study.

Otto Liedenbrock had no mischief in him, I willingly allow that; but unless he very considerably changes as he grows older, at the end he will be a most original character.

He was professor at the Johanneum, and was delivering a series of lectures on mineralogy, in the course of every one of which he broke into a passion once or twice at least. Not at all that he was overanxious about the improvement of his class, or about the degree of attention with which they listened to him, or the success which might eventually crown his labors. Such little matters of detail never troubled him much. His teaching was, as the German philosophy calls it, "subjective"; it was to benefit himself, not others. He was a learned egotist. He was a well of science, and the pulleys worked uneasily when you wanted to draw anything out of it. In a word, he was a learned miser.

Germany has not a few professors of this sort.

To his misfortune, my uncle was not gifted with a sufficiently rapid utterance; not, to be sure, when he was talking at home, but certainly in his public delivery; this is a want much to be deplored in a speaker. The fact is, that during the course of his lectures at the Johanneum, the professor often came to a complete standstill; he fought with willful words that refused to pass his struggling lips, such words as resist and distend the cheeks, and at last break out into the unasked-for shape of a round and most unscientific oath: then his fury would gradually abate.

Now in mineralogy there are many half-Greek and half-Latin terms, very hard to articulate, and which would be most trying to a poet's measures. I don't wish to say a word against so respectable a science, far be that from me. True, in the august presence of rhombohedral crystals, retinasphaltic resins, gehlenites, Fassaites, molybdenites, tungstates of manganese, and titanite of zirconium, why, the most facile of tongues may make a slip now and then.

It therefore happened that this venial fault of my uncle's came to be pretty well understood in time, and an unfair advantage was taken of it; the students laid wait for him in dangerous places, and when he began to stumble, loud was the laughter, which is not in good taste, not even in Germans. And if there was always a full audience to honor the Liedenbrock courses, I should be sorry to conjecture how many came to make merry at my uncle's expense.

Nevertheless my good uncle was a man of deep learning—a fact I am most anxious to assert and reassert. Sometimes he might irretrievably injure a specimen by his too great ardor in handling it; but still he united the genius of a true geologist with the keen eye of the mineralogist. Armed with his hammer, his steel pointer, his magnetic needles, his blowpipe, and his bottle of nitric acid, he was a powerful man of science. He would refer any mineral to its proper place among the six hundred elementary substances now enumerated, by its fracture, its appearance, its hardness, its fusibility, its sonorousness, its smell, and its taste.

The name of Liedenbrock was honorably mentioned in colleges and learned societies. Humphry Davy, Humboldt, Captain Sir John Franklin, General Sabine, never failed to call upon him on their way through Hamburg. Becquerel, Ebelman, Brewster, Dumas, Milne-Edwards, Saint-Claire-Deville frequently consulted him upon the most difficult problems in chemistry, a science which was indebted to him for considerable discoveries, for in 1853 there had appeared at Leipzig an imposing folio by Otto Liedenbrock, entitled *A Treatise upon Transcendental Chemistry*, with plates; a work, however, which failed to cover its expenses.

To all these titles to honor let me add that my uncle was the curator of the museum of mineralogy formed by M. Struve, the Russian ambassador; a most valuable collection, the fame of which is European.

Such was the gentleman who addressed me in that impetuous manner. Fancy a tall, spare man, of an iron constitution, and with a fair complexion which took off a good ten years from the fifty he must own to. His restless eyes were in incessant motion behind his full-sized spectacles. His long, thin nose was like a knife blade. Boys have been heard to remark that that organ was magnetized and attracted iron filings. But this was merely a mischievous report; it had no attraction except for snuff, which it seemed to draw to itself in great quantities.

When I have added, to complete my portrait, that my uncle walked by mathematical strides of a yard and a half, and that in walking he kept his fists firmly closed, a sure sign of an irritable temperament, I think I shall have said enough to disenchant anyone who should by mistake have coveted much of his company.

He lived in his own little house in Königstrasse, a structure half brick and half wood, with a gable cut into steps; it looked upon one of those winding canals which intersect each other in the middle of the ancient quarter of Hamburg, and which the great fire of 1842 had fortunately spared.

It is true that the old house stood slightly off the perpendicular, and bulged out a little toward the street; its roof sloped a little to one side, like the cap over the left ear of a Tugendbund student; its lines wanted accuracy; but after all, it stood firm, thanks to an old elm which buttressed it in front, and which often in spring sent its young sprays through the window panes.

My uncle was tolerably well off for a German professor. The house was his own, and everything in it. The living contents were his goddaughter Gräuben, a young Virlandaise of seventeen, Martha, and myself. As his nephew and an orphan, I became his laboratory assistant.

I freely confess that I was exceedingly fond of geology and all its kindred sciences; the blood of a mineralogist was in my veins, and in the midst of my specimens I was always happy.

In a word, a man might live happily enough in the little old house in the Königstrasse, in spite of the restless impatience of its master, for although he was a little too excitable—he was very fond of me. But the man had no notion how to wait; nature herself was too slow for him. In April, after he had planted in the terra-cotta pots outside his window seedling plants of mignonette and convolvulus, he would go and give them a little pull by their leaves to make them grow faster. In dealing with such a strange individual there was nothing for it but prompt obedience. I therefore rushed after him.

II

A MYSTERY TO BE SOLVED AT ANY PRICE

That study of his was a museum, and nothing else. Specimens of everything known in mineralogy lay there in their places in perfect order, and correctly named, divided into inflammable, metallic, and lithoid minerals.

How well I knew all these bits of science! Many a time, instead of enjoying the company of lads of my own age, I had preferred dusting these graphites, anthracites, coals, lignites, and peats! And there were bitumens, resins, organic salts, to be protected from the least grain of dust; and metals, from iron to gold, metals whose current value altogether disappeared in the presence of the republican equality of scientific specimens; and stones too, enough to rebuild entirely the house in Königstrasse, even with a handsome additional room, which would have suited me admirably.

But on entering this study now I thought of none of all these wonders; my uncle alone filled my thoughts. He had thrown himself into a velvet easy-chair, and was grasping between his hands a book over which he bent, pondering with intense admiration.

"Here's a remarkable book! What a wonderful book!" he was exclaiming.

These ejaculations brought to my mind the fact that my uncle was liable to occasional fits of bibliomania; but no old book had any value in his eyes unless it had the virtue of being nowhere else to be found, or, at any rate, of being illegible.

"Well, now; don't you see it yet? Why, I have got a priceless treasure, that I found his morning, in rummaging in old Hevelius's shop, the Jew."

"Magnificent!" I replied, with a good imitation of enthusiasm.

What was the good of all this fuss about an old quarto, bound in rough calf, a yellow, faded volume, with a ragged seal depending from it?

But for all that there was no lull yet in the admiring exclamations of the professor.

"See," he went on, both asking the questions and supplying the answers. "Isn't it a beauty? Yes; splendid! Did you ever see such a binding? Doesn't the book open easily? Yes; it stops open anywhere. But does it shut equally well? Yes; for the binding and the leaves are flush, all in a straight line, and no gaps or openings anywhere. And look at its back, after seven hundred years. Why, Bozerian, Closs, or Purgold might have been proud of such a binding!"

While rapidly making these comments my uncle kept opening and shutting the old tome. I really could do no less than ask a question about its contents, although I did not feel the slightest interest.

"And what is the title of this marvelous work?" I asked with an affected eagerness which he must have been very blind not to see through.

"This work," replied my uncle, firing up with renewed enthusiasm, "this work is the Heims Kringla of Snorre Turlleson, the most famous Icelandic author of the twelfth century! It is the chronicle of the Norwegian princes who ruled in Iceland."

"Indeed," I cried, keeping up wonderfully, "of course it is a German translation?"

"What!" sharply replied the professor. "A translation! What should I do with a translation? This is the Icelandic original, in the magnificent idiomatic vernacular, which is both rich and simple, and admits of an infinite variety of grammatical combinations and verbal modifications."

"Like German," I happily ventured.

"Yes," replied my uncle, shrugging his shoulders; "but, in addition to all this, the Icelandic has three numbers like the Greek, and irregular declensions of nouns proper like the Latin."

"Ah!" said I, a little moved out of my indifference. "And is the type good?"

"Type! What do you mean by talking of type, wretched Axel? Type! Do you take it for a printed book, you ignorant fool? It is a manuscript, a Runic manuscript."

"Runic?"

"Yes. Do you want me to explain what that is?"

"Of course not," I replied in the tone of an injured man. But my uncle persevered, and told me, against my will, of many things I cared nothing about.

"Runic characters were in use in Iceland in former ages. They were invented, it is said, by Odin himself. Look there, and wonder, impious young man, and admire these letters, the invention of the Scandinavian god!"

Well, well! Not knowing what to say, I was going to prostrate myself before this wonderful book, a way of answering equally pleasing to gods and kings, and which has the advantage of never giving them any embarrassment, when a little incident happened to divert conversation into another channel.

This was the appearance of a dirty slip of parchment, which slipped out of the volume and fell upon the floor.

My uncle pounced upon this shred with incredible avidity. An old document, enclosed an immemorial time within the folds of this old book, had for him an immeasurable value.

"What's this?" he cried.

And he laid out upon the table a piece of parchment, five inches by three, and along which were traced certain mysterious characters.

Here is the exact facsimile. I think it important to let these strange signs be publicly known, for they were the means of drawing on Professor Liedenbrock and his nephew to undertake the most wonderful expedition of the nineteenth century.

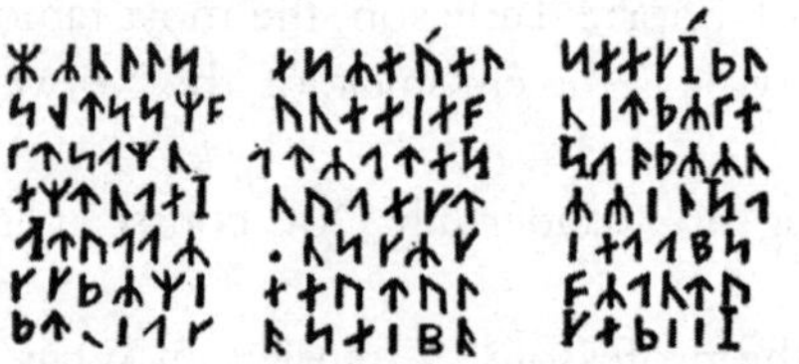

The professor mused a few moments over this series of characters; then raising his spectacles he pronounced:

"These are Runic letters; they are exactly like those of the manuscript of Snorre Turlleson. But, what on earth is their meaning?"

Runic letters appearing to my mind to be an invention of the learned to mystify this poor world, I was not sorry to see my uncle suffering the pangs of mystification. At least, so it seemed to me, judging from his fingers, which were beginning to work with terrible energy.

"It is certainly old Icelandic," he muttered between his teeth.

And Professor Liedenbrock must have known, for he was acknowledged to be quite a polyglot. Not that he could speak fluently in the two thousand languages and twelve thousand dialects which are spoken on the earth, but he knew at least his share of them.

So he was going, in the presence of this difficulty, to give way to all the impetuosity of his character, and I was preparing for a violent outbreak, when two o'clock struck by the little timepiece over the fireplace.

At that moment our good housekeeper Martha opened the study door, saying:

"Dinner is ready!"

I am afraid he sent that soup to where it would boil away to nothing, and Martha took to her heels for safety. I followed her, and hardly knowing how I got there I found myself seated in my usual place.

I waited a few minutes. No professor came. Never within my remembrance had he missed the important ceremonial of dinner. And yet what a good dinner it was! There was parsley soup, an omelette of ham garnished with spiced sorrel, a fillet of veal with compote of prunes; for dessert, crystallized fruit; the whole washed down with sweet Moselle.

All this my uncle was going to sacrifice to a bit of old parchment. As an affectionate and attentive nephew I considered it my duty to eat for him as well as for myself, which I did conscientiously.

"I have never known such a thing," said Martha. "M. Liedenbrock is not at table!"

"Who could have believed it?" I said, with my mouth full.

"Something serious is going to happen," said the servant, shaking her head.

My opinion was, that nothing more serious would happen than an awful scene when my uncle should have discovered that his dinner was devoured. I had come to the last of the fruit when a very loud voice tore me away from the pleasures of my dessert. With one spring I bounded out of the dining room into the study.

III

THE RUNIC WRITING EXERCISES THE PROFESSOR

"Undoubtedly it is Runic," said the professor, bending his brows; "but there is a secret in it, and I mean to discover the key."

A violent gesture finished the sentence.

"Sit there," he added, holding out his fist toward the table. "Sit there, and write."

I was seated in a trice.

"Now I will dictate to you every letter of our alphabet which corresponds with each of these Icelandic characters. We will see what that will give us. But, by St. Michael, if you should dare to deceive me—"

The dictation commenced. I did my best. Every letter was given me one after the other, with the following remarkable result:

mm.rnlls	esrevel	seecIde
sgtssmf	vnteief	niedrke
kt,samn	atrateS	saodrrn
emtnaeI	nvaect	rrilSa
Atsaar	.nvcrc	ieaabs
ccrmi	eevtVl	frAntv
dt,iac	oseibo	KediiI

When this work was ended my uncle tore the paper from me and examined it attentively for a long time.

"What does it all mean?" he kept repeating mechanically.

Upon my honor I could not have enlightened him. Besides he did not ask me, and he went on talking to himself.

"This is what is called a cryptogram, or cipher," he said, "in which letters are purposely thrown in confusion, which if properly arranged would reveal their sense. Only think that under this jargon there may lie concealed the clue to some great discovery!"

As for me, I was of opinion that there was nothing at all in it; though, of course, I took care not to say so.

Then the professor took the book and the parchment, and diligently compared them together.

"These two writings are not by the same hand," he said; "the cipher is of later date than the book, an undoubted proof of which I see in a moment. The first letter is a double m, a letter which is not to be found in Turlleson's book, and which was only added to the alphabet in the fourteenth century. Therefore there are two hundred years between the manuscript and the document."

I admitted that this was a strictly logical conclusion.

"I am therefore led to imagine," continued my uncle, "that some possessor of this book wrote these mysterious letters. But who was that possessor? Is his name nowhere to be found in the manuscript?"

My uncle raised his spectacles, took up a strong lens, and carefully examined the blank pages of the book. On the front of the second, the title page, he noticed a sort of stain which looked like an ink blot. But in looking at it very closely he thought he could distinguish some half-effaced letters. My uncle at once fastened upon this as the center of interest, and he labored at that blot, until by the help of his microscope he ended by making out the following Runic characters which he read without difficulty.

"Arne Saknussemm!" he cried in triumph. "Why, that is the name of another Icelander, a savant of the sixteenth century, a celebrated alchemist!"

I gazed at my uncle with satisfactory admiration.

"Those alchemists," he resumed, "Avicenna, Bacon, Lully, Paracelsus, were the real and only savants of their time. They made discoveries at which we are astonished. Has not this Saknussemm concealed under his cryptogram some surprising invention? It is so; it must be so!"

The professor's imagination took fire at this hypothesis.

"No doubt," I ventured to reply, "but what interest would he have in thus hiding so marvelous a discovery?"

"Why? Why? How can I tell? Did not Galileo do the same by Saturn? We shall see. I will get at the secret of this document, and I will neither sleep nor eat until I have found it out."

My comment on this was a half-suppressed "Oh!"

"Nor you either, Axel," he added.

"The deuce!" said I to myself. "Then it is lucky I have eaten two dinners today!"

"First of all we must find out the key to this cipher; that cannot be difficult."

At these words I quickly raised my head; but my uncle went on soliloquizing.

"There's nothing easier. In this document there are a hundred and thirty-two letters, viz., seventy-seven consonants and fifty-five vowels. This is the proportion found in southern languages, while northern tongues are much richer in consonants; therefore this is in a southern language."

These were very fair conclusions, I thought.

"But what language is it?"

Here I looked for a display of learning, but I met instead with profound analysis.

"This Saknussemm," he went on, "was a very well-informed man; now since he was not writing in his own mother tongue, he would naturally select that which was currently adopted by the choice spirits of the sixteenth century; I mean Latin. If I am mistaken, I can but try Spanish, French, Italian, Greek, or Hebrew. But the savants of the sixteenth century generally wrote in Latin. I am therefore entitled to pronounce this, *à priori*, to be Latin. It is Latin."

I jumped up in my chair. My Latin memories rose in revolt against the notion that these barbarous words could belong to the sweet language of Virgil.

"Yes, it is Latin," my uncle went on; "but it is Latin confused and in disorder; "*pertubata seu inordinata*," as Euclid has it."

"Very well," thought I, "if you can bring order out of that confusion, my dear uncle, you are a clever man."

"Let us examine carefully," said he again, taking up the leaf upon which I had written. "Here is a series of one hundred and thirty-two letters in apparent disorder. There are words consisting of consonants only, as *nrrlls*; others, on the other hand, in which vowels predominate, as for instance the fifth, *uneeief*, or the last but one, *oseibo*. Now this arrangement has evidently not been premeditated; it has arisen mathematically in obedience to the unknown law which has ruled in the succession of these letters. It appears to me a certainty that the original sentence was written in a proper manner, and afterward distorted by a law which we have yet to discover. Whoever possesses the key of this cipher will read it with fluency. What is that key? Axel, have you got it?"

I answered not a word, and for a very good reason. My eyes had fallen upon a charming picture, suspended against the wall, the portrait of Gräuben.

My uncle's ward was at that time at Altona, staying with a relation, and in her absence I was very downhearted; for I may confess it to you now, the pretty Virlandaise and the professor's nephew loved each other with a patience and a calmness entirely German. We had become engaged unknown to my uncle, who was too much taken up with geology to be able to enter into such feelings as ours. Gräuben was a lovely blue-eyed blonde, rather given to gravity and seriousness; but that did not prevent her from loving me very sincerely. As for me, I adored her, if there is such a word in the German language. Thus it happened that the pictufe of my pretty Virlandaise threw me in a moment out of the world of realities into that of memory and fancy.

There looked down upon me the faithful companion of my labors and my recreations. Every day she helped me to arrange my uncle's precious specimens; she and I labeled them together. Mademoiselle Gräuben was an accomplished mineralogist; she could have taught a few things to a savant. She was fond of investigating abstruse scientific questions. What pleasant hours we have spent in study; and how often I envied the very stones which she handled with her charming fingers.

Then, when our leisure hours came, we used to go out together and turn into the shady avenues by the Alster, and went happily side by side up to the old windmill, which forms such an improvement to the landscape at the head of the lake. On the road we chatted hand in hand; I told her amusing tales at which she laughed heartily. Then we reached the banks of the Elbe, and after having bid good-bye to the swan, sailing gracefully amid the white water lilies, we returned to the quay by the steamer.

That is just where I was in my dream, when my uncle with a vehement thump on the table dragged me back to the realities of life.

"Come," said he, "the very first idea which would come into anyone's head to confuse the letters of a sentence would be to write the words vertically instead of horizontally."

"Indeed!" said I.

"Now we must see what would be the effect of that, Axel; put down upon this paper any sentence you like, only instead of arranging the letters in the usual way, one after the other, place them in succession in vertical columns, so as to group them together in five or six vertical lines."

I caught his meaning, and immediately produced the following literary wonder:

I	y	l	o	a	u
l	o	l	w	r	b
o	u	,	n	G	e
v	w	m	d	r	n
e	e	y	e	a	!

"Good," said the professor, without reading them, "now set down those words in a horizontal line."

I obeyed, and with this result:

Iyloau lolwrb ou,nGe vwmdrn
eeyea!

"Excellent!" said my uncle, taking the paper hastily out of my hands. "This begins to look just like an ancient document: the vowels and the consonants are grouped together in equal disorder; there are even capitals in the middle of words, and commas too, just as in Saknussemm's parchment."

I considered these remarks very clever.

"Now," said my uncle, looking straight at me, "to read the sentence which you have just written, and with which I am wholly unacquainted, I shall only have to take the first letter of each word, then the second, the third, and so forth."

And my uncle, to his great astonishment, and my much greater, read:

"I love you well, my own dear Gräuben!"

"Hallo!" cried the professor.

Yes, indeed, without knowing what I was about, like an awkward and unlucky lover, I had compromised myself by writing this unfortunate sentence.

"Aha! You are in love with Gräuben?" he said, with the right look for a guardian.

"Yes; no!" I stammered.

"You love Gräuben," he went on once or twice dreamily. "Well, let us apply the process I have suggested to the document in question."

My uncle, falling back into his absorbing contemplations, had already forgotten my imprudent words. I merely say imprudent, for the great mind of so learned a man of course had no place for love affairs, and happily the grand business of the document gained me the victory.

Just as the moment of the supreme experiment arrived the professor's eyes flashed right through his spectacles. There was a quivering in his fingers as he grasped the old parchment. He was deeply moved. At last he gave a preliminary cough, and with profound gravity, naming in succession the first, then the second letter of each word, he dictated me the following:

mmessvnkaSenrA.icefdoK.segnittamvrtn
ecertserrette,rotaisadva,ednecsedsadne
lacartniiilvIsiratracSarbmvtabiledmek
meretarcsilvcoIsleffenSnI.

I confess I felt considerably excited in coming to the end; these letters named, one at a time, had carried no sense to my mind; I therefore waited for the professor with great pomp to unfold the magnificent but hidden Latin of this mysterious phrase.

But who could have foretold the result? A violent thump made the furniture rattle, and spilled some ink, and my pen dropped from between my fingers.

"That's not it," cried my uncle, "there's no sense in it."

Then darting out like a shot, bowling downstairs like an avalanche, he rushed into the Königstrasse and fled.

IV

THE ENEMY TO BE STARVED INTO SUBMISSION

"He is gone!" cried Martha, running out of her kitchen at the noise of the violent slamming of doors.

"Yes," I replied, "completely gone."

"Well; and how about his dinner?" said the old servant.

"He won't have any."

"And his supper?"

"He won't have any."

"What?" cried Martha, with clasped hands.

"No, my dear Martha, he will eat no more. No one in the house is to eat anything at all. Uncle Liedenbrock is going to make us all fast until he has succeeded in deciphering an undecipherable scrawl."

"Oh, my dear! Must we then all die of hunger?"

I hardly dared to confess that, with so absolute a ruler as my uncle, this fate was inevitable.

The old servant, visibly moved, returned to the kitchen, moaning piteously.

When I was alone, I thought I would go and tell Gräuben all about it. But how should I be able to escape from the house? The professor might return at any moment. And suppose he called me? And suppose he tackled me again with this logomachy, which might vainly have been set before ancient Oedipus. And if I did not obey his call, who could answer for what might happen?

The wisest course was to remain where I was. A mineralogist at Besançon had just sent us a collection of siliceous nodules, which I had to classify: so I set to work; I sorted, labeled, and arranged in their own glass case all these hollow specimens, in the cavity of each of which was a nest of little crystals.

But this work did not succeed in absorbing all my attention. That old document kept working in my brain. My head throbbed with excitement, and I felt an undefined uneasiness. I was possessed with a presentiment of coming evil.

In an hour my nodules were all arranged upon successive shelves. Then I dropped down into the old velvet armchair, my head thrown back and my hands joined over it. I lighted my long crooked pipe, with a painting on it of an idle-looking naiad; then I amused myself watching the process of the conversion of the tobacco into carbon, which was by slow degrees making my naiad into a negress. Now and then I listened to hear whether a well-known step was on the stairs. No. Where could my uncle be at that moment? I fancied him running under the noble trees which line the road to Altona, gesticulating, making shots with his cane, thrashing the long grass, cutting the heads off the thistles, and disturbing the contemplative storks in their peaceful solitude.

Would he return in triumph or in discouragement? Which would get the upper hand, he or the secret? I was thus asking myself questions, and mechanically taking between my fingers the sheet of paper mysteriously disfigured with the incomprehensible succession of letters I had written down; and I repeated to myself, "What does it all mean?"

I sought to group the letters so as to form words. Quite impossible! When I put them together by twos, threes, fives, or sixes, nothing came of it but nonsense. To be sure the fourteenth, fifteenth, and sixteenth letters made the English word "ice"; the eighty-third and two following made "sir"; and in the midst of the document, in the second and third lines, I observed the words "rots," "mutabile," "ira," "net," "atra."

"Come now," I thought, "these words seem to justify my uncle's view about the language of the document." In the fourth line appeared the word "luco," which means a sacred wood. It is true that in the third line was the word "tabiled," which looked like Hebrew, and in the last the purely French words "mer," "arc," "mère."

All this was enough to drive a poor fellow crazy. Four different languages in this ridiculous sentence! What connection could there possibly be between such words as ice, sir, anger, cruel, sacred wood, changeable, mother, bow, and sea? The first and the last might have something to do with each other; it was not at all surprising that in a document written in Iceland there should be mention of a sea of ice; but it was quite another thing to get to the end of this cryptogram with so small a clue. So I was struggling with an insurmountable difficulty; my brain got heated, my eyes watered over that sheet of paper; its hundred and thirty-two letters seemed to flutter and fly around me like those motes of mingled light and darkness which float in the air around the head when the blood is rushing upward with undue violence. I was a prey to a kind of hallucination; I was stifling; I wanted air. Unconsciously I fanned myself with the bit of paper, the back and front of which successively came before my eyes. What was my surprise when, in one of those rapid revolutions, at the moment when the back was turned to me I thought I caught sight of the Latin words "craterem," "terrestre," and others.

A sudden light burst in upon me; these hints alone gave me the first glimpse of the truth; I had discovered the key to the cipher. To read the document, it would not even be necessary to read it through the paper. Such as it was, just such as it had been dictated to me, so it might be spelled out with ease. All those ingenious professorial combinations were coming right. He was right as to the arrangement of the letters; he was right as to the language. He had been within a hair's breadth of reading this Latin document from end to end; but that hair's breadth, chance had given it to me!

You may be sure I felt stirred up. My eyes were dim, I could scarcely see. I had laid the paper upon the table. At a glance I could tell the whole secret.

At last I became more calm. I made a wise resolve to walk twice round the room quietly and settle my nerves, and then I returned into the deep gulf of the huge armchair.

"Now I'll read it," I cried, after having well distended my lungs with air.

I leaned over the table; I laid my finger successively upon every letter; and without a pause, without one moment's hesitation, I read off the whole sentence aloud.

Stupefaction! Terror! I sat overwhelmed as if with a sudden deadly blow. What! That which I read had actually, really been done! A mortal man had had the audacity to penetrate! . . .

"Ah!" I cried, springing up. "But no! No! My uncle shall never know it. He would insist upon doing it too. He would want to know all about it. Ropes could not hold him, such a determined geologist as he is! He would start, he would, in spite of everything and everybody, and he would take me with him, and we should never get back. No, never! Never!"

My overexcitement was beyond all description.

"No! No! It shall not be," I declared energetically; "and as it is in my power to prevent the knowledge of it coming into the mind of my tyrant, I will do it. By dint of turning this document round and round, he too might discover the key. I will destroy it."

There was a little fire left on the hearth. I seized not only the paper but Saknussemm's parchment; with a feverish hand I was about to fling it all upon the coals and utterly destroy and abolish this dangerous secret, when the study door opened, and my uncle appeared.

V

FAMINE, THEN VICTORY, FOLLOWED BY DISMAY

I had only just time to replace the unfortunate document upon the table.

Professor Liedenbrock seemed to be greatly abstracted.

The ruling thought gave him no rest. Evidently he had gone deeply into the matter, analytically and with profound scrutiny. He had brought all the resources of his mind to bear upon it during his walk, and he had come back to apply some new combination.

He sat in his armchair, and pen in hand he began what looked very much like algebraic formula: I followed with my eyes his trembling hands, I took count of every movement. Might not some unhoped-for result come of it? I trembled, too, very unnecessarily, since the true key was in my hands, and no other would open the secret.

For three long hours my uncle worked on without a word, without lifting his head; rubbing out, beginning again, then rubbing out again, and so on a hundred times.

I knew very well that if he succeeded in setting down these letters in every possible relative position, the sentence would come out. But I knew also that twenty letters alone could form two quintillions, four hundred and thirty-two quadrillions, nine hundred and two trillions, eight billions, a hundred and seventy-six millions, six hundred and forty thousand combinations. Now, here were a hundred and thirty-two letters in this sentence, and these hundred and thirty-two letters would give a number of different sentences, each made up of at least a hundred and thirty-three figures, a number which passed far beyond all calculation or conception.

So I felt reassured as far as regarded this heroic method of solving the difficulty.

But time was passing away; night came on; the street noises ceased; my uncle, bending over his task, noticed nothing, not even Martha half opening the door; he heard not a sound, not even that excellent woman saying:

"Will not monsieur take any supper tonight?"

And poor Martha had to go away unanswered. As for me, after long resistance, I was overcome by sleep, and fell off at the end of the sofa, while uncle Liedenbrock went on calculating and rubbing out his calculations.

When I awoke next morning that indefatigable worker was still at his post. His red eyes, his pale complexion, his hair tangled between his feverish fingers, the red spots on his cheeks, revealed his desperate struggle with impossibilities, and the weariness of spirit, the mental wrestlings he must have undergone all through that unhappy night.

To tell the plain truth, I pitied him. In spite of the reproaches which I considered I had a right to lay upon him, a certain feeling of compassion was beginning to gain upon me. The poor man was so entirely taken up with his one idea that he had even forgotten how to get angry. All the strength of his feelings was concentrated upon one point alone; and as their usual vent was closed, it was to be feared lest extreme tension should give rise to an explosion sooner or later.

I might with a word have loosened the screw of the steel vice that was crushing his brain; but that word I would not speak.

Yet I was not an ill-natured fellow. Why was I dumb at such a crisis? Why so insensible to my uncle's interests?

"No, no," I repeated, "I shall not speak. He would insist upon going; nothing on earth could stop him. His imagination is a volcano, and to do that which other geologists have never done he would risk his life. I will preserve silence. I will keep the secret which mere chance has revealed to me. To discover it, would be to kill Professor Liedenbrock! Let him find it out himself if he can. I will never have it laid to my door that I led him to his destruction."

Having formed this resolution, I folded my arms and waited. But I had not reckoned upon one little incident which turned up a few hours after.

When our good Martha wanted to go to Market, she found the door locked. The big key was gone. Who could have taken it out? Assuredly, it was my uncle, when he returned the night before from his hurried walk.

Was this done on purpose? Or was it a mistake? Did he want to reduce us by famine? This seemed like going rather too far! What! should Martha and I be victims of a position of things in which we had not the smallest interest? It was a fact that a few years before this, while my uncle was working at his great classification of minerals, he was forty-eight hours without eating, and all his household were obliged to share in this scientific fast. As for me, what I remember is, that I got severe cramps in my stomach, which hardly suited the constitution of a hungry, growing lad.

Now it appeared to me as if breakfast was going to be wanting, just as supper had been the night before. Yet I resolved to be a hero, and not to be conquered by the pangs of hunger. Martha took it very seriously, and, poor woman, was very much distressed. As for me, the impossibility of leaving the house distressed me a good deal more, and for a very good reason. A caged lover's feelings may easily be imagined.

My uncle went on working, his imagination went off rambling into the ideal world of combinations; he was far away from earth, and really far away from earthly wants.

About noon hunger began to stimulate me severely. Martha had, without thinking any harm, cleared out the larder the night before, so that now there was nothing left in the house. Still I held out; I made it a point of honor.

Two o'clock struck. This was becoming ridiculous; worse than that, unbearable. I began to say to myself that I was exaggerating the importance of the document; that my uncle would surely not believe in it, that he would set it down as a mere puzzle; that if it came to the worst, we should lay violent hands on him and keep him at home if he thought on venturing on the expedition; that, after all, he might himself discover the key of the cipher, and that then I should be clear at the mere expense of my involuntary abstinence.

These reasons seemed excellent to me, though on the night before I should have rejected them with indignation; I even went so far as to condemn myself for my absurdity in having waited so long, and I finally resolved to let it all out.

I was therefore meditating a proper introduction to the matter, so as not to seem too abrupt, when the professor jumped up, clapped on his hat, and prepared to go out.

Surely he was not going out, to shut us in again! No, never!

"Uncle!" I cried.

He seemed not to hear me.

"Uncle Liedenbrock!" I cried, lifting up my voice.

"Ay," he answered like a man suddenly waking.

"Uncle, that key!"

"What key? The door key?"

"No, no!" I cried. "The key of the document."

The professor stared at me over his spectacles; no doubt he saw something unusual in the expression of my countenance; for he laid hold of my arm, and speechlessly questioned me with his eyes. Yes, never was a question more forcibly put.

I nodded my head up and down.

He shook his pityingly, as if he was dealing with a lunatic. I gave a more affirmative gesture.

His eyes glistened and sparkled with live fire, his hand was shaken threateningly.

This mute conversation at such a momentous crisis would have riveted the attention of the most indifferent. And the fact really was that I dared not speak now, so intense was the excitement for fear lest my uncle should smother me in his first joyful embraces. But he became so urgent that I was at last compelled to answer.

"Yes, that key, chance—"

"What is that you are saying?" he shouted with indescribable emotion.

"There, read that!" I said, presenting a sheet of paper on which I had written.

"But there is nothing in this," he answered, crumpling up the paper.

"No, nothing until you proceed to read from the end to the beginning."

I had not finished my sentence when the professor broke out into a cry, nay, a roar. A new revelation burst in upon him. He was transformed!

"Aha, clever Saknussemm!" he cried. "You had first written out your sentence the wrong way."

And darting upon the paper, with eyes bedimmed, and voice choked with emotion, he read the whole document from the last letter to the first.

It was conceived in the following terms:

In Sneffels Joculis craterem quem delibat
Umbra Scartaris Julii intra calendas descende,
Audax viator, et terrestre centrum attinges.
Quod feci, Arne Saknussemm.

Which bad Latin may be translated thus:

"Descend, bold traveler, into the crater of the jokul of Sneffels, which the shadow of Scartaris touches before the kalends of July, and you will attain the center of the earth; which I have done, Arne Saknussemm."

In reading this, my uncle gave a spring as if he had touched a Leyden jar. His audacity, his joy, and his convictions were magnificent to behold. He came and he went; he seized his head between both his hands; he pushed the chairs out of their places, he piled up his books; incredible as it may seem, he rattled his precious nodules of flints together; he sent a kick here, a thump there. At last his nerves calmed down, and like a man exhausted by too lavish an expenditure of vital power, he sank back exhausted into his armchair.

"What o'clock is it?" he asked after a few moments of silence.

"Three o'clock," I replied.

"Is it really? The dinner hour is past, and I did not know it. I am half dead with hunger. Come on, and after dinner—"

"Well?"

"After dinner, pack up my trunk."

"What?" I cried.

"And yours!" replied the indefatigable professor, entering the dining room.

VI

EXCITING DISCUSSIONS ABOUT AN UNPARALLELED ENTERPRISE

At these words a cold shiver ran through me. Yet I controlled myself; I even resolved to put a good face upon it. Scientific arguments alone could have any weight with Professor Liedenbrock. Now there were good ones against the practicability of such a journey. Penetrate to the center of the earth! What nonsense! But I kept my dialectic battery in reserve for a suitable opportunity, and I interested myself in the prospect of my dinner, which was not yet forthcoming.

It is no use to tell of the rage and imprecations of my uncle before the empty table. Explanations were given, Martha was set at liberty, ran off to the market, and did her part so well that in an hour afterward my hunger was appeased, and I was able to return to the contemplation of the gravity of the situation.

During all dinner time my uncle was almost merry; he indulged in some of those learned jokes which never do anybody any harm. Dessert over, he beckoned me into his study.

I obeyed; he sat at one end of his table, I at the other.

"Axel," said he very mildly; "you are a very ingenious young man, you have done me a splendid service, at a moment when, wearied out with the struggle, I was going to abandon the contest. Where should I have lost myself? None can tell. Never, my lad, shall I forget it; and you shall have your share in the glory to which your discovery will lead."

"Oh, come!" thought I. "He is in a good way. Now is the time for discussing that same glory."

"Before all things," my uncle resumed, "I enjoin you to preserve the most inviolable secrecy: you understand? There are not a few in the scientific world who envy my success, and many would be ready to undertake this enterprise, to whom our return should be the first news of it."

"Do you really think there are many people bold enough?" said I.

"Certainly; who would hesitate to acquire such renown? If that document were divulged, a whole army of geologists would be ready to rush into the footsteps of Arne Saknussemm."

"I don't feel so very sure of that, uncle," I replied; "for we have no proof of the authenticity of this document."

"What! Not of the book, inside which we have discovered it?"

"Granted. I admit that Saknussemm may have written these lines. But does it follow that he has really accomplished such a journey? And may it not be that this old parchment is intended to mislead?"

I almost regretted having uttered this last word, which dropped from me in an unguarded moment. The professor bent his shaggy brows, and I feared I had seriously compromised my own safety. Happily no great harm came of it. A smile flitted across the lip of my severe companion, and he answered:

"That is what we shall see."

"Ah!" said I, rather put out. "But do let me exhaust all the possible objections against this document."

"Speak, my boy, don't be afraid. You are quite at liberty to express your opinions. You are no longer my nephew only, but my colleague. Pray go on."

"Well, in the first place, I wish to ask what are this Jokul, this Sneffels, and this Scartaris, names which I have never heard before?"

"Nothing easier. I received not long ago a map from my friend, Augustus Petermann, at Liepzig. Nothing could be more apropos. Take down the third atlas in the second shelf in the large bookcase, series Z, plate 4."

I rose, and with the help of such precise instructions could not fail to find the required atlas. My uncle opened it and said:

"Here is one of the best maps of Iceland, that of Handersen, and I believe this will solve the worst of our difficulties."

I bent over the map.

"You see this volcanic island," said the professor; "observe that all the volcanoes are called jokuls, a word which means glacier in Icelandic, and under the high latitude of Iceland nearly all the active volcanoes discharge through beds of ice. Hence this term of jokul is applied to all the eruptive mountains in Iceland."

"Very good," said I; "but what of Sneffels?"

I was hoping that this question would be unanswerable; but I was mistaken. My uncle replied:

"Follow my finger along the west coast of Iceland. Do you see Reyjkavik, the capital? You do. Well; ascend the innumerable fjords that indent those sea-beaten shores, and stop at the sixty-fifth degree of latitude. What do you see there?"

"I see a peninsula looking like a thigh bone with the knee bone at the end of it."

"A very fair comparison, my lad. Now do you see anything upon that knee bone?"

"Yes; a mountain rising out of the sea."

"Right. That is Snæfell."

"That Snæfell?"

"It is. It is a mountain five thousand feet high, one of the most remarkable in the world, if its crater leads down to the center of the earth."

"But that is impossible," I said shrugging my shoulders, and disgusted at such a ridiculous supposition.

"Impossible?" said the professor severely. "And why, pray?"

"Because this crater is evidently filled with lava and burning rocks, and therefore—"

"But suppose it is an extinct volcano?"

"Extinct?"

"Yes; the number of active volcanoes on the surface of the globe is at the present time only about three hundred. But there is a very much larger number of extinct ones. Now, Snæfell is one of these. Since historic times there has been but one eruption of this mountain, that of 1219; from that time it has quieted down more and more, and now it is no longer reckoned among active volcanoes."

To such positive statements I could make no reply. I therefore took refuge in other dark passages of the document.

"What is the meaning of this word Scartaris, and what have the kalends of July to do with it?"

My uncle took a few minutes to consider. For one short moment I felt a ray of hope, speedily to be extinguished. For he soon answered thus:

"What is darkness to you is light to me. This proves the ingenious care with which Saknussemm guarded and defined his discovery. Sneffels, or Snæfell, has several craters. It was therefore necessary to point out which of these leads to the center of the globe. What did the Icelandic sage do? He observed that at the approach of the kalends of July, that is to say in the last days of June, one of the peaks, called Scartaris, flung its shadow down the mouth of that particular crater, and he committed that fact to his document. Could there possibly have been a more exact guide? As soon as we have arrived at the summit of Snæfell we shall have no hesitation as to the proper road to take."

Decidedly, my uncle had answered every one of my objections. I saw that his position on the old parchment was impregnable. I therefore ceased to press him upon that part of the subject, and as above all things he must be convinced, I passed on to scientific objections, which in my opinion were far more serious.

"Well, then," I said, "I am forced to admit that Saknussemm's sentence is clear, and leaves no room for doubt. I will even allow that the document bears every mark and evidence of authenticity. That learned philosopher did get to the bottom of Sneffels, he has seen the shadow of Scartaris touch the edge of the crater before the kalends of July; he may even have heard the legendary stories told in his day about that crater reaching to the center of the world; but as for reaching it himself, as for performing the journey, and returning, if he ever went, I say no—he never, never did that."

"Now for your reason?" said my uncle ironically.

"All the theories of science demonstrate such a feat to be impracticable."

"The theories say that, do they?" replied the professor in the tone of a meek disciple. "Oh! Unpleasant theories! How the theories will hinder us, won't they?"

I saw that he was only laughing at me; but I went on all the same.

"Yes; it is perfectly well known that the internal temperature rises one degree for every 70 feet in depth; now, admitting this proportion to be constant, and the radius of the earth being fifteen hundred leagues, there must be a temperature of 360,032 degrees at the center of the earth. Therefore, all the substances that compose the body of this earth must exist there in a state of incandescent gas; for the metals that most resist the action of heat, gold, and platinum, and the hardest rocks, can never be either solid or liquid under such a temperature. I have therefore good reason for asking if it is possible to penetrate through such a medium."

"So, Axel, it is the heat that troubles you?"

"Of course it is. Were we to reach a depth of thirty miles we should have arrived at the limit of the terrestrial crust, for there the temperature will be more than 2,372 degrees."

"Are you afraid of being put into a state of fusion?"

"I will leave you to decide that question," I answered rather sullenly.

"This is my decision," replied Professor Liedenbrock, putting on one of his grandest airs. "Neither you nor anybody else knows with any certainty what is going on in the interior of this globe, since not the twelve thousandth part of its radius is known; science is eminently perfectible; and every new theory is soon routed by a newer. Was it not always believed until Fourier that the temperature of the interplanetary spaces decreased perpetually? And is it not known at the present time that the greatest cold of the ethereal regions is never lower than 40 degrees below zero Fahrenheit? Why should it not be the same with the internal heat? Why should it not, at a certain depth, attain an impassable limit, instead of rising to such a point as to fuse the most infusible metals?"

As my uncle was now taking his stand upon hypotheses, of course, there was nothing to be said.

"Well, I will tell you that true savants, among them Poisson, have demonstrated that if a heat of 360,000 degrees existed in the interior of the globe, the fiery gases arising from the fused matter would acquire an elastic force which the crust of the earth would be unable to resist, and that it would explode like the plates of a bursting boiler."

"That is Poisson's opinion, my uncle, nothing more."

"Granted. But it is likewise the creed adopted by other distinguished geologists, that the interior of the globe is neither gas nor water, nor any of the heaviest minerals known, for in none of these cases would the earth weigh what it does."

"Oh, with figures you may prove anything!"

"But is it the same with facts! Is it not known that the number of volcanoes has diminished since the first days of creation? And if there is central heat may we not thence conclude that it is in process of diminution?"

"My good uncle, if you will enter into the legion of speculation, I can discuss the matter no longer."

"But I have to tell you that the highest names have come to the support of my views. Do you remember a visit paid to me by the celebrated chemist Humphry Davy in 1825?"

"Not at all, for I was not born until nineteen years afterward."

"Well, Humphry Davy did call upon me on his way through Hamburg. We were long engaged in discussing, among other problems, the hypothesis of the liquid structure of the terrestrial nucleus. We were agreed that it could not be in a liquid state, for a reason which science has never been able to confute."

"What is that reason?" I said, rather astonished.

"Because this liquid mass would be subject, like the ocean, to the lunar attraction, and therefore twice every day there would be internal tides, which, upheaving the terrestrial crust, would cause periodical earthquakes!"

"Yet it is evident that the surface of the globe has been subject to the action of fire," I replied, "and it is quite reasonable to suppose that the external crust cooled down first, while the heat took refuge down to the center."

"Quite a mistake," my uncle answered. "The earth has been heated by combustion on its surface, that is all. Its surface was composed of a great number of metals, such as potassium and sodium, which have the peculiar property of igniting at the mere contact with air and water; these metals kindled when the atmospheric vapors fell in rain upon the soil; and by and by, when the waters penetrated into the fissures of the crust of the earth, they broke out into fresh combustion with explosions and eruptions. Such was the cause of the numerous volcanoes at the origin of the earth."

"Upon my word, this is a very clever hypothesis," I exclaimed, in spite rather of myself.

"And which Humphry Davy demonstrated to me by a simple experiment. He formed a small ball of the metals which I have named, and which was a very fair representation of our globe; whenever he caused a fine dew of rain to fall upon its surface, it heaved up into little monticules, it became oxidized and formed miniature mountains; a crater broke open at one of its summits; the eruption took place, and communicated to the whole of the ball such a heat that it could not be held in the hand."

In truth, I was beginning to be shaken by the professor's arguments, besides which he gave additional weight to them by his usual ardor and fervent enthusiasm.

"You see, Axel," he added, "the condition of the terrestrial nucleus has given rise to various hypotheses among geologists; there is no proof at all for this internal heat; my opinion is that there is no such thing, it cannot be; besides we shall see for ourselves, and, like Arne Saknussemm, we shall know exactly what to hold as truth concerning this grand question."

"Very well, we *shall* see," I replied, feeling myself carried off by his contagious enthusiasm. "Yes, we shall see; that is, if it is possible to see anything there."

"And why not? May we not depend upon electric phenomena to give us light? May we not even expect light from the atmosphere, the pressure of which may render it luminous as we approach the center?"

"Yes, yes," said I; "that is possible, too."

"It is certain," exclaimed my uncle in a tone of triumph. "But silence, do you hear me? Silence upon the whole subject; and let no one get before us in this design of discovering the center of the earth."

VII

A WOMAN'S COURAGE

Thus ended this memorable séance. That conversation threw me into a fever. I came out of my uncle's study as if I had been stunned, and as if there was not air enough in all the streets of Hamburg to put me right again. I therefore made for the banks of the Elbe, where the steamer lands her passengers, which forms the communication between the city and the Hamburg railway.

Was I convinced of the truth of what I had heard? Had I not bent under the iron rule of Professor Liedenbrock? Was I to believe him in earnest in his intention to penetrate to the center of this massive globe? Had I been listening to the mad speculations of a lunatic, or to the scientific conclusions of a lofty genius? Where did truth stop? Where did error begin?

I was all adrift among a thousand contradictory hypotheses, but I could not lay hold of one.

Yet I remembered that I had been convinced, although now my enthusiasm was beginning to cool down; but I felt a desire to start at once, and not to lose time and courage by calm reflection. I had at that moment quite courage enough to strap my knapsack to my shoulders and start.

But I must confess that in another hour this unnatural excitement abated, my nerves became unstrung, and from the depths of the abysses of this earth I ascended to its surface again.

"It is quite absurd!" I cried. "There is no sense about it. No sensible young man should for a moment entertain such a proposal. The whole thing is nonexistent. I have had a bad night, I have been dreaming of horrors."

But I had followed the banks of the Elbe and passed the town. After passing the port too, I had reached the Altona road. I was led by a presentiment, soon to be realized; for shortly I espied my little Gräuben bravely returning with her light step to Hamburg.

"Gräuben!" I cried from afar off.

The young girl stopped, rather frightened perhaps to hear her name called after her on the high road. Ten yards more, and I had joined her.

"Axel!" she cried surprised. "What! Have you come to meet me? Is this why you are here, sir?"

But when she had looked upon me, Gräuben could not fail to see the uneasiness and distress of my mind.

"What is the matter?" she said, holding out her hand.

"What is the matter, Gräuben?" I cried.

In a couple of minutes my pretty Virlandaise was fully informed of the position of affairs. For a time she was silent. Did her heart palpitate as mine did? I don't know about that, but I know that her hand did not tremble in mine. We went on a hundred yards without speaking.

At last she said, "Axel!"

"My dear Gräuben."

"That will be a splendid journey!"

I gave a bound at these words.

"Yes, Axel, a journey worthy of the nephew of a savant; it is a good thing for a man to be distinguished by some great enterprise."

"What, Gräuben, won't you dissuade me from such an undertaking?"

"No, my dear Axel, and I would willingly go with you, but that a poor girl would only be in your way."

"Is that quite true?"

"It is true."

Ah! Women and young girls, how incomprehensible are your feminine hearts! When you are not the timidest, you are the bravest of creatures. Reason has nothing to do with your actions. What! Did this child encourage me in such an expedition! Would she not be afraid to join it herself? And she was driving me to it, one whom she loved!

I was disconcerted, and, if I must tell the whole truth, I was ashamed.

"Gräuben, we will see whether you will say the same thing tomorrow."

"Tomorrow, dear Axel, I will say what I say today."

Gräuben and I, hand in hand, but in silence, pursued our way. The emotions of that day were breaking my heart.

After all, I thought, the kalends of July are a long way off, and between this and then many things may take place which will cure my uncle of his desire to travel underground.

It was night when we arrived at the house in Königstrasse. I expected to find all quiet there, my uncle in bed as was his custom, and Martha giving her last touches with the feather brush.

But I had not taken into account the professor's impatience. I found him shouting—and working himself up amid a crowd of porters and messengers who were all depositing various loads in the passage. Our old servant was at her wits' end.

"Come, Axel, come, you miserable wretch," my uncle cried from as far off as he could see me. "Your boxes are not packed, and my papers are not arranged; where's the key of my carpet bag? And what have you done with my gaiters?"

I stood thunderstruck. My voice failed. Scarcely could my lips utter the words:

"Are we really going?"

"Of course, you unhappy boy! Could I have dreamed that you would have gone out for a walk instead of hurrying your preparations forward?"

"Are we to go?" I asked again, with sinking hopes.

"Yes; the day after tomorrow, early."

I could hear no more. I fled for refuge into my own little room.

All hope was now at an end. My uncle had been all the morning making purchases of a part of the tools and apparatus required for this desperate undertaking. The passage was encumbered with rope ladders, knotted cords, torches, flasks, grappling irons, alpenstocks, pickaxes, iron shod sticks, enough to load ten men.

I spent an awful night. Next morning I was called early. I had quite decided I would not open the door. But how was I to resist the sweet voice which was always music to my ears, saying, "My dear Axel?"

I came out of my room. I thought my pale countenance and my red and sleepless eyes would work upon Gräuben's sympathies and change her mind.

"Ah! My dear Axel," she said. "I see you are better. A night's rest has done you good."

"Done me good!" I exclaimed.

I rushed to the glass. Well, in fact I did look better than I had expected. I could hardly believe my own eyes.

"Axel," she said, "I have had a long talk with my guardian. He is a bold philosopher, a man of immense courage, and you must remember that his blood flows in your veins. He has confided to me his plans, his hopes, and why and how he hopes to attain his object. He will no doubt succeed. My dear Axel, it is a grand thing to devote yourself to science! What honor will fall upon Herr Liedenbrock, and so be reflected upon his companion! When you return, Axel, you will be a man, his equal, free to speak and to act independently, and free to—"

The dear girl only finished this sentence by blushing. Her words revived me. Yet I refused to believe we should start. I drew Gräuben into the professor's study.

"Uncle, is it true that we are to go?"

"Why do you doubt?"

"Well, I don't doubt," I said, not to vex him; "but, I ask, what need is there to hurry?"

"Time, time, flying with irreparable rapidity."

"But it is only the 16th May, and until the end of June—"

"What, you monument of ignorance! Do you think you can get to Iceland in a couple of days? If you had not deserted me like a fool I should have taken you to the Copenhagen office, to Liffender & Co., and you would have learned then that there is only one trip every month from Copenhagen to Reykjavik, on the 22nd."

"Well?"

"Well, if we waited for the 22nd June we should be too late to see the shadow of Scartaris touch the crater of Sneffels. Therefore we must get to Copenhagen as fast as we can to secure our passage. Go and pack up."

There was no reply to this. I went up to my room. Gräuben followed me. She undertook to pack up all things necessary for my voyage. She was no more moved than if I had been starting for a little trip to Lübeck or Heligoland. Her little hands moved without haste. She talked quietly. She supplied me with sensible reasons for our expedition. She delighted me, and yet I was angry with her. Now and then I felt I ought to break out into a passion, but she took no notice and went on her way as methodically as ever.

Finally the last strap was buckled; I came downstairs. All that day the philosophical instrument makers and the electricians kept coming and going. Martha was distracted.

"Is master mad?" she asked.

I nodded my head.

"And is he going to take you with him?"

I nodded again.

"Where to?"

I pointed with my finger downward.

"Down into the cellar?" cried the old servant.

"No," I said. "Lower down than that."

Night came. But I knew nothing about the lapse of time.

"Tomorrow morning at six precisely," my uncle decreed, "we start."

At ten o'clock I fell upon my bed, a dead lump of inert matter. All through the night terror had hold of me. I spent it dreaming of abysses. I was a prey to delirium. I felt myself grasped by the professor's sinewy hand, dragged along, hurled down, shattered into little bits. I dropped down unfathomable precipices with the accelerating velocity of bodies falling through space. My life had become an endless fall. I awoke at five with shattered nerves, trembling and weary. I came downstairs. My uncle was at table, devouring his breakfast. I stared at him with horror and disgust. But dear Gräuben was there; so I said nothing, and could eat nothing.

At half-past five there was a rattle of wheels outside. A large carriage was there to take us to the Altona railway station. It was soon piled up with my uncle's multifarious preparations.

"Where's your box?" he cried.

"It is ready," I replied, with faltering voice.

"Then make haste down, or we shall lose the train."

It was now manifestly impossible to maintain the struggle against destiny. I went up again to my room, and rolling my portmanteaus downstairs I darted after him.

At that moment my uncle was solemnly investing Gräuben with the reins of government. My pretty Virlandaise was as calm and collected as was her wont. She kissed her guardian; but could not restrain a tear in touching my cheek with her gentle lips.

"Gräuben!" I murmured.

"Go, my dear Axel, go! I am now your betrothed; and when you come back I will be your wife."

I pressed her in my arms and took my place in the carriage. Martha and the young girl, standing at the door, waved their last farewell. Then the horses, roused by the driver's whistling, darted off at a gallop on the road to Altona.

VIII

SERIOUS PREPARATIONS FOR VERTICAL DESCENT

Altona, which is but a suburb of Hamburg, is the terminus of the Kiel railway, which was to carry us to the Belts. In twenty minutes we were in Holstein.

At half-past six the carriage stopped at the station; my uncle's numerous packages, his voluminous *impedimenta*, were unloaded, removed, labeled, weighed, put into the luggage vans, and at seven we were seated face-to-face in our compartment. The whistle sounded, the engine started, we were off.

Was I resigned? No, not yet. Yet the cool morning air and the scenes on the road, rapidly changed by the swiftness of the train, drew me away somewhat from my sad reflections.

As for the professor's reflections, they went far in advance of the swiftest express. We were alone in the carriage, but we sat in silence. My uncle examined all his pockets and his traveling bag with the minutest care. I saw that he had not forgotten the smallest matter of detail.

Among other documents, a sheet of paper, carefully folded, bore the heading of the Danish consulate with the signature of W. Christiensen, consul at Hamburg and the professor's friend. With this we possessed the proper introductions to the governor of Iceland.

I also observed the famous document most carefully laid up in a secret pocket in his portfolio. I bestowed a malediction upon it, and then proceeded to examine the country.

It was a very long succession of uninteresting loamy and fertile flats, a very easy country for the construction of railways, and propitious for the laying-down of these direct level lines so dear to railway companies.

I had no time to get tired of the monotony; for in three hours we stopped at Kiel, close to the sea.

The luggage being labeled for Copenhagen, we had no occasion to look after it. Yet the professor watched every article with jealous vigilance, until all were safe on board. There they disappeared in the hold.

My uncle, notwithstanding his hurry, had so well calculated the relations between the train and the steamer that we had a whole day to spare. The steamer *Ellenora* did not start until night. Thence sprang a feverish state of excitement in which the impatient irascible traveler devoted to perdition the railway directors and the steamboat companies and the governments which allowed such intolerable slowness. I was obliged to act chorus to him when he attacked the captain of the *Ellenora* upon this subject. The captain disposed of us summarily.

At Kiel, as elsewhere, we must do something to while away the time. What with walking on the verdant shores of the bay within which nestles the little town, exploring the thick woods which make it look like a nest embowered among thick foliage, admiring the villas, each provided with a little bathing house, and moving about and grumbling, at last ten o'clock came.

The heavy coils of smoke from the *Ellenora*'s funnel unrolled in the sky, the bridge shook with the quivering of the struggling steam; we were on board, and owners for the time of two berths, one over the other, in the only saloon cabin on board.

At a quarter past the moorings were loosed and the throbbing steamer pursued her way over the dark waters of the Great Belt.

The night was dark; there was a sharp breeze and a rough sea, a few lights appeared on shore through the thick darkness; later on, I cannot tell when, a dazzling light from some lighthouse threw a bright stream of fire along the waves; and this is all I can remember of this first portion of our sail.

At seven in the morning we landed at Korsor, a small town on the west coast of Zealand. There we were transferred from the boat to another line of railway, which took us by just as flat a country as the plain of Holstein.

Three hours' traveling brought us to the capital of Denmark. My uncle had not shut his eyes all night. In his impatience I believe he was trying to accelerate the train with his feet.

At last he discerned a stretch of sea.

"The Sound!" he cried.

At our left was a huge building that looked like a hospital.

"That's a lunatic asylum," said one of or traveling companions.

Very good! thought I, just the place we want to end our days in; and great as it is, that asylum is not big enough to contain all Professor Liedenbrock's madness!

At ten in the morning, at last, we set our feet in Copenhagen; the luggage was put upon a carriage and taken with ourselves to the Phoenix Hotel in Breda Gate. This took half an hour, for the station is out of the town. Then my uncle, after a hasty toilet, dragged me after him. The porter at the hotel could speak German and English; but the professor, as a polyglot, questioned him in good Danish, and it was in the same language that that personage directed him to the Museum of Northern Antiquities.

The curator of this curious establishment, in which wonders are gathered together out of which the ancient history of the country might be reconstructed by means of its stone weapons, its cups and its jewels, was a learned savant, the friend of the Danish consul at Hamburg, Professor Thomsen.

My uncle had a cordial letter of introduction to him. As a general rule one savant greets another with coolness. But here the case was different. M. Thomsen, like a good friend, gave Professor Liedenbrock a cordial greeting, and he even vouchsafed the same kindness to his nephew. It is hardly necessary to say the secret was sacredly kept from the excellent curator; we were simply disinterested travelers visiting Iceland out of harmless curiosity.

M. Thomsen placed his services at our disposal, and we visited the quays with the object of finding out the next vessel to sail.

I was yet in hopes that there would be no means of getting to Iceland. But there was no such luck. A small Danish schooner, the *Valkyria*, was to set sail for Reykjavik on the 2nd of June. The captain, M. Bjarne, was on board. His intending passenger was so joyful that he almost squeezed his hands till they ached. That good man was rather surprised at his energy. To him it seemed a very simple thing to go to Iceland, as that was his business; but to my uncle it was sublime. The worthy captain took advantage of his enthusiasm to charge double fares; but we did not trouble ourselves about mere trifles.

"You must be on board on Tuesday, at seven in the morning," said Captain Bjarne, after having pocketed more dollars than were his due.

Then we thanked M. Thomsen for his kindness, and we returned to the Phoenix Hotel.

"It's all right, it's all right," my uncle repeated. "How fortunate we are to have found this boat ready for sailing. Now let us have some breakfast and go about the town."

We went first to Kongens-nye-Torw, an irregular square in which are two innocent-looking guns, which need not alarm anyone. Close by, at No. 5, there was a French "restaurant," kept by a cook of the name of Vincent, where we had an ample breakfast for four marks each (2s. 4d.).

Then I took a childish pleasure in exploring the city; my uncle let me take him with me, but he took notice of nothing, neither the insignificant king's palace, nor the pretty seventeenth-century bridge, which spans the canal before the museum, nor that immense cenotaph of Thorwaldsen's, adorned with horrible mural painting, and containing within it a collection of the sculptor's works, nor in a fine park the toylike chateau of Rosenberg, nor the beautiful renaissance edifice of the Exchange, nor its spire composed of the twisted tails of four bronze dragons, nor the great windmill on the ramparts, whose huge arms dilated in the sea breeze like the sails of a ship.

What delicious walks we should have had together, my pretty Virlandaise and I, along the harbor where the two-deckers and the frigate slept peaceably by the red roofing of the warehouse, by the green banks of the strait, through the deep shades of the trees among which the fort is half concealed, where the guns are thrusting out their black throats between branches of alder and willow.

But, alas! Gräuben was far away; and I never hoped to see her again.

But if my uncle felt no attraction toward these romantic scenes he was very much struck with the aspect of a certain church spire situated in the island of Amak, which forms the southwest quarter of Copenhagen.

I was ordered to direct my feet that way; I embarked on a small steamer which plies on the canals, and in a few minutes she touched the quay of the dockyard.

After crossing a few narrow streets where some convicts, in trousers half yellow and half gray, were at work under the orders of the gangers, we arrived at the Vor Frelsers Kirk. There was nothing remarkable about the church; but there was a reason why its tall spire had attracted the professor's attention. Starting from the top of the tower, an external staircase wound around the spire, the spirals circling up into the sky.

"Let us get to the top," said my uncle.

"I shall be dizzy," I said.

"The more reason why we should go up; we must get used to it."

"But—"

"Come, I tell you; don't waste our time."

I had to obey. A keeper who lived at the other end of the street handed us the key, and the ascent began.

My uncle went ahead with a light step. I followed him not without alarm, for my head was very apt to feel dizzy; I possessed neither the equilibrium of an eagle nor his fearless nature.

As long as we were protected on the inside of the winding staircase up the tower, all was well enough; but after toiling up a hundred and fifty steps the fresh air came to salute my face, and we were on the leads of the tower. There the aerial staircase began its gyrations, only guarded by a thin iron rail, and the narrowing steps seemed to ascend into infinite space!

"Never shall I be able to do it," I said.

"Don't be a coward; come up, sir," said my uncle with the coldest cruelty.

I had to follow, clutching at every step. The keen air made me giddy; I felt the spire rocking with every gust of wind; my knees began to fail; soon I was crawling on my knees, then creeping on my stomach; I closed my eyes; I seemed to be lost in space.

At last I reached the apex, with the assistance of my uncle dragging me up by the collar.

"Look down!" he cried. "Look down well! You must take a lesson in abysses."

I opened my eyes. I saw houses squashed flat as if they had all fallen down from the skies; a smoke fog seemed to drown them. Over my head ragged clouds were drifting past, and by an optical inversion they seemed stationary, while the steeple, the ball, and I were all spinning along with fantastic speed. Far away on one side was the green country, on the other the sea sparkled, bathed in sunlight. The Sound stretched away to Elsinore, dotted with a few white sails, like seagulls' wings; and in the misty east and away to the northeast lay outstretched the faintly shadowed shores of Sweden. All this immensity of space whirled and wavered, fluctuating beneath my eyes.

But I was compelled to rise, to stand up, to look. My first lesson in dizziness lasted an hour. When I got permission to come down and feel the solid street pavements, I was afflicted with severe lumbago.

"Tomorrow we will do it again," said the professor.

And it was so; for five days in succession, I was obliged to undergo this antivertiginous exercise; and whether I would or not, I made some improvement in the art of "lofty contemplations."

IX

ICELAND! BUT WHAT NEXT?

The day for our departure arrived. The day before it our kind friend M. Thomsen brought us letters of introduction to Count Trampe, the governor of Iceland, M. Picturssen, the bishop's suffragan, and M. Finsen, mayor of Reykjavik. My uncle expressed his gratitude by tremendous compressions of both his hands.

On the 2nd, at six in the evening, all our precious baggage being safely on board the *Valkyria*, the captain took us into a very narrow cabin.

"Is the wind favorable?" my uncle asked.

"Excellent," replied Captain Bjarne; "a sou'easter. We shall pass down the Sound full speed, with all sails set."

In a few minutes the schooner, under her mizzen, brigantine, topsail, and topgallant sail, loosed from her moorings and made full sail through the straits. In an hour the capital of Denmark seemed to sink below the distant waves, and the *Valkyria* was skirting the coast by Elsinore. In my nervous frame of mind I expected to see the ghost of Hamlet wandering on the legendary castle terrace.

"Sublime madman!" I said. "No doubt you would approve of our expedition. Perhaps you would keep us company to the center of the globe, to find the solution of your eternal doubts."

But there was no ghostly shape upon the ancient walls. Indeed, the castle is much younger than the heroic prince of Denmark. It now answers the purpose of a sumptuous lodge for the doorkeeper of the straits of the Sound, before which every year there pass fifteen thousand ships of all nations.

The castle of Kronsberg soon disappeared in the mist, as well as the tower of Helsingborg, built on the Swedish coast, and the schooner passed lightly on her way urged by the breezes of the Cattegat.

The *Valkyria* was a splendid sailer, but on a sailing vessel you can place no dependence. She was taking to Reykjavik coal, household goods, earthenware, woolen clothing, and a cargo of wheat. The crew consisted of five men, all Danes.

"How long will the passage take?" my uncle asked.

"Ten days," the captain replied, "if we don't meet a nor'wester in passing the Faroes."

"But are you not subject to considerable delays?"

"No, M. Liedenbrock, don't be uneasy, we shall get there in very good time."

At evening the schooner doubled the Skaw at the northern point of Denmark, in the night passed the Skager Rack, skirted Norway by Cape Lindness, and entered the North Sea.

In two days more we sighted the coast of Scotland near Peterhead, and the *Valkyria* turned her lead toward the Faroe Islands, passing between the Orkneys and Shetlands.

Soon the schooner encountered the great Atlantic swell; she had to tack against the north wind, and reached the Faroes only with some difficulty. On the 8th the captain made out Myganness, the southernmost of these islands, and from that moment took a straight course for Cape Portland, the most southerly point of Iceland.

The passage was marked by nothing unusual. I bore the troubles of the sea pretty well; my uncle, to his own intense disgust, and his greater shame, was ill all through the voyage.

He therefore was unable to converse with the captain about Snæfell, the way to get to it, the facilities for transport, he was obliged to put off these inquiries until his arrival, and spent all his time at full length in his cabin, of which the timbers creaked and shook with every pitch she took. It must be confessed he was not undeserving of his punishment.

On the 11th we reached Cape Portland. The clear open weather gave us a good view of Myrdals jokul, which overhangs it. The cape is merely a low hill with steep sides, standing lonely by the beach.

The *Valkyria* kept at some distance from the coast, taking a westerly course amid great shoals of whales and sharks. Soon we came in sight of an enormous perforated rock, through which the sea dashed furiously. The Westman islets seemed to rise out of the ocean like a group of rocks in a liquid plain. From that time the schooner took a wide berth and swept at a great distance round Cape Rejkianess, which forms the western point of Iceland.

The rough sea prevented my uncle from coming on deck to admire these shattered and surf-beaten coasts.

Forty-eight hours after, coming out of a storm which forced the schooner to scud under bare poles, we sighted east of us the beacon on Cape Skagen, where dangerous rocks extend far away seaward. An Icelandic pilot came on board, and in three hours the *Valkyria* dropped her anchor before Reykjavik, in Faxa Bay.

The professor at last emerged from his cabin, rather pale and wretched-looking, but still full of enthusiasm, and with ardent satisfaction shining in his eyes.

The population of the town, wonderfully interested in the arrival of a vessel from which everyone expected something, formed in groups upon the quay.

My uncle left in haste his floating prison, or rather hospital. But before quitting the deck of the schooner he dragged me forward, and pointing with outstretched finger north of the bay at a distant mountain terminating in a double peak, a pair of cones covered with perpetual snow, he cried:

"Snæfell! Snæfell!"

Then recommending me, by an impressive gesture, to keep silence, he went into the boat which awaited him. I followed, and presently we were treading the soil of Iceland.

The first man we saw was a good-looking fellow enough, in a general's uniform. Yet he was not a general but a magistrate, the governor of the island, M. le Baron Trampe himself. The professor was soon aware of the presence he was in. He delivered him his letters from Copenhagen, and then followed a short conversation in the Danish language, the purport of which I was quite ignorant of, and for a very good reason. But the result of this first conversation was, that Baron Trampe placed himself entirely at the service of Professor Liedenbrock.

My uncle was just as courteously received by the mayor, M. Finsen, whose appearance was as military, and disposition and office as pacific, as the governor's.

As for the bishop's suffragan, M. Picturssen, he was at that moment engaged on an episcopal visitation in the north. For the time we must be resigned to wait for the honor of being presented to him. But M. Fridrikssen, professor of natural sciences at the school of Reykjavik, was a delightful man, and his friendship became very precious to me. This modest philosopher spoke only Danish and Latin. He came to proffer me his good offices in the language of Horace, and I felt that we were made to understand each other. In fact he was the only person in Iceland with whom I could converse at all.

This good-natured gentleman made over to us two of the three rooms which his house contained, and we were soon installed in it with all our luggage, the abundance of which rather astonished the good people of Reykjavik.

"Well, Axel," said my uncle, "we are getting on, and now the worst is over."

"The worst!" I said, astonished.

"To be sure, now we have nothing to do but go down."

"Oh, if that is all, you are quite right; but after all, when we have gone down, we shall have to get up again, I suppose?"

"Oh, I don't trouble myself about that. Come, there's no time to lose; I am going to the library. Perhaps there is some manuscript of Saknussemm's there, and I should be glad to consult it."

"Well, while you are there I will go into the town. Won't you?"

"Oh, that is very uninteresting to me. It is not what is upon this island, but what is underneath, that interests me."

I went out, and wandered wherever chance took me.

It would not be easy to lose your way in Reykjavik. I was therefore under no necessity to inquire the road, which exposes one to mistakes when the only medium of intercourse is gesture.

The town extends along a low and marshy level, between two hills. An immense bed of lava bounds it on one side, and falls gently toward the sea. On the other extends the vast bay of Faxa, shut in at the north by the enormous glacier of the Snæfell, and of which the *Valkyria* was for the time the only occupant. Usually the English and French conservators of fisheries moor in this bay, but just then they were cruising about the western coasts of the island.

The longest of the only two streets that Reykjavik possesses was parallel with the beach. Here live the merchants and traders, in wooden cabins made of red planks set horizontally; the other street, running west, ends at the little lake between the house of the bishop and other noncommercial people.

I had soon explored these melancholy ways; here and there I got a glimpse of faded turf, looking like a worn-out bit of carpet, or some appearance of a kitchen garden, the sparse vegetables of which (potatoes, cabbages, and lettuces) would have figured appropriately upon a Lilliputian table. A few sickly wallflowers were trying to enjoy the air and sunshine.

About the middle of the noncommercial street I found the public cemetery, enclosed with a mud wall, and where there seemed plenty of room.

Then a few steps brought me to the governor's house, a hut compared with the town hall of Hamburg, a palace in comparison with the cabins of the Icelandic population.

Between the little lake and the town the church is built in the Protestant style, of calcined stones extracted out of the volcanoes by *their* own labor and at *their* own expense; in high westerly winds it was manifest that the red tiles of the roof would be scattered in the air, to the great danger of the faithful worshipers.

On a neighboring hill I perceived the national school, where, as I was informed later by our host, were taught Hebrew, English, French, and Danish, four languages of which, with shame I confess it, I don't know a single word; after an examination I should have had to stand last of the forty scholars educated at this little college, and I should have been held unworthy to sleep along with them in one of those little double closets, where more delicate youths would have died of suffocation the very first night.

In three hours I had seen not only the town but its environs. The general aspect was wonderfully dull. No trees, and scarcely any vegetation. Everywhere bare rocks, signs of volcanic action. The Icelandic huts are made of earth and turf, and the walls slope inward; they rather resemble roofs placed on the ground. But then these roofs are meadows of comparative fertility. Thanks to the internal heat, the grass grows on them to some degree of perfection. It is carefully mown in the hay season; if it were not, the horses would come to pasture on these green abodes.

In my excursion I met but few people. On returning to the main street I found the greater part of the population busied in drying, salting, and putting on board codfish, their chief export. The men looked like robust but heavy, blond Germans with pensive eyes, conscious of being far removed from their fellow creatures, poor exiles relegated to this land of ice, poor creatures who should have been Esquimaux, since nature had condemned them to live only just outside the Arctic Circle! In vain did I try to detect a smile upon their lips; sometimes by a spasmodic and involuntary contraction of the muscles they seemed to laugh, but they never smiled.

Their costume consisted of a coarse jacket of black woolen cloth called in Scandinavian lands a "vadmel," a hat with a very broad brim, trousers with a narrow edge of red, and a bit of leather rolled round the foot for shoes.

The women looked as sad and as resigned as the men; their faces were agreeable but expressionless, and they wore gowns and petticoats of dark "vadmel"; as maidens, they wore over their braided hair a little knitted brown cap; when married, they put around their heads a colored handkerchief, crowned with a peak of white linen.

After a good walk I returned to M. Fridrikssen's house, where I found my uncle already in his host's company.

X

INTERESTING CONVERSATIONS WITH ICELANDIC SAVANTS

Dinner was ready. Professor Liedenbrock devoured his portion voraciously, for his compulsory fast on board had converted his stomach into a vast unfathomable gulf. There was nothing remarkable in the meal itself; but the hospitality of our host, more Danish than Icelandic, reminded me of the heroes of old. It was evident that we were more at home than he was himself.

The conversation was carried on in the vernacular tongue, which my uncle mixed with German and M. Fridrikssen with Latin for my benefit. It turned upon scientific questions as befits philosophers; but Professor Liedenbrock was excessively reserved, and at every sentence spoke to me with his eyes, enjoining the most absolute silence upon our plans.

In the first place M. Fridrikssen wanted to know what success my uncle had had at the library.

"Your library! Why, there is nothing but a few tattered books upon almost deserted shelves."

"Indeed!" replied M. Fridrikssen. "Why, we possess eight thousand volumes, many of them valuable and scarce, works in the old Scandinavian language, and we have all the novelties that Copenhagen sends us every year."

"Where do you keep your eight thousand volumes? For my part—"

"Oh, M. Liedenbrock, they are all over the country. In this icy region we are fond of study. There is not a farmer nor a fisherman that cannot read and does not read. Our principle is that books, instead of growing moldy behind an iron grating, should be worn out under the eyes of many readers. Therefore, these volumes are passed from one to another, read over and over, referred to again and again; and it often happens that they find their way back to their shelves only after an absence of a year or two."

"And in the meantime," said my uncle rather spitefully, "strangers—"

"Well, what would you have? Foreigners have their libraries at home, and the first essential for laboring people is that they should be educated. I repeat to you the love of reading runs in Icelandic blood. In 1816 we founded a prosperous literary society; learned strangers think themselves honored in becoming members of it. It publishes books which educate our fellow countrymen, and do the country great service. If you will consent to be a corresponding member, Herr Liedenbrock, you will be giving us great pleasure."

My uncle, who had already joined about a hundred learned societies, accepted with a grace, which evidently touched M. Fridrikssen.

"Now," said he, "will you be kind enough to tell me what books you hoped to find in our library, and I may perhaps enable you to consult them?"

My uncle's eyes and mine met. He hesitated. This direct question went to the root of the matter. But after a moment's reflection he decided on speaking.

"Monsieur Fridrikssen, I wished to know if among your ancient books you possessed any of the works of Arne Saknussemm?"

"Arne Saknussemm!" replied the Reykjavik professor. "You mean that learned sixteenth-century savant, a naturalist, a chemist, and a traveler?"

"Just so!"

"One of the glories of Icelandic literature and science?"

"That's the man."

"An illustrious man anywhere!"

"Quite so."

"And whose courage was equal to his genius!"

"I see that you know him well."

My uncle was bathed in delight at hearing his hero thus described. He feasted his eyes upon M. Fridrikssen's face.

"Well," he cried, "where are his works?"

"His works, we have them not."

"What—not in Iceland?"

"They are neither in Iceland nor anywhere else."

"Why is that?"

"Because Arne Saknussemm was persecuted for heresy, and in 1573 his books were burned by the hands of the common hangman."

"Very good! Excellent!" cried my uncle, to the great scandal of the professor of natural history.

"What!" he cried.

"Yes, yes; now it is all clear, now it is all unraveled; and I see why Saknussemm, put into the Index Expurgatorius, and compelled to hide the discoveries made by his genius, was obliged to bury in an incomprehensible cryptogram the secret—"

"What secret?" asked M. Fridrikssen, starting.

"Oh, just a secret which—" my uncle stammered.

"Have you some private document in your possession?" asked our host.

"No; I was only supposing a case."

"Oh, very well," answered M. Fridrikssen, who was kind enough not to pursue the subject when he had noticed the embarrassment of his friend. "I hope you will not leave our island until you have seen some of its mineralogical wealth."

"Certainly," replied my uncle; "but I am rather late; or have not others been here before me?"

"Yes, Herr Liedenbrock; the labors of MM. Olafsen and Povelsen, pursued by order of the king, the researches of Troïl the scientific mission of MM. Gaimard and Robert on the French corvette *La Recherche*,* and lately the observations of scientific men who came in the *Reine Hortense*, have added materially to our knowledge of Iceland. But I assure you there is plenty left."

"Do you think so?" said my uncle, pretending to look very modest, and trying to hide the curiosity was flashing out of his eyes.

"Oh, yes; how many mountains, glaciers, and volcanoes there are to study, which are as yet but imperfectly known! Then, without going any further, that mountain in the horizon. That is Snæfell."

"Ah!" said my uncle, as coolly as he was able. "Is that Snæfell?"

"Yes; one of the most curious volcanoes, and the crater of which has scarcely ever been visited."

"Is it extinct?"

"Oh, yes; more than five hundred years."

* The *Recherche* was sent out in 1835 by Admiral Duperré to learn the fate of the lost expedition of M. de Blosseville in the *Lilloise*, which has never been heard of.

"Well," replied my uncle, who was frantically locking his legs together to keep himself from jumping up in the air, "that is where I mean to begin my geological studies, there on that Seffel—Fessel—what do you call it?"

"Snæfell," replied the excellent M. Fridrikssen.

This part of the conversation was in Latin; I had understood every word of it, and I could hardly conceal my amusement at seeing my uncle trying to keep down the excitement and satisfaction which were brimming over in every limb and every feature. He tried hard to put on an innocent little expression of simplicity; but it looked like a diabolical grin.

"Yes," said he, "your words decide me. We will try to scale that Snæfell; perhaps even we may pursue our studies in its crater!"

"I am very sorry," said M. Fridrikssen, "that my engagements will not allow me to absent myself, or I would have accompanied you myself with both pleasure and profit."

"Oh, no, no!" replied my uncle with great animation. "We would not disturb anyone for the world, M. Fridrikssen. Still, I thank you with all my heart: the company of such a talented man would have been very serviceable, but the duties of your profession—"

I am glad to think that our host, in the innocence of his Icelandic soul, was blind to the transparent artifices of my uncle.

"I very much approve of your beginning with that volcano, M. Liedenbrock. You will gather a harvest of interesting observations. But, tell me, how do you expect to get to the peninsula of Snæfell?"

"By sea, crossing the bay. That's the most direct way."

"No doubt; but it is impossible."

"Why?"

"Because we don't possess a single boat at Reykjavik."

"You don't mean to say so?"

"You will have to go by land, following the shore. It will be longer, but more interesting."

"Very well, then; and now I shall have to see about a guide."

"I have one to offer you."

"A safe, intelligent man."

"Yes; an inhabitant of that peninsula. He is an eiderdown hunter, and very clever. He speaks Danish perfectly."

"When can I see him?"

"Tomorrow, if you like."

"Why not today?"

"Because he won't be here till tomorrow."

"Tomorrow, then," added my uncle with a sigh.

This momentous conversation ended in a few minutes with warm acknowledgments paid by the German to the Icelandic professor. At this dinner my uncle had just elicited important facts, among others, the history of Saknussemm, the reason of the mysterious document, that his host would not accompany him in his expedition, and that the very next day a guide would be waiting upon him.

XI

A GUIDE FOUND TO THE CENTER OF THE EARTH

In the evening I took a short walk on the beach and returned at night to my plank-bed, where I slept soundly all night.

When I awoke I heard my uncle talking at a great rate in the next room. I immediately dressed and joined him.

He was conversing in the Danish language with a tall man, of robust build. This fine fellow must have been possessed of great strength. His eyes, set in a large and ingenuous face, seemed to me very intelligent; they were of a dreamy sea-blue. Long hair, which would have been called red even in England, fell in long meshes upon his broad shoulders. The movements of this native were lithe and supple; but he made little use of his arms in speaking, like a man who knew nothing or cared nothing about the language of gestures. His whole appearance bespoke perfect calmness and self-possession, not indolence but tranquility. It was felt at once that he would be beholden to nobody, that he worked for his own convenience, and that nothing in this world could astonish or disturb his philosophic calmness.

I caught the shades of this Icelander's character by the way in which he listened to the impassioned flow of words which fell from the professor. He stood with arms crossed, perfectly unmoved by my uncle's incessant gesticulations. A negative was expressed by a slow movement of the head from left to right, an affirmative by a slight bend, so slight that his long hair scarcely moved. He carried economy of motion even to parsimony.

Certainly I should never have dreamed in looking at this man that he was a hunter; he did not look likely to frighten his game, nor did he seem as if he would even get near it. But the mystery was explained when M. Fridrikssen informed me that this tranquil personage was only a hunter of the eider duck, whose under plumage constitutes the chief wealth of the island. This is the celebrated eiderdown, and it requires no great rapidity of movement to get it.

Early in summer the female, a very pretty bird, goes to build her nest among the rocks of the fjords with which the coast is fringed. After building the nest she feathers it with down plucked from her own breast. Immediately the hunter, or rather the trader, comes and robs the nest, and the female recommences her work. This goes on as long as she has any down left. When she has stripped herself bare, the male takes his turn to pluck himself. But as the coarse and hard plumage of the male has no commercial value, the hunter does not take the trouble to rob the nest of this; the female therefore lays her eggs in the spoils of her mate, the young are hatched, and next year the harvest begins again.

Now, as the eider duck does not select steep cliffs for her nest, but rather the smooth terraced rocks which slope to the sea, the Icelandic hunter might exercise his calling without any inconvenient exertion. He was a farmer who was not obliged either to sow or reap his harvest, but merely to gather it in.

This grave, phlegmatic, and silent individual was called Hans Bjelke; and he came recommended by M. Fridrikssen. He was our future guide. His manners were a singular contrast with my uncle's.

Nevertheless, they soon came to understand each other. Neither looked at the amount of the payment: the one was ready to accept whatever was offered; the other was ready to give whatever was demanded. Never was bargain more readily concluded.

The result of the treaty was, that Hans engaged on his part to conduct us to the village of Stapi, on the south shore of the Snæfell peninsula, at the very foot of the volcano. By land this would be about twenty-two miles, to be done, said my uncle, in two days.

But when he learned that the Danish mile was 24,000 feet long, he was obliged to modify his calculations and allow seven or eight days for the march.

Four horses were to be placed at our disposal—two to carry him and me, two for the baggage. Hans, as was his custom, would go on foot. He knew all that part of the coast perfectly, and promised to take us the shortest way.

His engagement was not to terminate with our arrival at Stapi; he was to continue in my uncle's service for the whole period of his scientific researches, for the remuneration of three rixdales a week (about twelve shillings), but it was an express article of the covenant that his wages should be counted out to him every Saturday at six o'clock in the evening, which, according to him, was one indispensable part of the engagement.

The start was fixed for the 16th of June. My uncle wanted to pay the hunter a portion in advance, but he refused with one word:

"Efter," said he.

"After," said the professor for my edification.

The treaty concluded, Hans silently withdrew.

"A famous fellow," cried my uncle; "but he little thinks of the marvelous part he has to play in the future."

"So he is to go with us as far as—"

"As far as the center of the earth, Axel."

Forty-eight hours were left before our departure; to my great regret I had to employ them in preparations; for all our ingenuity was required to pack every article to the best advantage; instruments here, arms there, tools in this package, provisions in that: four sets of packages in all.

The instruments were:

1. An Eigel's centigrade thermometer, graduated up to 150 degrees (302 degrees Fahrenheit), which seemed to me too much or too little. Too much if the internal heat was to rise so high, for in this case we should be baked, not enough to measure the temperature of springs or any matter in a state of fusion.

2. An aneroid barometer, to indicate extreme pressures of the atmosphere. An ordinary barometer would not have answered the purpose, as the pressure would increase during our descent to a point which the mercurial barometer would not register.

3. A chronometer, made by Boissonnas, jun., of Geneva, accurately set to the meridian of Hamburg.

4. Two compasses, viz., a common compass and a dipping needle.

5. A night glass.

6. Two of Ruhmkorff's apparatus, which, by means of an electric current, supplied a safe and handy portable light.*

The arms consisted of two of Purdy's rifles and two brace of pistols. But what did we want arms for? We had neither savages nor wild beasts to fear, I supposed. But my uncle seemed to believe in his arsenal as in his instruments, and more especially in a considerable quantity of gun cotton, which is unaffected by moisture, and the explosive force of which exceeds that of gunpowder.

The tools comprised two pickaxes, two spades, a silk ropeladder, three iron-tipped sticks, a hatchet, a hammer, a dozen wedges and iron spikes, and a long knotted rope. Now this was a large load, for the ladder was 300 feet long.

And there were provisions too: this was not a large parcel, but it was comforting to know that of essence of beef and biscuits there were six months' consumption. Spirits were the only liquid, and of water we took none; but we had flasks, and my uncle depended on springs from which to fill them. Whatever objections I hazarded as to their quality, temperature, and even absence, remained ineffectual.

* Ruhmkorff's apparatus consists of a Bunsen pile worked with bichromate of potash, which makes no smell; an induction coil carries the electricity generated by the pile into communication with a lantern of peculiar construction; in this lantern there is a spiral glass tube from which the air has been excluded, and in which remains only a residuum of carbonic acid gas or of nitrogen. When the apparatus is put in action this gas becomes luminous, producing a white steady light. The pile and coil are placed in a leathern bag which the traveler carries over his shoulders; the lantern outside of the bag throws sufficient light into deep darkness; it enables one to venture without fear of explosions into the midst of the most inflammable gases, and is not extinguished even in the deepest waters. M. Ruhmkorff is a learned and most ingenious man of science; his great discovery is his induction coil, which produces a powerful stream of electricity. He obtained in 1864 the quinquennial prize of 50,000 francs reserved by the French government for the most ingenious application of electricity.

To complete the exact inventory of all our traveling accompaniments, I must not forget a pocket medicine chest, containing blunt scissors, splints for broken limbs, a piece of tape of unbleached linen, bandages and compresses, lint, a lancet for bleeding, all dreadful articles to take with one. Then there was a row of phials containing dextrine, alcoholic ether, liquid acetate of lead, vinegar, and ammonia drugs which afforded me no comfort. Finally, all the articles needful to supply Ruhmkorff's apparatus.

My uncle did not forget a supply of tobacco, coarse grained powder, and amadou, nor a leathern belt in which he carried a sufficient quantity of gold, silver, and paper money. Six pairs of boots and shoes, made waterproof with a composition of india rubber and naphtha, were packed among the tools.

"Clothed, shod, and equipped like this," said my uncle, "there is no telling how far we may go."

The 14th was wholly spent in arranging all our different articles. In the evening we dined with Baron Tramps; the mayor of Reykjavik and Dr. Hyaltalin, the first medical man of the place, being of the party. M. Fridrikssen was not there. I learned afterward that he and the governor disagreed upon some question of administration, and did not speak to each other. I therefore knew not a single word of all that was said at this semiofficial dinner; but I could not help noticing that my uncle talked the whole time.

On the 15th our preparations were all made. Our host gave the professor very great pleasure by presenting him with a map of Iceland far more complete than that of Hendersen. It was the map of M. Olaf Nikolas Olsen, in the proportion of 1 to 480,000 of the actual size of the island, and published by the Icelandic Literary Society. It was a precious document for a mineralogist.

Our last evening was spent in intimate conversation with M. Fridrikssen, with whom I felt the liveliest sympathy; then, after the talk, succeeded, for me, at any rate, a disturbed and restless night.

At five in the morning I was awoke by the neighing and pawing of four horses under my window. I dressed hastily and came down into the street. Hans was finishing our packing, almost as it were without moving a limb; and yet he did his work cleverly. My uncle made more noise than execution, and the guide seemed to pay very little attention to his energetic directions.

At six o'clock our preparations were over. M. Fridrikssen shook hands with us. My uncle thanked him heartily for his extreme kindness. I constructed a few fine Latin sentences to express my cordial farewell. Then we bestrode our steeds and with his last adieu M. Fridrikssen treated me to a line of Virgil eminently applicable to such uncertain wanderers as we were likely to be:

Et quacumque viam dedent fortuna sequamur.

Wherever fortune clears a way,
Thither our ready footsteps stray.

XII

A BARREN LAND

We had started under a sky overcast but calm. There was no fear of heat, none of disastrous rain. It was just the weather for tourists.

The pleasure of riding on horseback over an unknown country made me easy to be pleased at our first start. I threw myself wholly into the pleasure of the trip, and enjoyed the feeling of freedom and satisfied desire. I was beginning to take a real share in the enterprise.

"Besides," I said to myself, "where's the risk? Here we are traveling all through a most interesting country! We are about to climb a very remarkable mountain; at the worst we are going to scramble down an extinct crater. It is evident that Saknussemm did nothing more than this. As for a passage leading to the center of the globe, it is mere rubbish! Perfectly impossible! Very well, then; let us get all the good we can out of this expedition, and don't let us haggle about the chances."

This reasoning having settled my mind, we got out of Reykjavik.

Hans moved steadily on, keeping ahead of us at an even, smooth, and rapid pace. The baggage horses followed him without giving any trouble. Then came my uncle and myself, looking not so very ill-mounted on our small but hardy animals.

Iceland is one of the largest islands in Europe. Its surface is 14,000 square miles, and it contains but 16,000 inhabitants. Geographers have divided it into four quarters, and we were crossing diagonally the southwest quarter, called the "Sudvester Fjordungr."

On leaving Reykjavik Hans took us by the seashore. We passed lean pastures which were trying very hard, but in vain, to look green; yellow came out best. The rugged peaks of the trachyte rocks presented faint outlines on the eastern horizon; at times a few patches of snow, concentrating the vague light, glittered upon the slopes of the distant mountains; certain peaks, boldly uprising, passed through the gray clouds, and reappeared above the moving mists, like breakers emerging in the heavens.

Often these chains of barren rocks made a dip toward the sea, and encroached upon the scanty pasturage: but there was always enough room to pass. Besides, our horses instinctively chose the easiest places without ever slackening their pace. My uncle was refused even the satisfaction of stirring up his beast with whip or voice. He had no excuse for being impatient. I could not help smiling to see so tall a man on so small a pony, and as his long legs nearly touched the ground he looked like a six-legged centaur.

"Good horse! Good horse!" he kept saying. "You will see, Axel, that there is no more sagacious animal than the Icelandic horse. He is stopped by neither snow, nor storm, nor impassable roads, nor rocks, glaciers, or anything. He is courageous, sober, and surefooted. He never makes a false step, never shies. If there is a river or fjord to cross (and we shall meet with many) you will see him plunge in at once, just as if he were amphibious, and gain the opposite bank. But we must not hurry him; we must let him have his way, and we shall get on at the rate of thirty miles a day."

"*We* may; but how about our guide?"

"Oh, never mind him. People like him get over the ground without a thought. There is so little action in this man that he will never get tired; and besides, if he wants it, he shall have my horse. I shall get cramped if I don't have a little action. The arms are all right, but the legs want exercise."

We were advancing at a rapid pace. The country was already almost a desert. Here and there was a lonely farm, called a boër built either of wood, or of sods, or of pieces of lava, looking like a poor beggar by the wayside. These ruinous huts seemed to solicit charity from passersby; and on very small provocation we should have given alms for the relief of the poor inmates. In this country there were no roads and paths, and the poor vegetation, however slow, would soon efface the rare travelers' footsteps.

Yet this part of the province, at a very small distance from the capital, is reckoned among the inhabited and cultivated portions of Iceland. What, then, must other tracts be, more desert than this desert? In the first half mile we had not seen one farmer standing before his cabin door, nor one shepherd tending a flock less wild than himself, nothing but a few cows and sheep left to themselves. What then would be those convulsed regions upon which we were advancing, regions subject to the dire phenomena of eruptions, the offspring of volcanic explosions and subterranean convulsions?

We were to know them before long, but on consulting Olsen's map, I saw that they would be avoided by winding along the seashore. In fact, the great plutonic action is confined to the central portion of the island; there, rocks of the trappean and volcanic class, including trachyte, basalt, and tuffs and agglomerates associated with streams of lava, have made this a land of supernatural horrors. I had no idea of the spectacle which was awaiting us in the peninsula of Snæfell, where these ruins of a fiery nature have formed a frightful chaos.

In two hours from Reykjavik we arrived at the burgh of Gufunes, called

Aolkirkja, or principal church. There was nothing remarkable here but a few houses, scarcely enough for a German hamlet.

Hans stopped here half an hour. He shared with us our frugal breakfast; answering my uncle's questions about the road and our resting place that night with merely yes or no, except when he said "Gardär."

I consulted the map to see where Gardär was. I saw there was a small town of that name on the banks of the Hvalfjord, four miles from Reykjavik. I showed it to my uncle.

"Four miles only!" he exclaimed. "Four miles out of twenty-eight. What a nice little walk!"

He was about to make an observation to the guide, who without answering resumed his place at the head, and went on his way.

Three hours later, still treading on the colorless grass of the pasture land, we had to work round the Kolla fjord, a longer way but an easier one than across that inlet. We soon entered into a "pingstaoer," or parish, called Ejulberg, from whose steeple twelve o'clock would have struck, if Icelandic churches were rich enough to possess clocks. But they are like the parishioners who have no watches and do without.

There our horses were baited; then taking the narrow path to left between a chain of hills and the sea, they carried us to our next stage, the aolkirkja of Brantär and one mile farther on, to Saurboër "Annexia," a chapel of ease built on the south shore of the Hvalfjord.

It was now four o'clock, and we had gone four Icelandic miles, or twenty-four English miles.

In that place the fjord was at least three English miles wide; the waves rolled with a rushing din upon the sharp-pointed rocks; this inlet was confined between walls of rock, precipices crowned by sharp peaks 2,000 feet high, and remarkable for the brown strata which separated the beds of reddish tuff. However much I might respect the intelligence of our quadrupeds, I hardly cared to put it to the test by trusting myself to it on horseback across an arm of the sea.

If they are as intelligent as they are said to be, I thought, they won't try it. In any case, I will tax my intelligence to direct theirs.

But my uncle would not wait. He spurred on to the edge. His steed lowered his head to examine the nearest waves and stopped. My uncle, who had an instinct of his own, too, applied pressure, and was again refused by the animal significantly shaking his head. Then followed strong language, and the whip; but the brute answered these arguments with kicks and endeavors to throw his rider. At last the clever little pony, with a bend of his knees, started from under the professor's legs, and left him standing upon two boulders on the shore just like the colossus of Rhodes.

"Confounded brute!" cried the unhorsed horseman, suddenly degraded into a pedestrian, just as ashamed as a cavalry officer degraded to a foot soldier.

"*Färja*," said the guide, touching his shoulder.

"What! A boat?"

"*Der*," replied Hans, pointing to one.

"Yes," I cried; "there is a boat."

"Why did not you say so then? Well, let us go on."

"*Tidvatten*," said the guide.

"What is he saying?"

"He says tide," said my uncle, translating the Danish word.

"No doubt we must wait for the tide."

"*Förbida*," said my uncle.

"*Ja*," replied Hans.

My uncle stamped with his foot, while the horses went on to the boat.

I perfectly understood the necessity of abiding a particular moment of the tide to undertake the crossing of the fjord, when, the sea having reached its greatest height, it should be slack water. Then the ebb and flow have no sensible effect, and the boat does not risk being carried either to the bottom or out to sea.

That favorable moment arrived only with six o'clock; when my uncle, myself, the guide, two other passengers, and the four horses trusted ourselves to a somewhat fragile raft. Accustomed as I was to the swift and sure steamers on the Elbe, I found the oars of the rowers rather a slow means of propulsion. It took us more than an hour to cross the fjord; but the passage was effected without any mishap.

In another half hour we had reached the aolkirkja of Gardär.

XIII

HOSPITALITY UNDER THE ARCTIC CIRCLE

It ought to have been nighttime, but under the 65th parallel there was nothing surprising in the nocturnal polar light. In Iceland during the months of June and July the sun does not set.

But the temperature was much lower. I was cold and more hungry than cold. Welcome was the sight of the boër, which was hospitably opened to receive us.

It was a peasant's house, but in point of hospitality it was equal to a king's. On our arrival the master came with outstretched hands, and without more ceremony he beckoned us to follow him.

To accompany him down the long, narrow, dark passage would have been impossible. Therefore, we followed, as he bid us. The building was constructed of roughly squared timbers, with rooms on both sides, four in number, all opening out into the one passage: these were the kitchen, the weaving shop, the badstofa, or family sleeping room, and the visitors' room, which was the best of all. My uncle, whose height had not been thought of in building the house, of course hit his head several times against the beams that projected from the ceilings.

We were introduced into our apartment, a large room with a floor of earth stamped hard down, and lighted by a window, the panes of which were formed of sheep's bladder, not admitting too much light. The sleeping accommodation consisted of dry litter, thrown into two wooden frames painted red, and ornamented with Icelandic sentences. I was hardly expecting so much comfort; the only discomfort proceeded from the strong odor of dried fish, hung meat, and sour milk, of which my nose made bitter complaints.

When we had laid aside our traveling wraps, the voice of the host was heard inviting us to the kitchen, the only room where a fire was lighted even in the severest cold.

My uncle lost no time in obeying the friendly call, nor was I slack in following.

The kitchen chimney was constructed on the ancient pattern; in the middle of the room was a stone for a hearth, over it in the roof a hole to let the smoke escape. The kitchen was also a dining room.

At our entrance the host, as if he had never seen us, greeted us with the word "*Sællvertu*," which means "be happy," and came and kissed us on the cheek.

After him his wife pronounced the same words, accompanied with the same ceremonial; then the two placing their hands upon their hearts, inclined profoundly before us.

I hasten to inform the reader that this Icelandic lady was the mother of nineteen children, all, big and little, swarming in the midst of the dense wreaths of smoke with which the fire on the hearth filled the chamber. Every moment I noticed a fair-haired and rather melancholy face peeping out of the rolling volumes of smoke—they were a perfect cluster of unwashed angels.

My uncle and I treated this little tribe with kindness; and in a very short time we each had three or four of these brats on our shoulders, as many on our laps, and the rest between our knees. Those who could speak kept repeating "*Sællvertu*," in every conceivable tone; those that could not speak made up for that want by shrill cries.

This concert was brought to a close by the announcement of dinner. At that moment our hunter returned, who had been seeing his horses provided for; that is to say, he had economically let them loose in the fields, where the poor beasts had to content themselves with the scanty moss they could pull off the rocks and a few meager seaweeds, and the next day they would not fail to come of themselves and resume the labors of the previous day.

"*Sællvertu,*" said Hans.

Then calmly, automatically, and dispassionately he kissed the host, the hostess, and their nineteen children.

This ceremony over, we sat at table, twenty-four in number, and therefore one upon another. The luckiest had only two urchins upon their knees.

But silence reigned in all this little world at the arrival of the soup, and the national taciturnity resumed its empire even over the children. The host served out to us a soup made of lichen and by no means unpleasant, then an immense piece of dried fish floating in butter rancid with twenty years' keeping, and, therefore, according to Icelandic gastronomy, much preferable to fresh butter. Along with this, we had "skye," a sort of clotted milk, with biscuits, and a liquid prepared from juniper berries; for beverage we had a thin milk mixed with water, called in this country "blanda." It is not for me to decide whether this diet is wholesome or not; all I can say is that I was desperately hungry, and that at dessert I swallowed to the very last gulp of a thick broth made from buckwheat.

As soon as the meal was over the children disappeared, and their elders gathered round the peat fire, which also burned such miscellaneous fuel as briars, cow dung, and fish bones. After this little pinch of warmth the different groups retired to their respective rooms. Our hostess hospitably offered us her assistance in undressing, according to Icelandic usage; but on our gracefully declining, she insisted no longer, and I was able at last to curl myself up in my mossy bed.

At five next morning we bade our host farewell, my uncle with difficulty persuading him to accept a proper remuneration; and Hans signaled the start.

At a hundred yards from Gardär the soil began to change its aspect; it became boggy and less favorable to progress. On our right the chain of mountains was indefinitely prolonged like an immense system of natural fortifications, of which we were following the counterscarp, or lesser steep; often we were met by streams, which we had to ford with great care, not to wet our packages.

The desert became wider and more hideous; yet from time to time we seemed to descry a human figure that fled at our approach, sometimes a sharp turn would bring us suddenly within a short distance of one of these specters, and I was filled with loathing at the sight of a huge deformed head, the skin shining and hairless, and repulsive sores visible through the gaps in the poor creature's wretched rags.

The unhappy being forebore to approach us and offer his misshapen hand. He fled away, but not before Hans had saluted him with the customary "*Sællvertu.*"

"*Spetelsk*," said he.

"A leper!" my uncle repeated.

This word produced a repulsive effect. The horrible disease of leprosy is too common in Iceland; it is not contagious, but hereditary, and lepers are forbidden to marry.

These apparitions were not cheerful, and did not throw any charm over the less and less attractive landscapes. The last tufts of grass had disappeared from beneath our feet. Not a tree was to be seen, unless we except a few dwarf birches as low as brushwood. Not an animal but a few wandering ponies that their owners would not feed. Sometimes we could see a hawk balancing himself on his wings under the gray cloud, and then darting away south with rapid flight. I felt melancholy under this savage aspect of nature, and my thoughts went away to the cheerful scenes I had left in the far south.

We had to cross a few narrow fjords, and at last quite a wide gulf; the tide, then high, allowed us to pass over without delay, and to reach the hamlet of Alftanes, one mile beyond.

That evening, after having forded two rivers full of trout and pike, called Alfa and Heta, we were obliged to spend the night in a deserted building worthy to be haunted by all the elfins of Scandinavia. The ice king certainly held court here, and gave us all night long samples of what he could do.

No particular event marked the next day. Bogs, dead levels, melancholy desert tracks, wherever we traveled. By nightfall we had accomplished half our journey, and we lay at Krösolbt.

On the 19th of June, for about a mile, that is an Icelandic mile, we walked upon hardened lava; this ground is called in the country "hraun"; the writhen surface presented the appearance of distorted, twisted cables, sometimes stretched in length, sometimes contorted together; an immense torrent, once liquid, now solid, ran from the nearest mountains, now extinct volcanoes, but the ruins around revealed the violence of the past eruptions. Yet here and there were a few jets of steam from hot springs.

We had no time to watch these phenomena; we had to proceed on our way. Soon at the foot of the mountains the boggy land reappeared, intersected by little lakes. Our route now lay westward; we had turned the great bay of Faxa, and the twin peaks of Snæfell rose white into the cloudy sky at the distance of at least five miles.

The horses did their duty well, no difficulties stopped them in their steady career. I was getting tired; but my uncle was as firm and straight as he was at our first start. I could not help admiring his persistence, as well as the hunter's, who treated our expedition like a mere promenade.

June 20. At six p.m. we reached Büdir, a village on the seashore; and the guide there claiming his due, my uncle settled with him. It was Hans's own family, that is, his uncles and cousins, who gave us hospitality; we were kindly received, and without taxing too much the goodness of these folks, I would willingly have tarried here to recruit after my fatigues. But my uncle, who wanted no recruiting, would not hear of it, and the next morning we had to bestride our beasts again.

The soil told of the neighborhood of the mountain, whose granite foundations rose from the earth like the knotted roots of some huge oak. We were rounding the immense base of the volcano. The professor hardly took his eyes off it. He tossed up his arms and seemed to defy it, and to declare, "There stands the giant that I shall conquer." After about four hours' walking the horses stopped of their own accord at the door of the priest's house at Stapi.

XIV

BUT ARCTICS CAN BE INHOSPITABLE, TOO

Stapi is a village consisting of about thirty huts, built of lava, at the south side of the base of the volcano. It extends along the inner edge of a small fjord, enclosed between basaltic walls of the strangest construction.

Basalt is a brownish rock of igneous origin. It assumes regular forms, the arrangement of which is often very surprising. Here nature had done her work geometrically, with square and compass and plummet. Everywhere else her art consists alone in throwing down huge masses together in disorder. You see cones imperfectly formed, irregular pyramids, with a fantastic disarrangement of lines; but here, as if to exhibit an example of regularity, though in advance of the very earliest architects, she has created a severely simple order of architecture, never surpassed either by the splendors of Babylon or the wonders of Greece.

I had heard of the Giant's Causeway in Ireland, and Fingal's Cave in Staffa, one of the Hebrides; but I had never yet seen a basaltic formation.

At Stapi I beheld this phenomenon in all its beauty.

The wall that confined the fjord, like all the coast of the peninsula, was composed of a series of vertical columns thirty feet high. These straight shafts, of fair proportions, supported an architrave of horizontal slabs, the overhanging portion of which formed a semiarch over the sea. At intervals, under this natural shelter, there spread out vaulted entrances in beautiful curves, into which the waves came dashing with foam and spray. A few shafts of basalt, torn from their hold by the fury of tempests, lay along the soil like remains of an ancient temple, in ruins forever fresh, and over which centuries passed without leaving a trace of age upon them.

This was our last stage upon the earth. Hans had exhibited great intelligence, and it gave me some little comfort to think then that he was not going to leave us.

On arriving at the door of the rector's house, which was not different from the others, I saw a man shoeing a horse, hammer in hand, and with a leathern apron on.

"*Sællvertu*," said the hunter.

"*God dag*," said the blacksmith in good Danish.

"*Kyrkoherde*," said Hans, turning round to my uncle.

"The rector," repeated the professor. "It seems, Axel, that this good man is the rector."

Our guide in the meanwhile was making the "kyrkoherde" aware of the position of things; when the latter, suspending his labors for a moment, uttered a sound no doubt understood between horses and farriers, and immediately a tall and ugly hag appeared from the hut. She must have been six feet at the least. I was in great alarm lest she should treat me to the Icelandic kiss; but there was no occasion to fear, nor did she do the honors at all too gracefully.

The visitors' room seemed to me the worst in the whole cabin. It was close, dirty, and evil-smelling. But we had to be content. The rector did not to go in for antique hospitality. Very far from it. Before the day was over I saw that we had to do with a blacksmith, a fisherman, a hunter, a joiner, but not at all with a minister of the Gospel. To be sure, it was a weekday; perhaps on a Sunday he made amends.

I don't mean to say anything against these poor priests, who after all are very wretched. They receive from the Danish government a ridiculously small pittance, and they get from the parish the fourth part of the tithe, which does not come to sixty marks a year (about £4). Hence the necessity to work for their livelihood; but after fishing, hunting, and shoeing horses for any length of time, one soon gets into the ways and manners of fishermen, hunters, and farriers, and other rather rude and uncultivated people; and that evening I found out that temperance was not among the virtues that distinguished my host.

My uncle soon discovered what sort of a man he had to do with; instead of a good and learned man he found a rude and coarse peasant. He therefore resolved to commence the grand expedition at once, and to leave this inhospitable parsonage. He cared nothing about fatigue, and resolved to spend some days upon the mountain.

The preparations for our departure were therefore made the very day after our arrival at Stapi. Hans hired the services of three Icelanders to do the duty of the horses in the transport of the burdens; but as soon as we had arrived at the crater these natives were to turn back and leave us to our own devices. This was to be clearly understood.

My uncle now took the opportunity to explain to Hans that it was his intention to explore the interior of the volcano to its farthest limits.

Hans merely nodded. There or elsewhere, down in the bowels of the earth, or anywhere on the surface, all was alike to him. For my own part the incidents of the journey had hitherto kept me amused, and made me forgetful of coming evils; but now my fears again were beginning to get the better of me. But what could I do? The place to resist the professor would have been Hamburg, not the foot of Snæfell.

One thought, above all others, harassed and alarmed me; it was one calculated to shake firmer nerves than mine.

Now, thought I, here we are, about to climb Snæfell. Very good. We will explore the crater. Very good, too, others have done as much without dying for it. But that is not all. If there *is* a way to penetrate into the very bowels of the island, if that ill-advised Saknussemm has told a true tale, we shall lose our way amid the deep subterranean passages of this volcano. Now, there is no proof that Snæfell is extinct. Who can assure us that an eruption is not brewing at this very moment? Does it follow that because the monster has slept since 1229 he must therefore never awake again? And if he wakes up presently, where shall we be?

It was worthwhile debating this question, and I did debate it. I could not sleep for dreaming about eruptions. Now, the part of ejected scoriae and ashes seemed to my mind a very rough one to act.

So, at last, when I could hold out no longer, I resolved to lay the case before my uncle, as prudently and as cautiously as possible, just under the form of an almost impossible hypothesis.

I went to him. I communicated my fears to him, and drew back a step to give him room for the explosion which I knew must follow. But I was mistaken.

"I was thinking of that," he replied with great simplicity.

What could those words mean? Was he actually going to listen to reason? Was he contemplating the abandonment of his plans? This was too good to be true.

After a few moments' silence, during which I dared not question him, he resumed:

"I was thinking of that. Ever since we arrived at Stapi I have been occupied with the important question you have just opened, for we must not be guilty of imprudence."

"No, indeed!" I replied with forcible emphasis.

"For six hundred years Snæfell has been dumb; but he may speak again. Now, eruptions are always preceded by certain well-known phenomena. I have therefore examined the natives, I have studied external appearances, and I can assure you, Axel, that there will be no eruption."

At this positive affirmation I stood amazed and speechless.

"You don't doubt my word?" said my uncle. "Well, follow me."

I obeyed like an automaton. Coming out from the priest's house, the professor took a straight road, which, through an opening in the basaltic wall, led away from the sea. We were soon in the open country, if one may give that name to a vast extent of mounds of volcanic products. This tract seemed crushed under a rain of enormous ejected rocks of trap, basalt, granite, and all kinds of igneous rocks.

Here and there I could see puffs and jets of steam curling up into the air, called in Icelandic "reykir," issuing from thermal springs, and indicating by their motion the volcanic energy underneath. This seemed to justify my fears: But I fell from the height of my newborn hopes when my uncle said:

"You see all these volumes of steam, Axel; well, they demonstrate that we have nothing to fear from the fury of a volcanic eruption."

"Am I to believe that?" I cried.

"Understand this clearly," added the professor. "At the approach of an eruption these jets would redouble their activity, but disappear altogether during the period of the eruption. For the elastic fluids, being no longer under pressure, go off by way of the crater instead of escaping by their usual passages through the fissures in the soil. Therefore, if these vapors remain in their usual condition, if they display no augmentation of force, and if you add to this the observation that the wind and rain are not ceasing and being replaced by a still and heavy atmosphere, then you may affirm that no eruption is preparing."

"But—"

"No more; that is sufficient. When science has uttered her voice, let babblers hold their peace."

I returned to the parsonage, very crestfallen. My uncle had beaten me with the weapons of science. Still I had one hope left, and this was that when we had reached the bottom of the crater it would be impossible, for want of a passage, to go deeper, in spite of all the Saknussemm's in Iceland.

I spent that whole night in one constant nightmare; in the heart of a volcano, and from the deepest depths of the earth I saw myself tossed up among the interplanetary spaces under the form of an eruptive rock.

The next day, June 23, Hans was awaiting us with his companions carrying provisions, tools, and instruments; two iron-pointed sticks, two rifles, and two shot belts were for my uncle and myself. Hans, as a cautious man, had added to our luggage a leathern bottle full of water, which, with that in our flasks, would ensure us a supply of water for eight days.

It was nine in the morning. The priest and his tall Megaera were awaiting us at the door. We supposed they were standing there to bid us a kind farewell. But the farewell was put in the unexpected form of a heavy bill, in which everything was charged, even to the very air we breathed in the pastoral house, infected as it was. This worthy couple were fleecing us just as a Swiss innkeeper might have done, and estimated their imperfect hospitality at the highest price.

My uncle paid without a remark: a man who is starting for the center of the earth need not be particular about a few rix dollars.

This point being settled, Hans gave the signal, and we soon left Stapi behind us.

XV

SNÆFELL AT LAST

Snæfell is 5,000 feet high. Its double cone forms the limit of a trachytic belt which stands out distinctly in the mountain system of the island. From our starting point we could see the two peaks boldly projected against the dark gray sky; I could see an enormous cap of snow coming low down upon the giant's brow.

We walked in single file, headed by the hunter, who ascended by narrow tracks, where two could not have gone abreast. There was therefore no room for conversation.

After we had passed the basaltic wall of the fjord of Stapi we passed over a vegetable fibrous peat bog, left from the ancient vegetation of this peninsula. The vast quantity of this unworked fuel would be sufficient to warm the whole population of Iceland for a century; this vast turbary measured in certain ravines had in many places a depth of seventy feet, and presented layers of carbonized remains of vegetation alternating with thinner layers of tufaceous pumice.

As a true nephew of the professor Liedenbrock, and in spite of my dismal prospects, I could not help observing with interest the mineralogical curiosities which lay about me as in a vast museum, and I constructed for myself a complete geological account of Iceland.

This most curious island has evidently been projected from the bottom of the sea at a comparatively recent date. Possibly, it may still be subject to gradual elevation. If this is the case, its origin may well be attributed to subterranean fires. Therefore, in this case, the theory of Sir Humphry Davy, Saknussemm's document, and my uncle's theories would all go off in smoke. This hypothesis led me to examine with more attention the appearance of the surface, and I soon arrived at a conclusion as to the nature of the forces which presided at its birth.

Iceland, which is entirely devoid of alluvial soil, is wholly composed of volcanic tufa, that is to say, an agglomeration of porous rocks and stones. Before the volcanoes broke out it consisted of trap rocks slowly upraised to the level of the sea by the action of central forces. The internal fires had not yet forced their way through.

But at a later period a wide chasm formed diagonally from southwest to northeast, through which was gradually forced out the trachyte which was to form a mountain chain. No violence accompanied this change; the matter thrown out was in vast quantities, and the liquid material oozing out from the abysses of the earth slowly spread in extensive plains or in hillocky masses. To this period belong the feldspar, syenites, and porphyries.

But with the help of this outflow the thickness of the crust of the island increased materially, and therefore also its powers of resistance. It may easily be conceived what vast quantities of elastic gases, what masses of molten matter accumulated beneath its solid surface while no exit was practicable after the cooling of the trachytic crust. Therefore a time would come when the elastic and explosive forces of the imprisoned gases would upheave this ponderous cover and drive out for themselves openings through tall chimneys. Hence then the volcano would distend and lift up the crust, and then burst through a crater suddenly formed at the summit or thinnest part of the volcano.

To the eruption succeeded other volcanic phenomena. Through the outlets now made first escaped the ejected basalt of which the plain we had just left presented such marvelous specimens. We were moving over gray rocks of dense and massive formation, which in cooling had formed into hexagonal prisms. Everywhere around us we saw truncated cones, formerly so many fiery mouths.

After the exhaustion of the basalt, the volcano, the power of which grew by the extinction of the lesser craters, supplied an egress to lava, ashes, and scoriae, of which I could see lengthened screes streaming down the sides of the mountain like flowing hair.

Such was the succession of phenomena which produced Iceland, all arising from the action of internal fire; and to suppose that the mass within did not still exist in a state of liquid incandescence was absurd; and nothing could surpass the absurdity of fancying that it was possible to reach the earth's center.

So I felt a little comforted as we advanced to the assault of Snæfell.

The way was growing more and more arduous, the ascent steeper and steeper; the loose fragments of rock trembled beneath us, and the utmost care was needed to avoid dangerous falls.

Hans went on as quietly as if he were on level ground; sometimes he disappeared altogether behind the huge blocks, then a shrill whistle would direct us on our way to him. Sometimes he would halt, pick up a few bits of stone, build them up into a recognizable form, and thus made landmarks to guide us in our way back. A very wise precaution in itself, but, as things turned out, quite useless.

Three hours' fatiguing march had only brought us to the base of the mountain. There Hans bid us come to a halt, and a hasty breakfast was served out. My uncle swallowed two mouthfuls at a time to get on faster. But, whether he liked it or not, this was a rest as well as a breakfast hour and he had to wait till it pleased our guide to move on, which came to pass in an hour. The three Icelanders, just as taciturn as their comrade the hunter, never spoke, and ate their breakfasts in silence.

We were now beginning to scale the steep sides of Snæfell. Its snowy summit, by an optical illusion not infrequent in mountains, seemed close to us, and yet how many weary hours it took to reach it! The stones, adhering by no soil or fibrous roots of vegetation, rolled away from under our feet, and rushed down the precipice below with the swiftness of an avalanche.

At some places the flanks of the mountain formed an angle with the horizon of at least 36 degrees; it was impossible to climb them, and these stony cliffs had to be tacked round, not without great difficulty. Then we helped each other with our sticks.

I must admit that my uncle kept as close to me as he could; he never lost sight of me, and in many straits his arm furnished me with a powerful support. He himself seemed to possess an instinct for equilibrium, for he never stumbled. The Icelanders, though burdened with our loads, climbed with the agility of mountaineers.

To judge by the distant appearance of the summit of Snæfell, it would have seemed too steep to ascend on our side. Fortunately, after an hour of fatigue and athletic exercises, in the midst of the vast surface of snow presented by the hollow between the two peaks, a kind of staircase appeared unexpectedly, which greatly facilitated our ascent. It was formed by one of those torrents of stones flung up by the eruptions, called "sting" by the Icelanders. If this torrent had not been arrested in its fall by the formation of the sides of the mountain, it would have gone on to the sea and formed more islands.

Such as it was, it did us good service. The steepness increased, but these stone steps allowed us to rise with facility, and even with such rapidity that, having rested for a moment while my companions continued their ascent, I perceived them already reduced by distance to microscopic dimensions.

At seven we had ascended the two thousand steps of this grand staircase, and we had attained a bulge in the mountain, a kind of bed on which rested the cone proper of the crater.

Three thousand two hundred feet below us stretched the sea. We had passed the limit of perpetual snow, which, on account of the moisture of the climate, is at a greater elevation in Iceland than the high latitude would give reason to suppose. The cold was excessively keen. The wind was blowing violently. I was exhausted. The professor saw that my limbs were refusing to perform their office, and in spite of his impatience he decided on stopping. He therefore spoke to the hunter, who shook his head, saying:

"*Ofvanför.*"

"It seems we must go higher," said my uncle.

Then he asked Hans for his reason.

"*Mistour,*" replied the guide.

"*Ja Mistour,*" said one of the Icelanders in a tone of alarm.

"What does that word mean?" I asked uneasily.

"Look!" said my uncle.

I looked down upon the plain. An immense column of pulverized pumice, sand, and dust was rising with a whirling circular motion like a waterspout; the wind was lashing it onto that side of Snæfell where we were holding on; this dense veil, hung across the sun, threw a deep shadow over the mountain. If that huge revolving pillar sloped down, it would involve us in its whirling eddies. This phenomenon, which is not infrequent when the wind blows from the glaciers, is called in Icelandic "mistour."

"*Hastigt! Hastigt!*" cried our guide.

Without knowing Danish I understood at once that we must follow Hans at the top of our speed. He began to circle round the cone of the crater, but in a diagonal direction so as to facilitate our progress. Presently the dust storm fell upon the mountain, which quivered under the shock; the loose stones, caught with the irresistible blasts of wind, flew about in a perfect hail as in an eruption. Happily we were on the opposite side, and sheltered from all harm. But for the precaution of our guide, our mangled bodies, torn and pounded into fragments, would have been carried afar like the ruins hurled along by some unknown meteor.

Yet Hans did not think it prudent to spend the night upon the sides of the cone. We continued our zigzag climb. The fifteen hundred remaining feet took us five hours to clear; the circuitous route, the diagonal and the counter marches, must have measured at least three leagues. I could stand it no longer. I was yielding to the effects of hunger and cold. The rarefied air scarcely gave play to the action of my lungs.

At last, at eleven in the sunlit night, the summit of Snæfell was reached, and before going in for shelter into the crater I had time to observe the midnight sun, at his lowest point, gilding with his pale rays the island that slept at my feet.

XVI

BOLDLY DOWN THE CRATER

Supper was rapidly devoured, and the little company housed themselves as best they could. The bed was hard, the shelter not very substantial, and our position an anxious one, at five thousand feet above the sea level. Yet I slept particularly well; it was one of the best nights I had ever had, and I did not even dream.

Next morning we awoke half frozen by the sharp keen air, but with the light of a splendid sun. I rose from my granite bed and went out to enjoy the magnificent spectacle that lay unrolled before me.

I stood on the very summit of the southernmost of Snæfell's peaks. The range of the eye extended over the whole island. By an optical law which obtains at all great heights, the shores seemed raised and the center depressed. It seemed as if one of Helbesmer's raised maps lay at my feet. I could see deep valleys intersecting each other in every direction, precipices like low walls, lakes reduced to ponds, rivers abbreviated into streams. On my right were numberless glaciers and innumerable peaks, some plumed with feathery clouds of smoke. The undulating surface of these endless mountains, crested with sheets of snow, reminded one of a stormy sea. If I looked westward, there the ocean lay spread out in all its magnificence, like a mere continuation of those flocklike summits. The eye could hardly tell where the snowy ridges ended and the foaming waves began.

I was thus steeped in the marvelous ecstasy which all high summits develop in the mind; and now without giddiness, for I was beginning to be accustomed to these sublime aspects of nature. My dazzled eyes were bathed in the bright flood of the solar rays. I was forgetting where and who I was, to live the life of elves and sylphs, the fanciful creation of Scandinavian superstitions. I felt intoxicated with the sublime pleasure of lofty elevations without thinking of the profound abysses into which I was shortly to be plunged. But I was brought back to the realities of things by the arrival of Hans and the professor, who joined me on the summit.

My uncle pointed out to me in the far west a light steam or mist, a semblance of land, which bounded the distant horizon of waters.

"Greenland!" said he.

"Greenland?" I cried.

"Yes; we are only thirty-five leagues from it; and during thaws the white bears, borne by the ice fields from the north, are carried even into Iceland. But never mind that. Here we are at the top of Snæfell and here are two peaks, one north and one south. Hans will tell us the name of that on which we are now standing."

The question being put, Hans replied:

"Scartaris."

My uncle shot a triumphant glance at me.

"Now for the crater!" he cried.

The crater of Snæfell resembled an inverted cone, the opening of which might be half a league in diameter. Its depth appeared to be about two thousand feet. Imagine the aspect of such a reservoir, brim full and running over with liquid fire amid the rolling thunder. The bottom of the funnel was about 250 feet in circuit, so that the gentle slope allowed its lower brim to be reached without much difficulty. Involuntarily I compared the whole crater to an enormous erected mortar, and the comparison put me in a terrible fright.

"What madness," I thought, "to go down into a mortar, perhaps a loaded mortar, to be shot up into the air at a moment's notice!"

But I did not try to back out of it. Hans with perfect coolness resumed the lead, and I followed him without a word.

In order to facilitate the descent, Hans wound his way down the cone by a spiral path. Our route lay amid eruptive rocks, some of which, shaken out of their loosened beds, rushed bounding down the abyss, and in their fall awoke echoes remarkable for their loud and well-defined sharpness.

In certain parts of the cone there were glaciers. Here Hans advanced only with extreme precaution, sounding his way with his iron-pointed pole, to discover any crevasses in it. At particularly dubious passages we were obliged to connect ourselves with each other by a long cord, in order that any man who missed his footing might be held up by his companions. This solid formation was prudent, but did not remove all danger.

Yet, notwithstanding the difficulties of the descent, down steeps unknown to the guide, the journey was accomplished without accidents, except the loss of a coil of rope, which escaped from the hands of an Icelander, and took the shortest way to the bottom of the abyss.

At midday we arrived. I raised my head and saw straight above me the upper aperture of the cone, framing a bit of sky of very small circumference, but almost perfectly round. Just upon the edge appeared the snowy peak of Saris, standing out sharp and clear against endless space.

At the bottom of the crater were three chimneys, through which, in its eruptions, Snæfell had driven forth fire and lava from its central furnace. Each of these chimneys was a hundred feet in diameter. They gaped before us right in our path. I had not the courage to look down either of them. But Professor Liedenbrock had hastily surveyed all three; he was panting, running from one to the other, gesticulating, and uttering incoherent expressions. Hans and his comrades, seated upon loose lava rocks, looked at him with as much wonder as they knew how to express, and perhaps taking him for an escaped lunatic.

Suddenly my uncle uttered a cry. I thought his foot must have slipped and that he had fallen down one of the holes. But, no; I saw him, with arms outstretched and legs straddling wide apart, erect before a granite rock that stood in the center of the crater, just like a pedestal made ready to receive a statue of Pluto. He stood like a man stupefied, but the stupefaction soon gave way to delirious rapture.

"Axel, Axel," he cried. "Come, come!"

I ran. Hans and the Icelanders never stirred.

"Look!" cried the professor.

And, sharing his astonishment, but I think not his joy, I read on the western face of the block, in Runic characters, half moldered away with lapse of ages, this thrice-accursed name:

"Arne Saknussemm!" replied my uncle. "Do you yet doubt?"

I made no answer; and I returned in silence to my lava seat in a state of utter speechless consternation. Here was crushing evidence.

How long I remained plunged in agonizing reflections I cannot tell; all that I know is, that on raising my head again, I saw only my uncle and Hans at the bottom of the crater. The Icelanders had been dismissed, and they were now descending the outer slopes of Snæfell to return to Stapi.

Hans slept peaceably at the foot of a rock, in a lava bed, where he had found a suitable couch for himself; but my uncle was pacing around the bottom of the crater like a wild beast in a cage. I had neither the wish nor the strength to rise, and following the guide's example I went off into an unhappy slumber, fancying I could hear ominous noises or feel tremblings within the recesses of the mountain.

Thus the first night in the crater passed away.

The next morning, a gray, heavy, cloudy sky seemed to droop over the summit of the cone. I did not know this first from the appearances of nature, but I found it out by my uncle's impetuous wrath.

I soon found out the cause, and hope dawned again in my heart. For this reason.

Of the three ways open before us, one had been taken by Saknussemm. The indications of the learned Icelander hinted at in the cryptogram, pointed to this fact that the shadow of Scartaris came to touch that particular way during the latter days of the month of June.

That sharp peak might hence be considered as the gnomon of a vast sundial, the shadow projected from which on a certain day would point out the road to the center of the earth.

Now, no sun no shadow, and therefore no guide. Here was June 25. If the sun was clouded for six days we must postpone our visit till next year.

My limited powers of description would fail, were I to attempt a picture of the professor's angry impatience. The day wore on, and no shadow came to lay itself along the bottom of the crater. Hans did not move from the spot he had selected; yet he must be asking himself what were we waiting for, if he asked himself anything at all. My uncle spoke not a word to me. His gaze, ever directed upward, was lost in the gray and misty space beyond.

On the 26th nothing yet. Rain mingled with snow was falling all day long. Hans built a hut of pieces of lava. I felt a malicious pleasure in watching the thousand rills and cascades that came tumbling down the sides of the cone, and the deafening continuous din awaked by every stone against which they bounded.

My uncle's rage knew no bounds. It was enough to irritate a meeker man than he; for it was foundering almost within the port.

But Heaven never sends unmixed grief, and for Professor Liedenbrock there was a satisfaction in store proportioned to his desperate anxieties.

The next day the sky was again overcast; but on the 29th of June, the last day but one of the month, with the change of the moon came a change of weather. The sun poured a flood of light down the crater. Every hillock, every rock and stone, every projecting surface had its share of the beaming torrent, and threw its shadow on the ground. Among them all, Scartaris laid down his sharp-pointed angular shadow, which began to move slowly in the opposite direction to that of the radiant orb.

My uncle turned too, and followed it.

At noon, being at its least extent, it came and softly fell upon the edge of the middle chimney.

"There it is! There it is!" shouted the professor.

"Now for the center of the globe!" he added in Danish.

I looked at Hans, to hear what he would say.

"Forüt!" was his tranquil answer.

"Forward!" replied my uncle.

It was thirteen minutes past one.

XVII

VERTICAL DESCENT

Now began our real journey. Hitherto our toil had overcome all difficulties, now difficulties would spring up at every step.

I had not yet ventured to look down the bottomless pit into which I was about to take a plunge. The supreme hour had come. I might now either share in the enterprise or refuse to move forward. But I was ashamed to recoil in the presence of the hunter. Hans accepted the enterprise with such calmness, such indifference, such perfect disregard of any possible danger that I blushed at the idea of being less brave than he. If I had been alone I might have once more tried the effect of argument; but in the presence of the guide I held my peace; my heart flew back to my sweet Virlandaise, and I approached the central chimney.

I have already mentioned that it was a hundred feet in diameter, and three hundred feet round. I bent over a projecting rock and gazed down. My hair stood on end with terror. The bewildering feeling of vacuity laid hold upon me. I felt my center of gravity shifting its place, and giddiness mounting into my brain like drunkenness. There is nothing more treacherous than this attraction down deep abysses. I was just about to drop down, when a hand laid hold of me. It was that of Hans. I suppose I had not taken as many lessons on gulf exploration as I ought to have done in the Frelsers Kirk at Copenhagen.

But, however short was my examination of this well, I had taken some account of its conformation. Its almost perpendicular walls were bristling with innumerable projections which would facilitate the descent. But if there was no want of steps, still there was no rail. A rope fastened to the edge of the aperture might have helped us down. But how were we to unfasten it, when arrived at the other end?

My uncle employed a very simple expedient to obviate this difficulty. He uncoiled a cord of the thickness of a finger, and four hundred feet long; first he dropped half of it down, then he passed it round a lava block that projected conveniently, and threw the other half down the chimney. Each of us could then descend by holding with the hand both halves of the rope, which would not be able to unroll itself from its hold; when two hundred feet down, it would be easy to get possession of the whole of the rope by letting one end go and pulling down by the other. Then the exercise would go on again ad infinitum.

"Now," said my uncle, after having completed these preparations, "now let us look to our loads. I will divide them into three lots; each of us will strap one upon his back. I mean only fragile articles."

Of course, we were not included under that head.

"Hans," said he, "will take charge of the tools and a portion of the provisions; you, Axel, will take another third of the provisions, and the arms; and I will take the rest of the provisions and the delicate instruments."

"But," said I, "the clothes, and that mass of ladders and ropes, what is to become of them?"

"They will go down by themselves."

"How so?" I asked.

"You will see presently."

My uncle was always willing to employ magnificent resources. Obeying orders, Hans tied all the nonfragile articles in one bundle, corded them firmly, and sent them bodily down the gulf before us.

I listened to the dull thuds of the descending bale. My uncle, leaning over the abyss, followed the descent of the luggage with a satisfied nod, and only rose erect when he had quite lost sight of it.

"Very well, now it is our turn."

Now I ask any sensible man if it was possible to hear those words without a shudder.

The professor fastened his package of instruments upon his shoulders; Hans took the tools; I took the arms: and the descent commenced in the following order; Hans, my uncle, and myself. It was effected in profound silence, broken only by the descent of loosened stones down the dark gulf.

I dropped as it were, frantically clutching the double cord with one hand and buttressing myself from the wall with the other by means of my stick. One idea overpowered me almost, fear lest the rock should give way from which I was hanging. This cord seemed a fragile thing for three persons to be suspended from. I made as little use of it as possible, performing wonderful feats of equilibrium upon the lava projections which my foot seemed to catch hold of like a hand.

When one of these slippery steps shook under the heavier form of Hans, he said in his tranquil voice:

"Gif akt!"

"Attention!" repeated my uncle.

In half an hour we were standing upon the surface of a rock jammed in across the chimney from one side to the other.

Hans pulled the rope by one of its ends, the other rose in the air; after passing the higher rock it came down again, bringing with it a rather dangerous shower of bits of stone and lava.

Leaning over the edge of our narrow standing ground, I observed that the bottom of the hole was still invisible.

The same maneuver was repeated with the cord, and half an hour after we had descended another two hundred feet.

I don't suppose the maddest geologist under such circumstances would have studied the nature of the rocks that we were passing. I am sure I did trouble my head about them. Pliocene, Miocene, Eocene, Cretaceous, Jurassic, Triassic, Permian, Carboniferous, Devonian, Silurian, or primitive was all one to me. But the professor, no doubt, was pursuing his observations or taking notes, for in one of our halts he said to me:

"The farther I go the more confidence I feel. The order of these volcanic formations affords the strongest confirmation to the theories of Davy. We are now among the primitive rocks, upon which the chemical operations took place which are produced by the contact of elementary bases of metals with water. I repudiate the notion of central heat altogether. We shall see further proof of that very soon."

No variation, always the same conclusion. Of course, I was not inclined to argue. My silence was taken for consent and the descent went on.

Another three hours, and I saw no bottom to the chimney yet. When I lifted my head I perceived the gradual contraction of its aperture. Its walls, by a gentle incline, were drawing closer to each other, and it was beginning to grow darker.

Still we kept descending. It seemed to me that the falling stones were meeting with an earlier resistance, and that the concussion gave a more abrupt and deadened sound.

As I had taken care to keep an exact account of our maneuvers with the rope, which I knew that we had repeated fourteen times, each descent occupying half an hour, the conclusion was easy that we had been seven hours, plus fourteen quarters of rest, making ten hours and a half. We had started at one, it must therefore now be eleven o'clock; and the depth to which we had descended was fourteen times 200 feet, or 2,800 feet.

At this moment I heard the voice of Hans.

"Halt!" he cried.

I stopped short just as I was going to place my feet upon my uncle's head.

"We are there," he cried.

"Where?" said I, stepping near to him.

"At the bottom of the perpendicular chimney," he answered.

"Is there no way farther?"

"Yes; there is a sort of passage which inclines to the right. We will see about that tomorrow. Let us have our supper, and go to sleep."

The darkness was not yet complete. The provision case was opened; we refreshed ourselves, and went to sleep as well as we could upon a bed of stones and lava fragments.

When lying on my back, I opened my eyes and saw a bright sparkling point of light at the extremity of the gigantic tube 3,000 feet long, now a vast telescope.

It was a star which, seen from this depth, had lost all scintillation, and which by my computation should be 3 Ursa minor. Then I fell fast asleep.

XVIII

THE WONDERS OF TERRESTRIAL DEPTHS

At eight in the morning a ray of daylight came to wake us up. The thousand shining surfaces of lava on the walls received it on its passage, and scattered it like a shower of sparks.

There was light enough to distinguish surrounding objects.

"Well, Axel, what do you say to it?" cried my uncle, rubbing his hands. "Did you ever spend a quieter night in our little house at Königsberg? No noise of cart wheels, no cries of basket women, no boatmen shouting!"

"No doubt it is very quiet at the bottom of this well, but there is something alarming in the quietness itself."

"Now, come!" my uncle cried. "If you are frightened already, what will you be by and by? We have not gone a single inch yet into the bowels of the earth."

"What do you mean?"

"I mean that we have only reached the level of the island, long vertical tube, which terminates at the mouth of the crater, has its lower end only at the level of the sea."

"Are you sure of that?"

"Quite sure. Consult the barometer."

In fact, the mercury, which had risen in the instrument as fast as we descended, had stopped at twenty-nine inches.

"You see," said the professor, "we have now only the pressure of our atmosphere, and I shall be glad when the aneroid takes the place of the barometer."

And in truth this instrument would become useless as soon as the weight of the atmosphere should exceed the pressure ascertained at the level of the sea.

"But," I said, "is there not reason to fear that this ever-increasing pressure will become at last very painful to bear?"

"No; we shall descend at a slow rate, and our lungs will become inured to a denser atmosphere. Aeronauts find the want of air as they rise to high elevations, but we shall perhaps have too much: of the two, this is what I should prefer. Don't let us lose a moment. Where is the bundle we sent down before us?"

I then remembered that we had searched for it in vain the evening before. My uncle questioned Hans, who, after having examined attentively with the eye of a huntsman, replied:

"Der huppe!"

"Up there."

And so it was. The bundle had been caught by a projection a hundred feet above us. Immediately the Icelander climbed up like a cat, and in a few minutes the package was in our possession.

"Now," said my uncle, "let us breakfast; but we must lay in a good stock, for we don't know how long we may have to go on."

The biscuit and extract of meat were washed down with a draft of water mingled with a little gin.

Breakfast over, my uncle drew from his pocket a small notebook, intended for scientific observations. He consulted his instruments, and recorded:

"Monday, July 1.

"Chronometer, 8.17 a.m.; barometer, 297 in.; thermometer, 6° (43°F). Direction, E.S.E."

This last observation applied to the dark gallery, and was indicated by the compass.

"Now, Axel," cried the professor with enthusiasm, "now we are really going into the interior of the earth. At this precise moment the journey commences."

So saying, my uncle took in one hand Ruhmkorff's apparatus, which was hanging from his neck; and with the other he formed an electric communication with the coil in the lantern, and a sufficiently bright light dispersed the darkness of the passage.

Hans carried the other apparatus, which was also put into action. This ingenious application of electricity would enable us to go on for a long time by creating an artificial light even in the midst of the most inflammable gases.

"Now, march!" cried my uncle.

Each shouldered his package. Hans drove before him the load of cords and clothes; and, myself walking last, we entered the gallery.

At the moment of becoming engulfed in this dark gallery, I raised my head, and saw for the last time through the length of that vast tube the sky of Iceland, which I was never to behold again.

The lava, in the last eruption of 1229, had forced a passage through this tunnel. It still lined the walls with a thick and glistening coat. The electric light was here intensified a hundredfold by reflection.

The only difficulty in proceeding lay in not sliding too fast down an incline of about forty-five degrees; happily certain asperities and a few blisterings here and there formed steps, and we descended, letting our baggage slip before us from the end of a long rope.

But that which formed steps under our feet became stalactites overhead. The lava, which was porous in many places, had formed a surface covered with small rounded blisters; crystals of opaque quartz, set with limpid tears of glass, and hanging like clustered chandeliers from the vaulted roof, seemed as it were to kindle and form a sudden illumination as we passed on our way. It seemed as if the genii of the depths were lighting up their palace to receive their terrestrial guests.

"It is magnificent!" I cried spontaneously. "My uncle, what a sight! Don't you admire those blending hues of lava, passing from reddish-brown to bright yellow by imperceptible shades? And these crystals are just like globes of light."

"Ah, you think so, do you, Axel, my boy? Well, you will see greater splendors than these, I hope. Now let us march: march!"

He had better have said slide, for we did nothing but drop down the steep inclines. It was the *facifs descensus Averni* of Virgil. The compass, which I consulted frequently, gave our direction as southeast with inflexible steadiness. This lava stream deviated neither to the right nor to the left.

Yet there was no sensible increase of temperature. This justified Davy's theory, and more than once I consulted the thermometer with surprise. Two hours after our departure it only marked 10° (50°F), an increase of only 4°. This gave reason for believing that our descent was more horizontal than vertical. As for the exact depth reached, it was very easy to ascertain that; the professor measured accurately the angles of deviation and inclination on the road, but he kept the results to himself.

About eight in the evening he signaled to stop. Hans sat down at once. The lamps were hung upon a projection in the lava; we were in a sort of cavern where there was plenty of air. Certain puffs of air reached us. What atmospheric disturbance was the cause of them? I could not answer that question at the moment. Hunger and fatigue made me incapable of reasoning. A descent of seven hours consecutively is not made without considerable expenditure of strength. I was exhausted. The order to "halt" therefore gave me pleasure. Hans laid our provisions upon a block of lava, and we ate with a good appetite. But one thing troubled me, our supply of water was half consumed. My uncle reckoned upon a fresh supply from subterranean sources, but hitherto we had met with none. I could not help drawing his attention to this circumstance.

"Are you surprised at this want of springs?" he said.

"More than that, I am anxious about it; we have only water enough for five days."

"Don't be uneasy, Axel, we shall find more than we want."

"When?"

"When we have left this bed of lava behind us. How could springs break through such walls as these?"

"But perhaps this passage runs to a very great depth. It seems to me that we have made no great progress vertically."

"Why do you suppose that?"

"Because if we had gone deep into the crust of earth, we should have encountered greater heat."

"According to your system," said my uncle. "But what does the thermometer say?"

"Hardly fifteen degrees (59°F), nine degrees only since our departure."

"Well, what is your conclusion?"

"This is my conclusion. According to exact observations, the increase of temperature in the interior of the globe advances at the rate of one degree (1.8°F) for every hundred feet. But certain local conditions may modify this rate. Thus at Yakoutsk in Siberia the increase of a degree is ascertained to be reached every 36 feet. This difference depends upon the heat-conducting power of the rocks. Moreover, in the neighborhood of an extinct volcano, through gneiss, it has been observed that the increase of a degree is only attained at every 125 feet. Let us therefore assume this last hypothesis as the most suitable to our situation, and calculate."

"Well, do calculate, my boy."

"Nothing is easier," said I, putting down figures in my notebook. "Nine times a hundred and twenty-five feet gives a depth of eleven hundred and twenty-five feet."

"Very accurate indeed."

"Well?"

"By my observation we are at 10,000 feet below the level of the sea."

"Is that possible?"

"Yes, or figures are of no use."

The professor's calculations were quite correct. We had already attained a depth of six thousand feet beyond that hitherto reached by the foot of man, such as the mines of Kitz Bahl in Tyrol, and those of Wuttembourg in Bohemia.

The temperature, which ought to have been 81° (178°F) was scarcely 15° (59°F). Here was cause for reflection.

XIX

GEOLOGICAL STUDIES IN SITU

Next day, Tuesday, June 30, at 6 a.m., the descent began again.

We were still following the gallery of lava, a real natural staircase, and as gently sloping as those inclined planes which in some old houses are still found instead of flights of steps. And so we went on until 12:17, the precise moment when we overtook Hans, who had stopped.

"Ah! Here we are," exclaimed my uncle, "at the very end of the chimney."

I looked around me. We were standing at the intersection of two roads, both dark and narrow. Which were we to take? This was a difficulty.

Still my uncle refused to admit an appearance of hesitation, either before me or the guide; he pointed out the eastern tunnel, and we were soon all three in it.

Besides there would have been interminable hesitation before this choice of roads; for since there was no indication whatever to guide our choice, we were obliged to trust to chance.

The slope of this gallery was scarcely perceptible, and its sections very unequal. Sometimes we passed a series of arches succeeding each other like the majestic arcades of a Gothic cathedral. Here the architects of the Middle Ages might have found studies for every form of the sacred art which sprang from the development of the pointed arch. A mile farther we had to bow our heads under corniced elliptic arches in the Romanesque style; and massive pillars standing out from the wall bent under the spring of the vault that rested heavily upon them. In other places this magnificence gave way to narrow channels between low structures which looked like beaver's huts, and we had to creep along through extremely narrow passages.

The heat was perfectly bearable. Involuntarily I began to think of its heat when the lava thrown out by Snæfell was boiling and working through this now-silent road. I imagined the torrents of fire hurled back at every angle in the gallery, and the accumulation of intensely heated vapors in the midst of this confined channel.

I only hope, thought I, that this so-called extinct volcano won't take a fancy in his old age to begin his sports again!

I abstained from communicating these fears to Professor Liedenbrock. He would never have understood them at all. He had but one idea—forward! He walked, he slid, he scrambled, he tumbled, with a persistence which one could not but admire.

By six in the evening, after a not very fatiguing walk, we had gone two leagues south, but scarcely a quarter of a mile down.

My uncle said it was time to go to sleep. We ate without talking, and went to sleep without reflection.

Our arrangements for the night were very simple; a railway rug each, into which we rolled ourselves, was our sole covering. We had neither cold nor intrusive visits to fear. Travelers who penetrate into the wilds of central Africa, and into the pathless forests of the New World, are obliged to watch over each other by night. But we enjoyed absolute safety and utter seclusion; no savages or wild beasts infested these silent depths.

Next morning, we awoke fresh and in good spirits. The road was resumed. As the day before, we followed the path of the lava. It was impossible to tell what rocks we were passing: the tunnel, instead of tending lower, approached more and more nearly to a horizontal direction, I even fancied a slight rise. But about ten this upward tendency became so evident, and therefore so fatiguing, that I was obliged to slacken my pace.

"Well, Axel?" demanded the professor impatiently.

"Well, I cannot stand it any longer," I replied.

"What! After three hours' walk over such easy ground."

"It may be easy, but it is tiring all the same."

"What, when we have nothing to do but keep going down!"

"Going up, if you please."

"Going up!" said my uncle, with a shrug.

"No doubt, for the last half-hour the inclines have gone the other way, and at this rate we shall soon arrive upon the level soil of Iceland."

The professor nodded slowly and uneasily like a man that declines to be convinced. I tried to resume the conversation. He answered not a word, and gave the signal for a start. I saw that his silence was nothing but ill humor.

Still I had courageously shouldered my burden again, and was rapidly following Hans, whom my uncle preceded. I was anxious not to be left behind. My greatest care was not to lose sight of my companions. I shuddered at the thought of being lost in the mazes of this vast subterranean labyrinth.

Besides, if the ascending road did become steeper, I was comforted with the thought that it was bringing us nearer to the surface. There was hope in this. Every step confirmed me in it, and I was rejoicing at the thought of meeting my little Gräuben again.

By midday there was a change in the appearance of this wall of the gallery. I noticed it by a diminution of the amount of light reflected from the sides; solid rock was appearing in the place of the lava coating. The mass was composed of inclined and sometimes vertical strata. We were passing through rocks of the transition or Silurian system.

"It is evident," I cried, "the marine deposits formed in the second period, these shales, limestones, and sandstones. We are turning away from the primary granite. We are just as if we were people of Hamburg going to Lübeck by way of Hanover!"

I had better have kept my observations to myself. But my geological instinct was stronger than my prudence, and Uncle Liedenbrock heard my exclamation.

"What's that you are saying?" he asked.

"See," I said, pointing to the varied series of sandstones and limestones, and the first indication of slate.

"Well?"

"We are at the period when the first plants and animals appeared."

"Do you think so?"

"Look close, and examine."

I obliged the professor to move his lamp over the walls of the gallery. I expected some signs of astonishment; but he spoke not a word, and went on.

Had he understood me or not? Did he refuse to admit, out of self-love as an uncle and a philosopher, that he had mistaken his way when he chose the eastern tunnel? Or was he determined to examine this passage to its farthest extremity? It was evident that we had left the lava path, and that this road could not possibly lead to the extinct furnace of Snæfell.

Yet I asked myself if I was not depending too much on this change in the rock. Might I not myself be mistaken? Were we really crossing the layers of rock which overlie the granite foundation?

If I am right, I thought, I must soon find some fossil remains of primitive life; and then we must yield to evidence. I will look.

I had not gone a hundred paces before incontestable proofs presented themselves. It could not be otherwise, for in the Silurian age the seas contained at least fifteen hundred vegetable and animal species. My feet, which had become accustomed to the indurated lava floor, suddenly rested upon a dust composed of the debris of plants and shells. In the walls were distinct impressions of fucoids and lycopodites.

Professor Liedenbrock could not be mistaken, I thought, and yet he pushed on, with, I suppose, his eyes resolutely shut.

This was only invincible obstinacy. I could hold out no longer. I picked up a perfectly formed shell, which had belonged to an animal not unlike the woodlouse: then, joining my uncle, I said:

"Look at this!"

"Very well," said he quietly, "it is the shell of a crustacean, of an extinct species called a trilobite. Nothing more."

"But don't you conclude—?"

"Just what you conclude yourself. Yes; I do, perfectly. We have left the granite and the lava. It is possible that I may be mistaken. But I cannot be sure of that until I have reached the very end of this gallery."

"You are right in doing this, my uncle, and I should quite approve of your determination, if there were not a danger threatening us nearer and nearer."

"What danger?"

"The want of water."

"Well, Axel, we will put ourselves upon rations."

XX

THE FIRST SIGNS OF DISTRESS

In fact, we had to ration ourselves. Our provision of water could not last more than three days. I found that out for certain when supper time came. And, to our sorrow, we had little reason to expect to find a spring in these transition beds.

The whole of the next day the gallery opened before us its endless arcades. We moved on almost without a word. Hans's silence seemed to be infecting us.

The road was now not ascending, at least not perceptibly. Sometimes, even, it seemed to have a slight fall. But this tendency, which was very trifling, could not do anything to reassure the professor; for there was no change in the beds, and the transitional characteristics became more and more decided.

The electric light was reflected in sparkling splendor from the schist, limestone, and old red sandstone of the walls. It might have been thought that we were passing through a section of Wales, of which an ancient people gave its name to this system. Specimens of magnificent marbles clothed the walls, some of a grayish agate fantastically veined with white, others of rich crimson or yellow dashed with splotches of red; then came dark cherry-colored marbles relieved by the lighter tints of limestone.

The greater part of these bore impressions of primitive organisms. Creation had evidently advanced since the day before. Instead of rudimentary trilobites, I noticed remains of a more perfect order of beings, among others ganoid fishes and some of those sauroids in which paleontologists have discovered the earliest reptile forms. The Devonian seas were peopled by animals of these species, and deposited them by thousands in the rocks of the newer formation.

It was evident that we were ascending that scale of animal life in which man fills the highest place. But Professor Liedenbrock seemed not to notice it.

He was awaiting one of two events, either the appearance of a vertical well opening before his feet, down which our descent might be resumed, or that of some obstacle which should effectually turn us back on our own footsteps. But evening came and neither wish was gratified.

On Friday, after a night during which I felt pangs of thirst, our little troop again plunged into the winding passages of the gallery.

After ten hours' walking I observed a singular deadening of the reflection of our lamps from the side walls. The marble, the schist, the limestone, and the sandstone were giving way to a dark and lusterless lining. At one moment, the tunnel becoming very narrow, I leaned against the wall.

When I removed my hand it was black. I looked nearer, and found we were in a coal formation.

"A coal mine!" I cried.

"A mine without miners," my uncle replied.

"Who knows?" I asked.

"I know," the professor pronounced decidedly, "I am certain that this gallery driven through beds of coal was never pierced by the hand of man. But whether it be the hand of nature or not does not matter. Supper time is come; let us sup."

Hans prepared some food. I scarcely ate, and I swallowed down the few drops of water rationed out to me. One flask half full was all we had left to slake the thirst of three men.

After their meal my two companions laid themselves down upon their rugs, and found in sleep a solace for their fatigue. But I could not sleep, and I counted every hour until morning.

On Saturday, at six, we started afresh. In twenty minutes we reached a vast open space; I then knew that the hand of man had not hollowed out this mine; the vaults would have been shored up, and, as it was, they seemed to be held up by a miracle of equilibrium.

This cavern was about a hundred feet wide and a hundred and fifty in height. A large mass had been rent asunder by a subterranean disturbance. Yielding to some vast power from below it had broken asunder, leaving this great hollow into which human beings were now penetrating for the first time.

The whole history of the Carboniferous period was written upon these gloomy walls, and a geologist might with ease trace all its diverse phases. The beds of coal were separated by strata of sandstone or compact clays, and appeared crushed under the weight of overlying strata.

At the age of the world which preceded the secondary period, the earth was clothed with immense vegetable forms, the product of the double influence of tropical heat and constant moisture; a vapory atmosphere surrounded the earth, still veiling the direct rays of the sun.

Thence arises the conclusion that the high temperature then existing was due to some other source than the heat of the sun. Perhaps even the orb of day may not have been ready yet to play the splendid part he now acts. There were no "climates" as yet, and a torrid heat, equal from pole to equator, was spread over the whole surface of the globe. Whence this heat? Was it from the interior of the earth?

Notwithstanding the theories of Professor Liedenbrock, a violent heat did at that time brood within the body of the spheroid. Its action was felt to the very last coats of the terrestrial crust; the plants, unacquainted with the beneficent influences of the sun, yielded neither flowers nor scent. But their roots drew vigorous life from the burning soil of the early days of this planet.

There were but few trees. Herbaceous plants alone existed. There were tall grasses, ferns, lycopods, besides sigillaria, asterophyllites, now scarce plants, but then the species might be counted by thousands.

The coal measures owe their origin to this period of profuse vegetation. The yet elastic and yielding crust of the earth obeyed the fluid forces beneath. Thence innumerable fissures and depressions. The plants, sunk underneath the waters, formed by degrees into vast accumulated masses.

Then came the chemical action of nature; in the depths of the seas the vegetable accumulations first became peat; then, acted upon by generated gases and the heat of fermentation, they underwent a process of complete mineralization.

Thus were formed those immense coalfields, which nevertheless are not inexhaustible, and which three centuries at the present accelerated rate of consumption will exhaust unless the industrial world will devise a remedy.

These reflections came into my mind while I was contemplating the mineral wealth stored up in this portion of the globe. These no doubt, I thought, will never be discovered; the working of such deep mines would involve too large an outlay, and where would be the use as long as coal is yet spread far and wide near the surface? Such as my eyes behold these virgin stores, such they will be when this world comes to an end.

But still we marched on, and I alone was forgetting the length of the way by losing myself in the midst of geological contemplations. The temperature remained what it had been during our passage through the lava and schists. Only my sense of smell was forcibly affected by an odor of protocarburet of hydrogen. I immediately recognized in this gallery the presence of a considerable quantity of the dangerous gas called by miners firedamp, the explosion of which has often occasioned such dreadful catastrophes.

Happily, our light was from Ruhmkorff's ingenious apparatus. If unfortunately we had explored this gallery with torches, a terrible explosion would have put an end to traveling and travelers at one stroke.

This excursion through the coal mine lasted till night. My uncle scarcely could restrain his impatience at the horizontal road. The darkness, always deep twenty yards before us, prevented us from estimating the length of the gallery; and I was beginning to think it must be endless, when suddenly at six o'clock a wall very unexpectedly stood before us. Right or left, top or bottom, there was no road farther; we were at the end of a blind alley. "Very well, it's all right!" cried my uncle. "Now, at any rate, we shall know what we are about. We are not in Saknussemm's road, and all we have to do is to go back. Let us take a night's rest, and in three days we shall get to the fork in the road."

"Yes," said I, "if we have any strength left."

"Why not?"

"Because tomorrow we shall have no water."

"Nor courage either?" asked my uncle severely.

I dared make no answer.

XXI

COMPASSION FUSES THE PROFESSOR'S HEART

Next day we started early. We had to hasten forward. It was a three days' march to the crossroads.

I will not speak of the sufferings we endured in our return. My uncle bore them with the angry impatience of a man obliged to own his weakness; Hans with the resignation of his passive nature; I, I confess, with complaints and expressions of despair. I had no spirit to oppose this ill fortune.

As I had foretold, the water failed entirely by the end of the first day's retrograde march. Our fluid aliment was now nothing but gin; but this infernal fluid burned my throat, and I could not even endure the sight of it. I found the temperature and the air stifling. Fatigue paralyzed my limbs. More than once I dropped down motionless. Then there was a halt; and my uncle and the Icelander did their best to restore me. But I saw that the former was struggling painfully against excessive fatigue and the tortures of thirst.

At last, on Tuesday, July 8, we arrived on our hands and knees, and half dead, at the junction of the two roads. There I dropped like a lifeless lump, extended on the lava soil. It was ten in the morning.

Hans and my uncle, clinging to the wall, tried to nibble a few bits of biscuit. Long moans escaped from my swollen lips.

After some time my uncle approached me and raised me in his arms.

"Poor boy!" said he, in genuine tones of compassion.

I was touched with these words, not being accustomed to see the excitable professor in a softened mood. I grasped his trembling hands in mine. He let me hold them and looked at me. His eyes were moistened.

Then I saw him take the flask that was hanging at his side. To my amazement he placed it on my lips.

"Drink!" said he.

Had I heard him? Was my uncle beside himself? I stared at, him stupidly, and felt as if I could not understand him.

"Drink!" he said again.

And raising his flask he emptied it every drop between my lips.

Oh! Infinite pleasure! A slender sip of water came to moisten my burning mouth. It was but one sip, but it was enough to recall my ebbing life.

I thanked my uncle with clasped hands.

"Yes," he said, "a draft of water; but it is the very last—you hear!—the last. I had kept it as a precious treasure at the bottom of my flask. Twenty times, nay, a hundred times, have I fought against a frightful impulse to drink it off. But no, Axel, I kept it for you."

"My dear uncle," I said, while hot tears trickled down my face.

"Yes, my poor boy, I knew that as soon as you arrived at these crossroads you would drop half dead, and I kept my last drop of water to reanimate you."

"Thank you, thank you," I said. Although my thirst was only partially quenched, yet some strength had returned. The muscles of my throat, until then contracted, now relaxed again; and the inflammation of my lips abated somewhat; and I was now able to speak.

"Let us see," I said, "we have now but one thing to do. We have no water; we must go back."

While I spoke my uncle avoided looking at me; he hung his head down; his eyes avoided mine.

"We must return," I exclaimed vehemently; "we must go back on our way to Snæfell. May God give us strength to climb up the crater again!"

"Return!" said my uncle, as if he was rather answering himself than me.

"Yes, return, without the loss of a minute."

A long silence followed.

"So then, Axel," replied the professor ironically, "you have found no courage or energy in these few drops of water?"

"Courage?"

"I see you just as feeble-minded as you were before, and still expressing only despair!"

What sort of a man was this I had to do with, and what schemes was he now revolving in his fearless mind?

"What! You won't go back?"

"Should I renounce this expedition just when we have the fairest chance of success! Never!"

"Then must we resign ourselves to destruction?"

"No, Axel, no; go back. Hans will go with you. Leave me to myself!"

"Leave you here!"

"Leave me, I tell you. I have undertaken this expedition. I will carry it out to the end, and I will not return. Go, Axel, go!"

My uncle was in high state of excitement. His voice, which had for a moment been tender and gentle, had now become hard and threatening. He was struggling with gloomy resolutions against impossibilities. I would not leave him in this bottomless abyss, and on the other hand the instinct of self-preservation prompted me to fly.

The guide watched this scene with his usual phlegmatic unconcern. Yet he understood perfectly well what was going on between his two companions. The gestures themselves were sufficient to show that we were each bent on taking a different road; but Hans seemed to take no part in a question upon which depended his life. He was ready to start at a given signal, or to stay, if his master so willed it.

How I wished at this moment I could have made him understand me. My words, my complaints, my sorrow would have had some influence over that frigid nature. Those dangers which our guide could not understand I could have demonstrated and proved to him. Together we might have overruled the obstinate professor; if it were needed, we might perhaps have compelled him to regain the heights of Snæfell.

I drew near to Hans. I placed my hand upon his. He made no movement. My parted lips sufficiently revealed my sufferings. The Icelander slowly moved his head, and calmly pointing to my uncle said:

"Master."

"Master!" I shouted. "You madman! No, he is not the master of our life; we must fly, we must drag him. Do you hear me? Do you understand?"

I had seized Hans by the arm. I wished to oblige him to rise. I strove with him. My uncle interposed.

"Be calm, Axel! You will get nothing from that immovable servant. Therefore, listen to my proposal."

I crossed my arms, and confronted my uncle boldly.

"The want of water," he said, "is the only obstacle in our way. In this eastern gallery made up of lavas, schists, and coal, we have not met with a single particle of moisture. Perhaps we shall be more fortunate if we follow the western tunnel."

I shook my head incredulously.

"Hear me to the end," the professor went on with a firm voice. "While you were lying there motionless, I went to examine the conformation of that gallery. It penetrates directly downward, and in a few hours it will bring us to the granite rocks. There we must meet with abundant springs. The nature of the rock assures me of this, and instinct agrees with logic to support my conviction. Now, this is my proposal. When Columbus asked of his ships' crews for three days more to discover a new world, those crews, disheartened and sick as they were, recognized the justice of the claim, and he discovered America. I am the Columbus of this netherworld, and I only ask for one more day. If in a single day I have not met with the water that we want, I swear to you we will return to the surface of the earth."

In spite of my irritation I was moved with these words, as well as with the violence my uncle was doing to his own wishes in making so hazardous a proposal.

"Well," I said, "do as you will, and God reward your superhuman energy. You have now but a few hours to tempt fortune. Let us start!"

XXII

TOTAL FAILURE OF WATER

This time the descent commenced by the new gallery. Hans walked first as was his custom.

We had not gone a hundred yards when the professor, moving his lantern along the walls, cried:

"Here are primitive rocks. Now we are in the right way. Forward!"

When in its early stages the earth was slowly cooling, its contraction gave rise in its crust to disruptions, distortions, fissures, and chasms. The passage through which we were moving was such a fissure, through which at one time granite poured out in a molten state. Its thousands of windings formed an inextricable labyrinth through the primeval mass.

As fast as we descended, the succession of beds forming the primitive foundation came out with increasing distinctness. Geologists consider this primitive matter to be the base of the mineral crust of the earth, and have ascertained it to be composed of three different formations, schist, gneiss, and mica schist, resting upon that unchangeable foundation, the granite.

Never had mineralogists found themselves in so marvelous a situation to study nature in situ. What the boring machine, an insensible, inert instrument, was unable to bring to the surface of the inner structure of the globe, we were able to peruse with our own eyes and handle with our own hands.

Through the beds of schist, colored with delicate shades of green, ran in winding course threads of copper and manganese, with traces of platinum and gold. I thought, what riches are here buried at an unapproachable depth in the earth, hidden forever from the covetous eyes of the human race! These treasures have been buried at such a profound depth by the convulsions of primeval times that they run no chance of ever being molested by the pickaxe or the spade.

To the schists succeeded gneiss, partially stratified, remarkable for the parallelism and regularity of its lamina, then mica schists, laid in large plates or flakes, revealing their lamellated structure by the sparkle of the white shining mica.

The light from our apparatus, reflected from the small facets of quartz, shot sparkling rays at every angle, and I seemed to be moving through a diamond, within which the quickly darting rays broke across each other in a thousand flashing coruscations.

About six o'clock this brilliant fete of illuminations underwent a sensible abatement of splendor, then almost ceased. The walls assumed a crystallized though somber appearance; mica was more closely mingled with the feldspar and quartz to form the proper rocky foundations of the earth, which bears without distortion or crushing the weight of the four terrestrial systems. We were immured within prison walls of granite.

It was eight in the evening. No signs of water had yet appeared. I was suffering horribly. My uncle strode on. He refused to stop. He was listening anxiously for the murmur of distant springs. But, no, there was dead silence.

And now my limbs were failing beneath me. I resisted pain and torture, that I might not stop my uncle, which would have driven him to despair, for the day was drawing near to its end, and it was his last.

At last I failed utterly; I uttered a cry and fell.

"Come to me, I am dying."

My uncle retraced his steps. He gazed upon me with his arms crossed; then these muttered words passed his lips:

"It's all over!"

The last thing I saw was a fearful gesture of rage, and my eyes closed.

When I reopened them I saw my two companions motionless and rolled up in their coverings. Were they asleep? As for me, I could not get one moment's sleep. I was suffering too keenly, and what embittered my thoughts was that there was no remedy. My uncle's last words echoed painfully in my ears: "It's all over!" For in such a fearful state of debility, it was madness to think of ever reaching the upper world again.

We had above us a league and a half of terrestrial crust. The weight of it seemed to be crushing down upon my shoulders. I felt weighed down, and I exhausted myself with imaginary violent exertions to turn round upon my granite couch.

A few hours passed away. A deep silence reigned around us, the silence of the grave. No sound could reach us through walls, the thinnest of which were five miles thick.

Yet in the midst of my stupefaction I seemed to be aware of a noise. It was dark down the tunnel, but I seemed to see the Icelander vanishing from our sight with the lamp in his hand.

Why was he leaving us? Was Hans going to forsake us? My uncle was fast asleep. I wanted to shout, but my voice died upon my parched and swollen lips. The darkness became deeper, and the last sound died away in the far distance.

"Hans has abandoned us," I cried. "Hans! Hans!"

But these words were only spoken within me. They went no farther. Yet after the first moment of terror I felt ashamed of suspecting a man of such extraordinary faithfulness. Instead of ascending he was descending the gallery. An evil design would have taken him up, not down. This reflection restored me to calmness, and I turned to other thoughts. None but some weighty motive could have induced so quiet a man to forfeit his sleep. Was he on a journey of discovery? Had he during the silence of the night caught a sound, a murmuring of something in the distance, which had failed to affect my hearing?

XXIII

WATER DISCOVERED

For a whole hour I was trying to work out in my delirious brain the reasons which might have influenced this seemingly tranquil huntsman. The absurdest notions ran in utter confusion through my mind. I thought madness was coming on!

But at last a noise of footsteps was heard in the dark abyss. Hans was approaching. A flickering light was beginning to glimmer on the wall of our darksome prison; then it came out full at the mouth of the gallery. Hans appeared.

He drew close to my uncle, laid his hand upon his shoulder, and gently woke him. My uncle rose up.

"What is the matter?" he asked.

"Watten!" replied the huntsman.

No doubt under the inspiration of intense pain everybody becomes endowed with the gift of divers tongues. I did not know a word of Danish, yet instinctively I understood the word he had uttered.

"Water! Water!" I cried, clapping my hands and gesticulating like a madman.

"Water!" repeated my uncle. *"Hvar?"* he asked, in Icelandic.

"*Nedat*," replied Hans.

"Where? Down below!" I understood it all. I seized the hunter's hands, and pressed them while he looked on me without moving a muscle of his countenance.

The preparations for our departure were not long in making, and we were soon on our way down a passage inclining two feet in seven. In an hour we had gone a mile and a quarter, and descended two thousand feet.

Then I began to hear distinctly quite a new sound of something running within the thickness of the granite wall, a kind of dull, dead rumbling, like distant thunder. During the first part of our walk, not meeting with the promised spring, I felt my agony returning; but then my uncle acquainted me with the cause of the strange noise.

"Hans was not mistaken," he said. "What you hear is the rushing of a torrent."

"A torrent?" I exclaimed.

"There can be no doubt; a subterranean river is flowing around us."

We hurried forward in the greatest excitement. I was no longer sensible of my fatigue. This murmuring of waters close at hand was already refreshing me. It was audibly increasing. The torrent, after having for some time flowed over our heads, was now running within the left wall, roaring and rushing. Frequently I touched the wall, hoping to feel some indications of moisture: But there was no hope here.

Yet another half hour, another half league was passed.

Then it became clear that the hunter had gone no farther. Guided by an instinct peculiar to mountaineers, he had as it were felt this torrent through the rock; but he had certainly seen none of the precious liquid; he had drunk nothing himself.

Soon it became evident that if we continued our walk we should widen the distance between ourselves and the stream, the noise of which was becoming fainter.

We returned. Hans stopped where the torrent seemed closest. I sat near the wall, while the waters were flowing past me at a distance of two feet with extreme violence. But there was a thick granite wall between us and the object of our desires.

Without reflection, without asking if there were any means of procuring the water, I gave way to a movement of despair.

Hans glanced at me with, I thought, a smile of compassion.

He rose and took the lamp. I followed him. He moved toward the wall. I looked on. He applied his ear against the dry stone, and moved it slowly to and fro, listening intently. I perceived at once that he was examining to find the exact place where the torrent could be heard the loudest. He met with that point on the left side of the tunnel, at three feet from the ground.

I was stirred up with excitement. I hardly dared guess what the hunter was about to do. But I could not but understand, and applaud and cheer him on, when I saw him lay hold of the pickaxe to make an attack upon the rock.

"We are saved!" I cried.

"Yes," cried my uncle, almost frantic with excitement. "Hans is right. Capital fellow! Who but he would have thought of it?"

Yes; who but he? Such an expedient, however simple, would never have entered into our minds. True, it seemed most hazardous to strike a blow of the hammer in this part of the earth's structure. Suppose some displacement should occur and crush us all! Suppose the torrent, bursting through, should drown us in a sudden flood! There was nothing vain in these fancies. But still no fears of falling rocks or rushing floods could stay us now; and our thirst was so intense that, to satisfy it, we would have dared the waves of the North Atlantic.

Hans set about the task which my uncle and I together could not have accomplished. If our impatience had armed our hands with power, we should have shattered the rock into a thousand fragments. Not so Hans. Full of self-possession, he calmly wore his way through the rock with a steady succession of light and skillful strokes, working through an aperture six inches wide at the outside. I could hear a louder noise of flowing waters, and I fancied I could feel the delicious fluid refreshing my parched lips.

The pick had soon penetrated two feet into the granite partition, and our man had worked for above an hour. I was in an agony of impatience. My uncle wanted to employ stronger measures, and I had some difficulty in dissuading him; still he had just taken a pickaxe in his hand, when a sudden hissing was heard, and a jet of water spurted out with violence against the opposite wall.

Hans, almost thrown off his feet by the violence of the shock, uttered a cry of grief and disappointment, of which I soon understood the cause, when plunging my hands into the spouting torrent, I withdrew them in haste, for the water was scalding hot.

"The water is at the boiling point," I cried.

"Well, never mind, let it cool," my uncle replied.

The tunnel was filling with steam, while a stream was forming, which by degrees wandered away into subterranean windings, and soon we had the satisfaction of swallowing our first draft.

Could anything be more delicious than the sensation that our burning, intolerable thirst was passing away, and leaving us to enjoy comfort and pleasure? But where was this water from? No matter. It was water; and though still warm, it brought life back to the dying. I kept drinking without stopping, and almost without tasting.

At last after a most delightful time of reviving energy, I cried, "Why, this is a chalybeate spring!"

"Nothing could be better for the digestion," said my uncle. "It is highly impregnated with iron. It will be as good for us as going to the spa, or to Töplitz."

"Well, it is delicious!"

"Of course it is, water should be, found six miles underground. It has an inky flavor, which is not at all unpleasant. What a capital source of strength Hans has found for us here. We will call it after his name."

"Agreed," I cried.

And Hansbach it was from that moment.

Hans was none the prouder. After a moderate draft, he went quietly into a corner to rest.

"Now," I said, "we must not lose this water."

"What is the use of troubling ourselves?" my uncle replied. "I fancy it will never fail."

"Never mind, we cannot be sure; let us fill the water bottle and our flasks, and then stop up the opening."

My advice was followed so far as getting in a supply; but the stopping up of the hole was not so easy to accomplish. It was in vain that we took up fragments of granite, and stuffed them in with tow, we only scalded our hands without succeeding. The pressure was too great, and our efforts were fruitless.

"It is quite plain," said I, "that the higher body of this water is at a considerable elevation. The force of the jet shows that."

"No doubt," answered my uncle. "If this column of water is 32,000 feet high—that is, from the surface of the earth, it is equal to the weight of a thousand atmospheres. But I have got an idea."

"Well?"

"Why should we trouble ourselves to stop the stream from coming out at all?"

"Because—" Well, I could not assign a reason.

"When our flasks are empty, where shall we fill them again? Can we tell that?"

No; there was no certainty.

"Well, let us allow the water to run on. It will flow down, and will both guide and refresh us."

"That is well planned," I cried. "With this stream for our guide, there is no reason why we should not succeed in our undertaking."

"Ah, my boy! You agree with me now," cried the professor, laughing.

"I agree with you most heartily."

"Well, let us rest awhile; and then we will start again."

I was forgetting that it was night. The chronometer soon informed me of that fact; and in a very short time, refreshed and thankful, we all three fell into a sound sleep.

XXIV

WELL SAID, OLD MOLE! CANST THOU WORK I' THE GROUND SO FAST?

By the next day we had forgotten all our sufferings. At first, I was wondering that I was no longer thirsty, and I was for asking for the reason. The answer came in the murmuring of the stream at my feet.

We breakfasted, and drank of this excellent chalybeate water. I felt wonderfully stronger, and quite decided upon pushing on. Why should not so firmly convinced a man as my uncle, furnished with so industrious a guide as Hans, and accompanied by so determined a nephew as myself, go on to final success? Such were the magnificent plans which struggled for mastery within me. If it had been proposed to me to return to the summit of Snæfell, I should have indignantly declined.

Most fortunately, all we had to do was to descend.

"Let us start!" I cried, awakening by my shouts the echoes of the vaulted hollows of the earth.

On Thursday, at 8 a.m., we started afresh. The granite tunnel winding from side to side, earned us past unexpected turns, and seemed almost to form a labyrinth; but, on the whole, its direction seemed to be southeasterly. My uncle never ceased to consult his compass, to keep account of the ground gone over.

The gallery dipped down a very little way from the horizontal, scarcely more than two inches in a fathom, and the stream ran gently murmuring at our feet. I compared it to a friendly genius guiding us underground, and caressed with my hand the soft naiad, whose comforting voice accompanied our steps. With my reviving spirits these mythological notions seemed to come unbidden.

As for my uncle, he was beginning to storm against the horizontal road. He loved nothing better than a vertical path; but this way seemed indefinitely prolonged, and instead of sliding along the hypotenuse as we were now doing, he would willingly have dropped down the terrestrial radius. But there was no help for it, and as long as we were approaching the center at all we felt that we must not complain.

From time to time, a steeper path appeared; our naiad then began to tumble before us with a hoarser murmur, and we went down with her to a greater depth.

On the whole, that day and the next we made considerable way horizontally, very little vertically.

On Friday evening, the 10th of July, according to our calculations, we were thirty leagues southeast of Reykjavik, and at a depth of two leagues and a half.

At our feet there now opened a frightful abyss. My uncle, however, was not to be daunted, and he clapped his hands at the steepness of the descent.

"This will take us a long way," he cried, "and without much difficulty; for the projections in the rock form quite a staircase."

The ropes were so fastened by Hans as to guard against accident, and the descent commenced. I can hardly call it perilous, for I was beginning to be familiar with this kind of exercise.

This well, or abyss, was a narrow cleft in the mass of the granite, called by geologists a "fault," and caused by the unequal cooling of the globe of the earth. If it had at one time been a passage for eruptive matter thrown out by Snæfell, I still could not understand why no trace was left of its passage. We kept going down a kind of winding staircase, which seemed almost to have been made by the hand of man.

Every quarter of an hour we were obliged to halt, to take a little necessary repose and restore the action of our limbs. We then sat down upon a fragment of rock, and we talked as we ate and drank from the stream.

Of course, down this fault the Hansbach fell in a cascade, and lost some of its volume; but there was enough and to spare to slake our thirst. Besides, when the incline became more gentle, it would of course resume its peaceable course. At this moment it reminded me of my worthy uncle, in his frequent fits of impatience and anger, while below it ran with the calmness of the Icelandic hunter.

On the 6th and 7th of July we kept following the spiral curves of this singular well, penetrating in actual distance no more than two leagues; but being carried to a depth of five leagues below the level of the sea. But on the 8th, about noon, the fault took, toward the southeast, a much gentler slope, one of about forty-five degrees.

Then the road became monotonously easy. It could not be otherwise, for there was no landscape to vary the stages of our journey.

On Wednesday, the 15th, we were seven leagues underground, and had traveled fifty leagues away from Snæfell. Although we were tired, our health was perfect, and the medicine chest had not yet had occasion to be opened.

My uncle noted every hour the indications of the compass, the chronometer, the aneroid, and the thermometer the very same which he has published in his scientific report of our journey. It was therefore not difficult to know exactly our whereabouts. When he told me that we had gone fifty leagues horizontally, I could not repress an exclamation of astonishment, at the thought that we had now long left Iceland behind us.

"What is the matter?" he cried.

"I was reflecting that if your calculations are correct we are no longer under Iceland."

"Do you think so?"

"I am not mistaken," I said, and examining the map, I added, "We have passed Cape Portland, and those fifty leagues bring us under the wide expanse of ocean."

"Under the sea," my uncle repeated, rubbing his hands with delight.

"Can it be?" I said. "Is the ocean spread above our heads?"

"Of course, Axel. What can be more natural? At Newcastle are there not coal mines extending far under the sea?"

It was all very well for the professor to call this so simple, but I could not feel quite easy at the thought that the boundless ocean was rolling over my head. And yet it really mattered very little whether it was the plains and mountains that covered our heads, or the Atlantic waves, as long as we were arched over by solid granite. And, besides, I was getting used to this idea; for the tunnel, now running straight, now winding as capriciously in its inclines as in its turnings, but constantly preserving its southeasterly direction, and always running deeper, was gradually carrying us to very great depths indeed.

Four days later, Saturday, the 18th of July, in the evening, we arrived at a kind of vast grotto; and here my uncle paid Hans his weekly wages, and it was settled that the next day, Sunday, should be a day of rest.

XXV

DE PROFUNDIS

I therefore awoke next day relieved from the preoccupation of an immediate start. Although we were in the very deepest of known depths, there was something not unpleasant about it. And, besides, we were beginning to get accustomed to this troglodyte* life. I no longer thought of sun, moon, and stars, trees, houses, and towns, nor of any of those terrestrial superfluities which are necessaries of men who live upon the earth's surface. Being fossils, we looked upon all those things as mere jokes.

* **τρωγλη**, a hole; δύω, to creep into. The name of an Ethiopian tribe who lived in caves and holes.

The grotto was an immense apartment. Along its granite floor ran our faithful stream. At this distance from its spring the water was scarcely tepid, and we drank of it with pleasure.

After breakfast the professor gave a few hours to the arrangement of his daily notes.

"First," said he, "I will make a calculation to ascertain our exact position. I hope, after our return, to draw a map of our journey, which will be in reality a vertical section of the globe, containing the track of our expedition."

"That will be curious, uncle; but are your observations sufficiently accurate to enable you to do this correctly?"

"Yes; I have everywhere observed the angles and the inclines. I am sure there is no error. Let us see where we are now. Take your compass, and note the direction."

I looked, and replied carefully:

"Southeast by east."

"Well," answered the professor, after a rapid calculation, "I infer that we have gone eighty-five leagues since we started."

"Therefore we are under mid-Atlantic?"

"To be sure we are."

"And perhaps at this very moment there is a storm above, and ships over our heads are being rudely tossed by the tempest."

"Quite probable."

"And whales are lashing the roof of our prison with their tails?"

"It may be, Axel, but they won't shake us here. But let us go back to our calculation. Here we are eighty-five leagues southeast of Snæfell, and I reckon that we are at a depth of sixteen leagues."

"Sixteen leagues?" I cried.

"No doubt."

"Why, this is the very limit assigned by science to the thickness of the crust of the earth."

"I don't deny it."

"And here, according to the law of increasing temperature, there ought to be a heat of 2,732°F!"

"So there should, my lad."

"And all this solid granite ought to be running in fusion."

"You see that it is not so, and that, as so often happens, facts come to overthrow theories."

"I am obliged to agree; but, after all, it is surprising."

"What does the thermometer say?"

"Twenty-seven, six tenths (82°F)."

"Therefore the savants are wrong by 2,705°, and the proportional increase is a mistake. Therefore Humphry Davy was right, and I am not wrong in following him. What do you say now?"

"Nothing."

In truth, I had a good deal to say. I gave way in no respect to Davy's theory. I still held to the central heat, although I did not feel its effects. I preferred to admit in truth, that this chimney of an extinct volcano, lined with lavas, which are nonconductors of heat, did not suffer the heat to pass through its walls.

But without stopping to look up new arguments, I simply took up our situation such as it was.

"Well, admitting all your calculations to be quite correct, you must allow me to draw one rigid result therefrom."

"What is it? Speak freely."

"At the latitude of Iceland, where we now are, the radius of the earth, the distance from the center to the surface is about 1,583 leagues; let us say in round numbers 1,600 leagues, or 4,800 miles. Out of 1,600 leagues we have gone twelve!"

"So you say."

"And these twelve at a cost of 85 leagues diagonally?"

"Exactly so."

"In twenty days?"

"Yes."

"Now, sixteen leagues are the hundredth part of the earth's radius. At this rate we shall be two thousand days, or nearly five years and a half, in getting to the center."

No answer was vouchsafed to this rational conclusion. "Without reckoning, too, that if a vertical depth of sixteen leagues can be attained only by a diagonal descent of eighty-four, it follows that we must go eight thousand miles in a southeasterly direction; so that we shall emerge from some point in the earth's circumference instead of getting to the center!"

"Confusion to all your figures, and all your hypotheses besides," shouted my uncle in a sudden rage. "What is the basis of them all? How do you know that this passage does not run straight to our destination? Besides, there is a precedent. What one man has done, another may do."

"I hope so; but, still, I may be permitted—"

"You shall have my leave to hold your tongue, Axel, but not to talk in that irrational way."

I could see the awful professor bursting through my uncle's skin, and I took timely warning.

"Now look at your aneroid. What does that say?"

"It says we are under considerable pressure."

"Very good; so you see that by going gradually down, and getting accustomed to the density of the atmosphere, we don't suffer at all."

"Nothing, except a little pain in the ears."

"That's nothing, and you may get rid of even that by quick breathing whenever you feel the pain."

"Exactly so," I said, determined not to say a word that might cross my uncle's prejudices. "There is even positive pleasure in living in this dense atmosphere. Have you observed how intense sound is down here?"

"No doubt it is. A deaf man would soon learn to hear perfectly."

"But won't this density augment?"

"Yes; according to a rather obscure law. It is well known that the weight of bodies diminishes as fast as we descend. You know that it is at the surface of the globe that weight is most sensibly felt, and that at the center there is no weight at all."

"I am aware of that; but, tell me, will not air at last acquire the density of water?"

"Of course, under a pressure of seven hundred and ten atmospheres."

"And how, lower down still?"

"Lower down the density will still increase."

"But how shall we go down then?"

"Why, we must fill our pockets with stones."

"Well, indeed, my worthy uncle, you are never at a loss for an answer."

I dared venture no farther into the region of probabilities, for I might presently have stumbled upon an impossibility, which would have brought the professor on the scene when he was not wanted.

Still, it was evident that the air, under a pressure which might reach that of thousands of atmospheres, would at last reach the solid state, and then, even if our bodies could resist the strain, we should be stopped, and no reasonings would be able to get us on any farther.

But I did not advance this argument. My uncle would have met it with his inevitable Saknussemm, a precedent which possessed no weight with me; for even if the journey of the learned Icelander were really attested, there was one very simple answer, that in the sixteenth century there was neither barometer or aneroid and therefore Saknussemm could not tell how far he had gone.

But I kept this objection to myself, and waited the course of events.

The rest of the day was passed in calculations and in conversations. I remained a steadfast adherent of the opinions of Professor Liedenbrock, and I envied the stolid indifference of Hans, who, without going into causes and effects, went on with his eyes shut wherever his destiny guided him.

XXVI

THE WORST PERIL OF ALL

It must be confessed that hitherto things had not gone on so badly, and that I had small reason to complain. If our difficulties became no worse, we might hope to reach our end. And to what a height of scientific glory we should then attain! I had become quite a Liedenbrock in my reasonings; seriously I had. But would this state of things last in the strange place we had come to? Perhaps it might.

For several days steeper inclines, some even frightfully near to the perpendicular, brought us deeper and deeper into the mass of the interior of the earth. Some days we advanced nearer to the center by a league and a half, or nearly two leagues. These were perilous descents, in which the skill and marvelous coolness of Hans were invaluable to us. That unimpassioned Icelander devoted himself with incomprehensible deliberation; and, thanks to him, we crossed many a dangerous spot which we should never have cleared alone.

But his habit of silence gained upon him day by day, and was infecting us. External objects produce decided effects upon the brain. A man shut up between four walls soon loses the power to associate words and ideas together. How many prisoners in solitary confinement become idiots, if not mad, for want of exercise for the thinking faculty!

During the fortnight following our last conversation, no incident occurred worthy of being recorded. But I have good reason for remembering one very serious event which took place at this time, and of which I could scarcely now forget the smallest details.

By the 7th of August our successive descents had brought us to a depth of thirty leagues; that is, that for a space of thirty leagues there were over our heads solid beds of rock, ocean, continents, and towns. We must have been two hundred leagues from Iceland.

On that day the tunnel went down a gentle slope. I was ahead of the others. My uncle was carrying one of Ruhmkorff's lamps and I the other. I was examining the beds of granite.

Suddenly turning round I observed that I was alone.

Well, well, I thought; I have been going too fast, or Hans and my uncle have stopped on the way. Come, this won't do; I must join them. Fortunately there is not much of an ascent.

I retraced my steps. I walked for a quarter of an hour. I gazed into the darkness. I shouted. No reply: my voice was lost in the midst of the cavernous echoes which alone replied to my call.

I began to feel uneasy. A shudder ran through me.

"Calmly!" I said aloud to myself. "I am sure to find my companions again. There are not two roads. I was too far ahead. I will return!"

For half an hour I climbed up. I listened for a call, and in that dense atmosphere a voice could reach very far. But there was a dreary silence in all that long gallery. I stopped. I could not believe that I was lost. I was only bewildered for a time, not lost. I was sure I should find my way again.

"Come," I repeated, "since there is but one road, and they are on it, I must find them again. I have but to ascend still. Unless, indeed, missing me, and supposing me to be behind, they too should have gone back. But even in this case I have only to make the greater haste. I shall find them, I am sure."

I repeated these words in the fainter tones of a half-convinced man. Besides, to associate even such simple ideas with words, and reason with them, was a work of time.

A doubt then seized upon me. Was I indeed in advance when we became separated? Yes, to be sure I was. Hans was after me, preceding my uncle. He had even stopped for a while to strap his baggage better over his shoulders. I could remember this little incident. It was at that very moment that I must have gone on.

Besides, I thought, have not I a guarantee that I shall not lose my way, a clue in the labyrinth, that cannot be broken, my faithful stream? I have but to trace it back, and I must come upon them.

This conclusion revived my spirits, and I resolved to resume my march without loss of time.

How I then blessed my uncle's foresight in preventing the hunter from stopping up the hole in the granite. This beneficent spring, after having satisfied our thirst on the road, would now be my guide among the windings of the terrestrial crust.

Before starting afresh I thought a wash would do me good. I stooped to bathe my face in the Hansbach.

To my stupefaction and utter dismay my feet trod only—the rough dry granite. The stream was no longer at my feet.

XXVII

LOST IN THE BOWELS OF THE EARTH

To describe my despair would be impossible. No words could tell it. I was buried alive, with the prospect before me of dying of hunger and thirst.

Mechanically I swept the ground with my hands. How dry and hard the rock seemed to me!

But how had I left the course of the stream? For it was a terrible fact that it no longer ran at my side. Then I understood the reason of that fearful silence, when for the last time I listened to hear if any sound from my companions could reach my ears. At the moment when I left the right road I had not noticed the absence of the stream. It is evident that at that moment a deviation had presented itself before me, while the Hansbach, following the caprice of another incline, had gone with my companions away into unknown depths.

How was I to return? There was not a trace of their footsteps or of my own, for the foot left no mark upon the granite floor. I racked my brain for a solution of this impracticable problem. One word described my position. Lost!

Lost at an immeasurable depth! Thirty leagues of rock seemed to weigh upon my shoulders with a dreadful pressure. I felt crushed.

I tried to carry back my ideas to things on the surface of the earth. I could scarcely succeed. Hamburg, the house in the Königstrasse, my poor Gräuben, all that busy world underneath which I was wandering about, was passing in rapid confusion before my terrified memory. I could revive with vivid reality all the incidents of our voyage, Iceland, M. Fridrikssen, Snæfell. I said to myself that if, in such a position as I was now in, I was fool enough to cling to one glimpse of hope, it would be madness, and that the best thing I could do was to despair.

What human power could restore me to the light of the sun by rending asunder the huge arches of rock which united over my head, buttressing each other with impregnable strength? Who could place my feet on the right path, and bring me back to my company?

"Oh, my uncle!" burst from my lips in the tone of despair.

It was my only word of reproach, for I knew how much he must be suffering in seeking me, wherever he might be.

When I saw myself thus far removed from all earthly help, I had recourse to heavenly succour. The remembrance of my childhood, the recollection of my mother, whom I had only known in my tender early years, came back to me, and I knelt in prayer imploring for the divine help of which I was so little worthy.

This return of trust in God's providence allayed the turbulence of my fears, and I was enabled to concentrate upon my situation all the force of my intelligence.

I had three days' provisions with me and my flask was full. But I could not remain alone for long. Should I go up or down?

Up, of course; up continually.

I must thus arrive at the point where I had left the stream, that fatal turn in the road. With the stream at my feet, I might hope to regain the summit of Snæfell.

Why had I not thought of that sooner? Here was evidently a chance of safety. The most pressing duty was to find out again the course of the Hansbach. I rose, and leaning upon my iron-pointed stick I ascended the gallery. The slope was rather steep. I walked on without hope but without indecision, like a man who has made up his mind.

For half an hour I met with no obstacle. I tried to recognize my way by the form of the tunnel, by the projections of certain rocks, by the disposition of the fractures. But no particular sign appeared, and I soon saw that this gallery could not bring me back to the turning point. It came to an abrupt end. I struck against an impenetrable wall, and fell down upon the rock.

Unspeakable despair then seized upon me. I lay overwhelmed, aghast! My last hope was shattered against this granite wall.

Lost in this labyrinth, whose windings crossed each other in all directions, it was no use to think of flight any longer. Here I must die the most dreadful of deaths. And, strange to say, the thought came across me that when someday my petrified remains should be found thirty leagues below the surface in the bowels of the earth, the discovery might lead to grave scientific discussions.

I tried to speak aloud, but hoarse sounds alone passed my dry lips. I panted for breath.

In the midst of my agony a new terror laid hold of me. In falling my lamp had got wrong. I could not set it right, and its light was paling and would soon disappear altogether.

I gazed painfully upon the luminous current growing weaker and weaker in the wire coil. A dim procession of moving shadows seemed slowly unfolding down the darkening walls. I scarcely dared to shut my eyes for one moment, for fear of losing the least glimmer of this precious light. Every instant it seemed about to vanish and the dense blackness to come rolling in palpably upon me.

One last trembling glimmer shot feebly up. I watched it in trembling and anxiety; I drank it in as if I could preserve it, concentrating upon it the full power of my eyes, as upon the very last sensation of light which they were ever to experience, and the next moment I lay in the heavy gloom of deep, thick, unfathomable darkness.

A terrible cry of anguish burst from me. Upon earth, in the midst of the darkest night, light never abdicates its functions altogether. It is still subtle and diffusive, but whatever little there may be, the eye still catches that little. Here there was not an atom; the total darkness made me totally blind.

Then I began to lose my head. I arose with my arms stretched out before me, attempting painfully to feel my way. I began to run wildly, hurrying through the inextricable maze, still descending, still running through the substance of the earth's thick crust, a struggling denizen of geological "faults," crying, shouting, yelling, soon bruised by contact with the jagged rock, falling and rising again bleeding, trying to drink the blood which covered my face, and even waiting for some rock to shatter my skull against.

I shall never know whither my mad career took me. After the lapse of some hours, no doubt exhausted, I fell like a lifeless lump at the foot of the wall, and lost all consciousness.

XXVIII

THE RESCUE IN THE WHISPERING GALLERY

When I returned to partial life my face was wet with tears. How long that state of insensibility had lasted I cannot say. I had no means now of taking account of time. Never was solitude equal to this, never had any living being been so utterly forsaken.

After my fall I had lost a good deal of blood. I felt it flowing over me. Ah! How happy I should have been could I have died, and if death were not yet to be gone through. I would think no longer. I drove away every idea, and, conquered by my grief, I rolled myself to the foot of the opposite wall.

Already I was feeling the approach of another faint, and was hoping for complete annihilation, when a loud noise reached me. It was like the distant rumble of continuous thunder, and I could hear its sounding undulations rolling far away into the remote recesses of the abyss.

Whence could this noise proceed? It must be from some phenomenon proceeding in the great depths amid which I lay helpless. Was it an explosion of gas? Was it the fall of some mighty pillar of the globe?

I listened still. I wanted to know if the noise would be repeated. A quarter of an hour passed away. Silence reigned in this gallery. I could not hear even the beating of my heart.

Suddenly my ear, resting by chance against the wall, caught, or seemed to catch, certain vague, indescribable, distant, articulate sounds, as of words.

"This is a delusion," I thought.

But it was not. Listening more attentively, I heard in reality a murmuring of voices. But my weakness prevented me from understanding what the voices said. Yet it was language, I was sure of it.

For a moment I feared the words might be my own, brought back by the echo. Perhaps I had been crying out unknown to myself. I closed my lips firmly, and laid my ear against the wall again.

"Yes, truly, someone is speaking; those are words!"

Even a few feet from the wall I could hear distinctly. I succeeded in catching uncertain, strange, indistinguishable words. They came as if pronounced in low murmured whispers. The word "*forlorad*" was several times repeated in a tone of sympathy and sorrow.

"Help!" I cried with all my might. "Help!"

I listened, I watched in the darkness for an answer, a cry, a mere breath of sound, but nothing came. Some minutes passed. A whole world of ideas had opened in my mind. I thought that my weakened voice could never penetrate to my companions.

"It is they," I repeated. "What other men can be thirty leagues underground?"

I again began to listen. Passing my ear over the wall from one place to another, I found the point where the voices seemed to be best heard. The word "*forlorad*" again returned; then the rolling of thunder which had roused me from my lethargy.

"No," I said, "no; it is not through such a mass that a voice can be heard. I am surrounded by granite walls, and the loudest explosion could never be heard here! This noise comes along the gallery. There must be here some remarkable exercise of acoustic laws!"

I listened again, and this time, yes this time, I did distinctly hear my name pronounced across the wide interval.

It was my uncle's own voice! He was talking to the guide. And "*forlorad*" is a Danish word.

Then I understood it all. To make myself heard, I must speak along this wall, which would conduct the sound of my voice just as wire conducts electricity.

But there was no time to lose. If my companions moved but a few steps away, the acoustic phenomenon would cease. I therefore approached the wall, and pronounced these words as clearly as possible:

"Uncle Liedenbrock!"

I waited with the deepest anxiety. Sound does not travel with great velocity. Even increased density air has no effect upon its rate of traveling; it merely augments its intensity. Seconds, which seemed ages, passed away, and at last these words reached me:

"Axel! Axel! Is it you?"

. . .

"Yes, yes," I replied.

. . .

"My boy, where are you?"

. . .

"Lost, in the deepest darkness."

. . .

"Where is your lamp?"

. . .

"It is out."

. . .

"And the stream?"

. . .

"Disappeared."

. . .

"Axel, Axel, take courage!"

. . .

"Wait! I am exhausted! I can't answer. Speak to me!"

. . .

"Courage," resumed my uncle. "Don't speak. Listen to me. We have looked for you up the gallery and down the gallery. Could not find you. I wept for you, my poor boy. At last, supposing you were still on the Hansbach, we fired our guns. Our voices are audible to each other, but our hands cannot touch. But don't despair, Axel! It is a great thing that we can hear each other."

. . .

During this time I had been reflecting. A vague hope was returning to my heart. There was one thing I must know to begin with. I placed my lips close to the wall, saying:

"My uncle!"

. . .

"My boy!" came to me after a few seconds.

. . .

"We must know how far we are apart."

. . .

"That is easy."

. . .

"You have your chronometer?"

. . .

"Yes."

. . .

"Well, take it. Pronounce my name, noting exactly the second when you speak. I will repeat it as soon as it shall come to me, and you will observe the exact moment when you get my answer."

"Yes; and half the time between my call and your answer will exactly indicate that which my voice will take in coming to you."

. . .

"Just so, my uncle."

. . .

"Are you ready?"

. . .

"Yes."

. . .

"Now, attention. I am going to call your name."

. . .

I put my ear to the wall, and as soon as the name "Axel" came I immediately replied "Axel," then waited.

. . .

"Forty seconds," said my uncle. "Forty seconds between the two words; so the sound takes twenty seconds in coming. Now, at the rate of 1,120 feet in a second, this is 22,400 feet, or four miles and a quarter, nearly."

. . .

"Four miles and a quarter!" I murmured.

. . .

"It will soon be over, Axel."

. . .

"Must I go up or down?"

. . .

"Down—for this reason: We are in a vast chamber, with endless galleries. Yours must lead into it, for it seems as if all the clefts and fractures of the globe radiated round this vast cavern. So get up, and begin walking. Walk on, drag yourself along, if necessary slide down the steep places, and at the end you will find us ready to receive you. Now begin moving."

. . .

These words cheered me up.

"Good-bye, uncle." I cried. "I am going. There will be no more voices heard when once I have started. So good-bye!"

. . .

"Good-bye, Axel, *au revoir!*"

. . .

These were the last words I heard.

This wonderful underground conversation, carried on with a distance of four miles and a quarter between us, concluded with these words of hope. I thanked God from my heart, for it was He who had conducted me through those vast solitudes to the point where, alone of all others perhaps, the voices of my companions could have reached me.

This acoustic effect is easily explained on scientific grounds. It arose from the concave form of the gallery and the conducting power of the rock. There are many examples of this propagation of sounds which remain unheard in the intermediate space. I remember that a similar phenomenon has been observed in many places; among others, on the internal surface of the gallery of the dome of St. Paul's in London, and especially in the midst of the curious caverns among the quarries near Syracuse, the most wonderful of which is called Dionysus's Ear.

These remembrances came into my mind, and I clearly saw that since my uncle's voice really reached me, there could be no obstacle between us. Following the direction by which the sound came, of course I should arrive in his presence, if my strength did not fail me.

I therefore rose; I rather dragged myself than walked. The slope was rapid, and I slid down.

Soon the swiftness of the descent increased horribly, and threatened to become a fall. I no longer had the strength to stop myself.

Suddenly there was no ground under me. I felt myself revolving in air, striking and rebounding against the craggy projections of a vertical gallery, quite a well; my head struck against a sharp corner of the rock, and I became unconscious.

XXIX

THALATTA! THALATTA!

When I came to myself, I was stretched in half darkness, covered with thick coats and blankets. My uncle was watching over me, to discover the least sign of life. At my first sigh he took my hand; when I opened my eyes he uttered a cry of joy.

"He lives! He lives!" he cried.

"Yes, I am still alive," I answered feebly.

"My dear nephew," said my uncle, pressing me to his breast, "you are saved."

I was deeply touched with the tenderness of his manner as he uttered these words, and still more with the care with which he watched over me. But such trials were wanted to bring out the professor's tenderer qualities.

At this moment Hans came, he saw my hand in my uncle's, and I may safely say that there was joy in his countenance.

"*God dag*," said he.

"How do you do, Hans? How are you? And now, uncle, tell me where we are at the present moment."

"Tomorrow, Axel, tomorrow. Now you are too faint and weak. I have bandaged your head with compresses which must not be disturbed. Sleep now, and tomorrow I will tell you all."

"But do tell me what time it is, and what day."

"It is Sunday, the 8th of August, and it is ten at night. You must ask me no more questions until the 10th."

In truth I was very weak, and my eyes involuntarily closed. I wanted a good night's rest; and I therefore went off to sleep, with the knowledge that I had been four long days alone in the heart of the earth.

Next morning, on awakening, I looked round me. My couch, made up of all our traveling gear, was in a charming grotto, adorned with splendid stalactites, and the soil of which was a fine sand. It was half light. There was no torch, no lamp, yet certain mysterious glimpses of light came from without through a narrow opening in the grotto. I heard too a vague and indistinct noise, something like the murmuring of waves breaking upon a shingly shore, and at times I seemed to hear the whistling of wind.

I wondered whether I was awake, whether I was dreaming, whether my brain, crazed by my fall, was not affected by imaginary noises. Yet neither eyes nor ears could be so utterly deceived.

It is a ray of daylight, I thought, sliding in through this cleft in the rock! That is indeed the murmuring of waves! That is the rustling noise of wind. Am I quite mistaken, or have we returned to the surface of the earth? Has my uncle given up the expedition, or is it happily terminated?

I was asking myself these unanswerable questions when the professor entered.

"Good morning, Axel," he cried cheerily. "I feel sure you are better."

"Yes, I am indeed," said I, sitting up on my couch.

"You can hardly fail to be better, for you have slept quietly. Hans and I watched you by turns, and we have noticed you were evidently recovering."

"Indeed, I do feel a great deal better, and I will give you a proof of that presently if you will let me have my breakfast."

"You shall eat, lad. The fever has left you. Hans rubbed your wounds with some ointment or other of which the Icelanders keep the secret, and they have healed marvelously. Our hunter is a splendid fellow!"

While he went on talking, my uncle prepared a few provisions, which I devoured eagerly, notwithstanding his advice to the contrary. All the while I was overwhelming him with questions which he answered readily.

I then learned that my providential fall had brought me exactly to the extremity of an almost perpendicular shaft; and as I had landed in the midst of an accompanying torrent of stones, the least of which would have been enough to crush me, the conclusion was that a loose portion of the rock had come down with me. This frightful conveyance had thus carried me into the arms of my uncle, where I fell bruised, bleeding, and insensible.

"Truly it is wonderful that you have not been killed a hundred times over. But, for the love of God, don't let us ever separate again, or we many never see each other more."

"Not separate! Is the journey not over, then?" I opened a pair of astonished eyes, which immediately called for the question:

"What is the matter, Axel?"

"I have a question to ask you. You say that I am safe and sound?"

"No doubt you are."

"And all my limbs unbroken?"

"Certainly."

"And my head?"

"Your head, except for a few bruises, is all right; and it is on your shoulders, where it ought to be."

"Well, I am afraid my brain is affected."

"Your mind affected!"

"Yes, I fear so. Are we again on the surface of the globe?"

"No, certainly not."

"Then I must be mad; for don't I see the light of day, and don't I hear the wind blowing, and the sea breaking on the shore?"

"Ah! Is that all?"

"Do tell me all about it."

"I can't explain the inexplicable, but you will soon see and understand that geology has not yet learned all it has to learn."

"Then let us go," I answered quickly.

"No, Axel; the open air might be bad for you."

"Open air?"

"Yes; the wind is rather strong. You must not expose yourself."

"But I assure you I am perfectly well."

"A little patience, my nephew. A relapse might get us into trouble, and we have no time to lose, for the voyage may be a long one."

"The voyage!"

"Yes, rest today, and tomorrow we will set sail."

"Set sail!"—and I almost leaped up.

What did it all mean? Had we a river, a lake, a sea to depend upon? Was there a ship at our disposal in some underground harbor?

My curiosity was highly excited, my uncle vainly tried to restrain me. When he saw that my impatience was doing me harm, he yielded.

I dressed in haste. For greater safety I wrapped myself in a blanket, and came out of the grotto.

XXX

A NEW MARE INTERNUM

At first I could hardly see anything. My eyes, unaccustomed to the light, quickly closed. When I was able to reopen them, I stood more stupefied even than surprised.

"The sea!" I cried.

"Yes," my uncle replied, "the Liedenbrock Sea; and I don't suppose any other discoverer will ever dispute my claim to name it after myself as its first discoverer."

A vast sheet of water, the commencement of a lake or an ocean, spread far away beyond the range of the eye, reminding me forcibly of that open sea which drew from Xenophon's ten thousand Greeks, after their long retreat, the simultaneous cry, "Thalatta! Thalatta!" The sea! The sea! The deeply indented shore was lined with a breadth of fine shining sand, softly lapped by the waves, and strewn with the small shells which had been inhabited by the first of created beings. The waves broke on this shore with the hollow echoing murmur peculiar to vast enclosed spaces. A light foam flew over the waves before the breath of a moderate breeze, and some of the spray fell upon my face. On this slightly inclining shore, about a hundred fathoms from the limit of the waves, came down the foot of a huge wall of vast cliffs, which rose majestically to an enormous height. Some of these, dividing the beach with their sharp spurs, formed capes and promontories, worn away by the ceaseless action of the surf. Farther on, the eye discerned their massive outline sharply defined against the hazy distant horizon.

It was quite an ocean, with the irregular shores of earth, but desert and frightfully wild in appearance.

If my eyes were able to range afar over this great sea, it was because a peculiar light brought to view every detail of it. It was not the light of the sun, with his dazzling shafts of brightness and the splendor of his rays; nor was it the pale and uncertain shimmer of the moonbeams, the dim reflection of a nobler body of light. No; the illuminating power of this light, its trembling diffusiveness, its bright, clear whiteness, and its low temperature, showed that it must be of electric origin. It was like an aurora borealis, a continuous cosmical phenomenon, filling a cavern of sufficient extent to contain an ocean.

The vault that spanned the space above, the sky, if it could be called so, seemed composed of vast plains of cloud, shifting and variable vapors, which by their condensation must at certain times fall in torrents of rain. I should have thought that under so powerful a pressure of the atmosphere there could be no evaporation; and yet, under a law unknown to me, there were broad tracts of vapor suspended in the air. But then "the weather was fine." The play of the electric light produced singular effects upon the upper strata of cloud. Deep shadows reposed upon their lower wreaths; and often, between two separated fields of cloud, there glided down a ray of unspeakable luster. But it was not solar light, and there was no heat. The general effect was sad, supremely melancholy. Instead of the shining firmament, spangled with its innumerable stars, shining singly or in clusters, I felt that all these subdued and shaded lights were ribbed in by vast walls of granite, which seemed to overpower me with their weight, and that all this space, great as it was, would not be enough for the march of the humblest of satellites.

Then I remembered the theory of an English captain who likened the earth to a vast hollow sphere, in the interior of which the air became luminous because of the vast pressure that weighed upon it; while two stars, Pluto and Proserpine, rolled within upon the circuit of their mysterious orbits.

We were in reality shut up inside an immeasurable excavation. Its width could not be estimated, since the shore ran widening as far as eye could reach, nor could its length, for the dim horizon bounded the new. As for its height, it must have been several leagues. Where this vault rested upon its granite base no eye could tell; but there was a cloud hanging far above, the height of which we estimated at 12,000 feet, a greater height than that of any terrestrial vapor, and no doubt due to the great density of the air.

The word cavern does not convey any idea of this immense space; words of human tongue are inadequate to describe the discoveries of him who ventures into the deep abysses of earth.

Besides, I could not tell upon what geological theory to account for the existence of such an excavation. Had the cooling of the globe produced it? I knew of celebrated caverns from the descriptions of travelers, but had never heard of any of such dimensions as this.

If the grotto of Guachara, in Colombia, visited by Humboldt, had not given up the whole of the secret of its depth to the philosopher, who investigated it to the depth of 2,500 feet, it probably did not extend much farther. The immense mammoth cave in Kentucky is of gigantic proportions, since its vaulted roof rises five hundred feet above the level of an unfathomable lake and travelers have explored its ramifications to the extent of forty miles. But what were these cavities compared to that in which I stood with wonder and admiration, with its sky of luminous vapors, its bursts of electric light, and a vast sea filling its bed? My imagination fell powerless before such immensity.

I gazed upon these wonders in silence. Words failed me to express my feelings. I felt as if I was in some distant planet Uranus or Neptune—and in the presence of phenomena of which my terrestrial experience gave me no cognizance. For such novel sensations, new words were wanted; and my imagination failed to supply them. I gazed, I thought, I admired, with a stupefaction mingled with a certain amount of fear.

The unforeseen nature of this spectacle brought back the color to my cheeks. I was under a new course of treatment with the aid of astonishment, and my convalescence was promoted by this novel system of therapeutics; besides, the dense and breezy air invigorated me, supplying more oxygen to my lungs.

It will be easily conceived that after an imprisonment of forty-seven days in a narrow gallery, it was the height of physical enjoyment to breathe a moist air impregnated with saline particles.

I was delighted to leave my dark grotto. My uncle, already familiar with these wonders, had ceased to feel surprise.

"You feel strong enough to walk a little way now?" he asked.

"Yes, certainly; and nothing could be more delightful."

"Well, take my arm, Axel, and let us follow the windings of the shore."

I eagerly accepted, and we began to coast along this new sea. On the left huge pyramids of rock, piled one upon another, produced a prodigious titanic effect. Down their sides flowed numberless waterfalls, which went on their way in brawling but pellucid streams. A few light vapors, leaping from rock to rock, denoted the place of hot springs; and streams flowed softly down to the common basin, gliding down the gentle slopes with a softer murmur.

Among these streams I recognized our faithful traveling companion, the Hansbach, coming to lose its little volume quietly in the mighty sea, just as if it had done nothing else since the beginning of the world.

"We shall see it no more," I said, with a sigh.

"What matters," replied the philosopher, "whether this or another serves to guide us?"

I thought him rather ungrateful.

But at that moment my attention was drawn to an unexpected sight. At a distance of five hundred paces, at the turn of a high promontory, appeared a high, tufted, dense forest. It was composed of trees of moderate height, formed like umbrellas, with exact geometrical outlines. The currents of wind seemed to have had no effect upon their shape, and in the midst of the windy blasts they stood unmoved and firm, just like a clump of petrified cedars.

I hastened forward. I could not give any name to these singular creations. Were they some of the two hundred thousand species of vegetables known hitherto, and did they claim a place of their own in the lacustrine flora? No; when we arrived under their shade my surprise turned into admiration. There stood before me productions of earth, but of gigantic stature, which my uncle immediately named.

"It is only a forest of mushrooms," said he.

And he was right. Imagine the large development attained by these plants, which prefer a warm, moist climate. I knew that the *Lycopodon giganteum* attains, according to Bulliard, a circumference of eight or nine feet; but here were pale mushrooms, thirty to forty feet high, and crowned with a cap of equal diameter. There they stood in thousands. No light could penetrate between their huge cones, and complete darkness reigned beneath those giants; they formed settlements of domes placed in close array like the round, thatched roofs of a central African city.

Yet I wanted to penetrate farther underneath, though a chill fell upon me as soon as I came under those cellular vaults. For half an hour we wandered from side to side in the damp shades, and it was a comfortable and pleasant change to arrive once more upon the seashore.

But the subterranean vegetation was not confined to these fungi. Farther on rose groups of tall trees of colorless foliage and easy to recognize. They were lowly shrubs of earth, here attaining gigantic size; lycopodiums, a hundred feet high; the huge sigillaria, found in our coal mines; tree ferns, as tall as our fir trees in northern latitudes; lepidodendra, with cylindrical forked stems, terminated by long leaves, and bristling with rough hairs like those of the cactus.

"Wonderful, magnificent, splendid!" cried my uncle. "Here is the entire flora of the second period of the world—the transition period. These, humble garden plants with us, were tall trees in the early ages. Look, Axel, and admire it all. Never had botanist such a feast as this!"

"You are right, my uncle. Providence seems to have preserved in this immense conservatory the antediluvian plants which the wisdom of philosophers has so sagaciously put together again."

"It is a conservatory, Axel; but is it not also a menagerie?"

"Surely not a menagerie!"

"Yes; no doubt of it. Look at that dust under your feet; see the bones scattered on the ground."

"So there are!" I cried. "Bones of extinct animals."

I had rushed upon these remains, formed of indestructible phosphates of lime, and without hesitation I named these monstrous bones, which lay scattered about like decayed trunks of trees.

"Here is the lower jaw of a mastodon," I said. "These are the molar teeth of the deinotherium; this femur must have belonged to the greatest of those beasts, the megatherium. It certainly is a menagerie, for these remains were not brought here by a deluge. The animals to which they belonged roamed on the shores of this subterranean sea, under the shade of those arborescent trees. Here are entire skeletons. And yet I cannot understand the appearance of these quadrupeds in a granite cavern."

"Why?"

"Because animal life existed upon the earth only in the secondary period, when a sediment of soil had been deposited by the rivers, and taken the place of the incandescent rocks of the primitive period."

"Well, Axel, there is a very simple answer to your objection that this soil is alluvial."

"What! At such a depth below the surface of the earth?"

"No doubt; and there is a geological explanation of the fact. At a certain period the earth consisted only of an elastic crust or bark, alternately acted on by forces from above or below, according to the laws of attraction and gravitation. Probably there were subsidences of the outer crust, when a portion of the sedimentary deposits was carried down sudden openings."

"That may be," I replied; "but if there have been creatures now extinct in these underground regions, why may not some of those monsters be now roaming through these gloomy forests, or hidden behind the steep crags?"

And as this unpleasant notion got hold of me, I surveyed with anxious scrutiny the open spaces before me; but no living creature appeared upon the barren strand.

I felt rather tired, and went to sit down at the end of a promontory, at the foot of which the waves came and beat themselves into spray. Thence my eye could sweep every part of the bay; within its extremity a little harbor was formed between the pyramidal cliffs, where the still waters slept untouched by the boisterous winds. A brig and two or three schooners might have moored within it in safety. I almost fancied I should presently see some ship issue from it, full sail, and take to the open sea under the southern breeze.

But this illusion lasted a very short time. We were the only living creatures in this subterranean world. When the wind lulled, a deeper silence than that of the deserts fell upon the arid, naked rocks, and weighed upon the surface of the ocean. I then desired to pierce the distant haze, and to rend asunder the mysterious curtain that hung across the horizon. Anxious queries arose to my lips. Where did that sea terminate? Where did it lead to? Should we ever know anything about its opposite shores?

My uncle made no doubt about it at all; I both desired and feared.

After spending an hour in the contemplation of this marvelous spectacle, we returned to the shore to regain the grotto, and I fell asleep in the midst of the strangest thoughts.

XXXI

PREPARATIONS FOR A VOYAGE OF DISCOVERY

The next morning I awoke feeling perfectly well. I thought a bath would do me good, and I went to plunge for a few minutes into the waters of this Mediterranean Sea, for assuredly it better deserved this name than any other sea.

I came back to breakfast with a good appetite. Hans was a good caterer for our little household; he had water and fire at his disposal, so that he was able to vary our bill of fare now and then. For dessert he gave us a few cups of coffee, and never was coffee so delicious.

"Now," said my uncle, "now is the time for high tide, and we must not lose the opportunity to study this phenomenon."

"What! The tide!" I cried. "Can the influence of the sun and moon be felt down here?"

"Why not? Are not all bodies subject throughout their mass to the power of universal attraction? This mass of water cannot escape the general law. And in spite of the heavy atmospheric pressure on the surface, you will see it rise like the Atlantic itself."

At the same moment we reached the sand on the shore, and the waves were by slow degrees encroaching on the shore.

"Here is the tide rising," I cried.

"Yes, Axel; and judging by these ridges of foam, you may observe that the sea will rise about twelve feet."

"This is wonderful," I said.

"No; it is quite natural."

"You may say so, uncle; but to me it is most extraordinary, and I can hardly believe my eyes. Who would ever have imagined, under this terrestrial crust, an ocean with ebbing and flowing tides, with winds and storms?"

"Well," replied my uncle, "is there any scientific reason against it?"

"No; I see none, as soon as the theory of central heat is given up."

"So then, thus far," he answered, "the theory of Sir Humphry Davy is confirmed."

"Evidently it is; and now there is no reason why there should not be seas and continents in the interior of the earth."

"No doubt," said my uncle; "and inhabited too."

"To be sure," said I; "and why should not these waters yield to us fishes of unknown species?"

"At any rate," he replied, "we have not seen any yet."

"Well, let us make some lines, and see if the bait will draw here as it does in sublunary regions."

"We will try, Axel, for we must penetrate all secrets of these newly discovered regions."

"But where are we, uncle? For I have not yet asked you that question, and your instruments must be able to furnish the answer."

"Horizontally, three hundred and fifty leagues from Iceland."

"So much as that?"

"I am sure of not being a mile out of my reckoning."

"And does the compass still show southeast?"

"Yes; with a westerly deviation of nineteen degrees forty-five minutes, just as aboveground. As for its dip, a curious fact is coming to light, which I have observed carefully: that the needle, instead of dipping toward the pole as in the Northern Hemisphere, on the contrary, rises from it."

"Would you then conclude," I said, "that the magnetic pole is somewhere between the surface of the globe and the point where we are?"

"Exactly so; and it is likely enough that if we were to reach the spot beneath the polar regions, about that seventy-first degree where Sir James Ross has discovered the magnetic pole to be situated, we should see the needle point straight up. Therefore that mysterious center of attraction is at no great depth."

I remarked: "It is so; and here is a fact which science has scarcely suspected."

"Science, my lad, has been built upon many errors; but they are errors which it was good to fall into, for they led to the truth."

"What depth have we now reached?"

"We are thirty-five leagues below the surface."

"So," I said, examining the map, "the Highlands of Scotland are over our heads, and the Grampians are raising their rugged summits above us."

"Yes," answered the professor laughing. "It is rather a heavy weight to bear, but a solid arch spans over our heads. The great Architect has built it of the best materials; and never could man have given it so wide a stretch. What are the finest arches of bridges and the arcades of cathedrals, compared with this far-reaching vault, with a radius of three leagues, beneath which a wide and tempest-tossed ocean may flow at its ease?"

"Oh, I am not afraid that it will fall down upon my head. But now what are your plans? Are you not thinking of returning to the surface now?"

"Return! No, indeed! We will continue our journey, everything having gone on well so far."

"But how are we to get down below this liquid surface?"

"Oh, I am not going to dive head foremost. But if all oceans are properly speaking but lakes, since they are encompassed by land, of course this internal sea will be surrounded by a coast of granite, and on the opposite shores we shall find fresh passages opening."

"How long do you suppose this sea to be?"

"Thirty or forty leagues; so that we have no time to lose, and we shall set sail tomorrow."

I looked about for a ship.

"Set sail, shall we? But I should like to see my boat first."

"It will not be a boat at all, but a good, well-made raft."

"Why," I said, "a raft would be just as hard to make as a boat, and I don't see—"

"I know you don't see; but you might hear if you would listen. Don't you hear the hammer at work? Hans is already busy at it."

"What, has he already felled the trees?"

"Oh, the trees were already down. Come, and you will see for yourself."

After half an hour's walking, on the other side of the promontory which formed the little natural harbor, I perceived Hans at work. In a few more steps I was at his side. To my great surprise a half-finished raft was already lying on the sand, made of a peculiar kind of wood, and a great number of planks, straight and bent, and of frames, were covering the ground, enough almost for a little fleet.

"Uncle, what wood is this?" I cried.

"It is fir, pine, or birch, and other northern coniferae, mineralized by the action of the sea. It is called surturbrand, a variety of brown coal or lignite, found chiefly in Iceland."

"But surely, then, like other fossil wood, it must be as hard as stone, and cannot float?"

"Sometimes that may happen; some of these woods become true anthracites; but others, such as this, have only gone through the first stage of fossil transformation. Just look," added my uncle, throwing into the sea one of those precious waifs.

The bit of wood, after disappearing, returned to the surface and oscillated to and fro with the waves.

"Are you convinced?" said my uncle.

"I am quite convinced, although it is incredible!"

By next evening, thanks to the industry and skill of our guide, the raft was made. It was ten feet by five; the planks of surturbrand, braced strongly together with cords, presented an even surface, and when launched this improvised vessel floated easily upon the waves of the Liedenbrock Sea.

XXXII

WONDERS OF THE DEEP

On the 13th of August we awoke early. We were now to begin to adopt a mode of traveling both more expeditious and less fatiguing than hitherto.

A mast was made of two poles spliced together, a yard was made of a third, a blanket borrowed from our coverings made a tolerable sail. There was no want of cordage for the rigging, and everything was well and firmly made.

The provisions, the baggage, the instruments, the guns, and a good quantity of fresh water from the rocks around, all found their proper places on board; and at six the professor gave the signal to embark. Hans had fitted up a rudder to steer his vessel. He took the tiller, and unmoored; the sail was set, and we were soon afloat. At the moment of leaving the harbor, my uncle, who was tenaciously fond of naming his new discoveries, wanted to give it a name, and proposed mine among others.

"But I have a better to propose," I said: "Gräuben. Let it be called Port Gräuben; it will look very well upon the map."

"Port Gräuben let it be then."

And so the cherished remembrance of my Virlandaise became associated with our adventurous expedition.

The wind was from the northwest. We went with it at a high rate of speed. The dense atmosphere acted with great force and impelled us swiftly on.

In an hour my uncle had been able to estimate our progress. At this rate, he said, we shall make thirty leagues in twenty-four hours, and we shall soon come in sight of the opposite shore.

I made no answer, but went and sat forward. The northern shore was already beginning to dip under the horizon. The eastern and western strands spread wide as if to bid us farewell. Before our eyes lay far and wide a vast sea; shadows of great clouds swept heavily over its silver-gray surface; the glistening bluish rays of electric light, here and there reflected by the dancing drops of spray, shot out little sheaves of light from the track we left in our rear. Soon we entirely lost sight of land; no object was left for the eye to judge by, and but for the frothy track of the raft, I might have thought we were standing still.

About twelve, immense shoals of seaweeds came in sight. I was aware of the great powers of vegetation that characterize these plants, which grow at a depth of twelve thousand feet, reproduce themselves under a pressure of four hundred atmospheres, and sometimes form barriers strong enough to impede the course of a ship. But never, I think, were such seaweeds as those which we saw floating in immense waving lines upon the sea of Liedenbrock.

Our raft skirted the whole length of the fuci, three or four thousand feet long, undulating like vast serpents beyond the reach of sight; I found some amusement in tracing these endless waves, always thinking I should come to the end of them, and for hours my patience was vying with my surprise.

What natural force could have produced such plants, and what must have been the appearance of the earth in the first ages of its formation, when, under the action of heat and moisture, the vegetable kingdom alone was developing on its surface?

Evening came, and, as on the previous day, I perceived no change in the luminous condition of the air. It was a constant condition, the permanency of which might be relied upon.

After supper I laid myself down at the foot of the mast, and fell asleep in the midst of fantastic reveries.

Hans, keeping fast by the helm, let the raft run on, which, after all, needed no steering, the wind blowing directly aft.

Since our departure from Port Gräuben, Professor Liedenbrock had entrusted the log to my care; I was to register every observation, make entries of interesting phenomena, the direction of the wind, the rate of sailing, the way we made—in a word, every particular of our singular voyage.

I shall therefore reproduce here these daily notes, written, so to speak, as the course of events directed, in order to furnish an exact narrative of our passage.

Friday, August 14. Wind steady, N.W. The raft makes rapid way in a direct line. Coast thirty leagues to leeward. Nothing in sight before us. Intensity of light the same. Weather fine; that is to say, that the clouds are flying high, are light, and bathed in a white atmosphere resembling silver in a state of fusion. Therm. 89°F.

At noon Hans prepared a hook at the end of a line. He baited it with a small piece of meat and flung it into the sea. For two hours nothing was caught. Are these waters, then, bare of inhabitants? No, there's a pull at the line. Hans draws it in and brings out a struggling fish.

"A sturgeon," I cried; "a small sturgeon."

The professor eyes the creature attentively, and his opinion differs from mine.

The head of this fish was flat, but rounded in front, and the anterior part of its body was plated with bony, angular scales; it had no teeth, its pectoral fins were large, and of tail there was none. The animal belonged to the same order as the sturgeon, but differed from that fish in many essential particulars. After a short examination my uncle pronounced his opinion.

"This fish belongs to an extinct family, of which only fossil traces are found in the Devonian formations."

"What!" I cried. "Have we taken alive an inhabitant of the seas of primitive ages?"

"Yes; and you will observe that these fossil fishes have no identity with any living species. To have in one's possession a living specimen is a happy event for a naturalist."

"But to what family does it belong?"

"It is of the order of ganoids, of the family of the cephalaspidae; and a species of pterichthys. But this one displays a peculiarity confined to all fishes that inhabit subterranean waters. It is blind, and not only blind, but actually has no eyes at all."

I looked: nothing could be more certain. But supposing it might be a solitary case, we baited afresh, and threw out our line. Surely this ocean is well peopled with fish, for in another couple of hours we took a large quantity of pterichthydes, as well as of others belonging to the extinct family of the dipterides, but of which my uncle could not tell the species; none had organs of sight. This unhoped-for catch recruited our stock of provisions.

Thus it is evident that this sea contains none but species known to us in their fossil state, in which fishes as well as reptiles are the less perfectly and completely organized the farther back their date of creation.

Perhaps we may yet meet with some of those saurians which science has reconstructed out of a bit of bone or cartilage. I took up the telescope and scanned the whole horizon, and found it everywhere a desert sea. We are far away removed from the shores.

I gaze upward in the air. Why should not some of the strange birds restored by the immortal Cuvier again flap their "sail-broad vans" in this dense and heavy atmosphere? There are sufficient fish for their support. I survey the whole space that stretches overhead; it is as desert as the shore was.

Still my imagination carried me away among the wonderful speculations of paleontology. Though awake I fell into a dream. I thought I could see floating on the surface of the waters enormous chelonia, pre-Adamite tortoises, resembling floating islands. Over the dimly lighted strand there trod the huge mammals of the first ages of the world, the leptotherium (slender beast), found in the caverns of Brazil; the merycotherium (ruminating beast), found in the "drift" of ice-clad Siberia. Farther on, the pachydermatous lophiodon (crested toothed), a gigantic tapir, hides behind the rocks to dispute its prey with the anoplotherium (unarmed beast), a strange creature, which seemed a compound of horse, rhinoceros, camel, and hippopotamus. The colossal mastodon (nipple-toothed) twists and untwists his trunk, and brays and pounds with his huge tusks the fragments of rock that cover the shore; while the megatherium (huge beast), buttressed upon his enormous hinder paws, grubs in the soil, awaking the sonorous echoes of the granite rocks with his tremendous roarings. Higher up, the protopitheca—the first monkey that appeared on the globe—is climbing up the steep ascents. Higher yet, the pterodactyle (wing-fingered) darts in irregular zigzags to and fro in the heavy air. In the uppermost regions of the air immense birds, more powerful than the cassowary, and larger than the ostrich, spread their vast breadth of wings and strike with their heads the granite vault that bounds the sky.

All this fossil world rises to life again in my vivid imagination. I return to the scriptural periods or ages of the world, conventionally called "days," long before the appearance of man, when the unfinished world was as yet unfitted for his support. Then my dream backed even farther still into the ages before the creation of living beings. The mammals disappear, then the birds vanish, then the reptiles of the secondary period, and finally the fish, the crustaceans, mollusks, and articulated beings. Then the zoophytes of the transition period also return to nothing. I am the only living thing in the world: all life is concentrated in my beating heart alone. There are no more seasons; climates are no more; the heat of the globe continually increases and neutralizes that of the sun. Vegetation becomes accelerated. I glide like a shade among arborescent ferns, treading with unsteady feet the colored marls and the particolored clays; I lean for support against the trunks of immense conifers; I lie in the shade of sphenophylla (wedge-leaved), asterophylla (star-leaved), and lycopods, a hundred feet high.

Ages seem no more than days! I am passed, against my will, in retrograde order, through the long series of terrestrial changes. Plants disappear; granite rocks soften; intense heat converts solid bodies into thick fluids; the waters again cover the face of the earth; they boil, they rise in whirling eddies of steam; white and ghastly mists wrap round the shifting forms of the earth, which by imperceptible degrees dissolves into a gaseous mass, glowing fiery red and white, as large and as shining as the sun.

And I myself am floating with wild caprice in the midst of this nebulous mass of fourteen hundred thousand times the volume of the earth into which it will one day be condensed, and carried forward among the planetary bodies. My body is no longer firm and terrestrial; it is resolved into its constituent atoms, subtilized, volatilized. Sublimed into imponderable vapor, I mingle and am lost in the endless foods of those vast globular volumes of vaporous mists, which roll upon their flaming orbits through infinite space.

But is it not a dream? Whither is it carrying me? My feverish hand has vainly attempted to describe upon paper its strange and wonderful details. I have forgotten everything that surrounds me. The professor, the guide, the raft—are all gone out of my ken. An illusion has laid hold upon me.

"What is the matter?" my uncle breaks in.

My staring eyes are fixed vacantly upon him.

"Take care, Axel, or you will fall overboard."

At that moment I felt the sinewy hand of Hans seizing me vigorously. But for him, carried away by my dream, I should have thrown myself into the sea.

"Is he mad?" cried the professor.

"What is it all about?" at last I cried, returning to myself.

"Do you feel ill?" my uncle asked.

"No; but I have had a strange hallucination; it is over now. Is all going on right?"

"Yes, it is a fair wind and a fine sea; we are sailing rapidly along, and if I am not out in my reckoning, we shall soon land."

At these words I rose and gazed round upon the horizon, still everywhere bounded by clouds alone.

XXXIII

A BATTLE OF MONSTERS

Saturday, August 15. The sea unbroken all round. No land in sight. The horizon seems extremely distant.

My head is still stupefied with the vivid reality of my dream.

My uncle has had no dreams, but he is out of temper. He examines the horizon all round with his glass, and folds his arms with the air of an injured man.

I remark that Professor Liedenbrock has a tendency to relapse into an impatient mood, and I make a note of it in my log. All my danger and sufferings were needed to strike a spark of human feeling out of him; but now that I am well his nature has resumed its sway. And yet, what cause was there for anger? Is not the voyage prospering as favorably as possible under the circumstances? Is not the raft spinning along with marvelous speed?

"You seem anxious, my uncle," I said, seeing him continually with his glass to his eye.

"Anxious! No, not at all."

"Impatient, then?"

"One might be, with less reason than now."

"Yet we are going very fast."

"What does that signify? I am not complaining that the rate is slow, but that the sea is so wide."

I then remembered that the professor, before starting, had estimated the length of this underground sea at thirty leagues. Now we had made three times the distance, yet still the southern coast was not in sight.

"We are not descending as we ought to be," the professor declares. "We are losing time, and the fact is, I have not come all this way to take a little sail upon a pond on a raft."

He called this sea a pond, and our long voyage, taking a little sail!

"But," I remarked, "since we have followed the road that Saknussemm has shown us—"

"That is just the question. Have we followed that road? Did Saknussemm meet this sheet of water? Did he cross it? Has not the stream that we followed led us altogether astray?"

"At any rate we cannot feel sorry to have come so far. This prospect is magnificent, and—"

"But I don't care for prospects. I came with an object, and I mean to attain it. Therefore don't talk to me about views and prospects."

I take this as my answer, and I leave the professor to bite his lips with impatience. At six in the evening Hans asks for his wages, and his three rix dollars are counted out to him.

Sunday, August 16. Nothing new. Weather unchanged. The wind freshens. On awaking, my first thought was to observe the intensity of the light. I was possessed with an apprehension lest the electric light should grow dim, or fail altogether. But there seemed no reason to fear. The shadow of the raft was clearly outlined upon the surface of the waves.

Truly this sea is of infinite width. It must be as wide as the Mediterranean or the Atlantic—and why not?

My uncle took soundings several times. He tied the heaviest of our pickaxes to a long rope which he let down two hundred fathoms. No bottom yet; and we had some difficulty in hauling up our plummet.

But when the pick was shipped again, Hans pointed out on its surface deep prints as if it had been violently compressed between two hard bodies.

I looked at the hunter.

"*Tänder*," said he.

I could not understand him, and turned to my uncle who was entirely absorbed in his calculations. I had rather not disturb him while he is quiet. I return to the Icelander. He by a snapping motion of his jaws conveys his ideas to me.

"Teeth!" I cried, considering the iron bar with more attention.

Yes, indeed, those are the marks of teeth imprinted upon the metal! The jaws which they arm must be possessed of amazing strength. Is there some monster beneath us belonging to the extinct races, more voracious than the shark, more fearful in vastness than the whale? I could not take my eyes off this indented iron bar. Surely will my last night's dream be realized?

These thoughts agitated me all day, and my imagination scarcely calmed down after several hours' sleep.

Monday, August 17. I am trying to recall the peculiar instincts of the monsters of the pre-Adamite world, who, coming next in succession after the mollusks, the crustaceans, and the fishes, preceded the animals of mammalian race upon the earth. The world then belonged to reptiles. Those monsters held the mastery in the seas of the secondary period. They possessed a perfect organization, gigantic proportions, prodigious strength. The saurians of our day, the alligators and the crocodiles, are but feeble reproductions of their forefathers of primitive ages.

I shudder as I recall these monsters to my remembrance. No human eye has ever beheld them living. They burdened this earth a thousand ages before man appeared, but their fossil remains, found in the argillaceous limestone called by the English the lias, have enabled their colossal structure to be perfectly built up again and anatomically ascertained.

I saw at the Hamburg museum the skeleton of one of these creatures thirty feet in length. Am I then fated—I, a denizen of earth—to be placed face-to-face with these representatives of long-extinct families? No; surely it cannot be! Yet the deep marks of conical teeth upon the iron pick are certainly those of the crocodile.

My eyes are fearfully bent upon the sea. I dread to see one of these monsters darting forth from its submarine caverns. I suppose Professor Liedenbrock was of my opinion too, and even shared my fears, for after having examined the pick, his eyes traversed the ocean from side to side. What a very bad notion that was of his, I thought to myself, to take soundings just here! He has disturbed some monstrous beast in its remote den, and if we are not attacked on our voyage—

I look at our guns and see that they are all right. My uncle notices it, and looks on approvingly.

Already widely disturbed regions on the surface of the water indicate some commotion below. The danger is approaching. We must be on the lookout.

Tuesday, August 18. Evening came, or rather the time came when sleep weighs down the weary eyelids, for there is no night here, and the ceaseless light wearies the eyes with its persistence just as if we were sailing under an arctic sun. Hans was at the helm. During his watch I slept.

Two hours afterward a terrible shock awoke me. The raft was heaved up on a watery mountain and pitched down again, at a distance of twenty fathoms.

"What is the matter?" shouted my uncle. "Have we struck land?"

Hans pointed with his finger at a dark mass six hundred yards away, rising and falling alternately with heavy plunges. I looked and cried:

"It is an enormous porpoise."

"Yes," replied my uncle, "and there is a sea lizard of vast size."

"And farther on a monstrous crocodile. Look at its vast jaws and its rows of teeth! It is diving down!"

"There's a whale, a whale!" cried the professor. "I can see its great fins. See how he is throwing out air and water through his blowers."

And in fact two liquid columns were rising to a considerable height above the sea. We stood amazed, thunderstruck, at the presence of such a herd of marine monsters. They were of supernatural dimensions; the smallest of them would have crunched our raft, crew and all, at one snap of its huge jaws.

Hans wants to tack to get away from this dangerous neighborhood; but he sees on the other hand enemies not less terrible; a tortoise forty feet long, and a serpent of thirty, lifting its fearful head and gleaming eyes above the flood.

Flight was out of the question now. The reptiles rose; they wheeled around our little raft with a rapidity greater than that of express trains. They described around us gradually narrowing circles. I took up my rifle. But what could a ball do against the scaly armor with which these enormous beasts were clad?

We stood dumb with fear. They approach us close: on one side the crocodile, on the other the serpent. The remainder of the sea monsters have disappeared. I prepare to fire. Hans stops me by a gesture. The two monsters pass within a hundred and fifty yards of the raft, and hurl themselves the one upon the other, with a fury which prevents them from seeing us.

At three hundred yards from us the battle was fought. We could distinctly observe the two monsters engaged in deadly conflict. But it now seems to me as if the other animals were taking part in the fray—the porpoise, the whale, the lizard, the tortoise. Every moment I seem to see one or other of them. I point them to the Icelander. He shakes his head negatively.

"*Tva*," says he.

"What two? Does he mean that there are only two animals?"

"He is right," said my uncle, whose glass has never left his eye.

"Surely you must be mistaken," I cried.

"No: the first of those monsters has a porpoise's snout, a lizard's head, a crocodile's teeth; and hence our mistake. It is the ichthyosaurus (the fish lizard), the most terrible of the ancient monsters of the deep."

"And the other?"

"The other is a plesiosaurus (almost lizard), a serpent, armored with the carapace and the paddles of a turtle; he is the dreadful enemy of the other."

Hans had spoken truly. Two monsters only were creating all this commotion; and before my eyes are two reptiles of the primitive world. I can distinguish the eye of the ichthyosaurus glowing like a red-hot coal, and as large as a man's head. Nature has endowed it with an optical apparatus of extreme power, and capable of resisting the pressure of the great volume of water in the depths it inhabits. It has been appropriately called the saurian whale, for it has both the swiftness and the rapid movements of this monster of our own day. This one is not less than a hundred feet long, and I can judge of its size when it sweeps over the waters the vertical coils of its tail. Its jaw is enormous, and according to naturalists it is armed with no less than one hundred and eighty-two teeth.

The plesiosaurus, a serpent with a cylindrical body and a short tail, has four flappers or paddles to act like oars. Its body is entirely covered with a thick armor of scales, and its neck, as flexible as a swan's, rises thirty feet above the waves.

Those huge creatures attacked each other with the greatest animosity. They heaved around them liquid mountains, which rolled even to our raft and rocked it perilously. Twenty times we were near capsizing. Hissings of prodigious force are heard. The two beasts are fast locked together; I cannot distinguish the one from the other. The probable rage of the conqueror inspires us with intense fear.

One hour, two hours pass away. The struggle continues with unabated ferocity. The combatants alternately approach and recede from our raft. We remain motionless, ready to fire. Suddenly the ichthyosaurus and the plesiosaurus disappear below, leaving a whirlpool eddying in the water. Several minutes pass by while the fight goes on underwater.

All at once an enormous head is darted up, the head of the plesiosaurus. The monster is wounded to death. I no longer see his scaly armor. Only his long neck shoots up, drops again, coils and uncoils, droops, lashes the waters like a gigantic whip, and writhes like a worm that you tread on. The water is splashed for a long way around. The spray almost blinds us. But soon the reptile's agony draws to an end; its movements become fainter, its contortions cease to be so violent, and the long serpentine form lies a lifeless log on the laboring deep.

As for the ichthyosaurus—has he returned to his submarine cavern? Or will he reappear on the surface of the sea?

XXXIV

THE GREAT GEYSER

Wednesday, August 19. Fortunately the wind blows violently, and has enabled us to flee from the scene of the late terrible struggle. Hans keeps at his post at the helm. My uncle, whom the absorbing incidents of the combat had drawn away from his contemplations, began again to look impatiently around him.

The voyage resumes its uniform tenor, which I don't care to break with a repetition of such events as yesterday's.

Thursday, Aug. 20. Wind N.N.E., unsteady and fitful. Temperature high. Rate three and a half leagues an hour.

About noon a distant noise is heard. I note the fact without being able to explain it. It is a continuous roar.

"In the distance," says the professor, "there is a rock or islet, against which the sea is breaking."

Hans climbs up the mast, but sees no breakers. The ocean is smooth and unbroken to its farthest limit.

Three hours pass away. The roarings seem to proceed from a very distant waterfall.

I remark upon this to my uncle, who replies doubtfully: "Yes, I am convinced that I am right." Are we, then, speeding forward to some cataract which will cast us down an abyss? This method of getting on may please the professor, because it is vertical; but for my part I prefer the more ordinary modes of horizontal progression.

At any rate, some leagues to the windward there must be some noisy phenomenon, for now the roarings are heard with increasing loudness. Do they proceed from the sky or the ocean?

I look up to the atmospheric vapors, and try to fathom their depths. The sky is calm and motionless. The clouds have reached the utmost limit of the lofty vault, and there lie still bathed in the bright glare of the electric light. It is not there that we must seek for the cause of this phenomenon. Then I examine the horizon, which is unbroken and clear of all mist. There is no change in its aspect. But if this noise arises from a fall, a cataract, if all this ocean flows away headlong into a lower basin yet, if that deafening roar is produced by a mass of falling water, the current must needs accelerate, and its increasing speed will give me the measure of the peril that threatens us. I consult the current: there is none. I throw an empty bottle into the sea: it lies still.

About four Hans rises, lays hold of the mast, climbs to its top. Thence his eye sweeps a large area of sea, and it is fixed upon a point. His countenance exhibits no surprise, but his eye is immovably steady.

"He sees something," says my uncle.

"I believe he does."

Hans comes down, then stretches his arm to the south, saying:

"Dere nere!"

"Down there?" repeated my uncle.

Then, seizing his glass, he gazes attentively for a minute, which seems to me an age.

"Yes, yes!" he cried. "I see a vast inverted cone rising from the surface."

"Is it another sea beast?"

"Perhaps it is."

"Then let us steer farther westward, for we know something of the danger of coming across monsters of that sort."

"Let us go straight on," replied my uncle.

I appealed to Hans. He maintained his course inflexibly.

Yet, if at our present distance from the animal, a distance of twelve leagues at the least, the column of water driven through its blowers may be distinctly seen, it must needs be of vast size. The commonest prudence would counsel immediate flight; but we did not come so far to be prudent.

Imprudently, therefore, we pursue our way. The nearer we approach, the higher mounts the jet of water. What monster can possibly fill itself with such a quantity of water, and spurt it up so continuously?

At eight in the evening we are not two leagues distant from it. Its body—dusky, enormous, hillocky—lies spread upon the sea like an islet. Is it illusion or fear? Its length seems to me a couple of thousand yards. What can be this cetacean, which neither Cuvier nor Blumenbach knew anything about? It lies motionless, as if asleep; the sea seems unable to move it in the least; it is the waves that undulate upon its sides. The column of water thrown up to a height of five hundred feet falls in rain with a deafening uproar. And here are we scudding like lunatics before the wind, to get near to a monster that a hundred whales a day would not satisfy!

Terror seizes upon me. I refuse to go further. I will cut the halyards if necessary! I am in open mutiny against the professor, who vouchsafes no answer.

Suddenly Hans rises, and pointing with his finger at the menacing object, he says:

"*Holm*."

"An island!" cries my uncle.

"That's not an island!" I cried skeptically.

"It's nothing else," shouted the professor, with a loud laugh.

"But that column of water?"

"*Geyser*," said Hans.

"No doubt it is a geyser, like those in Iceland."

At first I protest against being so widely mistaken as to have taken an island for a marine monster. But the evidence is against me, and I have to confess my error. It is nothing worse than a natural phenomenon.

As we approach nearer, the dimensions of the liquid column become magnificent. The islet resembles, with a most deceiving likeness, an enormous cetacean, whose head dominates the waves at a height of twenty yards. The geyser, a word meaning "fury," rises majestically from its extremity. Deep and heavy explosions are heard from time to time, when the enormous jet, possessed with more furious violence, shakes its plumy crest, and springs with a bound till it reaches the lowest stratum of the clouds. It stands alone. No steam vents, no hot springs surround it, and all the volcanic power of the region is concentrated here. Sparks of electric fire mingle with the dazzling sheaf of lighted fluid, every drop of which refracts the prismatic colors.

"Let us land," said the professor.

"But we must carefully avoid this waterspout, which would sink our raft in a moment."

Hans, steering with his usual skill, brought us to the other extremity of the islet.

I leaped up on the rock; my uncle lightly followed, while our hunter remained at his post, like a man too wise ever to be astonished.

We walked upon granite mingled with siliceous tufa. The soil shivers and shakes under our feet, like the sides of an overheated boiler filled with steam struggling to get loose. We come in sight of a small central basin, out of which the geyser springs. I plunge a register thermometer into the boiling water. It marks an intense heat of 325°, which is far above the boiling point; therefore this water issues from an ardent furnace, which is not at all in harmony with Professor Liedenbrock's theories. I cannot help making the remark.

"Well," he replied, "how does that make against my doctrine?"

"Oh, nothing at all," I said, seeing that I was going in opposition to immovable obstinacy.

Still I am constrained to confess that hitherto we have been wonderfully favored, and that for some reason unknown to myself we have accomplished our journey under singularly favorable conditions of temperature. But it seems manifest to me that someday we shall reach a region where the central heat attains its highest limits, and goes beyond a point that can be registered by our thermometers.

"That is what we shall see." So says the professor, who, having named this volcanic islet after his nephew, gives the signal to embark again.

For some minutes I am still contemplating the geyser. I notice that it throws up its column of water with variable force: sometimes sending it to a great height, then again to a lower, which I attribute to the variable pressure of the steam accumulated in its reservoir.

At last we leave the island, rounding away past the low rocks on its southern shore. Hans has taken advantage of the halt to refit his rudder.

But before going any farther I make a few observations, to calculate the distance we have gone over, and note them in my journal. We have crossed two hundred and seventy leagues of sea since leaving Port Gräuben; and we are six hundred and twenty leagues from Iceland, under England.

XXXV

AN ELECTRIC STORM

Friday, August 21. On the morrow the magnificent geyser has disappeared. The wind has risen, and has rapidly carried us away from Axel Island. The roarings become lost in the distance.

The weather—if we may use that term—will change before long. The atmosphere is charged with vapors, pervaded with the electricity generated by the evaporation of saline waters. The clouds are sinking lower, and assume an olive hue. The electric light can scarcely penetrate through the dense curtain which has dropped over the theater on which the battle of the elements is about to be waged.

I feel peculiar sensations, like many creatures on earth at the approach of violent atmospheric changes. The heavily voluted cumulus clouds lower gloomily and threateningly; they wear that implacable look which I have sometimes noticed at the outbreak of a great storm. The air is heavy; the sea is calm.

In the distance the clouds resemble great bales of cotton, piled up in picturesque disorder. By degrees they dilate, and gain in huge size what they lose in number. Such is their ponderous weight that they cannot rise from the horizon; but, obeying an impulse from higher currents, their dense consistency slowly yields. The gloom upon them deepens; and they soon present to our view a ponderous mass of almost level surface. From time to time a fleecy tuft of mist, with yet some gleaming light left upon it, drops down upon the dense floor of gray, and loses itself in the opaque and impenetrable mass.

The atmosphere is evidently charged and surcharged with electricity. My whole body is saturated; my hair bristles just as when you stand upon an insulated stool under the action of an electrical machine. It seems to me as if my companions, the moment they touched me, would receive a severe shock like that from an electric eel.

At ten in the morning the symptoms of storm become aggravated. The wind never lulls but to acquire increased strength; the vast bank of heavy clouds is a huge reservoir of fearful windy gusts and rushing storms.

I am loath to believe these atmospheric menaces, and yet I cannot help muttering:

"Here's some very bad weather coming on."

The professor made no answer. His temper is awful, to judge from the working of his features, as he sees this vast length of ocean unrolling before him to an indefinite extent. He can only spare time to shrug his shoulders viciously.

"There's a heavy storm coming on," I cried, pointing toward the horizon. "Those clouds seem as if they were going to crush the sea."

A deep silence falls on all around. The lately roaring winds are hushed into a dead calm; nature seems to breathe no more, and to be sinking into the stillness of death. On the mast already I see the light play of a lambent St. Elmo's fire; the outstretched sail catches not a breath of wind, and hangs like a sheet of lead. The rudder stands motionless in a sluggish, waveless sea. But if we have now ceased to advance why do we yet leave that sail loose, which at the first shock of the tempest may capsize us in a moment?

"Let us reef the sail and cut the mast down!" I cried. "That will be safest."

"No, no! Never!" shouted my impetuous uncle. "Never! Let the wind catch us if it will! What I want is to get the least glimpse of rock or shore, even if our raft should be smashed into shivers!"

The words were hardly out of his mouth when a sudden change took place in the southern sky. The piled-up vapors condense into water; and the air, put into violent action to supply the vacuum left by the condensation of the mists, rouses itself into a whirlwind. It rushes on from the farthest recesses of the vast cavern. The darkness deepens; scarcely can I jot down a few hurried notes. The helm makes a bound. My uncle falls full length; I creep close to him. He has laid a firm hold upon a rope, and appears to watch with grim satisfaction this awful display of elemental strife.

Hans stirs not. His long hair blown by the pelting storm, and laid flat across his immovable countenance, makes him a strange figure; for the end of each lock of loose flowing hair is tipped with little luminous radiations. This frightful mask of electric sparks suggests to me, even in this dizzy excitement, a comparison with pre-Adamite man, the contemporary of the ichthyosaurus and the megatherium.

The mast yet holds firm. The sail stretches tight like a bubble ready to burst. The raft flies at a rate that I cannot reckon, but not so fast as the foaming clouds of spray which it dashes from side to side in its headlong speed.

"The sail! The sail!" I cry, motioning to lower it.

"No!" replies my uncle.

"Nej!" repeats Hans, leisurely shaking his head.

But now the rain forms a rushing cataract in front of that horizon toward which we are running with such maddening speed. But before it has reached us the rain cloud parts asunder, the sea boils, and the electric fires are brought into violent action by a mighty chemical power that descends from the higher regions. The most vivid flashes of lightning are mingled with the violent crash of continuous thunder. Ceaseless fiery arrows dart in and out among the flying thunderclouds; the vaporous mass soon glows with incandescent heat; hailstones rattle fiercely down, and as they dash upon our iron tools they too emit gleams and flashes of lurid light. The heaving waves resemble fiery volcanic hills, each belching forth its own interior flames, and every crest is plumed with dancing fire. My eyes fail under the dazzling light, my ears are stunned with the incessant crash of thunder. I must be bound to the mast, which bows like a reed before the mighty strength of the storm.

(Here my notes become vague and indistinct. I have only been able to find a few which I seem to have jotted down almost unconsciously. But their very brevity and their obscurity reveal the intensity of the excitement which dominated me, and describe the actual position even better than my memory could do.)

Sunday, August 23. Where are we? Driven forward with a swiftness that cannot be measured.

The night was fearful; no abatement of the storm. The din and uproar are incessant; our ears are bleeding; to exchange a word is impossible.

The lightning flashes with intense brilliancy, and never seems to cease for a moment. Zigzag streams of bluish-white fire dash down upon the sea and rebound, and then take an upward flight till they strike the granite vault that overarches our heads. Suppose that solid roof should crumble down upon our heads! Other flashes with incessant play cross their vivid fires, while others again roll themselves into balls of living fire which explode like bombshells, but the music of which scarcely adds to the din of the battle strife that almost deprives us of our senses of hearing and sight; the limit of intense loudness has been passed within which the human ear can distinguish one sound from another. If all the powder magazines in the world were to explode at once, we should hear no more than we do now.

From the undersurface of the clouds there are continual emissions of lurid light; electric matter is in continual evolution from their component molecules; the gaseous elements of the air need to be slaked with moisture; for innumerable columns of water rush upward into the air and fall back again in white foam.

Whither are we flying? My uncle lies full length across the raft.

The heat increases. I refer to the thermometer; it indicates . . . (the figure is obliterated).

Monday, August 24. Will there be an end to it? Is the atmospheric condition, having once reached this density, to become final?

We are prostrated and worn out with fatigue. But Hans is as usual. The raft bears on still to the southeast. We have made two hundred leagues since we left Axel Island.

At noon the violence of the storm redoubles. We are obliged to secure as fast as possible every article that belongs to our cargo. Each of us is lashed to some part of the raft. The waves rise above our heads.

For three days we have never been able to make each other hear a word. Our mouths open, our lips move, but not a word can be heard. We cannot even make ourselves heard by approaching our mouth close to the ear.

My uncle has drawn nearer to me. He has uttered a few words. They seem to be "We are lost"; but I am not sure.

At last I write down the words: "Let us lower the sail."

He nods his consent.

Scarcely has he lifted his head again before a ball of fire has bounded over the waves and lighted on board our raft. Mast and sail flew up in an instant together, and I saw them carried up to prodigious height, resembling in appearance a pterodactyl, one of those strong birds of the infant world.

We lay there, our blood running cold with unspeakable terror. The fireball, half of it white, half azure blue, and the size of a ten-inch shell, moved slowly about the raft, but revolving on its own axis with astonishing velocity, as if whipped round by the force of the whirlwind. Here it comes, there it glides, now it is up the ragged stump of the mast, thence it lightly leaps on the provision bag, descends with a light bound, and just skims the powder magazine. Horrible! We shall be blown up; but no, the dazzling disk of mysterious light nimbly leaps aside; it approaches Hans, who fixes his blue eye upon it steadily; it threatens the head of my uncle, who falls upon his knees with his head down to avoid it. And now my turn comes; pale and trembling under the blinding splendor and the melting heat, it drops at my feet, spinning silently round upon the deck; I try to move my foot away, but cannot.

A suffocating smell of nitrogen fills the air, it enters the throat, it fills the lungs. We suffer stifling pains.

Why am I unable to move my foot? Is it riveted to the planks? Alas! The fall upon our fated raft of this electric globe has magnetized every iron article on board. The instruments, the tools, our guns are clashing and clanking violently in their collisions with each other; the nails of my boots cling tenaciously to a plate of iron let into the timbers, and I cannot draw my foot away from the spot. At last by a violent effort I release myself at the instant when the ball in its gyrations was about to seize upon it, and carry me off my feet . . .

Ah! What a flood of intense and dazzling light! The globe has burst, and we are deluged with tongues of fire!

Then all the light disappears. I could just see my uncle at full length on the raft, and Hans still at his helm and spitting fire under the action of the electricity which has saturated him.

But where are we going to? Where?

* * * * *

Tuesday, August 25. I recover from a long swoon. The storm continues to roar and rage; the lightnings dash hither and thither, like broods of fiery serpents filling all the air. Are we still under the sea? Yes, we are borne at incalculable speed. We have been carried under England, under the Channel, under France, perhaps under the whole of Europe.

* * * * *

A fresh noise is heard! Surely it is the sea breaking upon the rocks! But then . . .

XXXVI

CALM PHILOSOPHIC DISCUSSIONS

Here I end what I may call my log, happily saved from the wreck, and I resume my narrative as before.

What happened when the raft was dashed upon the rocks is more than I can tell. I felt myself hurled into the waves; and if I escaped from death, and if my body was not torn over the sharp edges of the rocks, it was because the powerful arm of Hans came to my rescue.

The brave Icelander carried me out of the reach of the waves, over a burning sand where I found myself by the side of my uncle.

Then he returned to the rocks, against which the furious waves were beating, to save what he could. I was unable to speak. I was shattered with fatigue and excitement; I wanted a whole hour to recover even a little.

But a deluge of rain was still falling, though with that violence which generally denotes the near cessation of a storm. A few overhanging rocks afforded us some shelter from the storm. Hans prepared some food, which I could not touch; and each of us, exhausted with three sleepless nights, fell into a broken and painful sleep.

The next day the weather was splendid. The sky and the sea had sunk into sudden repose. Every trace of the awful storm had disappeared. The exhilarating voice of the professor fell upon my ears as I awoke; he was ominously cheerful.

"Well, my boy," he cried, "have you slept well?"

Would not anyone have thought that we were still in our cheerful little house on the Königstrasse and that I was only just coming down to breakfast, and that I was to be married to Gräuben that day?

Alas! If the tempest had but sent the raft a little more east, we should have passed under Germany, under my beloved town of Hamburg, under the very street where dwelt all that I loved most in the world. Then only forty leagues would have separated us! But they were forty leagues perpendicular of solid granite wall, and in reality we were a thousand leagues asunder!

All these painful reflections rapidly crossed my mind before I could answer my uncle's question.

"Well, now," he repeated, "won't you tell me how you have slept?"

"Oh, very well," I said. "I am only a little knocked up, but I shall soon be better."

"Oh," says my uncle, "that's nothing to signify. You are only a little bit tired."

"But you, uncle, you seem in very good spirits this morning."

"Delighted, my boy, delighted. We have got there."

"To our journey's end?"

"No; but we have got to the end of that endless sea. Now we shall go by land, and really begin to go down! Down! Down!"

"But, my dear uncle, do let me ask you one question."

"Of course, Axel."

"How about returning?"

"Returning? Why, you are talking about the return before the arrival."

"No, I only want to know how that is to be managed."

"In the simplest way possible. When we have reached the center of the globe, either we shall find some new way to get back, or we shall come back like decent folks the way we came. I feel pleased at the thought that it is sure not to be shut against us."

"But then we shall have to refit the raft."

"Of course."

"Then, as to provisions, have we enough to last?"

"Yes; to be sure we have. Hans is a clever fellow, and I am sure he must have saved a large part of our cargo. But still let us go and make sure."

We left this grotto which lay open to every wind. At the same time I cherished a trembling hope which was a fear as well. It seemed to me impossible that the terrible wreck of the raft should not have destroyed everything on board. On my arrival on the shore I found Hans surrounded by an assemblage of articles all arranged in good order. My uncle shook hands with him with a lively gratitude. This man, with almost superhuman devotion, had been at work all the while that we were asleep, and had saved the most precious of the articles at the risk of his life.

Not that we had suffered no losses. For instance, our firearms; but we might do without them. Our stock of powder had remained uninjured after having risked blowing up during the storm.

"Well," cried the professor, "as we have no guns we cannot hunt, that's all."

"Yes, but how about the instruments?"

"Here is the aneroid, the most useful of all, and for which I would have given all the others. By means of it I can calculate the depth and know when we have reached the center; without it we might very likely go beyond, and come out at the antipodes!"

Such high spirits as these were rather too strong.

"But where is the compass? I asked.

"Here it is, upon this rock, in perfect condition, as well as the thermometers and the chronometer. The hunter is a splendid fellow."

There was no denying it. We had all our instruments. As for tools and appliances, there they all lay on the ground—ladders, ropes, picks, spades, etc.

Still there was the question of provisions to be settled, and I asked, "How are we off for provisions?"

The boxes containing these were in a line upon the shore, in a perfect state of preservation; for the most part the sea had spared them, and what with biscuits, salt meat, spirits, and salt fish, we might reckon on four months' supply.

"Four months!" cried the professor. "We have time to go and to return; and with what is left I will give a grand dinner to my friends at the Johannæum."

I ought by this time to have been quite accustomed to my uncle's ways; yet there was always something fresh about him to astonish me.

"Now," said he, "we will replenish our supply of water with the rain which the storm has left in all these granite basins; therefore we shall have no reason to fear anything from thirst. As for the raft, I will recommend Hans to do his best to repair it, although I don't expect it will be of any further use to us."

"How so?" I cried.

"An idea of my own, my lad. I don't think we shall come out by the way that we went in."

I stared at the professor with a good deal of mistrust. I asked, was he not touched in the brain? And yet there was method in his madness.

"And now let us go to breakfast," said he.

I followed him to a headland, after he had given his instructions to the hunter. There preserved meat, biscuit, and tea made us an excellent meal, one of the best I ever remember. Hunger, the fresh air, the calm quiet weather, after the commotions we had gone through, all contributed to give me a good appetite.

While breakfasting I took the opportunity to put to my uncle the question where we were now.

"That seems to me," I said, "rather difficult to make out."

"Yes, it is difficult," he said, "to calculate exactly; perhaps even impossible, since during these three stormy days I have been unable to keep any account of the rate or direction of the raft; but still we may get an approximation."

"The last observation," I remarked, "was made on the island, when the geyser was—"

"You mean Axel Island. Don't decline the honor of having given your name to the first island ever discovered in the central parts of the globe."

"Well," said I, "let it be Axel Island. Then we had cleared two hundred and seventy leagues of sea, and we were six hundred leagues from Iceland."

"Very well," answered my uncle; "let us start from that point and count four days' storm, during which our rate cannot have been less than eighty leagues in the twenty-four hours."

"That is right; and this would make three hundred leagues more."

"Yes, and the Liedenbrock Sea would be six hundred leagues from shore to shore. Surely, Axel, it may vie in size with the Mediterranean itself."

"Especially," I replied, "if it happens that we have only crossed it in its narrowest part. And it is a curious circumstance," I added, "that if my computations are right, and we are nine hundred leagues from Reykjavik, we have now the Mediterranean above our head."

"That is a good long way, my friend. But whether we are under Turkey or the Atlantic depends very much upon the question in what direction we have been moving. Perhaps we have deviated."

"No, I think not. Our course has been the same all along, and I believe this shore is southeast of Port Gräuben."

"Well," replied my uncle, "we may easily ascertain this by consulting the compass. Let us go and see what it says."

The professor moved toward the rock upon which Hans had laid down the instruments. He was gay and full of spirits; he rubbed his hands, he studied his attitudes. I followed him, curious to know if I was right in my estimate. As soon as we had arrived at the rock my uncle took the compass, laid it horizontally, and questioned the needle, which, after a few oscillations, presently assumed a fixed position. My uncle looked, and looked, and looked again. He rubbed his eyes, and then turned to me thunderstruck with some unexpected discovery.

"What is the matter?" I asked.

He motioned to me to look. An exclamation of astonishment burst from me. The north pole of the needle was turned to what we supposed to be the south. It pointed to the shore instead of to the open sea! I shook the box, examined it again, it was in perfect condition. In whatever position I placed the box the needle pertinaciously returned to this unexpected quarter. Therefore there seemed no reason to doubt that during the storm there had been a sudden change of wind unperceived by us, which had brought our raft back to the shore which we thought we had left so long a distance behind us.

XXXVII

THE LIEDENBROCK MUSEUM OF GEOLOGY

How shall I describe the strange series of passions which in succession shook the breast of Professor Liedenbrock? First stupefaction, then incredulity, lastly a downright burst of rage. Never had I seen the man so put out of countenance and so disturbed. The fatigues of our passage across, the dangers met, had all to be begun over again. We had gone backward instead of forward!

But my uncle rapidly recovered himself.

"Aha! Will fate play tricks upon me? Will the elements lay plots against me? Shall fire, air, and water make a combined attack against me? Well, they shall know what a determined man can do. I will not yield. I will not stir a single foot backward, and it will be seen whether man or nature is to have the upper hand!"

Erect upon the rock, angry and threatening, Otto Liedenbrock was a rather grotesque fierce parody upon the fierce Achilles defying the lightning. But I thought it my duty to interpose and attempt to lay some restraint upon this unmeasured fanaticism.

"Just listen to me," I said firmly. "Ambition must have a limit somewhere; we cannot perform impossibilities; we are not at all fit for another sea voyage; who would dream of undertaking a voyage of five hundred leagues upon a heap of rotten planks, with a blanket in rags for a sail, a stick for a mast, and fierce winds in our teeth? We cannot steer; we shall be buffeted by the tempests, and we should be fools and madmen to attempt to cross a second time."

I was able to develop this series of unanswerable reasons for ten minutes without interruption; not that the professor was paying any respectful attention to his nephew's arguments, but because he was deaf to all my eloquence.

"To the raft!" he shouted.

Such was his only reply. It was no use for me to entreat, supplicate, get angry, or do anything else in the way of opposition; it would only have been opposing a will harder than the granite rock.

Hans was finishing the repairs of the raft. One would have thought that this strange being was guessing at my uncle's intentions. With a few more pieces of surturbrand he had refitted our vessel. A sail already hung from the new mast, and the wind was playing in its waving folds.

The professor said a few words to the guide, and immediately he put everything on board and arranged every necessary for our departure. The air was clear—and the northwest wind blew steadily.

What could I do? Could I stand against the two? It was impossible? If Hans had but taken my side! But no, it was not to be. The Icelander seemed to have renounced all will of his own and made a vow to forget and deny himself. I could get nothing out of a servant so feudalized, as it were, to his master. My only course was to proceed.

I was therefore going with as much resignation as I could find to resume my accustomed place on the raft, when my uncle laid his hand upon my shoulder.

"We shall not sail until tomorrow," he said.

I made a movement intended to express resignation.

"I must neglect nothing," he said; "and since my fate has driven me on this part of the coast, I will not leave it until I have examined it."

To understand what followed, it must be borne in mind that, through circumstances hereafter to be explained, we were not really where the professor supposed we were. In fact we were not upon the north shore of the sea.

"Now let us start upon fresh discoveries," I said.

And leaving Hans to his work, we started off together. The space between the water and the foot of the cliffs was considerable. It took half an hour to bring us to the wall of rock. We trampled under our feet numberless shells of all the forms and sizes which existed in the earliest ages of the world. I also saw immense carapaces more than fifteen feet in diameter. They had been the coverings of those gigantic glyptodons or armadillos of the Pleiocene period, of which the modern tortoise is but a miniature representative. The soil was besides this scattered with stony fragments, boulders rounded by water action, and ridged up in successive lines. I was therefore led to the conclusion that at one time the sea must have covered the ground on which we were treading. On the loose and scattered rocks, now out of the reach of the highest tides, the waves had left manifest traces of their power to wear their way in the hardest stone.

This might up to a certain point explain the existence of an ocean forty leagues beneath the surface of the globe. But in my opinion this liquid mass would be lost by degrees farther and farther within the interior of the earth, and it certainly had its origin in the waters of the ocean overhead, which had made their way hither through some fissure. Yet it must be believed that that fissure is now closed, and that all this cavern or immense reservoir was filled in a very short time. Perhaps even this water, subjected to the fierce action of central heat, had partly been resolved into vapor. This would explain the existence of those clouds suspended over our heads and the development of that electricity which raised such tempests within the bowels of the earth.

This theory of the phenomena we had witnessed seemed satisfactory to me; for however great and stupendous the phenomena of nature, fixed physical laws will or may always explain them.

We were therefore walking upon sedimentary soil, the deposits of the waters of former ages. The professor was carefully examining every little fissure in the rocks. Wherever he saw a hole he always wanted to know the depth of it. To him this was important.

We had traversed the shores of the Liedenbrock sea for a mile when we observed a sudden change in the appearance of the soil. It seemed upset, contorted, and convulsed by a violent upheaval of the lower strata. In many places depressions or elevations gave witness to some tremendous power effecting the dislocation of strata.

We moved with difficulty across these granite fissures and chasms mingled with silex, crystals of quartz, and alluvial deposits, when a field, nay, more than a field, a vast plain, of bleached bones lay spread before us. It seemed like an immense cemetery, where the remains of twenty ages mingled their dust together. Huge mounds of bony fragments rose stage after stage in the distance. They undulated away to the limits of the horizon, and melted in the distance in a faint haze. There within three square miles were accumulated the materials for a complete history of the animal life of ages, a history scarcely outlined in the too recent strata of the inhabited world.

But an impatient curiosity impelled our steps; crackling and rattling, our feet were trampling on the remains of prehistoric animals and interesting fossils, the possession of which is a matter of rivalry and contention between the museums of great cities. A thousand Cuviers could never have reconstructed the organic remains deposited in this magnificent and unparalleled collection.

I stood amazed. My uncle had uplifted his long arms to the vault which was our sky; his mouth gaping wide, his eyes flashing behind his shining spectacles, his head balancing with an up-and-down motion, his whole attitude denoted unlimited astonishment. Here he stood facing an immense collection of scattered leptotheria, mericotheria, lophiodia, anoplotheria, megatheria, mastodons, protopithecae, pterodactyls, and all sorts of extinct monsters here assembled together for his special satisfaction. Fancy an enthusiastic bibliomaniac suddenly brought into the midst of the famous Alexandrian library burned by Omar and restored by a miracle from its ashes! Just such a crazed enthusiast was my uncle, Professor Liedenbrock.

But more was to come, when, with a rush through clouds of bone dust, he laid his hand upon a bare skull, and cried with a voice trembling with excitement:

"Axel! Axel! A human head!"

"A human skull?" I cried, no less astonished.

"Yes, nephew. Aha! M. Milne-Edwards! Ah! M. de Quatrefages, how I wish you were standing here at the side of Otto Liedenbrock!"

XXXVIII

THE PROFESSOR IN HIS CHAIR AGAIN

To understand this apostrophe of my uncle's, made to absent French savants, it will be necessary to allude to an event of high importance in a paleontological point of view, which had occurred a little while before our departure.

On the 28th of March, 1863, some excavators working under the direction of M. Boucher de Perthes, in the stone quarries of Moulin Quignon, near Abbeville, in the department of Somme, found a human jawbone fourteen feet beneath the surface. It was the first fossil of this nature that had ever been brought to light. Not far distant were found stone hatchets and flint arrowheads stained and encased by lapse of time with a uniform coat of rust.

The noise of this discovery was very great, not in France alone, but in England and in Germany. Several savants of the French Institute, and among them MM. Milne-Edwards and de Quatrefages, saw at once the importance of this discovery, proved to demonstration the genuineness of the bone in question, and became the most ardent defendants in what the English called this "trial of a jawbone." To the geologists of the United Kingdom, who believed in the certainty of the fact—Messrs. Falconer, Busk, Carpenter, and others—scientific Germans were soon joined, and among them the forwardest, the most fiery, and the most enthusiastic, was my Uncle Liedenbrock.

Therefore the genuineness of a fossil human relic of the Quaternary period seemed to be incontestably proved and admitted.

It is true that this theory met with a most obstinate opponent in M. Elie de Beaumont. This high authority maintained that the soil of Moulin Quignon was not diluvial at all, but was of much more recent formation; and, agreeing in that with Cuvier, he refused to admit that the human species could be contemporary with the animals of the Quaternary period. My Uncle Liedenbrock, along with the great body of the geologists, had maintained his ground, disputed, and argued, until M. Elie de Beaumont stood almost alone in his opinion.

We knew all these details, but we were not aware that since our departure the question had advanced to farther stages. Other, similar maxillaries, though belonging to individuals of various types and different nations, were found in the loose gray soil of certain grottoes in France, Switzerland, and Belgium, as well as weapons, tools, earthen utensils, bones of children and adults. The existence therefore of man in the Quaternary period seemed to become daily more certain.

Nor was this all. Fresh discoveries of remains in the Pleiocene formation had emboldened other geologists to refer back the human species to a higher antiquity still. It is true that these remains were not human bones, but objects bearing the traces of his handiwork, such as fossil leg bones of animals, sculptured and carved evidently by the hand of man.

Thus, at one bound, the record of the existence of man receded far back into the history of the ages past; he was a predecessor of the mastodon; he was a contemporary of the southern elephant; he lived a hundred thousand years ago, when, according to geologists, the Pleiocene formation was in progress.

Such then was the state of paleontological science, and what we knew of it was sufficient to explain our behavior in the presence of this stupendous Golgotha. Anyone may now understand the frenzied excitement of my uncle, when, twenty yards farther on, he found himself face-to-face with a primitive man!

It was a perfectly recognizable human body. Had some particular soil, like that of the cemetery St. Michel, at Bordeaux, preserved it thus for so many ages? It might be so. But this dried corpse, with its parchmentlike skin drawn tightly over the bony frame, the limbs still preserving their shape, sound teeth, abundant hair, and finger- and toenails of frightful length, this desiccated mummy startled us by appearing just as it had lived countless ages ago. I stood mute before this apparition of remote antiquity. My uncle, usually so garrulous, was struck dumb likewise. We raised the body. We stood it up against a rock. It seemed to stare at us out of its empty orbits. We sounded with our knuckles his hollow frame.

After some moments' silence the professor was himself again. Otto Liedenbrock, yielding to his nature, forgot all the circumstances of our eventful journey, forgot where we were standing, forgot the vaulted cavern which contained us. No doubt he was in mind back again in his Johanneum, holding forth to his pupils, for he assumed his learned air; and addressing himself to an imaginary audience, he proceeded thus:

"Gentlemen, I have the honor to introduce to you a man of the Quaternary or post-Tertiary system. Eminent geologists have denied his existence, others no less eminent have affirmed it. The St. Thomases of paleontology, if they were here, might now touch him with their fingers, and would be obliged to acknowledge their error. I am quite aware that science has to be on its guard with discoveries of this kind. I know what capital enterprising individuals like Barnum have made out of fossil men. I have heard the tale of the kneepan of Ajax, the pretended body of Orestes claimed to have been found by the Spartans, and of the body of Asterius, ten cubits long, of which Pausanias speaks. I have read the reports of the skeleton of Trapani, found in the fourteenth century, and which was at the time identified as that of Polyphemus; and the history of the giant unearthed in the sixteenth century near Palermo. You know as well as I do, gentlemen, the analysis made at Lucerne in 1577 of those huge bones which the celebrated Dr. Felix Plater affirmed to be those of a giant nineteen feet high. I have gone through the treatises of Cassanion, and all those memoirs, pamphlets, answers, and rejoinders published respecting the skeleton of Teutobochus, the invader of Gaul, dug out of a sandpit in the Dauphiné, in 1613. In the eighteenth century I would have stood up for Scheuchzer's pre-Adamite man against Peter Campet. I have perused a writing, entitled Gigan—"

Here my uncle's unfortunate infirmity met him—that of being unable in public to pronounce hard words.

"The pamphlet entitled Gigan—"

He could get no further.

"Giganteo—"

It was not to be done. The unlucky word would not come out. At the Johanneum there would have been a laugh.

"Gigantostéologie," at last the professor burst out, between two words which I shall not record here.

Then rushing on with renewed vigor, and with great animation:

"Yes, gentlemen, I know all these things, and more. I know that Cuvier and Blumenbach have recognized in these bones nothing more remarkable than the bones of the mammoth and other mammals of the post-Tertiary period. But in the presence of this specimen, to doubt would be to insult science. There stands the body! You may see it, touch it. It is not a mere skeleton; it is an entire body, preserved for a purely anthropological end and purpose."

I was good enough not to contradict this startling assertion.

"If I could only wash it in a solution of sulfuric acid," pursued my uncle, "I should be able to clear it from all the earthy particles and the shells which are encrusted about it. But I do not possess that valuable solvent. Yet, such as it is, the body shall tell us its own wonderful story."

Here the professor laid hold of the fossil skeleton, and handled it with the skill of a dexterous showman.

"You see," he said, "that it is not six feet long, and that we are still separated by a long interval from the pretended race of giants. As for the family to which it belongs, it is evidently Caucasian. It is the white race, our own. The skull of this fossil is a regular oval, or rather ovoid. It exhibits no prominent cheekbones, no projecting jaws. It presents no appearance of that prognathism which diminishes the facial angle.* Measure that angle. It is nearly ninety degrees. But I will go further in my deductions, and I will affirm that this specimen of the human family is of the Japhetic race, which has since spread from the Indies to the Atlantic. Don't smile, gentlemen."

Nobody was smiling; but the learned professor was frequently disturbed by the broad smiles provoked by his learned eccentricities.

"Yes," he pursued with animation, "this is a fossil man, the contemporary of the mastodons whose remains fill this amphitheater. But if you ask me how he came there, how those strata on which he lay slipped down into this enormous hollow in the globe, I confess I cannot answer that question. No doubt in the post-Tertiary period considerable commotions were still disturbing the crust of the earth. The long-continued cooling of the globe produced chasms, fissures, clefts, and faults, into which, very probably, portions of the upper earth may have fallen. I make no rash assertions; but there is the man surrounded by his own works, by hatchets, by flint arrowheads, which are the characteristics of the Stone Age. And unless he came here, like myself, as a tourist on a visit and as a pioneer of science, I can entertain no doubt of the authenticity of his remote origin."

The professor ceased to speak, and the audience broke out into loud and unanimous applause. For of course my uncle was right, and wiser men than his nephew would have had some trouble to refute his statements.

Another remarkable thing. This fossil body was not the only one in this immense catacomb. We came upon other bodies at every step among this mortal dust, and my uncle might select the most curious of these specimens to demolish the incredulity of skeptics.

In fact it was a wonderful spectacle, that of these generations of men and animals commingled in a common cemetery. Then one very serious question arose presently which we scarcely dared to suggest. Had all those creatures slid through a great fissure in the crust of the earth, down to the shores of the Liedenbrock Sea, when they were dead and turning to dust, or had they lived and grown and died here in this subterranean world under a false sky,

* The facial angle is formed by two lines; one touching the brow and the front teeth, the other from the orifice of the ear to the lower line of the nostrils. The greater this angle, the higher intelligence denoted by the formation of the skull. Prognathism is that projection of the jawbones which sharpens or lessens this angle, and which is illustrated in the Negro countenance and in the lowest savages.

just like inhabitants of the upper earth? Until the present time we had seen alive only marine monsters and fishes. Might not some living man, some native of the abyss, be yet a wanderer below on this desert strand?

XXXIX

FOREST SCENERY ILLUMINATED BY ELECTRICITY

For another half hour we trod upon a pavement of bones. We pushed on, impelled by our burning curiosity. What other marvels did this cavern contain? What new treasures lay here for science to unfold? I was prepared for any surprise, my imagination was ready for any astonishment however astounding.

We had long lost sight of the seashore behind the hills of bones. The rash professor, careless of losing his way, hurried me forward. We advanced in silence, bathed in luminous electric fluid. By some phenomenon which I am unable to explain, it lighted up all sides of every object equally. Such was its diffusiveness, there being no central point from which the light emanated, that shadows no longer existed. You might have thought yourself under the rays of a vertical sun in a tropical region at noonday and the height of summer. No vapor was visible. The rocks, the distant mountains, a few isolated clumps of forest trees in the distance, presented a weird and wonderful aspect under these totally new conditions of a universal diffusion of light. We were like Hoffmann's shadowless man.

After walking a mile we reached the outskirts of a vast forest, but not one of those forests of fungi which bordered Port Gräuben.

Here was the vegetation of the tertiary period in its fullest blaze of magnificence. Tall palms, belonging to species no longer living, splendid palmacites, firs, yews, cypress trees, thujas, representatives of the conifers, were linked together by a tangled network of long climbing plants. A soft carpet of moss and hepaticas luxuriously clothed the soil. A few sparkling streams ran almost in silence under what would have been the shade of the trees, but that there was no shadow. On their banks grew tree ferns similar to those we grow in hothouses. But a remarkable feature was the total absence of color in all those trees, shrubs, and plants, growing without the life-giving heat and light of the sun. Everything seemed mixed-up and confounded in one uniform silver gray or light brown tint like that of fading and faded leaves. Not a green leaf anywhere, and the flowers—which were abundant enough in the Tertiary period, which first gave birth to flowers—looked like brown-paper flowers, without color or scent.

My Uncle Liedenbrock ventured to penetrate under this colossal grove.

I followed him, not without fear. Since nature had here provided vegetable nourishment, why should not the terrible mammals be there too? I perceived in the broad clearings left by fallen trees, decayed with age, leguminose plants, acerineae, rubiceae, and many other eatable shrubs, dear to ruminant animals at every period. Then I observed, mingled together in confusion, trees of countries far apart on the surface of the globe. The oak and the palm were growing side by side, the Australian eucalyptus leaned against the Norwegian pine, the birch tree of the north mingled its foliage with New Zealand kauris. It was enough to distract the most ingenious classifier of terrestrial botany.

Suddenly I halted. I drew back my uncle.

The diffused light revealed the smallest object in the dense and distant thickets. I had thought I saw—no! I did see, with my own eyes, vast colossal forms moving among the trees. They were gigantic animals; it was a herd of mastodons—not fossil remains, but living and resembling those the bones of which were found in the marshes of Ohio in 1801. I saw those huge elephants whose long, flexible trunks were grouting and turning up the soil under the trees like a legion of serpents. I could hear the crashing noise of their long ivory tusks boring into the old decaying trunks. The boughs cracked, and the leaves torn away by cartloads went down the cavernous throats of the vast brutes.

So, then, the dream in which I had had a vision of the prehistoric world, of the Tertiary and post-Tertiary periods, was now realized. And there we were alone, in the bowels of the earth, at the mercy of its wild inhabitants!

My uncle was gazing with intense and eager interest.

"Come on!" said he, seizing my arm. "Forward! Forward!"

"No, I will not!" I cried. "We have no firearms. What could we do in the midst of a herd of these four-footed giants? Come away, uncle—come! No human being may with safety dare the anger of these monstrous beasts."

"No human creature?" replied my uncle in a lower voice. "You are wrong, Axel. Look, look down there! I fancy I see a living creature similar to ourselves: it is a man!"

I looked, shaking my head incredulously. But though at first I was unbelieving, I had to yield to the evidence of my senses.

In fact, at a distance of a quarter of a mile, leaning against the trunk of a gigantic kauri, stood a human being, the Proteus of those subterranean regions, a new son of Neptune, watching this countless herd of mastodons.

*Immanis pecoris custos, immanior ipse.**

Yes, truly, huger still himself. It was no longer a fossil being like him whose dried remains we had easily lifted up in the field of bones; it was a giant, able

* "The shepherd of gigantic herds, and huger still himself."

to control those monsters. In stature he was at least twelve feet high. His head, huge and unshapely as a buffalo's, was half hidden in the thick and tangled growth of his unkempt hair. It most resembled the mane of the primitive elephant. In his hand he wielded with ease an enormous bough, a staff worthy of this shepherd of the geologic period.

We stood petrified and speechless with amazement. But he might see us! We must fly!

"Come, do come!" I said to my uncle, who for once allowed himself to be persuaded.

In another quarter of an hour our nimble heels had carried us beyond the reach of this horrible monster.

And yet, now that I can reflect quietly, now that my spirit has grown calm again, now that months have slipped by since this strange and supernatural meeting, what am I to think? What am I to believe? I must conclude that it was impossible that our senses had been deceived, that our eyes did not see what we supposed they saw. No human being lives in this subterranean world; no generation of men dwells in those inferior caverns of the globe, unknown to and unconnected with the inhabitants of its surface. It is absurd to believe it!

I had rather admit that it may have been some animal whose structure resembled the human, some ape or baboon of the early geological ages, some protopitheca, or some mesopitheca, some early or middle ape like that discovered by Mr. Lartet in the bone cave of Sansau. But this creature surpassed in stature all the measurements known in modern paleontology. But that a man, a living man, and therefore whole generations doubtless besides, should be buried there in the bowels of the earth, is impossible.

However, we had left behind us the luminous forest, dumb with astonishment, overwhelmed and struck down with a terror which amounted to stupefaction. We kept running on for fear the horrible monster might be on our track. It was a flight, a fall, like that fearful pulling and dragging which is peculiar to nightmare. Instinctively we got back to the Liedenbrock Sea, and I cannot say into what vagaries my mind would not have carried me but for a circumstance which brought me back to practical matters.

Although I was certain that we were now treading upon a soil not hitherto touched by our feet, I often perceived groups of rocks which reminded me of those about Port Gräuben. Besides, this seemed to confirm the indications of the needle, and to show that we had against our will returned to the north of the Liedenbrock Sea. Occasionally we felt quite convinced. Brooks and waterfalls were tumbling everywhere from the projections in the rocks. I thought I recognized the bed of surturbrand, our faithful Hansbach, and the grotto in which I had recovered life and consciousness. Then a few paces farther on, the arrangement of the cliffs, the appearance of an unrecognized stream, or the strange outline of a rock, came to throw me again into doubt.

I communicated my doubts to my uncle. Like myself, he hesitated; he could recognize nothing again amid this monotonous scene.

"Evidently," said I, "we have not landed again at our original starting point, but the storm has carried us a little higher, and if we follow the shore we shall find Port Gräuben."

"If that is the case it will be useless to continue our exploration, and we had better return to our raft. But, Axel, are you not mistaken?"

"It is difficult to speak decidedly, uncle, for all these rocks are so very much alike. Yet I think I recognize the promontory at the foot of which Hans constructed our launch. We must be very near the little port, if indeed this is not it," I added, examining a creek which I thought I recognized.

"No, Axel, we should at least find our own traces and I see nothing—"

"But I do see," I cried, darting upon an object lying on the sand.

And I showed my uncle a rusty dagger which I had just picked up.

"Come," said he, "had you this weapon with you?"

"I! No, certainly! But you, perhaps—"

"Not that I am aware," said the professor. "I have never had this object in my possession."

"Well, this is strange!"

"No, Axel, it is very simple. The Icelanders often wear arms of this kind. This must have belonged to Hans, and he has lost it."

I shook my head. Hans had never had an object like this in his possession.

"Did it not belong to some pre-Adamite warrior?" I cried, "to some living man, contemporary with the huge cattle-driver? But no. This is not a relic of the Stone Age. It is not even of the Iron Age. This blade is steel—"

My uncle stopped me abruptly on my way to a dissertation which would have taken me a long way, and said coolly:

"Be calm, Axel, and reasonable. This dagger belongs to the sixteenth century; it is a poniard, such as gentlemen carried in their belts to give the coup de grace. Its origin is Spanish. It was never either yours, or mine, or the hunter's, nor did it belong to any of those human beings who may or may not inhabit this inner world. See, it was never jagged like this by cutting men's throats; its blade is coated with a rust neither a day, nor a year, nor a hundred years old."

The professor was getting excited according to his wont, and was allowing his imagination to run away with him.

"Axel, we are on the way toward the grand discovery. This blade has been left on the strand for from one to three hundred years, and has blunted its edge upon the rocks that fringe this subterranean sea!"

"But it has not come alone. It has not twisted itself out of shape; some one has been here before us!

"Yes—a man has."

"And who was that man?"

"A man who has engraved his name somewhere with that dagger. That man wanted once more to mark the way to the center of the earth. Let us look about: look about!"

And, wonderfully interested, we peered all along the high wall, peeping into every fissure which might open out into a gallery.

And so we arrived at a place where the shore was much narrowed. Here the sea came to lap the foot of the steep cliff, leaving a passage no wider than a couple of yards. Between two boldly projecting rocks appeared the mouth of a dark tunnel.

There, upon a granite slab, appeared two mysterious graven letters, half eaten away by time. They were the initials of the bold and daring traveler:

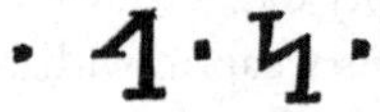

"A. S.," shouted my uncle. "Arne Saknussemm! Arne Saknussemm everywhere!"

XL

PREPARATIONS FOR BLASTING A PASSAGE TO THE CENTER OF THE EARTH

Since the start upon this marvelous pilgrimage I had been through so many astonishments that I might well be excused for thinking myself well hardened against any further surprise. Yet at the sight of these two letters, engraved on this spot three hundred years ago, I stood aghast in dumb amazement. Not only were the initials of the learned alchemist visible upon the living rock, but there lay the iron point with which the letters had been engraved. I could no longer doubt of the existence of that wonderful traveler and of the fact of his unparalleled journey, without the most glaring incredulity.

While these reflections were occupying me, Professor Liedenbrock had launched into a somewhat rhapsodical eulogium, of which Arne Saknussemm was, of course, the hero.

"Thou marvelous genius!" he cried. "Thou hast not forgotten one indication which might serve to lay open to mortals the road through the terrestrial crust; and thy fellow creatures may even now, after the lapse of three centuries, again trace thy footsteps through these deep and darksome ways. You reserved the contemplation of these wonders for other eyes besides your own. Your name, graven from stage to stage, leads the bold follower of your footsteps to the very center of our planet's core, and there again we shall find your own name written with your own hand. I too will inscribe my name upon this dark granite page. But forever henceforth let this cape that advances into the sea discovered by yourself be known by your own illustrious name—Cape Saknussemm."

Such were the glowing words of panegyric which fell upon my attentive ear, and I could not resist the sentiment of enthusiasm with which I too was infected. The fire of zeal kindled afresh in me. I forgot everything. I dismissed from my mind the past perils of the journey, the future danger of our return. That which another had done I supposed we might also do, and nothing that was not superhuman appeared impossible to me.

"Forward! Forward!" I cried.

I was already darting down the gloomy tunnel when the professor stopped me; he, the man of impulse, counseled patience and coolness.

"Let us first return to Hans," he said, "and bring the raft to this spot."

I obeyed, not without dissatisfaction, and passed out rapidly among the rocks on the shore.

I said, "Uncle, do you know it seems to me that circumstances have wonderfully befriended us hitherto?"

"You think so, Axel?"

"No doubt; even the tempest has put us on the right way. Blessings on that storm! It has brought us back to this coast from which fine weather would have carried us far away. Suppose we had touched with our prow (the prow of a rudder!) the southern shore of the Liedenbrock Sea, what would have become of us? We should never have seen the name of Saknussemm, and we should at this moment be imprisoned on a rockbound, impassable coast."

"Yes, Axel, it is providential that while supposing we were steering south we should have just got back north at Cape Saknussemm. I must say that this is astonishing, and that I feel I have no way to explain it."

"What does that signify, uncle? Our business is not to explain facts, but to use them!"

"Certainly; but—"

"Well, uncle, we are going to resume the northern route, and to pass under the north countries of Europe—under Sweden, Russia, Siberia: who knows where?—instead of burrowing under the deserts of Africa, or perhaps the waves of the Atlantic; and that is all I want to know."

"Yes, Axel, you are right. It is all for the best, since we have left that weary, horizontal sea, which led us nowhere. Now we shall go down, down, down! Do you know that it is now only 1,500 leagues to the center of the globe?"

"Is that all?" I cried. "Why, that's nothing. Let us start: march!"

All this crazy talk was going on still when we met the hunter. Everything was made ready for our instant departure. Every bit of cordage was put on board. We took our places, and with our sail set, Hans steered us along the coast to Cape Saknussemm.

The wind was unfavorable to a species of launch not calculated for shallow water. In many places we were obliged to push ourselves along with iron-pointed sticks. Often the sunken rocks just beneath the surface obliged us to deviate from our straight course. At last, after three hours' sailing, about six in the evening we reached a place suitable for our landing. I jumped ashore, followed by my uncle and the Icelander. This short passage had not served to cool my ardor. On the contrary, I even proposed to burn "our ship," to prevent the possibility of return; but my uncle would not consent to that. I thought him singularly lukewarm.

"At least," I said, "don't let us lose a minute."

"Yes, yes, lad," he replied; "but first let us examine this new gallery, to see if we shall require our ladders."

My uncle put his Ruhmkorff's apparatus in action; the raft moored to the shore was left alone; the mouth of the tunnel was not twenty yards from us; and our party, with myself at the head, made for it without a moment's delay.

The aperture, which was almost round, was about five feet in diameter; the dark passage was cut out in the live rock and lined with a coat of the eruptive matter which formerly issued from it; the interior was level with the ground outside, so that we were able to enter without difficulty. We were following a horizontal plane, when, only six paces in, our progress was interrupted by an enormous block just across our way.

"Accursed rock!" I cried in a passion, finding myself suddenly confronted by an impassable obstacle.

Right and left we searched in vain for a way, up and down, side to side; there was no getting any farther. I felt fearfully disappointed, and I would not admit that the obstacle was final. I stopped, I looked underneath the block: no opening. Above: granite still. Hans passed his lamp over every portion of the barrier in vain. We must give up all hope of passing it.

I sat down in despair. My uncle strode from side to side in the narrow passage.

"But how was it with Saknussemm?" I cried.

"Yes," said my uncle, "was he stopped by this stone barrier?"

"No, no," I replied with animation. "This fragment of rock has been shaken down by some shock or convulsion, or by one of those magnetic storms which agitate these regions, and has blocked up the passage which lay open to him. Many years have elapsed since the return of Saknussemm to the surface and the fall of this huge fragment. Is it not evident that this gallery was once the way open to the course of the lava, and that at that time there must have been a free passage? See here are recent fissures grooving and channeling the granite roof. This roof itself is formed of fragments of rock carried down, of enormous stones, as if by some giant's hand; but at one time the expulsive force was greater than usual, and this block, like the falling keystone of a ruined arch, has slipped down to the ground and blocked up the way. It is only an accidental obstruction, not met by Saknussemm, and if we don't destroy it we shall be unworthy to reach the center of the earth."

Such was my sentence! The soul of the professor had passed into me. The genius of discovery possessed me wholly. I forgot the past, I scorned the future. I gave not a thought to the things of the surface of this globe into which I had dived; its cities and its sunny plains, Hamburg and the Königstrasse, even poor Gräuben, who must have given us up for lost, all were for the time dismissed from the pages of my memory.

"Well," cried my uncle, "let us make a way with our pickaxes."

"Too hard for the pickaxe."

"Well, then, the spade."

"That would take us too long."

"What, then?"

"Why gunpowder, to be sure! Let us mine the obstacle and blow it up."

"Oh, yes, it is only a bit of rock to blast!"

"Hans, to work!" cried my uncle.

The Icelander returned to the raft and soon came back with an iron bar which he made use of to bore a hole for the charge. This was no easy work. A hole was to be made large enough to hold fifty pounds of guncotton, whose expansive force is four times that of gunpowder.

I was terribly excited. While Hans was at work I was actively helping my uncle to prepare a slow match of wetted powder encased in linen.

"This will do it," I said.

"It will," replied my uncle.

By midnight our mining preparations were over; the charge was rammed into the hole, and the slow match uncoiled along the gallery showed its end outside the opening.

A spark would now develop the whole of our preparations into activity.

"Tomorrow," said the professor.

I had to be resigned and to wait six long hours.

XLI

THE GREAT EXPLOSION AND THE RUSH DOWN BELOW

The next day, Thursday, August 27, is a well-remembered date in our subterranean journey. It never returns to my memory without sending through me a shudder of horror and a palpitation of the heart. From that hour we had no further occasion for the exercise of reason, or judgment, or skill, or contrivance. We were henceforth to be hurled along, the playthings of the fierce elements of the deep.

At six we were afoot. The moment drew near to clear a way by blasting through the opposing mass of granite.

I begged for the honor of lighting the fuse. This duty done, I was to join my companions on the raft, which had not yet been unloaded; we should then push off as far as we could and avoid the dangers arising from the explosion, the effects of which were not likely to be confined to the rock itself.

The fuse was calculated to burn ten minutes before setting fire to the mine. I therefore had sufficient time to get away to the raft.

I prepared to fulfill my task with some anxiety.

After a hasty meal, my uncle and the hunter embarked while I remained on shore. I was supplied with a lighted lantern to set fire to the fuse. "Now go," said my uncle, "and return immediately to us."

"Don't be uneasy," I replied. "I will not play by the way."

I immediately proceeded to the mouth of the tunnel. I opened my lantern. I laid hold of the end of the match.

The professor stood, chronometer in hand.

"Ready?" he cried.

"Ay."

"Fire!"

I instantly plunged the end of the fuse into the lantern. It spluttered and flamed, and I ran at the top of my speed to the raft.

"Come on board quickly, and let us push off."

Hans, with a vigorous thrust, sent us from the shore. The raft shot twenty fathoms out to sea.

It was a moment of intense excitement. The professor was watching the hand of the chronometer.

"Five minutes more!" he said. "Four! Three!"

My pulse beat half-seconds.

"Two! One! Down, granite rocks; down with you."

What took place at that moment? I believe I did not hear the dull roar of the explosion. But the rocks suddenly assumed a new arrangement: they rent asunder like a curtain. I saw a bottomless pit open on the shore. The sea, lashed into sudden fury, rose up in an enormous billow, on the ridge of which the unhappy raft was uplifted bodily in the air with all its crew and cargo.

We all three fell down flat. In less than a second we were in deep, unfathomable darkness. Then I felt as if not only myself but the raft also had no support beneath. I thought it was sinking; but it was not so. I wanted to speak to my uncle, but the roaring of the waves prevented him from hearing even the sound of my voice.

In spite of darkness, noise, astonishment, and terror, I then understood what had taken place.

On the other side of the blown-up rock was an abyss. The explosion had caused a kind of earthquake in this fissured and abysmal region; a great gulf had opened; and the sea, now changed into a torrent, was hurrying us along into it.

I gave myself up for lost.

An hour passed away—two hours, perhaps—I cannot tell. We clutched each other fast, to save ourselves from being thrown off the raft. We felt violent shocks whenever we were borne heavily against the craggy projections. Yet these shocks were not very frequent, from which I concluded that the gully was widening. It was no doubt the same road that Saknussemm had taken; but instead of walking peaceably down it, as he had done, we were carrying a whole sea along with us.

These ideas, it will be understood, presented themselves to my mind in a vague and undetermined form. I had difficulty in associating any ideas together during this headlong race, which seemed like a vertical descent. To judge by the air which was whistling past me and made a whizzing in my ears, we were moving faster than the fastest express trains. To light a torch under these conditions would have been impossible; and our last electric apparatus had been shattered by the force of the explosion.

I was therefore much surprised to see a clear light shining near me. It lighted up the calm and unmoved countenance of Hans. The skillful huntsman had succeeded in lighting the lantern; and although it flickered so much as to threaten to go out, it threw a fitful light across the awful darkness.

I was right in my supposition. It was a wide gallery. The dim light could not show us both its walls at once. The fall of the waters which were carrying us away exceeded that of the swiftest rapids in American rivers. Its surface seemed composed of a sheaf of arrows hurled with inconceivable force; I cannot convey my impressions by a better comparison. The raft, occasionally seized by an eddy, spun round as it still flew along. When it approached the walls of the gallery I threw on them the light of the lantern, and I could judge somewhat of the velocity of our speed by noticing how the jagged projections of the rocks spun into endless ribbons and bands, so that we seemed confined within a network of shifting lines. I supposed we were running at the rate of thirty leagues an hour.

My uncle and I gazed on each other with haggard eyes, clinging to the stump of the mast, which had snapped asunder at the first shock of our great catastrophe. We kept our backs to the wind, not to be stifled by the rapidity of a movement which no human power could check.

Hours passed away. No change in our situation; but a discovery came to complicate matters and make them worse.

In seeking to put our cargo into somewhat better order, I found that the greater part of the articles embarked had disappeared at the moment of the explosion, when the sea broke in upon us with such violence. I wanted to know exactly what we had saved, and with the lantern in my hand I began my examination. Of our instruments none were saved but the compass and the chronometer; our stock of ropes and ladders was reduced to the bit of cord rolled round the stump of the mast! Not a spade, not a pickaxe, not a hammer was left us; and, irreparable disaster! We had only one day's provisions left.

I searched every nook and corner, every crack and cranny in the raft. There was nothing. Our provisions were reduced to one bit of salt meat and a few biscuits.

I stared at our failing supplies stupidly. I refused to take in the gravity of our loss. And yet what was the use of troubling myself. If we had had provisions enough for months, how could we get out of the abyss into which we were being hurled by an irresistible torrent? Why should we fear the horrors of famine, when death was swooping down upon us in a multitude of other forms? Would there be time left to die of starvation?

Yet by an inexplicable play of the imagination I forgot my present dangers, to contemplate the threatening future. Was there any chance of escaping from the fury of this impetuous torrent, and of returning to the surface of the globe? I could not form the slightest conjecture how or when. But one chance in a thousand, or ten thousand, is still a chance; while death from starvation would leave us not the smallest hope in the world.

The thought came into my mind to declare the whole truth to my uncle, to show him the dreadful straits to which we were reduced, and to calculate how long we might yet expect to live. But I had the courage to preserve silence. I wished to leave him cool and self-possessed.

At that moment the light from our lantern began to sink by little and little, and then went out entirely. The wick had burned itself out. Black night reigned again; and there was no hope left of being able to dissipate the palpable darkness. We had yet a torch left, but we could not have kept it alight. Then, like a child, I closed my eyes firmly, not to see the darkness.

After a considerable lapse of time our speed redoubled. I could perceive it by the sharpness of the currents that blew past my face. The descent became steeper. I believe we were no longer sliding, but falling down. I had an impression that we were dropping vertically. My uncle's hand, and the vigorous arm of Hans, held me fast.

Suddenly, after a space of time that I could not measure, I felt a shock. The raft had not struck against any hard resistance, but had suddenly been checked in its fall. A waterspout, an immense liquid column, was beating upon the surface of the waters. I was suffocating! I was drowning!

But this sudden flood was not of long duration. In a few seconds I found myself in the air again, which I inhaled with all the force of my lungs. My uncle and Hans were still holding me fast by the arms; and the raft was still carrying us.

XLII

HEADLONG SPEED UPWARD THROUGH THE HORRORS OF DARKNESS

It might have been, as I guessed, about ten at night. The first of my senses which came into play after this last bout was that of hearing. All at once I could hear; and it was a real exercise of the sense of hearing. I could hear the silence in the gallery after the din which for hours had stunned me. At last these words of my uncle's came to me like a vague murmuring:

"We are going up."

"What do you mean?" I cried.

"Yes, we are going up—up!"

I stretched out my arm. I touched the wall, and drew back my hand bleeding. We were ascending with extreme rapidity.

"The torch! The torch!" cried the professor.

Not without difficulty Hans succeeded in lighting the torch; and the flame, preserving its upward tendency, threw enough light to show us what kind of a place we were in.

"Just as I thought," said the professor. "We are in a tunnel not four-and-twenty feet in diameter. The water had reached the bottom of the gulf. It is now rising to its level, and carrying us with it."

"Where to?"

"I cannot tell; but we must be ready for anything. We are mounting at a speed which seems to me of fourteen feet in a second, or ten miles an hour. At this rate we shall get on."

"Yes, if nothing stops us; if this well has an aperture. But suppose it to be stopped. If the air is condensed by the pressure of this column of water we shall be crushed."

"Axel," replied the professor with perfect coolness, "our situation is almost desperate; but there are some chances of deliverance, and it is these that I am considering. If at every instant we may perish, so at every instant we may be saved. Let us then be prepared to seize upon the smallest advantage."

"But what shall we do now?"

"Recruit our strength by eating."

At these words I fixed a haggard eye upon my uncle. That which I had been so unwilling to confess at last had to be told.

"Eat, did you say?"

"Yes, at once."

The professor added a few words in Danish, but Hans shook his head mournfully.

"What!" cried my uncle. "Have we lost our provisions?"

"Yes; here is all we have left; one bit of salt meat for the three."

My uncle stared at me as if he could not understand.

"Well," said I, "do you think we have any chance of being saved?"

My question was unanswered.

An hour passed away. I began to feel the pangs of a violent hunger. My companions were suffering too, and not one of us dared touch this wretched remnant of our goodly store.

But now we were mounting up with excessive speed. Sometimes the air would cut our breath short, as is experienced by aeronauts ascending too rapidly. But while they suffer from cold in proportion to their rise, we were beginning to feel a contrary effect. The heat was increasing in a manner to cause us the most fearful anxiety, and certainly the temperature was at this moment at the height of 100°F.

What could be the meaning of such a change? Up to this time facts had supported the theories of Davy and of Liedenbrock; until now particular conditions of nonconducting rocks, electricity, and magnetism had tempered the laws of nature, giving us only a moderately warm climate, for the theory of a central fire remained in my estimation the only one that was true and explicable. Were we then turning back to where the phenomena of central heat ruled in all their rigor and would reduce the most refractory rocks to the state of a molten liquid? I feared this, and said to the professor:

"If we are neither drowned, nor shattered to pieces, nor starved to death, there is still the chance that we may be burned alive and reduced to ashes."

At this he shrugged his shoulders and returned to his thoughts.

Another hour passed, and, except some slight increase in the temperature, nothing new had happened.

"Come," said he, "we must determine upon something."

"Determine on what?" said I.

"Yes, we must recruit our strength by carefully rationing ourselves, and so prolong our existence by a few hours. But we shall be reduced to very great weakness at last."

"And our last hour is not far off."

"Well, if there is a chance of safety, if a moment for active exertion presents itself, where should we find the required strength if we allowed ourselves to be enfeebled by hunger?"

"Well, uncle, when this bit of meat has been devoured, what shall we have left?"

"Nothing, Axel, nothing at all. But will it do you any more good to devour it with your eyes than with your teeth? Your reasoning has in it neither sense nor energy."

"Then don't you despair?" I cried irritably.

"No, certainly not," was the professor's firm reply.

"What! Do you think there is any chance of safety left?"

"Yes, I do; as long as the heart beats, as long as body and soul keep together, I cannot admit that any creature endowed with a will has need to despair of life."

Resolute words these! The man who could speak so, under such circumstances, was of no ordinary type.

"Finally, what do you mean to do?" I asked.

"Eat what is left to the last crumb, and recruit our fading strength. This meal will be our last, perhaps: so let it be! But at any rate we shall once more be men, and not exhausted, empty bags."

"Well, let us consume it then," I cried.

My uncle took the piece of meat and the few biscuits which had escaped from the general destruction. He divided them into three equal portions and gave one to each. This made about a pound of nourishment for each. The professor ate his greedily, with a kind of feverish rage. I ate without pleasure, almost with disgust; Hans quietly, moderately, masticating his small mouthfuls without any noise, and relishing them with the calmness of a man above all anxiety about the future. By diligent search he had found a flask of Hollands; he offered it to us each in turn, and this generous beverage cheered us up slightly.

"*Forträfflig*," said Hans, drinking in his turn.

"Excellent," replied my uncle.

A glimpse of hope had returned, although without cause. But our last meal was over, and it was now five in the morning.

Man is so constituted that health is a purely negative state. Hunger once satisfied, it is difficult for a man to imagine the horrors of starvation; they cannot be understood without being felt.

Therefore it was that after our long fast these few mouthfuls of meat and biscuit made us triumph over our past agonies.

But as soon as the meal was done, we each of us fell deep into thought. What was Hans thinking of—that man of the far West, but who seemed ruled by the fatalist doctrines of the East?

As for me, my thoughts were made up of remembrances, and they carried me up to the surface of the globe of which I ought never to have taken leave. The house in the Königstrasse, my poor dear Gräuben, that kind soul Martha, flitted like visions before my eyes, and in the dismal moanings which from time to time reached my ears I thought I could distinguish the roar of the traffic of the great cities upon earth.

My uncle still had his eye upon his work. Torch in hand, he tried to gather some idea of our situation from the observation of the strata. This calculation could, at best, be but a vague approximation; but a learned man is always a philosopher when he succeeds in remaining cool, and assuredly Professor Liedenbrock possessed this quality to a surprising degree.

I could hear him murmuring geological terms. I could understand them, and in spite of myself I felt interested in this last geological study.

"Eruptive granite," he was saying. "We are still in the primitive period. But we are going up, up, higher still. Who can tell?"

Ah! Who can tell? With his hand he was examining the perpendicular wall, and in a few more minutes he continued:

"This is gneiss! Here is mica schist! Ah! Presently we shall come to the transition period, and then—"

What did the professor mean? Could he be trying to measure the thickness of the crust of the earth that lay between us and the world above? Had he any means of making this calculation? No, he had not the aneroid, and no guessing could supply its place.

Still the temperature kept rising, and I felt myself steeped in a broiling atmosphere. I could only compare it to the heat of a furnace at the moment when the molten metal is running into the mold. Gradually we had been obliged to throw aside our coats and waistcoats, the lightest covering became uncomfortable and even painful.

"Are we rising into a fiery furnace?" I cried at one moment when the heat was redoubling.

"No," replied my uncle, "that is impossible—quite impossible!"

"Yet," I answered, feeling the wall, "this well is burning hot."

At the same moment, touching the water, I had to withdraw my hand in haste.

"The water is scalding," I cried.

This time the professor's only answer was an angry gesture.

Then an unconquerable terror seized upon me, from which I could no longer get free. I felt that a catastrophe was approaching before which the boldest spirit must quail. A dim, vague notion laid hold of my mind, but which was fast hardening into certainty. I tried to repel it, but it would return. I dared not express it in plain terms. Yet a few involuntary observations confirmed me in my view. By the flickering light of the torch I could distinguish contortions in the granite beds; a phenomenon was unfolding in which electricity would play the principal part; then this unbearable heat, this boiling water! I consulted the compass.

The compass had lost its properties! It had ceased to act properly!

XLIII

SHOT OUT OF A VOLCANO AT LAST!

Yes: our compass was no longer a guide; the needle flew from pole to pole with a kind of frenzied impulse; it ran round the dial, and spun hither and thither as if it were giddy or intoxicated.

I knew quite well that according to the best received theories the mineral covering of the globe is never at absolute rest; the changes brought about by the chemical decomposition of its component parts, the agitation caused by great liquid torrents, and the magnetic currents, are continually tending to disturb it—even when living beings upon its surface may fancy that all is quiet below. A phenomenon of this kind would not have greatly alarmed me, or at any rate it would not have given rise to dreadful apprehensions.

But other facts, other circumstances, of a peculiar nature, came to reveal to me by degrees the true state of the case. There came incessant and continuous explosions. I could only compare them to the loud rattle of a long train of chariots driven at full speed over the stones, or a roar of unintermitting thunder.

Then the disordered compass, thrown out of gear by the electric currents, confirmed me in a growing conviction. The mineral crust of the globe threatened to burst up, the granite foundations to come together with a crash, the fissure through which we were helplessly driven would be filled up, the void would be full of crushed fragments of rock, and we poor wretched mortals were to be buried and annihilated in this dreadful consummation.

"My uncle," I cried, "we are lost now, utterly lost!"

"What are you in a fright about now?" was the calm rejoinder. "What is the matter with you?"

"The matter? Look at those quaking walls! Look at those shivering rocks. Don't you feel the burning heat? Don't you see how the water boils and bubbles? Are you blind to the dense vapors and steam growing thicker and denser every minute? See this agitated compass needle. It is an earthquake that is threatening us."

My undaunted uncle calmly shook his head.

"Do you think," said he, "an earthquake is coming?"

"I do."

"Well, I think you are mistaken."

"What! Don't you recognize the symptoms?"

"Of an earthquake? No! I am looking out for something better."

"What can you mean? Explain?"

"It is an eruption, Axel."

"An eruption! Do you mean to affirm that we are running up the shaft of a volcano?"

"I believe we are," said the indomitable professor with an air of perfect self-possession; "and it is the best thing that could possibly happen to us under our circumstances."

The best thing! Was my uncle stark mad? What did the man mean? And what was the use of saying facetious things at a time like this?

"What!" I shouted. "Are we being taken up in an eruption? Our fate has flung us here among burning lavas, molten rocks, boiling waters, and all kinds of volcanic matter; we are going to be pitched out, expelled, tossed up, vomited, spit out high into the air, along with fragments of rock, showers of ashes and scoria, in the midst of a towering rush of smoke and flames; and it is the best thing that could happen to us!"

"Yes," replied the professor, eyeing me over his spectacles, "I don't see any other way of reaching the surface of the earth."

I pass rapidly over the thousand ideas which passed through my mind. My uncle was right, undoubtedly right; and never had he seemed to me more daring and more confirmed in his notions than at this moment when he was calmly contemplating the chances of being shot out of a volcano!

In the meantime up we went; the night passed away in continual ascent; the din and uproar around us became more and more intensified; I was stifled and stunned; I thought my last hour was approaching; and yet imagination is such a strong thing that even in this supreme hour I was occupied with strange and almost childish speculations. But I was the victim, not the master, of my own thoughts.

It was very evident that we were being hurried upward upon the crest of a wave of eruption; beneath our raft were boiling waters, and under these the more sluggish lava was working its way up in a heated mass, together with shoals of fragments of rock which, when they arrived at the crater, would be dispersed in all directions high and low. We were imprisoned in the shaft or chimney of some volcano. There was no room to doubt of that.

But this time, instead of Snæfell, an extinct volcano, we were inside one in full activity. I wondered, therefore, where could this mountain be, and in what part of the world we were to be shot out.

I made no doubt but that it would be in some northern region. Before its disorders set in, the needle had never deviated from that direction. From Cape Saknussemm we had been carried due north for hundreds of leagues. Were we under Iceland again? Were we destined to be thrown up out of Hecla, or by which of the seven other fiery craters in that island? Within a radius of five hundred leagues to the west I remembered under this parallel of latitude only the imperfectly known volcanoes of the northeast coast of America. To the east there was only one in the 80th degree of north latitude, the Esk in Jan Mayen Island, not far from Spitzbergen! Certainly there was no lack of craters, and there were some capacious enough to throw out a whole army! But I wanted to know which of them was to serve us for an exit from the inner world.

Toward morning the ascending movement became accelerated. If the heat increased, instead of diminishing, as we approached nearer to the surface of the globe, this effect was due to local causes alone, and those volcanic. The manner of our locomotion left no doubt in my mind. An enormous force, a force of hundreds of atmospheres, generated by the extreme pressure of confined vapors, was driving us irresistibly forward. But to what numberless dangers it exposed us!

Soon lurid lights began to penetrate the vertical gallery which widened as we went up. Right and left I could see deep channels, like huge tunnels, out of which escaped dense volumes of smoke; tongues of fire lapped the walls, which crackled and sputtered under the intense heat.

"See, see, my uncle!" I cried.

"Well, those are only sulfurous flames and vapors, which one must expect to see in an eruption. They are quite natural."

"But suppose they should wrap us round."

"But they won't wrap us round."

"But we shall be stifled."

"We shall not be stifled at all. The gallery is widening, and if it becomes necessary, we shall abandon the raft, and creep into a crevice."

"But the water—the rising water?"

"There is no more water, Axel; only a lava paste, which is bearing us up on its surface to the top of the crater."

The liquid column had indeed disappeared, to give place to dense and still boiling eruptive matter of all kinds. The temperature was becoming unbearable. A thermometer exposed to this atmosphere would have marked 150°. The perspiration streamed from my body. But for the rapidity of our ascent we should have been suffocated.

But the professor gave up his idea of abandoning the raft, and it was well he did. However roughly joined together, those planks afforded us a firmer support than we could have found anywhere else.

About eight in the morning a new incident occurred. The upward movement ceased. The raft lay motionless.

"What is this?" I asked, shaken by this sudden stoppage as if by a shock.

"It is a halt," replied my uncle.

"Is the eruption checked?" I asked.

"I hope not."

I rose, and tried to look around me. Perhaps the raft itself, stopped in its course by a projection, was staying the volcanic torrent. If this were the case, we should have to release it as soon as possible.

But it was not so. The blast of ashes, scorix, and rubbish had ceased to rise.

"Has the eruption stopped?" I cried.

"Ah!" said my uncle between his clenched teeth. "You are afraid. But don't alarm yourself—this lull cannot last long. It has lasted now five minutes, and in a short time we shall resume our journey to the mouth of the crater."

As he spoke, the professor continued to consult his chronometer, and he was again right in his prognostications. The raft was soon hurried and driven forward with a rapid but irregular movement, which lasted about ten minutes, and then stopped again.

"Very good," said my uncle; "in ten minutes more we shall be off again, for our present business lies with an intermittent volcano. It gives us time now and then to take breath."

This was perfectly true. When the ten minutes were over we started off again with renewed and increased speed. We were obliged to lay fast hold of the planks of the raft, not to be thrown off. Then again the paroxysm was over.

I have since reflected upon this singular phenomenon without being able to explain it. At any rate it was clear that we were not in the main shaft of the volcano, but in a lateral gallery where there were felt recurrent tunes of reaction.

How often this operation was repeated I cannot say. All I know is, that at each fresh impulse we were hurled forward with a greatly increased force, and we seemed as if we were mere projectiles. During the short halts we were stifled with the heat; while we were being projected forward the hot air almost stopped my breath. I thought for a moment how delightful it would be to find myself carried suddenly into the arctic regions, with a cold 30° below the freezing point. My overheated brain conjured up visions of white plains of cool snow, where I might roll and allay my feverish heat. Little by little my brain, weakened by so many constantly repeated shocks, seemed to be giving way altogether. But for the strong arm of Hans I should more than once have had my head broken against the granite roof of our burning dungeon.

I have therefore no exact recollection of what took place during the following hours. I have a confused impression left of continuous explosions, loud detonations, a general shaking of the rocks all around us, and of a spinning movement with which our raft was once whirled helplessly round. It rocked upon the lava torrent, amid a dense fall of ashes. Snorting flames darted their fiery tongues at us. There were wild, fierce puffs of stormy wind from below, resembling the blasts of vast iron furnaces blowing all at one time; and I caught a glimpse of the figure of Hans lighted up by the fire; and all the feeling I had left was just what I imagine must be the feeling of an unhappy criminal doomed to be blown away alive from the mouth of a cannon, just before the trigger is pulled, and the flying limbs and rags of flesh and skin fill the quivering air and spatter the bloodstained ground.

XLIV

SUNNY LANDS IN THE BLUE MEDITERRANEAN

When I opened my eyes again I felt myself grasped by the belt with the strong hand of our guide. With the other arm he supported my uncle. I was not seriously hurt, but I was shaken and bruised and battered all over. I found myself lying on the sloping side of a mountain only two yards from a gaping gulf, which would have swallowed me up had I leaned at all that way. Hans had saved me from death while I lay rolling on the edge of the crater.

"Where are we?" asked my uncle irascibly, as if he felt much injured by being landed upon the earth again.

The hunter shook his head in token of complete ignorance.

"Is it Iceland?" I asked.

"*Nej*," replied Hans.

"What! Not Iceland?" cried the professor.

"Hans must be mistaken," I said, raising myself up.

This was our final surprise after all the astonishing events of our wonderful journey. I expected to see a white cone covered with the eternal snow of ages rising from the midst of the barren deserts of the icy north, faintly lighted with the pale rays of the arctic sun, far away in the highest latitudes known; but contrary to all our expectations, my uncle, the Icelander, and myself were sitting halfway down a mountain baked under the burning rays of a southern sun, which was blistering us with the heat, and blinding us with the fierce light of his nearly vertical rays.

I could not believe my own eyes; but the heated air and the sensation of burning left me no room for doubt. We had come out of the crater half naked, and the radiant orb to which we had been strangers for two months was lavishing upon us out of his blazing splendors more of his light and heat than we were able to receive with comfort.

When my eyes had become accustomed to the bright light to which they had been so long strangers, I began to use them to set my imagination right. At least I would have it to be Spitzbergen, and I was in no humor to give up this notion.

The professor was the first to speak, and said:

"Well, this is not much like Iceland."

"But is it Jan Mayen?" I asked.

"Nor that either," he answered. "This is no northern mountain; here are no granite peaks capped with snow. Look, Axel, look!"

Above our heads, at a height of five hundred feet or more, we saw the crater of a volcano, through which, at intervals of fifteen minutes or so, there issued with loud explosions lofty columns of fire, mingled with pumice stones, ashes, and flowing lava. I could feel the heaving of the mountain, which seemed to breathe like a huge whale, and puff out fire and wind from its vast blowholes. Beneath, down a pretty steep declivity, ran streams of lava for eight or nine hundred feet, giving the mountain a height of about 1,300 or 1,400 feet. But the base of the mountain was hidden in a perfect bower of rich verdure, among which I was able to distinguish the olive, the fig, and vines, covered with their luscious purple bunches.

I was forced to confess that there was nothing arctic here.

When the eye passed beyond these green surroundings it rested on a wide, blue expanse of sea or lake, which appeared to enclose this enchanting island, within a compass of only a few leagues. Eastward lay a pretty little white seaport town or village, with a few houses scattered around it, and in the harbor of which a few vessels of peculiar rig were gently swayed by the softly swelling waves. Beyond it, groups of islets rose from the smooth, blue waters, but in such numbers that they seemed to dot the sea like a shoal. To the west distant coasts lined the dim horizon, on some rose blue mountains of smooth, undulating forms; on a more distant coast arose a prodigious cone crowned on its summit with a snowy plume of white cloud. To the northward lay spread a vast sheet of water, sparkling and dancing under the hot, bright rays, the uniformity broken here and there by the topmast of a gallant ship appearing above the horizon, or a swelling sail moving slowly before the wind.

This unforeseen spectacle was most charming to eyes long used to underground darkness.

"Where are we? Where are we?" I asked faintly.

Hans closed his eyes with lazy indifference. What did it matter to him? My uncle looked round with dumb surprise.

"Well, whatever mountain this may be," he said at last, "it is very hot here. The explosions are going on still, and I don't think it would look well to have come out by an eruption, and then to get our heads broken by bits of falling rock. Let us get down. Then we shall know better what we are about. Besides, I am starving, and parching with thirst."

Decidedly the professor was not given to contemplation. For my part, I could for another hour or two have forgotten my hunger and my fatigue to enjoy the lovely scene before me; but I had to follow my companions.

The slope of the volcano was in many places of great steepness. We slid down screes of ashes, carefully avoiding the lava streams which glided sluggishly by us like fiery serpents. As we went I chattered and asked all sorts of questions as to our whereabouts, for I was too much excited not to talk a great deal.

"We are in Asia," I cried, "on the coasts of India, in the Malay Islands, or in Oceania. We have passed through half the globe, and come out nearly at the antipodes."

"But the compass?" said my uncle.

"Ay, the compass!" I said, greatly puzzled. "According to the compass we have gone northward."

"Has it lied?"

"Surely not. Could it lie?"

"Unless, indeed, this is the North Pole!"

"Oh, no, it is not the pole; but—"

Well, here was something that baffled us completely. I could not tell what to say.

But now we were coming into that delightful greenery, and I was suffering greatly from hunger and thirst. Happily, after two hours' walking, a charming country lay open before us, covered with olive trees, pomegranate trees, and delicious vines, all of which seemed to belong to anybody who pleased to claim them. Besides, in our state of destitution and famine we were not likely to be particular. Oh, the inexpressible pleasure of pressing those cool, sweet fruits to our lips, and eating grapes by mouthfuls off the rich, full bunches! Not far off, in the grass, under the delicious shade of the trees, I discovered a spring of fresh, cool water, in which we luxuriously bathed our faces, hands, and feet.

While we were thus enjoying the sweets of repose a child appeared out of a grove of olive trees.

"Ah!" I cried. "Here is an inhabitant of this happy land!"

It was but a poor boy, miserably ill-clad, a sufferer from poverty, and our aspect seemed to alarm him a great deal; in fact, only half clothed, with ragged hair and beards, we were a suspicious-looking party; and if the people of the country knew anything about thieves, we were very likely to frighten them.

Just as the poor little wretch was going to take to his heels, Hans caught hold of him, and brought him to us, kicking and struggling.

My uncle began to encourage him as well as he could, and said to him in good German:

"Was heiszt diesen Berg, mein Knablein? Sage mir geschwind!" ("What is this mountain called, my little friend?")

The child made no answer.

"Very well," said my uncle. "I infer that we are not in Germany."

He put the same question in English.

We got no forwarder. I was a good deal puzzled.

"Is the child dumb?" cried the professor, who, proud of his knowledge of many languages, now tried French: *"Comment appellet-on cette montagne, mon enfant?"*

Silence still.

"Now let us try Italian," said my uncle; and he said: *"Dove noi siamo?"*

"Yes, where are we?" I impatiently repeated.

But there was no answer still.

"Will you speak when you are told?" exclaimed my uncle, shaking the urchin by the ears. *"Come si noma questa isola?"*

"Stromboli," replied the little herdboy, slipping out of Hans' hands and scudding into the plain across the olive trees.

We were hardly thinking of that. Stromboli! What an effect this unexpected name produced upon my mind! We were in the midst of the Mediterranean Sea, on an island of the Aeolian archipelago, in the ancient Strongyle, where Aeolus kept the winds and the storms chained up, to be let loose at his will. And those distant blue mountains in the east were the mountains of Calabria. And that threatening volcano far away in the south was the fierce Etna.

"Stromboli, Stromboli!" I repeated.

My uncle kept time to my exclamations with hands and feet, as well as with words. We seemed to be chanting in chorus!

What a journey we had accomplished! How marvelous! Having entered by one volcano, we had issued out of another more than two thousand miles from Snæfell and from that barren, faraway Iceland! The strange chances of our expedition had carried us into the heart of the fairest region in the world. We had exchanged the bleak regions of perpetual snow and of impenetrable barriers of ice for those of brightness and "the rich hues of all glorious things." We had left over our heads the murky sky and cold fogs of the frigid zone to revel under the azure sky of Italy!

After our delicious repast of fruits and cold, clear water we set off again to reach the port of Stromboli. It would not have been wise to tell how we came there. The superstitious Italians would have set us down for fire-devils vomited out of hell; so we presented ourselves in the humble guise of shipwrecked mariners. It was not so glorious, but it was safer.

On my way I could hear my uncle murmuring: "But the compass! That compass! It pointed due north. How are we to explain that fact?"

"My opinion is," I replied disdainfully, "that it is best not to explain it. That is the easiest way to shelve the difficulty."

"Indeed, sir! The occupant of a professorial chair at the Johanneum unable to explain the reason of a cosmical phenomenon! Why, it would be simply disgraceful!"

And as he spoke, my uncle, half undressed, in rags, a perfect scarecrow, with his leathern belt around him, settling his spectacles upon his nose and looking learned and imposing, was himself again, the terrible German professor of mineralogy.

One hour after we had left the grove of olives, we arrived at the little port of San Vicenzo, where Hans claimed his thirteen week's wages, which was counted out to him with a hearty shaking of hands all round.

At that moment, if he did not share our natural emotion, at least his countenance expanded in a manner very unusual with him, and while with the ends of his fingers he lightly pressed our hands, I believe he smiled.

XLV

ALL'S WELL THAT ENDS WELL

Such is the conclusion of a history which I cannot expect everybody to believe, for some people will believe nothing against the testimony of their own experience. However, I am indifferent to their incredulity, and they may believe as much or as little as they please.

The Strombolìotes received us kindly as shipwrecked mariners. They gave us food and clothing. After waiting forty-eight hours, on the 31st of August a small craft took us to Messina, where a few days' rest completely removed the effect of our fatigues.

On Friday, September the 4th, we embarked on the steamer Volturno, employed by the French Messageries Imperiales, and in three days more we were at Marseilles, having no care on our minds except that abominable deceitful compass, which we had mislaid somewhere and could not now examine; but its inexplicable behavior exercised my mind fearfully. On the 9th of September, in the evening, we arrived at Hamburg.

I cannot describe to you the astonishment of Martha or the joy of Gräuben.

"Now you are a hero, Axel," said to me my blushing fiancée, my betrothed, "you will not leave me again!"

I looked tenderly upon her, and she smiled through her tears.

How can I describe the extraordinary sensation produced by the return of Professor Liedenbrock? Thanks to Martha's ineradicable tattling, the news that the professor had gone to discover a way to the center of the earth had spread over the whole civilized world. People refused to believe it, and when they saw him they would not believe him any the more. Still, the appearance of Hans, and sundry pieces of intelligence derived from Iceland, tended to shake the confidence of the unbelievers.

Then my uncle became a great man, and I was now the nephew of a great man—which is not a privilege to be despised.

Hamburg gave a grand fete in our honor. A public audience was given to the professor at the Johanneum, at which he told all about our expedition, with only one omission, the unexplained and inexplicable behavior of our compass. On the same day, with much state, he deposited in the archives of the city the now-famous document of Saknussemm, and expressed his regret that circumstances over which he had no control had prevented him from following to the very center of the earth the track of the learned Icelander. He was modest notwithstanding his glory, and he was all the more famous for his humility.

So much honor could not but excite envy. There were those who envied him his fame; and as his theories, resting upon known facts, were in opposition to the systems of science upon the question of the central fire, he sustained with his pen and by his voice remarkable discussions with the learned of every country.

For my part I cannot agree with his theory of gradual cooling: in spite of what I have seen and felt, I believe, and always shall believe, in the central heat. But I admit that certain circumstances not yet sufficiently understood may tend to modify in places the action of natural phenomena.

While these questions were being debated with great animation, my uncle met with a real sorrow. Our faithful Hans, in spite of our entreaties, had left

Hamburg; the man to whom we owed all our success and our lives too would not suffer us to reward him as we could have wished. He was seized with the mal de pays, a complaint for which we have not even a name in English.

"*Farval*," said he one day; and with that simple word he left us and sailed for Reykjavik, which he reached in safety.

We were strongly attached to our brave eiderdown hunter; though far away in the remotest north, he will never be forgotten by those whose lives he protected, and certainly I shall not fail to endeavor to see him once more before I die.

To conclude, I have to add that this "Journey into the Interior of the Earth" created a wonderful sensation in the world. It was translated into all civilized languages. The leading newspapers extracted the most interesting passages, which were commented upon, picked to pieces, discussed, attacked, and defended with equal enthusiasm and determination, both by believers and skeptics. Rare privilege! My uncle enjoyed during his lifetime the glory he had deservedly won; and he may even boast the distinguished honor of an offer from Mr. Barnum, to exhibit him on most advantageous terms in all the principal cities in the United States!

But there was one "dead fly" amid all this glory and honor; one fact, one incident, of the journey remained a mystery. Now to a man eminent for his learning, an unexplained phenomenon is an unbearable hardship. Well! It was yet reserved for my uncle to be completely happy.

One day, while arranging a collection of minerals in his cabinet, I noticed in a corner this unhappy compass, which we had long lost sight of; I opened it, and began to watch it.

It had been in that corner for six months, little mindful of the trouble it was giving.

Suddenly, to my intense astonishment, I noticed a strange fact, and I uttered a cry of surprise.

"What is the matter?" my uncle asked.

"That compass!"

"Well?"

"See, its poles are reversed!"

"Reversed?"

"Yes, they point the wrong way."

My uncle looked, he compared, and the house shook with his triumphant leap of exultation.

A light broke in upon his spirit and mine.

"See there," he cried, as soon as he was able to speak. "After our arrival at Cape Saknussemm the north pole of the needle of this confounded compass began to point south instead of north."

"Evidently!"

"Here, then, is the explanation of our mistake. But what phenomenon could have caused this reversal of the poles?"

"The reason is evident, uncle."

"Tell me, then, Axel."

"During the electric storm on the Liedenbrock Sea, that ball of fire, which magnetized all the iron on board, reversed the poles of our magnet!"

"Aha! Aha!" shouted the professor with a loud laugh. "So it was just an electric joke!"

From that day forth the professor was the most glorious of savants, and I was the happiest of men; for my pretty Virlandaise, resigning her place as ward, took her position in the old house on the Königstrasse in the double capacity of niece to my uncle and wife to a certain happy youth. What is the need of adding that the illustrious Otto Liedenbrock, corresponding member of all the scientific, geographical, and mineralogical societies of all the civilized world, was now her uncle and mine?

LOOKING BACKWARD: 2000–1887

Edward Bellamy

AUTHOR'S PREFACE
HISTORICAL SECTION SHAWMUT COLLEGE, BOSTON
DECEMBER 26, 2000

Living as we do in the closing year of the twentieth century, enjoying the blessings of a social order at once so simple and logical that it seems but the triumph of common sense, it is no doubt difficult for those whose studies have not been largely historical to realize that the present organization of society is, in its completeness, less than a century old. No historical fact is, however, better established than that till nearly the end of the nineteenth century it was the general belief that the ancient industrial system, with all its shocking social consequences, was destined to last, with possibly a little patching, to the end of time. How strange and well-nigh incredible does it seem that so prodigious a moral and material transformation as has taken place since then could have been accomplished in so brief an interval! The readiness with which men accustom themselves, as matters of course, to improvements in their condition, which, when anticipated, seemed to leave nothing more to be desired, could not be more strikingly illustrated. What reflection could be better calculated to moderate the enthusiasm of reformers who count for their reward on the lively gratitude of future ages!

The object of this volume is to assist persons who, while desiring to gain a more definite idea of the social contrasts between the nineteenth and twentieth centuries, are daunted by the formal aspect of the histories which treat the subject. Warned by a teacher's experience that learning is accounted a weariness to the flesh, the author has sought to alleviate the instructive quality of the book by casting it in the form of a romantic narrative, which he would be glad to fancy not wholly devoid of interest on its own account.

The reader, to whom modern social institutions and their underlying principles are matters of course, may at times find Dr. Leete's explanations of them rather trite—but it must be remembered that to Dr. Leete's guest they were not matters of course, and that this book is written for the express purpose of inducing the reader to forget for the nonce that they are so to him. One word more. The almost universal theme of the writers and orators who have celebrated this bimillennial epoch has been the future rather than the past, not the advance that has been made, but the progress that shall be made, ever onward and upward, till the race shall achieve its ineffable destiny. This is well, wholly well, but it seems to me that nowhere can we find more solid ground for daring anticipations of human development during the next one thousand years, than by "Looking Backward" upon the progress of the last one hundred.

That this volume may be so fortunate as to find readers whose interest in the subject shall incline them to overlook the deficiencies of the treatment is the hope in which the author steps aside and leaves Mr. Julian West to speak for himself.

I

I first saw the light in the city of Boston in the year 1857. "What!" you say, "eighteen fifty-seven? That is an odd slip. He means nineteen fifty-seven, of course." I beg pardon, but there is no mistake. It was about four in the afternoon of December the 26th, one day after Christmas, in the year 1857, not 1957, that I first breathed the east wind of Boston, which, I assure the reader, was at that remote period marked by the same penetrating quality characterizing it in the present year of grace, 2000.

These statements seem so absurd on their face, especially when I add that I am a young man apparently of about thirty years of age, that no person can be blamed for refusing to read another word of what promises to be a mere imposition upon his credulity. Nevertheless I earnestly assure the reader that no imposition is intended, and will undertake, if he shall follow me a few pages, to entirely convince him of this. If I may, then, provisionally assume, with the pledge of justifying the assumption, that I know better than the reader when I was born, I will go on with my narrative. As every schoolboy knows, in the latter part of the nineteenth century the civilization of today, or anything like it, did not exist, although the elements which were to develop it were already in ferment. Nothing had, however, occurred to modify the immemorial division of society into the four classes, or nations, as they may be more fitly called, since the differences between them were far greater than those between any nations nowadays, of the rich and the poor, the educated and the ignorant. I myself was rich and also educated, and possessed, therefore, all the elements of happiness enjoyed by the most fortunate in that age. Living in luxury, and occupied only with the pursuit of the pleasures and refinements of life, I derived the means of my support from the labor of others, rendering no sort of service in return.

My parents and grandparents had lived in the same way, and I expected that my descendants, if I had any, would enjoy a like easy existence.

But how could I live without service to the world? you ask. Why should the world have supported in utter idleness one who was able to render service? The answer is that my great-grandfather had accumulated a sum of money on which his descendants had ever since lived. The sum, you will naturally infer, must have been very large not to have been exhausted in supporting three generations in idleness. This, however, was not the fact. The sum had been originally by no means large. It was, in fact, much larger now that three generations had been supported upon it in idleness, than it was at first. This mystery of use without consumption, of warmth without combustion, seems like magic, but was merely an ingenious application of the art now happily lost but carried to great perfection by your ancestors, of shifting the burden of one's support on the shoulders of others. The man who had accomplished this, and it was the end all sought, was said to live on the income of his investments. To explain at this point how the ancient methods of industry made this possible would delay us too much. I shall only stop now to say that interest on investments was a species of tax in perpetuity upon the product of those engaged in industry which a person possessing or inheriting money was able to levy. It must not be supposed that an arrangement which seems so unnatural and preposterous according to modern notions was never criticized by your ancestors. It had been the effort of lawgivers and prophets from the earliest ages to abolish interest, or at least to limit it to the smallest possible rate. All these efforts had, however, failed, as they necessarily must so long as the ancient social organizations prevailed. At the time of which I write, the latter part of the nineteenth century, governments had generally given up trying to regulate the subject at all.

By way of attempting to give the reader some general impression of the way people lived together in those days, and especially of the relations of the rich and poor to one another, perhaps I cannot do better than to compare society as it then was to a prodigious coach which the masses of humanity were harnessed to and dragged toilsomely along a very hilly and sandy road. The driver was hunger, and permitted no lagging, though the pace was necessarily very slow. Despite the difficulty of drawing the coach at all along so hard a road, the top was covered with passengers who never got down, even at the steepest ascents. These seats on top were very breezy and comfortable. Well up out of the dust, their occupants could enjoy the scenery at their leisure, or critically discuss the merits of the straining team. Naturally such places were in great demand and the competition for them was keen, every one seeking as the first end in life to secure a seat on the coach for himself and to leave it to his child after him. By the rule of the coach a man could leave his seat to whom he wished, but on the other hand there were many accidents by which it might at any time be wholly lost. For all that they were so easy, the seats were very insecure, and at every sudden jolt of the coach persons were slipping out of them and falling to the ground, where they were instantly compelled to take hold of the rope and help to drag the coach on which they had before ridden so pleasantly. It was naturally regarded as a terrible misfortune to lose one's seat, and the apprehension that this might happen to them or their friends was a constant cloud upon the happiness of those who rode.

But did they think only of themselves? you ask. Was not their very luxury rendered intolerable to them by comparison with the lot of their brothers and sisters in the harness, and the knowledge that their own weight added to their toil? Had they no compassion for fellow beings from whom fortune only distinguished them? Oh, yes; commiseration was frequently expressed by those who rode for those who had to pull the coach, especially when the vehicle came to a bad place in the road, as it was constantly doing, or to a particularly steep hill. At such times, the desperate straining of the team, their agonized leaping and plunging under the pitiless lashing of hunger, the many who fainted at the rope and were trampled in the mire, made a very distressing spectacle, which often called forth highly creditable displays of feeling on the top of the coach. At such times the passengers would call down encouragingly to the toilers of the rope, exhorting them to patience, and holding out hopes of possible compensation in another world for the hardness of their lot, while others contributed to buy salves and liniments for the crippled and injured. It was agreed that it was a great pity that the coach should be so hard to pull, and there was a sense of general relief when the specially bad piece of road was gotten over. This relief was not, indeed, wholly on account of the team, for there was always some danger at these bad places of a general overturn in which all would lose their seats.

It must in truth be admitted that the main effect of the spectacle of the misery of the toilers at the rope was to enhance the passengers' sense of the value of their seats upon the coach, and to cause them to hold on to them more desperately than before. If the passengers could only have felt assured that neither they nor their friends would ever fall from the top, it is probable that, beyond contributing to the funds for liniments and bandages, they would have troubled themselves extremely little about those who dragged the coach.

I am well aware that this will appear to the men and women of the twentieth century an incredible inhumanity, but there are two facts, both very curious, which partly explain it. In the first place, it was firmly and sincerely believed that there was no other way in which Society could get along, except the many pulled at the rope and the few rode, and not only this, but that no very radical improvement even was possible, either in the harness, the coach, the roadway, or the distribution of the toil. It had always been as it was, and it always would be so. It was a pity, but it could not be helped, and philosophy forbade wasting compassion on what was beyond remedy.

The other fact is yet more curious, consisting in a singular hallucination which those on the top of the coach generally shared, that they were not exactly like their brothers and sisters who pulled at the rope, but of finer clay, in some way belonging to a higher order of beings who might justly expect to be drawn. This seems unaccountable, but, as I once rode on this very coach and shared that very hallucination, I ought to be believed. The strangest thing about the hallucination was that those who had but just climbed up from the ground, before they had outgrown the marks of the rope upon their hands, began to fall under its influence. As for those whose parents and grandparents before them had been so fortunate as to keep their seats on the top, the conviction they cherished of the essential difference between their sort of humanity and the common article was absolute. The effect of such a delusion in moderating fellow feeling for the sufferings of the mass of men into a distant and philosophical compassion is obvious. To it I refer as the only extenuation I can offer for the indifference which, at the period I write of, marked my own attitude toward the misery of my brothers.

In 1887 I came to my thirtieth year. Although still unmarried, I was engaged to wed Edith Bartlett. She, like myself, rode on the top of the coach. That is to say, not to encumber ourselves further with an illustration which has, I hope, served its purpose of giving the reader some general impression of how we lived then, her family was wealthy. In that age, when money alone commanded all that was agreeable and refined in life, it was enough for a woman to be rich to have suitors; but Edith Bartlett was beautiful and graceful also.

My lady readers, I am aware, will protest at this. "Handsome she might have been," I hear them saying, "but graceful never, in the costumes which were the fashion at that period, when the head covering was a dizzy structure a foot tall, and the almost incredible extension of the skirt behind by means of artificial contrivances more thoroughly dehumanized the form than any former device of dressmakers. Fancy any one graceful in such a costume!" The point is certainly well taken, and I can only reply that while the ladies of the twentieth century are lovely demonstrations of the effect of appropriate drapery in accenting feminine graces, my recollection of their great-grandmothers enables me to maintain that no deformity of costume can wholly disguise them.

Our marriage only waited on the completion of the house which I was building for our occupancy in one of the most desirable parts of the city, that is to say, a part chiefly inhabited by the rich. For it must be understood that the comparative desirability of different parts of Boston for residence depended then, not on natural features, but on the character of the neighboring population. Each class or nation lived by itself, in quarters of its own. A rich man living among the poor, an educated man among the uneducated, was like one living in isolation among a jealous and alien race. When the house had been begun, its completion by the winter of 1886 had been expected. The spring of the following year found it, however, yet incomplete, and my marriage still a thing of the future. The cause of a delay calculated to be particularly exasperating to an ardent lover was a series of strikes, that is to say, concerted refusals to work on the part of the brick-layers, masons, carpenters, painters, plumbers, and other trades concerned in house building. What the specific causes of these strikes were I do not remember. Strikes had become so common at that period that people had ceased to inquire into their particular grounds. In one department of industry or another, they had been nearly incessant ever since the great business crisis of 1873. In fact it had come to be the exceptional thing to see any class of laborers pursue their avocation steadily for more than a few months at a time.

The reader who observes the dates alluded to will of course recognize in these disturbances of industry the first and incoherent phase of the great movement which ended in the establishment of the modern industrial system with all its social consequences. This is all so plain in the retrospect that a child can understand it, but not being prophets, we of that day had no clear idea what was happening to us. What we did see was that industrially the country was in a very queer way. The relation between the workingman and the employer, between labor and capital, appeared in some unaccountable manner to have become dislocated. The working classes had quite suddenly and very generally become infected with a profound discontent with their condition, and an idea that it could be greatly bettered if they only knew how to go about it. On every side, with one accord, they preferred demands for higher pay, shorter hours, better dwellings, better educational advantages, and a share in the refinements and luxuries of life, demands which it was impossible to see the way to granting unless the world were to become a great deal richer than it then was. Though they knew something of what they wanted, they knew nothing of how to accomplish it, and the eager enthusiasm with which they thronged about any one who seemed likely to give them any light on the subject lent sudden reputation to many would-be leaders, some of whom had little enough light to give. However chimerical the aspirations of the laboring classes might be deemed, the devotion with which they supported one another in the strikes, which were their chief weapon, and the sacrifices which they underwent to carry them out left no doubt of their dead earnestness.

As to the final outcome of the labor troubles, which was the phrase by which the movement I have described was most commonly referred to, the opinions of the people of my class differed according to individual temperament. The sanguine argued very forcibly that it was in the very nature of things impossible that the new hopes of the workingmen could be satisfied, simply because the world had not the wherewithal to satisfy them. It was only because the masses worked very hard and lived on short commons that the race did not starve outright, and no considerable improvement in their condition was possible while the world, as a whole, remained so poor. It was not the capitalists whom the laboring men were contending with, these maintained, but the iron-bound environment of humanity, and it was merely a question of the thickness of their skulls when they would discover the fact and make up their minds to endure what they could not cure.

The less sanguine admitted all this. Of course the workingmen's aspirations were impossible of fulfillment for natural reasons, but there were grounds to fear that they would not discover this fact until they had made a sad mess of society. They had the votes and the power to do so if they pleased, and their leaders meant they should. Some of these desponding observers went so far as to predict an impending social cataclysm. Humanity, they argued, having climbed to the top round of the ladder of civilization, was about to take a header into chaos, after which it would doubtless pick itself up, turn round, and begin to climb again. Repeated experiences of this sort in historic and prehistoric times possibly accounted for the puzzling bumps on the human cranium. Human history, like all great movements, was cyclical, and returned to the point of beginning. The idea of indefinite progress in a right line was a chimera of the imagination, with no analogue in nature. The parabola of a comet was perhaps a yet better illustration of the career of humanity. Tending upward and sunward from the aphelion of barbarism, the race attained the perihelion of civilization only to plunge downward once more to its nether goal in the regions of chaos.

This, of course, was an extreme opinion, but I remember serious men among my acquaintances who, in discussing the signs of the times, adopted a very similar tone. It was no doubt the common opinion of thoughtful men that society was approaching a critical period which might result in great changes. The labor troubles, their causes, course, and cure, took lead of all other topics in the public prints, and in serious conversation.

The nervous tension of the public mind could not have been more strikingly illustrated than it was by the alarm resulting from the talk of a small band of men who called themselves anarchists, and proposed to terrify the American people into adopting their ideas by threats of violence, as if a mighty nation which had but just put down a rebellion of half its own numbers, in order to maintain its political system, were likely to adopt a new social system out of fear.

As one of the wealthy, with a large stake in the existing order of things, I naturally shared the apprehensions of my class. The particular grievance I had against the working classes at the time of which I write, on account of the effect of their strikes in postponing my wedded bliss, no doubt lent a special animosity to my feeling toward them.

II

The thirtieth day of May, 1887, fell on a Monday. It was one of the annual holidays of the nation in the latter third of the nineteenth century, being set apart under the name of Decoration Day, for doing honor to the memory of the soldiers of the North who took part in the war for the preservation of the union of the States. The survivors of the war, escorted by military and civic processions and bands of music, were wont on this occasion to visit the cemeteries and lay wreaths of flowers upon the graves of their dead comrades, the ceremony being a very solemn and touching one. The eldest brother of Edith Bartlett had fallen in the war, and on Decoration Day the family was in the habit of making a visit to Mount Auburn, where he lay.

I had asked permission to make one of the party, and, on our return to the city at nightfall, remained to dine with the family of my betrothed. In the drawing-room, after dinner, I picked up an evening paper and read of a fresh strike in the building trades, which would probably still further delay the completion of my unlucky house. I remember distinctly how exasperated I was at this, and the objurgations, as forcible as the presence of the ladies permitted, which I lavished upon workmen in general, and these strikers in particular. I had abundant sympathy from those about me, and the remarks made in the desultory conversation which followed, upon the unprincipled conduct of the labor agitators, were calculated to make those gentlemen's ears tingle. It was agreed that affairs were going from bad to worse very fast, and that there was no telling what we should come to soon. "The worst of it," I remember Mrs. Bartlett's saying, "is that the working classes all over the world seem to be going crazy at once. In Europe it is far worse even than here. I'm sure I should not dare to live there at all. I asked Mr. Bartlett the other day where we should emigrate to if all the terrible things took place which those socialists threaten. He said he did not know any place now where society could be called stable except Greenland, Patagonia, and the Chinese Empire." "Those Chinamen knew what they were about," somebody added, "when they refused to let in our western civilization. They knew what it would lead to better than we did. They saw it was nothing but dynamite in disguise."

After this, I remember drawing Edith apart and trying to persuade her that it would be better to be married at once without waiting for the completion of the house, spending the time in travel till our home was ready for us. She was remarkably handsome that evening, the mourning costume that she wore in recognition of the day setting off to great advantage the purity of her complexion. I can see her even now with my mind's eye just as she looked that night. When I took my leave she followed me into the hall and I kissed her good-by as usual. There was no circumstance out of the common to distinguish this parting from previous occasions when we had bade each other good-by for a night or a day. There was absolutely no premonition in my mind, or I am sure in hers, that this was more than an ordinary separation.

Ah, well!

The hour at which I had left my betrothed was a rather early one for a lover, but the fact was no reflection on my devotion. I was a confirmed sufferer from insomnia, and although otherwise perfectly well had been completely fagged out that day, from having slept scarcely at all the two previous nights. Edith knew this and had insisted on sending me home by nine o'clock, with strict orders to go to bed at once.

The house in which I lived had been occupied by three generations of the family of which I was the only living representative in the direct line. It was a large, ancient wooden mansion, very elegant in an old-fashioned way within, but situated in a quarter that had long since become undesirable for residence, from its invasion by tenement houses and manufactories. It was not a house to which I could think of bringing a bride, much less so dainty a one as Edith Bartlett. I had advertised it for sale, and meanwhile merely used it for sleeping purposes, dining at my club. One servant, a faithful colored man by the name of Sawyer, lived with me and attended to my few wants. One feature of the house I expected to miss greatly when I should leave it, and this was the sleeping chamber which I had built under the foundations. I could not have slept in the city at all, with its never ceasing nightly noises, if I had been obliged to use an upstairs chamber. But to this subterranean room no murmur from the upper world ever penetrated. When I had entered it and closed the door, I was surrounded by the silence of the tomb. In order to prevent the dampness of the subsoil from penetrating the chamber, the walls had been laid in hydraulic cement and were very thick, and the floor was likewise protected. In order that the room might serve also as a vault equally proof against violence and flames, for the storage of valuables, I had roofed it with stone slabs hermetically sealed, and the outer door was of iron with a thick coating of asbestos. A small pipe, communicating with a wind-mill on the top of the house, insured the renewal of air.

It might seem that the tenant of such a chamber ought to be able to command slumber, but it was rare that I slept well, even there, two nights in succession. So accustomed was I to wakefulness that I minded little the loss of one night's rest. A second night, however, spent in my reading chair instead of my bed, tired me out, and I never allowed myself to go longer than that without slumber, from fear of nervous disorder. From this statement it will be inferred that I had at my command some artificial means for inducing sleep in the last resort, and so in fact I had. If after two sleepless nights I found myself on the approach of the third without sensations of drowsiness, I called in Dr. Pillsbury.

He was a doctor by courtesy only, what was called in those days an "irregular" or "quack" doctor. He called himself a "Professor of Animal Magnetism." I had come across him in the course of some amateur investigations into the phenomena of animal magnetism. I don't think he knew anything about medicine, but he was certainly a remarkable mesmerist. It was for the purpose of being put to sleep by his manipulations that I used to send for him when I found a third night of sleeplessness impending. Let my nervous excitement or mental preoccupation be however great, Dr. Pillsbury never failed, after a short time, to leave me in a deep slumber, which continued till I was aroused by a reversal of the mesmerizing process. The process for awaking the sleeper was much simpler than that for putting him to sleep, and for convenience I had made Dr. Pillsbury teach Sawyer how to do it.

My faithful servant alone knew for what purpose Dr. Pillsbury visited me, or that he did so at all. Of course, when Edith became my wife I should have to tell her my secrets. I had not hitherto told her this, because there was unquestionably a slight risk in the mesmeric sleep, and I knew she would set her face against my practice. The risk, of course, was that it might become too profound and pass into a trance beyond the mesmerizer's power to break, ending in death. Repeated experiments had fully convinced me that the risk was next to nothing if reasonable precautions were exercised, and of this I hoped, though doubtingly, to convince Edith. I went directly home after leaving her, and at once sent Sawyer to fetch Dr. Pillsbury. Meanwhile I sought my subterranean sleeping chamber, and exchanging my costume for a comfortable dressing-gown, sat down to read the letters by the evening mail which Sawyer had laid on my reading table.

One of them was from the builder of my new house, and confirmed what I had inferred from the newspaper item. The new strikes, he said, had postponed indefinitely the completion of the contract, as neither masters nor workmen would concede the point at issue without a long struggle. Caligula wished that the Roman people had but one neck that he might cut it off, and as I read this letter I am afraid that for a moment I was capable of wishing the same thing concerning the laboring classes of America. The return of Sawyer with the doctor interrupted my gloomy meditations.

It appeared that he had with difficulty been able to secure his services, as he was preparing to leave the city that very night. The doctor explained that since he had seen me last he had learned of a fine professional opening in a distant city, and decided to take prompt advantage of it. On my asking, in some panic, what I was to do for some one to put me to sleep, he gave me the names of several mesmerizers in Boston who, he averred, had quite as great powers as he.

Somewhat relieved on this point, I instructed Sawyer to rouse me at nine o'clock next morning, and, lying down on the bed in my dressing-gown, assumed a comfortable attitude, and surrendered myself to the manipulations of the mesmerizer. Owing, perhaps, to my unusually nervous state, I was slower than common in losing consciousness, but at length a delicious drowsiness stole over me.

III

"He is going to open his eyes. He had better see but one of us at first."

"Promise me, then, that you will not tell him."

The first voice was a man's, the second a woman's, and both spoke in whispers.

"I will see how he seems," replied the man.

"No, no, promise me," persisted the other.

"Let her have her way," whispered a third voice, also a woman.

"Well, well, I promise, then," answered the man. "Quick, go! He is coming out of it."

There was a rustle of garments and I opened my eyes. A fine looking man of perhaps sixty was bending over me, an expression of much benevolence mingled with great curiosity upon his features. He was an utter stranger. I raised myself on an elbow and looked around. The room was empty. I certainly had never been in it before, or one furnished like it. I looked back at my companion. He smiled.

"How do you feel?" he inquired.

"Where am I?" I demanded.

"You are in my house," was the reply.

"How came I here?"

"We will talk about that when you are stronger. Meanwhile, I beg you will feel no anxiety. You are among friends and in good hands. How do you feel?"

"A bit queerly," I replied, "but I am well, I suppose. Will you tell me how I came to be indebted to your hospitality? What has happened to me? How came I here? It was in my own house that I went to sleep."

"There will be time enough for explanations later," my unknown host replied, with a reassuring smile. "It will be better to avoid agitating talk until you are a little more yourself. Will you oblige me by taking a couple of swallows of this mixture? It will do you good. I am a physician."

I repelled the glass with my hand and sat up on the couch, although with an effort, for my head was strangely light.

"I insist upon knowing at once where I am and what you have been doing with me," I said.

"My dear sir," responded my companion, "let me beg that you will not agitate yourself. I would rather you did not insist upon explanations so soon, but if you do, I will try to satisfy you, provided you will first take this draught, which will strengthen you somewhat."

I thereupon drank what he offered me. Then he said, "It is not so simple a matter as you evidently suppose to tell you how you came here. You can tell me quite as much on that point as I can tell you. You have just been roused from a deep sleep, or, more properly, trance. So much I can tell you. You say you were in your own house when you fell into that sleep. May I ask you when that was?"

"When?" I replied, "when? Why, last evening, of course, at about ten o'clock. I left my man Sawyer orders to call me at nine o'clock. What has become of Sawyer?"

"I can't precisely tell you that," replied my companion, regarding me with a curious expression, "but I am sure that he is excusable for not being here. And now can you tell me a little more explicitly when it was that you fell into that sleep, the date, I mean?"

"Why, last night, of course; I said so, didn't I? That is, unless I have overslept an entire day. Great heavens! that cannot be possible; and yet I have an odd sensation of having slept a long time. It was Decoration Day that I went to sleep."

"Decoration Day?"

"Yes, Monday, the 30th."

"Pardon me, the 30th of what?"

"Why, of this month, of course, unless I have slept into June, but that can't be."

"This month is September."

"September! You don't mean that I've slept since May! God in heaven! Why, it is incredible."

"We shall see," replied my companion; "you say that it was May 30th when you went to sleep?"

"Yes."

"May I ask of what year?"

I stared blankly at him, incapable of speech, for some moments.

"Of what year?" I feebly echoed at last.

"Yes, of what year, if you please? After you have told me that I shall be able to tell you how long you have slept."

"It was the year 1887," I said.

My companion insisted that I should take another draught from the glass, and felt my pulse.

"My dear sir," he said, "your manner indicates that you are a man of culture, which I am aware was by no means the matter of course in your day it now is. No doubt, then, you have yourself made the observation that nothing in this world can be truly said to be more wonderful than anything else. The causes of all phenomena are equally adequate, and the results equally matters of course. That you should be startled by what I shall tell you is to be expected; but I am confident that you will not permit it to affect your equanimity unduly. Your appearance is that of a young man of barely thirty, and your bodily condition seems not greatly different from that of one just roused from a somewhat too long and profound sleep, and yet this is the tenth day of September in the year 2000, and you have slept exactly one hundred and thirteen years, three months, and eleven days."

Feeling partially dazed, I drank a cup of some sort of broth at my companion's suggestion, and, immediately afterward becoming very drowsy, went off into a deep sleep.

When I awoke it was broad daylight in the room, which had been lighted artificially when I was awake before. My mysterious host was sitting near. He was not looking at me when I opened my eyes, and I had a good opportunity to study him and meditate upon my extraordinary situation, before he observed that I was awake. My giddiness was all gone, and my mind perfectly clear. The story that I had been asleep one hundred and thirteen years, which, in my former weak and bewildered condition, I had accepted without question, recurred to me now only to be rejected as a preposterous attempt at an imposture, the motive of which it was impossible remotely to surmise.

Something extraordinary had certainly happened to account for my waking up in this strange house with this unknown companion, but my fancy was utterly impotent to suggest more than the wildest guess as to what that something might have been. Could it be that I was the victim of some sort of conspiracy? It looked so, certainly; and yet, if human lineaments ever gave true evidence, it was certain that this man by my side, with a face so refined and ingenuous, was no party to any scheme of crime or outrage. Then it occurred to me to question if I might not be the butt of some elaborate practical joke on the part of friends who had somehow learned the secret of my underground chamber and taken this means of impressing me with the peril of mesmeric experiments. There were great difficulties in the way of this theory; Sawyer would never have betrayed me, nor had I any friends at all likely to undertake such an enterprise; nevertheless the supposition that I was the victim of a practical joke seemed on the whole the only one tenable. Half expecting to catch a glimpse of some familiar face grinning from behind a chair or curtain, I looked carefully about the room. When my eyes next rested on my companion, he was looking at me.

"You have had a fine nap of twelve hours," he said briskly, "and I can see that it has done you good. You look much better. Your color is good and your eyes are bright. How do you feel?"

"I never felt better," I said, sitting up.

"You remember your first waking, no doubt," he pursued, "and your surprise when I told you how long you had been asleep?"

"You said, I believe, that I had slept one hundred and thirteen years."

"Exactly."

"You will admit," I said, with an ironical smile, "that the story was rather an improbable one."

"Extraordinary, I admit," he responded, "but given the proper conditions, not improbable nor inconsistent with what we know of the trance state. When complete, as in your case, the vital functions are absolutely suspended, and there is no waste of the tissues. No limit can be set to the possible duration of a trance when the external conditions protect the body from physical injury. This trance of yours is indeed the longest of which there is any positive record, but there is no known reason wherefore, had you not been discovered and had the chamber in which we found you continued intact, you might not have remained in a state of suspended animation till, at the end of indefinite ages, the gradual refrigeration of the earth had destroyed the bodily tissues and set the spirit free."

I had to admit that, if I were indeed the victim of a practical joke, its authors had chosen an admirable agent for carrying out their imposition. The impressive and even eloquent manner of this man would have lent dignity to an argument that the moon was made of cheese. The smile with which I had regarded him as he advanced his trance hypothesis did not appear to confuse him in the slightest degree.

"Perhaps," I said, "you will go on and favor me with some particulars as to the circumstances under which you discovered this chamber of which you speak, and its contents. I enjoy good fiction."

"In this case," was the grave reply, "no fiction could be so strange as the truth. You must know that these many years I have been cherishing the idea of building a laboratory in the large garden beside this house, for the purpose of chemical experiments for which I have a taste. Last Thursday the excavation for the cellar was at last begun. It was completed by that night, and Friday the masons were to have come. Thursday night we had a tremendous deluge of rain, and Friday morning I found my cellar a frog-pond and the walls quite washed down. My daughter, who had come out to view the disaster with me, called my attention to a corner of masonry laid bare by the crumbling away of one of the walls. I cleared a little earth from it, and, finding that it seemed part of a large mass, determined to investigate it. The workmen I sent for unearthed an oblong vault some eight feet below the surface, and set in the corner of what had evidently been the foundation walls of an ancient house. A layer of ashes and charcoal on the top of the vault showed that the house above had perished by fire. The vault itself was perfectly intact, the cement being as good as when first applied. It had a door, but this we could not force, and found entrance by removing one of the flagstones which formed the roof. The air which came up was stagnant but pure, dry and not cold. Descending with a lantern, I found myself in an apartment fitted up as a bedroom in the style of the nineteenth century. On the bed lay a young man. That he was dead and must have been dead a century was of course to be taken for granted; but the extraordinary state of preservation of the body struck me and the medical colleagues whom I had summoned with amazement. That the art of such embalming as this had ever been known we should not have believed, yet here seemed conclusive testimony that our immediate ancestors had possessed it. My medical colleagues, whose curiosity was highly excited, were at once for undertaking experiments to test the nature of the process employed, but I withheld them. My motive in so doing, at least the only motive I now need speak of, was the recollection of something I once had read about the extent to which your contemporaries had cultivated the subject of animal magnetism. It had occurred to me as just conceivable that you might be in a trance, and that the secret of your bodily integrity after so long a time was not the craft of an embalmer, but life. So extremely fanciful did this idea seem, even to me, that I did not risk the ridicule of my fellow physicians by mentioning it, but gave some other reason for postponing their experiments. No sooner, however, had they left me, than I set on foot a systematic attempt at resuscitation, of which you know the result."

Had its theme been yet more incredible, the circumstantiality of this narrative, as well as the impressive manner and personality of the narrator, might have staggered a listener, and I had begun to feel very strangely, when, as he closed, I chanced to catch a glimpse of my reflection in a mirror hanging on the wall of the room. I rose and went up to it. The face I saw was the face to a hair and a line and not a day older than the one I had looked at as I tied my cravat before going to Edith that Decoration Day, which, as this man would have me believe, was celebrated one hundred and thirteen years before. At this, the colossal character of the fraud which was being attempted on me, came over me afresh. Indignation mastered my mind as I realized the outrageous liberty that had been taken.

"You are probably surprised," said my companion, "to see that, although you are a century older than when you lay down to sleep in that underground chamber, your appearance is unchanged. That should not amaze you. It is by virtue of the total arrest of the vital functions that you have survived this great period of time. If your body could have undergone any change during your trance, it would long ago have suffered dissolution."

"Sir," I replied, turning to him, "what your motive can be in reciting to me with a serious face this remarkable farrago, I am utterly unable to guess; but you are surely yourself too intelligent to suppose that anybody but an imbecile could be deceived by it. Spare me any more of this elaborate nonsense and once for all tell me whether you refuse to give me an intelligible account of where I am and how I came here. If so, I shall proceed to ascertain my whereabouts for myself, whoever may hinder."

"You do not, then, believe that this is the year 2000?"

"Do you really think it necessary to ask me that?" I returned.

"Very well," replied my extraordinary host. "Since I cannot convince you, you shall convince yourself. Are you strong enough to follow me upstairs?"

"I am as strong as I ever was," I replied angrily, "as I may have to prove if this jest is carried much farther."

"I beg, sir," was my companion's response, "that you will not allow yourself to be too fully persuaded that you are the victim of a trick, lest the reaction, when you are convinced of the truth of my statements, should be too great."

The tone of concern, mingled with commiseration, with which he said this, and the entire absence of any sign of resentment at my hot words, strangely daunted me, and I followed him from the room with an extraordinary mixture of emotions. He led the way up two flights of stairs and then up a shorter one, which landed us upon a belvedere on the house-top. "Be pleased to look around you," he said, as we reached the platform, "and tell me if this is the Boston of the nineteenth century."

At my feet lay a great city. Miles of broad streets, shaded by trees and lined with fine buildings, for the most part not in continuous blocks but set in larger or smaller inclosures, stretched in every direction. Every quarter contained large open squares filled with trees, among which statues glistened and fountains flashed in the late afternoon sun. Public buildings of a colossal size and an architectural grandeur unparalleled in my day raised their stately piles on every side. Surely I had never seen this city nor one comparable to it before. Raising my eyes at last towards the horizon, I looked westward. That blue ribbon winding away to the sunset, was it not the sinuous Charles? I looked east; Boston harbor stretched before me within its headlands, not one of its green islets missing.

I knew then that I had been told the truth concerning the prodigious thing which had befallen me.

IV

I did not faint, but the effort to realize my position made me very giddy, and I remember that my companion had to give me a strong arm as he conducted me from the roof to a roomy apartment on the upper floor of the house, where he insisted on my drinking a glass or two of good wine and partaking of a light repast.

"I think you are going to be all right now," he said cheerily. "I should not have taken so abrupt a means to convince you of your position if your course, while perfectly excusable under the circumstances, had not rather obliged me to do so. I confess," he added laughing, "I was a little apprehensive at one time that I should undergo what I believe you used to call a knockdown in the nineteenth century, if I did not act rather promptly. I remembered that the Bostonians of your day were famous pugilists, and thought best to lose no time. I take it you are now ready to acquit me of the charge of hoaxing you."

"If you had told me," I replied, profoundly awed, "that a thousand years instead of a hundred had elapsed since I last looked on this city, I should now believe you."

"Only a century has passed," he answered, "but many a millennium in the world's history has seen changes less extraordinary."

"And now," he added, extending his hand with an air of irresistible cordiality, "let me give you a hearty welcome to the Boston of the twentieth century and to this house. My name is Leete, Dr. Leete they call me."

"My name," I said as I shook his hand, "is Julian West."

"I am most happy in making your acquaintance, Mr. West," he responded. "Seeing that this house is built on the site of your own, I hope you will find it easy to make yourself at home in it."

After my refreshment Dr. Leete offered me a bath and a change of clothing, of which I gladly availed myself.

It did not appear that any very startling revolution in men's attire had been among the great changes my host had spoken of, for, barring a few details, my new habiliments did not puzzle me at all.

Physically, I was now myself again. But mentally, how was it with me, the reader will doubtless wonder. What were my intellectual sensations, he may wish to know, on finding myself so suddenly dropped as it were into a new world. In reply let me ask him to suppose himself suddenly, in the twinkling of an eye, transported from earth, say, to Paradise or Hades. What does he fancy would be his own experience? Would his thoughts return at once to the earth he had just left, or would he, after the first shock, well-nigh forget his former life for a while, albeit to be remembered later, in the interest excited by his new surroundings? All I can say is, that if his experience were at all like mine in the transition I am describing, the latter hypothesis would prove the correct one. The impressions of amazement and curiosity which my new surroundings produced occupied my mind, after the first shock, to the exclusion of all other thoughts. For the time the memory of my former life was, as it were, in abeyance.

No sooner did I find myself physically rehabilitated through the kind offices of my host, than I became eager to return to the house-top; and presently we were comfortably established there in easy chairs, with the city beneath and around us. After Dr. Leete had responded to numerous questions on my part, as to the ancient landmarks I missed and the new ones which had replaced them, he asked me what point of the contrast between the new and the old city struck me most forcibly.

"To speak of small things before great," I responded, "I really think that the complete absence of chimneys and their smoke is the detail that first impressed me."

"Ah!" ejaculated my companion with an air of much interest, "I had forgotten the chimneys, it is so long since they went out of use. It is nearly a century since the crude method of combustion on which you depended for heat became obsolete."

"In general," I said, "what impresses me most about the city is the material prosperity on the part of the people which its magnificence implies."

"I would give a great deal for just one glimpse of the Boston of your day," replied Dr. Leete. "No doubt, as you imply, the cities of that period were rather shabby affairs. If you had the taste to make them splendid, which I would not be so rude as to question, the general poverty resulting from your extraordinary industrial system would not have given you the means. Moreover, the excessive individualism which then prevailed was inconsistent with much public spirit. What little wealth you had seems almost wholly to have been lavished in private luxury. Nowadays, on the contrary, there is no destination of the surplus wealth so popular as the adornment of the city, which all enjoy in equal degree."

The sun had been setting as we returned to the house-top, and as we talked night descended upon the city.

"It is growing dark," said Dr. Leete. "Let us descend into the house; I want to introduce my wife and daughter to you."

His words recalled to me the feminine voices which I had heard whispering about me as I was coming back to conscious life; and, most curious to learn what the ladies of the year 2000 were like, I assented with alacrity to the proposition. The apartment in which we found the wife and daughter of my host, as well as the entire interior of the house, was filled with a mellow light, which I knew must be artificial, although I could not discover the source from which it was diffused. Mrs. Leete was an exceptionally fine-looking and well-preserved woman of about her husband's age, while the daughter, who was in the first blush of womanhood, was the most beautiful girl I had ever seen. Her face was as bewitching as deep blue eyes, delicately tinted complexion, and perfect features could make it, but even had her countenance lacked special charms, the faultless luxuriance of her figure would have given her place as a beauty among the women of the nineteenth century. Feminine softness and delicacy were in this lovely creature deliciously combined with an appearance of health and abounding physical vitality too often lacking in the maidens with whom alone I could compare her. It was a coincidence trifling in comparison with the general strangeness of the situation, but still striking, that her name should be Edith.

The evening that followed was certainly unique in the history of social intercourse, but to suppose that our conversation was peculiarly strained or difficult would be a great mistake. I believe indeed that it is under what may be called unnatural, in the sense of extraordinary, circumstances that people behave most naturally, for the reason, no doubt, that such circumstances banish artificiality. I know at any rate that my intercourse that evening with these representatives of another age and world was marked by an ingenuous sincerity and frankness such as but rarely crown long acquaintance. No doubt the exquisite tact of my entertainers had much to do with this. Of course there was nothing we could talk of but the strange experience by virtue of which I was there, but they talked of it with an interest so naive and direct in its expression as to relieve the subject to a great degree of the element of the weird and the uncanny which might so easily have been overpowering. One would have supposed that they were quite in the habit of entertaining waifs from another century, so perfect was their tact.

For my own part, never do I remember the operations of my mind to have been more alert and acute than that evening, or my intellectual sensibilities more keen. Of course I do not mean that the consciousness of my amazing situation was for a moment out of mind, but its chief effect thus far was to produce a feverish elation, a sort of mental intoxication.*

Edith Leete took little part in the conversation, but when several times the

* In accounting for this state of mind it must be remembered that, except for the topic of our conversations, there was in my surroundings next to nothing to suggest what had befallen me. Within a block of my home in the old Boston I could have found social circles vastly more foreign to me. The speech of the Bostonians of the twentieth century differs even less from that of their cultured ancestors of the nineteenth than did that of the latter from the language of Washington and Franklin, while the differences between the style of dress and furniture of the two epochs are not more marked than I have known fashion to make in the time of one generation.

magnetism of her beauty drew my glance to her face, I found her eyes fixed on me with an absorbed intensity, almost like fascination. It was evident that I had excited her interest to an extraordinary degree, as was not astonishing, supposing her to be a girl of imagination. Though I supposed curiosity was the chief motive of her interest, it could but affect me as it would not have done had she been less beautiful.

Dr. Leete, as well as the ladies, seemed greatly interested in my account of the circumstances under which I had gone to sleep in the underground chamber. All had suggestions to offer to account for my having been forgotten there, and the theory which we finally agreed on offers at least a plausible explanation, although whether it be in its details the true one, nobody, of course, will ever know. The layer of ashes found above the chamber indicated that the house had been burned down. Let it be supposed that the conflagration had taken place the night I fell asleep. It only remains to assume that Sawyer lost his life in the fire or by some accident connected with it, and the rest follows naturally enough. No one but he and Dr. Pillsbury either knew of the existence of the chamber or that I was in it, and Dr. Pillsbury, who had gone that night to New Orleans, had probably never heard of the fire at all. The conclusion of my friends, and of the public, must have been that I had perished in the flames. An excavation of the ruins, unless thorough, would not have disclosed the recess in the foundation walls connecting with my chamber. To be sure, if the site had been again built upon, at least immediately, such an excavation would have been necessary, but the troublous times and the undesirable character of the locality might well have prevented rebuilding. The size of the trees in the garden now occupying the site indicated, Dr. Leete said, that for more than half a century at least it had been open ground.

V

When, in the course of the evening the ladies retired, leaving Dr. Leete and myself alone, he sounded me as to my disposition for sleep, saying that if I felt like it my bed was ready for me; but if I was inclined to wakefulness nothing would please him better than to bear me company. "I am a late bird, myself," he said, "and, without suspicion of flattery, I may say that a companion more interesting than yourself could scarcely be imagined. It is decidedly not often that one has a chance to converse with a man of the nineteenth century."

Now I had been looking forward all the evening with some dread to the time when I should be alone, on retiring for the night. Surrounded by these most friendly strangers, stimulated and supported by their sympathetic interest, I had been able to keep my mental balance. Even then, however, in pauses of the conversation I had had glimpses, vivid as lightning flashes, of the horror of strangeness that was waiting to be faced when I could no longer command diversion. I knew I could not sleep that night, and as for lying awake and thinking, it argues no cowardice, I am sure, to confess that I was afraid of it. When, in reply to my host's question, I frankly told him this, he replied that it would be strange if I did not feel just so, but that I need have no anxiety about sleeping; whenever I wanted to go to bed, he would give me a dose which would insure me a sound night's sleep without fail. Next morning, no doubt, I would awake with the feeling of an old citizen.

"Before I acquired that," I replied, "I must know a little more about the sort of Boston I have come back to. You told me when we were upon the house-top that though a century only had elapsed since I fell asleep, it had been marked by greater changes in the conditions of humanity than many a previous millennium. With the city before me I could well believe that, but I am very curious to know what some of the changes have been. To make a beginning somewhere, for the subject is doubtless a large one, what solution, if any, have you found for the labor question? It was the Sphinx's riddle of the nineteenth century, and when I dropped out the Sphinx was threatening to devour society, because the answer was not forthcoming. It is well worth sleeping a hundred years to learn what the right answer was, if, indeed, you have found it yet."

"As no such thing as the labor question is known nowadays," replied Dr. Leete, "and there is no way in which it could arise, I suppose we may claim to have solved it. Society would indeed have fully deserved being devoured if it had failed to answer a riddle so entirely simple. In fact, to speak by the book, it was not necessary for society to solve the riddle at all. It may be said to have solved itself. The solution came as the result of a process of industrial evolution which could not have terminated otherwise. All that society had to do was to recognize and cooperate with that evolution, when its tendency had become unmistakable."

"I can only say," I answered, "that at the time I fell asleep no such evolution had been recognized."

"It was in 1887 that you fell into this sleep, I think you said."

"Yes, May 30th, 1887."

My companion regarded me musingly for some moments. Then he observed, "And you tell me that even then there was no general recognition of the nature of the crisis which society was nearing? Of course, I fully credit your statement. The singular blindness of your contemporaries to the signs of the times is a phenomenon commented on by many of our historians, but few facts of history are more difficult for us to realize, so obvious and unmistakable as we look back seem the indications, which must also have come under your eyes, of the transformation about to come to pass. I should be interested, Mr. West, if you would give me a little more definite idea of the view which you and men of your grade of intellect took of the state and prospects of society in 1887. You must, at least, have realized that the widespread industrial and social troubles, and the underlying dissatisfaction of all classes with the inequalities of society, and the general misery of mankind, were portents of great changes of some sort."

"We did, indeed, fully realize that," I replied. "We felt that society was dragging anchor and in danger of going adrift. Whither it would drift nobody could say, but all feared the rocks."

"Nevertheless," said Dr. Leete, "the set of the current was perfectly perceptible if you had but taken pains to observe it, and it was not toward the rocks, but toward a deeper channel."

"We had a popular proverb," I replied, "that 'hindsight is better than foresight,' the force of which I shall now, no doubt, appreciate more fully than ever. All I can say is, that the prospect was such when I went into that long sleep that I should not have been surprised had I looked down from your house-top today on a heap of charred and moss-grown ruins instead of this glorious city."

Dr. Leete had listened to me with close attention and nodded thoughtfully as I finished speaking. "What you have said," he observed, "will be regarded as a most valuable vindication of Storiot, whose account of your era has been generally thought exaggerated in its picture of the gloom and confusion of men's minds. That a period of transition like that should be full of excitement and agitation was indeed to be looked for; but seeing how plain was the tendency of the forces in operation, it was natural to believe that hope rather than fear would have been the prevailing temper of the popular mind."

"You have not yet told me what was the answer to the riddle which you found," I said. "I am impatient to know by what contradiction of natural sequence the peace and prosperity which you now seem to enjoy could have been the outcome of an era like my own."

"Excuse me," replied my host, "but do you smoke?" It was not till our cigars were lighted and drawing well that he resumed. "Since you are in the humor to talk rather than to sleep, as I certainly am, perhaps I cannot do better than to try to give you enough idea of our modern industrial system to dissipate at least the impression that there is any mystery about the process of its evolution. The Bostonians of your day had the reputation of being great askers of questions, and I am going to show my descent by asking you one to begin with. What should you name as the most prominent feature of the labor troubles of your day?"

"Why, the strikes, of course," I replied.

"Exactly; but what made the strikes so formidable?"

"The great labor organizations."

"And what was the motive of these great organizations?"

"The workmen claimed they had to organize to get their rights from the big corporations," I replied.

"That is just it," said Dr. Leete; "the organization of labor and the strikes were an effect, merely, of the concentration of capital in greater masses than had ever been known before. Before this concentration began, while as yet commerce and industry were conducted by innumerable petty concerns with small capital, instead of a small number of great concerns with vast capital, the individual workman was relatively important and independent in his relations to the employer. Moreover, when a little capital or a new idea was enough to start a man in business for himself, workingmen were constantly becoming employers and there was no hard and fast line between the two classes. Labor unions were needless then, and general strikes out of the question. But when the era of small concerns with small capital was succeeded by that of the great aggregations of capital, all this was changed. The individual laborer, who had been relatively important to the small employer, was reduced to insignificance and powerlessness over against the great corporation, while at the same time the way upward to the grade of employer was closed to him. Self-defense drove him to union with his fellows.

"The records of the period show that the outcry against the concentration of capital was furious. Men believed that it threatened society with a form of tyranny more abhorrent than it had ever endured. They believed that the great corporations were preparing for them the yoke of a baser servitude than had ever been imposed on the race, servitude not to men but to soulless machines incapable of any motive but insatiable greed. Looking back, we cannot wonder at their desperation, for certainly humanity was never confronted with a fate more sordid and hideous than would have been the era of corporate tyranny which they anticipated.

"Meanwhile, without being in the smallest degree checked by the clamor against it, the absorption of business by ever larger monopolies continued. In the United States there was not, after the beginning of the last quarter of the century, any opportunity whatever for individual enterprise in any important field of industry, unless backed by a great capital. During the last decade of the century, such small businesses as still remained were fast-failing survivals of a past epoch, or mere parasites on the great corporations, or else existed in fields too small to attract the great capitalists. Small businesses, as far as they still remained, were reduced to the condition of rats and mice, living in holes and corners, and counting on evading notice for the enjoyment of existence. The railroads had gone on combining till a few great syndicates controlled every rail in the land. In manufactories, every important staple was controlled by a syndicate. These syndicates, pools, trusts, or whatever their name, fixed prices and crushed all competition except when combinations as vast as themselves arose. Then a struggle, resulting in a still greater consolidation, ensued. The great city bazaar crushed its country rivals with branch stores, and in the city itself absorbed its smaller rivals till the business of a whole quarter was concentrated under one roof, with a hundred former proprietors of shops serving as clerks. Having no business of his own to put his money in, the small capitalist, at the same time that he took service under the corporation, found no other investment for his money but its stocks and bonds, thus becoming doubly dependent upon it.

"The fact that the desperate popular opposition to the consolidation of business in a few powerful hands had no effect to check it proves that there must have been a strong economical reason for it. The small capitalists, with their innumerable petty concerns, had in fact yielded the field to the great aggregations of capital, because they belonged to a day of small things and were totally incompetent to the demands of an age of steam and telegraphs and the gigantic scale of its enterprises. To restore the former order of things, even if possible, would have involved returning to the day of stagecoaches. Oppressive and intolerable as was the regime of the great consolidations of capital, even its victims, while they cursed it, were forced to admit the prodigious increase of efficiency which had been imparted to the national industries, the vast economies effected by concentration of management and unity of organization, and to confess that since the new system had taken the place of the old the wealth of the world had increased at a rate before undreamed of. To be sure this vast increase had gone chiefly to make the rich richer, increasing the gap between them and the poor; but the fact remained that, as a means merely of producing wealth, capital had been proved efficient in proportion to its consolidation. The restoration of the old system with the subdivision of capital, if it were possible, might indeed bring back a greater equality of conditions, with more individual dignity and freedom, but it would be at the price of general poverty and the arrest of material progress.

"Was there, then, no way of commanding the services of the mighty wealth-producing principle of consolidated capital without bowing down to a plutocracy like that of Carthage? As soon as men began to ask themselves these questions, they found the answer ready for them. The movement toward the conduct of business by larger and larger aggregations of capital, the tendency toward monopolies, which had been so desperately and vainly resisted, was recognized at last, in its true significance, as a process which only needed to complete its logical evolution to open a golden future to humanity.

"Early in the last century the evolution was completed by the final consolidation of the entire capital of the nation. The industry and commerce of the country, ceasing to be conducted by a set of irresponsible corporations and syndicates of private persons at their caprice and for their profit, were intrusted to a single syndicate representing the people, to be conducted in the common interest for the common profit. The nation, that is to say, organized as the one great business corporation in which all other corporations were absorbed; it became the one capitalist in the place of all other capitalists, the sole employer, the final monopoly in which all previous and lesser monopolies were swallowed up, a monopoly in the profits and economies of which all citizens shared. The epoch of trusts had ended in The Great Trust. In a word, the people of the United States concluded to assume the conduct of their own business, just as one hundred odd years before they had assumed the conduct of their own government, organizing now for industrial purposes on precisely the same grounds that they had then organized for political purposes. At last, strangely late in the world's history, the obvious fact was perceived that no business is so essentially the public business as the industry and commerce on which the people's livelihood depends, and that to entrust it to private persons to be managed for private profit is a folly similar in kind, though vastly greater in magnitude, to that of surrendering the functions of political government to kings and nobles to be conducted for their personal glorification."

"Such a stupendous change as you describe," said I, "did not, of course, take place without great bloodshed and terrible convulsions."

"On the contrary," replied Dr. Leete, "there was absolutely no violence. The change had been long foreseen. Public opinion had become fully ripe for it, and the whole mass of the people was behind it. There was no more possibility of opposing it by force than by argument. On the other hand the popular sentiment toward the great corporations and those identified with them had ceased to be one of bitterness, as they came to realize their necessity as a link, a transition phase, in the evolution of the true industrial system. The most violent foes of the great private monopolies were now forced to recognize how invaluable and indispensable had been their office in educating the people up to the point of assuming control of their own business. Fifty years before, the consolidation of the industries of the country under national control would have seemed a very daring experiment to the most sanguine. But by a series of object lessons, seen and studied by all men, the great corporations had taught the people an entirely new set of ideas on this subject. They had seen for many years syndicates handling revenues greater than those of states, and directing the labors of hundreds of thousands of men with an efficiency and economy unattainable in smaller operations. It had come to be recognized as an axiom that the larger the business the simpler the principles that can be applied to it; that, as the machine is truer than the hand, so the system, which in a great concern does the work of the master's eye in a small business, turns out more accurate results. Thus it came about that, thanks to the corporations themselves, when it was proposed that the nation should assume their functions, the suggestion implied nothing which seemed impracticable even to the timid. To be sure it was a step beyond any yet taken, a broader generalization, but the very fact that the nation would be the sole corporation in the field would, it was seen, relieve the undertaking of many difficulties with which the partial monopolies had contended."

VI

Dr. Leete ceased speaking, and I remained silent, endeavoring to form some general conception of the changes in the arrangements of society implied in the tremendous revolution which he had described.

Finally I said, "The idea of such an extension of the functions of government is, to say the least, rather overwhelming."

"Extension!" he repeated, "where is the extension?"

"In my day," I replied, "it was considered that the proper functions of government, strictly speaking, were limited to keeping the peace and defending the people against the public enemy, that is, to the military and police powers."

"And, in heaven's name, who are the public enemies?" exclaimed Dr. Leete. "Are they France, England, Germany, or hunger, cold, and nakedness? In your day governments were accustomed, on the slightest international misunderstanding, to seize upon the bodies of citizens and deliver them over by hundreds of thousands to death and mutilation, wasting their treasures the while like water; and all this oftenest for no imaginable profit to the victims. We have no wars now, and our governments no war powers, but in order to protect every citizen against hunger, cold, and nakedness, and provide for all his physical and mental needs, the function is assumed of directing his industry for a term of years. No, Mr. West, I am sure on reflection you will perceive that it was in your age, not in ours, that the extension of the functions of governments was extraordinary. Not even for the best ends would men now allow their governments such powers as were then used for the most maleficent."

"Leaving comparisons aside," I said, "the demagoguery and corruption of our public men would have been considered, in my day, insuperable objections to any assumption by government of the charge of the national industries. We should have thought that no arrangement could be worse than to entrust the politicians with control of the wealth-producing machinery of the country. Its material interests were quite too much the football of parties as it was."

"No doubt you were right," rejoined Dr. Leete, "but all that is changed now. We have no parties or politicians, and as for demagoguery and corruption, they are words having only an historical significance."

"Human nature itself must have changed very much," I said.

"Not at all," was Dr. Leete's reply, "but the conditions of human life have changed, and with them the motives of human action. The organization of society with you was such that officials were under a constant temptation to misuse their power for the private profit of themselves or others. Under such circumstances it seems almost strange that you dared entrust them with any of your affairs. Nowadays, on the contrary, society is so constituted that there is absolutely no way in which an official, however ill-disposed, could possibly make any profit for himself or any one else by a misuse of his power. Let him be as bad an official as you please, he cannot be a corrupt one. There is no motive to be. The social system no longer offers a premium on dishonesty. But these are matters which you can only understand as you come, with time, to know us better."

"But you have not yet told me how you have settled the labor problem. It is the problem of capital which we have been discussing," I said. "After the nation had assumed conduct of the mills, machinery, railroads, farms, mines, and capital in general of the country, the labor question still remained. In assuming the responsibilities of capital the nation had assumed the difficulties of the capitalist's position."

"The moment the nation assumed the responsibilities of capital those difficulties vanished," replied Dr. Leete. "The national organization of labor under one direction was the complete solution of what was, in your day and under your system, justly regarded as the insoluble labor problem. When the nation became the sole employer, all the citizens, by virtue of their citizenship, became employees, to be distributed according to the needs of industry."

"That is," I suggested, "you have simply applied the principle of universal military service, as it was understood in our day, to the labor question."

"Yes," said Dr. Leete, "that was something which followed as a matter of course as soon as the nation had become the sole capitalist. The people were already accustomed to the idea that the obligation of every citizen, not physically disabled, to contribute his military services to the defense of the nation was equal and absolute. That it was equally the duty of every citizen to contribute his quota of industrial or intellectual services to the maintenance of the nation was equally evident, though it was not until the nation became the employer of labor that citizens were able to render this sort of service with any pretense either of universality or equity. No organization of labor was possible when the employing power was divided among hundreds or thousands of individuals and corporations, between which concert of any kind was neither desired, nor indeed feasible. It constantly happened then that vast numbers who desired to labor could find no opportunity, and on the other hand, those who desired to evade a part or all of their debt could easily do so."

"Service, now, I suppose, is compulsory upon all," I suggested.

"It is rather a matter of course than of compulsion," replied Dr. Leete. "It is regarded as so absolutely natural and reasonable that the idea of its being compulsory has ceased to be thought of. He would be thought to be an incredibly contemptible person who should need compulsion in such a case. Nevertheless, to speak of service being compulsory would be a weak way to state its absolute inevitableness. Our entire social order is so wholly based upon and deduced from it that if it were conceivable that a man could escape it, he would be left with no possible way to provide for his existence. He would have excluded himself from the world, cut himself off from his kind, in a word, committed suicide."

"Is the term of service in this industrial army for life?"

"Oh, no; it both begins later and ends earlier than the average working period in your day. Your workshops were filled with children and old men, but we hold the period of youth sacred to education, and the period of maturity, when the physical forces begin to flag, equally sacred to ease and agreeable relaxation. The period of industrial service is twenty-four years, beginning at the close of the course of education at twenty-one and terminating at forty-five. After forty-five, while discharged from labor, the citizen still remains liable to special calls, in case of emergencies causing a sudden great increase in the demand for labor, till he reaches the age of fifty-five, but such calls are rarely, in fact almost never, made. The fifteenth day of October of every year is what we call Muster Day, because those who have reached the age of twenty-one are then mustered into the industrial service, and at the same time those who, after twenty-four years' service, have reached the age of forty-five, are honorably mustered out. It is the great day of the year with us, whence we reckon all other events, our Olympiad, save that it is annual."

VII

"It is after you have mustered your industrial army into service," I said, "that I should expect the chief difficulty to arise, for there its analogy with a military army must cease. Soldiers have all the same thing, and a very simple thing, to do, namely, to practice the manual of arms, to march and stand guard. But the industrial army must learn and follow two or three hundred diverse trades and avocations. What administrative talent can be equal to determining wisely what trade or business every individual in a great nation shall pursue?"

"The administration has nothing to do with determining that point."

"Who does determine it, then?" I asked.

"Every man for himself in accordance with his natural aptitude, the utmost pains being taken to enable him to find out what his natural aptitude really is. The principle on which our industrial army is organized is that a man's natural endowments, mental and physical, determine what he can work at most profitably to the nation and most satisfactorily to himself. While the obligation of service in some form is not to be evaded, voluntary election, subject only to necessary regulation, is depended on to determine the particular sort of service every man is to render. As an individual's satisfaction during his term of service depends on his having an occupation to his taste, parents and teachers watch from early years for indications of special aptitudes in children. A thorough study of the national industrial system, with the history and rudiments of all the great trades, is an essential part of our educational system. While manual training is not allowed to encroach on the general intellectual culture to which our schools are devoted, it is carried far enough to give our youth, in addition to their theoretical knowledge of the national industries, mechanical and agricultural, a certain familiarity with their tools and methods. Our schools are constantly visiting our workshops, and often are taken on long excursions to inspect particular industrial enterprises. In your day a man was not ashamed to be grossly ignorant of all trades except his own, but such ignorance would not be consistent with our idea of placing every one in a position to select intelligently the occupation for which he has most taste. Usually long before he is mustered into service a young man has found out the pursuit he wants to follow, has acquired a great deal of knowledge about it, and is waiting impatiently the time when he can enlist in its ranks."

"Surely," I said, "it can hardly be that the number of volunteers for any trade is exactly the number needed in that trade. It must be generally either under or over the demand."

"The supply of volunteers is always expected to fully equal the demand," replied Dr. Leete. "It is the business of the administration to see that this is the case. The rate of volunteering for each trade is closely watched. If there be a noticeably greater excess of volunteers over men needed in any trade, it is inferred that the trade offers greater attractions than others. On the other hand, if the number of volunteers for a trade tends to drop below the demand, it is inferred that it is thought more arduous. It is the business of the administration to seek constantly to equalize the attractions of the trades, so far as the conditions of labor in them are concerned, so that all trades shall be equally attractive to persons having natural tastes for them. This is done by making the hours of labor in different trades to differ according to their arduousness. The lighter trades, prosecuted under the most agreeable circumstances, have in this way the longest hours, while an arduous trade, such as mining, has very short hours. There is no theory, no a priori rule, by which the respective attractiveness of industries is determined. The administration, in taking burdens off one class of workers and adding them to other classes, simply follows the fluctuations of opinion among the workers themselves as indicated by the rate of volunteering. The principle is that no man's work ought to be, on the whole, harder for him than any other man's for him, the workers themselves to be the judges. There are no limits to the application of this rule. If any particular occupation is in itself so arduous or so oppressive that, in order to induce volunteers, the day's work in it had to be reduced to ten minutes, it would be done. If, even then, no man was willing to do it, it would remain undone. But of course, in point of fact, a moderate reduction in the hours of labor, or addition of other privileges, suffices to secure all needed volunteers for any occupation necessary to men. If, indeed, the unavoidable difficulties and dangers of such a necessary pursuit were so great that no inducement of compensating advantages would overcome men's repugnance to it, the administration would only need to take it out of the common order of occupations by declaring it 'extra hazardous,' and those who pursued it especially worthy of the national gratitude, to be overrun with volunteers. Our young men are very greedy of honor, and do not let slip such opportunities. Of course you will see that dependence on the purely voluntary choice of avocations involves the abolition in all of anything like unhygienic conditions or special peril to life and limb. Health and safety are conditions common to all industries. The nation does not maim and slaughter its workmen by thousands, as did the private capitalists and corporations of your day."

"When there are more who want to enter a particular trade than there is room for, how do you decide between the applicants?" I inquired.

"Preference is given to those who have acquired the most knowledge of the trade they wish to follow. No man, however, who through successive years remains persistent in his desire to show what he can do at any particular trade, is in the end denied an opportunity. Meanwhile, if a man cannot at first win entrance into the business he prefers, he has usually one or more alternative preferences, pursuits for which he has some degree of aptitude, although not the highest. Every one, indeed, is expected to study his aptitudes so as to have not only a first choice as to occupation, but a second or third, so that if, either at the outset of his career or subsequently, owing to the progress of invention or changes in demand, he is unable to follow his first vocation, he can still find reasonably congenial employment. This principle of secondary choices as to occupation is quite important in our system. I should add, in reference to the counter-possibility of some sudden failure of volunteers in a particular trade, or some sudden necessity of an increased force, that the administration, while depending on the voluntary system for filling up the trades as a rule, holds always in reserve the power to call for special volunteers, or draft any force needed from any quarter. Generally, however, all needs of this sort can be met by details from the class of unskilled or common laborers."

"How is this class of common laborers recruited?" I asked. "Surely nobody voluntarily enters that."

"It is the grade to which all new recruits belong for the first three years of their service. It is not till after this period, during which he is assignable to any work at the discretion of his superiors, that the young man is allowed to elect a special avocation. These three years of stringent discipline none are exempt from, and very glad our young men are to pass from this severe school into the comparative liberty of the trades. If a man were so stupid as to have no choice as to occupation, he would simply remain a common laborer; but such cases, as you may suppose, are not common."

"Having once elected and entered on a trade or occupation," I remarked, "I suppose he has to stick to it the rest of his life."

"Not necessarily," replied Dr. Leete; "while frequent and merely capricious changes of occupation are not encouraged or even permitted, every worker is allowed, of course, under certain regulations and in accordance with the exigencies of the service, to volunteer for another industry which he thinks would suit him better than his first choice. In this case his application is received just as if he were volunteering for the first time, and on the same terms. Not only this, but a worker may likewise, under suitable regulations and not too frequently, obtain a transfer to an establishment of the same industry in another part of the country which for any reason he may prefer. Under your system a discontented man could indeed leave his work at will, but he left his means of support at the same time, and took his chances as to future livelihood. We find that the number of men who wish to abandon an accustomed occupation for a new one, and old friends and associations for strange ones, is small. It is only the poorer sort of workmen who desire to change even as frequently as our regulations permit. Of course transfers or discharges, when health demands them, are always given."

"As an industrial system, I should think this might be extremely efficient," I said, "but I don't see that it makes any provision for the professional classes, the men who serve the nation with brains instead of hands. Of course you can't get along without the brain-workers. How, then, are they selected from those who are to serve as farmers and mechanics? That must require a very delicate sort of sifting process, I should say."

"So it does," replied Dr. Leete; "the most delicate possible test is needed here, and so we leave the question whether a man shall be a brain or hand worker entirely to him to settle. At the end of the term of three years as a common laborer, which every man must serve, it is for him to choose, in accordance to his natural tastes, whether he will fit himself for an art or profession, or be a farmer or mechanic. If he feels that he can do better work with his brains than his muscles, he finds every facility provided for testing the reality of his supposed bent, of cultivating it, and if fit of pursuing it as his avocation. The schools of technology, of medicine, of art, of music, of histrionics, and of higher liberal learning are always open to aspirants without condition."

"Are not the schools flooded with young men whose only motive is to avoid work?"

Dr. Leete smiled a little grimly.

"No one is at all likely to enter the professional schools for the purpose of avoiding work, I assure you," he said. "They are intended for those with special aptitude for the branches they teach, and any one without it would find it easier to do double hours at his trade than try to keep up with the classes. Of course many honestly mistake their vocation, and, finding themselves unequal to the requirements of the schools, drop out and return to the industrial service; no discredit attaches to such persons, for the public policy is to encourage all to develop suspected talents which only actual tests can prove the reality of. The professional and scientific schools of your day depended on the patronage of their pupils for support, and the practice appears to have been common of giving diplomas to unfit persons, who afterwards found their way into the professions. Our schools are national institutions, and to have passed their tests is a proof of special abilities not to be questioned.

"This opportunity for a professional training," the doctor continued, "remains open to every man till the age of thirty is reached, after which students are not received, as there would remain too brief a period before the age of discharge in which to serve the nation in their professions. In your day young men had to choose their professions very young, and therefore, in a large proportion of instances, wholly mistook their vocations. It is recognized nowadays that the natural aptitudes of some are later than those of others in developing, and therefore, while the choice of profession may be made as early as twenty-four, it remains open for six years longer."

A question which had a dozen times before been on my lips now found utterance, a question which touched upon what, in my time, had been regarded the most vital difficulty in the way of any final settlement of the industrial problem. "It is an extraordinary thing," I said, "that you should not yet have said a word about the method of adjusting wages. Since the nation is the sole employer, the government must fix the rate of wages and determine just how much everybody shall earn, from the doctors to the diggers. All I can say is, that this plan would never have worked with us, and I don't see how it can now unless human nature has changed. In my day, nobody was satisfied with his wages or salary. Even if he felt he received enough, he was sure his neighbor had too much, which was as bad. If the universal discontent on this subject, instead of being dissipated in curses and strikes directed against innumerable employers, could have been concentrated upon one, and that the government, the strongest ever devised would not have seen two pay days."

Dr. Leete laughed heartily.

"Very true, very true," he said, "a general strike would most probably have followed the first pay day, and a strike directed against a government is a revolution."

"How, then, do you avoid a revolution every pay day?" if demanded. "Has some prodigious philosopher devised a new system of calculus satisfactory to all for determining the exact and comparative value of all sorts of service, whether by brawn or brain, by hand or voice, by ear or eye? Or has human nature itself changed, so that no man looks upon his own things but 'every man on the things of his neighbor'? One or the other of these events must be the explanation."

"Neither one nor the other, however, is," was my host's laughing response. "And now, Mr. West," he continued, "you must remember that you are my patient as well as my guest, and permit me to prescribe sleep for you before we have any more conversation. It is after three o'clock."

"The prescription is, no doubt, a wise one," I said; "I only hope it can be filled."

"I will see to that," the doctor replied, and he did, for he gave me a wineglass of something or other which sent me to sleep as soon as my head touched the pillow.

VIII

When I awoke I felt greatly refreshed, and lay a considerable time in a dozing state, enjoying the sensation of bodily comfort. The experiences of the day previous, my waking to find myself in the year 2000, the sight of the new Boston, my host and his family, and the wonderful things I had heard, were a blank in my memory. I thought I was in my bed-chamber at home, and the half-dreaming, half-waking fancies which passed before my mind related to the incidents and experiences of my former life. Dreamily I reviewed the incidents of Decoration Day, my trip in company with Edith and her parents to Mount Auburn, and my dining with them on our return to the city. I recalled how extremely well Edith had looked, and from that fell to thinking of our marriage; but scarcely had my imagination begun to develop this delightful theme than my waking dream was cut short by the recollection of the letter I had received the night before from the builder announcing that the new strikes might postpone indefinitely the completion of the new house. The chagrin which this recollection brought with it effectually roused me. I remembered that I had an appointment with the builder at eleven o'clock, to discuss the strike, and opening my eyes, looked up at the clock at the foot of my bed to see what time it was. But no clock met my glance, and what was more, I instantly perceived that I was not in my room. Starting up on my couch, I stared wildly round the strange apartment.

I think it must have been many seconds that I sat up thus in bed staring about, without being able to regain the clew to my personal identity. I was no more able to distinguish myself from pure being during those moments than we may suppose a soul in the rough to be before it has received the earmarks, the individualizing touches which make it a person. Strange that the sense of this inability should be such anguish! But so we are constituted. There are no words for the mental torture I endured during this helpless, eyeless groping for myself in a boundless void. No other experience of the mind gives probably anything like the sense of absolute intellectual arrest from the loss of a mental fulcrum, a starting point of thought, which comes during such a momentary obscuration of the sense of one's identity. I trust I may never know what it is again.

I do not know how long this condition had lasted—it seemed an interminable time—when, like a flash, the recollection of everything came back to me. I remembered who and where I was, and how I had come here, and that these scenes as of the life of yesterday which had been passing before my mind concerned a generation long, long ago mouldered to dust. Leaping from bed, I stood in the middle of the room clasping my temples with all my might between my hands to keep them from bursting. Then I fell prone on the couch, and, burying my face in the pillow, lay without motion. The reaction which was inevitable, from the mental elation, the fever of the intellect that had been the first effect of my tremendous experience, had arrived. The emotional crisis which had awaited the full realization of my actual position, and all that it implied, was upon me, and with set teeth and laboring chest, gripping the bedstead with frenzied strength, I lay there and fought for my sanity. In my mind, all had broken loose, habits of feeling, associations of thought, ideas of persons and things, all had dissolved and lost coherence and were seething together in apparently irretrievable chaos. There were no rallying points, nothing was left stable. There only remained the will, and was any human will strong enough to say to such a weltering sea, "Peace, be still"? I dared not think. Every effort to reason upon what had befallen me, and realize what it implied, set up an intolerable swimming of the brain. The idea that I was two persons, that my identity was double, began to fascinate me with its simple solution of my experience.

I knew that I was on the verge of losing my mental balance. If I lay there thinking, I was doomed. Diversion of some sort I must have, at least the diversion of physical exertion. I sprang up, and, hastily dressing, opened the door of my room and went down-stairs. The hour was very early, it being not yet fairly light, and I found no one in the lower part of the house. There was a hat in the hall, and, opening the front door, which was fastened with a slightness indicating that burglary was not among the perils of the modern Boston, I found myself on the street. For two hours I walked or ran through the streets of the city, visiting most quarters of the peninsular part of the town. None but an antiquarian who knows something of the contrast which the Boston of today offers to the Boston of the nineteenth century can begin to appreciate what a series of bewildering surprises I underwent during that time. Viewed from the house-top the day before, the city had indeed appeared strange to me, but that was only in its general aspect. How complete the change had been I first realized now that I walked the streets. The few old landmarks which still remained only intensified this effect, for without them I might have imagined myself in a foreign town. A man may leave his native city in childhood, and return fifty years later, perhaps, to find it transformed in many features. He is astonished, but he is not bewildered. He is aware of a great lapse of time, and of changes likewise occurring in himself meanwhile. He but dimly recalls the city as he knew it when a child. But remember that there was no sense of any lapse of time with me. So far as my consciousness was concerned, it was but yesterday, but a few hours, since I had walked these streets in which scarcely a feature had escaped a complete metamorphosis. The mental image of the old city was so fresh and strong that it did not yield to the impression of the actual city, but contended with it, so that it was first one and then the other which seemed the more unreal. There was nothing I saw which was not blurred in this way, like the faces of a composite photograph.

Finally, I stood again at the door of the house from which I had come out. My feet must have instinctively brought me back to the site of my old home, for I had no clear idea of returning thither. It was no more homelike to me than any other spot in this city of a strange generation, nor were its inmates less utterly and necessarily strangers than all the other men and women now on the earth. Had the door of the house been locked, I should have been reminded by its resistance that I had no object in entering, and turned away, but it yielded to my hand, and advancing with uncertain steps through the hall, I entered one of the apartments opening from it. Throwing myself into a chair, I covered my burning eyeballs with my hands to shut out the horror of strangeness. My mental confusion was so intense as to produce actual nausea. The anguish of those moments, during which my brain seemed melting, or the abjectness of my sense of helplessness, how can I describe? In my despair I groaned aloud. I began to feel that unless some help should come I was about to lose my mind. And just then it did come. I heard the rustle of drapery, and looked up. Edith Leete was standing before me. Her beautiful face was full of the most poignant sympathy.

"Oh, what is the matter, Mr. West?" she said. "I was here when you came in. I saw how dreadfully distressed you looked, and when I heard you groan, I could not keep silent. What has happened to you? Where have you been? Can't I do something for you?"

Perhaps she involuntarily held out her hands in a gesture of compassion as she spoke. At any rate I had caught them in my own and was clinging to them with an impulse as instinctive as that which prompts the drowning man to seize upon and cling to the rope which is thrown him as he sinks for the last time. As I looked up into her compassionate face and her eyes moist with pity, my brain ceased to whirl. The tender human sympathy which thrilled in the soft pressure of her fingers had brought me the support I needed. Its effect to calm and soothe was like that of some wonder-working elixir.

"God bless you," I said, after a few moments. "He must have sent you to me just now. I think I was in danger of going crazy if you had not come." At this the tears came into her eyes.

"Oh, Mr. West!" she cried. "How heartless you must have thought us! How could we leave you to yourself so long! But it is over now, is it not? You are better, surely."

"Yes," I said, "thanks to you. If you will not go away quite yet, I shall be myself soon."

"Indeed I will not go away," she said, with a little quiver of her face, more expressive of her sympathy than a volume of words. "You must not think us so heartless as we seemed in leaving you so by yourself. I scarcely slept last night, for thinking how strange your waking would be this morning; but father said you would sleep till late. He said that it would be better not to show too much sympathy with you at first, but to try to divert your thoughts and make you feel that you were among friends."

"You have indeed made me feel that," I answered. "But you see it is a good deal of a jolt to drop a hundred years, and although I did not seem to feel it so much last night, I have had very odd sensations this morning." While I held her hands and kept my eyes on her face, I could already even jest a little at my plight.

"No one thought of such a thing as your going out in the city alone so early in the morning," she went on. "Oh, Mr. West, where have you been?"

Then I told her of my morning's experience, from my first waking till the moment I had looked up to see her before me, just as I have told it here. She was overcome by distressful pity during the recital, and, though I had released one of her hands, did not try to take from me the other, seeing, no doubt, how much good it did me to hold it. "I can think a little what this feeling must have been like," she said. "It must have been terrible. And to think you were left alone to struggle with it! Can you ever forgive us?"

"But it is gone now. You have driven it quite away for the present," I said.

"You will not let it return again," she queried anxiously.

"I can't quite say that," I replied. "It might be too early to say that, considering how strange everything will still be to me."

"But you will not try to contend with it alone again, at least," she persisted. "Promise that you will come to us, and let us sympathize with you, and try to help you. Perhaps we can't do much, but it will surely be better than to try to bear such feelings alone."

"I will come to you if you will let me," I said.

"Oh yes, yes, I beg you will," she said eagerly. "I would do anything to help you that I could."

"All you need do is to be sorry for me, as you seem to be now," I replied.

"It is understood, then," she said, smiling with wet eyes, "that you are to come and tell me next time, and not run all over Boston among strangers."

This assumption that we were not strangers seemed scarcely strange, so near within these few minutes had my trouble and her sympathetic tears brought us.

"I will promise, when you come to me," she added, with an expression of charming archness, passing, as she continued, into one of enthusiasm, "to seem as sorry for you as you wish, but you must not for a moment suppose that I am really sorry for you at all, or that I think you will long be sorry for yourself. I know, as well as I know that the world now is heaven compared with what it was in your day, that the only feeling you will have after a little while will be one of thankfulness to God that your life in that age was so strangely cut off, to be returned to you in this."

IX

Dr. and Mrs. Leete were evidently not a little startled to learn, when they presently appeared, that I had been all over the city alone that morning, and it was apparent that they were agreeably surprised to see that I seemed so little agitated after the experience.

"Your stroll could scarcely have failed to be a very interesting one," said Mrs. Leete, as we sat down to table soon after. "You must have seen a good many new things."

"I saw very little that was not new," I replied. "But I think what surprised me as much as anything was not to find any stores on Washington Street, or any banks on State. What have you done with the merchants and bankers? Hung them all, perhaps, as the anarchists wanted to do in my day?"

"Not so bad as that," replied Dr. Leete. "We have simply dispensed with them. Their functions are obsolete in the modern world."

"Who sells you things when you want to buy them?" I inquired.

"There is neither selling nor buying nowadays; the distribution of goods is effected in another way. As to the bankers, having no money we have no use for those gentry."

"Miss Leete," said I, turning to Edith, "I am afraid that your father is making sport of me. I don't blame him, for the temptation my innocence offers must be extraordinary. But, really, there are limits to my credulity as to possible alterations in the social system."

"Father has no idea of jesting, I am sure," she replied, with a reassuring smile.

The conversation took another turn then, the point of ladies' fashions in the nineteenth century being raised, if I remember rightly, by Mrs. Leete, and it was not till after breakfast, when the doctor had invited me up to the house-top, which appeared to be a favorite resort of his, that he recurred to the subject.

"You were surprised," he said, "at my saying that we got along without money or trade, but a moment's reflection will show that trade existed and money was needed in your day simply because the business of production was left in private hands, and that, consequently, they are superfluous now."

"I do not at once see how that follows," I replied.

"It is very simple," said Dr. Leete. "When innumerable different and independent persons produced the various things needful to life and comfort, endless exchanges between individuals were requisite in order that they might supply themselves with what they desired. These exchanges constituted trade, and money was essential as their medium. But as soon as the nation became the sole producer of all sorts of commodities, there was no need of exchanges between individuals that they might get what they required. Everything was procurable from one source, and nothing could be procured anywhere else. A system of direct distribution from the national storehouses took the place of trade, and for this money was unnecessary."

"How is this distribution managed?" I asked.

"On the simplest possible plan," replied Dr. Leete. "A credit corresponding to his share of the annual product of the nation is given to every citizen on the public books at the beginning of each year, and a credit card issued him with which he procures at the public storehouses, found in every community, whatever he desires whenever he desires it. This arrangement, you will see, totally obviates the necessity for business transactions of any sort between individuals and consumers. Perhaps you would like to see what our credit cards are like.

"You observe," he pursued as I was curiously examining the piece of pasteboard he gave me, "that this card is issued for a certain number of dollars. We have kept the old word, but not the substance. The term, as we use it, answers to no real thing, but merely serves as an algebraical symbol for comparing the values of products with one another. For this purpose they are all priced in dollars and cents, just as in your day. The value of what I procure on this card is checked off by the clerk, who pricks out of these tiers of squares the price of what I order."

"If you wanted to buy something of your neighbor, could you transfer part of your credit to him as consideration?" I inquired.

"In the first place," replied Dr. Leete, "our neighbors have nothing to sell us, but in any event our credit would not be transferable, being strictly personal. Before the nation could even think of honoring any such transfer as you speak of, it would be bound to inquire into all the circumstances of the transaction, so as to be able to guarantee its absolute equity. It would have been reason enough, had there been no other, for abolishing money, that its possession was no indication of rightful title to it. In the hands of the man who had stolen it or murdered for it, it was as good as in those which had earned it by industry. People nowadays interchange gifts and favors out of friendship, but buying and selling is considered absolutely inconsistent with the mutual benevolence and disinterestedness which should prevail between citizens and the sense of community of interest which supports our social system. According to our ideas, buying and selling is essentially anti-social in all its tendencies. It is an education in self-seeking at the expense of others, and no society whose citizens are trained in such a school can possibly rise above a very low grade of civilization."

"What if you have to spend more than your card in any one year?" I asked.

"The provision is so ample that we are more likely not to spend it all," replied Dr. Leete. "But if extraordinary expenses should exhaust it, we can obtain a limited advance on the next year's credit, though this practice is not encouraged, and a heavy discount is charged to check it. Of course if a man showed himself a reckless spendthrift he would receive his allowance monthly or weekly instead of yearly, or if necessary not be permitted to handle it all."

"If you don't spend your allowance, I suppose it accumulates?"

"That is also permitted to a certain extent when a special outlay is anticipated. But unless notice to the contrary is given, it is presumed that the citizen who does not fully expend his credit did not have occasion to do so, and the balance is turned into the general surplus."

"Such a system does not encourage saving habits on the part of citizens," I said.

"It is not intended to," was the reply. "The nation is rich, and does not wish the people to deprive themselves of any good thing. In your day, men were bound to lay up goods and money against coming failure of the means of support and for their children. This necessity made parsimony a virtue. But now it would have no such laudable object, and, having lost its utility, it has ceased to be regarded as a virtue. No man any more has any care for the morrow, either for himself or his children, for the nation guarantees the nurture, education, and comfortable maintenance of every citizen from the cradle to the grave."

"That is a sweeping guarantee!" I said. "What certainty can there be that the value of a man's labor will recompense the nation for its outlay on him? On the whole, society may be able to support all its members, but some must earn less than enough for their support, and others more; and that brings us back once more to the wages question, on which you have hitherto said nothing. It was at just this point, if you remember, that our talk ended last evening; and I say again, as I did then, that here I should suppose a national industrial system like yours would find its main difficulty. How, I ask once more, can you adjust satisfactorily the comparative wages or remuneration of the multitude of avocations, so unlike and so incommensurable, which are necessary for the service of society? In our day the market rate determined the price of labor of all sorts, as well as of goods. The employer paid as little as he could, and the worker got as much. It was not a pretty system ethically, I admit; but it did, at least, furnish us a rough and ready formula for settling a question which must be settled ten thousand times a day if the world was ever going to get forward. There seemed to us no other practicable way of doing it."

"Yes," replied Dr. Leete, "it was the only practicable way under a system which made the interests of every individual antagonistic to those of every other; but it would have been a pity if humanity could never have devised a better plan, for yours was simply the application to the mutual relations of men of the devil's maxim, 'Your necessity is my opportunity.' The reward of any service depended not upon its difficulty, danger, or hardship, for throughout the world it seems that the most perilous, severe, and repulsive labor was done by the worst paid classes; but solely upon the strait of those who needed the service."

"All that is conceded," I said. "But, with all its defects, the plan of settling prices by the market rate was a practical plan; and I cannot conceive what satisfactory substitute you can have devised for it. The government being the only possible employer, there is of course no labor market or market rate. Wages of all sorts must be arbitrarily fixed by the government. I cannot imagine a more complex and delicate function than that must be, or one, however performed, more certain to breed universal dissatisfaction."

"I beg your pardon," replied Dr. Leete, "but I think you exaggerate the difficulty. Suppose a board of fairly sensible men were charged with settling the wages for all sorts of trades under a system which, like ours, guaranteed employment to all, while permitting the choice of avocations. Don't you see that, however unsatisfactory the first adjustment might be, the mistakes would soon correct themselves? The favored trades would have too many volunteers, and those discriminated against would lack them till the errors were set right. But this is aside from the purpose, for, though this plan would, I fancy, be practicable enough, it is no part of our system."

"How, then, do you regulate wages?" I once more asked.

Dr. Leete did not reply till after several moments of meditative silence. "I know, of course," he finally said, "enough of the old order of things to understand just what you mean by that question; and yet the present order is so utterly different at this point that I am a little at loss how to answer you best. You ask me how we regulate wages; I can only reply that there is no idea in the modern social economy which at all corresponds with what was meant by wages in your day."

"I suppose you mean that you have no money to pay wages in," said I. "But the credit given the worker at the government storehouse answers to his wages with us. How is the amount of the credit given respectively to the workers in different lines determined? By what title does the individual claim his particular share? What is the basis of allotment?"

"His title," replied Dr. Leete, "is his humanity. The basis of his claim is the fact that he is a man."

"The fact that he is a man!" I repeated, incredulously. "Do you possibly mean that all have the same share?"

"Most assuredly."

The readers of this book never having practically known any other arrangement, or perhaps very carefully considered the historical accounts of former epochs in which a very different system prevailed, cannot be expected to appreciate the stupor of amazement into which Dr. Leete's simple statement plunged me.

"You see," he said, smiling, "that it is not merely that we have no money to pay wages in, but, as I said, we have nothing at all answering to your idea of wages."

By this time I had pulled myself together sufficiently to voice some of the criticisms which, man of the nineteenth century as I was, came uppermost in my mind, upon this to me astounding arrangement. "Some men do twice the work of others!" I exclaimed. "Are the clever workmen content with a plan that ranks them with the indifferent?"

"We leave no possible ground for any complaint of injustice," replied Dr. Leete, "by requiring precisely the same measure of service from all."

"How can you do that, I should like to know, when no two men's powers are the same?"

"Nothing could be simpler," was Dr. Leete's reply. "We require of each that he shall make the same effort; that is, we demand of him the best service it is in his power to give."

"And supposing all do the best they can," I answered, "the amount of the product resulting is twice greater from one man than from another."

"Very true," replied Dr. Leete; "but the amount of the resulting product has nothing whatever to do with the question, which is one of desert. Desert is a moral question, and the amount of the product a material quantity. It would be an extraordinary sort of logic which should try to determine a moral question by a material standard. The amount of the effort alone is pertinent to the question of desert. All men who do their best, do the same. A man's endowments, however godlike, merely fix the measure of his duty. The man of great endowments who does not do all he might, though he may do more than a man of small endowments who does his best, is deemed a less deserving worker than the latter, and dies a debtor to his fellows. The Creator sets men's tasks for them by the faculties he gives them; we simply exact their fulfillment."

"No doubt that is very fine philosophy," I said; "nevertheless it seems hard that the man who produces twice as much as another, even if both do their best, should have only the same share."

"Does it, indeed, seem so to you?" responded Dr. Leete. "Now, do you know, that seems very curious to me? The way it strikes people nowadays is, that a man who can produce twice as much as another with the same effort, instead of being rewarded for doing so, ought to be punished if he does not do so. In the nineteenth century, when a horse pulled a heavier load than a goat, I suppose you rewarded him. Now, we should have whipped him soundly if he had not, on the ground that, being much stronger, he ought to. It is singular how ethical standards change." The doctor said this with such a twinkle in his eye that I was obliged to laugh.

"I suppose," I said, "that the real reason that we rewarded men for their endowments, while we considered those of horses and goats merely as fixing the service to be severally required of them, was that the animals, not being reasoning beings, naturally did the best they could, whereas men could only be induced to do so by rewarding them according to the amount of their product. That brings me to ask why, unless human nature has mightily changed in a hundred years, you are not under the same necessity."

"We are," replied Dr. Leete. "I don't think there has been any change in human nature in that respect since your day. It is still so constituted that special incentives in the form of prizes, and advantages to be gained, are requisite to call out the best endeavors of the average man in any direction."

"But what inducement," I asked, "can a man have to put forth his best endeavors when, however much or little he accomplishes, his income remains the same? High characters may be moved by devotion to the common welfare under such a system, but does not the average man tend to rest back on his oar, reasoning that it is of no use to make a special effort, since the effort will not increase his income, nor its withholding diminish it?"

"Does it then really seem to you," answered my companion, "that human nature is insensible to any motives save fear of want and love of luxury, that you should expect security and equality of livelihood to leave them without possible incentives to effort? Your contemporaries did not really think so, though they might fancy they did. When it was a question of the grandest class of efforts, the most absolute self-devotion, they depended on quite other incentives. Not higher wages, but honor and the hope of men's gratitude, patriotism and the inspiration of duty, were the motives which they set before their soldiers when it was a question of dying for the nation, and never was there an age of the world when those motives did not call out what is best and noblest in men. And not only this, but when you come to analyze the love of money which was the general impulse to effort in your day, you find that the dread of want and desire of luxury was but one of several motives which the pursuit of money represented; the others, and with many the more influential, being desire of power, of social position, and reputation for ability and success. So you see that though we have abolished poverty and the fear of it, and inordinate luxury with the hope of it, we have not touched the greater part of the motives which underlay the love of money in former times, or any of those which prompted the supremer sorts of effort. The coarser motives, which no longer move us, have been replaced by higher motives wholly unknown to the mere wage earners of your age. Now that industry of whatever sort is no longer self-service, but service of the nation, patriotism, passion for humanity, impel the worker as in your day they did the soldier. The army of industry is an army, not alone by virtue of its perfect organization, but by reason also of the ardor of self-devotion which animates its members.

"But as you used to supplement the motives of patriotism with the love of glory, in order to stimulate the valor of your soldiers, so do we. Based as our industrial system is on the principle of requiring the same unit of effort from every man, that is, the best he can do, you will see that the means by which we spur the workers to do their best must be a very essential part of our scheme. With us, diligence in the national service is the sole and certain way to public repute, social distinction, and official power. The value of a man's services to society fixes his rank in it. Compared with the effect of our social arrangements in impelling men to be zealous in business, we deem the object-lessons of biting poverty and wanton luxury on which you depended a device as weak and uncertain as it was barbaric. The lust of honor even in your sordid day notoriously impelled men to more desperate effort than the love of money could."

"I should be extremely interested," I said, "to learn something of what these social arrangements are."

"The scheme in its details," replied the doctor, "is of course very elaborate, for it underlies the entire organization of our industrial army; but a few words will give you a general idea of it."

At this moment our talk was charmingly interrupted by the emergence upon the aerial platform where we sat of Edith Leete. She was dressed for the street, and had come to speak to her father about some commission she was to do for him.

"By the way, Edith," he exclaimed, as she was about to leave us to ourselves, "I wonder if Mr. West would not be interested in visiting the store with you? I have been telling him something about our system of distribution, and perhaps he might like to see it in practical operation."

"My daughter," he added, turning to me, "is an indefatigable shopper, and can tell you more about the stores than I can."

The proposition was naturally very agreeable to me, and Edith being good enough to say that she should be glad to have my company, we left the house together.

X

"If I am going to explain our way of shopping to you," said my companion, as we walked along the street, "you must explain your way to me. I have never been able to understand it from all I have read on the subject. For example, when you had such a vast number of shops, each with its different assortment, how could a lady ever settle upon any purchase till she had visited all the shops? For, until she had, she could not know what there was to choose from."

"It was as you suppose; that was the only way she could know," I replied.

"Father calls me an indefatigable shopper, but I should soon be a very fatigued one if I had to do as they did," was Edith's laughing comment.

"The loss of time in going from shop to shop was indeed a waste which the busy bitterly complained of," I said; "but as for the ladies of the idle class, though they complained also, I think the system was really a godsend by furnishing a device to kill time."

"But say there were a thousand shops in a city, hundreds, perhaps, of the same sort, how could even the idlest find time to make their rounds?"

"They really could not visit all, of course," I replied. "Those who did a great deal of buying, learned in time where they might expect to find what they wanted. This class had made a science of the specialties of the shops, and bought at advantage, always getting the most and best for the least money. It required, however, long experience to acquire this knowledge. Those who were too busy, or bought too little to gain it, took their chances and were generally unfortunate, getting the least and worst for the most money. It was the merest chance if persons not experienced in shopping received the value of their money."

"But why did you put up with such a shockingly inconvenient arrangement when you saw its faults so plainly?" Edith asked me.

"It was like all our social arrangements," I replied. "You can see their faults scarcely more plainly than we did, but we saw no remedy for them."

"Here we are at the store of our ward," said Edith, as we turned in at the great portal of one of the magnificent public buildings I had observed in my morning walk. There was nothing in the exterior aspect of the edifice to suggest a store to a representative of the nineteenth century. There was no display of goods in the great windows, or any device to advertise wares, or attract custom. Nor was there any sort of sign or legend on the front of the building to indicate the character of the business carried on there; but instead, above the portal, standing out from the front of the building, a majestic life-size group of statuary, the central figure of which was a female ideal of Plenty, with her cornucopia. Judging from the composition of the throng passing in and out, about the same proportion of the sexes among shoppers obtained as in the nineteenth century. As we entered, Edith said that there was one of these great distributing establishments in each ward of the city, so that no residence was more than five or ten minutes' walk from one of them. It was the first interior of a twentieth-century public building that I had ever beheld, and the spectacle naturally impressed me deeply. I was in a vast hall full of light, received not alone from the windows on all sides, but from the dome, the point of which was a hundred feet above. Beneath it, in the center of the hall, a magnificent fountain played, cooling the atmosphere to a delicious freshness with its spray. The walls and ceiling were frescoed in mellow tints, calculated to soften without absorbing the light which flooded the interior. Around the fountain was a space occupied with chairs and sofas, on which many persons were seated conversing. Legends on the walls all about the hall indicated to what classes of commodities the counters below were devoted. Edith directed her steps towards one of these, where samples of muslin of a bewildering variety were displayed, and proceeded to inspect them.

"Where is the clerk?" I asked, for there was no one behind the counter, and no one seemed coming to attend to the customer.

"I have no need of the clerk yet," said Edith; "I have not made my selection."

"It was the principal business of clerks to help people to make their selections in my day," I replied.

"What! To tell people what they wanted?"

"Yes; and oftener to induce them to buy what they didn't want."

"But did not ladies find that very impertinent?" Edith asked, wonderingly. "What concern could it possibly be to the clerks whether people bought or not?"

"It was their sole concern," I answered. "They were hired for the purpose of getting rid of the goods, and were expected to do their utmost, short of the use of force, to compass that end."

"Ah, yes! How stupid I am to forget!" said Edith. "The storekeeper and his clerks depended for their livelihood on selling the goods in your day. Of course that is all different now. The goods are the nation's. They are here for those who want them, and it is the business of the clerks to wait on people and take their orders; but it is not the interest of the clerk or the nation to dispose of a yard or a pound of anything to anybody who does not want it." She smiled as she added, "How exceedingly odd it must have seemed to have clerks trying to induce one to take what one did not want, or was doubtful about!"

"But even a twentieth-century clerk might make himself useful in giving you information about the goods, though he did not tease you to buy them," I suggested.

"No," said Edith, "that is not the business of the clerk. These printed cards, for which the government authorities are responsible, give us all the information we can possibly need."

I saw then that there was fastened to each sample a card containing in succinct form a complete statement of the make and materials of the goods and all its qualities, as well as price, leaving absolutely no point to hang a question on.

"The clerk has, then, nothing to say about the goods he sells?" I said.

"Nothing at all. It is not necessary that he should know or profess to know anything about them. Courtesy and accuracy in taking orders are all that are required of him."

"What a prodigious amount of lying that simple arrangement saves!" I ejaculated.

"Do you mean that all the clerks misrepresented their goods in your day?" Edith asked.

"God forbid that I should say so!" I replied, "for there were many who did not, and they were entitled to especial credit, for when one's livelihood and that of his wife and babies depended on the amount of goods he could dispose of, the temptation to deceive the customer—or let him deceive himself—was well-nigh overwhelming. But, Miss Leete, I am distracting you from your task with my talk."

"Not at all. I have made my selections." With that she touched a button, and in a moment a clerk appeared. He took down her order on a tablet with a pencil which made two copies, of which he gave one to her, and enclosing the counterpart in a small receptacle, dropped it into a transmitting tube.

"The duplicate of the order," said Edith as she turned away from the counter, after the clerk had punched the value of her purchase out of the credit card she gave him, "is given to the purchaser, so that any mistakes in filling it can be easily traced and rectified."

"You were very quick about your selections," I said. "May I ask how you knew that you might not have found something to suit you better in some of the other stores? But probably you are required to buy in your own district."

"Oh, no," she replied. "We buy where we please, though naturally most often near home. But I should have gained nothing by visiting other stores. The assortment in all is exactly the same, representing as it does in each case samples of all the varieties produced or imported by the United States. That is why one can decide quickly, and never need visit two stores."

"And is this merely a sample store? I see no clerks cutting off goods or marking bundles."

"All our stores are sample stores, except as to a few classes of articles. The goods, with these exceptions, are all at the great central warehouse of the city, to which they are shipped directly from the producers. We order from the sample and the printed statement of texture, make, and qualities. The orders are sent to the warehouse, and the goods distributed from there."

"That must be a tremendous saving of handling," I said. "By our system, the manufacturer sold to the wholesaler, the wholesaler to the retailer, and the retailer to the consumer, and the goods had to be handled each time. You avoid one handling of the goods, and eliminate the retailer altogether, with his big profit and the army of clerks it goes to support. Why, Miss Leete, this store is merely the order department of a wholesale house, with no more than a wholesaler's complement of clerks. Under our system of handling the goods, persuading the customer to buy them, cutting them off, and packing them, ten clerks would not do what one does here. The saving must be enormous."

"I suppose so," said Edith, "but of course we have never known any other way. But, Mr. West, you must not fail to ask father to take you to the central warehouse some day, where they receive the orders from the different sample houses all over the city and parcel out and send the goods to their destinations. He took me there not long ago, and it was a wonderful sight. The system is certainly perfect; for example, over yonder in that sort of cage is the dispatching clerk. The orders, as they are taken by the different departments in the store, are sent by transmitters to him. His assistants sort them and enclose each class in a carrier-box by itself. The dispatching clerk has a dozen pneumatic transmitters before him answering to the general classes of goods, each communicating with the corresponding department at the warehouse. He drops the box of orders into the tube it calls for, and in a few moments later it drops on the proper desk in the warehouse, together with all the orders of the same sort from the other sample stores. The orders are read off, recorded, and sent to be filled, like lightning. The filling I thought the most interesting part. Bales of cloth are placed on spindles and turned by machinery, and the cutter, who also has a machine, works right through one bale after another till exhausted, when another man takes his place; and it is the same with those who fill the orders in any other staple. The packages are then delivered by larger tubes to the city districts, and thence distributed to the houses. You may understand how quickly it is all done when I tell you that my order will probably be at home sooner than I could have carried it from here."

"How do you manage in the thinly settled rural districts?" I asked.

"The system is the same," Edith explained; "the village sample shops are connected by transmitters with the central county warehouse, which may be twenty miles away. The transmission is so swift, though, that the time lost on the way is trifling. But, to save expense, in many counties one set of tubes connect several villages with the warehouse, and then there is time lost waiting for one another. Sometimes it is two or three hours before goods ordered are received. It was so where I was staying last summer, and I found it quite inconvenient."*

"There must be many other respects also, no doubt, in which the country stores are inferior to the city stores," I suggested.

"No," Edith answered, "they are otherwise precisely as good. The sample shop of the smallest village, just like this one, gives you your choice of all the varieties of goods the nation has, for the county warehouse draws on the same source as the city warehouse."

As we walked home I commented on the great variety in the size and cost of the houses. "How is it," I asked, "that this difference is consistent with the fact that all citizens have the same income?"

"Because," Edith explained, "although the income is the same, personal taste determines how the individual shall spend it. Some like fine horses; others, like myself, prefer pretty clothes; and still others want an elaborate table. The rents which the nation receives for these houses vary, according to size, elegance, and location, so that everybody can find something to suit. The larger houses are usually occupied by large families, in which there are several to contribute to the rent; while small families, like ours, find smaller houses more convenient and economical. It is a matter of taste and convenience wholly. I have read that in old times people often kept up establishments and did other things which they could not afford for ostentation, to make people think them richer than they were. Was it really so, Mr. West?"

"I shall have to admit that it was," I replied.

"Well, you see, it could not be so nowadays; for everybody's income is known, and it is known that what is spent one way must be saved another."

XI

When we arrived home, Dr. Leete had not yet returned, and Mrs. Leete was not visible. "Are you fond of music, Mr. West?" Edith asked.

I assured her that it was half of life, according to my notion.

"I ought to apologize for inquiring," she said. "It is not a question that we ask one another nowadays; but I have read that in your day, even among the cultured class, there were some who did not care for music."

"You must remember, in excuse," I said, "that we had some rather absurd kinds of music."

* I am informed since the above is in type that this lack of perfection in the distributing service of some of the country districts is to be remedied, and that soon every village will have its own set of tubes.

"Yes," she said, "I know that; I am afraid I should not have fancied it all myself. Would you like to hear some of ours now, Mr. West?"

"Nothing would delight me so much as to listen to you," I said.

"To me!" she exclaimed, laughing. "Did you think I was going to play or sing to you?"

"I hoped so, certainly," I replied.

Seeing that I was a little abashed, she subdued her merriment and explained. "Of course, we all sing nowadays as a matter of course in the training of the voice, and some learn to play instruments for their private amusement; but the professional music is so much grander and more perfect than any performance of ours, and so easily commanded when we wish to hear it, that we don't think of calling our singing or playing music at all. All the really fine singers and players are in the musical service, and the rest of us hold our peace for the main part. But would you really like to hear some music?"

I assured her once more that I would.

"Come, then, into the music room," she said, and I followed her into an apartment finished, without hangings, in wood, with a floor of polished wood. I was prepared for new devices in musical instruments, but I saw nothing in the room which by any stretch of imagination could be conceived as such. It was evident that my puzzled appearance was affording intense amusement to Edith.

"Please look at today's music," she said, handing me a card, "and tell me what you would prefer. It is now five o'clock, you will remember."

The card bore the date "September 12, 2000," and contained the longest programme of music I had ever seen. It was as various as it was long, including a most extraordinary range of vocal and instrumental solos, duets, quartettes, and various orchestral combinations. I remained bewildered by the prodigious list until Edith's pink finger tip indicated a particular section of it, where several selections were bracketed, with the words "5 P.M." against them; then I observed that this prodigious programme was an all-day one, divided into twenty-four sections answering to the hours. There were but a few pieces of music in the "5 P.M." section, and I indicated an organ piece as my preference.

"I am so glad you like the organ," said she. "I think there is scarcely any music that suits my mood oftener."

She made me sit down comfortably, and, crossing the room, so far as I could see, merely touched one or two screws, and at once the room was filled with the music of a grand organ anthem; filled, not flooded, for, by some means, the volume of melody had been perfectly graduated to the size of the apartment. I listened, scarcely breathing, to the close. Such music, so perfectly rendered, I had never expected to hear.

"Grand!" I cried, as the last great wave of sound broke and ebbed away into silence. "Bach must be at the keys of that organ; but where is the organ?"

"Wait a moment, please," said Edith; "I want to have you listen to this waltz before you ask any questions. I think it is perfectly charming"; and as she spoke the sound of violins filled the room with the witchery of a summer night. When this had also ceased, she said: "There is nothing in the least mysterious about the music, as you seem to imagine. It is not made by fairies or genii, but by good, honest, and exceedingly clever human hands. We have simply carried the idea of labor saving by cooperation into our musical service as into everything else. There are a number of music rooms in the city, perfectly adapted acoustically to the different sorts of music. These halls are connected by telephone with all the houses of the city whose people care to pay the small fee, and there are none, you may be sure, who do not. The corps of musicians attached to each hall is so large that, although no individual performer, or group of performers, has more than a brief part, each day's programme lasts through the twenty-four hours. There are on that card for today, as you will see if you observe closely, distinct programmes of four of these concerts, each of a different order of music from the others, being now simultaneously performed, and any one of the four pieces now going on that you prefer, you can hear by merely pressing the button which will connect your house-wire with the hall where it is being rendered. The programmes are so coordinated that the pieces at any one time simultaneously proceeding in the different halls usually offer a choice, not only between instrumental and vocal, and between different sorts of instruments; but also between different motives from grave to gay, so that all tastes and moods can be suited."

"It appears to me, Miss Leete," I said, "that if we could have devised an arrangement for providing everybody with music in their homes, perfect in quality, unlimited in quantity, suited to every mood, and beginning and ceasing at will, we should have considered the limit of human felicity already attained, and ceased to strive for further improvements."

"I am sure I never could imagine how those among you who depended at all on music managed to endure the old-fashioned system for providing it," replied Edith. "Music really worth hearing must have been, I suppose, wholly out of the reach of the masses, and attainable by the most favored only occasionally, at great trouble, prodigious expense, and then for brief periods, arbitrarily fixed by somebody else, and in connection with all sorts of undesirable circumstances. Your concerts, for instance, and operas! How perfectly exasperating it must have been, for the sake of a piece or two of music that suited you, to have to sit for hours listening to what you did not care for! Now, at a dinner one can skip the courses one does not care for. Who would ever dine, however hungry, if required to eat everything brought on the table? And I am sure one's hearing is quite as sensitive as one's taste. I suppose it was these difficulties in the way of commanding really good music which made you endure so much playing and singing in your homes by people who had only the rudiments of the art."

"Yes," I replied, "it was that sort of music or none for most of us.

"Ah, well," Edith sighed, "when one really considers, it is not so strange that people in those days so often did not care for music. I dare say I should have detested it, too."

"Did I understand you rightly," I inquired, "that this musical programme covers the entire twenty-four hours? It seems to on this card, certainly; but who is there to listen to music between say midnight and morning?"

"Oh, many," Edith replied. "Our people keep all hours; but if the music were provided from midnight to morning for no others, it still would be for the sleepless, the sick, and the dying. All our bedchambers have a telephone attachment at the head of the bed by which any person who may be sleepless can command music at pleasure, of the sort suited to the mood."

"Is there such an arrangement in the room assigned to me?"

"Why, certainly; and how stupid, how very stupid, of me not to think to tell you of that last night! Father will show you about the adjustment before you go to bed to-night, however; and with the receiver at your ear, I am quite sure you will be able to snap your fingers at all sorts of uncanny feelings if they trouble you again."

That evening Dr. Leete asked us about our visit to the store, and in the course of the desultory comparison of the ways of the nineteenth century and the twentieth, which followed, something raised the question of inheritance. "I suppose," I said, "the inheritance of property is not now allowed."

"On the contrary," replied Dr. Leete, "there is no interference with it. In fact, you will find, Mr. West, as you come to know us, that there is far less interference of any sort with personal liberty nowadays than you were accustomed to. We require, indeed, by law that every man shall serve the nation for a fixed period, instead of leaving him his choice, as you did, between working, stealing, or starving. With the exception of this fundamental law, which is, indeed, merely a codification of the law of nature—the edict of Eden—by which it is made equal in its pressure on men, our system depends in no particular upon legislation, but is entirely voluntary, the logical outcome of the operation of human nature under rational conditions. This question of inheritance illustrates just that point. The fact that the nation is the sole capitalist and land-owner of course restricts the individual's possessions to his annual credit, and what personal and household belongings he may have procured with it. His credit, like an annuity in your day, ceases on his death, with the allowance of a fixed sum for funeral expenses. His other possessions he leaves as he pleases."

"What is to prevent, in course of time, such accumulations of valuable goods and chattels in the hands of individuals as might seriously interfere with equality in the circumstances of citizens?" I asked.

"That matter arranges itself very simply," was the reply. "Under the present organization of society, accumulations of personal property are merely burdensome the moment they exceed what adds to the real comfort. In your day, if a man had a house crammed full with gold and silver plate, rare china, expensive furniture, and such things, he was considered rich, for these things represented money, and could at any time be turned into it. Nowadays a man whom the legacies of a hundred relatives, simultaneously dying, should place in a similar position, would be considered very unlucky. The articles, not being salable, would be of no value to him except for their actual use or the enjoyment of their beauty. On the other hand, his income remaining the same, he would have to deplete his credit to hire houses to store the goods in, and still further to pay for the service of those who took care of them. You may be very sure that such a man would lose no time in scattering among his friends possessions which only made him the poorer, and that none of those friends would accept more of them than they could easily spare room for and time to attend to. You see, then, that to prohibit the inheritance of personal property with a view to prevent great accumulations would be a superfluous precaution for the nation. The individual citizen can be trusted to see that he is not overburdened. So careful is he in this respect, that the relatives usually waive claim to most of the effects of deceased friends, reserving only particular objects. The nation takes charge of the resigned chattels, and turns such as are of value into the common stock once more."

"You spoke of paying for service to take care of your houses," said I. "That suggests a question I have several times been on the point of asking. How have you disposed of the problem of domestic service? Who are willing to be domestic servants in a community where all are social equals? Our ladies found it hard enough to find such even when there was little pretense of social equality."

"It is precisely because we are all social equals whose equality nothing can compromise, and because service is honorable, in a society whose fundamental principle is that all in turn shall serve the rest, that we could easily provide a corps of domestic servants such as you never dreamed of, if we needed them," replied Dr. Leete. "But we do not need them."

"Who does your housework, then?" I asked.

"There is none to do," said Mrs. Leete, to whom I had addressed this question. "Our washing is all done at public laundries at excessively cheap rates, and our cooking at public kitchens. The making and repairing of all we wear are done outside in public shops. Electricity, of course, takes the place of all fires and lighting. We choose houses no larger than we need, and furnish them so as to involve the minimum of trouble to keep them in order. We have no use for domestic servants."

"The fact," said Dr. Leete, "that you had in the poorer classes a boundless supply of serfs on whom you could impose all sorts of painful and disagreeable tasks, made you indifferent to devices to avoid the necessity for them. But now that we all have to do in turn whatever work is done for society, every individual in the nation has the same interest, and a personal one, in devices for lightening the burden. This fact has given a prodigious impulse to labor-saving inventions in all sorts of industry, of which the combination of the maximum of comfort and minimum of trouble in household arrangements was one of the earliest results.

"In case of special emergencies in the household," pursued Dr. Leete, "such as extensive cleaning or renovation, or sickness in the family, we can always secure assistance from the industrial force."

"But how do you recompense these assistants, since you have no money?"

"We do not pay them, of course, but the nation for them. Their services can be obtained by application at the proper bureau, and their value is pricked off the credit card of the applicant."

"What a paradise for womankind the world must be now!" I exclaimed. "In my day, even wealth and unlimited servants did not enfranchise their possessors from household cares, while the women of the merely well-to-do and poorer classes lived and died martyrs to them."

"Yes," said Mrs. Leete, "I have read something of that; enough to convince me that, badly off as the men, too, were in your day, they were more fortunate than their mothers and wives."

"The broad shoulders of the nation," said Dr. Leete, "bear now like a feather the burden that broke the backs of the women of your day. Their misery came, with all your other miseries, from that incapacity for cooperation which followed from the individualism on which your social system was founded, from your inability to perceive that you could make ten times more profit out of your fellow men by uniting with them than by contending with them. The wonder is, not that you did not live more comfortably, but that you were able to live together at all, who were all confessedly bent on making one another your servants, and securing possession of one another's goods.

"There, there, father, if you are so vehement, Mr. West will think you are scolding him," laughingly interposed Edith.

"When you want a doctor," I asked, "do you simply apply to the proper bureau and take any one that may be sent?"

"That rule would not work well in the case of physicians," replied Dr. Leete. "The good a physician can do a patient depends largely on his acquaintance with his constitutional tendencies and condition. The patient must be able, therefore, to call in a particular doctor, and he does so just as patients did in your day. The only difference is that, instead of collecting his fee for himself, the doctor collects it for the nation by pricking off the amount, according to a regular scale for medical attendance, from the patient's credit card."

"I can imagine," I said, "that if the fee is always the same, and a doctor may not turn away patients, as I suppose he may not, the good doctors are called constantly and the poor doctors left in idleness."

"In the first place, if you will overlook the apparent conceit of the remark from a retired physician," replied Dr. Leete, with a smile, "we have no poor doctors. Anybody who pleases to get a little smattering of medical terms is not now at liberty to practice on the bodies of citizens, as in your day. None but students who have passed the severe tests of the schools, and clearly proved their vocation, are permitted to practice. Then, too, you will observe that there is nowadays no attempt of doctors to build up their practice at the expense of other doctors. There would be no motive for that. For the rest, the doctor has to render regular reports of his work to the medical bureau, and if he is not reasonably well employed, work is found for him."

XII

The questions which I needed to ask before I could acquire even an outline acquaintance with the institutions of the twentieth century being endless, and Dr. Leete's good-nature appearing equally so, we sat up talking for several hours after the ladies left us. Reminding my host of the point at which our talk had broken off that morning, I expressed my curiosity to learn how the organization of the industrial army was made to afford a sufficient stimulus to diligence in the lack of any anxiety on the worker's part as to his livelihood.

"You must understand in the first place," replied the doctor, "that the supply of incentives to effort is but one of the objects sought in the organization we have adopted for the army. The other, and equally important, is to secure for the file-leaders and captains of the force, and the great officers of the nation, men of proven abilities, who are pledged by their own careers to hold their followers up to their highest standard of performance and permit no lagging. With a view to these two ends the industrial army is organized. First comes the unclassified grade of common laborers, men of all work, to which all recruits during their first three years belong. This grade is a sort of school, and a very strict one, in which the young men are taught habits of obedience, subordination, and devotion to duty. While the miscellaneous nature of the work done by this force prevents the systematic grading of the workers which is afterwards possible, yet individual records are kept, and excellence receives distinction corresponding with the penalties that negligence incurs. It is not, however, policy with us to permit youthful recklessness or indiscretion, when not deeply culpable, to handicap the future careers of young men, and all who have passed through the unclassified grade without serious disgrace have an equal opportunity to choose the life employment they have most liking for. Having selected this, they enter upon it as apprentices. The length of the apprenticeship naturally differs in different occupations. At the end of it the apprentice becomes a full workman, and a member of his trade or guild. Now not only are the individual records of the apprentices for ability and industry strictly kept, and excellence distinguished by suitable distinctions, but upon the average of his record during apprenticeship the standing given the apprentice among the full workmen depends.

"While the internal organizations of different industries, mechanical and agricultural, differ according to their peculiar conditions, they agree in a general division of their workers into first, second, and third grades, according to ability, and these grades are in many cases subdivided into first and second classes. According to his standing as an apprentice a young man is assigned his place as a first, second, or third grade worker. Of course only men of unusual ability pass directly from apprenticeship into the first grade of the workers. The most fall into the lower grades, working up as they grow more experienced, at the periodical regradings. These regradings take place in each industry at intervals corresponding with the length of the apprenticeship to that industry, so that merit never need wait long to rise, nor can any rest on past achievements unless they would drop into a lower rank. One of the notable advantages of a high grading is the privilege it gives the worker in electing which of the various branches or processes of his industry he will follow as his specialty. Of course it is not intended that any of these processes shall be disproportionately arduous, but there is often much difference between them, and the privilege of election is accordingly highly prized. So far as possible, indeed, the preferences even of the poorest workmen are considered in assigning them their line of work, because not only their happiness but their usefulness is thus enhanced. While, however, the wish of the lower grade man is consulted so far as the exigencies of the service permit, he is considered only after the upper grade men have been provided for, and often he has to put up with second or third choice, or even with an arbitrary assignment when help is needed. This privilege of election attends every regrading, and when a man loses his grade he also risks having to exchange the sort of work he likes for some other less to his taste. The results of each regrading, giving the standing of every man in his industry, are gazetted in the public prints, and those who have won promotion since the last regrading receive the nation's thanks and are publicly invested with the badge of their new rank."

"What may this badge be?" I asked.

"Every industry has its emblematic device," replied Dr. Leete, "and this, in the shape of a metallic badge so small that you might not see it unless you knew where to look, is all the insignia which the men of the army wear, except where public convenience demands a distinctive uniform. This badge is the same in form for all grades of industry, but while the badge of the third grade is iron, that of the second grade is silver, and that of the first is gilt.

"Apart from the grand incentive to endeavor afforded by the fact that the high places in the nation are open only to the highest class men, and that rank in the army constitutes the only mode of social distinction for the vast majority who are not aspirants in art, literature, and the professions, various incitements of a minor, but perhaps equally effective, sort are provided in the form of special privileges and immunities in the way of discipline, which the superior class men enjoy. These, while intended to be as little as possible invidious to the less successful, have the effect of keeping constantly before every man's mind the great desirability of attaining the grade next above his own.

"It is obviously important that not only the good but also the indifferent and poor workmen should be able to cherish the ambition of rising. Indeed, the number of the latter being so much greater, it is even more essential that the ranking system should not operate to discourage them than that it should stimulate the others. It is to this end that the grades are divided into classes. The grades as well as the classes being made numerically equal at each regrading, there is not at any time, counting out the officers and the unclassified and apprentice grades, over one-ninth of the industrial army in the lowest class, and most of this number are recent apprentices, all of whom expect to rise. Those who remain during the entire term of service in the lowest class are but a trifling fraction of the industrial army, and likely to be as deficient in sensibility to their position as in ability to better it.

"It is not even necessary that a worker should win promotion to a higher grade to have at least a taste of glory. While promotion requires a general excellence of record as a worker, honorable mention and various sorts of prizes are awarded for excellence less than sufficient for promotion, and also for special feats and single performances in the various industries. There are many minor distinctions of standing, not only within the grades but within the classes, each of which acts as a spur to the efforts of a group. It is intended that no form of merit shall wholly fail of recognition.

"As for actual neglect of work, positively bad work, or other overt remissness on the part of men incapable of generous motives, the discipline of the industrial army is far too strict to allow anything whatever of the sort. A man able to do duty, and persistently refusing, is sentenced to solitary imprisonment on bread and water till he consents.

"The lowest grade of the officers of the industrial army, that of assistant foremen or lieutenants, is appointed out of men who have held their place for two years in the first class of the first grade. Where this leaves too large a range of choice, only the first group of this class are eligible. No one thus comes to the point of commanding men until he is about thirty years old. After a man becomes an officer, his rating of course no longer depends on the efficiency of his own work, but on that of his men. The foremen are appointed from among the assistant foremen, by the same exercise of discretion limited to a small eligible class. In the appointments to the still higher grades another principle is introduced, which it would take too much time to explain now.

"Of course such a system of grading as I have described would have been impracticable applied to the small industrial concerns of your day, in some of which there were hardly enough employees to have left one apiece for the classes. You must remember that, under the national organization of labor, all industries are carried on by great bodies of men, many of your farms or shops being combined as one. It is also owing solely to the vast scale on which each industry is organized, with co-ordinate establishments in every part of the country, that we are able by exchanges and transfers to fit every man so nearly with the sort of work he can do best.

"And now, Mr. West, I will leave it to you, on the bare outline of its features which I have given, if those who need special incentives to do their best are likely to lack them under our system. Does it not seem to you that men who found themselves obliged, whether they wished or not, to work, would under such a system be strongly impelled to do their best?"

I replied that it seemed to me the incentives offered were, if any objection were to be made, too strong; that the pace set for the young men was too hot; and such, indeed, I would add with deference, still remains my opinion, now that by longer residence among you I become better acquainted with the whole subject.

Dr. Leete, however, desired me to reflect, and I am ready to say that it is perhaps a sufficient reply to my objection, that the worker's livelihood is in no way dependent on his ranking, and anxiety for that never embitters his disappointments; that the working hours are short, the vacations regular, and that all emulation ceases at forty-five, with the attainment of middle life.

"There are two or three other points I ought to refer to," he added, "to prevent your getting mistaken impressions. In the first place, you must understand that this system of preferment given the more efficient workers over the less so, in no way contravenes the fundamental idea of our social system, that all who do their best are equally deserving, whether that best be great or small. I have shown that the system is arranged to encourage the weaker as well as the stronger with the hope of rising, while the fact that the stronger are selected for the leaders is in no way a reflection upon the weaker, but in the interest of the common weal.

"Do not imagine, either, because emulation is given free play as an incentive under our system, that we deem it a motive likely to appeal to the nobler sort of men, or worthy of them. Such as these find their motives within, not without, and measure their duty by their own endowments, not by those of others. So long as their achievement is proportioned to their powers, they would consider it preposterous to expect praise or blame because it chanced to be great or small. To such natures emulation appears philosophically absurd, and despicable in a moral aspect by its substitution of envy for admiration, and exultation for regret, in one's attitude toward the successes and the failures of others.

"But all men, even in the last year of the twentieth century, are not of this high order, and the incentives to endeavor requisite for those who are not must be of a sort adapted to their inferior natures. For these, then, emulation of the keenest edge is provided as a constant spur. Those who need this motive will feel it. Those who are above its influence do not need it.

"I should not fail to mention," resumed the doctor, "that for those too deficient in mental or bodily strength to be fairly graded with the main body of workers, we have a separate grade, unconnected with the others—a sort of invalid corps, the members of which are provided with a light class of tasks fitted to their strength. All our sick in mind and body, all our deaf and dumb, and lame and blind and crippled, and even our insane, belong to this invalid corps, and bear its insignia. The strongest often do nearly a man's work, the feeblest, of course, nothing; but none who can do anything are willing quite to give up. In their lucid intervals, even our insane are eager to do what they can."

"That is a pretty idea of the invalid corps," I said. "Even a barbarian from the nineteenth century can appreciate that. It is a very graceful way of disguising charity, and must be grateful to the feelings of its recipients."

"Charity!" repeated Dr. Leete. "Did you suppose that we consider the incapable class we are talking of objects of charity?"

"Why, naturally," I said, "inasmuch as they are incapable of self-support."

But here the doctor took me up quickly.

"Who is capable of self-support?" he demanded. "There is no such thing in a civilized society as self-support. In a state of society so barbarous as not even to know family cooperation, each individual may possibly support himself, though even then for a part of his life only; but from the moment that men begin to live together, and constitute even the rudest sort of society, self-support becomes impossible. As men grow more civilized, and the subdivision of occupations and services is carried out, a complex mutual dependence becomes the universal rule. Every man, however solitary may seem his occupation, is a member of a vast industrial partnership, as large as the nation, as large as humanity. The necessity of mutual dependence should imply the duty and guarantee of mutual support; and that it did not in your day constituted the essential cruelty and unreason of your system."

"That may all be so," I replied, "but it does not touch the case of those who are unable to contribute anything to the product of industry."

"Surely I told you this morning, at least I thought I did," replied Dr. Leete, "that the right of a man to maintenance at the nation's table depends on the fact that he is a man, and not on the amount of health and strength he may have, so long as he does his best."

"You said so," I answered, "but I supposed the rule applied only to the workers of different ability. Does it also hold of those who can do nothing at all?"

"Are they not also men?"

"I am to understand, then, that the lame, the blind, the sick, and the impotent, are as well off as the most efficient and have the same income?"

"Certainly," was the reply.

"The idea of charity on such a scale," I answered, "would have made our most enthusiastic philanthropists gasp."

"If you had a sick brother at home," replied Dr. Leete, "unable to work, would you feed him on less dainty food, and lodge and clothe him more poorly, than yourself? More likely far, you would give him the preference; nor would you think of calling it charity. Would not the word, in that connection, fill you with indignation?"

"Of course," I replied; "but the cases are not parallel. There is a sense, no doubt, in which all men are brothers; but this general sort of brotherhood is not to be compared, except for rhetorical purposes, to the brotherhood of blood, either as to its sentiment or its obligations."

"There speaks the nineteenth century!" exclaimed Dr. Leete. "Ah, Mr. West, there is no doubt as to the length of time that you slept. If I were to give you, in one sentence, a key to what may seem the mysteries of our civilization as compared with that of your age, I should say that it is the fact that the solidarity of the race and the brotherhood of man, which to you were but fine phrases, are, to our thinking and feeling, ties as real and as vital as physical fraternity.

"But even setting that consideration aside, I do not see why it so surprises you that those who cannot work are conceded the full right to live on the produce of those who can. Even in your day, the duty of military service for the protection of the nation, to which our industrial service corresponds, while obligatory on those able to discharge it, did not operate to deprive of the privileges of citizenship those who were unable. They stayed at home, and were protected by those who fought, and nobody questioned their right to be, or thought less of them. So, now, the requirement of industrial service from those able to render it does not operate to deprive of the privileges of citizenship, which now implies the citizen's maintenance, him who cannot work. The worker is not a citizen because he works, but works because he is a citizen. As you recognize the duty of the strong to fight for the weak, we, now that fighting is gone by, recognize his duty to work for him.

"A solution which leaves an unaccounted-for residuum is no solution at all; and our solution of the problem of human society would have been none at all had it left the lame, the sick, and the blind outside with the beasts, to fare as they might. Better far have left the strong and well unprovided for than these burdened ones, toward whom every heart must yearn, and for whom ease of mind and body should be provided, if for no others. Therefore it is, as I told you this morning, that the title of every man, woman, and child to the means of existence rests on no basis less plain, broad, and simple than the fact that they are fellows of one race-members of one human family. The only coin current is the image of God, and that is good for all we have.

"I think there is no feature of the civilization of your epoch so repugnant to modern ideas as the neglect with which you treated your dependent classes. Even if you had no pity, no feeling of brotherhood, how was it that you did not see that you were robbing the incapable class of their plain right in leaving them unprovided for?"

"I don't quite follow you there," I said. "I admit the claim of this class to our pity, but how could they who produced nothing claim a share of the product as a right?"

"How happened it," was Dr. Leete's reply, "that your workers were able to produce more than so many savages would have done? Was it not wholly on account of the heritage of the past knowledge and achievements of the race, the machinery of society, thousands of years in contriving, found by you ready-made to your hand? How did you come to be possessors of this knowledge and this machinery, which represent nine parts to one contributed by yourself in the value of your product? You inherited it, did you not? And were not these others, these unfortunate and crippled brothers whom you cast out, joint inheritors, co-heirs with you? What did you do with their share? Did you not rob them when you put them off with crusts, who were entitled to sit with the heirs, and did you not add insult to robbery when you called the crusts charity?

"Ah, Mr. West," Dr. Leete continued, as I did not respond, "what I do not understand is, setting aside all considerations either of justice or brotherly feeling toward the crippled and defective, how the workers of your day could have had any heart for their work, knowing that their children, or grand-children, if unfortunate, would be deprived of the comforts and even necessities of life. It is a mystery how men with children could favor a system under which they were rewarded beyond those less endowed with bodily strength or mental power. For, by the same discrimination by which the father profited, the son, for whom he would give his life, being perchance weaker than others, might be reduced to crusts and beggary. How men dared leave children behind them, I have never been able to understand."

Note: Although in his talk on the previous evening Dr. Leete had emphasized the pains taken to enable every man to ascertain and follow his natural bent in choosing an occupation, it was not till I learned that the worker's income is the same in all occupations that I realized how absolutely he may be counted on to do so, and thus, by selecting the harness which sets most lightly on himself, find that in which he can pull best. The failure of my age in any systematic or effective way to develop and utilize the natural aptitudes of men for the industries and intellectual avocations was one of the great wastes, as well as one of the most common causes of unhappiness in that time. The vast majority of my contemporaries, though nominally free to do so, never really chose their occupations at all, but were forced by circumstances into work for which they were relatively inefficient, because not naturally fitted for it. The rich, in this respect, had little advantage over the poor. The latter, indeed, being generally deprived of education, had no opportunity even to ascertain the natural aptitudes they might have, and on account of their poverty were unable to develop them by cultivation even when ascertained. The liberal and technical professions, except by favorable accident, were shut to them, to their own great loss and that of the nation. On the other hand, the well-to-do, although they could command education and opportunity, were scarcely less hampered by social prejudice, which forbade them to pursue manual avocations, even when adapted to them, and destined them, whether fit or unfit, to the professions, thus wasting many an excellent handicraftsman. Mercenary considerations, tempting men to pursue money-making occupations for which they were unfit, instead of less remunerative employments for which they were fit, were responsible for another vast perversion of talent. All these things now are changed. Equal education and opportunity must needs bring to light whatever aptitudes a man has, and neither social prejudices nor mercenary considerations hamper him in the choice of his life work.

XIII

As Edith had promised he should do, Dr. Leete accompanied me to my bedroom when I retired, to instruct me as to the adjustment of the musical telephone. He showed how, by turning a screw, the volume of the music could be made to fill the room, or die away to an echo so faint and far that one could scarcely be sure whether he heard or imagined it. If, of two persons side by side, one desired to listen to music and the other to sleep, it could be made audible to one and inaudible to another.

"I should strongly advise you to sleep if you can tonight, Mr. West, in preference to listening to the finest tunes in the world," the doctor said, after explaining these points. "In the trying experience you are just now passing through, sleep is a nerve tonic for which there is no substitute."

Mindful of what had happened to me that very morning, I promised to heed his counsel.

"Very well," he said, "then I will set the telephone at eight o'clock."

"What do you mean?" I asked.

He explained that, by a clockwork combination, a person could arrange to be awakened at any hour by the music.

It began to appear, as has since fully proved to be the case, that I had left my tendency to insomnia behind me with the other discomforts of existence in the nineteenth century; for though I took no sleeping draught this time, yet, as the night before, I had no sooner touched the pillow than I was asleep.

I dreamed that I sat on the throne of the Abencerrages in the banqueting hall of the Alhambra, feasting my lords and generals, who next day were to follow the crescent against the Christian dogs of Spain. The air, cooled by the spray of fountains, was heavy with the scent of flowers. A band of nautch girls, round-limbed and luscious-lipped, danced with voluptuous grace to the music of brazen and stringed instruments. Looking up to the latticed galleries, one caught a gleam now and then from the eye of some beauty of the royal harem, looking down upon the assembled flower of Moorish chivalry. Louder and louder clashed the cymbals, wilder and wilder grew the strain, till the blood of the desert race could no longer resist the martial delirium, and the swart nobles leaped to their feet; a thousand scimitars were bared, and the cry, "Allah il Allah!" shook the hall and awoke me, to find it broad daylight, and the room tingling with the electric music of the "Turkish Reveille."

At the breakfast-table, when I told my host of my morning's experience, I learned that it was not a mere chance that the piece of music which awakened me was a reveille. The airs played at one of the halls during the waking hours of the morning were always of an inspiring type.

"By the way," I said, "I have not thought to ask you anything about the state of Europe. Have the societies of the Old World also been remodeled?"

"Yes," replied Dr. Leete, "the great nations of Europe as well as Australia, Mexico, and parts of South America, are now organized industrially like the United States, which was the pioneer of the evolution. The peaceful relations of these nations are assured by a loose form of federal union of worldwide extent. An international council regulates the mutual intercourse and commerce of the members of the union and their joint policy toward the more backward races, which are gradually being educated up to civilized institutions. Complete autonomy within its own limits is enjoyed by every nation."

"How do you carry on commerce without money?" I said. "In trading with other nations, you must use some sort of money, although you dispense with it in the internal affairs of the nation."

"Oh, no; money is as superfluous in our foreign as in our internal relations. When foreign commerce was conducted by private enterprise, money was necessary to adjust it on account of the multifarious complexity of the transactions; but nowadays it is a function of the nations as units. There are thus only a dozen or so merchants in the world, and their business being supervised by the international council, a simple system of book accounts serves perfectly to regulate their dealings. Customs duties of every sort are of course superfluous. A nation simply does not import what its government does not think requisite for the general interest. Each nation has a bureau of foreign exchange, which manages its trading. For example, the American bureau, estimating such and such quantities of French goods necessary to America for a given year, sends the order to the French bureau, which in turn sends its order to our bureau. The same is done mutually by all the nations."

"But how are the prices of foreign goods settled, since there is no competition?"

"The price at which one nation supplies another with goods," replied Dr. Leete, "must be that at which it supplies its own citizens. So you see there is no danger of misunderstanding. Of course no nation is theoretically bound to supply another with the product of its own labor, but it is for the interest of all to exchange some commodities. If a nation is regularly supplying another with certain goods, notice is required from either side of any important change in the relation."

"But what if a nation, having a monopoly of some natural product, should refuse to supply it to the others, or to one of them?"

"Such a case has never occurred, and could not without doing the refusing party vastly more harm than the others," replied Dr. Leete. "In the fist place, no favoritism could be legally shown. The law requires that each nation shall deal with the others, in all respects, on exactly the same footing. Such a course as you suggest would cut off the nation adopting it from the remainder of the earth for all purposes whatever. The contingency is one that need not give us much anxiety."

"But," said I, "supposing a nation, having a natural monopoly in some product of which it exports more than it consumes, should put the price away up, and thus, without cutting off the supply, make a profit out of its neighbors' necessities? Its own citizens would of course have to pay the higher price on that commodity, but as a body would make more out of foreigners than they would be out of pocket themselves."

"When you come to know how prices of all commodities are determined nowadays, you will perceive how impossible it is that they could be altered, except with reference to the amount or arduousness of the work required respectively to produce them," was Dr. Leete's reply. "This principle is an international as well as a national guarantee; but even without it the sense of community of interest, international as well as national, and the conviction of the folly of selfishness, are too deep nowadays to render possible such a piece of sharp practice as you apprehend. You must understand that we all look forward to an eventual unification of the world as one nation. That, no doubt, will be the ultimate form of society, and will realize certain economic advantages over the present federal system of autonomous nations. Meanwhile, however, the present system works so nearly perfectly that we are quite content to leave to posterity the completion of the scheme. There are, indeed, some who hold that it never will be completed, on the ground that the federal plan is not merely a provisional solution of the problem of human society, but the best ultimate solution."

"How do you manage," I asked, "when the books of any two nations do not balance? Supposing we import more from France than we export to her."

"At the end of each year," replied the doctor, "the books of every nation are examined. If France is found in our debt, probably we are in the debt of some nation which owes France, and so on with all the nations. The balances that remain after the accounts have been cleared by the international council should not be large under our system. Whatever they may be, the council requires them to be settled every few years, and may require their settlement at any time if they are getting too large; for it is not intended that any nation shall run largely in debt to another, lest feelings unfavorable to amity should be engendered. To guard further against this, the international council inspects the commodities interchanged by the nations, to see that they are of perfect quality."

"But what are the balances finally settled with, seeing that you have no money?"

"In national staples; a basis of agreement as to what staples shall be accepted, and in what proportions, for settlement of accounts, being a preliminary to trade relations."

"Emigration is another point I want to ask you about," said I. "With every nation organized as a close industrial partnership, monopolizing all means of production in the country, the emigrant, even if he were permitted to land, would starve. I suppose there is no emigration nowadays."

"On the contrary, there is constant emigration, by which I suppose you mean removal to foreign countries for permanent residence," replied Dr. Leete. "It is arranged on a simple international arrangement of indemnities. For example, if a man at twenty-one emigrates from England to America, England loses all the expense of his maintenance and education, and America gets a workman for nothing. America accordingly makes England an allowance. The same principle, varied to suit the case, applies generally. If the man is near the term of his labor when he emigrates, the country receiving him has the allowance. As to imbecile persons, it is deemed best that each nation should be responsible for its own, and the emigration of such must be under full guarantees of support by his own nation. Subject to these regulations, the right of any man to emigrate at any time is unrestricted."

"But how about mere pleasure trips; tours of observation? How can a stranger travel in a country whose people do not receive money, and are themselves supplied with the means of life on a basis not extended to him? His own credit card cannot, of course, be good in other lands. How does he pay his way?"

"An American credit card," replied Dr. Leete, "is just as good in Europe as American gold used to be, and on precisely the same condition, namely, that it be exchanged into the currency of the country you are traveling in. An American in Berlin takes his credit card to the local office of the international council, and receives in exchange for the whole or part of it a German credit card, the amount being charged against the United States in favor of Germany on the international account."

"Perhaps Mr. West would like to dine at the Elephant today," said Edith, as we left the table.

"That is the name we give to the general dining-house in our ward," explained her father. "Not only is our cooking done at the public kitchens, as I told you last night, but the service and quality of the meals are much more satisfactory if taken at the dining-house. The two minor meals of the day are usually taken at home, as not worth the trouble of going out; but it is general to go out to dine. We have not done so since you have been with us, from a notion that it would be better to wait till you had become a little more familiar with our ways. What do you think? Shall we take dinner at the dining-house today?"

I said that I should be very much pleased to do so.

Not long after, Edith came to me, smiling, and said:

"Last night, as I was thinking what I could do to make you feel at home until you came to be a little more used to us and our ways, an idea occurred to me. What would you say if I were to introduce you to some very nice people of your own times, whom I am sure you used to be well acquainted with?"

I replied, rather vaguely, that it would certainly be very agreeable, but I did not see how she was going to manage it.

"Come with me," was her smiling reply, "and see if I am not as good as my word."

My susceptibility to surprise had been pretty well exhausted by the numerous shocks it had received, but it was with some wonderment that I followed her into a room which I had not before entered. It was a small, cozy apartment, walled with cases filled with books.

"Here are your friends," said Edith, indicating one of the cases, and as my eye glanced over the names on the backs of the volumes, Shakespeare, Milton, Wordsworth, Shelley, Tennyson, Defoe, Dickens, Thackeray, Hugo, Hawthorne, Irving, and a score of other great writers of my time and all time, I understood her meaning. She had indeed made good her promise in a sense compared with which its literal fulfillment would have been a disappointment. She had introduced me to a circle of friends whom the century that had elapsed since last I communed with them had aged as little as it had myself. Their spirit was as high, their wit as keen, their laughter and their tears as contagious, as when their speech had whiled away the hours of a former century. Lonely I was not and could not be more, with this goodly companionship, however wide the gulf of years that gaped between me and my old life.

"You are glad I brought you here," exclaimed Edith, radiant, as she read in my face the success of her experiment. "It was a good idea, was it not, Mr. West? How stupid in me not to think of it before! I will leave you now with your old friends, for I know there will be no company for you like them just now; but remember you must not let old friends make you quite forget new ones!" and with that smiling caution she left me.

Attracted by the most familiar of the names before me, I laid my hand on a volume of Dickens, and sat down to read. He had been my prime favorite among the bookwriters of the century—I mean the nineteenth century—and a week had rarely passed in my old life during which I had not taken up some volume of his works to while away an idle hour. Any volume with which I had been familiar would have produced an extraordinary impression, read under my present circumstances, but my exceptional familiarity with Dickens, and his consequent power to call up the associations of my former life, gave to his writings an effect no others could have had, to intensify, by force of contrast, my appreciation of the strangeness of my present environment. However new and astonishing one's surroundings, the tendency is to become a part of them so soon that almost from the first the power to see them objectively and fully measure their strangeness, is lost. That power, already dulled in my case, the pages of Dickens restored by carrying me back through their associations to the standpoint of my former life.

With a clearness which I had not been able before to attain, I saw now the past and present, like contrasting pictures, side by side.

The genius of the great novelist of the nineteenth century, like that of Homer, might indeed defy time; but the setting of his pathetic tales, the misery of the poor, the wrongs of power, the pitiless cruelty of the system of society, had passed away as utterly as Circe and the sirens, Charybdis and Cyclops.

During the hour or two that I sat there with Dickens open before me, I did not actually read more than a couple of pages. Every paragraph, every phrase, brought up some new aspect of the world-transformation which had taken place, and led my thoughts on long and widely ramifying excursions. As meditating thus in Dr. Leete's library I gradually attained a more clear and coherent idea of the prodigious spectacle which I had been so strangely enabled to view, I was filled with a deepening wonder at the seeming capriciousness of the fate that had given to one who so little deserved it, or seemed in any way set apart for it, the power alone among his contemporaries to stand upon the earth in this latter day. I had neither foreseen the new world nor toiled for it, as many about me had done regardless of the scorn of fools or the misconstruction of the good. Surely it would have been more in accordance with the fitness of things had one of those prophetic and strenuous souls been enabled to see the travail of his soul and be satisfied; he, for example, a thousand times rather than I, who, having beheld in a vision the world I looked on, sang of it in words that again and again, during these last wondrous days, had rung in my mind:

For I dipped into the future, far as human eye could see,
Saw the vision of the world, and all the wonder that would be;
Till the war-drum throbbed no longer, and the battle-flags were furled.
In the Parliament of man, the Federation of the world.

Then the common sense of most shall hold a fretful realm in awe,
And the kindly earth shall slumber, lapped in universal law.
Yet I doubt not through the ages one increasing purpose runs,
And the thoughts of men are widened with the process of the suns.*

* Tennyson, "Locksley Hall"

What though, in his old age, he momentarily lost faith in his own prediction, as prophets in their hours of depression and doubt generally do; the words had remained eternal testimony to the seership of a poet's heart, the insight that is given to faith.

I was still in the library when some hours later Dr. Leete sought me there. "Edith told me of her idea," he said, "and I thought it an excellent one. I had a little curiosity what writer you would first turn to. Ah, Dickens! You admired him, then! That is where we moderns agree with you. Judged by our standards, he overtops all the writers of his age, not because his literary genius was highest, but because his great heart beat for the poor, because he made the cause of the victims of society his own, and devoted his pen to exposing its cruelties and shams. No man of his time did so much as he to turn men's minds to the wrong and wretchedness of the old order of things, and open their eyes to the necessity of the great change that was coming, although he himself did not clearly foresee it."

XIV

A heavy rainstorm came up during the day, and I had concluded that the condition of the streets would be such that my hosts would have to give up the idea of going out to dinner, although the dining hall I had understood to be quite near. I was much surprised when at the dinner hour the ladies appeared prepared to go out, but without either rubbers or umbrellas.

The mystery was explained when we found ourselves on the street, for a continuous waterproof covering had been let down so as to enclose the sidewalk and turn it into a well lighted and perfectly dry corridor, which was filled with a stream of ladies and gentlemen dressed for dinner. At the comers the entire open space was similarly roofed in. Edith Leete, with whom I walked, seemed much interested in learning what appeared to be entirely new to her, that in the stormy weather the streets of the Boston of my day had been impassable, except to persons protected by umbrellas, boots, and heavy clothing. "Were sidewalk coverings not used at all?" she asked. They were used, I explained, but in a scattered and utterly unsystematic way, being private enterprises. She said to me that at the present time all the streets were provided against inclement weather in the manner I saw, the apparatus being rolled out of the way when it was unnecessary. She intimated that it would be considered an extraordinary imbecility to permit the weather to have any effect on the social movements of the people.

Dr. Leete, who was walking ahead, overhearing something of our talk, turned to say that the difference between the age of individualism and that of concert was well characterized by the fact that, in the nineteenth century, when it rained, the people of Boston put up three hundred thousand umbrellas over as many heads, and in the twentieth century they put up one umbrella over all the heads.

As we walked on, Edith said, "The private umbrella is father's favorite figure to illustrate the old way when everybody lived for himself and his family. There is a nineteenth century painting at the Art Gallery representing a crowd of people in the rain, each one holding his umbrella over himself and his wife, and giving his neighbors the drippings, which he claims must have been meant by the artist as a satire on his times."

We now entered a large building into which a stream of people was pouring. I could not see the front, owing to the awning, but, if in correspondence with the interior, which was even finer than the store I visited the day before, it would have been magnificent. My companion said that the sculptured group over the entrance was especially admired. Going up a grand staircase we walked some distance along a broad corridor with many doors opening upon it. At one of these, which bore my host's name, we turned in, and I found myself in an elegant dining-room containing a table for four. Windows opened on a courtyard where a fountain played to a great height and music made the air electric.

"You seem at home here," I said, as we seated ourselves at table, and Dr. Leete touched an annunciator.

"This is, in fact, a part of our house, slightly detached from the rest," he replied. "Every family in the ward has a room set apart in this great building for its permanent and exclusive use for a small annual rental. For transient guests and individuals there is accommodation on another floor. If we expect to dine here, we put in our orders the night before, selecting anything in market, according to the daily reports in the papers. The meal is as expensive or as simple as we please, though of course everything is vastly cheaper as well as better than it would be prepared at home. There is actually nothing which our people take more interest in than the perfection of the catering and cooking done for them, and I admit that we are a little vain of the success that has been attained by this branch of the service. Ah, my dear Mr. West, though other aspects of your civilization were more tragical, I can imagine that none could have been more depressing than the poor dinners you had to eat, that is, all of you who had not great wealth."

"You would have found none of us disposed to disagree with you on that point," I said.

The waiter, a fine-looking young fellow, wearing a slightly distinctive uniform, now made his appearance. I observed him closely, as it was the first time I had been able to study particularly the bearing of one of the enlisted members of the industrial army. This young man, I knew from what I had been told, must be highly educated, and the equal, socially and in all respects, of those he served. But it was perfectly evident that to neither side was the situation in the slightest degree embarrassing. Dr. Leete addressed the young man in a tone devoid, of course, as any gentleman's would be, of superciliousness, but at the same time not in any way deprecatory, while the manner of the young man was simply that of a person intent on discharging correctly the task he was engaged in, equally without familiarity or obsequiousness. It was, in fact, the manner of a soldier on duty, but without the military stiffness. As the youth left the room, I said, "I cannot get over my wonder at seeing a young man like that serving so contentedly in a menial position."

"What is that word 'menial'? I never heard it," said Edith.

"It is obsolete now," remarked her father. "If I understand it rightly, it applied to persons who performed particularly disagreeable and unpleasant tasks for others, and carried with it an implication of contempt. Was it not so, Mr. West?"

"That is about it," I said. "Personal service, such as waiting on tables, was considered menial, and held in such contempt, in my day, that persons of culture and refinement would suffer hardship before condescending to it."

"What a strangely artificial idea," exclaimed Mrs. Leete wonderingly.

"And yet these services had to be rendered," said Edith.

"Of course," I replied. "But we imposed them on the poor, and those who had no alternative but starvation."

"And increased the burden you imposed on them by adding your contempt," remarked Dr. Leete.

"I don't think I clearly understand," said Edith. "Do you mean that you permitted people to do things for you which you despised them for doing, or that you accepted services from them which you would have been unwilling to render them? You can't surely mean that, Mr. West?"

I was obliged to tell her that the fact was just as she had stated. Dr. Leete, however, came to my relief.

"To understand why Edith is surprised," he said, "you must know that nowadays it is an axiom of ethics that to accept a service from another which we would be unwilling to return in kind, if need were, is like borrowing with the intention of not repaying, while to enforce such a service by taking advantage of the poverty or necessity of a person would be an outrage like forcible robbery. It is the worst thing about any system which divides men, or allows them to be divided, into classes and castes, that it weakens the sense of a common humanity. Unequal distribution of wealth, and, still more effectually, unequal opportunities of education and culture, divided society in your day into classes which in many respects regarded each other as distinct races. There is not, after all, such a difference as might appear between our ways of looking at this question of service. Ladies and gentlemen of the cultured class in your day would no more have permitted persons of their own class to render them services they would scorn to return than we would permit anybody to do so. The poor and the uncultured, however, they looked upon as of another kind from themselves. The equal wealth and equal opportunities of culture which all persons now enjoy have simply made us all members of one class, which corresponds to the most fortunate class with you. Until this equality of condition had come to pass, the idea of the solidarity of humanity, the brotherhood of all men, could never have become the real conviction and practical principle of action it is nowadays. In your day the same phrases were indeed used, but they were phrases merely."

"Do the waiters, also, volunteer?"

"No," replied Dr. Leete. "The waiters are young men in the unclassified grade of the industrial army who are assignable to all sorts of miscellaneous occupations not requiring special skill. Waiting on table is one of these, and every young recruit is given a taste of it. I myself served as a waiter for several months in this very dining-house some forty years ago. Once more you must remember that there is recognized no sort of difference between the dignity of the different sorts of work required by the nation. The individual is never regarded, nor regards himself, as the servant of those he serves, nor is he in any way dependent upon them. It is always the nation which he is serving. No difference is recognized between a waiter's functions and those of any other worker. The fact that his is a personal service is indifferent from our point of view. So is a doctor's. I should as soon expect our waiter today to look down on me because I served him as a doctor, as think of looking down on him because he serves me as a waiter."

After dinner my entertainers conducted me about the building, of which the extent, the magnificent architecture and richness of embellishment, astonished me. It seemed that it was not merely a dining hall, but likewise a great pleasure-house and social rendezvous of the quarter, and no appliance of entertainment or recreation seemed lacking.

"You find illustrated here," said Dr. Leete, when I had expressed my admiration, "what I said to you in our first conversation, when you were looking out over the city, as to the splendor of our public and common life as compared with the simplicity of our private and home life, and the contrast which, in this respect, the twentieth bears to the nineteenth century. To save ourselves useless burdens, we have as little gear about us at home as is consistent with comfort, but the social side of our life is ornate and luxurious beyond anything the world ever knew before. All the industrial and professional guilds have clubhouses as extensive as this, as well as country, mountain, and seaside houses for sport and rest in vacations."

Note: In the latter part of the nineteenth century it became a practice of needy young men at some of the colleges of the country to earn a little money for their term bills by serving as waiters on tables at hotels during the long summer vacation. It was claimed, in reply to critics who expressed the prejudices of the time in asserting that persons voluntarily following such an occupation could not be gentlemen, that they were entitled to praise for vindicating, by their example, the dignity of all honest and necessary labor. The use of this argument illustrates a common confusion in thought on the part of my former contemporaries. The business of waiting on tables was in no more need of defense than most of the other ways of getting a living in that day, but to talk of dignity attaching to labor of any sort under the system then prevailing was absurd. There is no way in which selling labor for the highest price it will fetch is more dignified than selling goods for what can be got. Both were commercial transactions to be judged by the commercial standard. By setting a price in money on his service, the worker accepted the money measure for it, and renounced all clear claim to be judged by any other. The sordid taint which this necessity imparted to the noblest and the highest sorts of service was bitterly resented by generous souls, but there was no evading it. There was no exemption, however transcendent the quality of one's service, from the necessity of haggling for its price in the market-place. The physician must sell his healing and the apostle his preaching like the rest. The prophet, who had guessed the meaning of God, must dicker for the price of the revelation, and the poet hawk his visions in printers' row. If I were asked to name the most distinguishing felicity of this age, as compared to that in which I first saw the light, I should say that to me it seems to consist in the dignity you have given to labor by refusing to set a price upon it and abolishing the market-place forever. By requiring of every man his best you have made God his task-master, and by making honor the sole reward of achievement you have imparted to all service the distinction peculiar in my day to the soldier's.

XV

When, in the course of our tour of inspection, we came to the library, we succumbed to the temptation of the luxurious leather chairs with which it was furnished, and sat down in one of the book-lined alcoves to rest and chat awhile.*

"Edith tells me that you have been in the library all the morning," said

* I cannot sufficiently celebrate the glorious liberty that reigns in the public libraries of the twentieth century as compared with the intolerable management of those of the nineteenth century, in which the books were jealously railed away from the people, and obtainable only at an expenditure of time and red tape calculated to discourage any ordinary taste for literature.

Mrs. Leete. "Do you know, it seems to me, Mr. West, that you are the most enviable of mortals."

"I should like to know just why," I replied.

"Because the books of the last hundred years will be new to you," she answered. "You will have so much of the most absorbing literature to read as to leave you scarcely time for meals these five years to come. Ah, what would I give if I had not already read Berrian's novels."

"Or Nesmyth's, mamma," added Edith.

"Yes, or Oates' poems, or 'Past and Present,' or, 'In the Beginning,' or—oh, I could name a dozen books, each worth a year of one's life," declared Mrs. Leete, enthusiastically.

"I judge, then, that there has been some notable literature produced in this century."

"Yes," said Dr. Leete. "It has been an era of unexampled intellectual splendor. Probably humanity never before passed through a moral and material evolution, at once so vast in its scope and brief in its time of accomplishment, as that from the old order to the new in the early part of this century. When men came to realize the greatness of the felicity which had befallen them, and that the change through which they had passed was not merely an improvement in details of their condition, but the rise of the race to a new plane of existence with an illimitable vista of progress, their minds were affected in all their faculties with a stimulus, of which the outburst of the mediaeval renaissance offers a suggestion but faint indeed. There ensued an era of mechanical invention, scientific discovery, art, musical and literary productiveness to which no previous age of the world offers anything comparable."

"By the way," said I, "talking of literature, how are books published now? Is that also done by the nation?"

"Certainly."

"But how do you manage it? Does the government publish everything that is brought it as a matter of course, at the public expense, or does it exercise a censorship and print only what it approves?"

"Neither way. The printing department has no censorial powers. It is bound to print all that is offered it, but prints it only on condition that the author defray the first cost out of his credit. He must pay for the privilege of the public ear, and if he has any message worth hearing we consider that he will be glad to do it. Of course, if incomes were unequal, as in the old times, this rule would enable only the rich to be authors, but the resources of citizens being equal, it merely measures the strength of the author's motive. The cost of an edition of an average book can be saved out of a year's credit by the practice of economy and some sacrifices. The book, on being published, is placed on sale by the nation."

"The author receiving a royalty on the sales as with us, I suppose," I suggested.

"Not as with you, certainly," replied Dr. Leete, "but nevertheless in one way. The price of every book is made up of the cost of its publication with a royalty for the author. The author fixes this royalty at any figure he pleases. Of course if he puts it unreasonably high it is his own loss, for the book will not sell. The amount of this royalty is set to his credit and he is discharged from other service to the nation for so long a period as this credit at the rate of allowance for the support of citizens shall suffice to support him. If his book be moderately successful, he has thus a furlough for several months, a year, two or three years, and if he in the mean time produces other successful work, the remission of service is extended so far as the sale of that may justify. An author of much acceptance succeeds in supporting himself by his pen during the entire period of service, and the degree of any writer's literary ability, as determined by the popular voice, is thus the measure of the opportunity given him to devote his time to literature. In this respect the outcome of our system is not very dissimilar to that of yours, but there are two notable differences. In the first place, the universally high level of education nowadays gives the popular verdict a conclusiveness on the real merit of literary work which in your day it was as far as possible from having. In the second place, there is no such thing now as favoritism of any sort to interfere with the recognition of true merit. Every author has precisely the same facilities for bringing his work before the popular tribunal. To judge from the complaints of the writers of your day, this absolute equality of opportunity would have been greatly prized."

"In the recognition of merit in other fields of original genius, such as music, art, invention, design," I said, "I suppose you follow a similar principle."

"Yes," he replied, "although the details differ. In art, for example, as in literature, the people are the sole judges. They vote upon the acceptance of statues and paintings for the public buildings, and their favorable verdict carries with it the artist's remission from other tasks to devote himself to his vocation. On copies of his work disposed of, he also derives the same advantage as the author on sales of his books. In all these lines of original genius the plan pursued is the same to offer a free field to aspirants, and as soon as exceptional talent is recognized to release it from all trammels and let it have free course. The remission of other service in these cases is not intended as a gift or reward, but as the means of obtaining more and higher service. Of course there are various literary, art, and scientific institutes to which membership comes to the famous and is greatly prized. The highest of all honors in the nation, higher than the presidency, which calls merely for good sense and devotion to duty, is the red ribbon awarded by the vote of the people to the great authors, artists, engineers, physicians, and inventors of the generation. Not over a certain number wear it at any one time, though every bright young fellow in the country loses innumerable nights' sleep dreaming of it. I even did myself."

"Just as if mamma and I would have thought any more of you with it," exclaimed Edith; "not that it isn't, of course, a very fine thing to have."

"You had no choice, my dear, but to take your father as you found him and make the best of him," Dr. Leete replied; "but as for your mother, there, she would never have had me if I had not assured her that I was bound to get the red ribbon or at least the blue."

On this extravagance Mrs. Leete's only comment was a smile.

"How about periodicals and newspapers?" I said. "I won't deny that your book publishing system is a considerable improvement on ours, both as to its tendency to encourage a real literary vocation, and, quite as important, to discourage mere scribblers; but I don't see how it can be made to apply to magazines and newspapers. It is very well to make a man pay for publishing a book, because the expense will be only occasional; but no man could afford the expense of publishing a newspaper every day in the year. It took the deep pockets of our private capitalists to do that, and often exhausted even them before the returns came in. If you have newspapers at all, they must, I fancy, be published by the government at the public expense, with government editors, reflecting government opinions. Now, if your system is so perfect that there is never anything to criticize in the conduct of affairs, this arrangement may answer. Otherwise I should think the lack of an independent unofficial medium for the expression of public opinion would have most unfortunate results. Confess, Dr. Leete, that a free newspaper press, with all that it implies, was a redeeming incident of the old system when capital was in private hands, and that you have to set off the loss of that against your gains in other respects."

"I am afraid I can't give you even that consolation," replied Dr. Leete, laughing. "In the first place, Mr. West, the newspaper press is by no means the only or, as we look at it, the best vehicle for serious criticism of public affairs. To us, the judgments of your newspapers on such themes seem generally to have been crude and flippant, as well as deeply tinctured with prejudice and bitterness. In so far as they may be taken as expressing public opinion, they give an unfavorable impression of the popular intelligence, while so far as they may have formed public opinion, the nation was not to be felicitated. Nowadays, when a citizen desires to make a serious impression upon the public mind as to any aspect of public affairs, he comes out with a book or pamphlet, published as other books are. But this is not because we lack newspapers and magazines, or that they lack the most absolute freedom. The newspaper press is organized so as to be a more perfect expression of public opinion than it possibly could be in your day, when private capital controlled and managed it primarily as a money-making business, and secondarily only as a mouthpiece for the people."

"But," said I, "if the government prints the papers at the public expense, how can it fail to control their policy? Who appoints the editors, if not the government?"

"The government does not pay the expense of the papers, nor appoint their editors, nor in any way exert the slightest influence on their policy," replied Dr. Leete. "The people who take the paper pay the expense of its publication, choose its editor, and remove him when unsatisfactory. You will scarcely say, I think, that such a newspaper press is not a free organ of popular opinion."

"Decidedly I shall not," I replied, "but how is it practicable?"

"Nothing could be simpler. Supposing some of my neighbors or myself think we ought to have a newspaper reflecting our opinions, and devoted especially to our locality, trade, or profession. We go about among the people till we get the names of such a number that their annual subscriptions will meet the cost of the paper, which is little or big according to the largeness of its constituency. The amount of the subscriptions marked off the credits of the citizens guarantees the nation against loss in publishing the paper, its business, you understand, being that of a publisher purely, with no option to refuse the duty required. The subscribers to the paper now elect somebody as editor, who, if he accepts the office, is discharged from other service during his incumbency. Instead of paying a salary to him, as in your day, the subscribers pay the nation an indemnity equal to the cost of his support for taking him away from the general service. He manages the paper just as one of your editors did, except that he has no counting-room to obey, or interests of private capital as against the public good to defend. At the end of the first year, the subscribers for the next either re-elect the former editor or choose any one else to his place. An able editor, of course, keeps his place indefinitely. As the subscription list enlarges, the funds of the paper increase, and it is improved by the securing of more and better contributors, just as your papers were."

"How is the staff of contributors recompensed, since they cannot be paid in money?"

"The editor settles with them the price of their wares. The amount is transferred to their individual credit from the guarantee credit of the paper, and a remission of service is granted the contributor for a length of time corresponding to the amount credited him, just as to other authors. As to magazines, the system is the same. Those interested in the prospectus of a new periodical pledge enough subscriptions to run it for a year; select their editor, who recompenses his contributors just as in the other case, the printing bureau furnishing the necessary force and material for publication, as a matter of course. When an editor's services are no longer desired, if he cannot earn the right to his time by other literary work, he simply resumes his place in the industrial army. I should add that, though ordinarily the editor is elected only at the end of the year, and as a rule is continued in office for a term of years, in case of any sudden change he should give to the tone of the paper, provision is made for taking the sense of the subscribers as to his removal at any time."

"However earnestly a man may long for leisure for purposes of study or meditation," I remarked, "he cannot get out of the harness, if I understand you rightly, except in these two ways you have mentioned. He must either by literary, artistic, or inventive productiveness indemnify the nation for the loss of his services, or must get a sufficient number of other people to contribute to such an indemnity."

"It is most certain," replied Dr. Leete, "that no able-bodied man nowadays can evade his share of work and live on the toil of others, whether he calls himself by the fine name of student or confesses to being simply lazy. At the same time our system is elastic enough to give free play to every instinct of human nature which does not aim at dominating others or living on the fruit of others' labor. There is not only the remission by indemnification but the remission by abnegation. Any man in his thirty-third year, his term of service being then half done, can obtain an honorable discharge from the army, provided he accepts for the rest of his life one half the rate of maintenance other citizens receive. It is quite possible to live on this amount, though one must forego the luxuries and elegancies of life, with some, perhaps, of its comforts."

When the ladies retired that evening, Edith brought me a book and said:

"If you should be wakeful to-night, Mr. West, you might be interested in looking over this story by Berrian. It is considered his masterpiece, and will at least give you an idea what the stories nowadays are like."

I sat up in my room that night reading "Penthesilia" till it grew gray in the east, and did not lay it down till I had finished it. And yet let no admirer of the great romancer of the twentieth century resent my saying that at the first reading what most impressed me was not so much what was in the book as what was left out of it. The story-writers of my day would have deemed the making of bricks without straw a light task compared with the construction of a romance from which should be excluded all effects drawn from the contrasts of wealth and poverty, education and ignorance, coarseness and refinement, high and low, all motives drawn from social pride and ambition, the desire of being richer or the fear of being poorer, together with sordid anxieties of any sort for one's self or others; a romance in which there should, indeed, be love galore, but love unfretted by artificial barriers created by differences of station or possessions, owning no other law but that of the heart. The reading of "Penthesilia" was of more value than almost any amount of explanation would have been in giving me something like a general impression of the social aspect of the twentieth century. The information Dr. Leete had imparted was indeed extensive as to facts, but they had affected my mind as so many separate impressions, which I had as yet succeeded but imperfectly in making cohere. Berrian put them together for me in a picture.

XVI

Next morning I rose somewhat before the breakfast hour. As I descended the stairs, Edith stepped into the hall from the room which had been the scene of the morning interview between us described some chapters back.

"Ah!" she exclaimed, with a charmingly arch expression, "you thought to slip out unbeknown for another of those solitary morning rambles which have such nice effects on you. But you see I am up too early for you this time. You are fairly caught."

"You discredit the efficacy of your own cure," I said, "by supposing that such a ramble would now be attended with bad consequences."

"I am very glad to hear that," she said. "I was in here arranging some flowers for the breakfast table when I heard you come down, and fancied I detected something surreptitious in your step on the stairs."

"You did me injustice," I replied. "I had no idea of going out at all."

Despite her effort to convey an impression that my interception was purely accidental, I had at the time a dim suspicion of what I afterwards learned to be the fact, namely, that this sweet creature, in pursuance of her self-assumed guardianship over me, had risen for the last two or three mornings at an unheard-of hour, to insure against the possibility of my wandering off alone in case I should be affected as on the former occasion. Receiving permission to assist her in making up the breakfast bouquet, I followed her into the room from which she had emerged.

"Are you sure," she asked, "that you are quite done with those terrible sensations you had that morning?"

"I can't say that I do not have times of feeling decidedly queer," I replied, "moments when my personal identity seems an open question. It would be too much to expect after my experience that I should not have such sensations occasionally, but as for being carried entirely off my feet, as I was on the point of being that morning, I think the danger is past."

"I shall never forget how you looked that morning," she said.

"If you had merely saved my life," I continued, "I might, perhaps, find words to express my gratitude, but it was my reason you saved, and there are no words that would not belittle my debt to you." I spoke with emotion, and her eyes grew suddenly moist.

"It is too much to believe all this," she said, "but it is very delightful to hear you say it. What I did was very little. I was very much distressed for you, I know. Father never thinks anything ought to astonish us when it can be explained scientifically, as I suppose this long sleep of yours can be, but even to fancy myself in your place makes my head swim. I know that I could not have borne it at all."

"That would depend," I replied, "on whether an angel came to support you with her sympathy in the crisis of your condition, as one came to me." If my face at all expressed the feelings I had a right to have toward this sweet and lovely young girl, who had played so angelic a role toward me, its expression must have been very worshipful just then. The expression or the words, or both together, caused her now to drop her eyes with a charming blush.

"For the matter of that," I said, "if your experience has not been as startling as mine, it must have been rather overwhelming to see a man belonging to a strange century, and apparently a hundred years dead, raised to life."

"It seemed indeed strange beyond any describing at first," she said, "but when we began to put ourselves in your place, and realize how much stranger it must seem to you, I fancy we forgot our own feelings a good deal, at least I know I did. It seemed then not so much astounding as interesting and touching beyond anything ever heard of before."

"But does it not come over you as astounding to sit at table with me, seeing who I am?"

"You must remember that you do not seem so strange to us as we must to you," she answered. "We belong to a future of which you could not form an idea, a generation of which you knew nothing until you saw us. But you belong to a generation of which our forefathers were a part. We know all about it; the names of many of its members are household words with us. We have made a study of your ways of living and thinking; nothing you say or do surprises us, while we say and do nothing which does not seem strange to you. So you see, Mr. West, that if you feel that you can, in time, get accustomed to us, you must not be surprised that from the first we have scarcely found you strange at all."

"I had not thought of it in that way," I replied. "There is indeed much in what you say. One can look back a thousand years easier than forward fifty. A century is not so very long a retrospect. I might have known your great-grandparents. Possibly I did. Did they live in Boston?"

"I believe so."

"You are not sure, then?"

"Yes," she replied. "Now I think, they did."

"I had a very large circle of acquaintances in the city," I said. "It is not unlikely that I knew or knew of some of them. Perhaps I may have known them well. Wouldn't it be interesting if I should chance to be able to tell you all about your great-grandfather, for instance?"

"Very interesting."

"Do you know your genealogy well enough to tell me who your forbears were in the Boston of my day?"

"Oh, yes."

"Perhaps, then, you will some time tell me what some of their names were."

She was engrossed in arranging a troublesome spray of green, and did not reply at once. Steps upon the stairway indicated that the other members of the family were descending.

"Perhaps, some time," she said.

After breakfast, Dr. Leete suggested taking me to inspect the central warehouse and observe actually in operation the machinery of distribution, which Edith had described to me. As we walked away from the house I said, "It is now several days that I have been living in your household on a most extraordinary footing, or rather on none at all. I have not spoken of this aspect of my position before because there were so many other aspects yet more extraordinary. But now that I am beginning a little to feel my feet under me, and to realize that, however I came here, I am here, and must make the best of it, I must speak to you on this point."

"As for your being a guest in my house," replied Dr. Leete, "I pray you not to begin to be uneasy on that point, for I mean to keep you a long time yet. With all your modesty, you can but realize that such a guest as yourself is an acquisition not willingly to be parted with."

"Thanks, doctor," I said. "It would be absurd, certainly, for me to affect any oversensitiveness about accepting the temporary hospitality of one to whom I owe it that I am not still awaiting the end of the world in a living tomb. But if I am to be a permanent citizen of this century I must have some standing in it. Now, in my time a person more or less entering the world, however he got in, would not be noticed in the unorganized throng of men, and might make a place for himself anywhere he chose if he were strong enough. But nowadays everybody is a part of a system with a distinct place and function. I am outside the system, and don't see how I can get in; there seems no way to get in, except to be born in or to come in as an emigrant from some other system."

Dr. Leete laughed heartily.

"I admit," he said, "that our system is defective in lacking provision for cases like yours, but you see nobody anticipated additions to the world except by the usual process. You need, however, have no fear that we shall be unable to provide both a place and occupation for you in due time. You have as yet been brought in contact only with the members of my family, but you must not suppose that I have kept your secret. On the contrary, your case, even before your resuscitation, and vastly more since has excited the profoundest interest in the nation. In view of your precarious nervous condition, it was thought best that I should take exclusive charge of you at first, and that you should, through me and my family, receive some general idea of the sort of world you had come back to before you began to make the acquaintance generally of its inhabitants. As to finding a function for you in society, there was no hesitation as to what that would be. Few of us have it in our power to confer so great a service on the nation as you will be able to when you leave my roof, which, however, you must not think of doing for a good time yet."

"What can I possibly do?" I asked. "Perhaps you imagine I have some trade, or art, or special skill. I assure you I have none whatever. I never earned a dollar in my life, or did an hour's work. I am strong, and might be a common laborer, but nothing more."

"If that were the most efficient service you were able to render the nation, you would find that avocation considered quite as respectable as any other," replied Dr. Leete; "but you can do something else better. You are easily the master of all our historians on questions relating to the social condition of the latter part of the nineteenth century, to us one of the most absorbingly interesting periods of history: and whenever in due time you have sufficiently familiarized yourself with our institutions, and are willing to teach us something concerning those of your day, you will find an historical lectureship in one of our colleges awaiting you."

"Very good! Very good indeed," I said, much relieved by so practical a suggestion on a point which had begun to trouble me. "If your people are really so much interested in the nineteenth century, there will indeed be an occupation ready-made for me. I don't think there is anything else that I could possibly earn my salt at, but I certainly may claim without conceit to have some special qualifications for such a post as you describe."

XVII

I found the processes at the warehouse quite as interesting as Edith had described them, and became even enthusiastic over the truly remarkable illustration which is seen there of the prodigiously multiplied efficiency which perfect organization can give to labor. It is like a gigantic mill, into the hopper of which goods are being constantly poured by the train-load and shipload, to issue at the other end in packages of pounds and ounces, yards and inches, pints and gallons, corresponding to the infinitely complex personal needs of half a million people. Dr. Leete, with the assistance of data furnished by me as to the way goods were sold in my day, figured out some astounding results in the way of the economies effected by the modern system.

As we set out homeward, I said: "After what I have seen today, together with what you have told me, and what I learned under Miss Leete's tutelage at the sample store, I have a tolerably clear idea of your system of distribution, and how it enables you to dispense with a circulating medium. But I should like very much to know something more about your system of production. You have told me in general how your industrial army is levied and organized, but who directs its efforts? What supreme authority determines what shall be done in every department, so that enough of everything is produced and yet no labor wasted? It seems to me that this must be a wonderfully complex and difficult function, requiring very unusual endowments."

"Does it indeed seem so to you?" responded Dr. Leete. "I assure you that it is nothing of the kind, but on the other hand so simple, and depending on principles so obvious and easily applied, that the functionaries at Washington to whom it is trusted require to be nothing more than men of fair abilities to discharge it to the entire satisfaction of the nation. The machine which they direct is indeed a vast one, but so logical in its principles and direct and simple in its workings, that it all but runs itself; and nobody but a fool could derange it, as I think you will agree after a few words of explanation. Since you already have a pretty good idea of the working of the distributive system, let us begin at that end. Even in your day statisticians were able to tell you the number of yards of cotton, velvet, woolen, the number of barrels of flour, potatoes, butter, number of pairs of shoes, hats, and umbrellas annually consumed by the nation. Owing to the fact that production was in private hands, and that there was no way of getting statistics of actual distribution, these figures were not exact, but they were nearly so. Now that every pin which is given out from a national warehouse is recorded, of course the figures of consumption for any week, month, or year, in the possession of the department of distribution at the end of that period, are precise. On these figures, allowing for tendencies to increase or decrease and for any special causes likely to affect demand, the estimates, say for a year ahead, are based. These estimates, with a proper margin for security, having been accepted by the general administration, the responsibility of the distributive department ceases until the goods are delivered to it. I speak of the estimates being furnished for an entire year ahead, but in reality they cover that much time only in case of the great staples for which the demand can be calculated on as steady. In the great majority of smaller industries for the product of which popular taste fluctuates, and novelty is frequently required, production is kept barely ahead of consumption, the distributive department furnishing frequent estimates based on the weekly state of demand.

"Now the entire field of productive and constructive industry is divided into ten great departments, each representing a group of allied industries, each particular industry being in turn represented by a subordinate bureau, which has a complete record of the plant and force under its control, of the present product, and means of increasing it. The estimates of the distributive department, after adoption by the administration, are sent as mandates to the ten great departments, which allot them to the subordinate bureaus representing the particular industries, and these set the men at work. Each bureau is responsible for the task given it, and this responsibility is enforced by departmental oversight and that of the administration; nor does the distributive department accept the product without its own inspection; while even if in the hands of the consumer an article turns out unfit, the system enables the fault to be traced back to the original workman. The production of the commodities for actual public consumption does not, of course, require by any means all the national force of workers. After the necessary contingents have been detailed for the various industries, the amount of labor left for other employment is expended in creating fixed capital, such as buildings, machinery, engineering works, and so forth."

"One point occurs to me," I said, "on which I should think there might be dissatisfaction. Where there is no opportunity for private enterprise, how is there any assurance that the claims of small minorities of the people to have articles produced, for which there is no wide demand, will be respected? An official decree at any moment may deprive them of the means of gratifying some special taste, merely because the majority does not share it."

"That would be tyranny indeed," replied Dr. Leete, "and you may be very sure that it does not happen with us, to whom liberty is as dear as equality or fraternity. As you come to know our system better, you will see that our officials are in fact, and not merely in name, the agents and servants of the people. The administration has no power to stop the production of any commodity for which there continues to be a demand. Suppose the demand for any article declines to such a point that its production becomes very costly. The price has to be raised in proportion, of course, but as long as the consumer cares to pay it, the production goes on. Again, suppose an article not before produced is demanded. If the administration doubts the reality of the demand, a popular petition guaranteeing a certain basis of consumption compels it to produce the desired article. A government, or a majority, which should undertake to tell the people, or a minority, what they were to eat, drink, or wear, as I believe governments in America did in your day, would be regarded as a curious anachronism indeed. Possibly you had reasons for tolerating these infringements of personal independence, but we should not think them endurable. I am glad you raised this point, for it has given me a chance to show you how much more direct and efficient is the control over production exercised by the individual citizen now than it was in your day, when what you called private initiative prevailed, though it should have been called capitalist initiative, for the average private citizen had little enough share in it."

"You speak of raising the price of costly articles," I said. "How can prices be regulated in a country where there is no competition between buyers or sellers?"

"Just as they were with you," replied Dr. Leete. "You think that needs explaining," he added, as I looked incredulous, "but the explanation need not be long; the cost of the labor which produced it was recognized as the legitimate basis of the price of an article in your day, and so it is in ours. In your day, it was the difference in wages that made the difference in the cost of labor; now it is the relative number of hours constituting a day's work in different trades, the maintenance of the worker being equal in all cases. The cost of a man's work in a trade so difficult that in order to attract volunteers the hours have to be fixed at four a day is twice as great as that in a trade where the men work eight hours. The result as to the cost of labor, you see, is just the same as if the man working four hours were paid, under your system, twice the wages the others get. This calculation applied to the labor employed in the various processes of a manufactured article gives its price relatively to other articles. Besides the cost of production and transportation, the factor of scarcity affects the prices of some commodities. As regards the great staples of life, of which an abundance can always be secured, scarcity is eliminated as a factor. There is always a large surplus kept on hand from which any fluctuations of demand or supply can be corrected, even in most cases of bad crops. The prices of the staples grow less year by year, but rarely, if ever, rise. There are, however, certain classes of articles permanently, and others temporarily, unequal to the demand, as, for example, fresh fish or dairy products in the latter category, and the products of high skill and rare materials in the other. All that can be done here is to equalize the inconvenience of the scarcity. This is done by temporarily raising the price if the scarcity be temporary, or fixing it high if it be permanent. High prices in your day meant restriction of the articles affected to the rich, but nowadays, when the means of all are the same, the effect is only that those to whom the articles seem most desirable are the ones who purchase them. Of course the nation, as any other caterer for the public needs must be, is frequently left with small lots of goods on its hands by changes in taste, unseasonable weather and various other causes. These it has to dispose of at a sacrifice just as merchants often did in your day, charging up the loss to the expenses of the business. Owing, however, to the vast body of consumers to which such lots can be simultaneously offered, there is rarely any difficulty in getting rid of them at trifling loss. I have given you now some general notion of our system of production; as well as distribution. Do you find it as complex as you expected?"

I admitted that nothing could be much simpler.

"I am sure," said Dr. Leete, "that it is within the truth to say that the head of one of the myriad private businesses of your day, who had to maintain sleepless vigilance against the fluctuations of the market, the machinations of his rivals, and the failure of his debtors, had a far more trying task than the group of men at Washington who nowadays direct the industries of the entire nation. All this merely shows, my dear fellow, how much easier it is to do things the right way than the wrong. It is easier for a general up in a balloon, with perfect survey of the field, to maneuver a million men to victory than for a sergeant to manage a platoon in a thicket."

"The general of this army, including the flower of the manhood of the nation, must be the foremost man in the country, really greater even than the President of the United States," I said.

"He is the President of the United States," replied Dr. Leete, "or rather the most important function of the presidency is the headship of the industrial army."

"How is he chosen?" I asked.

"I explained to you before," replied Dr. Leete, "when I was describing the force of the motive of emulation among all grades of the industrial army, that the line of promotion for the meritorious lies through three grades to the officer's grade, and thence up through the lieutenancies to the captaincy or foremanship, and superintendency or colonel's rank. Next, with an intervening grade in some of the larger trades, comes the general of the guild, under whose immediate control all the operations of the trade are conducted. This officer is at the head of the national bureau representing his trade, and is responsible for its work to the administration. The general of his guild holds a splendid position, and one which amply satisfies the ambition of most men, but above his rank, which may be compared—to follow the military analogies familiar to you—to that of a general of division or major-general, is that of the chiefs of the ten great departments, or groups of allied trades. The chiefs of these ten grand divisions of the industrial army may be compared to your commanders of army corps, or lieutenant-generals, each having from a dozen to a score of generals of separate guilds reporting to him. Above these ten great officers, who form his council, is the general-in-chief, who is the President of the United States.

"The general-in-chief of the industrial army must have passed through all the grades below him, from the common laborers up. Let us see how he rises. As I have told you, it is simply by the excellence of his record as a worker that one rises through the grades of the privates and becomes a candidate for a lieutenancy. Through the lieutenancies he rises to the colonelcy, or superintendent's position, by appointment from above, strictly limited to the candidates of the best records. The general of the guild appoints to the ranks under him, but he himself is not appointed, but chosen by suffrage."

"By suffrage!" I exclaimed. "Is not that ruinous to the discipline of the guild, by tempting the candidates to intrigue for the support of the workers under them?"

"So it would be, no doubt," replied Dr. Leete, "if the workers had any suffrage to exercise, or anything to say about the choice. But they have nothing. Just here comes in a peculiarity of our system. The general of the guild is chosen from among the superintendents by vote of the honorary members of the guild, that is, of those who have served their time in the guild and received their discharge. As you know, at the age of forty-five we are mustered out of the army of industry, and have the residue of life for the pursuit of our own improvement or recreation. Of course, however, the associations of our active lifetime retain a powerful hold on us. The companionships we formed then remain our companionships till the end of life. We always continue honorary members of our former guilds, and retain the keenest and most jealous interest in their welfare and repute in the hands of the following generation. In the clubs maintained by the honorary members of the several guilds, in which we meet socially, there are no topics of conversation so common as those which relate to these matters, and the young aspirants for guild leadership who can pass the criticism of us old fellows are likely to be pretty well equipped. Recognizing this fact, the nation entrusts to the honorary members of each guild the election of its general, and I venture to claim that no previous form of society could have developed a body of electors so ideally adapted to their office, as regards absolute impartiality, knowledge of the special qualifications and record of candidates, solicitude for the best result, and complete absence of self-interest.

"Each of the ten lieutenant-generals or heads of departments is himself elected from among the generals of the guilds grouped as a department, by vote of the honorary members of the guilds thus grouped. Of course there is a tendency on the part of each guild to vote for its own general, but no guild of any group has nearly enough votes to elect a man not supported by most of the others. I assure you that these elections are exceedingly lively."

"The President, I suppose, is selected from among the ten heads of the great departments," I suggested.

"Precisely, but the heads of departments are not eligible to the presidency till they have been a certain number of years out of office. It is rarely that a man passes through all the grades to the headship of a department much before he is forty, and at the end of a five years' term he is usually forty-five. If more, he still serves through his term, and if less, he is nevertheless discharged from the industrial army at its termination. It would not do for him to return to the ranks. The interval before he is a candidate for the presidency is intended to give time for him to recognize fully that he has returned into the general mass of the nation, and is identified with it rather than with the industrial army. Moreover, it is expected that he will employ this period in studying the general condition of the army, instead of that of the special group of guilds of which he was the head. From among the former heads of departments who may be eligible at the time, the President is elected by vote of all the men of the nation who are not connected with the industrial army."

"The army is not allowed to vote for President?"

"Certainly not. That would be perilous to its discipline, which it is the business of the President to maintain as the representative of the nation at large. His right hand for this purpose is the inspectorate, a highly important department of our system; to the inspectorate come all complaints or information as to defects in goods, insolence or inefficiency of officials, or dereliction of any sort in the public service. The inspectorate, however, does not wait for complaints. Not only is it on the alert to catch and sift every rumor of a fault in the service, but it is its business, by systematic and constant oversight and inspection of every branch of the army, to find out what is going wrong before anybody else does. The President is usually not far from fifty when elected, and serves five years, forming an honorable exception to the rule of retirement at forty-five. At the end of his term of office, a national Congress is called to receive his report and approve or condemn it. If it is approved, Congress usually elects him to represent the nation for five years more in the international council. Congress, I should also say, passes on the reports of the outgoing heads of departments, and a disapproval renders any one of them ineligible for President. But it is rare, indeed, that the nation has occasion for other sentiments than those of gratitude toward its high officers. As to their ability, to have risen from the ranks, by tests so various and severe, to their positions, is proof in itself of extraordinary qualities, while as to faithfulness, our social system leaves them absolutely without any other motive than that of winning the esteem of their fellow citizens. Corruption is impossible in a society where there is neither poverty to be bribed nor wealth to bribe, while as to demagoguery or intrigue for office, the conditions of promotion render them out of the question."

"One point I do not quite understand," I said. "Are the members of the liberal professions eligible to the presidency? And if so, how are they ranked with those who pursue the industries proper?"

"They have no ranking with them," replied Dr. Leete. "The members of the technical professions, such as engineers and architects, have a ranking with the constructive guilds; but the members of the liberal professions, the doctors and teachers, as well as the artists and men of letters who obtain remissions of industrial service, do not belong to the industrial army. On this ground they vote for the President, but are not eligible to his office. One of its main duties being the control and discipline of the industrial army, it is essential that the President should have passed through all its grades to understand his business."

"That is reasonable," I said; "but if the doctors and teachers do not know enough of industry to be President, neither, I should think, can the President know enough of medicine and education to control those departments."

"No more does he," was the reply. "Except in the general way that he is responsible for the enforcement of the laws as to all classes, the President has nothing to do with the faculties of medicine and education, which are controlled by boards of regents of their own, in which the President is ex-officio chairman, and has the casting vote. These regents, who, of course, are responsible to Congress, are chosen by the honorary members of the guilds of education and medicine, the retired teachers and doctors of the country."

"Do you know," I said, "the method of electing officials by votes of the retired members of the guilds is nothing more than the application on a national scale of the plan of government by alumni, which we used to a slight extent occasionally in the management of our higher educational institutions."

"Did you, indeed?" exclaimed Dr. Leete, with animation. "That is quite new to me, and I fancy will be to most of us, and of much interest as well. There has been great discussion as to the germ of the idea, and we fancied that there was for once something new under the sun. Well! well! In your higher educational institutions! that is interesting indeed. You must tell me more of that."

"Truly, there is very little more to tell than I have told already," I replied. "If we had the germ of your idea, it was but as a germ."

XVIII

That evening I sat up for some time after the ladies had retired, talking with Dr. Leete about the effect of the plan of exempting men from further service to the nation after the age of forty-five, a point brought up by his account of the part taken by the retired citizens in the government.

"At forty-five," said I, "a man still has ten years of good manual labor in him, and twice ten years of good intellectual service. To be superannuated at that age and laid on the shelf must be regarded rather as a hardship than a favor by men of energetic dispositions."

"My dear Mr. West," exclaimed Dr. Leete, beaming upon me, "you cannot have any idea of the piquancy your nineteenth-century ideas have for us of this day, the rare quaintness of their effect. Know, O child of another race and yet the same, that the labor we have to render as our part in securing for the nation the means of a comfortable physical existence is by no means regarded as the most important, the most interesting, or the most dignified employment of our powers. We look upon it as a necessary duty to be discharged before we can fully devote ourselves to the higher exercise of our faculties, the intellectual and spiritual enjoyments and pursuits which alone mean life. Everything possible is indeed done by the just distribution of burdens, and by all manner of special attractions and incentives to relieve our labor of irksomeness, and, except in a comparative sense, it is not usually irksome, and is often inspiring. But it is not our labor, but the higher and larger activities which the performance of our task will leave us free to enter upon, that are considered the main business of existence.

"Of course not all, nor the majority, have those scientific, artistic, literary, or scholarly interests which make leisure the one thing valuable to their possessors. Many look upon the last half of life chiefly as a period for enjoyment of other sorts; for travel, for social relaxation in the company of their lifetime friends; a time for the cultivation of all manner of personal idiosyncrasies and special tastes, and the pursuit of every imaginable form of recreation; in a word, a time for the leisurely and unperturbed appreciation of the good things of the world which they have helped to create. But, whatever the differences between our individual tastes as to the use we shall put our leisure to, we all agree in looking forward to the date of our discharge as the time when we shall first enter upon the full enjoyment of our birthright, the period when we shall first really attain our majority and become enfranchised from discipline and control, with the fee of our lives vested in ourselves. As eager boys in your day anticipated twenty-one, so men nowadays look forward to forty-five. At twenty-one we become men, but at forty-five we renew youth. Middle age and what you would have called old age are considered, rather than youth, the enviable time of life. Thanks to the better conditions of existence nowadays, and above all the freedom of every one from care, old age approaches many years later and has an aspect far more benign than in past times. Persons of average constitution usually live to eighty-five or ninety, and at forty-five we are physically and mentally younger, I fancy, than you were at thirty-five. It is a strange reflection that at forty-five, when we are just entering upon the most enjoyable period of life, you already began to think of growing old and to look backward. With you it was the forenoon, with us it is the afternoon, which is the brighter half of life."

After this I remember that our talk branched into the subject of popular sports and recreations at the present time as compared with those of the nineteenth century.

"In one respect," said Dr. Leete, "there is a marked difference. The professional sportsmen, which were such a curious feature of your day, we have nothing answering to, nor are the prizes for which our athletes contend money prizes, as with you. Our contests are always for glory only. The generous rivalry existing between the various guilds, and the loyalty of each worker to his own, afford a constant stimulation to all sorts of games and matches by sea and land, in which the young men take scarcely more interest than the honorary guildsmen who have served their time. The guild yacht races off Marblehead take place next week, and you will be able to judge for yourself of the popular enthusiasm which such events nowadays call out as compared with your day. The demand for *panem ef circenses* preferred by the Roman populace is recognized nowadays as a wholly reasonable one. If bread is the first necessity of life, recreation is a close second, and the nation caters for both. Americans of the nineteenth century were as unfortunate in lacking an adequate provision for the one sort of need as for the other. Even if the people of that period had enjoyed larger leisure, they would, I fancy, have often been at a loss how to pass it agreeably. We are never in that predicament."

XIX

In the course of an early morning constitutional I visited Charlestown. Among the changes, too numerous to attempt to indicate, which mark the lapse of a century in that quarter, I particularly noted the total disappearance of the old state prison.

"That went before my day, but I remember hearing about it," said Dr. Leete, when I alluded to the fact at the breakfast table. "We have no jails nowadays. All cases of atavism are treated in the hospitals."

"Of atavism!" I exclaimed, staring.

"Why, yes," replied Dr. Leete. "The idea of dealing punitively with those unfortunates was given up at least fifty years ago, and I think more."

"I don't quite understand you," I said. "Atavism in my day was a word applied to the cases of persons in whom some trait of a remote ancestor recurred in a noticeable manner. Am I to understand that crime is nowadays looked upon as the recurrence of an ancestral trait?"

"I beg your pardon," said Dr. Leete with a smile half humorous, half deprecating, "but since you have so explicitly asked the question, I am forced to say that the fact is precisely that."

After what I had already learned of the moral contrasts between the nineteenth and the twentieth centuries, it was doubtless absurd in me to begin to develop sensitiveness on the subject, and probably if Dr. Leete had not spoken with that apologetic air and Mrs. Leete and Edith shown a corresponding embarrassment, I should not have flushed, as I was conscious I did.

"I was not in much danger of being vain of my generation before," I said; "but, really—"

"This is your generation, Mr. West," interposed Edith. "It is the one in which you are living, you know, and it is only because we are alive now that we call it ours."

"Thank you. I will try to think of it so," I said, and as my eyes met hers their expression quite cured my senseless sensitiveness. "After all," I said, with a laugh, "I was brought up a Calvinist, and ought not to be startled to hear crime spoken of as an ancestral trait."

"In point of fact," said Dr. Leete, "our use of the word is no reflection at all on your generation, if, begging Edith's pardon, we may call it yours, so far as seeming to imply that we think ourselves, apart from our circumstances, better than you were. In your day fully nineteen twentieths of the crime, using the word broadly to include all sorts of misdemeanors, resulted from the inequality in the possessions of individuals; want tempted the poor, lust of greater gains, or the desire to preserve former gains, tempted the well-to-do. Directly or indirectly, the desire for money, which then meant every good thing, was the motive of all this crime, the taproot of a vast poison growth, which the machinery of law, courts, and police could barely prevent from choking your civilization outright. When we made the nation the sole trustee of the wealth of the people, and guaranteed to all abundant maintenance, on the one hand abolishing want, and on the other checking the accumulation of riches, we cut this root, and the poison tree that overshadowed your society withered, like Jonah's gourd, in a day. As for the comparatively small class of violent crimes against persons, unconnected with any idea of gain, they were almost wholly confined, even in your day, to the ignorant and bestial; and in these days, when education and good manners are not the monopoly of a few, but universal, such atrocities are scarcely ever heard of. You now see why the word 'atavism' is used for crime. It is because nearly all forms of crime known to you are motiveless now, and when they appear can only be explained as the outcropping of ancestral traits. You used to call persons who stole, evidently without any rational motive, kleptomaniacs, and when the case was clear deemed it absurd to punish them as thieves. Your attitude toward the genuine kleptomaniac is precisely ours toward the victim of atavism, an attitude of compassion and firm but gentle restraint."

"Your courts must have an easy time of it," I observed. "With no private property to speak of, no disputes between citizens over business relations, no real estate to divide or debts to collect, there must be absolutely no civil business at all for them; and with no offenses against property, and mighty few of any sort to provide criminal cases, I should think you might almost do without judges and lawyers altogether."

"We do without the lawyers, certainly," was Dr. Leete's reply. "It would not seem reasonable to us, in a case where the only interest of the nation is to find out the truth, that persons should take part in the proceedings who had an acknowledged motive to color it."

"But who defends the accused?"

"If he is a criminal he needs no defense, for he pleads guilty in most instances," replied Dr. Leete. "The plea of the accused is not a mere formality with us, as with you. It is usually the end of the case."

"You don't mean that the man who pleads not guilty is thereupon discharged?"

"No, I do not mean that. He is not accused on light grounds, and if he denies his guilt, must still be tried. But trials are few, for in most cases the guilty man pleads guilty. When he makes a false plea and is clearly proved guilty, his penalty is doubled. Falsehood is, however, so despised among us that few offenders would lie to save themselves."

"That is the most astounding thing you have yet told me," I exclaimed. "If lying has gone out of fashion, this is indeed the 'new heavens and the new earth wherein dwelleth righteousness,' which the prophet foretold."

"Such is, in fact, the belief of some persons nowadays," was the doctor's answer. "They hold that we have entered upon the millennium, and the theory from their point of view does not lack plausibility. But as to your astonishment at finding that the world has outgrown lying, there is really no ground for it. Falsehood, even in your day, was not common between gentlemen and ladies, social equals. The lie of fear was the refuge of cowardice, and the lie of fraud the device of the cheat. The inequalities of men and the lust of acquisition offered a constant premium on lying at that time. Yet even then, the man who neither feared another nor desired to defraud him scorned falsehood. Because we are now all social equals, and no man either has anything to fear from another or can gain anything by deceiving him, the contempt of falsehood is so universal that it is rarely, as I told you, that even a criminal in other respects will be found willing to lie. When, however, a plea of not guilty is returned, the judge appoints two colleagues to state the opposite sides of the case. How far these men are from being like your hired advocates and prosecutors, determined to acquit or convict, may appear from the fact that unless both agree that the verdict found is just, the case is tried over, while anything like bias in the tone of either of the judges stating the case would be a shocking scandal."

"Do I understand," I said, "that it is a judge who states each side of the case as well as a judge who hears it?"

"Certainly. The judges take turns in serving on the bench and at the bar, and are expected to maintain the judicial temper equally whether in stating or deciding a case. The system is indeed in effect that of trial by three judges occupying different points of view as to the case. When they agree upon a verdict, we believe it to be as near to absolute truth as men well can come."

"You have given up the jury system, then?"

"It was well enough as a corrective in the days of hired advocates, and a bench sometimes venal, and often with a tenure that made it dependent, but is needless now. No conceivable motive but justice could actuate our judges."

"How are these magistrates selected?"

"They are an honorable exception to the rule which discharges all men from service at the age of forty-five. The President of the nation appoints the necessary judges year by year from the class reaching that age. The number appointed is, of course, exceedingly few, and the honor so high that it is held an offset to the additional term of service which follows, and though a judge's appointment may be declined, it rarely is. The term is five years, without eligibility to reappointment. The members of the Supreme Court, which is the guardian of the constitution, are selected from among the lower judges. When a vacancy in that court occurs, those of the lower judges, whose terms expire that year, select, as their last official act, the one of their colleagues left on the bench whom they deem fittest to fill it."

"There being no legal profession to serve as a school for judges," I said, "they must, of course, come directly from the law school to the bench."

"We have no such things as law schools," replied the doctor smiling. "The law as a special science is obsolete. It was a system of casuistry which the elaborate artificiality of the old order of society absolutely required to interpret it, but only a few of the plainest and simplest legal maxims have any application to the existing state of the world. Everything touching the relations of men to one another is now simpler, beyond any comparison, than in your day. We should have no sort of use for the hair-splitting experts who presided and argued in your courts. You must not imagine, however, that we have any disrespect for those ancient worthies because we have no use for them. On the contrary, we entertain an unfeigned respect, amounting almost to awe, for the men who alone understood and were able to expound the interminable complexity of the rights of property, and the relations of commercial and personal dependence involved in your system. What, indeed, could possibly give a more powerful impression of the intricacy and artificiality of that system than the fact that it was necessary to set apart from other pursuits the cream of the intellect of every generation, in order to provide a body of pundits able to make it even vaguely intelligible to those whose fates it determined. The treatises of your great lawyers, the works of Blackstone and Chitty, of Story and Parsons, stand in our museums, side by side with the tomes of Duns Scotus and his fellow scholastics, as curious monuments of intellectual subtlety devoted to subjects equally remote from the interests of modern men. Our judges are simply widely informed, judicious, and discreet men of ripe years.

"I should not fail to speak of one important function of the minor judges," added Dr. Leete. "This is to adjudicate all cases where a private of the industrial army makes a complaint of unfairness against an officer. All such questions are heard and settled without appeal by a single judge, three judges being required only in graver cases. The efficiency of industry requires the strictest discipline in the army of labor, but the claim of the workman to just and considerate treatment is backed by the whole power of the nation. The officer commands and the private obeys, but no officer is so high that he would dare display an overbearing manner toward a workman of the lowest class. As for churlishness or rudeness by an official of any sort, in his relations to the public, not one among minor offenses is more sure of a prompt penalty than this. Not only justice but civility is enforced by our judges in all sorts of intercourse. No value of service is accepted as a set-off to boorish or offensive manners."

It occurred to me, as Dr. Leete was speaking, that in all his talk I had heard much of the nation and nothing of the state governments. Had the organization of the nation as an industrial unit done away with the states? I asked.

"Necessarily," he replied. "The state governments would have interfered with the control and discipline of the industrial army, which, of course, required to be central and uniform. Even if the state governments had not become inconvenient for other reasons, they were rendered superfluous by the prodigious simplification in the task of government since your day. Almost the sole function of the administration now is that of directing the industries of the country. Most of the purposes for which governments formerly existed no longer remain to be subserved. We have no army or navy, and no military organization. We have no departments of state or treasury, no excise or revenue services, no taxes or tax collectors. The only function proper of government, as known to you, which still remains, is the judiciary and police system. I have already explained to you how simple is our judicial system as compared with your huge and complex machine. Of course the same absence of crime and temptation to it, which make the duties of judges so light, reduces the number and duties of the police to a minimum."

"But with no state legislatures, and Congress meeting only once in five years, how do you get your legislation done?"

"We have no legislation," replied Dr. Leete, "that is, next to none. It is rarely that Congress, even when it meets, considers any new laws of consequence, and then it only has power to commend them to the following Congress, lest anything be done hastily. If you will consider a moment, Mr. West, you will see that we have nothing to make laws about. The fundamental principles on which our society is founded settle for all time the strifes and misunderstandings which in your day called for legislation.

"Fully ninety-nine hundredths of the laws of that time concerned the definition and protection of private property and the relations of buyers and sellers. There is neither private property, beyond personal belongings, now, nor buying and selling, and therefore the occasion of nearly all the legislation formerly necessary has passed away. Formerly, society was a pyramid poised on its apex. All the gravitations of human nature were constantly tending to topple it over, and it could be maintained upright, or rather upwrong (if you will pardon the feeble witticism), by an elaborate system of constantly renewed props and buttresses and guy-ropes in the form of laws. A central Congress and forty state legislatures, turning out some twenty thousand laws a year, could not make new props fast enough to take the place of those which were constantly breaking down or becoming ineffectual through some shifting of the strain. Now society rests on its base, and is in as little need of artificial supports as the everlasting hills."

"But you have at least municipal governments besides the one central authority?"

"Certainly, and they have important and extensive functions in looking out for the public comfort and recreation, and the improvement and embellishment of the villages and cities."

"But having no control over the labor of their people, or means of hiring it, how can they do anything?"

"Every town or city is conceded the right to retain, for its own public works, a certain proportion of the quota of labor its citizens contribute to the nation. This proportion, being assigned it as so much credit, can be applied in any way desired."

XX

That afternoon Edith casually inquired if I had yet revisited the underground chamber in the garden in which I had been found.

"Not yet," I replied. "To be frank, I have shrunk thus far from doing so, lest the visit might revive old associations rather too strongly for my mental equilibrium."

"Ah, yes!" she said, "I can imagine that you have done well to stay away. I ought to have thought of that."

"No," I said, "I am glad you spoke of it. The danger, if there was any, existed only during the first day or two. Thanks to you, chiefly and always, I feel my footing now so firm in this new world, that if you will go with me to keep the ghosts off, I should really like to visit the place this afternoon."

Edith demurred at first, but, finding that I was in earnest, consented to accompany me. The rampart of earth thrown up from the excavation was visible among the trees from the house, and a few steps brought us to the spot. All remained as it was at the point when work was interrupted by the discovery of the tenant of the chamber, save that the door had been opened and the slab from the roof replaced. Descending the sloping sides of the excavation, we went in at the door and stood within the dimly lighted room.

Everything was just as I had beheld it last on that evening one hundred and thirteen years previous, just before closing my eyes for that long sleep. I stood for some time silently looking about me. I saw that my companion was furtively regarding me with an expression of awed and sympathetic curiosity. I put out my hand to her and she placed hers in it, the soft fingers responding with a reassuring pressure to my clasp. Finally she whispered, "Had we not better go out now? You must not try yourself too far. Oh, how strange it must be to you!"

"On the contrary," I replied, "it does not seem strange; that is the strangest part of it."

"Not strange?" she echoed.

"Even so," I replied. "The emotions with which you evidently credit me, and which I anticipated would attend this visit, I simply do not feel. I realize all that these surroundings suggest, but without the agitation I expected. You can't be nearly as much surprised at this as I am myself. Ever since that terrible morning when you came to my help, I have tried to avoid thinking of my former life, just as I have avoided coming here, for fear of the agitating effects. I am for all the world like a man who has permitted an injured limb to lie motionless under the impression that it is exquisitely sensitive, and on trying to move it finds that it is paralyzed."

"Do you mean your memory is gone?"

"Not at all. I remember everything connected with my former life, but with a total lack of keen sensation. I remember it for clearness as if it had been but a day since then, but my feelings about what I remember are as faint as if to my consciousness, as well as in fact, a hundred years had intervened. Perhaps it is possible to explain this, too. The effect of change in surroundings is like that of lapse of time in making the past seem remote. When I first woke from that trance, my former life appeared as yesterday, but now, since I have learned to know my new surroundings, and to realize the prodigious changes that have transformed the world, I no longer find it hard, but very easy, to realize that I have slept a century. Can you conceive of such a thing as living a hundred years in four days? It really seems to me that I have done just that, and that it is this experience which has given so remote and unreal an appearance to my former life. Can you see how such a thing might be?"

"I can conceive it," replied Edith, meditatively, "and I think we ought all to be thankful that it is so, for it will save you much suffering, I am sure."

"Imagine," I said, in an effort to explain, as much to myself as to her, the strangeness of my mental condition, "that a man first heard of a bereavement many, many years, half a lifetime perhaps, after the event occurred. I fancy his feeling would be perhaps something as mine is. When I think of my friends in the world of that former day, and the sorrow they must have felt for me, it is with a pensive pity, rather than keen anguish, as of a sorrow long, long ago ended."

"You have told us nothing yet of your friends," said Edith. "Had you many to mourn you?"

"Thank God, I had very few relatives, none nearer than cousins," I replied. "But there was one, not a relative, but dearer to me than any kin of blood. She had your name. She was to have been my wife soon. Ah me!"

"Ah me!" sighed the Edith by my side. "Think of the heartache she must have had."

Something in the deep feeling of this gentle girl touched a chord in my benumbed heart. My eyes, before so dry, were flooded with the tears that had till now refused to come. When I had regained my composure, I saw that she too had been weeping freely.

"God bless your tender heart," I said. "Would you like to see her picture?"

A small locket with Edith Bartlett's picture, secured about my neck with a gold chain, had lain upon my breast all through that long sleep, and removing this I opened and gave it to my companion. She took it with eagerness, and after poring long over the sweet face, touched the picture with her lips.

"I know that she was good and lovely enough to well deserve your tears," she said; "but remember her heartache was over long ago, and she has been in heaven for nearly a century."

It was indeed so. Whatever her sorrow had once been, for nearly a century she had ceased to weep, and, my sudden passion spent, my own tears dried away. I had loved her very dearly in my other life, but it was a hundred years ago! I do not know but some may find in this confession evidence of lack of feeling, but I think, perhaps, that none can have had an experience sufficiently like mine to enable them to judge me. As we were about to leave the chamber, my eye rested upon the great iron safe which stood in one corner. Calling my companion's attention to it, I said:

"This was my strong room as well as my sleeping room. In the safe yonder are several thousand dollars in gold, and any amount of securities. If I had known when I went to sleep that night just how long my nap would be, I should still have thought that the gold was a safe provision for my needs in any country or any century, however distant. That a time would ever come when it would lose its purchasing power, I should have considered the wildest of fancies. Nevertheless, here I wake up to find myself among a people of whom a cartload of gold will not procure a loaf of bread."

As might be expected, I did not succeed in impressing Edith that there was anything remarkable in this fact. "Why in the world should it?" she merely asked.

XXI

It had been suggested by Dr. Leete that we should devote the next morning to an inspection of the schools and colleges of the city, with some attempt on his own part at an explanation of the educational system of the twentieth century.

"You will see," said he, as we set out after breakfast, "many very important differences between our methods of education and yours, but the main difference is that nowadays all persons equally have those opportunities of higher education which in your day only an infinitesimal portion of the population enjoyed. We should think we had gained nothing worth speaking of, in equalizing the physical comfort of men, without this educational equality."

"The cost must be very great," I said.

"If it took half the revenue of the nation, nobody would grudge it," replied Dr. Leete, "nor even if it took it all save a bare pittance. But in truth the expense of educating ten thousand youth is not ten nor five times that of educating one thousand. The principle which makes all operations on a large scale proportionally cheaper than on a small scale holds as to education also."

"College education was terribly expensive in my day," said I.

"If I have not been misinformed by our historians," Dr. Leete answered, "it was not college education but college dissipation and extravagance which cost so highly. The actual expense of your colleges appears to have been very low, and would have been far lower if their patronage had been greater. The higher education nowadays is as cheap as the lower, as all grades of teachers, like all other workers, receive the same support. We have simply added to the common school system of compulsory education, in vogue in Massachusetts a hundred years ago, a half dozen higher grades, carrying the youth to the age of twenty-one and giving him what you used to call the education of a gentleman, instead of turning him loose at fourteen or fifteen with no mental equipment beyond reading, writing, and the multiplication table."

"Setting aside the actual cost of these additional years of education," I replied, "we should not have thought we could afford the loss of time from industrial pursuits. Boys of the poorer classes usually went to work at sixteen or younger, and knew their trade at twenty."

"We should not concede you any gain even in material product by that plan," Dr. Leete replied. "The greater efficiency which education gives to all sorts of labor, except the rudest, makes up in a short period for the time lost in acquiring it."

"We should also have been afraid," said I, "that a high education, while it adapted men to the professions, would set them against manual labor of all sorts."

"That was the effect of high education in your day, I have read," replied the doctor; "and it was no wonder, for manual labor meant association with a rude, coarse, and ignorant class of people. There is no such class now. It was inevitable that such a feeling should exist then, for the further reason that all men receiving a high education were understood to be destined for the professions or for wealthy leisure, and such an education in one neither rich nor professional was a proof of disappointed aspirations, an evidence of failure, a badge of inferiority rather than superiority. Nowadays, of course, when the highest education is deemed necessary to fit a man merely to live, without any reference to the sort of work he may do, its possession conveys no such implication."

"After all," I remarked, "no amount of education can cure natural dullness or make up for original mental deficiencies. Unless the average natural mental capacity of men is much above its level in my day, a high education must be pretty nearly thrown away on a large element of the population. We used to hold that a certain amount of susceptibility to educational influences is required to make a mind worth cultivating, just as a certain natural fertility in soil is required if it is to repay tilling."

"Ah," said Dr. Leete, "I am glad you used that illustration, for it is just the one I would have chosen to set forth the modern view of education. You say that land so poor that the product will not repay the labor of tilling is not cultivated. Nevertheless, much land that does not begin to repay tilling by its product was cultivated in your day and is in ours. I refer to gardens, parks, lawns, and, in general, to pieces of land so situated that, were they left to grow up to weeds and briers, they would be eyesores and inconveniencies to all about. They are therefore tilled, and though their product is little, there is yet no land that, in a wider sense, better repays cultivation. So it is with the men and women with whom we mingle in the relations of society, whose voices are always in our ears, whose behavior in innumerable ways affects our enjoyment—who are, in fact, as much conditions of our lives as the air we breathe, or any of the physical elements on which we depend. If, indeed, we could not afford to educate everybody, we should choose the coarsest and dullest by nature, rather than the brightest, to receive what education we could give. The naturally refined and intellectual can better dispense with aids to culture than those less fortunate in natural endowments.

"To borrow a phrase which was often used in your day, we should not consider life worth living if we had to be surrounded by a population of ignorant, boorish, coarse, wholly uncultivated men and women, as was the plight of the few educated in your day. Is a man satisfied, merely because he is perfumed himself, to mingle with a malodorous crowd? Could he take more than a very limited satisfaction, even in a palatial apartment, if the windows on all four sides opened into stable yards? And yet just that was the situation of those considered most fortunate as to culture and refinement in your day. I know that the poor and ignorant envied the rich and cultured then; but to us the latter, living as they did, surrounded by squalor and brutishness, seem little better off than the former. The cultured man in your age was like one up to the neck in a nauseous bog solacing himself with a smelling bottle. You see, perhaps, now, how we look at this question of universal high education. No single thing is so important to every man as to have for neighbors intelligent, companionable persons. There is nothing, therefore, which the nation can do for him that will enhance so much his own happiness as to educate his neighbors. When it fails to do so, the value of his own education to him is reduced by half, and many of the tastes he has cultivated are made positive sources of pain.

"To educate some to the highest degree, and leave the mass wholly uncultivated, as you did, made the gap between them almost like that between different natural species, which have no means of communication. What could be more inhuman than this consequence of a partial enjoyment of education! Its universal and equal enjoyment leaves, indeed, the differences between men as to natural endowments as marked as in a state of nature, but the level of the lowest is vastly raised. Brutishness is eliminated. All have some inkling of the humanities, some appreciation of the things of the mind, and an admiration for the still higher culture they have fallen short of. They have become capable of receiving and imparting, in various degrees, but all in some measure, the pleasures and inspirations of a refined social life. The cultured society of the nineteenth century—what did it consist of but here and there a few microscopic oases in a vast, unbroken wilderness? The proportion of individuals capable of intellectual sympathies or refined intercourse, to the mass of their contemporaries, used to be so infinitesimal as to be in any broad view of humanity scarcely worth mentioning. One generation of the world today represents a greater volume of intellectual life than any five centuries ever did before.

"There is still another point I should mention in stating the grounds on which nothing less than the universality of the best education could now be tolerated," continued Dr. Leete, "and that is, the interest of the coming generation in having educated parents. To put the matter in a nutshell, there are three main grounds on which our educational system rests: first, the right of every man to the completest education the nation can give him on his own account, as necessary to his enjoyment of himself; second, the right of his fellow-citizens to have him educated, as necessary to their enjoyment of his society; third, the right of the unborn to be guaranteed an intelligent and refined parentage."

I shall not describe in detail what I saw in the schools that day. Having taken but slight interest in educational matters in my former life, I could offer few comparisons of interest. Next to the fact of the universality of the higher as well as the lower education, I was most struck with the prominence given to physical culture, and the fact that proficiency in athletic feats and games as well as in scholarship had a place in the rating of the youth.

"The faculty of education," Dr. Leete explained, "is held to the same responsibility for the bodies as for the minds of its charges. The highest possible physical, as well as mental, development of every one is the double object of a curriculum which lasts from the age of six to that of twenty-one."

The magnificent health of the young people in the schools impressed me strongly. My previous observations, not only of the notable personal endowments of the family of my host, but of the people I had seen in my walks abroad, had already suggested the idea that there must have been something like a general improvement in the physical standard of the race since my day, and now, as I compared these stalwart young men and fresh, vigorous maidens with the young people I had seen in the schools of the nineteenth century, I was moved to impart my thought to Dr. Leete. He listened with great interest to what I said.

"Your testimony on this point," he declared, "is invaluable. We believe that there has been such an improvement as you speak of, but of course it could only be a matter of theory with us. It is an incident of your unique position that you alone in the world of today can speak with authority on this point. Your opinion, when you state it publicly, will, I assure you, make a profound sensation. For the rest it would be strange, certainly, if the race did not show an improvement. In your day, riches debauched one class with idleness of mind and body, while poverty sapped the vitality of the masses by overwork, bad food, and pestilent homes. The labor required of children, and the burdens laid on women, enfeebled the very springs of life. Instead of these maleficent circumstances, all now enjoy the most favorable conditions of physical life; the young are carefully nurtured and studiously cared for; the labor which is required of all is limited to the period of greatest bodily vigor, and is never excessive; care for one's self and one's family, anxiety as to livelihood, the strain of a ceaseless battle for life—all these influences, which once did so much to wreck the minds and bodies of men and women, are known no more. Certainly, an improvement of the species ought to follow such a change. In certain specific respects we know, indeed, that the improvement has taken place. Insanity, for instance, which in the nineteenth century was so terribly common a product of your insane mode of life, has almost disappeared, with its alternative, suicide."

XXII

We had made an appointment to meet the ladies at the dining hall for dinner, after which, having some engagement, they left us sitting at table there, discussing our wine and cigars with a multitude of other matters.

"Doctor," said I, in the course of our talk, "morally speaking, your social system is one which I should be insensate not to admire in comparison with any previously in vogue in the world, and especially with that of my own most unhappy century. If I were to fall into a mesmeric sleep tonight as lasting as that other and meanwhile the course of time were to take a turn backward instead of forward, and I were to wake up again in the nineteenth century, when I had told my friends what I had seen, they would every one admit that your world was a paradise of order, equity, and felicity. But they were a very practical people, my contemporaries, and after expressing their admiration for the moral beauty and material splendor of the system, they would presently begin to cipher and ask how you got the money to make everybody so happy; for certainly, to support the whole nation at a rate of comfort, and even luxury, such as I see around me, must involve vastly greater wealth than the nation produced in my day. Now, while I could explain to them pretty nearly everything else of the main features of your system, I should quite fail to answer this question, and failing there, they would tell me, for they were very close cipherers, that I had been dreaming; nor would they ever believe anything else. In my day, I know that the total annual product of the nation, although it might have been divided with absolute equality, would not have come to more than three or four hundred dollars per head, not very much more than enough to supply the necessities of life with few or any of its comforts. How is it that you have so much more?"

"That is a very pertinent question, Mr. West," replied Dr. Leete, "and I should not blame your friends, in the case you supposed, if they declared your story all moonshine, failing a satisfactory reply to it. It is a question which I cannot answer exhaustively at any one sitting, and as for the exact statistics to bear out my general statements, I shall have to refer you for them to books in my library, but it would certainly be a pity to leave you to be put to confusion by your old acquaintances, in case of the contingency you speak of, for lack of a few suggestions.

"Let us begin with a number of small items wherein we economize wealth as compared with you. We have no national, state, county, or municipal debts, or payments on their account. We have no sort of military or naval expenditures for men or materials, no army, navy, or militia. We have no revenue service, no swarm of tax assessors and collectors. As regards our judiciary, police, sheriffs, and jailers, the force which Massachusetts alone kept on foot in your day far more than suffices for the nation now. We have no criminal class preying upon the wealth of society as you had. The number of persons, more or less absolutely lost to the working force through physical disability, of the lame, sick, and debilitated, which constituted such a burden on the able-bodied in your day, now that all live under conditions of health and comfort, has shrunk to scarcely perceptible proportions, and with every generation is becoming more completely eliminated.

"Another item wherein we save is the disuse of money and the thousand occupations connected with financial operations of all sorts, whereby an army of men was formerly taken away from useful employments. Also consider that the waste of the very rich in your day on inordinate personal luxury has ceased, though, indeed, this item might easily be over-estimated. Again, consider that there are no idlers now, rich or poor—no drones.

"A very important cause of former poverty was the vast waste of labor and materials which resulted from domestic washing and cooking, and the performing separately of innumerable other tasks to which we apply the cooperative plan.

"A larger economy than any of these—yes, of all together—is effected by the organization of our distributing system, by which the work done once by the merchants, traders, storekeepers, with their various grades of jobbers, wholesalers, retailers, agents, commercial travelers, and middlemen of all sorts, with an excessive waste of energy in needless transportation and interminable handlings, is performed by one tenth the number of hands and an unnecessary turn of not one wheel. Something of what our distributing system is like you know. Our statisticians calculate that one eightieth part of our workers suffices for all the processes of distribution which in your day required one eighth of the population, so much being withdrawn from the force engaged in productive labor."

"I begin to see," I said, "where you get your greater wealth."

"I beg your pardon," replied Dr. Leete, "but you scarcely do as yet. The economies I have mentioned thus far, in the aggregate, considering the labor they would save directly and indirectly through saving of material, might possibly be equivalent to the addition to your annual production of wealth of one half its former total. These items are, however, scarcely worth mentioning in comparison with other prodigious wastes, now saved, which resulted inevitably from leaving the industries of the nation to private enterprise. However great the economies your contemporaries might have devised in the consumption of products, and however marvelous the progress of mechanical invention, they could never have raised themselves out of the slough of poverty so long as they held to that system.

"No mode more wasteful for utilizing human energy could be devised, and for the credit of the human intellect it should be remembered that the system never was devised, but was merely a survival from the rude ages when the lack of social organization made any sort of cooperation impossible."

"I will readily admit," I said, "that our industrial system was ethically very bad, but as a mere wealth-making machine, apart from moral aspects, it seemed to us admirable."

"As I said," responded the doctor, "the subject is too large to discuss at length now, but if you are really interested to know the main criticisms which we moderns make on your industrial system as compared with our own, I can touch briefly on some of them.

"The wastes which resulted from leaving the conduct of industry to irresponsible individuals, wholly without mutual understanding or concert, were mainly four: first, the waste by mistaken undertakings; second, the waste from the competition and mutual hostility of those engaged in industry; third, the waste by periodical gluts and crises, with the consequent interruptions of industry; fourth, the waste from idle capital and labor, at all times. Any one of these four great leaks, were all the others stopped, would suffice to make the difference between wealth and poverty on the part of a nation.

"Take the waste by mistaken undertakings, to begin with. In your day the production and distribution of commodities being without concert or organization, there was no means of knowing just what demand there was for any class of products, or what was the rate of supply. Therefore, any enterprise by a private capitalist was always a doubtful experiment. The projector having no general view of the field of industry and consumption, such as our government has, could never be sure either what the people wanted, or what arrangements other capitalists were making to supply them. In view of this, we are not surprised to learn that the chances were considered several to one in favor of the failure of any given business enterprise, and that it was common for persons who at last succeeded in making a hit to have failed repeatedly. If a shoemaker, for every pair of shoes he succeeded in completing, spoiled the leather of four or five pair, besides losing the time spent on them, he would stand about the same chance of getting rich as your contemporaries did with their system of private enterprise, and its average of four or five failures to one success.

"The next of the great wastes was that from competition. The field of industry was a battlefield as wide as the world, in which the workers wasted, in assailing one another, energies which, if expended in concerted effort, as today, would have enriched all. As for mercy or quarter in this warfare, there was absolutely no suggestion of it. To deliberately enter a field of business and destroy the enterprises of those who had occupied it previously, in order to plant one's own enterprise on their ruins, was an achievement which never failed to command popular admiration. Nor is there any stretch of fancy in comparing this sort of struggle with actual warfare, so far as concerns the mental agony and physical suffering which attended the struggle, and the misery which overwhelmed the defeated and those dependent on them. Now nothing about your age is, at first sight, more astounding to a man of modern times than the fact that men engaged in the same industry, instead of fraternizing as comrades and co-laborers to a common end, should have regarded each other as rivals and enemies to be throttled and overthrown. This certainly seems like sheer madness, a scene from bedlam. But more closely regarded, it is seen to be no such thing. Your contemporaries, with their mutual throat-cutting, knew very well what they were at. The producers of the nineteenth century were not, like ours, working together for the maintenance of the community, but each solely for his own maintenance at the expense of the community. If, in working to this end, he at the same time increased the aggregate wealth, that was merely incidental. It was just as feasible and as common to increase one's private hoard by practices injurious to the general welfare. One's worst enemies were necessarily those of his own trade, for, under your plan of making private profit the motive of production, a scarcity of the article he produced was what each particular producer desired. It was for his interest that no more of it should be produced than he himself could produce. To secure this consummation as far as circumstances permitted, by killing off and discouraging those engaged in his line of industry, was his constant effort. When he had killed off all he could, his policy was to combine with those he could not kill, and convert their mutual warfare into a warfare upon the public at large by cornering the market, as I believe you used to call it, and putting up prices to the highest point people would stand before going without the goods. The daydream of the nineteenth-century producer was to gain absolute control of the supply of some necessity of life, so that he might keep the public at the verge of starvation, and always command famine prices for what he supplied. This, Mr. West, is what was called in the nineteenth century a system of production. I will leave it to you if it does not seem, in some of its aspects, a great deal more like a system for preventing production. Some time when we have plenty of leisure I am going to ask you to sit down with me and try to make me comprehend, as I never yet could, though I have studied the matter a great deal how such shrewd fellows as your contemporaries appear to have been in many respects ever came to entrust the business of providing for the community to a class whose interest it was to starve it. I assure you that the wonder with us is, not that the world did not get rich under such a system, but that it did not perish outright from want. This wonder increases as we go on to consider some of the other prodigious wastes that characterized it.

"Apart from the waste of labor and capital by misdirected industry, and that from the constant bloodletting of your industrial warfare, your system was liable to periodical convulsions, overwhelming alike the wise and unwise, the successful cut-throat as well as his victim. I refer to the business crises at intervals of five to ten years, which wrecked the industries of the nation, prostrating all weak enterprises and crippling the strongest, and were followed by long periods, often of many years, of so-called dull times, during which the capitalists slowly regathered their dissipated strength while the laboring classes starved and rioted. Then would ensue another brief season of prosperity, followed in turn by another crisis and the ensuing years of exhaustion. As commerce developed, making the nations mutually dependent, these crises became worldwide, while the obstinacy of the ensuing state of collapse increased with the area affected by the convulsions, and the consequent lack of rallying centers. In proportion as the industries of the world multiplied and became complex, and the volume of capital involved was increased, these business cataclysms became more frequent, till, in the latter part of the nineteenth century, there were two years of bad times to one of good, and the system of industry, never before so extended or so imposing, seemed in danger of collapsing by its own weight. After endless discussions, your economists appear by that time to have settled down to the despairing conclusion that there was no more possibility of preventing or controlling these crises than if they had been drouths or hurricanes. It only remained to endure them as necessary evils, and when they had passed over to build up again the shattered structure of industry, as dwellers in an earthquake country keep on rebuilding their cities on the same site.

"So far as considering the causes of the trouble inherent in their industrial system, your contemporaries were certainly correct. They were in its very basis, and must needs become more and more maleficent as the business fabric grew in size and complexity. One of these causes was the lack of any common control of the different industries, and the consequent impossibility of their orderly and coordinate development. It inevitably resulted from this lack that they were continually getting out of step with one another and out of relation with the demand.

"Of the latter there was no criterion such as organized distribution gives us, and the first notice that it had been exceeded in any group of industries was a crash of prices, bankruptcy of producers, stoppage of production, reduction of wages, or discharge of workmen. This process was constantly going on in many industries, even in what were called good times, but a crisis took place only when the industries affected were extensive. The markets then were glutted with goods, of which nobody wanted beyond a sufficiency at any price. The wages and profits of those making the glutted classes of goods being reduced or wholly stopped, their purchasing power as consumers of other classes of goods, of which there were no natural glut, was taken away, and, as a consequence, goods of which there was no natural glut became artificially glutted, till their prices also were broken down, and their makers thrown out of work and deprived of income. The crisis was by this time fairly under way, and nothing could check it till a nation's ransom had been wasted.

"A cause, also inherent in your system, which often produced and always terribly aggravated crises, was the machinery of money and credit. Money was essential when production was in many private hands, and buying and selling was necessary to secure what one wanted. It was, however, open to the obvious objection of substituting for food, clothing, and other things a merely conventional representative of them. The confusion of mind which this favored, between goods and their representative, led the way to the credit system and its prodigious illusions. Already accustomed to accept money for commodities, the people next accepted promises for money, and ceased to look at all behind the representative for the thing represented. Money was a sign of real commodities, but credit was but the sign of a sign. There was a natural limit to gold and silver, that is, money proper, but none to credit, and the result was that the volume of credit, that is, the promises of money, ceased to bear any ascertainable proportion to the money, still less to the commodities, actually in existence. Under such a system, frequent and periodical crises were necessitated by a law as absolute as that which brings to the ground a structure overhanging its center of gravity. It was one of your fictions that the government and the banks authorized by it alone issued money; but everybody who gave a dollar's credit issued money to that extent, which was as good as any to swell the circulation till the next crises. The great extension of the credit system was a characteristic of the latter part of the nineteenth century, and accounts largely for the almost incessant business crises which marked that period. Perilous as credit was, you could not dispense with its use, for, lacking any national or other public organization of the capital of the country, it was the only means you had for concentrating and directing it upon industrial enterprises. It was in this way a most potent means for exaggerating the chief peril of the private enterprise system of industry by enabling particular industries to absorb disproportionate amounts of the disposable capital of the country, and thus prepare disaster. Business enterprises were always vastly in debt for advances of credit, both to one another and to the banks and capitalists, and the prompt withdrawal of this credit at the first sign of a crisis was generally the precipitating cause of it.

"It was the misfortune of your contemporaries that they had to cement their business fabric with a material which an accident might at any moment turn into an explosive. They were in the plight of a man building a house with dynamite for mortar, for credit can be compared with nothing else.

"If you would see how needless were these convulsions of business which I have been speaking of, and how entirely they resulted from leaving industry to private and unorganized management, just consider the working of our system. Overproduction in special lines, which was the great hobgoblin of your day, is impossible now, for by the connection between distribution and production supply is geared to demand like an engine to the governor which regulates its speed. Even suppose by an error of judgment an excessive production of some commodity. The consequent slackening or cessation of production in that line throws nobody out of employment. The suspended workers are at once found occupation in some other department of the vast workshop and lose only the time spent in changing, while, as for the glut, the business of the nation is large enough to carry any amount of product manufactured in excess of demand till the latter overtakes it. In such a case of over-production, as I have supposed, there is not with us, as with you, any complex machinery to get out of order and magnify a thousand times the original mistake. Of course, having not even money, we still less have credit. All estimates deal directly with the real things, the flour, iron, wood, wool, and labor, of which money and credit were for you the very misleading representatives. In our calculation of cost there can be no mistakes. Out of the annual product the amount necessary for the support of the people is taken, and the requisite labor to produce the next year's consumption provided for. The residue of the material and labor represents what can be safely expended in improvements. If the crops are bad, the surplus for that year is less than usual, that is all. Except for slight occasional effects of such natural causes, there are no fluctuations of business; the material prosperity of the nation flows on uninterruptedly from generation to generation, like an ever broadening and deepening river.

"Your business crises, Mr. West," continued the doctor, "like either of the great wastes I mentioned before, were enough, alone, to have kept your noses to the grindstone forever; but I have still to speak of one other great cause of your poverty, and that was the idleness of a great part of your capital and labor. With us it is the business of the administration to keep in constant employment every ounce of available capital and labor in the country. In your day there was no general control of either capital or labor, and a large part of both failed to find employment. 'Capital,' you used to say, 'is naturally timid,' and it would certainly have been reckless if it had not been timid in an epoch when there was a large preponderance of probability that any particular business venture would end in failure. There was no time when, if security could have been guaranteed it, the amount of capital devoted to productive industry could not have been greatly increased. The proportion of it so employed underwent constant extraordinary fluctuations, according to the greater or less feeling of uncertainty as to the stability of the industrial situation, so that the output of the national industries greatly varied in different years. But for the same reason that the amount of capital employed at times of special insecurity was far less than at times of somewhat greater security, a very large proportion was never employed at all, because the hazard of business was always very great in the best of times.

"It should be also noted that the great amount of capital always seeking employment where tolerable safety could be insured terribly embittered the competition between capitalists when a promising opening presented itself. The idleness of capital, the result of its timidity, of course meant the idleness of labor in corresponding degree. Moreover, every change in the adjustments of business, every slightest alteration in the condition of commerce or manufactures, not to speak of the innumerable business failures that took place yearly, even in the best of times, were constantly throwing a multitude of men out of employment for periods of weeks or months, or even years. A great number of these seekers after employment were constantly traversing the country, becoming in time professional vagabonds, then criminals. 'Give us work!' was the cry of an army of the unemployed at nearly all seasons, and in seasons of dullness in business this army swelled to a host so vast and desperate as to threaten the stability of the government. Could there conceivably be a more conclusive demonstration of the imbecility of the system of private enterprise as a method for enriching a nation than the fact that, in an age of such general poverty and want of everything, capitalists had to throttle one another to find a safe chance to invest their capital and workmen rioted and burned because they could find no work to do?

"Now, Mr. West," continued Dr. Leete, "I want you to bear in mind that these points of which I have been speaking indicate only negatively the advantages of the national organization of industry by showing certain fatal defects and prodigious imbecilities of the systems of private enterprise which are not found in it. These alone, you must admit, would pretty well explain why the nation is so much richer than in your day. But the larger half of our advantage over you, the positive side of it, I have yet barely spoken of. Supposing the system of private enterprise in industry were without any of the great leaks I have mentioned; that there were no waste on account of misdirected effort growing out of mistakes as to the demand, and inability to command a general view of the industrial field. Suppose, also, there were no neutralizing and duplicating of effort from competition. Suppose, also, there were no waste from business panics and crises through bankruptcy and long interruptions of industry, and also none from the idleness of capital and labor. Supposing these evils, which are essential to the conduct of industry by capital in private hands, could all be miraculously prevented, and the system yet retained; even then the superiority of the results attained by the modern industrial system of national control would remain overwhelming.

"You used to have some pretty large textile manufacturing establishments, even in your day, although not comparable with ours. No doubt you have visited these great mills in your time, covering acres of ground, employing thousands of hands, and combining under one roof, under one control, the hundred distinct processes between, say, the cotton bale and the bale of glossy calicoes. You have admired the vast economy of labor as of mechanical force resulting from the perfect interworking with the rest of every wheel and every hand. No doubt you have reflected how much less the same force of workers employed in that factory would accomplish if they were scattered, each man working independently. Would you think it an exaggeration to say that the utmost product of those workers, working thus apart, however amicable their relations might be, was increased not merely by a percentage, but many fold, when their efforts were organized under one control? Well now, Mr. West, the organization of the industry of the nation under a single control, so that all its processes interlock, has multiplied the total product over the utmost that could be done under the former system, even leaving out of account the four great wastes mentioned, in the same proportion that the product of those millworkers was increased by cooperation. The effectiveness of the working force of a nation, under the myriad-headed leadership of private capital, even if the leaders were not mutual enemies, as compared with that which it attains under a single head, may be likened to the military efficiency of a mob, or a horde of barbarians with a thousand petty chiefs, as compared with that of a disciplined army under one general—such a fighting machine, for example, as the German army in the time of Von Moltke."

"After what you have told me," I said, "I do not so much wonder that the nation is richer now than then, but that you are not all Croesuses."

"Well," replied Dr. Leete, "we are pretty well off. The rate at which we live is as luxurious as we could wish. The rivalry of ostentation, which in your day led to extravagance in no way conducive to comfort, finds no place, of course, in a society of people absolutely equal in resources, and our ambition stops at the surroundings which minister to the enjoyment of life. We might, indeed, have much larger incomes, individually, if we chose so to use the surplus of our product, but we prefer to expend it upon public works and pleasures in which all share, upon public halls and buildings, art galleries, bridges, statuary, means of transit, and the conveniences of our cities, great musical and theatrical exhibitions, and in providing on a vast scale for the recreations of the people. You have not begun to see how we live yet, Mr. West. At home we have comfort, but the splendor of our life is, on its social side, that which we share with our fellows. When you know more of it you will see where the money goes, as you used to say, and I think you will agree that we do well so to expend it."

"I suppose," observed Dr. Leete, as we strolled homeward from the dining hall, "that no reflection would have cut the men of your wealth-worshiping century more keenly than the suggestion that they did not know how to make money. Nevertheless that is just the verdict history has passed on them. Their system of unorganized and antagonistic industries was as absurd economically as it was morally abominable. Selfishness was their only science, and in industrial production selfishness is suicide. Competition, which is the instinct of selfishness, is another word for dissipation of energy, while combination is the secret of efficient production; and not till the idea of increasing the individual hoard gives place to the idea of increasing the common stock can industrial combination be realized, and the acquisition of wealth really begin. Even if the principle of share and share alike for all men were not the only humane and rational basis for a society, we should still enforce it as economically expedient, seeing that until the disintegrating influence of self-seeking is suppressed no true concert of industry is possible."

XXIII

That evening, as I sat with Edith in the music room, listening to some pieces in the programme of that day which had attracted my notice, I took advantage of an interval in the music to say, "I have a question to ask you which I fear is rather indiscreet."

"I am quite sure it is not that," she replied, encouragingly.

"I am in the position of an eavesdropper," I continued, "who, having overheard a little of a matter not intended for him, though seeming to concern him, has the impudence to come to the speaker for the rest."

"An eavesdropper!" she repeated, looking puzzled.

"Yes," I said, "but an excusable one, as I think you will admit."

"This is very mysterious," she replied.

"Yes," said I, "so mysterious that often I have doubted whether I really overheard at all what I am going to ask you about, or only dreamed it. I want you to tell me. The matter is this: When I was coming out of that sleep of a century, the first impression of which I was conscious was of voices talking around me, voices that afterwards I recognized as your father's, your mother's, and your own. First, I remember your father's voice saying, "He is going to open his eyes. He had better see but one person at first." Then you said, if I did not dream it all, "Promise me, then, that you will not tell him." Your father seemed to hesitate about promising, but you insisted, and your mother interposing, he finally promised, and when I opened my eyes I saw only him."

I had been quite serious when I said that I was not sure that I had not dreamed the conversation I fancied I had overheard, so incomprehensible was it that these people should know anything of me, a contemporary of their great-grandparents, which I did not know myself. But when I saw the effect of my words upon Edith, I knew that it was no dream, but another mystery, and a more puzzling one than any I had before encountered. For from the moment that the drift of my question became apparent, she showed indications of the most acute embarrassment. Her eyes, always so frank and direct in expression, had dropped in a panic before mine, while her face crimsoned from neck to forehead.

"Pardon me," I said, as soon as I had recovered from bewilderment at the extraordinary effect of my words. "It seems, then, that I was not dreaming. There is some secret, something about me, which you are withholding from me. Really, doesn't it seem a little hard that a person in my position should not be given all the information possible concerning himself?"

"It does not concern you—that is, not directly. It is not about you exactly," she replied, scarcely audibly.

"But it concerns me in some way," I persisted. "It must be something that would interest me."

"I don't know even that," she replied, venturing a momentary glance at my face, furiously blushing, and yet with a quaint smile flickering about her lips which betrayed a certain perception of humor in the situation despite its embarrassment—"I am not sure that it would even interest you."

"Your father would have told me," I insisted, with an accent of reproach. "It was you who forbade him. He thought I ought to know."

She did not reply. She was so entirely charming in her confusion that I was now prompted, as much by the desire to prolong the situation as by my original curiosity, to importune her further.

"Am I never to know? Will you never tell me?" I said.

"It depends," she answered, after a long pause.

"On what?" I persisted.

"Ah, you ask too much," she replied. Then, raising to mine a face which inscrutable eyes, flushed cheeks, and smiling lips combined to render perfectly bewitching, she added, "What should you think if I said that it depended on—yourself?"

"On myself?" I echoed. "How can that possibly be?"

"Mr. West, we are losing some charming music," was her only reply to this, and turning to the telephone, at a touch of her finger she set the air to swaying to the rhythm of an adagio. After that she took good care that the music should leave no opportunity for conversation. She kept her face averted from me, and pretended to be absorbed in the airs, but that it was a mere pretense the crimson tide standing at flood in her cheeks sufficiently betrayed.

When at length she suggested that I might have heard all I cared to, for that time, and we rose to leave the room, she came straight up to me and said, without raising her eyes, "Mr. West, you say I have been good to you. I have not been particularly so, but if you think I have, I want you to promise me that you will not try again to make me tell you this thing you have asked to-night, and that you will not try to find it out from any one else—my father or mother, for instance."

To such an appeal there was but one reply possible. "Forgive me for distressing you. Of course I will promise," I said. "I would never have asked you if I had fancied it could distress you. But do you blame me for being curious?"

"I do not blame you at all."

"And some time," I added, "if I do not tease you, you may tell me of your own accord. May I not hope so?"

"Perhaps," she murmured.

"Only perhaps?"

Looking up, she read my face with a quick, deep glance. "Yes," she said, "I think I may tell you—some time": and so our conversation ended, for she gave me no chance to say anything more.

That night I don't think even Dr. Pillsbury could have put me to sleep, till toward morning at least. Mysteries had been my accustomed food for days now, but none had before confronted me at once so mysterious and so fascinating as this, the solution of which Edith Leete had forbidden me even to seek. It was a double mystery. How, in the first place, was it conceivable that she should know any secret about me, a stranger from a strange age? In the second place, even if she should know such a secret, how account for the agitating effect which the knowledge of it seemed to have upon her? There are puzzles so difficult that one cannot even get so far as a conjecture as to the solution, and this seemed one of them. I am usually of too practical a turn to waste time on such conundrums; but the difficulty of a riddle embodied in a beautiful young girl does not detract from its fascination. In general, no doubt, maidens' blushes may be safely assumed to tell the same tale to young men in all ages and races, but to give that interpretation to Edith's crimson cheeks would, considering my position and the length of time I had known her, and still more the fact that this mystery dated from before I had known her at all, be a piece of utter fatuity. And yet she was an angel, and I should not have been a young man if reason and common sense had been able quite to banish a roseate tinge from my dreams that night.

XXIV

In the morning I went down stairs early in the hope of seeing Edith alone. In this, however, I was disappointed. Not finding her in the house, I sought her in the garden, but she was not there. In the course of my wanderings I visited the underground chamber, and sat down there to rest. Upon the reading table in the chamber several periodicals and newspapers lay, and thinking that Dr. Leete might be interested in glancing over a Boston daily of 1887, I brought one of the papers with me into the house when I came.

At breakfast I met Edith. She blushed as she greeted me, but was perfectly self-possessed. As we sat at table, Dr. Leete amused himself with looking over the paper I had brought in. There was in it, as in all the newspapers of that date, a great deal about the labor troubles, strikes, lockouts, boycotts, the programmes of labor parties, and the wild threats of the anarchists.

"By the way," said I, as the doctor read aloud to us some of these items, "what part did the followers of the red flag take in the establishment of the new order of things? They were making considerable noise the last thing that I knew."

"They had nothing to do with it except to hinder it, of course," replied Dr. Leete. "They did that very effectually while they lasted, for their talk so disgusted people as to deprive the best considered projects for social reform of a hearing. The subsidizing of those fellows was one of the shrewdest moves of the opponents of reform."

"Subsidizing them!" I exclaimed in astonishment.

"Certainly," replied Dr. Leete. "No historical authority nowadays doubts that they were paid by the great monopolies to wave the red flag and talk about burning, sacking, and blowing people up, in order, by alarming the timid, to head off any real reforms. What astonishes me most is that you should have fallen into the trap so unsuspectingly."

"What are your grounds for believing that the red flag party was subsidized?" I inquired.

"Why simply because they must have seen that their course made a thousand enemies of their professed cause to one friend. Not to suppose that they were hired for the work is to credit them with an inconceivable folly.* In the United States, of all countries, no party could intelligently expect to carry its point without first winning over to its ideas a majority of the nation, as the national party eventually did."

"The national party!" I exclaimed. "That must have arisen after my day. I suppose it was one of the labor parties."

"Oh no!" replied the doctor. "The labor parties, as such, never could have accomplished anything on a large or permanent scale. For purposes of national scope, their basis as merely class organizations was too narrow. It was not till a rearrangement of the industrial and social system on a higher ethical basis, and for the more efficient production of wealth, was recognized as the interest, not of one class, but equally of all classes, of rich and poor, cultured and ignorant, old and young, weak and strong, men and women, that there was any prospect that it would be achieved. Then the national party arose to carry it out by political methods. It probably took that name because its aim was to nationalize the functions of production and distribution. Indeed, it could not well have had any other name, for its purpose was to realize the idea of the nation with a grandeur and completeness never before conceived, not as an association of men for certain merely political functions affecting their happiness only remotely and superficially, but as a family, a vital union, a common life, a mighty heaven-touching tree whose leaves are its people, fed from its veins, and feeding it in turn. The most patriotic of all possible parties, it sought to justify patriotism and raise it from an instinct to a rational

* I fully admit the difficulty of accounting for the course of the anarchists on any other theory than that they were subsidized by the capitalists, but at the same time, there is no doubt that the theory is wholly erroneous. It certainly was not held at the time by any one, though it may seem so obvious in the retrospect.

devotion, by making the native land truly a father land, a father who kept the people alive and was not merely an idol for which they were expected to die."

XXV

The personality of Edith Leete had naturally impressed me strongly ever since I had come, in so strange a manner, to be an inmate of her father's house, and it was to be expected that after what had happened the night previous, I should be more than ever preoccupied with thoughts of her. From the first I had been struck with the air of serene frankness and ingenuous directness, more like that of a noble and innocent boy than any girl I had ever known, which characterized her. I was curious to know how far this charming quality might be peculiar to herself, and how far possibly a result of alterations in the social position of women which might have taken place since my time. Finding an opportunity that day, when alone with Dr. Leete, I turned the conversation in that direction.

"I suppose," I said, "that women nowadays, having been relieved of the burden of housework, have no employment but the cultivation of their charms and graces."

"So far as we men are concerned," replied Dr. Leete, "we should consider that they amply paid their way, to use one of your forms of expression, if they confined themselves to that occupation, but you may be very sure that they have quite too much spirit to consent to be mere beneficiaries of society, even as a return for ornamenting it. They did, indeed, welcome their riddance from housework, because that was not only exceptionally wearing in itself, but also wasteful, in the extreme, of energy, as compared with the cooperative plan; but they accepted relief from that sort of work only that they might contribute in other and more effectual, as well as more agreeable, ways to the common weal. Our women, as well as our men, are members of the industrial army, and leave it only when maternal duties claim them. The result is that most women, at one time or another of their lives, serve industrially some five or ten or fifteen years, while those who have no children fill out the full term."

"A woman does not, then, necessarily leave the industrial service on marriage?" I queried.

"No more than a man," replied the doctor. "Why on earth should she? Married women have no housekeeping responsibilities now, you know, and a husband is not a baby that he should be cared for."

"It was thought one of the most grievous features of our civilization that we required so much toil from women," I said; "but it seems to me you get more out of them than we did."

Dr. Leete laughed. "Indeed we do, just as we do out of our men. Yet the women of this age are very happy, and those of the nineteenth century, unless contemporary references greatly mislead us, were very miserable. The reason that women nowadays are so much more efficient colaborers with the men, and at the same time are so happy, is that, in regard to their work as well as men's, we follow the principle of providing every one the kind of occupation he or she is best adapted to. Women being inferior in strength to men, and further disqualified industrially in special ways, the kinds of occupation reserved for them, and the conditions under which they pursue them, have reference to these facts. The heavier sorts of work are everywhere reserved for men, the lighter occupations for women. Under no circumstances is a woman permitted to follow any employment not perfectly adapted, both as to kind and degree of labor, to her sex. Moreover, the hours of women's work are considerably shorter than those of men's, more frequent vacations are granted, and the most careful provision is made for rest when needed. The men of this day so well appreciate that they owe to the beauty and grace of women the chief zest of their lives and their main incentive to effort, that they permit them to work at all only because it is fully understood that a certain regular requirement of labor, of a sort adapted to their powers, is well for body and mind, during the period of maximum physical vigor. We believe that the magnificent health which distinguishes our women from those of your day, who seem to have been so generally sickly, is owing largely to the fact that all alike are furnished with healthful and inspiriting occupation."

"I understood you," I said, "that the women-workers belong to the army of industry, but how can they be under the same system of ranking and discipline with the men, when the conditions of their labor are so different?"

"They are under an entirely different discipline," replied Dr. Leete, "and constitute rather an allied force than an integral part of the army of the men. They have a woman general-in-chief and are under exclusively feminine regime. This general, as also the higher officers, is chosen by the body of women who have passed the time of service, in correspondence with the manner in which the chiefs of the masculine army and the President of the nation are elected. The general of the women's army sits in the cabinet of the President and has a veto on measures respecting women's work, pending appeals to Congress. I should have said, in speaking of the judiciary, that we have women on the bench, appointed by the general of the women, as well as men. Causes in which both parties are women are determined by women judges, and where a man and a woman are parties to a case, a judge of either sex must consent to the verdict."

"Womanhood seems to be organized as a sort of *imperium in imperio* in your system," I said.

"To some extent," Dr. Leete replied; "but the inner *imperium* is one from which you will admit there is not likely to be much danger to the nation. The lack of some such recognition of the distinct individuality of the sexes was one of the innumerable defects of your society. The passional attraction between men and women has too often prevented a perception of the profound differences which make the members of each sex in many things strange to the other, and capable of sympathy only with their own. It is in giving full play to the differences of sex rather than in seeking to obliterate them, as was apparently the effort of some reformers in your day, that the enjoyment of each by itself and the piquancy which each has for the other, are alike enhanced. In your day there was no career for women except in an unnatural rivalry with men. We have given them a world of their own, with its emulations, ambitions, and careers, and I assure you they are very happy in it. It seems to us that women were more than any other class the victims of your civilization. There is something which, even at this distance of time, penetrates one with pathos in the spectacle of their ennuied, undeveloped lives, stunted at marriage, their narrow horizon, bounded so often, physically, by the four walls of home, and morally by a petty circle of personal interests. I speak now, not of the poorer classes, who were generally worked to death, but also of the well-to-do and rich. From the great sorrows, as well as the petty frets of life, they had no refuge in the breezy outdoor world of human affairs, nor any interests save those of the family. Such an existence would have softened men's brains or driven them mad. All that is changed today. No woman is heard nowadays wishing she were a man, nor parents desiring boy rather than girl children. Our girls are as full of ambition for their careers as our boys. Marriage, when it comes, does not mean incarceration for them, nor does it separate them in any way from the larger interests of society, the bustling life of the world. Only when maternity fills a woman's mind with new interests does she withdraw from the world for a time. Afterward, and at any time, she may return to her place among her comrades, nor need she ever lose touch with them. Women are a very happy race nowadays, as compared with what they ever were before in the world's history, and their power of giving happiness to men has been of course increased in proportion."

"I should imagine it possible," I said, "that the interest which girls take in their careers as members of the industrial army and candidates for its distinctions might have an effect to deter them from marriage."

Dr. Leete smiled. "Have no anxiety on that score, Mr. West," he replied. "The Creator took very good care that whatever other modifications the dispositions of men and women might with time take on, their attraction for each other should remain constant. The mere fact that in an age like yours, when the struggle for existence must have left people little time for other thoughts, and the future was so uncertain that to assume parental responsibilities must have often seemed like a criminal risk, there was even then marrying and giving in marriage, should be conclusive on this point. As for love nowadays, one of our authors says that the vacuum left in the minds of men and women by the absence of care for one's livelihood has been entirely taken up by the tender passion. That, however, I beg you to believe, is something of an exaggestion. For the rest, so far is marriage from being an interference with a woman's career, that the higher positions in the feminine army of industry are intrusted only to women who have been both wives and mothers, as they alone fully represent their sex."

"Are credit cards issued to the women just as to the men?"

"Certainly."

"The credits of the women, I suppose, are for smaller sums, owing to the frequent suspension of their labor on account of family responsibilities."

"Smaller!" exclaimed Dr. Leete. "Oh, no! The maintenance of all our people is the same. There are no exceptions to that rule, but if any difference were made on account of the interruptions you speak of, it would be by making the woman's credit larger, not smaller. Can you think of any service constituting a stronger claim on the nation's gratitude than bearing and nursing the nation's children? According to our view, none deserve so well of the world as good parents. There is no task so unselfish, so necessarily without return, though the heart is well rewarded, as the nurture of the children who are to make the world for one another when we are gone."

"It would seem to follow, from what you have said, that wives are in no way dependent on their husbands for maintenance."

"Of course they are not," replied Dr. Leete, "nor children on their parents either, that is, for means of support, though of course they are for the offices of affection. The child's labor, when he grows up, will go to increase the common stock, not his parents', who will be dead, and therefore he is properly nurtured out of the common stock. The account of every person, man, woman, and child, you must understand, is always with the nation directly, and never through any intermediary, except, of course, that parents, to a certain extent, act for children as their guardians. You see that it is by virtue of the relation of individuals to the nation, of their membership in it, that they are entitled to support; and this title is in no way connected with or affected by their relations to other individuals who are fellow members of the nation with them. That any person should be dependent for the means of support upon another would be shocking to the moral sense as well as indefensible on any rational social theory. What would become of personal liberty and dignity under such an arrangement? I am aware that you called yourselves free in the nineteenth century. The meaning of the word could not then, however, have been at all what it is at present, or you certainly would not have applied it to a society of which nearly every member was in a position of galling personal dependence upon others as to the very means of life, the poor upon the rich, or employed upon employer, women upon men, children upon parents. Instead of distributing the product of the nation directly to its members, which would seem the most natural and obvious method, it would actually appear that you had given your minds to devising a plan of hand to hand distribution, involving the maximum of personal humiliation to all classes of recipients.

"As regards the dependence of women upon men for support, which then was usual, of course, natural attraction in case of marriages of love may often have made it endurable, though for spirited women I should fancy it must always have remained humiliating. What, then, must it have been in the innumerable cases where women, with or without the form of marriage, had to sell themselves to men to get their living? Even your contemporaries, callous as they were to most of the revolting aspects of their society, seem to have had an idea that this was not quite as it should be; but, it was still only for pity's sake that they deplored the lot of the women. It did not occur to them that it was robbery as well as cruelty when men seized for themselves the whole product of the world and left women to beg and wheedle for their share. Why—but bless me, Mr. West, I am really running on at a remarkable rate, just as if the robbery, the sorrow, and the shame which those poor women endured were not over a century since, or as if you were responsible for what you no doubt deplored as much as I do."

"I must bear my share of responsibility for the world as it then was," I replied. "All I can say in extenuation is that until the nation was ripe for the present system of organized production and distribution, no radical improvement in the position of woman was possible. The root of her disability, as you say, was her personal dependence upon man for her livelihood, and I can imagine no other mode of social organization than that you have adopted, which would have set woman free of man at the same time that it set men free of one another. I suppose, by the way, that so entire a change in the position of women cannot have taken place without affecting in marked ways the social relations of the sexes. That will be a very interesting study for me."

"The change you will observe," said Dr. Leete, "will chiefly be, I think, the entire frankness and unconstraint which now characterizes those relations, as compared with the artificiality which seems to have marked them in your time. The sexes now meet with the ease of perfect equals, suitors to each other for nothing but love. In your time the fact that women were dependent for support on men made the woman in reality the one chiefly benefited by marriage. This fact, so far as we can judge from contemporary records, appears to have been coarsely enough recognized among the lower classes, while among the more polished it was glossed over by a system of elaborate conventionalities which aimed to carry the precisely opposite meaning, namely, that the man was the party chiefly benefited. To keep up this convention it was essential that he should always seem the suitor. Nothing was therefore considered more shocking to the proprieties than that a woman should betray a fondness for a man before he had indicated a desire to marry her. Why, we actually have in our libraries books, by authors of your day, written for no other purpose than to discuss the question whether, under any conceivable circumstances, a woman might, without discredit to her sex, reveal an unsolicited love. All this seems exquisitely absurd to us, and yet we know that, given your circumstances, the problem might have a serious side. When for a woman to proffer her love to a man was in effect to invite him to assume the burden of her support, it is easy to see that pride and delicacy might well have checked the promptings of the heart. When you go out into our society, Mr. West, you must be prepared to be often cross-questioned on this point by our young people, who are naturally much interested in this aspect of old-fashioned manners."*

"And so the girls of the twentieth century tell their love."

"If they choose," replied Dr. Leete. "There is no more pretense of a concealment of feeling on their part than on the part of their lovers. Coquetry would be as much despised in a girl as in a man. Affected coldness, which in your day rarely deceived a lover, would deceive him wholly now, for no one thinks of practicing it."

"One result which must follow from the independence of women I can see for myself," I said. "There can be no marriages now except those of inclination."

"That is a matter of course," replied Dr. Leete.

"Think of a world in which there are nothing but matches of pure love! Ah me, Dr. Leete, how far you are from being able to understand what an astonishing phenomenon such a world seems to a man of the nineteenth century!"

"I can, however, to some extent, imagine it," replied the doctor. "But the fact you celebrate, that there are nothing but love matches, means even more, perhaps, than you probably at first realize. It means that for the first time in human history the principle of sexual selection, with its tendency to preserve and transmit the better types of the race, and let the inferior types drop out, has unhindered operation. The necessities of poverty, the need of having a home, no longer tempt women to accept as the fathers of their children

*I may say that Dr. Leete's warning has been fully justified by my experience. The amount and intensity of amusement which the young people of this day, and the young women especially, are able to extract from what they are pleased to call the oddities of courtship in the nineteenth century, appear unlimited.

men whom they neither can love nor respect. Wealth and rank no longer divert attention from personal qualities. Gold no longer 'gilds the straitened forehead of the fool.' The gifts of person, mind, and disposition; beauty, wit, eloquence, kindness, generosity, geniality, courage, are sure of transmission to posterity. Every generation is sifted through a little finer mesh than the last. The attributes that human nature admires are preserved, those that repel it are left behind. There are, of course, a great many women who with love must mingle admiration, and seek to wed greatly, but these not the less obey the same law, for to wed greatly now is not to marry men of fortune or title, but those who have risen above their fellows by the solidity or brilliance of their services to humanity. These form nowadays the only aristocracy with which alliance is distinction.

"You were speaking, a day or two ago, of the physical superiority of our people to your contemporaries. Perhaps more important than any of the causes I mentioned then as tending to race purification has been the effect of untrammeled sexual selection upon the quality of two or three successive generations. I believe that when you have made a fuller study of our people you will find in them not only a physical, but a mental and moral improvement. It would be strange if it were not so, for not only is one of the great laws of nature now freely working out the salvation of the race, but a profound moral sentiment has come to its support. Individualism, which in your day was the animating idea of society, not only was fatal to any vital sentiment of brotherhood and common interest among living men, but equally to any realization of the responsibility of the living for the generation to follow. Today this sense of responsibility, practically unrecognized in all previous ages, has become one of the great ethical ideas of the race, reinforcing, with an intense conviction of duty, the natural impulse to seek in marriage the best and noblest of the other sex. The result is, that not all the encouragements and incentives of every sort which we have provided to develop industry, talent, genius, excellence of whatever kind, are comparable in their effect on our young men with the fact that our women sit aloft as judges of the race and reserve themselves to reward the winners. Of all the whips, and spurs, and baits, and prizes, there is none like the thought of the radiant faces which the laggards will find averted.

"Celibates nowadays are almost invariably men who have failed to acquit themselves creditably in the work of life. The woman must be a courageous one, with a very evil sort of courage, too, whom pity for one of these unfortunates should lead to defy the opinion of her generation—for otherwise she is free—so far as to accept him for a husband. I should add that, more exacting and difficult to resist than any other element in that opinion, she would find the sentiment of her own sex. Our women have risen to the full height of their responsibility as the wardens of the world to come, to whose keeping the keys of the future are confided. Their feeling of duty in this respect amounts to a sense of religious consecration. It is a cult in which they educate their daughters from childhood."

After going to my room that night, I sat up late to read a romance of Berrian, handed me by Dr. Leete, the plot of which turned on a situation suggested by his last words, concerning the modern view of parental responsibility. A similar situation would almost certainly have been treated by a nineteenth century romancist so as to excite the morbid sympathy of the reader with the sentimental selfishness of the lovers, and his resentment toward the unwritten law which they outraged. I need not describe—for who has not read "Ruth Elton"?—how different is the course which Berrian takes, and with what tremendous effect he enforces the principle which he states: "Over the unborn our power is that of God, and our responsibility like His toward us. As we acquit ourselves toward them, so let Him deal with us."

XXVI

I think if a person were ever excusable for losing track of the days of the week, the circumstances excused me. Indeed, if I had been told that the method of reckoning time had been wholly changed and the days were now counted in lots of five, ten, or fifteen instead of seven, I should have been in no way surprised after what I had already heard and seen of the twentieth century. The first time that any inquiry as to the days of the week occurred to me was the morning following the conversation related in the last chapter. At the breakfast table Dr. Leete asked me if I would care to hear a sermon.

"Is it Sunday, then?" I exclaimed.

"Yes," he replied. "It was on Friday, you see, when we made the lucky discovery of the buried chamber to which we owe your society this morning. It was on Saturday morning, soon after midnight, that you first awoke, and Sunday afternoon when you awoke the second time with faculties fully regained."

"So you still have Sundays and sermons," I said. "We had prophets who foretold that long before this time the world would have dispensed with both. I am very curious to know how the ecclesiastical systems fit in with the rest of your social arrangements. I suppose you have a sort of national church with official clergymen."

Dr. Leete laughed, and Mrs. Leete and Edith seemed greatly amused.

"Why, Mr. West," Edith said, "what odd people you must think us. You were quite done with national religious establishments in the nineteenth century, and did you fancy we had gone back to them?"

"But how can voluntary churches and an unofficial clerical profession be reconciled with national ownership of all buildings, and the industrial service required of all men?" I answered.

"The religious practices of the people have naturally changed considerably in a century," replied Dr. Leete; "but supposing them to have remained unchanged, our social system would accommodate them perfectly. The nation supplies any person or number of persons with buildings on guarantee of the rent, and they remain tenants while they pay it. As for the clergymen, if a number of persons wish the services of an individual for any particular end of their own, apart from the general service of the nation, they can always secure it, with that individual's own consent, of course, just as we secure the service of our editors, by contributing from their credit cards an indemnity to the nation for the loss of his services in general industry. This indemnity paid the nation for the individual answers to the salary in your day paid to the individual himself; and the various applications of this principle leave private initiative full play in all details to which national control is not applicable. Now, as to hearing a sermon today, if you wish to do so, you can either go to a church to hear it or stay at home."

"How am I to hear it if I stay at home?"

"Simply by accompanying us to the music room at the proper hour and selecting an easy chair. There are some who still prefer to hear sermons in church, but most of our preaching, like our musical performances, is not in public, but delivered in acoustically prepared chambers, connected by wire with subscribers' houses. If you prefer to go to a church I shall be glad to accompany you, but I really don't believe you are likely to hear anywhere a better discourse than you will at home. I see by the paper that Mr. Barton is to preach this morning, and he preaches only by telephone, and to audiences often reaching 150,000."

"The novelty of the experience of hearing a sermon under such circumstances would incline me to be one of Mr. Barton's hearers, if for no other reason," I said.

An hour or two later, as I sat reading in the library, Edith came for me, and I followed her to the music room, where Dr. and Mrs. Leete were waiting. We had not more than seated ourselves comfortably when the tinkle of a bell was heard, and a few moments after the voice of a man, at the pitch of ordinary conversation, addressed us, with an effect of proceeding from an invisible person in the room. This was what the voice said:

MR. BARTON'S SERMON

"We have had among us, during the past week, a critic from the nineteenth century, a living representative of the epoch of our great-grandparents.

It would be strange if a fact so extraordinary had not somewhat strongly affected our imaginations. Perhaps most of us have been stimulated to some effort to realize the society of a century ago, and figure to ourselves what it must have been like to live then. In inviting you now to consider certain reflections upon this subject which have occurred to me, I presume that I shall rather follow than divert the course of your own thoughts."

Edith whispered something to her father at this point, to which he nodded assent and turned to me.

"Mr. West," he said, "Edith suggests that you may find it slightly embarrassing to listen to a discourse on the lines Mr. Barton is laying down, and if so, you need not be cheated out of a sermon. She will connect us with Mr. Sweetser's speaking room if you say so, and I can still promise you a very good discourse."

"No, no," I said. "Believe me, I would much rather hear what Mr. Barton has to say."

"As you please," replied my host.

When her father spoke to me Edith had touched a screw, and the voice of Mr. Barton had ceased abruptly. Now at another touch the room was once more filled with the earnest sympathetic tones which had already impressed me most favorably.

"I venture to assume that one effect has been common with us as a result of this effort at retrospection, and that it has been to leave us more than ever amazed at the stupendous change which one brief century has made in the material and moral conditions of humanity.

"Still, as regards the contrast between the poverty of the nation and the world in the nineteenth century and their wealth now, it is not greater, possibly, than had been before seen in human history, perhaps not greater, for example, than that between the poverty of this country during the earliest colonial period of the seventeenth century and the relatively great wealth it had attained at the close of the nineteenth, or between the England of William the Conqueror and that of Victoria. Although the aggregate riches of a nation did not then, as now, afford any accurate criterion of the masses of its people, yet instances like these afford partial parallels for the merely material side of the contrast between the nineteenth and the twentieth centuries. It is when we contemplate the moral aspect of that contrast that we find ourselves in the presence of a phenomenon for which history offers no precedent, however far back we may cast our eye. One might almost be excused who should exclaim, 'Here, surely, is something like a miracle!' Nevertheless, when we give over idle wonder, and begin to examine the seeming prodigy critically, we find it no prodigy at all, much less a miracle. It is not necessary to suppose a moral new birth of humanity, or a wholesale destruction of the wicked and survival of the good, to account for the fact before us. It finds its simple and obvious explanation in the reaction of a changed environment upon human nature. It means merely that a form of society which was founded on the pseudo self-interest of selfishness, and appealed solely to the anti-social and brutal side of human nature, has been replaced by institutions based on the true self-interest of a rational unselfishness, and appealing to the social and generous instincts of men.

"My friends, if you would see men again the beasts of prey they seemed in the nineteenth century, all you have to do is to restore the old social and industrial system, which taught them to view their natural prey in their fellow-men, and find their gain in the loss of others. No doubt it seems to you that no necessity, however dire, would have tempted you to subsist on what superior skill or strength enabled you to wrest from others equally needy. But suppose it were not merely your own life that you were responsible for. I know well that there must have been many a man among our ancestors who, if it had been merely a question of his own life, would sooner have given it up than nourished it by bread snatched from others. But this he was not permitted to do. He had dear lives dependent on him. Men loved women in those days, as now. God knows how they dared be fathers, but they had babies as sweet, no doubt, to them as ours to us, whom they must feed, clothe, educate. The gentlest creatures are fierce when they have young to provide for, and in that wolfish society the struggle for bread borrowed a peculiar desperation from the tenderest sentiments. For the sake of those dependent on him, a man might not choose, but must plunge into the foul fight—cheat, overreach, supplant, defraud, buy below worth and sell above, break down the business by which his neighbor fed his young ones, tempt men to buy what they ought not and to sell what they should not, grind his laborers, sweat his debtors, cozen his creditors. Though a man sought it carefully with tears, it was hard to find a way in which he could earn a living and provide for his family except by pressing in before some weaker rival and taking the food from his mouth. Even the ministers of religion were not exempt from this cruel necessity. While they warned their flocks against the love of money, regard for their families compelled them to keep an outlook for the pecuniary prizes of their calling. Poor fellows, theirs was indeed a trying business, preaching to men a generosity and unselfishness which they and everybody knew would, in the existing state of the world, reduce to poverty those who should practice them, laying down laws of conduct which the law of self-preservation compelled men to break. Looking on the inhuman spectacle of society, these worthy men bitterly bemoaned the depravity of human nature; as if angelic nature would not have been debauched in such a devil's school! Ah, my friends, believe me, it is not now in this happy age that humanity is proving the divinity within it. It was rather in those evil days when not even the fight for life with one another, the struggle for mere existence, in which mercy was folly, could wholly banish generosity and kindness from the earth.

"It is not hard to understand the desperation with which men and women, who under other conditions would have been full of gentleness and truth, fought and tore each other in the scramble for gold, when we realize what it meant to miss it, what poverty was in that day. For the body it was hunger and thirst, torment by heat and frost, in sickness neglect, in health unremitting toil; for the moral nature it meant oppression, contempt, and the patient endurance of indignity, brutish associations from infancy, the loss of all the innocence of childhood, the grace of womanhood, the dignity of manhood; for the mind it meant the death of ignorance, the torpor of all those faculties which distinguish us from brutes, the reduction of life to a round of bodily functions.

"Ah, my friends, if such a fate as this were offered you and your children as the only alternative of success in the accumulation of wealth, how long do you fancy would you be in sinking to the moral level of your ancestors?

"Some two or three centuries ago an act of barbarity was committed in India, which, though the number of lives destroyed was but a few score, was attended by such peculiar horrors that its memory is likely to be perpetual. A number of English prisoners were shut up in a room containing not enough air to supply one-tenth their number. The unfortunates were gallant men, devoted comrades in service, but, as the agonies of suffocation began to take hold on them, they forgot all else, and became involved in a hideous struggle, each one for himself, and against all others, to force a way to one of the small apertures of the prison at which alone it was possible to get a breath of air. It was a struggle in which men became beasts, and the recital of its horrors by the few survivors so shocked our forefathers that for a century later we find it a stock reference in their literature as a typical illustration of the extreme possibilities of human misery, as shocking in its moral as its physical aspect. They could scarcely have anticipated that to us the Black Hole of Calcutta, with its press of maddened men tearing and trampling one another in the struggle to win a place at the breathing holes, would seem a striking type of the society of their age. It lacked something of being a complete type, however, for in the Calcutta Black Hole there were no tender women, no little children and old men and women, no cripples. They were at least all men, strong to bear, who suffered.

"When we reflect that the ancient order of which I have been speaking was prevalent up to the end of the nineteenth century, while to us the new order which succeeded it already seems antique, even our parents having known no other, we cannot fail to be astounded at the suddenness with which a transition so profound beyond all previous experience of the race must have been effected. Some observation of the state of men's minds during the last quarter of the nineteenth century will, however, in great measure, dissipate this astonishment. Though general intelligence in the modern sense could not be said to exist in any community at that time, yet, as compared with previous generations, the one then on the stage was intelligent. The inevitable consequence of even this comparative degree of intelligence had been a perception of the evils of society, such as had never before been general. It is quite true that these evils had been even worse, much worse, in previous ages. It was the increased intelligence of the masses which made the difference, as the dawn reveals the squalor of surroundings which in the darkness may have seemed tolerable. The keynote of the literature of the period was one of compassion for the poor and unfortunate, and indignant outcry against the failure of the social machinery to ameliorate the miseries of men. It is plain from these outbursts that the moral hideousness of the spectacle about them was, at least by flashes, fully realized by the best of the men of that time, and that the lives of some of the more sensitive and generous hearted of them were rendered well nigh unendurable by the intensity of their sympathies.

"Although the idea of the vital unity of the family of mankind, the reality of human brotherhood, was very far from being apprehended by them as the moral axiom it seems to us, yet it is a mistake to suppose that there was no feeling at all corresponding to it. I could read you passages of great beauty from some of their writers which show that the conception was clearly attained by a few, and no doubt vaguely by many more. Moreover, it must not be forgotten that the nineteenth century was in name Christian, and the fact that the entire commercial and industrial frame of society was the embodiment of the anti-Christian spirit must have had some weight, though I admit it was strangely little, with the nominal followers of Jesus Christ.

"When we inquire why it did not have more, why, in general, long after a vast majority of men had agreed as to the crying abuses of the existing social arrangement, they still tolerated it, or contented themselves with talking of petty reforms in it, we come upon an extraordinary fact. It was the sincere belief of even the best of men at that epoch that the only stable elements in human nature, on which a social system could be safely founded, were its worst propensities. They had been taught and believed that greed and self-seeking were all that held mankind together, and that all human associations would fall to pieces if anything were done to blunt the edge of these motives or curb their operation. In a word, they believed—even those who longed to believe otherwise—the exact reverse of what seems to us self-evident; they believed, that is, that the anti-social qualities of men, and not their social qualities, were what furnished the cohesive force of society.

It seemed reasonable to them that men lived together solely for the purpose of overreaching and oppressing one another, and of being overreached and oppressed, and that while a society that gave full scope to these propensities could stand, there would be little chance for one based on the idea of cooperation for the benefit of all. It seems absurd to expect any one to believe that convictions like these were ever seriously entertained by men; but that they were not only entertained by our great-grandfathers, but were responsible for the long delay in doing away with the ancient order, after a conviction of its intolerable abuses had become general, is as well established as any fact in history can be. Just here you will find the explanation of the profound pessimism of the literature of the last quarter of the nineteenth century, the note of melancholy in its poetry, and the cynicism of its humor.

"Feeling that the condition of the race was unendurable, they had no clear hope of anything better. They believed that the evolution of humanity had resulted in leading it into a cul de sac, and that there was no way of getting forward. The frame of men's minds at this time is strikingly illustrated by treatises which have come down to us, and may even now be consulted in our libraries by the curious, in which laborious arguments are pursued to prove that despite the evil plight of men, life was still, by some slight preponderance of considerations, probably better worth living than leaving. Despising themselves, they despised their Creator. There was a general decay of religious belief. Pale and watery gleams, from skies thickly veiled by doubt and dread, alone lighted up the chaos of earth. That men should doubt Him whose breath is in their nostrils, or dread the hands that molded them, seems to us indeed a pitiable insanity; but we must remember that children who are brave by day have sometimes foolish fears at night. The dawn has come since then. It is very easy to believe in the fatherhood of God in the twentieth century.

"Briefly, as must needs be in a discourse of this character, I have adverted to some of the causes which had prepared men's minds for the change from the old to the new order, as well as some causes of the conservatism of despair which for a while held it back after the time was ripe. To wonder at the rapidity with which the change was completed after its possibility was first entertained is to forget the intoxicating effect of hope upon minds long accustomed to despair. The sunburst, after so long and dark a night, must needs have had a dazzling effect. From the moment men allowed themselves to believe that humanity after all had not been meant for a dwarf, that its squat stature was not the measure of its possible growth, but that it stood upon the verge of an avatar of limitless development, the reaction must needs have been overwhelming. It is evident that nothing was able to stand against the enthusiasm which the new faith inspired.

"Here, at last, men must have felt, was a cause compared with which the grandest of historic causes had been trivial. It was doubtless because it could have commanded millions of martyrs, that none were needed. The change of a dynasty in a petty kingdom of the old world often cost more lives than did the revolution which set the feet of the human race at last in the right way.

"Doubtless it ill beseems one to whom the boon of life in our resplendent age has been vouchsafed to wish his destiny other, and yet I have often thought that I would fain exchange my share in this serene and golden day for a place in that stormy epoch of transition, when heroes burst the barred gate of the future and revealed to the kindling gaze of a hopeless race, in place of the blank wall that had closed its path, a vista of progress whose end, for very excess of light, still dazzles us. Ah, my friends! Who will say that to have lived then, when the weakest influence was a lever to whose touch the centuries trembled, was not worth a share even in this era of fruition?

"You know the story of that last, greatest, and most bloodless of revolutions. In the time of one generation men laid aside the social traditions and practices of barbarians, and assumed a social order worthy of rational and human beings. Ceasing to be predatory in their habits, they became co-workers, and found in fraternity, at once, the science of wealth and happiness. 'What shall I eat and drink, and wherewithal shall I be clothed?' stated as a problem beginning and ending in self, had been an anxious and an endless one. But when once it was conceived, not from the individual, but the fraternal standpoint, 'What shall we eat and drink, and wherewithal shall we be clothed?'—its difficulties vanished.

"Poverty with servitude had been the result, for the mass of humanity, of attempting to solve the problem of maintenance from the individual standpoint, but no sooner had the nation become the sole capitalist and employer than not alone did plenty replace poverty, but the last vestige of the serfdom of man to man disappeared from earth. Human slavery, so often vainly scotched, at last was killed. The means of subsistence no longer doled out by men to women, by employer to employed, by rich to poor, was distributed from a common stock as among children at the father's table. It was impossible for a man any longer to use his fellow-men as tools for his own profit. His esteem was the only sort of gain he could thenceforth make out of him. There was no more either arrogance or servility in the relations of human beings to one another. For the first time since the creation every man stood up straight before God. The fear of want and the lust of gain became extinct motives when abundance was assured to all and immoderate possessions made impossible of attainment. There were no more beggars nor almoners. Equity left charity without an occupation. The ten commandments became well nigh obsolete in a world where there was no temptation to theft, no occasion to lie either for fear or favor, no room for envy where all were equal, and little provocation to violence where men were disarmed of power to injure one another. Humanity's ancient dream of liberty, equality, fraternity, mocked by so many ages, at last was realized.

"As in the old society the generous, the just, the tender-hearted had been placed at a disadvantage by the possession of those qualities; so in the new society the cold-hearted, the greedy, and self-seeking found themselves out of joint with the world. Now that the conditions of life for the first time ceased to operate as a forcing process to develop the brutal qualities of human nature, and the premium which had heretofore encouraged selfishness was not only removed, but placed upon unselfishness, it was for the first time possible to see what unperverted human nature really was like. The depraved tendencies, which had previously overgrown and obscured the better to so large an extent, now withered like cellar fungi in the open air, and the nobler qualities showed a sudden luxuriance which turned cynics into panegyrists and for the first time in human history tempted mankind to fall in love with itself. Soon was fully revealed, what the divines and philosophers of the old world never would have believed, that human nature in its essential qualities is good, not bad, that men by their natural intention and structure are generous, not selfish, pitiful, not cruel, sympathetic, not arrogant, godlike in aspirations, instinct with divinest impulses of tenderness and self-sacrifice, images of God indeed, not the travesties upon Him they had seemed. The constant pressure, through numberless generations, of conditions of life which might have perverted angels, had not been able to essentially alter the natural nobility of the stock, and these conditions once removed, like a bent tree, it had sprung back to its normal uprightness.

"To put the whole matter in the nutshell of a parable, let me compare humanity in the olden time to a rosebush planted in a swamp, watered with black bog-water, breathing miasmatic fogs by day, and chilled with poison dews at night. Innumerable generations of gardeners had done their best to make it bloom, but beyond an occasional half-opened bud with a worm at the heart, their efforts had been unsuccessful. Many, indeed, claimed that the bush was no rosebush at all, but a noxious shrub, fit only to be uprooted and burned. The gardeners, for the most part, however, held that the bush belonged to the rose family, but had some ineradicable taint about it, which prevented the buds from coming out, and accounted for its generally sickly condition. There were a few, indeed, who maintained that the stock was good enough, that the trouble was in the bog, and that under more favorable conditions the plant might be expected to do better. But these persons were not regular gardeners, and being condemned by the latter as mere theorists and daydreamers, were, for the most part, so regarded by the people. Moreover, urged some eminent moral philosophers, even conceding for the sake of the argument that the bush might possibly do better elsewhere, it was a more valuable discipline for the buds to try to bloom in a bog than it would be under more favorable conditions. The buds that succeeded in opening might indeed be very rare, and the flowers pale and scentless, but they represented far more moral effort than if they had bloomed spontaneously in a garden.

"The regular gardeners and the moral philosophers had their way. The bush remained rooted in the bog, and the old course of treatment went on. Continually new varieties of forcing mixtures were applied to the roots, and more recipes than could be numbered, each declared by its advocates the best and only suitable preparation, were used to kill the vermin and remove the mildew. This went on a very long time. Occasionally some one claimed to observe a slight improvement in the appearance of the bush, but there were quite as many who declared that it did not look so well as it used to. On the whole there could not be said to be any marked change. Finally, during a period of general despondency as to the prospects of the bush where it was, the idea of transplanting it was again mooted, and this time found favor. 'Let us try it,' was the general voice. 'Perhaps it may thrive better elsewhere, and here it is certainly doubtful if it be worth cultivating longer.' So it came about that the rosebush of humanity was transplanted, and set in sweet, warm, dry earth, where the sun bathed it, the stars wooed it, and the south wind caressed it. Then it appeared that it was indeed a rosebush. The vermin and the mildew disappeared, and the bush was covered with most beautiful red roses, whose fragrance filled the world.

"It is a pledge of the destiny appointed for us that the Creator has set in our hearts an infinite standard of achievement, judged by which our past attainments seem always insignificant, and the goal never nearer. Had our forefathers conceived a state of society in which men should live together like brethren dwelling in unity, without strifes or envying, violence or overreaching, and where, at the price of a degree of labor not greater than health demands, in their chosen occupations, they should be wholly freed from care for the morrow and left with no more concern for their livelihood than trees which are watered by unfailing streams—had they conceived such a condition, I say, it would have seemed to them nothing less than paradise. They would have confounded it with their idea of heaven, nor dreamed that there could possibly lie further beyond anything to be desired or striven for.

"But how is it with us who stand on this height which they gazed up to? Already we have well nigh forgotten, except when it is especially called to our minds by some occasion like the present, that it was not always with men as it is now. It is a strain on our imaginations to conceive the social arrangements of our immediate ancestors. We find them grotesque. The solution of the problem of physical maintenance so as to banish care and crime, so far from seeming to us an ultimate attainment, appears but as a preliminary to anything like real human progress. We have but relieved ourselves of an impertinent and needless harassment which hindered our ancestor from undertaking the real ends of existence. We are merely stripped for the race; no more. We are like a child which has just learned to stand upright and to walk. It is a great event, from the child's point of view, when he first walks. Perhaps he fancies that there can be little beyond that achievement, but a year later he has forgotten that he could not always walk. His horizon did but widen when he rose, and enlarge as he moved. A great event indeed, in one sense, was his first step, but only as a beginning, not as the end. His true career was but then first entered on. The enfranchisement of humanity in the last century, from mental and physical absorption in working and scheming for the mere bodily necessities, may be regarded as a species of second birth of the race, without which its first birth to an existence that was but a burden would forever have remained unjustified, but whereby it is now abundantly vindicated. Since then, humanity has entered on a new phase of spiritual development, an evolution of higher faculties, the very existence of which in human nature our ancestors scarcely suspected. In place of the dreary hopelessness of the nineteenth century, its profound pessimism as to the future of humanity, the animating idea of the present age is an enthusiastic conception of the opportunities of our earthly existence, and the unbounded possibilities of human nature. The betterment of mankind from generation to generation, physically, mentally, morally, is recognized as the one great object supremely worthy of effort and of sacrifice. We believe the race for the first time to have entered on the realization of God's ideal of it, and each generation must now be a step upward.

"Do you ask what we look for when unnumbered generations shall have passed away? I answer, the way stretches far before us, but the end is lost in light. For twofold is the return of man to God 'who is our home,' the return of the individual by the way of death, and the return of the race by the fulfillment of the evolution, when the divine secret hidden in the germ shall be perfectly unfolded. With a tear for the dark past, turn we then to the dazzling future, and, veiling our eyes, press forward. The long and weary winter of the race is ended. Its summer has begun. Humanity has burst the chrysalis. The heavens are before it."

XXVII

I never could tell just why, but Sunday afternoon during my old life had been a time when I was peculiarly subject to melancholy, when the color unaccountably faded out of all the aspects of life, and everything appeared pathetically uninteresting. The hours, which in general were wont to bear me easily on their wings, lost the power of flight, and toward the close of the day, drooping quite to earth, had fairly to be dragged along by main strength. Perhaps it was partly owing to the established association of ideas that, despite the utter change in my circumstances, I fell into a state of profound depression on the afternoon of this my first Sunday in the twentieth century.

It was not, however, on the present occasion a depression without specific cause, the mere vague melancholy I have spoken of, but a sentiment suggested and certainly quite justified by my position. The sermon of Mr. Barton, with its constant implication of the vast moral gap between the century to which I belonged and that in which I found myself, had had an effect strongly to accentuate my sense of loneliness in it. Considerately and philosophically as he had spoken, his words could scarcely have failed to leave upon my mind a strong impression of the mingled pity, curiosity, and aversion which I, as a representative of an abhorred epoch, must excite in all around me.

The extraordinary kindness with which I had been treated by Dr. Leete and his family, and especially the goodness of Edith, had hitherto prevented my fully realizing that their real sentiment toward me must necessarily be that of the whole generation to which they belonged. The recognition of this, as regarded Dr. Leete and his amiable wife, however painful, I might have endured, but the conviction that Edith must share their feeling was more than I could bear.

The crushing effect with which this belated perception of a fact so obvious came to me opened my eyes fully to something which perhaps the reader has already suspected—I loved Edith.

Was it strange that I did? The affecting occasion on which our intimacy had begun, when her hands had drawn me out of the whirlpool of madness; the fact that her sympathy was the vital breath which had set me up in this new life and enabled me to support it; my habit of looking to her as the mediator between me and the world around in a sense that even her father was not—these were circumstances that had predetermined a result which her remarkable loveliness of person and disposition would alone have accounted for. It was quite inevitable that she should have come to seem to me, in a sense quite different from the usual experience of lovers, the only woman in this world. Now that I had become suddenly sensible of the fatuity of the hopes I had begun to cherish, I suffered not merely what another lover might, but in addition a desolate loneliness, an utter forlornness, such as no other lover, however unhappy, could have felt.

My hosts evidently saw that I was depressed in spirits, and did their best to divert me. Edith especially, I could see, was distressed for me, but according to the usual perversity of lovers, having once been so mad as to dream of receiving something more from her, there was no longer any virtue for me in a kindness that I knew was only sympathy.

Toward nightfall, after secluding myself in my room most of the afternoon, I went into the garden to walk about. The day was overcast, with an autumnal flavor in the warm, still air. Finding myself near the excavation, I entered the subterranean chamber and sat down there. "This," I muttered to myself, "is the only home I have. Let me stay here, and not go forth any more." Seeking aid from the familiar surroundings, I endeavored to find a sad sort of consolation in reviving the past and summoning up the forms and faces that were about me in my former life. It was in vain. There was no longer any life in them. For nearly one hundred years the stars had been looking down on Edith Bartlett's grave, and the graves of all my generation.

The past was dead, crushed beneath a century's weight, and from the present I was shut out. There was no place for me anywhere. I was neither dead nor properly alive.

"Forgive me for following you."

I looked up. Edith stood in the door of the subterranean room, regarding me smilingly, but with eyes full of sympathetic distress.

"Send me away if I am intruding on you," she said; "but we saw that you were out of spirits, and you know you promised to let me know if that were so. You have not kept your word."

I rose and came to the door, trying to smile, but making, I fancy, rather sorry work of it, for the sight of her loveliness brought home to me the more poignantly the cause of my wretchedness.

"I was feeling a little lonely, that is all," I said. "Has it never occurred to you that my position is so much more utterly alone than any human being's ever was before that a new word is really needed to describe it?"

"Oh, you must not talk that way—you must not let yourself feel that way—you must not!" she exclaimed, with moistened eyes. "Are we not your friends? It is your own fault if you will not let us be. You need not be lonely."

"You are good to me beyond my power of understanding," I said, "but don't you suppose that I know it is pity merely, sweet pity, but pity only. I should be a fool not to know that I cannot seem to you as other men of your own generation do, but as some strange uncanny being, a stranded creature of an unknown sea, whose forlornness touches your compassion despite its grotesqueness. I have been so foolish, you were so kind, as to almost forget that this must needs be so, and to fancy I might in time become naturalized, as we used to say, in this age, so as to feel like one of you and to seem to you like the other men about you. But Mr. Barton's sermon taught me how vain such a fancy is, how great the gulf between us must seem to you."

"Oh that miserable sermon!" she exclaimed, fairly crying now in her sympathy, "I wanted you not to hear it. What does he know of you? He has read in old musty books about your times, that is all. What do you care about him, to let yourself be vexed by anything he said? Isn't it anything to you, that we who know you feel differently? Don't you care more about what we think of you than what he does who never saw you? Oh, Mr. West! you don't know, you can't think, how it makes me feel to see you so forlorn. I can't have it so. What can I say to you? How can I convince you how different our feeling for you is from what you think?"

As before, in that other crisis of my fate when she had come to me, she extended her hands toward me in a gesture of helpfulness, and, as then, I caught and held them in my own; her bosom heaved with strong emotion, and little tremors in the fingers which I clasped emphasized the depth of her feeling. In her face, pity contended in a sort of divine spite against the obstacles which reduced it to impotence. Womanly compassion surely never wore a guise more lovely.

Such beauty and such goodness quite melted me, and it seemed that the only fitting response I could make was to tell her just the truth. Of course I had not a spark of hope, but on the other hand I had no fear that she would be angry. She was too pitiful for that. So I said presently, "It is very ungrateful in me not to be satisfied with such kindness as you have shown me, and are showing me now. But are you so blind as not to see why they are not enough to make me happy? Don't you see that it is because I have been mad enough to love you?"

At my last words she blushed deeply and her eyes fell before mine, but she made no effort to withdraw her hands from my clasp. For some moments she stood so, panting a little. Then blushing deeper than ever, but with a dazzling smile, she looked up.

"Are you sure it is not you who are blind?" she said.

That was all, but it was enough, for it told me that, unaccountable, incredible as it was, this radiant daughter of a golden age had bestowed upon me not alone her pity, but her love. Still, I half believed I must be under some blissful hallucination even as I clasped her in my arms. "If I am beside myself," I cried, "let me remain so."

"It is I whom you must think beside myself," she panted, escaping from my arms when I had barely tasted the sweetness of her lips. "Oh! oh! what must you think of me almost to throw myself in the arms of one I have known but a week? I did not mean that you should find it out so soon, but I was so sorry for you I forgot what I was saying. No, no; you must not touch me again till you know who I am. After that, sir, you shall apologize to me very humbly for thinking, as I know you do, that I have been over quick to fall in love with you. After you know who I am, you will be bound to confess that it was nothing less than my duty to fall in love with you at first sight, and that no girl of proper feeling in my place could do otherwise."

As may be supposed, I would have been quite content to waive explanations, but Edith was resolute that there should be no more kisses until she had been vindicated from all suspicion of precipitancy in the bestowal of her affections, and I was fain to follow the lovely enigma into the house. Having come where her mother was, she blushingly whispered something in her ear and ran away, leaving us together.

It then appeared that, strange as my experience had been, I was now first to know what was perhaps its strangest feature. From Mrs. Leete I learned that Edith was the great-granddaughter of no other than my lost love, Edith Bartlett. After mourning me for fourteen years, she had made a marriage of esteem, and left a son who had been Mrs. Leete's father. Mrs. Leete had never seen her grandmother, but had heard much of her, and, when her daughter was born, gave her the name of Edith. This fact might have tended to increase the interest which the girl took, as she grew up, in all that concerned her ancestress, and especially the tragic story of the supposed death of the lover, whose wife she expected to be, in the conflagration of his house. It was a tale well calculated to touch the sympathy of a romantic girl, and the fact that the blood of the unfortunate heroine was in her own veins naturally heightened Edith's interest in it. A portrait of Edith Bartlett and some of her papers, including a packet of my own letters, were among the family heirlooms. The picture represented a very beautiful young woman about whom it was easy to imagine all manner of tender and romantic things. My letters gave Edith some material for forming a distinct idea of my personality, and both together sufficed to make the sad old story very real to her. She used to tell her parents, half jestingly, that she would never marry till she found a lover like Julian West, and there were none such nowadays.

Now all this, of course, was merely the daydreaming of a girl whose mind had never been taken up by a love affair of her own, and would have had no serious consequence but for the discovery that morning of the buried vault in her father's garden and the revelation of the identity of its inmate. For when the apparently lifeless form had been borne into the house, the face in the locket found upon the breast was instantly recognized as that of Edith Bartlett, and by that fact, taken in connection with the other circumstances, they knew that I was no other than Julian West. Even had there been no thought, as at first there was not, of my resuscitation, Mrs. Leete said she believed that this event would have affected her daughter in a critical and life-long manner. The presumption of some subtle ordering of destiny, involving her fate with mine, would under all circumstances have possessed an irresistible fascination for almost any woman.

Whether when I came back to life a few hours afterward, and from the first seemed to turn to her with a peculiar dependence and to find a special solace in her company, she had been too quick in giving her love at the first sign of mine, I could now, her mother said, judge for myself. If I thought so, I must remember that this, after all, was the twentieth and not the nineteenth century, and love was, no doubt, now quicker in growth, as well as franker in utterance than then.

From Mrs. Leete I went to Edith. When I found her, it was first of all to take her by both hands and stand a long time in rapt contemplation of her face. As I gazed, the memory of that other Edith, which had been affected as with a benumbing shock by the tremendous experience that had parted us, revived, and my heart was dissolved with tender and pitiful emotions, but also very blissful ones. For she who brought to me so poignantly the sense of my loss was to make that loss good. It was as if from her eyes Edith Bartlett looked into mine, and smiled consolation to me. My fate was not alone the strangest, but the most fortunate that ever befell a man. A double miracle had been wrought for me. I had not been stranded upon the shore of this strange world to find myself alone and companionless. My love, whom I had dreamed lost, had been reembodied for my consolation. When at last, in an ecstasy of gratitude and tenderness, I folded the lovely girl in my arms, the two Ediths were blended in my thought, nor have they ever since been clearly distinguished. I was not long in finding that on Edith's part there was a corresponding confusion of identities. Never, surely, was there between freshly united lovers a stranger talk than ours that afternoon. She seemed more anxious to have me speak of Edith Bartlett than of herself, of how I had loved her than how I loved herself, rewarding my fond words concerning another woman with tears and tender smiles and pressures of the hand.

"You must not love me too much for myself," she said. "I shall be very jealous for her. I shall not let you forget her. I am going to tell you something which you may think strange. Do you not believe that spirits sometimes come back to the world to fulfill some work that lay near their hearts? What if I were to tell you that I have sometimes thought that her spirit lives in me—that Edith Bartlett, not Edith Leete, is my real name. I cannot know it; of course none of us can know who we really are; but I can feel it. Can you wonder that I have such a feeling, seeing how my life was affected by her and by you, even before you came. So you see you need not trouble to love me at all, if only you are true to her. I shall not be likely to be jealous."

Dr. Leete had gone out that afternoon, and I did not have an interview with him till later. He was not, apparently, wholly unprepared for the intelligence I conveyed, and shook my hand heartily.

"Under any ordinary circumstances, Mr. West, I should say that this step had been taken on rather short acquaintance; but these are decidedly not ordinary circumstances. In fairness, perhaps I ought to tell you," he added smilingly, "that while I cheerfully consent to the proposed arrangement, you must not feel too much indebted to me, as I judge my consent is a mere formality. From the moment the secret of the locket was out, it had to be, I fancy. Why, bless me, if Edith had not been there to redeem her great-grandmother's pledge, I really apprehend that Mrs. Leete's loyalty to me would have suffered a severe strain."

That evening the garden was bathed in moonlight, and till midnight Edith and I wandered to and fro there, trying to grow accustomed to our happiness.

"What should I have done if you had not cared for me?" she exclaimed. "I was afraid you were not going to. What should I have done then, when I felt I was consecrated to you! As soon as you came back to life, I was as sure as if she had told me that I was to be to you what she could not be, but that could only be if you would let me. Oh, how I wanted to tell you that morning, when you felt so terribly strange among us, who I was, but dared not open my lips about that, or let father or mother—"

"That must have been what you would not let your father tell me!" I exclaimed, referring to the conversation I had overheard as I came out of my trance.

"Of course it was," Edith laughed. "Did you only just guess that? Father being only a man, thought that it would make you feel among friends to tell you who we were. He did not think of me at all. But mother knew what I meant, and so I had my way. I could never have looked you in the face if you had known who I was. It would have been forcing myself on you quite too boldly. I am afraid you think I did that today, as it was. I am sure I did not mean to, for I know girls were expected to hide their feelings in your day, and I was dreadfully afraid of shocking you. Ah me, how hard it must have been for them to have always had to conceal their love like a fault. Why did they think it such a shame to love any one till they had been given permission? It is so odd to think of waiting for permission to fall in love. Was it because men in those days were angry when girls loved them? That is not the way women would feel, I am sure, or men either, I think, now. I don't understand it at all. That will be one of the curious things about the women of those days that you will have to explain to me. I don't believe Edith Bartlett was so foolish as the others."

After sundry ineffectual attempts at parting, she finally insisted that we must say good night. I was about to imprint upon her lips the positively last kiss, when she said, with an indescribable archness:

"One thing troubles me. Are you sure that you quite forgive Edith Bartlett for marrying any one else? The books that have come down to us make out lovers of your time more jealous than fond, and that is what makes me ask. It would be a great relief to me if I could feel sure that you were not in the least jealous of my great-grandfather for marrying your sweetheart. May I tell my great-grandmother's picture when I go to my room that you quite forgive her for proving false to you?"

Will the reader believe it, this coquettish quip, whether the speaker herself had any idea of it or not, actually touched and with the touching cured a preposterous ache of something like jealousy which I had been vaguely conscious of ever since Mrs. Leete had told me of Edith Bartlett's marriage. Even while I had been holding Edith Bartlett's great-granddaughter in my arms, I had not, till this moment, so illogical are some of our feelings, distinctly realized that but for that marriage I could not have done so. The absurdity of this frame of mind could only be equalled by the abruptness with which it dissolved as Edith's roguish query cleared the fog from my perceptions. I laughed as I kissed her.

"You may assure her of my entire forgiveness," I said, "although if it had been any man but your great-grandfather whom she married, it would have been a very different matter."

On reaching my chamber that night I did not open the musical telephone that I might be lulled to sleep with soothing tunes, as had become my habit. For once my thoughts made better music than even twentieth century orchestras discourse, and it held me enchanted till well toward morning, when I fell asleep.

XXVIII

"It's a little after the time you told me to wake you, sir. You did not come out of it as quick as common, sir."

The voice was the voice of my man Sawyer. I started bolt upright in bed and stared around. I was in my underground chamber. The mellow light of the lamp which always burned in the room when I occupied it illumined the familiar walls and furnishings. By my bedside, with the glass of sherry in his hand which Dr. Pillsbury prescribed on first rousing from a mesmeric sleep, by way of awakening the torpid physical functions, stood Sawyer.

"Better take this right off, sir," he said, as I stared blankly at him. "You look kind of flushed like, sir, and you need it."

I tossed off the liquor and began to realize what had happened to me. It was, of course, very plain. All that about the twentieth century had been a dream. I had but dreamed of that enlightened and care-free race of men and their ingeniously simple institutions, of the glorious new Boston with its domes and pinnacles, its gardens and fountains, and its universal reign of comfort. The amiable family which I had learned to know so well, my genial host and Mentor, Dr. Leete, his wife, and their daughter, the second and more beauteous Edith, my betrothed—these, too, had been but figments of a vision.

For a considerable time I remained in the attitude in which this conviction had come over me, sitting up in bed gazing at vacancy, absorbed in recalling the scenes and incidents of my fantastic experience. Sawyer, alarmed at my looks, was meanwhile anxiously inquiring what was the matter with me. Roused at length by his importunities to a recognition of my surroundings, I pulled myself together with an effort and assured the faithful fellow that I was all right. "I have had an extraordinary dream, that's all, Sawyer," I said, "a most-ex-traor-dinary dream."

I dressed in a mechanical way, feeling light-headed and oddly uncertain of myself, and sat down to the coffee and rolls which Sawyer was in the habit of providing for my refreshment before I left the house. The morning newspaper lay by the plate. I took it up, and my eye fell on the date, May 31, 1887. I had known, of course, from the moment I opened my eyes that my long and detailed experience in another century had been a dream, and yet it was startling to have it so conclusively demonstrated that the world was but a few hours older than when I had lain down to sleep.

Glancing at the table of contents at the head of the paper, which reviewed the news of the morning, I read the following summary:

FOREIGN AFFAIRS: The impending war between France and Germany. The French Chambers asked for new military credits to meet Germany's increase of her army. Probability that all Europe will be involved in case of war. Great suffering among the unemployed in London. They demand work. Monster demonstration to be made. The authorities uneasy. Great strikes in Belgium. The government preparing to repress outbreaks. Shocking facts in regard to the employment of girls in Belgium coal mines. Wholesale evictions in Ireland.

"HOME AFFAIRS: The epidemic of fraud unchecked. Embezzlement of half a million in New York. Misappropriation of a trust fund by executors. Orphans left penniless. Clever system of thefts by a bank teller; $50,000 gone. The coal barons decide to advance the price of coal and reduce production. Speculators engineering a great wheat corner at Chicago. A clique forcing up the price of coffee. Enormous land-grabs of Western syndicates. Revelations of shocking corruption among Chicago officials. Systematic bribery. The trials of the Boodle aldermen to go on at New York. Large failures of business houses. Fears of a business crisis. A large grist of burglaries and larcenies. A woman murdered in cold blood for her money at New Haven. A householder shot by a burglar in this city last night. A man shoots himself in Worcester because he could not get work. A large family left destitute.

An aged couple in New Jersey commit suicide rather than go to the poorhouse. Pitiable destitution among the women wage-workers in the great cities. Startling growth of illiteracy in Massachusetts. More insane asylums wanted. Decoration Day addresses. Professor Brown's oration on the moral grandeur of nineteenth century civilization."

It was indeed the nineteenth century to which I had awaked; there could be no kind of doubt about that. Its complete microcosm this summary of the day's news had presented, even to that last unmistakable touch of fatuous self-complacency. Coming after such a damning indictment of the age as that one day's chronicle of worldwide bloodshed, greed, and tyranny, was a bit of cynicism worthy of Mephistopheles, and yet of all whose eyes it had met this morning I was, perhaps, the only one who perceived the cynicism, and but yesterday I should have perceived it no more than the others. That strange dream it was which had made all the difference. For I know not how long, I forgot my surroundings after this, and was again in fancy moving in that vivid dream-world, in that glorious city, with its homes of simple comfort and its gorgeous public palaces. Around me were again faces unmarred by arrogance or servility, by envy or greed, by anxious care or feverish ambition, and stately forms of men and women who had never known fear of a fellow man or depended on his favor, but always, in the words of that sermon which still rang in my ears, had "stood up straight before God."

With a profound sigh and a sense of irreparable loss, not the less poignant that it was a loss of what had never really been, I roused at last from my reverie, and soon after left the house.

A dozen times between my door and Washington Street I had to stop and pull myself together, such power had been in that vision of the Boston of the future to make the real Boston strange. The squalor and malodorousness of the town struck me, from the moment I stood upon the street, as facts I had never before observed. But yesterday, moreover, it had seemed quite a matter of course that some of my fellow-citizens should wear silks, and others rags, that some should look well fed, and others hungry. Now on the contrary the glaring disparities in the dress and condition of the men and women who brushed each other on the sidewalks shocked me at every step, and yet more the entire indifference which the prosperous showed to the plight of the unfortunate. Were these human beings, who could behold the wretchedness of their fellows without so much as a change of countenance? And yet, all the while, I knew well that it was I who had changed, and not my contemporaries. I had dreamed of a city whose people fared all alike as children of one family and were one another's keepers in all things.

Another feature of the real Boston, which assumed the extraordinary effect of strangeness that marks familiar things seen in a new light, was the prevalence of advertising. There had been no personal advertising in the Boston of the twentieth century, because there was no need of any, but here the walls of the buildings, the windows, the broadsides of the newspapers in every hand, the very pavements, everything in fact in sight, save the sky, were covered with the appeals of individuals who sought, under innumerable pretexts, to attract the contributions of others to their support. However the wording might vary, the tenor of all these appeals was the same:

"Help John Jones. Never mind the rest. They are frauds. I, John Jones, am the right one. Buy of me. Employ me. Visit me. Hear me, John Jones. Look at me. Make no mistake, John Jones is the man and nobody else. Let the rest starve, but for God's sake remember John Jones!"

Whether the pathos or the moral repulsiveness of the spectacle most impressed me, so suddenly become a stranger in my own city, I know not. Wretched men, I was moved to cry, who, because they will not learn to be helpers of one another, are doomed to be beggars of one another from the least to the greatest! This horrible babel of shameless self-assertion and mutual depreciation, this stunning clamor of conflicting boasts, appeals, and adjurations, this stupendous system of brazen beggary, what was it all but the necessity of a society in which the opportunity to serve the world according to his gifts, instead of being secured to every man as the first object of social organization, had to be fought for!

I reached Washington Street at the busiest point, and there I stood and laughed aloud, to the scandal of the passers-by. For my life I could not have helped it, with such a mad humor was I moved at sight of the interminable rows of stores on either side, up and down the street so far as I could see—scores of them, to make the spectacle more utterly preposterous, within a stone's throw devoted to selling the same sort of goods. Stores! Stores! Stores! Miles of stores! Ten thousand stores to distribute the goods needed by this one city, which in my dream had been supplied with all things from a single warehouse, as they were ordered through one great store in every quarter, where the buyer, without waste of time or labor, found under one roof the world's assortment in whatever line he desired. There the labor of distribution had been so slight as to add but a scarcely perceptible fraction to the cost of commodities to the user. The cost of production was virtually all he paid. But here the mere distribution of the goods, their handling alone, added a fourth, a third, a half and more, to the cost. All these ten thousand plants must be paid for, their rent, their staffs of superintendence, their platoons of salesmen, their ten thousand sets of accountants, jobbers, and business dependents, with all they spent in advertising themselves and fighting one another, and the consumers must do the paying. What a famous process for beggaring a nation!

Were these serious men I saw about me, or children, who did their business on such a plan? Could they be reasoning beings, who did not see the folly which, when the product is made and ready for use, wastes so much of it in getting it to the user? If people eat with a spoon that leaks half its contents between bowl and lip, are they not likely to go hungry?

I had passed through Washington Street thousands of times before and viewed the ways of those who sold merchandise, but my curiosity concerning them was as if I had never gone by their way before. I took wondering note of the show windows of the stores, filled with goods arranged with a wealth of pains and artistic device to attract the eye. I saw the throngs of ladies looking in, and the proprietors eagerly watching the effect of the bait. I went within and noted the hawk-eyed floor-walker watching for business, overlooking the clerks, keeping them up to their task of inducing the customers to buy, buy, buy, for money if they had it, for credit if they had it not, to buy what they wanted not, more than they wanted, what they could not afford. At times I momentarily lost the clue and was confused by the sight. Why this effort to induce people to buy? Surely that had nothing to do with the legitimate business of distributing products to those who needed them. Surely it was the sheerest waste to force upon people what they did not want, but what might be useful to another. The nation was so much the poorer for every such achievement. What were these clerks thinking of? Then I would remember that they were not acting as distributors like those in the store I had visited in the dream Boston. They were not serving the public interest, but their immediate personal interest, and it was nothing to them what the ultimate effect of their course on the general prosperity might be, if but they increased their own hoard, for these goods were their own, and the more they sold and the more they got for them, the greater their gain. The more wasteful the people were, the more articles they did not want which they could be induced to buy, the better for these sellers. To encourage prodigality was the express aim of the ten thousand stores of Boston.

Nor were these storekeepers and clerks a whit worse men than any others in Boston. They must earn a living and support their families, and how were they to find a trade to do it by which did not necessitate placing their individual interests before those of others and that of all? They could not be asked to starve while they waited for an order of things such as I had seen in my dream, in which the interest of each and that of all were identical. But, God in heaven! what wonder, under such a system as this about me—what wonder that the city was so shabby, and the people so meanly dressed, and so many of them ragged and hungry!

Some time after this it was that I drifted over into South Boston and found myself among the manufacturing establishments. I had been in this quarter of the city a hundred times before, just as I had been on Washington Street, but here, as well as there, I now first perceived the true significance of what I witnessed. Formerly I had taken pride in the fact that, by actual count, Boston had some four thousand independent manufacturing establishments; but in this very multiplicity and independence I recognized now the secret of the insignificant total product of their industry.

If Washington Street had been like a lane in Bedlam, this was a spectacle as much more melancholy as production is a more vital function than distribution. For not only were these four thousand establishments not working in concert, and for that reason alone operating at prodigious disadvantage, but, as if this did not involve a sufficiently disastrous loss of power, they were using their utmost skill to frustrate one another's effort, praying by night and working by day for the destruction of one another's enterprises.

The roar and rattle of wheels and hammers resounding from every side was not the hum of a peaceful industry, but the clangor of swords wielded by foemen. These mills and shops were so many forts, each under its own flag, its guns trained on the mills and shops about it, and its sappers busy below, undermining them.

Within each one of these forts the strictest organization of industry was insisted on; the separate gangs worked under a single central authority. No interference and no duplicating of work were permitted. Each had his allotted task, and none were idle. By what hiatus in the logical faculty, by what lost link of reasoning, account, then, for the failure to recognize the necessity of applying the same principle to the organization of the national industries as a whole, to see that if lack of organization could impair the efficiency of a shop, it must have effects as much more disastrous in disabling the industries of the nation at large as the latter are vaster in volume and more complex in the relationship of their parts.

People would be prompt enough to ridicule an army in which there were neither companies, battalions, regiments, brigades, divisions, or army corps—no unit of organization, in fact, larger than the corporal's squad, with no officer higher than a corporal, and all the corporals equal in authority. And yet just such an army were the manufacturing industries of nineteenth century Boston, an army of four thousand independent squads led by four thousand independent corporals, each with a separate plan of campaign.

Knots of idle men were to be seen here and there on every side, some idle because they could find no work at any price, others because they could not get what they thought a fair price. I accosted some of the latter, and they told me their grievances. It was very little comfort I could give them. "I am sorry for you," I said. "You get little enough, certainly, and yet the wonder to me is, not that industries conducted as these are do not pay you living wages, but that they are able to pay you any wages at all."

Making my way back again after this to the peninsular city, toward three o'clock I stood on State Street, staring, as if I had never seen them before, at the banks and brokers' offices, and other financial institutions, of which there had been in the State Street of my vision no vestige. Business men, confidential clerks, and errand boys were thronging in and out of the banks, for it wanted but a few minutes of the closing hour. Opposite me was the bank where I did business, and presently I crossed the street, and, going in with the crowd, stood in a recess of the wall looking on at the army of clerks handling money, and the cues of depositors at the tellers' windows. An old gentleman whom I knew, a director of the bank, passing me and observing my contemplative attitude, stopped a moment.

"Interesting sight, isn't it, Mr. West," he said. "Wonderful piece of mechanism; I find it so myself. I like sometimes to stand and look on at it just as you are doing. It's a poem, sir, a poem, that's what I call it. Did you ever think, Mr. West, that the bank is the heart of the business system? From it and to it, in endless flux and reflux, the life blood goes. It is flowing in now. It will flow out again in the morning"; and pleased with his little conceit, the old man passed on smiling.

Yesterday I should have considered the simile apt enough, but since then I had visited a world incomparably more affluent than this, in which money was unknown and without conceivable use. I had learned that it had a use in the world around me only because the work of producing the nation's livelihood, instead of being regarded as the most strictly public and common of all concerns, and as such conducted by the nation, was abandoned to the hap-hazard efforts of individuals. This original mistake necessitated endless exchanges to bring about any sort of general distribution of products. These exchanges money effected—how equitably, might be seen in a walk from the tenement house districts to the Back Bay—at the cost of an army of men taken from productive labor to manage it, with constant ruinous breakdowns of its machinery, and a generally debauching influence on mankind which had justified its description, from ancient time, as the "root of all evil."

Alas for the poor old bank director with his poem! He had mistaken the throbbing of an abscess for the beating of the heart. What he called "a wonderful piece of mechanism" was an imperfect device to remedy an unnecessary defect, the clumsy crutch of a self-made cripple.

After the banks had closed I wandered aimlessly about the business quarter for an hour or two, and later sat a while on one of the benches of the Common, finding an interest merely in watching the throngs that passed, such as one has in studying the populace of a foreign city, so strange since yesterday had my fellow citizens and their ways become to me. For thirty years I had lived among them, and yet I seemed to have never noted before how drawn and anxious were their faces, of the rich as of the poor, the refined, acute faces of the educated as well as the dull masks of the ignorant. And well it might be so, for I saw now, as never before I had seen so plainly, that each as he walked constantly turned to catch the whispers of a specter at his ear, the specter of Uncertainty. "Do your work never so well," the specter was whispering—"rise early and toil till late, rob cunningly or serve faithfully, you shall never know security. Rich you may be now and still come to poverty at last. Leave never so much wealth to your children, you cannot buy the assurance that your son may not be the servant of your servant, or that your daughter will not have to sell herself for bread."

A man passing by thrust an advertising card in my hand, which set forth the merits of some new scheme of life insurance. The incident reminded me of the only device, pathetic in its admission of the universal need it so poorly supplied, which offered these tired and hunted men and women even a partial protection from uncertainty. By this means, those already well-to-do, I remembered, might purchase a precarious confidence that after their death their loved ones would not, for a while at least, be trampled under the feet of men. But this was all, and this was only for those who could pay well for it. What idea was possible to these wretched dwellers in the land of Ishmael, where every man's hand was against each and the hand of each against every other, of true life insurance as I had seen it among the people of that dream land, each of whom, by virtue merely of his membership in the national family, was guaranteed against need of any sort, by a policy underwritten by one hundred million fellow countrymen.

Some time after this it was that I recall a glimpse of myself standing on the steps of a building on Tremont Street, looking at a military parade. A regiment was passing. It was the first sight in that dreary day which had inspired me with any other emotions than wondering pity and amazement. Here at last were order and reason, an exhibition of what intelligent cooperation can accomplish. The people who stood looking on with kindling faces—could it be that the sight had for them no more than but a spectacular interest? Could they fail to see that it was their perfect concert of action, their organization under one control, which made these men the tremendous engine they were, able to vanquish a mob ten times as numerous? Seeing this so plainly, could they fail to compare the scientific manner in which the nation went to war with the unscientific manner in which it went to work? Would they not query since what time the killing of men had been a task so much more important than feeding and clothing them, that a trained army should be deemed alone adequate to the former, while the latter was left to a mob?

It was now toward nightfall, and the streets were thronged with the workers from the stores, the shops, and mills. Carried along with the stronger part of the current, I found myself, as it began to grow dark, in the midst of a scene of squalor and human degradation such as only the South Cove tenement district could present. I had seen the mad wasting of human labor; here I saw in direst shape the want that waste had bred.

From the black doorways and windows of the rookeries on every side came gusts of fetid air. The streets and alleys reeked with the effluvia of a slave ship's between-decks. As I passed I had glimpses within of pale babies gasping out their lives amid sultry stenches, of hopeless-faced women deformed by hardship, retaining of womanhood no trait save weakness, while from the windows leered girls with brows of brass. Like the starving bands of mongrel curs that infest the streets of Moslem towns, swarms of half-clad brutalized children filled the air with shrieks and curses as they fought and tumbled among the garbage that littered the court-yards.

There was nothing in all this that was new to me. Often had I passed through this part of the city and witnessed its sights with feelings of disgust mingled with a certain philosophical wonder at the extremities mortals will endure and still cling to life. But not alone as regarded the economical follies of this age, but equally as touched its moral abominations, scales had fallen from my eyes since that vision of another century. No more did I look upon the woeful dwellers in this Inferno with a callous curiosity as creatures scarcely human. I saw in them my brothers and sisters, my parents, my children, flesh of my flesh, blood of my blood. The festering mass of human wretchedness about me offended not now my senses merely, but pierced my heart like a knife, so that I could not repress sighs and groans. I not only saw but felt in my body all that I saw.

Presently, too, as I observed the wretched beings about me more closely, I perceived that they were all quite dead. Their bodies were so many living sepulchers. On each brutal brow was plainly written the *hic jacet* of a soul dead within.

As I looked, horror struck, from one death's head to another, I was affected by a singular hallucination. Like a wavering translucent spirit face superimposed upon each of these brutish masks I saw the ideal, the possible face that would have been the actual if mind and soul had lived. It was not till I was aware of these ghostly faces, and of the reproach that could not be gainsaid which was in their eyes, that the full piteousness of the ruin that had been wrought was revealed to me. I was moved with contrition as with a strong agony, for I had been one of those who had endured that these things should be. I had been one of those who, well knowing that they were, had not desired to hear or be compelled to think much of them, but had gone on as if they were not, seeking my own pleasure and profit. Therefore now I found upon my garments the blood of this great multitude of strangled souls of my brothers. The voice of their blood cried out against me from the ground. Every stone of the reeking pavements, every brick of the pestilential rookeries, found a tongue and called after me as I fled: What hast thou done with thy brother Abel?

I have no clear recollection of anything after this till I found myself standing on the carved stone steps of the magnificent home of my betrothed in Commonwealth Avenue. Amid the tumult of my thoughts that day, I had scarcely once thought of her, but now obeying some unconscious impulse my feet had found the familiar way to her door. I was told that the family were at dinner, but word was sent out that I should join them at table. Besides the family, I found several guests present, all known to me. The table glittered with plate and costly china. The ladies were sumptuously dressed and wore the jewels of queens. The scene was one of costly elegance and lavish luxury. The company was in excellent spirits, and there was plentiful laughter and a running fire of jests.

To me it was as if, in wandering through the place of doom, my blood turned to tears by its sights, and my spirit attuned to sorrow, pity, and despair, I had happened in some glade upon a merry party of roisterers. I sat in silence until Edith began to rally me upon my somber looks, What ailed me? The others presently joined in the playful assault, and I became a target for quips and jests. Where had I been, and what had I seen to make such a dull fellow of me?

"I have been in Golgotha," at last I answered. "I have seen Humanity hanging on a cross! Do none of you know what sights the sun and stars look down on in this city, that you can think and talk of anything else? Do you not know that close to your doors a great multitude of men and women, flesh of your flesh, live lives that are one agony from birth to death? Listen! Their dwellings are so near that if you hush your laughter you will hear their grievous voices, the piteous crying of the little ones that suckle poverty, the hoarse curses of men sodden in misery turned half-way back to brutes, the chaffering of an army of women selling themselves for bread. With what have you stopped your ears that you do not hear these doleful sounds? For me, I can hear nothing else."

Silence followed my words. A passion of pity had shaken me as I spoke, but when I looked around upon the company, I saw that, far from being stirred as I was, their faces expressed a cold and hard astonishment, mingled in Edith's with extreme mortification, in her father's with anger. The ladies were exchanging scandalized looks, while one of the gentlemen had put up his eyeglass and was studying me with an air of scientific curiosity. When

I saw that things which were to me so intolerable moved them not at all, that words that melted my heart to speak had only offended them with the speaker, I was at first stunned and then overcome with a desperate sickness and faintness at the heart. What hope was there for the wretched, for the world, if thoughtful men and tender women were not moved by things like these! Then I bethought myself that it must be because I had not spoken aright. No doubt I had put the case badly. They were angry because they thought I was berating them, when God knew I was merely thinking of the horror of the fact without any attempt to assign the responsibility for it.

I restrained my passion, and tried to speak calmly and logically that I might correct this impression. I told them that I had not meant to accuse them, as if they, or the rich in general, were responsible for the misery of the world. True indeed it was, that the superfluity which they wasted would, otherwise bestowed, relieve much bitter suffering. These costly viands, these rich wines, these gorgeous fabrics and glistening jewels represented the ransom of many lives. They were verily not without the guiltiness of those who waste in a land stricken with famine. Nevertheless, all the waste of all the rich, were it saved, would go but a little way to cure the poverty of the world. There was so little to divide that even if the rich went share and share with the poor, there would be but a common fare of crusts, albeit made very sweet then by brotherly love.

The folly of men, not their hard-heartedness, was the great cause of the world's poverty. It was not the crime of man, nor of any class of men, that made the race so miserable, but a hideous, ghastly mistake, a colossal world-darkening blunder. And then I showed them how four fifths of the labor of men was utterly wasted by the mutual warfare, the lack of organization and concert among the workers. Seeking to make the matter very plain, I instanced the case of arid lands where the soil yielded the means of life only by careful use of the watercourses for irrigation. I showed how in such countries it was counted the most important function of the government to see that the water was not wasted by the selfishness or ignorance of individuals, since otherwise there would be famine. To this end its use was strictly regulated and systematized, and individuals of their mere caprice were not permitted to dam it or divert it, or in any way to tamper with it.

The labor of men, I explained, was the fertilizing stream which alone rendered earth habitable. It was but a scanty stream at best, and its use required to be regulated by a system which expended every drop to the best advantage, if the world were to be supported in abundance. But how far from any system was the actual practice! Every man wasted the precious fluid as he wished, animated only by the equal motives of saving his own crop and spoiling his neighbor's, that his might sell the better. What with greed and what with spite some fields were flooded while others were parched, and half the water ran wholly to waste. In such a land, though a few by strength or cunning might win the means of luxury, the lot of the great mass must be poverty, and of the weak and ignorant bitter want and perennial famine.

Let but the famine-stricken nation assume the function it had neglected, and regulate for the common good the course of the life-giving stream, and the earth would bloom like one garden, and none of its children lack any good thing. I described the physical felicity, mental enlightenment, and moral elevation which would then attend the lives of all men. With fervency I spoke of that new world, blessed with plenty, purified by justice and sweetened by brotherly kindness, the world of which I had indeed but dreamed, but which might so easily be made real. But when I had expected now surely the faces around me to light up with emotions akin to mine, they grew ever more dark, angry, and scornful. Instead of enthusiasm, the ladies showed only aversion and dread, while the men interrupted me with shouts of reprobation and contempt. "Madman!" "Pestilent fellow!" "Fanatic!" "Enemy of society!" were some of their cries, and the one who had before taken his eyeglass to me exclaimed, "He says we are to have no more poor. Ha! Ha!"

"Put the fellow out!" exclaimed the father of my betrothed, and at the signal the men sprang from their chairs and advanced upon me.

It seemed to me that my heart would burst with the anguish of finding that what was to me so plain and so all important was to them meaningless, and that I was powerless to make it other. So hot had been my heart that I had thought to melt an iceberg with its glow, only to find at last the overmastering chill seizing my own vitals. It was not enmity that I felt toward them as they thronged me, but pity only, for them and for the world.

Although despairing, I could not give over. Still I strove with them. Tears poured from my eyes. In my vehemence I became inarticulate. I panted, I sobbed, I groaned, and immediately afterward found myself sitting upright in bed in my room in Dr. Leete's house, and the morning sun shining through the open window into my eyes. I was gasping. The tears were streaming down my face, and I quivered in every nerve.

As with an escaped convict who dreams that he has been recaptured and brought back to his dark and reeking dungeon, and opens his eyes to see the heaven's vault spread above him, so it was with me, as I realized that my return to the nineteenth century had been the dream, and my presence in the twentieth was the reality.

The cruel sights which I had witnessed in my vision, and could so well confirm from the experience of my former life, though they had, alas! once been, and must in the retrospect to the end of time move the compassionate to tears, were, God be thanked, forever gone by. Long ago oppressor and oppressed, prophet and scorner, had been dust. For generations, rich and poor had been forgotten words.

But in that moment, while yet I mused with unspeakable thankfulness upon the greatness of the world's salvation and my privilege in beholding it, there suddenly pierced me like a knife a pang of shame, remorse, and wondering self-reproach, that bowed my head upon my breast and made me wish the grave had hid me with my fellows from the sun. For I had been a man of that former time. What had I done to help on the deliverance whereat I now presumed to rejoice? I who had lived in those cruel, insensate days, what had I done to bring them to an end? I had been every whit as indifferent to the wretchedness of my brothers, as cynically incredulous of better things, as besotted a worshiper of Chaos and Old Night, as any of my fellows. So far as my personal influence went, it had been exerted rather to hinder than to help forward the enfranchisement of the race which was even then preparing. What right had I to hail a salvation which reproached me, to rejoice in a day whose dawning I had mocked?

"Better for you, better for you," a voice within me rang, "had this evil dream been the reality, and this fair reality the dream; better your part pleading for crucified humanity with a scoffing generation, than here, drinking of wells you digged not, and eating of trees whose husbandmen you stoned"; and my spirit answered, "Better, truly."

When at length I raised my bowed head and looked forth from the window, Edith, fresh as the morning, had come into the garden and was gathering flowers. I hastened to descend to her. Kneeling before her, with my face in the dust, I confessed with tears how little was my worth to breathe the air of this golden century, and how infinitely less to wear upon my breast its consummate flower. Fortunate is he who, with a case so desperate as mine, finds a judge so merciful.

THE WAR OF THE WORLDS

H. G. Wells

But who shall dwell in these worlds if they be inhabited? . . . Are we or they Lords of the World? . . . And how are all things made for man?

KEPLER (quoted in *The Anatomy of Melancholy*)

BOOK I: THE COMING OF THE MARTIANS

I

THE EVE OF THE WAR

No one would have believed in the last years of the nineteenth century that this world was being watched keenly and closely by intelligences greater than man's and yet as mortal as his own; that as men busied themselves about their various concerns they were scrutinised and studied, perhaps almost as narrowly as a man with a microscope might scrutinise the transient creatures that swarm and multiply in a drop of water. With infinite complacency men went to and fro over this globe about their little affairs, serene in their assurance of their empire over matter. It is possible that the infusoria under the microscope do the same. No one gave a thought to the older worlds of space as sources of human danger, or thought of them only to dismiss the idea of life upon them as impossible or improbable. It is curious to recall some of the mental habits of those departed days. At most terrestrial men fancied there might be other men upon Mars, perhaps inferior to themselves and ready to welcome a missionary enterprise. Yet across the gulf of space, minds that are to our minds as ours are to those of the beasts that perish, intellects vast and cool and unsympathetic, regarded this earth with envious eyes, and slowly and surely drew their plans against us. And early in the twentieth century came the great disillusionment.

The planet Mars, I scarcely need remind the reader, revolves about the sun at a mean distance of 140,000,000 miles, and the light and heat it receives from the sun is barely half of that received by this world. It must be, if the nebular hypothesis has any truth, older than our world; and long before this earth ceased to be molten, life upon its surface must have begun its course. The fact that it is scarcely one-seventh of the volume of the earth must have accelerated its cooling to the temperature at which life could begin. It has air and water and all that is necessary for the support of animated existence.

Yet so vain is man, and so blinded by his vanity, that no writer, up to the very end of the nineteenth century, expressed any idea that intelligent life might have developed there far, or indeed at all, beyond its earthly level. Nor was it generally understood that since Mars is older than our earth, with scarcely a quarter of the superficial area and remoter from the sun, it necessarily follows that it is not only more distant from time's beginning but nearer its end.

The secular cooling that must someday overtake our planet has already gone far indeed with our neighbour. Its physical condition is still largely a mystery, but we know now that even in its equatorial region the midday temperature barely approaches that of our coldest winter. Its air is much more attenuated than ours, its oceans have shrunk until they cover but a third of its surface, and as its slow seasons change huge snowcaps gather and melt about either pole and periodically inundate its temperate zones. That last stage of exhaustion, which to us is still incredibly remote, has become a present-day problem for the inhabitants of Mars. The immediate pressure of necessity has brightened their intellects, enlarged their powers, and hardened their hearts. And looking across space with instruments, and intelligences such as we have scarcely dreamed of, they see, at its nearest distance only 35,000,000 of miles sunward of them, a morning star of hope, our own warmer planet, green with vegetation and grey with water, with a cloudy atmosphere eloquent of fertility, with glimpses through its drifting cloud wisps of broad stretches of populous country and narrow, navy-crowded seas.

And we men, the creatures who inhabit this earth, must be to them at least as alien and lowly as are the monkeys and lemurs to us. The intellectual side of man already admits that life is an incessant struggle for existence, and it would seem that this too is the belief of the minds upon Mars. Their world is far gone in its cooling and this world is still crowded with life, but crowded only with what they regard as inferior animals. To carry warfare sunward is, indeed, their only escape from the destruction that, generation after generation, creeps upon them.

And before we judge of them too harshly we must remember what ruthless and utter destruction our own species has wrought, not only upon animals, such as the vanished bison and the dodo, but upon its inferior races. The Tasmanians, in spite of their human likeness, were entirely swept out of existence in a war of extermination waged by European immigrants, in the space of fifty years. Are we such apostles of mercy as to complain if the Martians warred in the same spirit?

The Martians seem to have calculated their descent with amazing subtlety—their mathematical learning is evidently far in excess of ours—and to have carried out their preparations with a well-nigh perfect unanimity. Had our instruments permitted it, we might have seen the gathering trouble far back in the nineteenth century. Men like Schiaparelli watched the red planet—it is odd, by the by, that for countless centuries Mars has been the star of war—but failed to interpret the fluctuating appearances of the markings they mapped so well. All that time the Martians must have been getting ready.

During the opposition of 1894 a great light was seen on the illuminated part of the disk, first at the Lick Observatory, then by Perrotin of Nice, and then by other observers. English readers heard of it first in the issue of *Nature* dated August 2nd. I am inclined to think that this blaze may have been the casting of the huge gun, in the vast pit sunk into their planet, from which their shots were fired at us. Peculiar markings, as yet unexplained, were seen near the site of that outbreak during the next two oppositions.

The storm burst upon us six years ago now. As Mars approached opposition, Lavelle of Java set the wires of the astronomical exchange palpitating with the amazing intelligence of a huge outbreak of incandescent gas upon the planet. It had occurred towards midnight of the twelfth; and the spectroscope, to which he had at once resorted, indicated a mass of flaming gas, chiefly hydrogen, moving with an enormous velocity towards this earth. This jet of fire had become invisible about a quarter past twelve. He compared it to a colossal puff of flame suddenly and violently squirted out of the planet, "as flaming gases rushed out of a gun."

A singularly appropriate phrase it proved. Yet the next day there was nothing of this in the papers except a little note in the *Daily Telegraph*, and the world went in ignorance of one of the gravest dangers that ever threatened the human race. I might not have heard of the eruption at all had I not met Ogilvy, the well-known astronomer, at Ottershaw. He was immensely excited at the news, and in the excess of his feelings invited me up to take a turn with him that night in a scrutiny of the red planet.

In spite of all that has happened since, I still remember that vigil very distinctly: the black and silent observatory, the shadowed lantern throwing a feeble glow upon the floor in the corner, the steady ticking of the clockwork of the telescope, the little slit in the roof—an oblong profundity with the stardust streaked across it. Ogilvy moved about, invisible but audible. Looking through the telescope, one saw a circle of deep blue and the little round planet swimming in the field. It seemed such a little thing, so bright and small and still, faintly marked with transverse stripes, and slightly flattened from the perfect round. But so little it was, so silvery warm—a pin's-head of light!

It was as if it quivered, but really this was the telescope vibrating with the activity of the clockwork that kept the planet in view.

As I watched, the planet seemed to grow larger and smaller and to advance and recede, but that was simply that my eye was tired. Forty millions of miles it was from us—more than forty millions of miles of void. Few people realise the immensity of vacancy in which the dust of the material universe swims.

Near it in the field, I remember, were three faint points of light, three telescopic stars infinitely remote, and all around it was the unfathomable darkness of empty space. You know how that blackness looks on a frosty starlight night. In a telescope it seems far profounder. And invisible to me because it was so remote and small, flying swiftly and steadily towards me across that incredible distance, drawing nearer every minute by so many thousands of miles, came the Thing they were sending us, the Thing that was to bring so much struggle and calamity and death to the earth. I never dreamed of it then as I watched; no one on earth dreamed of that unerring missile.

That night, too, there was another jetting out of gas from the distant planet. I saw it. A reddish flash at the edge, the slightest projection of the outline just as the chronometer struck midnight; and at that I told Ogilvy and he took my place. The night was warm and I was thirsty, and I went stretching my legs clumsily and feeling my way in the darkness, to the little table where the siphon stood, while Ogilvy exclaimed at the streamer of gas that came out towards us.

That night another invisible missile started on its way to the earth from Mars, just a second or so under twenty-four hours after the first one. I remember how I sat on the table there in the blackness, with patches of green and crimson swimming before my eyes. I wished I had a light to smoke by, little suspecting the meaning of the minute gleam I had seen and all that it would presently bring me. Ogilvy watched till one, and then gave it up; and we lit the lantern and walked over to his house. Down below in the darkness were Ottershaw and Chertsey and all their hundreds of people, sleeping in peace.

He was full of speculation that night about the condition of Mars, and scoffed at the vulgar idea of its having inhabitants who were signalling us. His idea was that meteorites might be falling in a heavy shower upon the planet, or that a huge volcanic explosion was in progress. He pointed out to me how unlikely it was that organic evolution had taken the same direction in the two adjacent planets.

"The chances against anything man-like on Mars are a million to one," he said.

Hundreds of observers saw the flame that night and the night after about midnight, and again the night after; and so for ten nights, a flame each night. Why the shots ceased after the tenth no one on earth has attempted to explain. It may be the gases of the firing caused the Martians inconvenience. Dense clouds of smoke or dust, visible through a powerful telescope on earth as little grey, fluctuating patches, spread through the clearness of the planet's atmosphere and obscured its more familiar features.

Even the daily papers woke up to the disturbances at last, and popular notes appeared here, there, and everywhere concerning the volcanoes upon Mars. The seriocomic periodical *Punch*, I remember, made a happy use of it in the political cartoon. And, all unsuspected, those missiles the Martians had fired at us drew earthward, rushing now at a pace of many miles a second through the empty gulf of space, hour by hour and day by day, nearer and nearer. It seems to me now almost incredibly wonderful that, with that swift fate hanging over us, men could go about their petty concerns as they did. I remember how jubilant Markham was at securing a new photograph of the planet for the illustrated paper he edited in those days. People in these latter times scarcely realise the abundance and enterprise of our nineteenth-century papers. For my own part, I was much occupied in learning to ride the bicycle, and busy upon a series of papers discussing the probable developments of moral ideas as civilisation progressed.

One night (the first missile then could scarcely have been 10,000,000 miles away) I went for a walk with my wife. It was starlight and I explained the Signs of the Zodiac to her, and pointed out Mars, a bright dot of light creeping zenithward, towards which so many telescopes were pointed. It was a warm night. Coming home, a party of excursionists from Chertsey or Isleworth passed us singing and playing music. There were lights in the upper windows of the houses as the people went to bed. From the railway station in the distance came the sound of shunting trains, ringing and rumbling, softened almost into melody by the distance. My wife pointed out to me the brightness of the red, green, and yellow signal lights hanging in a framework against the sky. It seemed so safe and tranquil.

II

THE FALLING-STAR

Then came the night of the first falling-star. It was seen early in the morning, rushing over Winchester eastward, a line of flame high in the atmosphere. Hundreds must have seen it, and taken it for an ordinary falling-star. Albin described it as leaving a greenish streak behind it that glowed for some seconds. Denning, our greatest authority on meteorites, stated that the height of its first appearance was about ninety or one hundred miles. It seemed to him that it fell to earth about one hundred miles east of him.

I was at home at that hour and writing in my study; and although my French windows face towards Ottershaw and the blind was up (for I loved in those days to look up at the night sky), I saw nothing of it. Yet this strangest of all things that ever came to earth from outer space must have fallen while I was sitting there, visible to me had I only looked up as it passed. Some of those who saw its flight say it travelled with a hissing sound. I myself heard nothing of that. Many people in Berkshire, Surrey, and Middlesex must have seen the fall of it, and, at most, have thought that another meteorite had descended. No one seems to have troubled to look for the fallen mass that night.

But very early in the morning poor Ogilvy, who had seen the shooting star and who was persuaded that a meteorite lay somewhere on the common between Horsell, Ottershaw, and Woking, rose early with the idea of finding it. Find it he did, soon after dawn, and not far from the sand pits. An enormous hole had been made by the impact of the projectile, and the sand and gravel had been flung violently in every direction over the heath, forming heaps visible a mile and a half away. The heather was on fire eastward, and a thin blue smoke rose against the dawn.

The Thing itself lay almost entirely buried in sand, amidst the scattered splinters of a fir tree it had shivered to fragments in its descent. The uncovered part had the appearance of a huge cylinder, caked over and its outline softened by a thick scaly dun-coloured incrustation. It had a diameter of about thirty yards. He approached the mass, surprised at the size and more so at the shape, since most meteorites are rounded more or less completely. It was, however, still so hot from its flight through the air as to forbid his near approach. A stirring noise within its cylinder he ascribed to the unequal cooling of its surface; for at that time it had not occurred to him that it might be hollow.

He remained standing at the edge of the pit that the Thing had made for itself, staring at its strange appearance, astonished chiefly at its unusual shape and colour, and dimly perceiving even then some evidence of design in its arrival. The early morning was wonderfully still, and the sun, just clearing the pine trees towards Weybridge, was already warm. He did not remember hearing any birds that morning, there was certainly no breeze stirring, and the only sounds were the faint movements from within the cindery cylinder. He was all alone on the common.

Then suddenly he noticed with a start that some of the grey clinker, the ashy incrustation that covered the meteorite, was falling off the circular edge of the end. It was dropping off in flakes and raining down upon the sand. A large piece suddenly came off and fell with a sharp noise that brought his heart into his mouth.

For a minute he scarcely realised what this meant, and, although the heat was excessive, he clambered down into the pit close to the bulk to see the Thing more clearly. He fancied even then that the cooling of the body might account for this, but what disturbed that idea was the fact that the ash was falling only from the end of the cylinder.

And then he perceived that, very slowly, the circular top of the cylinder was rotating on its body. It was such a gradual movement that he discovered it only through noticing that a black mark that had been near him five minutes ago was now at the other side of the circumference. Even then he scarcely understood what this indicated, until he heard a muffled grating sound and saw the black mark jerk forward an inch or so. Then the thing came upon him in a flash. The cylinder was artificial—hollow—with an end that screwed out! Something within the cylinder was unscrewing the top!

"Good heavens!" said Ogilvy. "There's a man in it—men in it! Half roasted to death! Trying to escape!"

At once, with a quick mental leap, he linked the Thing with the flash upon Mars.

The thought of the confined creature was so dreadful to him that he forgot the heat and went forward to the cylinder to help turn. But luckily the dull radiation arrested him before he could burn his hands on the still-glowing metal. At that he stood irresolute for a moment, then turned, scrambled out of the pit, and set off running wildly into Woking. The time then must have been somewhere about six o'clock. He met a waggoner and tried to make him understand, but the tale he told and his appearance were so wild—his hat had fallen off in the pit—that the man simply drove on. He was equally unsuccessful with the potman who was just unlocking the doors of the public-house by Horsell Bridge. The fellow thought he was a lunatic at large and made an unsuccessful attempt to shut him into the taproom. That sobered him a little; and when he saw Henderson, the London journalist, in his garden, he called over the palings and made himself understood.

"Henderson," he called, "you saw that shooting star last night?"

"Well?" said Henderson.

"It's out on Horsell Common now."

"Good Lord!" said Henderson. "Fallen meteorite! That's good."

"But it's something more than a meteorite. It's a cylinder—an artificial cylinder, man! And there's something inside."

Henderson stood up with his spade in his hand.

"What's that?" he said. He was deaf in one ear.

Ogilvy told him all that he had seen. Henderson was a minute or so taking it in. Then he dropped his spade, snatched up his jacket, and came out into the road. The two men hurried back at once to the common, and found the cylinder still lying in the same position. But now the sounds inside had ceased, and a thin circle of bright metal showed between the top and the body of the cylinder. Air was either entering or escaping at the rim with a thin, sizzling sound.

They listened, rapped on the scaly burnt metal with a stick, and, meeting with no response, they both concluded the man or men inside must be insensible or dead.

Of course the two were quite unable to do anything. They shouted consolation and promises, and went off back to the town again to get help. One can imagine them, covered with sand, excited and disordered, running up the little street in the bright sunlight just as the shop folks were taking down their shutters and people were opening their bedroom windows. Henderson went into the railway station at once, in order to telegraph the news to London. The newspaper articles had prepared men's minds for the reception of the idea.

By eight o'clock a number of boys and unemployed men had already started for the common to see the "dead men from Mars." That was the form the story took. I heard of it first from my newspaper boy about a quarter to nine when I went out to get my *Daily Chronicle*. I was naturally startled, and lost no time in going out and across the Ottershaw bridge to the sand pits.

III

ON HORSELL COMMON

I found a little crowd of perhaps twenty people surrounding the huge hole in which the cylinder lay. I have already described the appearance of that colossal bulk, embedded in the ground. The turf and gravel about it seemed charred as if by a sudden explosion. No doubt its impact had caused a flash of fire. Henderson and Ogilvy were not there. I think they perceived that nothing was to be done for the present, and had gone away to breakfast at Henderson's house.

There were four or five boys sitting on the edge of the Pit, with their feet dangling, and amusing themselves—until I stopped them—by throwing stones at the giant mass. After I had spoken to them about it, they began playing at "touch" in and out of the group of bystanders.

Among these were a couple of cyclists, a jobbing gardener I employed sometimes, a girl carrying a baby, Gregg the butcher and his little boy, and two or three loafers and golf caddies who were accustomed to hang about the railway station. There was very little talking. Few of the common people in England had anything but the vaguest astronomical ideas in those days. Most of them were staring quietly at the big table-like end of the cylinder, which was still as Ogilvy and Henderson had left it. I fancy the popular expectation of a heap of charred corpses was disappointed at this inanimate bulk. Some went away while I was there, and other people came. I clambered into the pit and fancied I heard a faint movement under my feet. The top had certainly ceased to rotate.

It was only when I got thus close to it that the strangeness of this object was at all evident to me. At the first glance it was really no more exciting than an overturned carriage or a tree blown across the road. Not so much so, indeed. It looked like a rusty gas float. It required a certain amount of scientific education to perceive that the grey scale of the Thing was no common oxide, that the yellowish-white metal that gleamed in the crack between the lid and the cylinder had an unfamiliar hue. "Extraterrestrial" had no meaning for most of the onlookers.

At that time it was quite clear in my own mind that the Thing had come from the planet Mars, but I judged it improbable that it contained any living creature. I thought the unscrewing might be automatic. In spite of Ogilvy, I still believed that there were men in Mars. My mind ran fancifully on the possibilities of its containing manuscript, on the difficulties in translation that might arise, whether we should find coins and models in it, and so forth. Yet it was a little too large for assurance on this idea. I felt an impatience to see it opened. About eleven, as nothing seemed happening, I walked back, full of such thought, to my home in Maybury. But I found it difficult to get to work upon my abstract investigations.

In the afternoon the appearance of the common had altered very much. The early editions of the evening papers had startled London with enormous headlines:

> A MESSAGE RECEIVED FROM MARS.
> "REMARKABLE STORY FROM WOKING,"

and so forth. In addition, Ogilvy's wire to the Astronomical Exchange had roused every observatory in the three kingdoms.

There were half a dozen flies or more from the Woking station standing in the road by the sand pits, a basket-chaise from Chobham, and a rather lordly carriage. Besides that, there was quite a heap of bicycles. In addition, a large number of people must have walked, in spite of the heat of the day, from Woking and Chertsey, so that there was altogether quite a considerable crowd—one or two gaily dressed ladies among the others.

It was glaringly hot, not a cloud in the sky nor a breath of wind, and the only shadow was that of the few scattered pine trees. The burning heather had been extinguished, but the level ground towards Ottershaw was blackened as far as one could see, and still giving off vertical streamers of smoke. An enterprising sweet-stuff dealer in the Chobham Road had sent up his son with a barrow-load of green apples and ginger-beer.

Going to the edge of the pit, I found it occupied by a group of about half a dozen men—Henderson, Ogilvy, and a tall, fair-haired man that I afterwards learned was Stent, the Astronomer Royal, with several workmen wielding spades and pickaxes. Stent was giving directions in a clear, high-pitched voice. He was standing on the cylinder, which was now evidently much cooler; his face was crimson and streaming with perspiration, and something seemed to have irritated him.

A large portion of the cylinder had been uncovered, though its lower end was still embedded. As soon as Ogilvy saw me among the staring crowd on the edge of the pit he called to me to come down, and asked me if I would mind going over to see Lord Hilton, the lord of the manor.

The growing crowd, he said, was becoming a serious impediment to their excavations, especially the boys. They wanted a light railing put up, and help to keep the people back. He told me that a faint stirring was occasionally still audible within the case, but that the workmen had failed to unscrew the top, as it afforded no grip to them. The case appeared to be enormously thick, and it was possible that the faint sounds we heard represented a noisy tumult in the interior.

I was very glad to do as he asked, and so become one of the privileged spectators within the contemplated enclosure. I failed to find Lord Hilton at his house, but I was told he was expected from London by the six o'clock train from Waterloo; and as it was then about a quarter past five, I went home, had some tea, and walked up to the station to waylay him.

IV

THE CYLINDER OPENS

When I returned to the common the sun was setting. Scattered groups were hurrying from the direction of Woking, and one or two persons were returning. The crowd about the pit had increased, and stood out black against the lemon yellow of the sky—a couple of hundred people, perhaps. There were raised voices, and some sort of struggle appeared to be going on about the pit. Strange imaginings passed through my mind. As I drew nearer I heard Stent's voice:

"Keep back! Keep back!"

A boy came running towards me.

"It's a-movin'," he said to me as he passed; "a-screwin' and a-screwin' out. I don't like it. I'm a-goin' 'ome, I am."

I went on to the crowd. There were really, I should think, two or three hundred people elbowing and jostling one another, the one or two ladies there being by no means the least active.

"He's fallen in the pit!" cried someone.

"Keep back!" said several.

The crowd swayed a little, and I elbowed my way through. Everyone seemed greatly excited. I heard a peculiar humming sound from the pit.

"I say!" said Ogilvy. "Help keep these idiots back. We don't know what's in the confounded thing, you know!"

I saw a young man, a shop assistant in Woking I believe he was, standing on the cylinder and trying to scramble out of the hole again. The crowd had pushed him in.

The end of the cylinder was being screwed out from within. Nearly two feet of shining screw projected. Somebody blundered against me, and I narrowly missed being pitched onto the top of the screw. I turned, and as I did so the screw must have come out, for the lid of the cylinder fell upon the gravel with a ringing concussion. I stuck my elbow into the person behind me, and turned my head towards the Thing again. For a moment that circular cavity seemed perfectly black. I had the sunset in my eyes.

I think everyone expected to see a man emerge—possibly something a little unlike us terrestrial men, but in all essentials a man. I know I did. But, looking, I presently saw something stirring within the shadow: greyish billowy movements, one above another, and then two luminous disks—like eyes. Then something resembling a little grey snake, about the thickness of a walking stick, coiled up out of the writhing middle, and wriggled in the air towards me—and then another.

A sudden chill came over me. There was a loud shriek from a woman behind. I half turned, keeping my eyes fixed upon the cylinder still, from which other tentacles were now projecting, and began pushing my way back from the edge of the pit. I saw astonishment giving place to horror on the faces of the people about me. I heard inarticulate exclamations on all sides. There was a general movement backwards. I saw the shopman struggling still on the edge of the pit. I found myself alone, and saw the people on the other side of the pit running off, Stent among them. I looked again at the cylinder, and ungovernable terror gripped me. I stood petrified and staring.

A big greyish rounded bulk, the size, perhaps, of a bear, was rising slowly and painfully out of the cylinder. As it bulged up and caught the light, it glistened like wet leather.

Two large dark-coloured eyes were regarding me steadfastly. The mass that framed them, the head of the thing, was rounded, and had, one might say, a face. There was a mouth under the eyes, the lipless brim of which quivered and panted, and dropped saliva. The whole creature heaved and pulsated convulsively. A lank tentacular appendage gripped the edge of the cylinder, another swayed in the air.

Those who have never seen a living Martian can scarcely imagine the strange horror of its appearance. The peculiar V-shaped mouth with its pointed upper lip, the absence of brow ridges, the absence of a chin beneath the wedge-like lower lip, the incessant quivering of this mouth, the Gorgon groups of tentacles, the tumultuous breathing of the lungs in a strange atmosphere, the evident heaviness and painfulness of movement due to the greater gravitational energy of the earth—above all, the extraordinary intensity of the immense eyes—were at once vital, intense, inhuman, crippled and monstrous. There was something fungoid in the oily brown skin, something in the clumsy deliberation of the tedious movements unspeakably nasty. Even at this first encounter, this first glimpse, I was overcome with disgust and dread.

Suddenly the monster vanished. It had toppled over the brim of the cylinder and fallen into the pit, with a thud like the fall of a great mass of leather. I heard it give a peculiar thick cry, and forthwith another of these creatures appeared darkly in the deep shadow of the aperture.

I turned and, running madly, made for the first group of trees, perhaps a hundred yards away; but I ran slantingly and stumbling, for I could not avert my face from these things.

There, among some young pine trees and furze bushes, I stopped, panting, and waited further developments. The common round the sand pits was dotted with people, standing like myself in a half-fascinated terror, staring at these creatures, or rather at the heaped gravel at the edge of the pit in which they lay. And then, with a renewed horror, I saw a round, black object bobbing up and down on the edge of the pit. It was the head of the shopman who had fallen in, but showing as a little black object against the hot western sun. Now he got his shoulder and knee up, and again he seemed to slip back until only his head was visible. Suddenly he vanished, and I could have fancied a faint shriek had reached me. I had a momentary impulse to go back and help him that my fears overruled.

Everything was then quite invisible, hidden by the deep pit and the heap of sand that the fall of the cylinder had made. Anyone coming along the road from Chobham or Woking would have been amazed at the sight—a dwindling multitude of perhaps a hundred people or more standing in a great irregular circle, in ditches, behind bushes, behind gates and hedges, saying little to one another and that in short, excited shouts, and staring, staring hard at a few heaps of sand. The barrow of ginger beer stood, a queer derelict, black against the burning sky, and in the sand pits was a row of deserted vehicles with their horses feeding out of nosebags or pawing the ground.

V

THE HEAT-RAY

After the glimpse I had had of the Martians emerging from the cylinder in which they had come to the earth from their planet, a kind of fascination paralysed my actions. I remained standing knee-deep in the heather, staring at the mound that hid them. I was a battleground of fear and curiosity.

I did not dare to go back towards the pit, but I felt a passionate longing to peer into it. I began walking, therefore, in a big curve, seeking some point of vantage and continually looking at the sand heaps that hid these newcomers to our earth. Once a leash of thin black whips, like the arms of an octopus, flashed across the sunset and was immediately withdrawn, and afterwards a thin rod rose up, joint by joint, bearing at its apex a circular disk that spun with a wobbling motion. What could be going on there?

Most of the spectators had gathered in one or two groups—one a little crowd towards Woking, the other a knot of people in the direction of Chobham. Evidently they shared my mental conflict. There were few near me. One man I approached—he was, I perceived, a neighbour of mine, though I did not know his name—and accosted. But it was scarcely a time for articulate conversation.

"What ugly *brutes!*" he said. "Good God! What ugly brutes!" He repeated this over and over again.

"Did you see a man in the pit?" I said; but he made no answer to that. We became silent, and stood watching for a time side by side, deriving, I fancy, a certain comfort in one another's company. Then I shifted my position to a little knoll that gave me the advantage of a yard or more of elevation and when I looked for him presently he was walking towards Woking.

The sunset faded to twilight before anything further happened. The crowd far away on the left, towards Woking, seemed to grow, and I heard now a faint murmur from it. The little knot of people towards Chobham dispersed. There was scarcely an intimation of movement from the pit.

It was this, as much as anything, that gave people courage, and I suppose the new arrivals from Woking also helped to restore confidence. At any rate, as the dusk came on a slow, intermittent movement upon the sand pits began, a movement that seemed to gather force as the stillness of the evening about the cylinder remained unbroken. Vertical black figures in twos and threes would advance, stop, watch, and advance again, spreading out as they did so in a thin irregular crescent that promised to enclose the pit in its attenuated horns. I, too, on my side began to move towards the pit.

Then I saw some cabmen and others had walked boldly into the sand pits, and heard the clatter of hoofs and the gride of wheels. I saw a lad trundling off the barrow of apples. And then, within thirty yards of the pit, advancing from the direction of Horsell, I noted a little black knot of men, the foremost of whom was waving a white flag.

This was the Deputation. There had been a hasty consultation, and since the Martians were evidently, in spite of their repulsive forms, intelligent creatures, it had been resolved to show them, by approaching them with signals, that we too were intelligent.

Flutter, flutter, went the flag, first to the right, then to the left. It was too far for me to recognise anyone there, but afterwards I learned that Ogilvy, Stent, and Henderson were with others in this attempt at communication. This little group had in its advance dragged inward, so to speak, the circumference of the now almost complete circle of people, and a number of dim black figures followed it at discreet distances.

Suddenly there was a flash of light, and a quantity of luminous greenish smoke came out of the pit in three distinct puffs, which drove up, one after the other, straight into the still air.

This smoke (or flame, perhaps, would be the better word for it) was so bright that the deep blue sky overhead and the hazy stretches of brown common towards Chertsey, set with black pine trees, seemed to darken abruptly as these puffs arose, and to remain the darker after their dispersal. At the same time a faint hissing sound became audible.

Beyond the pit stood the little wedge of people with the white flag at its apex, arrested by these phenomena, a little knot of small vertical black shapes upon the black ground. As the green smoke arose, their faces flashed out pallid green, and faded again as it vanished. Then slowly the hissing passed into a humming, into a long, loud, droning noise. Slowly a humped shape rose out of the pit, and the ghost of a beam of light seemed to flicker out from it.

Forthwith flashes of actual flame, a bright glare leaping from one to another, sprang from the scattered group of men. It was as if some invisible jet impinged upon them and flashed into white flame. It was as if each man were suddenly and momentarily turned to fire.

Then, by the light of their own destruction, I saw them staggering and falling, and their supporters turning to run.

I stood staring, not as yet realising that this was death leaping from man to man in that little distant crowd. All I felt was that it was something very strange. An almost noiseless and blinding flash of light, and a man fell headlong and lay still; and as the unseen shaft of heat passed over them, pine trees burst into fire, and every dry furze bush became with one dull thud a mass of flames. And far away towards Knaphill I saw the flashes of trees and hedges and wooden buildings suddenly set alight.

It was sweeping round swiftly and steadily, this flaming death, this invisible, inevitable sword of heat. I perceived it coming towards me by the flashing bushes it touched, and was too astounded and stupefied to stir. I heard the crackle of fire in the sand pits and the sudden squeal of a horse that was as suddenly stilled. Then it was as if an invisible yet intensely heated finger were drawn through the heather between me and the Martians, and all along a curving line beyond the sand pits the dark ground smoked and crackled. Something fell with a crash far away to the left where the road from Woking station opens out on the common. Forthwith the hissing and humming ceased, and the black, dome-like object sank slowly out of sight into the pit.

All this had happened with such swiftness that I had stood motionless, dumbfounded and dazzled by the flashes of light. Had that death swept through a full circle, it must inevitably have slain me in my surprise. But it passed and spared me, and left the night about me suddenly dark and unfamiliar.

The undulating common seemed now dark almost to blackness, except where its roadways lay grey and pale under the deep blue sky of the early night. It was dark, and suddenly void of men. Overhead the stars were mustering, and in the west the sky was still a pale, bright, almost greenish blue. The tops of the pine trees and the roofs of Horsell came out sharp and black against the western afterglow. The Martians and their appliances were altogether invisible, save for that thin mast upon which their restless mirror wobbled. Patches of bush and isolated trees here and there smoked and glowed still, and the houses towards Woking station were sending up spires of flame into the stillness of the evening air.

Nothing was changed save for that and a terrible astonishment. The little group of black specks with the flag of white had been swept out of existence, and the stillness of the evening, so it seemed to me, had scarcely been broken.

It came to me that I was upon this dark common, helpless, unprotected, and alone. Suddenly, like a thing falling upon me from without, came—fear.

With an effort I turned and began a stumbling run through the heather.

The fear I felt was no rational fear, but a panic terror not only of the Martians, but of the dusk and stillness all about me. Such an extraordinary effect in unmanning me it had that I ran weeping silently as a child might do. Once I had turned, I did not dare to look back.

I remember I felt an extraordinary persuasion that I was being played with, that presently, when I was upon the very verge of safety, this mysterious death—as swift as the passage of light—would leap after me from the pit about the cylinder and strike me down.

VI

THE HEAT-RAY IN THE CHOBHAM ROAD

It is still a matter of wonder how the Martians are able to slay men so swiftly and so silently. Many think that in some way they are able to generate an intense heat in a chamber of practically absolute non-conductivity. This intense heat they project in a parallel beam against any object they choose, by means of a polished parabolic mirror of unknown composition, much as the parabolic mirror of a lighthouse projects a beam of light. But no one has absolutely proved these details. However it is done, it is certain that a beam of heat is the essence of the matter. Heat, and invisible, instead of visible, light. Whatever is combustible flashes into flame at its touch, lead runs like water, it softens iron, cracks and melts glass, and when it falls upon water, incontinently that explodes into steam.

That night nearly forty people lay under the starlight about the pit, charred and distorted beyond recognition, and all night long the common from Horsell to Maybury was deserted and brightly ablaze.

The news of the massacre probably reached Chobham, Woking, and Ottershaw about the same time. In Woking the shops had closed when the tragedy happened, and a number of people, shop people and so forth, attracted by the stories they had heard, were walking over the Horsell Bridge and along the road between the hedges that runs out at last upon the common. You may imagine the young people brushed up after the labours of the day, and making this novelty, as they would make any novelty, the excuse for walking together and enjoying a trivial flirtation. You may figure to yourself the hum of voices along the road in the gloaming . . .

As yet, of course, few people in Woking even knew that the cylinder had opened, though poor Henderson had sent a messenger on a bicycle to the post office with a special wire to an evening paper.

As these folks came out by twos and threes upon the open, they found little knots of people talking excitedly and peering at the spinning mirror over the sand pits, and the newcomers were, no doubt, soon infected by the excitement of the occasion.

By half past eight, when the Deputation was destroyed, there may have been a crowd of three hundred people or more at this place, besides those who had left the road to approach the Martians nearer. There were three policemen too, one of whom was mounted, doing their best, under instructions from Stent, to keep the people back and deter them from approaching the cylinder. There was some booing from those more thoughtless and excitable souls to whom a crowd is always an occasion for noise and horseplay.

Stent and Ogilvy, anticipating some possibilities of a collision, had telegraphed from Horsell to the barracks as soon as the Martians emerged, for the help of a company of soldiers to protect these strange creatures from violence. After that they returned to lead that ill-fated advance. The description of their death, as it was seen by the crowd, tallies very closely with my own impressions: the three puffs of green smoke, the deep humming note, and the flashes of flame.

But that crowd of people had a far narrower escape than mine. Only the fact that a hummock of heathery sand intercepted the lower part of the Heat-Ray saved them. Had the elevation of the parabolic mirror been a few yards higher, none could have lived to tell the tale. They saw the flashes and the men falling and an invisible hand, as it were, lit the bushes as it hurried towards them through the twilight. Then, with a whistling note that rose above the droning of the pit, the beam swung close over their heads, lighting the tops of the beech trees that line the road, and splitting the bricks, smashing the windows, firing the window frames, and bringing down in crumbling ruin a portion of the gable of the house nearest the corner.

In the sudden thud, hiss, and glare of the igniting trees, the panic-stricken crowd seems to have swayed hesitatingly for some moments. Sparks and burning twigs began to fall into the road, and single leaves like puffs of flame. Hats and dresses caught fire. Then came a crying from the common. There were shrieks and shouts, and suddenly a mounted policeman came galloping through the confusion with his hands clasped over his head, screaming.

"They're coming!" a woman shrieked, and incontinently everyone was turning and pushing at those behind, in order to clear their way to Woking again. They must have bolted as blindly as a flock of sheep. Where the road grows narrow and black between the high banks the crowd jammed, and a desperate struggle occurred. All that crowd did not escape; three persons at least, two women and a little boy, were crushed and trampled there, and left to die amid the terror and the darkness.

VII

HOW I REACHED HOME

For my own part, I remember nothing of my flight except the stress of blundering against trees and stumbling through the heather. All about me gathered the invisible terrors of the Martians; that pitiless sword of heat seemed whirling to and fro, flourishing overhead before it descended and smote me out of life. I came into the road between the crossroads and Horsell, and ran along this to the crossroads.

At last I could go no further; I was exhausted with the violence of my emotion and of my flight, and I staggered and fell by the wayside. That was near the bridge that crosses the canal by the gasworks. I fell and lay still.

I must have remained there some time.

I sat up, strangely perplexed. For a moment, perhaps, I could not clearly understand how I came there. My terror had fallen from me like a garment. My hat had gone, and my collar had burst away from its fastener. A few minutes before, there had only been three real things before me—the immensity of the night and space and nature, my own feebleness and anguish, and the near approach of death. Now it was as if something turned over, and the point of view altered abruptly. There was no sensible transition from one state of mind to the other. I was immediately the self of every day again—a decent, ordinary citizen. The silent common, the impulse of my flight, the starting flames, were as if they had been in a dream. I asked myself had these latter things indeed happened? I could not credit it.

I rose and walked unsteadily up the steep incline of the bridge. My mind was blank wonder. My muscles and nerves seemed drained of their strength. I daresay I staggered drunkenly. A head rose over the arch, and the figure of a workman carrying a basket appeared. Beside him ran a little boy. He passed me, wishing me good night. I was minded to speak to him, but did not. I answered his greeting with a meaningless mumble and went on over the bridge.

Over the Maybury arch a train, a billowing tumult of white, firelit smoke, and a long caterpillar of lighted windows, went flying south—clatter, clatter, clap, rap, and it had gone. A dim group of people talked in the gate of one of the houses in the pretty little row of gables that was called Oriental Terrace. It was all so real and so familiar. And that behind me! It was frantic, fantastic! Such things, I told myself, could not be.

Perhaps I am a man of exceptional moods. I do not know how far my experience is common. At times I suffer from the strangest sense of detachment from myself and the world about me; I seem to watch it all from the outside, from somewhere inconceivably remote, out of time, out of space, out of the stress and tragedy of it all. This feeling was very strong upon me that night. Here was another side to my dream.

But the trouble was the blank incongruity of this serenity and the swift death flying yonder, not two miles away. There was a noise of business from the gasworks, and the electric lamps were all alight. I stopped at the group of people.

"What news from the common?" said I.

There were two men and a woman at the gate.

"Eh?" said one of the men, turning.

"What news from the common?" I said.

"'Ain't yer just *been* there?" asked the men.

"People seem fair silly about the common," said the woman over the gate. "What's it all abart?"

"Haven't you heard of the men from Mars?" said I. "The creatures from Mars?"

"Quite enough," said the woman over the gate. "Thenks"; and all three of them laughed.

I felt foolish and angry. I tried and found I could not tell them what I had seen. They laughed again at my broken sentences.

"You'll hear more yet," I said, and went on to my home.

I startled my wife at the doorway, so haggard was I. I went into the dining room, sat down, drank some wine, and so soon as I could collect myself sufficiently I told her the things I had seen. The dinner, which was a cold one, had already been served, and remained neglected on the table while I told my story.

"There is one thing," I said, to allay the fears I had aroused; "they are the most sluggish things I ever saw crawl. They may keep the pit and kill people who come near them, but they cannot get out of it . . . But the horror of them!"

"Don't, dear!" said my wife, knitting her brows and putting her hand on mine.

"Poor Ogilvy!" I said. "To think he may be lying dead there!"

My wife at least did not find my experience incredible. When I saw how deadly white her face was, I ceased abruptly.

"They may come here," she said again and again.

I pressed her to take wine, and tried to reassure her.

"They can scarcely move," I said.

I began to comfort her and myself by repeating all that Ogilvy had told me of the impossibility of the Martians establishing themselves on the earth. In particular I laid stress on the gravitational difficulty. On the surface of the earth the force of gravity is three times what it is on the surface of Mars. A

Martian, therefore, would weigh three times more than on Mars, albeit his muscular strength would be the same. His own body would be a cope of lead to him. That, indeed, was the general opinion. Both the *Times* and the *Daily Telegraph*, for instance, insisted on it the next morning, and both overlooked, just as I did, two obvious modifying influences.

The atmosphere of the earth, we now know, contains far more oxygen or far less argon (whichever way one likes to put it) than does Mars. The invigorating influences of this excess of oxygen upon the Martians indisputably did much to counterbalance the increased weight of their bodies. And, in the second place, we all overlooked the fact that such mechanical intelligence as the Martian possessed was quite able to dispense with muscular exertion at a pinch.

But I did not consider these points at the time, and so my reasoning was dead against the chances of the invaders. With wine and food, the confidence of my own table, and the necessity of reassuring my wife, I grew by insensible degrees courageous and secure.

"They have done a foolish thing," said I, fingering my wineglass. "They are dangerous because, no doubt, they are mad with terror. Perhaps they expected to find no living things—certainly no intelligent living things."

"A shell in the pit" said I, "if the worst comes to the worst, will kill them all."

The intense excitement of the events had no doubt left my perceptive powers in a state of erethism. I remember that dinner table with extraordinary vividness even now. My dear wife's sweet anxious face peering at me from under the pink lamp shade, the white cloth with its silver and glass table furniture—for in those days even philosophical writers had many little luxuries—the crimson-purple wine in my glass, are photographically distinct. At the end of it I sat, tempering nuts with a cigarette, regretting Ogilvy's rashness, and denouncing the shortsighted timidity of the Martians.

So some respectable dodo in the Mauritius might have lorded it in his nest, and discussed the arrival of that shipful of pitiless sailors in want of animal food. "We will peck them to death tomorrow, my dear."

I did not know it, but that was the last civilised dinner I was to eat for very many strange and terrible days.

VIII

FRIDAY NIGHT

The most extraordinary thing to my mind, of all the strange and wonderful things that happened upon that Friday, was the dovetailing of the commonplace habits of our social order with the first beginnings of the series of events that was to topple that social order headlong. If on Friday night you had taken a pair of compasses and drawn a circle with a radius of five miles round the Woking sand pits, I doubt if you would have had one human being outside it, unless it were some relation of Stent or of the three or four cyclists or London people lying dead on the common, whose emotions or habits were at all affected by the newcomers. Many people had heard of the cylinder, of course, and talked about it in their leisure, but it certainly did not make the sensation that an ultimatum to Germany would have done.

In London that night poor Henderson's telegram describing the gradual unscrewing of the shot was judged to be a canard, and his evening paper, after wiring for authentication from him and receiving no reply—the man was killed—decided not to print a special edition.

Even within the five-mile circle the great majority of people were inert. I have already described the behaviour of the men and women to whom I spoke. All over the district people were dining and supping; working men were gardening after the labours of the day, children were being put to bed, young people were wandering through the lanes love-making, students sat over their books.

Maybe there was a murmur in the village streets, a novel and dominant topic in the public-houses, and here and there a messenger, or even an eye-witness of the later occurrences, caused a whirl of excitement, a shouting, and a running to and fro; but for the most part the daily routine of working, eating, drinking, sleeping, went on as it had done for countless years—as though no planet Mars existed in the sky. Even at Woking station and Horsell and Chobham that was the case.

In Woking junction, until a late hour, trains were stopping and going on, others were shunting on the sidings, passengers were alighting and waiting, and everything was proceeding in the most ordinary way. A boy from the town, trenching on Smith's monopoly, was selling papers with the afternoon's news. The ringing impact of trucks, the sharp whistle of the engines from the junction, mingled with their shouts of "Men from Mars!" Excited men came into the station about nine o'clock with incredible tidings, and caused no more disturbance than drunkards might have done. People rattling Londonwards peered into the darkness outside the carriage windows, and saw only a rare, flickering, vanishing spark dance up from the direction of Horsell, a red glow and a thin veil of smoke driving across the stars, and thought that nothing more serious than a heath fire was happening. It was only round the edge of the common that any disturbance was perceptible. There were half a dozen villas burning on the Woking border. There were lights in all the houses on the common side of the three villages, and the people there kept awake till dawn.

A curious crowd lingered restlessly, people coming and going but the crowd remaining, both on the Chobham and Horsell bridges. One or two adventurous souls, it was afterwards found, went into the darkness and crawled quite near the Martians; but they never returned, for now and again a light-ray, like the beam of a warship's searchlight swept the common, and the Heat-Ray was ready to follow. Save for such, that big area of common was silent and desolate, and the charred bodies lay about on it all night under the stars, and all the next day. A noise of hammering from the pit was heard by many people.

So you have the state of things on Friday night. In the centre, sticking into the skin of our old planet Earth like a poisoned dart, was this cylinder. But the poison was scarcely working yet. Around it was a patch of silent common, smouldering in places, and with a few dark, dimly seen objects lying in contorted attitudes here and there. Here and there was a burning bush or tree. Beyond was a fringe of excitement, and farther than that fringe the inflammation had not crept as yet. In the rest of the world the stream of life still flowed as it had flowed for immemorial years. The fever of war that would presently clog vein and artery, deaden nerve and destroy brain, had still to develop.

All night long the Martians were hammering and stirring, sleepless, indefatigable, at work upon the machines they were making ready, and ever and again a puff of greenish-white smoke whirled up to the starlit sky.

About eleven a company of soldiers came through Horsell, and deployed along the edge of the common to form a cordon. Later a second company marched through Chobham to deploy on the north side of the common. Several officers from the Inkerman barracks had been on the common earlier in the day, and one, Major Eden, was reported to be missing. The colonel of the regiment came to the Chobham bridge and was busy questioning the crowd at midnight. The military authorities were certainly alive to the seriousness of the business. About eleven, the next morning's papers were able to say, a squadron of hussars, two Maxims, and about four hundred men of the Cardigan regiment started from Aldershot.

A few seconds after midnight the crowd in the Chertsey road, Woking, saw a star fall from heaven into the pine woods to the northwest. It had a greenish colour, and caused a silent brightness like summer lightning. This was the second cylinder.

IX

THE FIGHTING BEGINS

Saturday lives in my memory as a day of suspense. It was a day of lassitude too, hot and close, with, I am told, a rapidly fluctuating barometer. I had slept but little, though my wife had succeeded in sleeping, and I rose early. I went into my garden before breakfast and stood listening, but towards the common there was nothing stirring but a lark.

The milkman came as usual. I heard the rattle of his chariot and I went round to the side gate to ask the latest news. He told me that during the night the Martians had been surrounded by troops, and that guns were expected. Then—a familiar, reassuring note—I heard a train running towards Woking.

"They aren't to be killed," said the milkman, "if that can possibly be avoided."

I saw my neighbour gardening, chatted with him for a time, and then strolled in to breakfast. It was a most unexceptional morning. My neighbour was of opinion that the troops would be able to capture or to destroy the Martians during the day.

"It's a pity they make themselves so unapproachable," he said. "It would be curious to know how they live on another planet; we might learn a thing or two."

He came up to the fence and extended a handful of strawberries, for his gardening was as generous as it was enthusiastic. At the same time he told me of the burning of the pine woods about the Byfleet Golf Links.

"They say," said he, "that there's another of those blessed things fallen there—number two. But one's enough, surely. This lot'll cost the insurance people a pretty penny before everything's settled." He laughed with an air of the greatest good humour as he said this. The woods, he said, were still burning, and pointed out a haze of smoke to me. "They will be hot under foot for days, on account of the thick soil of pine needles and turf," he said, and then grew serious over "poor Ogilvy."

After breakfast, instead of working, I decided to walk down towards the common. Under the railway bridge I found a group of soldiers—sappers, I think, men in small round caps, dirty red jackets unbuttoned, and showing their blue shirts, dark trousers, and boots coming to the calf. They told me no one was allowed over the canal, and, looking along the road towards the bridge, I saw one of the Cardigan men standing sentinel there. I talked with these soldiers for a time; I told them of my sight of the Martians on the previous evening. None of them had seen the Martians, and they had but the vaguest ideas of them, so that they plied me with questions. They said that they did not know who had authorised the movements of the troops; their idea was that a dispute had arisen at the Horse Guards. The ordinary sapper is a great deal better educated than the common soldier, and they discussed the peculiar conditions of the possible fight with some acuteness. I described the Heat-Ray to them, and they began to argue among themselves.

"Crawl up under cover and rush 'em, say I," said one.

"Get aht!" said another. "What's cover against this 'ere 'eat? Sticks to cook yer! What we got to do is to go as near as the ground'll let us, and then drive a trench."

"Blow yer trenches! You always want trenches; you ought to ha' been born a rabbit, Snippy."

"Ain't they got any necks, then?" said a third, abruptly—a little, contemplative, dark man, smoking a pipe.

I repeated my description.

"Octopuses," said he, "that's what I calls 'em. Talk about fishers of men—fighters of fish it is this time!"

"It ain't no murder killing beasts like that," said the first speaker.

"Why not shell the darned things strite off and finish 'em?" said the little dark man. "You carn tell what they might do."

"Where's your shells?" said the first speaker. "There ain't no time. Do it in a rush, that's my tip, and do it at once."

So they discussed it. After a while I left them, and went on to the railway station to get as many morning papers as I could.

But I will not weary the reader with a description of that long morning and of the longer afternoon. I did not succeed in getting a glimpse of the common, for even Horsell and Chobham church towers were in the hands of the military authorities. The soldiers I addressed didn't know anything; the officers were mysterious as well as busy. I found people in the town quite secure again in the presence of the military, and I heard for the first time from Marshall, the tobacconist, that his son was among the dead on the common. The soldiers had made the people on the outskirts of Horsell lock up and leave their houses.

I got back to lunch about two, very tired for, as I have said, the day was extremely hot and dull; and in order to refresh myself I took a cold bath in the afternoon. About half past four I went up to the railway station to get an evening paper, for the morning papers had contained only a very inaccurate description of the killing of Stent, Henderson, Ogilvy, and the others. But there was little I didn't know. The Martians did not show an inch of themselves. They seemed busy in their pit, and there was a sound of hammering and an almost continuous streamer of smoke. Apparently they were busy getting ready for a struggle. "Fresh attempts have been made to signal, but without success," was the stereotyped formula of the papers. A sapper told me it was done by a man in a ditch with a flag on a long pole. The Martians took as much notice of such advances as we should of the lowing of a cow.

I must confess the sight of all this armament, all this preparation, greatly excited me. My imagination became belligerent, and defeated the invaders in a dozen striking ways; something of my schoolboy dreams of battle and heroism came back. It hardly seemed a fair fight to me at that time. They seemed very helpless in that pit of theirs.

About three o'clock there began the thud of a gun at measured intervals from Chertsey or Addlestone. I learned that the smouldering pine wood into which the second cylinder had fallen was being shelled, in the hope of destroying that object before it opened. It was only about five, however, that a field gun reached Chobham for use against the first body of Martians.

About six in the evening, as I sat at tea with my wife in the summerhouse talking vigorously about the battle that was lowering upon us, I heard a muffled detonation from the common, and immediately after a gust of firing. Close on the heels of that came a violent rattling crash, quite close to us, that shook the ground; and, starting out upon the lawn, I saw the tops of the trees about the Oriental College burst into smoky red flame, and the tower of the little church beside it slide down into ruin. The pinnacle of the mosque had vanished, and the roof line of the college itself looked as if a hundred-ton gun had been at work upon it. One of our chimneys cracked as if a shot had hit it, flew, and a piece of it came clattering down the tiles and made a heap of broken red fragments upon the flower bed by my study window.

I and my wife stood amazed. Then I realised that the crest of Maybury Hill must be within range of the Martians' Heat-Ray now that the college was cleared out of the way.

At that I gripped my wife's arm, and without ceremony ran her out into the road. Then I fetched out the servant, telling her I would go upstairs myself for the box she was clamouring for.

"We can't possibly stay here," I said; and as I spoke the firing reopened for a moment upon the common.

"But where are we to go?" said my wife in terror.

I thought perplexed. Then I remembered her cousins at Leatherhead.

"Leatherhead!" I shouted above the sudden noise.

She looked away from me downhill. The people were coming out of their houses, astonished.

"How are we to get to Leatherhead?" she said.

Down the hill I saw a bevy of hussars ride under the railway bridge; three galloped through the open gates of the Oriental College; two others dismounted, and began running from house to house. The sun, shining through the smoke that drove up from the tops of the trees, seemed blood-red, and threw an unfamiliar lurid light upon everything.

"Stop here," said I; "you are safe here"; and I started off at once for the Spotted Dog, for I knew the landlord had a horse and dog cart. I ran, for I perceived that in a moment everyone upon this side of the hill would be moving. I found him in his bar, quite unaware of what was going on behind his house. A man stood with his back to me, talking to him.

"I must have a pound," said the landlord, "and I've no one to drive it."

"I'll give you two," said I, over the stranger's shoulder.

"What for?"

"And I'll bring it back by midnight," I said.

"Lord!" said the landlord. "What's the hurry? I'm selling my bit of a pig. Two pounds, and you bring it back? What's going on now?"

I explained hastily that I had to leave my home, and so secured the dog cart. At the time it did not seem to me nearly so urgent that the landlord should leave his. I took care to have the cart there and then, drove it off down the road, and, leaving it in charge of my wife and servant, rushed into my house and packed a few valuables, such plate as we had, and so forth. The beech trees below the house were burning while I did this, and the palings up the road glowed red. While I was occupied in this way, one of the dismounted hussars came running up. He was going from house to house, warning people to leave. He was going on as I came out of my front door, lugging my treasures, done up in a tablecloth. I shouted after him:

"What news?"

He turned, stared, bawled something about "crawling out in a thing like a dish cover," and ran on to the gate of the house at the crest. A sudden whirl of black smoke driving across the road hid him for a moment. I ran to my neighbour's door and rapped to satisfy myself of what I already knew, that his wife had gone to London with him and had locked up their house. I went in again, according to my promise, to get my servant's box, lugged it out, clapped it beside her on the tail of the dog cart, and then caught the reins and jumped up into the driver's seat beside my wife. In another moment we were clear of the smoke and noise, and spanking down the opposite slope of Maybury Hill towards Old Woking.

In front was a quiet sunny landscape, a wheat field ahead on either side of the road, and the Maybury Inn with its swinging sign. I saw the doctor's cart ahead of me. At the bottom of the hill I turned my head to look at the hillside I was leaving. Thick streamers of black smoke shot with threads of red fire were driving up into the still air, and throwing dark shadows upon the green treetops eastward. The smoke already extended far away to the east and west—to the Byfleet pine woods eastward, and to Woking on the west. The road was dotted with people running towards us. And very faint now, but very distinct through the hot, quiet air, one heard the whirr of a machine-gun that was presently stilled, and an intermittent cracking of rifles. Apparently the Martians were setting fire to everything within range of their Heat-Ray.

I am not an expert driver, and I had immediately to turn my attention to the horse. When I looked back again the second hill had hidden the black smoke. I slashed the horse with the whip, and gave him a loose rein until Woking and Send lay between us and that quivering tumult. I overtook and passed the doctor between Woking and Send.

X

IN THE STORM

Leatherhead is about twelve miles from Maybury Hill. The scent of hay was in the air through the lush meadows beyond Pyrford, and the hedges on either side were sweet and gay with multitudes of dog-roses. The heavy firing that had broken out while we were driving down Maybury Hill ceased as abruptly as it began, leaving the evening very peaceful and still. We got to Leatherhead without misadventure about nine o'clock, and the horse had an hour's rest while I took supper with my cousins and commended my wife to their care.

My wife was curiously silent throughout the drive, and seemed oppressed with forebodings of evil. I talked to her reassuringly, pointing out that the Martians were tied to the Pit by sheer heaviness, and at the utmost could but crawl a little out of it; but she answered only in monosyllables. Had it not been for my promise to the innkeeper, she would, I think, have urged me to stay in Leatherhead that night. Would that I had! Her face, I remember, was very white as we parted.

For my own part, I had been feverishly excited all day. Something very like the war fever that occasionally runs through a civilised community had got into my blood, and in my heart I was not so very sorry that I had to return to Maybury that night. I was even afraid that that last fusillade I had heard might mean the extermination of our invaders from Mars. I can best express my state of mind by saying that I wanted to be in at the death.

It was nearly eleven when I started to return. The night was unexpectedly dark; to me, walking out of the lighted passage of my cousins' house, it seemed indeed black, and it was as hot and close as the day. Overhead the clouds were driving fast, albeit not a breath stirred the shrubs about us. My cousins' man lit both lamps. Happily, I knew the road intimately. My wife stood in the light of the doorway, and watched me until I jumped up into the dog cart. Then abruptly she turned and went in, leaving my cousins side by side wishing me good hap.

I was a little depressed at first with the contagion of my wife's fears, but very soon my thoughts reverted to the Martians. At that time I was absolutely in the dark as to the course of the evening's fighting. I did not know even the circumstances that had precipitated the conflict. As I came through Ockham (for that was the way I returned, and not through Send and Old Woking) I saw along the western horizon a blood-red glow, which as I drew nearer, crept slowly up the sky. The driving clouds of the gathering thunderstorm mingled there with masses of black and red smoke.

Ripley Street was deserted, and except for a lighted window or so the village showed not a sign of life; but I narrowly escaped an accident at the corner of the road to Pyrford, where a knot of people stood with their backs to me. They said nothing to me as I passed. I do not know what they knew of the things happening beyond the hill, nor do I know if the silent houses I passed on my way were sleeping securely, or deserted and empty, or harassed and watching against the terror of the night.

From Ripley until I came through Pyrford I was in the valley of the Wey, and the red glare was hidden from me. As I ascended the little hill beyond Pyrford Church the glare came into view again, and the trees about me shivered with the first intimation of the storm that was upon me. Then I heard midnight pealing out from Pyrford Church behind me, and then came the silhouette of Maybury Hill, with its treetops and roofs black and sharp against the red.

Even as I beheld this a lurid green glare lit the road about me and showed the distant woods towards Addlestone. I felt a tug at the reins. I saw that the driving clouds had been pierced as it were by a thread of green fire, suddenly lighting their confusion and falling into the field to my left. It was the third falling-star!

Close on its apparition, and blindingly violet by contrast, danced out the first lightning of the gathering storm, and the thunder burst like a rocket overhead. The horse took the bit between his teeth and bolted.

A moderate incline runs towards the foot of Maybury Hill, and down this we clattered. Once the lightning had begun, it went on in as rapid a succession of flashes as I have ever seen. The thunderclaps, treading one on the heels of another and with a strange crackling accompaniment, sounded more like the working of a gigantic electric machine than the usual detonating reverberations. The flickering light was blinding and confusing, and a thin hail smote gustily at my face as I drove down the slope.

At first I regarded little but the road before me, and then abruptly my attention was arrested by something that was moving rapidly down the opposite slope of Maybury Hill. At first I took it for the wet roof of a house, but one flash following another showed it to be in swift rolling movement. It was an elusive vision—a moment of bewildering darkness, and then, in a flash like daylight, the red masses of the Orphanage near the crest of the hill, the green tops of the pine trees, and this problematical object came out clear and sharp and bright.

And this Thing I saw! How can I describe it? A monstrous tripod, higher than many houses, striding over the young pine trees, and smashing them aside in its career; a walking engine of glittering metal, striding now across the heather; articulate ropes of steel dangling from it, and the clattering tumult of its passage mingling with the riot of the thunder. A flash, and it came out vividly, heeling over one way with two feet in the air, to vanish and reappear almost instantly as it seemed, with the next flash, a hundred yards nearer. Can you imagine a milking stool tilted and bowled violently along the ground? That was the impression those instant flashes gave. But instead of a milking stool imagine it a great body of machinery on a tripod stand.

Then suddenly the trees in the pine wood ahead of me were parted, as brittle reeds are parted by a man thrusting through them; they were snapped off and driven headlong, and a second huge tripod appeared, rushing, as it seemed, headlong towards me. And I was galloping hard to meet it! At the sight of the second monster my nerve went altogether. Not stopping to look again, I wrenched the horse's head hard round to the right and in another moment the dog cart had heeled over upon the horse; the shafts smashed noisily, and I was flung sideways and fell heavily into a shallow pool of water.

I crawled out almost immediately, and crouched, my feet still in the water, under a clump of furze. The horse lay motionless (his neck was broken, poor brute!) and by the lightning flashes I saw the black bulk of the overturned dog cart and the silhouette of the wheel still spinning slowly. In another moment the colossal mechanism went striding by me, and passed uphill towards Pyrford.

Seen nearer, the Thing was incredibly strange, for it was no mere insensate machine driving on its way. Machine it was, with a ringing metallic pace, and long, flexible, glittering tentacles (one of which gripped a young pine tree) swinging and rattling about its strange body. It picked its road as it went striding along, and the brazen hood that surmounted it moved to and fro with the inevitable suggestion of a head looking about. Behind the main body was a huge mass of white metal like a gigantic fisherman's basket, and puffs of green smoke squirted out from the joints of the limbs as the monster swept by me. And in an instant it was gone.

So much I saw then, all vaguely for the flickering of the lightning, in blinding highlights and dense black shadows.

As it passed it set up an exultant deafening howl that drowned the thunder—"Aloo! Aloo!"—and in another minute it was with its companion, half a mile away, stooping over something in the field. I have no doubt this Thing in the field was the third of the ten cylinders they had fired at us from Mars.

For some minutes I lay there in the rain and darkness watching, by the intermittent light, these monstrous beings of metal moving about in the distance over the hedge tops. A thin hail was now beginning, and as it came and went their figures grew misty and then flashed into clearness again. Now and then came a gap in the lightning, and the night swallowed them up.

I was soaked with hail above and puddle water below. It was some time before my blank astonishment would let me struggle up the bank to a drier position, or think at all of my imminent peril.

Not far from me was a little one-roomed squatter's hut of wood, surrounded by a patch of potato garden. I struggled to my feet at last, and, crouching and making use of every chance of cover, I made a run for this. I hammered at the door, but I could not make the people hear (if there were any people inside), and after a time I desisted, and, availing myself of a ditch for the greater part of the way, succeeded in crawling, unobserved by these monstrous machines, into the pine woods towards Maybury.

Under cover of this I pushed on, wet and shivering now, towards my own house. I walked among the trees trying to find the footpath. It was very dark indeed in the wood, for the lightning was now becoming infrequent, and the hail, which was pouring down in a torrent, fell in columns through the gaps in the heavy foliage.

If I had fully realised the meaning of all the things I had seen I should have immediately worked my way round through Byfleet to Street Cobham, and so gone back to rejoin my wife at Leatherhead. But that night the strangeness of things about me, and my physical wretchedness, prevented me, for I was bruised, weary, wet to the skin, deafened and blinded by the storm.

I had a vague idea of going on to my own house, and that was as much motive as I had. I staggered through the trees, fell into a ditch and bruised my knees against a plank, and finally splashed out into the lane that ran down from the College Arms. I say splashed, for the storm water was sweeping the sand down the hill in a muddy torrent. There in the darkness a man blundered into me and sent me reeling back.

He gave a cry of terror, sprang sideways, and rushed on before I could gather my wits sufficiently to speak to him. So heavy was the stress of the storm just at this place that I had the hardest task to win my way up the hill. I went close up to the fence on the left and worked my way along its palings.

Near the top I stumbled upon something soft, and, by a flash of lightning, saw between my feet a heap of black broadcloth and a pair of boots. Before I could distinguish clearly how the man lay, the flicker of light had passed. I stood over him waiting for the next flash. When it came, I saw that he was a sturdy man, cheaply but not shabbily dressed; his head was bent under his body, and he lay crumpled up close to the fence, as though he had been flung violently against it.

Overcoming the repugnance natural to one who had never before touched a dead body, I stooped and turned him over to feel for his heart. He was quite dead. Apparently his neck had been broken. The lightning flashed for a third time, and his face leaped upon me. I sprang to my feet. It was the landlord of the Spotted Dog, whose conveyance I had taken.

I stepped over him gingerly and pushed on up the hill. I made my way by the police station and the College Arms towards my own house. Nothing was burning on the hillside, though from the common there still came a red glare and a rolling tumult of ruddy smoke beating up against the drenching hail. So far as I could see by the flashes, the houses about me were mostly uninjured. By the College Arms a dark heap lay in the road.

Down the road towards Maybury Bridge there were voices and the sound of feet, but I had not the courage to shout or to go to them. I let myself in with my latchkey, closed, locked and bolted the door, staggered to the foot of the staircase, and sat down. My imagination was full of those striding metallic monsters, and of the dead body smashed against the fence.

I crouched at the foot of the staircase with my back to the wall, shivering violently.

XI

AT THE WINDOW

I have already said that my storms of emotion have a trick of exhausting themselves. After a time I discovered that I was cold and wet, and with little pools of water about me on the stair carpet. I got up almost mechanically, went into the dining room and drank some whiskey, and then I was moved to change my clothes.

After I had done that I went upstairs to my study, but why I did so I do not know. The window of my study looks over the trees and the railway towards Horsell Common. In the hurry of our departure this window had been left open. The passage was dark, and, by contrast with the picture the window frame enclosed, the side of the room seemed impenetrably dark. I stopped short in the doorway.

The thunderstorm had passed. The towers of the Oriental College and the pine trees about it had gone, and very far away, lit by a vivid red glare, the common about the sand pits was visible. Across the light huge black shapes, grotesque and strange, moved busily to and fro.

It seemed indeed as if the whole country in that direction was on fire—a broad hillside set with minute tongues of flame, swaying and writhing with the gusts of the dying storm, and throwing a red reflection upon the cloud-scud above. Every now and then a haze of smoke from some nearer conflagration drove across the window and hid the Martian shapes. I could not see what they were doing, nor the clear form of them, nor recognise the black objects they were busied upon. Neither could I see the nearer fire, though the reflections of it danced on the wall and ceiling of the study. A sharp, resinous tang of burning was in the air.

I closed the door noiselessly and crept towards the window. As I did so, the view opened out until, on the one hand, it reached to the houses about Woking station, and on the other to the charred and blackened pine woods of Byfleet. There was a light down below the hill, on the railway, near the arch, and several of the houses along the Maybury road and the streets near the station were glowing ruins. The light upon the railway puzzled me at first; there were a black heap and a vivid glare, and to the right of that a row of yellow oblongs. Then I perceived this was a wrecked train, the forepart smashed and on fire, the hinder carriages still upon the rails.

Between these three main centres of light—the houses, the train, and the burning county towards Chobham—stretched irregular patches of dark country, broken here and there by intervals of dimly glowing and smoking ground. It was the strangest spectacle, that black expanse set with fire. It reminded me, more than anything else, of the Potteries at night. At first I could distinguish no people at all, though I peered intently for them. Later I saw against the light of Woking station a number of black figures hurrying one after the other across the line.

And this was the little world in which I had been living securely for years, this fiery chaos! What had happened in the last seven hours I still did not know; nor did I know, though I was beginning to guess, the relation between these mechanical colossi and the sluggish lumps I had seen disgorged from the cylinder. With a queer feeling of impersonal interest I turned my desk chair to the window, sat down, and stared at the blackened country, and particularly at the three gigantic black things that were going to and fro in the glare about the sand pits.

They seemed amazingly busy. I began to ask myself what they could be. Were they intelligent mechanisms? Such a thing I felt was impossible. Or did a Martian sit within each, ruling, directing, using, much as a man's brain sits and rules in his body? I began to compare the things to human machines, to ask myself for the first time in my life how an ironclad or a steam engine would seem to an intelligent lower animal.

The storm had left the sky clear, and over the smoke of the burning land the little fading pinpoint of Mars was dropping into the west, when a soldier came into my garden. I heard a slight scraping at the fence, and rousing myself from the lethargy that had fallen upon me, I looked down and saw him dimly, clambering over the palings. At the sight of another human being my torpor passed, and I leaned out of the window eagerly.

"Hist!" said I, in a whisper.

He stopped astride of the fence in doubt. Then he came over and across the lawn to the corner of the house. He bent down and stepped softly.

"Who's there?" he said, also whispering, standing under the window and peering up.

"Where are you going?" I asked.

"God knows."

"Are you trying to hide?"

"That's it."

"Come into the house," I said.

I went down, unfastened the door, and let him in, and locked the door again. I could not see his face. He was hatless, and his coat was unbuttoned.

"My God!" he said, as I drew him in.

"What has happened?" I asked.

"What hasn't?" In the obscurity I could see he made a gesture of despair. "They wiped us out—simply wiped us out," he repeated again and again.

He followed me, almost mechanically, into the dining room.

"Take some whiskey," I said, pouring out a stiff dose.

He drank it. Then abruptly he sat down before the table, put his head on his arms, and began to sob and weep like a little boy, in a perfect passion of emotion, while I, with a curious forgetfulness of my own recent despair, stood beside him, wondering.

It was a long time before he could steady his nerves to answer my questions, and then he answered perplexingly and brokenly. He was a driver in the artillery, and had only come into action about seven. At that time firing was going on across the common, and it was said the first party of Martians were crawling slowly towards their second cylinder under cover of a metal shield.

Later this shield staggered up on tripod legs and became the first of the fighting-machines I had seen. The gun he drove had been unlimbered near Horsell, in order to command the sand pits, and its arrival it was that had precipitated the action. As the limber gunners went to the rear, his horse trod in a rabbit hole and came down, throwing him into a depression of the ground. At the same moment the gun exploded behind him, the ammunition blew up, there was fire all about him, and he found himself lying under a heap of charred dead men and dead horses.

"I lay still," he said, "scared out of my wits, with the forequarter of a horse atop of me. We'd been wiped out. And the smell—good God! Like burnt meat! I was hurt across the back by the fall of the horse, and there I had to lie until I felt better. Just like parade it had been a minute before—then stumble, bang, swish!"

"Wiped out!" he said.

He had hid under the dead horse for a long time, peeping out furtively across the common. The Cardigan men had tried a rush, in skirmishing order, at the pit, simply to be swept out of existence. Then the monster had risen to its feet and had begun to walk leisurely to and fro across the common among the few fugitives, with its head-like hood turning about exactly like the head of a cowled human being. A kind of arm carried a complicated metallic case, about which green flashes scintillated, and out of the funnel of this there smoked the Heat-Ray.

In a few minutes there was, so far as the soldier could see, not a living thing left upon the common, and every bush and tree upon it that was not already a blackened skeleton was burning. The hussars had been on the road beyond the curvature of the ground, and he saw nothing of them. He heard the Martians rattle for a time and then become still. The giant saved Woking station and its cluster of houses until the last; then in a moment the Heat-Ray was brought to bear, and the town became a heap of fiery ruins. Then the Thing shut off the Heat-Ray, and turning its back upon the artilleryman, began to waddle away towards the smouldering pine woods that sheltered the second cylinder. As it did so a second glittering Titan built itself up out of the pit.

The second monster followed the first, and at that the artilleryman began to crawl very cautiously across the hot heather ash towards Horsell. He managed to get alive into the ditch by the side of the road, and so escaped to Woking. There his story became ejaculatory. The place was impassable. It seems there were a few people alive there, frantic for the most part and many burned and scalded. He was turned aside by the fire, and hid among some almost scorching heaps of broken wall as one of the Martian giants returned. He saw this one pursue a man, catch him up in one of its steely tentacles, and knock his head against the trunk of a pine tree. At last, after nightfall, the artilleryman made a rush for it and got over the railway embankment.

Since then he had been skulking along towards Maybury, in the hope of getting out of danger Londonward. People were hiding in trenches and cellars, and many of the survivors had made off towards Woking village and Send. He had been consumed with thirst until he found one of the water mains near the railway arch smashed, and the water bubbling out like a spring upon the road.

That was the story I got from him, bit by bit. He grew calmer telling me and trying to make me see the things he had seen. He had eaten no food since midday, he told me early in his narrative, and I found some mutton and bread in the pantry and brought it into the room. We lit no lamp for fear of attracting the Martians, and ever and again our hands would touch upon bread or meat. As he talked, things about us came darkly out of the darkness, and the trampled bushes and broken rose trees outside the window grew distinct. It would seem that a number of men or animals had rushed across the lawn. I began to see his face, blackened and haggard, as no doubt mine was also.

When we had finished eating we went softly upstairs to my study, and I looked again out of the open window. In one night the valley had become a valley of ashes. The fires had dwindled now. Where flames had been there were now streamers of smoke; but the countless ruins of shattered and gutted houses and blasted and blackened trees that the night had hidden stood out now gaunt and terrible in the pitiless light of dawn. Yet here and there some object had had the luck to escape—a white railway signal here, the end of a greenhouse there, white and fresh amid the wreckage. Never before in the history of warfare had destruction been so indiscriminate and so universal. And shining with the growing light of the east, three of the metallic giants stood about the pit, their cowls rotating as though they were surveying the desolation they had made.

It seemed to me that the pit had been enlarged, and ever and again puffs of vivid green vapour streamed up and out of it towards the brightening dawn—streamed up, whirled, broke, and vanished.

Beyond were the pillars of fire about Chobham. They became pillars of bloodshot smoke at the first touch of day.

XII

WHAT I SAW OF THE DESTRUCTION OF WEYBRIDGE AND SHEPPERTON

As the dawn grew brighter we withdrew from the window from which we had watched the Martians, and went very quietly downstairs.

The artilleryman agreed with me that the house was no place to stay in. He proposed, he said, to make his way Londonward, and thence rejoin his battery—No. 12, of the Horse Artillery. My plan was to return at once to Leatherhead; and so greatly had the strength of the Martians impressed me that I had determined to take my wife to Newhaven, and go with her out of the country forthwith. For I already perceived clearly that the country about London must inevitably be the scene of a disastrous struggle before such creatures as these could be destroyed.

Between us and Leatherhead, however, lay the third cylinder, with its guarding giants. Had I been alone, I think I should have taken my chance and struck across country. But the artilleryman dissuaded me: "It's no kindness to the right sort of wife," he said, "to make her a widow"; and in the end I agreed to go with him, under cover of the woods, northward as far as Street Cobham before I parted with him. Thence I would make a big detour by Epsom to reach Leatherhead.

I should have started at once, but my companion had been in active service and he knew better than that. He made me ransack the house for a flask, which he filled with whiskey; and we lined every available pocket with packets of biscuits and slices of meat. Then we crept out of the house, and ran as quickly as we could down the ill-made road by which I had come overnight. The houses seemed deserted. In the road lay a group of three charred bodies close together, struck dead by the Heat-Ray; and here and there were things that people had dropped—a clock, a slipper, a silver spoon, and the like poor valuables. At the corner turning up towards the post office a little cart, filled with boxes and furniture, and horseless, heeled over on a broken wheel. A cash box had been hastily smashed open and thrown under the debris.

Except the lodge at the Orphanage, which was still on fire, none of the houses had suffered very greatly here. The Heat-Ray had shaved the chimney tops and passed. Yet, save ourselves, there did not seem to be a living soul on Maybury Hill. The majority of the inhabitants had escaped, I suppose, by way of the Old Woking road—the road I had taken when I drove to Leatherhead—or they had hidden.

We went down the lane, by the body of the man in black, sodden now from the overnight hail, and broke into the woods at the foot of the hill. We pushed through these towards the railway without meeting a soul. The woods across the line were but the scarred and blackened ruins of woods; for the most part the trees had fallen, but a certain proportion still stood, dismal grey stems, with dark brown foliage instead of green.

On our side the fire had done no more than scorch the nearer trees; it had failed to secure its footing. In one place the woodmen had been at work on Saturday; trees, felled and freshly trimmed, lay in a clearing, with heaps of sawdust by the sawing-machine and its engine. Hard by was a temporary hut, deserted. There was not a breath of wind this morning, and everything was strangely still. Even the birds were hushed, and as we hurried along I and the artilleryman talked in whispers and looked now and again over our shoulders. Once or twice we stopped to listen.

After a time we drew near the road, and as we did so we heard the clatter of hoofs and saw through the tree stems three cavalry soldiers riding slowly towards Woking. We hailed them, and they halted while we hurried towards them. It was a lieutenant and a couple of privates of the 8th Hussars, with a stand like a theodolite, which the artilleryman told me was a heliograph.

"You are the first men I've seen coming this way this morning," said the lieutenant. "What's brewing?"

His voice and face were eager. The men behind him stared curiously. The artilleryman jumped down the bank into the road and saluted.

"Gun destroyed last night, sir. Have been hiding. Trying to rejoin battery, sir. You'll come in sight of the Martians, I expect, about half a mile along this road."

"What the dickens are they like?" asked the lieutenant.

"Giants in armour, sir. Hundred feet high. Three legs and a body like 'luminium, with a mighty great head in a hood, sir."

"Get out!" said the lieutenant. "What confounded nonsense!"

"You'll see, sir. They carry a kind of box, sir, that shoots fire and strikes you dead."

"What d'ye mean—a gun?"

"No, sir," and the artilleryman began a vivid account of the Heat-Ray. Halfway through, the lieutenant interrupted him and looked up at me. I was still standing on the bank by the side of the road.

"It's perfectly true," I said.

"Well," said the lieutenant, "I suppose it's my business to see it too. Look here"—to the artilleryman—"we're detailed here clearing people out of their houses. You'd better go along and report yourself to Brigadier-General Marvin, and tell him all you know. He's at Weybridge. Know the way?"

"I do," I said; and he turned his horse southward again.

"Half a mile, you say?" said he.

"At most," I answered, and pointed over the treetops southward. He thanked me and rode on, and we saw them no more.

Farther along we came upon a group of three women and two children in the road, busy clearing out a labourer's cottage. They had got hold of a little hand truck, and were piling it up with unclean-looking bundles and shabby furniture. They were all too assiduously engaged to talk to us as we passed.

By Byfleet station we emerged from the pine trees, and found the country calm and peaceful under the morning sunlight. We were far beyond the range of the Heat-Ray there, and had it not been for the silent desertion of some of the houses, the stirring movement of packing in others, and the knot of soldiers standing on the bridge over the railway and staring down the line towards Woking, the day would have seemed very like any other Sunday.

Several farm waggons and carts were moving creakily along the road to Addlestone, and suddenly through the gate of a field we saw, across a stretch of flat meadow, six twelve-pounders standing neatly at equal distances pointing towards Woking. The gunners stood by the guns waiting, and the ammunition waggons were at a business-like distance. The men stood almost as if under inspection.

"That's good!" said I. "They will get one fair shot, at any rate."

The artilleryman hesitated at the gate.

"I shall go on," he said.

Farther on towards Weybridge, just over the bridge, there were a number of men in white fatigue jackets throwing up a long rampart, and more guns behind.

"It's bows and arrows against the lightning, anyhow," said the artilleryman. "They 'aven't seen that fire-beam yet."

The officers who were not actively engaged stood and stared over the treetops southwestward, and the men digging would stop every now and again to stare in the same direction.

Byfleet was in a tumult; people packing, and a score of hussars, some of them dismounted, some on horseback, were hunting them about. Three or four black government waggons, with crosses in white circles, and an old omnibus, among other vehicles, were being loaded in the village street. There were scores of people, most of them sufficiently sabbatical to have assumed their best clothes. The soldiers were having the greatest difficulty in making them realise the gravity of their position. We saw one shrivelled old fellow with a huge box and a score or more of flower pots containing orchids, angrily expostulating with the corporal who would leave them behind. I stopped and gripped his arm.

"Do you know what's over there?" I said, pointing at the pine tops that hid the Martians.

"Eh?" said he, turning. "I was explainin' these is vallyble."

"Death!" I shouted. "Death is coming! Death!" and leaving him to digest that if he could, I hurried on after the artillery-man. At the corner I looked back. The soldier had left him, and he was still standing by his box, with the pots of orchids on the lid of it, and staring vaguely over the trees.

No one in Weybridge could tell us where the headquarters were established; the whole place was in such confusion as I had never seen in any town before. Carts, carriages everywhere, the most astonishing miscellany of conveyances and horseflesh. The respectable inhabitants of the place, men in golf and boating costumes, wives prettily dressed, were packing, river-side loafers energetically helping, children excited, and, for the most part, highly delighted at this astonishing variation of their Sunday experiences. In the midst of it all the worthy vicar was very pluckily holding an early celebration, and his bell was jangling out above the excitement.

I and the artilleryman, seated on the step of the drinking fountain, made a very passable meal upon what we had brought with us. Patrols of soldiers—here no longer hussars, but grenadiers in white—were warning people to move now or to take refuge in their cellars as soon as the firing began. We saw as we crossed the railway bridge that a growing crowd of people had assembled in and about the railway station, and the swarming platform was piled with boxes and packages. The ordinary traffic had been stopped, I believe, in order to allow of the passage of troops and guns to Chertsey, and I have heard since that a savage struggle occurred for places in the special trains that were put on at a later hour.

We remained at Weybridge until midday, and at that hour we found ourselves at the place near Shepperton Lock where the Wey and Thames join. Part of the time we spent helping two old women to pack a little cart. The Wey has a treble mouth, and at this point boats are to be hired, and there was a ferry across the river. On the Shepperton side was an inn with a lawn, and beyond that the tower of Shepperton Church—it has been replaced by a spire—rose above the trees.

Here we found an excited and noisy crowd of fugitives. As yet the flight had not grown to a panic, but there were already far more people than all the boats going to and fro could enable to cross. People came panting along under heavy burdens; one husband and wife were even carrying a small outhouse door between them, with some of their household goods piled thereon. One man told us he meant to try to get away from Shepperton station.

There was a lot of shouting, and one man was even jesting. The idea people seemed to have here was that the Martians were simply formidable human beings, who might attack and sack the town, to be certainly destroyed in the end. Every now and then people would glance nervously across the Wey, at the meadows towards Chertsey, but everything over there was still.

Across the Thames, except just where the boats landed, everything was quiet, in vivid contrast with the Surrey side. The people who landed there from the boats went tramping off down the lane. The big ferryboat had just made a journey. Three or four soldiers stood on the lawn of the inn, staring and jesting at the fugitives, without offering to help. The inn was closed, as it was now within prohibited hours.

"What's that?" cried a boatman, and "Shut up, you fool!" said a man near me to a yelping dog. Then the sound came again, this time from the direction of Chertsey, a muffled thud—the sound of a gun.

The fighting was beginning. Almost immediately unseen batteries across the river to our right, unseen because of the trees, took up the chorus, firing heavily one after the other. A woman screamed. Everyone stood arrested by the sudden stir of battle, near us and yet invisible to us. Nothing was to be seen save flat meadows, cows feeding unconcernedly for the most part, and silvery pollard willows motionless in the warm sunlight.

"The sojers'll stop 'em," said a woman beside me, doubtfully. A haziness rose over the treetops.

Then suddenly we saw a rush of smoke far away up the river, a puff of smoke that jerked up into the air and hung; and forthwith the ground heaved under foot and a heavy explosion shook the air, smashing two or three windows in the houses near, and leaving us astonished.

"Here they are!" shouted a man in a blue jersey. "Yonder! D'yer see them? Yonder!"

Quickly, one after the other, one, two, three, four of the armoured Martians appeared, far away over the little trees, across the flat meadows that stretched towards Chertsey, and striding hurriedly towards the river. Little cowled figures they seemed at first, going with a rolling motion and as fast as flying birds.

Then, advancing obliquely towards us, came a fifth. Their armoured bodies glittered in the sun as they swept swiftly forward upon the guns, growing rapidly larger as they drew nearer. One on the extreme left, the remotest that is, flourished a huge case high in the air, and the ghostly, terrible Heat-Ray I had already seen on Friday night smote towards Chertsey, and struck the town.

At sight of these strange, swift, and terrible creatures the crowd near the water's edge seemed to me to be for a moment horror-struck. There was no screaming or shouting, but a silence. Then a hoarse murmur and a movement of feet—a splashing from the water. A man, too frightened to drop the portmanteau he carried on his shoulder, swung round and sent me staggering with a blow from the corner of his burden. A woman thrust at me with her hand and rushed past me. I turned with the rush of the people, but I was not too terrified for thought. The terrible Heat-Ray was in my mind. To get under water! That was it!

"Get under water!" I shouted, unheeded.

I faced about again, and rushed towards the approaching Martian, rushed right down the gravelly beach and headlong into the water. Others did the same. A boatload of people putting back came leaping out as I rushed past. The stones under my feet were muddy and slippery, and the river was so low that I ran perhaps twenty feet scarcely waist-deep. Then, as the Martian towered overhead scarcely a couple of hundred yards away, I flung myself forward under the surface. The splashes of the people in the boats leaping into the river sounded like thunderclaps in my ears. People were landing hastily on both sides of the river.

But the Martian machine took no more notice for the moment of the people running this way and that than a man would of the confusion of ants in a nest against which his foot has kicked. When, half suffocated, I raised my head above water, the Martian's hood pointed at the batteries that were still firing across the river, and as it advanced it swung loose what must have been the generator of the Heat-Ray.

In another moment it was on the bank, and in a stride wading halfway across. The knees of its foremost legs bent at the farther bank, and in another moment it had raised itself to its full height again, close to the village of Shepperton. Forthwith the six guns which, unknown to anyone on the right bank, had been hidden behind the outskirts of that village, fired simultaneously. The sudden near concussion, the last close upon the first, made my heart jump. The monster was already raising the case generating the Heat-Ray as the first shell burst six yards above the hood.

I gave a cry of astonishment. I saw and thought nothing of the other four Martian monsters; my attention was riveted upon the nearer incident. Simultaneously two other shells burst in the air near the body as the hood twisted round in time to receive, but not in time to dodge, the fourth shell.

The shell burst clean in the face of the Thing. The hood bulged, flashed, was whirled off in a dozen tattered fragments of red flesh and glittering metal.

"Hit!" shouted I, with something between a scream and a cheer.

I heard answering shouts from the people in the water about me. I could have leaped out of the water with that momentary exultation.

The decapitated colossus reeled like a drunken giant; but it did not fall over. It recovered its balance by a miracle, and, no longer heeding its steps and with the camera that fired the Heat-Ray now rigidly upheld, it reeled swiftly upon Shepperton. The living intelligence, the Martian within the hood, was slain and splashed to the four winds of heaven, and the Thing was now but a mere intricate device of metal whirling to destruction. It drove along in a straight line, incapable of guidance. It struck the tower of Shepperton Church, smashing it down as the impact of a battering ram might have done, swerved aside, blundered on and collapsed with tremendous force into the river out of my sight.

A violent explosion shook the air, and a spout of water, steam, mud, and shattered metal shot far up into the sky. As the camera of the Heat-Ray hit the water, the latter had immediately flashed into steam. In another moment a huge wave, like a muddy tidal bore but almost scaldingly hot, came sweeping round the bend upstream. I saw people struggling shorewards, and heard their screaming and shouting faintly above the seething and roar of the Martian's collapse.

For a moment I heeded nothing of the heat, forgot the patent need of self-preservation. I splashed through the tumultuous water, pushing aside a man in black to do so, until I could see round the bend. Half a dozen deserted boats pitched aimlessly upon the confusion of the waves. The fallen Martian came into sight downstream, lying across the river, and for the most part submerged.

Thick clouds of steam were pouring off the wreckage, and through the tumultuously whirling wisps I could see, intermittently and vaguely, the gigantic limbs churning the water and flinging a splash and spray of mud and froth into the air. The tentacles swayed and struck like living arms, and, save for the helpless purposelessness of these movements, it was as if some wounded thing were struggling for its life amid the waves. Enormous quantities of a ruddy-brown fluid were spurting up in noisy jets out of the machine.

My attention was diverted from this death flurry by a furious yelling, like that of the thing called a siren in our manufacturing towns. A man, knee-deep near the towing path, shouted inaudibly to me and pointed. Looking back, I saw the other Martians advancing with gigantic strides down the riverbank from the direction of Chertsey. The Shepperton guns spoke this time unavailingly.

At that I ducked at once under water, and, holding my breath until movement was an agony, blundered painfully ahead under the surface as long as I could. The water was in a tumult about me, and rapidly growing hotter.

When for a moment I raised my head to take breath and throw the hair and water from my eyes, the steam was rising in a whirling white fog that at first hid the Martians altogether. The noise was deafening. Then I saw them dimly, colossal figures of grey, magnified by the mist. They had passed by me, and two were stooping over the frothing, tumultuous ruins of their comrade.

The third and fourth stood beside him in the water, one perhaps two hundred yards from me, the other towards Laleham. The generators of the Heat-Rays waved high, and the hissing beams smote down this way and that.

The air was full of sound, a deafening and confusing conflict of noises—the clangorous din of the Martians, the crash of falling houses, the thud of trees, fences, sheds flashing into flame, and the crackling and roaring of fire. Dense black smoke was leaping up to mingle with the steam from the river, and as the Heat-Ray went to and fro over Weybridge its impact was marked by flashes of incandescent white, that gave place at once to a smoky dance of lurid flames. The nearer houses still stood intact, awaiting their fate, shadowy, faint and pallid in the steam, with the fire behind them going to and fro.

For a moment perhaps I stood there, breast-high in the almost boiling water, dumbfounded at my position, hopeless of escape. Through the reek

I could see the people who had been with me in the river scrambling out of the water through the reeds, like little frogs hurrying through grass from the advance of a man, or running to and fro in utter dismay on the towing path.

Then suddenly the white flashes of the Heat-Ray came leaping towards me. The houses caved in as they dissolved at its touch, and darted out flames; the trees changed to fire with a roar. The Ray flickered up and down the towing path, licking off the people who ran this way and that, and came down to the water's edge not fifty yards from where I stood. It swept across the river to Shepperton, and the water in its track rose in a boiling weal crested with steam. I turned shoreward.

In another moment the huge wave, well-nigh at the boiling-point had rushed upon me. I screamed aloud, and scalded, half blinded, agonised, I staggered through the leaping, hissing water towards the shore. Had my foot stumbled, it would have been the end. I fell helplessly, in full sight of the Martians, upon the broad, bare gravelly spit that runs down to mark the angle of the Wey and Thames. I expected nothing but death.

I have a dim memory of the foot of a Martian coming down within a score of yards of my head, driving straight into the loose gravel, whirling it this way and that and lifting again; of a long suspense, and then of the four carrying the debris of their comrade between them, now clear and then presently faint through a veil of smoke, receding interminably, as it seemed to me, across a vast space of river and meadow. And then, very slowly, I realised that by a miracle I had escaped.

XII

HOW I FELL IN WITH THE CURATE

After getting this sudden lesson in the power of terrestrial weapons, the Martians retreated to their original position upon Horsell Common; and in their haste, and encumbered with the debris of their smashed companion, they no doubt overlooked many such a stray and negligible victim as myself. Had they left their comrade and pushed on forthwith, there was nothing at that time between them and London but batteries of twelve-pounder guns, and they would certainly have reached the capital in advance of the tidings of their approach; as sudden, dreadful, and destructive their advent would have been as the earthquake that destroyed Lisbon a century ago.

But they were in no hurry. Cylinder followed cylinder on its interplanetary flight; every twenty-four hours brought them reinforcement. And meanwhile the military and naval authorities, now fully alive to the tremendous power of their antagonists, worked with furious energy. Every minute a fresh gun came into position until, before twilight, every copse, every row of suburban villas on the hilly slopes about Kingston and Richmond, masked an expectant black muzzle. And through the charred and desolated area—perhaps twenty square miles altogether—that encircled the Martian encampment on Horsell Common, through charred and ruined villages among the green trees, through the blackened and smoking arcades that had been but a day ago pine spinneys, crawled the devoted scouts with the heliographs that were presently to warn the gunners of the Martian approach. But the Martians now understood our command of artillery and the danger of human proximity, and not a man ventured within a mile of either cylinder, save at the price of his life.

It would seem that these giants spent the earlier part of the afternoon in going to and fro, transferring everything from the second and third cylinders—the second in Addlestone Golf Links and the third at Pyrford—to their original pit on Horsell Common. Over that, above the blackened heather and ruined buildings that stretched far and wide, stood one as sentinel, while the rest abandoned their vast fighting-machines and descended into the pit. They were hard at work there far into the night, and the towering pillar of dense green smoke that rose therefrom could be seen from the hills about Merrow, and even, it is said, from Banstead and Epsom Downs.

And while the Martians behind me were thus preparing for their next sally, and in front of me Humanity gathered for the battle, I made my way with infinite pains and labour from the fire and smoke of burning Weybridge towards London.

I saw an abandoned boat, very small and remote, drifting down-stream; and throwing off the most of my sodden clothes, I went after it, gained it, and so escaped out of that destruction. There were no oars in the boat, but I contrived to paddle, as well as my parboiled hands would allow, down the river towards Halliford and Walton, going very tediously and continually looking behind me, as you may well understand. I followed the river, because I considered that the water gave me my best chance of escape should these giants return.

The hot water from the Martian's overthrow drifted downstream with me, so that for the best part of a mile I could see little of either bank. Once, however, I made out a string of black figures hurrying across the meadows from the direction of Weybridge. Halliford, it seemed, was deserted, and several of the houses facing the river were on fire. It was strange to see the place quite tranquil, quite desolate under the hot blue sky, with the smoke and little threads of flame going straight up into the heat of the afternoon. Never before had I seen houses burning without the accompaniment of an obstructive crowd. A little farther on the dry reeds up the bank were smoking and glowing, and a line of fire inland was marching steadily across a late field of hay.

For a long time I drifted, so painful and weary was I after the violence I had been through, and so intense the heat upon the water. Then my fears got the better of me again, and I resumed my paddling. The sun scorched my bare back. At last, as the bridge at Walton was coming into sight round the bend, my fever and faintness overcame my fears, and I landed on the Middlesex bank and lay down, deadly sick, amid the long grass. I suppose the time was then about four or five o'clock. I got up presently, walked perhaps half a mile without meeting a soul, and then lay down again in the shadow of a hedge. I seem to remember talking, wanderingly, to myself during that last spurt. I was also very thirsty, and bitterly regretful I had drunk no more water. It is a curious thing that I felt angry with my wife; I cannot account for it, but my impotent desire to reach Leatherhead worried me excessively.

I do not clearly remember the arrival of the curate, so that probably I dozed. I became aware of him as a seated figure in soot-smudged shirt sleeves, and with his upturned, clean-shaven face staring at a faint flickering that danced over the sky. The sky was what is called a mackerel sky—rows and rows of faint down-plumes of cloud, just tinted with the midsummer sunset.

I sat up, and at the rustle of my motion he looked at me quickly.

"Have you any water?" I asked abruptly.

He shook his head.

"You have been asking for water for the last hour," he said.

For a moment we were silent, taking stock of each other. I daresay he found me a strange enough figure, naked, save for my water-soaked trousers and socks, scalded, and my face and shoulders blackened by the smoke. His face was a fair weakness, his chin retreated, and his hair lay in crisp, almost flaxen curls on his low forehead; his eyes were rather large, pale blue, and blankly staring. He spoke abruptly, looking vacantly away from me.

"What does it mean?" he said. "What do these things mean?"

I stared at him and made no answer.

He extended a thin white hand and spoke in almost a complaining tone.

"Why are these things permitted? What sins have we done? The morning service was over, I was walking through the roads to clear my brain for the afternoon, and then—fire, earthquake, death! As if it were Sodom and Gomorrah! All our work undone, all the work—what are these Martians?"

"What are we?" I answered, clearing my throat.

He gripped his knees and turned to look at me again. For half a minute, perhaps, he stared silently.

"I was walking through the roads to clear my brain," he said. "And suddenly—fire, earthquake, death!"

He relapsed into silence, with his chin now sunken almost to his knees.

Presently he began waving his hand.

"All the work—all the Sunday schools—what have we done—what has Weybridge done? Everything gone—everything destroyed. The church! We rebuilt it only three years ago. Gone! Swept out of existence! Why?"

Another pause, and he broke out again like one demented.

"The smoke of her burning goeth up forever and ever!" he shouted.

His eyes flamed, and he pointed a lean finger in the direction of Weybridge.

By this time I was beginning to take his measure. The tremendous tragedy in which he had been involved—it was evident he was a fugitive from Weybridge—had driven him to the very verge of his reason.

"Are we far from Sunbury?" I said, in a matter-of-fact tone.

"What are we to do?" he asked. "Are these creatures everywhere? Has the earth been given over to them?"

"Are we far from Sunbury?"

"Only this morning I officiated at early celebration—"

"Things have changed," I said, quietly. "You must keep your head. There is still hope."

"Hope!"

"Yes. Plentiful hope—for all this destruction!"

I began to explain my view of our position. He listened at first, but as I went on the interest dawning in his eyes gave place to their former stare, and his regard wandered from me.

"This must be the beginning of the end," he said, interrupting me. "The end! The great and terrible day of the Lord! When men shall call upon the mountains and the rocks to fall upon them and hide them—hide them from the face of Him that sitteth upon the throne!"

I began to understand the position. I ceased my laboured reasoning, struggled to my feet, and, standing over him, laid my hand on his shoulder.

"Be a man!" said I. "You are scared out of your wits! What good is religion if it collapses under calamity? Think of what earthquakes and floods, wars and volcanoes, have done before to men! Did you think God had exempted Weybridge? He is not an insurance agent."

For a time he sat in blank silence.

"But how can we escape?" he asked, suddenly. "They are invulnerable, they are pitiless."

"Neither the one nor, perhaps, the other," I answered. "And the mightier they are the more sane and wary should we be. One of them was killed yonder not three hours ago."

"Killed!" he said, staring about him. "How can God's ministers be killed?"

"I saw it happen." I proceeded to tell him. "We have chanced to come in for the thick of it," said I, "and that is all."

"What is that flicker in the sky?" he asked abruptly.

I told him it was the heliograph signalling—that it was the sign of human help and effort in the sky.

"We are in the midst of it," I said, "quiet as it is. That flicker in the sky tells of the gathering storm. Yonder, I take it are the Martians, and Londonward, where those hills rise about Richmond and Kingston and the trees give cover, earthworks are being thrown up and guns are being placed. Presently the Martians will be coming this way again."

And even as I spoke he sprang to his feet and stopped me by a gesture.

"Listen!" he said.

From beyond the low hills across the water came the dull resonance of distant guns and a remote weird crying. Then everything was still. A cockchafer came droning over the hedge and past us. High in the west the crescent moon hung faint and pale above the smoke of Weybridge and Shepperton and the hot, still splendour of the sunset.

"We had better follow this path," I said, "northward."

XIV

IN LONDON

My younger brother was in London when the Martians fell at Woking. He was a medical student working for an imminent examination, and he heard nothing of the arrival until Saturday morning. The morning papers on Saturday contained, in addition to lengthy special articles on the planet Mars, on life in the planets, and so forth, a brief and vaguely worded telegram, all the more striking for its brevity.

The Martians, alarmed by the approach of a crowd, had killed a number of people with a quick-firing gun, so the story ran. The telegram concluded with the words: "Formidable as they seem to be, the Martians have not moved from the pit into which they have fallen, and, indeed, seem incapable of doing so. Probably this is due to the relative strength of the earth's gravitational energy." On that last text their leader-writer expanded very comfortingly.

Of course all the students in the crammer's biology class, to which my brother went that day, were intensely interested, but there were no signs of any unusual excitement in the streets. The afternoon papers puffed scraps of news under big headlines. They had nothing to tell beyond the movements of troops about the common, and the burning of the pine woods between Woking and Weybridge, until eight. Then the *St. James's Gazette*, in an extra-special edition, announced the bare fact of the interruption of telegraphic communication. This was thought to be due to the falling of burning pine trees across the line. Nothing more of the fighting was known that night, the night of my drive to Leatherhead and back.

My brother felt no anxiety about us, as he knew from the description in the papers that the cylinder was a good two miles from my house. He made up his mind to run down that night to me, in order, as he says, to see the Things before they were killed. He dispatched a telegram, which never reached me, about four o'clock, and spent the evening at a music hall.

In London, also, on Saturday night there was a thunderstorm, and my brother reached Waterloo in a cab. On the platform from which the midnight train usually starts he learned, after some waiting, that an accident prevented trains from reaching Woking that night. The nature of the accident he could not ascertain; indeed, the railway authorities did not clearly know at that time. There was very little excitement in the station, as the officials, failing to realise that anything further than a breakdown between Byfleet and Woking junction had occurred, were running the theatre trains which usually passed through Woking round by Virginia Water or Guildford. They were busy making the necessary arrangements to alter the route of the Southampton and Portsmouth Sunday League excursions. A nocturnal newspaper reporter, mistaking my brother for the traffic manager, to whom he bears a slight resemblance, waylaid and tried to interview him. Few people, excepting the railway officials, connected the breakdown with the Martians.

I have read, in another account of these events, that on Sunday morning "all London was electrified by the news from Woking." As a matter of fact, there was nothing to justify that very extravagant phrase. Plenty of Londoners did not hear of the Martians until the panic of Monday morning. Those who did took some time to realise all that the hastily worded telegrams in the Sunday papers conveyed. The majority of people in London do not read Sunday papers.

The habit of personal security, moreover, is so deeply fixed in the Londoner's mind, and startling intelligence so much a matter of course in the papers, that they could read without any personal tremors: "About seven o'clock last night the Martians came out of the cylinder, and, moving about under an armour of metallic shields, have completely wrecked Woking station with the adjacent houses, and massacred an entire battalion of the Cardigan Regiment. No details are known. Maxims have been absolutely useless against their armour; the field guns have been disabled by them. Flying hussars have been galloping into Chertsey. The Martians appear to be moving slowly towards Chertsey or Windsor. Great anxiety prevails in West Surrey, and earthworks are being thrown up to check the advance Londonward." That was how the Sunday *Sun* put it, and a clever and remarkably prompt "handbook" article in the *Referee* compared the affair to a menagerie suddenly let loose in a village.

No one in London knew positively of the nature of the armoured Martians, and there was still a fixed idea that these monsters must be sluggish: "crawling," "creeping painfully"—such expressions occurred in almost all the earlier reports. None of the telegrams could have been written by an eyewitness of their advance. The Sunday papers printed separate editions as further news came to hand, some even in default of it. But there was practically nothing more to tell people until late in the afternoon, when the authorities gave the press agencies the news in their possession. It was stated that the people of Walton and Weybridge, and all the district were pouring along the roads Londonward, and that was all.

My brother went to church at the Foundling Hospital in the morning, still in ignorance of what had happened on the previous night. There he heard allusions made to the invasion, and a special prayer for peace. Coming out, he bought a *Referee.* He became alarmed at the news in this, and went again to Waterloo station to find out if communication were restored. The omnibuses, carriages, cyclists, and innumerable people walking in their best clothes seemed scarcely affected by the strange intelligence that the news venders were disseminating. People were interested, or, if alarmed, alarmed only on account of the local residents. At the station he heard for the first time that the Windsor and Chertsey lines were now interrupted. The porters told him that several remarkable telegrams had been received in the morning from Byfleet and Chertsey stations, but that these had abruptly ceased. My brother could get very little precise detail out of them. "There's fighting going on about Weybridge" was the extent of their information.

The train service was now very much disorganised. Quite a number of people who had been expecting friends from places on the South-Western network were standing about the station. One grey-headed old gentleman came and abused the South-Western Company bitterly to my brother. "It wants showing up," he said.

One or two trains came in from Richmond, Putney, and Kingston, containing people who had gone out for a day's boating and found the locks closed and a feeling of panic in the air. A man in a blue-and-white blazer addressed my brother, full of strange tidings.

"There's hosts of people driving into Kingston in traps and carts and things, with boxes of valuables and all that," he said. "They come from Molesey and Weybridge and Walton, and they say there's been guns heard at Chertsey, heavy firing, and that mounted soldiers have told them to get off at once because the Martians are coming. *We* heard guns firing at Hampton Court station, but we thought it was thunder. What the dickens does it all mean? The Martians can't get out of their pit, can they?"

My brother could not tell him.

Afterwards he found that the vague feeling of alarm had spread to the clients of the underground railway, and that the Sunday excursionists began to return from all over the South-Western "lung"—Barnes, Wimbledon, Richmond Park, Kew, and so forth—at unnaturally early hours; but not a soul had anything more than vague hearsay to tell of. Everyone connected with the terminus seemed ill-tempered.

About five o'clock the gathering crowd in the station was immensely excited by the opening of the line of communication, which is almost invariably closed, between the South-Eastern and the South-Western stations, and the passage of carriage trucks bearing huge guns and carriages crammed with soldiers. These were the guns that were brought up from Woolwich and Chatham to cover Kingston. There was an exchange of pleasantries: "You'll get eaten!" "We're the beast-tamers!" and so forth. A little while after that a squad of police came into the station and began to clear the public off the platforms, and my brother went out into the street again.

The church bells were ringing for evensong, and a squad of Salvation Army lassies came singing down Waterloo Road. On the bridge a number of loafers were watching a curious brown scum that came drifting down the stream in patches. The sun was just setting, and the Clock Tower and the Houses of Parliament rose against one of the most peaceful skies it is possible to imagine, a sky of gold, barred with long transverse stripes of reddish-purple cloud. There was talk of a floating body. One of the men there, a reservist he said he was, told my brother he had seen the heliograph flickering in the west.

In Wellington Street my brother met a couple of sturdy roughs who had just been rushed out of Fleet Street with still-wet newspapers and staring placards. "Dreadful catastrophe!" they bawled one to the other down Wellington Street. "Fighting at Weybridge! Full description! Repulse of the Martians! London in Danger!" He had to give threepence for a copy of that paper.

Then it was, and then only, that he realised something of the full power and terror of these monsters. He learned that they were not merely a handful of small sluggish creatures, but that they were minds swaying vast mechanical bodies; and that they could move swiftly and smite with such power that even the mightiest guns could not stand against them.

They were described as "vast spider-like machines, nearly a hundred feet high, capable of the speed of an express train, and able to shoot out a beam of intense heat." Masked batteries, chiefly of field guns, had been planted in the country about Horsell Common, and especially between the Woking district and London. Five of the machines had been seen moving towards the Thames, and one, by a happy chance, had been destroyed. In the other cases the shells had missed, and the batteries had been at once annihilated by the Heat-Rays. Heavy losses of soldiers were mentioned, but the tone of the dispatch was optimistic.

The Martians had been repulsed; they were not invulnerable. They had retreated to their triangle of cylinders again, in the circle about Woking. Signallers with heliographs were pushing forward upon them from all sides. Guns were in rapid transit from Windsor, Portsmouth, Aldershot, Woolwich—even from the north; among others, long wire-guns of ninety-five tons from Woolwich. Altogether one hundred and sixteen were in position or being hastily placed, chiefly covering London. Never before in England had there been such a vast or rapid concentration of military material.

Any further cylinders that fell, it was hoped, could be destroyed at once by high explosives, which were being rapidly manufactured and distributed. No doubt, ran the report, the situation was of the strangest and gravest description, but the public was exhorted to avoid and discourage panic. No doubt the Martians were strange and terrible in the extreme, but at the outside there could not be more than twenty of them against our millions.

The authorities had reason to suppose, from the size of the cylinders, that at the outside there could not be more than five in each cylinder—fifteen altogether. And one at least was disposed of—perhaps more. The public would be fairly warned of the approach of danger, and elaborate measures were being taken for the protection of the people in the threatened southwestern suburbs. And so, with reiterated assurances of the safety of London and the ability of the authorities to cope with the difficulty, this quasi-proclamation closed.

This was printed in enormous type on paper so fresh that it was still wet, and there had been no time to add a word of comment. It was curious, my brother said, to see how ruthlessly the usual contents of the paper had been hacked and taken out to give this place.

All down Wellington Street people could be seen fluttering out the pink sheets and reading, and the Strand was suddenly noisy with the voices of an army of hawkers following these pioneers. Men came scrambling off buses to secure copies. Certainly this news excited people intensely, whatever their previous apathy. The shutters of a map shop in the Strand were being taken down, my brother said, and a man in his Sunday raiment, lemon-yellow gloves even, was visible inside the window hastily fastening maps of Surrey to the glass.

Going on along the Strand to Trafalgar Square, the paper in his hand, my brother saw some of the fugitives from West Surrey. There was a man with his wife and two boys and some articles of furniture in a cart such as greengrocers use. He was driving from the direction of Westminster Bridge; and close behind him came a hay waggon with five or six respectable-looking people in it, and some boxes and bundles. The faces of these people were haggard, and their entire appearance contrasted conspicuously with the Sabbath-best appearance of the people on the omnibuses. People in fashionable clothing peeped at them out of cabs. They stopped at the Square as if undecided which way to take, and finally turned eastward along the Strand. Some way behind these came a man in workday clothes, riding one of those old-fashioned tricycles with a small front wheel. He was dirty and white in the face.

My brother turned down towards Victoria, and met a number of such people. He had a vague idea that he might see something of me. He noticed an unusual number of police regulating the traffic. Some of the refugees were exchanging news with the people on the omnibuses. One was professing to have seen the Martians. "Boilers on stilts, I tell you, striding along like men." Most of them were excited and animated by their strange experience.

Beyond Victoria the public-houses were doing a lively trade with these arrivals. At all the street corners groups of people were reading papers, talking excitedly, or staring at these unusual Sunday visitors. They seemed to increase as night drew on, until at last the roads, my brother said, were like Epsom High Street on a Derby Day. My brother addressed several of these fugitives and got unsatisfactory answers from most.

None of them could tell him any news of Woking except one man, who assured him that Woking had been entirely destroyed on the previous night.

"I come from Byfleet," he said; "man on a bicycle came through the place in the early morning, and ran from door to door warning us to come away. Then came soldiers. We went out to look, and there were clouds of smoke to the south—nothing but smoke, and not a soul coming that way. Then we heard the guns at Chertsey, and folks coming from Weybridge. So I've locked up my house and come on."

At the time there was a strong feeling in the streets that the authorities were to blame for their incapacity to dispose of the invaders without all this inconvenience.

About eight o'clock a noise of heavy firing was distinctly audible all over the south of London. My brother could not hear it for the traffic in the main thoroughfares, but by striking through the quiet back streets to the river he was able to distinguish it quite plainly.

He walked from Westminster to his apartments near Regent's Park, about two. He was now very anxious on my account, and disturbed at the evident magnitude of the trouble. His mind was inclined to run, even as mine had run on Saturday, on military details. He thought of all those silent, expectant guns, of the suddenly nomadic countryside; he tried to imagine "boilers on stilts" a hundred feet high.

There were one or two cartloads of refugees passing along Oxford Street, and several in the Marylebone Road, but so slowly was the news spreading that Regent Street and Portland Place were full of their usual Sunday-night promenaders, albeit they talked in groups, and along the edge of Regent's Park there were as many silent couples "walking out" together under the scattered gas lamps as ever there had been. The night was warm and still, and a little oppressive; the sound of guns continued intermittently, and after midnight there seemed to be sheet lightning in the south.

He read and reread the paper, fearing the worst had happened to me. He was restless, and after supper prowled out again aimlessly. He returned and tried in vain to divert his attention to his examination notes. He went to bed a little after midnight, and was awakened from lurid dreams in the small hours of Monday by the sound of door knockers, feet running in the street, distant drumming, and a clamour of bells. Red reflections danced on the ceiling. For a moment he lay astonished, wondering whether day had come or the world gone mad. Then he jumped out of bed and ran to the window.

His room was an attic and as he thrust his head out, up and down the street there were a dozen echoes to the noise of his window sash, and heads in every kind of night disarray appeared. Enquiries were being shouted. "They are coming!" bawled a policeman, hammering at the door, "The Martians are coming!" and hurried to the next door.

The sound of drumming and trumpeting came from the Albany Street Barracks, and every church within earshot was hard at work killing sleep with a vehement disorderly tocsin. There was a noise of doors opening, and window after window in the houses opposite flashed from darkness into yellow illumination.

Up the street came galloping a closed carriage, bursting abruptly into noise at the corner, rising to a clattering climax under the window, and dying away slowly in the distance. Close on the rear of this came a couple of cabs, the forerunners of a long procession of flying vehicles, going for the most part to Chalk Farm station, where the North-Western special trains were loading up, instead of coming down the gradient into Euston.

For a long time my brother stared out of the window in blank astonishment, watching the policemen hammering at door after door, and delivering their incomprehensible message. Then the door behind him opened, and the man who lodged across the landing came in, dressed only in shirt, trousers, and slippers, his braces loose about his waist, his hair disordered from his pillow.

"What the devil is it?" he asked. "A fire? What a devil of a row!"

They both craned their heads out of the window, straining to hear what the policemen were shouting. People were coming out of the side streets, and standing in groups at the corners talking.

"What the devil is it all about?" said my brother's fellow lodger.

My brother answered him vaguely and began to dress, running with each garment to the window in order to miss nothing of the growing excitement. And presently men selling unnaturally early newspapers came bawling into the street:

"London in danger of suffocation! The Kingston and Richmond defences forced! Fearful massacres in the Thames Valley!"

And all about him—in the rooms below, in the houses on each side and across the road, and behind in the Park Terraces and in the hundred other streets of that part of Marylebone, and the Westbourne Park district and St. Pancras, and westward and northward in Kilburn and St. John's Wood and Hampstead, and eastward in Shoreditch and Highbury and Haggerston and Hoxton, and, indeed, through all the vastness of London from Ealing to East Ham—people were rubbing their eyes, and opening windows to stare out and ask aimless questions, dressing hastily as the first breath of the coming storm of Fear blew through the streets. It was the dawn of the great panic. London, which had gone to bed on Sunday night oblivious and inert, was awakened, in the small hours of Monday morning, to a vivid sense of danger.

Unable from his window to learn what was happening, my brother went down and out into the street, just as the sky between the parapets of the houses grew pink with the early dawn. The flying people on foot and in vehicles grew more numerous every moment. "Black Smoke!" he heard people crying, and again "Black Smoke!" The contagion of such a unanimous fear was inevitable. As my brother hesitated on the door-step, he saw another news vender approaching, and got a paper forthwith. The man was running away with the rest, and selling his papers for a shilling each as he ran—a grotesque mingling of profit and panic.

And from this paper my brother read that catastrophic dispatch of the Commander-in-Chief:

"The Martians are able to discharge enormous clouds of a black and poisonous vapour by means of rockets. They have smothered our batteries, destroyed Richmond, Kingston, and Wimbledon, and are advancing slowly towards London, destroying everything on the way. It is impossible to stop them. There is no safety from the Black Smoke but in instant flight."

That was all, but it was enough. The whole population of the great six-million city was stirring, slipping, running; presently it would be pouring en masse northward.

"Black Smoke!" the voices cried. "Fire!"

The bells of the neighbouring church made a jangling tumult, a cart carelessly driven smashed, amid shrieks and curses, against the water trough up the street. Sickly yellow lights went to and fro in the houses, and some of the passing cabs flaunted unextinguished lamps. And overhead the dawn was growing brighter, clear and steady and calm.

He heard footsteps running to and fro in the rooms, and up and down stairs behind him. His landlady came to the door, loosely wrapped in dressing gown and shawl; her husband followed ejaculating.

As my brother began to realise the import of all these things, he turned hastily to his own room, put all his available money—some ten pounds altogether—into his pockets, and went out again into the streets.

XV

WHAT HAD HAPPENED IN SURREY

It was while the curate had sat and talked so wildly to me under the hedge in the flat meadows near Halliford, and while my brother was watching the fugitives stream over Westminster Bridge, that the Martians had resumed the offensive. So far as one can ascertain from the conflicting accounts that have been put forth, the majority of them remained busied with preparations in the Horsell pit until nine that night, hurrying on some operation that disengaged huge volumes of green smoke.

But three certainly came out about eight o'clock and, advancing slowly and cautiously, made their way through Byfleet and Pyrford towards Ripley and Weybridge, and so came in sight of the expectant batteries against the setting sun. These Martians did not advance in a body, but in a line, each perhaps a mile and a half from his nearest fellow. They communicated with one another by means of siren-like howls, running up and down the scale from one note to another.

It was this howling and firing of the guns at Ripley and St. George's Hill that we had heard at Upper Halliford. The Ripley gunners, unseasoned artillery volunteers who ought never to have been placed in such a position, fired one wild, premature, ineffectual volley, and bolted on horse and foot through the deserted village, while the Martian, without using his Heat-Ray, walked serenely over their guns, stepped gingerly among them, passed in front of them, and so came unexpectedly upon the guns in Painshill Park, which he destroyed.

The St. George's Hill men, however, were better led or of a better mettle. Hidden by a pine wood as they were, they seem to have been quite unsuspected by the Martian nearest to them. They laid their guns as deliberately as if they had been on parade, and fired at about a thousand yards' range.

The shells flashed all round him, and he was seen to advance a few paces, stagger, and go down. Everybody yelled together, and the guns were reloaded in frantic haste. The overthrown Martian set up a prolonged ululation, and immediately a second glittering giant, answering him, appeared over the trees to the south. It would seem that a leg of the tripod had been smashed by one of the shells. The whole of the second volley flew wide of the Martian on the ground, and, simultaneously, both his companions brought their Heat-Rays to bear on the battery. The ammunition blew up, the pine trees all about the guns flashed into fire, and only one or two of the men who were already running over the crest of the hill escaped.

After this it would seem that the three took counsel together and halted, and the scouts who were watching them report that they remained absolutely stationary for the next half hour. The Martian who had been overthrown crawled tediously out of his hood, a small brown figure, oddly suggestive from that distance of a speck of blight, and apparently engaged in the repair of his support. About nine he had finished, for his cowl was then seen above the trees again.

It was a few minutes past nine that night when these three sentinels were joined by four other Martians, each carrying a thick black tube. A similar tube was handed to each of the three, and the seven proceeded to distribute themselves at equal distances along a curved line between St. George's Hill, Weybridge, and the village of Send, southwest of Ripley.

A dozen rockets sprang out of the hills before them so soon as they began to move, and warned the waiting batteries about Ditton and Esher. At the same time four of their fighting machines, similarly armed with tubes, crossed the river, and two of them, black against the western sky, came into sight of myself and the curate as we hurried wearily and painfully along the road that runs northward out of Halliford. They moved, as it seemed to us, upon a cloud, for a milky mist covered the fields and rose to a third of their height.

At this sight the curate cried faintly in his throat, and began running; but I knew it was no good running from a Martian, and I turned aside and crawled through dewy nettles and brambles into the broad ditch by the side of the road. He looked back, saw what I was doing, and turned to join me.

The two halted, the nearer to us standing and facing Sunbury, the remoter being a grey indistinctness towards the evening star, away towards Staines.

The occasional howling of the Martians had ceased; they took up their positions in the huge crescent about their cylinders in absolute silence. It was a crescent with twelve miles between its horns. Never since the devising of gunpowder was the beginning of a battle so still. To us and to an observer about Ripley it would have had precisely the same effect—the Martians seemed in solitary possession of the darkling night, lit only as it was by the slender moon, the stars, the afterglow of the daylight, and the ruddy glare from St. George's Hill and the woods of Painshill.

But facing that crescent everywhere—at Staines, Hounslow, Ditton, Esher, Ockham, behind hills and woods south of the river, and across the flat grass meadows to the north of it, wherever a cluster of trees or village houses gave sufficient cover—the guns were waiting. The signal rockets burst and rained their sparks through the night and vanished, and the spirit of all those watching batteries rose to a tense expectation. The Martians had but to advance into the line of fire, and instantly those motionless black forms of men, those guns glittering so darkly in the early night, would explode into a thunderous fury of battle.

No doubt the thought that was uppermost in a thousand of those vigilant minds, even as it was uppermost in mine, was the riddle—how much they understood of us. Did they grasp that we in our millions were organized, disciplined, working together? Or did they interpret our spurts of fire, the sudden stinging of our shells, our steady investment of their encampment, as we should the furious unanimity of onslaught in a disturbed hive of bees? Did they dream they might exterminate us? (At that time no one knew what food they needed.) A hundred such questions struggled together in my mind as I watched that vast sentinel shape. And in the back of my mind was the sense of all the huge unknown and hidden forces Londonward. Had they prepared pitfalls? Were the powder mills at Hounslow ready as a snare? Would the Londoners have the heart and courage to make a greater Moscow of their mighty province of houses?

Then, after an interminable time, as it seemed to us, crouching and peering through the hedge, came a sound like the distant concussion of a gun. Another nearer, and then another. And then the Martian beside us raised his tube on high and discharged it, gunwise, with a heavy report that made the ground heave. The one towards Staines answered him. There was no flash, no smoke, simply that loaded detonation.

I was so excited by these heavy minute guns following one another that I so far forgot my personal safety and my scalded hands as to clamber up into the hedge and stare towards Sunbury. As I did so a second report followed, and a big projectile hurtled overhead towards Hounslow. I expected at least to see smoke or fire, or some such evidence of its work. But all I saw was the deep blue sky above, with one solitary star, and the white mist spreading wide and low beneath. And there had been no crash, no answering explosion. The silence was restored; the minute lengthened to three.

"What has happened?" said the curate, standing up beside me.

"Heaven knows!" said I.

A bat flickered by and vanished. A distant tumult of shouting began and ceased. I looked again at the Martian, and saw he was now moving eastward along the riverbank, with a swift, rolling motion.

Every moment I expected the fire of some hidden battery to spring upon him; but the evening calm was unbroken. The figure of the Martian grew smaller as he receded, and presently the mist and the gathering night had swallowed him up. By a common impulse we clambered higher. Towards Sunbury was a dark appearance, as though a conical hill had suddenly come into being there, hiding our view of the farther country; and then, remoter across the river, over Walton, we saw another such summit. These hill-like forms grew lower and broader even as we stared.

Moved by a sudden thought, I looked northward, and there I perceived a third of these cloudy black kopjes had risen.

Everything had suddenly become very still. Far away to the southeast, marking the quiet, we heard the Martians hooting to one another, and then the air quivered again with the distant thud of their guns. But the earthly artillery made no reply.

Now at the time we could not understand these things, but later I was to learn the meaning of these ominous kopjes that gathered in the twilight. Each of the Martians, standing in the great crescent I have described, had discharged, by means of the gun-like tube he carried, a huge canister over whatever hill, copse, cluster of houses, or other possible cover for guns, chanced to be in front of him. Some fired only one of these, some two—as in the case of the one we had seen; the one at Ripley is said to have discharged no fewer than five at that time. These canisters smashed on striking the ground—they did not explode—and incontinently disengaged an enormous volume of heavy, inky vapour, coiling and pouring upward in a huge and ebony cumulus cloud, a gaseous hill that sank and spread itself slowly over the surrounding country. And the touch of that vapour, the inhaling of its pungent wisps, was death to all that breathes.

It was heavy, this vapour, heavier than the densest smoke, so that, after the first tumultuous uprush and outflow of its impact, it sank down through the air and poured over the ground in a manner rather liquid than gaseous, abandoning the hills, and streaming into the valleys and ditches and watercourses even as I have heard the carbonic-acid gas that pours from volcanic clefts is wont to do. And where it came upon water some chemical action occurred, and the surface would be instantly covered with a powdery scum that sank slowly and made way for more. The scum was absolutely insoluble, and it is a strange thing, seeing the instant effect of the gas, that one could drink without hurt the water from which it had been strained. The vapour did not diffuse as a true gas would do. It hung together in banks, flowing sluggishly down the slope of the land and driving reluctantly before the wind, and very slowly it combined with the mist and moisture of the air, and sank to the earth in the form of dust. Save that an unknown element giving a group of four lines in the blue of the spectrum is concerned, we are still entirely ignorant of the nature of this substance.

Once the tumultuous upheaval of its dispersion was over, the black smoke clung so closely to the ground, even before its precipitation, that fifty feet up in the air, on the roofs and upper stories of high houses and on great trees, there was a chance of escaping its poison altogether, as was proved even that night at Street Cobham and Ditton.

The man who escaped at the former place tells a wonderful story of the strangeness of its coiling flow, and how he looked down from the church spire and saw the houses of the village rising like ghosts out of its inky nothingness. For a day and a half he remained there, weary, starving and sun-scorched, the earth under the blue sky and against the prospect of the distant hills a velvet-black expanse, with red roofs, green trees, and, later, black-veiled shrubs and gates, barns, outhouses, and walls, rising here and there into the sunlight.

But that was at Street Cobham, where the black vapour was allowed to remain until it sank of its own accord into the ground. As a rule the Martians, when it had served its purpose, cleared the air of it again by wading into it and directing a jet of steam upon it.

This they did with the vapour banks near us, as we saw in the starlight from the window of a deserted house at Upper Halliford, whither we had returned. From there we could see the searchlights on Richmond Hill and Kingston Hill going to and fro, and about eleven the windows rattled, and we heard the sound of the huge siege guns that had been put in position there. These continued intermittently for the space of a quarter of an hour, sending chance shots at the invisible Martians at Hampton and Ditton, and then the pale beams of the electric light vanished, and were replaced by a bright red glow.

Then the fourth cylinder fell—a brilliant green meteor—as I learned afterwards, in Bushey Park. Before the guns on the Richmond and Kingston line of hills began, there was a fitful cannonade far away in the southwest, due, I believe, to guns being fired haphazard before the black vapour could overwhelm the gunners.

So, setting about it as methodically as men might smoke out a wasps' nest, the Martians spread this strange stifling vapour over the Londonward country. The horns of the crescent slowly moved apart, until at last they formed a line from Hanwell to Coombe and Malden. All night through their destructive tubes advanced. Never once, after the Martian at St. George's Hill was brought down, did they give the artillery the ghost of a chance against them. Wherever there was a possibility of guns being laid for them unseen, a fresh canister of the black vapour was discharged, and where the guns were openly displayed the Heat-Ray was brought to bear.

By midnight the blazing trees along the slopes of Richmond Park and the glare of Kingston Hill threw their light upon a network of black smoke, blotting out the whole valley of the Thames and extending as far as the eye could reach. And through this two Martians slowly waded, and turned their hissing steam jets this way and that.

They were sparing of the Heat-Ray that night, either because they had but a limited supply of material for its production or because they did not wish to destroy the country but only to crush and overawe the opposition they had aroused. In the latter aim they certainly succeeded. Sunday night was the end of the organised opposition to their movements. After that no body of men would stand against them, so hopeless was the enterprise. Even the crews of the torpedo-boats and destroyers that had brought their quick-firers up the Thames refused to stop, mutinied, and went down again. The only offensive operation men ventured upon after that night was the preparation of mines and pitfalls, and even in that their energies were frantic and spasmodic.

One has to imagine, as well as one may, the fate of those batteries towards Esher, waiting so tensely in the twilight. Survivors there were none. One may picture the orderly expectation, the officers alert and watchful, the gunners ready, the ammunition piled to hand, the limber gunners with their horses and waggons, the groups of civilian spectators standing as near as they were permitted, the evening stillness, the ambulances and hospital tents with the burned and wounded from Weybridge; then the dull resonance of the shots the Martians fired, and the clumsy projectile whirling over the trees and houses and smashing amid the neighbouring fields.

One may picture, too, the sudden shifting of the attention, the swiftly spreading coils and bellyings of that blackness advancing headlong, towering heavenward, turning the twilight to a palpable darkness, a strange and horrible antagonist of vapour striding upon its victims, men and horses near it seen dimly, running, shrieking, falling headlong, shouts of dismay, the guns suddenly abandoned, men choking and writhing on the ground, and the swift broadening-out of the opaque cone of smoke. And then night and extinction—nothing but a silent mass of impenetrable vapour hiding its dead.

Before dawn the black vapour was pouring through the streets of Richmond, and the disintegrating organism of government was, with a last expiring effort, rousing the population of London to the necessity of flight.

XVI

THE EXODUS FROM LONDON

So you understand the roaring wave of fear that swept through the greatest city in the world just as Monday was dawning—the stream of flight rising swiftly to a torrent, lashing in a foaming tumult round the railway stations, banked up into a horrible struggle about the shipping in the Thames, and hurrying by every available channel northward and eastward. By ten o'clock the police organisation, and by midday even the railway organisations, were losing coherency, losing shape and efficiency, guttering, softening, running at last in that swift liquefaction of the social body.

All the railway lines north of the Thames and the South-Eastern people at Cannon Street had been warned by midnight on Sunday, and trains were being filled. People were fighting savagely for standing-room in the carriages even at two o'clock. By three, people were being trampled and crushed even in Bishopsgate Street, a couple of hundred yards or more from Liverpool Street station; revolvers were fired, people stabbed, and the policemen who had been sent to direct the traffic, exhausted and infuriated, were breaking the heads of the people they were called out to protect.

And as the day advanced and the engine drivers and stokers refused to return to London, the pressure of the flight drove the people in an ever-thickening multitude away from the stations and along the northward-running roads. By midday a Martian had been seen at Barnes, and a cloud of slowly sinking black vapour drove along the Thames and across the flats of Lambeth, cutting off all escape over the bridges in its sluggish advance. Another bank drove over Ealing, and surrounded a little island of survivors on Castle Hill, alive, but unable to escape.

After a fruitless struggle to get aboard a North-Western train at Chalk Farm—the engines of the trains that had loaded in the goods yard there *ploughed* through shrieking people, and a dozen stalwart men fought to keep the crowd from crushing the driver against his furnace—my brother emerged upon the Chalk Farm road, dodged across through a hurrying swarm of vehicles, and had the luck to be foremost in the sack of a cycle shop. The front tire of the machine he got was punctured in dragging it through the window, but he got up and off, notwithstanding, with no further injury than a cut wrist. The steep foot of Haverstock Hill was impassable owing to several overturned horses, and my brother struck into Belsize Road.

So he got out of the fury of the panic, and, skirting the Edgware Road, reached Edgware about seven, fasting and wearied, but well ahead of the crowd. Along the road people were standing in the roadway, curious, wondering. He was passed by a number of cyclists, some horsemen, and two motor cars. A mile from Edgware the rim of the wheel broke, and the machine became unridable. He left it by the roadside and trudged through the village. There were shops half opened in the main street of the place, and people crowded on the pavement and in the doorways and windows, staring astonished at this extraordinary procession of fugitives that was beginning. He succeeded in getting some food at an inn.

For a time he remained in Edgware not knowing what next to do. The flying people increased in number. Many of them, like my brother, seemed inclined to loiter in the place. There was no fresh news of the invaders from Mars.

At that time the road was crowded, but as yet far from congested. Most of the fugitives at that hour were mounted on cycles, but there were soon motor cars, hansom cabs, and carriages hurrying along, and the dust hung in heavy clouds along the road to St. Albans.

It was perhaps a vague idea of making his way to Chelmsford, where some friends of his lived, that at last induced my brother to strike into a quiet lane running eastward. Presently he came upon a stile, and, crossing it, followed a footpath northeastward. He passed near several farmhouses and some little places whose names he did not learn. He saw few fugitives until, in a grass lane towards High Barnet, he happened upon two ladies who became his fellow travellers. He came upon them just in time to save them.

He heard their screams, and, hurrying round the corner, saw a couple of men struggling to drag them out of the little pony-chaise in which they had been driving, while a third with difficulty held the frightened pony's head. One of the ladies, a short woman dressed in white, was simply screaming; the other, a dark, slender figure, slashed at the man who gripped her arm with a whip she held in her disengaged hand.

My brother immediately grasped the situation, shouted, and hurried towards the struggle. One of the men desisted and turned towards him, and my brother, realising from his antagonist's face that a fight was unavoidable, and being an expert boxer, went into him forthwith and sent him down against the wheel of the chaise.

It was no time for pugilistic chivalry and my brother laid him quiet with a kick, and gripped the collar of the man who pulled at the slender lady's arm. He heard the clatter of hoofs, the whip stung across his face, a third antagonist struck him between the eyes, and the man he held wrenched himself free and made off down the lane in the direction from which he had come.

Partly stunned, he found himself facing the man who had held the horse's head, and became aware of the chaise receding from him down the lane, swaying from side to side, and with the women in it looking back. The man before him, a burly rough, tried to close, and he stopped him with a blow in the face. Then, realising that he was deserted, he dodged round and made off down the lane after the chaise, with the sturdy man close behind him, and the fugitive, who had turned now, following remotely.

Suddenly he stumbled and fell; his immediate pursuer went headlong, and he rose to his feet to find himself with a couple of antagonists again. He would have had little chance against them had not the slender lady very pluckily pulled up and returned to his help. It seems she had had a revolver all this time, but it had been under the seat when she and her companion were attacked. She fired at six yards' distance, narrowly missing my brother. The less courageous of the robbers made off, and his companion followed him, cursing his cowardice. They both stopped in sight down the lane, where the third man lay insensible.

"Take this!" said the slender lady, and she gave my brother her revolver.

"Go back to the chaise," said my brother, wiping the blood from his split lip.

She turned without a word—they were both panting—and they went back to where the lady in white struggled to hold back the frightened pony.

The robbers had evidently had enough of it. When my brother looked again they were retreating.

"I'll sit here," said my brother, "if I may"; and he got upon the empty front seat. The lady looked over her shoulder.

"Give me the reins," she said, and laid the whip along the pony's side. In another moment a bend in the road hid the three men from my brother's eyes.

So, quite unexpectedly, my brother found himself, panting, with a cut mouth, a bruised jaw, and bloodstained knuckles, driving along an unknown lane with these two women.

He learned they were the wife and the younger sister of a surgeon living at Stanmore, who had come in the small hours from a dangerous case at Pinner, and heard at some railway station on his way of the Martian advance. He had hurried home, roused the women—their servant had left them two days before—packed some provisions, put his revolver under the seat—luckily for my brother—and told them to drive on to Edgware, with the idea of getting a train there. He stopped behind to tell the neighbours. He would overtake them, he said, at about half past four in the morning, and now it was nearly nine and they had seen nothing of him. They could not stop in Edgware because of the growing traffic through the place, and so they had come into this side lane.

That was the story they told my brother in fragments when presently they stopped again, nearer to New Barnet. He promised to stay with them, at least until they could determine what to do, or until the missing man arrived, and professed to be an expert shot with the revolver—a weapon strange to him—in order to give them confidence.

They made a sort of encampment by the wayside, and the pony became happy in the hedge. He told them of his own escape out of London, and all that he knew of these Martians and their ways. The sun crept higher in the sky, and after a time their talk died out and gave place to an uneasy state of anticipation. Several wayfarers came along the lane, and of these my brother gathered such news as he could. Every broken answer he had deepened his impression of the great disaster that had come on humanity, deepened his persuasion of the immediate necessity for prosecuting this flight. He urged the matter upon them.

"We have money," said the slender woman, and hesitated.

Her eyes met my brother's, and her hesitation ended.

"So have I," said my brother.

She explained that they had as much as thirty pounds in gold, besides a five-pound note, and suggested that with that they might get upon a train at St. Albans or New Barnet. My brother thought that was hopeless, seeing the fury of the Londoners to crowd upon the trains, and broached his own idea of striking across Essex towards Harwich and thence escaping from the country altogether.

Mrs. Elphinstone—that was the name of the woman in white—would listen to no reasoning, and kept calling upon "George"; but her sister-in-law was astonishingly quiet and deliberate, and at last agreed to my brother's suggestion. So, designing to cross the Great North Road, they went on towards Barnet, my brother leading the pony to save it as much as possible. As the sun crept up the sky the day became excessively hot, and under foot a thick, whitish sand grew burning and blinding, so that they travelled only very slowly. The hedges were grey with dust. And as they advanced towards Barnet a tumultuous murmuring grew stronger.

They began to meet more people. For the most part these were staring before them, murmuring indistinct questions, jaded, haggard, unclean. One man in evening dress passed them on foot, his eyes on the ground. They heard his voice, and, looking back at him, saw one hand clutched in his hair and the other beating invisible things. His paroxysm of rage over, he went on his way without once looking back.

As my brother's party went on towards the crossroads to the south of Barnet they saw a woman approaching the road across some fields on their left, carrying a child and with two other children; and then passed a man in dirty black, with a thick stick in one hand and a small portmanteau in the other. Then round the corner of the lane, from between the villas that guarded it at its confluence with the high road, came a little cart drawn by a sweating black pony and driven by a sallow youth in a bowler hat, grey with dust. There were three girls, East End factory girls, and a couple of little children crowded in the cart.

"This'll tike us rahnd Edgware?" asked the driver, wild-eyed, white-faced; and when my brother told him it would if he turned to the left, he whipped up at once without the formality of thanks.

My brother noticed a pale grey smoke or haze rising among the houses in front of them, and veiling the white facade of a terrace beyond the road that appeared between the backs of the villas. Mrs. Elphinstone suddenly cried out at a number of tongues of smoky red flame leaping up above the houses in front of them against the hot, blue sky. The tumultuous noise resolved itself now into the disorderly mingling of many voices, the gride of many wheels, the creaking of waggons, and the staccato of hoofs. The lane came round sharply not fifty yards from the crossroads.

"Good heavens!" cried Mrs. Elphinstone. "What is this you are driving us into?"

My brother stopped.

For the main road was a boiling stream of people, a torrent of human beings rushing northward, one pressing on another. A great bank of dust, white and luminous in the blaze of the sun, made everything within twenty feet of the ground grey and indistinct and was perpetually renewed by the hurrying feet of a dense crowd of horses and of men and women on foot, and by the wheels of vehicles of every description.

"Way!" my brother heard voices crying. "Make way!"

It was like riding into the smoke of a fire to approach the meeting point of the lane and road; the crowd roared like a fire, and the dust was hot and pungent. And, indeed, a little way up the road a villa was burning and sending rolling masses of black smoke across the road to add to the confusion.

Two men came past them. Then a dirty woman, carrying a heavy bundle and weeping. A lost retriever dog, with hanging tongue, circled dubiously round them, scared and wretched, and fled at my brother's threat.

So much as they could see of the road Londonward between the houses to the right was a tumultuous stream of dirty, hurrying people, pent in between the villas on either side; the black heads, the crowded forms, grew into distinctness as they rushed towards the corner, hurried past, and merged their individuality again in a receding multitude that was swallowed up at last in a cloud of dust.

"Go on! Go on!" cried the voices. "Way! Way!"

One man's hands pressed on the back of another. My brother stood at the pony's head. Irresistibly attracted, he advanced slowly, pace by pace, down the lane.

Edgware had been a scene of confusion, Chalk Farm a riotous tumult, but this was a whole population in movement. It is hard to imagine that host. It had no character of its own. The figures poured out past the corner, and receded with their backs to the group in the lane. Along the margin came those who were on foot threatened by the wheels, stumbling in the ditches, blundering into one another.

The carts and carriages crowded close upon one another, making little way for those swifter and more impatient vehicles that darted forward every now and then when an opportunity showed itself of doing so, sending the people scattering against the fences and gates of the villas.

"Push on!" was the cry. "Push on! They are coming!"

In one cart stood a blind man in the uniform of the Salvation Army, gesticulating with his crooked fingers and bawling, "Eternity! Eternity!" His voice was hoarse and very loud so that my brother could hear him long after he was lost to sight in the dust. Some of the people who crowded in the carts whipped stupidly at their horses and quarrelled with other drivers; some sat motionless, staring at nothing with miserable eyes; some gnawed their hands with thirst, or lay prostrate in the bottoms of their conveyances. The horses' bits were covered with foam, their eyes bloodshot.

There were cabs, carriages, shop cars, waggons, beyond counting; a mail cart, a road-cleaner's cart marked "Vestry of St. Pancras," a huge timber waggon crowded with roughs. A brewer's dray rumbled by with its two near wheels splashed with fresh blood.

"Clear the way!" cried the voices. "Clear the way!"

"Eter-nity! Eter-nity!" came echoing down the road.

There were sad, haggard women tramping by, well dressed, with children that cried and stumbled, their dainty clothes smothered in dust, their weary faces smeared with tears. With many of these came men, sometimes helpful, sometimes lowering and savage. Fighting side by side with them pushed some weary street outcast in faded black rags, wide-eyed, loud-voiced, and foul-mouthed. There were sturdy workmen thrusting their way along, wretched, unkempt men, clothed like clerks or shopmen, struggling spasmodically; a wounded soldier my brother noticed, men dressed in the clothes of railway porters, one wretched creature in a nightshirt with a coat thrown over it.

But varied as its composition was, certain things all that host had in common. There were fear and pain on their faces, and fear behind them. A tumult up the road, a quarrel for a place in a waggon, sent the whole host of them quickening their pace; even a man so scared and broken that his knees bent under him was galvanised for a moment into renewed activity. The heat and dust had already been at work upon this multitude. Their skins were dry, their lips black and cracked. They were all thirsty, weary, and footsore. And amid the various cries one heard disputes, reproaches, groans of weariness and fatigue; the voices of most of them were hoarse and weak. Through it all ran a refrain:

"Way! Way! The Martians are coming!"

Few stopped and came aside from that flood. The lane opened slantingly into the main road with a narrow opening, and had a delusive appearance of coming from the direction of London. Yet a kind of eddy of people drove into its mouth; weaklings elbowed out of the stream, who for the most part rested but a moment before plunging into it again. A little way down the lane, with two friends bending over him, lay a man with a bare leg, wrapped about with bloody rags. He was a lucky man to have friends.

A little old man, with a grey military moustache and a filthy black frock coat, limped out and sat down beside the trap, removed his boot—his sock was blood-stained—shook out a pebble, and hobbled on again; and then a little girl of eight or nine, all alone, threw herself under the hedge close by my brother, weeping.

"I can't go on! I can't go on!"

My brother woke from his torpor of astonishment and lifted her up, speaking gently to her, and carried her to Miss Elphinstone. So soon as my brother touched her she became quite still, as if frightened.

"Ellen!" shrieked a woman in the crowd, with tears in her voice—"Ellen!" And the child suddenly darted away from my brother, crying "Mother!"

"They are coming," said a man on horseback, riding past along the lane.

"Out of the way, there!" bawled a coachman, towering high; and my brother saw a closed carriage turning into the lane.

The people crushed back on one another to avoid the horse. My brother pushed the pony and chaise back into the hedge, and the man drove by and stopped at the turn of the way. It was a carriage, with a pole for a pair of horses, but only one was in the traces. My brother saw dimly through the dust that two men lifted out something on a white stretcher and put it gently on the grass beneath the privet hedge.

One of the men came running to my brother.

"Where is there any water?" he said. "He is dying fast, and very thirsty. It is Lord Garrick."

"Lord Garrick!" said my brother; "the Chief Justice?"

"The water?" he said.

"There may be a tap," said my brother, "in some of the houses. We have no water. I dare not leave my people."

The man pushed against the crowd towards the gate of the corner house.

"Go on!" said the people, thrusting at him. "They are coming! Go on!"

Then my brother's attention was distracted by a bearded, eagle-faced man lugging a small handbag, which split even as my brother's eyes rested on it and disgorged a mass of sovereigns that seemed to break up into separate coins as it struck the ground. They rolled hither and thither among the struggling feet of men and horses. The man stopped and looked stupidly at the heap, and the shaft of a cab struck his shoulder and sent him reeling. He gave a shriek and dodged back, and a cartwheel shaved him narrowly.

"Way!" cried the men all about him. "Make way!"

So soon as the cab had passed, he flung himself, with both hands open, upon the heap of coins, and began thrusting handfuls in his pocket. A horse rose close upon him, and in another moment, half rising, he had been borne down under the horse's hoofs.

"Stop!" screamed my brother, and pushing a woman out of his way, tried to clutch the bit of the horse.

Before he could get to it, he heard a scream under the wheels, and saw through the dust the rim passing over the poor wretch's back. The driver of the cart slashed his whip at my brother, who ran round behind the cart. The multitudinous shouting confused his ears. The man was writhing in the dust among his scattered money, unable to rise, for the wheel had broken his back, and his lower limbs lay limp and dead. My brother stood up and yelled at the next driver, and a man on a black horse came to his assistance.

"Get him out of the road," said he; and, clutching the man's collar with his free hand, my brother lugged him sideways. But he still clutched after his money, and regarded my brother fiercely, hammering at his arm with a handful of gold. "Go on! Go on!" shouted angry voices behind. "Way! Way!"

There was a smash as the pole of a carriage crashed into the cart that the man on horseback stopped. My brother looked up, and the man with the gold twisted his head round and bit the wrist that held his collar. There was a concussion, and the black horse came staggering sideways, and the carthorse pushed beside it. A hoof missed my brother's foot by a hair's breadth. He released his grip on the fallen man and jumped back. He saw anger change to terror on the face of the poor wretch on the ground, and in a moment he was hidden and my brother was borne backward and carried past the entrance of the lane, and had to fight hard in the torrent to recover it.

He saw Miss Elphinstone covering her eyes, and a little child, with all a child's want of sympathetic imagination, staring with dilated eyes at a dusty something that lay black and still, ground and crushed under the rolling wheels. "Let us go back!" he shouted, and began turning the pony round. "We cannot cross this—hell," he said and they went back a hundred yards the way they had come, until the fighting crowd was hidden. As they passed the bend in the lane my brother saw the face of the dying man in the ditch under the privet, deadly white and drawn, and shining with perspiration. The two women sat silent, crouching in their seat and shivering.

Then beyond the bend my brother stopped again. Miss Elphinstone was white and pale, and her sister-in-law sat weeping, too wretched even to call upon "George." My brother was horrified and perplexed. So soon as they had retreated he realised how urgent and unavoidable it was to attempt this crossing. He turned to Miss Elphinstone, suddenly resolute.

"We must go that way," he said, and led the pony round again.

For the second time that day this girl proved her quality. To force their way into the torrent of people, my brother plunged into the traffic and held back a cab horse, while she drove the pony across its head. A waggon locked wheels for a moment and ripped a long splinter from the chaise. In another moment they were caught and swept forward by the stream. My brother, with the cabman's whip marks red across his face and hands, scrambled into the chaise and took the reins from her.

"Point the revolver at the man behind," he said, giving it to her, "if he presses us too hard. No—point it at his horse!"

Then he began to look out for a chance of edging to the right across the road. But once in the stream he seemed to lose volition, to become a part of that dusty rout. They swept through Chipping Barnet with the torrent; they were nearly a mile beyond the centre of the town before they had fought across to the opposite side of the way. It was din and confusion indescribable; but in and beyond the town the road forks repeatedly, and this to some extent relieved the stress.

They struck eastward through Hadley, and there on either side of the road, and at another place farther on they came upon a great multitude of people drinking at the stream, some fighting to come at the water. And farther on, from a lull near East Barnet, they saw two trains running slowly one after the other without signal or order—trains swarming with people, with men even among the coals behind the engines—going northward along the Great Northern Railway. My brother supposes they must have filled outside London, for at that time the furious terror of the people had rendered the central termini impossible.

Near this place they halted for the rest of the afternoon, for the violence of the day had already utterly exhausted all three of them. They began to suffer the beginnings of hunger; the night was cold, and none of them dared to sleep. And in the evening many people came hurrying along the road nearby their stopping place, fleeing from unknown dangers before them, and going in the direction from which my brother had come.

XVII

THE *THUNDER CHILD*

Had the Martians aimed only at destruction, they might on Monday have annihilated the entire population of London, as it spread itself slowly through the home counties. Not only along the road through Barnet, but also through Edgware and Waltham Abbey, and along the roads eastward to Southend and Shoeburyness, and south of the Thames to Deal and Broadstairs, poured the same frantic rout. If one could have hung that June morning in a balloon in the blazing blue above London every northward and eastward road running out of the tangled maze of streets would have seemed stippled black with the streaming fugitives, each dot a human agony of terror and physical distress. I have set forth at length in the last chapter my brother's account of the road through Chipping Barnet, in order that my readers may realise how that swarming of black dots appeared to one of those concerned. Never before in the history of the world had such a mass of human beings moved and suffered together. The legendary hosts of Goths and Huns, the hugest armies Asia has ever seen, would have been but a drop in that current. And this was no disciplined march; it was a stampede—a stampede gigantic and terrible—without order and without a goal, six million people unarmed and unprovisioned, driving headlong. It was the beginning of the rout of civilisation, of the massacre of mankind.

Directly below him the balloonist would have seen the network of streets far and wide, houses, churches, squares, crescents, gardens—already derelict—spread out like a huge map, and in the southward *blotted*. Over Ealing, Richmond, Wimbledon, it would have seemed as if some monstrous pen had flung ink upon the chart. Steadily, incessantly, each black splash grew and spread, shooting out ramifications this way and that, now banking itself against rising ground, now pouring swiftly over a crest into a newfound valley, exactly as a gout of ink would spread itself upon blotting paper.

And beyond, over the blue hills that rise southward of the river, the glittering Martians went to and fro, calmly and methodically spreading their poison cloud over this patch of country and then over that, laying it again with their steam jets when it had served its purpose, and taking possession of the conquered country. They do not seem to have aimed at extermination so much as at complete demoralisation and the destruction of any opposition. They exploded any stores of powder they came upon, cut every telegraph, and wrecked the railways here and there. They were hamstringing mankind. They seemed in no hurry to extend the field of their operations, and did not come beyond the central part of London all that day. It is possible that a very considerable number of people in London stuck to their houses through Monday morning. Certain it is that many died at home suffocated by the Black Smoke.

Until about midday the Pool of London was an astonishing scene. Steamboats and shipping of all sorts lay there, tempted by the enormous sums of money offered by fugitives, and it is said that many who swam out to these vessels were thrust off with boathooks and drowned. About one o'clock in the afternoon the thinning remnant of a cloud of the black vapour appeared between the arches of Blackfriars Bridge. At that the Pool became a scene of mad confusion, fighting, and collision, and for some time a multitude of boats and barges jammed in the northern arch of the Tower Bridge, and the sailors and lightermen had to fight savagely against the people who swarmed upon them from the riverfront. People were actually clambering down the piers of the bridge from above.

When, an hour later, a Martian appeared beyond the Clock Tower and waded down the river, nothing but wreckage floated above Limehouse.

Of the falling of the fifth cylinder I have presently to tell. The sixth star fell at Wimbledon. My brother, keeping watch beside the women in the chaise in a meadow, saw the green flash of it far beyond the hills. On Tuesday the little party, still set upon getting across the sea, made its way through the swarming country towards Colchester. The news that the Martians were now in possession of the whole of London was confirmed. They had been seen at Highgate, and even, it was said, at Neasden. But they did not come into my brother's view until the morrow.

That day the scattered multitudes began to realise the urgent need of provisions. As they grew hungry the rights of property ceased to be regarded. Farmers were out to defend their cattle-sheds, granaries, and ripening root crops with arms in their hands. A number of people now, like my brother, had their faces eastward, and there were some desperate souls even going back towards London to get food. These were chiefly people from the northern suburbs, whose knowledge of the Black Smoke came by hearsay. He heard that about half the members of the government had gathered at Birmingham, and that enormous quantities of high explosives were being prepared to be used in automatic mines across the Midland counties.

He was also told that the Midland Railway Company had replaced the desertions of the first day's panic, had resumed traffic, and was running northward trains from St. Albans to relieve the congestion of the home counties. There was also a placard in Chipping Ongar announcing that large stores of flour were available in the northern towns and that within twenty-four hours bread would be distributed among the starving people in the neighbourhood. But this intelligence did not deter him from the plan of escape he had formed, and the three pressed eastward all day, and heard no more of the bread distribution than this promise. Nor, as a matter of fact, did anyone else hear more of it. That night fell the seventh star, falling upon Primrose Hill. It fell while Miss Elphinstone was watching, for she took that duty alternately with my brother. She saw it.

On Wednesday the three fugitives—they had passed the night in a field of unripe wheat—reached Chelmsford, and there a body of the inhabitants, calling itself the Committee of Public Supply, seized the pony as provisions, and would give nothing in exchange for it but the promise of a share in it the next day. Here there were rumours of Martians at Epping, and news of the destruction of Waltham Abbey Powder Mills in a vain attempt to blow up one of the invaders.

People were watching for Martians here from the church towers. My brother, very luckily for him as it chanced, preferred to push on at once to the coast rather than wait for food, although all three of them were very hungry. By midday they passed through Tillingham, which, strangely enough, seemed to be quite silent and deserted, save for a few furtive plunderers hunting for food. Near Tillingham they suddenly came in sight of the sea, and the most amazing crowd of shipping of all sorts that it is possible to imagine.

For after the sailors could no longer come up the Thames, they came on to the Essex coast, to Harwich and Walton and Clacton, and afterwards to Foulness and Shoebury, to bring off the people. They lay in a huge sickle-shaped curve that vanished into mist at last towards the Naze. Close inshore was a multitude of fishing smacks—English, Scotch, French, Dutch, and Swedish; steam launches from the Thames, yachts, electric boats; and beyond were ships of large burden, a multitude of filthy colliers, trim merchantmen, cattle ships, passenger boats, petroleum tanks, ocean tramps, an old white transport even, neat white and grey liners from Southampton and Hamburg; and along the blue coast across the Blackwater my brother could make out dimly a dense swarm of boats chaffering with the people on the beach, a swarm which also extended up the Blackwater almost to Maldon.

About a couple of miles out lay an ironclad, very low in the water, almost, to my brother's perception, like a water-logged ship. This was the ram *Thunder Child*. It was the only warship in sight, but far away to the right over the smooth surface of the sea—for that day there was a dead calm—lay a serpent of black smoke to mark the next ironclads of the Channel Fleet, which hovered in an extended line, steam up and ready for action, across the Thames estuary during the course of the Martian conquest, vigilant and yet powerless to prevent it.

At the sight of the sea, Mrs. Elphinstone, in spite of the assurances of her sister-in-law, gave way to panic. She had never been out of England before, she would rather die than trust herself friendless in a foreign country, and so forth. She seemed, poor woman, to imagine that the French and the Martians might prove very similar. She had been growing increasingly hysterical, fearful, and depressed during the two days' journeyings. Her great idea was to return to Stanmore. Things had been always well and safe at Stanmore. They would find George at Stanmore.

It was with the greatest difficulty they could get her down to the beach, where presently my brother succeeded in attracting the attention of some men on a paddle steamer from the Thames. They sent a boat and drove a bargain for thirty-six pounds for the three. The steamer was going, these men said, to Ostend.

It was about two o'clock when my brother, having paid their fares at the gangway, found himself safely aboard the steamboat with his charges. There was food aboard, albeit at exorbitant prices, and the three of them contrived to eat a meal on one of the seats forward.

There were already a couple of score of passengers aboard, some of whom had expended their last money in securing a passage, but the captain lay off the Blackwater until five in the afternoon, picking up passengers until the seated decks were even dangerously crowded. He would probably have remained longer had it not been for the sound of guns that began about that hour in the south. As if in answer, the ironclad seaward fired a small gun and hoisted a string of flags. A jet of smoke sprang out of her funnels.

Some of the passengers were of opinion that this firing came from Shoeburyness, until it was noticed that it was growing louder. At the same time, far away in the southeast the masts and upperworks of three ironclads rose one after the other out of the sea, beneath clouds of black smoke. But my brother's attention speedily reverted to the distant firing in the south. He fancied he saw a column of smoke rising out of the distant grey haze.

The little steamer was already flapping her way eastward of the big crescent of shipping, and the low Essex coast was growing blue and hazy, when a Martian appeared, small and faint in the remote distance, advancing along the muddy coast from the direction of Foulness. At that the captain on the bridge swore at the top of his voice with fear and anger at his own delay, and the paddles seemed infected with his terror. Every soul aboard stood at the bulwarks or on the seats of the steamer and stared at that distant shape, higher than the trees or church towers inland, and advancing with a leisurely parody of a human stride.

It was the first Martian my brother had seen, and he stood, more amazed than terrified, watching this Titan advancing deliberately towards the shipping, wading farther and farther into the water as the coast fell away. Then, far away beyond the Crouch, came another, striding over some stunted trees, and then yet another, still farther off, wading deeply through a shiny mudflat that seemed to hang halfway up between sea and sky. They were all stalking seaward, as if to intercept the escape of the multitudinous vessels that were crowded between Foulness and the Naze. In spite of the throbbing exertions of the engines of the little paddle-boat, and the pouring foam that her wheels flung behind her, she receded with terrifying slowness from this ominous advance.

Glancing northwestward, my brother saw the large crescent of shipping already writhing with the approaching terror; one ship passing behind another, another coming round from broadside to end on, steamships whistling and giving off volumes of steam, sails being let out, launches rushing hither and thither. He was so fascinated by this and by the creeping danger away to the left that he had no eyes for anything seaward. And then a swift movement of the steamboat (she had suddenly come round to avoid being run down) flung him headlong from the seat upon which he was standing. There was a shouting all about him, a trampling of feet, and a cheer that seemed to be answered faintly. The steamboat lurched and rolled him over upon his hands.

He sprang to his feet and saw to starboard, and not a hundred yards from their heeling, pitching boat, a vast iron bulk like the blade of a plough tearing through the water, tossing it on either side in huge waves of foam that leaped towards the steamer, flinging her paddles helplessly in the air, and then sucking her deck down almost to the waterline.

A douche of spray blinded my brother for a moment. When his eyes were clear again he saw the monster had passed and was rushing landward. Big iron upperworks rose out of this headlong structure, and from that twin funnels projected and spat a smoking blast shot with fire. It was the torpedo ram, *Thunder Child*, steaming headlong, coming to the rescue of the threatened shipping.

Keeping his footing on the heaving deck by clutching the bulwarks, my brother looked past this charging leviathan at the Martians again, and he saw the three of them now close together, and standing so far out to sea that their tripod supports were almost entirely submerged. Thus sunken, and seen in remote perspective, they appeared far less formidable than the huge iron bulk in whose wake the steamer was pitching so helplessly. It would seem they were regarding this new antagonist with astonishment. To their intelligence, it may be, the giant was even such another as themselves. The *Thunder Child* fired no gun, but simply drove full speed towards them. It was probably her not firing that enabled her to get so near the enemy as she did. They did not know what to make of her. One shell, and they would have sent her to the bottom forthwith with the Heat-Ray.

She was steaming at such a pace that in a minute she seemed halfway between the steamboat and the Martians—a diminishing black bulk against the receding horizontal expanse of the Essex coast.

Suddenly the foremost Martian lowered his tube and discharged a canister of the black gas at the ironclad. It hit her larboard side and glanced off in an inky jet that rolled away to seaward, an unfolding torrent of Black Smoke, from which the ironclad drove clear. To the watchers from the steamer, low in the water and with the sun in their eyes, it seemed as though she were already among the Martians.

They saw the gaunt figures separating and rising out of the water as they retreated shoreward, and one of them raised the camera-like generator of the Heat-Ray. He held it pointing obliquely downward, and a bank of steam sprang from the water at its touch. It must have driven through the iron of the ship's side like a white-hot iron rod through paper.

A flicker of flame went up through the rising steam, and then the Martian reeled and staggered. In another moment he was cut down, and a great body of water and steam shot high in the air. The guns of the *Thunder Child* sounded through the reek, going off one after the other, and one shot splashed the water high close by the steamer, ricocheted towards the other flying ships to the north, and smashed a smack to matchwood.

But no one heeded that very much. At the sight of the Martian's collapse the captain on the bridge yelled inarticulately, and all the crowding passengers on the steamer's stern shouted together. And then they yelled again. For, surging out beyond the white tumult, drove something long and black, the flames streaming from its middle parts, its ventilators and funnels spouting fire.

She was alive still; the steering gear, it seems, was intact and her engines working. She headed straight for a second Martian, and was within a hundred yards of him when the Heat-Ray came to bear. Then with a violent thud, a blinding flash, her decks, her funnels, leaped upward. The Martian staggered with the violence of her explosion, and in another moment the flaming wreckage, still driving forward with the impetus of its pace, had struck him and crumpled him up like a thing of cardboard. My brother shouted involuntarily. A boiling tumult of steam hid everything again.

"Two!" yelled the captain.

Everyone was shouting. The whole steamer from end to end rang with frantic cheering that was taken up first by one and then by all in the crowding multitude of ships and boats that was driving out to sea.

The steam hung upon the water for many minutes, hiding the third Martian and the coast altogether. And all this time the boat was paddling steadily out to sea and away from the fight; and when at last the confusion cleared, the drifting bank of black vapour intervened, and nothing of the *Thunder Child* could be made out, nor could the third Martian be seen. But the ironclads to seaward were now quite close and standing in towards shore past the steamboat.

The little vessel continued to beat its way seaward, and the ironclads receded slowly towards the coast, which was hidden still by a marbled bank of vapour, part steam, part black gas, eddying and combining in the strangest way. The fleet of refugees was scattering to the northeast; several smacks were sailing between the ironclads and the steamboat. After a time, and before they reached the sinking cloud bank, the warships turned northward, and then abruptly went about and passed into the thickening haze of evening southward. The coast grew faint, and at last indistinguishable amid the low banks of clouds that were gathering about the sinking sun.

Then suddenly out of the golden haze of the sunset came the vibration of guns, and a form of black shadows moving. Everyone struggled to the rail of the steamer and peered into the blinding furnace of the west, but nothing was to be distinguished clearly. A mass of smoke rose slanting and barred the face of the sun. The steamboat throbbed on its way through an interminable suspense.

The sun sank into grey clouds, the sky flushed and darkened, the evening star trembled into sight. It was deep twilight when the captain cried out and pointed. My brother strained his eyes. Something rushed up into the sky out of the greyness—rushed slantingly upward and very swiftly into the luminous clearness above the clouds in the western sky; something flat and broad, and very large, that swept round in a vast curve, grew smaller, sank slowly, and vanished again into the grey mystery of the night. And as it flew it rained down darkness upon the land.

BOOK II: THE EARTH UNDER THE MARTIANS

I

UNDERFOOT

In the first book I have wandered so much from my own adventures to tell of the experiences of my brother that all through the last two chapters I and the curate have been lurking in the empty house at Halliford whither we fled to escape the Black Smoke. There I will resume. We stopped there all Sunday night and all the next day—the day of the panic—in a little island of daylight, cut off by the Black Smoke from the rest of the world. We could do nothing but wait in aching inactivity during those two weary days.

My mind was occupied by anxiety for my wife. I figured her at Leatherhead, terrified, in danger, mourning me already as a dead man. I paced the rooms and cried aloud when I thought of how I was cut off from her, of all that might happen to her in my absence. My cousin I knew was brave enough for any emergency, but he was not the sort of man to realise danger quickly, to rise promptly. What was needed now was not bravery, but circumspection. My only consolation was to believe that the Martians were moving Londonward and away from her. Such vague anxieties keep the mind sensitive and painful. I grew very weary and irritable with the curate's perpetual ejaculations; I tired of the sight of his selfish despair. After some ineffectual remonstrance I kept away from him, staying in a room—evidently a children's schoolroom—containing globes, forms, and copybooks. When he followed me thither, I went to a box room at the top of the house and, in order to be alone with my aching miseries, locked myself in.

We were hopelessly hemmed in by the Black Smoke all that day and the morning of the next. There were signs of people in the next house on Sunday evening—a face at a window and moving lights, and later the slamming of a door. But I do not know who these people were, nor what became of them. We saw nothing of them next day. The Black Smoke drifted slowly riverward all through Monday morning, creeping nearer and nearer to us, driving at last along the roadway outside the house that hid us.

A Martian came across the fields about midday, laying the stuff with a jet of superheated steam that hissed against the walls, smashed all the windows it touched, and scalded the curate's hand as he fled out of the front room. When at last we crept across the sodden rooms and looked out again, the country northward was as though a black snowstorm had passed over it. Looking towards the river, we were astonished to see an unaccountable redness mingling with the black of the scorched meadows.

For a time we did not see how this change affected our position, save that we were relieved of our fear of the Black Smoke. But later I perceived that we were no longer hemmed in, that now we might get away. So soon as I realised that the way of escape was open, my dream of action returned. But the curate was lethargic, unreasonable.

"We are safe here," he repeated; "safe here."

I resolved to leave him—would that I had! Wiser now for the artilleryman's teaching, I sought out food and drink. I had found oil and rags for my burns, and I also took a hat and a flannel shirt that I found in one of the bedrooms. When it was clear to him that I meant to go alone—had reconciled myself to going alone—he suddenly roused himself to come. And all being quiet throughout the afternoon, we started about five o'clock, as I should judge, along the blackened road to Sunbury.

In Sunbury, and at intervals along the road, were dead bodies lying in contorted attitudes, horses as well as men, overturned carts and luggage, all covered thickly with black dust. That pall of cindery powder made me think of what I had read of the destruction of Pompeii. We got to Hampton Court without misadventure, our minds full of strange and unfamiliar appearances, and at Hampton Court our eyes were relieved to find a patch of green that had escaped the suffocating drift. We went through Bushey Park, with its deer going to and fro under the chestnuts, and some men and women hurrying in the distance towards Hampton, and so we came to Twickenham. These were the first people we saw.

Away across the road the woods beyond Ham and Petersham were still afire. Twickenham was uninjured by either Heat-Ray or Black Smoke, and there were more people about here, though none could give us news. For the most part they were like ourselves, taking advantage of a lull to shift their quarters. I have an impression that many of the houses here were still occupied by scared inhabitants, too frightened even for flight. Here too the evidence of a hasty rout was abundant along the road. I remember most vividly three smashed bicycles in a heap, pounded into the road by the wheels of subsequent carts. We crossed Richmond Bridge about half past eight. We hurried across the exposed bridge, of course, but I noticed floating down the stream a number of red masses, some many feet across. I did not know what these were—there was no time for scrutiny—and I put a more horrible interpretation on them than they deserved. Here again on the Surrey side were black dust that had once been smoke, and dead bodies—a heap near the approach to the station; but we had no glimpse of the Martians until we were some way towards Barnes.

We saw in the blackened distance a group of three people running down a side street towards the river, but otherwise it seemed deserted. Up the hill Richmond town was burning briskly; outside the town of Richmond there was no trace of the Black Smoke.

Then suddenly, as we approached Kew, came a number of people running, and the upperworks of a Martian fighting-machine loomed in sight over the housetops, not a hundred yards away from us. We stood aghast at our danger, and had the Martian looked down we must immediately have perished. We were so terrified that we dared not go on, but turned aside and hid in a shed in a garden. There the curate crouched, weeping silently, and refusing to stir again.

But my fixed idea of reaching Leatherhead would not let me rest, and in the twilight I ventured out again. I went through a shrubbery, and along a passage beside a big house standing in its own grounds, and so emerged upon the road towards Kew. The curate I left in the shed, but he came hurrying after me.

That second start was the most foolhardy thing I ever did. For it was manifest the Martians were about us. No sooner had the curate overtaken me than we saw either the fighting-machine we had seen before or another, far away across the meadows in the direction of Kew Lodge. Four or five little black figures hurried before it across the green-grey of the field, and in a moment it was evident this Martian pursued them. In three strides he was among them, and they ran radiating from his feet in all directions. He used no Heat-Ray to destroy them, but picked them up one by one. Apparently he tossed them into the great metallic carrier which projected behind him, much as a workman's basket hangs over his shoulder.

It was the first time I realised that the Martians might have any other purpose than destruction with defeated humanity. We stood for a moment petrified, then turned and fled through a gate behind us into a walled garden, fell into, rather than found, a fortunate ditch, and lay there, scarce daring to whisper to each other until the stars were out.

I suppose it was nearly eleven o'clock before we gathered courage to start again, no longer venturing into the road, but sneaking along hedgerows and through plantations, and watching keenly through the darkness, he on the right and I on the left, for the Martians, who seemed to be all about us. In one place we blundered upon a scorched and blackened area, now cooling and ashen, and a number of scattered dead bodies of men, burned horribly about the heads and trunks but with their legs and boots mostly intact; and of dead horses, fifty feet, perhaps, behind a line of four ripped guns and smashed gun carriages.

Sheen, it seemed, had escaped destruction, but the place was silent and deserted. Here we happened on no dead, though the night was too dark for us to see into the side roads of the place. In Sheen my companion suddenly complained of faintness and thirst, and we decided to try one of the houses.

The first house we entered, after a little difficulty with the window, was a small semi-detached villa, and I found nothing eatable left in the place but some mouldy cheese. There was, however, water to drink; and I took a hatchet, which promised to be useful in our next house-breaking.

We then crossed to a place where the road turns towards Mortlake. Here there stood a white house within a walled garden, and in the pantry of this domicile we found a store of food—two loaves of bread in a pan, an uncooked steak, and the half of a ham. I give this catalogue so precisely because, as it happened, we were destined to subsist upon this store for the next fortnight. Bottled beer stood under a shelf, and there were two bags of haricot beans and some limp lettuces. This pantry opened into a kind of wash-up kitchen, and in this was firewood; there was also a cupboard, in which we found nearly a dozen of burgundy, tinned soups and salmon, and two tins of biscuits.

We sat in the adjacent kitchen in the dark—for we dared not strike a light—and ate bread and ham, and drank beer out of the same bottle. The curate, who was still timorous and restless, was now, oddly enough, for pushing on, and I was urging him to keep up his strength by eating when the thing happened that was to imprison us.

"It can't be midnight yet," I said, and then came a blinding glare of vivid green light. Everything in the kitchen leaped out, clearly visible in green and black, and vanished again. And then followed such a concussion as I have never heard before or since. So close on the heels of this as to seem instantaneous came a thud behind me, a clash of glass, a crash and rattle of falling masonry all about us, and the plaster of the ceiling came down upon us, smashing into a multitude of fragments upon our heads. I was knocked headlong across the floor against the oven handle and stunned. I was insensible for a long time, the curate told me, and when I came to we were in darkness again, and he, with a face wet, as I found afterwards, with blood from a cut forehead, was dabbing water over me.

For some time I could not recollect what had happened. Then things came to me slowly. A bruise on my temple asserted itself.

"Are you better?" asked the curate in a whisper.

At last I answered him. I sat up.

"Don't move," he said. "The floor is covered with smashed crockery from the dresser. You can't possibly move without making a noise, and I fancy they are outside."

We both sat quite silent, so that we could scarcely hear each other breathing. Everything seemed deadly still, but once something near us, some plaster or broken brickwork, slid down with a rumbling sound. Outside and very near was an intermittent, metallic rattle.

"That!" said the curate, when presently it happened again.

"Yes," I said. "But what is it?"

"A Martian!" said the curate.

I listened again.

"It was not like the Heat-Ray," I said, and for a time I was inclined to think one of the great fighting-machines had stumbled against the house, as I had seen one stumble against the tower of Shepperton Church.

Our situation was so strange and incomprehensible that for three or four hours, until the dawn came, we scarcely moved. And then the light filtered in, not through the window, which remained black, but through a triangular aperture between a beam and a heap of broken bricks in the wall behind us. The interior of the kitchen we now saw greyly for the first time.

The window had been burst in by a mass of garden mould, which flowed over the table upon which we had been sitting and lay about our feet. Outside, the soil was banked high against the house. At the top of the window frame we could see an uprooted drainpipe. The floor was littered with smashed hardware; the end of the kitchen towards the house was broken into, and since the daylight shone in there, it was evident the greater part of the house had collapsed. Contrasting vividly with this ruin was the neat dresser, stained in the fashion, pale green, and with a number of copper and tin vessels below it, the wallpaper imitating blue and white tiles, and a couple of coloured supplements fluttering from the walls above the kitchen range.

As the dawn grew clearer, we saw through the gap in the wall the body of a Martian, standing sentinel, I suppose, over the still glowing cylinder. At the sight of that we crawled as circumspectly as possible out of the twilight of the kitchen into the darkness of the scullery.

Abruptly the right interpretation dawned upon my mind.

"The fifth cylinder," I whispered, "the fifth shot from Mars, has struck this house and buried us under the ruins!"

For a time the curate was silent, and then he whispered:

"God have mercy upon us!"

I heard him presently whimpering to himself.

Save for that sound we lay quite still in the scullery; I for my part scarce dared breathe, and sat with my eyes fixed on the faint light of the kitchen door. I could just see the curate's face, a dim, oval shape, and his collar and cuffs. Outside there began a metallic hammering, then a violent hooting, and then again, after a quiet interval, a hissing like the hissing of an engine. These noises, for the most part problematical, continued intermittently, and seemed if anything to increase in number as time wore on. Presently a measured thudding and a vibration that made everything about us quiver and the vessels in the pantry ring and shift, began and continued. Once the light was eclipsed, and the ghostly kitchen doorway became absolutely dark. For many hours we must have crouched there, silent and shivering, until our tired attention failed . . .

At last I found myself awake and very hungry. I am inclined to believe we must have spent the greater portion of a day before that awakening. My hunger was at a stride so insistent that it moved me to action. I told the curate I was going to seek food, and felt my way towards the pantry. He made me no answer, but so soon as I began eating the faint noise I made stirred him up and I heard him crawling after me.

II

WHAT WE SAW FROM THE RUINED HOUSE

After eating we crept back to the scullery, and there I must have dozed again, for when presently I looked round I was alone. The thudding vibration continued with wearisome persistence. I whispered for the curate several times, and at last felt my way to the door of the kitchen. It was still daylight, and I perceived him across the room, lying against the triangular hole that looked out upon the Martians. His shoulders were hunched, so that his head was hidden from me.

I could hear a number of noises almost like those in an engine shed; and the place rocked with that beating thud. Through the aperture in the wall I could see the top of a tree touched with gold and the warm blue of a tranquil evening sky. For a minute or so I remained watching the curate, and then I advanced, crouching and stepping with extreme care amid the broken crockery that littered the floor.

I touched the curate's leg, and he started so violently that a mass of plaster went sliding down outside and fell with a loud impact. I gripped his arm, fearing he might cry out, and for a long time we crouched motionless. Then I turned to see how much of our rampart remained. The detachment of the plaster had left a vertical slit open in the debris, and by raising myself cautiously across a beam I was able to see out of this gap into what had been overnight a quiet suburban roadway. Vast, indeed, was the change that we beheld.

The fifth cylinder must have fallen right into the midst of the house we had first visited. The building had vanished, completely smashed, pulverised, and dispersed by the blow. The cylinder lay now far beneath the original foundations—deep in a hole, already vastly larger than the pit I had looked into at Woking. The earth all round it had splashed under that tremendous impact—"splashed" is the only word—and lay in heaped piles that hid the masses of the adjacent houses. It had behaved exactly like mud under the violent blow of a hammer. Our house had collapsed backward; the front portion, even on the ground floor, had been destroyed completely; by a chance the kitchen and scullery had escaped, and stood buried now under soil and ruins, closed in by tons of earth on every side save towards the cylinder. Over that aspect we hung now on the very edge of the great circular pit the Martians were engaged in making. The heavy beating sound was evidently just behind us, and ever and again a bright green vapour drove up like a veil across our peephole.

The cylinder was already opened in the centre of the pit, and on the farther edge of the pit, amid the smashed and gravel-heaped shrubbery, one of the great fighting-machines, deserted by its occupant, stood stiff and tall against the evening sky. At first I scarcely noticed the pit and the cylinder, although it has been convenient to describe them first, on account of the extraordinary glittering mechanism I saw busy in the excavation, and on account of the strange creatures that were crawling slowly and painfully across the heaped mould near it.

The mechanism it certainly was that held my attention first. It was one of those complicated fabrics that have since been called handling-machines, and the study of which has already given such an enormous impetus to terrestrial invention. As it dawned upon me first, it presented a sort of metallic spider with five jointed, agile legs, and with an extraordinary number of jointed levers, bars, and reaching and clutching tentacles about its body. Most of its arms were retracted, but with three long tentacles it was fishing out a number of rods, plates, and bars which lined the covering and apparently strengthened the walls of the cylinder. These, as it extracted them, were lifted out and deposited upon a level surface of earth behind it.

Its motion was so swift, complex, and perfect that at first I did not see it as a machine, in spite of its metallic glitter. The fighting-machines were coordinated and animated to an extraordinary pitch, but nothing to compare with this. People who have never seen these structures, and have only the ill-imagined efforts of artists or the imperfect descriptions of such eye-witnesses as myself to go upon, scarcely realise that living quality.

I recall particularly the illustration of one of the first pamphlets to give a consecutive account of the war. The artist had evidently made a hasty study of one of the fighting-machines, and there his knowledge ended. He presented them as tilted, stiff tripods, without either flexibility or subtlety, and with an altogether misleading monotony of effect. The pamphlet containing these renderings had a considerable vogue, and I mention them here simply to warn the reader against the impression they may have created. They were no more like the Martians I saw in action than a Dutch doll is like a human being. To my mind, the pamphlet would have been much better without them.

At first, I say, the handling-machine did not impress me as a machine, but as a crab-like creature with a glittering integument, the controlling Martian whose delicate tentacles actuated its movements seeming to be simply the equivalent of the crab's cerebral portion. But then I perceived the resemblance of its grey-brown, shiny, leathery integument to that of the other sprawling bodies beyond, and the true nature of this dexterous workman dawned upon me. With that realisation my interest shifted to those other creatures, the real Martians. Already I had had a transient impression of these, and the first nausea no longer obscured my observation. Moreover, I was concealed and motionless, and under no urgency of action.

They were, I now saw, the most unearthly creatures it is possible to conceive. They were huge round bodies—or, rather, heads—about four feet in diameter, each body having in front of it a face. This face had no nostrils—indeed, the Martians do not seem to have had any sense of smell, but it had a pair of very large dark-coloured eyes, and just beneath this a kind of fleshy beak. In the back of this head or body—I scarcely know how to speak of it—was the single tight tympanic surface, since known to be anatomically an ear, though it must have been almost useless in our dense air. In a group round the mouth were sixteen slender, almost whip-like tentacles, arranged in two bunches of eight each. These bunches have since been named rather aptly, by that distinguished anatomist, Professor Howes, the *hands*. Even as I saw these Martians for the first time they seemed to be endeavouring to raise themselves on these hands, but of course, with the increased weight of terrestrial conditions, this was impossible. There is reason to suppose that on Mars they may have progressed upon them with some facility.

The internal anatomy, I may remark here, as dissection has since shown, was almost equally simple. The greater part of the structure was the brain, sending enormous nerves to the eyes, ear, and tactile tentacles. Besides this were the bulky lungs, into which the mouth opened, and the heart and its vessels. The pulmonary distress caused by the denser atmosphere and greater gravitational attraction was only too evident in the convulsive movements of the outer skin.

And this was the sum of the Martian organs. Strange as it may seem to a human being, all the complex apparatus of digestion, which makes up the bulk of our bodies, did not exist in the Martians. They were heads—merely heads. Entrails they had none. They did not eat, much less digest. Instead, they took the fresh, living blood of other creatures, and *injected* it into their own veins. I have myself seen this being done, as I shall mention in its place. But, squeamish as I may seem, I cannot bring myself to describe what I could not endure even to continue watching. Let it suffice to say, blood obtained from a still living animal, in most cases from a human being, was run directly by means of a little pipette into the recipient canal . . .

The bare idea of this is no doubt horribly repulsive to us, but at the same time I think that we should remember how repulsive our carnivorous habits would seem to an intelligent rabbit.

The physiological advantages of the practice of injection are undeniable, if one thinks of the tremendous waste of human time and energy occasioned by eating and the digestive process. Our bodies are half made up of glands and tubes and organs, occupied in turning heterogeneous food into blood. The digestive processes and their reaction upon the nervous system sap our strength and colour our minds. Men go happy or miserable as they have healthy or unhealthy livers, or sound gastric glands. But the Martians were lifted above all these organic fluctuations of mood and emotion.

Their undeniable preference for men as their source of nourishment is partly explained by the nature of the remains of the victims they had brought with them as provisions from Mars. These creatures, to judge from the shrivelled remains that have fallen into human hands, were bipeds with flimsy, silicious skeletons (almost like those of the silicious sponges) and feeble musculature, standing about six feet high and having round, erect heads, and large eyes in flinty sockets. Two or three of these seem to have been brought in each cylinder, and all were killed before earth was reached. It was just as well for them, for the mere attempt to stand upright upon our planet would have broken every bone in their bodies.

And while I am engaged in this description, I may add in this place certain further details which, although they were not all evident to us at the time, will enable the reader who is unacquainted with them to form a clearer picture of these offensive creatures.

In three other points their physiology differed strangely from ours. Their organisms did not sleep, any more than the heart of man sleeps. Since they had no extensive muscular mechanism to recuperate, that periodical extinction was unknown to them. They had little or no sense of fatigue, it would seem. On earth they could never have moved without effort, yet even to the last they kept in action. In twenty-four hours they did twenty-four hours of work, as even on earth is perhaps the case with the ants.

In the next place, wonderful as it seems in a sexual world, the Martians were absolutely without sex, and therefore without any of the tumultuous emotions that arise from that difference among men. A young Martian, there can now be no dispute, was really born upon earth during the war, and it was found attached to its parent, partially *budded* off, just as young lilybulbs bud off, or like the young animals in the fresh-water polyp.

In man, in all the higher terrestrial animals, such a method of increase has disappeared; but even on this earth it was certainly the primitive method. Among the lower animals, up even to those first cousins of the vertebrated animals, the Tunicates, the two processes occur side by side, but finally the sexual method superseded its competitor altogether. On Mars, however, just the reverse has apparently been the case.

It is worthy of remark that a certain speculative writer of quasi-scientific repute, writing long before the Martian invasion, did forecast for man a final structure not unlike the actual Martian condition. His prophecy, I remember, appeared in November or December, 1893, in a long-defunct publication, the *Pall Mall Budget*, and I recall a caricature of it in a pre-Martian periodical called *Punch*. He pointed out—writing in a foolish, facetious tone—that the perfection of mechanical appliances must ultimately supersede limbs; the perfection of chemical devices, digestion; that such organs as hair, external nose, teeth, ears, and chin were no longer essential parts of the human being, and that the tendency of natural selection would lie in the direction of their steady diminution through the coming ages. The brain alone remained a cardinal necessity. Only one other part of the body had a strong case for survival, and that was the hand, "teacher and agent of the brain." While the rest of the body dwindled, the hands would grow larger.

There is many a true word written in jest, and here in the Martians we have beyond dispute the actual accomplishment of such a suppression of the animal side of the organism by the intelligence. To me it is quite credible that the Martians may be descended from beings not unlike ourselves, by a gradual development of brain and hands (the latter giving rise to the two bunches of delicate tentacles at last) at the expense of the rest of the body. Without the body the brain would, of course, become a mere selfish intelligence, without any of the emotional substratum of the human being.

The last salient point in which the systems of these creatures differed from ours was in what one might have thought a very trivial particular. Micro-organisms, which cause so much disease and pain on earth, have either never appeared upon Mars or Martian sanitary science eliminated them ages ago. A hundred diseases, all the fevers and contagions of human life, consumption, cancers, tumours and such morbidities, never enter the scheme of their life. And speaking of the differences between the life on Mars and terrestrial life, I may allude here to the curious suggestions of the red weed.

Apparently the vegetable kingdom in Mars, instead of having green for a dominant colour, is of a vivid blood-red tint. At any rate, the seeds which the Martians (intentionally or accidentally) brought with them gave rise in all cases to red-coloured growths. Only that known popularly as the red weed, however, gained any footing in competition with terrestrial forms. The red creeper was quite a transitory growth, and few people have seen it growing. For a time, however, the red weed grew with astonishing vigour and luxuriance. It spread up the sides of the pit by the third or fourth day of our imprisonment, and its cactus-like branches formed a carmine fringe to the edges of our triangular window. And afterwards I found it broadcast throughout the country, and especially wherever there was a stream of water.

The Martians had what appears to have been an auditory organ, a single round drum at the back of the head-body, and eyes with a visual range not very different from ours except that, according to Philips, blue and violet were as black to them. It is commonly supposed that they communicated by sounds and tentacular gesticulations; this is asserted, for instance, in the able but hastily compiled pamphlet (written evidently by someone not an eyewitness of Martian actions) to which I have already alluded, and which, so far, has been the chief source of information concerning them. Now no surviving human being saw so much of the Martians in action as I did. I take no credit to myself for an accident, but the fact is so. And I assert that I watched them closely time after time, and that I have seen four, five, and (once) six of them sluggishly performing the most elaborately complicated operations together without either sound or gesture. Their peculiar hooting invariably preceded feeding; it had no modulation, and was, I believe, in no sense a signal, but merely the expiration of air preparatory to the suctional operation. I have a certain claim to at least an elementary knowledge of psychology, and in this matter I am convinced—as firmly as I am convinced of anything—that the Martians interchanged thoughts without any physical intermediation. And I have been convinced of this in spite of strong preconceptions. Before the Martian invasion, as an occasional reader here or there may remember, I had written with some little vehemence against the telepathic theory.

The Martians wore no clothing. Their conceptions of ornament and decorum were necessarily different from ours; and not only were they evidently much less sensible of changes of temperature than we are, but changes of pressure do not seem to have affected their health at all seriously. Yet though they wore no clothing, it was in the other artificial additions to their bodily resources that their great superiority over man lay. We men, with our bicycles and road-skates, our Lilienthal soaring-machines, our guns and sticks and so forth, are just in the beginning of the evolution that the Martians have worked out. They have become practically mere brains, wearing different bodies according to their needs just as men wear suits of clothes and take a bicycle in a hurry or an umbrella in the wet. And of their appliances, perhaps nothing is more wonderful to a man than the curious fact that what is the dominant feature of almost all human devices in mechanism is absent—the *wheel* is absent; among all the things they brought to earth there is no trace or suggestion of their use of wheels. One would have at least expected it in locomotion. And in this connection it is curious to remark that even on this earth Nature has never hit upon the wheel, or has preferred other expedients to its development. And not only did the Martians either not know of (which is incredible), or abstain from, the wheel, but in their apparatus singularly little use is made of the fixed pivot or relatively fixed pivot, with circular motions thereabout confined to one plane. Almost all the joints of the machinery present a complicated system of sliding parts moving over small but beautifully curved friction bearings. And while upon this matter of detail, it is remarkable that the long leverages of their machines are in most cases actuated by a sort of sham musculature of the disks in an elastic sheath; these disks become polarised and drawn closely and powerfully together when traversed by a current of electricity. In this way the curious parallelism to animal motions, which was so striking and disturbing to the human beholder, was attained. Such quasi-muscles abounded in the crab-like handling-machine which, on my first peeping out of the slit, I watched unpacking the cylinder. It seemed infinitely more alive than the actual Martians lying beyond it in the sunset light, panting, stirring ineffectual tentacles, and moving feebly after their vast journey across space.

While I was still watching their sluggish motions in the sunlight, and noting each strange detail of their form, the curate reminded me of his presence by pulling violently at my arm. I turned to a scowling face, and silent, eloquent lips. He wanted the slit, which permitted only one of us to peep through; and so I had to forego watching them for a time while he enjoyed that privilege.

When I looked again, the busy handling-machine had already put together several of the pieces of apparatus it had taken out of the cylinder into a shape having an unmistakable likeness to its own; and down on the left a busy little digging mechanism had come into view, emitting jets of green vapour and working its way round the pit, excavating and embanking in a methodical and discriminating manner. This it was which had caused the regular beating noise, and the rhythmic shocks that had kept our ruinous refuge quivering. It piped and whistled as it worked. So far as I could see, the thing was without a directing Martian at all.

III

THE DAYS OF IMPRISONMENT

The arrival of a second fighting-machine drove us from our peephole into the scullery, for we feared that from his elevation the Martian might see down upon us behind our barrier. At a later date we began to feel less in danger of their eyes, for to an eye in the dazzle of the sunlight outside our refuge must have been blank blackness, but at first the slightest suggestion of approach drove us into the scullery in heart-throbbing retreat. Yet terrible as was the danger we incurred, the attraction of peeping was for both of us irresistible. And I recall now with a sort of wonder that, in spite of the infinite danger in which we were between starvation and a still more terrible death, we could yet struggle bitterly for that horrible privilege of sight. We would race across the kitchen in a grotesque way between eagerness and the dread of making a noise, and strike each other, and thrust and kick, within a few inches of exposure.

The fact is that we had absolutely incompatible dispositions and habits of thought and action, and our danger and isolation only accentuated the incompatibility. At Halliford I had already come to hate the curate's trick of helpless exclamation, his stupid rigidity of mind. His endless muttering monologue vitiated every effort I made to think out a line of action, and drove me at times, thus pent up and intensified, almost to the verge of craziness. He was as lacking in restraint as a silly woman. He would weep for hours together, and I verily believe that to the very end this spoiled child of life thought his weak tears in some way efficacious. And I would sit in the darkness unable to keep my mind off him by reason of his importunities. He ate more than I did, and it was in vain I pointed out that our only chance of life was to stop in the house until the Martians had done with their pit, that in that long patience a time might presently come when we should need food. He ate and drank impulsively in heavy meals at long intervals. He slept little.

As the days wore on, his utter carelessness of any consideration so intensified our distress and danger that I had, much as I loathed doing it, to resort to threats, and at last to blows. That brought him to reason for a time. But he was one of those weak creatures, void of pride, timorous, anaemic, hateful souls, full of shifty cunning, who face neither God nor man, who face not even themselves.

It is disagreeable for me to recall and write these things, but I set them down that my story may lack nothing. Those who have escaped the dark and terrible aspects of life will find my brutality, my flash of rage in our final tragedy, easy enough to blame; for they know what is wrong as well as any, but not what is possible to tortured men. But those who have been under the shadow, who have gone down at last to elemental things, will have a wider charity.

And while within we fought out our dark, dim contest of whispers, snatched food and drink, and gripping hands and blows, without, in the pitiless sunlight of that terrible June, was the strange wonder, the unfamiliar routine of the Martians in the pit. Let me return to those first new experiences of mine. After a long time I ventured back to the peephole, to find that the newcomers had been reinforced by the occupants of no fewer than three of the fighting-machines. These last had brought with them certain fresh appliances that stood in an orderly manner about the cylinder. The second handling-machine was now completed, and was busied in serving one of the novel contrivances the big machine had brought. This was a body resembling a milk can in its general form, above which oscillated a pear-shaped receptacle, and from which a stream of white powder flowed into a circular basin below.

The oscillatory motion was imparted to this by one tentacle of the handling-machine. With two spatulate hands the handling-machine was digging out and flinging masses of clay into the pear-shaped receptacle above, while with another arm it periodically opened a door and removed rusty and blackened clinkers from the middle part of the machine. Another steely tentacle directed the powder from the basin along a ribbed channel towards some receiver that was hidden from me by the mound of bluish dust. From this unseen receiver a little thread of green smoke rose vertically into the quiet air. As I looked, the handling-machine, with a faint and musical clinking, extended, telescopic fashion, a tentacle that had been a moment before a mere blunt projection, until its end was hidden behind the mound of clay. In another second it had lifted a bar of white aluminium into sight, untarnished as yet, and shining dazzlingly, and deposited it in a growing stack of bars that stood at the side of the pit. Between sunset and starlight this dexterous machine must have made more than a hundred such bars out of the crude clay, and the mound of bluish dust rose steadily until it topped the side of the pit.

The contrast between the swift and complex movements of these contrivances and the inert panting clumsiness of their masters was acute, and for days I had to tell myself repeatedly that these latter were indeed the living of the two things.

The curate had possession of the slit when the first men were brought to the pit. I was sitting below, huddled up, listening with all my ears. He made a sudden movement backward, and I, fearful that we were observed, crouched in a spasm of terror. He came sliding down the rubbish and crept beside me in the darkness, inarticulate, gesticulating, and for a moment I shared his panic. His gesture suggested a resignation of the slit, and after a little while my curiosity gave me courage, and I rose up, stepped across him, and clambered up to it. At first I could see no reason for his frantic behaviour. The twilight had now come, the stars were little and faint, but the pit was illuminated by the flickering green fire that came from the aluminium-making. The whole picture was a flickering scheme of green gleams and shifting rusty black shadows, strangely trying to the eyes. Over and through it all went the bats, heeding it not at all. The sprawling Martians were no longer to be seen, the mound of blue-green powder had risen to cover them from sight, and a fighting-machine, with its legs contracted, crumpled, and abbreviated, stood across the corner of the pit. And then, amid the clangour of the machinery, came a drifting suspicion of human voices, that I entertained at first only to dismiss.

I crouched, watching this fighting-machine closely, satisfying myself now for the first time that the hood did indeed contain a Martian. As the green flames lifted I could see the oily gleam of his integument and the brightness of his eyes. And suddenly I heard a yell, and saw a long tentacle reaching over the shoulder of the machine to the little cage that hunched upon its back. Then something—something struggling violently—was lifted high against the sky, a black, vague enigma against the starlight; and as this black object came down again, I saw by the green brightness that it was a man. For an instant he was clearly visible. He was a stout, ruddy, middle-aged man, well dressed; three days before, he must have been walking the world, a man of considerable consequence. I could see his staring eyes and gleams of light on his studs and watch chain. He vanished behind the mound, and for a moment there was silence. And then began a shrieking and a sustained and cheerful hooting from the Martians.

I slid down the rubbish, struggled to my feet, clapped my hands over my ears, and bolted into the scullery. The curate, who had been crouching silently with his arms over his head, looked up as I passed, cried out quite loudly at my desertion of him, and came running after me.

That night, as we lurked in the scullery, balanced between our horror and the terrible fascination this peeping had, although I felt an urgent need of action I tried in vain to conceive some plan of escape; but afterwards, during the second day, I was able to consider our position with great clearness. The curate, I found, was quite incapable of discussion; this new and culminating atrocity had robbed him of all vestiges of reason or forethought. Practically he had already sunk to the level of an animal. But as the saying goes, I gripped myself with both hands. It grew upon my mind, once I could face the facts, that terrible as our position was, there was as yet no justification for absolute despair. Our chief chance lay in the possibility of the Martians making the pit nothing more than a temporary encampment. Or even if they kept it permanently, they might not consider it necessary to guard it, and a chance of escape might be afforded us. I also weighed very carefully the possibility of our digging a way out in a direction away from the pit, but the chances of our emerging within sight of some sentinel fighting-machine seemed at first too great. And I should have had to do all the digging myself. The curate would certainly have failed me.

It was on the third day, if my memory serves me right, that I saw the lad killed. It was the only occasion on which I actually saw the Martians feed. After that experience I avoided the hole in the wall for the better part of a day. I went into the scullery, removed the door, and spent some hours digging with my hatchet as silently as possible; but when I had made a hole about a couple of feet deep the loose earth collapsed noisily, and I did not dare continue. I lost heart, and lay down on the scullery floor for a long time, having no spirit even to move. And after that I abandoned altogether the idea of escaping by excavation.

It says much for the impression the Martians had made upon me that at first I entertained little or no hope of our escape being brought about by their overthrow through any human effort. But on the fourth or fifth night I heard a sound like heavy guns.

It was very late in the night, and the moon was shining brightly. The Martians had taken away the excavating-machine, and, save for a fighting-machine that stood in the remoter bank of the pit and a handling-machine that was buried out of my sight in a corner of the pit immediately beneath my peephole, the place was deserted by them. Except for the pale glow from the handling-machine and the bars and patches of white moonlight the pit was in darkness, and, except for the clinking of the handling-machine, quite still. That night was a beautiful serenity; save for one planet, the moon seemed to have the sky to herself. I heard a dog howling, and that familiar sound it was that made me listen. Then I heard quite distinctly a booming exactly like the sound of great guns. Six distinct reports I counted, and after a long interval six again. And that was all.

IV

THE DEATH OF THE CURATE

It was on the sixth day of our imprisonment that I peeped for the last time, and presently found myself alone. Instead of keeping close to me and trying to oust me from the slit, the curate had gone back into the scullery. I was struck by a sudden thought. I went back quickly and quietly into the scullery. In the darkness I heard the curate drinking. I snatched in the darkness, and my fingers caught a bottle of burgundy.

For a few minutes there was a tussle. The bottle struck the floor and broke, and I desisted and rose. We stood panting and threatening each other. In the end I planted myself between him and the food, and told him of my determination to begin a discipline. I divided the food in the pantry, into rations to last us ten days. I would not let him eat anymore that day. In the afternoon he made a feeble effort to get at the food. I had been dozing, but in an instant I was awake. All day and all night we sat face to face, I weary but resolute, and he weeping and complaining of his immediate hunger. It was, I know, a night and a day, but to me it seemed—it seems now—an interminable length of time.

And so our widened incompatibility ended at last in open conflict. For two vast days we struggled in undertones and wrestling contests. There were times when I beat and kicked him madly, times when I cajoled and persuaded him, and once I tried to bribe him with the last bottle of burgundy, for there was a rain-water pump from which I could get water. But neither force nor kindness availed; he was indeed beyond reason. He would neither desist from his attacks on the food nor from his noisy babbling to himself. The rudimentary precautions to keep our imprisonment endurable he would not observe. Slowly I began to realise the complete overthrow of his intelligence, to perceive that my sole companion in this close and sickly darkness was a man insane.

From certain vague memories I am inclined to think my own mind wandered at times. I had strange and hideous dreams whenever I slept. It sounds paradoxical, but I am inclined to think that the weakness and insanity of the curate warned me, braced me, and kept me a sane man.

On the eighth day he began to talk aloud instead of whispering, and nothing I could do would moderate his speech.

"It is just, O God!" he would say, over and over again. "It is just. On me and mine be the punishment laid. We have sinned, we have fallen short. There was poverty, sorrow; the poor were trodden in the dust, and I held my peace. I preached acceptable folly—my God, what folly! When I should have stood up, though I died for it, and called upon them to repent—repent! . . . Oppressors of the poor and needy! . . . The wine-press of God!"

Then he would suddenly revert to the matter of the food I withheld from him, praying, begging, weeping, at last threatening. He began to raise his voice—I prayed him not to. He perceived a hold on me—he threatened he would shout and bring the Martians upon us. For a time that scared me; but any concession would have shortened our chance of escape beyond estimating. I defied him, although I felt no assurance that he might not do this thing. But that day, at any rate, he did not. He talked with his voice rising slowly, through the greater part of the eighth and ninth days—threats, entreaties, mingled with a torrent of half-sane and always frothy repentance for his vacant sham of God's service, such as made me pity him. Then he slept awhile, and began again with renewed strength, so loudly that I must needs make him desist.

"Be still!" I implored.

He rose to his knees, for he had been sitting in the darkness near the copper.

"I have been still too long," he said, in a tone that must have reached the pit, "and now I must bear my witness. Woe unto this unfaithful city! Woe! Woe! Woe! Woe! Woe! To the inhabitants of the earth by reason of the other voices of the trumpet—"

"Shut up!" I said, rising to my feet, and in a terror lest the Martians should hear us. "For God's sake—"

"Nay," shouted the curate, at the top of his voice, standing likewise and extending his arms. "Speak! The word of the Lord is upon me!"

In three strides he was at the door leading into the kitchen.

"I must bear my witness! I go! It has already been too long delayed."

I put out my hand and felt the meat chopper hanging to the wall. In a flash I was after him. I was fierce with fear. Before he was halfway across the kitchen I had overtaken him. With one last touch of humanity I turned the blade back and struck him with the butt. He went headlong forward and lay stretched on the ground. I stumbled over him and stood panting. He lay still.

Suddenly I heard a noise without, the run and smash of slipping plaster, and the triangular aperture in the wall was darkened. I looked up and saw the lower surface of a handling-machine coming slowly across the hole. One of its gripping limbs curled amid the debris; another limb appeared, feeling its way over the fallen beams. I stood petrified, staring. Then I saw through a sort of glass plate near the edge of the body the face, as we may call it, and the large dark eyes of a Martian, peering, and then a long metallic snake of tentacle came feeling slowly through the hole.

I turned by an effort, stumbled over the curate, and stopped at the scullery door. The tentacle was now some way, two yards or more, in the room, and twisting and turning, with queer sudden movements, this way and that. For a while I stood fascinated by that slow, fitful advance. Then, with a faint, hoarse cry, I forced myself across the scullery. I trembled violently; I could scarcely stand upright. I opened the door of the coal cellar, and stood there in the darkness staring at the faintly lit doorway into the kitchen, and listening. Had the Martian seen me? What was it doing now?

Something was moving to and fro there, very quietly; every now and then it tapped against the wall, or started on its movements with a faint metallic ringing, like the movements of keys on a split-ring. Then a heavy body—I knew too well what—was dragged across the floor of the kitchen towards the opening. Irresistibly attracted, I crept to the door and peeped into the kitchen. In the triangle of bright outer sunlight I saw the Martian, in its Briareus of a handling-machine, scrutinizing the curate's head. I thought at once that it would infer my presence from the mark of the blow I had given him.

I crept back to the coal cellar, shut the door, and began to cover myself up as much as I could, and as noiselessly as possible in the darkness, among the firewood and coal therein. Every now and then I paused, rigid, to hear if the Martian had thrust its tentacles through the opening again.

Then the faint metallic jingle returned. I traced it slowly feeling over the kitchen. Presently I heard it nearer—in the scullery, as I judged. I thought that its length might be insufficient to reach me. I prayed copiously. It passed, scraping faintly across the cellar door. An age of almost intolerable suspense intervened; then I heard it fumbling at the latch! It had found the door! The Martians understood doors!

It worried at the catch for a minute, perhaps, and then the door opened.

In the darkness I could just see the thing—like an elephant's trunk more than anything else—waving towards me and touching and examining the wall, coals, wood and ceiling. It was like a black worm swaying its blind head to and fro.

Once, even, it touched the heel of my boot. I was on the verge of screaming; I bit my hand. For a time the tentacle was silent. I could have fancied it had been withdrawn. Presently, with an abrupt click, it gripped something—I thought it had me!—and seemed to go out of the cellar again. For a minute I was not sure. Apparently it had taken a lump of coal to examine.

I seized the opportunity of slightly shifting my position, which had become cramped, and then listened. I whispered passionate prayers for safety.

Then I heard the slow, deliberate sound creeping towards me again. Slowly, slowly it drew near, scratching against the walls and tapping the furniture.

While I was still doubtful, it rapped smartly against the cellar door and closed it. I heard it go into the pantry, and the biscuit-tins rattled and a bottle smashed, and then came a heavy bump against the cellar door. Then silence that passed into an infinity of suspense.

Had it gone?

At last I decided that it had.

It came into the scullery no more; but I lay all the tenth day in the close darkness, buried among coals and firewood, not daring even to crawl out for the drink for which I craved. It was the eleventh day before I ventured so far from my security.

V

THE STILLNESS

My first act before I went into the pantry was to fasten the door between the kitchen and the scullery. But the pantry was empty; every scrap of food had gone. Apparently, the Martian had taken it all on the previous day. At that discovery I despaired for the first time. I took no food, or no drink either, on the eleventh or the twelfth day.

At first my mouth and throat were parched, and my strength ebbed sensibly. I sat about in the darkness of the scullery, in a state of despondent wretchedness. My mind ran on eating. I thought I had become deaf, for the noises of movement I had been accustomed to hear from the pit had ceased absolutely. I did not feel strong enough to crawl noiselessly to the peephole, or I would have gone there.

On the twelfth day my throat was so painful that, taking the chance of alarming the Martians, I attacked the creaking rain-water pump that stood by the sink, and got a couple of glassfuls of blackened and tainted rain water. I was greatly refreshed by this, and emboldened by the fact that no enquiring tentacle followed the noise of my pumping.

During these days, in a rambling, inconclusive way, I thought much of the curate and of the manner of his death.

On the thirteenth day I drank some more water, and dozed and thought disjointedly of eating and of vague impossible plans of escape. Whenever I dozed I dreamt of horrible phantasms, of the death of the curate, or of sumptuous dinners; but, asleep or awake, I felt a keen pain that urged me to drink again and again. The light that came into the scullery was no longer grey, but red. To my disordered imagination it seemed the colour of blood.

On the fourteenth day I went into the kitchen, and I was surprised to find that the fronds of the red weed had grown right across the hole in the wall, turning the half-light of the place into a crimson-coloured obscurity.

It was early on the fifteenth day that I heard a curious, familiar sequence of sounds in the kitchen, and, listening, identified it as the snuffing and scratching of a dog. Going into the kitchen, I saw a dog's nose peering in through a break among the ruddy fronds. This greatly surprised me. At the scent of me he barked shortly.

I thought if I could induce him to come into the place quietly I should be able, perhaps, to kill and eat him; and in any case, it would be advisable to kill him, lest his actions attracted the attention of the Martians.

I crept forward, saying "Good dog!" very softly; but he suddenly withdrew his head and disappeared.

I listened—I was not deaf—but certainly the pit was still. I heard a sound like the flutter of a bird's wings, and a hoarse croaking, but that was all.

For a long while I lay close to the peephole, but not daring to move aside the red plants that obscured it. Once or twice I heard a faint pitter-patter like the feet of the dog going hither and thither on the sand far below me, and there were more bird-like sounds, but that was all. At length, encouraged by the silence, I looked out.

Except in the corner, where a multitude of crows hopped and fought over the skeletons of the dead the Martians had consumed, there was not a living thing in the pit.

I stared about me, scarcely believing my eyes. All the machinery had gone. Save for the big mound of greyish-blue powder in one corner, certain bars of aluminium in another, the black birds, and the skeletons of the killed, the place was merely an empty circular pit in the sand.

Slowly I thrust myself out through the red weed, and stood upon the mound of rubble. I could see in any direction save behind me, to the north, and neither Martians nor sign of Martians were to be seen. The pit dropped sheerly from my feet, but a little way along the rubbish afforded a practicable slope to the summit of the ruins. My chance of escape had come. I began to tremble.

I hesitated for some time, and then, in a gust of desperate resolution, and with a heart that throbbed violently, I scrambled to the top of the mound in which I had been buried so long.

I looked about again. To the northward, too, no Martian was visible.

When I had last seen this part of Sheen in the daylight it had been a straggling street of comfortable white and red houses, interspersed with abundant shady trees. Now I stood on a mound of smashed brickwork, clay, and gravel, over which spread a multitude of red cactus-shaped plants, knee-high, without a solitary terrestrial growth to dispute their footing. The trees near me were dead and brown, but further a network of red thread scaled the still living stems.

The neighbouring houses had all been wrecked, but none had been burned; their walls stood, sometimes to the second story, with smashed windows and shattered doors. The red weed grew tumultuously in their roofless rooms. Below me was the great pit, with the crows struggling for its refuse. A number of other birds hopped about among the ruins. Far away I saw a gaunt cat slink crouchingly along a wall, but traces of men there were none.

The day seemed, by contrast with my recent confinement, dazzlingly bright, the sky a glowing blue. A gentle breeze kept the red weed that covered every scrap of unoccupied ground gently swaying. And oh! The sweetness of the air!

VI

THE WORK OF FIFTEEN DAYS

For some time I stood tottering on the mound regardless of my safety. Within that noisome den from which I had emerged I had thought with a narrow intensity only of our immediate security. I had not realised what had been happening to the world, had not anticipated this startling vision of unfamiliar things. I had expected to see Sheen in ruins—I found about me the landscape, weird and lurid, of another planet.

For that moment I touched an emotion beyond the common range of men, yet one that the poor brutes we dominate know only too well. I felt as a rabbit might feel returning to his burrow and suddenly confronted by the work of a dozen busy navvies digging the foundations of a house. I felt the first inkling of a thing that presently grew quite clear in my mind, that oppressed me for many days, a sense of dethronement, a persuasion that I was no longer a master, but an animal among the animals, under the Martian heel. With us it would be as with them, to lurk and watch, to run and hide; the fear and empire of man had passed away.

But so soon as this strangeness had been realised it passed, and my dominant motive became the hunger of my long and dismal fast. In the direction away from the pit I saw, beyond a red-covered wall, a patch of garden ground unburied. This gave me a hint, and I went knee-deep, and sometimes neck-deep, in the red weed. The density of the weed gave me a reassuring sense of hiding. The wall was some six feet high, and when I attempted to clamber it I found I could not lift my feet to the crest. So I went along by the side of it, and came to a corner and a rockwork that enabled me to get to the top, and tumble into the garden I coveted. Here I found some young onions, a couple of gladiolus bulbs, and a quantity of immature carrots, all of which I secured, and, scrambling over a ruined wall, went on my way through scarlet and crimson trees towards Kew—it was like walking through an avenue of gigantic blood drops—possessed with two ideas: to get more food, and to limp, as soon and as far as my strength permitted, out of this accursed unearthly region of the pit.

Some way farther, in a grassy place, was a group of mushrooms which also I devoured, and then I came upon a brown sheet of flowing shallow water, where meadows used to be. These fragments of nourishment served only to whet my hunger. At first I was surprised at this flood in a hot, dry summer, but afterwards I discovered that it was caused by the tropical exuberance of the red weed. Directly this extraordinary growth encountered water it straightway became gigantic and of unparalleled fecundity. Its seeds were simply poured down into the water of the Wey and Thames, and its swiftly growing and Titanic water fronds speedily choked both those rivers.

At Putney, as I afterwards saw, the bridge was almost lost in a tangle of this weed, and at Richmond, too, the Thames water poured in a broad and shallow stream across the meadows of Hampton and Twickenham. As the water spread the weed followed them, until the ruined villas of the Thames valley were for a time lost in this red swamp, whose margin I explored, and much of the desolation the Martians had caused was concealed.

In the end the red weed succumbed almost as quickly as it had spread. A cankering disease, due, it is believed, to the action of certain bacteria, presently seized upon it. Now by the action of natural selection, all terrestrial plants have acquired a resisting power against bacterial diseases—they never succumb without a severe struggle, but the red weed rotted like a thing already dead. The fronds became bleached, and then shrivelled and brittle. They broke off at the least touch, and the waters that had stimulated their early growth carried their last vestiges out to sea.

My first act on coming to this water was, of course, to slake my thirst. I drank a great deal of it and, moved by an impulse, gnawed some fronds of red weed; but they were watery, and had a sickly, metallic taste. I found the water was sufficiently shallow for me to wade securely, although the red weed impeded my feet a little; but the flood evidently got deeper towards the river, and I turned back to Mortlake. I managed to make out the road by means of occasional ruins of its villas and fences and lamps, and so presently I got out of this spate and made my way to the hill going up towards Roehampton and came out on Putney Common.

Here the scenery changed from the strange and unfamiliar to the wreckage of the familiar: patches of ground exhibited the devastation of a cyclone, and in a few score yards I would come upon perfectly undisturbed spaces, houses with their blinds trimly drawn and doors closed, as if they had been left for a day by the owners, or as if their inhabitants slept within. The red weed was less abundant; the tall trees along the lane were free from the red creeper. I hunted for food among the trees, finding nothing, and I also raided a couple of silent houses, but they had already been broken into and ransacked. I rested for the remainder of the daylight in a shrubbery, being, in my enfeebled condition, too fatigued to push on.

All this time I saw no human beings, and no signs of the Martians. I encountered a couple of hungry-looking dogs, but both hurried circuitously away from the advances I made them. Near Roehampton I had seen two human skeletons—not bodies, but skeletons, picked clean—and in the wood by me I found the crushed and scattered bones of several cats and rabbits and the skull of a sheep. But though I gnawed parts of these in my mouth, there was nothing to be got from them.

After sunset I struggled on along the road towards Putney, where I think the Heat-Ray must have been used for some reason. And in the garden beyond Roehampton I got a quantity of immature potatoes, sufficient to stay my hunger. From this garden one looked down upon Putney and the river. The aspect of the place in the dusk was singularly desolate: blackened trees, blackened, desolate ruins, and down the hill the sheets of the flooded river, red-tinged with the weed. And over all—silence. It filled me with indescribable terror to think how swiftly that desolating change had come.

For a time I believed that mankind had been swept out of existence, and that I stood there alone, the last man left alive. Hard by the top of Putney Hill I came upon another skeleton, with the arms dislocated and removed several yards from the rest of the body. As I proceeded I became more and more convinced that the extermination of mankind was, save for such stragglers as myself, already accomplished in this part of the world. The Martians, I thought, had gone on and left the country desolated, seeking food elsewhere. Perhaps even now they were destroying Berlin or Paris, or it might be they had gone northward.

VII

THE MAN ON PUTNEY HILL

I spent that night in the inn that stands at the top of Putney Hill, sleeping in a made bed for the first time since my flight to Leatherhead. I will not tell the needless trouble I had breaking into that house—afterwards I found the front door was on the latch—nor how I ransacked every room for food, until just on the verge of despair, in what seemed to me to be a servant's bedroom, I found a rat-gnawed crust and two tins of pineapple. The place had been already searched and emptied. In the bar I afterwards found some biscuits and sandwiches that had been overlooked. The latter I could not eat, they were too rotten, but the former not only stayed my hunger, but filled my pockets. I lit no lamps, fearing some Martian might come beating that part of London for food in the night. Before I went to bed I had an interval of restlessness, and prowled from window to window, peering out for some sign of these monsters. I slept little. As I lay in bed I found myself thinking consecutively—a thing I do not remember to have done since my last argument with the curate. During all the intervening time my mental condition had been a hurrying succession of vague emotional states or a sort of stupid receptivity. But in the night my brain, reinforced, I suppose, by the food I had eaten, grew clear again, and I thought.

Three things struggled for possession of my mind: the killing of the curate, the whereabouts of the Martians, and the possible fate of my wife. The former gave me no sensation of horror or remorse to recall; I saw it simply as a thing done, a memory infinitely disagreeable but quite without the quality of remorse. I saw myself then as I see myself now, driven step by step towards that hasty blow, the creature of a sequence of accidents leading inevitably to that. I felt no condemnation; yet the memory, static, unprogressive, haunted me. In the silence of the night, with that sense of the nearness of God that sometimes comes into the stillness and the darkness, I stood my trial, my only trial, for that moment of wrath and fear. I retraced every step of our conversation from the moment when I had found him crouching beside me, heedless of my thirst, and pointing to the fire and smoke that streamed up from the ruins of Weybridge. We had been incapable of co-operation—grim chance had taken no heed of that. Had I foreseen, I should have left him at Halliford. But I did not foresee; and crime is to foresee and do. And I set this down as I have set all this story down, as it was. There were no witnesses—all these things I might have concealed. But I set it down, and the reader must form his judgment as he will.

And when, by an effort, I had set aside that picture of a prostrate body, I faced the problem of the Martians and the fate of my wife. For the former I had no data; I could imagine a hundred things, and so, unhappily, I could for the latter. And suddenly that night became terrible. I found myself sitting up in bed, staring at the dark. I found myself praying that the Heat-Ray might have suddenly and painlessly struck her out of being. Since the night of my return from Leatherhead I had not prayed. I had uttered prayers, fetish prayers, had prayed as heathens mutter charms when I was in extremity; but now I prayed indeed, pleading steadfastly and sanely, face to face with the darkness of God. Strange night! Strangest in this, that so soon as dawn had come, I, who had talked with God, crept out of the house like a rat leaving its hiding place—a creature scarcely larger, an inferior animal, a thing that for any passing whim of our masters might be hunted and killed. Perhaps they also prayed confidently to God. Surely, if we have learned nothing else, this war has taught us pity—pity for those witless souls that suffer our dominion.

The morning was bright and fine, and the eastern sky glowed pink, and was fretted with little golden clouds. In the road that runs from the top of Putney Hill to Wimbledon was a number of poor vestiges of the panic torrent that must have poured Londonward on the Sunday night after the fighting began. There was a little two-wheeled cart inscribed with the name of Thomas Lobb, Greengrocer, New Malden, with a smashed wheel and an abandoned tin trunk; there was a straw hat trampled into the now hardened mud, and at the top of West Hill a lot of blood-stained glass about the overturned water trough. My movements were languid, my plans of the vaguest. I had an idea of going to Leatherhead, though I knew that there I had the poorest chance of finding my wife. Certainly, unless death had overtaken them suddenly, my cousins and she would have fled thence; but it seemed to me I might find or learn there whither the Surrey people had fled. I knew I wanted to find my wife, that my heart ached for her and the world of men, but I had no clear idea how the finding might be done. I was also sharply aware now of my intense loneliness. From the corner I went, under cover of a thicket of trees and bushes, to the edge of Wimbledon Common, stretching wide and far.

That dark expanse was lit in patches by yellow gorse and broom; there was no red weed to be seen, and as I prowled, hesitating, on the verge of the open, the sun rose, flooding it all with light and vitality. I came upon a busy swarm of little frogs in a swampy place among the trees. I stopped to look at them, drawing a lesson from their stout resolve to live. And presently, turning suddenly, with an odd feeling of being watched, I beheld something crouching amid a clump of bushes. I stood regarding this. I made a step towards it, and it rose up and became a man armed with a cutlass. I approached him slowly. He stood silent and motionless, regarding me.

As I drew nearer I perceived he was dressed in clothes as dusty and filthy as my own; he looked, indeed, as though he had been dragged through a culvert. Nearer, I distinguished the green slime of ditches mixing with the pale drab of dried clay and shiny, coaly patches. His black hair fell over his eyes, and his face was dark and dirty and sunken, so that at first I did not recognise him. There was a red cut across the lower part of his face.

"Stop!" he cried, when I was within ten yards of him, and I stopped. His voice was hoarse. "Where do you come from?" he said.

I thought, surveying him.

"I come from Mortlake," I said. "I was buried near the pit the Martians made about their cylinder. I have worked my way out and escaped."

"There is no food about here," he said. "This is my country. All this hill down to the river, and back to Clapham, and up to the edge of the common. There is only food for one. Which way are you going?"

I answered slowly.

"I don't know," I said. "I have been buried in the ruins of a house thirteen or fourteen days. I don't know what has happened."

He looked at me doubtfully, then started, and looked with a changed expression.

"I've no wish to stop about here," said I. "I think I shall go to Leatherhead, for my wife was there."

He shot out a pointing finger.

"It is you," said he; "the man from Woking. And you weren't killed at Weybridge?"

I recognised him at the same moment.

"You are the artilleryman who came into my garden."

"Good luck!" he said. "We are lucky ones! Fancy you!" He put out a hand, and I took it. "I crawled up a drain," he said. "But they didn't kill everyone. And after they went away I got off towards Walton across the fields. But—it's not sixteen days altogether—and your hair is grey." He looked over his shoulder suddenly. "Only a rook," he said. "One gets to know that birds have shadows these days. This is a bit open. Let us crawl under those bushes and talk."

"Have you seen any Martians?" I said. "Since I crawled out—"

"They've gone away across London," he said. "I guess they've got a bigger camp there. Of a night, all over there, Hampstead way, the sky is alive with their lights. It's like a great city, and in the glare you can just see them moving. By daylight you can't. But nearer—I haven't seen them—" (he counted on his fingers) "five days. Then I saw a couple across Hammersmith way carrying something big. And the night before last"—he stopped and spoke impressively—"it was just a matter of lights, but it was something up in the air. I believe they've built a flying-machine, and are learning to fly."

I stopped, on hands and knees, for we had come to the bushes.

"Fly!"

"Yes," he said, "fly."

I went on into a little bower, and sat down.

"It is all over with humanity," I said. "If they can do that they will simply go round the world."

He nodded.

"They will. But— it will relieve things over here a bit. And besides—" He looked at me. "Aren't you satisfied it *is* up with humanity? I am. We're down; we're beat."

I stared. Strange as it may seem, I had not arrived at this fact—a fact perfectly obvious so soon as he spoke. I had still held a vague hope; rather, I had kept a lifelong habit of mind. He repeated his words, "We're beat." They carried absolute conviction.

"It's all over," he said. "They've lost *one*—just *one*. And they've made their footing good and crippled the greatest power in the world. They've walked over us. The death of that one at Weybridge was an accident. And these are only pioneers. They kept on coming. These green stars—I've seen none these five or six days, but I've no doubt they're falling somewhere every night. Nothing's to be done. We're under! We're beat!"

I made him no answer. I sat staring before me, trying in vain to devise some countervailing thought.

"This isn't a war," said the artilleryman. "It never was a war, any more than there's war between man and ants."

Suddenly I recalled the night in the observatory.

"After the tenth shot they fired no more—at least, until the first cylinder came."

"How do you know?" said the artilleryman. I explained. He thought. "Something wrong with the gun," he said. "But what if there is? They'll get it right again. And even if there's a delay, how can it alter the end? It's just men and ants. There's the ants builds their cities, live their lives, have wars, revolutions, until the men want them out of the way, and then they go out of the way. That's what we are now—just ants. Only—"

"Yes," I said.

"We're eatable ants."

We sat looking at each other.

"And what will they do with us?" I said.

"That's what I've been thinking," he said; "that's what I've been thinking. After Weybridge I went south—thinking. I saw what was up. Most of the people were hard at it squealing and exciting themselves. But I'm not so fond of squealing. I've been in sight of death once or twice; I'm not an ornamental soldier, and at the best and worst, death—it's just death. And it's the man that keeps on thinking comes through. I saw everyone tracking away south. Says I, 'Food won't last this way,' and I turned right back. I went for the Martians like a sparrow goes for man. All round"—he waved a hand to the horizon—"they're starving in heaps, bolting, treading on each other . . ."

He saw my face, and halted awkwardly.

"No doubt lots who had money have gone away to France," he said. He seemed to hesitate whether to apologise, met my eyes, and went on: "There's food all about here. Canned things in shops; wines, spirits, mineral waters; and the water mains and drains are empty. Well, I was telling you what I was thinking. 'Here's intelligent things,' I said, 'and it seems they want us for food. First, they'll smash us up—ships, machines, guns, cities, all the order and organisation. All that will go. If we were the size of ants we might pull through. But we're not. It's all too bulky to stop. That's the first certainty.' Eh?"

I assented.

"It is; I've thought it out. Very well, then—next; at present we're caught as we're wanted. A Martian has only to go a few miles to get a crowd on the run. And I saw one, one day, out by Wandsworth, picking houses to pieces and routing among the wreckage. But they won't keep on doing that. So soon as they've settled all our guns and ships, and smashed our railways, and done all the things they are doing over there, they will begin catching us systematic, picking the best and storing us in cages and things. That's what they will start doing in a bit. Lord! They haven't begun on us yet. Don't you see that?"

"Not begun!" I exclaimed.

"Not begun. All that's happened so far is through our not having the sense to keep quiet—worrying them with guns and such foolery. And losing our heads, and rushing off in crowds to where there wasn't any more safety than where we were. They don't want to bother us yet. They're making their things—making all the things they couldn't bring with them, getting things ready for the rest of their people. Very likely that's why the cylinders have stopped for a bit, for fear of hitting those who are here. And instead of our rushing about blind, on the howl, or getting dynamite on the chance of busting them up, we've got to fix ourselves up according to the new state of affairs. That's how I figure it out. It isn't quite according to what a man wants for his species, but it's about what the facts point to. And that's the principle I acted upon. Cities, nations, civilisation, progress—it's all over. That game's up. We're beat."

"But if that is so, what is there to live for?"

The artilleryman looked at me for a moment.

"There won't be any more blessed concerts for a million years or so; there won't be any Royal Academy of Arts, and no nice little feeds at restaurants. If it's amusement you're after, I reckon the game is up. If you've got any drawing-room manners or a dislike to eating peas with a knife or dropping aitches, you'd better chuck 'em away. They ain't no further use."

"You mean—"

"I mean that men like me are going on living—for the sake of the breed. I tell you, I'm grim set on living. And if I'm not mistaken, you'll show what insides you've got, too, before long. We aren't going to be exterminated. And I don't mean to be caught either, and tamed and fattened and bred like a thundering ox. Ugh! Fancy those brown creepers!"

"You don't mean to say—"

"I do. I'm going on, under their feet. I've got it planned; I've thought it out. We men are beat. We don't know enough. We've got to learn before we've got a chance. And we've got to live and keep independent while we learn. See! That's what has to be done."

I stared, astonished, and stirred profoundly by the man's resolution.

"Great God!" cried I. "But you are a man indeed!" And suddenly I gripped his hand.

"Eh!" he said, with his eyes shining. "I've thought it out, eh?"

"Go on," I said.

"Well, those who mean to escape their catching must get ready. I'm getting ready. Mind you, it isn't all of us that are made for wild beasts; and that's what it's got to be. That's why I watched you. I had my doubts. You're slender. I didn't know that it was you, you see, or just how you'd been buried. All these—the sort of people that lived in these houses, and all those damn little clerks that used to live down that way—they'd be no good. They haven't any spirit in them—no proud dreams and no proud lusts; and a man who hasn't one or the other—Lord! What is he but funk and precautions? They just used to skedaddle off to work—I've seen hundreds of 'em, bit of breakfast in hand, running wild and shining to catch their little season-ticket train, for fear they'd get dismissed if they didn't; working at businesses they were afraid to take the trouble to understand; skedaddling back for fear they wouldn't be in time for dinner; keeping indoors after dinner for fear of the back streets, and sleeping with the wives they married, not because they wanted them, but because they had a bit of money that would make for safety in their one little miserable skedaddle through the world. Lives insured and a bit invested for fear of accidents. And on Sundays—fear of the hereafter. As if hell was built for rabbits! Well, the Martians will just be a godsend to these. Nice roomy cages, fattening food, careful breeding, no worry. After a week or so chasing about the fields and lands on empty stomachs, they'll come and be caught cheerful. They'll be quite glad after a bit. They'll wonder what people did before there were Martians to take care of them. And the bar loafers, and mashers, and singers—I can imagine them. I can imagine them," he said, with a sort of sombre gratification. "There'll be any amount of sentiment and religion loose among them. There's hundreds of things I saw with my eyes that I've only begun to see clearly these last few days. There's lots will take things as they are—fat and stupid; and lots will be worried by a sort of feeling that it's all wrong, and that they ought to be doing something. Now whenever things are so that a lot of people feel they ought to be doing something, the weak, and those who go weak with a lot of complicated thinking, always make for a sort of do-nothing religion, very pious and superior, and submit to persecution and the will of the Lord. Very likely you've seen the same thing. It's energy in a gale of funk, and turned clean inside out. These cages will be full of psalms and hymns and piety. And those of a less simple sort will work in a bit of—what is it?—eroticism."

He paused.

"Very likely these Martians will make pets of some of them; train them to do tricks—who knows?—get sentimental over the pet boy who grew up and had to be killed. And some, maybe, they will train to hunt us."

"No," I cried, "that's impossible! No human being—"

"What's the good of going on with such lies?" said the artilleryman. "There's men who'd do it cheerful. What nonsense to pretend there isn't!"

And I succumbed to his conviction.

"If they come after me," he said; "Lord, if they come after me!" and subsided into a grim meditation.

I sat contemplating these things. I could find nothing to bring against this man's reasoning. In the days before the invasion no one would have questioned my intellectual superiority to his—I, a professed and recognised writer on philosophical themes, and he, a common soldier; and yet he had already formulated a situation that I had scarcely realised.

"What are you doing?" I said presently. "What plans have you made?"

He hesitated.

"Well, it's like this," he said. "What have we to do? We have to invent a sort of life where men can live and breed, and be sufficiently secure to bring the children up. Yes—wait a bit, and I'll make it clearer what I think ought to be done. The tame ones will go like all tame beasts; in a few generations they'll be big, beautiful, rich-blooded, stupid—rubbish! The risk is that we who keep wild will go savage—degenerate into a sort of big, savage rat . . . You see, how I mean to live is underground. I've been thinking about the drains. Of course those who don't know drains think horrible things; but under this London are miles and miles—hundreds of miles—and a few days' rain and London empty will leave them sweet and clean. The main drains are big enough and airy enough for anyone. Then there's cellars, vaults, stores, from which bolting passages may be made to the drains. And the railway tunnels and subways. Eh? You begin to see? And we form a band—able-bodied, clean-minded men. We're not going to pick up any rubbish that drifts in. Weaklings go out again."

"As you meant me to go?"

"Well—I parleyed, didn't I?"

"We won't quarrel about that. Go on."

"Those who stop obey orders. Able-bodied, clean-minded women we want also—mothers and teachers. No lackadaisical ladies—no blasted rolling eyes. We can't have any weak or silly. Life is real again, and the useless and cumbersome and mischievous have to die. They ought to die. They ought to be willing to die. It's a sort of disloyalty, after all, to live and taint the race. And they can't be happy. Moreover, dying's none so dreadful; it's the funking makes it bad. And in all those places we shall gather. Our district will be London. And we may even be able to keep a watch, and run about in the open when the Martians keep away. Play cricket, perhaps. That's how we shall save the race. Eh? It's a possible thing? But saving the race is nothing in itself. As I say, that's only being rats. It's saving our knowledge and adding to it is the thing. There men like you come in. There's books, there's models. We must make great safe places down deep, and get all the books we can; not novels and poetry swipes, but ideas, science books. That's where men like you come in. We must go to the British Museum and pick all those books through. Especially we must keep up our science—learn more. We must watch these Martians. Some of us must go as spies. When it's all working, perhaps I will. Get caught, I mean. And the great thing is, we must leave the Martians alone. We mustn't even steal. If we get in their way, we clear out. We must show them we mean no harm. Yes, I know. But they're intelligent things, and they won't hunt us down if they have all they want, and think we're just harmless vermin."

The artilleryman paused and laid a brown hand upon my arm.

"After all, it may not be so much we may have to learn before—Just imagine this: four or five of their fighting machines suddenly starting off—Heat-Rays right and left, and not a Martian in 'em. Not a Martian in 'em, but men—men who have learned the way how. It may be in my time, even—those men. Fancy having one of them lovely things, with its Heat-Ray wide and free! Fancy having it in control! What would it matter if you smashed to smithereens at the end of the run, after a bust like that? I reckon the Martians'll open their beautiful eyes! Can't you see them, man? Can't you see them hurrying, hurrying—puffing and blowing and hooting to their other mechanical affairs? Something out of gear in every case. And swish, bang, rattle, swish! Just as they are fumbling over it, swish comes the Heat-Ray, and, behold! Man has come back to his own."

For a while the imaginative daring of the artilleryman, and the tone of assurance and courage he assumed, completely dominated my mind. I believed unhesitatingly both in his forecast of human destiny and in the practicability of his astonishing scheme, and the reader who thinks me susceptible and foolish must contrast his position, reading steadily with all his thoughts about his subject, and mine, crouching fearfully in the bushes and listening, distracted by apprehension. We talked in this manner through the early morning time, and later crept out of the bushes, and, after scanning the sky for Martians, hurried precipitately to the house on Putney Hill where he had made his lair. It was the coal cellar of the place, and when I saw the work he had spent a week upon—it was a burrow scarcely ten yards long, which he designed to reach to the main drain on Putney Hill—I had my first inkling of the gulf between his dreams and his powers. Such a hole I could have dug in a day. But I believed in him sufficiently to work with him all that morning until past midday at his digging. We had a garden barrow and shot the earth we removed against the kitchen range. We refreshed ourselves with a tin of mock-turtle soup and wine from the neighbouring pantry. I found a curious relief from the aching strangeness of the world in this steady labour. As we worked, I turned his project over in my mind, and presently objections and doubts began to arise; but I worked there all the morning, so glad was I to find myself with a purpose again. After working an hour I began to speculate on the distance one had to go before the cloaca was reached, the chances we had of missing it altogether. My immediate trouble was why we should dig this long tunnel, when it was possible to get into the drain at once down one of the manholes, and work back to the house. It seemed to me, too, that the house was inconveniently chosen, and required a needless length of tunnel. And just as I was beginning to face these things, the artilleryman stopped digging, and looked at me.

"We're working well," he said. He put down his spade. "Let us knock off a bit," he said. "I think it's time we reconnoitred from the roof of the house."

I was for going on, and after a little hesitation he resumed his spade; and then suddenly I was struck by a thought. I stopped, and so did he at once.

"Why were you walking about the common," I said, "instead of being here?"

"Taking the air," he said. "I was coming back. It's safer by night."

"But the work?"

"Oh, one can't always work," he said, and in a flash I saw the man plain. He hesitated, holding his spade. "We ought to reconnoitre now," he said, "because if any come near they may hear the spades and drop upon us unawares."

I was no longer disposed to object. We went together to the roof and stood on a ladder peeping out of the roof door. No Martians were to be seen, and we ventured out on the tiles, and slipped down under shelter of the parapet.

From this position a shrubbery hid the greater portion of Putney, but we could see the river below, a bubbly mass of red weed, and the low parts of Lambeth flooded and red. The red creeper swarmed up the trees about the old palace, and their branches stretched gaunt and dead, and set with shrivelled leaves, from amid its clusters. It was strange how entirely dependent both these things were upon flowing water for their propagation. About us neither had gained a footing; laburnums, pink mays, snowballs, and trees of arbor-vitae, rose out of laurels and hydrangeas, green and brilliant into the sunlight. Beyond Kensington dense smoke was rising, and that and a blue haze hid the northward hills.

The artilleryman began to tell me of the sort of people who still remained in London.

"One night last week," he said, "some fools got the electric light in order, and there was all Regent Street and the Circus ablaze, crowded with painted and ragged drunkards, men and women, dancing and shouting till dawn. A man who was there told me. And as the day came they became aware of a fighting-machine standing near by the Langham and looking down at them. Heaven knows how long he had been there. It must have given some of them a nasty turn. He came down the road towards them, and picked up nearly a hundred too drunk or frightened to run away."

Grotesque gleam of a time no history will ever fully describe!

From that, in answer to my questions, he came round to his grandiose plans again. He grew enthusiastic. He talked so eloquently of the possibility of capturing a fighting-machine that I more than half believed in him again. But now that I was beginning to understand something of his quality, I could divine the stress he laid on doing nothing precipitately. And I noted that now there was no question that he personally was to capture and fight the great machine.

After a time we went down to the cellar. Neither of us seemed disposed to resume digging, and when he suggested a meal, I was nothing loath. He became suddenly very generous, and when we had eaten he went away and returned with some excellent cigars. We lit these, and his optimism glowed. He was inclined to regard my coming as a great occasion.

"There's some champagne in the cellar," he said.

"We can dig better on this Thames-side burgundy," said I.

"No," said he; "I am host today. Champagne! Great God! We've a heavy enough task before us! Let us take a rest and gather strength while we may. Look at these blistered hands!"

And pursuant to this idea of a holiday, he insisted upon playing cards after we had eaten. He taught me euchre, and after dividing London between us, I taking the northern side and he the southern, we played for parish points. Grotesque and foolish as this will seem to the sober reader, it is absolutely true, and what is more remarkable, I found the card game and several others we played extremely interesting.

Strange mind of man! That, with our species upon the edge of extermination or appalling degradation, with no clear prospect before us but the chance of a horrible death, we could sit following the chance of this painted pasteboard, and playing the "joker" with vivid delight. Afterwards he taught me poker, and I beat him at three tough chess games. When dark came we decided to take the risk, and lit a lamp.

After an interminable string of games, we supped, and the artilleryman finished the champagne. We went on smoking the cigars. He was no longer the energetic regenerator of his species I had encountered in the morning. He was still optimistic, but it was a less kinetic, a more thoughtful optimism. I remember he wound up with my health, proposed in a speech of small variety and considerable intermittence. I took a cigar, and went upstairs to look at the lights of which he had spoken that blazed so greenly along the Highgate hills.

At first I stared unintelligently across the London valley. The northern hills were shrouded in darkness; the fires near Kensington glowed redly, and now and then an orange-red tongue of flame flashed up and vanished in the deep blue night. All the rest of London was black. Then, nearer, I perceived a strange light, a pale, violet-purple fluorescent glow, quivering under the night breeze. For a space I could not understand it, and then I knew that it must be the red weed from which this faint irradiation proceeded. With that realisation my dormant sense of wonder, my sense of the proportion of things, awoke again. I glanced from that to Mars, red and clear, glowing high in the west, and then gazed long and earnestly at the darkness of Hampstead and Highgate.

I remained a very long time upon the roof, wondering at the grotesque changes of the day. I recalled my mental states from the midnight prayer to the foolish card-playing. I had a violent revulsion of feeling. I remember I flung away the cigar with a certain wasteful symbolism. My folly came to me with glaring exaggeration. I seemed a traitor to my wife and to my kind; I was filled with remorse. I resolved to leave this strange undisciplined dreamer of great things to his drink and gluttony, and to go on into London. There, it seemed to me, I had the best chance of learning what the Martians and my fellow men were doing. I was still upon the roof when the late moon rose.

VIII

DEAD LONDON

After I had parted from the artilleryman, I went down the hill, and by the High Street across the bridge to Fulham. The red weed was tumultuous at that time, and nearly choked the bridge roadway; but its fronds were already whitened in patches by the spreading disease that presently removed it so swiftly.

At the corner of the lane that runs to Putney Bridge station I found a man lying. He was as black as a sweep with the black dust, alive, but helplessly and speechlessly drunk. I could get nothing from him but curses and furious lunges at my head. I think I should have stayed by him but for the brutal expression of his face.

There was black dust along the roadway from the bridge onwards, and it grew thicker in Fulham. The streets were horribly quiet. I got food—sour, hard, and mouldy, but quite eatable—in a baker's shop here. Some way towards Walham Green the streets became clear of powder, and I passed a white terrace of houses on fire; the noise of the burning was an absolute relief. Going on towards Brompton, the streets were quiet again.

Here I came once more upon the black powder in the streets and upon dead bodies. I saw altogether about a dozen in the length of the Fulham Road. They had been dead many days, so that I hurried quickly past them. The black powder covered them over, and softened their outlines. One or two had been disturbed by dogs.

Where there was no black powder, it was curiously like a Sunday in the City, with the closed shops, the houses locked up and the blinds drawn, the desertion, and the stillness. In some places plunderers had been at work, but rarely at other than the provision and wine shops. A jeweller's window had been broken open in one place, but apparently the thief had been disturbed, and a number of gold chains and a watch lay scattered on the pavement. I did not trouble to touch them. Farther on was a tattered woman in a heap on a doorstep; the hand that hung over her knee was gashed and bled down her rusty brown dress, and a smashed magnum of champagne formed a pool across the pavement. She seemed asleep, but she was dead.

The farther I penetrated into London, the profounder grew the stillness. But it was not so much the stillness of death—it was the stillness of suspense, of expectation. At any time the destruction that had already singed the northwestern borders of the metropolis, and had annihilated Ealing and Kilburn, might strike among these houses and leave them smoking ruins. It was a city condemned and derelict . . .

In South Kensington the streets were clear of dead and of black powder. It was near South Kensington that I first heard the howling. It crept almost imperceptibly upon my senses. It was a sobbing alternation of two notes, "Ulla, ulla, ulla, ulla," keeping on perpetually. When I passed streets that ran northward it grew in volume, and houses and buildings seemed to deaden and cut it off again. It came in a full tide down Exhibition Road. I stopped, staring towards Kensington Gardens, wondering at this strange, remote wailing. It was as if that mighty desert of houses had found a voice for its fear and solitude.

"Ulla, ulla, ulla, ulla," wailed that superhuman note—great waves of sound sweeping down the broad, sunlit roadway, between the tall buildings on each side. I turned northwards, marvelling, towards the iron gates of Hyde Park. I had half a mind to break into the Natural History Museum and find my way up to the summits of the towers, in order to see across the park. But I decided to keep to the ground, where quick hiding was possible, and so went on up the Exhibition Road. All the large mansions on each side of the road were empty and still, and my footsteps echoed against the sides of the houses. At the top, near the park gate, I came upon a strange sight—a bus overturned, and the skeleton of a horse picked clean. I puzzled over this for a time, and then went on to the bridge over the Serpentine. The voice grew stronger and stronger, though I could see nothing above the housetops on the north side of the park, save a haze of smoke to the northwest.

"Ulla, ulla, ulla, ulla," cried the voice, coming, as it seemed to me, from the district about Regent's Park. The desolating cry worked upon my mind. The mood that had sustained me passed. The wailing took possession of me. I found I was intensely weary, footsore, and now again hungry and thirsty.

It was already past noon. Why was I wandering alone in this city of the dead? Why was I alone when all London was lying in state, and in its black shroud? I felt intolerably lonely. My mind ran on old friends that I had forgotten for years. I thought of the poisons in the chemists' shops, of the liquors the wine merchants stored; I recalled the two sodden creatures of despair, who so far as I knew, shared the city with myself . . .

I came into Oxford Street by the Marble Arch, and here again were black powder and several bodies, and an evil, ominous smell from the gratings of the cellars of some of the houses. I grew very thirsty after the heat of my long walk. With infinite trouble I managed to break into a public-house and get food and drink. I was weary after eating, and went into the parlour behind the bar, and slept on a black horsehair sofa I found there.

I awoke to find that dismal howling still in my ears, "Ulla, ulla, ulla, ulla." It was now dusk, and after I had routed out some biscuits and a cheese in the bar—there was a meat safe, but it contained nothing but maggots—I wandered on through the silent residential squares to Baker Street—Portman Square is the only one I can name—and so came out at last upon Regent's Park. And as I emerged from the top of Baker Street, I saw far away over the trees in the clearness of the sunset the hood of the Martian giant from which this howling proceeded. I was not terrified. I came upon him as if it were a matter of course. I watched him for some time, but he did not move. He appeared to be standing and yelling, for no reason that I could discover.

I tried to formulate a plan of action. That perpetual sound of "Ulla, ulla, ulla, ulla" confused my mind. Perhaps I was too tired to be very fearful. Certainly I was more curious to know the reason of this monotonous crying than afraid. I turned back away from the park and struck into Park Road, intending to skirt the park, went along under the shelter of the terraces, and got a view of this stationary, howling Martian from the direction of St. John's Wood. A couple of hundred yards out of Baker Street I heard a yelping chorus, and saw, first a dog with a piece of putrescent red meat in his jaws coming headlong towards me, and then a pack of starving mongrels in pursuit of him. He made a wide curve to avoid me, as though he feared I might prove a fresh competitor. As the yelping died away down the silent road, the wailing sound of "Ulla, ulla, ulla, ulla" reasserted itself.

I came upon the wrecked handling-machine halfway to St. John's Wood station. At first I thought a house had fallen across the road. It was only as I clambered among the ruins that I saw, with a start, this mechanical Samson lying, with its tentacles bent and smashed and twisted, among the ruins it had made. The forepart was shattered. It seemed as if it had driven blindly straight at the house, and had been overwhelmed in its overthrow. It seemed to me then that this might have happened by a handling-machine escaping from the guidance of its Martian. I could not clamber among the ruins to see it, and the twilight was now so far advanced that the blood with which its seat was smeared, and the gnawed gristle of the Martian that the dogs had left, were invisible to me.

Wondering still more at all that I had seen, I pushed on towards Primrose Hill. Far away, through a gap in the trees, I saw a second Martian, as motionless as the first, standing in the park towards the Zoological Gardens, and silent. A little beyond the ruins about the smashed handling-machine I came upon the red weed again, and found the Regent's Canal, a spongy mass of dark-red vegetation.

As I crossed the bridge, the sound of "Ulla, ulla, ulla, ulla" ceased. It was, as it were, cut off. The silence came like a thunderclap.

The dusky houses about me stood faint and tall and dim; the trees towards the park were growing black. All about me the red weed clambered among the ruins, writhing to get above me in the dimness. Night, the mother of fear and mystery, was coming upon me. But while that voice sounded the solitude, the desolation, had been endurable; by virtue of it London had still seemed alive, and the sense of life about me had upheld me. Then suddenly a change, the passing of something—I knew not what—and then a stillness that could be felt. Nothing but this gaunt quiet.

London about me gazed at me spectrally. The windows in the white houses were like the eye sockets of skulls. About me my imagination found a thousand noiseless enemies moving. Terror seized me, a horror of my temerity. In front of me the road became pitchy black as though it was tarred, and I saw a contorted shape lying across the pathway. I could not bring myself to go on. I turned down St. John's Wood Road, and ran headlong from this unendurable stillness towards Kilburn. I hid from the night and the silence, until long after midnight, in a cabmen's shelter in Harrow Road. But before the dawn my courage returned, and while the stars were still in the sky I turned once more towards Regent's Park. I missed my way among the streets, and presently saw down a long avenue, in the half-light of the early dawn, the curve of Primrose Hill. On the summit, towering up to the fading stars, was a third Martian, erect and motionless like the others.

An insane resolve possessed me. I would die and end it. And I would save myself even the trouble of killing myself. I marched on recklessly towards this Titan, and then, as I drew nearer and the light grew, I saw that a multitude of black birds was circling and clustering about the hood. At that my heart gave a bound, and I began running along the road.

I hurried through the red weed that choked St. Edmund's Terrace (I waded breast-high across a torrent of water that was rushing down from the waterworks towards the Albert Road), and emerged upon the grass before the rising of the sun. Great mounds had been heaped about the crest of the hill, making a huge redoubt of it—it was the final and largest place the Martians had made—and from behind these heaps there rose a thin smoke against the sky. Against the sky line an eager dog ran and disappeared. The thought that had flashed into my mind grew real, grew credible. I felt no fear, only a wild, trembling exultation, as I ran up the hill towards the motionless monster. Out of the hood hung lank shreds of brown, at which the hungry birds pecked and tore.

In another moment I had scrambled up the earthen rampart and stood upon its crest, and the interior of the redoubt was below me. A mighty space it was, with gigantic machines here and there within it, huge mounds of material and strange shelter places. And scattered about it, some in their overturned war-machines, some in the now rigid handling-machines, and a dozen of them stark and silent and laid in a row, were the Martians—*dead!*—slain by the putrefactive and disease bacteria against which their systems were unprepared; slain as the red weed was being slain; slain, after all man's devices had failed, by the humblest things that God, in his wisdom, has put upon this earth.

For so it had come about, as indeed I and many men might have foreseen had not terror and disaster blinded our minds. These germs of disease have taken toll of humanity since the beginning of things—taken toll of our prehuman ancestors since life began here. But by virtue of this natural selection of our kind we have developed resisting power; to no germs do we succumb without a struggle, and to many—those that cause putrefaction in dead matter, for instance—our living frames are altogether immune. But there are no bacteria in Mars, and directly these invaders arrived, directly they drank and fed, our microscopic allies began to work their overthrow. Already when I watched them they were irrevocably doomed, dying and rotting even as they went to and fro. It was inevitable. By the toll of a billion deaths man has bought his birthright of the earth, and it is his against all comers; it would still be his were the Martians ten times as mighty as they are. For neither do men live nor die in vain.

Here and there they were scattered, nearly fifty altogether, in that great gulf they had made, overtaken by a death that must have seemed to them as incomprehensible as any death could be. To me also at that time this death was incomprehensible. All I knew was that these things that had been alive and so terrible to men were dead. For a moment I believed that the destruction of Sennacherib had been repeated, that God had repented, that the Angel of Death had slain them in the night.

I stood staring into the pit, and my heart lightened gloriously, even as the rising sun struck the world to fire about me with his rays. The pit was still in darkness; the mighty engines, so great and wonderful in their power and complexity, so unearthly in their tortuous forms, rose weird and vague and strange out of the shadows towards the light. A multitude of dogs, I could hear, fought over the bodies that lay darkly in the depth of the pit, far below me. Across the pit on its farther lip, flat and vast and strange, lay the great flying-machine with which they had been experimenting upon our denser atmosphere when decay and death arrested them. Death had come not a day too soon. At the sound of a cawing overhead I looked up at the huge fighting-machine that would fight no more forever, at the tattered red shreds of flesh that dripped down upon the overturned seats on the summit of Primrose Hill.

I turned and looked down the slope of the hill to where, enhaloed now in birds, stood those other two Martians that I had seen overnight, just as death had overtaken them. The one had died, even as it had been crying to its companions; perhaps it was the last to die, and its voice had gone on perpetually until the force of its machinery was exhausted. They glittered now, harmless tripod towers of shining metal, in the brightness of the rising sun.

All about the pit, and saved as by a miracle from everlasting destruction, stretched the great Mother of Cities. Those who have only seen London veiled in her sombre robes of smoke can scarcely imagine the naked clearness and beauty of the silent wilderness of houses.

Eastward, over the blackened ruins of the Albert Terrace and the splintered spire of the church, the sun blazed dazzling in a clear sky, and here and there some facet in the great wilderness of roofs caught the light and glared with a white intensity.

Northward were Kilburn and Hampsted, blue and crowded with houses; westward the great city was dimmed; and southward, beyond the Martians, the green waves of Regent's Park, the Langham Hotel, the dome of the Albert Hall, the Imperial Institute, and the giant mansions of the Brompton Road came out clear and little in the sunrise, the jagged ruins of Westminster rising hazily beyond. Far away and blue were the Surrey hills, and the towers of the Crystal Palace glittered like two silver rods. The dome of St. Paul's was dark against the sunrise, and injured, I saw for the first time, by a huge gaping cavity on its western side.

And as I looked at this wide expanse of houses and factories and churches, silent and abandoned; as I thought of the multitudinous hopes and efforts, the innumerable hosts of lives that had gone to build this human reef, and of the swift and ruthless destruction that had hung over it all; when I realised that the shadow had been rolled back, and that men might still live in the streets, and this dear vast dead city of mine be once more alive and powerful, I felt a wave of emotion that was near akin to tears.

The torment was over. Even that day the healing would begin. The survivors of the people scattered over the country—leaderless, lawless, foodless, like sheep without a shepherd—the thousands who had fled by sea, would begin to return; the pulse of life, growing stronger and stronger, would beat again in the empty streets and pour across the vacant squares. Whatever destruction was done, the hand of the destroyer was stayed. All the gaunt wrecks, the blackened skeletons of houses that stared so dismally at the sunlit grass of the hill, would presently be echoing with the hammers of the restorers and ringing with the tapping of their trowels. At the thought I extended my hands towards the sky and began thanking God. In a year, thought I—in a year . . .

With overwhelming force came the thought of myself, of my wife, and the old life of hope and tender helpfulness that had ceased forever.

IX

WRECKAGE

And now comes the strangest thing in my story. Yet, perhaps, it is not altogether strange. I remember, clearly and coldly and vividly, all that I did that day until the time that I stood weeping and praising God upon the summit of Primrose Hill. And then I forget.

Of the next three days I know nothing. I have learned since that, so far from my being the first discoverer of the Martian overthrow, several such wanderers as myself had already discovered this on the previous night. One man—the first—had gone to St. Martin's-le-Grand, and, while I sheltered in the cabmen's hut, had contrived to telegraph to Paris. Thence the joyful news had flashed all over the world; a thousand cities, chilled by ghastly apprehensions, suddenly flashed into frantic illuminations; they knew of it in Dublin, Edinburgh, Manchester, Birmingham, at the time when I stood upon the verge of the pit. Already men, weeping with joy, as I have heard, shouting and staying their work to shake hands and shout, were making up trains, even as near as Crewe, to descend upon London. The church bells that had ceased a fortnight since suddenly caught the news, until all England was bell-ringing. Men on cycles, lean-faced, unkempt, scorched along every country lane shouting of unhoped deliverance, shouting to gaunt, staring figures of despair. And for the food! Across the Channel, across the Irish Sea, across the Atlantic, corn, bread, and meat were tearing to our relief. All the shipping in the world seemed going Londonward in those days. But of all this I have no memory. I drifted—a demented man. I found myself in a house of kindly people, who had found me on the third day wandering, weeping, and raving through the streets of St. John's Wood. They have told me since that I was singing some insane doggerel about "The Last Man Left Alive! Hurrah! The Last Man Left Alive!" Troubled as they were with their own affairs, these people, whose name, much as I would like to express my gratitude to them, I may not even give here, nevertheless cumbered themselves with me, sheltered me, and protected me from myself. Apparently they had learned something of my story from me during the days of my lapse.

Very gently, when my mind was assured again, did they break to me what they had learned of the fate of Leatherhead. Two days after I was imprisoned it had been destroyed, with every soul in it, by a Martian. He had swept it out of existence, as it seemed, without any provocation, as a boy might crush an ant hill, in the mere wantonness of power.

I was a lonely man, and they were very kind to me. I was a lonely man and a sad one, and they bore with me. I remained with them four days after my recovery. All that time I felt a vague, a growing craving to look once more on whatever remained of the little life that seemed so happy and bright in my past. It was a mere hopeless desire to feast upon my misery. They dissuaded me. They did all they could to divert me from this morbidity. But at last I could resist the impulse no longer, and, promising faithfully to return to them, and parting, as I will confess, from these four-day friends with tears, I went out again into the streets that had lately been so dark and strange and empty.

Already they were busy with returning people; in places even there were shops open, and I saw a drinking fountain running water.

I remember how mockingly bright the day seemed as I went back on my melancholy pilgrimage to the little house at Woking, how busy the streets and vivid the moving life about me. So many people were abroad everywhere, busied in a thousand activities, that it seemed incredible that any great proportion of the population could have been slain. But then I noticed how yellow were the skins of the people I met, how shaggy the hair of the men, how large and bright their eyes, and that every other man still wore his dirty rags. Their faces seemed all with one of two expressions—a leaping exultation and energy or a grim resolution. Save for the expression of the faces, London seemed a city of tramps. The vestries were indiscriminately distributing bread sent us by the French government. The ribs of the few horses showed dismally. Haggard special constables with white badges stood at the corners of every street. I saw little of the mischief wrought by the Martians until I reached Wellington Street, and there I saw the red weed clambering over the buttresses of Waterloo Bridge.

At the corner of the bridge, too, I saw one of the common contrasts of that grotesque time—a sheet of paper flaunting against a thicket of the red weed, transfixed by a stick that kept it in place. It was the placard of the first newspaper to resume publication—the *Daily Mail.* I bought a copy for a blackened shilling I found in my pocket. Most of it was in blank, but the solitary compositor who did the thing had amused himself by making a grotesque scheme of advertisement stereo on the back page. The matter he printed was emotional; the news organisation had not as yet found its way back. I learned nothing fresh except that already in one week the examination of the Martian mechanisms had yielded astonishing results. Among other things, the article assured me what I did not believe at the time, that the "Secret of Flying" was discovered. At Waterloo I found the free trains that were taking people to their homes. The first rush was already over. There were few people in the train, and I was in no mood for casual conversation. I got a compartment to myself, and sat with folded arms, looking greyly at the sunlit devastation that flowed past the windows. And just outside the terminus the train jolted over temporary rails, and on either side of the railway the houses were blackened ruins. To Clapham Junction the face of London was grimy with powder of the Black Smoke, in spite of two days of thunderstorms and rain, and at Clapham Junction the line had been wrecked again; there were hundreds of out-of-work clerks and shopmen working side by side with the customary navvies, and we were jolted over a hasty relaying.

All down the line from there the aspect of the country was gaunt and unfamiliar; Wimbledon particularly had suffered. Walton, by virtue of its unburned pine woods, seemed the least hurt of any place along the line. The Wandle, the Mole, every little stream, was a heaped mass of red weed, in appearance between butcher's meat and pickled cabbage. The Surrey pine woods were too dry, however, for the festoons of the red climber. Beyond Wimbledon, within sight of the line, in certain nursery grounds, were the heaped masses of earth about the sixth cylinder. A number of people were standing about it, and some sappers were busy in the midst of it. Over it flaunted a Union Jack, flapping cheerfully in the morning breeze. The nursery grounds were everywhere crimson with the weed, a wide expanse of livid colour cut with purple shadows, and very painful to the eye. One's gaze went with infinite relief from the scorched greys and sullen reds of the foreground to the blue-green softness of the eastward hills.

The line on the London side of Woking station was still undergoing repair, so I descended at Byfleet station and took the road to Maybury, past the place where I and the artilleryman had talked to the hussars, and on by the spot where the Martian had appeared to me in the thunderstorm. Here, moved by curiosity, I turned aside to find, among a tangle of red fronds, the warped and broken dog cart with the whitened bones of the horse scattered and gnawed. For a time I stood regarding these vestiges . . .

Then I returned through the pine wood, neck-high with red weed here and there, to find the landlord of the Spotted Dog had already found burial, and so came home past the College Arms. A man standing at an open cottage door greeted me by name as I passed.

I looked at my house with a quick flash of hope that faded immediately. The door had been forced; it was unfast and was opening slowly as I approached.

It slammed again. The curtains of my study fluttered out of the open window from which I and the artilleryman had watched the dawn. No one had closed it since. The smashed bushes were just as I had left them nearly four weeks ago. I stumbled into the hall, and the house felt empty. The stair carpet was ruffled and discoloured where I had crouched, soaked to the skin from the thunderstorm the night of the catastrophe. Our muddy footsteps I saw still went up the stairs.

I followed them to my study, and found lying on my writing-table still, with the selenite paper weight upon it, the sheet of work I had left on the afternoon of the opening of the cylinder. For a space I stood reading over my abandoned arguments. It was a paper on the probable development of Moral Ideas with the development of the civilising process; and the last sentence was the opening of a prophecy: "In about two hundred years," I had written, "we may expect—" The sentence ended abruptly. I remembered my inability to fix my mind that morning, scarcely a month gone by, and how I had broken off to get my *Daily Chronicle* from the newsboy. I remembered how I went down to the garden gate as he came along, and how I had listened to his odd story of "Men from Mars."

I came down and went into the dining room. There were the mutton and the bread, both far gone now in decay, and a beer bottle overturned, just as I and the artilleryman had left them. My home was desolate. I perceived the folly of the faint hope I had cherished so long. And then a strange thing occurred. "It is no use," said a voice. "The house is deserted. No one has been here these ten days. Do not stay here to torment yourself. No one escaped but you."

I was startled. Had I spoken my thought aloud? I turned, and the French window was open behind me. I made a step to it, and stood looking out.

And there, amazed and afraid, even as I stood amazed and afraid, were my cousin and my wife—my wife white and tearless. She gave a faint cry.

"I came," she said. "I knew—knew—"

She put her hand to her throat—swayed. I made a step forward, and caught her in my arms.

X

THE EPILOGUE

I cannot but regret, now that I am concluding my story, how little I am able to contribute to the discussion of the many debatable questions which are still unsettled. In one respect I shall certainly provoke criticism. My particular province is speculative philosophy. My knowledge of comparative physiology is confined to a book or two, but it seems to me that Carver's suggestions as to the reason of the rapid death of the Martians is so probable as to be regarded almost as a proven conclusion. I have assumed that in the body of my narrative.

At any rate, in all the bodies of the Martians that were examined after the war, no bacteria except those already known as terrestrial species were found. That they did not bury any of their dead, and the reckless slaughter they perpetrated, point also to an entire ignorance of the putrefactive process. But probable as this seems, it is by no means a proven conclusion.

Neither is the composition of the Black Smoke known, which the Martians used with such deadly effect, and the generator of the Heat-Rays remains a puzzle. The terrible disasters at the Ealing and South Kensington laboratories have disinclined analysts for further investigations upon the latter. Spectrum analysis of the black powder points unmistakably to the presence of an unknown element with a brilliant group of three lines in the green, and it is possible that it combines with argon to form a compound which acts at once with deadly effect upon some constituent in the blood. But such unproven speculations will scarcely be of interest to the general reader, to whom this story is addressed. None of the brown scum that drifted down the Thames after the destruction of Shepperton was examined at the time, and now none is forthcoming.

The results of an anatomical examination of the Martians, so far as the prowling dogs had left such an examination possible, I have already given. But everyone is familiar with the magnificent and almost complete specimen in spirits at the Natural History Museum, and the countless drawings that have been made from it; and beyond that the interest of their physiology and structure is purely scientific.

A question of graver and universal interest is the possibility of another attack from the Martians. I do not think that nearly enough attention is being given to this aspect of the matter. At present the planet Mars is in conjunction, but with every return to opposition I, for one, anticipate a renewal of their adventure. In any case, we should be prepared. It seems to me that it should be possible to define the position of the gun from which the shots are discharged, to keep a sustained watch upon this part of the planet, and to anticipate the arrival of the next attack.

In that case the cylinder might be destroyed with dynamite or artillery before it was sufficiently cool for the Martians to emerge, or they might be butchered by means of guns so soon as the screw opened. It seems to me that they have lost a vast advantage in the failure of their first surprise. Possibly they see it in the same light.

Lessing has advanced excellent reasons for supposing that the Martians have actually succeeded in effecting a landing on the planet Venus. Seven months ago now, Venus and Mars were in alignment with the sun; that is to say, Mars was in opposition from the point of view of an observer on Venus. Subsequently a peculiar luminous and sinuous marking appeared on the unillumined half of the inner planet, and almost simultaneously a faint dark mark of a similar sinuous character was detected upon a photograph of the Martian disk. One needs to see the drawings of these appearances in order to appreciate fully their remarkable resemblance in character.

At any rate, whether we expect another invasion or not, our views of the human future must be greatly modified by these events. We have learned now that we cannot regard this planet as being fenced in and a secure abiding place for Man; we can never anticipate the unseen good or evil that may come upon us suddenly out of space. It may be that in the larger design of the universe this invasion from Mars is not without its ultimate benefit for men; it has robbed us of that serene confidence in the future which is the most fruitful source of decadence, the gifts to human science it has brought are enormous, and it has done much to promote the conception of the commonweal of mankind. It may be that across the immensity of space the Martians have watched the fate of these pioneers of theirs and learned their lesson, and that on the planet Venus they have found a securer settlement. Be that as it may, for many years yet there will certainly be no relaxation of the eager scrutiny of the Martian disk, and those fiery darts of the sky, the shooting stars, will bring with them as they fall an unavoidable apprehension to all the sons of men.

The broadening of men's views that has resulted can scarcely be exaggerated. Before the cylinder fell there was a general persuasion that through all the deep of space no life existed beyond the petty surface of our minute sphere. Now we see further. If the Martians can reach Venus, there is no reason to suppose that the thing is impossible for men, and when the slow cooling of the sun makes this earth uninhabitable, as at last it must do, it may be that the thread of life that has begun here will have streamed out and caught our sister planet within its toils.

Dim and wonderful is the vision I have conjured up in my mind of life spreading slowly from this little seed bed of the solar system throughout the inanimate vastness of sidereal space. But that is a remote dream. It may be, on the other hand, that the destruction of the Martians is only a reprieve. To them, and not to us, perhaps, is the future ordained.

I must confess the stress and danger of the time have left an abiding sense of doubt and insecurity in my mind. I sit in my study writing by lamplight, and suddenly I see again the healing valley below set with writhing flames, and feel the house behind and about me empty and desolate. I go out into the Byfleet Road, and vehicles pass me, a butcher boy in a cart, a cabful of visitors, a workman on a bicycle, children going to school, and suddenly they become vague and unreal, and I hurry again with the artilleryman through the hot, brooding silence. Of a night I see the black powder darkening the silent streets, and the contorted bodies shrouded in that layer; they rise upon me tattered and dog-bitten. They gibber and grow fiercer, paler, uglier, mad distortions of humanity at last, and I wake, cold and wretched, in the darkness of the night.

I go to London and see the busy multitudes in Fleet Street and the

Strand, and it comes across my mind that they are but the ghosts of the past, haunting the streets that I have seen silent and wretched, going to and fro, phantasms in a dead city, the mockery of life in a galvanised body. And strange, too, it is to stand on Primrose Hill, as I did but a day before writing this last chapter, to see the great province of houses, dim and blue through the haze of the smoke and mist, vanishing at last into the vague lower sky, to see the people walking to and fro among the flower beds on the hill, to see the sightseers about the Martian machine that stands there still, to hear the tumult of playing children, and to recall the time when I saw it all bright and clear-cut, hard and silent, under the dawn of that last great day . . .

And strangest of all is it to hold my wife's hand again, and to think that I have counted her, and that she has counted me, among the dead.

A PRINCESS OF MARS

Edgar Rice Burroughs

FOREWORD

To the Reader of this Work:

In submitting Captain Carter's strange manuscript to you in book form, I believe that a few words relative to this remarkable personality will be of interest.

My first recollection of Captain Carter is of the few months he spent at my father's home in Virginia, just prior to the opening of the civil war. I was then a child of but five years, yet I well remember the tall, dark, smooth-faced, athletic man whom I called Uncle Jack.

He seemed always to be laughing; and he entered into the sports of the children with the same hearty good fellowship he displayed toward those pastimes in which the men and women of his own age indulged; or he would sit for an hour at a time entertaining my old grandmother with stories of his strange, wild life in all parts of the world. We all loved him, and our slaves fairly worshipped the ground he trod.

He was a splendid specimen of manhood, standing a good two inches over six feet, broad of shoulder and narrow of hip, with the carriage of the trained fighting man. His features were regular and clear cut, his hair black and closely cropped, while his eyes were of a steel gray, reflecting a strong and loyal character, filled with fire and initiative. His manners were perfect, and his courtliness was that of a typical southern gentleman of the highest type.

His horsemanship, especially after hounds, was a marvel and delight even in that country of magnificent horsemen. I have often heard my father caution him against his wild recklessness, but he would only laugh, and say that the tumble that killed him would be from the back of a horse yet unfoaled.

When the war broke out he left us, nor did I see him again for some fifteen or sixteen years. When he returned it was without warning, and I was much surprised to note that he had not aged apparently a moment, nor had he changed in any other outward way. He was, when others were with him, the same genial, happy fellow we had known of old, but when he thought himself alone I have seen him sit for hours gazing off into space, his face set in a look of wistful longing and hopeless misery; and at night he would sit thus looking up into the heavens, at what I did not know until I read his manuscript years afterward.

He told us that he had been prospecting and mining in Arizona part of the time since the war; and that he had been very successful was evidenced by the unlimited amount of money with which he was supplied. As to the details of his life during these years he was very reticent, in fact he would not talk of them at all.

He remained with us for about a year and then went to New York, where he purchased a little place on the Hudson, where I visited him once a year on the occasions of my trips to the New York market—my father and I owning and operating a string of general stores throughout Virginia at that time. Captain Carter had a small but beautiful cottage, situated on a bluff overlooking the river, and during one of my last visits, in the winter of 1885, I observed he was much occupied in writing, I presume now, upon this manuscript.

He told me at this time that if anything should happen to him he wished me to take charge of his estate, and he gave me a key to a compartment in the safe which stood in his study, telling me I would find his will there and some personal instructions which he had me pledge myself to carry out with absolute fidelity.

After I had retired for the night I have seen him from my window standing in the moonlight on the brink of the bluff overlooking the Hudson with his arms stretched out to the heavens as though in appeal. I thought at the time that he was praying, although I never understood that he was in the strict sense of the term a religious man.

Several months after I had returned home from my last visit, the first of March, 1886, I think, I received a telegram from him asking me to come to him at once. I had always been his favorite among the younger generation of Carters and so I hastened to comply with his demand.

I arrived at the little station, about a mile from his grounds, on the morning of March 4, 1886, and when I asked the livery man to drive me out to Captain Carter's he replied that if I was a friend of the Captain's he had some very bad news for me; the Captain had been found dead shortly after daylight that very morning by the watchman attached to an adjoining property.

For some reason this news did not surprise me, but I hurried out to his place as quickly as possible, so that I could take charge of the body and of his affairs.

I found the watchman who had discovered him, together with the local police chief and several townspeople, assembled in his little study. The watchman related the few details connected with the finding of the body, which he said had been still warm when he came upon it. It lay, he said, stretched full length in the snow with the arms outstretched above the head toward the edge of the bluff, and when he showed me the spot it flashed upon me that it was the identical one where I had seen him on those other nights, with his arms raised in supplication to the skies.

There were no marks of violence on the body, and with the aid of a local physician the coroner's jury quickly reached a decision of death from heart failure. Left alone in the study, I opened the safe and withdrew the contents of the drawer in which he had told me I would find my instructions. They were in part peculiar indeed, but I have followed them to each last detail as faithfully as I was able.

He directed that I remove his body to Virginia without embalming, and that he be laid in an open coffin within a tomb which he previously had had constructed and which, as I later learned, was well ventilated. The instructions impressed upon me that I must personally see that this was carried out just as he directed, even in secrecy if necessary.

His property was left in such a way that I was to receive the entire income for twenty-five years, when the principal was to become mine. His further instructions related to this manuscript which I was to retain sealed and unread, just as I found it, for eleven years; nor was I to divulge its contents until twenty-one years after his death.

A strange feature about the tomb, where his body still lies, is that the massive door is equipped with a single, huge gold-plated spring lock which can be opened *only from the inside.*

Yours very sincerely,
Edgar Rice Burroughs

I

ON THE ARIZONA HILLS

I am a very old man; how old I do not know. Possibly I am a hundred, possibly more; but I cannot tell because I have never aged as other men, nor do I remember any childhood. So far as I can recollect I have always been a man, a man of about thirty. I appear today as I did forty years and more ago, and yet I feel that I cannot go on living forever; that some day I shall die the real death from which there is no resurrection. I do not know why I should fear death, I who have died twice and am still alive; but yet I have the same horror of it as you who have never died, and it is because of this terror of death, I believe, that I am so convinced of my mortality.

And because of this conviction I have determined to write down the story of the interesting periods of my life and of my death. I cannot explain the phenomena; I can only set down here in the words of an ordinary soldier of fortune a chronicle of the strange events that befell me during the ten years that my dead body lay undiscovered in an Arizona cave.

I have never told this story, nor shall mortal man see this manuscript until after I have passed over for eternity. I know that the average human mind will not believe what it cannot grasp, and so I do not purpose being pilloried by the public, the pulpit, and the press, and held up as a colossal liar when I am but telling the simple truths which some day science will substantiate. Possibly the suggestions which I gained upon Mars, and the knowledge which I can set down in this chronicle, will aid in an earlier understanding of the mysteries of our sister planet; mysteries to you, but no longer mysteries to me.

My name is John Carter; I am better known as Captain Jack Carter of Virginia. At the close of the Civil War I found myself possessed of several hundred thousand dollars (Confederate) and a captain's commission in the cavalry arm of an army which no longer existed; the servant of a state which had vanished with the hopes of the South. Masterless, penniless, and with my only means of livelihood, fighting, gone, I determined to work my way to the southwest and attempt to retrieve my fallen fortunes in a search for gold.

I spent nearly a year prospecting in company with another Confederate officer, Captain James K. Powell of Richmond. We were extremely fortunate, for late in the winter of 1865, after many hardships and privations, we located the most remarkable gold-bearing quartz vein that our wildest dreams had ever pictured. Powell, who was a mining engineer by education, stated that we had uncovered over a million dollars worth of ore in a trifle over three months.

As our equipment was crude in the extreme we decided that one of us must return to civilization, purchase the necessary machinery and return with a sufficient force of men properly to work the mine.

As Powell was familiar with the country, as well as with the mechanical requirements of mining we determined that it would be best for him to make the trip. It was agreed that I was to hold down our claim against the remote possibility of its being jumped by some wandering prospector.

On March 3, 1866, Powell and I packed his provisions on two of our burros, and bidding me good-bye he mounted his horse, and started down the mountainside toward the valley, across which led the first stage of his journey.

The morning of Powell's departure was, like nearly all Arizona mornings, clear and beautiful; I could see him and his little pack animals picking their way down the mountainside toward the valley, and all during the morning I would catch occasional glimpses of them as they topped a hog back or came out upon a level plateau. My last sight of Powell was about three in the afternoon as he entered the shadows of the range on the opposite side of the valley.

Some half hour later I happened to glance casually across the valley and was much surprised to note three little dots in about the same place I had last seen my friend and his two pack animals. I am not given to needless worrying, but the more I tried to convince myself that all was well with Powell, and that the dots I had seen on his trail were antelope or wild horses, the less I was able to assure myself.

Since we had entered the territory we had not seen a hostile Indian, and we had, therefore, become careless in the extreme, and were wont to ridicule the stories we had heard of the great numbers of these vicious marauders that were supposed to haunt the trails, taking their toll in lives and torture of every white party which fell into their merciless clutches.

Powell, I knew, was well armed and, further, an experienced Indian fighter; but I too had lived and fought for years among the Sioux in the North, and I knew that his chances were small against a party of cunning trailing Apaches. Finally I could endure the suspense no longer, and, arming myself with my two Colt revolvers and a carbine, I strapped two belts of cartridges about me and catching my saddle horse, started down the trail taken by Powell in the morning.

As soon as I reached comparatively level ground I urged my mount into a canter and continued this, where the going permitted, until, close upon dusk, I discovered the point where other tracks joined those of Powell. They were the tracks of unshod ponies, three of them, and the ponies had been galloping.

I followed rapidly until, darkness shutting down, I was forced to await the rising of the moon, and given an opportunity to speculate on the question of the wisdom of my chase. Possibly I had conjured up impossible dangers, like some nervous old housewife, and when I should catch up with Powell would get a good laugh for my pains. However, I am not prone to sensitiveness, and the following of a sense of duty, wherever it may lead, has always been a kind of fetich with me throughout my life; which may account for the honors bestowed upon me by three republics and the decorations and friendships of an old and powerful emperor and several lesser kings, in whose service my sword has been red many a time.

About nine o'clock the moon was sufficiently bright for me to proceed on my way and I had no difficulty in following the trail at a fast walk, and in some places at a brisk trot until, about midnight, I reached the water hole where Powell had expected to camp. I came upon the spot unexpectedly, finding it entirely deserted, with no signs of having been recently occupied as a camp.

I was interested to note that the tracks of the pursuing horsemen, for such

I was now convinced they must be, continued after Powell with only a brief stop at the hole for water; and always at the same rate of speed as his.

I was positive now that the trailers were Apaches and that they wished to capture Powell alive for the fiendish pleasure of the torture, so I urged my horse onward at a most dangerous pace, hoping against hope that I would catch up with the red rascals before they attacked him.

Further speculation was suddenly cut short by the faint report of two shots far ahead of me. I knew that Powell would need me now if ever, and I instantly urged my horse to his topmost speed up the narrow and difficult mountain trail.

I had forged ahead for perhaps a mile or more without hearing further sounds, when the trail suddenly debouched onto a small, open plateau near the summit of the pass. I had passed through a narrow, overhanging gorge just before entering suddenly upon this table land, and the sight which met my eyes filled me with consternation and dismay.

The little stretch of level land was white with Indian tepees, and there were probably half a thousand red warriors clustered around some object near the center of the camp. Their attention was so wholly riveted to this point of interest that they did not notice me, and I easily could have turned back into the dark recesses of the gorge and made my escape with perfect safety. The fact, however, that this thought did not occur to me until the following day removes any possible right to a claim to heroism to which the narration of this episode might possibly otherwise entitle me.

I do not believe that I am made of the stuff which constitutes heroes, because, in all of the hundreds of instances that my voluntary acts have placed me face to face with death, I cannot recall a single one where any alternative step to that I took occurred to me until many hours later. My mind is evidently so constituted that I am subconsciously forced into the path of duty without recourse to tiresome mental processes. However that may be, I have never regretted that cowardice is not optional with me.

In this instance I was, of course, positive that Powell was the center of attraction, but whether I thought or acted first I do not know, but within an instant from the moment the scene broke upon my view I had whipped out my revolvers and was charging down upon the entire army of warriors, shooting rapidly, and whooping at the top of my lungs. Singlehanded, I could not have pursued better tactics, for the red men, convinced by sudden surprise that not less than a regiment of regulars was upon them, turned and fled in every direction for their bows, arrows, and rifles.

The view which their hurried routing disclosed filled me with apprehension and with rage. Under the clear rays of the Arizona moon lay Powell, his body fairly bristling with the hostile arrows of the braves. That he was already dead I could not but be convinced, and yet I would have saved his body from mutilation at the hands of the Apaches as quickly as I would have saved the man himself from death.

Riding close to him I reached down from the saddle, and grasping his cartridge belt drew him up across the withers of my mount. A backward glance convinced me that to return by the way I had come would be more hazardous than to continue across the plateau, so, putting spurs to my poor beast, I made a dash for the opening to the pass which I could distinguish on the far side of the table land.

The Indians had by this time discovered that I was alone and I was pursued with imprecations, arrows, and rifle balls. The fact that it is difficult to aim anything but imprecations accurately by moonlight, that they were upset by the sudden and unexpected manner of my advent, and that I was a rather rapidly moving target saved me from the various deadly projectiles of the enemy and permitted me to reach the shadows of the surrounding peaks before an orderly pursuit could be organized.

My horse was traveling practically unguided as I knew that I had probably less knowledge of the exact location of the trail to the pass than he, and thus it happened that he entered a defile which led to the summit of the range and not to the pass which I had hoped would carry me to the valley and to safety. It is probable, however, that to this fact I owe my life and the remarkable experiences and adventures which befell me during the following ten years.

My first knowledge that I was on the wrong trail came when I heard the yells of the pursuing savages suddenly grow fainter and fainter far off to my left.

I knew then that they had passed to the left of the jagged rock formation at the edge of the plateau, to the right of which my horse had borne me and the body of Powell.

I drew rein on a little level promontory overlooking the trail below and to my left, and saw the party of pursuing savages disappearing around the point of a neighboring peak.

I knew the Indians would soon discover that they were on the wrong trail and that the search for me would be renewed in the right direction as soon as they located my tracks.

I had gone but a short distance further when what seemed to be an excellent trail opened up around the face of a high cliff. The trail was level and quite broad and led upward and in the general direction I wished to go. The cliff arose for several hundred feet on my right, and on my left was an equal and nearly perpendicular drop to the bottom of a rocky ravine.

I had followed this trail for perhaps a hundred yards when a sharp turn to the right brought me to the mouth of a large cave. The opening was about four feet in height and three to four feet wide, and at this opening the trail ended.

It was now morning, and, with the customary lack of dawn which is a startling characteristic of Arizona, it had become daylight almost without warning.

Dismounting, I laid Powell upon the ground, but the most painstaking examination failed to reveal the faintest spark of life. I forced water from my canteen between his dead lips, bathed his face and rubbed his hands, working over him continuously for the better part of an hour in the face of the fact that I knew him to be dead.

I was very fond of Powell; he was thoroughly a man in every respect; a polished southern gentleman; a staunch and true friend; and it was with a feeling of the deepest grief that I finally gave up my crude endeavors at resuscitation.

Leaving Powell's body where it lay on the ledge I crept into the cave to reconnoiter. I found a large chamber, possibly a hundred feet in diameter and thirty or forty feet in height; a smooth and well-worn floor, and many other evidences that the cave had, at some remote period, been inhabited. The back of the cave was so lost in dense shadow that I could not distinguish whether there were openings into other apartments or not.

As I was continuing my examination I commenced to feel a pleasant drowsiness creeping over me which I attributed to the fatigue of my long and strenuous ride, and the reaction from the excitement of the fight and the pursuit. I felt comparatively safe in my present location as I knew that one man could defend the trail to the cave against an army.

I soon became so drowsy that I could scarcely resist the strong desire to throw myself on the floor of the cave for a few moments' rest, but I knew that this would never do, as it would mean certain death at the hands of my red friends, who might be upon me at any moment. With an effort I started toward the opening of the cave only to reel drunkenly against a side wall, and from there slip prone upon the floor.

II

THE ESCAPE OF THE DEAD

A sense of delicious dreaminess overcame me, my muscles relaxed, and I was on the point of giving way to my desire to sleep when the sound of approaching horses reached my ears. I attempted to spring to my feet but was horrified to discover that my muscles refused to respond to my will. I was now thoroughly awake, but as unable to move a muscle as though turned to stone. It was then, for the first time, that I noticed a slight vapor filling the cave. It was extremely tenuous and only noticeable against the opening which led to daylight. There also came to my nostrils a faintly pungent odor, and I could only assume that I had been overcome by some poisonous gas, but why I should retain my mental faculties and yet be unable to move I could not fathom.

I lay facing the opening of the cave and where I could see the short stretch of trail which lay between the cave and the turn of the cliff around which the trail led. The noise of the approaching horses had ceased, and I judged the Indians were creeping stealthily upon me along the little ledge which led to my living tomb. I remember that I hoped they would make short work of me as I did not particularly relish the thought of the innumerable things they might do to me if the spirit prompted them.

I had not long to wait before a stealthy sound apprised me of their nearness, and then a war-bonneted, paint-streaked face was thrust cautiously around the shoulder of the cliff, and savage eyes looked into mine. That he could see me in the dim light of the cave I was sure for the early morning sun was falling full upon me through the opening.

The fellow, instead of approaching, merely stood and stared; his eyes bulging and his jaw dropped. And then another savage face appeared, and a third and fourth and fifth, craning their necks over the shoulders of their fellows whom they could not pass upon the narrow ledge. Each face was the picture of awe and fear, but for what reason I did not know, nor did I learn until ten years later. That there were still other braves behind those who regarded me was apparent from the fact that the leaders passed back whispered word to those behind them.

Suddenly a low but distinct moaning sound issued from the recesses of the cave behind me, and, as it reached the ears of the Indians, they turned and fled in terror, panic-stricken. So frantic were their efforts to escape from the unseen thing behind me that one of the braves was hurled headlong from the cliff to the rocks below. Their wild cries echoed in the canyon for a short time, and then all was still once more.

The sound which had frightened them was not repeated, but it had been sufficient as it was to start me speculating on the possible horror which lurked in the shadows at my back. Fear is a relative term and so I can only measure my feelings at that time by what I had experienced in previous positions of danger and by those that I have passed through since; but I can say without shame that if the sensations I endured during the next few minutes were fear, then may God help the coward, for cowardice is of a surety its own punishment.

To be held paralyzed, with one's back toward some horrible and unknown danger from the very sound of which the ferocious Apache warriors turn in wild stampede, as a flock of sheep would madly flee from a pack of wolves, seems to me the last word in fearsome predicaments for a man who had ever been used to fighting for his life with all the energy of a powerful physique.

Several times I thought I heard faint sounds behind me as of somebody moving cautiously, but eventually even these ceased, and I was left to the contemplation of my position without interruption. I could but vaguely conjecture the cause of my paralysis, and my only hope lay in that it might pass off as suddenly as it had fallen upon me.

Late in the afternoon my horse, which had been standing with dragging rein before the cave, started slowly down the trail, evidently in search of food and water, and I was left alone with my mysterious unknown companion and the dead body of my friend, which lay just within my range of vision upon the ledge where I had placed it in the early morning.

From then until possibly midnight all was silence, the silence of the dead; then, suddenly, the awful moan of the morning broke upon my startled ears, and there came again from the black shadows the sound of a moving thing, and a faint rustling as of dead leaves. The shock to my already overstrained nervous system was terrible in the extreme, and with a superhuman effort I strove to break my awful bonds. It was an effort of the mind, of the will, of the nerves; not muscular, for I could not move even so much as my little finger, but none the less mighty for all that. And then something gave, there was a momentary feeling of nausea, a sharp click as of the snapping of a steel wire, and I stood with my back against the wall of the cave facing my unknown foe.

And then the moonlight flooded the cave, and there before me lay my own body as it had been lying all these hours, with the eyes staring toward the open ledge and the hands resting limply upon the ground. I looked first at my lifeless clay there upon the floor of the cave and then down at myself in utter bewilderment; for there I lay clothed, and yet here I stood but naked as at the minute of my birth.

The transition had been so sudden and so unexpected that it left me for a moment forgetful of aught else than my strange metamorphosis. My first thought was, is this then death! Have I indeed passed over forever into that other life! But I could not well believe this, as I could feel my heart pounding against my ribs from the exertion of my efforts to release myself from the anaesthesis which had held me. My breath was coming in quick, short gasps, cold sweat stood out from every pore of my body, and the ancient experiment of pinching revealed the fact that I was anything other than a wraith.

Again was I suddenly recalled to my immediate surroundings by a repetition of the weird moan from the depths of the cave. Naked and unarmed as I was, I had no desire to face the unseen thing which menaced me.

My revolvers were strapped to my lifeless body which, for some unfathomable reason, I could not bring myself to touch. My carbine was in its boot, strapped to my saddle, and as my horse had wandered off I was left without means of defense. My only alternative seemed to lie in flight and my decision was crystallized by a recurrence of the rustling sound from the thing which now seemed, in the darkness of the cave and to my distorted imagination, to be creeping stealthily upon me.

Unable longer to resist the temptation to escape this horrible place I leaped quickly through the opening into the starlight of a clear Arizona night. The crisp, fresh mountain air outside the cave acted as an immediate tonic and I felt new life and new courage coursing through me. Pausing upon the brink of the ledge I upbraided myself for what now seemed to me wholly unwarranted apprehension. I reasoned with myself that I had lain helpless for many hours within the cave, yet nothing had molested me, and my better judgment, when permitted the direction of clear and logical reasoning, convinced me that the noises I had heard must have resulted from purely natural and harmless causes; probably the conformation of the cave was such that a slight breeze had caused the sounds I heard.

I decided to investigate, but first I lifted my head to fill my lungs with the pure, invigorating night air of the mountains. As I did so I saw stretching far below me the beautiful vista of rocky gorge, and level, cacti-studded flat, wrought by the moonlight into a miracle of soft splendor and wondrous enchantment.

Few western wonders are more inspiring than the beauties of an Arizona moonlit landscape; the silvered mountains in the distance, the strange lights and shadows upon hog back and arroyo, and the grotesque details of the stiff, yet beautiful cacti form a picture at once enchanting and inspiring; as though one were catching for the first time a glimpse of some dead and forgotten world, so different is it from the aspect of any other spot upon our earth.

As I stood thus meditating, I turned my gaze from the landscape to the heavens where the myriad stars formed a gorgeous and fitting canopy for the wonders of the earthly scene. My attention was quickly riveted by a large red star close to the distant horizon. As I gazed upon it I felt a spell of overpowering fascination—it was Mars, the god of war, and for me, the fighting man, it had always held the power of irresistible enchantment. As I gazed at it on that far-gone night it seemed to call across the unthinkable void, to lure me to it, to draw me as the lodestone attracts a particle of iron.

My longing was beyond the power of opposition; I closed my eyes, stretched out my arms toward the god of my vocation and felt myself drawn with the suddenness of thought through the trackless immensity of space. There was an instant of extreme cold and utter darkness.

III

MY ADVENT ON MARS

I opened my eyes upon a strange and weird landscape. I knew that I was on Mars; not once did I question either my sanity or my wakefulness. I was not asleep, no need for pinching here; my inner consciousness told me as plainly that I was upon Mars as your conscious mind tells you that you are upon Earth. You do not question the fact; neither did I.

I found myself lying prone upon a bed of yellowish, mosslike vegetation which stretched around me in all directions for interminable miles. I seemed to be lying in a deep, circular basin, along the outer verge of which I could distinguish the irregularities of low hills.

It was midday, the sun was shining full upon me and the heat of it was rather intense upon my naked body, yet no greater than would have been true under similar conditions on an Arizona desert. Here and there were slight outcroppings of quartz-bearing rock which glistened in the sunlight; and a little to my left, perhaps a hundred yards, appeared a low, walled enclosure about four feet in height. No water, and no other vegetation than the moss was in evidence, and as I was somewhat thirsty I determined to do a little exploring.

Springing to my feet I received my first Martian surprise, for the effort, which on Earth would have brought me standing upright, carried me into the Martian air to the height of about three yards. I alighted softly upon the ground, however, without appreciable shock or jar. Now commenced a series of evolutions which even then seemed ludicrous in the extreme. I found that I must learn to walk all over again, as the muscular exertion which carried me easily and safely upon Earth played strange antics with me upon Mars.

Instead of progressing in a sane and dignified manner, my attempts to walk resulted in a variety of hops which took me clear of the ground a couple of feet at each step and landed me sprawling upon my face or back at the end of each second or third hop. My muscles, perfectly attuned and accustomed to the force of gravity on Earth, played the mischief with me in attempting for the first time to cope with the lesser gravitation and lower air pressure on Mars.

I was determined, however, to explore the low structure which was the only evidence of habitation in sight, and so I hit upon the unique plan of reverting to first principles in locomotion, creeping. I did fairly well at this and in a few moments had reached the low, encircling wall of the enclosure.

There appeared to be no doors or windows upon the side nearest me, but as the wall was but about four feet high I cautiously gained my feet and peered over the top upon the strangest sight it had ever been given me to see.

The roof of the enclosure was of solid glass about four or five inches in thickness, and beneath this were several hundred large eggs, perfectly round and snowy white. The eggs were nearly uniform in size being about two and one-half feet in diameter.

Five or six had already hatched and the grotesque caricatures which sat blinking in the sunlight were enough to cause me to doubt my sanity. They seemed mostly head, with little scrawny bodies, long necks and six legs, or, as I afterward learned, two legs and two arms, with an intermediary pair of limbs which could be used at will either as arms or legs. Their eyes were set at the extreme sides of their heads a trifle above the center and protruded in such a manner that they could be directed either forward or back and also independently of each other, thus permitting this queer animal to look in any direction, or in two directions at once, without the necessity of turning the head.

The ears, which were slightly above the eyes and closer together, were small, cup-shaped antennae, protruding not more than an inch on these young specimens. Their noses were but longitudinal slits in the center of their faces, midway between their mouths and ears.

There was no hair on their bodies, which were of a very light yellowish-green color. In the adults, as I was to learn quite soon, this color deepens to an olive green and is darker in the male than in the female. Further, the heads of the adults are not so out of proportion to their bodies as in the case of the young.

The iris of the eyes is blood red, as in Albinos, while the pupil is dark. The eyeball itself is very white, as are the teeth. These latter add a most ferocious appearance to an otherwise fearsome and terrible countenance, as the lower tusks curve upward to sharp points which end about where the eyes of earthly human beings are located. The whiteness of the teeth is not that of ivory, but of the snowiest and most gleaming of china. Against the dark background of their olive skins their tusks stand out in a most striking manner, making these weapons present a singularly formidable appearance.

Most of these details I noted later, for I was given but little time to speculate on the wonders of my new discovery. I had seen that the eggs were in the process of hatching, and as I stood watching the hideous little monsters break from their shells I failed to note the approach of a score of full-grown Martians from behind me.

Coming, as they did, over the soft and soundless moss, which covers practically the entire surface of Mars with the exception of the frozen areas at the poles and the scattered cultivated districts, they might have captured me easily, but their intentions were far more sinister. It was the rattling of the accouterments of the foremost warrior which warned me.

On such a little thing my life hung that I often marvel that I escaped so easily. Had not the rifle of the leader of the party swung from its fastenings beside his saddle in such a way as to strike against the butt of his great metal-shod spear I should have snuffed out without ever knowing that death was near me. But the little sound caused me to turn, and there upon me, not ten feet from my breast, was the point of that huge spear, a spear forty feet long, tipped with gleaming metal, and held low at the side of a mounted replica of the little devils I had been watching.

But how puny and harmless they now looked beside this huge and terrific incarnation of hate, of vengeance and of death. The man himself, for such I may call him, was fully fifteen feet in height and, on Earth, would have weighed some four hundred pounds. He sat his mount as we sit a horse, grasping the animal's barrel with his lower limbs, while the hands of his two right arms held his immense spear low at the side of his mount; his two left arms were outstretched laterally to help preserve his balance, the thing he rode having neither bridle or reins of any description for guidance.

And his mount! How can earthly words describe it! It towered ten feet at the shoulder; had four legs on either side; a broad flat tail, larger at the tip than at the root, and which it held straight out behind while running; a gaping mouth which split its head from its snout to its long, massive neck.

Like its master, it was entirely devoid of hair, but was of a dark slate color and exceeding smooth and glossy. Its belly was white, and its legs shaded from the slate of its shoulders and hips to a vivid yellow at the feet. The feet themselves were heavily padded and nailless, which fact had also contributed to the noiselessness of their approach, and, in common with a multiplicity of legs, is a characteristic feature of the fauna of Mars. The highest type of man and one other animal, the only mammal existing on Mars, alone have well-formed nails, and there are absolutely no hoofed animals in existence there.

Behind this first charging demon trailed nineteen others, similar in all respects, but, as I learned later, bearing individual characteristics peculiar to themselves; precisely as no two of us are identical although we are all cast in a similar mold. This picture, or rather materialized nightmare, which I have described at length, made but one terrible and swift impression on me as I turned to meet it.

Unarmed and naked as I was, the first law of nature manifested itself in the only possible solution of my immediate problem, and that was to get out of the vicinity of the point of the charging spear. Consequently I gave a very earthly and at the same time superhuman leap to reach the top of the Martian incubator, for such I had determined it must be.

My effort was crowned with a success which appalled me no less than it seemed to surprise the Martian warriors, for it carried me fully thirty feet into the air and landed me a hundred feet from my pursuers and on the opposite side of the enclosure.

I alighted upon the soft moss easily and without mishap, and turning saw my enemies lined up along the further wall. Some were surveying me with expressions which I afterward discovered marked extreme astonishment, and the others were evidently satisfying themselves that I had not molested their young.

They were conversing together in low tones, and gesticulating and pointing toward me. Their discovery that I had not harmed the little Martians, and that I was unarmed, must have caused them to look upon me with less ferocity; but, as I was to learn later, the thing which weighed most in my favor was my exhibition of hurdling.

While the Martians are immense, their bones are very large and they are muscled only in proportion to the gravitation which they must overcome. The result is that they are infinitely less agile and less powerful, in proportion to their weight, than an Earth man, and I doubt that were one of them suddenly to be transported to Earth he could lift his own weight from the ground; in fact, I am convinced that he could not do so.

My feat then was as marvelous upon Mars as it would have been upon Earth, and from desiring to annihilate me they suddenly looked upon me as a wonderful discovery to be captured and exhibited among their fellows.

The respite my unexpected agility had given me permitted me to formulate plans for the immediate future and to note more closely the appearance of the warriors, for I could not disassociate these people in my mind from those other warriors who, only the day before, had been pursuing me.

I noted that each was armed with several other weapons in addition to the huge spear which I have described. The weapon which caused me to decide against an attempt at escape by flight was what was evidently a rifle of some description, and which I felt, for some reason, they were peculiarly efficient in handling.

These rifles were of a white metal stocked with wood, which I learned later was a very light and intensely hard growth much prized on Mars, and entirely unknown to us denizens of Earth. The metal of the barrel is an alloy composed principally of aluminum and steel which they have learned to temper to a hardness far exceeding that of the steel with which we are familiar. The weight of these rifles is comparatively little, and with the small caliber, explosive, radium projectiles which they use, and the great length of the barrel, they are deadly in the extreme and at ranges which would be unthinkable on Earth. The theoretic effective radius of this rifle is three hundred miles, but the best they can do in actual service when equipped with their wireless finders and sighters is but a trifle over two hundred miles.

This is quite far enough to imbue me with great respect for the Martian firearm, and some telepathic force must have warned me against an attempt to escape in broad daylight from under the muzzles of twenty of these death-dealing machines.

The Martians, after conversing for a short time, turned and rode away in the direction from which they had come, leaving one of their number alone by the enclosure. When they had covered perhaps two hundred yards they halted, and turning their mounts toward us sat watching the warrior by the enclosure.

He was the one whose spear had so nearly transfixed me, and was evidently the leader of the band, as I had noted that they seemed to have moved to their present position at his direction. When his force had come to a halt he dismounted, threw down his spear and small arms, and came around the end of the incubator toward me, entirely unarmed and as naked as I, except for the ornaments strapped upon his head, limbs, and breast.

When he was within about fifty feet of me he unclasped an enormous metal armlet, and holding it toward me in the open palm of his hand, addressed me in a clear, resonant voice, but in a language, it is needless to say, I could not understand. He then stopped as though waiting for my reply, pricking up his antennae-like ears and cocking his strange-looking eyes still further toward me.

As the silence became painful I concluded to hazard a little conversation on my own part, as I had guessed that he was making overtures of peace. The throwing down of his weapons and the withdrawing of his troop before his advance toward me would have signified a peaceful mission anywhere on Earth, so why not, then, on Mars!

Placing my hand over my heart I bowed low to the Martian and explained to him that while I did not understand his language, his actions spoke for the peace and friendship that at the present moment were most dear to my heart. Of course I might have been a babbling brook for all the intelligence my speech carried to him, but he understood the action with which I immediately followed my words.

Stretching my hand toward him, I advanced and took the armlet from his open palm, clasping it about my arm above the elbow; smiled at him and stood waiting. His wide mouth spread into an answering smile, and locking one of his intermediary arms in mine we turned and walked back toward his mount. At the same time he motioned his followers to advance. They started toward us on a wild run, but were checked by a signal from him. Evidently he feared that were I to be really frightened again I might jump entirely out of the landscape.

He exchanged a few words with his men, motioned to me that I would ride behind one of them, and then mounted his own animal. The fellow designated reached down two or three hands and lifted me up behind him on the glossy back of his mount, where I hung on as best I could by the belts and straps which held the Martian's weapons and ornaments.

The entire cavalcade then turned and galloped away toward the range of hills in the distance.

IV

A PRISONER

We had gone perhaps ten miles when the ground began to rise very rapidly. We were, as I was later to learn, nearing the edge of one of Mars' long-dead seas, in the bottom of which my encounter with the Martians had taken place.

In a short time we gained the foot of the mountains, and after traversing a narrow gorge came to an open valley, at the far extremity of which was a low table land upon which I beheld an enormous city. Toward this we galloped, entering it by what appeared to be a ruined roadway leading out from the city, but only to the edge of the table land, where it ended abruptly in a flight of broad steps.

Upon closer observation I saw as we passed them that the buildings were deserted, and while not greatly decayed had the appearance of not having been tenanted for years, possibly for ages. Toward the center of the city was a large plaza, and upon this and in the buildings immediately surrounding it were camped some nine or ten hundred creatures of the same breed as my captors, for such I now considered them despite the suave manner in which I had been trapped.

With the exception of their ornaments all were naked. The women varied in appearance but little from the men, except that their tusks were much larger in proportion to their height, in some instances curving nearly to their high-set ears. Their bodies were smaller and lighter in color, and their fingers and toes bore the rudiments of nails, which were entirely lacking among the males. The adult females ranged in height from ten to twelve feet.

The children were light in color, even lighter than the women, and all looked precisely alike to me, except that some were taller than others; older, I presumed.

I saw no signs of extreme age among them, nor is there any appreciable difference in their appearance from the age of maturity, about forty, until, at about the age of one thousand years, they go voluntarily upon their last strange pilgrimage down the river Iss, which leads no living Martian knows whither and from whose bosom no Martian has ever returned, or would be allowed to live did he return after once embarking upon its cold, dark waters.

Only about one Martian in a thousand dies of sickness or disease, and possibly about twenty take the voluntary pilgrimage. The other nine hundred and seventy-nine die violent deaths in duels, in hunting, in aviation and in war; but perhaps by far the greatest death loss comes during the age of childhood, when vast numbers of the little Martians fall victims to the great white apes of Mars.

The average life expectancy of a Martian after the age of maturity is about three hundred years, but would be nearer the one-thousand mark were it not for the various means leading to violent death. Owing to the waning resources of the planet it evidently became necessary to counteract the increasing longevity which their remarkable skill in therapeutics and surgery produced, and so human life has come to be considered but lightly on Mars, as is evidenced by their dangerous sports and the almost continual warfare between the various communities.

There are other and natural causes tending toward a diminution of population, but nothing contributes so greatly to this end as the fact that no male or female Martian is ever voluntarily without a weapon of destruction.

As we neared the plaza and my presence was discovered we were immediately surrounded by hundreds of the creatures who seemed anxious to pluck me from my seat behind my guard. A word from the leader of the party stilled their clamor, and we proceeded at a trot across the plaza to the entrance of as magnificent an edifice as mortal eye has rested upon.

The building was low, but covered an enormous area. It was constructed of gleaming white marble inlaid with gold and brilliant stones which sparkled and scintillated in the sunlight. The main entrance was some hundred feet in width and projected from the building proper to form a huge canopy above the entrance hall. There was no stairway, but a gentle incline to the first floor of the building opened into an enormous chamber encircled by galleries.

On the floor of this chamber, which was dotted with highly carved wooden desks and chairs, were assembled about forty or fifty male Martians around the steps of a rostrum. On the platform proper squatted an enormous warrior heavily loaded with metal ornaments, gay-colored feathers and beautifully wrought leather trappings ingeniously set with precious stones. From his shoulders depended a short cape of white fur lined with brilliant scarlet silk.

What struck me as most remarkable about this assemblage and the hall in which they were congregated was the fact that the creatures were entirely out of proportion to the desks, chairs, and other furnishings; these being of a size adapted to human beings such as I, whereas the great bulks of the Martians could scarcely have squeezed into the chairs, nor was there room beneath the desks for their long legs. Evidently, then, there were other denizens on Mars than the wild and grotesque creatures into whose hands I had fallen, but the evidences of extreme antiquity which showed all around me indicated that these buildings might have belonged to some long-extinct and forgotten race in the dim antiquity of Mars.

Our party had halted at the entrance to the building, and at a sign from the leader I had been lowered to the ground. Again locking his arm in mine, we had proceeded into the audience chamber. There were few formalities observed in approaching the Martian chieftain. My captor merely strode up to the rostrum, the others making way for him as he advanced. The chieftain rose to his feet and uttered the name of my escort who, in turn, halted and repeated the name of the ruler followed by his title.

At the time, this ceremony and the words they uttered meant nothing to me, but later I came to know that this was the customary greeting between green Martians. Had the men been strangers, and therefore unable to exchange names, they would have silently exchanged ornaments, had their missions been peaceful—otherwise they would have exchanged shots, or have fought out their introduction with some other of their various weapons.

My captor, whose name was Tars Tarkas, was virtually the vice-chieftain of the community, and a man of great ability as a statesman and warrior. He evidently explained briefly the incidents connected with his expedition, including my capture, and when he had concluded the chieftain addressed me at some length.

I replied in our good old English tongue merely to convince him that neither of us could understand the other; but I noticed that when I smiled slightly on concluding, he did likewise. This fact, and the similar occurrence during my first talk with Tars Tarkas, convinced me that we had at least something in common; the ability to smile, therefore to laugh; denoting a sense of humor. But I was to learn that the Martian smile is merely perfunctory, and that the Martian laugh is a thing to cause strong men to blanch in horror.

The ideas of humor among the green men of Mars are widely at variance with our conceptions of incitants to merriment. The death agonies of a fellow being are, to these strange creatures, provocative of the wildest hilarity, while their chief form of commonest amusement is to inflict death on their prisoners of war in various ingenious and horrible ways.

The assembled warriors and chieftains examined me closely, feeling my muscles and the texture of my skin. The principal chieftain then evidently signified a desire to see me perform, and, motioning me to follow, he started with Tars Tarkas for the open plaza.

Now, I had made no attempt to walk, since my first signal failure, except while tightly grasping Tars Tarkas' arm, and so now I went skipping and flitting about among the desks and chairs like some monstrous grasshopper. After bruising myself severely, much to the amusement of the Martians, I again had recourse to creeping, but this did not suit them and I was roughly jerked to my feet by a towering fellow who had laughed most heartily at my misfortunes.

As he banged me down upon my feet his face was bent close to mine and I did the only thing a gentleman might do under the circumstances of brutality, boorishness, and lack of consideration for a stranger's rights; I swung my fist squarely to his jaw and he went down like a felled ox. As he sunk to the floor I wheeled around with my back toward the nearest desk, expecting to be overwhelmed by the vengeance of his fellows, but determined to give them as good a battle as the unequal odds would permit before I gave up my life.

My fears were groundless, however, as the other Martians, at first struck dumb with wonderment, finally broke into wild peals of laughter and applause. I did not recognize the applause as such, but later, when I had become acquainted with their customs, I learned that I had won what they seldom accord, a manifestation of approbation.

The fellow whom I had struck lay where he had fallen, nor did any of his mates approach him. Tars Tarkas advanced toward me, holding out one of his arms, and we thus proceeded to the plaza without further mishap. I did not, of course, know the reason for which we had come to the open, but I was not long in being enlightened. They first repeated the word "sak" a number of times, and then Tars Tarkas made several jumps, repeating the same word before each leap; then, turning to me, he said, "sak!" I saw what they were after, and gathering myself together I "sakked" with such marvelous success that I cleared a good hundred and fifty feet; nor did I, this time, lose my equilibrium, but landed squarely upon my feet without falling. I then returned by easy jumps of twenty-five or thirty feet to the little group of warriors.

My exhibition had been witnessed by several hundred lesser Martians, and they immediately broke into demands for a repetition, which the chieftain then ordered me to make; but I was both hungry and thirsty, and determined on the spot that my only method of salvation was to demand the consideration from these creatures which they evidently would not voluntarily accord. I therefore ignored the repeated commands to "sak," and each time they were made I motioned to my mouth and rubbed my stomach.

Tars Tarkas and the chief exchanged a few words, and the former, calling to a young female among the throng, gave her some instructions and motioned me to accompany her. I grasped her proffered arm and together we crossed the plaza toward a large building on the far side.

My fair companion was about eight feet tall, having just arrived at maturity, but not yet to her full height. She was of a light olive-green color, with a smooth, glossy hide. Her name, as I afterward learned, was Sola, and she belonged to the retinue of Tars Tarkas. She conducted me to a spacious chamber in one of the buildings fronting on the plaza, and which, from the litter of silks and furs upon the floor, I took to be the sleeping quarters of several of the natives.

The room was well lighted by a number of large windows and was beautifully decorated with mural paintings and mosaics, but upon all there seemed to rest that indefinable touch of the finger of antiquity which convinced me that the architects and builders of these wondrous creations had nothing in common with the crude half-brutes which now occupied them.

Sola motioned me to be seated upon a pile of silks near the center of the room, and, turning, made a peculiar hissing sound, as though signaling to someone in an adjoining room. In response to her call I obtained my first sight of a new Martian wonder. It waddled in on its ten short legs, and squatted down before the girl like an obedient puppy. The thing was about the size of a Shetland pony, but its head bore a slight resemblance to that of a frog, except that the jaws were equipped with three rows of long, sharp tusks.

V

I ELUDE MY WATCH DOG

Sola stared into the brute's wicked-looking eyes, muttered a word or two of command, pointed to me, and left the chamber. I could not but wonder what this ferocious-looking monstrosity might do when left alone in such close proximity to such a relatively tender morsel of meat; but my fears were groundless, as the beast, after surveying me intently for a moment, crossed the room to the only exit which led to the street, and lay down full length across the threshold.

This was my first experience with a Martian watch dog, but it was destined not to be my last, for this fellow guarded me carefully during the time I remained a captive among these green men; twice saving my life, and never voluntarily being away from me a moment.

While Sola was away I took occasion to examine more minutely the room in which I found myself captive. The mural painting depicted scenes of rare and wonderful beauty; mountains, rivers, lake, ocean, meadow, trees and flowers, winding roadways, sun-kissed gardens—scenes which might have portrayed earthly views but for the different colorings of the vegetation. The work had evidently been wrought by a master hand, so subtle the atmosphere, so perfect the technique; yet nowhere was there a representation of a living animal, either human or brute, by which I could guess at the likeness of these other and perhaps extinct denizens of Mars.

While I was allowing my fancy to run riot in wild conjecture on the possible explanation of the strange anomalies which I had so far met with on Mars, Sola returned bearing both food and drink. These she placed on the floor beside me, and seating herself a short ways off regarded me intently. The food consisted of about a pound of some solid substance of the consistency of cheese and almost tasteless, while the liquid was apparently milk from some animal. It was not unpleasant to the taste, though slightly acid, and I learned in a short time to prize it very highly. It came, as I later discovered, not from an animal, as there is only one mammal on Mars and that one very rare indeed, but from a large plant which grows practically without water, but seems to distill its plentiful supply of milk from the products of the soil, the moisture of the air, and the rays of the sun. A single plant of this species will give eight or ten quarts of milk per day.

After I had eaten I was greatly invigorated, but feeling the need of rest I stretched out upon the silks and was soon asleep. I must have slept several hours, as it was dark when I awoke, and I was very cold. I noticed that someone had thrown a fur over me, but it had become partially dislodged and in the darkness I could not see to replace it. Suddenly a hand reached out and pulled the fur over me, shortly afterwards adding another to my covering.

I presumed that my watchful guardian was Sola, nor was I wrong. This girl alone, among all the green Martians with whom I came in contact, disclosed characteristics of sympathy, kindliness, and affection; her ministrations to my bodily wants were unfailing, and her solicitous care saved me from much suffering and many hardships.

As I was to learn, the Martian nights are extremely cold, and as there is practically no twilight or dawn, the changes in temperature are sudden and most uncomfortable, as are the transitions from brilliant daylight to darkness. The nights are either brilliantly illumined or very dark, for if neither of the two moons of Mars happen to be in the sky almost total darkness results, since the lack of atmosphere, or, rather, the very thin atmosphere, fails to diffuse the starlight to any great extent; on the other hand, if both of the moons are in the heavens at night the surface of the ground is brightly illuminated.

Both of Mars' moons are vastly nearer her than is our moon to Earth; the nearer moon being but about five thousand miles distant, while the further is but little more than fourteen thousand miles away, against the nearly one-quarter million miles which separate us from our moon. The nearer moon of Mars makes a complete revolution around the planet in a little over seven and one-half hours, so that she may be seen hurtling through the sky like some huge meteor two or three times each night, revealing all her phases during each transit of the heavens.

The further moon revolves about Mars in something over thirty and one-quarter hours, and with her sister satellite makes a nocturnal Martian scene one of splendid and weird grandeur. And it is well that nature has so graciously and abundantly lighted the Martian night, for the green men of Mars, being a nomadic race without high intellectual development, have but crude means for artificial lighting; depending principally upon torches, a kind of candle, and a peculiar oil lamp which generates a gas and burns without a wick.

This last device produces an intensely brilliant far-reaching white light, but as the natural oil which it requires can only be obtained by mining in one of several widely separated and remote localities it is seldom used by these creatures whose only thought is for today, and whose hatred for manual labor has kept them in a semi-barbaric state for countless ages.

After Sola had replenished my coverings I again slept, nor did I awaken until daylight. The other occupants of the room, five in number, were all females, and they were still sleeping, piled high with a motley array of silks and furs. Across the threshold lay stretched the sleepless guardian brute, just as I had last seen him on the preceding day; apparently he had not moved a muscle; his eyes were fairly glued upon me, and I fell to wondering just what might befall me should I endeavor to escape.

I have ever been prone to seek adventure and to investigate and experiment where wiser men would have left well enough alone. It therefore now occurred to me that the surest way of learning the exact attitude of this beast toward me would be to attempt to leave the room. I felt fairly secure in my belief that I could escape him should he pursue me once I was outside the building, for I had begun to take great pride in my ability as a jumper. Furthermore, I could see from the shortness of his legs that the brute himself was no jumper and probably no runner.

Slowly and carefully, therefore, I gained my feet, only to see that my watcher did the same; cautiously I advanced toward him, finding that by moving with a shuffling gait I could retain my balance as well as make reasonably rapid progress. As I neared the brute he backed cautiously away from me, and when I had reached the open he moved to one side to let me pass. He then fell in behind me and followed about ten paces in my rear as I made my way along the deserted street.

Evidently his mission was to protect me only, I thought, but when we reached the edge of the city he suddenly sprang before me, uttering strange sounds and baring his ugly and ferocious tusks. Thinking to have some amusement at his expense, I rushed toward him, and when almost upon him sprang into the air, alighting far beyond him and away from the city. He wheeled instantly and charged me with the most appalling speed I had ever beheld. I had thought his short legs a bar to swiftness, but had he been coursing with greyhounds the latter would have appeared as though asleep on a door mat. As I was to learn, this is the fleetest animal on Mars, and owing to its intelligence, loyalty, and ferocity is used in hunting, in war, and as the protector of the Martian man.

I quickly saw that I would have difficulty in escaping the fangs of the beast on a straightaway course, and so I met his charge by doubling in my tracks and leaping over him as he was almost upon me. This maneuver gave me a considerable advantage, and I was able to reach the city quite a bit ahead of him, and as he came tearing after me I jumped for a window about thirty feet from the ground in the face of one of the buildings overlooking the valley.

Grasping the sill I pulled myself up to a sitting posture without looking into the building, and gazed down at the baffled animal beneath me. My exultation was short-lived, however, for scarcely had I gained a secure seat upon the sill than a huge hand grasped me by the neck from behind and dragged me violently into the room. Here I was thrown upon my back, and beheld standing over me a colossal ape-like creature, white and hairless except for an enormous shock of bristly hair upon its head.

VI

A FIGHT THAT WON FRIENDS

The thing, which more nearly resembled our earthly men than it did the Martians I had seen, held me pinioned to the ground with one huge foot, while it jabbered and gesticulated at some answering creature behind me. This other, which was evidently its mate, soon came toward us, bearing a mighty stone cudgel with which it evidently intended to brain me.

The creatures were about ten or fifteen feet tall, standing erect, and had, like the green Martians, an intermediary set of arms or legs, midway between their upper and lower limbs. Their eyes were close together and non-protruding; their ears were high set, but more laterally located than those of the Martians, while their snouts and teeth were strikingly like those of our African gorilla. Altogether they were not unlovely when viewed in comparison with the green Martians.

The cudgel was swinging in the arc which ended upon my upturned face when a bolt of myriad-legged horror hurled itself through the doorway full upon the breast of my executioner. With a shriek of fear the ape which held me leaped through the open window, but its mate closed in a terrific death struggle with my preserver, which was nothing less than my faithful watch-thing; I cannot bring myself to call so hideous a creature a dog.

As quickly as possible I gained my feet and backing against the wall I witnessed such a battle as it is vouchsafed few beings to see. The strength, agility, and blind ferocity of these two creatures is approached by nothing known to earthly man. My beast had an advantage in his first hold, having sunk his mighty fangs far into the breast of his adversary; but the great arms and paws of the ape, backed by muscles far transcending those of the Martian men I had seen, had locked the throat of my guardian and slowly were choking out his life, and bending back his head and neck upon his body, where I momentarily expected the former to fall limp at the end of a broken neck.

In accomplishing this the ape was tearing away the entire front of its breast, which was held in the vise-like grip of the powerful jaws. Back and forth upon the floor they rolled, neither one emitting a sound of fear or pain. Presently I saw the great eyes of my beast bulging completely from their sockets and blood flowing from its nostrils. That he was weakening perceptibly was evident, but so also was the ape, whose struggles were growing momentarily less.

Suddenly I came to myself and, with that strange instinct which seems ever to prompt me to my duty, I seized the cudgel, which had fallen to the floor at the commencement of the battle, and swinging it with all the power of my earthly arms I crashed it full upon the head of the ape, crushing his skull as though it had been an eggshell.

Scarcely had the blow descended when I was confronted with a new danger. The ape's mate, recovered from its first shock of terror, had returned to the scene of the encounter by way of the interior of the building. I glimpsed him just before he reached the doorway and the sight of him, now roaring as he perceived his lifeless fellow stretched upon the floor, and frothing at the mouth, in the extremity of his rage, filled me, I must confess, with dire forebodings.

I am ever willing to stand and fight when the odds are not too overwhelmingly against me, but in this instance I perceived neither glory nor profit in pitting my relatively puny strength against the iron muscles and brutal ferocity of this enraged denizen of an unknown world; in fact, the only outcome of such an encounter, so far as I might be concerned, seemed sudden death.

I was standing near the window and I knew that once in the street I might gain the plaza and safety before the creature could overtake me; at least there was a chance for safety in flight, against almost certain death should I remain and fight however desperately.

It is true I held the cudgel, but what could I do with it against his four great arms? Even should I break one of them with my first blow, for I figured that he would attempt to ward off the cudgel, he could reach out and annihilate me with the others before I could recover for a second attack.

In the instant that these thoughts passed through my mind I had turned to make for the window, but my eyes alighting on the form of my erstwhile guardian threw all thoughts of flight to the four winds. He lay gasping upon the floor of the chamber, his great eyes fastened upon me in what seemed a pitiful appeal for protection. I could not withstand that look, nor could I, on second thought, have deserted my rescuer without giving as good an account of myself in his behalf as he had in mine.

Without more ado, therefore, I turned to meet the charge of the infuriated bull ape. He was now too close upon me for the cudgel to prove of any effective assistance, so I merely threw it as heavily as I could at his advancing bulk. It struck him just below the knees, eliciting a howl of pain and rage, and so throwing him off his balance that he lunged full upon me with arms wide stretched to ease his fall.

Again, as on the preceding day, I had recourse to earthly tactics, and swinging my right fist full upon the point of his chin I followed it with a smashing left to the pit of his stomach. The effect was marvelous, for, as I lightly sidestepped, after delivering the second blow, he reeled and fell upon the floor doubled up with pain and gasping for wind. Leaping over his prostrate body, I seized the cudgel and finished the monster before he could regain his feet.

As I delivered the blow a low laugh rang out behind me, and, turning, I beheld Tars Tarkas, Sola, and three or four warriors standing in the doorway of the chamber. As my eyes met theirs I was, for the second time, the recipient of their zealously guarded applause.

My absence had been noted by Sola on her awakening, and she had quickly informed Tars Tarkas, who had set out immediately with a handful of warriors to search for me. As they had approached the limits of the city they had witnessed the actions of the bull ape as he bolted into the building, frothing with rage.

They had followed immediately behind him, thinking it barely possible that his actions might prove a clew to my whereabouts and had witnessed my short but decisive battle with him. This encounter, together with my set-to with the Martian warrior on the previous day and my feats of jumping placed me upon a high pinnacle in their regard. Evidently devoid of all the finer sentiments of friendship, love, or affection, these people fairly worship physical prowess and bravery, and nothing is too good for the object of their adoration as long as he maintains his position by repeated examples of his skill, strength, and courage.

Sola, who had accompanied the searching party of her own volition, was the only one of the Martians whose face had not been twisted in laughter as I battled for my life. She, on the contrary, was sober with apparent solicitude and, as soon as I had finished the monster, rushed to me and carefully examined my body for possible wounds or injuries. Satisfying herself that I had come off unscathed she smiled quietly, and, taking my hand, started toward the door of the chamber.

Tars Tarkas and the other warriors had entered and were standing over the now rapidly reviving brute which had saved my life, and whose life I, in turn, had rescued. They seemed to be deep in argument, and finally one of them addressed me, but remembering my ignorance of his language turned back to Tars Tarkas, who, with a word and gesture, gave some command to the fellow and turned to follow us from the room.

There seemed something menacing in their attitude toward my beast, and I hesitated to leave until I had learned the outcome. It was well I did so, for the warrior drew an evil looking pistol from its holster and was on the point of putting an end to the creature when I sprang forward and struck up his arm. The bullet striking the wooden casing of the window exploded, blowing a hole completely through the wood and masonry.

I then knelt down beside the fearsome-looking thing, and raising it to its feet motioned for it to follow me. The looks of surprise which my actions elicited from the Martians were ludicrous; they could not understand, except in a feeble and childish way, such attributes as gratitude and compassion. The warrior whose gun I had struck up looked enquiringly at Tars Tarkas, but the latter signed that I be left to my own devices, and so we returned to the plaza with my great beast following close at heel, and Sola grasping me tightly by the arm.

I had at least two friends on Mars; a young woman who watched over me with motherly solicitude, and a dumb brute which, as I later came to know, held in its poor ugly carcass more love, more loyalty, more gratitude than could have been found in the entire five million green Martians who rove the deserted cities and dead sea bottoms of Mars.

VII

CHILD-RAISING ON MARS

After a breakfast, which was an exact replica of the meal of the preceding day and an index of practically every meal which followed while I was with the green men of Mars, Sola escorted me to the plaza, where I found the entire community engaged in watching or helping at the harnessing of huge mastodonian animals to great three-wheeled chariots. There were about two hundred and fifty of these vehicles, each drawn by a single animal, any one of which, from their appearance, might easily have drawn the entire wagon train when fully loaded.

The chariots themselves were large, commodious, and gorgeously decorated. In each was seated a female Martian loaded with ornaments of metal, with jewels and silks and furs, and upon the back of each of the beasts which drew the chariots was perched a young Martian driver. Like the animals upon which the warriors were mounted, the heavier draft animals wore neither bit nor bridle, but were guided entirely by telepathic means.

This power is wonderfully developed in all Martians, and accounts largely for the simplicity of their language and the relatively few spoken words exchanged even in long conversations. It is the universal language of Mars, through the medium of which the higher and lower animals of this world of paradoxes are able to communicate to a greater or less extent, depending upon the intellectual sphere of the species and the development of the individual.

As the cavalcade took up the line of march in single file, Sola dragged me into an empty chariot and we proceeded with the procession toward the point by which I had entered the city the day before. At the head of the caravan rode some two hundred warriors, five abreast, and a like number brought up the rear, while twenty-five or thirty outriders flanked us on either side.

Every one but myself—men, women, and children—were heavily armed, and at the tail of each chariot trotted a Martian hound, my own beast following closely behind ours; in fact, the faithful creature never left me voluntarily during the entire ten years I spent on Mars. Our way led out across the little valley before the city, through the hills, and down into the dead sea bottom which I had traversed on my journey from the incubator to the plaza. The incubator, as it proved, was the terminal point of our journey this day, and, as the entire cavalcade broke into a mad gallop as soon as we reached the level expanse of sea bottom, we were soon within sight of our goal.

On reaching it the chariots were parked with military precision on the four sides of the enclosure, and half a score of warriors, headed by the enormous chieftain, and including Tars Tarkas and several other lesser chiefs, dismounted and advanced toward it. I could see Tars Tarkas explaining something to the principal chieftain, whose name, by the way, was, as nearly as I can translate it into English, Lorquas Ptomel, Jed; jed being his title.

I was soon appraised of the subject of their conversation, as, calling to Sola, Tars Tarkas signed for her to send me to him. I had by this time mastered the intricacies of walking under Martian conditions, and quickly responding to his command I advanced to the side of the incubator where the warriors stood.

As I reached their side a glance showed me that all but a very few eggs had hatched, the incubator being fairly alive with the hideous little devils. They ranged in height from three to four feet, and were moving restlessly about the enclosure as though searching for food.

As I came to a halt before him, Tars Tarkas pointed over the incubator and said, "Sak." I saw that he wanted me to repeat my performance of yesterday for the edification of Lorquas Ptomel, and, as I must confess that my prowess gave me no little satisfaction, I responded quickly, leaping entirely over the parked chariots on the far side of the incubator. As I returned, Lorquas Ptomel grunted something at me, and turning to his warriors gave a few words of command relative to the incubator. They paid no further attention to me and I was thus permitted to remain close and watch their operations, which consisted in breaking an opening in the wall of the incubator large enough to permit of the exit of the young Martians.

On either side of this opening the women and the younger Martians, both male and female, formed two solid walls leading out through the chariots and quite away into the plain beyond. Between these walls the little Martians scampered, wild as deer; being permitted to run the full length of the aisle, where they were captured one at a time by the women and older children; the last in the line capturing the first little one to reach the end of the gauntlet, her opposite in the line capturing the second, and so on until all the little fellows had left the enclosure and been appropriated by some youth or female. As the women caught the young they fell out of line and returned to their respective chariots, while those who fell into the hands of the young men were later turned over to some of the women.

I saw that the ceremony, if it could be dignified by such a name, was over, and seeking out Sola I found her in our chariot with a hideous little creature held tightly in her arms.

The work of rearing young, green Martians consists solely in teaching them to talk, and to use the weapons of warfare with which they are loaded down from the very first year of their lives. Coming from eggs in which they have lain for five years, the period of incubation, they step forth into the world perfectly developed except in size. Entirely unknown to their mothers, who, in turn, would have difficulty in pointing out the fathers with any degree of accuracy, they are the common children of the community, and their education devolves upon the females who chance to capture them as they leave the incubator.

Their foster mothers may not even have had an egg in the incubator, as was the case with Sola, who had not commenced to lay, until less than a year before she became the mother of another woman's offspring. But this counts for little among the green Martians, as parental and filial love is as unknown to them as it is common among us. I believe this horrible system which has been carried on for ages is the direct cause of the loss of all the finer feelings and higher humanitarian instincts among these poor creatures. From birth they know no father or mother love, they know not the meaning of the word home; they are taught that they are only suffered to live until they can demonstrate by their physique and ferocity that they are fit to live. Should they prove deformed or defective in any way they are promptly shot; nor do they see a tear shed for a single one of the many cruel hardships they pass through from earliest infancy.

I do not mean that the adult Martians are unnecessarily or intentionally cruel to the young, but theirs is a hard and pitiless struggle for existence upon a dying planet, the natural resources of which have dwindled to a point where the support of each additional life means an added tax upon the community into which it is thrown.

By careful selection they rear only the hardiest specimens of each species, and with almost supernatural foresight they regulate the birth rate to merely offset the loss by death.

Each adult Martian female brings forth about thirteen eggs each year, and those which meet the size, weight, and specific gravity tests are hidden in the recesses of some subterranean vault where the temperature is too low for incubation. Every year these eggs are carefully examined by a council of twenty chieftains, and all but about one hundred of the most perfect are destroyed out of each yearly supply. At the end of five years about five hundred almost perfect eggs have been chosen from the thousands brought forth. These are then placed in the almost air-tight incubators to be hatched by the sun's rays after a period of another five years. The hatching which we had witnessed today was a fairly representative event of its kind, all but about one per cent of the eggs hatching in two days. If the remaining eggs ever hatched we knew nothing of the fate of the little Martians. They were not wanted, as their offspring might inherit and transmit the tendency to prolonged incubation, and thus upset the system which has maintained for ages and which permits the adult Martians to figure the proper time for return to the incubators, almost to an hour.

The incubators are built in remote fastnesses, where there is little or no likelihood of their being discovered by other tribes. The result of such a catastrophe would mean no children in the community for another five years. I was later to witness the results of the discovery of an alien incubator.

The community of which the green Martians with whom my lot was cast formed a part was composed of some thirty thousand souls. They roamed an enormous tract of arid and semi-arid land between forty and eighty degrees south latitude, and bounded on the east and west by two large fertile tracts. Their headquarters lay in the southwest corner of this district, near the crossing of two of the so-called Martian canals.

As the incubator had been placed far north of their own territory in a supposedly uninhabited and unfrequented area, we had before us a tremendous journey, concerning which I, of course, knew nothing.

After our return to the dead city I passed several days in comparative idleness. On the day following our return all the warriors had ridden forth early in the morning and had not returned until just before darkness fell. As I later learned, they had been to the subterranean vaults in which the eggs were kept and had transported them to the incubator, which they had then walled up for another five years, and which, in all probability, would not be visited again during that period.

The vaults which hid the eggs until they were ready for the incubator were located many miles south of the incubator, and would be visited yearly by the council of twenty chieftains. Why they did not arrange to build their vaults and incubators nearer home has always been a mystery to me, and, like many other Martian mysteries, unsolved and unsolvable by earthly reasoning and customs.

Sola's duties were now doubled, as she was compelled to care for the young Martian as well as for me, but neither one of us required much attention, and as we were both about equally advanced in Martian education, Sola took it upon herself to train us together.

Her prize consisted in a male about four feet tall, very strong and physically perfect; also, he learned quickly, and we had considerable amusement, at least I did, over the keen rivalry we displayed. The Martian language, as I have said, is extremely simple, and in a week I could make all my wants known and understand nearly everything that was said to me. Likewise, under Sola's tutelage, I developed my telepathic powers so that I shortly could sense practically everything that went on around me.

What surprised Sola most in me was that while I could catch telepathic messages easily from others, and often when they were not intended for me, no one could read a jot from my mind under any circumstances. At first this vexed me, but later I was very glad of it, as it gave me an undoubted advantage over the Martians.

VIII

A FAIR CAPTIVE FROM THE SKY

The third day after the incubator ceremony we set forth toward home, but scarcely had the head of the procession debouched into the open ground before the city than orders were given for an immediate and hasty return. As though trained for years in this particular evolution, the green Martians melted like mist into the spacious doorways of the nearby buildings, until, in less than three minutes, the entire cavalcade of chariots, mastodons and mounted warriors was nowhere to be seen.

Sola and I had entered a building upon the front of the city, in fact, the same one in which I had had my encounter with the apes, and, wishing to see what had caused the sudden retreat, I mounted to an upper floor and peered from the window out over the valley and the hills beyond; and there I saw the cause of their sudden scurrying to cover. A huge craft, long, low, and gray-painted, swung slowly over the crest of the nearest hill. Following it came another, and another, and another, until twenty of them, swinging low above the ground, sailed slowly and majestically toward us.

Each carried a strange banner swung from stem to stern above the upper works, and upon the prow of each was painted some odd device that gleamed in the sunlight and showed plainly even at the distance at which we were from the vessels. I could see figures crowding the forward decks and upper works of the air craft. Whether they had discovered us or simply were looking at the deserted city I could not say, but in any event they received a rude reception, for suddenly and without warning the green Martian warriors fired a terrific volley from the windows of the buildings facing the little valley across which the great ships were so peacefully advancing.

Instantly the scene changed as by magic; the foremost vessel swung broadside toward us, and bringing her guns into play returned our fire, at the same time moving parallel to our front for a short distance and then turning back with the evident intention of completing a great circle which would bring her up to position once more opposite our firing line; the other vessels followed in her wake, each one opening upon us as she swung into position. Our own fire never diminished, and I doubt if twenty-five per cent of our shots went wild. It had never been given me to see such deadly accuracy of aim, and it seemed as though a little figure on one of the craft dropped at the explosion of each bullet, while the banners and upper works dissolved in spurts of flame as the irresistible projectiles of our warriors mowed through them.

The fire from the vessels was most ineffectual, owing, as I afterward learned, to the unexpected suddenness of the first volley, which caught the ship's crews entirely unprepared and the sighting apparatus of the guns unprotected from the deadly aim of our warriors.

It seems that each green warrior has certain objective points for his fire under relatively identical circumstances of warfare. For example, a proportion of them, always the best marksmen, direct their fire entirely upon the wireless finding and sighting apparatus of the big guns of an attacking naval force; another detail attends to the smaller guns in the same way; others pick off the gunners; still others the officers; while certain other quotas concentrate their attention upon the other members of the crew, upon the upper works, and upon the steering gear and propellers.

Twenty minutes after the first volley the great fleet swung trailing off in the direction from which it had first appeared. Several of the craft were limping perceptibly, and seemed but barely under the control of their depleted crews. Their fire had ceased entirely and all their energies seemed focused upon escape. Our warriors then rushed up to the roofs of the buildings which we occupied and followed the retreating armada with a continuous fusillade of deadly fire.

One by one, however, the ships managed to dip below the crests of the outlying hills until only one barely moving craft was in sight. This had received the brunt of our fire and seemed to be entirely unmanned, as not a moving figure was visible upon her decks. Slowly she swung from her course, circling back toward us in an erratic and pitiful manner. Instantly the warriors ceased firing, for it was quite apparent that the vessel was entirely helpless, and, far from being in a position to inflict harm upon us, she could not even control herself sufficiently to escape.

As she neared the city the warriors rushed out upon the plain to meet her, but it was evident that she still was too high for them to hope to reach her decks. From my vantage point in the window I could see the bodies of her crew strewn about, although I could not make out what manner of creatures they might be. Not a sign of life was manifest upon her as she drifted slowly with the light breeze in a southeasterly direction.

She was drifting some fifty feet above the ground, followed by all but some hundred of the warriors who had been ordered back to the roofs to cover the possibility of a return of the fleet, or of reinforcements. It soon became evident that she would strike the face of the buildings about a mile south of our position, and as I watched the progress of the chase I saw a number of warriors gallop ahead, dismount and enter the building she seemed destined to touch.

As the craft neared the building, and just before she struck, the Martian warriors swarmed upon her from the windows, and with their great spears eased the shock of the collision, and in a few moments they had thrown out grappling hooks and the big boat was being hauled to ground by their fellows below.

After making her fast, they swarmed the sides and searched the vessel from stem to stern. I could see them examining the dead sailors, evidently for signs of life, and presently a party of them appeared from below dragging a little figure among them. The creature was considerably less than half as tall as the green Martian warriors, and from my balcony I could see that it walked erect upon two legs and surmised that it was some new and strange Martian monstrosity with which I had not as yet become acquainted.

They removed their prisoner to the ground and then commenced a systematic rifling of the vessel. This operation required several hours, during which time a number of the chariots were requisitioned to transport the loot, which consisted in arms, ammunition, silks, furs, jewels, strangely carved stone vessels, and a quantity of solid foods and liquids, including many casks of water, the first I had seen since my advent upon Mars.

After the last load had been removed the warriors made lines fast to the craft and towed her far out into the valley in a southwesterly direction. A few of them then boarded her and were busily engaged in what appeared, from my distant position, as the emptying of the contents of various carboys upon the dead bodies of the sailors and over the decks and works of the vessel.

This operation concluded, they hastily clambered over her sides, sliding down the guy ropes to the ground. The last warrior to leave the deck turned and threw something back upon the vessel, waiting an instant to note the outcome of his act. As a faint spurt of flame rose from the point where the missile struck he swung over the side and was quickly upon the ground. Scarcely had he alighted than the guy ropes were simultaneously released, and the great warship, lightened by the removal of the loot, soared majestically into the air, her decks and upper works a mass of roaring flames.

Slowly she drifted to the southeast, rising higher and higher as the flames ate away her wooden parts and diminished the weight upon her. Ascending to the roof of the building I watched her for hours, until finally she was lost in the dim vistas of the distance. The sight was awe-inspiring in the extreme as one contemplated this mighty floating funeral pyre, drifting unguided and unmanned through the lonely wastes of the Martian heavens; a derelict of death and destruction, typifying the life story of these strange and ferocious creatures into whose unfriendly hands fate had carried it.

Much depressed, and, to me, unaccountably so, I slowly descended to the street. The scene I had witnessed seemed to mark the defeat and annihilation of the forces of a kindred people, rather than the routing by our green warriors of a horde of similar, though unfriendly, creatures. I could not fathom the seeming hallucination, nor could I free myself from it; but somewhere in the innermost recesses of my soul I felt a strange yearning toward these unknown foemen, and a mighty hope surged through me that the fleet would return and demand a reckoning from the green warriors who had so ruthlessly and wantonly attacked it.

Close at my heel, in his now accustomed place, followed Woola, the hound, and as I emerged upon the street Sola rushed up to me as though I had been the object of some search on her part. The cavalcade was returning to the plaza, the homeward march having been given up for that day; nor, in fact, was it recommenced for more than a week, owing to the fear of a return attack by the air craft.

Lorquas Ptomel was too astute an old warrior to be caught upon the open plains with a caravan of chariots and children, and so we remained at the deserted city until the danger seemed passed.

As Sola and I entered the plaza a sight met my eyes which filled my whole being with a great surge of mingled hope, fear, exultation, and depression, and yet most dominant was a subtle sense of relief and happiness; for just as we neared the throng of Martians I caught a glimpse of the prisoner from the battle craft who was being roughly dragged into a nearby building by a couple of green Martian females.

And the sight which met my eyes was that of a slender, girlish figure, similar in every detail to the earthly women of my past life. She did not see me at first, but just as she was disappearing through the portal of the building which was to be her prison she turned, and her eyes met mine. Her face was oval and beautiful in the extreme, her every feature was finely chiseled and exquisite, her eyes large and lustrous and her head surmounted by a mass of coal black, waving hair, caught loosely into a strange yet becoming coiffure. Her skin was of a light reddish copper color, against which the crimson glow of her cheeks and the ruby of her beautifully molded lips shone with a strangely enhancing effect.

She was as destitute of clothes as the green Martians who accompanied her; indeed, save for her highly wrought ornaments she was entirely naked, nor could any apparel have enhanced the beauty of her perfect and symmetrical figure.

As her gaze rested on me her eyes opened wide in astonishment, and she made a little sign with her free hand; a sign which I did not, of course, understand. Just a moment we gazed upon each other, and then the look of hope and renewed courage which had glorified her face as she discovered me, faded into one of utter dejection, mingled with loathing and contempt. I realized I had not answered her signal, and ignorant as I was of Martian customs, I intuitively felt that she had made an appeal for succor and protection which my unfortunate ignorance had prevented me from answering. And then she was dragged out of my sight into the depths of the deserted edifice.

IX

I LEARN THE LANGUAGE

As I came back to myself I glanced at Sola, who had witnessed this encounter and I was surprised to note a strange expression upon her usually expressionless countenance. What her thoughts were I did not know, for as yet I had learned but little of the Martian tongue; enough only to suffice for my daily needs.

As I reached the doorway of our building a strange surprise awaited me. A warrior approached bearing the arms, ornaments, and full accouterments of his kind. These he presented to me with a few unintelligible words, and a bearing at once respectful and menacing.

Later, Sola, with the aid of several of the other women, remodeled the trappings to fit my lesser proportions, and after they completed the work I went about garbed in all the panoply of war.

From then on Sola instructed me in the mysteries of the various weapons, and with the Martian young I spent several hours each day practicing upon the plaza. I was not yet proficient with all the weapons, but my great familiarity with similar earthly weapons made me an unusually apt pupil, and I progressed in a very satisfactory manner.

The training of myself and the young Martians was conducted solely by the women, who not only attend to the education of the young in the arts of individual defense and offense, but are also the artisans who produce every manufactured article wrought by the green Martians. They make the powder, the cartridges, the firearms; in fact everything of value is produced by the females. In time of actual warfare they form a part of the reserves, and when the necessity arises fight with even greater intelligence and ferocity than the men.

The men are trained in the higher branches of the art of war; in strategy and the maneuvering of large bodies of troops. They make the laws as they are needed; a new law for each emergency. They are unfettered by precedent in the administration of justice. Customs have been handed down by ages of repetition, but the punishment for ignoring a custom is a matter for individual treatment by a jury of the culprit's peers, and I may say that justice seldom misses fire, but seems rather to rule in inverse ratio to the ascendency of law. In one respect at least the Martians are a happy people; they have no lawyers.

I did not see the prisoner again for several days subsequent to our first encounter, and then only to catch a fleeting glimpse of her as she was being conducted to the great audience chamber where I had had my first meeting with Lorquas Ptomel. I could not but note the unnecessary harshness and brutality with which her guards treated her; so different from the almost maternal kindliness which Sola manifested toward me, and the respectful attitude of the few green Martians who took the trouble to notice me at all.

I had observed on the two occasions when I had seen her that the prisoner exchanged words with her guards, and this convinced me that they spoke, or at least could make themselves understood by a common language. With this added incentive I nearly drove Sola distracted by my importunities to hasten on my education and within a few more days I had mastered the Martian tongue sufficiently well to enable me to carry on a passable conversation and to fully understand practically all that I heard.

At this time our sleeping quarters were occupied by three or four females and a couple of the recently hatched young, beside Sola and her youthful ward, myself, and Woola the hound. After they had retired for the night it was customary for the adults to carry on a desultory conversation for a short time before lapsing into sleep, and now that I could understand their language I was always a keen listener, although I never proffered any remarks myself.

On the night following the prisoner's visit to the audience chamber the conversation finally fell upon this subject, and I was all ears on the instant. I had feared to question Sola relative to the beautiful captive, as I could not but recall the strange expression I had noted upon her face after my first encounter with the prisoner. That it denoted jealousy I could not say, and yet, judging all things by mundane standards as I still did, I felt it safer to affect indifference in the matter until I learned more surely Sola's attitude toward the object of my solicitude.

Sarkoja, one of the older women who shared our domicile, had been present at the audience as one of the captive's guards, and it was toward her the question turned.

"When," asked one of the women, "will we enjoy the death throes of the red one? or does Lorquas Ptomel, Jed, intend holding her for ransom?"

"They have decided to carry her with us back to Thark, and exhibit her last agonies at the great games before Tal Hajus," replied Sarkoja.

"What will be the manner of her going out?" inquired Sola. "She is very small and very beautiful; I had hoped that they would hold her for ransom."

Sarkoja and the other women grunted angrily at this evidence of weakness on the part of Sola. "It is sad, Sola, that you were not born a million years ago," snapped Sarkoja, "when all the hollows of the land were filled with water, and the peoples were as soft as the stuff they sailed upon. In our day we have progressed to a point where such sentiments mark weakness and atavism. It will not be well for you to permit Tars Tarkas to learn that you hold such degenerate sentiments, as I doubt that he would care to entrust such as you with the grave responsibilities of maternity."

"I see nothing wrong with my expression of interest in this red woman," retorted Sola. "She has never harmed us, nor would she should we have fallen into her hands. It is only the men of her kind who war upon us, and I have ever thought that their attitude toward us is but the reflection of ours toward them. They live at peace with all their fellows, except when duty calls upon them to make war, while we are at peace with none; forever warring among our own kind as well as upon the red men, and even in our own communities the individuals fight amongst themselves. Oh, it is one continual, awful period of bloodshed from the time we break the shell until we gladly embrace the bosom of the river of mystery, the dark and ancient Iss which carries us to an unknown, but at least no more frightful and terrible existence! Fortunate indeed is he who meets his end in an early death. Say what you please to Tars Tarkas, he can mete out no worse fate to me than a continuation of the horrible existence we are forced to lead in this life."

This wild outbreak on the part of Sola so greatly surprised and shocked the other women, that, after a few words of general reprimand, they all lapsed into silence and were soon asleep. One thing the episode had accomplished was to assure me of Sola's friendliness toward the poor girl, and also to convince me that I had been extremely fortunate in falling into her hands rather than those of some of the other females. I knew that she was fond of me, and now that I had discovered that she hated cruelty and barbarity I was confident that I could depend upon her to aid me and the girl captive to escape, provided of course that such a thing was within the range of possibilities.

I did not even know that there were any better conditions to escape to, but I was more than willing to take my chances among people fashioned after my own mold rather than to remain longer among the hideous and bloodthirsty green men of Mars. But where to go, and how, was as much of a puzzle to me as the age-old search for the spring of eternal life has been to earthly men since the beginning of time.

I decided that at the first opportunity I would take Sola into my confidence and openly ask her to aid me, and with this resolution strong upon me I turned among my silks and furs and slept the dreamless and refreshing sleep of Mars.

X

CHAMPION AND CHIEF

Early the next morning I was astir. Considerable freedom was allowed me, as Sola had informed me that so long as I did not attempt to leave the city I was free to go and come as I pleased. She had warned me, however, against venturing forth unarmed, as this city, like all other deserted metropolises of an ancient Martian civilization, was peopled by the great white apes of my second day's adventure.

In advising me that I must not leave the boundaries of the city Sola had explained that Woola would prevent this anyway should I attempt it, and she warned me most urgently not to arouse his fierce nature by ignoring his warnings should I venture too close to the forbidden territory. His nature was such, she said, that he would bring me back into the city dead or alive should I persist in opposing him; "preferably dead," she added.

On this morning I had chosen a new street to explore when suddenly I found myself at the limits of the city. Before me were low hills pierced by narrow and inviting ravines. I longed to explore the country before me, and, like the pioneer stock from which I sprang, to view what the landscape beyond the encircling hills might disclose from the summits which shut out my view.

It also occurred to me that this would prove an excellent opportunity to test the qualities of Woola. I was convinced that the brute loved me; I had seen more evidences of affection in him than in any other Martian animal, man or beast, and I was sure that gratitude for the acts that had twice saved his life would more than outweigh his loyalty to the duty imposed upon him by cruel and loveless masters.

As I approached the boundary line Woola ran anxiously before me, and thrust his body against my legs. His expression was pleading rather than ferocious, nor did he bare his great tusks or utter his fearful guttural warnings. Denied the friendship and companionship of my kind, I had developed considerable affection for Woola and Sola, for the normal earthly man must have some outlet for his natural affections, and so I decided upon an appeal to a like instinct in this great brute, sure that I would not be disappointed.

I had never petted nor fondled him, but now I sat upon the ground and putting my arms around his heavy neck I stroked and coaxed him, talking in my newly acquired Martian tongue as I would have to my hound at home, as I would have talked to any other friend among the lower animals. His response to my manifestation of affection was remarkable to a degree; he stretched his great mouth to its full width, baring the entire expanse of his upper rows of tusks and wrinkling his snout until his great eyes were almost hidden by the folds of flesh. If you have ever seen a collie smile you may have some idea of Woola's facial distortion.

He threw himself upon his back and fairly wallowed at my feet; jumped up and sprang upon me, rolling me upon the ground by his great weight; then wriggling and squirming around me like a playful puppy presenting its back for the petting it craves. I could not resist the ludicrousness of the spectacle, and holding my sides I rocked back and forth in the first laughter which had passed my lips in many days; the first, in fact, since the morning Powell had left camp when his horse, long unused, had precipitately and unexpectedly bucked him off headforemost into a pot of frijoles.

My laughter frightened Woola, his antics ceased and he crawled pitifully toward me, poking his ugly head far into my lap; and then I remembered what laughter signified on Mars—torture, suffering, death. Quieting myself, I rubbed the poor old fellow's head and back, talked to him for a few minutes, and then in an authoritative tone commanded him to follow me, and arising started for the hills.

There was no further question of authority between us; Woola was my devoted slave from that moment hence, and I his only and undisputed master. My walk to the hills occupied but a few minutes, and I found nothing of particular interest to reward me. Numerous brilliantly colored and strangely formed wild flowers dotted the ravines and from the summit of the first hill I saw still other hills stretching off toward the north, and rising, one range above another, until lost in mountains of quite respectable dimensions; though I afterward found that only a few peaks on all Mars exceed four thousand feet in height; the suggestion of magnitude was merely relative.

My morning's walk had been large with importance to me for it had resulted in a perfect understanding with Woola, upon whom Tars Tarkas relied for my safe keeping. I now knew that while theoretically a prisoner I was virtually free, and I hastened to regain the city limits before the defection of Woola could be discovered by his erstwhile masters. The adventure decided me never again to leave the limits of my prescribed stamping grounds until I was ready to venture forth for good and all, as it would certainly result in a curtailment of my liberties, as well as the probable death of Woola, were we to be discovered.

On regaining the plaza I had my third glimpse of the captive girl. She was standing with her guards before the entrance to the audience chamber, and as I approached she gave me one haughty glance and turned her back full upon me. The act was so womanly, so earthly womanly, that though it stung my pride it also warmed my heart with a feeling of companionship; it was good to know that someone else on Mars beside myself had human instincts of a civilized order, even though the manifestation of them was so painful and mortifying.

Had a green Martian woman desired to show dislike or contempt she would, in all likelihood, have done it with a sword thrust or a movement of her trigger finger; but as their sentiments are mostly atrophied it would have required a serious injury to have aroused such passions in them. Sola, let me add, was an exception; I never saw her perform a cruel or uncouth act, or fail in uniform kindliness and good nature. She was indeed, as her fellow Martian had said of her, an atavism; a dear and precious reversion to a former type of loved and loving ancestor.

Seeing that the prisoner seemed the center of attraction I halted to view the proceedings. I had not long to wait for presently Lorquas Ptomel and his retinue of chieftains approached the building and, signing the guards to follow with the prisoner entered the audience chamber. Realizing that I was a somewhat favored character, and also convinced that the warriors did not know of my proficiency in their language, as I had plead with Sola to keep this a secret on the grounds that I did not wish to be forced to talk with the men until I had perfectly mastered the Martian tongue, I chanced an attempt to enter the audience chamber and listen to the proceedings.

The council squatted upon the steps of the rostrum, while below them stood the prisoner and her two guards. I saw that one of the women was Sarkoja, and thus understood how she had been present at the hearing of the preceding day, the results of which she had reported to the occupants of our dormitory last night. Her attitude toward the captive was most harsh and brutal. When she held her, she sunk her rudimentary nails into the poor girl's flesh, or twisted her arm in a most painful manner. When it was necessary to move from one spot to another she either jerked her roughly, or pushed her headlong before her. She seemed to be venting upon this poor defenseless creature all the hatred, cruelty, ferocity, and spite of her nine hundred years, backed by unguessable ages of fierce and brutal ancestors.

The other woman was less cruel because she was entirely indifferent; if the prisoner had been left to her alone, and fortunately she was at night, she would have received no harsh treatment, nor, by the same token would she have received any attention at all.

As Lorquas Ptomel raised his eyes to address the prisoner they fell on me and he turned to Tars Tarkas with a word, and gesture of impatience. Tars Tarkas made some reply which I could not catch, but which caused Lorquas Ptomel to smile; after which they paid no further attention to me.

"What is your name?" asked Lorquas Ptomel, addressing the prisoner.

"Dejah Thoris, daughter of Mors Kajak of Helium."

"And the nature of your expedition?" he continued.

"It was a purely scientific research party sent out by my father's father, the Jeddak of Helium, to rechart the air currents, and to take atmospheric density tests," replied the fair prisoner, in a low, well-modulated voice.

"We were unprepared for battle," she continued, "as we were on a peaceful mission, as our banners and the colors of our craft denoted. The work we were doing was as much in your interests as in ours, for you know full well that were it not for our labors and the fruits of our scientific operations there would not be enough air or water on Mars to support a single human life. For ages we have maintained the air and water supply at practically the same point without an appreciable loss, and we have done this in the face of the brutal and ignorant interference of you green men.

"Why, oh, why will you not learn to live in amity with your fellows? Must you ever go on down the ages to your final extinction but little above the plane of the dumb brutes that serve you! A people without written language, without art, without homes, without love; the victims of eons of the horrible community idea. Owning everything in common, even to your women and children, has resulted in your owning nothing in common. You hate each other as you hate all else except yourselves. Come back to the ways of our common ancestors, come back to the light of kindliness and fellowship. The way is open to you, you will find the hands of the red men stretched out to aid you. Together we may do still more to regenerate our dying planet. The granddaughter of the greatest and mightiest of the red jeddaks has asked you. Will you come?"

Lorquas Ptomel and the warriors sat looking silently and intently at the young woman for several moments after she had ceased speaking. What was passing in their minds no man may know, but that they were moved I truly believe, and if one man high among them had been strong enough to rise above custom, that moment would have marked a new and mighty era for Mars.

I saw Tars Tarkas rise to speak, and on his face was such an expression as I had never seen upon the countenance of a green Martian warrior. It bespoke an inward and mighty battle with self, with heredity, with age-old custom, and as he opened his mouth to speak, a look almost of benignity, of kindliness, momentarily lighted up his fierce and terrible countenance.

What words of moment were to have fallen from his lips were never spoken, as just then a young warrior, evidently sensing the trend of thought among the older men, leaped down from the steps of the rostrum, and striking the frail captive a powerful blow across the face, which felled her to the floor, placed his foot upon her prostrate form and turning toward the assembled council broke into peals of horrid, mirthless laughter.

For an instant I thought Tars Tarkas would strike him dead, nor did the aspect of Lorquas Ptomel augur any too favorably for the brute, but the mood passed, their old selves reasserted their ascendency, and they smiled. It was portentous however that they did not laugh aloud, for the brute's act constituted a side-splitting witticism according to the ethics which rule green Martian humor.

That I have taken moments to write down a part of what occurred as that blow fell does not signify that I remained inactive for any such length of time. I think I must have sensed something of what was coming, for I realize now that I was crouched as for a spring as I saw the blow aimed at her beautiful, upturned, pleading face, and ere the hand descended I was halfway across the hall.

Scarcely had his hideous laugh rang out but once, when I was upon him. The brute was twelve feet in height and armed to the teeth, but I believe that I could have accounted for the whole roomful in the terrific intensity of my rage. Springing upward, I struck him full in the face as he turned at my warning cry and then as he drew his short-sword I drew mine and sprang up again upon his breast, hooking one leg over the butt of his pistol and grasping one of his huge tusks with my left hand while I delivered blow after blow upon his enormous chest.

He could not use his short-sword to advantage because I was too close to him, nor could he draw his pistol, which he attempted to do in direct opposition to Martian custom which says that you may not fight a fellow warrior in private combat with any other than the weapon with which you are attacked. In fact he could do nothing but make a wild and futile attempt to dislodge me. With all his immense bulk he was little if any stronger than I, and it was but the matter of a moment or two before he sank, bleeding and lifeless, to the floor.

Dejah Thoris had raised herself upon one elbow and was watching the battle with wide, staring eyes. When I had regained my feet I raised her in my arms and bore her to one of the benches at the side of the room.

Again no Martian interfered with me, and tearing a piece of silk from my cape I endeavored to staunch the flow of blood from her nostrils. I was soon successful as her injuries amounted to little more than an ordinary nosebleed, and when she could speak she placed her hand upon my arm and looking up into my eyes, said:

"Why did you do it? You who refused me even friendly recognition in the first hour of my peril! And now you risk your life and kill one of your companions for my sake. I cannot understand. What strange manner of man are you, that you consort with the green men, though your form is that of my race, while your color is little darker than that of the white ape? Tell me, are you human, or are you more than human?"

"It is a strange tale," I replied, "too long to attempt to tell you now, and one which I so much doubt the credibility of myself that I fear to hope that others will believe it. Suffice it, for the present, that I am your friend, and, so far as our captors will permit, your protector and your servant."

"Then you too are a prisoner? But why, then, those arms and the regalia of a Tharkian chieftain? What is your name? Where your country?"

"Yes, Dejah Thoris, I too am a prisoner; my name is John Carter, and I claim Virginia, one of the United States of America, Earth, as my home; but why I am permitted to wear arms I do not know, nor was I aware that my regalia was that of a chieftain."

We were interrupted at this juncture by the approach of one of the warriors, bearing arms, accoutrements and ornaments, and in a flash one of her questions was answered and a puzzle cleared up for me. I saw that the body of my dead antagonist had been stripped, and I read in the menacing yet respectful attitude of the warrior who had brought me these trophies of the kill the same demeanor as that evinced by the other who had brought me my original equipment, and now for the first time I realized that my blow, on the occasion of my first battle in the audience chamber had resulted in the death of my adversary.

The reason for the whole attitude displayed toward me was now apparent; I had won my spurs, so to speak, and in the crude justice, which always marks Martian dealings, and which, among other things, has caused me to call her the planet of paradoxes, I was accorded the honors due a conqueror; the trappings and the position of the man I killed. In truth, I was a Martian chieftain, and this I learned later was the cause of my great freedom and my toleration in the audience chamber.

As I had turned to receive the dead warrior's chattels I had noticed that Tars Tarkas and several others had pushed forward toward us, and the eyes of the former rested upon me in a most quizzical manner. Finally he addressed me:

"You speak the tongue of Barsoom quite readily for one who was deaf and dumb to us a few short days ago. Where did you learn it, John Carter?"

"You, yourself, are responsible, Tars Tarkas," I replied, "in that you furnished me with an instructress of remarkable ability; I have to thank Sola for my learning."

"She has done well," he answered, "but your education in other respects needs considerable polish. Do you know what your unprecedented temerity would have cost you had you failed to kill either of the two chieftains whose metal you now wear?"

"I presume that that one whom I had failed to kill, would have killed me," I answered, smiling.

"No, you are wrong. Only in the last extremity of self-defense would a Martian warrior kill a prisoner; we like to save them for other purposes," and his face bespoke possibilities that were not pleasant to dwell upon.

"But one thing can save you now," he continued. "Should you, in recognition of your remarkable valor, ferocity, and prowess, be considered by Tal Hajus as worthy of his service you may be taken into the community and become a full-fledged Tharkian. Until we reach the headquarters of Tal Hajus it is the will of Lorquas Ptomel that you be accorded the respect your acts have earned you. You will be treated by us as a Tharkian chieftain, but you must not forget that every chief who ranks you is responsible for your safe delivery to our mighty and most ferocious ruler. I am done."

"I hear you, Tars Tarkas," I answered. "As you know I am not of Barsoom; your ways are not my ways, and I can only act in the future as I have in the past, in accordance with the dictates of my conscience and guided by the standards of mine own people. If you will leave me alone I will go in peace, but if not, let the individual Barsoomians with whom I must deal either respect my rights as a stranger among you, or take whatever consequences may befall. Of one thing let us be sure, whatever may be your ultimate intentions toward this unfortunate young woman, whoever would offer her injury or insult in the future must figure on making a full accounting to me. I understand that you belittle all sentiments of generosity and kindliness, but I do not, and I can convince your most doughty warrior that these characteristics are not incompatible with an ability to fight."

Ordinarily I am not given to long speeches, nor ever before had I descended to bombast, but I had guessed at the keynote which would strike an answering chord in the breasts of the green Martians, nor was I wrong, for my harangue evidently deeply impressed them, and their attitude toward me thereafter was still further respectful.

Tars Tarkas himself seemed pleased with my reply, but his only comment was more or less enigmatical—"And I think I know Tal Hajus, Jeddak of Thark."

I now turned my attention to Dejah Thoris, and assisting her to her feet I turned with her toward the exit, ignoring her hovering guardian harpies as well as the inquiring glances of the chieftains. Was I not now a chieftain also! Well, then, I would assume the responsibilities of one. They did not molest us, and so Dejah Thoris, Princess of Helium, and John Carter, gentleman of Virginia, followed by the faithful Woola, passed through utter silence from the audience chamber of Lorquas Ptomel, Jed among the Tharks of Barsoom.

XI

WITH DEJAH THORIS

As we reached the open the two female guards who had been detailed to watch over Dejah Thoris hurried up and made as though to assume custody of her once more. The poor child shrank against me and I felt her two little hands fold tightly over my arm. Waving the women away, I informed them that Sola would attend the captive hereafter, and I further warned Sarkoja that any more of her cruel attentions bestowed upon Dejah Thoris would result in Sarkoja's sudden and painful demise.

My threat was unfortunate and resulted in more harm than good to Dejah Thoris, for, as I learned later, men do not kill women upon Mars, nor women, men. So Sarkoja merely gave us an ugly look and departed to hatch up deviltries against us.

I soon found Sola and explained to her that I wished her to guard Dejah Thoris as she had guarded me; that I wished her to find other quarters where they would not be molested by Sarkoja, and I finally informed her that I myself would take up my quarters among the men.

Sola glanced at the accouterments which were carried in my hand and slung across my shoulder.

"You are a great chieftain now, John Carter," she said, "and I must do your bidding, though indeed I am glad to do it under any circumstances. The man whose metal you carry was young, but he was a great warrior, and had by his promotions and kills won his way close to the rank of Tars Tarkas, who, as you know, is second to Lorquas Ptomel only. You are eleventh, there are but ten chieftains in this community who rank you in prowess."

"And if I should kill Lorquas Ptomel?" I asked.

"You would be first, John Carter; but you may only win that honor by the will of the entire council that Lorquas Ptomel meet you in combat, or should he attack you, you may kill him in self-defense, and thus win first place."

I laughed, and changed the subject. I had no particular desire to kill Lorquas Ptomel, and less to be a jed among the Tharks.

I accompanied Sola and Dejah Thoris in a search for new quarters, which we found in a building nearer the audience chamber and of far more pretentious architecture than our former habitation. We also found in this building real sleeping apartments with ancient beds of highly wrought metal swinging from enormous gold chains depending from the marble ceilings. The decoration of the walls was most elaborate, and, unlike the frescoes in the other buildings I had examined, portrayed many human figures in the compositions. These were of people like myself, and of a much lighter color than Dejah Thoris. They were clad in graceful, flowing robes, highly ornamented with metal and jewels, and their luxuriant hair was of a beautiful golden and reddish bronze. The men were beardless and only a few wore arms. The scenes depicted for the most part, a fair-skinned, fair-haired people at play.

Dejah Thoris clasped her hands with an exclamation of rapture as she gazed upon these magnificent works of art, wrought by a people long extinct; while Sola, on the other hand, apparently did not see them.

We decided to use this room, on the second floor and overlooking the plaza, for Dejah Thoris and Sola, and another room adjoining and in the rear for the cooking and supplies. I then dispatched Sola to bring the bedding and such food and utensils as she might need, telling her that I would guard Dejah Thoris until her return.

As Sola departed Dejah Thoris turned to me with a faint smile.

"And whereto, then, would your prisoner escape should you leave her, unless it was to follow you and crave your protection, and ask your pardon for the cruel thoughts she has harbored against you these past few days?"

"You are right," I answered, "there is no escape for either of us unless we go together."

"I heard your challenge to the creature you call Tars Tarkas, and I think I understand your position among these people, but what I cannot fathom is your statement that you are not of Barsoom."

"In the name of my first ancestor, then," she continued, "where may you be from? You are like unto my people, and yet so unlike. You speak my language, and yet I heard you tell Tars Tarkas that you had but learned it recently. All Barsoomians speak the same tongue from the ice-clad south to the ice-clad north, though their written languages differ. Only in the valley Dor, where the river Iss empties into the lost sea of Korus, is there supposed to be a different language spoken, and, except in the legends of our ancestors, there is no record of a Barsoomian returning up the river Iss, from the shores of Korus in the valley of Dor. Do not tell me that you have thus returned! They would kill you horribly anywhere upon the surface of Barsoom if that were true; tell me it is not!"

Her eyes were filled with a strange, weird light; her voice was pleading, and her little hands, reached up upon my breast, were pressed against me as though to wring a denial from my very heart.

"I do not know your customs, Dejah Thoris, but in my own Virginia a gentleman does not lie to save himself; I am not of Dor; I have never seen the mysterious Iss; the lost sea of Korus is still lost, so far as I am concerned. Do you believe me?"

And then it struck me suddenly that I was very anxious that she should believe me. It was not that I feared the results which would follow a general belief that I had returned from the Barsoomian heaven or hell, or whatever it was. Why was it, then! Why should I care what she thought? I looked down at her; her beautiful face upturned, and her wonderful eyes opening up the very depth of her soul; and as my eyes met hers I knew why, and—I shuddered.

A similar wave of feeling seemed to stir her; she drew away from me with a sigh, and with her earnest, beautiful face turned up to mine, she whispered: "I believe you, John Carter; I do not know what a 'gentleman' is, nor have I ever heard before of Virginia; but on Barsoom no man lies; if he does not wish to speak the truth he is silent. Where is this Virginia, your country, John Carter?" she asked, and it seemed that this fair name of my fair land had never sounded more beautiful than as it fell from those perfect lips on that far-gone day.

"I am of another world," I answered, "the great planet Earth, which revolves about our common sun and next within the orbit of your Barsoom, which we know as Mars. How I came here I cannot tell you, for I do not know; but here I am, and since my presence has permitted me to serve Dejah Thoris I am glad that I am here."

She gazed at me with troubled eyes, long and questioningly. That it was difficult to believe my statement I well knew, nor could I hope that she would do so however much I craved her confidence and respect. I would much rather not have told her anything of my antecedents, but no man could look into the depth of those eyes and refuse her slightest behest.

Finally she smiled, and, rising, said: "I shall have to believe even though I cannot understand. I can readily perceive that you are not of the Barsoom of today; you are like us, yet different—but why should I trouble my poor head with such a problem, when my heart tells me that I believe because I wish to believe!"

It was good logic, good, earthly, feminine logic, and if it satisfied her I certainly could pick no flaws in it. As a matter of fact it was about the only kind of logic that could be brought to bear upon my problem. We fell into a general conversation then, asking and answering many questions on each side. She was curious to learn of the customs of my people and displayed a remarkable knowledge of events on Earth. When I questioned her closely on this seeming familiarity with earthly things she laughed, and cried out:

"Why, every school boy on Barsoom knows the geography, and much concerning the fauna and flora, as well as the history of your planet fully as well as of his own. Can we not see everything which takes place upon Earth, as you call it; is it not hanging there in the heavens in plain sight?"

This baffled me, I must confess, fully as much as my statements had confounded her; and I told her so. She then explained in general the instruments her people had used and been perfecting for ages, which permit them to throw upon a screen a perfect image of what is transpiring upon any planet and upon many of the stars. These pictures are so perfect in detail that, when photographed and enlarged, objects no greater than a blade of grass may be distinctly recognized. I afterward, in Helium, saw many of these pictures, as well as the instruments which produced them.

"If, then, you are so familiar with earthly things," I asked, "why is it that you do not recognize me as identical with the inhabitants of that planet?"

She smiled again as one might in bored indulgence of a questioning child.

"Because, John Carter," she replied, "nearly every planet and star having atmospheric conditions at all approaching those of Barsoom, shows forms of animal life almost identical with you and me; and, further, Earth men, almost without exception, cover their bodies with strange, unsightly pieces of cloth, and their heads with hideous contraptions the purpose of which we have been unable to conceive; while you, when found by the Tharkian warriors, were entirely undisfigured and unadorned.

"The fact that you wore no ornaments is a strong proof of your un-Barsoomian origin, while the absence of grotesque coverings might cause a doubt as to your earthliness."

I then narrated the details of my departure from the Earth, explaining that my body there lay fully clothed in all the, to her, strange garments of mundane dwellers. At this point Sola returned with our meager belongings and her young Martian protege, who, of course, would have to share the quarters with them.

Sola asked us if we had had a visitor during her absence, and seemed much surprised when we answered in the negative. It seemed that as she had mounted the approach to the upper floors where our quarters were located, she had met Sarkoja descending. We decided that she must have been eavesdropping, but as we could recall nothing of importance that had passed between us we dismissed the matter as of little consequence, merely promising ourselves to be warned to the utmost caution in the future.

Dejah Thoris and I then fell to examining the architecture and decorations of the beautiful chambers of the building we were occupying. She told me that these people had presumably flourished over a hundred thousand years before. They were the early progenitors of her race, but had mixed with the other great race of early Martians, who were very dark, almost black, and also with the reddish yellow race which had flourished at the same time.

These three great divisions of the higher Martians had been forced into a mighty alliance as the drying up of the Martian seas had compelled them to seek the comparatively few and always diminishing fertile areas, and to defend themselves, under new conditions of life, against the wild hordes of green men.

Ages of close relationship and intermarrying had resulted in the race of red men, of which Dejah Thoris was a fair and beautiful daughter. During the ages of hardships and incessant warring between their own various races, as well as with the green men, and before they had fitted themselves to the changed conditions, much of the high civilization and many of the arts of the fair-haired Martians had become lost; but the red race of today has reached a point where it feels that it has made up in new discoveries and in a more practical civilization for all that lies irretrievably buried with the ancient Barsoomians, beneath the countless intervening ages.

These ancient Martians had been a highly cultivated and literary race, but during the vicissitudes of those trying centuries of readjustment to new conditions, not only did their advancement and production cease entirely, but practically all their archives, records, and literature were lost.

Dejah Thoris related many interesting facts and legends concerning this lost race of noble and kindly people. She said that the city in which we were camping was supposed to have been a center of commerce and culture known as Korad. It had been built upon a beautiful, natural harbor, landlocked by magnificent hills. The little valley on the west front of the city, she explained, was all that remained of the harbor, while the pass through the hills to the old sea bottom had been the channel through which the shipping passed up to the city's gates.

The shores of the ancient seas were dotted with just such cities, and lesser ones, in diminishing numbers, were to be found converging toward the center of the oceans, as the people had found it necessary to follow the receding waters until necessity had forced upon them their ultimate salvation, the so-called Martian canals.

We had been so engrossed in exploration of the building and in our conversation that it was late in the afternoon before we realized it. We were brought back to a realization of our present conditions by a messenger bearing a summons from Lorquas Ptomel directing me to appear before him forthwith. Bidding Dejah Thoris and Sola farewell, and commanding Woola to remain on guard, I hastened to the audience chamber, where I found Lorquas Ptomel and Tars Tarkas seated upon the rostrum.

XII

A PRISONER WITH POWER

As I entered and saluted, Lorquas Ptomel signaled me to advance, and, fixing his great, hideous eyes upon me, addressed me thus:

"You have been with us a few days, yet during that time you have by your prowess won a high position among us. Be that as it may, you are not one of us; you owe us no allegiance.

"Your position is a peculiar one," he continued; "you are a prisoner and yet you give commands which must be obeyed; you are an alien and yet you are a Tharkian chieftain; you are a midget and yet you can kill a mighty warrior with one blow of your fist. And now you are reported to have been plotting to escape with another prisoner of another race; a prisoner who, from her own admission, half believes you are returned from the valley of Dor. Either one of these accusations, if proved, would be sufficient grounds for your execution, but we are a just people and you shall have a trial on our return to Thark, if Tal Hajus so commands.

"But," he continued, in his fierce guttural tones, "if you run off with the red girl it is I who shall have to account to Tal Hajus; it is I who shall have to face Tars Tarkas, and either demonstrate my right to command, or the metal from my dead carcass will go to a better man, for such is the custom of the Tharks.

"I have no quarrel with Tars Tarkas; together we rule supreme the greatest of the lesser communities among the green men; we do not wish to fight between ourselves; and so if you were dead, John Carter, I should be glad. Under two conditions only, however, may you be killed by us without orders from Tal Hajus; in personal combat in self-defense, should you attack one of us, or were you apprehended in an attempt to escape.

"As a matter of justice I must warn you that we only await one of these two excuses for ridding ourselves of so great a responsibility. The safe delivery of the red girl to Tal Hajus is of the greatest importance. Not in a thousand years have the Tharks made such a capture; she is the granddaughter of the greatest of the red jeddaks, who is also our bitterest enemy. I have spoken. The red girl told us that we were without the softer sentiments of humanity, but we are a just and truthful race. You may go."

Turning, I left the audience chamber. So this was the beginning of Sarkoja's persecution! I knew that none other could be responsible for this report which had reached the ears of Lorquas Ptomel so quickly, and now I recalled those portions of our conversation which had touched upon escape and upon my origin.

Sarkoja was at this time Tars Tarkas' oldest and most trusted female. As such she was a mighty power behind the throne, for no warrior had the confidence of Lorquas Ptomel to such an extent as did his ablest lieutenant, Tars Tarkas.

However, instead of putting thoughts of possible escape from my mind, my audience with Lorquas Ptomel only served to center my every faculty on this subject. Now, more than before, the absolute necessity for escape, in so far as Dejah Thoris was concerned, was impressed upon me, for I was convinced that some horrible fate awaited her at the headquarters of Tal Hajus.

As described by Sola, this monster was the exaggerated personification of all the ages of cruelty, ferocity, and brutality from which he had descended. Cold, cunning, calculating; he was, also, in marked contrast to most of his fellows, a slave to that brute passion which the waning demands for procreation upon their dying planet has almost stilled in the Martian breast.

The thought that the divine Dejah Thoris might fall into the clutches of such an abysmal atavism started the cold sweat upon me. Far better that we save friendly bullets for ourselves at the last moment, as did those brave frontier women of my lost land, who took their own lives rather than fall into the hands of the Indian braves.

As I wandered about the plaza lost in my gloomy forebodings Tars Tarkas approached me on his way from the audience chamber. His demeanor toward me was unchanged, and he greeted me as though we had not just parted a few moments before.

"Where are your quarters, John Carter?" he asked.

"I have selected none," I replied. "It seemed best that I quartered either by myself or among the other warriors, and I was awaiting an opportunity to ask your advice. As you know," and I smiled, "I am not yet familiar with all the customs of the Tharks."

"Come with me," he directed, and together we moved off across the plaza to a building which I was glad to see adjoined that occupied by Sola and her charges.

"My quarters are on the first floor of this building," he said, "and the second floor also is fully occupied by warriors, but the third floor and the floors above are vacant; you may take your choice of these.

"I understand," he continued, "that you have given up your woman to the red prisoner. Well, as you have said, your ways are not our ways, but you can fight well enough to do about as you please, and so, if you wish to give your woman to a captive, it is your own affair; but as a chieftain you should have those to serve you, and in accordance with our customs you may select any or all the females from the retinues of the chieftains whose metal you now wear."

I thanked him, but assured him that I could get along very nicely without assistance except in the matter of preparing food, and so he promised to send women to me for this purpose and also for the care of my arms and the manufacture of my ammunition, which he said would be necessary. I suggested that they might also bring some of the sleeping silks and furs which belonged to me as spoils of combat, for the nights were cold and I had none of my own.

He promised to do so, and departed. Left alone, I ascended the winding corridor to the upper floors in search of suitable quarters. The beauties of the other buildings were repeated in this, and, as usual, I was soon lost in a tour of investigation and discovery.

I finally chose a front room on the third floor, because this brought me nearer to Dejah Thoris, whose apartment was on the second floor of the adjoining building, and it flashed upon me that I could rig up some means of communication whereby she might signal me in case she needed either my services or my protection.

Adjoining my sleeping apartment were baths, dressing rooms, and other sleeping and living apartments, in all some ten rooms on this floor. The windows of the back rooms overlooked an enormous court, which formed the center of the square made by the buildings which faced the four contiguous streets, and which was now given over to the quartering of the various animals belonging to the warriors occupying the adjoining buildings.

While the court was entirely overgrown with the yellow, moss-like vegetation which blankets practically the entire surface of Mars, yet numerous fountains, statuary, benches, and pergola-like contraptions bore witness to the beauty which the court must have presented in bygone times, when graced by the fair-haired, laughing people whom stern and unalterable cosmic laws had driven not only from their homes, but from all except the vague legends of their descendants.

One could easily picture the gorgeous foliage of the luxuriant Martian vegetation which once filled this scene with life and color; the graceful figures of the beautiful women, the straight and handsome men; the happy frolicking children—all sunlight, happiness and peace.

It was difficult to realize that they had gone; down through ages of darkness, cruelty, and ignorance, until their hereditary instincts of culture and humanitarianism had risen ascendant once more in the final composite race which now is dominant upon Mars.

My thoughts were cut short by the advent of several young females bearing loads of weapons, silks, furs, jewels, cooking utensils, and casks of food and drink, including considerable loot from the air craft. All this, it seemed, had been the property of the two chieftains I had slain, and now, by the customs of the Tharks, it had become mine. At my direction they placed the stuff in one of the back rooms, and then departed, only to return with a second load, which they advised me constituted the balance of my goods. On the second trip they were accompanied by ten or fifteen other women and youths, who, it seemed, formed the retinues of the two chieftains.

They were not their families, nor their wives, nor their servants; the relationship was peculiar, and so unlike anything known to us that it is most difficult to describe. All property among the green Martians is owned in common by the community, except the personal weapons, ornaments and sleeping silks and furs of the individuals. These alone can one claim undisputed right to, nor may he accumulate more of these than are required for his actual needs. The surplus he holds merely as custodian, and it is passed on to the younger members of the community as necessity demands.

The women and children of a man's retinue may be likened to a military unit for which he is responsible in various ways, as in matters of instruction, discipline, sustenance, and the exigencies of their continual roamings and their unending strife with other communities and with the red Martians. His women are in no sense wives. The green Martians use no word corresponding in meaning with this earthly word. Their mating is a matter of community interest solely, and is directed without reference to natural selection. The council of chieftains of each community control the matter as surely as the owner of a Kentucky racing stud directs the scientific breeding of his stock for the improvement of the whole.

In theory it may sound well, as is often the case with theories, but the results of ages of this unnatural practice, coupled with the community interest in the offspring being held paramount to that of the mother, is shown in the cold, cruel creatures, and their gloomy, loveless, mirthless existence.

It is true that the green Martians are absolutely virtuous, both men and women, with the exception of such degenerates as Tal Hajus; but better far a finer balance of human characteristics even at the expense of a slight and occasional loss of chastity.

Finding that I must assume responsibility for these creatures, whether I would or not, I made the best of it and directed them to find quarters on the upper floors, leaving the third floor to me. One of the girls I charged with the duties of my simple cuisine, and directed the others to take up the various activities which had formerly constituted their vocations. Thereafter I saw little of them, nor did I care to.

XIII

LOVE-MAKING ON MARS

Following the battle with the air ships, the community remained within the city for several days, abandoning the homeward march until they could feel reasonably assured that the ships would not return; for to be caught on the open plains with a cavalcade of chariots and children was far from the desire of even so warlike a people as the green Martians.

During our period of inactivity, Tars Tarkas had instructed me in many of the customs and arts of war familiar to the Tharks, including lessons in riding and guiding the great beasts which bore the warriors. These creatures, which are known as thoats, are as dangerous and vicious as their masters, but when once subdued are sufficiently tractable for the purposes of the green Martians.

Two of these animals had fallen to me from the warriors whose metal I wore, and in a short time I could handle them quite as well as the native warriors. The method was not at all complicated. If the thoats did not respond with sufficient celerity to the telepathic instructions of their riders they were dealt a terrific blow between the ears with the butt of a pistol, and if they showed fight this treatment was continued until the brutes either were subdued, or had unseated their riders.

In the latter case it became a life and death struggle between the man and the beast. If the former were quick enough with his pistol he might live to ride again, though upon some other beast; if not, his torn and mangled body was gathered up by his women and burned in accordance with Tharkian custom.

My experience with Woola determined me to attempt the experiment of kindness in my treatment of my thoats. First I taught them that they could not unseat me, and even rapped them sharply between the ears to impress upon them my authority and mastery. Then, by degrees, I won their confidence in much the same manner as I had adopted countless times with my many mundane mounts. I was ever a good hand with animals, and by inclination, as well as because it brought more lasting and satisfactory results, I was always kind and humane in my dealings with the lower orders. I could take a human life, if necessary, with far less compunction than that of a poor, unreasoning, irresponsible brute.

In the course of a few days my thoats were the wonder of the entire community. They would follow me like dogs, rubbing their great snouts against my body in awkward evidence of affection, and respond to my every command with an alacrity and docility which caused the Martian warriors to ascribe to me the possession of some earthly power unknown on Mars.

"How have you bewitched them?" asked Tars Tarkas one afternoon, when he had seen me run my arm far between the great jaws of one of my thoats which had wedged a piece of stone between two of his teeth while feeding upon the moss-like vegetation within our court yard.

"By kindness," I replied. "You see, Tars Tarkas, the softer sentiments have their value, even to a warrior. In the height of battle as well as upon the march I know that my thoats will obey my every command, and therefore my fighting efficiency is enhanced, and I am a better warrior for the reason that I am a kind master. Your other warriors would find it to the advantage of themselves as well as of the community to adopt my methods in this respect. Only a few days since you, yourself, told me that these great brutes, by the uncertainty of their tempers, often were the means of turning victory into defeat, since, at a crucial moment, they might elect to unseat and rend their riders."

"Show me how you accomplish these results," was Tars Tarkas' only rejoinder.

And so I explained as carefully as I could the entire method of training I had adopted with my beasts, and later he had me repeat it before Lorquas Ptomel and the assembled warriors. That moment marked the beginning of a new existence for the poor thoats, and before I left the community of Lorquas Ptomel I had the satisfaction of observing a regiment of as tractable and docile mounts as one might care to see. The effect on the precision and celerity of the military movements was so remarkable that Lorquas Ptomel presented me with a massive anklet of gold from his own leg, as a sign of his appreciation of my service to the horde.

On the seventh day following the battle with the air craft we again took up the march toward Thark, all probability of another attack being deemed remote by Lorquas Ptomel.

During the days just preceding our departure I had seen but little of Dejah Thoris, as I had been kept very busy by Tars Tarkas with my lessons in the art of Martian warfare, as well as in the training of my thoats. The few times I had visited her quarters she had been absent, walking upon the streets with Sola, or investigating the buildings in the near vicinity of the plaza. I had warned them against venturing far from the plaza for fear of the great white apes, whose ferocity I was only too well acquainted with. However, since Woola accompanied them on all their excursions, and as Sola was well armed, there was comparatively little cause for fear.

On the evening before our departure I saw them approaching along one of the great avenues which lead into the plaza from the east. I advanced to meet them, and telling Sola that I would take the responsibility for Dejah Thoris' safekeeping, I directed her to return to her quarters on some trivial errand. I liked and trusted Sola, but for some reason I desired to be alone with Dejah Thoris, who represented to me all that I had left behind upon Earth in agreeable and congenial companionship. There seemed bonds of mutual interest between us as powerful as though we had been born under the same roof rather than upon different planets, hurtling through space some forty-eight million miles apart.

That she shared my sentiments in this respect I was positive, for on my approach the look of pitiful hopelessness left her sweet countenance to be replaced by a smile of joyful welcome, as she placed her little right hand upon my left shoulder in true red Martian salute.

"Sarkoja told Sola that you had become a true Thark," she said, "and that I would now see no more of you than of any of the other warriors."

"Sarkoja is a liar of the first magnitude," I replied, "notwithstanding the proud claim of the Tharks to absolute verity."

Dejah Thoris laughed.

"I knew that even though you became a member of the community you would not cease to be my friend; 'A warrior may change his metal, but not his heart,' as the saying is upon Barsoom.

"I think they have been trying to keep us apart," she continued, "for whenever you have been off duty one of the older women of Tars Tarkas' retinue has always arranged to trump up some excuse to get Sola and me out of sight. They have had me down in the pits below the buildings helping them mix their awful radium powder, and make their terrible projectiles. You know that these have to be manufactured by artificial light, as exposure to sunlight always results in an explosion. You have noticed that their bullets explode when they strike an object? Well, the opaque, outer coating is broken by the impact, exposing a glass cylinder, almost solid, in the forward end of which is a minute particle of radium powder. The moment the sunlight, even though diffused, strikes this powder it explodes with a violence which nothing can withstand. If you ever witness a night battle you will note the absence of these explosions, while the morning following the battle will be filled at sunrise with the sharp detonations of exploding missiles fired the preceding night. As a rule, however, non-exploding projectiles are used at night."

While I was much interested in Dejah Thoris' explanation of this wonderful adjunct to Martian warfare, I was more concerned by the immediate problem of their treatment of her. That they were keeping her away from me was not a matter for surprise, but that they should subject her to dangerous and arduous labor filled me with rage.

"Have they ever subjected you to cruelty and ignominy, Dejah Thoris?" I asked, feeling the hot blood of my fighting ancestors leap in my veins as I awaited her reply.

"Only in little ways, John Carter," she answered. "Nothing that can harm me outside my pride. They know that I am the daughter of ten thousand jeddaks, that I trace my ancestry straight back without a break to the builder of the first great waterway, and they, who do not even know their own mothers, are jealous of me. At heart they hate their horrid fates, and so wreak their poor spite on me who stand for everything they have not, and for all they most crave and never can attain. Let us pity them, my chieftain, for even though we die at their hands we can afford them pity, since we are greater than they and they know it."

Had I known the significance of those words "my chieftain," as applied by a red Martian woman to a man, I should have had the surprise of my life, but I did not know at that time, nor for many months thereafter. Yes, I still had much to learn upon Barsoom.

"I presume it is the better part of wisdom that we bow to our fate with as good grace as possible, Dejah Thoris; but I hope, nevertheless, that I may be present the next time that any Martian, green, red, pink, or violet, has the temerity to even so much as frown on you, my princess."

Dejah Thoris caught her breath at my last words, and gazed upon me with dilated eyes and quickening breath, and then, with an odd little laugh, which brought roguish dimples to the corners of her mouth, she shook her head and cried:

"What a child! A great warrior and yet a stumbling little child."

"What have I done now?" I asked, in sore perplexity.

"Some day you shall know, John Carter, if we live; but I may not tell you. And I, the daughter of Mors Kajak, son of Tardos Mors, have listened without anger," she soliloquized in conclusion.

Then she broke out again into one of her gay, happy, laughing moods; joking with me on my prowess as a Thark warrior as contrasted with my soft heart and natural kindliness.

"I presume that should you accidentally wound an enemy you would take him home and nurse him back to health," she laughed.

"That is precisely what we do on Earth," I answered. "At least among civilized men."

This made her laugh again. She could not understand it, for, with all her tenderness and womanly sweetness, she was still a Martian, and to a Martian the only good enemy is a dead enemy; for every dead foeman means so much more to divide between those who live.

I was very curious to know what I had said or done to cause her so much perturbation a moment before and so I continued to importune her to enlighten me.

"No," she exclaimed, "it is enough that you have said it and that I have listened. And when you learn, John Carter, and if I be dead, as likely I shall be ere the further moon has circled Barsoom another twelve times, remember that I listened and that I—smiled."

It was all Greek to me, but the more I begged her to explain the more positive became her denials of my request, and, so, in very hopelessness, I desisted.

Day had now given away to night and as we wandered along the great avenue lighted by the two moons of Barsoom, and with Earth looking down upon us out of her luminous green eye, it seemed that we were alone in the universe, and I, at least, was content that it should be so.

The chill of the Martian night was upon us, and removing my silks I threw them across the shoulders of Dejah Thoris. As my arm rested for an instant upon her I felt a thrill pass through every fiber of my being such as contact with no other mortal had even produced; and it seemed to me that she had leaned slightly toward me, but of that I was not sure. Only I knew that as my arm rested there across her shoulders longer than the act of adjusting the silk required she did not draw away, nor did she speak. And so, in silence, we walked the surface of a dying world, but in the breast of one of us at least had been born that which is ever oldest, yet ever new.

I loved Dejah Thoris. The touch of my arm upon her naked shoulder had spoken to me in words I would not mistake, and I knew that I had loved her since the first moment that my eyes had met hers that first time in the plaza of the dead city of Korad.

XIV

A DUEL TO THE DEATH

My first impulse was to tell her of my love, and then I thought of the helplessness of her position wherein I alone could lighten the burdens of her captivity, and protect her in my poor way against the thousands of hereditary enemies she must face upon our arrival at Thark. I could not chance causing her additional pain or sorrow by declaring a love which, in all probability she did not return. Should I be so indiscreet, her position would be even more unbearable than now, and the thought that she might feel that I was taking advantage of her helplessness, to influence her decision was the final argument which sealed my lips.

"Why are you so quiet, Dejah Thoris?" I asked. "Possibly you would rather return to Sola and your quarters."

"No," she murmured, "I am happy here. I do not know why it is that I should always be happy and contented when you, John Carter, a stranger, are with me; yet at such times it seems that I am safe and that, with you, I shall soon return to my father's court and feel his strong arms about me and my mother's tears and kisses on my cheek."

"Do people kiss, then, upon Barsoom?" I asked, when she had explained the word she used, in answer to my inquiry as to its meaning.

"Parents, brothers, and sisters, yes; and," she added in a low, thoughtful tone, "lovers."

"And you, Dejah Thoris, have parents and brothers and sisters?"

"Yes."

"And a—lover?"

She was silent, nor could I venture to repeat the question.

"The man of Barsoom," she finally ventured, "does not ask personal questions of women, except his mother, and the woman he has fought for and won."

"But I have fought—" I started, and then I wished my tongue had been cut from my mouth; for she turned even as I caught myself and ceased, and drawing my silks from her shoulder she held them out to me, and without a word, and with head held high, she moved with the carriage of the queen she was toward the plaza and the doorway of her quarters.

I did not attempt to follow her, other than to see that she reached the building in safety, but, directing Woola to accompany her, I turned disconsolately and entered my own house. I sat for hours cross-legged, and cross-tempered, upon my silks meditating upon the queer freaks chance plays upon us poor devils of mortals.

So this was love! I had escaped it for all the years I had roamed the five continents and their encircling seas; in spite of beautiful women and urging opportunity; in spite of a half-desire for love and a constant search for my ideal, it had remained for me to fall furiously and hopelessly in love with a creature from another world, of a species similar possibly, yet not identical with mine. A woman who was hatched from an egg, and whose span of life might cover a thousand years; whose people had strange customs and ideas; a woman whose hopes, whose pleasures, whose standards of virtue and of right and wrong might vary as greatly from mine as did those of the green Martians.

Yes, I was a fool, but I was in love, and though I was suffering the greatest misery I had ever known I would not have had it otherwise for all the riches of Barsoom. Such is love, and such are lovers wherever love is known.

To me, Dejah Thoris was all that was perfect; all that was virtuous and beautiful and noble and good. I believed that from the bottom of my heart, from the depth of my soul on that night in Korad as I sat cross-legged upon my silks while the nearer moon of Barsoom raced through the western sky toward the horizon, and lighted up the gold and marble, and jeweled mosaics of my world-old chamber, and I believe it today as I sit at my desk in the little study overlooking the Hudson. Twenty years have intervened; for ten of them I lived and fought for Dejah Thoris and her people, and for ten I have lived upon her memory.

The morning of our departure for Thark dawned clear and hot, as do all Martian mornings except for the six weeks when the snow melts at the poles.

I sought out Dejah Thoris in the throng of departing chariots, but she turned her shoulder to me, and I could see the red blood mount to her cheek. With the foolish inconsistency of love I held my peace when I might have pled ignorance of the nature of my offense, or at least the gravity of it, and so have effected, at worst, a half conciliation.

My duty dictated that I must see that she was comfortable, and so I glanced into her chariot and rearranged her silks and furs. In doing so I noted with horror that she was heavily chained by one ankle to the side of the vehicle.

"What does this mean?" I cried, turning to Sola.

"Sarkoja thought it best," she answered, her face betokening her disapproval of the procedure.

Examining the manacles I saw that they fastened with a massive spring lock.

"Where is the key, Sola? Let me have it."

"Sarkoja wears it, John Carter," she answered.

I turned without further word and sought out Tars Tarkas, to whom I vehemently objected to the unnecessary humiliations and cruelties, as they seemed to my lover's eyes, that were being heaped upon Dejah Thoris.

"John Carter," he answered, "if ever you and Dejah Thoris escape the Tharks it will be upon this journey. We know that you will not go without her. You have shown yourself a mighty fighter, and we do not wish to manacle you, so we hold you both in the easiest way that will yet ensure security. I have spoken."

I saw the strength of his reasoning at a flash, and knew that it was futile to appeal from his decision, but I asked that the key be taken from Sarkoja and that she be directed to leave the prisoner alone in future.

"This much, Tars Tarkas, you may do for me in return for the friendship that, I must confess, I feel for you."

"Friendship?" he replied. "There is no such thing, John Carter; but have your will. I shall direct that Sarkoja cease to annoy the girl, and I myself will take the custody of the key."

"Unless you wish me to assume the responsibility," I said, smiling.

He looked at me long and earnestly before he spoke.

"Were you to give me your word that neither you nor Dejah Thoris would attempt to escape until after we have safely reached the court of Tal Hajus you might have the key and throw the chains into the river Iss."

"It was better that you held the key, Tars Tarkas," I replied.

He smiled, and said no more, but that night as we were making camp I saw him unfasten Dejah Thoris' fetters himself.

With all his cruel ferocity and coldness there was an undercurrent of something in Tars Tarkas which he seemed ever battling to subdue. Could it be a vestige of some human instinct come back from an ancient forbear to haunt him with the horror of his people's ways!

As I was approaching Dejah Thoris' chariot I passed Sarkoja, and the black, venomous look she accorded me was the sweetest balm I had felt for many hours. Lord, how she hated me! It bristled from her so palpably that one might almost have cut it with a sword.

A few moments later I saw her deep in conversation with a warrior named Zad; a big, hulking, powerful brute, but one who had never made a kill among his own chieftains, and so was still an *o mad*, or man with one name; he could win a second name only with the metal of some chieftain. It was this custom which entitled me to the names of either of the chieftains I had killed; in fact, some of the warriors addressed me as Dotar Sojat, a combination of the surnames of the two warrior chieftains whose metal I had taken, or, in other words, whom I had slain in fair fight.

As Sarkoja talked with Zad he cast occasional glances in my direction, while she seemed to be urging him very strongly to some action. I paid little attention to it at the time, but the next day I had good reason to recall the circumstances, and at the same time gain a slight insight into the depths of Sarkoja's hatred and the lengths to which she was capable of going to wreak her horrid vengeance on me.

Dejah Thoris would have none of me again on this evening, and though I spoke her name she neither replied, nor conceded by so much as the flutter of an eyelid that she realized my existence. In my extremity I did what most other lovers would have done; I sought word from her through an intimate. In this instance it was Sola whom I intercepted in another part of camp.

"What is the matter with Dejah Thoris?" I blurted out at her. "Why will she not speak to me?"

Sola seemed puzzled herself, as though such strange actions on the part of two humans were quite beyond her, as indeed they were, poor child.

"She says you have angered her, and that is all she will say, except that she is the daughter of a jed and the granddaughter of a jeddak and she has been humiliated by a creature who could not polish the teeth of her grandmother's sorak."

I pondered over this report for some time, finally asking, "What might a sorak be, Sola?"

"A little animal about as big as my hand, which the red Martian women keep to play with," explained Sola.

Not fit to polish the teeth of her grandmother's cat! I must rank pretty low in the consideration of Dejah Thoris, I thought; but I could not help laughing at the strange figure of speech, so homely and in this respect so earthly. It made me homesick, for it sounded very much like "not fit to polish her shoes." And then commenced a train of thought quite new to me. I began to wonder what my people at home were doing. I had not seen them for years. There was a family of Carters in Virginia who claimed close relationship with me; I was supposed to be a great uncle, or something of the kind equally foolish. I could pass anywhere for twenty-five to thirty years of age, and to be a great uncle always seemed the height of incongruity, for my thoughts and feelings were those of a boy. There were two little kiddies in the Carter family whom I had loved and who had thought there was no one on Earth like Uncle Jack; I could see them just as plainly, as I stood there under the moonlit skies of Barsoom, and I longed for them as I had never longed for any mortals before. By nature a wanderer, I had never known the true meaning of the word home, but the great hall of the Carters had always stood for all that the word did mean to me, and now my heart turned toward it from the cold and unfriendly peoples I had been thrown amongst. For did not even Dejah Thoris despise me! I was a low creature, so low in fact that I was not even fit to polish the teeth of her grandmother's cat; and then my saving sense of humor came to my rescue, and laughing I turned into my silks and furs and slept upon the moon-haunted ground the sleep of a tired and healthy fighting man.

We broke camp the next day at an early hour and marched with only a single halt until just before dark. Two incidents broke the tediousness of the march. About noon we espied far to our right what was evidently an incubator, and Lorquas Ptomel directed Tars Tarkas to investigate it. The latter took a dozen warriors, including myself, and we raced across the velvety carpeting of moss to the little enclosure.

It was indeed an incubator, but the eggs were very small in comparison with those I had seen hatching in ours at the time of my arrival on Mars.

Tars Tarkas dismounted and examined the enclosure minutely, finally announcing that it belonged to the green men of Warhoon and that the cement was scarcely dry where it had been walled up.

"They cannot be a day's march ahead of us," he exclaimed, the light of battle leaping to his fierce face.

The work at the incubator was short indeed. The warriors tore open the entrance and a couple of them, crawling in, soon demolished all the eggs with their short-swords. Then remounting we dashed back to join the cavalcade. During the ride I took occasion to ask Tars Tarkas if these Warhoons whose eggs we had destroyed were a smaller people than his Tharks.

"I noticed that their eggs were so much smaller than those I saw hatching in your incubator," I added.

He explained that the eggs had just been placed there; but, like all green Martian eggs, they would grow during the five-year period of incubation until they obtained the size of those I had seen hatching on the day of my arrival on Barsoom. This was indeed an interesting piece of information, for it had always seemed remarkable to me that the green Martian women, large as they were, could bring forth such enormous eggs as I had seen the four-foot infants emerging from. As a matter of fact, the new-laid egg is but little larger than an ordinary goose egg, and as it does not commence to grow until subjected to the light of the sun the chieftains have little difficulty in transporting several hundreds of them at one time from the storage vaults to the incubators.

Shortly after the incident of the Warhoon eggs we halted to rest the animals, and it was during this halt that the second of the day's interesting episodes occurred. I was engaged in changing my riding cloths from one of my thoats to the other, for I divided the day's work between them, when Zad approached me, and without a word struck my animal a terrific blow with his long-sword.

I did not need a manual of green Martian etiquette to know what reply to make, for, in fact, I was so wild with anger that I could scarcely refrain from drawing my pistol and shooting him down for the brute he was; but he stood waiting with drawn long-sword, and my only choice was to draw my own and meet him in fair fight with his choice of weapons or a lesser one.

This latter alternative is always permissible, therefore I could have used my short-sword, my dagger, my hatchet, or my fists had I wished, and been entirely within my rights, but I could not use firearms or a spear while he held only his long-sword.

I chose the same weapon he had drawn because I knew he prided himself upon his ability with it, and I wished, if I worsted him at all, to do it with his own weapon. The fight that followed was a long one and delayed the resumption of the march for an hour. The entire community surrounded us, leaving a clear space about one hundred feet in diameter for our battle.

Zad first attempted to rush me down as a bull might a wolf, but I was much too quick for him, and each time I side-stepped his rushes he would go lunging past me, only to receive a nick from my sword upon his arm or back. He was soon streaming blood from a half dozen minor wounds, but I could not obtain an opening to deliver an effective thrust. Then he changed his tactics, and fighting warily and with extreme dexterity, he tried to do by science what he was unable to do by brute strength. I must admit that he was a magnificent swordsman, and had it not been for my greater endurance and the remarkable agility the lesser gravitation of Mars lent me I might not have been able to put up the creditable fight I did against him.

We circled for some time without doing much damage on either side; the long, straight, needle-like swords flashing in the sunlight, and ringing out upon the stillness as they crashed together with each effective parry. Finally Zad, realizing that he was tiring more than I, evidently decided to close in and end the battle in a final blaze of glory for himself; just as he rushed me a blinding flash of light struck full in my eyes, so that I could not see his approach and could only leap blindly to one side in an effort to escape the mighty blade that it seemed I could already feel in my vitals. I was only partially successful, as a sharp pain in my left shoulder attested, but in the sweep of my glance as I sought to again locate my adversary, a sight met my astonished gaze which paid me well for the wound the temporary blindness had caused me. There, upon Dejah Thoris' chariot stood three figures, for the purpose evidently of witnessing the encounter above the heads of the intervening Tharks. There were Dejah Thoris, Sola, and Sarkoja, and as my fleeting glance swept over them a little tableau was presented which will stand graven in my memory to the day of my death.

As I looked, Dejah Thoris turned upon Sarkoja with the fury of a young tigress and struck something from her upraised hand; something which flashed in the sunlight as it spun to the ground. Then I knew what had blinded me at that crucial moment of the fight, and how Sarkoja had found a way to kill me without herself delivering the final thrust. Another thing I saw, too, which almost lost my life for me then and there, for it took my mind for the fraction of an instant entirely from my antagonist; for, as Dejah Thoris struck the tiny mirror from her hand, Sarkoja, her face livid with hatred and baffled rage, whipped out her dagger and aimed a terrific blow at Dejah Thoris; and then Sola, our dear and faithful Sola, sprang between them; the last I saw was the great knife descending upon her shielding breast.

My enemy had recovered from his thrust and was making it extremely interesting for me, so I reluctantly gave my attention to the work in hand, but my mind was not upon the battle.

We rushed each other furiously time after time, 'til suddenly, feeling the sharp point of his sword at my breast in a thrust I could neither parry nor escape, I threw myself upon him with outstretched sword and with all the weight of my body, determined that I would not die alone if I could prevent it. I felt the steel tear into my chest, all went black before me, my head whirled in dizziness, and I felt my knees giving beneath me.

XV

SOLA TELLS ME HER STORY

When consciousness returned, and, as I soon learned, I was down but a moment, I sprang quickly to my feet searching for my sword, and there I found it, buried to the hilt in the green breast of Zad, who lay stone dead upon the ochre moss of the ancient sea bottom. As I regained my full senses I found his weapon piercing my left breast, but only through the flesh and muscles which cover my ribs, entering near the center of my chest and coming out below the shoulder. As I had lunged I had turned so that his sword merely passed beneath the muscles, inflicting a painful but not dangerous wound.

Removing the blade from my body I also regained my own, and turning my back upon his ugly carcass, I moved, sick, sore, and disgusted, toward the chariots which bore my retinue and my belongings. A murmur of Martian applause greeted me, but I cared not for it.

Bleeding and weak I reached my women, who, accustomed to such happenings, dressed my wounds, applying the wonderful healing and remedial agents which make only the most instantaneous of death blows fatal. Give a Martian woman a chance and death must take a back seat. They soon had me patched up so that, except for weakness from loss of blood and a little soreness around the wound, I suffered no great distress from this thrust which, under earthly treatment, undoubtedly would have put me flat on my back for days.

As soon as they were through with me I hastened to the chariot of Dejah Thoris, where I found my poor Sola with her chest swathed in bandages, but apparently little the worse for her encounter with Sarkoja, whose dagger it seemed had struck the edge of one of Sola's metal breast ornaments and, thus deflected, had inflicted but a slight flesh wound.

As I approached I found Dejah Thoris lying prone upon her silks and furs, her lithe form wracked with sobs. She did not notice my presence, nor did she hear me speaking with Sola, who was standing a short distance from the vehicle.

"Is she injured?" I asked of Sola, indicating Dejah Thoris by an inclination of my head.

"No," she answered, "she thinks that you are dead."

"And that her grandmother's cat may now have no one to polish its teeth?" I queried, smiling.

"I think you wrong her, John Carter," said Sola. "I do not understand either her ways or yours, but I am sure the granddaughter of ten thousand jeddaks would never grieve like this over any who held but the highest claim upon her affections. They are a proud race, but they are just, as are all Barsoomians, and you must have hurt or wronged her grievously that she will not admit your existence living, though she mourns you dead.

"Tears are a strange sight upon Barsoom," she continued, "and so it is difficult for me to interpret them. I have seen but two people weep in all my life, other than Dejah Thoris; one wept from sorrow, the other from baffled rage. The first was my mother, years ago before they killed her; the other was Sarkoja, when they dragged her from me today."

"Your mother!" I exclaimed, "but, Sola, you could not have known your mother, child."

"But I did. And my father also," she added. "If you would like to hear the strange and un-Barsoomian story come to the chariot tonight, John Carter, and I will tell you that of which I have never spoken in all my life before. And now the signal has been given to resume the march, you must go."

"I will come tonight, Sola," I promised. "Be sure to tell Dejah Thoris I am alive and well. I shall not force myself upon her, and be sure that you do not let her know I saw her tears. If she would speak with me I but await her command."

Sola mounted the chariot, which was swinging into its place in line, and I hastened to my waiting thoat and galloped to my station beside Tars Tarkas at the rear of the column.

We made a most imposing and awe-inspiring spectacle as we strung out across the yellow landscape; the two hundred and fifty ornate and brightly colored chariots, preceded by an advance guard of some two hundred mounted warriors and chieftains riding five abreast and one hundred yards apart, and followed by a like number in the same formation, with a score or more of flankers on either side; the fifty extra mastodons, or heavy draught animals, known as zitidars, and the five or six hundred extra thoats of the warriors running loose within the hollow square formed by the surrounding warriors. The gleaming metal and jewels of the gorgeous ornaments of the men and women, duplicated in the trappings of the zitidars and thoats, and interspersed with the flashing colors of magnificent silks and furs and feathers, lent a barbaric splendor to the caravan which would have turned an East Indian potentate green with envy.

The enormous broad tires of the chariots and the padded feet of the animals brought forth no sound from the moss-covered sea bottom; and so we moved in utter silence, like some huge phantasmagoria, except when the stillness was broken by the guttural growling of a goaded zitidar, or the squealing of fighting thoats. The green Martians converse but little, and then usually in monosyllables, low and like the faint rumbling of distant thunder.

We traversed a trackless waste of moss which, bending to the pressure of broad tire or padded foot, rose up again behind us, leaving no sign that we had passed. We might indeed have been the wraiths of the departed dead upon the dead sea of that dying planet for all the sound or sign we made in passing. It was the first march of a large body of men and animals I had ever witnessed which raised no dust and left no spoor; for there is no dust upon Mars except in the cultivated districts during the winter months, and even then the absence of high winds renders it almost unnoticeable.

We camped that night at the foot of the hills we had been approaching for two days and which marked the southern boundary of this particular sea. Our animals had been two days without drink, nor had they had water for nearly two months, not since shortly after leaving Thark; but, as Tars Tarkas explained to me, they require but little and can live almost indefinitely upon the moss which covers Barsoom, and which, he told me, holds in its tiny stems sufficient moisture to meet the limited demands of the animals.

After partaking of my evening meal of cheese-like food and vegetable milk I sought out Sola, whom I found working by the light of a torch upon some of Tars Tarkas' trappings. She looked up at my approach, her face lighting with pleasure and with welcome.

"I am glad you came," she said; "Dejah Thoris sleeps and I am lonely. Mine own people do not care for me, John Carter; I am too unlike them. It is a sad fate, since I must live my life amongst them, and I often wish that I were a true green Martian woman, without love and without hope; but I have known love and so I am lost.

"I promised to tell you my story, or rather the story of my parents. From what I have learned of you and the ways of your people I am sure that the tale will not seem strange to you, but among green Martians it has no parallel within the memory of the oldest living Thark, nor do our legends hold many similar tales.

"My mother was rather small, in fact too small to be allowed the responsibilities of maternity, as our chieftains breed principally for size. She was also less cold and cruel than most green Martian women, and caring little for their society, she often roamed the deserted avenues of Thark alone, or went and sat among the wild flowers that deck the nearby hills, thinking thoughts and wishing wishes which I believe I alone among Tharkian women today may understand, for am I not the child of my mother?

"And there among the hills she met a young warrior, whose duty it was to guard the feeding zitidars and thoats and see that they roamed not beyond the hills. They spoke at first only of such things as interest a community of Tharks, but gradually, as they came to meet more often, and, as was now quite evident to both, no longer by chance, they talked about themselves, their likes, their ambitions and their hopes. She trusted him and told him of the awful repugnance she felt for the cruelties of their kind, for the hideous, loveless lives they must ever lead, and then she waited for the storm of denunciation to break from his cold, hard lips; but instead he took her in his arms and kissed her.

"They kept their love a secret for six long years. She, my mother, was of the retinue of the great Tal Hajus, while her lover was a simple warrior, wearing only his own metal. Had their defection from the traditions of the Tharks been discovered both would have paid the penalty in the great arena before Tal Hajus and the assembled hordes.

"The egg from which I came was hidden beneath a great glass vessel upon the highest and most inaccessible of the partially ruined towers of ancient Thark. Once each year my mother visited it for the five long years it lay there in the process of incubation. She dared not come oftener, for in the mighty guilt of her conscience she feared that her every move was watched. During this period my father gained great distinction as a warrior and had taken the metal from several chieftains. His love for my mother had never diminished, and his own ambition in life was to reach a point where he might wrest the metal from Tal Hajus himself, and thus, as ruler of the Tharks, be free to claim her as his own, as well as, by the might of his power, protect the child which otherwise would be quickly dispatched should the truth become known.

"It was a wild dream, that of wresting the metal from Tal Hajus in five short years, but his advance was rapid, and he soon stood high in the councils of Thark. But one day the chance was lost forever, in so far as it could come in time to save his loved ones, for he was ordered away upon a long expedition to the ice-clad south, to make war upon the natives there and despoil them of their furs, for such is the manner of the green Barsoomian; he does not labor for what he can wrest in battle from others.

"He was gone for four years, and when he returned all had been over for three; for about a year after his departure, and shortly before the time for the return of an expedition which had gone forth to fetch the fruits of a community incubator, the egg had hatched. Thereafter my mother continued to keep me in the old tower, visiting me nightly and lavishing upon me the love the community life would have robbed us both of. She hoped, upon the return of the expedition from the incubator, to mix me with the other young assigned to the quarters of Tal Hajus, and thus escape the fate which would surely follow discovery of her sin against the ancient traditions of the green men.

"She taught me rapidly the language and customs of my kind, and one night she told me the story I have told to you up to this point, impressing upon me the necessity for absolute secrecy and the great caution I must exercise after she had placed me with the other young Tharks to permit no one to guess that I was further advanced in education than they, nor by any sign to divulge in the presence of others my affection for her, or my knowledge of my parentage; and then drawing me close to her she whispered in my ear the name of my father.

"And then a light flashed out upon the darkness of the tower chamber, and there stood Sarkoja, her gleaming, baleful eyes fixed in a frenzy of loathing and contempt upon my mother. The torrent of hatred and abuse she poured out upon her turned my young heart cold in terror. That she had heard the entire story was apparent, and that she had suspected something wrong from my mother's long nightly absences from her quarters accounted for her presence there on that fateful night.

"One thing she had not heard, nor did she know, the whispered name of my father. This was apparent from her repeated demands upon my mother to disclose the name of her partner in sin, but no amount of abuse or threats could wring this from her, and to save me from needless torture she lied, for she told Sarkoja that she alone knew nor would she ever tell her child.

"With final imprecations, Sarkoja hastened away to Tal Hajus to report her discovery, and while she was gone my mother, wrapping me in the silks and furs of her night coverings, so that I was scarcely noticeable, descended to the streets and ran wildly away toward the outskirts of the city, in the direction which led to the far south, out toward the man whose protection she might not claim, but on whose face she wished to look once more before she died.

"As we neared the city's southern extremity a sound came to us from across the mossy flat, from the direction of the only pass through the hills which led to the gates, the pass by which caravans from either north or south or east or west would enter the city. The sounds we heard were the squealing of thoats and the grumbling of zitidars, with the occasional clank of arms which announced the approach of a body of warriors. The thought uppermost in her mind was that it was my father returned from his expedition, but the cunning of the Thark held her from headlong and precipitate flight to greet him.

"Retreating into the shadows of a doorway she awaited the coming of the cavalcade which shortly entered the avenue, breaking its formation and thronging the thoroughfare from wall to wall. As the head of the procession passed us the lesser moon swung clear of the overhanging roofs and lit up the scene with all the brilliancy of her wondrous light. My mother shrank further back into the friendly shadows, and from her hiding place saw that the expedition was not that of my father, but the returning caravan bearing the young Tharks. Instantly her plan was formed, and as a great chariot swung close to our hiding place she slipped stealthily in upon the trailing tailboard, crouching low in the shadow of the high side, straining me to her bosom in a frenzy of love.

"She knew, what I did not, that never again after that night would she hold me to her breast, nor was it likely we would ever look upon each other's face again. In the confusion of the plaza she mixed me with the other children, whose guardians during the journey were now free to relinquish their responsibility. We were herded together into a great room, fed by women who had not accompanied the expedition, and the next day we were parceled out among the retinues of the chieftains.

"I never saw my mother after that night. She was imprisoned by Tal Hajus, and every effort, including the most horrible and shameful torture, was brought to bear upon her to wring from her lips the name of my father; but she remained steadfast and loyal, dying at last amidst the laughter of Tal Hajus and his chieftains during some awful torture she was undergoing.

"I learned afterwards that she told them that she had killed me to save me from a like fate at their hands, and that she had thrown my body to the white apes. Sarkoja alone disbelieved her, and I feel to this day that she suspects my true origin, but does not dare expose me, at the present, at all events, because she also guesses, I am sure, the identity of my father.

"When he returned from his expedition and learned the story of my mother's fate I was present as Tal Hajus told him; but never by the quiver of a muscle did he betray the slightest emotion; only he did not laugh as Tal

Hajus gleefully described her death struggles. From that moment on he was the cruelest of the cruel, and I am awaiting the day when he shall win the goal of his ambition, and feel the carcass of Tal Hajus beneath his foot, for I am as sure that he but waits the opportunity to wreak a terrible vengeance, and that his great love is as strong in his breast as when it first transfigured him nearly forty years ago, as I am that we sit here upon the edge of a world-old ocean while sensible people sleep, John Carter."

"And your father, Sola, is he with us now?" I asked.

"Yes," she replied, "but he does not know me for what I am, nor does he know who betrayed my mother to Tal Hajus. I alone know my father's name, and only I and Tal Hajus and Sarkoja know that it was she who carried the tale that brought death and torture upon her he loved."

We sat silent for a few moments, she wrapped in the gloomy thoughts of her terrible past, and I in pity for the poor creatures whom the heartless, senseless customs of their race had doomed to loveless lives of cruelty and of hate. Presently she spoke.

"John Carter, if ever a real man walked the cold, dead bosom of Barsoom you are one. I know that I can trust you, and because the knowledge may someday help you or him or Dejah Thoris or myself, I am going to tell you the name of my father, nor place any restrictions or conditions upon your tongue. When the time comes, speak the truth if it seems best to you. I trust you because I know that you are not cursed with the terrible trait of absolute and unswerving truthfulness, that you could lie like one of your own Virginia gentlemen if a lie would save others from sorrow or suffering. My father's name is Tars Tarkas."

XVI

WE PLAN ESCAPE

The remainder of our journey to Thark was uneventful. We were twenty days upon the road, crossing two sea bottoms and passing through or around a number of ruined cities, mostly smaller than Korad. Twice we crossed the famous Martian waterways, or canals, so-called by our earthly astronomers. When we approached these points a warrior would be sent far ahead with a powerful field glass, and if no great body of red Martian troops was in sight we would advance as close as possible without chance of being seen and then camp until dark, when we would slowly approach the cultivated tract, and, locating one of the numerous, broad highways which cross these areas at regular intervals, creep silently and stealthily across to the arid lands upon the other side. It required five hours to make one of these crossings without a single halt, and the other consumed the entire night, so that we were just leaving the confines of the high-walled fields when the sun broke out upon us.

Crossing in the darkness, as we did, I was unable to see but little, except as the nearer moon, in her wild and ceaseless hurtling through the Barsoomian heavens, lit up little patches of the landscape from time to time, disclosing walled fields and low, rambling buildings, presenting much the appearance of earthly farms. There were many trees, methodically arranged, and some of them were of enormous height; there were animals in some of the enclosures, and they announced their presence by terrified squealings and snortings as they scented our queer, wild beasts and wilder human beings.

Only once did I perceive a human being, and that was at the intersection of our crossroad with the wide, white turnpike which cuts each cultivated district longitudinally at its exact center. The fellow must have been sleeping beside the road, for, as I came abreast of him, he raised upon one elbow and after a single glance at the approaching caravan leaped shrieking to his feet and fled madly down the road, scaling a nearby wall with the agility of a scared cat. The Tharks paid him not the slightest attention; they were not out upon the warpath, and the only sign that I had that they had seen him was a quickening of the pace of the caravan as we hastened toward the bordering desert which marked our entrance into the realm of Tal Hajus.

Not once did I have speech with Dejah Thoris, as she sent no word to me that I would be welcome at her chariot, and my foolish pride kept me from making any advances. I verily believe that a man's way with women is in inverse ratio to his prowess among men. The weakling and the saphead have often great ability to charm the fair sex, while the fighting man who can face a thousand real dangers unafraid, sits hiding in the shadows like some frightened child.

Just thirty days after my advent upon Barsoom we entered the ancient city of Thark, from whose long-forgotten people this horde of green men have stolen even their name. The hordes of Thark number some thirty thousand souls, and are divided into twenty-five communities. Each community has its own jed and lesser chieftains, but all are under the rule of Tal Hajus, Jeddak of Thark. Five communities make their headquarters at the city of Thark, and the balance are scattered among other deserted cities of ancient Mars throughout the district claimed by Tal Hajus.

We made our entry into the great central plaza early in the afternoon. There were no enthusiastic friendly greetings for the returned expedition. Those who chanced to be in sight spoke the names of warriors or women with whom they came in direct contact, in the formal greeting of their kind, but when it was discovered that they brought two captives a greater interest was aroused, and Dejah Thoris and I were the centers of inquiring groups.

We were soon assigned to new quarters, and the balance of the day was devoted to settling ourselves to the changed conditions. My home now was upon an avenue leading into the plaza from the south, the main artery down which we had marched from the gates of the city. I was at the far end of the square and had an entire building to myself. The same grandeur of architecture which was so noticeable a characteristic of Korad was in evidence here, only, if that were possible, on a larger and richer scale. My quarters would have been suitable for housing the greatest of earthly emperors, but to these queer creatures nothing about a building appealed to them but its size and the enormity of its chambers; the larger the building, the more desirable; and so Tal Hajus occupied what must have been an enormous public building, the largest in the city, but entirely unfitted for residence purposes; the next largest was reserved for Lorquas Ptomel, the next for the jed of a lesser rank, and so on to the bottom of the list of five jeds. The warriors occupied the buildings with the chieftains to whose retinues they belonged; or, if they preferred, sought shelter among any of the thousands of untenanted buildings in their own quarter of town; each community being assigned a certain section of the city. The selection of building had to be made in accordance with these divisions, except in so far as the jeds were concerned, they all occupying edifices which fronted upon the plaza.

When I had finally put my house in order, or rather seen that it had been done, it was nearing sunset, and I hastened out with the intention of locating Sola and her charges, as I had determined upon having speech with Dejah Thoris and trying to impress on her the necessity of our at least patching up a truce until I could find some way of aiding her to escape. I searched in vain until the upper rim of the great red sun was just disappearing behind the horizon and then I spied the ugly head of Woola peering from a second-story window on the opposite side of the very street where I was quartered, but nearer the plaza.

Without waiting for a further invitation I bolted up the winding runway which led to the second floor, and entering a great chamber at the front of the building was greeted by the frenzied Woola, who threw his great carcass upon me, nearly hurling me to the floor; the poor old fellow was so glad to see me that I thought he would devour me, his head split from ear to ear, showing his three rows of tusks in his hobgoblin smile.

Quieting him with a word of command and a caress, I looked hurriedly through the approaching gloom for a sign of Dejah Thoris, and then, not seeing her, I called her name. There was an answering murmur from the far corner of the apartment, and with a couple of quick strides I was standing beside her where she crouched among the furs and silks upon an ancient carved wooden seat. As I waited she rose to her full height and looking me straight in the eye said:

"What would Dotar Sojat, Thark, of Dejah Thoris his captive?"

"Dejah Thoris, I do not know how I have angered you. It was furtherest from my desire to hurt or offend you, whom I had hoped to protect and comfort. Have none of me if it is your will, but that you must aid me in effecting your escape, if such a thing be possible, is not my request, but my command. When you are safe once more at your father's court you may do with me as you please, but from now on until that day I am your master, and you must obey and aid me."

She looked at me long and earnestly and I thought that she was softening toward me.

"I understand your words, Dotar Sojat," she replied, "but you I do not understand. You are a queer mixture of child and man, of brute and noble. I only wish that I might read your heart."

"Look down at your feet, Dejah Thoris; it lies there now where it has lain since that other night at Korad, and where it will ever lie beating alone for you until death stills it forever."

She took a little step toward me, her beautiful hands outstretched in a strange, groping gesture.

"What do you mean, John Carter?" she whispered. "What are you saying to me?"

"I am saying what I had promised myself that I would not say to you, at least until you were no longer a captive among the green men; what from your attitude toward me for the past twenty days I had thought never to say to you; I am saying, Dejah Thoris, that I am yours, body and soul, to serve you, to fight for you, and to die for you. Only one thing I ask of you in return, and that is that you make no sign, either of condemnation or of approbation of my words until you are safe among your own people, and that whatever sentiments you harbor toward me they be not influenced or colored by gratitude; whatever I may do to serve you will be prompted solely from selfish motives, since it gives me more pleasure to serve you than not."

"I will respect your wishes, John Carter, because I understand the motives which prompt them, and I accept your service no more willingly than I bow to your authority; your word shall be my law. I have twice wronged you in my thoughts and again I ask your forgiveness."

Further conversation of a personal nature was prevented by the entrance of Sola, who was much agitated and wholly unlike her usual calm and possessed self.

"That horrible Sarkoja has been before Tal Hajus," she cried, "and from what I heard upon the plaza there is little hope for either of you."

"What do they say?" inquired Dejah Thoris.

"That you will be thrown to the wild calots [dogs] in the great arena as soon as the hordes have assembled for the yearly games."

"Sola," I said, "you are a Thark, but you hate and loathe the customs of your people as much as we do. Will you not accompany us in one supreme effort to escape? I am sure that Dejah Thoris can offer you a home and protection among her people, and your fate can be no worse among them than it must ever be here."

"Yes," cried Dejah Thoris, "come with us, Sola, you will be better off among the red men of Helium than you are here, and I can promise you not only a home with us, but the love and affection your nature craves and which must always be denied you by the customs of your own race. Come with us, Sola; we might go without you, but your fate would be terrible if they thought you had connived to aid us. I know that even that fear would not tempt you to interfere in our escape, but we want you with us, we want you to come to a land of sunshine and happiness, amongst a people who know the meaning of love, of sympathy, and of gratitude. Say that you will, Sola; tell me that you will."

"The great waterway which leads to Helium is but fifty miles to the south," murmured Sola, half to herself; "a swift thoat might make it in three hours; and then to Helium it is five hundred miles, most of the way through thinly settled districts. They would know and they would follow us. We might hide among the great trees for a time, but the chances are small indeed for escape. They would follow us to the very gates of Helium, and they would take toll of life at every step; you do not know them."

"Is there no other way we might reach Helium?" I asked. "Can you not draw me a rough map of the country we must traverse, Dejah Thoris?"

"Yes," she replied, and taking a great diamond from her hair she drew upon the marble floor the first map of Barsoomian territory I had ever seen. It was crisscrossed in every direction with long straight lines, sometimes running parallel and sometimes converging toward some great circle. The lines, she said, were waterways; the circles, cities; and one far to the northwest of us she pointed out as Helium. There were other cities closer, but she said she feared to enter many of them, as they were not all friendly toward Helium.

Finally, after studying the map carefully in the moonlight which now flooded the room, I pointed out a waterway far to the north of us which also seemed to lead to Helium.

"Does not this pierce your grandfather's territory?" I asked.

"Yes," she answered, "but it is two hundred miles north of us; it is one of the waterways we crossed on the trip to Thark."

"They would never suspect that we would try for that distant waterway," I answered, "and that is why I think that it is the best route for our escape."

Sola agreed with me, and it was decided that we should leave Thark this same night; just as quickly, in fact, as I could find and saddle my thoats. Sola was to ride one and Dejah Thoris and I the other; each of us carrying sufficient food and drink to last us for two days, since the animals could not be urged too rapidly for so long a distance.

I directed Sola to proceed with Dejah Thoris along one of the less frequented avenues to the southern boundary of the city, where I would overtake them with the thoats as quickly as possible; then, leaving them to gather what food, silks, and furs we were to need, I slipped quietly to the rear of the first floor, and entered the courtyard, where our animals were moving restlessly about, as was their habit, before settling down for the night.

In the shadows of the buildings and out beneath the radiance of the Martian moons moved the great herd of thoats and zitidars, the latter grunting their low gutturals and the former occasionally emitting the sharp squeal which denotes the almost habitual state of rage in which these creatures passed their existence. They were quieter now, owing to the absence of man, but as they scented me they became more restless and their hideous noise increased. It was risky business, this entering a paddock of thoats alone and at night; first, because their increasing noisiness might warn the nearby warriors that something was amiss, and also because for the slightest cause, or for no cause at all some great bull thoat might take it upon himself to lead a charge upon me.

Having no desire to awaken their nasty tempers upon such a night as this, where so much depended upon secrecy and dispatch, I hugged the shadows of the buildings, ready at an instant's warning to leap into the safety of a nearby door or window. Thus I moved silently to the great gates which opened upon the street at the back of the court, and as I neared the exit I called softly to my two animals. How I thanked the kind providence which had given me the foresight to win the love and confidence of these wild dumb brutes, for presently from the far side of the court I saw two huge bulks forcing their way toward me through the surging mountains of flesh.

They came quite close to me, rubbing their muzzles against my body and nosing for the bits of food it was always my practice to reward them with. Opening the gates I ordered the two great beasts to pass out, and then slipping quietly after them I closed the portals behind me.

I did not saddle or mount the animals there, but instead walked quietly in the shadows of the buildings toward an unfrequented avenue which led toward the point I had arranged to meet Dejah Thoris and Sola. With the noiselessness of disembodied spirits we moved stealthily along the deserted streets, but not until we were within sight of the plain beyond the city did I commence to breathe freely. I was sure that Sola and Dejah Thoris would find no difficulty in reaching our rendezvous undetected, but with my great thoats I was not so sure for myself, as it was quite unusual for warriors to leave the city after dark; in fact there was no place for them to go within any but a long ride.

I reached the appointed meeting place safely, but as Dejah Thoris and Sola were not there I led my animals into the entrance hall of one of the large buildings. Presuming that one of the other women of the same household may have come in to speak to Sola, and so delayed their departure, I did not feel any undue apprehension until nearly an hour had passed without a sign of them, and by the time another half hour had crawled away I was becoming filled with grave anxiety. Then there broke upon the stillness of the night the sound of an approaching party, which, from the noise, I knew could be no fugitives creeping stealthily toward liberty. Soon the party was near me, and from the black shadows of my entranceway I perceived a score of mounted warriors, who, in passing, dropped a dozen words that fetched my heart clean into the top of my head.

"He would likely have arranged to meet them just without the city, and so—" I heard no more, they had passed on; but it was enough. Our plan had been discovered, and the chances for escape from now on to the fearful end would be small indeed. My one hope now was to return undetected to the quarters of Dejah Thoris and learn what fate had overtaken her, but how to do it with these great monstrous thoats upon my hands, now that the city probably was aroused by the knowledge of my escape was a problem of no mean proportions.

Suddenly an idea occurred to me, and acting on my knowledge of the construction of the buildings of these ancient Martian cities with a hollow court within the center of each square, I groped my way blindly through the dark chambers, calling the great thoats after me. They had difficulty in negotiating some of the doorways, but as the buildings fronting the city's principal exposures were all designed upon a magnificent scale, they were able to wriggle through without sticking fast; and thus we finally made the inner court where I found, as I had expected, the usual carpet of moss-like vegetation which would prove their food and drink until I could return them to their own enclosure. That they would be as quiet and contented here as elsewhere I was confident, nor was there but the remotest possibility that they would be discovered, as the green men had no great desire to enter these outlying buildings, which were frequented by the only thing, I believe, which caused them the sensation of fear—the great white apes of Barsoom.

Removing the saddle trappings, I hid them just within the rear doorway of the building through which we had entered the court, and, turning the beasts loose, quickly made my way across the court to the rear of the buildings upon the further side, and thence to the avenue beyond. Waiting in the doorway of the building until I was assured that no one was approaching, I hurried across to the opposite side and through the first doorway to the court beyond; thus, crossing through court after court with only the slight chance of detection which the necessary crossing of the avenues entailed, I made my way in safety to the courtyard in the rear of Dejah Thoris' quarters.

Here, of course, I found the beasts of the warriors who quartered in the adjacent buildings, and the warriors themselves I might expect to meet within if I entered; but, fortunately for me, I had another and safer method of reaching the upper story where Dejah Thoris should be found, and, after first determining as nearly as possible which of the buildings she occupied, for I had never observed them before from the court side, I took advantage of my relatively great strength and agility and sprang upward until I grasped the sill of a second-story window which I thought to be in the rear of her apartment. Drawing myself inside the room I moved stealthily toward the front of the building, and not until I had quite reached the doorway of her room was I made aware by voices that it was occupied.

I did not rush headlong in, but listened without to assure myself that it was Dejah Thoris and that it was safe to venture within. It was well indeed that I took this precaution, for the conversation I heard was in the low gutturals of men, and the words which finally came to me proved a most timely warning. The speaker was a chieftain and he was giving orders to four of his warriors.

"And when he returns to this chamber," he was saying, "as he surely will when he finds she does not meet him at the city's edge, you four are to spring upon him and disarm him. It will require the combined strength of all of you to do it if the reports they bring back from Korad are correct. When you have him fast bound bear him to the vaults beneath the jeddak's quarters and chain him securely where he may be found when Tal Hajus wishes him. Allow him to speak with none, nor permit any other to enter this apartment before he comes. There will be no danger of the girl returning, for by this time she is safe in the arms of Tal Hajus, and may all her ancestors have pity upon her, for Tal Hajus will have none; the great Sarkoja has done a noble night's work. I go, and if you fail to capture him when he comes, I commend your carcasses to the cold bosom of Iss."

XVII

A COSTLY RECAPTURE

As the speaker ceased he turned to leave the apartment by the door where I was standing, but I needed to wait no longer; I had heard enough to fill my soul with dread, and stealing quietly away I returned to the courtyard by the way I had come. My plan of action was formed upon the instant, and crossing the square and the bordering avenue upon the opposite side I soon stood within the courtyard of Tal Hajus.

The brilliantly lighted apartments of the first floor told me where first to seek, and advancing to the windows I peered within. I soon discovered that my approach was not to be the easy thing I had hoped, for the rear rooms bordering the court were filled with warriors and women. I then glanced up at the stories above, discovering that the third was apparently unlighted, and so decided to make my entrance to the building from that point. It was the work of but a moment for me to reach the windows above, and soon I had drawn myself within the sheltering shadows of the unlighted third floor.

Fortunately the room I had selected was untenanted, and creeping noiselessly to the corridor beyond I discovered a light in the apartments ahead of me. Reaching what appeared to be a doorway I discovered that it was but an opening upon an immense inner chamber which towered from the first floor, two stories below me, to the dome-like roof of the building, high above my head. The floor of this great circular hall was thronged with chieftains, warriors and women, and at one end was a great raised platform upon which squatted the most hideous beast I had ever put my eyes upon. He had all the cold, hard, cruel, terrible features of the green warriors, but accentuated and debased by the animal passions to which he had given himself over for many years. There was not a mark of dignity or pride upon his bestial countenance, while his enormous bulk spread itself out upon the platform where he squatted like some huge devil fish, his six limbs accentuating the similarity in a horrible and startling manner.

But the sight that froze me with apprehension was that of Dejah Thoris and Sola standing there before him, and the fiendish leer of him as he let his great protruding eyes gloat upon the lines of her beautiful figure. She was speaking, but I could not hear what she said, nor could I make out the low grumbling of his reply. She stood there erect before him, her head high held, and even at the distance I was from them I could read the scorn and disgust upon her face as she let her haughty glance rest without sign of fear upon him. She was indeed the proud daughter of a thousand jeddaks, every inch of her dear, precious little body; so small, so frail beside the towering warriors around her, but in her majesty dwarfing them into insignificance; she was the mightiest figure among them and I verily believe that they felt it.

Presently Tal Hajus made a sign that the chamber be cleared, and that the prisoners be left alone before him. Slowly the chieftains, the warriors and the women melted away into the shadows of the surrounding chambers, and Dejah Thoris and Sola stood alone before the jeddak of the Tharks.

One chieftain alone had hesitated before departing; I saw him standing in the shadows of a mighty column, his fingers nervously toying with the hilt of his great-sword and his cruel eyes bent in implacable hatred upon Tal Hajus. It was Tars Tarkas, and I could read his thoughts as they were an open book for the undisguised loathing upon his face. He was thinking of that other woman who, forty years ago, had stood before this beast, and could I have spoken a word into his ear at that moment the reign of Tal Hajus would have been over; but finally he also strode from the room, not knowing that he left his own daughter at the mercy of the creature he most loathed.

Tal Hajus arose, and I, half fearing, half anticipating his intentions, hurried to the winding runway which led to the floors below. No one was near to intercept me, and I reached the main floor of the chamber unobserved, taking my station in the shadow of the same column that Tars Tarkas had but just deserted. As I reached the floor Tal Hajus was speaking.

"Princess of Helium, I might wring a mighty ransom from your people would I but return you to them unharmed, but a thousand times rather would I watch that beautiful face writhe in the agony of torture; it shall be long drawn out, that I promise you; ten days of pleasure were all too short to show the love I harbor for your race. The terrors of your death shall haunt the slumbers of the red men through all the ages to come; they will shudder in the shadows of the night as their fathers tell them of the awful vengeance of the green men; of the power and might and hate and cruelty of Tal Hajus. But before the torture you shall be mine for one short hour, and word of that too shall go forth to Tardos Mors, Jeddak of Helium, your grandfather, that he may grovel upon the ground in the agony of his sorrow. Tomorrow the torture will commence; tonight thou art Tal Hajus'; come!"

He sprang down from the platform and grasped her roughly by the arm, but scarcely had he touched her than I leaped between them. My short-sword, sharp and gleaming was in my right hand; I could have plunged it into his putrid heart before he realized that I was upon him; but as I raised my arm to strike I thought of Tars Tarkas, and, with all my rage, with all my hatred, I could not rob him of that sweet moment for which he had lived and hoped all these long, weary years, and so, instead, I swung my good right fist full upon the point of his jaw. Without a sound he slipped to the floor as one dead.

In the same deathly silence I grasped Dejah Thoris by the hand, and motioning Sola to follow we sped noiselessly from the chamber and to the floor above. Unseen we reached a rear window and with the straps and leather of my trappings I lowered, first Sola and then Dejah Thoris to the ground below. Dropping lightly after them I drew them rapidly around the court in the shadows of the buildings, and thus we returned over the same course I had so recently followed from the distant boundary of the city.

We finally came upon my thoats in the courtyard where I had left them, and placing the trappings upon them we hastened through the building to the avenue beyond. Mounting, Sola upon one beast, and Dejah Thoris behind me upon the other, we rode from the city of Thark through the hills to the south.

Instead of circling back around the city to the northwest and toward the nearest waterway which lay so short a distance from us, we turned to the northeast and struck out upon the mossy waste across which, for two hundred dangerous and weary miles, lay another main artery leading to Helium.

No word was spoken until we had left the city far behind, but I could hear the quiet sobbing of Dejah Thoris as she clung to me with her dear head resting against my shoulder.

"If we make it, my chieftain, the debt of Helium will be a mighty one; greater than she can ever pay you; and should we not make it," she continued, "the debt is no less, though Helium will never know, for you have saved the last of our line from worse than death."

I did not answer, but instead reached to my side and pressed the little fingers of her I loved where they clung to me for support, and then, in unbroken silence, we sped over the yellow, moonlit moss; each of us occupied with his own thoughts. For my part I could not be other than joyful had I tried, with Dejah Thoris' warm body pressed close to mine, and with all our unpassed danger my heart was singing as gaily as though we were already entering the gates of Helium.

Our earlier plans had been so sadly upset that we now found ourselves without food or drink, and I alone was armed. We therefore urged our beasts to a speed that must tell on them sorely before we could hope to sight the ending of the first stage of our journey.

We rode all night and all the following day with only a few short rests. On the second night both we and our animals were completely fagged, and so we lay down upon the moss and slept for some five or six hours, taking up the journey once more before daylight. All the following day we rode, and when, late in the afternoon we had sighted no distant trees, the mark of the great waterways throughout all Barsoom, the terrible truth flashed upon us—we were lost.

Evidently we had circled, but which way it was difficult to say, nor did it seem possible with the sun to guide us by day and the moons and stars by night. At any rate no waterway was in sight, and the entire party was almost ready to drop from hunger, thirst and fatigue. Far ahead of us and a trifle to the right we could distinguish the outlines of low mountains. These we decided to attempt to reach in the hope that from some ridge we might discern the missing waterway. Night fell upon us before we reached our goal, and, almost fainting from weariness and weakness, we lay down and slept.

I was awakened early in the morning by some huge body pressing close to mine, and opening my eyes with a start I beheld my blessed old Woola snuggling close to me; the faithful brute had followed us across that trackless waste to share our fate, whatever it might be. Putting my arms about his neck I pressed my cheek close to his, nor am I ashamed that I did it, nor of the tears that came to my eyes as I thought of his love for me. Shortly after this Dejah Thoris and Sola awakened, and it was decided that we push on at once in an effort to gain the hills.

We had gone scarcely a mile when I noticed that my thoat was commencing to stumble and stagger in a most pitiful manner, although we had not attempted to force them out of a walk since about noon of the preceding day. Suddenly he lurched wildly to one side and pitched violently to the ground. Dejah Thoris and I were thrown clear of him and fell upon the soft moss with scarcely a jar; but the poor beast was in a pitiable condition, not even being able to rise, although relieved of our weight. Sola told me that the coolness of the night, when it fell, together with the rest would doubtless revive him, and so I decided not to kill him, as was my first intention, as I had thought it cruel to leave him alone there to die of hunger and thirst. Relieving him of his trappings, which I flung down beside him, we left the poor fellow to his fate, and pushed on with the one thoat as best we could. Sola and I walked, making Dejah Thoris ride, much against her will. In this way we had progressed to within about a mile of the hills we were endeavoring to reach when Dejah Thoris, from her point of vantage upon the thoat, cried out that she saw a great party of mounted men filing down from a pass in the hills several miles away. Sola and I both looked in the direction she indicated, and there, plainly discernible, were several hundred mounted warriors. They seemed to be headed in a southwesterly direction, which would take them away from us.

They doubtless were Thark warriors who had been sent out to capture us, and we breathed a great sigh of relief that they were traveling in the opposite direction. Quickly lifting Dejah Thoris from the thoat, I commanded the animal to lie down and we three did the same, presenting as small an object as possible for fear of attracting the attention of the warriors toward us.

We could see them as they filed out of the pass, just for an instant, before they were lost to view behind a friendly ridge; to us a most providential ridge; since, had they been in view for any great length of time, they scarcely could have failed to discover us. As what proved to be the last warrior came into view from the pass, he halted and, to our consternation, threw his small but powerful fieldglass to his eye and scanned the sea bottom in all directions. Evidently he was a chieftain, for in certain marching formations among the green men a chieftain brings up the extreme rear of the column. As his glass swung toward us our hearts stopped in our breasts, and I could feel the cold sweat start from every pore in my body.

Presently it swung full upon us and—stopped. The tension on our nerves was near the breaking point, and I doubt if any of us breathed for the few moments he held us covered by his glass; and then he lowered it and we could see him shout a command to the warriors who had passed from our sight behind the ridge. He did not wait for them to join him, however, instead he wheeled his thoat and came tearing madly in our direction.

There was but one slight chance and that we must take quickly. Raising my strange Martian rifle to my shoulder I sighted and touched the button which controlled the trigger; there was a sharp explosion as the missile reached its goal, and the charging chieftain pitched backward from his flying mount.

Springing to my feet I urged the thoat to rise, and directed Sola to take Dejah Thoris with her upon him and make a mighty effort to reach the hills before the green warriors were upon us. I knew that in the ravines and gullies they might find a temporary hiding place, and even though they died there of hunger and thirst it would be better so than that they fell into the hands of the Tharks. Forcing my two revolvers upon them as a slight means of protection, and, as a last resort, as an escape for themselves from the horrid death which recapture would surely mean, I lifted Dejah Thoris in my arms and placed her upon the thoat behind Sola, who had already mounted at my command.

"Good-bye, my princess," I whispered, "we may meet in Helium yet. I have escaped from worse plights than this," and I tried to smile as I lied.

"What," she cried, "are you not coming with us?"

"How may I, Dejah Thoris? Someone must hold these fellows off for a while, and I can better escape them alone than could the three of us together."

She sprang quickly from the thoat and, throwing her dear arms about my neck, turned to Sola, saying with quiet dignity: "Fly, Sola! Dejah Thoris remains to die with the man she loves."

Those words are engraved upon my heart. Ah, gladly would I give up my life a thousand times could I only hear them once again; but I could not then give even a second to the rapture of her sweet embrace, and pressing my lips to hers for the first time, I picked her up bodily and tossed her to her seat behind Sola again, commanding the latter in peremptory tones to hold her there by force, and then, slapping the thoat upon the flank, I saw them borne away; Dejah Thoris struggling to the last to free herself from Sola's grasp.

Turning, I beheld the green warriors mounting the ridge and looking for their chieftain. In a moment they saw him, and then me; but scarcely had they discovered me than I commenced firing, lying flat upon my belly in the moss. I had an even hundred rounds in the magazine of my rifle, and another hundred in the belt at my back, and I kept up a continuous stream of fire until I saw all of the warriors who had been first to return from behind the ridge either dead or scurrying to cover.

My respite was short-lived however, for soon the entire party, numbering some thousand men, came charging into view, racing madly toward me. I fired until my rifle was empty and they were almost upon me, and then a glance showing me that Dejah Thoris and Sola had disappeared among the hills, I sprang up, throwing down my useless gun, and started away in the direction opposite to that taken by Sola and her charge.

If ever Martians had an exhibition of jumping, it was granted those astonished warriors on that day long years ago, but while it led them away from Dejah Thoris it did not distract their attention from endeavoring to capture me.

They raced wildly after me until, finally, my foot struck a projecting piece of quartz, and down I went sprawling upon the moss. As I looked up they were upon me, and although I drew my long-sword in an attempt to sell my life as dearly as possible, it was soon over. I reeled beneath their blows which fell upon me in perfect torrents; my head swam; all was black, and I went down beneath them to oblivion.

XVIII

CHAINED IN WARHOON

It must have been several hours before I regained consciousness and I well remember the feeling of surprise which swept over me as I realized that I was not dead.

I was lying among a pile of sleeping silks and furs in the corner of a small room in which were several green warriors, and bending over me was an ancient and ugly female.

As I opened my eyes she turned to one of the warriors, saying,

"He will live, O Jed."

" 'Tis well," replied the one so addressed, rising and approaching my couch, "he should render rare sport for the great games."

And now as my eyes fell upon him, I saw that he was no Thark, for his ornaments and metal were not of that horde. He was a huge fellow, terribly scarred about the face and chest, and with one broken tusk and a missing ear. Strapped on either breast were human skulls and depending from these a number of dried human hands.

His reference to the great games of which I had heard so much while among the Tharks convinced me that I had but jumped from purgatory into gehenna.

After a few more words with the female, during which she assured him that I was now fully fit to travel, the jed ordered that we mount and ride after the main column.

I was strapped securely to as wild and unmanageable a thoat as I had ever seen, and, with a mounted warrior on either side to prevent the beast from bolting, we rode forth at a furious pace in pursuit of the column. My wounds gave me but little pain, so wonderfully and rapidly had the applications and injections of the female exercised their therapeutic powers, and so deftly had she bound and plastered the injuries.

Just before dark we reached the main body of troops shortly after they had made camp for the night. I was immediately taken before the leader, who proved to be the jeddak of the hordes of Warhoon.

Like the jed who had brought me, he was frightfully scarred, and also decorated with the breastplate of human skulls and dried dead hands which seemed to mark all the greater warriors among the Warhoons, as well as to indicate their awful ferocity, which greatly transcends even that of the Tharks.

The jeddak, Bar Comas, who was comparatively young, was the object of the fierce and jealous hatred of his old lieutenant, Dak Kova, the jed who had captured me, and I could not but note the almost studied efforts which the latter made to affront his superior.

He entirely omitted the usual formal salutation as we entered the presence of the jeddak, and as he pushed me roughly before the ruler he exclaimed in a loud and menacing voice.

"I have brought a strange creature wearing the metal of a Thark whom it is my pleasure to have battle with a wild thoat at the great games."

"He will die as Bar Comas, your jeddak, sees fit, if at all," replied the young ruler, with emphasis and dignity.

"If at all?" roared Dak Kova. "By the dead hands at my throat but he shall die, Bar Comas. No maudlin weakness on your part shall save him. O, would that Warhoon were ruled by a real jeddak rather than by a water-hearted weakling from whom even old Dak Kova could tear the metal with his bare hands!"

Bar Comas eyed the defiant and insubordinate chieftain for an instant, his expression one of haughty, fearless contempt and hate, and then without drawing a weapon and without uttering a word he hurled himself at the throat of his defamer.

I never before had seen two green Martian warriors battle with nature's weapons and the exhibition of animal ferocity which ensued was as fearful a thing as the most disordered imagination could picture. They tore at each others' eyes and ears with their hands and with their gleaming tusks repeatedly slashed and gored until both were cut fairly to ribbons from head to foot.

Bar Comas had much the better of the battle as he was stronger, quicker and more intelligent. It soon seemed that the encounter was done saving only the final death thrust when Bar Comas slipped in breaking away from a clinch. It was the one little opening that Dak Kova needed, and hurling himself at the body of his adversary he buried his single mighty tusk in Bar Comas' groin and with a last powerful effort ripped the young jeddak wide open the full length of his body, the great tusk finally wedging in the bones of Bar Comas' jaw. Victor and vanquished rolled limp and lifeless upon the moss, a huge mass of torn and bloody flesh.

Bar Comas was stone dead, and only the most herculean efforts on the part of Dak Kova's females saved him from the fate he deserved. Three days later he walked without assistance to the body of Bar Comas which, by custom, had not been moved from where it fell, and placing his foot upon the neck of his erstwhile ruler he assumed the title of Jeddak of Warhoon.

The dead jeddak's hands and head were removed to be added to the ornaments of his conqueror, and then his women cremated what remained, amid wild and terrible laughter.

The injuries to Dak Kova had delayed the march so greatly that it was decided to give up the expedition, which was a raid upon a small Thark community in retaliation for the destruction of the incubator, until after the great games, and the entire body of warriors, ten thousand in number, turned back toward Warhoon.

My introduction to these cruel and bloodthirsty people was but an index to the scenes I witnessed almost daily while with them. They are a smaller horde than the Tharks but much more ferocious. Not a day passed but that some members of the various Warhoon communities met in deadly combat. I have seen as high as eight mortal duels within a single day.

We reached the city of Warhoon after some three days march and I was immediately cast into a dungeon and heavily chained to the floor and walls. Food was brought me at intervals but owing to the utter darkness of the place I do not know whether I lay there days, or weeks, or months. It was the most horrible experience of all my life and that my mind did not give way to the terrors of that inky blackness has been a wonder to me ever since. The place was filled with creeping, crawling things; cold, sinuous bodies passed over me when I lay down, and in the darkness I occasionally caught glimpses of gleaming, fiery eyes, fixed in horrible intentness upon me. No sound reached me from the world above and no word would my jailer vouchsafe when my food was brought to me, although I at first bombarded him with questions.

Finally all the hatred and maniacal loathing for these awful creatures who had placed me in this horrible place was centered by my tottering reason upon this single emissary who represented to me the entire horde of Warhoons.

I had noticed that he always advanced with his dim torch to where he could place the food within my reach and as he stooped to place it upon the floor his head was about on a level with my breast. So, with the cunning of a madman, I backed into the far corner of my cell when next I heard him approaching and gathering a little slack of the great chain which held me in my hand I waited his coming, crouching like some beast of prey. As he stooped to place my food upon the ground I swung the chain above my head and crashed the links with all my strength upon his skull. Without a sound he slipped to the floor, stone dead.

Laughing and chattering like the idiot I was fast becoming I fell upon his prostrate form my fingers feeling for his dead throat. Presently they came in contact with a small chain at the end of which dangled a number of keys. The touch of my fingers on these keys brought back my reason with the suddenness of thought. No longer was I a jibbering idiot, but a sane, reasoning man with the means of escape within my very hands.

As I was groping to remove the chain from about my victim's neck I glanced up into the darkness to see six pairs of gleaming eyes fixed, unwinking, upon me. Slowly they approached and slowly I shrank back from the awful horror of them. Back into my corner I crouched holding my hands palms out, before me, and stealthily on came the awful eyes until they reached the dead body at my feet. Then slowly they retreated but this time with a strange grating sound and finally they disappeared in some black and distant recess of my dungeon.

XIX

BATTLING IN THE ARENA

Slowly I regained my composure and finally essayed again to attempt to remove the keys from the dead body of my former jailer. But as I reached out into the darkness to locate it I found to my horror that it was gone. Then the truth flashed on me; the owners of those gleaming eyes had dragged my prize away from me to be devoured in their neighboring lair; as they had been waiting for days, for weeks, for months, through all this awful eternity of my imprisonment to drag my dead carcass to their feast.

For two days no food was brought me, but then a new messenger appeared and my incarceration went on as before, but not again did I allow my reason to be submerged by the horror of my position.

Shortly after this episode another prisoner was brought in and chained near me. By the dim torch light I saw that he was a red Martian and I could scarcely await the departure of his guards to address him. As their retreating footsteps died away in the distance, I called out softly the Martian word of greeting, *kaor*.

"Who are you who speaks out of the darkness?" he answered

"John Carter, a friend of the red men of Helium."

"I am of Helium," he said, "but I do not recall your name."

And then I told him my story as I have written it here, omitting only any reference to my love for Dejah Thoris. He was much excited by the news of Helium's princess and seemed quite positive that she and Sola could easily have reached a point of safety from where they left me. He said that he knew the place well because the defile through which the Warhoon warriors had passed when they discovered us was the only one ever used by them when marching to the south.

"Dejah Thoris and Sola entered the hills not five miles from a great waterway and are now probably quite safe," he assured me.

My fellow prisoner was Kantos Kan, a padwar (lieutenant) in the navy of Helium. He had been a member of the ill-fated expedition which had fallen into the hands of the Tharks at the time of Dejah Thoris' capture, and he briefly related the events which followed the defeat of the battleships.

Badly injured and only partially manned they had limped slowly toward Helium, but while passing near the city of Zodanga, the capital of Helium's hereditary enemies among the red men of Barsoom, they had been attacked by a great body of war vessels and all but the craft to which Kantos Kan belonged were either destroyed or captured. His vessel was chased for days by three of the Zodangan war ships but finally escaped during the darkness of a moonless night.

Thirty days after the capture of Dejah Thoris, or about the time of our coming to Thark, his vessel had reached Helium with about ten survivors of the original crew of seven hundred officers and men. Immediately seven great fleets, each of one hundred mighty war ships, had been dispatched to search for Dejah Thoris, and from these vessels two thousand smaller craft had been kept out continuously in futile search for the missing princess.

Two green Martian communities had been wiped off the face of Barsoom by the avenging fleets, but no trace of Dejah Thoris had been found. They had been searching among the northern hordes, and only within the past few days had they extended their quest to the south.

Kantos Kan had been detailed to one of the small one-man fliers and had had the misfortune to be discovered by the Warhoons while exploring their city. The bravery and daring of the man won my greatest respect and admiration. Alone he had landed at the city's boundary and on foot had penetrated to the buildings surrounding the plaza. For two days and nights he had explored their quarters and their dungeons in search of his beloved princess only to fall into the hands of a party of Warhoons as he was about to leave, after assuring himself that Dejah Thoris was not a captive there.

During the period of our incarceration Kantos Kan and I became well acquainted, and formed a warm personal friendship. A few days only elapsed, however, before we were dragged forth from our dungeon for the great games. We were conducted early one morning to an enormous amphitheater, which instead of having been built upon the surface of the ground was excavated below the surface. It had partially filled with debris so that how large it had originally been was difficult to say. In its present condition it held the entire twenty thousand Warhoons of the assembled hordes.

The arena was immense but extremely uneven and unkempt. Around it the Warhoons had piled building stone from some of the ruined edifices of the ancient city to prevent the animals and the captives from escaping into the audience, and at each end had been constructed cages to hold them until their turns came to meet some horrible death upon the arena.

Kantos Kan and I were confined together in one of the cages. In the others were wild calots, thoats, mad zitidars, green warriors, and women of other hordes, and many strange and ferocious wild beasts of Barsoom which I had never before seen. The din of their roaring, growling and squealing was deafening and the formidable appearance of any one of them was enough to make the stoutest heart feel grave forebodings.

Kantos Kan explained to me that at the end of the day one of these prisoners would gain freedom and the others would lie dead about the arena. The winners in the various contests of the day would be pitted against each other until only two remained alive; the victor in the last encounter being set free, whether animal or man. The following morning the cages would be filled with a new consignment of victims, and so on throughout the ten days of the games.

Shortly after we had been caged the amphitheater began to fill and within an hour every available part of the seating space was occupied. Dak Kova, with his jeds and chieftains, sat at the center of one side of the arena upon a large raised platform.

At a signal from Dak Kova the doors of two cages were thrown open and a dozen green Martian females were driven to the center of the arena. Each was given a dagger and then, at the far end, a pack of twelve calots, or wild dogs were loosed upon them.

As the brutes, growling and foaming, rushed upon the almost defenseless women I turned my head that I might not see the horrid sight. The yells and laughter of the green horde bore witness to the excellent quality of the sport and when I turned back to the arena, as Kantos Kan told me it was over, I saw three victorious calots, snarling and growling over the bodies of their prey. The women had given a good account of themselves.

Next a mad zitidar was loosed among the remaining dogs, and so it went throughout the long, hot, horrible day.

During the day I was pitted against first men and then beasts, but as I was armed with a long-sword and always outclassed my adversary in agility and generally in strength as well, it proved but child's play to me. Time and time again I won the applause of the bloodthirsty multitude, and toward the end there were cries that I be taken from the arena and be made a member of the hordes of Warhoon.

Finally there were but three of us left, a great green warrior of some far northern horde, Kantos Kan, and myself.

The other two were to battle and then I to fight the conqueror for the liberty which was accorded the final winner.

Kantos Kan had fought several times during the day and like myself had always proven victorious, but occasionally by the smallest of margins, especially when pitted against the green warriors. I had little hope that he could best his giant adversary who had mowed down all before him during the day. The fellow towered nearly sixteen feet in height, while Kantos Kan was some inches under six feet. As they advanced to meet one another I saw for the first time a trick of Martian swordsmanship which centered Kantos Kan's every hope of victory and life on one cast of the dice, for, as he came to within about twenty feet of the huge fellow he threw his sword arm far behind him over his shoulder and with a mighty sweep hurled his weapon point foremost at the green warrior. It flew true as an arrow and piercing the poor devil's heart laid him dead upon the arena.

Kantos Kan and I were now pitted against each other but as we approached to the encounter I whispered to him to prolong the battle until nearly dark in the hope that we might find some means of escape. The horde evidently guessed that we had no hearts to fight each other and so they howled in rage as neither of us placed a fatal thrust. Just as I saw the sudden coming of dark I whispered to Kantos Kan to thrust his sword between my left arm and my body. As he did so I staggered back clasping the sword tightly with my arm and thus fell to the ground with his weapon apparently protruding from my chest. Kantos Kan perceived my coup and stepping quickly to my side he placed his foot upon my neck and withdrawing his sword from my body gave me the final death blow through the neck which is supposed to sever the jugular vein, but in this instance the cold blade slipped harmlessly into the sand of the arena. In the darkness which had now fallen none could tell but that he had really finished me. I whispered to him to go and claim his freedom and then look for me in the hills east of the city, and so he left me.

When the amphitheater had cleared I crept stealthily to the top and as the great excavation lay far from the plaza and in an untenanted portion of the great dead city I had little trouble in reaching the hills beyond.

XX

IN THE ATMOSPHERE FACTORY

For two days I waited there for Kantos Kan, but as he did not come I started off on foot in a northwesterly direction toward a point where he had told me lay the nearest waterway. My only food consisted of vegetable milk from the plants which gave so bounteously of this priceless fluid.

Through two long weeks I wandered, stumbling through the nights guided only by the stars and hiding during the days behind some protruding rock or among the occasional hills I traversed. Several times I was attacked by wild beasts; strange, uncouth monstrosities that leaped upon me in the dark, so that I had ever to grasp my long-sword in my hand that I might be ready for them. Usually my strange, newly acquired telepathic power warned me in ample time, but once I was down with vicious fangs at my jugular and a hairy face pressed close to mine before I knew that I was even threatened.

What manner of thing was upon me I did not know, but that it was large and heavy and many-legged I could feel. My hands were at its throat before the fangs had a chance to bury themselves in my neck, and slowly I forced the hairy face from me and closed my fingers, vise-like, upon its windpipe.

Without sound we lay there, the beast exerting every effort to reach me with those awful fangs, and I straining to maintain my grip and choke the life from it as I kept it from my throat. Slowly my arms gave to the unequal struggle, and inch by inch the burning eyes and gleaming tusks of my antagonist crept toward me, until, as the hairy face touched mine again, I realized that all was over. And then a living mass of destruction sprang from the surrounding darkness full upon the creature that held me pinioned to the ground. The two rolled growling upon the moss, tearing and rending one another in a frightful manner, but it was soon over and my preserver stood with lowered head above the throat of the dead thing which would have killed me.

The nearer moon, hurtling suddenly above the horizon and lighting up the Barsoomian scene, showed me that my preserver was Woola, but from whence he had come, or how found me, I was at a loss to know. That I was glad of his companionship it is needless to say, but my pleasure at seeing him was tempered by anxiety as to the reason of his leaving Dejah Thoris. Only her death I felt sure, could account for his absence from her, so faithful I knew him to be to my commands.

By the light of the now brilliant moons I saw that he was but a shadow of his former self, and as he turned from my caress and commenced greedily to devour the dead carcass at my feet I realized that the poor fellow was more than half starved. I, myself, was in but little better plight but I could not bring myself to eat the uncooked flesh and I had no means of making a fire. When Woola had finished his meal I again took up my weary and seemingly endless wandering in quest of the elusive waterway.

At daybreak of the fifteenth day of my search I was overjoyed to see the high trees that denoted the object of my search. About noon I dragged myself wearily to the portals of a huge building which covered perhaps four square miles and towered two hundred feet in the air. It showed no aperture in the mighty walls other than the tiny door at which I sank exhausted, nor was there any sign of life about it.

I could find no bell or other method of making my presence known to the inmates of the place, unless a small round hole in the wall near the door was for that purpose. It was of about the bigness of a lead pencil and thinking that it might be in the nature of a speaking tube I put my mouth to it and was about to call into it when a voice issued from it asking me whom I might be, where from, and the nature of my errand.

I explained that I had escaped from the Warhoons and was dying of starvation and exhaustion.

"You wear the metal of a green warrior and are followed by a calot, yet you are of the figure of a red man. In color you are neither green nor red. In the name of the ninth ray, what manner of creature are you?"

"I am a friend of the red men of Barsoom and I am starving. In the name of humanity open to us," I replied.

Presently the door commenced to recede before me until it had sunk into the wall fifty feet, then it stopped and slid easily to the left, exposing a short, narrow corridor of concrete, at the further end of which was another door, similar in every respect to the one I had just passed. No one was in sight, yet immediately we passed the first door it slid gently into place behind us and receded rapidly to its original position in the front wall of the building. As the door had slipped aside I had noted its great thickness, fully twenty feet, and as it reached its place once more after closing behind us, great cylinders of steel had dropped from the ceiling behind it and fitted their lower ends into apertures countersunk in the floor.

A second and third door receded before me and slipped to one side as the first, before I reached a large inner chamber where I found food and drink set out upon a great stone table. A voice directed me to satisfy my hunger and to feed my calot, and while I was thus engaged my invisible host put me through a severe and searching cross-examination.

"Your statements are most remarkable," said the voice, on concluding its questioning, "but you are evidently speaking the truth, and it is equally evident that you are not of Barsoom. I can tell that by the conformation of your brain and the strange location of your internal organs and the shape and size of your heart."

"Can you see through me?" I exclaimed.

"Yes, I can see all but your thoughts, and were you a Barsoomian I could read those."

Then a door opened at the far side of the chamber and a strange, dried up, little mummy of a man came toward me. He wore but a single article of clothing or adornment, a small collar of gold from which depended upon his chest a great ornament as large as a dinner plate set solid with huge diamonds, except for the exact center which was occupied by a strange stone, an inch in diameter, that scintillated nine different and distinct rays; the seven colors of our earthly prism and two beautiful rays which, to me, were new and nameless. I cannot describe them any more than you could describe red to a blind man. I only know that they were beautiful in the extreme.

The old man sat and talked with me for hours, and the strangest part of our intercourse was that I could read his every thought while he could not fathom an iota from my mind unless I spoke.

I did not apprise him of my ability to sense his mental operations, and thus I learned a great deal which proved of immense value to me later and which I would never have known had he suspected my strange power, for the Martians have such perfect control of their mental machinery that they are able to direct their thoughts with absolute precision.

The building in which I found myself contained the machinery which produces that artificial atmosphere which sustains life on Mars. The secret of the entire process hinges on the use of the ninth ray, one of the beautiful scintillations which I had noted emanating from the great stone in my host's diadem.

This ray is separated from the other rays of the sun by means of finely adjusted instruments placed upon the roof of the huge building, three-quarters of which is used for reservoirs in which the ninth ray is stored. This product is then treated electrically, or rather certain proportions of refined electric vibrations are incorporated with it, and the result is then pumped to the five principal air centers of the planet where, as it is released, contact with the ether of space transforms it into atmosphere.

There is always sufficient reserve of the ninth ray stored in the great building to maintain the present Martian atmosphere for a thousand years, and the only fear, as my new friend told me, was that some accident might befall the pumping apparatus.

He led me to an inner chamber where I beheld a battery of twenty radium pumps any one of which was equal to the task of furnishing all Mars with the atmosphere compound. For eight hundred years, he told me, he had watched these pumps which are used alternately a day each at a stretch, or a little over twenty-four and one-half Earth hours. He has one assistant who divides the watch with him. Half a Martian year, about three hundred and forty-four of our days, each of these men spend alone in this huge, isolated plant.

Every red Martian is taught during earliest childhood the principles of the manufacture of atmosphere, but only two at one time ever hold the secret of ingress to the great building, which, built as it is with walls a hundred and fifty feet thick, is absolutely unassailable, even the roof being guarded from assault by air craft by a glass covering five feet thick.

The only fear they entertain of attack is from the green Martians or some demented red man, as all Barsoomians realize that the very existence of every form of life of Mars is dependent upon the uninterrupted working of this plant.

One curious fact I discovered as I watched his thoughts was that the outer doors are manipulated by telepathic means. The locks are so finely adjusted that the doors are released by the action of a certain combination of thought waves. To experiment with my new-found toy I thought to surprise him into revealing this combination and so I asked him in a casual manner how he had managed to unlock the massive doors for me from the inner chambers of the building. As quick as a flash there leaped to his mind nine Martian sounds, but as quickly faded as he answered that this was a secret he must not divulge.

From then on his manner toward me changed as though he feared that he had been surprised into divulging his great secret, and I read suspicion and fear in his looks and thoughts, though his words were still fair.

Before I retired for the night he promised to give me a letter to a nearby agricultural officer who would help me on my way to Zodanga, which he said, was the nearest Martian city.

"But be sure that you do not let them know you are bound for Helium as they are at war with that country. My assistant and I are of no country, we belong to all Barsoom and this talisman which we wear protects us in all lands, even among the green men—though we do not trust ourselves to their hands if we can avoid it," he added.

"And so good-night, my friend," he continued, "may you have a long and restful sleep—yes, a long sleep."

And though he smiled pleasantly I saw in his thoughts the wish that he had never admitted me, and then a picture of him standing over me in the night, and the swift thrust of a long dagger and the half formed words, "I am sorry, but it is for the best good of Barsoom."

As he closed the door of my chamber behind him his thoughts were cut off from me as was the sight of him, which seemed strange to me in my little knowledge of thought transference.

What was I to do? How could I escape through these mighty walls? Easily could I kill him now that I was warned, but once he was dead I could no more escape, and with the stopping of the machinery of the great plant I should die with all the other inhabitants of the planet—all, even Dejah Thoris were she not already dead. For the others I did not give the snap of my finger, but the thought of Dejah Thoris drove from my mind all desire to kill my mistaken host.

Cautiously I opened the door of my apartment and, followed by Woola, sought the inner of the great doors. A wild scheme had come to me; I would attempt to force the great locks by the nine thought waves I had read in my host's mind.

Creeping stealthily through corridor after corridor and down winding runways which turned hither and thither I finally reached the great hall in which I had broken my long fast that morning. Nowhere had I seen my host, nor did I know where he kept himself by night.

I was on the point of stepping boldly out into the room when a slight noise behind me warned me back into the shadows of a recess in the corridor. Dragging Woola after me I crouched low in the darkness.

Presently the old man passed close by me, and as he entered the dimly lighted chamber which I had been about to pass through I saw that he held a long thin dagger in his hand and that he was sharpening it upon a stone. In his mind was the decision to inspect the radium pumps, which would take about thirty minutes, and then return to my bed chamber and finish me.

As he passed through the great hall and disappeared down the runway which led to the pump-room, I stole stealthily from my hiding place and crossed to the great door, the inner of the three which stood between me and liberty.

Concentrating my mind upon the massive lock I hurled the nine thought waves against it. In breathless expectancy I waited, when finally the great door moved softly toward me and slid quietly to one side. One after the other the remaining mighty portals opened at my command and Woola and I stepped forth into the darkness, free, but little better off than we had been before, other than that we had full stomachs.

Hastening away from the shadows of the formidable pile I made for the first crossroad, intending to strike the central turnpike as quickly as possible. This I reached about morning and entering the first enclosure I came to I searched for some evidences of a habitation.

There were low rambling buildings of concrete barred with heavy impassable doors, and no amount of hammering and hallooing brought any response. Weary and exhausted from sleeplessness I threw myself upon the ground commanding Woola to stand guard.

Some time later I was awakened by his frightful growlings and opened my eyes to see three red Martians standing a short distance from us and covering me with their rifles.

"I am unarmed and no enemy," I hastened to explain. "I have been a prisoner among the green men and am on my way to Zodanga. All I ask is food and rest for myself and my calot and the proper directions for reaching my destination."

They lowered their rifles and advanced pleasantly toward me placing their right hands upon my left shoulder, after the manner of their custom of salute, and asking me many questions about myself and my wanderings. They then took me to the house of one of them which was only a short distance away.

The buildings I had been hammering at in the early morning were occupied only by stock and farm produce, the house proper standing among a grove of enormous trees, and, like all red-Martian homes, had been raised at night some forty or fifty feet from the ground on a large round metal shaft which slid up or down within a sleeve sunk in the ground, and was operated by a tiny radium engine in the entrance hall of the building. Instead of bothering with bolts and bars for their dwellings, the red Martians simply run them up out of harm's way during the night. They also have private means for lowering or raising them from the ground without if they wish to go away and leave them.

These brothers, with their wives and children, occupied three similar houses on this farm. They did no work themselves, being government officers in charge. The labor was performed by convicts, prisoners of war, delinquent debtors and confirmed bachelors who were too poor to pay the high celibate tax which all red-Martian governments impose.

They were the personification of cordiality and hospitality and I spent several days with them, resting and recuperating from my long and arduous experiences.

When they had heard my story—I omitted all reference to Dejah Thoris and the old man of the atmosphere plant—they advised me to color my body to more nearly resemble their own race and then attempt to find employment in Zodanga, either in the army or the navy.

"The chances are small that your tale will be believed until after you have proven your trustworthiness and won friends among the higher nobles of the court. This you can most easily do through military service, as we are a warlike people on Barsoom," explained one of them, "and save our richest favors for the fighting man."

When I was ready to depart they furnished me with a small domestic bull thoat, such as is used for saddle purposes by all red Martians. The animal is about the size of a horse and quite gentle, but in color and shape an exact replica of his huge and fierce cousin of the wilds.

The brothers had supplied me with a reddish oil with which I anointed my entire body and one of them cut my hair, which had grown quite long, in the prevailing fashion of the time, square at the back and banged in front, so that I could have passed anywhere upon Barsoom as a full-fledged red Martian. My metal and ornaments were also renewed in the style of a Zodangan gentleman, attached to the house of Ptor, which was the family name of my benefactors.

They filled a little sack at my side with Zodangan money. The medium of exchange upon Mars is not dissimilar from our own except that the coins are oval. Paper money is issued by individuals as they require it and redeemed twice yearly. If a man issues more than he can redeem, the government pays his creditors in full and the debtor works out the amount upon the farms or in mines, which are all owned by the government. This suits everybody except the debtor as it has been a difficult thing to obtain sufficient voluntary labor to work the great isolated farm lands of Mars, stretching as they do like narrow ribbons from pole to pole, through wild stretches peopled by wild animals and wilder men.

When I mentioned my inability to repay them for their kindness to me they assured me that I would have ample opportunity if I lived long upon Barsoom, and bidding me farewell they watched me until I was out of sight upon the broad white turnpike.

XXI

AN AIR SCOUT FOR ZODANGA

As I proceeded on my journey toward Zodanga many strange and interesting sights arrested my attention, and at the several farm houses where I stopped I learned a number of new and instructive things concerning the methods and manners of Barsoom.

The water which supplies the farms of Mars is collected in immense underground reservoirs at either pole from the melting ice caps, and pumped through long conduits to the various populated centers. Along either side of these conduits, and extending their entire length, lie the cultivated districts. These are divided into tracts of about the same size, each tract being under the supervision of one or more government officers.

Instead of flooding the surface of the fields, and thus wasting immense quantities of water by evaporation, the precious liquid is carried underground through a vast network of small pipes directly to the roots of the vegetation. The crops upon Mars are always uniform, for there are no droughts, no rains, no high winds, and no insects, or destroying birds.

On this trip I tasted the first meat I had eaten since leaving Earth—large, juicy steaks and chops from the well-fed domestic animals of the farms. Also I enjoyed luscious fruits and vegetables, but not a single article of food which was exactly similar to anything on Earth. Every plant and flower and vegetable and animal has been so refined by ages of careful, scientific cultivation and breeding that the like of them on Earth dwindled into pale, gray, characterless nothingness by comparison.

At a second stop I met some highly cultivated people of the noble class and while in conversation we chanced to speak of Helium. One of the older men had been there on a diplomatic mission several years before and spoke with regret of the conditions which seemed destined ever to keep these two countries at war.

"Helium," he said, "rightly boasts the most beautiful women of Barsoom, and of all her treasures the wondrous daughter of Mors Kajak, Dejah Thoris, is the most exquisite flower.

"Why," he added, "the people really worship the ground she walks upon and since her loss on that ill-starred expedition all Helium has been draped in mourning.

"That our ruler should have attacked the disabled fleet as it was returning to Helium was but another of his awful blunders which I fear will sooner or later compel Zodanga to elevate a wiser man to his place.

"Even now, though our victorious armies are surrounding Helium, the people of Zodanga are voicing their displeasure, for the war is not a popular one, since it is not based on right or justice. Our forces took advantage of the absence of the principal fleet of Helium on their search for the princess, and so we have been able easily to reduce the city to a sorry plight. It is said she will fall within the next few passages of the further moon."

"And what, think you, may have been the fate of the princess, Dejah Thoris?" I asked as casually as possible.

"She is dead," he answered. "This much was learned from a green warrior recently captured by our forces in the south. She escaped from the hordes of Thark with a strange creature of another world, only to fall into the hands of the Warhoons. Their thoats were found wandering upon the sea bottom and evidences of a bloody conflict were discovered nearby."

While this information was in no way reassuring, neither was it at all conclusive proof of the death of Dejah Thoris, and so I determined to make every effort possible to reach Helium as quickly as I could and carry to Tardos Mors such news of his granddaughter's possible whereabouts as lay in my power.

Ten days after leaving the three Ptor brothers I arrived at Zodanga. From the moment that I had come in contact with the red inhabitants of Mars

I had noticed that Woola drew a great amount of unwelcome attention to me, since the huge brute belonged to a species which is never domesticated by the red men. Were one to stroll down Broadway with a Numidian lion at his heels the effect would be somewhat similar to that which I should have produced had I entered Zodanga with Woola.

The very thought of parting with the faithful fellow caused me so great regret and genuine sorrow that I put it off until just before we arrived at the city's gates; but then, finally, it became imperative that we separate. Had nothing further than my own safety or pleasure been at stake no argument could have prevailed upon me to turn away the one creature upon Barsoom that had never failed in a demonstration of affection and loyalty; but as I would willingly have offered my life in the service of her in search of whom I was about to challenge the unknown dangers of this, to me, mysterious city, I could not permit even Woola's life to threaten the success of my venture, much less his momentary happiness, for I doubted not he soon would forget me. And so I bade the poor beast an affectionate farewell, promising him, however, that if I came through my adventure in safety that in some way I should find the means to search him out.

He seemed to understand me fully, and when I pointed back in the direction of Thark he turned sorrowfully away, nor could I bear to watch him go; but resolutely set my face toward Zodanga and with a touch of heartsickness approached her frowning walls.

The letter I bore from them gained me immediate entrance to the vast, walled city. It was still very early in the morning and the streets were practically deserted. The residences, raised high upon their metal columns, resembled huge rookeries, while the uprights themselves presented the appearance of steel tree trunks. The shops as a rule were not raised from the ground nor were their doors bolted or barred, since thievery is practically unknown upon Barsoom. Assassination is the ever-present fear of all Barsoomians, and for this reason alone their homes are raised high above the ground at night, or in times of danger.

The Ptor brothers had given me explicit directions for reaching the point of the city where I could find living accommodations and be near the offices of the government agents to whom they had given me letters. My way led to the central square or plaza, which is a characteristic of all Martian cities.

The plaza of Zodanga covers a square mile and is bounded by the palaces of the jeddak, the jeds, and other members of the royalty and nobility of Zodanga, as well as by the principal public buildings, cafes, and shops.

As I was crossing the great square lost in wonder and admiration of the magnificent architecture and the gorgeous scarlet vegetation which carpeted the broad lawns I discovered a red Martian walking briskly toward me from one of the avenues. He paid not the slightest attention to me, but as he came abreast I recognized him, and turning I placed my hand upon his shoulder, calling out:

"Kaor, Kantos Kan!"

Like lightning he wheeled and before I could so much as lower my hand the point of his long-sword was at my breast.

"Who are you?" he growled, and then as a backward leap carried me fifty feet from his sword he dropped the point to the ground and exclaimed, laughing,

"I do not need a better reply, there is but one man upon all Barsoom who can bounce about like a rubber ball. By the mother of the further moon, John Carter, how came you here, and have you become a Darseen that you can change your color at will?

"You gave me a bad half minute my friend," he continued, after I had briefly outlined my adventures since parting with him in the arena at Warhoon. "Were my name and city known to the Zodangans I would shortly be sitting on the banks of the lost sea of Korus with my revered and departed ancestors. I am here in the interest of Tardos Mors, Jeddak of Helium, to discover the whereabouts of Dejah Thoris, our princess. Sab Than, prince of Zodanga, has her hidden in the city and has fallen madly in love with her. His father, Than Kosis, Jeddak of Zodanga, has made her voluntary marriage to his son the price of peace between our countries, but Tardos Mors will not accede to the demands and has sent word that he and his people would rather look upon the dead face of their princess than see her wed to any than her own choice, and that personally he would prefer being engulfed in the ashes of a lost and burning Helium to joining the metal of his house with that of Than Kosis. His reply was the deadliest affront he could have put upon Than Kosis and the Zodangans, but his people love him the more for it and his strength in Helium is greater today than ever.

"I have been here three days," continued Kantos Kan, "but I have not yet found where Dejah Thoris is imprisoned. Today I join the Zodangan navy as an air scout and I hope in this way to win the confidence of Sab Than, the prince, who is commander of this division of the navy, and thus learn the whereabouts of Dejah Thoris. I am glad that you are here, John Carter, for I know your loyalty to my princess and two of us working together should be able to accomplish much."

The plaza was now commencing to fill with people going and coming upon the daily activities of their duties. The shops were opening and the cafes filling with early morning patrons. Kantos Kan led me to one of these gorgeous eating places where we were served entirely by mechanical apparatus. No hand touched the food from the time it entered the building in its raw state until it emerged hot and delicious upon the tables before the guests, in response to the touching of tiny buttons to indicate their desires.

After our meal, Kantos Kan took me with him to the headquarters of the air-scout squadron and introducing me to his superior asked that I be enrolled as a member of the corps. In accordance with custom an examination was necessary, but Kantos Kan had told me to have no fear on this score as he would attend to that part of the matter. He accomplished this by taking my order for examination to the examining officer and representing himself as John Carter.

"This ruse will be discovered later," he cheerfully explained, "when they check up my weights, measurements, and other personal identification data, but it will be several months before this is done and our mission should be accomplished or have failed long before that time."

The next few days were spent by Kantos Kan in teaching me the intricacies of flying and of repairing the dainty little contrivances which the Martians use for this purpose. The body of the one-man air craft is about sixteen feet long, two feet wide and three inches thick, tapering to a point at each end. The driver sits on top of this plane upon a seat constructed over the small, noiseless radium engine which propels it. The medium of buoyancy is contained within the thin metal walls of the body and consists of the eighth Barsoomian ray, or ray of propulsion, as it may be termed in view of its properties.

This ray, like the ninth ray, is unknown on Earth, but the Martians have discovered that it is an inherent property of all light no matter from what source it emanates. They have learned that it is the solar eighth ray which propels the light of the sun to the various planets, and that it is the individual eighth ray of each planet which "reflects," or propels the light thus obtained out into space once more. The solar eighth ray would be absorbed by the surface of Barsoom, but the Barsoomian eighth ray, which tends to propel light from Mars into space, is constantly streaming out from the planet constituting a force of repulsion of gravity which when confined is able to lift enormous weights from the surface of the ground.

It is this ray which has enabled them to so perfect aviation that battle ships far outweighing anything known upon Earth sail as gracefully and lightly through the thin air of Barsoom as a toy balloon in the heavy atmosphere of Earth.

During the early years of the discovery of this ray many strange accidents occurred before the Martians learned to measure and control the wonderful power they had found. In one instance, some nine hundred years before, the first great battle ship to be built with eighth ray reservoirs was stored with too great a quantity of the rays and she had sailed up from Helium with five hundred officers and men, never to return.

Her power of repulsion for the planet was so great that it had carried her far into space, where she can be seen today, by the aid of powerful telescopes, hurtling through the heavens ten thousand miles from Mars; a tiny satellite that will thus encircle Barsoom to the end of time.

The fourth day after my arrival at Zodanga I made my first flight, and as a result of it I won a promotion which included quarters in the palace of Than Kosis.

As I rose above the city I circled several times, as I had seen Kantos Kan do, and then throwing my engine into top speed I raced at terrific velocity toward the south, following one of the great waterways which enter Zodanga from that direction.

I had traversed perhaps two hundred miles in a little less than an hour when I descried far below me a party of three green warriors racing madly toward a small figure on foot which seemed to be trying to reach the confines of one of the walled fields.

Dropping my machine rapidly toward them, and circling to the rear of the warriors, I soon saw that the object of their pursuit was a red Martian wearing the metal of the scout squadron to which I was attached. A short distance away lay his tiny flier, surrounded by the tools with which he had evidently been occupied in repairing some damage when surprised by the green warriors.

They were now almost upon him; their flying mounts charging down on the relatively puny figure at terrific speed, while the warriors leaned low to the right, with their great metal-shod spears. Each seemed striving to be the first to impale the poor Zodangan and in another moment his fate would have been sealed had it not been for my timely arrival.

Driving my fleet air craft at high speed directly behind the warriors I soon overtook them and without diminishing my speed I rammed the prow of my little flier between the shoulders of the nearest. The impact sufficient to have torn through inches of solid steel, hurled the fellow's headless body into the air over the head of his thoat, where it fell sprawling upon the moss. The mounts of the other two warriors turned squealing in terror, and bolted in opposite directions.

Reducing my speed I circled and came to the ground at the feet of the astonished Zodangan. He was warm in his thanks for my timely aid and promised that my day's work would bring the reward it merited, for it was none other than a cousin of the jeddak of Zodanga whose life I had saved.

We wasted no time in talk as we knew that the warriors would surely return as soon as they had gained control of their mounts. Hastening to his damaged machine we were bending every effort to finish the needed repairs and had almost completed them when we saw the two green monsters returning at top speed from opposite sides of us. When they had approached within a hundred yards their thoats again became unmanageable and absolutely refused to advance further toward the air craft which had frightened them.

The warriors finally dismounted and hobbling their animals advanced toward us on foot with drawn long-swords.

I advanced to meet the larger, telling the Zodangan to do the best he could with the other. Finishing my man with almost no effort, as had now from much practice become habitual with me, I hastened to return to my new acquaintance whom I found indeed in desperate straits.

He was wounded and down with the huge foot of his antagonist upon his throat and the great long-sword raised to deal the final thrust. With a bound I cleared the fifty feet intervening between us, and with outstretched point drove my sword completely through the body of the green warrior. His sword fell, harmless, to the ground and he sank limply upon the prostrate form of the Zodangan.

A cursory examination of the latter revealed no mortal injuries and after a brief rest he asserted that he felt fit to attempt the return voyage. He would have to pilot his own craft, however, as these frail vessels are not intended to convey but a single person.

Quickly completing the repairs we rose together into the still, cloudless Martian sky, and at great speed and without further mishap returned to Zodanga.

As we neared the city we discovered a mighty concourse of civilians and troops assembled upon the plain before the city. The sky was black with naval vessels and private and public pleasure craft, flying long streamers of gay-colored silks, and banners and flags of odd and picturesque design.

My companion signaled that I slow down, and running his machine close beside mine suggested that we approach and watch the ceremony, which, he said, was for the purpose of conferring honors on individual officers and men for bravery and other distinguished service. He then unfurled a little ensign which denoted that his craft bore a member of the royal family of Zodanga, and together we made our way through the maze of low-lying air vessels until we hung directly over the jeddak of Zodanga and his staff. All were mounted upon the small domestic bull thoats of the red Martians, and their trappings and ornamentation bore such a quantity of gorgeously colored feathers that I could not but be struck with the startling resemblance the concourse bore to a band of the red Indians of my own Earth.

One of the staff called the attention of Than Kosis to the presence of my companion above them and the ruler motioned for him to descend. As they waited for the troops to move into position facing the jeddak the two talked earnestly together, the jeddak and his staff occasionally glancing up at me. I could not hear their conversation and presently it ceased and all dismounted, as the last body of troops had wheeled into position before their emperor. A member of the staff advanced toward the troops, and calling the name of a soldier commanded him to advance. The officer then recited the nature of the heroic act which had won the approval of the jeddak, and the latter advanced and placed a metal ornament upon the left arm of the lucky man.

Ten men had been so decorated when the aide called out,

"John Carter, air scout!"

Never in my life had I been so surprised, but the habit of military discipline is strong within me, and I dropped my little machine lightly to the ground and advanced on foot as I had seen the others do. As I halted before the officer, he addressed me in a voice audible to the entire assemblage of troops and spectators.

"In recognition, John Carter," he said, "of your remarkable courage and skill in defending the person of the cousin of the jeddak Than Kosis and, singlehanded, vanquishing three green warriors, it is the pleasure of our jeddak to confer on you the mark of his esteem."

Than Kosis then advanced toward me and placing an ornament upon me, said:

"My cousin has narrated the details of your wonderful achievement, which seems little short of miraculous, and if you can so well defend a cousin of the jeddak how much better could you defend the person of the jeddak himself. You are therefore appointed a padwar of The Guards and will be quartered in my palace hereafter."

I thanked him, and at his direction joined the members of his staff. After the ceremony I returned my machine to its quarters on the roof of the barracks of the air-scout squadron, and with an orderly from the palace to guide me I reported to the officer in charge of the palace.

XXII

I FIND DEJAH

The major-domo to whom I reported had been given instructions to station me near the person of the jeddak, who, in time of war, is always in great danger of assassination, as the rule that all is fair in war seems to constitute the entire ethics of Martian conflict.

He therefore escorted me immediately to the apartment in which Than Kosis then was. The ruler was engaged in conversation with his son, Sab Than, and several courtiers of his household, and did not perceive my entrance.

The walls of the apartment were completely hung with splendid tapestries which hid any windows or doors which may have pierced them. The room was lighted by imprisoned rays of sunshine held between the ceiling proper and what appeared to be a ground-glass false ceiling a few inches below.

My guide drew aside one of the tapestries, disclosing a passage which encircled the room, between the hangings and the walls of the chamber. Within this passage I was to remain, he said, so long as Than Kosis was in the apartment. When he left I was to follow. My only duty was to guard the ruler and keep out of sight as much as possible. I would be relieved after a period of four hours. The major-domo then left me.

The tapestries were of a strange weaving which gave the appearance of heavy solidity from one side, but from my hiding place I could perceive all that took place within the room as readily as though there had been no curtain intervening.

Scarcely had I gained my post than the tapestry at the opposite end of the chamber separated and four soldiers of The Guard entered, surrounding a female figure. As they approached Than Kosis the soldiers fell to either side and there standing before the jeddak and not ten feet from me, her beautiful face radiant with smiles, was Dejah Thoris.

Sab Than, Prince of Zodanga, advanced to meet her, and hand in hand they approached close to the jeddak. Than Kosis looked up in surprise, and, rising, saluted her.

"To what strange freak do I owe this visit from the Princess of Helium, who, two days ago, with rare consideration for my pride, assured me that she would prefer Tal Hajus, the green Thark, to my son?"

Dejah Thoris only smiled the more and with the roguish dimples playing at the corners of her mouth she made answer:

"From the beginning of time upon Barsoom it has been the prerogative of woman to change her mind as she listed and to dissemble in matters concerning her heart. That you will forgive, Than Kosis, as has your son. Two days ago I was not sure of his love for me, but now I am, and I have come to beg of you to forget my rash words and to accept the assurance of the Princess of Helium that when the time comes she will wed Sab Than, Prince of Zodanga."

"I am glad that you have so decided," replied Than Kosis. "It is far from my desire to push war further against the people of Helium, and, your promise shall be recorded and a proclamation to my people issued forthwith."

"It were better, Than Kosis," interrupted Dejah Thoris, "that the proclamation wait the ending of this war. It would look strange indeed to my people and to yours were the Princess of Helium to give herself to her country's enemy in the midst of hostilities."

"Cannot the war be ended at once?" spoke Sab Than. "It requires but the word of Than Kosis to bring peace. Say it, my father, say the word that will hasten my happiness, and end this unpopular strife."

"We shall see," replied Than Kosis, "how the people of Helium take to peace. I shall at least offer it to them."

Dejah Thoris, after a few words, turned and left the apartment, still followed by her guards.

Thus was the edifice of my brief dream of happiness dashed, broken, to the ground of reality. The woman for whom I had offered my life, and from whose lips I had so recently heard a declaration of love for me, had lightly forgotten my very existence and smilingly given herself to the son of her people's most hated enemy.

Although I had heard it with my own ears I could not believe it. I must search out her apartments and force her to repeat the cruel truth to me alone before I would be convinced, and so I deserted my post and hastened through the passage behind the tapestries toward the door by which she had left the chamber. Slipping quietly through this opening I discovered a maze of winding corridors, branching and turning in every direction.

Running rapidly down first one and then another of them I soon became hopelessly lost and was standing panting against a side wall when I heard voices near me. Apparently they were coming from the opposite side of the partition against which I leaned and presently I made out the tones of Dejah Thoris. I could not hear the words but I knew that I could not possibly be mistaken in the voice.

Moving on a few steps I discovered another passageway at the end of which lay a door. Walking boldly forward I pushed into the room only to find myself in a small antechamber in which were the four guards who had accompanied her. One of them instantly arose and accosted me, asking the nature of my business.

"I am from Than Kosis," I replied, "and wish to speak privately with Dejah Thoris, Princess of Helium."

"And your order?" asked the fellow.

I did not know what he meant, but replied that I was a member of The Guard, and without waiting for a reply from him I strode toward the opposite door of the antechamber, behind which I could hear Dejah Thoris conversing.

But my entrance was not to be so easily accomplished. The guardsman stepped before me, saying,

"No one comes from Than Kosis without carrying an order or the password. You must give me one or the other before you may pass."

"The only order I require, my friend, to enter where I will, hangs at my side," I answered, tapping my long-sword; "will you let me pass in peace or no?"

For reply he whipped out his own sword, calling to the others to join him, and thus the four stood, with drawn weapons, barring my further progress.

"You are not here by the order of Than Kosis," cried the one who had first addressed me, "and not only shall you not enter the apartments of the Princess of Helium but you shall go back to Than Kosis under guard to explain this unwarranted temerity. Throw down your sword; you cannot hope to overcome four of us," he added with a grim smile.

My reply was a quick thrust which left me but three antagonists and I can assure you that they were worthy of my metal. They had me backed against the wall in no time, fighting for my life. Slowly I worked my way to a corner of the room where I could force them to come at me only one at a time, and thus we fought upward of twenty minutes; the clanging of steel on steel producing a veritable bedlam in the little room.

The noise had brought Dejah Thoris to the door of her apartment, and there she stood throughout the conflict with Sola at her back peering over her shoulder. Her face was set and emotionless and I knew that she did not recognize me, nor did Sola.

Finally a lucky cut brought down a second guardsman and then, with only two opposing me, I changed my tactics and rushed them down after the fashion of my fighting that had won me many a victory. The third fell within ten seconds after the second, and the last lay dead upon the bloody floor a few moments later. They were brave men and noble fighters, and it grieved me that I had been forced to kill them, but I would have willingly depopulated all Barsoom could I have reached the side of my Dejah Thoris in no other way.

Sheathing my bloody blade I advanced toward my Martian Princess, who still stood mutely gazing at me without sign of recognition.

"Who are you, Zodangan?" she whispered. "Another enemy to harass me in my misery?"

"I am a friend," I answered, "a once cherished friend."

"No friend of Helium's princess wears that metal," she replied, "and yet the voice! I have heard it before; it is not—it cannot be—no, for he is dead."

"It is, though, my Princess, none other than John Carter," I said. "Do you not recognize, even through paint and strange metal, the heart of your chieftain?"

As I came close to her she swayed toward me with outstretched hands, but as I reached to take her in my arms she drew back with a shudder and a little moan of misery.

"Too late, too late," she grieved. "O my chieftain that was, and whom I thought dead, had you but returned one little hour before—but now it is too late, too late."

"What do you mean, Dejah Thoris?" I cried. "That you would not have promised yourself to the Zodangan prince had you known that I lived?"

"Think you, John Carter, that I would give my heart to you yesterday and today to another? I thought that it lay buried with your ashes in the pits of Warhoon, and so today I have promised my body to another to save my people from the curse of a victorious Zodangan army."

"But I am not dead, my princess. I have come to claim you, and all Zodanga cannot prevent it."

"It is too late, John Carter, my promise is given, and on Barsoom that is final. The ceremonies which follow later are but meaningless formalities. They make the fact of marriage no more certain than does the funeral cortege of a jeddak again place the seal of death upon him. I am as good as married, John Carter. No longer may you call me your princess. No longer are you my chieftain."

"I know but little of your customs here upon Barsoom, Dejah Thoris, but I do know that I love you, and if you meant the last words you spoke to me that day as the hordes of Warhoon were charging down upon us, no other man shall ever claim you as his bride. You meant them then, my princess, and you mean them still! Say that it is true."

"I meant them, John Carter," she whispered. "I cannot repeat them now for I have given myself to another. Ah, if you had only known our ways, my friend," she continued, half to herself, "the promise would have been yours long months ago, and you could have claimed me before all others. It might have meant the fall of Helium, but I would have given my empire for my Tharkian chief."

Then aloud she said: "Do you remember the night when you offended me? You called me your princess without having asked my hand of me, and then you boasted that you had fought for me. You did not know, and I should not have been offended; I see that now. But there was no one to tell you what I could not, that upon Barsoom there are two kinds of women in the cities of the red men. The one they fight for that they may ask them in marriage; the other kind they fight for also, but never ask their hands. When a man has won a woman he may address her as his princess, or in any of the several terms which signify possession. You had fought for me, but had never asked me in marriage, and so when you called me your princess, you see," she faltered, "I was hurt, but even then, John Carter, I did not repulse you, as I should have done, until you made it doubly worse by taunting me with having won me through combat."

"I do not need ask your forgiveness now, Dejah Thoris," I cried. "You must know that my fault was of ignorance of your Barsoomian customs. What I failed to do, through implicit belief that my petition would be presumptuous and unwelcome, I do now, Dejah Thoris; I ask you to be my wife, and by all the Virginian fighting blood that flows in my veins you shall be."

"No, John Carter, it is useless," she cried, hopelessly, "I may never be yours while Sab Than lives."

"You have sealed his death warrant, my princess—Sab Than dies."

"Nor that either," she hastened to explain. "I may not wed the man who slays my husband, even in self-defense. It is custom. We are ruled by custom upon Barsoom. It is useless, my friend. You must bear the sorrow with me. That at least we may share in common. That, and the memory of the brief days among the Tharks. You must go now, nor ever see me again. Good-bye, my chieftain that was."

Disheartened and dejected, I withdrew from the room, but I was not entirely discouraged, nor would I admit that Dejah Thoris was lost to me until the ceremony had actually been performed.

As I wandered along the corridors, I was as absolutely lost in the mazes of winding passageways as I had been before I discovered Dejah Thoris' apartments.

I knew that my only hope lay in escape from the city of Zodanga, for the matter of the four dead guardsmen would have to be explained, and as I could never reach my original post without a guide, suspicion would surely rest on me so soon as I was discovered wandering aimlessly through the palace.

Presently I came upon a spiral runway leading to a lower floor, and this I followed downward for several stories until I reached the doorway of a large apartment in which were a number of guardsmen. The walls of this room were hung with transparent tapestries behind which I secreted myself without being apprehended.

The conversation of the guardsmen was general, and awakened no interest in me until an officer entered the room and ordered four of the men to relieve the detail who were guarding the Princess of Helium. Now, I knew, my troubles would commence in earnest and indeed they were upon me all too soon, for it seemed that the squad had scarcely left the guardroom before one of their number burst in again breathlessly, crying that they had found their four comrades butchered in the antechamber.

In a moment the entire palace was alive with people. Guardsmen, officers, courtiers, servants, and slaves ran helter-skelter through the corridors and apartments carrying messages and orders, and searching for signs of the assassin.

This was my opportunity and slim as it appeared I grasped it, for as a number of soldiers came hurrying past my hiding place I fell in behind them and followed through the mazes of the palace until, in passing through a great hall, I saw the blessed light of day coming in through a series of larger windows.

Here I left my guides, and, slipping to the nearest window, sought for an avenue of escape. The windows opened upon a great balcony which overlooked one of the broad avenues of Zodanga. The ground was about thirty feet below, and at a like distance from the building was a wall fully twenty feet high, constructed of polished glass about a foot in thickness. To a red Martian escape by this path would have appeared impossible, but to me, with my earthly strength and agility, it seemed already accomplished. My only fear was in being detected before darkness fell, for I could not make the leap in broad daylight while the court below and the avenue beyond were crowded with Zodangans.

Accordingly I searched for a hiding place and finally found one by accident, inside a huge hanging ornament which swung from the ceiling of the hall, and about ten feet from the floor. Into the capacious bowl-like vase I sprang with ease, and scarcely had I settled down within it than I heard a number of people enter the apartment. The group stopped beneath my hiding place and I could plainly overhear their every word.

"It is the work of Heliumites," said one of the men.

"Yes, O Jeddak, but how had they access to the palace? I could believe that even with the diligent care of your guardsmen a single enemy might reach the inner chambers, but how a force of six or eight fighting men could have done so unobserved is beyond me. We shall soon know, however, for here comes the royal psychologist."

Another man now joined the group, and, after making his formal greetings to his ruler, said:

"O mighty Jeddak, it is a strange tale I read in the dead minds of your faithful guardsmen. They were felled not by a number of fighting men, but by a single opponent."

He paused to let the full weight of this announcement impress his hearers, and that his statement was scarcely credited was evidenced by the impatient exclamation of incredulity which escaped the lips of Than Kosis.

"What manner of weird tale are you bringing me, Notan?" he cried.

"It is the truth, my Jeddak," replied the psychologist. "In fact the impressions were strongly marked on the brain of each of the four guardsmen. Their antagonist was a very tall man, wearing the metal of one of your own guardsmen, and his fighting ability was little short of marvelous for he fought fair against the entire four and vanquished them by his surpassing skill and superhuman strength and endurance. Though he wore the metal of Zodanga, my Jeddak, such a man was never seen before in this or any other country upon Barsoom.

"The mind of the Princess of Helium whom I have examined and questioned was a blank to me, she has perfect control, and I could not read one iota of it. She said that she witnessed a portion of the encounter, and that when she looked there was but one man engaged with the guardsmen; a man whom she did not recognize as ever having seen."

"Where is my erstwhile savior?" spoke another of the party, and I recognized the voice of the cousin of Than Kosis, whom I had rescued from the green warriors. "By the metal of my first ancestor," he went on, "but the description fits him to perfection, especially as to his fighting ability."

"Where is this man?" cried Than Kosis. "Have him brought to me at once. What know you of him, cousin? It seemed strange to me now that I think upon it that there should have been such a fighting man in Zodanga, of whose name, even, we were ignorant before today. And his name too, John Carter, who ever heard of such a name upon Barsoom!"

Word was soon brought that I was nowhere to be found, either in the palace or at my former quarters in the barracks of the air-scout squadron. Kantos Kan, they had found and questioned, but he knew nothing of my whereabouts, and as to my past, he had told them he knew as little, since he had but recently met me during our captivity among the Warhoons.

"Keep your eyes on this other one," commanded Than Kosis. "He also is a stranger and likely as not they both hail from Helium, and where one is we shall sooner or later find the other. Quadruple the air patrol, and let every man who leaves the city by air or ground be subjected to the closest scrutiny."

Another messenger now entered with word that I was still within the palace walls.

"The likeness of every person who has entered or left the palace grounds today has been carefully examined," concluded the fellow, "and not one approaches the likeness of this new padwar of the guards, other than that which was recorded of him at the time he entered."

"Then we will have him shortly," commented Than Kosis contentedly, "and in the meanwhile we will repair to the apartments of the Princess of Helium and question her in regard to the affair. She may know more than she cared to divulge to you, Notan. Come."

They left the hall, and, as darkness had fallen without, I slipped lightly from my hiding place and hastened to the balcony. Few were in sight, and choosing a moment when none seemed near I sprang quickly to the top of the glass wall and from there to the avenue beyond the palace grounds.

XXIII

LOST IN THE SKY

Without effort at concealment I hastened to the vicinity of our quarters, where I felt sure I should find Kantos Kan. As I neared the building I became more careful, as I judged, and rightly, that the place would be guarded. Several men in civilian metal loitered near the front entrance and in the rear were others. My only means of reaching, unseen, the upper story where our apartments were situated was through an adjoining building, and after considerable maneuvering I managed to attain the roof of a shop several doors away.

Leaping from roof to roof, I soon reached an open window in the building where I hoped to find the Heliumite, and in another moment I stood in the room before him. He was alone and showed no surprise at my coming, saying he had expected me much earlier, as my tour of duty must have ended some time since.

I saw that he knew nothing of the events of the day at the palace, and when I had enlightened him he was all excitement. The news that Dejah Thoris had promised her hand to Sab Than filled him with dismay.

"It cannot be," he exclaimed. "It is impossible! Why no man in all Helium but would prefer death to the selling of our loved princess to the ruling house of Zodanga. She must have lost her mind to have assented to such an atrocious bargain. You, who do not know how we of Helium love the members of our ruling house, cannot appreciate the horror with which I contemplate such an unholy alliance.

"What can be done, John Carter?" he continued. "You are a resourceful man. Can you not think of some way to save Helium from this disgrace?"

"If I can come within sword's reach of Sab Than," I answered, "I can solve the difficulty in so far as Helium is concerned, but for personal reasons I would prefer that another struck the blow that frees Dejah Thoris."

Kantos Kan eyed me narrowly before he spoke.

"You love her!" he said. "Does she know it?"

"She knows it, Kantos Kan, and repulses me only because she is promised to Sab Than."

The splendid fellow sprang to his feet, and grasping me by the shoulder raised his sword on high, exclaiming:

"And had the choice been left to me I could not have chosen a more fitting mate for the first princess of Barsoom. Here is my hand upon your shoulder, John Carter, and my word that Sab Than shall go out at the point of my sword for the sake of my love for Helium, for Dejah Thoris, and for you. This very night I shall try to reach his quarters in the palace."

"How?" I asked. "You are strongly guarded and a quadruple force patrols the sky."

He bent his head in thought a moment, then raised it with an air of confidence.

"I only need to pass these guards and I can do it," he said at last. "I know a secret entrance to the palace through the pinnacle of the highest tower. I fell upon it by chance one day as I was passing above the palace on patrol duty. In this work it is required that we investigate any unusual occurrence we may witness, and a face peering from the pinnacle of the high tower of the palace was, to me, most unusual. I therefore drew near and discovered that the possessor of the peering face was none other than Sab Than. He was slightly put out at being detected and commanded me to keep the matter to myself, explaining that the passage from the tower led directly to his apartments, and was known only to him. If I can reach the roof of the barracks and get my machine I can be in Sab Than's quarters in five minutes; but how am I to escape from this building, guarded as you say it is?"

"How well are the machine sheds at the barracks guarded?" I asked.

"There is usually but one man on duty there at night upon the roof."

"Go to the roof of this building, Kantos Kan, and wait me there."

Without stopping to explain my plans I retraced my way to the street and hastened to the barracks. I did not dare to enter the building, filled as it was with members of the air-scout squadron, who, in common with all Zodanga, were on the lookout for me.

The building was an enormous one, rearing its lofty head fully a thousand feet into the air. But few buildings in Zodanga were higher than these barracks, though several topped it by a few hundred feet; the docks of the great battleships of the line standing some fifteen hundred feet from the ground, while the freight and passenger stations of the merchant squadrons rose nearly as high.

It was a long climb up the face of the building, and one fraught with much danger, but there was no other way, and so I essayed the task. The fact that Barsoomian architecture is extremely ornate made the feat much simpler than I had anticipated, since I found ornamental ledges and projections which fairly formed a perfect ladder for me all the way to the eaves of the building. Here I met my first real obstacle. The eaves projected nearly twenty feet from the wall to which I clung, and though I encircled the great building I could find no opening through them.

The top floor was alight, and filled with soldiers engaged in the pastimes of their kind; I could not, therefore, reach the roof through the building.

There was one slight, desperate chance, and that I decided I must take—it was for Dejah Thoris, and no man has lived who would not risk a thousand deaths for such as she.

Clinging to the wall with my feet and one hand, I unloosened one of the long leather straps of my trappings at the end of which dangled a great hook by which air sailors are hung to the sides and bottoms of their craft for various purposes of repair, and by means of which landing parties are lowered to the ground from the battleships.

I swung this hook cautiously to the roof several times before it finally found lodgment; gently I pulled on it to strengthen its hold, but whether it would bear the weight of my body I did not know. It might be barely caught upon the very outer verge of the roof, so that as my body swung out at the end of the strap it would slip off and launch me to the pavement a thousand feet below.

An instant I hesitated, and then, releasing my grasp upon the supporting ornament, I swung out into space at the end of the strap. Far below me lay the brilliantly lighted streets, the hard pavements, and death. There was a little jerk at the top of the supporting eaves, and a nasty slipping, grating sound which turned me cold with apprehension; then the hook caught and I was safe.

Clambering quickly aloft I grasped the edge of the eaves and drew myself to the surface of the roof above. As I gained my feet I was confronted by the sentry on duty, into the muzzle of whose revolver I found myself looking.

"Who are you and whence came you?" he cried.

"I am an air scout, friend, and very near a dead one, for just by the merest chance I escaped falling to the avenue below," I replied.

"But how came you upon the roof, man? No one has landed or come up from the building for the past hour. Quick, explain yourself, or I call the guard."

"Look you here, sentry, and you shall see how I came and how close a shave I had to not coming at all," I answered, turning toward the edge of the roof, where, twenty feet below, at the end of my strap, hung all my weapons.

The fellow, acting on impulse of curiosity, stepped to my side and to his undoing, for as he leaned to peer over the eaves I grasped him by his throat and his pistol arm and threw him heavily to the roof. The weapon dropped from his grasp, and my fingers choked off his attempted cry for assistance. I gagged and bound him and then hung him over the edge of the roof as I myself had hung a few moments before. I knew it would be morning before he would be discovered, and I needed all the time that I could gain.

Donning my trappings and weapons I hastened to the sheds, and soon had out both my machine and Kantos Kan's. Making his fast behind mine I started my engine, and skimming over the edge of the roof I dove down into the streets of the city far below the plane usually occupied by the air patrol. In less than a minute I was settling safely upon the roof of our apartment beside the astonished Kantos Kan.

I lost no time in explanation, but plunged immediately into a discussion of our plans for the immediate future. It was decided that I was to try to make Helium while Kantos Kan was to enter the palace and dispatch Sab Than. If successful he was then to follow me. He set my compass for me, a clever little device which will remain steadfastly fixed upon any given point on the surface of Barsoom, and bidding each other farewell we rose together and sped in the direction of the palace which lay in the route which I must take to reach Helium.

As we neared the high tower a patrol shot down from above, throwing its piercing searchlight full upon my craft, and a voice roared out a command to halt, following with a shot as I paid no attention to his hail. Kantos Kan dropped quickly into the darkness, while I rose steadily and at terrific speed raced through the Martian sky followed by a dozen of the air-scout craft which had joined the pursuit, and later by a swift cruiser carrying a hundred men and a battery of rapid-fire guns. By twisting and turning my little machine, now rising and now falling, I managed to elude their search-lights most of the time, but I was also losing ground by these tactics, and so I decided to hazard everything on a straight-away course and leave the result to fate and the speed of my machine.

Kantos Kan had shown me a trick of gearing, which is known only to the navy of Helium, that greatly increased the speed of our machines, so that I felt sure I could distance my pursuers if I could dodge their projectiles for a few moments.

As I sped through the air the screeching of the bullets around me convinced me that only by a miracle could I escape, but the die was cast, and throwing on full speed I raced a straight course toward Helium. Gradually I left my pursuers further and further behind, and I was just congratulating myself on my lucky escape, when a well-directed shot from the cruiser exploded at the prow of my little craft. The concussion nearly capsized her, and with a sickening plunge she hurtled downward through the dark night.

How far I fell before I regained control of the plane I do not know, but I must have been very close to the ground when I started to rise again, as I plainly heard the squealing of animals below me. Rising again I scanned the heavens for my pursuers, and finally making out their lights far behind me, saw that they were landing, evidently in search of me.

Not until their lights were no longer discernible did I venture to flash my little lamp upon my compass, and then I found to my consternation that a fragment of the projectile had utterly destroyed my only guide, as well as my speedometer. It was true I could follow the stars in the general direction of Helium, but without knowing the exact location of the city or the speed at which I was traveling my chances for finding it were slim.

Helium lies a thousand miles southwest of Zodanga, and with my compass intact I should have made the trip, barring accidents, in between four and five hours. As it turned out, however, morning found me speeding over a vast expanse of dead sea bottom after nearly six hours of continuous flight at high speed. Presently a great city showed below me, but it was not Helium, as that alone of all Barsoomian metropolises consists in two immense circular walled cities about seventy-five miles apart and would have been easily distinguishable from the altitude at which I was flying.

Believing that I had come too far to the north and west, I turned back in a southeasterly direction, passing during the forenoon several other large cities, but none resembling the description which Kantos Kan had given me of Helium. In addition to the twin-city formation of Helium, another distinguishing feature is the two immense towers, one of vivid scarlet rising nearly a mile into the air from the center of one of the cities, while the other, of bright yellow and of the same height, marks her sister.

XXIV

TARS TARKAS FINDS A FRIEND

About noon I passed low over a great dead city of ancient Mars, and as I skimmed out across the plain beyond I came full upon several thousand green warriors engaged in a terrific battle. Scarcely had I seen them than a volley of shots was directed at me, and with the almost unfailing accuracy of their aim my little craft was instantly a ruined wreck, sinking erratically to the ground.

I fell almost directly in the center of the fierce combat, among warriors who had not seen my approach so busily were they engaged in life and death struggles. The men were fighting on foot with long-swords, while an occasional shot from a sharpshooter on the outskirts of the conflict would bring down a warrior who might for an instant separate himself from the entangled mass.

As my machine sank among them I realized that it was fight or die, with good chances of dying in any event, and so I struck the ground with drawn long-sword ready to defend myself as I could.

I fell beside a huge monster who was engaged with three antagonists, and as I glanced at his fierce face, filled with the light of battle, I recognized Tars Tarkas the Thark. He did not see me, as I was a trifle behind him, and just then the three warriors opposing him, and whom I recognized as Warhoons, charged simultaneously. The mighty fellow made quick work of one of them, but in stepping back for another thrust he fell over a dead body behind him and was down and at the mercy of his foes in an instant. Quick as lightning they were upon him, and Tars Tarkas would have been gathered to his fathers in short order had I not sprung before his prostrate form and engaged his adversaries. I had accounted for one of them when the mighty Thark regained his feet and quickly settled the other.

He gave me one look, and a slight smile touched his grim lip as, touching my shoulder, he said,

"I would scarcely recognize you, John Carter, but there is no other mortal upon Barsoom who would have done what you have for me. I think I have learned that there is such a thing as friendship, my friend."

He said no more, nor was there opportunity, for the Warhoons were closing in about us, and together we fought, shoulder to shoulder, during all that long, hot afternoon, until the tide of battle turned and the remnant of the fierce Warhoon horde fell back upon their thoats, and fled into the gathering darkness.

Ten thousand men had been engaged in that titanic struggle, and upon the field of battle lay three thousand dead. Neither side asked or gave quarter, nor did they attempt to take prisoners.

On our return to the city after the battle we had gone directly to Tars Tarkas' quarters, where I was left alone while the chieftain attended the customary council which immediately follows an engagement.

As I sat awaiting the return of the green warrior I heard something move in an adjoining apartment, and as I glanced up there rushed suddenly upon me a huge and hideous creature which bore me backward upon the pile of silks and furs upon which I had been reclining. It was Woola—faithful, loving Woola. He had found his way back to Thark and, as Tars Tarkas later told me, had gone immediately to my former quarters where he had taken up his pathetic and seemingly hopeless watch for my return.

"Tal Hajus knows that you are here, John Carter," said Tars Tarkas, on his return from the jeddak's quarters; "Sarkoja saw and recognized you as we were returning. Tal Hajus has ordered me to bring you before him tonight. I have ten thoats, John Carter; you may take your choice from among them, and I will accompany you to the nearest waterway that leads to Helium. Tars Tarkas may be a cruel green warrior, but he can be a friend as well. Come, we must start."

"And when you return, Tars Tarkas?" I asked.

"The wild calots, possibly, or worse," he replied. "Unless I should chance to have the opportunity I have so long waited of battling with Tal Hajus."

"We will stay, Tars Tarkas, and see Tal Hajus tonight. You shall not sacrifice yourself, and it may be that tonight you can have the chance you wait."

He objected strenuously, saying that Tal Hajus often flew into wild fits of passion at the mere thought of the blow I had dealt him, and that if ever he laid his hands upon me I would be subjected to the most horrible tortures.

While we were eating I repeated to Tars Tarkas the story which Sola had told me that night upon the sea bottom during the march to Thark.

He said but little, but the great muscles of his face worked in passion and in agony at recollection of the horrors which had been heaped upon the only thing he had ever loved in all his cold, cruel, terrible existence.

He no longer demurred when I suggested that we go before Tal Hajus, only saying that he would like to speak to Sarkoja first. At his request I accompanied him to her quarters, and the look of venomous hatred she cast upon me was almost adequate recompense for any future misfortunes this accidental return to Thark might bring me.

"Sarkoja," said Tars Tarkas, "forty years ago you were instrumental in bringing about the torture and death of a woman named Gozava. I have just discovered that the warrior who loved that woman has learned of your part in the transaction. He may not kill you, Sarkoja, it is not our custom, but there is nothing to prevent him tying one end of a strap about your neck and the other end to a wild thoat, merely to test your fitness to survive and help perpetuate our race. Having heard that he would do this on the morrow, I thought it only right to warn you, for I am a just man. The river Iss is but a short pilgrimage, Sarkoja. Come, John Carter."

The next morning Sarkoja was gone, nor was she ever seen after.

In silence we hastened to the jeddak's palace, where we were immediately admitted to his presence; in fact, he could scarcely wait to see me and was standing erect upon his platform glowering at the entrance as I came in.

"Strap him to that pillar," he shrieked. "We shall see who it is dares strike the mighty Tal Hajus. Heat the irons; with my own hands I shall burn the eyes from his head that he may not pollute my person with his vile gaze."

"Chieftains of Thark," I cried, turning to the assembled council and ignoring Tal Hajus, "I have been a chief among you, and today I have fought for Thark shoulder to shoulder with her greatest warrior. You owe me, at least, a hearing. I have won that much today. You claim to be a just people—"

"Silence," roared Tal Hajus. "Gag the creature and bind him as I command."

"Justice, Tal Hajus," exclaimed Lorquas Ptomel. "Who are you to set aside the customs of ages among the Tharks?"

"Yes, justice!" echoed a dozen voices, and so, while Tal Hajus fumed and frothed, I continued.

"You are a brave people and you love bravery, but where was your mighty jeddak during the fighting today? I did not see him in the thick of battle; he was not there. He rends defenseless women and little children in his lair, but how recently has one of you seen him fight with men? Why, even I, a midget beside him, felled him with a single blow of my fist. Is it of such that the Tharks fashion their jeddaks? There stands beside me now a great Thark, a mighty warrior and a noble man. Chieftains, how sounds, Tars Tarkas, Jeddak of Thark?"

A roar of deep-toned applause greeted this suggestion.

"It but remains for this council to command, and Tal Hajus must prove his fitness to rule. Were he a brave man he would invite Tars Tarkas to combat, for he does not love him, but Tal Hajus is afraid; Tal Hajus, your jeddak, is a coward. With my bare hands I could kill him, and he knows it."

After I ceased there was tense silence, as all eyes were riveted upon Tal Hajus. He did not speak or move, but the blotchy green of his countenance turned livid, and the froth froze upon his lips.

"Tal Hajus," said Lorquas Ptomel in a cold, hard voice, "never in my long life have I seen a jeddak of the Tharks so humiliated. There could be but one answer to this arraignment. We wait it." And still Tal Hajus stood as though petrified.

"Chieftains," continued Lorquas Ptomel, "shall the jeddak, Tal Hajus, prove his fitness to rule over Tars Tarkas?"

There were twenty chieftains about the rostrum, and twenty swords flashed high in assent.

There was no alternative. That decree was final, and so Tal Hajus drew his long-sword and advanced to meet Tars Tarkas.

The combat was soon over, and, with his foot upon the neck of the dead monster, Tars Tarkas became jeddak among the Tharks.

His first act was to make me a full-fledged chieftain with the rank I had won by my combats the first few weeks of my captivity among them.

Seeing the favorable disposition of the warriors toward Tars Tarkas, as well as toward me, I grasped the opportunity to enlist them in my cause against Zodanga. I told Tars Tarkas the story of my adventures, and in a few words had explained to him the thought I had in mind.

"John Carter has made a proposal," he said, addressing the council, "which meets with my sanction. I shall put it to you briefly. Dejah Thoris, the Princess of Helium, who was our prisoner, is now held by the jeddak of Zodanga, whose son she must wed to save her country from devastation at the hands of the Zodangan forces.

"John Carter suggests that we rescue her and return her to Helium. The loot of Zodanga would be magnificent, and I have often thought that had we an alliance with the people of Helium we could obtain sufficient assurance of sustenance to permit us to increase the size and frequency of our hatchings, and thus become unquestionably supreme among the green men of all Barsoom. What say you?"

It was a chance to fight, an opportunity to loot, and they rose to the bait as a speckled trout to a fly.

For Tharks they were wildly enthusiastic, and before another half hour had passed twenty mounted messengers were speeding across dead sea bottoms to call the hordes together for the expedition.

In three days we were on the march toward Zodanga, one hundred thousand strong, as Tars Tarkas had been able to enlist the services of three smaller hordes on the promise of the great loot of Zodanga.

At the head of the column I rode beside the great Thark while at the heels of my mount trotted my beloved Woola.

We traveled entirely by night, timing our marches so that we camped during the day at deserted cities where, even to the beasts, we were all kept indoors during the daylight hours. On the march Tars Tarkas, through his remarkable ability and statesmanship, enlisted fifty thousand more warriors from various hordes, so that, ten days after we set out we halted at midnight outside the great walled city of Zodanga, one hundred and fifty thousand strong.

The fighting strength and efficiency of this horde of ferocious green monsters was equivalent to ten times their number of red men. Never in the history of Barsoom, Tars Tarkas told me, had such a force of green warriors marched to battle together. It was a monstrous task to keep even a semblance of harmony among them, and it was a marvel to me that he got them to the city without a mighty battle among themselves.

But as we neared Zodanga their personal quarrels were submerged by their greater hatred for the red men, and especially for the Zodangans, who had for years waged a ruthless campaign of extermination against the green men, directing special attention toward despoiling their incubators.

Now that we were before Zodanga the task of obtaining entry to the city devolved upon me, and directing Tars Tarkas to hold his forces in two divisions out of earshot of the city, with each division opposite a large gateway, I took twenty dismounted warriors and approached one of the small gates that pierced the walls at short intervals. These gates have no regular guard, but are covered by sentries, who patrol the avenue that encircles the city just within the walls as our metropolitan police patrol their beats.

The walls of Zodanga are seventy-five feet in height and fifty feet thick. They are built of enormous blocks of carborundum, and the task of entering the city seemed, to my escort of green warriors, an impossibility. The fellows who had been detailed to accompany me were of one of the smaller hordes, and therefore did not know me.

Placing three of them with their faces to the wall and arms locked, I commanded two more to mount to their shoulders, and a sixth I ordered to climb upon the shoulders of the upper two. The head of the topmost warrior towered over forty feet from the ground.

In this way, with ten warriors, I built a series of three steps from the ground to the shoulders of the topmost man. Then starting from a short distance behind them I ran swiftly up from one tier to the next, and with a final bound from the broad shoulders of the highest I clutched the top of the great wall and quietly drew myself to its broad expanse. After me I dragged six lengths of leather from an equal number of my warriors. These lengths we had previously fastened together, and passing one end to the topmost warrior I lowered the other end cautiously over the opposite side of the wall toward the avenue below. No one was in sight, so, lowering myself to the end of my leather strap, I dropped the remaining thirty feet to the pavement below.

I had learned from Kantos Kan the secret of opening these gates, and in another moment my twenty great fighting men stood within the doomed city of Zodanga.

I found to my delight that I had entered at the lower boundary of the enormous palace grounds. The building itself showed in the distance a blaze of glorious light, and on the instant I determined to lead a detachment of warriors directly within the palace itself, while the balance of the great horde was attacking the barracks of the soldiery.

Dispatching one of my men to Tars Tarkas for a detail of fifty Tharks, with word of my intentions, I ordered ten warriors to capture and open one of the great gates while with the nine remaining I took the other. We were to do our work quietly, no shots were to be fired and no general advance made until I had reached the palace with my fifty Tharks. Our plans worked to perfection. The two sentries we met were dispatched to their fathers upon the banks of the lost sea of Korus, and the guards at both gates followed them in silence.

XXV

THE LOOTING OF ZODANGA

As the great gate where I stood swung open my fifty Tharks, headed by Tars Tarkas himself, rode in upon their mighty thoats. I led them to the palace walls, which I negotiated easily without assistance. Once inside, however, the gate gave me considerable trouble, but I finally was rewarded by seeing it swing upon its huge hinges, and soon my fierce escort was riding across the gardens of the jeddak of Zodanga.

As we approached the palace I could see through the great windows of the first floor into the brilliantly illuminated audience chamber of Than Kosis. The immense hall was crowded with nobles and their women, as though some important function was in progress. There was not a guard in sight without the palace, due, I presume, to the fact that the city and palace walls were considered impregnable, and so I came close and peered within.

At one end of the chamber, upon massive golden thrones encrusted with diamonds, sat Than Kosis and his consort, surrounded by officers and dignitaries of state. Before them stretched a broad aisle lined on either side with soldiery, and as I looked there entered this aisle at the far end of the hall, the head of a procession which advanced to the foot of the throne.

First there marched four officers of the jeddak's Guard bearing a huge salver on which reposed, upon a cushion of scarlet silk, a great golden chain with a collar and padlock at each end. Directly behind these officers came four others carrying a similar salver which supported the magnificent ornaments of a prince and princess of the reigning house of Zodanga.

At the foot of the throne these two parties separated and halted, facing each other at opposite sides of the aisle. Then came more dignitaries, and the officers of the palace and of the army, and finally two figures entirely muffled in scarlet silk, so that not a feature of either was discernible. These two stopped at the foot of the throne, facing Than Kosis. When the balance of the procession had entered and assumed their stations Than Kosis addressed the couple standing before him. I could not hear his words, but presently two officers advanced and removed the scarlet robe from one of the figures, and I saw that Kantos Kan had failed in his mission, for it was Sab Than, Prince of Zodanga, who stood revealed before me.

Than Kosis now took a set of the ornaments from one of the salvers and placed one of the collars of gold about his son's neck, springing the padlock fast. After a few more words addressed to Sab Than he turned to the other figure, from which the officers now removed the enshrouding silks, disclosing to my now comprehending view Dejah Thoris, Princess of Helium.

The object of the ceremony was clear to me; in another moment Dejah Thoris would be joined forever to the Prince of Zodanga. It was an impressive and beautiful ceremony, I presume, but to me it seemed the most fiendish sight I had ever witnessed, and as the ornaments were adjusted upon her beautiful figure and her collar of gold swung open in the hands of Than Kosis I raised my long-sword above my head, and, with the heavy hilt, I shattered the glass of the great window and sprang into the midst of the astonished assemblage. With a bound I was on the steps of the platform beside Than Kosis, and as he stood riveted with surprise I brought my long-sword down upon the golden chain that would have bound Dejah Thoris to another.

In an instant all was confusion; a thousand drawn swords menaced me from every quarter, and Sab Than sprang upon me with a jeweled dagger he had drawn from his nuptial ornaments. I could have killed him as easily as I might a fly, but the age-old custom of Barsoom stayed my hand, and grasping his wrist as the dagger flew toward my heart I held him as though in a vise and with my long-sword pointed to the far end of the hall.

"Zodanga has fallen," I cried. "Look!"

All eyes turned in the direction I had indicated, and there, forging through the portals of the entranceway rode Tars Tarkas and his fifty warriors on their great thoats.

A cry of alarm and amazement broke from the assemblage, but no word of fear, and in a moment the soldiers and nobles of Zodanga were hurling themselves upon the advancing Tharks.

Thrusting Sab Than headlong from the platform, I drew Dejah Thoris to my side. Behind the throne was a narrow doorway and in this Than Kosis now stood facing me, with drawn long-sword. In an instant we were engaged, and I found no mean antagonist.

As we circled upon the broad platform I saw Sab Than rushing up the steps to aid his father, but, as he raised his hand to strike, Dejah Thoris sprang before him and then my sword found the spot that made Sab Than jeddak of Zodanga. As his father rolled dead upon the floor the new jeddak tore himself free from Dejah Thoris' grasp, and again we faced each other. He was soon joined by a quartet of officers, and, with my back against a golden throne, I fought once again for Dejah Thoris. I was hard pressed to defend myself and yet not strike down Sab Than and, with him, my last chance to win the woman I loved. My blade was swinging with the rapidity of lightning as I sought to parry the thrusts and cuts of my opponents. Two I had disarmed, and one was down, when several more rushed to the aid of their new ruler, and to avenge the death of the old.

As they advanced there were cries of "The woman! The woman! Strike her down; it is her plot. Kill her! Kill her!"

Calling to Dejah Thoris to get behind me I worked my way toward the little doorway back of the throne, but the officers realized my intentions, and three of them sprang in behind me and blocked my chances for gaining a position where I could have defended Dejah Thoris against an army of swordsmen.

The Tharks were having their hands full in the center of the room, and I began to realize that nothing short of a miracle could save Dejah Thoris and myself, when I saw Tars Tarkas surging through the crowd of pygmies that swarmed about him. With one swing of his mighty longsword he laid a dozen corpses at his feet, and so he hewed a pathway before him until in another moment he stood upon the platform beside me, dealing death and destruction right and left.

The bravery of the Zodangans was awe-inspiring, not one attempted to escape, and when the fighting ceased it was because only Tharks remained alive in the great hall, other than Dejah Thoris and myself.

Sab Than lay dead beside his father, and the corpses of the flower of Zodangan nobility and chivalry covered the floor of the bloody shambles.

My first thought when the battle was over was for Kantos Kan, and leaving Dejah Thoris in charge of Tars Tarkas I took a dozen warriors and hastened to the dungeons beneath the palace. The jailers had all left to join the fighters in the throne room, so we searched the labyrinthine prison without opposition.

I called Kantos Kan's name aloud in each new corridor and compartment, and finally I was rewarded by hearing a faint response. Guided by the sound, we soon found him helpless in a dark recess.

He was overjoyed at seeing me, and to know the meaning of the fight, faint echoes of which had reached his prison cell. He told me that the air patrol had captured him before he reached the high tower of the palace, so that he had not even seen Sab Than.

We discovered that it would be futile to attempt to cut away the bars and chains which held him prisoner, so, at his suggestion I returned to search the bodies on the floor above for keys to open the padlocks of his cell and of his chains.

Fortunately among the first I examined I found his jailer, and soon we had Kantos Kan with us in the throne room.

The sounds of heavy firing, mingled with shouts and cries, came to us from the city's streets, and Tars Tarkas hastened away to direct the fighting without. Kantos Kan accompanied him to act as guide, the green warriors commencing a thorough search of the palace for other Zodangans and for loot, and Dejah Thoris and I were left alone.

She had sunk into one of the golden thrones, and as I turned to her she greeted me with a wan smile.

"Was there ever such a man!" she exclaimed. "I know that Barsoom has never before seen your like. Can it be that all Earth men are as you? Alone, a stranger, hunted, threatened, persecuted, you have done in a few short months what in all the past ages of Barsoom no man has ever done: joined together the wild hordes of the sea bottoms and brought them to fight as allies of a red Martian people."

"The answer is easy, Dejah Thoris," I replied smiling. "It was not I who did it, it was love, love for Dejah Thoris, a power that would work greater miracles than this you have seen."

A pretty flush overspread her face and she answered,

"You may say that now, John Carter, and I may listen, for I am free."

"And more still I have to say, ere it is again too late," I returned. "I have done many strange things in my life, many things that wiser men would not have dared, but never in my wildest fancies have I dreamed of winning a Dejah Thoris for myself—for never had I dreamed that in all the universe dwelt such a woman as the Princess of Helium. That you are a princess does not abash me, but that you are you is enough to make me doubt my sanity as I ask you, my princess, to be mine."

"He does not need to be abashed who so well knew the answer to his plea before the plea were made," she replied, rising and placing her dear hands upon my shoulders, and so I took her in my arms and kissed her.

And thus in the midst of a city of wild conflict, filled with the alarms of war; with death and destruction reaping their terrible harvest around her, did Dejah Thoris, Princess of Helium, true daughter of Mars, the God of War, promise herself in marriage to John Carter, Gentleman of Virginia.

XXVI

THROUGH CARNAGE TO JOY

Sometime later Tars Tarkas and Kantos Kan returned to report that Zodanga had been completely reduced. Her forces were entirely destroyed or captured, and no further resistance was to be expected from within. Several battleships had escaped, but there were thousands of war and merchant vessels under guard of Thark warriors.

The lesser hordes had commenced looting and quarreling among themselves, so it was decided that we collect what warriors we could, man as many vessels as possible with Zodangan prisoners and make for Helium without further loss of time.

Five hours later we sailed from the roofs of the dock buildings with a fleet of two hundred and fifty battleships, carrying nearly one hundred thousand green warriors, followed by a fleet of transports with our thoats.

Behind us we left the stricken city in the fierce and brutal clutches of some forty thousand green warriors of the lesser hordes. They were looting, murdering, and fighting amongst themselves. In a hundred places they had applied the torch, and columns of dense smoke were rising above the city as though to blot out from the eye of heaven the horrid sights beneath.

In the middle of the afternoon we sighted the scarlet and yellow towers of Helium, and a short time later a great fleet of Zodangan battleships rose from the camps of the besiegers without the city, and advanced to meet us.

The banners of Helium had been strung from stem to stern of each of our mighty craft, but the Zodangans did not need this sign to realize that we were enemies, for our green Martian warriors had opened fire upon them almost as they left the ground. With their uncanny marksmanship they raked the on-coming fleet with volley after volley.

The twin cities of Helium, perceiving that we were friends, sent out hundreds of vessels to aid us, and then began the first real air battle I had ever witnessed.

The vessels carrying our green warriors were kept circling above the contending fleets of Helium and Zodanga, since their batteries were useless in the hands of the Tharks who, having no navy, have no skill in naval gunnery. Their small-arm fire, however, was most effective, and the final outcome of the engagement was strongly influenced, if not wholly determined, by their presence.

At first the two forces circled at the same altitude, pouring broadside after broadside into each other. Presently a great hole was torn in the hull of one of the immense battle craft from the Zodangan camp; with a lurch she turned completely over, the little figures of her crew plunging, turning and twisting toward the ground a thousand feet below; then with sickening velocity she tore after them, almost completely burying herself in the soft loam of the ancient sea bottom.

A wild cry of exultation arose from the Heliumite squadron, and with redoubled ferocity they fell upon the Zodangan fleet. By a pretty maneuver two of the vessels of Helium gained a position above their adversaries, from which they poured upon them from their keel bomb batteries a perfect torrent of exploding bombs.

Then, one by one, the battleships of Helium succeeded in rising above the Zodangans, and in a short time a number of the beleaguering battleships were drifting hopeless wrecks toward the high scarlet tower of greater Helium. Several others attempted to escape, but they were soon surrounded by thousands of tiny individual fliers, and above each hung a monster battleship of Helium ready to drop boarding parties upon their decks.

Within but little more than an hour from the moment the victorious Zodangan squadron had risen to meet us from the camp of the besiegers the battle was over, and the remaining vessels of the conquered Zodangans were headed toward the cities of Helium under prize crews.

There was an extremely pathetic side to the surrender of these mighty fliers, the result of an age-old custom which demanded that surrender should be signalized by the voluntary plunging to earth of the commander of the vanquished vessel. One after another the brave fellows, holding their colors high above their heads, leaped from the towering bows of their mighty craft to an awful death.

Not until the commander of the entire fleet took the fearful plunge, thus indicating the surrender of the remaining vessels, did the fighting cease, and the useless sacrifice of brave men come to an end.

We now signaled the flagship of Helium's navy to approach, and when she was within hailing distance I called out that we had the Princess Dejah Thoris on board, and that we wished to transfer her to the flagship that she might be taken immediately to the city.

As the full import of my announcement bore in upon them a great cry arose from the decks of the flagship, and a moment later the colors of the Princess of Helium broke from a hundred points upon her upper works. When the other vessels of the squadron caught the meaning of the signals flashed them they took up the wild acclaim and unfurled her colors in the gleaming sunlight.

The flagship bore down upon us, and as she swung gracefully to and touched our side a dozen officers sprang upon our decks. As their astonished gaze fell upon the hundreds of green warriors, who now came forth from the fighting shelters, they stopped aghast, but at sight of Kantos Kan, who advanced to meet them, they came forward, crowding about him.

Dejah Thoris and I then advanced, and they had no eyes for other than her. She received them gracefully, calling each by name, for they were men high in the esteem and service of her grandfather, and she knew them well.

"Lay your hands upon the shoulder of John Carter," she said to them, turning toward me, "the man to whom Helium owes her princess as well as her victory today."

They were very courteous to me and said many kind and complimentary things, but what seemed to impress them most was that I had won the aid of the fierce Tharks in my campaign for the liberation of Dejah Thoris, and the relief of Helium.

"You owe your thanks more to another man than to me," I said, "and here he is; meet one of Barsoom's greatest soldiers and statesmen, Tars Tarkas, Jeddak of Thark."

With the same polished courtesy that had marked their manner toward me they extended their greetings to the great Thark, nor, to my surprise, was he much behind them in ease of bearing or in courtly speech. Though not a garrulous race, the Tharks are extremely formal, and their ways lend themselves amazingly to dignified and courtly manners.

Dejah Thoris went aboard the flagship, and was much put out that I would not follow, but, as I explained to her, the battle was but partly won; we still had the land forces of the besieging Zodangans to account for, and I would not leave Tars Tarkas until that had been accomplished.

The commander of the naval forces of Helium promised to arrange to have the armies of Helium attack from the city in conjunction with our land attack, and so the vessels separated and Dejah Thoris was borne in triumph back to the court of her grandfather, Tardos Mors, Jeddak of Helium.

In the distance lay our fleet of transports, with the thoats of the green warriors, where they had remained during the battle. Without landing stages it was to be a difficult matter to unload these beasts upon the open plain, but there was nothing else for it, and so we put out for a point about ten miles from the city and began the task.

It was necessary to lower the animals to the ground in slings and this work occupied the remainder of the day and half the night. Twice we were attacked by parties of Zodangan cavalry, but with little loss, however, and after darkness shut down they withdrew.

As soon as the last thoat was unloaded Tars Tarkas gave the command to advance, and in three parties we crept upon the Zodangan camp from the north, the south and the east.

About a mile from the main camp we encountered their outposts and, as had been prearranged, accepted this as the signal to charge. With wild, ferocious cries and amidst the nasty squealing of battle-enraged thoats we bore down upon the Zodangans.

We did not catch them napping, but found a well-entrenched battle line confronting us. Time after time we were repulsed until, toward noon, I began to fear for the result of the battle.

The Zodangans numbered nearly a million fighting men, gathered from pole to pole, wherever stretched their ribbon-like waterways, while pitted against them were less than a hundred thousand green warriors. The forces from Helium had not arrived, nor could we receive any word from them.

Just at noon we heard heavy firing all along the line between the Zodangans and the cities, and we knew then that our much-needed reinforcements had come.

Again Tars Tarkas ordered the charge, and once more the mighty thoats bore their terrible riders against the ramparts of the enemy. At the same moment the battle line of Helium surged over the opposite breastworks of the Zodangans and in another moment they were being crushed as between two millstones. Nobly they fought, but in vain.

The plain before the city became a veritable shambles ere the last Zodangan surrendered, but finally the carnage ceased, the prisoners were marched back to Helium, and we entered the greater city's gates, a huge triumphal procession of conquering heroes.

The broad avenues were lined with women and children, among which were the few men whose duties necessitated that they remain within the city during the battle. We were greeted with an endless round of applause and showered with ornaments of gold, platinum, silver, and precious jewels. The city had gone mad with joy.

My fierce Tharks caused the wildest excitement and enthusiasm. Never before had an armed body of green warriors entered the gates of Helium, and that they came now as friends and allies filled the red men with rejoicing.

That my poor services to Dejah Thoris had become known to the Heliumites was evidenced by the loud crying of my name, and by the loads of ornaments that were fastened upon me and my huge thoat as we passed up the avenues to the palace, for even in the face of the ferocious appearance of Woola the populace pressed close about me.

As we approached this magnificent pile we were met by a party of officers who greeted us warmly and requested that Tars Tarkas and his jeds with the jeddaks and jeds of his wild allies, together with myself, dismount and accompany them to receive from Tardos Mors an expression of his gratitude for our services.

At the top of the great steps leading up to the main portals of the palace stood the royal party, and as we reached the lower steps one of their number descended to meet us.

He was an almost perfect specimen of manhood; tall, straight as an arrow, superbly muscled and with the carriage and bearing of a ruler of men. I did not need to be told that he was Tardos Mors, Jeddak of Helium.

The first member of our party he met was Tars Tarkas and his first words sealed forever the new friendship between the races.

"That Tardos Mors," he said, earnestly, "may meet the greatest living warrior of Barsoom is a priceless honor, but that he may lay his hand on the shoulder of a friend and ally is a far greater boon."

"Jeddak of Helium," returned Tars Tarkas, "it has remained for a man of another world to teach the green warriors of Barsoom the meaning of friendship; to him we owe the fact that the hordes of Thark can understand you; that they can appreciate and reciprocate the sentiments so graciously expressed."

Tardos Mors then greeted each of the green jeddaks and jeds, and to each spoke words of friendship and appreciation.

As he approached me he laid both hands upon my shoulders.

"Welcome, my son," he said; "that you are granted, gladly, and without one word of opposition, the most precious jewel in all Helium, yes, on all Barsoom, is sufficient earnest of my esteem."

We were then presented to Mors Kajak, Jed of lesser Helium, and father of Dejah Thoris. He had followed close behind Tardos Mors and seemed even more affected by the meeting than had his father.

He tried a dozen times to express his gratitude to me, but his voice choked with emotion and he could not speak, and yet he had, as I was to later learn, a reputation for ferocity and fearlessness as a fighter that was remarkable even upon warlike Barsoom. In common with all Helium he worshiped his daughter, nor could he think of what she had escaped without deep emotion.

XXVII

FROM JOY TO DEATH

For ten days the hordes of Thark and their wild allies were feasted and entertained, and, then, loaded with costly presents and escorted by ten thousand soldiers of Helium commanded by Mors Kajak, they started on the return journey to their own lands. The jed of lesser Helium with a small party of nobles accompanied them all the way to Thark to cement more closely the new bonds of peace and friendship.

Sola also accompanied Tars Tarkas, her father, who before all his chieftains had acknowledged her as his daughter.

Three weeks later, Mors Kajak and his officers, accompanied by Tars Tarkas and Sola, returned upon a battleship that had been dispatched to Thark to fetch them in time for the ceremony which made Dejah Thoris and John Carter one.

For nine years I served in the councils and fought in the armies of Helium as a prince of the house of Tardos Mors. The people seemed never to tire of heaping honors upon me, and no day passed that did not bring some new proof of their love for my princess, the incomparable Dejah Thoris.

In a golden incubator upon the roof of our palace lay a snow-white egg. For nearly five years ten soldiers of the jeddak's Guard had constantly stood over it, and not a day passed when I was in the city that Dejah Thoris and I did not stand hand in hand before our little shrine planning for the future, when the delicate shell should break.

Vivid in my memory is the picture of the last night as we sat there talking in low tones of the strange romance which had woven our lives together and of this wonder which was coming to augment our happiness and fulfill our hopes.

In the distance we saw the bright-white light of an approaching airship, but we attached no special significance to so common a sight. Like a bolt of lightning it raced toward Helium until its very speed bespoke the unusual.

Flashing the signals which proclaimed it a dispatch bearer for the jeddak, it circled impatiently awaiting the tardy patrol boat which must convoy it to the palace docks.

Ten minutes after it touched at the palace a message called me to the council chamber, which I found filling with the members of that body.

On the raised platform of the throne was Tardos Mors, pacing back and forth with tense-drawn face. When all were in their seats he turned toward us.

"This morning," he said, "word reached the several governments of Barsoom that the keeper of the atmosphere plant had made no wireless report for two days, nor had almost ceaseless calls upon him from a score of capitals elicited a sign of response.

"The ambassadors of the other nations asked us to take the matter in hand and hasten the assistant keeper to the plant. All day a thousand cruisers have been searching for him until just now one of them returns bearing his dead body, which was found in the pits beneath his house horribly mutilated by some assassin.

"I do not need to tell you what this means to Barsoom. It would take months to penetrate those mighty walls, in fact the work has already commenced, and there would be little to fear were the engine of the pumping plant to run as it should and as they all have for hundreds of years; but the worst, we fear, has happened. The instruments show a rapidly decreasing air pressure on all parts of Barsoom—the engine has stopped."

"My gentlemen," he concluded, "we have at best three days to live."

There was absolute silence for several minutes, and then a young noble arose, and with his drawn sword held high above his head addressed Tardos Mors.

"The men of Helium have prided themselves that they have ever shown Barsoom how a nation of red men should live, now is our opportunity to show them how they should die. Let us go about our duties as though a thousand useful years still lay before us."

The chamber rang with applause and as there was nothing better to do than to allay the fears of the people by our example we went our ways with smiles upon our faces and sorrow gnawing at our hearts.

When I returned to my palace I found that the rumor already had reached Dejah Thoris, so I told her all that I had heard.

"We have been very happy, John Carter," she said, "and I thank whatever fate overtakes us that it permits us to die together."

The next two days brought no noticeable change in the supply of air, but on the morning of the third day breathing became difficult at the higher altitudes of the rooftops. The avenues and plazas of Helium were filled with people. All business had ceased. For the most part the people looked bravely into the face of their unalterable doom. Here and there, however, men and women gave way to quiet grief.

Toward the middle of the day many of the weaker commenced to succumb and within an hour the people of Barsoom were sinking by thousands into the unconsciousness which precedes death by asphyxiation.

Dejah Thoris and I with the other members of the royal family had collected in a sunken garden within an inner courtyard of the palace. We conversed in low tones, when we conversed at all, as the awe of the grim shadow of death crept over us. Even Woola seemed to feel the weight of the impending calamity, for he pressed close to Dejah Thoris and to me, whining pitifully.

The little incubator had been brought from the roof of our palace at request of Dejah Thoris and she sat gazing longingly upon the unknown little life that now she would never know.

As it was becoming perceptibly difficult to breathe Tardos Mors arose, saying,

"Let us bid each other farewell. The days of the greatness of Barsoom are over. Tomorrow's sun will look down upon a dead world which through all eternity must go swinging through the heavens peopled not even by memories. It is the end."

He stooped and kissed the women of his family, and laid his strong hand upon the shoulders of the men.

As I turned sadly from him my eyes fell upon Dejah Thoris. Her head was drooping upon her breast, to all appearances she was lifeless. With a cry I sprang to her and raised her in my arms.

Her eyes opened and looked into mine.

"Kiss me, John Carter," she murmured. "I love you! I love you! It is cruel that we must be torn apart who were just starting upon a life of love and happiness."

As I pressed her dear lips to mine the old feeling of unconquerable power and authority rose in me. The fighting blood of Virginia sprang to life in my veins.

"It shall not be, my princess," I cried. "There is, there must be some way, and John Carter, who has fought his way through a strange world for love of you, will find it."

And with my words there crept above the threshold of my conscious mind a series of nine long forgotten sounds. Like a flash of lightning in the darkness their full purport dawned upon me—the key to the three great doors of the atmosphere plant!

Turning suddenly toward Tardos Mors as I still clasped my dying love to my breast I cried, "A flier, Jeddak! Quick! Order your swiftest flier to the palace top. I can save Barsoom yet."

He did not wait to question, but in an instant a guard was racing to the nearest dock and though the air was thin and almost gone at the rooftop they managed to launch the fastest one-man, air-scout machine that the skill of Barsoom had ever produced.

Kissing Dejah Thoris a dozen times and commanding Woola, who would have followed me, to remain and guard her, I bounded with my old agility and strength to the high ramparts of the palace, and in another moment I was headed toward the goal of the hopes of all Barsoom.

I had to fly low to get sufficient air to breathe, but I took a straight course across an old sea bottom and so had to rise only a few feet above the ground.

I traveled with awful velocity for my errand was a race against time with death. The face of Dejah Thoris hung always before me. As I turned for a last look as I left the palace garden I had seen her stagger and sink upon the ground beside the little incubator. That she had dropped into the last coma which would end in death, if the air supply remained unreplenished, I well knew, and so, throwing caution to the winds, I flung overboard everything but the engine and compass, even to my ornaments, and lying on my belly along the deck with one hand on the steering wheel and the other pushing the speed lever to its last notch I split the thin air of dying Mars with the speed of a meteor.

An hour before dark the great walls of the atmosphere plant loomed suddenly before me, and with a sickening thud I plunged to the ground before the small door which was withholding the spark of life from the inhabitants of an entire planet.

Beside the door a great crew of men had been laboring to pierce the wall, but they had scarcely scratched the flint-like surface, and now most of them lay in the last sleep from which not even air would awaken them.

Conditions seemed much worse here than at Helium, and it was with difficulty that I breathed at all. There were a few men still conscious, and to one of these I spoke.

"If I can open these doors is there a man who can start the engines?" I asked.

"I can," he replied, "if you open quickly. I can last but a few moments more. But it is useless, they are both dead and no one else upon Barsoom knew the secret of these awful locks. For three days men crazed with fear have surged about this portal in vain attempts to solve its mystery."

I had no time to talk, I was becoming very weak and it was with difficulty that I controlled my mind at all.

But, with a final effort, as I sank weakly to my knees I hurled the nine thought waves at that awful thing before me. The Martian had crawled to my side and with staring eyes fixed on the single panel before us we waited in the silence of death.

Slowly the mighty door receded before us. I attempted to rise and follow it but I was too weak.

"After it," I cried to my companion, "and if you reach the pump room turn loose all the pumps. It is the only chance Barsoom has to exist tomorrow!"

From where I lay I opened the second door, and then the third, and as I saw the hope of Barsoom crawling weakly on hands and knees through the last doorway I sank unconscious upon the ground.

XXVIII

AT THE ARIZONA CAVE

It was dark when I opened my eyes again. Strange, stiff garments were upon my body; garments that cracked and powdered away from me as I rose to a sitting posture.

I felt myself over from head to foot and from head to foot I was clothed, though when I fell unconscious at the little doorway I had been naked. Before me was a small patch of moonlit sky which showed through a ragged aperture.

As my hands passed over my body they came in contact with pockets and in one of these a small parcel of matches wrapped in oiled paper. One of these matches I struck, and its dim flame lighted up what appeared to be a huge cave, toward the back of which I discovered a strange, still figure huddled over a tiny bench. As I approached it I saw that it was the dead and mummified remains of a little old woman with long black hair, and the thing it leaned over was a small charcoal burner upon which rested a round copper vessel containing a small quantity of greenish powder.

Behind her, depending from the roof upon rawhide thongs, and stretching entirely across the cave, was a row of human skeletons. From the thong which held them stretched another to the dead hand of the little old woman; as I touched the cord the skeletons swung to the motion with a noise as of the rustling of dry leaves.

It was a most grotesque and horrid tableau and I hastened out into the fresh air; glad to escape from so gruesome a place.

The sight that met my eyes as I stepped out upon a small ledge which ran before the entrance of the cave filled me with consternation.

A new heaven and a new landscape met my gaze. The silvered mountains in the distance, the almost stationary moon hanging in the sky, the cacti-studded valley below me were not of Mars. I could scarce believe my eyes, but the truth slowly forced itself upon me—I was looking upon Arizona from the same ledge from which ten years before I had gazed with longing upon Mars.

Burying my head in my arms I turned, broken, and sorrowful, down the trail from the cave.

Above me shone the red eye of Mars holding her awful secret, forty-eight million miles away.

Did the Martian reach the pump room? Did the vitalizing air reach the people of that distant planet in time to save them? Was my Dejah Thoris alive, or did her beautiful body lie cold in death beside the tiny golden incubator in the sunken garden of the inner courtyard of the palace of Tardos Mors, the jeddak of Helium?

For ten years I have waited and prayed for an answer to my questions. For ten years I have waited and prayed to be taken back to the world of my lost love. I would rather lie dead beside her there than live on Earth all those millions of terrible miles from her.

The old mine, which I found untouched, has made me fabulously wealthy; but what care I for wealth!

As I sit here tonight in my little study overlooking the Hudson, just twenty years have elapsed since I first opened my eyes upon Mars.

I can see her shining in the sky through the little window by my desk, and tonight she seems calling to me again as she has not called before since that long dead night, and I think I can see, across that awful abyss of space, a beautiful black-haired woman standing in the garden of a palace, and at her side is a little boy who puts his arm around her as she points into the sky toward the planet Earth, while at their feet is a huge and hideous creature with a heart of gold.

I believe that they are waiting there for me, and something tells me that I shall soon know.

THE LOST WORLD

Arthur Conan Doyle

I have wrought my simple plan
If I give one hour of joy
To the boy who's half a man,
Or the man who's half a boy.

FOREWORD

Mr. E. D. Malone desires to state that both the injunction for restraint and the libel action have been withdrawn unreservedly by Professor G. E. Challenger, who, being satisfied that no criticism or comment in this book is meant in an offensive spirit, has guaranteed that he will place no impediment to its publication and circulation.

I

"THERE ARE HEROISMS ALL ROUND US"

Mr. Hungerton, her father, really was the most tactless person upon earth—a fluffy, feathery, untidy cockatoo of a man, perfectly good-natured, but absolutely centered upon his own silly self. If anything could have driven me from Gladys, it would have been the thought of such a father-in-law. I am convinced that he really believed in his heart that I came round to the Chestnuts three days a week for the pleasure of his company, and very especially to hear his views upon bimetallism, a subject upon which he was by way of being an authority.

For an hour or more that evening I listened to his monotonous chirrup about bad money driving out good, the token value of silver, the depreciation of the rupee, and the true standards of exchange.

"Suppose," he cried with feeble violence, "that all the debts in the world were called up simultaneously, and immediate payment insisted upon—what under our present conditions would happen then?"

I gave the self-evident answer that I should be a ruined man, upon which he jumped from his chair, reproved me for my habitual levity, which made it impossible for him to discuss any reasonable subject in my presence, and bounced off out of the room to dress for a Masonic meeting.

At last I was alone with Gladys, and the moment of Fate had come! All that evening I had felt like the soldier who awaits the signal which will send him on a forlorn hope; hope of victory and fear of repulse alternating in his mind.

She sat with that proud, delicate profile of hers outlined against the red curtain. How beautiful she was! And yet how aloof! We had been friends, quite good friends; but never could I get beyond the same comradeship which I might have established with one of my fellow-reporters upon the *Gazette*—perfectly frank, perfectly kindly, and perfectly unsexual. My instincts are all against a woman being too frank and at her ease with me. It is no compliment to a man. Where the real sex feeling begins, timidity and distrust are its companions, heritage from old wicked days when love and violence went often hand in hand. The bent head, the averted eye, the faltering voice, the wincing figure—these, and not the unshrinking gaze and frank reply, are the true signals of passion. Even in my short life I had learned as much as that—or had inherited it in that race memory which we call instinct.

Gladys was full of every womanly quality. Some judged her to be cold and hard; but such a thought was treason. That delicately bronzed skin, almost oriental in its coloring, that raven hair, the large liquid eyes, the full but exquisite lips—all the stigmata of passion were there. But I was sadly conscious that up to now I had never found the secret of drawing it forth. However, come what might, I should have done with suspense and bring matters to a head tonight. She could but refuse me, and better be a repulsed lover than an accepted brother.

So far my thoughts had carried me, and I was about to break the long and uneasy silence, when two critical, dark eyes looked round at me, and the proud head was shaken in smiling reproof. "I have a presentiment that you are going to propose, Ned. I do wish you wouldn't; for things are so much nicer as they are."

I drew my chair a little nearer. "Now, how did you know that I was going to propose?" I asked in genuine wonder.

"Don't women always know? Do you suppose any woman in the world was ever taken unawares? But—oh, Ned, our friendship has been so good and so pleasant! What a pity to spoil it! Don't you feel how splendid it is that a young man and a young woman should be able to talk face to face as we have talked?"

"I don't know, Gladys. You see, I can talk face to face with—with the station-master." I can't imagine how that official came into the matter; but in he trotted, and set us both laughing. "That does not satisfy me in the least. I want my arms round you, and your head on my breast, and—oh, Gladys, I want—"

She had sprung from her chair, as she saw signs that I proposed to demonstrate some of my wants. "You've spoiled everything, Ned," she said. "It's all so beautiful and natural until this kind of thing comes in! It is such a pity! Why can't you control yourself?"

"I didn't invent it," I pleaded. "It's nature. It's love."

"Well, perhaps if both love, it may be different. I have never felt it."

"But you must—you, with your beauty, with your soul! Oh, Gladys, you were made for love! You must love!"

"One must wait till it comes."

"But why can't you love me, Gladys? Is it my appearance, or what?"

She did unbend a little. She put forward a hand—such a gracious, stooping attitude it was—and she pressed back my head. Then she looked into my upturned face with a very wistful smile.

"No it isn't that," she said at last. "You're not a conceited boy by nature, and so I can safely tell you it is not that. It's deeper."

"My character?"

She nodded severely.

"What can I do to mend it? Do sit down and talk it over. No, really, I won't if you'll only sit down!"

She looked at me with a wondering distrust which was much more to my mind than her whole-hearted confidence. How primitive and bestial it looks when you put it down in black and white! And perhaps after all it is only a feeling peculiar to myself. Anyhow, she sat down.

"Now tell me what's amiss with me?"

"I'm in love with somebody else," said she.

It was my turn to jump out of my chair.

"It's nobody in particular," she explained, laughing at the expression of my face: "only an ideal. I've never met the kind of man I mean."

"Tell me about him. What does he look like?"

"Oh, he might look very much like you."

"How dear of you to say that! Well, what is it that he does that I don't do? Just say the word—teetotal, vegetarian, aeronaut, theosophist, superman. I'll have a try at it, Gladys, if you will only give me an idea what would please you."

She laughed at the elasticity of my character. "Well, in the first place, I don't think my ideal would speak like that," said she. "He would be a harder, sterner man, not so ready to adapt himself to a silly girl's whim. But, above all, he must be a man who could do, who could act, who could look Death in the face and have no fear of him, a man of great deeds and strange experiences.

It is never a man that I should love, but always the glories he had won; for they would be reflected upon me. Think of Richard Burton! When I read his wife's life of him I could so understand her love! And Lady Stanley! Did you ever read the wonderful last chapter of that book about her husband? These are the sort of men that a woman could worship with all her soul, and yet be the greater, not the less, on account of her love, honored by all the world as the inspirer of noble deeds."

She looked so beautiful in her enthusiasm that I nearly brought down the whole level of the interview. I gripped myself hard, and went on with the argument.

"We can't all be Stanleys and Burtons," said I; "besides, we don't get the chance—at least, I never had the chance. If I did, I should try to take it."

"But chances are all around you. It is the mark of the kind of man I mean that he makes his own chances. You can't hold him back. I've never met him, and yet I seem to know him so well. There are heroisms all round us waiting to be done. It's for men to do them, and for women to reserve their love as a reward for such men. Look at that young Frenchman who went up last week in a balloon. It was blowing a gale of wind; but because he was announced to go he insisted on starting. The wind blew him fifteen hundred miles in twenty-four hours, and he fell in the middle of Russia. That was the kind of man I mean. Think of the woman he loved, and how other women must have envied her! That's what I should like to be—envied for my man."

"I'd have done it to please you."

"But you shouldn't do it merely to please me. You should do it because you can't help yourself, because it's natural to you, because the man in you is crying out for heroic expression. Now, when you described the Wigan coal explosion last month, could you not have gone down and helped those people, in spite of the choke-damp?"

"I did."

"You never said so."

"There was nothing worth bucking about."

"I didn't know." She looked at me with rather more interest. "That was brave of you."

"I had to. If you want to write good copy, you must be where the things are."

"What a prosaic motive! It seems to take all the romance out of it. But, still, whatever your motive, I am glad that you went down that mine." She gave me her hand; but with such sweetness and dignity that I could only stoop and kiss it. "I dare say I am merely a foolish woman with a young girl's fancies. And yet it is so real with me, so entirely part of my very self, that I cannot help acting upon it. If I marry, I do want to marry a famous man!"

"Why should you not?" I cried. "It is women like you who brace men up.

Give me a chance, and see if I will take it! Besides, as you say, men ought to make their own chances, and not wait until they are given. Look at Clive—just a clerk, and he conquered India! By George! I'll do something in the world yet!"

She laughed at my sudden Irish effervescence. "Why not?" she said. "You have everything a man could have—youth, health, strength, education, energy. I was sorry you spoke. And now I am glad—so glad—if it wakens these thoughts in you!"

"And if I do—"

Her dear hand rested like warm velvet upon my lips. "Not another word, Sir! You should have been at the office for evening duty half an hour ago; only I hadn't the heart to remind you. Some day, perhaps, when you have won your place in the world, we shall talk it over again."

And so it was that I found myself that foggy November evening pursuing the Camberwell tram with my heart glowing within me, and with the eager determination that not another day should elapse before I should find some deed which was worthy of my lady. But who—who in all this wide world could ever have imagined the incredible shape which that deed was to take, or the strange steps by which I was led to the doing of it?

And, after all, this opening chapter will seem to the reader to have nothing to do with my narrative; and yet there would have been no narrative without it, for it is only when a man goes out into the world with the thought that there are heroisms all round him, and with the desire all alive in his heart to follow any which may come within sight of him, that he breaks away as I did from the life he knows, and ventures forth into the wonderful mystic twilight land where lie the great adventures and the great rewards. Behold me, then, at the office of the *Daily Gazette*, on the staff of which I was a most insignificant unit, with the settled determination that very night, if possible, to find the quest which should be worthy of my Gladys! Was it hardness, was it selfishness, that she should ask me to risk my life for her own glorification? Such thoughts may come to middle age; but never to ardent three-and-twenty in the fever of his first love.

II

"TRY YOUR LUCK WITH PROFESSOR CHALLENGER"

I always liked McArdle, the crabbed, old, round-backed, red-headed news editor, and I rather hoped that he liked me. Of course, Beaumont was the real boss; but he lived in the rarefied atmosphere of some Olympian height from which he could distinguish nothing smaller than an international crisis or a split in the Cabinet. Sometimes we saw him passing in lonely majesty to his inner sanctum, with his eyes staring vaguely and his mind hovering over the Balkans or the Persian Gulf. He was above and beyond us. But McArdle was his first lieutenant, and it was he that we knew. The old man nodded as I entered the room, and he pushed his spectacles far up on his bald forehead.

"Well, Mr. Malone, from all I hear, you seem to be doing very well," said he in his kindly Scotch accent.

I thanked him.

"The colliery explosion was excellent. So was the Southwark fire. You have the true descreeptive touch. What did you want to see me about?"

"To ask a favor."

He looked alarmed, and his eyes shunned mine. "Tut, tut! What is it?"

"Do you think, Sir, that you could possibly send me on some mission for the paper? I would do my best to put it through and get you some good copy."

"What sort of meesion had you in your mind, Mr. Malone?"

"Well, Sir, anything that had adventure and danger in it. I really would do my very best. The more difficult it was, the better it would suit me."

"You seem very anxious to lose your life."

"To justify my life, Sir."

"Dear me, Mr. Malone, this is very—very exalted. I'm afraid the day for this sort of thing is rather past. The expense of the 'special meesion' business hardly justifies the result, and, of course, in any case it would only be an experienced man with a name that would command public confidence who would get such an order. The big blank spaces in the map are all being filled in, and there's no room for romance anywhere. Wait a bit, though!" he added, with a sudden smile upon his face. "Talking of the blank spaces of the map gives me an idea. What about exposing a fraud—a modern Munchausen—and making him rideeculous? You could show him up as the liar that he is! Eh, man, it would be fine. How does it appeal to you?"

"Anything—anywhere—I care nothing."

McArdle was plunged in thought for some minutes.

"I wonder whether you could get on friendly—or at least on talking terms with the fellow," he said, at last. "You seem to have a sort of genius for establishing relations with people—seempathy, I suppose, or animal magnetism, or youthful vitality, or something. I am conscious of it myself."

"You are very good, sir."

"So why should you not try your luck with Professor Challenger, of Enmore Park?"

I dare say I looked a little startled.

"Challenger!" I cried. "Professor Challenger, the famous zoologist! Wasn't he the man who broke the skull of Blundell, of the *Telegraph*?"

The news editor smiled grimly.

"Do you mind? Didn't you say it was adventures you were after?"

"It is all in the way of business, sir," I answered.

"Exactly. I don't suppose he can always be so violent as that. I'm thinking that Blundell got him at the wrong moment, maybe, or in the wrong fashion. You may have better luck, or more tact in handling him. There's something in your line there, I am sure, and the *Gazette* should work it."

"I really know nothing about him," said I. "I only remember his name in connection with the police-court proceedings, for striking Blundell."

"I have a few notes for your guidance, Mr. Malone. I've had my eye on the Professor for some little time." He took a paper from a drawer. "Here is a summary of his record. I give it you briefly:

" 'Challenger, George Edward. *Born:* Largs, N. B., 1863. *Educ.:* Largs Academy; Edinburgh University. British Museum Assistant, 1892. Assistant-Keeper of Comparative Anthropology Department, 1893. Resigned after acrimonious correspondence same year. Winner of Crayston Medal for Zoological Research. Foreign Member of'—well, quite a lot of things, about two inches of small type—'Société Belge, American Academy of Sciences, La Plata, etc., etc. Ex-President Palaeontological Society. Section H, British Association'—so on, so on!—'*Publications:* "Some Observations Upon a Series of Kalmuck Skulls"; "Outlines of Vertebrate Evolution"; and numerous papers, including "The underlying fallacy of Weissmannism," which caused heated discussion at the Zoological Congress of Vienna. *Recreations:* Walking, Alpine climbing. *Address:* Enmore Park, Kensington, W.'

"There, take it with you. I've nothing more for you tonight."

I pocketed the slip of paper.

"One moment, sir," I said, as I realized that it was a pink bald head, and not a red face, which was fronting me. "I am not very clear yet why I am to interview this gentleman. What has he done?"

The face flashed back again.

"Went to South America on a solitary expedeetion two years ago. Came back last year. Had undoubtedly been to South America, but refused to say exactly where. Began to tell his adventures in a vague way, but somebody started to pick holes, and he just shut up like an oyster. Something wonderful happened—or the man's a champion liar, which is the more probable supposeetion. Had some damaged photographs, said to be fakes. Got so touchy that he assaults anyone who asks questions, and heaves reporters down the stairs. In my opinion he's just a homicidal megalomaniac with a turn for science. That's your man, Mr. Malone. Now, off you run, and see what you can make of him. You're big enough to look after yourself. Anyway, you are all safe. Employers' Liability Act, you know."

A grinning red face turned once more into a pink oval, fringed with gingery fluff; the interview was at an end.

I walked across to the Savage Club, but instead of turning into it I leaned upon the railings of Adelphi Terrace and gazed thoughtfully for a long time at the brown, oily river. I can always think most sanely and clearly in the open air. I took out the list of Professor Challenger's exploits, and I read it over under the electric lamp. Then I had what I can only regard as an inspiration. As a Pressman, I felt sure from what I had been told that I could never hope to get into touch with this cantankerous Professor. But these recriminations, twice mentioned in his skeleton biography, could only mean that he was a fanatic in science. Was there not an exposed margin there upon which he might be accessible? I would try.

I entered the club. It was just after eleven, and the big room was fairly full, though the rush had not yet set in. I noticed a tall, thin, angular man seated in an armchair by the fire. He turned as I drew my chair up to him. It was the man of all others whom I should have chosen—Tarp Henry, of the staff of *Nature*, a thin, dry, leathery creature, who was full, to those who knew him, of kindly humanity. I plunged instantly into my subject.

"What do you know of Professor Challenger?"

"Challenger?" He gathered his brows in scientific disapproval. "Challenger was the man who came with some cock-and-bull story from South America."

"What story?"

"Oh, it was rank nonsense about some queer animals he had discovered. I believe he has retracted since. Anyhow, he has suppressed it all. He gave an interview to Reuter's, and there was such a howl that he saw it wouldn't do. It was a discreditable business. There were one or two folk who were inclined to take him seriously, but he soon choked them off."

"How?"

"Well, by his insufferable rudeness and impossible behavior. There was poor old Wadley, of the Zoological Institute. Wadley sent a message: 'The President of the Zoological Institute presents his compliments to Professor Challenger, and would take it as a personal favor if he would do them the honor to come to their next meeting.' The answer was unprintable."

"You don't say?"

"Well, a bowdlerized version of it would run: 'Professor Challenger presents his compliments to the President of the Zoological Institute, and would take it as a personal favor if he would go to the devil.' "

"Good Lord!"

"Yes, I expect that's what old Wadley said. I remember his wail at the meeting, which began: 'In fifty years experience of scientific intercourse—' It quite broke the old man up."

"Anything more about Challenger?"

"Well, I'm a bacteriologist, you know. I live in a nine-hundred-diameter microscope. I can hardly claim to take serious notice of anything that I can see with my naked eye. I'm a frontiersman from the extreme edge of the Knowable, and I feel quite out of place when I leave my study and come into touch with all you great, rough, hulking creatures. I'm too detached to talk scandal, and yet at scientific conversaziones I have heard something of Challenger, for he is one of those men whom nobody can ignore. He's as clever as they make 'em—a full-charged battery of force and vitality, but a quarrelsome, ill-conditioned faddist, and unscrupulous at that. He had gone the length of faking some photographs over the South American business."

"You say he is a faddist. What is his particular fad?"

"He has a thousand, but the latest is something about Weissmann and Evolution. He had a fearful row about it in Vienna, I believe."

"Can't you tell me the point?"

"Not at the moment, but a translation of the proceedings exists. We have it filed at the office. Would you care to come?"

"It's just what I want. I have to interview the fellow, and I need some lead up to him. It's really awfully good of you to give me a lift. I'll go with you now, if it is not too late."

Half an hour later I was seated in the newspaper office with a huge tome in front of me, which had been opened at the article "Weissmann *versus* Darwin," with the sub heading, "Spirited Protest at Vienna. Lively Proceedings." My scientific education having been somewhat neglected, I was unable to follow the whole argument, but it was evident that the English Professor had handled his subject in a very aggressive fashion, and had thoroughly annoyed his Continental colleagues. "Protests," "Uproar," and "General appeal to the Chairman" were three of the first brackets which caught my eye. Most of the matter might have been written in Chinese for any definite meaning that it conveyed to my brain.

"I wish you could translate it into English for me," I said, pathetically, to my help-mate.

"Well, it is a translation."

"Then I'd better try my luck with the original."

"It is certainly rather deep for a layman."

"If I could only get a single good, meaty sentence which seemed to convey some sort of definite human idea, it would serve my turn. Ah, yes, this one will do. I seem in a vague way almost to understand it. I'll copy it out. This shall be my link with the terrible Professor."

"Nothing else I can do?"

"Well, yes; I propose to write to him. If I could frame the letter here, and use your address it would give atmosphere."

"We'll have the fellow round here making a row and breaking the furniture."

"No, no; you'll see the letter—nothing contentious, I assure you."

"Well, that's my chair and desk. You'll find paper there. I'd like to censor it before it goes."

It took some doing, but I flatter myself that it wasn't such a bad job when it was finished. I read it aloud to the critical bacteriologist with some pride in my handiwork.

"DEAR PROFESSOR CHALLENGER," it said, "As a humble student of Nature, I have always taken the most profound interest in your speculations as to the differences between Darwin and Weissmann. I have recently had occasion to refresh my memory by re-reading—"

"You infernal liar!" murmured Tarp Henry.

"—by re-reading your masterly address at Vienna. That lucid and admirable statement seems to be the last word in the matter. There is one sentence in it, however—namely: 'I protest strongly against the insufferable and entirely dogmatic assertion that each separate *id* is a microcosm possessed of an historical architecture elaborated slowly through the series of generations.' Have you no desire, in view of later research, to modify this statement? Do you not think that it is over-accentuated? With your permission, I would ask the favor of an interview, as I feel strongly upon the subject, and have certain suggestions which I could only elaborate in a personal conversation. With your consent, I trust to have the honor of calling at eleven o'clock the day after tomorrow (Wednesday) morning.

"I remain, Sir, with assurances of profound respect, yours very truly, EDWARD D. MALONE."

"How's that?" I asked, triumphantly.

"Well if your conscience can stand it—"

"It has never failed me yet."

"But what do you mean to do?"

"To get there. Once I am in his room I may see some opening. I may even go the length of open confession. If he is a sportsman he will be tickled."

"Tickled, indeed! He's much more likely to do the tickling. Chain mail, or an American football suit—that's what you'll want. Well, good-bye. I'll have the answer for you here on Wednesday morning—if he ever deigns to answer you. He is a violent, dangerous, cantankerous character, hated by everyone who comes across him, and the butt of the students, so far as they dare take a liberty with him. Perhaps it would be best for you if you never heard from the fellow at all."

III

"HE IS A PERFECTLY IMPOSSIBLE PERSON"

My friend's fear or hope was not destined to be realized. When I called on Wednesday there was a letter with the West Kensington postmark upon it, and my name scrawled across the envelope in a handwriting which looked like a barbed-wire railing. The contents were as follows:

"Enmore Park, W.

"Sir—I have duly received your note, in which you claim to endorse my views, although I am not aware that they are dependent upon endorsement either from you or anyone else. You have ventured to use the word 'speculation' with regard to my statement upon the subject of Darwinism, and I would call your attention to the fact that such a word in such a connection is offensive to a degree. The context convinces me, however, that you have sinned rather through ignorance and tactlessness than through malice, so I am content to pass the matter by. You quote an isolated sentence from my lecture, and appear to have some difficulty in understanding it. I should have thought that only a sub-human intelligence could have failed to grasp the point, but if it really needs amplification I shall consent to see you at the hour named, though visits and visitors of every sort are exceeding distasteful to me. As to your suggestion that I may modify my opinion, I would have you know that it is not my habit to do so after a deliberate expression of my mature views. You will kindly show the envelope of this letter to my man, Austin, when you call, as he has to take every precaution to shield me from the intrusive rascals who call themselves 'journalists.'

"Yours faithfully,
George Edward Challenger."

This was the letter that I read aloud to Tarp Henry, who had come down early to hear the result of my venture. His only remark was, "There's some new stuff, cuticura or something, which is better than arnica." Some people have such extraordinary notions of humor.

It was nearly half-past ten before I had received my message, but a taxicab took me round in good time for my appointment. It was an imposing porticoed house at which we stopped, and the heavily-curtained windows gave every indication of wealth upon the part of this formidable Professor. The door was opened by an odd, swarthy, dried-up person of uncertain age, with a dark pilot jacket and brown leather gaiters. I found afterwards that he was the chauffeur, who filled the gaps left by a succession of fugitive butlers. He looked me up and down with a searching light blue eye.

"Expected?" he asked.

"An appointment."

"Got your letter?"

I produced the envelope.

"Right!" He seemed to be a person of few words. Following him down the passage I was suddenly interrupted by a small woman, who stepped out from what proved to be the dining room door. She was a bright, vivacious, dark-eyed lady, more French than English in her type.

"One moment," she said. "You can wait, Austin. Step in here, sir. May I ask if you have met my husband before?"

"No, madam, I have not had the honor."

"Then I apologize to you in advance. I must tell you that he is a perfectly impossible person—absolutely impossible. If you are forewarned you will be the more ready to make allowances."

"It is most considerate of you, madam."

"Get quickly out of the room if he seems inclined to be violent. Don't wait to argue with him. Several people have been injured through doing that. Afterwards there is a public scandal and it reflects upon me and all of us. I suppose it wasn't about South America you wanted to see him?"

I could not lie to a lady.

"Dear me! That is his most dangerous subject. You won't believe a word he says—I'm sure I don't wonder. But don't tell him so, for it makes him very violent. Pretend to believe him, and you may get through all right. Remember he believes it himself. Of that you may be assured. A more honest man never lived. Don't wait any longer or he may suspect. If you find him dangerous—really dangerous—ring the bell and hold him off until I come. Even at his worst I can usually control him."

With these encouraging words the lady handed me over to the taciturn Austin, who had waited like a bronze statue of discretion during our short interview, and I was conducted to the end of the passage. There was a tap at a door, a bull's bellow from within, and I was face to face with the Professor.

He sat in a rotating chair behind a broad table, which was covered with books, maps, and diagrams. As I entered, his seat spun round to face me. His appearance made me gasp. I was prepared for something strange, but not for so overpowering a personality as this. It was his size which took one's breath away—his size and his imposing presence. His head was enormous, the largest I have ever seen upon a human being. I am sure that his top-hat, had I ever ventured to don it, would have slipped over me entirely and rested on my shoulders. He had the face and beard which I associate with an Assyrian bull; the former florid, the latter so black as almost to have a suspicion of blue, spade-shaped and rippling down over his chest. The hair was peculiar, plastered down in front in a long, curving wisp over his massive forehead. The eyes were blue-gray under great black tufts, very clear, very critical, and very masterful. A huge spread of shoulders and a chest like a barrel were the other parts of him which appeared above the table, save for two enormous hands covered with long black hair. This and a bellowing, roaring, rumbling voice made up my first impression of the notorious Professor Challenger.

"Well?" said he, with a most insolent stare. "What now?"

I must keep up my deception for at least a little time longer, otherwise here was evidently an end of the interview.

"You were good enough to give me an appointment, sir," said I, humbly, producing his envelope.

He took my letter from his desk and laid it out before him.

"Oh, you are the young person who cannot understand plain English, are you? My general conclusions you are good enough to approve, as I understand?"

"Entirely, sir—entirely!" I was very emphatic.

"Dear me! That strengthens my position very much, does it not? Your age and appearance make your support doubly valuable. Well, at least you are better than that herd of swine in Vienna, whose gregarious grunt is, however, not more offensive than the isolated effort of the British hog." He glared at me as the present representative of the beast.

"They seem to have behaved abominably," said I.

"I assure you that I can fight my own battles, and that I have no possible need of your sympathy. Put me alone, sir, and with my back to the wall. G. E. C. is happiest then. Well, sir, let us do what we can to curtail this visit, which can hardly be agreeable to you, and is inexpressibly irksome to me. You had, as I have been led to believe, some comments to make upon the proposition which I advanced in my thesis."

There was a brutal directness about his methods which made evasion difficult. I must still make play and wait for a better opening. It had seemed simple enough at a distance. Oh, my Irish wits, could they not help me now, when I needed help so sorely? He transfixed me with two sharp, steely eyes. "Come, come!" he rumbled.

"I am, of course, a mere student," said I, with a fatuous smile, "hardly more, I might say, than an earnest inquirer. At the same time, it seemed to me that you were a little severe upon Weissmann in this matter. Has not the general evidence since that date tended to—well, to strengthen his position?"

"What evidence?" He spoke with a menacing calm.

"Well, of course, I am aware that there is not any what you might call definite evidence. I alluded merely to the trend of modern thought and the general scientific point of view, if I might so express it."

He leaned forward with great earnestness.

"I suppose you are aware," said he, checking off points upon his fingers, "that the cranial index is a constant factor?"

"Naturally," said I.

"And that telegony is still *sub judice?*"

"Undoubtedly."

"And that the germ plasm is different from the parthenogenetic egg?"

"Why, surely!" I cried, and gloried in my own audacity.

"But what does that prove?" he asked, in a gentle, persuasive voice.

"Ah, what indeed?" I murmured. "What does it prove?"

"Shall I tell you?" he cooed.

"Pray do."

"It proves," he roared, with a sudden blast of fury, "that you are the damnedest imposter in London—a vile, crawling journalist, who has no more science than he has decency in his composition!"

He had sprung to his feet with a mad rage in his eyes. Even at that moment of tension I found time for amazement at the discovery that he was quite a short man, his head not higher than my shoulder—a stunted Hercules whose tremendous vitality had all run to depth, breadth, and brain.

"Gibberish!" he cried, leaning forward, with his fingers on the table and his face projecting. "That's what I have been talking to you, sir—scientific gibberish! Did you think you could match cunning with me—you with your walnut of a brain? You think you are omnipotent, you infernal scribblers, don't you? That your praise can make a man and your blame can break him? We must all bow to you, and try to get a favorable word, must we? This man shall have a leg up, and this man shall have a dressing down! Creeping vermin, I know you! You've got out of your station. Time was when your ears were clipped. You've lost your sense of proportion. Swollen gas-bags! I'll keep you in your proper place. Yes, sir, you haven't got over G. E. C. There's one man who is still your master. He warned you off, but if you WILL come, by the Lord you do it at your own risk. Forfeit, my good Mr. Malone, I claim forfeit! You have played a rather dangerous game, and it strikes me that you have lost it."

"Look here, sir," said I, backing to the door and opening it; "you can be as abusive as you like. But there is a limit. You shall not assault me."

"Shall I not?" He was slowly advancing in a peculiarly menacing way, but he stopped now and put his big hands into the side-pockets of a rather boyish short jacket which he wore. "I have thrown several of you out of the house. You will be the fourth or fifth. Three pound fifteen each—that is how it averaged. Expensive, but very necessary. Now, sir, why should you not follow your brethren? I rather think you must." He resumed his unpleasant and stealthy advance, pointing his toes as he walked, like a dancing master.

I could have bolted for the hall door, but it would have been too ignominious. Besides, a little glow of righteous anger was springing up within me. I had been hopelessly in the wrong before, but this man's menaces were putting me in the right.

"I'll trouble you to keep your hands off, sir. I'll not stand it."

"Dear me!" His black moustache lifted and a white fang twinkled in a sneer. "You won't stand it, eh?"

"Don't be such a fool, Professor!" I cried. "What can you hope for? I'm fifteen stone, as hard as nails, and play center three-quarter every Saturday for the London Irish. I'm not the man—"

It was at that moment that he rushed me. It was lucky that I had opened the door, or we should have gone through it. We did a Catharine-wheel together down the passage. Somehow we gathered up a chair upon our way, and bounded on with it towards the street. My mouth was full of his beard, our arms were locked, our bodies intertwined, and that infernal chair radiated its legs all round us. The watchful Austin had thrown open the hall door. We went with a back somersault down the front steps. I have seen the two Macs attempt something of the kind at the halls, but it appears to take some practise to do it without hurting oneself. The chair went to matchwood at the bottom, and we rolled apart into the gutter. He sprang to his feet, waving his fists and wheezing like an asthmatic.

"Had enough?" he panted.

"You infernal bully!" I cried, as I gathered myself together.

Then and there we should have tried the thing out, for he was effervescing with fight, but fortunately I was rescued from an odious situation. A policeman was beside us, his notebook in his hand.

"What's all this? You ought to be ashamed" said the policeman. It was the most rational remark which I had heard in Enmore Park. "Well," he insisted, turning to me, "what is it, then?"

"This man attacked me," said I.

"Did you attack him?" asked the policeman.

The Professor breathed hard and said nothing.

"It's not the first time, either," said the policeman, severely, shaking his head. "You were in trouble last month for the same thing. You've blackened this young man's eye. Do you give him in charge, sir?"

I relented.

"No," said I, "I do not."

"What's that?" said the policeman.

"I was to blame myself. I intruded upon him. He gave me fair warning."

The policeman snapped up his notebook.

"Don't let us have any more such goings-on," said he. "Now, then! Move on, there, move on!" This to a butcher's boy, a maid, and one or two loafers who had collected. He clumped heavily down the street, driving this little flock before him. The Professor looked at me, and there was something humorous at the back of his eyes.

"Come in!" said he. "I've not done with you yet."

The speech had a sinister sound, but I followed him nonetheless into the house. The man-servant, Austin, like a wooden image, closed the door behind us.

IV

"IT'S JUST THE VERY BIGGEST THING IN THE WORLD"

Hardly was it shut when Mrs. Challenger darted out from the dining room. The small woman was in a furious temper. She barred her husband's way like an enraged chicken in front of a bulldog. It was evident that she had seen my exit, but had not observed my return.

"You brute, George!" she screamed. "You've hurt that nice young man."

He jerked backwards with his thumb.

"Here he is, safe and sound behind me."

She was confused, but not unduly so.

"I am so sorry, I didn't see you."

"I assure you, madam, that it is all right."

"He has marked your poor face! Oh, George, what a brute you are! Nothing but scandals from one end of the week to the other. Everyone hating and making fun of you. You've finished my patience. This ends it."

"Dirty linen," he rumbled.

"It's not a secret," she cried. "Do you suppose that the whole street—the whole of London, for that matter— Get away, Austin, we don't want you here. Do you suppose they don't all talk about you? Where is your dignity? You, a man who should have been Regius Professor at a great University with a thousand students all revering you. Where is your dignity, George?"

"How about yours, my dear?"

"You try me too much. A ruffian—a common brawling ruffian—that's what you have become."

"Be good, Jessie."

"A roaring, raging bully!"

"That's done it! Stool of penance!" said he.

To my amazement he stooped, picked her up, and placed her sitting upon a high pedestal of black marble in the angle of the hall. It was at least seven feet high, and so thin that she could hardly balance upon it. A more absurd object than she presented cocked up there with her face convulsed with anger, her feet dangling, and her body rigid for fear of an upset, I could not imagine.

"Let me down!" she wailed.

"Say 'please.' "

"You brute, George! Let me down this instant!"

"Come into the study, Mr. Malone."

"Really, sir—!" said I, looking at the lady.

"Here's Mr. Malone pleading for you, Jessie. Say 'please,' and down you come."

"Oh, you brute! Please! Please!"

He took her down as if she had been a canary.

"You must behave yourself, dear. Mr. Malone is a Pressman. He will have it all in his rag tomorrow, and sell an extra dozen among our neighbors. 'Strange story of high life'—you felt fairly high on that pedestal, did you not? Then a sub-title, 'Glimpse of a singular menage.' He's a foul feeder, is Mr. Malone, a carrion eater, like all of his kind—*porcus ex grege diaboli*—a swine from the devil's herd. That's it, Malone—what?"

"You are really intolerable!" said I, hotly.

He bellowed with laughter.

"We shall have a coalition presently," he boomed, looking from his wife to me and puffing out his enormous chest. Then, suddenly altering his tone, "Excuse this frivolous family badinage, Mr. Malone. I called you back for some more serious purpose than to mix you up with our little domestic pleasantries. Run away, little woman, and don't fret." He placed a huge hand upon each of her shoulders. "All that you say is perfectly true. I should be a better man if I did what you advise, but I shouldn't be quite George Edward Challenger. There are plenty of better men, my dear, but only one G. E. C. So make the best of him." He suddenly gave her a resounding kiss, which embarrassed me even more than his violence had done. "Now, Mr. Malone," he continued, with a great accession of dignity, "this way, if you please."

* * * * *

We re-entered the room which we had left so tumultuously ten minutes before. The Professor closed the door carefully behind us, motioned me into an arm-chair, and pushed a cigar-box under my nose.

"Real San Juan Colorado," he said. "Excitable people like you are the better for narcotics. Heavens! Don't bite it! Cut—and cut with reverence! Now lean back, and listen attentively to whatever I may care to say to you. If any remark should occur to you, you can reserve it for some more opportune time.

"First of all, as to your return to my house after your most justifiable expulsion"—he protruded his beard, and stared at me as one who challenges and invites contradiction—"after, as I say, your well-merited expulsion. The reason lay in your answer to that most officious policeman, in which I seemed to discern some glimmering of good feeling upon your part—more, at any rate, than I am accustomed to associate with your profession. In admitting that the fault of the incident lay with you, you gave some evidence of a certain mental detachment and breadth of view which attracted my favorable notice. The sub-species of the human race to which you unfortunately belong has always been below my mental horizon. Your words brought you suddenly above it. You swam up into my serious notice. For this reason I asked you to return with me, as I was minded to make your further acquaintance. You will kindly deposit your ash in the small Japanese tray on the bamboo table which stands at your left elbow."

All this he boomed forth like a professor addressing his class. He had swung round his revolving chair so as to face me, and he sat all puffed out like an enormous bull-frog, his head laid back and his eyes half-covered by supercilious lids. Now he suddenly turned himself sideways, and all I could see of him was tangled hair with a red, protruding ear. He was scratching about among the litter of papers upon his desk. He faced me presently with what looked like a very tattered sketchbook in his hand.

"I am going to talk to you about South America," said he. "No comments if you please. First of all, I wish you to understand that nothing I tell you now is to be repeated in any public way unless you have my express permission. That permission will, in all human probability, never be given. Is that clear?"

"It is very hard," said I. "Surely a judicious account—"

He replaced the notebook upon the table.

"That ends it," said he. "I wish you a very good morning."

"No, no!" I cried. "I submit to any conditions. So far as I can see, I have no choice."

"None in the world," said he.

"Well, then, I promise."

"Word of honor?"

"Word of honor."

He looked at me with doubt in his insolent eyes.

"After all, what do I know about your honor?" said he.

"Upon my word, sir," I cried, angrily, "you take very great liberties! I have never been so insulted in my life."

He seemed more interested than annoyed at my outbreak.

"Round-headed," he muttered. "Brachycephalic, gray-eyed, black-haired, with suggestion of the negroid. Celtic, I presume?"

"I am an Irishman, sir."

"Irish Irish?"

"Yes, sir."

"That, of course, explains it. Let me see; you have given me your promise that my confidence will be respected? That confidence, I may say, will be far from complete. But I am prepared to give you a few indications which will be of interest. In the first place, you are probably aware that two years ago I made a journey to South America—one which will be classical in the scientific history of the world? The object of my journey was to verify some conclusions of Wallace and of Bates, which could only be done by observing their reported facts under the same conditions in which they had themselves noted them. If my expedition had no other results it would still have been noteworthy, but a curious incident occurred to me while there which opened up an entirely fresh line of inquiry.

"You are aware—or probably, in this half-educated age, you are not aware—that the country round some parts of the Amazon is still only partially explored, and that a great number of tributaries, some of them entirely uncharted, run into the main river. It was my business to visit this little-known back-country and to examine its fauna, which furnished me with the materials for several chapters for that great and monumental work upon zoology which will be my life's justification. I was returning, my work accomplished, when I had occasion to spend a night at a small Indian village at a point where a certain tributary—the name and position of which I withhold—opens into the main river. The natives were Cucama Indians, an amiable but degraded race, with mental powers hardly superior to the average Londoner. I had effected some cures among them upon my way up the river, and had impressed them considerably with my personality, so that I was not surprised to find myself eagerly awaited upon my return. I gathered from their signs that someone had urgent need of my medical services, and I followed the chief to one of his huts. When I entered I found that the sufferer to whose aid I had been summoned had that instant expired. He was, to my surprise, no Indian, but a white man; indeed, I may say a very white man, for he was flaxen-haired and had some characteristics of an albino. He was clad in rags, was very emaciated, and bore every trace of prolonged hardship. So far as I could understand the account of the natives, he was a complete stranger to them, and had come upon their village through the woods alone and in the last stage of exhaustion.

"The man's knapsack lay beside the couch, and I examined the contents. His name was written upon a tab within it—Maple White, Lake Avenue, Detroit, Michigan. It is a name to which I am prepared always to lift my hat. It is not too much to say that it will rank level with my own when the final credit of this business comes to be apportioned.

"From the contents of the knapsack it was evident that this man had been an artist and poet in search of effects. There were scraps of verse. I do not profess to be a judge of such things, but they appeared to me to be singularly wanting in merit. There were also some rather commonplace pictures of river scenery, a paint-box, a box of colored chalks, some brushes, that curved bone which lies upon my inkstand, a volume of Baxter's 'Moths and Butterflies,' a cheap revolver, and a few cartridges. Of personal equipment he either had none or he had lost it in his journey. Such were the total effects of this strange American Bohemian.

"I was turning away from him when I observed that something projected from the front of his ragged jacket. It was this sketchbook, which was as dilapidated then as you see it now. Indeed, I can assure you that a first folio of Shakespeare could not be treated with greater reverence than this relic has been since it came into my possession. I hand it to you now, and I ask you to take it page by page and to examine the contents."

He helped himself to a cigar and leaned back with a fiercely critical pair of eyes, taking note of the effect which this document would produce.

I had opened the volume with some expectation of a revelation, though of what nature I could not imagine. The first page was disappointing, however, as it contained nothing but the picture of a very fat man in a pea-jacket, with the legend, "Jimmy Colver on the Mail-boat," written beneath it. There followed several pages which were filled with small sketches of Indians and their ways. Then came a picture of a cheerful and corpulent ecclesiastic in a shovel hat, sitting opposite a very thin European, and the inscription: "Lunch with Fra Cristofero at Rosario." Studies of women and babies accounted for several more pages, and then there was an unbroken series of animal drawings with such explanations as "Manatee upon Sandbank," "Turtles and Their Eggs," "Black Ajouti under a Miriti Palm"—the matter disclosing some sort of pig-like animal; and finally came a double page of studies of long-snouted and very unpleasant saurians. I could make nothing of it, and said so to the Professor.

"Surely these are only crocodiles?"

"Alligators! Alligators! There is hardly such a thing as a true crocodile in South America. The distinction between them—"

"I meant that I could see nothing unusual—nothing to justify what you have said."

He smiled serenely.

"Try the next page," said he.

I was still unable to sympathize. It was a full-page sketch of a landscape roughly tinted in color—the kind of painting which an open-air artist takes as a guide to a future more elaborate effort. There was a pale-green foreground of feathery vegetation, which sloped upwards and ended in a line of cliffs dark red in color, and curiously ribbed like some basaltic formations which I have seen. They extended in an unbroken wall right across the background. At one point was an isolated pyramidal rock, crowned by a great tree, which appeared to be separated by a cleft from the main crag. Behind it all, a blue tropical sky. A thin green line of vegetation fringed the summit of the ruddy cliff.

"Well?" he asked.

"It is no doubt a curious formation," said I "but I am not geologist enough to say that it is wonderful."

"Wonderful!" he repeated. "It is unique. It is incredible. No one on earth has ever dreamed of such a possibility. Now the next."

I turned it over, and gave an exclamation of surprise. There was a full-page picture of the most extraordinary creature that I had ever seen. It was the wild dream of an opium smoker, a vision of delirium. The head was like that of a fowl, the body that of a bloated lizard, the trailing tail was furnished with upward-turned spikes, and the curved back was edged with a high serrated fringe, which looked like a dozen cocks' wattles placed behind each other. In front of this creature was an absurd mannikin, or dwarf, in human form, who stood staring at it.

"Well, what do you think of that?" cried the Professor, rubbing his hands with an air of triumph.

"It is monstrous—grotesque."

"But what made him draw such an animal?"

"Trade gin, I should think."

"Oh, that's the best explanation you can give, is it?"

"Well, sir, what is yours?"

"The obvious one that the creature exists. That is actually sketched from the life."

I should have laughed only that I had a vision of our doing another Catharine-wheel down the passage.

"No doubt," said I, "no doubt," as one humors an imbecile. "I confess, however," I added, "that this tiny human figure puzzles me. If it were an Indian we could set it down as evidence of some pigmy race in America, but it appears to be a European in a sun-hat."

The Professor snorted like an angry buffalo. "You really touch the limit," said he. "You enlarge my view of the possible. Cerebral paresis! Mental inertia! Wonderful!"

He was too absurd to make me angry. Indeed, it was a waste of energy, for if you were going to be angry with this man you would be angry all the time. I contented myself with smiling wearily. "It struck me that the man was small," said I.

"Look here!" he cried, leaning forward and dabbing a great hairy sausage of a finger on to the picture. "You see that plant behind the animal; I suppose you thought it was a dandelion or a Brussels sprout—what? Well, it is a vegetable ivory palm, and they run to about fifty or sixty feet. Don't you see that the man is put in for a purpose? He couldn't really have stood in front of that brute and lived to draw it. He sketched himself in to give a scale of heights. He was, we will say, over five feet high. The tree is ten times bigger, which is what one would expect."

"Good heavens!" I cried. "Then you think the beast was— Why, Charing Cross station would hardly make a kennel for such a brute!"

"Apart from exaggeration, he is certainly a well-grown specimen," said the Professor, complacently.

"But," I cried, "surely the whole experience of the human race is not to be set aside on account of a single sketch"—I had turned over the leaves and ascertained that there was nothing more in the book—"a single sketch by a wandering American artist who may have done it under hashish, or in the delirium of fever, or simply in order to gratify a freakish imagination. You can't, as a man of science, defend such a position as that."

For answer the Professor took a book down from a shelf.

"This is an excellent monograph by my gifted friend, Ray Lankester!" said he. "There is an illustration here which would interest you. Ah, yes, here it is! The inscription beneath it runs: 'Probable appearance in life of the Jurassic Dinosaur Stegosaurus. The hind leg alone is twice as tall as a full-grown man.' Well, what do you make of that?"

He handed me the open book. I started as I looked at the picture. In this reconstructed animal of a dead world there was certainly a very great resemblance to the sketch of the unknown artist.

"That is certainly remarkable," said I.

"But you won't admit that it is final?"

"Surely it might be a coincidence, or this American may have seen a picture of the kind and carried it in his memory. It would be likely to recur to a man in a delirium."

"Very good," said the Professor, indulgently; "we leave it at that. I will now ask you to look at this bone." He handed over the one which he had already described as part of the dead man's possessions. It was about six inches long, and thicker than my thumb, with some indications of dried cartilage at one end of it.

"To what known creature does that bone belong?" asked the Professor.

I examined it with care and tried to recall some half-forgotten knowledge.

"It might be a very thick human collarbone," I said.

My companion waved his hand in contemptuous deprecation.

"The human collarbone is curved. This is straight. There is a groove upon its surface showing that a great tendon played across it, which could not be the case with a clavicle."

"Then I must confess that I don't know what it is."

"You need not be ashamed to expose your ignorance, for I don't suppose the whole South Kensington staff could give a name to it." He took a little bone the size of a bean out of a pill-box. "So far as I am a judge this human bone is the analogue of the one which you hold in your hand. That will give you some idea of the size of the creature. You will observe from the cartilage that this is no fossil specimen, but recent. What do you say to that?"

"Surely in an elephant—"

He winced as if in pain.

"Don't! Don't talk of elephants in South America. Even in these days of Board schools—"

"Well," I interrupted, "any large South American animal—a tapir, for example."

"You may take it, young man, that I am versed in the elements of my business. This is not a conceivable bone either of a tapir or of any other creature known to zoology. It belongs to a very large, a very strong, and, by all analogy, a very fierce animal which exists upon the face of the earth, but has not yet come under the notice of science. You are still unconvinced?"

"I am at least deeply interested."

"Then your case is not hopeless. I feel that there is reason lurking in you somewhere, so we will patiently grope round for it. We will now leave the dead American and proceed with my narrative. You can imagine that I could hardly come away from the Amazon without probing deeper into the matter. There were indications as to the direction from which the dead traveler had come. Indian legends would alone have been my guide, for I found that rumors of a strange land were common among all the riverine tribes. You have heard, no doubt, of Curupuri?"

"Never."

"Curupuri is the spirit of the woods, something terrible, something malevolent, something to be avoided. None can describe its shape or nature, but it is a word of terror along the Amazon. Now all tribes agree as to the direction in which Curupuri lives. It was the same direction from which the American had come. Something terrible lay that way. It was my business to find out what it was."

"What did you do?" My flippancy was all gone. This massive man compelled one's attention and respect.

"I overcame the extreme reluctance of the natives—a reluctance which extends even to talk upon the subject—and by judicious persuasion and gifts, aided, I will admit, by some threats of coercion, I got two of them to act as guides. After many adventures which I need not describe, and after traveling a distance which I will not mention, in a direction which I withhold, we came at last to a tract of country which has never been described, nor, indeed, visited save by my unfortunate predecessor. Would you kindly look at this?"

He handed me a photograph—half-plate size.

"The unsatisfactory appearance of it is due to the fact," said he, "that on descending the river the boat was upset and the case which contained the undeveloped films was broken, with disastrous results. Nearly all of them were totally ruined—an irreparable loss. This is one of the few which partially escaped. This explanation of deficiencies or abnormalities you will kindly accept. There was talk of faking. I am not in a mood to argue such a point."

The photograph was certainly very off-colored. An unkind critic might easily have misinterpreted that dim surface. It was a dull gray landscape, and as I gradually deciphered the details of it I realized that it represented a long and enormously high line of cliffs exactly like an immense cataract seen in the distance, with a sloping, tree-clad plain in the foreground.

"I believe it is the same place as the painted picture," said I.

"It *is* the same place," the Professor answered. "I found traces of the fellow's camp. Now look at this."

It was a nearer view of the same scene, though the photograph was extremely defective. I could distinctly see the isolated, tree-crowned pinnacle of rock which was detached from the crag.

"I have no doubt of it at all," said I.

"Well, that is something gained," said he. "We progress, do we not? Now, will you please look at the top of that rocky pinnacle? Do you observe something there?"

"An enormous tree."

"But on the tree?"

"A large bird," said I.

He handed me a lens.

"Yes," I said, peering through it, "a large bird stands on the tree. It appears to have a considerable beak. I should say it was a pelican."

"I cannot congratulate you upon your eyesight," said the Professor. "It is not a pelican, nor, indeed, is it a bird. It may interest you to know that I succeeded in shooting that particular specimen. It was the only absolute proof of my experiences which I was able to bring away with me."

"You have it, then?" Here at last was tangible corroboration.

"I had it. It was unfortunately lost with so much else in the same boat accident which ruined my photographs. I clutched at it as it disappeared in the swirl of the rapids, and part of its wing was left in my hand. I was insensible when washed ashore, but the miserable remnant of my superb specimen was still intact; I now lay it before you."

From a drawer he produced what seemed to me to be the upper portion of the wing of a large bat. It was at least two feet in length, a curved bone, with a membranous veil beneath it.

"A monstrous bat!" I suggested.

"Nothing of the sort," said the Professor, severely. "Living, as I do, in an educated and scientific atmosphere, I could not have conceived that the first principles of zoology were so little known. Is it possible that you do not know the elementary fact in comparative anatomy, that the wing of a bird is really the forearm, while the wing of a bat consists of three elongated fingers with membranes between? Now, in this case, the bone is certainly not the forearm, and you can see for yourself that this is a single membrane hanging upon a single bone, and therefore that it cannot belong to a bat. But if it is neither bird nor bat, what is it?"

My small stock of knowledge was exhausted.

"I really do not know," said I.

He opened the standard work to which he had already referred me.

"Here," said he, pointing to the picture of an extraordinary flying monster, "is an excellent reproduction of the dimorphodon, or pterodactyl, a flying reptile of the Jurassic period. On the next page is a diagram of the mechanism of its wing. Kindly compare it with the specimen in your hand."

A wave of amazement passed over me as I looked. I was convinced. There could be no getting away from it. The cumulative proof was overwhelming. The sketch, the photographs, the narrative, and now the actual specimen—the evidence was complete. I said so—I said so warmly, for I felt that the Professor was an ill-used man. He leaned back in his chair with drooping eyelids and a tolerant smile, basking in this sudden gleam of sunshine.

"It's just the very biggest thing that I ever heard of!" said I, though it was my journalistic rather than my scientific enthusiasm that was roused. "It is colossal.

You are a Columbus of science who has discovered a lost world. I'm awfully sorry if I seemed to doubt you. It was all so unthinkable. But I understand evidence when I see it, and this should be good enough for anyone."

The Professor purred with satisfaction.

"And then, sir, what did you do next?"

"It was the wet season, Mr. Malone, and my stores were exhausted. I explored some portion of this huge cliff, but I was unable to find any way to scale it. The pyramidal rock upon which I saw and shot the pterodactyl was more accessible. Being something of a cragsman, I did manage to get half way to the top of that. From that height I had a better idea of the plateau upon the top of the crags. It appeared to be very large; neither to east nor to west could I see any end to the vista of green-capped cliffs. Below, it is a swampy, jungly region, full of snakes, insects, and fever. It is a natural protection to this singular country."

"Did you see any other trace of life?"

"No, sir, I did not; but during the week that we lay encamped at the base of the cliff we heard some very strange noises from above."

"But the creature that the American drew? How do you account for that?"

"We can only suppose that he must have made his way to the summit and seen it there. We know, therefore, that there is a way up. We know equally that it must be a very difficult one, otherwise the creatures would have come down and overrun the surrounding country. Surely that is clear?"

"But how did they come to be there?"

"I do not think that the problem is a very obscure one," said the Professor; "there can only be one explanation. South America is, as you may have heard, a granite continent. At this single point in the interior there has been, in some far distant age, a great, sudden volcanic upheaval. These cliffs, I may remark, are basaltic, and therefore plutonic. An area, as large perhaps as Sussex, has been lifted up en bloc with all its living contents, and cut off by perpendicular precipices of a hardness which defies erosion from all the rest of the continent. What is the result? Why, the ordinary laws of Nature are suspended. The various checks which influence the struggle for existence in the world at large are all neutralized or altered. Creatures survive which would otherwise disappear. You will observe that both the pterodactyl and the stegosaurus are Jurassic, and therefore of a great age in the order of life. They have been artificially conserved by those strange accidental conditions."

"But surely your evidence *is* conclusive. You have only to lay it before the proper authorities."

"So in my simplicity, I had imagined," said the Professor, bitterly. "I can only tell you that it was not so, that I was met at every turn by incredulity, born partly of stupidity and partly of jealousy. It is not my nature, sir, to cringe to any man, or to seek to prove a fact if my word has been doubted. After the first I have not condescended to show such corroborative proofs as I possess. The subject became hateful to me—I would not speak of it. When men like yourself, who represent the foolish curiosity of the public, came to disturb my privacy I was unable to meet them with dignified reserve. By nature I am, I admit, somewhat fiery, and under provocation I am inclined to be violent. I fear you may have remarked it."

I nursed my eye and was silent.

"My wife has frequently remonstrated with me upon the subject, and yet I fancy that any man of honor would feel the same. Tonight, however, I propose to give an extreme example of the control of the will over the emotions. I invite you to be present at the exhibition." He handed me a card from his desk. "You will perceive that Mr. Percival Waldron, a naturalist of some popular repute, is announced to lecture at eight-thirty at the Zoological Institute's Hall upon 'The Record of the Ages.' I have been specially invited to be present upon the platform, and to move a vote of thanks to the lecturer. While doing so, I shall make it my business, with infinite tact and delicacy, to throw out a few remarks which may arouse the interest of the audience and cause some of them to desire to go more deeply into the matter. Nothing contentious, you understand, but only an indication that there are greater deeps beyond. I shall hold myself strongly in leash, and see whether by this self-restraint I attain a more favorable result."

"And I may come?" I asked eagerly.

"Why, surely," he answered, cordially. He had an enormously massive genial manner, which was almost as overpowering as his violence. His smile of benevolence was a wonderful thing, when his cheeks would suddenly bunch into two red apples, between his half-closed eyes and his great black beard. "By all means, come. It will be a comfort to me to know that I have one ally in the hall, however inefficient and ignorant of the subject he may be. I fancy there will be a large audience, for Waldron, though an absolute charlatan, has a considerable popular following. Now, Mr. Malone, I have given you rather more of my time than I had intended. The individual must not monopolize what is meant for the world. I shall be pleased to see you at the lecture tonight. In the meantime, you will understand that no public use is to be made of any of the material that I have given you."

"But Mr. McArdle—my news editor, you know—will want to know what I have done."

"Tell him what you like. You can say, among other things, that if he sends anyone else to intrude upon me I shall call upon him with a riding-whip. But I leave it to you that nothing of all this appears in print. Very good. Then the Zoological Institute's Hall at eight-thirty tonight." I had a last impression of red cheeks, blue rippling beard, and intolerant eyes, as he waved me out of the room.

V

"QUESTION!"

What with the physical shocks incidental to my first interview with Professor Challenger and the mental ones which accompanied the second, I was a somewhat demoralized journalist by the time I found myself in Enmore Park once more. In my aching head the one thought was throbbing that there really was truth in this man's story, that it was of tremendous consequence, and that it would work up into inconceivable copy for the *Gazette* when I could obtain permission to use it. A taxicab was waiting at the end of the road, so I sprang into it and drove down to the office. McArdle was at his post as usual.

"Well," he cried, expectantly, "what may it run to? I'm thinking, young man, you have been in the wars. Don't tell me that he assaulted you."

"We had a little difference at first."

"What a man it is! What did you do?"

"Well, he became more reasonable and we had a chat. But I got nothing out of him—nothing for publication."

"I'm not so sure about that. You got a black eye out of him, and that's for publication. We can't have this reign of terror, Mr. Malone. We must bring the man to his bearings. I'll have a leaderette on him tomorrow that will raise a blister. Just give me the material and I will engage to brand the fellow forever. Professor Munchausen—how's that for an inset headline? Sir John Mandeville redivivus—Cagliostro—all the imposters and bullies in history. I'll show him up for the fraud he is."

"I wouldn't do that, sir."

"Why not?"

"Because he is not a fraud at all."

"What!" roared McArdle. "You don't mean to say you really believe this stuff of his about mammoths and mastodons and great sea sairpents?"

"Well, I don't know about that. I don't think he makes any claims of that kind. But I do believe he has got something new."

"Then for Heaven's sake, man, write it up!"

"I'm longing to, but all I know he gave me in confidence and on condition that I didn't." I condensed into a few sentences the Professor's narrative. "That's how it stands."

McArdle looked deeply incredulous.

"Well, Mr. Malone," he said at last, "about this scientific meeting tonight; there can be no privacy about that, anyhow. I don't suppose any paper will want to report it, for Waldron has been reported already a dozen times, and no one is aware that Challenger will speak. We may get a scoop, if we are lucky. You'll be there in any case, so you'll just give us a pretty full report. I'll keep space up to midnight."

My day was a busy one, and I had an early dinner at the Savage Club with Tarp Henry, to whom I gave some account of my adventures. He listened with a sceptical smile on his gaunt face, and roared with laughter on hearing that the Professor had convinced me.

"My dear chap, things don't happen like that in real life. People don't stumble upon enormous discoveries and then lose their evidence. Leave that to the novelists. The fellow is as full of tricks as the monkey-house at the Zoo. It's all bosh."

"But the American poet?"

"He never existed."

"I saw his sketchbook."

"Challenger's sketchbook."

"You think he drew that animal?"

"Of course he did. Who else?"

"Well, then, the photographs?"

"There was nothing in the photographs. By your own admission you only saw a bird."

"A pterodactyl."

"That's what *he* says. He put the pterodactyl into your head."

"Well, then, the bones?"

"First one out of an Irish stew. Second one vamped up for the occasion. If you are clever and know your business you can fake a bone as easily as you can a photograph."

I began to feel uneasy. Perhaps, after all, I had been premature in my acquiescence. Then I had a sudden happy thought.

"Will you come to the meeting?" I asked.

Tarp Henry looked thoughtful.

"He is not a popular person, the genial Challenger," said he. "A lot of people have accounts to settle with him. I should say he is about the best-hated man in London. If the medical students turn out there will be no end of a rag. I don't want to get into a bear-garden."

"You might at least do him the justice to hear him state his own case."

"Well, perhaps it's only fair. All right. I'm your man for the evening."

When we arrived at the hall we found a much greater concourse than I had expected. A line of electric broughams discharged their little cargoes of white-bearded professors, while the dark stream of humbler pedestrians, who crowded through the arched doorway, showed that the audience would be popular as well as scientific. Indeed, it became evident to us as soon as we had taken our seats that a youthful and even boyish spirit was abroad in the gallery and the back portions of the hall. Looking behind me, I could see rows of faces of the familiar medical student type. Apparently the great hospitals had each sent down their contingent. The behavior of the audience at present was good-humored, but mischievous. Scraps of popular songs were chorused with an enthusiasm which was a strange prelude to a scientific lecture, and there was already a tendency to personal chaff which promised a jovial evening to others, however embarrassing it might be to the recipients of these dubious honors.

Thus, when old Doctor Meldrum, with his well-known curly-brimmed opera-hat, appeared upon the platform, there was such a universal query of "Where *did* you get that tile?" that he hurriedly removed it, and concealed it furtively under his chair. When gouty Professor Wadley limped down to his seat there were general affectionate inquiries from all parts of the hall as to the exact state of his poor toe, which caused him obvious embarrassment. The greatest demonstration of all, however, was at the entrance of my new acquaintance, Professor Challenger, when he passed down to take his place at the extreme end of the front row of the platform. Such a yell of welcome broke forth when his black beard first protruded round the corner that I began to suspect Tarp Henry was right in his surmise, and that this assemblage was there not merely for the sake of the lecture, but because it had got rumored abroad that the famous Professor would take part in the proceedings.

There was some sympathetic laughter on his entrance among the front benches of well-dressed spectators, as though the demonstration of the students in this instance was not unwelcome to them. That greeting was, indeed, a frightful outburst of sound, the uproar of the carnivora cage when the step of the bucket-bearing keeper is heard in the distance. There was an offensive tone in it, perhaps, and yet in the main it struck me as mere riotous outcry, the noisy reception of one who amused and interested them, rather than of one they disliked or despised. Challenger smiled with weary and tolerant contempt, as a kindly man would meet the yapping of a litter of puppies. He sat slowly down, blew out his chest, passed his hand caressingly down his beard, and looked with drooping eyelids and supercilious eyes at the crowded hall before him. The uproar of his advent had not yet died away when Professor Ronald Murray, the chairman, and Mr. Waldron, the lecturer, threaded their way to the front, and the proceedings began.

Professor Murray will, I am sure, excuse me if I say that he has the common fault of most Englishmen of being inaudible. Why on earth people who have something to say which is worth hearing should not take the slight trouble to learn how to make it heard is one of the strange mysteries of modern life. Their methods are as reasonable as to try to pour some precious stuff from the spring to the reservoir through a non-conducting pipe, which could by the least effort be opened. Professor Murray made several profound remarks to his white tie and to the water-carafe upon the table, with a humorous, twinkling aside to the silver candlestick upon his right. Then he sat down, and Mr. Waldron, the famous popular lecturer, rose amid a general murmur of applause. He was a stern, gaunt man, with a harsh voice, and an aggressive manner, but he had the merit of knowing how to assimilate the ideas of other men, and to pass them on in a way which was intelligible and even interesting to the lay public, with a happy knack of being funny about the most unlikely objects, so that the precession of the Equinox or the formation of a vertebrate became a highly humorous process as treated by him.

It was a bird's-eye view of creation, as interpreted by science, which, in language always clear and sometimes picturesque, he unfolded before us. He told us of the globe, a huge mass of flaming gas, flaring through the heavens. Then he pictured the solidification, the cooling, the wrinkling which formed the mountains, the steam which turned to water, the slow preparation of the stage upon which was to be played the inexplicable drama of life. On the origin of life itself he was discreetly vague. That the germs of it could hardly have survived the original roasting was, he declared, fairly certain. Therefore it had come later. Had it built itself out of the cooling, inorganic elements of the globe? Very likely. Had the germs of it arrived from outside upon a meteor? It was hardly conceivable. On the whole, the wisest man was the least dogmatic upon the point. We could not—or at least we had not succeeded up to date in making organic life in our laboratories out of inorganic materials. The gulf between the dead and the living was something which our chemistry could not as yet bridge. But there was a higher and subtler chemistry of Nature, which, working with great forces over long epochs, might well produce results which were impossible for us. There the matter must be left.

This brought the lecturer to the great ladder of animal life, beginning low down in molluscs and feeble sea creatures, then up rung by rung through reptiles and fishes, till at last we came to a kangaroo-rat, a creature which brought forth its young alive, the direct ancestor of all mammals, and presumably, therefore, of everyone in the audience. ("No, no," from a sceptical student in the back row.) If the young gentleman in the red tie who cried "No, no," and who presumably claimed to have been hatched out of an egg, would wait upon him after the lecture, he would be glad to see such a curiosity. (Laughter.) It was strange to think that the climax of all the age-long process of Nature had been the creation of that gentleman in the red tie. But had the process stopped? Was this gentleman to be taken as the final type—the be-all and end-all of development? He hoped that he would not hurt the feelings of the gentleman in the red tie if he maintained that, whatever virtues that gentleman might possess in private life, still the vast processes of the universe were not fully justified if they were to end entirely in his production. Evolution was not a spent force, but one still working, and even greater achievements were in store.

Having thus, amid a general titter, played very prettily with his interrupter, the lecturer went back to his picture of the past, the drying of the seas, the emergence of the sand-bank, the sluggish, viscous life which lay upon their margins, the overcrowded lagoons, the tendency of the sea creatures to take refuge upon the mud-flats, the abundance of food awaiting them, their consequent enormous growth. "Hence, ladies and gentlemen," he added, "that frightful brood of saurians which still affright our eyes when seen in the Wealden or in the Solenhofen slates, but which were fortunately extinct long before the first appearance of mankind upon this planet."

"Question!" boomed a voice from the platform.

Mr. Waldron was a strict disciplinarian with a gift of acid humor, as exemplified upon the gentleman with the red tie, which made it perilous to interrupt him. But this interjection appeared to him so absurd that he was at a loss how to deal with it. So looks the Shakespearean who is confronted by a rancid Baconian, or the astronomer who is assailed by a flat-earth fanatic. He paused for a moment, and then, raising his voice, repeated slowly the words: "Which were extinct before the coming of man."

"Question!" boomed the voice once more.

Waldron looked with amazement along the line of professors upon the platform until his eyes fell upon the figure of Challenger, who leaned back in his chair with closed eyes and an amused expression, as if he were smiling in his sleep.

"I see!" said Waldron, with a shrug. "It is my friend Professor Challenger," and amid laughter he renewed his lecture as if this was a final explanation and no more need be said.

But the incident was far from being closed. Whatever path the lecturer took amid the wilds of the past seemed invariably to lead him to some assertion as to extinct or prehistoric life which instantly brought the same bulls' bellow from the Professor. The audience began to anticipate it and to roar with delight when it came. The packed benches of students joined in, and every time Challenger's beard opened, before any sound could come forth, there was a yell of "Question!" from a hundred voices, and an answering counter cry of "Order!" and "Shame!" from as many more. Waldron, though a hardened lecturer and a strong man, became rattled. He hesitated, stammered, repeated himself, got snarled in a long sentence, and finally turned furiously upon the cause of his troubles.

"This is really intolerable!" he cried, glaring across the platform. "I must ask you, Professor Challenger, to cease these ignorant and unmannerly interruptions."

There was a hush over the hall, the students rigid with delight at seeing the high gods on Olympus quarrelling among themselves. Challenger levered his bulky figure slowly out of his chair.

"I must in turn ask you, Mr. Waldron," he said, "to cease to make assertions which are not in strict accordance with scientific fact."

The words unloosed a tempest. "Shame! Shame!" "Give him a hearing!" "Put him out!" "Shove him off the platform!" "Fair play!" emerged from a general roar of amusement or execration. The chairman was on his feet flapping both his hands and bleating excitedly. "Professor Challenger—personal—views—later," were the solid peaks above his clouds of inaudible mutter. The interrupter bowed, smiled, stroked his beard, and relapsed into his chair. Waldron, very flushed and warlike, continued his observations. Now and then, as he made an assertion, he shot a venomous glance at his opponent, who seemed to be slumbering deeply, with the same broad, happy smile upon his face.

At last the lecture came to an end—I am inclined to think that it was a premature one, as the peroration was hurried and disconnected. The thread of the argument had been rudely broken, and the audience was restless and expectant. Waldron sat down, and, after a chirrup from the chairman, Professor Challenger rose and advanced to the edge of the platform. In the interests of my paper I took down his speech verbatim.

"Ladies and Gentlemen," he began, amid a sustained interruption from the back. "I beg pardon—Ladies, Gentlemen, and Children—I must apologize, I had inadvertently omitted a considerable section of this audience" (tumult, during which the Professor stood with one hand raised and his enormous head nodding sympathetically, as if he were bestowing a pontifical blessing upon the crowd), "I have been selected to move a vote of thanks to Mr. Waldron for the very picturesque and imaginative address to which we have just listened. There are points in it with which I disagree, and it has been my duty to indicate them as they arose, but, nonetheless, Mr. Waldron has accomplished his object well, that object being to give a simple and interesting account of what he conceives to have been the history of our planet. Popular lectures are the easiest to listen to, but Mr. Waldron" (here he beamed and blinked at the lecturer) "will excuse me when I say that they are necessarily both superficial and misleading, since they have to be graded to the comprehension of an ignorant audience." (Ironical cheering.) "Popular lecturers are in their nature parasitic." (Angry gesture of protest from Mr. Waldron.) "They exploit for fame or cash the work which has been done by their indigent and unknown brethren. One smallest new fact obtained in the laboratory, one brick built into the temple of science, far outweighs any second-hand exposition which passes an idle hour, but can leave no useful result behind it. I put forward this obvious reflection, not out of any desire to disparage Mr. Waldron in particular, but that you may not lose your sense of proportion and mistake the acolyte for the high priest." (At this point Mr. Waldron whispered to the chairman, who half rose and said something severely to his water-carafe.) "But enough of this!" (Loud and prolonged cheers.) "Let me pass to some subject of wider interest. What is the particular point upon which I, as an original investigator, have challenged our lecturer's accuracy? It is upon the permanence of certain types of animal life upon the earth. I do not speak upon this subject as an amateur, nor, I may add, as a popular lecturer, but I speak as one whose scientific conscience compels him to adhere closely to facts, when I say that Mr. Waldron is very wrong in supposing that because he has never himself seen a so-called prehistoric animal, therefore these creatures no longer exist. They are indeed, as he has said, our ancestors, but they are, if I may use the expression, our contemporary ancestors, who can still be found with all their hideous and formidable characteristics if one has but the energy and hardihood to seek their haunts. Creatures which were supposed to be Jurassic, monsters who would hunt down and devour our largest and fiercest mammals, still exist." (Cries of "Bosh!" "Prove it!" "How do you know?" "Question!") "How do I know, you ask me? I know because I have visited their secret haunts. I know because I have seen some of them." (Applause, uproar, and a voice, "Liar!") "Am I a liar?" (General hearty and noisy assent.) "Did I hear someone say that I was a liar? Will the person who called me a liar kindly stand up that I may know him?" (A voice, "Here he is, sir!" and an inoffensive little person in spectacles, struggling violently, was held up among a group of students.) "Did you venture to call me a liar?" ("No, sir, no!" shouted the accused, and disappeared like a jack-in-the-box.) "If any person in this hall dares to doubt my veracity, I shall be glad to have a few words with him after the lecture." ("Liar!") "Who said that?" (Again the inoffensive one plunging desperately, was elevated high into the air.) "If I come down among you—" (General chorus of "Come, love, come!" which interrupted the proceedings for some moments, while the chairman, standing up and waving both his arms, seemed to be conducting the music. The Professor, with his face flushed, his nostrils dilated, and his beard bristling, was now in a proper Berserk mood.) "Every great discoverer has been met with the same incredulity—the sure brand of a generation of fools. When great facts are laid before you, you have not the intuition, the imagination which would help you to understand them. You can only throw mud at the men who have risked their lives to open new fields to science. You persecute the prophets! Galileo! Darwin, and I—" (Prolonged cheering and complete interruption.)

All this is from my hurried notes taken at the time, which give little notion of the absolute chaos to which the assembly had by this time been reduced. So terrific was the uproar that several ladies had already beaten a hurried retreat. Grave and reverend seniors seemed to have caught the prevailing spirit as badly as the students, and I saw white-bearded men rising and shaking their fists at the obdurate Professor. The whole great audience seethed and simmered like a boiling pot. The Professor took a step forward and raised both his hands. There was something so big and arresting and virile in the man that the clatter and shouting died gradually away before his commanding gesture and his masterful eyes. He seemed to have a definite message. They hushed to hear it.

"I will not detain you," he said. "It is not worth it. Truth is truth, and the noise of a number of foolish young men—and, I fear I must add, of their equally foolish seniors—cannot affect the matter. I claim that I have opened a new field of science. You dispute it." (Cheers.) "Then I put you to the test. Will you accredit one or more of your own number to go out as your representatives and test my statement in your name?"

Mr. Summerlee, the veteran Professor of Comparative Anatomy, rose among the audience, a tall, thin, bitter man, with the withered aspect of a theologian. He wished, he said, to ask Professor Challenger whether the results to which he had alluded in his remarks had been obtained during a journey to the headwaters of the Amazon made by him two years before.

Professor Challenger answered that they had.

Mr. Summerlee desired to know how it was that Professor Challenger claimed to have made discoveries in those regions which had been overlooked by Wallace, Bates, and other previous explorers of established scientific repute.

Professor Challenger answered that Mr. Summerlee appeared to be confusing the Amazon with the Thames; that it was in reality a somewhat larger river; that Mr. Summerlee might be interested to know that with the

Orinoco, which communicated with it, some fifty thousand miles of country were opened up, and that in so vast a space it was not impossible for one person to find what another had missed.

Mr. Summerlee declared, with an acid smile, that he fully appreciated the difference between the Thames and the Amazon, which lay in the fact that any assertion about the former could be tested, while about the latter it could not. He would be obliged if Professor Challenger would give the latitude and the longitude of the country in which prehistoric animals were to be found.

Professor Challenger replied that he reserved such information for good reasons of his own, but would be prepared to give it with proper precautions to a committee chosen from the audience. Would Mr. Summerlee serve on such a committee and test his story in person?

Mr. Summerlee: "Yes, I will." (Great cheering.)

Professor Challenger: "Then I guarantee that I will place in your hands such material as will enable you to find your way. It is only right, however, since Mr. Summerlee goes to check my statement that I should have one or more with him who may check his. I will not disguise from you that there are difficulties and dangers. Mr. Summerlee will need a younger colleague. May I ask for volunteers?"

It is thus that the great crisis of a man's life springs out at him. Could I have imagined when I entered that hall that I was about to pledge myself to a wilder adventure than had ever come to me in my dreams? But Gladys—was it not the very opportunity of which she spoke? Gladys would have told me to go. I had sprung to my feet. I was speaking, and yet I had prepared no words. Tarp Henry, my companion, was plucking at my skirts and I heard him whispering, "Sit down, Malone! Don't make a public ass of yourself." At the same time I was aware that a tall, thin man, with dark gingery hair, a few seats in front of me, was also upon his feet. He glared back at me with hard angry eyes, but I refused to give way.

"I will go, Mr. Chairman," I kept repeating over and over again.

"Name! Name!" cried the audience.

"My name is Edward Dunn Malone. I am the reporter of the *Daily Gazette*. I claim to be an absolutely unprejudiced witness."

"What is your name, sir?" the chairman asked of my tall rival.

"I am Lord John Roxton. I have already been up the Amazon, I know all the ground, and have special qualifications for this investigation."

"Lord John Roxton's reputation as a sportsman and a traveler is, of course, world-famous," said the chairman; "at the same time it would certainly be as well to have a member of the Press upon such an expedition."

"Then I move," said Professor Challenger, "that both these gentlemen be elected, as representatives of this meeting, to accompany Professor Summerlee upon his journey to investigate and to report upon the truth of my statements."

And so, amid shouting and cheering, our fate was decided, and I found myself borne away in the human current which swirled towards the door, with my mind half stunned by the vast new project which had risen so suddenly before it. As I emerged from the hall I was conscious for a moment of a rush of laughing students—down the pavement, and of an arm wielding a heavy umbrella, which rose and fell in the midst of them. Then, amid a mixture of groans and cheers, Professor Challenger's electric brougham slid from the curb, and I found myself walking under the silvery lights of Regent Street, full of thoughts of Gladys and of wonder as to my future.

Suddenly there was a touch at my elbow. I turned, and found myself looking into the humorous, masterful eyes of the tall, thin man who had volunteered to be my companion on this strange quest.

"Mr. Malone, I understand," said he. "We are to be companions—what? My rooms are just over the road, in the Albany. Perhaps you would have the kindness to spare me half an hour, for there are one or two things that I badly want to say to you."

VI

"I WAS THE FLAIL OF THE LORD"

Lord John Roxton and I turned down Vigo Street together and through the dingy portals of the famous aristocratic rookery. At the end of a long drab passage my new acquaintance pushed open a door and turned on an electric switch. A number of lamps shining through tinted shades bathed the whole great room before us in a ruddy radiance. Standing in the doorway and glancing round me, I had a general impression of extraordinary comfort and elegance combined with an atmosphere of masculine virility. Everywhere there were mingled the luxury of the wealthy man of taste and the careless untidiness of the bachelor. Rich furs and strange iridescent mats from some Oriental bazaar were scattered upon the floor. Pictures and prints which even my unpractised eyes could recognize as being of great price and rarity hung thick upon the walls. Sketches of boxers, of ballet-girls, and of racehorses alternated with a sensuous Fragonard, a martial Girardet, and a dreamy Turner. But amid these varied ornaments there were scattered the trophies which brought back strongly to my recollection the fact that Lord John Roxton was one of the great all-round sportsmen and athletes of his day. A dark-blue oar crossed with a cherry-pink one above his mantelpiece spoke of the old Oxonian and Leander man, while the foils and boxing-gloves above and below them were the tools of a man who had won supremacy with each. Like a dado round the room was the jutting line of splendid heavy game-heads, the best of their sort from every quarter of the world, with the rare white rhinoceros of the Lado Enclave drooping its supercilious lip above them all.

In the center of the rich red carpet was a black and gold Louis Quinze table, a lovely antique, now sacrilegiously desecrated with marks of glasses and the scars of cigar-stumps. On it stood a silver tray of smokables and a burnished spirit-stand, from which and an adjacent siphon my silent host proceeded to charge two high glasses. Having indicated an armchair to me and placed my refreshment near it, he handed me a long, smooth Havana. Then, seating himself opposite to me, he looked at me long and fixedly with his strange, twinkling, reckless eyes—eyes of a cold light blue, the color of a glacier lake.

Through the thin haze of my cigar-smoke I noted the details of a face which was already familiar to me from many photographs—the strongly-curved nose, the hollow, worn cheeks, the dark, ruddy hair, thin at the top, the crisp, virile moustaches, the small, aggressive tuft upon his projecting chin. Something there was of Napoleon III., something of Don Quixote, and yet again something which was the essence of the English country gentleman, the keen, alert, open-air lover of dogs and of horses. His skin was of a rich flower-pot red from sun and wind. His eyebrows were tufted and overhanging, which gave those naturally cold eyes an almost ferocious aspect, an impression which was increased by his strong and furrowed brow. In figure he was spare, but very strongly built—indeed, he had often proved that there were few men in England capable of such sustained exertions. His height was a little over six feet, but he seemed shorter on account of a peculiar rounding of the shoulders. Such was the famous Lord John Roxton as he sat opposite to me, biting hard upon his cigar and watching me steadily in a long and embarrassing silence.

"Well," said he, at last, "we've gone and done it, young fellah my lad." (This curious phrase he pronounced as if it were all one word—"young-fellah-me-lad.") "Yes, we've taken a jump, you an' me. I suppose, now, when you went into that room there was no such notion in your head—what?"

"No thought of it."

"The same here. No thought of it. And here we are, up to our necks in the tureen. Why, I've only been back three weeks from Uganda, and taken a place in Scotland, and signed the lease and all. Pretty goin's on—what? How does it hit you?"

"Well, it is all in the main line of my business. I am a journalist on the *Gazette*."

"Of course—you said so when you took it on. By the way, I've got a small job for you, if you'll help me."

"With pleasure."

"Don't mind takin' a risk, do you?"

"What is the risk?"

"Well, it's Ballinger—he's the risk. You've heard of him?"

"No."

"Why, young fellah, where have you lived? Sir John Ballinger is the best gentleman jock in the north country. I could hold him on the flat at my best, but over jumps he's my master. Well, it's an open secret that when he's out of trainin' he drinks hard—strikin' an average, he calls it. He got delirium on Toosday, and has been ragin' like a devil ever since. His room is above this. The doctors say that it is all up with the old dear unless some food is got into him, but as he lies in bed with a revolver on his coverlet, and swears he will put six of the best through anyone that comes near him, there's been a bit of a strike among the serving-men. He's a hard nail, is Jack, and a dead shot, too, but you can't leave a Grand National winner to die like that—what?"

"What do you mean to do, then?" I asked.

"Well, my idea was that you and I could rush him. He may be dozin', and at the worst he can only wing one of us, and the other should have him. If we can get his bolster-cover round his arms and then 'phone up a stomach-pump, we'll give the old dear the supper of his life."

It was a rather desperate business to come suddenly into one's day's work. I don't think that I am a particularly brave man. I have an Irish imagination which makes the unknown and the untried more terrible than they are. On the other hand, I was brought up with a horror of cowardice and with a terror of such a stigma. I dare say that I could throw myself over a precipice, like the Hun in the history books, if my courage to do it were questioned, and yet it would surely be pride and fear, rather than courage, which would be my inspiration. Therefore, although every nerve in my body shrank from the whisky-maddened figure which I pictured in the room above, I still answered, in as careless a voice as I could command, that I was ready to go. Some further remark of Lord Roxton's about the danger only made me irritable.

"Talking won't make it any better," said I. "Come on."

I rose from my chair and he from his. Then with a little confidential chuckle of laughter, he patted me two or three times on the chest, finally pushing me back into my chair.

"All right, sonny my lad—you'll do," said he. I looked up in surprise.

"I saw after Jack Ballinger myself this mornin'. He blew a hole in the skirt of my kimono, bless his shaky old hand, but we got a jacket on him, and he's to be all right in a week. I say, young fellah, I hope you don't mind—what? You see, between you an' me close-tiled, I look on this South American business as a mighty serious thing, and if I have a pal with me I want a man I can bank on. So I sized you down, and I'm bound to say that you came well out of it. You see, it's all up to you and me, for this old Summerlee man will want dry-nursin' from the first. By the way, are you by any chance the Malone who is expected to get his Rugby cap for Ireland?"

"A reserve, perhaps."

"I thought I remembered your face. Why, I was there when you got that try against Richmond—as fine a swervin' run as I saw the whole season. I never miss a Rugby match if I can help it, for it is the manliest game we have left. Well, I didn't ask you in here just to talk sport. We've got to fix our business. Here are the sailin's, on the first page of the Times. There's a Booth boat for Para next Wednesday week, and if the Professor and you can work it, I think we should take it—what? Very good, I'll fix it with him. What about your outfit?"

"My paper will see to that."

"Can you shoot?"

"About average Territorial standard."

"Good Lord! As bad as that? It's the last thing you young fellahs think of learnin'. You're all bees without stings, so far as lookin' after the hive goes. You'll look silly, some o' these days, when someone comes along an' sneaks the honey. But you'll need to hold your gun straight in South America, for, unless our friend the Professor is a madman or a liar, we may see some queer things before we get back. What gun have you?"

He crossed to an oaken cupboard, and as he threw it open I caught a glimpse of glistening rows of parallel barrels, like the pipes of an organ.

"I'll see what I can spare you out of my own battery," said he.

One by one he took out a succession of beautiful rifles, opening and shutting them with a snap and a clang, and then patting them as he put them back into the rack as tenderly as a mother would fondle her children.

"This is a Bland's .577 axite express," said he. "I got that big fellow with it." He glanced up at the white rhinoceros. "Ten more yards, and he'd would have added me to his collection.

"'On that conical bullet his one chance hangs,
'Tis the weak one's advantage fair.'

"Hope you know your Gordon, for he's the poet of the horse and the gun and the man that handles both. Now, here's a useful tool—.470, telescopic sight, double ejector, point-blank up to three-fifty. That's the rifle I used against the Peruvian slave-drivers three years ago. I was the flail of the Lord up in those parts, I may tell you, though you won't find it in any Blue-book. There are times, young fellah, when every one of us must make a stand for human right and justice, or you never feel clean again. That's why I made a little war on my own. Declared it myself, waged it myself, ended it myself. Each of those nicks is for a slave murderer—a good row of them—what? That big one is for Pedro Lopez, the king of them all, that I killed in a backwater of the Putomayo River. Now, here's something that would do for you." He took out a beautiful brown-and-silver rifle. "Well rubbered at the stock, sharply sighted, five cartridges to the clip. You can trust your life to that." He handed it to me and closed the door of his oak cabinet.

"By the way," he continued, coming back to his chair, "what do you know of this Professor Challenger?"

"I never saw him till today."

"Well, neither did I. It's funny we should both sail under sealed orders from a man we don't know. He seemed an uppish old bird. His brothers of science don't seem too fond of him, either. How came you to take an interest in the affair?"

I told him shortly my experiences of the morning, and he listened intently. Then he drew out a map of South America and laid it on the table.

"I believe every single word he said to you was the truth," said he, earnestly, "and, mind you, I have something to go on when I speak like that. South America is a place I love, and I think, if you take it right through from Darien to Fuego, it's the grandest, richest, most wonderful bit of earth upon this planet. People don't know it yet, and don't realize what it may become. I've been up an' down it from end to end, and had two dry seasons in those very parts, as I told you when I spoke of the war I made on the slave-dealers. Well, when I was up there I heard some yarns of the same kind—traditions of Indians and the like, but with somethin' behind them, no doubt. The more you knew of that country, young fellah, the more you would understand that anythin' was possible—*anythin'*. There are just some narrow water-lanes along which folk travel, and outside that it is all darkness. Now, down here in the Matto Grande"—he swept his cigar over a part of the map—"or up in this corner where three countries meet, nothin' would surprise me. As that chap said tonight, there are fifty-thousand miles of water-way runnin' through a forest that is very near the size of Europe. You and I could be as far away from each other as Scotland is from Constantinople, and yet each of us be in the same great Brazilian forest. Man has just made a track here and a scrape there in the maze. Why, the river rises and falls the best part of forty feet, and half the country is a morass that you can't pass over. Why shouldn't somethin' new and wonderful lie in such a country? And why shouldn't we be the men to find it out? Besides," he added, his queer, gaunt face shining with delight, "there's a sportin' risk in every mile of it. I'm like an old golf-ball—I've had all the white paint knocked off me long ago. Life can whack me about now, and it can't leave a mark. But a sportin' risk, young fellah, that's the salt of existence. Then it's worth livin' again. We're all gettin' a deal too soft and dull and comfy. Give me the great waste lands and the wide spaces, with a gun in my fist and somethin' to look for that's worth findin'. I've tried war and steeplechasin' and aeroplanes, but this huntin' of beasts that look like a lobster-supper dream is a brand-new sensation." He chuckled with glee at the prospect.

Perhaps I have dwelt too long upon this new acquaintance, but he is to be my comrade for many a day, and so I have tried to set him down as I first saw him, with his quaint personality and his queer little tricks of speech and of thought. It was only the need of getting in the account of my meeting which drew me at last from his company. I left him seated amid his pink radiance, oiling the lock of his favorite rifle, while he still chuckled to himself at the thought of the adventures which awaited us. It was very clear to me that if dangers lay before us I could not in all England have found a cooler head or a braver spirit with which to share them.

That night, wearied as I was after the wonderful happenings of the day, I sat late with McArdle, the news editor, explaining to him the whole situation, which he thought important enough to bring next morning before the notice of Sir George Beaumont, the chief. It was agreed that I should write home full accounts of my adventures in the shape of successive letters to McArdle, and that these should either be edited for the *Gazette* as they arrived, or held back to be published later, according to the wishes of Professor Challenger, since we could not yet know what conditions he might attach to those directions which should guide us to the unknown land. In response to a telephone inquiry, we received nothing more definite than a fulmination against the Press, ending up with the remark that if we would notify our boat he would hand us any directions which he might think it proper to give us at the moment of starting. A second question from us failed to elicit any answer at all, save a plaintive bleat from his wife to the effect that her husband was in a very violent temper already, and that she hoped we would do nothing to make it worse. A third attempt, later in the day, provoked a terrific crash, and a subsequent message from the Central Exchange that Professor Challenger's receiver had been shattered. After that we abandoned all attempt at communication.

* * * * *

And now my patient readers, I can address you directly no longer. From now onwards (if, indeed, any continuation of this narrative should ever reach you) it can only be through the paper which I represent. In the hands of the editor I leave this account of the events which have led up to one of the most remarkable expeditions of all time, so that if I never return to England there shall be some record as to how the affair came about. I am writing these last lines in the saloon of the Booth liner *Francisca*, and they will go back by the pilot to the keeping of Mr. McArdle. Let me draw one last picture before I close the notebook—a picture which is the last memory of the old country which I bear away with me. It is a wet, foggy morning in the late spring; a thin, cold rain is falling. Three shining mackintoshed figures are walking down the quay, making for the gang-plank of the great liner from which the blue-peter is flying. In front of them a porter pushes a trolley piled high with trunks, wraps, and gun-cases. Professor Summerlee, a long, melancholy figure, walks with dragging steps and drooping head, as one who is already profoundly sorry for himself. Lord John Roxton steps briskly, and his thin, eager face beams forth between his hunting-cap and his muffler. As for myself, I am glad to have got the bustling days of preparation and the pangs of leave-taking behind me, and I have no doubt that I show it in my bearing. Suddenly, just as we reach the vessel, there is a shout behind us. It is Professor Challenger, who had promised to see us off. He runs after us, a puffing, red-faced, irascible figure.

"No thank you," says he; "I should much prefer not to go aboard. I have only a few words to say to you, and they can very well be said where we are. I beg you not to imagine that I am in any way indebted to you for making this journey. I would have you to understand that it is a matter of perfect indifference to me, and I refuse to entertain the most remote sense of personal obligation. Truth is truth, and nothing which you can report can affect it in any way, though it may excite the emotions and allay the curiosity of a number of very ineffectual people. My directions for your instruction and guidance are in this sealed envelope. You will open it when you reach a town upon the Amazon which is called Manaos, but not until the date and hour which is marked upon the outside. Have I made myself clear? I leave the strict observance of my conditions entirely to your honor. No, Mr. Malone, I will place no restriction upon your correspondence, since the ventilation of the facts is the object of your journey; but I demand that you shall give no particulars as to your exact destination, and that nothing be actually published until your return. Good-bye, sir. You have done something to mitigate my feelings for the loathsome profession to which you unhappily belong. Good-bye, Lord John. Science is, as I understand, a sealed book to you; but you may congratulate yourself upon the hunting-field which awaits you. You will, no doubt, have the opportunity of describing in the Field how you brought down the rocketing dimorphodon. And good-bye to you also, Professor Summerlee. If you are still capable of self-improvement, of which I am frankly unconvinced, you will surely return to London a wiser man."

So he turned upon his heel, and a minute later from the deck I could see his short, squat figure bobbing about in the distance as he made his way back to his train. Well, we are well down Channel now. There's the last bell for letters, and it's good-bye to the pilot. We'll be "down, hull-down, on the old trail" from now on. God bless all we leave behind us, and send us safely back.

VII

"TOMORROW WE DISAPPEAR INTO THE UNKNOWN"

I will not bore those whom this narrative may reach by an account of our luxurious voyage upon the Booth liner, nor will I tell of our week's stay at Para (save that I should wish to acknowledge the great kindness of the Pereira da Pinta Company in helping us to get together our equipment). I will also allude very briefly to our river journey, up a wide, slow-moving, clay-tinted stream, in a steamer which was little smaller than that which had carried us across the Atlantic. Eventually we found ourselves through the narrows of Obidos and reached the town of Manaos. Here we were rescued from the limited attractions of the local inn by Mr. Shortman, the representative of the British and Brazilian Trading Company. In his hospital Fazenda we spent our time until the day when we were empowered to open the letter of instructions given to us by Professor Challenger. Before I reach the surprising events of that date I would desire to give a clearer sketch of my comrades in this enterprise, and of the associates whom we had already gathered together in South America. I speak freely, and I leave the use of my material to your own discretion, Mr. McArdle, since it is through your hands that this report must pass before it reaches the world.

The scientific attainments of Professor Summerlee are too well known for me to trouble to recapitulate them. He is better equipped for a rough expedition of this sort than one would imagine at first sight. His tall, gaunt, stringy figure is insensible to fatigue, and his dry, half-sarcastic, and often wholly unsympathetic manner is uninfluenced by any change in his surroundings. Though in his sixty-sixth year, I have never heard him express any dissatisfaction at the occasional hardships which we have had to encounter. I had regarded his presence as an encumbrance to the expedition, but, as a matter of fact, I am now well convinced that his power of endurance is as great as my own. In temper he is naturally acid and sceptical. From the beginning he has never concealed his belief that Professor Challenger is an absolute fraud, that we are all embarked upon an absurd wild-goose chase and that we are likely to reap nothing but disappointment and danger in South America, and corresponding ridicule in England. Such are the views which, with much passionate distortion of his thin features and wagging of his thin, goat-like beard, he poured into our ears all the way from Southampton to Manaos. Since landing from the boat he has obtained some consolation from the beauty and variety of the insect and bird life around him, for he is absolutely whole-hearted in his devotion to science. He spends his days flitting through the woods with his shotgun and his butterfly-net, and his evenings in mounting the many specimens he has acquired. Among his minor peculiarities are that he is careless as to his attire, unclean in his person, exceedingly absent-minded in his habits, and addicted to smoking a short briar pipe, which is seldom out of his mouth. He has been upon several scientific expeditions in his youth (he was with Robertson in Papua), and the life of the camp and the canoe is nothing fresh to him.

Lord John Roxton has some points in common with Professor Summerlee, and others in which they are the very antithesis to each other. He is twenty years younger, but has something of the same spare, scraggy physique. As to his appearance, I have, as I recollect, described it in that portion of my narrative which I have left behind me in London. He is exceedingly neat and prim in his ways, dresses always with great care in white drill suits and high brown mosquito-boots, and shaves at least once a day. Like most men of action, he is laconic in speech, and sinks readily into his own thoughts, but he is always quick to answer a question or join in a conversation, talking in a queer, jerky, half-humorous fashion. His knowledge of the world, and very especially of South America, is surprising, and he has a whole-hearted belief in the possibilities of our journey which is not to be dashed by the sneers of Professor Summerlee. He has a gentle voice and a quiet manner, but behind his twinkling blue eyes there lurks a capacity for furious wrath and implacable resolution, the more dangerous because they are held in leash. He spoke little of his own exploits in Brazil and Peru, but it was a revelation to me to find the excitement which was caused by his presence among the riverine natives, who looked upon him as their champion and protector. The exploits of the Red Chief, as they called him, had become legends among them, but the real facts, as far as I could learn them, were amazing enough.

These were that Lord John had found himself some years before in that no-man's-land which is formed by the half-defined frontiers between Peru,

Brazil, and Columbia. In this great district the wild rubber tree flourishes, and has become, as in the Congo, a curse to the natives which can only be compared to their forced labor under the Spaniards upon the old silver mines of Darien. A handful of villainous half-breeds dominated the country, armed such Indians as would support them, and turned the rest into slaves, terrorizing them with the most inhuman tortures in order to force them to gather the india-rubber, which was then floated down the river to Para. Lord John Roxton expostulated on behalf of the wretched victims, and received nothing but threats and insults for his pains. He then formally declared war against Pedro Lopez, the leader of the slave-drivers, enrolled a band of runaway slaves in his service, armed them, and conducted a campaign, which ended by his killing with his own hands the notorious half-breed and breaking down the system which he represented.

No wonder that the ginger-headed man with the silky voice and the free and easy manners was now looked upon with deep interest upon the banks of the great South American river, though the feelings he inspired were naturally mixed, since the gratitude of the natives was equaled by the resentment of those who desired to exploit them. One useful result of his former experiences was that he could talk fluently in the Lingoa Geral, which is the peculiar talk, one-third Portuguese and two-thirds Indian, which is current all over Brazil.

I have said before that Lord John Roxton was a South Americomaniac. He could not speak of that great country without ardor, and this ardor was infectious, for, ignorant as I was, he fixed my attention and stimulated my curiosity. How I wish I could reproduce the glamour of his discourses, the peculiar mixture of accurate knowledge and of racy imagination which gave them their fascination, until even the Professor's cynical and sceptical smile would gradually vanish from his thin face as he listened. He would tell the history of the mighty river so rapidly explored (for some of the first conquerors of Peru actually crossed the entire continent upon its waters), and yet so unknown in regard to all that lay behind its ever-changing banks.

"What is there?" he would cry, pointing to the north. "Wood and marsh and unpenetrated jungle. Who knows what it may shelter? And there to the south? A wilderness of swampy forest, where no white man has ever been. The unknown is up against us on every side. Outside the narrow lines of the rivers what does anyone know? Who will say what is possible in such a country? Why should old man Challenger not be right?" At which direct defiance the stubborn sneer would reappear upon Professor Summerlee's face, and he would sit, shaking his sardonic head in unsympathetic silence, behind the cloud of his briar-root pipe.

* * * * *

So much, for the moment, for my two white companions, whose characters and limitations will be further exposed, as surely as my own, as this narrative proceeds. But already we have enrolled certain retainers who may play no small part in what is to come. The first is a gigantic negro named Zambo, who is a black Hercules, as willing as any horse, and about as intelligent. Him we enlisted at Para, on the recommendation of the steamship company, on whose vessels he had learned to speak a halting English.

It was at Para also that we engaged Gomez and Manuel, two half-breeds from up the river, just come down with a cargo of redwood. They were swarthy fellows, bearded and fierce, as active and wiry as panthers. Both of them had spent their lives in those upper waters of the Amazon which we were about to explore, and it was this recommendation which had caused Lord John to engage them. One of them, Gomez, had the further advantage that he could speak excellent English. These men were willing to act as our personal servants, to cook, to row, or to make themselves useful in any way at a payment of fifteen dollars a month. Besides these, we had engaged three Mojo Indians from Bolivia, who are the most skilful at fishing and boat work of all the river tribes. The chief of these we called Mojo, after his tribe, and the others are known as Jose and Fernando. Three white men, then, two half-breeds, one negro, and three Indians made up the personnel of the little expedition which lay waiting for its instructions at Manaos before starting upon its singular quest.

At last, after a weary week, the day had come and the hour. I ask you to picture the shaded sitting-room of the Fazenda St. Ignatio, two miles inland from the town of Manaos. Outside lay the yellow, brassy glare of the sunshine, with the shadows of the palm trees as black and definite as the trees themselves. The air was calm, full of the eternal hum of insects, a tropical chorus of many octaves, from the deep drone of the bee to the high, keen pipe of the mosquito. Beyond the veranda was a small cleared garden, bounded with cactus hedges and adorned with clumps of flowering shrubs, round which the great blue butterflies and the tiny humming-birds fluttered and darted in crescents of sparkling light. Within we were seated round the cane table, on which lay a sealed envelope. Inscribed upon it, in the jagged handwriting of Professor Challenger, were the words:

> "Instructions to Lord John Roxton and party. To be opened at Manaos upon July 15th, at 12 o'clock precisely."

Lord John had placed his watch upon the table beside him.

"We have seven more minutes," said he. "The old dear is very precise."

Professor Summerlee gave an acid smile as he picked up the envelope in his gaunt hand.

"What can it possibly matter whether we open it now or in seven minutes?" said he. "It is all part and parcel of the same system of quackery and nonsense, for which I regret to say that the writer is notorious."

"Oh, come, we must play the game accordin' to rules," said Lord John. "It's old man Challenger's show and we are here by his good will, so it would be rotten bad form if we didn't follow his instructions to the letter."

"A pretty business it is!" cried the Professor, bitterly. "It struck me as preposterous in London, but I'm bound to say that it seems even more so upon closer acquaintance. I don't know what is inside this envelope, but, unless it is something pretty definite, I shall be much tempted to take the next down-river boat and catch the *Bolivia* at Para. After all, I have some more responsible work in the world than to run about disproving the assertions of a lunatic. Now, Roxton, surely it is time."

"Time it is," said Lord John. "You can blow the whistle." He took up the envelope and cut it with his penknife. From it he drew a folded sheet of paper. This he carefully opened out and flattened on the table. It was a blank sheet. He turned it over. Again it was blank. We looked at each other in a bewildered silence, which was broken by a discordant burst of derisive laughter from Professor Summerlee.

"It is an open admission," he cried. "What more do you want? The fellow is a self-confessed humbug. We have only to return home and report him as the brazen imposter that he is."

"Invisible ink!" I suggested.

"I don't think!" said Lord Roxton, holding the paper to the light. "No, young fellah my lad, there is no use deceiving yourself. I'll go bail for it that nothing has ever been written upon this paper."

"May I come in?" boomed a voice from the veranda.

The shadow of a squat figure had stolen across the patch of sunlight. That voice! That monstrous breadth of shoulder! We sprang to our feet with a gasp of astonishment as Challenger, in a round, boyish straw-hat with a colored ribbon—Challenger, with his hands in his jacket-pockets and his canvas shoes daintily pointing as he walked—appeared in the open space before us. He threw back his head, and there he stood in the golden glow with all his old Assyrian luxuriance of beard, all his native insolence of drooping eyelids and intolerant eyes.

"I fear," said he, taking out his watch, "that I am a few minutes too late. When I gave you this envelope I must confess that I had never intended that you should open it, for it had been my fixed intention to be with you before the hour. The unfortunate delay can be apportioned between a blundering pilot and an intrusive sandbank. I fear that it has given my colleague, Professor Summerlee, occasion to blaspheme."

"I am bound to say, sir," said Lord John, with some sternness of voice, "that your turning up is a considerable relief to us, for our mission seemed to have come to a premature end. Even now I can't for the life of me understand why you should have worked it in so extraordinary a manner."

Instead of answering, Professor Challenger entered, shook hands with myself and Lord John, bowed with ponderous insolence to Professor Summerlee, and sank back into a basket-chair, which creaked and swayed beneath his weight.

"Is all ready for your journey?" he asked.

"We can start tomorrow."

"Then so you shall. You need no chart of directions now, since you will have the inestimable advantage of my own guidance. From the first I had determined that I would myself preside over your investigation. The most elaborate charts would, as you will readily admit, be a poor substitute for my own intelligence and advice. As to the small ruse which I played upon you in the matter of the envelope, it is clear that, had I told you all my intentions, I should have been forced to resist unwelcome pressure to travel out with you."

"Not from me, sir!" exclaimed Professor Summerlee, heartily. "So long as there was another ship upon the Atlantic."

Challenger waved him away with his great hairy hand.

"Your common sense will, I am sure, sustain my objection and realize that it was better that I should direct my own movements and appear only at the exact moment when my presence was needed. That moment has now arrived. You are in safe hands. You will not now fail to reach your destination. From henceforth I take command of this expedition, and I must ask you to complete your preparations tonight, so that we may be able to make an early start in the morning. My time is of value, and the same thing may be said, no doubt, in a lesser degree of your own. I propose, therefore, that we push on as rapidly as possible, until I have demonstrated what you have come to see."

Lord John Roxton has chartered a large steam launch, the *Esmeralda*, which was to carry us up the river. So far as climate goes, it was immaterial what time we chose for our expedition, as the temperature ranges from seventy-five to ninety degrees both summer and winter, with no appreciable difference in heat. In moisture, however, it is otherwise; from December to May is the period of the rains, and during this time the river slowly rises until it attains a height of nearly forty feet above its low-water mark. It floods the banks, extends in great lagoons over a monstrous waste of country, and forms a huge district, called locally the Gapo, which is for the most part too marshy for foot-travel and too shallow for boating. About June the waters begin to fall, and are at their lowest at October or November. Thus our expedition was at the time of the dry season, when the great river and its tributaries were more or less in a normal condition.

The current of the river is a slight one, the drop being not greater than eight inches in a mile. No stream could be more convenient for navigation, since the prevailing wind is south-east, and sailing boats may make a continuous progress to the Peruvian frontier, dropping down again with the current. In our own case the excellent engines of the Esmeralda could disregard the sluggish flow of the stream, and we made as rapid progress as if we were navigating a stagnant lake. For three days we steamed north-westwards up a stream which even here, a thousand miles from its mouth, was still so enormous that from its center the two banks were mere shadows upon the distant skyline. On the fourth day after leaving Manaos we turned into a tributary which at its mouth was little smaller than the main stream. It narrowed rapidly, however, and after two more days' steaming we reached an Indian village, where the Professor insisted that we should land, and that the Esmeralda should be sent back to Manaos. We should soon come upon rapids, he explained, which would make its further use impossible. He added privately that we were now approaching the door of the unknown country, and that the fewer whom we took into our confidence the better it would be. To this end also he made each of us give our word of honor that we would publish or say nothing which would give any exact clue as to the whereabouts of our travels, while the servants were all solemnly sworn to the same effect. It is for this reason that I am compelled to be vague in my narrative, and I would warn my readers that in any map or diagram which I may give the relation of places to each other may be correct, but the points of the compass are carefully confused, so that in no way can it be taken as an actual guide to the country. Professor Challenger's reasons for secrecy may be valid or not, but we had no choice but to adopt them, for he was prepared to abandon the whole expedition rather than modify the conditions upon which he would guide us.

It was August 2nd when we snapped our last link with the outer world by bidding farewell to the *Esmeralda.* Since then four days have passed, during which we have engaged two large canoes from the Indians, made of so light a material (skins over a bamboo framework) that we should be able to carry them round any obstacle. These we have loaded with all our effects, and have engaged two additional Indians to help us in the navigation. I understand that they are the very two—Ataca and Ipetu by name—who accompanied

Professor Challenger upon his previous journey. They appeared to be terrified at the prospect of repeating it, but the chief has patriarchal powers in these countries, and if the bargain is good in his eyes the clansman has little choice in the matter.

So tomorrow we disappear into the unknown. This account I am transmitting down the river by canoe, and it may be our last word to those who are interested in our fate. I have, according to our arrangement, addressed it to you, my dear Mr. McArdle, and I leave it to your discretion to delete, alter, or do what you like with it. From the assurance of Professor Challenger's manner—and in spite of the continued scepticism of Professor Summerlee—I have no doubt that our leader will make good his statement, and that we are really on the eve of some most remarkable experiences.

VIII

"THE OUTLYING PICKETS OF THE NEW WORLD"

Our friends at home may well rejoice with us, for we are at our goal, and up to a point, at least, we have shown that the statement of Professor Challenger can be verified. We have not, it is true, ascended the plateau, but it lies before us, and even Professor Summerlee is in a more chastened mood. Not that he will for an instant admit that his rival could be right, but he is less persistent in his incessant objections, and has sunk for the most part into an observant silence. I must hark back, however, and continue my narrative from where I dropped it. We are sending home one of our local Indians who is injured, and I am committing this letter to his charge, with considerable doubts in my mind as to whether it will ever come to hand.

When I wrote last we were about to leave the Indian village where we had been deposited by the *Esmeralda.* I have to begin my report by bad news, for the first serious personal trouble (I pass over the incessant bickerings between the Professors) occurred this evening, and might have had a tragic ending. I have spoken of our English-speaking half-breed, Gomez—a fine worker and a willing fellow, but afflicted, I fancy, with the vice of curiosity, which is common enough among such men. On the last evening he seems to have hid himself near the hut in which we were discussing our plans, and, being observed by our huge negro Zambo, who is as faithful as a dog and has the hatred which all his race bear to the half-breeds, he was dragged out and carried into our presence. Gomez whipped out his knife, however, and but for the huge strength of his captor, which enabled him to disarm him with one hand, he would certainly have stabbed him. The matter has ended in reprimands, the opponents have been compelled to shake hands, and there is every hope that all will be well. As to the feuds of the two learned men, they are continuous and bitter. It must be admitted that Challenger is provocative in the last degree, but Summerlee has an acid tongue, which makes matters worse. Last night Challenger said that he never cared to walk on the Thames Embankment and look up the river, as it was always sad to see one's own eventual goal. He is convinced, of course, that he is destined for Westminster Abbey. Summerlee rejoined, however, with a sour smile, by saying that he understood that Millbank Prison had been pulled down. Challenger's conceit is too colossal to allow him to be really annoyed. He only smiled in his beard and repeated "Really! Really!" in the pitying tone one would use to a child. Indeed, they are children both—the one wizened and cantankerous, the other formidable and overbearing, yet each with a brain which has put him in the front rank of his scientific age. Brain, character, soul—only as one sees more of life does one understand how distinct is each.

The very next day we did actually make our start upon this remarkable expedition. We found that all our possessions fitted very easily into the two canoes, and we divided our personnel, six in each, taking the obvious precaution in the interests of peace of putting one Professor into each canoe. Personally, I was with Challenger, who was in a beatific humor, moving about as one in a silent ecstasy and beaming benevolence from every feature. I have had some experience of him in other moods, however, and shall be the less surprised when the thunderstorms suddenly come up amidst the sunshine. If it is impossible to be at your ease, it is equally impossible to be dull in his company, for one is always in a state of half-tremulous doubt as to what sudden turn his formidable temper may take.

For two days we made our way up a good-sized river some hundreds of yards broad, and dark in color, but transparent, so that one could usually see the bottom. The affluents of the Amazon are, half of them, of this nature, while the other half are whitish and opaque, the difference depending upon the class of country through which they have flowed. The dark indicate vegetable decay, while the others point to clayey soil. Twice we came across rapids, and in each case made a portage of half a mile or so to avoid them. The woods on either side were primeval, which are more easily penetrated than woods of the second growth, and we had no great difficulty in carrying our canoes through them. How shall I ever forget the solemn mystery of it? The height of the trees and the thickness of the boles exceeded anything which I in my town-bred life could have imagined, shooting upwards in magnificent columns until, at an enormous distance above our heads, we could dimly discern the spot where they threw out their side-branches into Gothic upward curves which coalesced to form one great matted roof of verdure, through which only an occasional golden ray of sunshine shot downwards to trace a thin dazzling line of light amidst the majestic obscurity. As we walked noiselessly amid the thick, soft carpet of decaying vegetation the hush fell upon our souls which comes upon us in the twilight of the Abbey, and even Professor Challenger's full-chested notes sank into a whisper. Alone, I should have been ignorant of the names of these giant growths, but our men of science pointed out the cedars, the great silk cotton trees, and the redwood trees, with all that profusion of various plants which has made this continent the chief supplier to the human race of those gifts of Nature which depend upon the vegetable world, while it is the most backward in those products which come from animal life. Vivid orchids and wonderful colored lichens smoldered upon the swarthy tree-trunks and where a wandering shaft of light fell full upon the golden allamanda, the scarlet star-clusters of the tacsonia, or the rich deep blue of ipomaea, the effect was as a dream of fairyland. In these great wastes of forest, life, which abhors darkness, struggles ever upwards to the light. Every plant, even the smaller ones, curls and writhes to the green surface, twining itself round its stronger and taller brethren in the effort. Climbing plants are monstrous and luxuriant, but others which have never been known to climb elsewhere learn the art as an escape from that somber shadow, so that the common nettle, the jasmine, and even the jacitara palm tree can be seen circling the stems of the cedars and striving to reach their crowns. Of animal life there was no movement amid the majestic vaulted aisles which stretched from us as we walked, but a constant movement far above our heads told of that multitudinous world of snake and monkey, bird and sloth, which lived in the sunshine, and looked down in wonder at our tiny, dark, stumbling figures in the obscure depths immeasurably below them. At dawn and at sunset the howler monkeys screamed together and the parakeets broke into shrill chatter, but during the hot hours of the day only the full drone of insects, like the beat of a distant surf, filled the ear, while nothing moved amid the solemn vistas of stupendous trunks, fading away into the darkness which held us in. Once some bandy-legged, lurching creature, an anteater or a bear, scuttled clumsily amid the shadows. It was the only sign of earth life which I saw in this great Amazonian forest.

And yet there were indications that even human life itself was not far from us in those mysterious recesses. On the third day out we were aware of a singular deep throbbing in the air, rhythmic and solemn, coming and going fitfully throughout the morning. The two boats were paddling within a few yards of each other when first we heard it, and our Indians remained motionless, as if they had been turned to bronze, listening intently with expressions of terror upon their faces.

"What is it, then?" I asked.

"Drums," said Lord John, carelessly; "war drums. I have heard them before."

"Yes, sir, war drums," said Gomez, the half-breed. "Wild Indians, bravos, not mansos; they watch us every mile of the way; kill us if they can."

"How can they watch us?" I asked, gazing into the dark, motionless void.

The half-breed shrugged his broad shoulders.

"The Indians know. They have their own way. They watch us. They talk the drum talk to each other. Kill us if they can."

By the afternoon of that day—my pocket diary shows me that it was Tuesday, August 18th—at least six or seven drums were throbbing from various points. Sometimes they beat quickly, sometimes slowly, sometimes in obvious question and answer, one far to the east breaking out in a high staccato rattle, and being followed after a pause by a deep roll from the north. There was something indescribably nerve-shaking and menacing in that constant mutter, which seemed to shape itself into the very syllables of the half-breed, endlessly repeated, "We will kill you if we can. We will kill you if we can." No one ever moved in the silent woods. All the peace and soothing of quiet Nature lay in that dark curtain of vegetation, but away from behind there came ever the one message from our fellow-man. "We will kill you if we can," said the men in the east. "We will kill you if we can," said the men in the north.

All day the drums rumbled and whispered, while their menace reflected itself in the faces of our colored companions. Even the hardy, swaggering half-breed seemed cowed. I learned, however, that day once for all that both Summerlee and Challenger possessed that highest type of bravery, the bravery of the scientific mind. Theirs was the spirit which upheld Darwin among the gauchos of the Argentine or Wallace among the head-hunters of Malaya. It is decreed by a merciful Nature that the human brain cannot think of two things simultaneously, so that if it be steeped in curiosity as to science it has no room for merely personal considerations. All day amid that incessant and mysterious menace our two Professors watched every bird upon the wing, and every shrub upon the bank, with many a sharp wordy contention, when the snarl of Summerlee came quick upon the deep growl of Challenger, but with no more sense of danger and no more reference to drum-beating Indians than if they were seated together in the smoking-room of the Royal Society's Club in St. James's Street. Once only did they condescend to discuss them.

"Miranha or Amajuaca cannibals," said Challenger, jerking his thumb towards the reverberating wood.

"No doubt, sir," Summerlee answered. "Like all such tribes, I shall expect to find them of polysynthetic speech and of Mongolian type."

"Polysynthetic certainly," said Challenger, indulgently. "I am not aware that any other type of language exists in this continent, and I have notes of more than a hundred. The Mongolian theory I regard with deep suspicion."

"I should have thought that even a limited knowledge of comparative anatomy would have helped to verify it," said Summerlee, bitterly.

Challenger thrust out his aggressive chin until he was all beard and hat-rim. "No doubt, sir, a limited knowledge would have that effect. When one's knowledge is exhaustive, one comes to other conclusions." They glared at each other in mutual defiance, while all round rose the distant whisper, "We will kill you—we will kill you if we can."

That night we moored our canoes with heavy stones for anchors in the center of the stream, and made every preparation for a possible attack. Nothing came, however, and with the dawn we pushed upon our way, the drum-beating dying out behind us. About three o'clock in the afternoon we came to a very steep rapid, more than a mile long—the very one in which Professor Challenger had suffered disaster upon his first journey. I confess that the sight of it consoled me, for it was really the first direct corroboration, slight as it was, of the truth of his story. The Indians carried first our canoes and then our stores through the brushwood, which is very thick at this point, while we four whites, our rifles on our shoulders, walked between them and any danger coming from the woods. Before evening we had successfully passed the rapids, and made our way some ten miles above them, where we anchored for the night. At this point I reckoned that we had come not less than a hundred miles up the tributary from the main stream.

It was in the early forenoon of the next day that we made the great departure. Since dawn Professor Challenger had been acutely uneasy, continually scanning each bank of the river. Suddenly he gave an exclamation of satisfaction and pointed to a single tree, which projected at a peculiar angle over the side of the stream.

"What do you make of that?" he asked.

"It is surely an Assai palm," said Summerlee.

"Exactly. It was an Assai palm which I took for my landmark. The secret opening is half a mile onwards upon the other side of the river. There is no break in the trees. That is the wonder and the mystery of it. There where you see light-green rushes instead of dark-green undergrowth, there between the great cotton woods, that is my private gate into the unknown. Push through, and you will understand."

It was indeed a wonderful place. Having reached the spot marked by a line of light-green rushes, we poled out two canoes through them for some hundreds of yards, and eventually emerged into a placid and shallow stream, running clear and transparent over a sandy bottom. It may have been twenty yards across, and was banked in on each side by most luxuriant vegetation. No one who had not observed that for a short distance reeds had taken the place of shrubs, could possibly have guessed the existence of such a stream or dreamed of the fairyland beyond.

For a fairyland it was—the most wonderful that the imagination of man could conceive. The thick vegetation met overhead, interlacing into a natural pergola, and through this tunnel of verdure in a golden twilight flowed the green, pellucid river, beautiful in itself, but marvelous from the strange tints thrown by the vivid light from above filtered and tempered in its fall. Clear as crystal, motionless as a sheet of glass, green as the edge of an iceberg, it stretched in front of us under its leafy archway, every stroke of our paddles sending a thousand ripples across its shining surface. It was a fitting avenue to a land of wonders. All sign of the Indians had passed away, but animal life was more frequent, and the tameness of the creatures showed that they knew nothing of the hunter. Fuzzy little black-velvet monkeys, with snow-white teeth and gleaming, mocking eyes, chattered at us as we passed. With a dull, heavy splash an occasional caiman plunged in from the bank. Once a dark, clumsy tapir stared at us from a gap in the bushes, and then lumbered away through the forest; once, too, the yellow, sinuous form of a great puma whisked amid the brushwood, and its green, baleful eyes glared hatred at us over its tawny shoulder. Bird life was abundant, especially the wading birds, stork, heron, and ibis gathering in little groups, blue, scarlet, and white, upon every log which jutted from the bank, while beneath us the crystal water was alive with fish of every shape and color.

For three days we made our way up this tunnel of hazy green sunshine. On the longer stretches one could hardly tell as one looked ahead where the distant green water ended and the distant green archway began. The deep peace of this strange waterway was unbroken by any sign of man.

"No Indian here. Too much afraid. Curupuri," said Gomez.

"Curupuri is the spirit of the woods," Lord John explained. "It's a name for any kind of devil. The poor beggars think that there is something fearsome in this direction, and therefore they avoid it."

On the third day it became evident that our journey in the canoes could not last much longer, for the stream was rapidly growing more shallow. Twice in as many hours we stuck upon the bottom. Finally we pulled the boats up among the brushwood and spent the night on the bank of the river. In the morning Lord John and I made our way for a couple of miles through the forest, keeping parallel with the stream; but as it grew ever shallower we returned and reported, what Professor Challenger had already suspected, that we had reached the highest point to which the canoes could be brought. We drew them up, therefore, and concealed them among the bushes, blazing a tree with our axes, so that we should find them again. Then we distributed the various burdens among us—guns, ammunition, food, a tent, blankets, and the rest—and, shouldering our packages, we set forth upon the more laborious stage of our journey.

An unfortunate quarrel between our pepper-pots marked the outset of our new stage. Challenger had from the moment of joining us issued directions to the whole party, much to the evident discontent of Summerlee. Now, upon his assigning some duty to his fellow-Professor (it was only the carrying of an aneroid barometer), the matter suddenly came to a head.

"May I ask, sir," said Summerlee, with vicious calm, "in what capacity you take it upon yourself to issue these orders?"

Challenger glared and bristled.

"I do it, Professor Summerlee, as leader of this expedition."

"I am compelled to tell you, sir, that I do not recognize you in that capacity."

"Indeed!" Challenger bowed with unwieldy sarcasm. "Perhaps you would define my exact position."

"Yes, sir. You are a man whose veracity is upon trial, and this committee is here to try it. You walk, sir, with your judges."

"Dear me!" said Challenger, seating himself on the side of one of the canoes. "In that case you will, of course, go on your way, and I will follow at my leisure. If I am not the leader you cannot expect me to lead."

Thank heaven that there were two sane men—Lord John Roxton and myself—to prevent the petulance and folly of our learned Professors from sending us back empty-handed to London. Such arguing and pleading and explaining before we could get them mollified! Then at last Summerlee, with his sneer and his pipe, would move forwards, and Challenger would come rolling and grumbling after. By some good fortune we discovered about this time that both our savants had the very poorest opinion of Dr. Illingworth of Edinburgh. Thenceforward that was our one safety, and every strained situation was relieved by our introducing the name of the Scotch zoologist, when both our Professors would form a temporary alliance and friendship in their detestation and abuse of this common rival.

Advancing in single file along the bank of the stream, we soon found that it narrowed down to a mere brook, and finally that it lost itself in a great green morass of sponge-like mosses, into which we sank up to our knees. The place was horribly haunted by clouds of mosquitoes and every form of flying pest, so we were glad to find solid ground again and to make a circuit among the trees, which enabled us to outflank this pestilent morass, which droned like an organ in the distance, so loud was it with insect life.

On the second day after leaving our canoes we found that the whole character of the country changed. Our road was persistently upwards, and as we ascended the woods became thinner and lost their tropical luxuriance. The huge trees of the alluvial Amazonian plain gave place to the Phoenix and coco palms, growing in scattered clumps, with thick brushwood between. In the damper hollows the Mauritia palms threw out their graceful drooping fronds. We traveled entirely by compass, and once or twice there were differences of opinion between Challenger and the two Indians, when, to quote the Professor's indignant words, the whole party agreed to "trust the fallacious instincts of undeveloped savages rather than the highest product of modern European culture." That we were justified in doing so was shown upon the third day, when Challenger admitted that he recognized several landmarks of his former journey, and in one spot we actually came upon four fire-blackened stones, which must have marked a camping-place.

The road still ascended, and we crossed a rock-studded slope which took two days to traverse. The vegetation had again changed, and only the vegetable ivory tree remained, with a great profusion of wonderful orchids, among which I learned to recognize the rare *Nuttonia Vexillaria* and the glorious pink and scarlet blossoms of Cattleya and odontoglossum. Occasional brooks with pebbly bottoms and fern-draped banks gurgled down the shallow gorges in the hill, and offered good camping-grounds every evening on the banks of some rock-studded pool, where swarms of little blue-backed fish, about the size and shape of English trout, gave us a delicious supper.

On the ninth day after leaving the canoes, having done, as I reckon, about a hundred and twenty miles, we began to emerge from the trees, which had grown smaller until they were mere shrubs. Their place was taken by an immense wilderness of bamboo, which grew so thickly that we could only penetrate it by cutting a pathway with the machetes and billhooks of the Indians. It took us a long day, traveling from seven in the morning till eight at night, with only two breaks of one hour each, to get through this obstacle. Anything more monotonous and wearying could not be imagined, for, even at the most open places, I could not see more than ten or twelve yards, while usually my vision was limited to the back of Lord John's cotton jacket in front of me, and to the yellow wall within a foot of me on either side. From above came one thin knife-edge of sunshine, and fifteen feet over our heads one saw the tops of the reeds swaying against the deep blue sky. I do not know what kind of creatures inhabit such a thicket, but several times we heard the plunging of large, heavy animals quite close to us. From their sounds Lord John judged them to be some form of wild cattle. Just as night fell we cleared the belt of bamboos, and at once formed our camp, exhausted by the interminable day.

Early next morning we were again afoot, and found that the character of the country had changed once again. Behind us was the wall of bamboo, as definite as if it marked the course of a river. In front was an open plain, sloping slightly upwards and dotted with clumps of tree-ferns, the whole curving before us until it ended in a long, whale-backed ridge. This we reached about midday, only to find a shallow valley beyond, rising once again into a gentle incline which led to a low, rounded sky-line. It was here, while we crossed the first of these hills, that an incident occurred which may or may not have been important.

Professor Challenger, who with the two local Indians was in the van of the party, stopped suddenly and pointed excitedly to the right. As he did so we saw, at the distance of a mile or so, something which appeared to be a huge gray bird flap slowly up from the ground and skim smoothly off, flying very low and straight, until it was lost among the tree-ferns.

"Did you see it?" cried Challenger, in exultation. "Summerlee, did you see it?"

His colleague was staring at the spot where the creature had disappeared.

"What do you claim that it was?" he asked.

"To the best of my belief, a pterodactyl."

Summerlee burst into derisive laughter "A pter-fiddlestick!" said he. "It was a stork, if ever I saw one."

Challenger was too furious to speak. He simply swung his pack upon his back and continued upon his march. Lord John came abreast of me, however, and his face was more grave than was his wont. He had his Zeiss glasses in his hand.

"I focused it before it got over the trees," said he. "I won't undertake to say what it was, but I'll risk my reputation as a sportsman that it wasn't any bird that ever I clapped eyes on in my life."

So there the matter stands. Are we really just at the edge of the unknown, encountering the outlying pickets of this lost world of which our leader speaks? I give you the incident as it occurred and you will know as much as I do. It stands alone, for we saw nothing more which could be called remarkable.

And now, my readers, if ever I have any, I have brought you up the broad river, and through the screen of rushes, and down the green tunnel, and up the long slope of palm trees, and through the bamboo brake, and across the plain of tree-ferns. At last our destination lay in full sight of us. When we had crossed the second ridge we saw before us an irregular, palm-studded plain, and then the line of high red cliffs which I have seen in the picture. There it lies, even as I write, and there can be no question that it is the same.

At the nearest point it is about seven miles from our present camp, and it curves away, stretching as far as I can see. Challenger struts about like a prize peacock, and Summerlee is silent, but still sceptical. Another day should bring some of our doubts to an end. Meanwhile, as Jose, whose arm was pierced by a broken bamboo, insists upon returning, I send this letter back in his charge, and only hope that it may eventually come to hand. I will write again as the occasion serves. I have enclosed with this a rough chart of our journey, which may have the effect of making the account rather easier to understand.

IX

"WHO COULD HAVE FORESEEN IT?"

A dreadful thing has happened to us. Who could have foreseen it? I cannot foresee any end to our troubles. It may be that we are condemned to spend our whole lives in this strange, inaccessible place. I am still so confused that I can hardly think clearly of the facts of the present or of the chances of the future. To my astounded senses the one seems most terrible and the other as black as night.

No men have ever found themselves in a worse position; nor is there any use in disclosing to you our exact geographical situation and asking our friends for a relief party. Even if they could send one, our fate will in all human probability be decided long before it could arrive in South America.

We are, in truth, as far from any human aid as if we were in the moon. If we are to win through, it is only our own qualities which can save us. I have as companions three remarkable men, men of great brain-power and of unshaken courage. There lies our one and only hope. It is only when I look upon the untroubled faces of my comrades that I see some glimmer through the darkness. Outwardly I trust that I appear as unconcerned as they. Inwardly I am filled with apprehension.

Let me give you, with as much detail as I can, the sequence of events which have led us to this catastrophe.

When I finished my last letter I stated that we were within seven miles from an enormous line of ruddy cliffs, which encircled, beyond all doubt, the plateau of which Professor Challenger spoke. Their height, as we approached them, seemed to me in some places to be greater than he had stated—running up in parts to at least a thousand feet—and they were curiously striated, in a manner which is, I believe, characteristic of basaltic upheavals. Something of the sort is to be seen in Salisbury Crags at Edinburgh. The summit showed every sign of a luxuriant vegetation, with bushes near the edge, and farther back many high trees. There was no indication of any life that we could see.

That night we pitched our camp immediately under the cliff—a most wild and desolate spot. The crags above us were not merely perpendicular, but curved outwards at the top, so that ascent was out of the question. Close to us was the high thin pinnacle of rock which I believe I mentioned earlier in this narrative. It is like a broad red church spire, the top of it being level with the plateau, but a great chasm gaping between. On the summit of it there grew one high tree. Both pinnacle and cliff were comparatively low—some five or six hundred feet, I should think.

"It was on that," said Professor Challenger, pointing to this tree, "that the pterodactyl was perched. I climbed halfway up the rock before I shot him. I am inclined to think that a good mountaineer like myself could ascend the rock to the top, though he would, of course, be no nearer to the plateau when he had done so."

As Challenger spoke of his pterodactyl I glanced at Professor Summerlee, and for the first time I seemed to see some signs of a dawning credulity and repentance. There was no sneer upon his thin lips, but, on the contrary, a gray, drawn look of excitement and amazement. Challenger saw it, too, and reveled in the first taste of victory.

"Of course," said he, with his clumsy and ponderous sarcasm, "Professor Summerlee will understand that when I speak of a pterodactyl I mean a stork—only it is the kind of stork which has no feathers, a leathery skin, membranous wings, and teeth in its jaws." He grinned and blinked and bowed until his colleague turned and walked away.

In the morning, after a frugal breakfast of coffee and manioc—we had to be economical of our stores—we held a council of war as to the best method of ascending to the plateau above us.

Challenger presided with a solemnity as if he were the Lord Chief Justice on the Bench. Picture him seated upon a rock, his absurd boyish straw hat tilted on the back of his head, his supercilious eyes dominating us from under his drooping lids, his great black beard wagging as he slowly defined our present situation and our future movements.

Beneath him you might have seen the three of us—myself, sunburnt, young, and vigorous after our open-air tramp; Summerlee, solemn but still critical, behind his eternal pipe; Lord John, as keen as a razor-edge, with his supple, alert figure leaning upon his rifle, and his eager eyes fixed eagerly upon the speaker. Behind us were grouped the two swarthy half-breeds and the little knot of Indians, while in front and above us towered those huge, ruddy ribs of rocks which kept us from our goal.

"I need not say," said our leader, "that on the occasion of my last visit I exhausted every means of climbing the cliff, and where I failed I do not think that anyone else is likely to succeed, for I am something of a mountaineer. I had none of the appliances of a rock-climber with me, but I have taken the precaution to bring them now. With their aid I am positive I could climb that detached pinnacle to the summit; but so long as the main cliff overhangs, it is vain to attempt ascending that. I was hurried upon my last visit by the approach of the rainy season and by the exhaustion of my supplies. These considerations limited my time, and I can only claim that I have surveyed about six miles of the cliff to the east of us, finding no possible way up. What, then, shall we now do?"

"There seems to be only one reasonable course," said Professor Summerlee. "If you have explored the east, we should travel along the base of the cliff to the west, and seek for a practicable point for our ascent."

"That's it," said Lord John. "The odds are that this plateau is of no great size, and we shall travel round it until we either find an easy way up it, or come back to the point from which we started."

"I have already explained to our young friend here," said Challenger (he has a way of alluding to me as if I were a school child ten years old), "that it is quite impossible that there should be an easy way up anywhere, for the simple reason that if there were the summit would not be isolated, and those conditions would not obtain which have effected so singular an interference with the general laws of survival. Yet I admit that there may very well be places where an expert human climber may reach the summit, and yet a cumbrous and heavy animal be unable to descend. It is certain that there is a point where an ascent is possible."

"How do you know that, sir?" asked Summerlee, sharply.

"Because my predecessor, the American Maple White, actually made such an ascent. How otherwise could he have seen the monster which he sketched in his notebook?"

"There you reason somewhat ahead of the proved facts," said the stubborn Summerlee. "I admit your plateau, because I have seen it; but I have not as yet satisfied myself that it contains any form of life whatever."

"What you admit, sir, or what you do not admit, is really of inconceivably small importance. I am glad to perceive that the plateau itself has actually obtruded itself upon your intelligence." He glanced up at it, and then, to our amazement, he sprang from his rock, and, seizing Summerlee by the neck, he tilted his face into the air. "Now sir!" he shouted, hoarse with excitement. "Do I help you to realize that the plateau contains some animal life?"

I have said that a thick fringe of green overhung the edge of the cliff. Out of this there had emerged a black, glistening object. As it came slowly forth and overhung the chasm, we saw that it was a very large snake with a peculiar flat, spade-like head. It wavered and quivered above us for a minute, the morning sun gleaming upon its sleek, sinuous coils. Then it slowly drew inwards and disappeared.

Summerlee had been so interested that he had stood unresisting while Challenger tilted his head into the air. Now he shook his colleague off and came back to his dignity.

"I should be glad, Professor Challenger," said he, "if you could see your way to make any remarks which may occur to you without seizing me by the chin. Even the appearance of a very ordinary rock python does not appear to justify such a liberty."

"But there is life upon the plateau all the same," his colleague replied in triumph. "And now, having demonstrated this important conclusion so that it is clear to anyone, however prejudiced or obtuse, I am of opinion that we cannot do better than break up our camp and travel to westward until we find some means of ascent."

The ground at the foot of the cliff was rocky and broken so that the going was slow and difficult. Suddenly we came, however, upon something which cheered our hearts. It was the site of an old encampment, with several empty Chicago meat tins, a bottle labeled "Brandy," a broken tin-opener, and a quantity of other travelers' *débris.* A crumpled, disintegrated newspaper revealed itself as the *Chicago Democrat*, though the date had been obliterated.

"Not mine," said Challenger. "It must be Maple White's."

Lord John had been gazing curiously at a great tree-fern which overshadowed the encampment. "I say, look at this," said he. "I believe it is meant for a sign-post."

A slip of hard wood had been nailed to the tree in such a way as to point to the westward.

"Most certainly a sign-post," said Challenger. "What else? Finding himself upon a dangerous errand, our pioneer has left this sign so that any party which follows him may know the way he has taken. Perhaps we shall come upon some other indications as we proceed."

We did indeed, but they were of a terrible and most unexpected nature. Immediately beneath the cliff there grew a considerable patch of high bamboo, like that which we had traversed in our journey. Many of these stems were twenty feet high, with sharp, strong tops, so that even as they stood they made formidable spears. We were passing along the edge of this cover when my eye was caught by the gleam of something white within it. Thrusting in my head between the stems, I found myself gazing at a fleshless skull. The whole skeleton was there, but the skull had detached itself and lay some feet nearer to the open.

With a few blows from the machetes of our Indians we cleared the spot and were able to study the details of this old tragedy. Only a few shreds of clothes could still be distinguished, but there were the remains of boots upon the bony feet, and it was very clear that the dead man was a European. A gold watch by Hudson, of New York, and a chain which held a stylographic pen, lay among the bones. There was also a silver cigarette-case, with "J. C., from A. E. S.," upon the lid. The state of the metal seemed to show that the catastrophe had occurred no great time before.

"Who can he be?" asked Lord John. "Poor devil! Every bone in his body seems to be broken."

"And the bamboo grows through his smashed ribs," said Summerlee. "It is a fast-growing plant, but it is surely inconceivable that this body could have been here while the canes grew to be twenty feet in length."

"As to the man's identity," said Professor Challenger, "I have no doubt whatever upon that point. As I made my way up the river before I reached you at the fazenda I instituted very particular inquiries about Maple White. At Para they knew nothing. Fortunately, I had a definite clue, for there was a particular picture in his sketchbook which showed him taking lunch with a certain ecclesiastic at Rosario. This priest I was able to find, and though he proved a very argumentative fellow, who took it absurdly amiss that I should point out to him the corrosive effect which modern science must have upon his beliefs, he nonetheless gave me some positive information. Maple White passed Rosario four years ago, or two years before I saw his dead body. He was not alone at the time, but there was a friend, an American named James Colver, who remained in the boat and did not meet this ecclesiastic. I think, therefore, that there can be no doubt that we are now looking upon the remains of this James Colver."

"Nor," said Lord John, "is there much doubt as to how he met his death. He has fallen or been chucked from the top, and so been impaled. How else could he come by his broken bones, and how could he have been stuck through by these canes with their points so high above our heads?"

A hush came over us as we stood round these shattered remains and realized the truth of Lord John Roxton's words. The beetling head of the cliff projected over the cane-brake. Undoubtedly he had fallen from above. But *had* he fallen? Had it been an accident? Or—already ominous and terrible possibilities began to form round that unknown land.

We moved off in silence, and continued to coast round the line of cliffs, which were as even and unbroken as some of those monstrous Antarctic ice-fields which I have seen depicted as stretching from horizon to horizon and towering high above the mast-heads of the exploring vessel.

* * * * *

In five miles we saw no rift or break. And then suddenly we perceived something which filled us with new hope. In a hollow of the rock, protected from rain, there was drawn a rough arrow in chalk, pointing still to the westwards.

"Maple White again," said Professor Challenger. "He had some presentiment that worthy footsteps would follow close behind him."

"He had chalk, then?"

"A box of colored chalks was among the effects I found in his knapsack. I remember that the white one was worn to a stump."

"That is certainly good evidence," said Summerlee. "We can only accept his guidance and follow on to the westward."

We had proceeded some five more miles when again we saw a white arrow upon the rocks. It was at a point where the face of the cliff was for the first time split into a narrow cleft. Inside the cleft was a second guidance mark, which pointed right up it with the tip somewhat elevated, as if the spot indicated were above the level of the ground.

It was a solemn place, for the walls were so gigantic and the slit of blue sky so narrow and so obscured by a double fringe of verdure, that only a dim and shadowy light penetrated to the bottom. We had had no food for many hours, and were very weary with the stony and irregular journey, but our nerves were too strung to allow us to halt. We ordered the camp to be pitched, however, and, leaving the Indians to arrange it, we four, with the two half-breeds, proceeded up the narrow gorge.

It was not more than forty feet across at the mouth, but it rapidly closed until it ended in an acute angle, too straight and smooth for an ascent. Certainly it was not this which our pioneer had attempted to indicate. We made our way back—the whole gorge was not more than a quarter of a mile deep—and then suddenly the quick eyes of Lord John fell upon what we were seeking. High up above our heads, amid the dark shadows, there was one circle of deeper gloom. Surely it could only be the opening of a cave.

The base of the cliff was heaped with loose stones at the spot, and it was not difficult to clamber up. When we reached it, all doubt was removed. Not only was it an opening into the rock, but on the side of it there was marked once again the sign of the arrow. Here was the point, and this the means by which Maple White and his ill-fated comrade had made their ascent.

We were too excited to return to the camp, but must make our first exploration at once. Lord John had an electric torch in his knapsack, and this had to serve us as light. He advanced, throwing his little clear circlet of yellow radiance before him, while in single file we followed at his heels.

The cave had evidently been water-worn, the sides being smooth and the floor covered with rounded stones. It was of such a size that a single man could just fit through by stooping. For fifty yards it ran almost straight into the rock, and then it ascended at an angle of forty-five. Presently this incline became even steeper, and we found ourselves climbing upon hands and knees among loose rubble which slid from beneath us. Suddenly an exclamation broke from Lord Roxton.

"It's blocked!" said he.

Clustering behind him we saw in the yellow field of light a wall of broken basalt which extended to the ceiling.

"The roof has fallen in!"

In vain we dragged out some of the pieces. The only effect was that the larger ones became detached and threatened to roll down the gradient and crush us. It was evident that the obstacle was far beyond any efforts which we could make to remove it. The road by which Maple White had ascended was no longer available.

Too much cast down to speak, we stumbled down the dark tunnel and made our way back to the camp.

One incident occurred, however, before we left the gorge, which is of importance in view of what came afterwards.

We had gathered in a little group at the bottom of the chasm, some forty feet beneath the mouth of the cave, when a huge rock rolled suddenly downwards—and shot past us with tremendous force. It was the narrowest escape for one or all of us. We could not ourselves see whence the rock had come, but our half-breed servants, who were still at the opening of the cave, said that it had flown past them, and must therefore have fallen from the summit. Looking upwards, we could see no sign of movement above us amidst the green jungle which topped the cliff. There could be little doubt, however, that the stone was aimed at us, so the incident surely pointed to humanity—and malevolent humanity—upon the plateau.

We withdrew hurriedly from the chasm, our minds full of this new development and its bearing upon our plans. The situation was difficult enough before, but if the obstructions of Nature were increased by the deliberate opposition of man, then our case was indeed a hopeless one. And yet, as we looked up at that beautiful fringe of verdure only a few hundreds of feet above our heads, there was not one of us who could conceive the idea of returning to London until we had explored it to its depths.

On discussing the situation, we determined that our best course was to continue to coast round the plateau in the hope of finding some other means of reaching the top. The line of cliffs, which had decreased considerably in height, had already begun to trend from west to north, and if we could take this as representing the arc of a circle, the whole circumference could not be very great. At the worst, then, we should be back in a few days at our starting-point.

We made a march that day which totaled some two-and-twenty miles, without any change in our prospects. I may mention that our aneroid shows us that in the continual incline which we have ascended since we abandoned our canoes we have risen to no less than three thousand feet above sea-level. Hence there is a considerable change both in the temperature and in the vegetation. We have shaken off some of that horrible insect life which is the bane of tropical travel. A few palms still survive, and many tree-ferns, but the Amazonian trees have been all left behind. It was pleasant to see the convolvulus, the passionflower, and the begonia, all reminding me of home, here among these inhospitable rocks. There was a red begonia just the same color as one that is kept in a pot in the window of a certain villa in Streatham—but I am drifting into private reminiscence.

That night—I am still speaking of the first day of our circumnavigation of the plateau—a great experience awaited us, and one which forever set at rest any doubt which we could have had as to the wonders so near us.

You will realize as you read it, my dear Mr. McArdle, and possibly for the first time that the paper has not sent me on a wild-goose chase, and that there is inconceivably fine copy waiting for the world whenever we have the Professor's leave to make use of it. I shall not dare to publish these articles unless I can bring back my proofs to England, or I shall be hailed as the journalistic Munchausen of all time. I have no doubt that you feel the same way yourself, and that you would not care to stake the whole credit of the *Gazette* upon this adventure until we can meet the chorus of criticism and scepticism which such articles must of necessity elicit. So this wonderful incident, which would make such a headline for the old paper, must still wait its turn in the editorial drawer.

And yet it was all over in a flash, and there was no sequel to it, save in our own convictions.

What occurred was this. Lord John had shot an ajouti—which is a small, pig-like animal—and, half of it having been given to the Indians, we were cooking the other half upon our fire. There is a chill in the air after dark, and we had all drawn close to the blaze. The night was moonless, but there were some stars, and one could see for a little distance across the plain. Well, suddenly out of the darkness, out of the night, there swooped something with a swish like an aeroplane. The whole group of us were covered for an instant by a canopy of leathery wings, and I had a momentary vision of a long, snake-like neck, a fierce, red, greedy eye, and a great snapping beak, filled, to my amazement, with little, gleaming teeth. The next instant it was gone—and so was our dinner. A huge black shadow, twenty feet across, skimmed up into the air; for an instant the monster wings blotted out the stars, and then it vanished over the brow of the cliff above us. We all sat in amazed silence round the fire, like the heroes of Virgil when the Harpies came down upon them. It was Summerlee who was the first to speak.

"Professor Challenger," said he, in a solemn voice, which quavered with emotion, "I owe you an apology. Sir, I am very much in the wrong, and I beg that you will forget what is past."

It was handsomely said, and the two men for the first time shook hands. So much we have gained by this clear vision of our first pterodactyl. It was worth a stolen supper to bring two such men together.

But if prehistoric life existed upon the plateau it was not superabundant, for we had no further glimpse of it during the next three days. During this time we traversed a barren and forbidding country, which alternated between stony desert and desolate marshes full of many wildfowl, upon the north and east of the cliffs. From that direction the place is really inaccessible, and, were it not for a hardish ledge which runs at the very base of the precipice, we should have had to turn back. Many times we were up to our waists in the slime and blubber of an old, semi-tropical swamp. To make matters worse, the place seemed to be a favorite breeding-place of the Jaracaca snake, the most venomous and aggressive in South America. Again and again these horrible creatures came writhing and springing towards us across the surface of this putrid bog, and it was only by keeping our shotguns forever ready that we could feel safe from them. One funnel-shaped depression in the morass, of a livid green in color from some lichen which festered in it, will always remain as a nightmare memory in my mind. It seems to have been a special nest of these vermins, and the slopes were alive with them, all writhing in our direction, for it is a peculiarity of the Jaracaca that he will always attack man at first sight. There were too many for us to shoot, so we fairly took to our heels and ran until we were exhausted. I shall always remember as we looked back how far behind we could see the heads and necks of our horrible pursuers rising and falling amid the reeds. Jaracaca Swamp we named it in the map which we are constructing.

The cliffs upon the farther side had lost their ruddy tint, being chocolate-brown in color; the vegetation was more scattered along the top of them, and they had sunk to three or four hundred feet in height, but in no place did we find any point where they could be ascended. If anything, they were more impossible than at the first point where we had met them. Their absolute steepness is indicated in the photograph which I took over the stony desert.

"Surely," said I, as we discussed the situation, "the rain must find its way down somehow. There are bound to be water-channels in the rocks."

"Our young friend has glimpses of lucidity," said Professor Challenger, patting me upon the shoulder.

"The rain must go somewhere," I repeated.

"He keeps a firm grip upon actuality. The only drawback is that we have conclusively proved by ocular demonstration that there are no water channels down the rocks."

"Where, then, does it go?" I persisted.

"I think it may be fairly assumed that if it does not come outwards it must run inwards."

"Then there is a lake in the center."

"So I should suppose."

"It is more than likely that the lake may be an old crater," said Summerlee. "The whole formation is, of course, highly volcanic. But, however that may be, I should expect to find the surface of the plateau slope inwards with a considerable sheet of water in the center, which may drain off, by some subterranean channel, into the marshes of the Jaracaca Swamp."

"Or evaporation might preserve an equilibrium," remarked Challenger, and the two learned men wandered off into one of their usual scientific arguments, which were as comprehensible as Chinese to the layman.

On the sixth day we completed our first circuit of the cliffs, and found ourselves back at the first camp, beside the isolated pinnacle of rock. We were a disconsolate party, for nothing could have been more minute than our investigation, and it was absolutely certain that there was no single point where the most active human being could possibly hope to scale the cliff. The place which Maple White's chalk-marks had indicated as his own means of access was now entirely impassable.

What were we to do now? Our stores of provisions, supplemented by our guns, were holding out well, but the day must come when they would need replenishment. In a couple of months the rains might be expected, and we should be washed out of our camp. The rock was harder than marble, and any attempt at cutting a path for so great a height was more than our time or resources would admit. No wonder that we looked gloomily at each other that night, and sought our blankets with hardly a word exchanged. I remember that as I dropped off to sleep my last recollection was that Challenger was squatting, like a monstrous bull-frog, by the fire, his huge head in his hands, sunk apparently in the deepest thought, and entirely oblivious to the good-night which I wished him.

But it was a very different Challenger who greeted us in the morning—a

Challenger with contentment and self-congratulation shining from his whole person. He faced us as we assembled for breakfast with a deprecating false modesty in his eyes, as who should say, "I know that I deserve all that you can say, but I pray you to spare my blushes by not saying it." His beard bristled exultantly, his chest was thrown out, and his hand was thrust into the front of his jacket. So, in his fancy, may he see himself sometimes, gracing the vacant pedestal in Trafalgar Square, and adding one more to the horrors of the London streets.

"Eureka!" he cried, his teeth shining through his beard. "Gentlemen, you may congratulate me and we may congratulate each other. The problem is solved."

"You have found a way up?"

"I venture to think so."

"And where?"

For answer he pointed to the spire-like pinnacle upon our right.

Our faces—or mine, at least—fell as we surveyed it. That it could be climbed we had our companion's assurance. But a horrible abyss lay between it and the plateau.

"We can never get across," I gasped.

"We can at least all reach the summit," said he. "When we are up I may be able to show you that the resources of an inventive mind are not yet exhausted."

After breakfast we unpacked the bundle in which our leader had brought his climbing accessories. From it he took a coil of the strongest and lightest rope, a hundred and fifty feet in length, with climbing irons, clamps, and other devices. Lord John was an experienced mountaineer, and Summerlee had done some rough climbing at various times, so that I was really the novice at rock-work of the party; but my strength and activity may have made up for my want of experience.

It was not in reality a very stiff task, though there were moments which made my hair bristle upon my head. The first half was perfectly easy, but from there upwards it became continually steeper until, for the last fifty feet, we were literally clinging with our fingers and toes to tiny ledges and crevices in the rock. I could not have accomplished it, nor could Summerlee, if Challenger had not gained the summit (it was extraordinary to see such activity in so unwieldy a creature) and there fixed the rope round the trunk of the considerable tree which grew there. With this as our support, we were soon able to scramble up the jagged wall until we found ourselves upon the small grassy platform, some twenty-five feet each way, which formed the summit.

The first impression which I received when I had recovered my breath was of the extraordinary view over the country which we had traversed. The whole Brazilian plain seemed to lie beneath us, extending away and away until it ended in dim blue mists upon the farthest skyline. In the foreground was the long slope, strewn with rocks and dotted with tree-ferns; farther off in the middle distance, looking over the saddle-back hill, I could just see the yellow and green mass of bamboos through which we had passed; and then, gradually, the vegetation increased until it formed the huge forest which extended as far as the eyes could reach, and for a good two thousand miles beyond.

I was still drinking in this wonderful panorama when the heavy hand of the Professor fell upon my shoulder.

"This way, my young friend," said he; "*vestigia nulla retrorsum.* Never look rearwards, but always to our glorious goal."

The level of the plateau, when I turned, was exactly that on which we stood, and the green bank of bushes, with occasional trees, was so near that it was difficult to realize how inaccessible it remained. At a rough guess the gulf was forty feet across, but, so far as I could see, it might as well have been forty miles. I placed one arm round the trunk of the tree and leaned over the abyss. Far down were the small dark figures of our servants, looking up at us. The wall was absolutely precipitous, as was that which faced me.

"This is indeed curious," said the creaking voice of Professor Summerlee.

I turned, and found that he was examining with great interest the tree to which I clung. That smooth bark and those small, ribbed leaves seemed familiar to my eyes. "Why," I cried, "it's a beech!"

"Exactly," said Summerlee. "A fellow-countryman in a far land."

"Not only a fellow-countryman, my good sir," said Challenger, "but also, if I may be allowed to enlarge your simile, an ally of the first value. This beech tree will be our saviour."

"By George!" cried Lord John, "a bridge!"

"Exactly, my friends, a bridge! It is not for nothing that I expended an hour last night in focusing my mind upon the situation. I have some recollection of once remarking to our young friend here that G. E. C. is at his best when his back is to the wall. Last night you will admit that all our backs were to the wall. But where will-power and intellect go together, there is always a way out. A drawbridge had to be found which could be dropped across the abyss. Behold it!"

It was certainly a brilliant idea. The tree was a good sixty feet in height, and if it only fell the right way it would easily cross the chasm. Challenger had slung the camp axe over his shoulder when he ascended. Now he handed it to me.

"Our young friend has the thews and sinews," said he. "I think he will be the most useful at this task. I must beg, however, that you will kindly refrain from thinking for yourself, and that you will do exactly what you are told."

Under his direction I cut such gashes in the sides of the trees as would ensure that it should fall as we desired. It had already a strong, natural tilt in the direction of the plateau, so that the matter was not difficult. Finally I set to work in earnest upon the trunk, taking turn and turn with Lord John. In a little over an hour there was a loud crack, the tree swayed forward, and then crashed over, burying its branches among the bushes on the farther side. The severed trunk rolled to the very edge of our platform, and for one terrible second we all thought it was over. It balanced itself, however, a few inches from the edge, and there was our bridge to the unknown.

All of us, without a word, shook hands with Professor Challenger, who raised his straw hat and bowed deeply to each in turn.

"I claim the honor," said he, "to be the first to cross to the unknown land—a fitting subject, no doubt, for some future historical painting."

He had approached the bridge when Lord John laid his hand upon his coat.

"My dear chap," said he, "I really cannot allow it."

"Cannot allow it, sir!" The head went back and the beard forward.

"When it is a matter of science, don't you know, I follow your lead because you are by way of bein' a man of science. But it's up to you to follow me when you come into my department."

"Your department, sir?"

"We all have our professions, and soldierin' is mine. We are, accordin' to my ideas, invadin' a new country, which may or may not be chock-full of enemies of sorts. To barge blindly into it for want of a little common sense and patience isn't my notion of management."

The remonstrance was too reasonable to be disregarded. Challenger tossed his head and shrugged his heavy shoulders.

"Well, sir, what do you propose?"

"For all I know there may be a tribe of cannibals waitin' for lunch-time among those very bushes," said Lord John, looking across the bridge. "It's better to learn wisdom before you get into a cookin'-pot; so we will content ourselves with hopin' that there is no trouble waitin' for us, and at the same time we will act as if there were. Malone and I will go down again, therefore, and we will fetch up the four rifles, together with Gomez and the other. One man can then go across and the rest will cover him with guns, until he sees that it is safe for the whole crowd to come along."

Challenger sat down upon the cut stump and groaned his impatience; but Summerlee and I were of one mind that Lord John was our leader when such practical details were in question. The climb was a more simple thing now that the rope dangled down the face of the worst part of the ascent. Within an hour we had brought up the rifles and a shotgun. The half-breeds had ascended also, and under Lord John's orders they had carried up a bale of provisions in case our first exploration should be a long one. We had each bandoliers of cartridges.

"Now, Challenger, if you really insist upon being the first man in," said Lord John, when every preparation was complete.

"I am much indebted to you for your gracious permission," said the angry Professor; for never was a man so intolerant of every form of authority. "Since you are good enough to allow it, I shall most certainly take it upon myself to act as pioneer upon this occasion."

Seating himself with a leg overhanging the abyss on each side, and his hatchet slung upon his back, Challenger hopped his way across the trunk and was soon at the other side. He clambered up and waved his arms in the air.

"At last!" he cried; "at last!"

I gazed anxiously at him, with a vague expectation that some terrible fate would dart at him from the curtain of green behind him. But all was quiet, save that a strange, many-colored bird flew up from under his feet and vanished among the trees.

Summerlee was the second. His wiry energy is wonderful in so frail a frame. He insisted upon having two rifles slung upon his back, so that both Professors were armed when he had made his transit. I came next, and tried hard not to look down into the horrible gulf over which I was passing. Summerlee held out the butt-end of his rifle, and an instant later I was able to grasp his hand. As to Lord John, he walked across—actually walked without support! He must have nerves of iron.

And there we were, the four of us, upon the dreamland, the lost world, of Maple White. To all of us it seemed the moment of our supreme triumph. Who could have guessed that it was the prelude to our supreme disaster? Let me say in a few words how the crushing blow fell upon us.

We had turned away from the edge, and had penetrated about fifty yards of close brushwood, when there came a frightful rending crash from behind us. With one impulse we rushed back the way that we had come. The bridge was gone!

Far down at the base of the cliff I saw, as I looked over, a tangled mass of branches and splintered trunk. It was our beech tree. Had the edge of the platform crumbled and let it through? For a moment this explanation was in all our minds. The next, from the farther side of the rocky pinnacle before us a swarthy face, the face of Gomez the half-breed, was slowly protruded. Yes, it was Gomez, but no longer the Gomez of the demure smile and the mask-like expression. Here was a face with flashing eyes and distorted features, a face convulsed with hatred and with the mad joy of gratified revenge.

"Lord Roxton!" he shouted. "Lord John Roxton!"

"Well," said our companion, "here I am."

A shriek of laughter came across the abyss.

"Yes, there you are, you English dog, and there you will remain! I have waited and waited, and now has come my chance. You found it hard to get up; you will find it harder to get down. You cursed fools, you are trapped, every one of you!"

We were too astounded to speak. We could only stand there staring in amazement. A great broken bough upon the grass showed whence he had gained his leverage to tilt over our bridge. The face had vanished, but presently it was up again, more frantic than before.

"We nearly killed you with a stone at the cave," he cried; "but this is better. It is slower and more terrible. Your bones will whiten up there, and none will know where you lie or come to cover them. As you lie dying, think of Lopez, whom you shot five years ago on the Putomayo River. I am his brother, and, come what will I will die happy now, for his memory has been avenged." A furious hand was shaken at us, and then all was quiet.

Had the half-breed simply wrought his vengeance and then escaped, all might have been well with him. It was that foolish, irresistible Latin impulse to be dramatic which brought his own downfall. Roxton, the man who had earned himself the name of the Flail of the Lord through three countries, was not one who could be safely taunted. The half-breed was descending on the farther side of the pinnacle; but before he could reach the ground Lord John had run along the edge of the plateau and gained a point from which he could see his man. There was a single crack of his rifle, and, though we saw nothing, we heard the scream and then the distant thud of the falling body. Roxton came back to us with a face of granite.

"I have been a blind simpleton," said he, bitterly, "It's my folly that has brought you all into this trouble. I should have remembered that these people have long memories for blood-feuds, and have been more upon my guard."

"What about the other one? It took two of them to lever that tree over the edge."

"I could have shot him, but I let him go. He may have had no part in it. Perhaps it would have been better if I had killed him, for he must, as you say, have lent a hand."

Now that we had the clue to his action, each of us could cast back and remember some sinister act upon the part of the half-breed—his constant desire to know our plans, his arrest outside our tent when he was over-hearing them, the furtive looks of hatred which from time to time one or other of us had surprised. We were still discussing it, endeavoring to adjust our minds to these new conditions, when a singular scene in the plain below arrested our attention.

A man in white clothes, who could only be the surviving half-breed, was running as one does run when Death is the pacemaker. Behind him, only a few yards in his rear, bounded the huge ebony figure of Zambo, our devoted negro. Even as we looked, he sprang upon the back of the fugitive and flung his arms round his neck. They rolled on the ground together. An instant afterwards Zambo rose, looked at the prostrate man, and then, waving his hand joyously to us, came running in our direction. The white figure lay motionless in the middle of the great plain.

Our two traitors had been destroyed, but the mischief that they had done lived after them. By no possible means could we get back to the pinnacle. We had been natives of the world; now we were natives of the plateau. The two things were separate and apart. There was the plain which led to the canoes. Yonder, beyond the violet, hazy horizon, was the stream which led back to civilization. But the link between was missing. No human ingenuity could suggest a means of bridging the chasm which yawned between ourselves and our past lives. One instant had altered the whole conditions of our existence.

It was at such a moment that I learned the stuff of which my three comrades were composed. They were grave, it is true, and thoughtful, but of an invincible serenity. For the moment we could only sit among the bushes in patience and wait the coming of Zambo. Presently his honest black face topped the rocks and his Herculean figure emerged upon the top of the pinnacle.

"What I do now?" he cried. "You tell me and I do it."

It was a question which it was easier to ask than to answer. One thing only was clear. He was our one trusty link with the outside world. On no account must he leave us.

"No no!" he cried. "I not leave you. Whatever come, you always find me here. But no able to keep Indians. Already they say too much Curupuri live on this place, and they go home. Now you leave them me no able to keep them."

It was a fact that our Indians had shown in many ways of late that they were weary of their journey and anxious to return. We realized that Zambo spoke the truth, and that it would be impossible for him to keep them.

"Make them wait till tomorrow, Zambo," I shouted; "then I can send letter back by them."

"Very good, sarr! I promise they wait till tomorrow," said the negro. "But what I do for you now?"

There was plenty for him to do, and admirably the faithful fellow did it.

First of all, under our directions, he undid the rope from the tree-stump and threw one end of it across to us. It was not thicker than a clothesline, but it was of great strength, and though we could not make a bridge of it, we might well find it invaluable if we had any climbing to do. He then fastened his end of the rope to the package of supplies which had been carried up, and we were able to drag it across. This gave us the means of life for at least a week, even if we found nothing else. Finally he descended and carried up two other packets of mixed goods—a box of ammunition and a number of other things, all of which we got across by throwing our rope to him and hauling it back. It was evening when he at last climbed down, with a final assurance that he would keep the Indians till next morning.

And so it is that I have spent nearly the whole of this our first night upon the plateau writing up our experiences by the light of a single candle-lantern.

We supped and camped at the very edge of the cliff, quenching our thirst with two bottles of Apollinaris which were in one of the cases. It is vital to us to find water, but I think even Lord John himself had had adventures enough for one day, and none of us felt inclined to make the first push into the unknown. We forbore to light a fire or to make any unnecessary sound.

Tomorrow (or today, rather, for it is already dawn as I write) we shall make our first venture into this strange land. When I shall be able to write again—or if I ever shall write again—I know not. Meanwhile, I can see that the Indians are still in their place, and I am sure that the faithful Zambo will be here presently to get my letter. I only trust that it will come to hand.

P.S.—The more I think the more desperate does our position seem. I see no possible hope of our return. If there were a high tree near the edge of the plateau we might drop a return bridge across, but there is none within fifty yards. Our united strength could not carry a trunk which would serve our purpose. The rope, of course, is far too short that we could descend by it. No, our position is hopeless—hopeless!

X

"THE MOST WONDERFUL THINGS HAVE HAPPENED"

The most wonderful things have happened and are continually happening to us. All the paper that I possess consists of five old note-books and a lot of scraps, and I have only the one stylographic pencil; but so long as I can move my hand I will continue to set down our experiences and impressions, for, since we are the only men of the whole human race to see such things, it is of enormous importance that I should record them whilst they are fresh in my memory and before that fate which seems to be constantly impending does actually overtake us. Whether Zambo can at last take these letters to the river, or whether I shall myself in some miraculous way carry them back with me, or, finally, whether some daring explorer, coming upon our tracks with the advantage, perhaps, of a perfected monoplane, should find this bundle of manuscript, in any case I can see that what I am writing is destined to immortality as a classic of true adventure.

On the morning after our being trapped upon the plateau by the villainous Gomez we began a new stage in our experiences. The first incident in it was not such as to give me a very favorable opinion of the place to which we had wandered. As I roused myself from a short nap after day had dawned, my eyes fell upon a most singular appearance upon my own leg. My trouser had slipped up, exposing a few inches of my skin above my sock. On this there rested a large, purplish grape. Astonished at the sight, I leaned forward to pick it off, when, to my horror, it burst between my finger and thumb, squirting blood in every direction. My cry of disgust had brought the two professors to my side.

"Most interesting," said Summerlee, bending over my shin. "An enormous blood-tick, as yet, I believe, unclassified."

"The first-fruits of our labors," said Challenger in his booming, pedantic fashion. "We cannot do less than call it *Ixodes Maloni.* The very small inconvenience of being bitten, my young friend, cannot, I am sure, weigh with you as against the glorious privilege of having your name inscribed in the deathless roll of zoology. Unhappily you have crushed this fine specimen at the moment of satiation."

"Filthy vermin!" I cried.

Professor Challenger raised his great eyebrows in protest, and placed a soothing paw upon my shoulder.

"You should cultivate the scientific eye and the detached scientific mind," said he. "To a man of philosophic temperament like myself the blood-tick, with its lancet-like proboscis and its distending stomach, is as beautiful a work of Nature as the peacock or, for that matter, the aurora borealis. It pains me to hear you speak of it in so unappreciative a fashion. No doubt, with due diligence, we can secure some other specimen."

"There can be no doubt of that," said Summerlee, grimly, "for one has just disappeared behind your shirt-collar."

Challenger sprang into the air bellowing like a bull, and tore frantically at his coat and shirt to get them off. Summerlee and I laughed so that we could hardly help him. At last we exposed that monstrous torso (fifty-four inches, by the tailor's tape). His body was all matted with black hair, out of which jungle we picked the wandering tick before it had bitten him. But the bushes round were full of the horrible pests, and it was clear that we must shift our camp.

But first of all it was necessary to make our arrangements with the faithful negro, who appeared presently on the pinnacle with a number of tins of cocoa and biscuits, which he tossed over to us. Of the stores which remained below he was ordered to retain as much as would keep him for two months. The Indians were to have the remainder as a reward for their services and as payment for taking our letters back to the Amazon. Some hours later we saw them in single file far out upon the plain, each with a bundle on his head, making their way back along the path we had come. Zambo occupied our little tent at the base of the pinnacle, and there he remained, our one link with the world below.

And now we had to decide upon our immediate movements. We shifted our position from among the tick-laden bushes until we came to a small clearing thickly surrounded by trees upon all sides. There were some flat slabs of rock in the center, with an excellent well close by, and there we sat in cleanly comfort while we made our first plans for the invasion of this new country. Birds were calling among the foliage—especially one with a peculiar whooping cry which was new to us—but beyond these sounds there were no signs of life.

Our first care was to make some sort of list of our own stores, so that we might know what we had to rely upon. What with the things we had ourselves brought up and those which Zambo had sent across on the rope, we were fairly well supplied. Most important of all, in view of the dangers which might surround us, we had our four rifles and one thousand three hundred rounds, also a shotgun, but not more than a hundred and fifty medium pellet cartridges. In the matter of provisions we had enough to last for several weeks, with a sufficiency of tobacco and a few scientific implements, including a large telescope and a good field-glass. All these things we collected together in the clearing, and as a first precaution, we cut down with our hatchet and knives a number of thorny bushes, which we piled round in a circle some fifteen yards in diameter. This was to be our headquarters for the time—our place of refuge against sudden danger and the guard-house for our stores. Fort Challenger, we called it.

It was midday before we had made ourselves secure, but the heat was not oppressive, and the general character of the plateau, both in its temperature and in its vegetation, was almost temperate. The beech, the oak, and even the birch were to be found among the tangle of trees which girt us in. One huge gingko tree, topping all the others, shot its great limbs and maidenhair foliage over the fort which we had constructed. In its shade we continued our discussion, while Lord John, who had quickly taken command in the hour of action, gave us his views.

"So long as neither man nor beast has seen or heard us, we are safe," said he. "From the time they know we are here our troubles begin. There are no signs that they have found us out as yet. So our game surely is to lie low for a time and spy out the land. We want to have a good look at our neighbors before we get on visitin' terms."

"But we must advance," I ventured to remark.

"By all means, sonny my boy! We will advance. But with common sense. We must never go so far that we can't get back to our base. Above all, we must never, unless it is life or death, fire off our guns."

"But you fired yesterday," said Summerlee.

"Well, it couldn't be helped. However, the wind was strong and blew outwards. It is not likely that the sound could have traveled far into the plateau. By the way, what shall we call this place? I suppose it is up to us to give it a name?"

There were several suggestions, more or less happy, but Challenger's was final.

"It can only have one name," said he. "It is called after the pioneer who discovered it. It is Maple White Land."

Maple White Land it became, and so it is named in that chart which has become my special task. So it will, I trust, appear in the atlas of the future.

The peaceful penetration of Maple White Land was the pressing subject before us. We had the evidence of our own eyes that the place was inhabited by some unknown creatures, and there was that of Maple White's sketchbook to show that more dreadful and more dangerous monsters might still appear. That there might also prove to be human occupants and that they were of a malevolent character was suggested by the skeleton impaled upon the bamboos, which could not have got there had it not been dropped from above. Our situation, stranded without possibility of escape in such a land, was clearly full of danger, and our reasons endorsed every measure of caution which Lord John's experience could suggest. Yet it was surely impossible that we should halt on the edge of this world of mystery when our very souls were tingling with impatience to push forward and to pluck the heart from it.

We therefore blocked the entrance to our zareba by filling it up with several thorny bushes, and left our camp with the stores entirely surrounded by this protecting hedge. We then slowly and cautiously set forth into the unknown, following the course of the little stream which flowed from our spring, as it should always serve us as a guide on our return.

* * * * *

Hardly had we started when we came across signs that there were indeed wonders awaiting us. After a few hundred yards of thick forest, containing many trees which were quite unknown to me, but which Summerlee, who was the botanist of the party, recognized as forms of conifera and of cycadaceous plants which have long passed away in the world below, we entered a region where the stream widened out and formed a considerable bog. High reeds of a peculiar type grew thickly before us, which were pronounced to be equisetacea, or mare's-tails, with tree-ferns scattered amongst them, all of them swaying in a brisk wind. Suddenly Lord John, who was walking first, halted with uplifted hand.

"Look at this!" said he. "By George, this must be the trail of the father of all birds!"

An enormous three-toed track was imprinted in the soft mud before us. The creature, whatever it was, had crossed the swamp and had passed on into the forest. We all stopped to examine that monstrous spoor. If it were indeed a bird—and what animal could leave such a mark?—its foot was so much larger than an ostrich's that its height upon the same scale must be enormous. Lord John looked eagerly round him and slipped two cartridges into his elephant-gun.

"I'll stake my good name as a shikarree," said he, "that the track is a fresh one. The creature has not passed ten minutes. Look how the water is still oozing into that deeper print! By Jove! See, here is the mark of a little one!"

Sure enough, smaller tracks of the same general form were running parallel to the large ones.

"But what do you make of this?" cried Professor Summerlee, triumphantly, pointing to what looked like the huge print of a five-fingered human hand appearing among the three-toed marks.

"Wealden!" cried Challenger, in an ecstasy. "I've seen them in the Wealden clay. It is a creature walking erect upon three-toed feet, and occasionally putting one of its five-fingered forepaws upon the ground. Not a bird, my dear Roxton—not a bird."

"A beast?"

"No; a reptile—a dinosaur. Nothing else could have left such a track. They puzzled a worthy Sussex doctor some ninety years ago; but who in the world could have hoped—hoped—to have seen a sight like that?"

His words died away into a whisper, and we all stood in motionless amazement. Following the tracks, we had left the morass and passed through a screen of brushwood and trees. Beyond was an open glade, and in this were five of the most extraordinary creatures that I have ever seen. Crouching down among the bushes, we observed them at our leisure.

There were, as I say, five of them, two being adults and three young ones. In size they were enormous. Even the babies were as big as elephants, while the two large ones were far beyond all creatures I have ever seen. They had slate-colored skin, which was scaled like a lizard's and shimmered where the sun shone upon it. All five were sitting up, balancing themselves upon their broad, powerful tails and their huge three-toed hind-feet, while with their small five-fingered front-feet they pulled down the branches upon which they browsed. I do not know that I can bring their appearance home to you better than by saying that they looked like monstrous kangaroos, twenty feet in length, and with skins like black crocodiles.

I do not know how long we stayed motionless gazing at this marvelous spectacle. A strong wind blew towards us and we were well concealed, so there was no chance of discovery. From time to time the little ones played round their parents in unwieldy gambols, the great beasts bounding into the air and falling with dull thuds upon the earth. The strength of the parents seemed to be limitless, for one of them, having some difficulty in reaching a bunch of foliage which grew upon a considerable-sized tree, put his fore-legs round the trunk and tore it down as if it had been a sapling. The action seemed, as I thought, to show not only the great development of its muscles, but also the small one of its brain, for the whole weight came crashing down upon the top of it, and it uttered a series of shrill yelps to show that, big as it was, there was a limit to what it could endure. The incident made it think, apparently, that the neighborhood was dangerous, for it slowly lurched off through the wood, followed by its mate and its three enormous infants. We saw the shimmering slaty gleam of their skins between the tree-trunks, and their heads undulating high above the brushwood. Then they vanished from our sight.

I looked at my comrades. Lord John was standing at gaze with his finger on the trigger of his elephant-gun, his eager hunter's soul shining from his fierce eyes. What would he not give for one such head to place between the two crossed oars above the mantelpiece in his snuggery at the Albany! And yet his reason held him in, for all our exploration of the wonders of this unknown land depended upon our presence being concealed from its inhabitants. The two professors were in silent ecstasy. In their excitement they had unconsciously seized each other by the hand, and stood like two little children in the presence of a marvel, Challenger's cheeks bunched up into a seraphic smile, and Summerlee's sardonic face softening for the moment into wonder and reverence.

"Nunc dimittis!" he cried at last. "What will they say in England of this?"

"My dear Summerlee, I will tell you with great confidence exactly what they will say in England," said Challenger. "They will say that you are an infernal liar and a scientific charlatan, exactly as you and others said of me."

"In the face of photographs?"

"Faked, Summerlee! Clumsily faked!"

"In the face of specimens?"

"Ah, there we may have them! Malone and his filthy Fleet Street crew may be all yelping our praises yet. August the twenty-eighth—the day we saw five live iguanodons in a glade of Maple White Land. Put it down in your diary, my young friend, and send it to your rag."

"And be ready to get the toe-end of the editorial boot in return," said Lord John. "Things look a bit different from the latitude of London, young fellah my lad. There's many a man who never tells his adventures, for he can't hope to be believed. Who's to blame them? For this will seem a bit of a dream to ourselves in a month or two. *What* did you say they were?"

"Iguanodons," said Summerlee. "You'll find their footmarks all over the Hastings sands, in Kent, and in Sussex. The South of England was alive with them when there was plenty of good lush green-stuff to keep them going. Conditions have changed, and the beasts died. Here it seems that the conditions have not changed, and the beasts have lived."

"If ever we get out of this alive, I must have a head with me," said Lord John. "Lord, how some of that Somaliland-Uganda crowd would turn a beautiful pea-green if they saw it! I don't know what you chaps think, but it strikes me that we are on mighty thin ice all this time."

I had the same feeling of mystery and danger around us. In the gloom of the trees there seemed a constant menace and as we looked up into their shadowy foliage vague terrors crept into one's heart. It is true that these monstrous creatures which we had seen were lumbering, inoffensive brutes which were unlikely to hurt anyone, but in this world of wonders what other survivals might there not be—what fierce, active horrors ready to pounce upon us from their lair among the rocks or brushwood? I knew little of prehistoric life, but I had a clear remembrance of one book which I had read in which it spoke of creatures who would live upon our lions and tigers as a cat lives upon mice. What if these also were to be found in the woods of Maple White Land!

It was destined that on this very morning—our first in the new country—we were to find out what strange hazards lay around us. It was a loathsome adventure, and one of which I hate to think. If, as Lord John said, the glade of the iguanodons will remain with us as a dream, then surely the swamp of the pterodactyls will forever be our nightmare. Let me set down exactly what occurred.

We passed very slowly through the woods, partly because Lord Roxton acted as scout before he would let us advance, and partly because at every second step one or other of our professors would fall, with a cry of wonder, before some flower or insect which presented him with a new type. We may have traveled two or three miles in all, keeping to the right of the line of the stream, when we came upon a considerable opening in the trees. A belt of brushwood led up to a tangle of rocks—the whole plateau was strewn with boulders. We were walking slowly towards these rocks, among bushes which reached over our waists, when we became aware of a strange low gabbling and whistling sound, which filled the air with a constant clamor and appeared to come from some spot immediately before us. Lord John held up his hand as a signal for us to stop, and he made his way swiftly, stooping and running, to the line of rocks. We saw him peep over them and give a gesture of amazement. Then he stood staring as if forgetting us, so utterly entranced was he by what he saw. Finally he waved us to come on, holding up his hand as a signal for caution. His whole bearing made me feel that something wonderful but dangerous lay before us.

Creeping to his side, we looked over the rocks. The place into which we gazed was a pit, and may, in the early days, have been one of the smaller volcanic blow-holes of the plateau. It was bowl-shaped and at the bottom, some hundreds of yards from where we lay, were pools of green-scummed, stagnant water, fringed with bullrushes. It was a weird place in itself, but its occupants made it seem like a scene from the Seven Circles of Dante. The place was a rookery of pterodactyls. There were hundreds of them congregated within view. All the bottom area round the water-edge was alive with their young ones, and with hideous mothers brooding upon their leathery, yellowish eggs. From this crawling flapping mass of obscene reptilian life came the shocking clamor which filled the air and the mephitic, horrible, musty odor which turned us sick. But above, perched each upon its own stone, tall, gray, and withered, more like dead and dried specimens than actual living creatures, sat the horrible males, absolutely motionless save for the rolling of their red eyes or an occasional snap of their rat-trap beaks as a dragon-fly went past them. Their huge, membranous wings were closed by folding their forearms, so that they sat like gigantic old women, wrapped in hideous web-colored shawls, and with their ferocious heads protruding above them. Large and small, not less than a thousand of these filthy creatures lay in the hollow before us.

Our professors would gladly have stayed there all day, so entranced were they by this opportunity of studying the life of a prehistoric age. They pointed out the fish and dead birds lying about among the rocks as proving the nature of the food of these creatures, and I heard them congratulating each other on having cleared up the point why the bones of this flying dragon are found in such great numbers in certain well-defined areas, as in the Cambridge Green-sand, since it was now seen that, like penguins, they lived in gregarious fashion.

Finally, however, Challenger, bent upon proving some point which Summerlee had contested, thrust his head over the rock and nearly brought destruction upon us all. In an instant the nearest male gave a shrill, whistling cry, and flapped its twenty-foot span of leathery wings as it soared up into the air. The females and young ones huddled together beside the water, while the whole circle of sentinels rose one after the other and sailed off into the sky. It was a wonderful sight to see at least a hundred creatures of such enormous size and hideous appearance all swooping like swallows with swift, shearing wing-strokes above us; but soon we realized that it was not one on which we could afford to linger. At first the great brutes flew round in a huge ring, as if to make sure what the exact extent of the danger might be. Then, the flight grew lower and the circle narrower, until they were whizzing round and round us, the dry, rustling flap of their huge slate-colored wings filling the air with a volume of sound that made me think of Hendon aerodrome upon a race day.

"Make for the wood and keep together," cried Lord John, clubbing his rifle. "The brutes mean mischief."

The moment we attempted to retreat the circle closed in upon us, until the tips of the wings of those nearest to us nearly touched our faces. We beat at them with the stocks of our guns, but there was nothing solid or vulnerable to strike. Then suddenly out of the whizzing, slate-colored circle a long neck shot out, and a fierce beak made a thrust at us. Another and another followed. Summerlee gave a cry and put his hand to his face, from which the blood was streaming. I felt a prod at the back of my neck, and turned dizzy with the shock. Challenger fell, and as I stooped to pick him up I was again struck from behind and dropped on the top of him. At the same instant I heard the crash of Lord John's elephant-gun, and, looking up, saw one of the creatures with a broken wing struggling upon the ground, spitting and gurgling at us with a wide-opened beak and blood-shot, goggled eyes, like some devil in a medieval picture. Its comrades had flown higher at the sudden sound, and were circling above our heads.

"Now," cried Lord John, "now for our lives!"

We staggered through the brushwood, and even as we reached the trees the harpies were on us again. Summerlee was knocked down, but we tore him up and rushed among the trunks. Once there we were safe, for those huge wings had no space for their sweep beneath the branches. As we limped homewards, sadly mauled and discomfited, we saw them for a long time flying at a great height against the deep blue sky above our heads, soaring round and round, no bigger than wood-pigeons, with their eyes no doubt still following our progress. At last, however, as we reached the thicker woods they gave up the chase, and we saw them no more.

"A most interesting and convincing experience," said Challenger, as we halted beside the brook and he bathed a swollen knee. "We are exceptionally well informed, Summerlee, as to the habits of the enraged pterodactyl."

Summerlee was wiping the blood from a cut in his forehead, while I was tying up a nasty stab in the muscle of the neck. Lord John had the shoulder of his coat torn away, but the creature's teeth had only grazed the flesh.

"It is worth noting," Challenger continued, "that our young friend has received an undoubted stab, while Lord John's coat could only have been torn by a bite. In my own case, I was beaten about the head by their wings, so we have had a remarkable exhibition of their various methods of offence."

"It has been touch and go for our lives," said Lord John, gravely, "and I could not think of a more rotten sort of death than to be outed by such filthy vermin. I was sorry to fire my rifle, but, by Jove! There was no great choice."

"We should not be here if you hadn't," said I, with conviction.

"It may do no harm," said he. "Among these woods there must be many loud cracks from splitting or falling trees which would be just like the sound of a gun. But now, if you are of my opinion, we have had thrills enough for one day, and had best get back to the surgical box at the camp for some carbolic. Who knows what venom these beasts may have in their hideous jaws?"

But surely no men ever had just such a day since the world began. Some fresh surprise was ever in store for us. When, following the course of our brook, we at last reached our glade and saw the thorny barricade of our camp, we thought that our adventures were at an end. But we had something more to think of before we could rest. The gate of Fort Challenger had been untouched, the walls were unbroken, and yet it had been visited by some strange and powerful creature in our absence. No footmark showed a trace of its nature, and only the overhanging branch of the enormous gingko tree suggested how it might have come and gone; but of its malevolent strength there was ample evidence in the condition of our stores. They were strewn at random all over the ground, and one tin of meat had been crushed into pieces so as to extract the contents. A case of cartridges had been shattered into matchwood, and one of the brass shells lay shredded into pieces beside it. Again the feeling of vague horror came upon our souls, and we gazed round with frightened eyes at the dark shadows which lay around us, in all of which some fearsome shape might be lurking. How good it was when we were hailed by the voice of Zambo, and, going to the edge of the plateau, saw him sitting grinning at us upon the top of the opposite pinnacle.

"All well, Massa Challenger, all well!" he cried. "Me stay here. No fear. You always find me when you want."

His honest black face, and the immense view before us, which carried us halfway back to the affluent of the Amazon, helped us to remember that we really were upon this earth in the twentieth century, and had not by some magic been conveyed to some raw planet in its earliest and wildest state. How difficult it was to realize that the violet line upon the far horizon was well advanced to that great river upon which huge steamers ran, and folk talked of the small affairs of life, while we, marooned among the creatures of a bygone age, could but gaze towards it and yearn for all that it meant!

One other memory remains with me of this wonderful day, and with it I will close this letter. The two professors, their tempers aggravated no doubt by their injuries, had fallen out as to whether our assailants were of the genus pterodactylus or dimorphodon, and high words had ensued. To avoid their wrangling I moved some little way apart, and was seated smoking upon the trunk of a fallen tree, when Lord John strolled over in my direction.

"I say, Malone," said he, "do you remember that place where those beasts were?"

"Very clearly."

"A sort of volcanic pit, was it not?"

"Exactly," said I.

"Did you notice the soil?"

"Rocks."

"But round the water—where the reeds were?"

"It was a bluish soil. It looked like clay."

"Exactly. A volcanic tube full of blue clay."

"What of that?" I asked.

"Oh, nothing, nothing," said he, and strolled back to where the voices of the contending men of science rose in a prolonged duet, the high, strident note of Summerlee rising and falling to the sonorous bass of Challenger. I should have thought no more of Lord John's remark were it not that once again that night I heard him mutter to himself: "Blue clay—clay in a volcanic tube!" They were the last words I heard before I dropped into an exhausted sleep.

XI

"FOR ONCE I WAS THE HERO"

Lord John Roxton was right when he thought that some specially toxic quality might lie in the bite of the horrible creatures which had attacked us.

On the morning after our first adventure upon the plateau, both Summerlee and I were in great pain and fever, while Challenger's knee was so bruised that he could hardly limp. We kept to our camp all day, therefore, Lord John busying himself, with such help as we could give him, in raising the height and thickness of the thorny walls which were our only defense. I remember that during the whole long day I was haunted by the feeling that we were closely observed, though by whom or whence I could give no guess.

So strong was the impression that I told Professor Challenger of it, who put it down to the cerebral excitement caused by my fever. Again and again I glanced round swiftly, with the conviction that I was about to see something, but only to meet the dark tangle of our hedge or the solemn and cavernous gloom of the great trees which arched above our heads. And yet the feeling grew ever stronger in my own mind that something observant and something malevolent was at our very elbow. I thought of the Indian superstition of the Curupuri—the dreadful, lurking spirit of the woods—and I could have imagined that his terrible presence haunted those who had invaded his most remote and sacred retreat.

That night (our third in Maple White Land) we had an experience which left a fearful impression upon our minds, and made us thankful that Lord John had worked so hard in making our retreat impregnable. We were all sleeping round our dying fire when we were aroused—or, rather, I should say, shot out of our slumbers—by a succession of the most frightful cries and screams to which I have ever listened. I know no sound to which I could compare this amazing tumult, which seemed to come from some spot within a few hundred yards of our camp. It was as ear-splitting as any whistle of a railway-engine; but whereas the whistle is a clear, mechanical, sharp-edged sound, this was far deeper in volume and vibrant with the uttermost strain of agony and horror. We clapped our hands to our ears to shut out that nerve-shaking appeal. A cold sweat broke out over my body, and my heart turned sick at the misery of it. All the woes of tortured life, all its stupendous indictment of high heaven, its innumerable sorrows, seemed to be centered and condensed into that one dreadful, agonized cry. And then, under this high-pitched, ringing sound there was another, more intermittent, a low, deep-chested laugh, a growling, throaty gurgle of merriment which formed a grotesque accompaniment to the shriek with which it was blended. For three or four minutes on end the fearsome duet continued, while all the foliage rustled with the rising of startled birds. Then it shut off as suddenly as it began. For a long time we sat in horrified silence. Then Lord John threw a bundle of twigs upon the fire, and their red glare lit up the intent faces of my companions and flickered over the great boughs above our heads.

"What was it?" I whispered.

"We shall know in the morning," said Lord John. "It was close to us—not farther than the glade."

"We have been privileged to overhear a prehistoric tragedy, the sort of drama which occurred among the reeds upon the border of some Jurassic lagoon, when the greater dragon pinned the lesser among the slime," said Challenger, with more solemnity than I had ever heard in his voice. "It was surely well for man that he came late in the order of creation. There were powers abroad in earlier days which no courage and no mechanism of his could have met. What could his sling, his throwing-stick, or his arrow avail him against such forces as have been loose tonight? Even with a modern rifle it would be all odds on the monster."

"I think I should back my little friend," said Lord John, caressing his Express. "But the beast would certainly have a good sporting chance."

Summerlee raised his hand.

"Hush!" he cried. "Surely I hear something?"

From the utter silence there emerged a deep, regular pat-pat. It was the tread of some animal—the rhythm of soft but heavy pads placed cautiously upon the ground. It stole slowly round the camp, and then halted near our gateway. There was a low, sibilant rise and fall—the breathing of the creature. Only our feeble hedge separated us from this horror of the night. Each of us had seized his rifle, and Lord John had pulled out a small bush to make an embrasure in the hedge.

"By George!" he whispered. "I think I can see it!"

I stooped and peered over his shoulder through the gap. Yes, I could see it, too. In the deep shadow of the tree there was a deeper shadow yet, black, inchoate, vague—a crouching form full of savage vigor and menace. It was no higher than a horse, but the dim outline suggested vast bulk and strength. That hissing pant, as regular and full-volumed as the exhaust of an engine, spoke of a monstrous organism. Once, as it moved, I thought I saw the glint of two terrible, greenish eyes. There was an uneasy rustling, as if it were crawling slowly forward.

"I believe it is going to spring!" said I, cocking my rifle.

"Don't fire! Don't fire!" whispered Lord John. "The crash of a gun in this silent night would be heard for miles. Keep it as a last card."

"If it gets over the hedge we're done," said Summerlee, and his voice crackled into a nervous laugh as he spoke.

"No, it must not get over," cried Lord John; "but hold your fire to the last. Perhaps I can make something of the fellow. I'll chance it, anyhow."

It was as brave an act as ever I saw a man do. He stooped to the fire, picked up a blazing branch, and slipped in an instant through a sallyport which he had made in our gateway. The thing moved forward with a dreadful snarl. Lord John never hesitated, but, running towards it with a quick, light step, he dashed the flaming wood into the brute's face. For one moment I had a vision of a horrible mask like a giant toad's, of a warty, leprous skin, and of a loose mouth all beslobbered with fresh blood. The next, there was a crash in the underwood and our dreadful visitor was gone.

"I thought he wouldn't face the fire," said Lord John, laughing, as he came back and threw his branch among the faggots.

"You should not have taken such a risk!" we all cried.

"There was nothin' else to be done. If he had got among us we should have shot each other in tryin' to down him. On the other hand, if we had fired through the hedge and wounded him he would soon have been on the top of us—to say nothin' of giving ourselves away. On the whole, I think that we are jolly well out of it. What was he, then?"

Our learned men looked at each other with some hesitation.

"Personally, I am unable to classify the creature with any certainty," said Summerlee, lighting his pipe from the fire.

"In refusing to commit yourself you are but showing a proper scientific reserve," said Challenger, with massive condescension. "I am not myself prepared to go farther than to say in general terms that we have almost certainly been in contact tonight with some form of carnivorous dinosaur. I have already expressed my anticipation that something of the sort might exist upon this plateau."

"We have to bear in mind," remarked Summerlee, "that there are many prehistoric forms which have never come down to us. It would be rash to suppose that we can give a name to all that we are likely to meet."

"Exactly. A rough classification may be the best that we can attempt. Tomorrow some further evidence may help us to an identification. Meantime we can only renew our interrupted slumbers."

"But not without a sentinel," said Lord John, with decision. "We can't afford to take chances in a country like this. Two-hour spells in the future, for each of us."

"Then I'll just finish my pipe in starting the first one," said Professor Summerlee; and from that time onwards we never trusted ourselves again without a watchman.

In the morning it was not long before we discovered the source of the hideous uproar which had aroused us in the night. The iguanodon glade was the scene of a horrible butchery. From the pools of blood and the enormous lumps of flesh scattered in every direction over the green sward we imagined at first that a number of animals had been killed, but on examining the remains more closely we discovered that all this carnage came from one of these unwieldy monsters, which had been literally torn to pieces by some creature not larger, perhaps, but far more ferocious, than itself.

Our two professors sat in absorbed argument, examining piece after piece, which showed the marks of savage teeth and of enormous claws.

"Our judgment must still be in abeyance," said Professor Challenger, with a huge slab of whitish-colored flesh across his knee. "The indications would be consistent with the presence of a saber-toothed tiger, such as are still found among the breccia of our caverns; but the creature actually seen was undoubtedly of a larger and more reptilian character. Personally, I should pronounce for allosaurus."

"Or megalosaurus," said Summerlee.

"Exactly. Any one of the larger carnivorous dinosaurs would meet the case. Among them are to be found all the most terrible types of animal life that have ever cursed the earth or blessed a museum." He laughed sonorously at his own conceit, for, though he had little sense of humor, the crudest pleasantry from his own lips moved him always to roars of appreciation.

"The less noise the better," said Lord Roxton, curtly. "We don't know who or what may be near us. If this fellah comes back for his breakfast and catches us here we won't have so much to laugh at. By the way, what is this mark upon the iguanodon's hide?"

On the dull, scaly, slate-colored skin somewhere above the shoulder, there was a singular black circle of some substance which looked like asphalt. None of us could suggest what it meant, though Summerlee was of opinion that he had seen something similar upon one of the young ones two days before. Challenger said nothing, but looked pompous and puffy, as if he could if he would, so that finally Lord John asked his opinion direct.

"If your lordship will graciously permit me to open my mouth, I shall be happy to express my sentiments," said he, with elaborate sarcasm. "I am not in the habit of being taken to task in the fashion which seems to be customary with your lordship. I was not aware that it was necessary to ask your permission before smiling at a harmless pleasantry."

It was not until he had received his apology that our touchy friend would suffer himself to be appeased. When at last his ruffled feelings were at ease, he addressed us at some length from his seat upon a fallen tree, speaking, as his habit was, as if he were imparting most precious information to a class of a thousand.

"With regard to the marking," said he, "I am inclined to agree with my friend and colleague, Professor Summerlee, that the stains are from asphalt.

As this plateau is, in its very nature, highly volcanic, and as asphalt is a substance which one associates with Plutonic forces, I cannot doubt that it exists in the free liquid state, and that the creatures may have come in contact with it. A much more important problem is the question as to the existence of the carnivorous monster which has left its traces in this glade. We know roughly that this plateau is not larger than an average English county. Within this confined space a certain number of creatures, mostly types which have passed away in the world below, have lived together for innumerable years. Now, it is very clear to me that in so long a period one would have expected that the carnivorous creatures, multiplying unchecked, would have exhausted their food supply and have been compelled to either modify their flesh-eating habits or die of hunger. This we see has not been so. We can only imagine, therefore, that the balance of Nature is preserved by some check which limits the numbers of these ferocious creatures. One of the many interesting problems, therefore, which await our solution is to discover what that check may be and how it operates. I venture to trust that we may have some future opportunity for the closer study of the carnivorous dinosaurs."

"And I venture to trust we may not," I observed.

The Professor only raised his great eyebrows, as the schoolmaster meets the irrelevant observation of the naughty boy.

"Perhaps Professor Summerlee may have an observation to make," he said, and the two savants ascended together into some rarefied scientific atmosphere, where the possibilities of a modification of the birth-rate were weighed against the decline of the food supply as a check in the struggle for existence.

That morning we mapped out a small portion of the plateau, avoiding the swamp of the pterodactyls, and keeping to the east of our brook instead of to the west. In that direction the country was still thickly wooded, with so much undergrowth that our progress was very slow.

I have dwelt up to now upon the terrors of Maple White Land; but there was another side to the subject, for all that morning we wandered among lovely flowers—mostly, as I observed, white or yellow in color, these being, as our professors explained, the primitive flower-shades. In many places the ground was absolutely covered with them, and as we walked ankle-deep on that wonderful yielding carpet, the scent was almost intoxicating in its sweetness and intensity. The homely English bee buzzed everywhere around us. Many of the trees under which we passed had their branches bowed down with fruit, some of which were of familiar sorts, while other varieties were new. By observing which of them were pecked by the birds we avoided all danger of poison and added a delicious variety to our food reserve. In the jungle which we traversed were numerous hard-trodden paths made by the wild beasts, and in the more marshy places we saw a profusion of strange footmarks, including many of the iguanodon. Once in a grove we observed several of these great creatures grazing, and Lord John, with his glass, was able to report that they also were spotted with asphalt, though in a different place to the one which we had examined in the morning. What this phenomenon meant we could not imagine.

We saw many small animals, such as porcupines, a scaly ant-eater, and a wild pig, piebald in color and with long curved tusks. Once, through a break in the trees, we saw a clear shoulder of green hill some distance away, and across this a large dun-colored animal was traveling at a considerable pace. It passed so swiftly that we were unable to say what it was; but if it were a deer, as was claimed by Lord John, it must have been as large as those monstrous Irish elk which are still dug up from time to time in the bogs of my native land.

Ever since the mysterious visit which had been paid to our camp we always returned to it with some misgivings. However, on this occasion we found everything in order.

That evening we had a grand discussion upon our present situation and future plans, which I must describe at some length, as it led to a new departure by which we were enabled to gain a more complete knowledge of Maple White Land than might have come in many weeks of exploring. It was Summerlee who opened the debate. All day he had been querulous in manner, and now some remark of Lord John's as to what we should do on the morrow brought all his bitterness to a head.

"What we ought to be doing today, tomorrow, and all the time," said he, "is finding some way out of the trap into which we have fallen. You are all turning your brains towards getting into this country. I say that we should be scheming how to get out of it."

"I am surprised, sir," boomed Challenger, stroking his majestic beard, "that any man of science should commit himself to so ignoble a sentiment. You are in a land which offers such an inducement to the ambitious naturalist as none ever has since the world began, and you suggest leaving it before we have acquired more than the most superficial knowledge of it or of its contents. I expected better things of you, Professor Summerlee."

"You must remember," said Summerlee, sourly, "that I have a large class in London who are at present at the mercy of an extremely inefficient *locum tenens*. This makes my situation different from yours, Professor Challenger, since, so far as I know, you have never been entrusted with any responsible educational work."

"Quite so," said Challenger. "I have felt it to be a sacrilege to divert a brain which is capable of the highest original research to any lesser object. That is why I have sternly set my face against any proffered scholastic appointment."

"For example?" asked Summerlee, with a sneer; but Lord John hastened to change the conversation.

"I must say," said he, "that I think it would be a mighty poor thing to go back to London before I know a great deal more of this place than I do at present."

"I could never dare to walk into the back office of my paper and face old McArdle," said I. (You will excuse the frankness of this report, will you not, sir?) "He'd never forgive me for leaving such unexhausted copy behind me. Besides, so far as I can see it is not worth discussing, since we can't get down, even if we wanted."

"Our young friend makes up for many obvious mental lacunae by some measure of primitive common sense," remarked Challenger. "The interests of his deplorable profession are immaterial to us; but, as he observes, we cannot get down in any case, so it is a waste of energy to discuss it."

"It is a waste of energy to do anything else," growled Summerlee from behind his pipe. "Let me remind you that we came here upon a perfectly definite mission, entrusted to us at the meeting of the Zoological Institute in London. That mission was to test the truth of Professor Challenger's statements. Those statements, as I am bound to admit, we are now in a position to endorse. Our ostensible work is therefore done. As to the detail which remains to be worked out upon this plateau, it is so enormous that only a large expedition, with a very special equipment, could hope to cope with it. Should we attempt to do so ourselves, the only possible result must be that we shall never return with the important contribution to science which we have already gained. Professor Challenger has devised means for getting us on to this plateau when it appeared to be inaccessible; I think that we should now call upon him to use the same ingenuity in getting us back to the world from which we came."

I confess that as Summerlee stated his view it struck me as altogether reasonable. Even Challenger was affected by the consideration that his enemies would never stand confuted if the confirmation of his statements should never reach those who had doubted them.

"The problem of the descent is at first sight a formidable one," said he, "and yet I cannot doubt that the intellect can solve it. I am prepared to agree with our colleague that a protracted stay in Maple White Land is at present inadvisable, and that the question of our return will soon have to be faced. I absolutely refuse to leave, however, until we have made at least a superficial examination of this country, and are able to take back with us something in the nature of a chart."

Professor Summerlee gave a snort of impatience.

"We have spent two long days in exploration," said he, "and we are no wiser as to the actual geography of the place than when we started. It is clear that it is all thickly wooded, and it would take months to penetrate it and to learn the relations of one part to another. If there were some central peak it would be different, but it all slopes downwards, so far as we can see. The farther we go the less likely it is that we will get any general view."

It was at that moment that I had my inspiration. My eyes chanced to light upon the enormous gnarled trunk of the gingko tree which cast its huge branches over us. Surely, if its bole exceeded that of all others, its height must do the same. If the rim of the plateau was indeed the highest point, then why should this mighty tree not prove to be a watchtower which commanded the whole country? Now, ever since I ran wild as a lad in Ireland I have been a bold and skilled tree-climber. My comrades might be my masters on the rocks, but I knew that I would be supreme among those branches. Could I only get my legs on to the lowest of the giant off-shoots, then it would be strange indeed if I could not make my way to the top. My comrades were delighted at my idea.

"Our young friend," said Challenger, bunching up the red apples of his cheeks, "is capable of acrobatic exertions which would be impossible to a man of a more solid, though possibly of a more commanding, appearance. I applaud his resolution."

"By George, young fellah, you've put your hand on it!" said Lord John, clapping me on the back. "How we never came to think of it before I can't imagine! There's not more than an hour of daylight left, but if you take your notebook you may be able to get some rough sketch of the place. If we put these three ammunition cases under the branch, I will soon hoist you on to it."

He stood on the boxes while I faced the trunk, and was gently raising me when Challenger sprang forward and gave me such a thrust with his huge hand that he fairly shot me into the tree. With both arms clasping the branch, I scrambled hard with my feet until I had worked, first my body, and then my knees, onto it. There were three excellent off-shoots, like huge rungs of a ladder, above my head, and a tangle of convenient branches beyond, so that I clambered onwards with such speed that I soon lost sight of the ground and had nothing but foliage beneath me. Now and then I encountered a check, and once I had to shin up a creeper for eight or ten feet, but I made excellent progress, and the booming of Challenger's voice seemed to be a great distance beneath me. The tree was, however, enormous, and, looking upwards, I could see no thinning of the leaves above my head. There was some thick, bush-like clump which seemed to be a parasite upon a branch up which I was swarming. I leaned my head round it in order to see what was beyond, and I nearly fell out of the tree in my surprise and horror at what I saw.

A face was gazing into mine—at the distance of only a foot or two. The creature that owned it had been crouching behind the parasite, and had looked round it at the same instant that I did. It was a human face—or at least it was far more human than any monkey's that I have ever seen. It was long, whitish, and blotched with pimples, the nose flattened, and the lower jaw projecting, with a bristle of coarse whiskers round the chin. The eyes, which were under thick and heavy brows, were bestial and ferocious, and as it opened its mouth to snarl what sounded like a curse at me I observed that it had curved, sharp canine teeth. For an instant I read hatred and menace in the evil eyes. Then, as quick as a flash, came an expression of overpowering fear. There was a crash of broken boughs as it dived wildly down into the tangle of green. I caught a glimpse of a hairy body like that of a reddish pig, and then it was gone amid a swirl of leaves and branches.

"What's the matter?" shouted Roxton from below. "Anything wrong with you?"

"Did you see it?" I cried, with my arms round the branch and all my nerves tingling.

"We heard a row, as if your foot had slipped. What was it?"

I was so shocked at the sudden and strange appearance of this ape-man that I hesitated whether I should not climb down again and tell my experience to my companions. But I was already so far up the great tree that it seemed a humiliation to return without having carried out my mission.

After a long pause, therefore, to recover my breath and my courage, I continued my ascent. Once I put my weight upon a rotten branch and swung for a few seconds by my hands, but in the main it was all easy climbing. Gradually the leaves thinned around me, and I was aware, from the wind upon my face, that I had topped all the trees of the forest. I was determined, however, not to look about me before I had reached the very highest point, so I scrambled on until I had got so far that the topmost branch was bending beneath my weight. There I settled into a convenient fork, and, balancing myself securely, I found myself looking down at a most wonderful panorama of this strange country in which we found ourselves.

The sun was just above the western skyline, and the evening was a particularly bright and clear one, so that the whole extent of the plateau was visible beneath me. It was, as seen from this height, of an oval contour, with a breadth of about thirty miles and a width of twenty. Its general shape was that of a shallow funnel, all the sides sloping down to a considerable lake in the center. This lake may have been ten miles in circumference, and lay very green and beautiful in the evening light, with a thick fringe of reeds at its edges, and with its surface broken by several yellow sandbanks, which gleamed golden in the mellow sunshine. A number of long dark objects, which were too large for alligators and too long for canoes, lay upon the edges of these patches of sand. With my glass I could clearly see that they were alive, but what their nature might be I could not imagine.

From the side of the plateau on which we were, slopes of woodland, with occasional glades, stretched down for five or six miles to the central lake. I could see at my very feet the glade of the iguanodons, and farther off was a round opening in the trees which marked the swamp of the pterodactyls. On the side facing me, however, the plateau presented a very different aspect. There the basalt cliffs of the outside were reproduced upon the inside, forming an escarpment about two hundred feet high, with a woody slope beneath it. Along the base of these red cliffs, some distance above the ground, I could see a number of dark holes through the glass, which I conjectured to be the mouths of caves. At the opening of one of these something white was shimmering, but I was unable to make out what it was. I sat charting the country until the sun had set and it was so dark that I could no longer distinguish details. Then I climbed down to my companions waiting for me so eagerly at the bottom of the great tree. For once I was the hero of the expedition. Alone I had thought of it, and alone I had done it; and here was the chart which would save us a month's blind groping among unknown dangers. Each of them shook me solemnly by the hand.

But before they discussed the details of my map I had to tell them of my encounter with the ape-man among the branches.

"He has been there all the time," said I.

"How do you know that?" asked Lord John.

"Because I have never been without that feeling that something malevolent was watching us. I mentioned it to you, Professor Challenger."

"Our young friend certainly said something of the kind. He is also the one among us who is endowed with that Celtic temperament which would make him sensitive to such impressions."

"The whole theory of telepathy—" began Summerlee, filling his pipe.

"Is too vast to be now discussed," said Challenger, with decision. "Tell me, now," he added, with the air of a bishop addressing a Sunday school, "did you happen to observe whether the creature could cross its thumb over its palm?"

"No, indeed."

"Had it a tail?"

"No."

"Was the foot prehensile?"

"I do not think it could have made off so fast among the branches if it could not get a grip with its feet."

"In South America there are, if my memory serves me—you will check the observation, Professor Summerlee—some thirty-six species of monkeys, but the anthropoid ape is unknown. It is clear, however, that he exists in this country, and that he is not the hairy, gorilla-like variety, which is never seen out of Africa or the East." (I was inclined to interpolate, as I looked at him, that I had seen his first cousin in Kensington.) "This is a whiskered and colorless type, the latter characteristic pointing to the fact that he spends his days in arboreal seclusion. The question which we have to face is whether he approaches more closely to the ape or the man. In the latter case, he may well approximate to what the vulgar have called the 'missing link.' The solution of this problem is our immediate duty."

"It is nothing of the sort," said Summerlee, abruptly. "Now that, through the intelligence and activity of Mr. Malone" (I cannot help quoting the words), "we have got our chart, our one and only immediate duty is to get ourselves safe and sound out of this awful place."

"The flesh-pots of civilization," groaned Challenger.

"The ink-pots of civilization, sir. It is our task to put on record what we have seen, and to leave the further exploration to others. You all agreed as much before Mr. Malone got us the chart."

"Well," said Challenger, "I admit that my mind will be more at ease when I am assured that the result of our expedition has been conveyed to our friends. How we are to get down from this place I have not as yet an idea. I have never yet encountered any problem, however, which my inventive brain was unable to solve, and I promise you that tomorrow I will turn my attention to the question of our descent." And so the matter was allowed to rest.

But that evening, by the light of the fire and of a single candle, the first map of the lost world was elaborated. Every detail which I had roughly noted from my watch-tower was drawn out in its relative place. Challenger's pencil hovered over the great blank which marked the lake.

"What shall we call it?" he asked.

"Why should you not take the chance of perpetuating your own name?" said Summerlee, with his usual touch of acidity.

"I trust, sir, that my name will have other and more personal claims upon posterity," said Challenger, severely. "Any ignoramus can hand down his worthless memory by imposing it upon a mountain or a river. I need no such monument."

Summerlee, with a twisted smile, was about to make some fresh assault when Lord John hastened to intervene.

"It's up to you, young fellah, to name the lake," said he. "You saw it first, and, by George, if you choose to put 'Lake Malone' on it, no one has a better right."

"By all means. Let our young friend give it a name," said Challenger.

"Then," said I, blushing, I dare say, as I said it, "let it be named Lake Gladys."

"Don't you think the Central Lake would be more descriptive?" remarked Summerlee.

"I should prefer Lake Gladys."

Challenger looked at me sympathetically, and shook his great head in mock disapproval. "Boys will be boys," said he. "Lake Gladys let it be."

XII

"IT WAS DREADFUL IN THE FOREST"

I have said—or perhaps I have not said, for my memory plays me sad tricks these days—that I glowed with pride when three such men as my comrades thanked me for having saved, or at least greatly helped, the situation. As the youngster of the party, not merely in years, but in experience, character, knowledge, and all that goes to make a man, I had been overshadowed from the first. And now I was coming into my own. I warmed at the thought. Alas! for the pride which goes before a fall! That little glow of self-satisfaction, that added measure of self-confidence, were to lead me on that very night to the most dreadful experience of my life, ending with a shock which turns my heart sick when I think of it.

It came about in this way. I had been unduly excited by the adventure of the tree, and sleep seemed to be impossible. Summerlee was on guard, sitting hunched over our small fire, a quaint, angular figure, his rifle across his knees and his pointed, goat-like beard wagging with each weary nod of his head. Lord John lay silent, wrapped in the South American poncho which he wore, while Challenger snored with a roll and rattle which reverberated through the woods. The full moon was shining brightly, and the air was crisply cold. What a night for a walk! And then suddenly came the thought, "Why not?" Suppose I stole softly away, suppose I made my way down to the central lake, suppose I was back at breakfast with some record of the place—would I not in that case be thought an even more worthy associate? Then, if Summerlee carried the day and some means of escape were found, we should return to London with first-hand knowledge of the central mystery of the plateau, to which I alone, of all men, would have penetrated. I thought of Gladys, with her "There are heroisms all round us." I seemed to hear her voice as she said it. I thought also of McArdle. What a three-column article for the paper! What a foundation for a career! A correspondentship in the next great war might be within my reach. I clutched at a gun—my pockets were full of cartridges—and, parting the thorn bushes at the gate of our zareba, quickly slipped out. My last glance showed me the unconscious Summerlee, most futile of sentinels, still nodding away like a queer mechanical toy in front of the smouldering fire.

I had not gone a hundred yards before I deeply repented my rashness. I may have said somewhere in this chronicle that I am too imaginative to be a really courageous man, but that I have an overpowering fear of seeming afraid. This was the power which now carried me onwards. I simply could not slink back with nothing done. Even if my comrades should not have missed me, and should never know of my weakness, there would still remain some intolerable self-shame in my own soul. And yet I shuddered at the position in which I found myself, and would have given all I possessed at that moment to have been honorably free of the whole business.

It was dreadful in the forest. The trees grew so thickly and their foliage spread so widely that I could see nothing of the moonlight save that here and there the high branches made a tangled filigree against the starry sky. As the eyes became more used to the obscurity one learned that there were different degrees of darkness among the trees—that some were dimly visible, while between and among them there were coal-black shadowed patches, like the mouths of caves, from which I shrank in horror as I passed. I thought of the despairing yell of the tortured iguanodon—that dreadful cry which had echoed through the woods. I thought, too, of the glimpse I had in the light of Lord John's torch of that bloated, warty, blood-slavering muzzle. Even now I was on its hunting-ground. At any instant it might spring upon me from the shadows—this nameless and horrible monster. I stopped, and, picking a cartridge from my pocket, I opened the breech of my gun. As I touched the lever my heart leaped within me. It was the shotgun, not the rifle, which I had taken!

Again the impulse to return swept over me. Here, surely, was a most excellent reason for my failure—one for which no one would think the less of me. But again the foolish pride fought against that very word. I could not—must not—fail. After all, my rifle would probably have been as useless as a shotgun against such dangers as I might meet. If I were to go back to camp to change my weapon I could hardly expect to enter and to leave again without being seen. In that case there would be explanations, and my attempt would no longer be all my own. After a little hesitation, then, I screwed up my courage and continued upon my way, my useless gun under my arm.

* * * * *

The darkness of the forest had been alarming, but even worse was the white, still flood of moonlight in the open glade of the iguanodons. Hid among the bushes, I looked out at it. None of the great brutes were in sight. Perhaps the tragedy which had befallen one of them had driven them from their feeding-ground. In the misty, silvery night I could see no sign of any living thing. Taking courage, therefore, I slipped rapidly across it, and among the jungle on the farther side I picked up once again the brook which was my guide. It was a cheery companion, gurgling and chuckling as it ran, like the dear old trout-stream in the West Country where I have fished at night in my boyhood. So long as I followed it down I must come to the lake, and so long as I followed it back I must come to the camp. Often I had to lose sight of it on account of the tangled brushwood, but I was always within earshot of its tinkle and splash.

As one descended the slope the woods became thinner, and bushes, with occasional high trees, took the place of the forest. I could make good progress, therefore, and I could see without being seen. I passed close to the pterodactyl swamp, and as I did so, with a dry, crisp, leathery rattle of wings, one of these great creatures—it was twenty feet at least from tip to tip—rose up from somewhere near me and soared into the air. As it passed across the face of the moon the light shone clearly through the membranous wings, and it looked like a flying skeleton against the white, tropical radiance. I crouched low among the bushes, for I knew from past experience that with a single cry the creature could bring a hundred of its loathsome mates about my ears. It was not until it had settled again that I dared to steal onwards upon my journey.

The night had been exceedingly still, but as I advanced I became conscious of a low, rumbling sound, a continuous murmur, somewhere in front of me. This grew louder as I proceeded, until at last it was clearly quite close to me. When I stood still the sound was constant, so that it seemed to come from some stationary cause. It was like a boiling kettle or the bubbling of some great pot. Soon I came upon the source of it, for in the center of a small clearing I found a lake—or a pool, rather, for it was not larger than the basin of the Trafalgar Square fountain—of some black, pitch-like stuff, the surface of which rose and fell in great blisters of bursting gas. The air above it was shimmering with heat, and the ground round was so hot that I could hardly bear to lay my hand on it. It was clear that the great volcanic outburst which had raised this strange plateau so many years ago had not yet entirely spent its forces. Blackened rocks and mounds of lava I had already seen everywhere peeping out from amid the luxuriant vegetation which draped them, but this asphalt pool in the jungle was the first sign that we had of actual existing activity on the slopes of the ancient crater. I had no time to examine it further for I had need to hurry if I were to be back in camp in the morning.

It was a fearsome walk, and one which will be with me so long as memory holds. In the great moonlight clearings I slunk along among the shadows on the margin. In the jungle I crept forward, stopping with a beating heart whenever I heard, as I often did, the crash of breaking branches as some wild beast went past. Now and then great shadows loomed up for an instant and were gone—great, silent shadows which seemed to prowl upon padded feet. How often I stopped with the intention of returning, and yet every time my pride conquered my fear, and sent me on again until my object should be attained.

At last (my watch showed that it was one in the morning) I saw the gleam of water amid the openings of the jungle, and ten minutes later I was among the reeds upon the borders of the central lake. I was exceedingly dry, so I lay down and took a long draught of its waters, which were fresh and cold. There was a broad pathway with many tracks upon it at the spot which I had found, so that it was clearly one of the drinking-places of the animals. Close to the water's edge there was a huge isolated block of lava. Up this I climbed, and, lying on the top, I had an excellent view in every direction.

The first thing which I saw filled me with amazement. When I described the view from the summit of the great tree, I said that on the farther cliff I could see a number of dark spots, which appeared to be the mouths of caves. Now, as I looked up at the same cliffs, I saw discs of light in every direction, ruddy, clearly-defined patches, like the port-holes of a liner in the darkness. For a moment I thought it was the lava-glow from some volcanic action; but this could not be so. Any volcanic action would surely be down in the hollow and not high among the rocks. What, then, was the alternative? It was wonderful, and yet it must surely be. These ruddy spots must be the reflection of fires within the caves—fires which could only be lit by the hand of man. There were human beings, then, upon the plateau. How gloriously my expedition was justified! Here was news indeed for us to bear back with us to London!

For a long time I lay and watched these red, quivering blotches of light. I suppose they were ten miles off from me, yet even at that distance one could observe how, from time to time, they twinkled or were obscured as someone passed before them. What would I not have given to be able to crawl up to them, to peep in, and to take back some word to my comrades as to the appearance and character of the race who lived in so strange a place! It was out of the question for the moment, and yet surely we could not leave the plateau until we had some definite knowledge upon the point.

Lake Gladys—my own lake—lay like a sheet of quicksilver before me, with a reflected moon shining brightly in the center of it. It was shallow, for in many places I saw low sandbanks protruding above the water. Everywhere upon the still surface I could see signs of life, sometimes mere rings and ripples in the water, sometimes the gleam of a great silver-sided fish in the air, sometimes the arched, slate-colored back of some passing monster. Once upon a yellow sandbank I saw a creature like a huge swan, with a clumsy body and a high, flexible neck, shuffling about upon the margin. Presently it plunged in, and for some time I could see the arched neck and darting head undulating over the water. Then it dived, and I saw it no more.

My attention was soon drawn away from these distant sights and brought back to what was going on at my very feet. Two creatures like large armadillos had come down to the drinking-place, and were squatting at the edge of the water, their long, flexible tongues like red ribbons shooting in and out as they lapped. A huge deer, with branching horns, a magnificent creature which carried itself like a king, came down with its doe and two fawns and drank beside the armadillos. No such deer exist anywhere else upon earth, for the moose or elks which I have seen would hardly have reached its shoulders. Presently it gave a warning snort, and was off with its family among the reeds, while the armadillos also scuttled for shelter. A newcomer, a most monstrous animal, was coming down the path.

For a moment I wondered where I could have seen that ungainly shape, that arched back with triangular fringes along it, that strange bird-like head held close to the ground. Then it came back, to me. It was the stegosaurus—the very creature which Maple White had preserved in his sketchbook, and which had been the first object which arrested the attention of Challenger! There he was—perhaps the very specimen which the American artist had encountered. The ground shook beneath his tremendous weight, and his gulpings of water resounded through the still night. For five minutes he was so close to my rock that by stretching out my hand I could have touched the hideous waving hackles upon his back. Then he lumbered away and was lost among the boulders.

Looking at my watch, I saw that it was half-past two o'clock, and high time, therefore, that I started upon my homeward journey. There was no difficulty about the direction in which I should return for all along I had kept the little brook upon my left, and it opened into the central lake within a stone's-throw of the boulder upon which I had been lying. I set off, therefore, in high spirits, for I felt that I had done good work and was bringing back a fine budget of news for my companions. Foremost of all, of course, were the sight of the fiery caves and the certainty that some troglodytic race inhabited them. But besides that I could speak from experience of the central lake. I could testify that it was full of strange creatures, and I had seen several land forms of primeval life which we had not before encountered. I reflected as I walked that few men in the world could have spent a stranger night or added more to human knowledge in the course of it.

I was plodding up the slope, turning these thoughts over in my mind, and had reached a point which may have been half-way to home, when my mind was brought back to my own position by a strange noise behind me. It was something between a snore and a growl, low, deep, and exceedingly menacing. Some strange creature was evidently near me, but nothing could be seen, so I hastened more rapidly upon my way. I had traversed half a mile or so when suddenly the sound was repeated, still behind me, but louder and more menacing than before. My heart stood still within me as it flashed across me that the beast, whatever it was, must surely be after me.

My skin grew cold and my hair rose at the thought. That these monsters should tear each other to pieces was a part of the strange struggle for existence, but that they should turn upon modern man, that they should deliberately track and hunt down the predominant human, was a staggering and fearsome thought. I remembered again the blood-beslobbered face which we had seen in the glare of Lord John's torch, like some horrible vision from the deepest circle of Dante's hell. With my knees shaking beneath me, I stood and glared with starting eyes down the moonlit path which lay behind me. All was quiet as in a dream landscape. Silver clearings and the black patches of the bushes—nothing else could I see. Then from out of the silence, imminent and threatening, there came once more that low, throaty croaking, far louder and closer than before. There could no longer be a doubt. Something was on my trail, and was closing in upon me every minute.

I stood like a man paralyzed, still staring at the ground which I had traversed. Then suddenly I saw it. There was movement among the bushes at the far end of the clearing which I had just traversed. A great dark shadow disengaged itself and hopped out into the clear moonlight. I say "hopped" advisedly, for the beast moved like a kangaroo, springing along in an erect position upon its powerful hind legs, while its front ones were held bent in front of it. It was of enormous size and power, like an erect elephant, but its movements, in spite of its bulk, were exceedingly alert. For a moment, as I saw its shape, I hoped that it was an iguanodon, which I knew to be harmless, but, ignorant as I was, I soon saw that this was a very different creature. Instead of the gentle, deer-shaped head of the great three-toed leaf-eater, this beast had a broad, squat, toad-like face like that which had alarmed us in our camp. His ferocious cry and the horrible energy of his pursuit both assured me that this was surely one of the great flesh-eating dinosaurs, the most terrible beasts which have ever walked this earth. As the huge brute loped along it dropped forward upon its forepaws and brought its nose to the ground every twenty yards or so. It was smelling out my trail. Sometimes, for an instant, it was at fault. Then it would catch it up again and come bounding swiftly along the path I had taken.

Even now when I think of that nightmare the sweat breaks out upon my brow. What could I do? My useless fowling-piece was in my hand. What help could I get from that? I looked desperately round for some rock or tree, but I was in a bushy jungle with nothing higher than a sapling within sight, while I knew that the creature behind me could tear down an ordinary tree as though it were a reed. My only possible chance lay in flight. I could not move swiftly over the rough, broken ground, but as I looked round me in despair I saw a well-marked, hard-beaten path which ran across in front of me. We had seen several of the sort, the runs of various wild beasts, during our expeditions. Along this I could perhaps hold my own, for I was a fast runner, and in excellent condition. Flinging away my useless gun, I set myself to do such a half-mile as I have never done before or since. My limbs ached, my chest heaved, I felt that my throat would burst for want of air, and yet with that horror behind me I ran and I ran and ran. At last I paused, hardly able to move. For a moment I thought that I had thrown him off. The path lay still behind me. And then suddenly, with a crashing and a rending, a thudding of giant feet and a panting of monster lungs the beast was upon me once more. He was at my very heels. I was lost.

Madman that I was to linger so long before I fled! Up to then he had hunted by scent, and his movement was slow. But he had actually seen me as I started to run. From then onwards he had hunted by sight, for the path showed him where I had gone. Now, as he came round the curve, he was springing in great bounds. The moonlight shone upon his huge projecting eyes, the row of enormous teeth in his open mouth, and the gleaming fringe of claws upon his short, powerful forearms. With a scream of terror I turned and rushed wildly down the path. Behind me the thick, gasping breathing of the creature sounded louder and louder. His heavy footfall was beside me. Every instant I expected to feel his grip upon my back. And then suddenly there came a crash—I was falling through space, and everything beyond was darkness and rest.

As I emerged from my unconsciousness—which could not, I think, have lasted more than a few minutes—I was aware of a most dreadful and penetrating smell. Putting out my hand in the darkness I came upon something which felt like a huge lump of meat, while my other hand closed upon a large bone. Up above me there was a circle of starlit sky, which showed me that I was lying at the bottom of a deep pit. Slowly I staggered to my feet and felt myself all over. I was stiff and sore from head to foot, but there was no limb which would not move, no joint which would not bend. As the circumstances of my fall came back into my confused brain, I looked up in terror, expecting to see that dreadful head silhouetted against the paling sky. There was no sign of the monster, however, nor could I hear any sound from above. I began to walk slowly round, therefore, feeling in every direction to find out what this strange place could be into which I had been so opportunely precipitated.

It was, as I have said, a pit, with sharply sloping walls and a level bottom about twenty feet across. This bottom was littered with great gobbets of flesh, most of which was in the last state of putridity. The atmosphere was poisonous and horrible. After tripping and stumbling over these lumps of decay, I came suddenly against something hard, and I found that an upright post was firmly fixed in the center of the hollow. It was so high that I could not reach the top of it with my hand, and it appeared to be covered with grease.

Suddenly I remembered that I had a tin box of wax-vestas in my pocket. Striking one of them, I was able at last to form some opinion of this place into which I had fallen. There could be no question as to its nature. It was a trap—made by the hand of man. The post in the center, some nine feet long, was sharpened at the upper end, and was black with the stale blood of the creatures who had been impaled upon it. The remains scattered about were fragments of the victims, which had been cut away in order to clear the stake for the next who might blunder in. I remembered that Challenger had declared that man could not exist upon the plateau, since with his feeble weapons he could not hold his own against the monsters who roamed over it. But now it was clear enough how it could be done. In their narrow-mouthed caves the natives, whoever they might be, had refuges into which the huge saurians could not penetrate, while with their developed brains they were capable of setting such traps, covered with branches, across the paths which marked the run of the animals as would destroy them in spite of all their strength and activity. Man was always the master.

The sloping wall of the pit was not difficult for an active man to climb, but I hesitated long before I trusted myself within reach of the dreadful creature which had so nearly destroyed me. How did I know that he was not lurking in the nearest clump of bushes, waiting for my reappearance? I took heart, however, as I recalled a conversation between Challenger and Summerlee upon the habits of the great saurians. Both were agreed that the monsters were practically brainless, that there was no room for reason in their tiny cranial cavities, and that if they have disappeared from the rest of the world it was assuredly on account of their own stupidity, which made it impossible for them to adapt themselves to changing conditions.

To lie in wait for me now would mean that the creature had appreciated what had happened to me, and this in turn would argue some power connecting cause and effect. Surely it was more likely that a brainless creature, acting solely by vague predatory instinct, would give up the chase when I disappeared, and, after a pause of astonishment, would wander away in search of some other prey? I clambered to the edge of the pit and looked over. The stars were fading, the sky was whitening, and the cold wind of morning blew pleasantly upon my face. I could see or hear nothing of my enemy. Slowly I climbed out and sat for a while upon the ground, ready to spring back into my refuge if any danger should appear. Then, reassured by the absolute stillness and by the growing light, I took my courage in both hands and stole back along the path which I had come. Some distance down it I picked up my gun, and shortly afterwards struck the brook which was my guide. So, with many a frightened backward glance, I made for home.

And suddenly there came something to remind me of my absent companions. In the clear, still morning air there sounded far away the sharp, hard note of a single rifle-shot. I paused and listened, but there was nothing more. For a moment I was shocked at the thought that some sudden danger might have befallen them. But then a simpler and more natural explanation came to my mind. It was now broad daylight. No doubt my absence had been noticed. They had imagined, that I was lost in the woods, and had fired this shot to guide me home. It is true that we had made a strict resolution against firing, but if it seemed to them that I might be in danger they would not hesitate. It was for me now to hurry on as fast as possible, and so to reassure them.

I was weary and spent, so my progress was not so fast as I wished; but at last I came into regions which I knew. There was the swamp of the pterodactyls upon my left; there in front of me was the glade of the iguanodons. Now I was in the last belt of trees which separated me from Fort Challenger. I raised my voice in a cheery shout to allay their fears. No answering greeting came back to me. My heart sank at that ominous stillness. I quickened my pace into a run. The zareba rose before me, even as I had left it, but the gate was open. I rushed in. In the cold, morning light it was a fearful sight which met my eyes. Our effects were scattered in wild confusion over the ground; my comrades had disappeared, and close to the smouldering ashes of our fire the grass was stained crimson with a hideous pool of blood.

I was so stunned by this sudden shock that for a time I must have nearly lost my reason. I have a vague recollection, as one remembers a bad dream, of rushing about through the woods all round the empty camp, calling wildly for my companions. No answer came back from the silent shadows. The horrible thought that I might never see them again, that I might find myself abandoned all alone in that dreadful place, with no possible way of descending into the world below, that I might live and die in that nightmare country, drove me to desperation. I could have torn my hair and beaten my head in my despair. Only now did I realize how I had learned to lean upon my companions, upon the serene self-confidence of Challenger, and upon the masterful, humorous coolness of Lord John Roxton. Without them I was like a child in the dark, helpless and powerless. I did not know which way to turn or what I should do first.

After a period, during which I sat in bewilderment, I set myself to try and discover what sudden misfortune could have befallen my companions. The whole disordered appearance of the camp showed that there had been some sort of attack, and the rifle-shot no doubt marked the time when it had occurred. That there should have been only one shot showed that it had been all over in an instant. The rifles still lay upon the ground, and one of them—Lord John's—had the empty cartridge in the breech. The blankets of Challenger and of Summerlee beside the fire suggested that they had been asleep at the time. The cases of ammunition and of food were scattered about in a wild litter, together with our unfortunate cameras and plate-carriers, but none of them were missing. On the other hand, all the exposed provisions—and I remembered that there were a considerable quantity of them—were gone. They were animals, then, and not natives, who had made the inroad, for surely the latter would have left nothing behind.

But if animals, or some single terrible animal, then what had become of my comrades? A ferocious beast would surely have destroyed them and left their remains. It is true that there was that one hideous pool of blood, which told of violence. Such a monster as had pursued me during the night could have carried away a victim as easily as a cat would a mouse. In that case the others would have followed in pursuit. But then they would assuredly have taken their rifles with them. The more I tried to think it out with my confused and weary brain the less could I find any plausible explanation. I searched round in the forest, but could see no tracks which could help me to a conclusion. Once I lost myself, and it was only by good luck, and after an hour of wandering, that I found the camp once more.

Suddenly a thought came to me and brought some little comfort to my heart. I was not absolutely alone in the world. Down at the bottom of the cliff, and within call of me, was waiting the faithful Zambo. I went to the edge of the plateau and looked over. Sure enough, he was squatting among his blankets beside his fire in his little camp. But, to my amazement, a second man was seated in front of him. For an instant my heart leaped for joy, as I thought that one of my comrades had made his way safely down. But a second glance dispelled the hope. The rising sun shone red upon the man's skin. He was an Indian. I shouted loudly and waved my handkerchief. Presently Zambo looked up, waved his hand, and turned to ascend the pinnacle. In a short time he was standing close to me and listening with deep distress to the story which I told him.

"Devil got them for sure, Massa Malone," said he. "You got into the devil's country, sah, and he take you all to himself. You take advice, Massa Malone, and come down quick, else he get you as well."

"How can I come down, Zambo?"

"You get creepers from trees, Massa Malone. Throw them over here. I make fast to this stump, and so you have bridge."

"We have thought of that. There are no creepers here which could bear us."

"Send for ropes, Massa Malone."

"Who can I send, and where?"

"Send to Indian villages, sah. Plenty hide rope in Indian village. Indian down below; send him."

"Who is he?

"One of our Indians. Other ones beat him and take away his pay. He come back to us. Ready now to take letter, bring rope—anything."

To take a letter! Why not? Perhaps he might bring help; but in any case he would ensure that our lives were not spent for nothing, and that news of all that we had won for Science should reach our friends at home. I had two completed letters already waiting. I would spend the day in writing a third, which would bring my experiences absolutely up to date. The Indian could bear this back to the world. I ordered Zambo, therefore, to come again in the evening, and I spent my miserable and lonely day in recording my own adventures of the night before. I also drew up a note, to be given to any white merchant or captain of a steam-boat whom the Indian could find, imploring them to see that ropes were sent to us, since our lives must depend upon it. These documents I threw to Zambo in the evening, and also my purse, which contained three English sovereigns. These were to be given to the Indian, and he was promised twice as much if he returned with the ropes.

So now you will understand, my dear Mr. McArdle, how this communication reaches you, and you will also know the truth, in case you never hear again from your unfortunate correspondent. Tonight I am too weary and too depressed to make my plans. Tomorrow I must think out some way by which I shall keep in touch with this camp, and yet search round for any traces of my unhappy friends.

XIII

"A SIGHT WHICH I SHALL NEVER FORGET"

Just as the sun was setting upon that melancholy night I saw the lonely figure of the Indian upon the vast plain beneath me, and I watched him, our one faint hope of salvation, until he disappeared in the rising mists of evening which lay, rose-tinted from the setting sun, between the far-off river and me.

It was quite dark when I at last turned back to our stricken camp, and my last vision as I went was the red gleam of Zambo's fire, the one point of light in the wide world below, as was his faithful presence in my own shadowed soul. And yet I felt happier than I had done since this crushing blow had fallen upon me, for it was good to think that the world should know what we had done, so that at the worst our names should not perish with our bodies, but should go down to posterity associated with the result of our labors.

It was an awesome thing to sleep in that ill-fated camp; and yet it was even more unnerving to do so in the jungle. One or the other it must be. Prudence, on the one hand, warned me that I should remain on guard, but exhausted Nature, on the other, declared that I should do nothing of the kind. I climbed up on to a limb of the great gingko tree, but there was no secure perch on its rounded surface, and I should certainly have fallen off and broken my neck the moment I began to doze. I got down, therefore, and pondered over what I should do. Finally, I closed the door of the zareba, lit three separate fires in a triangle, and having eaten a hearty supper dropped off into a profound sleep, from which I had a strange and most welcome awakening. In the early morning, just as day was breaking, a hand was laid upon my arm, and starting up, with all my nerves in a tingle and my hand feeling for a rifle, I gave a cry of joy as in the cold gray light I saw Lord John Roxton kneeling beside me.

It was he—and yet it was not he. I had left him calm in his bearing, correct in his person, prim in his dress. Now he was pale and wild-eyed, gasping as he breathed like one who has run far and fast. His gaunt face was scratched and bloody, his clothes were hanging in rags, and his hat was gone. I stared in amazement, but he gave me no chance for questions. He was grabbing at our stores all the time he spoke.

"Quick, young fellah! Quick!" he cried. "Every moment counts. Get the rifles, both of them. I have the other two. Now, all the cartridges you can gather. Fill up your pockets. Now, some food. Half a dozen tins will do. That's all right! Don't wait to talk or think. Get a move on, or we are done!"

Still half-awake, and unable to imagine what it all might mean, I found myself hurrying madly after him through the wood, a rifle under each arm and a pile of various stores in my hands. He dodged in and out through the thickest of the scrub until he came to a dense clump of brushwood. Into this he rushed, regardless of thorns, and threw himself into the heart of it, pulling me down by his side.

"There!" he panted. "I think we are safe here. They'll make for the camp as sure as fate. It will be their first idea. But this should puzzle 'em."

"What is it all?" I asked, when I had got my breath. "Where are the professors? And who is it that is after us?"

"The ape-men," he cried. "My God, what brutes! Don't raise your voice, for they have long ears—sharp eyes, too, but no power of scent, so far as I could judge, so I don't think they can sniff us out. Where have you been, young fellah? You were well out of it."

In a few sentences I whispered what I had done.

"Pretty bad," said he, when he had heard of the dinosaur and the pit. "It isn't quite the place for a rest cure. What? But I had no idea what its possibilities were until those devils got hold of us. The man-eatin' Papuans had me once, but they are Chesterfields compared to this crowd."

"How did it happen?" I asked.

"It was in the early mornin'. Our learned friends were just stirrin'. Hadn't even begun to argue yet. Suddenly it rained apes. They came down as thick as apples out of a tree. They had been assemblin' in the dark, I suppose, until that great tree over our heads was heavy with them. I shot one of them through the belly, but before we knew where we were they had us spread-eagled on our backs. I call them apes, but they carried sticks and stones in their hands and jabbered talk to each other, and ended up by tyin' our hands with creepers, so they are ahead of any beast that I have seen in my wanderin's. Ape-men—that's what they are—Missin' Links, and I wish they had stayed missin'. They carried off their wounded comrade—he was bleedin' like a pig—and then they sat around us, and if ever I saw frozen murder it was in their faces. They were big fellows, as big as a man and a deal stronger. Curious glassy gray eyes they have, under red tufts, and they just sat and gloated and gloated. Challenger is no chicken, but even he was cowed. He managed to struggle to his feet, and yelled out at them to have done with it and get it over. I think he had gone a bit off his head at the suddenness of it, for he raged and cursed at them like a lunatic. If they had been a row of his favorite Pressmen he could not have slanged them worse."

"Well, what did they do?" I was enthralled by the strange story which my companion was whispering into my ear, while all the time his keen eyes were shooting in every direction and his hand grasping his cocked rifle.

"I thought it was the end of us, but instead of that it started them on a new line. They all jabbered and chattered together. Then one of them stood out beside Challenger. You'll smile, young fellah, but 'pon my word they might have been kinsmen. I couldn't have believed it if I hadn't seen it with my own eyes. This old ape-man—he was their chief—was a sort of red Challenger, with every one of our friend's beauty points, only just a trifle more so. He had the short body, the big shoulders, the round chest, no neck, a great ruddy frill of a beard, the tufted eyebrows, the 'What do you want, damn you!' look about the eyes, and the whole catalogue. When the ape-man stood by Challenger and put his paw on his shoulder, the thing was complete. Summerlee was a bit hysterical, and he laughed till he cried. The ape-men laughed too—or at least they put up the devil of a cacklin'—and they set to work to drag us off through the forest. They wouldn't touch the guns and things—thought them dangerous, I expect—but they carried away all our loose food. Summerlee and I got some rough handlin' on the way—there's my skin and my clothes to prove it—for they took us a beeline through the brambles, and their own hides are like leather. But Challenger was all right. Four of them carried him shoulder high, and he went like a Roman emperor. What's that?"

It was a strange clicking noise in the distance not unlike castanets.

"There they go!" said my companion, slipping cartridges into the second double-barreled Express. "Load them all up, young fellah my lad, for we're not going to be taken alive, and don't you think it! That's the row they make when they are excited. By George! They'll have something to excite them if they put us up. The 'Last Stand of the Grays' won't be in it. 'With their rifles grasped in their stiffened hands, mid a ring of the dead and dyin',' as some fathead sings. Can you hear them now?"

"Very far away."

"That little lot will do no good, but I expect their search parties are all over the wood. Well, I was telling you my tale of woe. They got us soon to this town of theirs—about a thousand huts of branches and leaves in a great grove of trees near the edge of the cliff. It's three or four miles from here. The filthy beasts fingered me all over, and I feel as if I should never be clean again. They tied us up—the fellow who handled me could tie like a bosun—and there we lay with our toes up, beneath a tree, while a great brute stood guard over us with a club in his hand. When I say 'we' I mean Summerlee and myself. Old Challenger was up a tree, eatin' pines and havin' the time of his life. I'm bound to say that he managed to get some fruit to us, and with his own hands he loosened our bonds. If you'd seen him sitting up in that tree hob-nobbin' with his twin brother—and singin' in that rollin' bass of his, 'Ring out, wild bells,' cause music of any kind seemed to put 'em in a good humor, you'd have smiled; but we weren't in much mood for laughin', as you can guess. They were inclined, within limits, to let him do what he liked, but they drew the line pretty sharply at us. It was a mighty consolation to us all to know that you were runnin' loose and had the archives in your keepin'.

"Well, now, young fellah, I'll tell you what will surprise you. You say you saw signs of men, and fires, traps, and the like. Well, we have seen the natives themselves. Poor devils they were, down-faced little chaps, and had enough to make them so. It seems that the humans hold one side of this plateau—over yonder, where you saw the caves—and the ape-men hold this side, and there is bloody war between them all the time. That's the situation, so far as I could follow it. Well, yesterday the ape-men got hold of a dozen of the humans and brought them in as prisoners. You never heard such a jabberin' and shriekin' in your life. The men were little red fellows, and had been bitten and clawed so that they could hardly walk. The ape-men put two of them to death there and then—fairly pulled the arm off one of them—it was perfectly beastly. Plucky little chaps they are, and hardly gave a squeak. But it turned us absolutely sick. Summerlee fainted, and even Challenger had as much as he could stand. I think they have cleared, don't you?"

We listened intently, but nothing save the calling of the birds broke the deep peace of the forest. Lord Roxton went on with his story.

"I think you have had the escape of your life, young fellah my lad. It was catchin' those Indians that put you clean out of their heads, else they would have been back to the camp for you as sure as fate and gathered you in. Of course, as you said, they have been watchin' us from the beginnin' out of that tree, and they knew perfectly well that we were one short. However, they could think only of this new haul; so it was I, and not a bunch of apes, that dropped in on you in the morning. Well, we had a horrid business afterwards. My God! What a nightmare the whole thing is! You remember the great bristle of sharp canes down below where we found the skeleton of the American? Well, that is just under ape-town, and that's the jumpin'-off place of their prisoners. I expect there's heaps of skeletons there, if we looked for 'em. They have a sort of clear parade-ground on the top, and they make a proper ceremony about it. One by one the poor devils have to jump, and the game is to see whether they are merely dashed to pieces or whether they get skewered on the canes. They took us out to see it, and the whole tribe lined up on the edge. Four of the Indians jumped, and the canes went through 'em like knittin' needles through a pat of butter. No wonder we found that poor Yankee's skeleton with the canes growin' between his ribs. It was horrible—but it was doocedly interestin' too. We were all fascinated to see them take the dive, even when we thought it would be our turn next on the springboard.

"Well, it wasn't. They kept six of the Indians up for today—that's how I understood it—but I fancy we were to be the star performers in the show.

Challenger might get off, but Summerlee and I were in the bill. Their language is more than half signs, and it was not hard to follow them. So I thought it was time we made a break for it. I had been plottin' it out a bit, and had one or two things clear in my mind. It was all on me, for Summerlee was useless and Challenger not much better. The only time they got together they got slangin' because they couldn't agree upon the scientific classification of these red-headed devils that had got hold of us. One said it was the dryopithecus of Java, the other said it was pithecanthropus. Madness, I call it—Loonies, both. But, as I say, I had thought out one or two points that were helpful. One was that these brutes could not run as fast as a man in the open. They have short, bandy legs, you see, and heavy bodies. Even Challenger could give a few yards in a hundred to the best of them, and you or I would be a perfect Shrubb. Another point was that they knew nothin' about guns. I don't believe they ever understood how the fellow I shot came by his hurt. If we could get at our guns there was no sayin' what we could do.

"So I broke away early this mornin', gave my guard a kick in the tummy that laid him out, and sprinted for the camp. There I got you and the guns, and here we are."

"But the professors!" I cried, in consternation.

"Well, we must just go back and fetch 'em. I couldn't bring 'em with me. Challenger was up the tree, and Summerlee was not fit for the effort. The only chance was to get the guns and try a rescue. Of course they may scupper them at once in revenge. I don't think they would touch Challenger, but I wouldn't answer for Summerlee. But they would have had him in any case. Of that I am certain. So I haven't made matters any worse by boltin'. But we are honor bound to go back and have them out or see it through with them. So you can make up your soul, young fellah my lad, for it will be one way or the other before evenin'."

I have tried to imitate here Lord Roxton's jerky talk, his short, strong sentences, the half-humorous, half-reckless tone that ran through it all. But he was a born leader. As danger thickened his jaunty manner would increase, his speech become more racy, his cold eyes glitter into ardent life, and his Don Quixote moustache bristle with joyous excitement. His love of danger, his intense appreciation of the drama of an adventure—all the more intense for being held tightly in—his consistent view that every peril in life is a form of sport, a fierce game betwixt you and Fate, with Death as a forfeit, made him a wonderful companion at such hours. If it were not for our fears as to the fate of our companions, it would have been a positive joy to throw myself with such a man into such an affair. We were rising from our brushwood hiding-place when suddenly I felt his grip upon my arm.

"By George!" he whispered, "here they come!"

From where we lay we could look down a brown aisle, arched with green, formed by the trunks and branches. Along this a party of the ape-men were passing. They went in single file, with bent legs and rounded backs, their hands occasionally touching the ground, their heads turning to left and right as they trotted along. Their crouching gait took away from their height, but I should put them at five feet or so, with long arms and enormous chests. Many of them carried sticks, and at the distance they looked like a line of very hairy and deformed human beings. For a moment I caught this clear glimpse of them. Then they were lost among the bushes.

"Not this time," said Lord John, who had caught up his rifle. "Our best chance is to lie quiet until they have given up the search. Then we shall see whether we can't get back to their town and hit 'em where it hurts most. Give 'em an hour and we'll march."

We filled in the time by opening one of our food tins and making sure of our breakfast. Lord Roxton had had nothing but some fruit since the morning before and ate like a starving man. Then, at last, our pockets bulging with cartridges and a rifle in each hand, we started off upon our mission of rescue. Before leaving it we carefully marked our little hiding-place among the brushwood and its bearing to Fort Challenger, that we might find it again if we needed it. We slunk through the bushes in silence until we came to the very edge of the cliff, close to the old camp. There we halted, and Lord John gave me some idea of his plans.

"So long as we are among the thick trees these swine are our masters," said he. "They can see us and we cannot see them. But in the open it is different. There we can move faster than they. So we must stick to the open all we can. The edge of the plateau has fewer large trees than further inland. So that's our line of advance. Go slowly, keep your eyes open and your rifle ready. Above all, never let them get you prisoner while there is a cartridge left—that's my last word to you, young fellah."

When we reached the edge of the cliff I looked over and saw our good old black Zambo sitting smoking on a rock below us. I would have given a great deal to have hailed him and told him how we were placed, but it was too dangerous, lest we should be heard. The woods seemed to be full of the ape-men; again and again we heard their curious clicking chatter. At such times we plunged into the nearest clump of bushes and lay still until the sound had passed away. Our advance, therefore, was very slow, and two hours at least must have passed before I saw by Lord John's cautious movements that we must be close to our destination. He motioned to me to lie still, and he crawled forward himself. In a minute he was back again, his face quivering with eagerness.

"Come!" said he. "Come quick! I hope to the Lord we are not too late already!"

I found myself shaking with nervous excitement as I scrambled forward and lay down beside him, looking out through the bushes at a clearing which stretched before us.

It was a sight which I shall never forget until my dying day—so weird, so impossible, that I do not know how I am to make you realize it, or how in a few years I shall bring myself to believe in it if I live to sit once more on a lounge in the Savage Club and look out on the drab solidity of the Embankment. I know that it will seem then to be some wild nightmare, some delirium of fever. Yet I will set it down now, while it is still fresh in my memory, and one at least, the man who lay in the damp grasses by my side, will know if I have lied.

A wide, open space lay before us—some hundreds of yards across—all green turf and low bracken growing to the very edge of the cliff. Round this clearing there was a semi-circle of trees with curious huts built of foliage piled one above the other among the branches. A rookery, with every nest a little house, would best convey the idea. The openings of these huts and the branches of the trees were thronged with a dense mob of ape-people, whom from their size I took to be the females and infants of the tribe. They formed the background of the picture, and were all looking out with eager interest at the same scene which fascinated and bewildered us.

In the open, and near the edge of the cliff, there had assembled a crowd of some hundred of these shaggy, red-haired creatures, many of them of immense size, and all of them horrible to look upon. There was a certain discipline among them, for none of them attempted to break the line which had been formed. In front there stood a small group of Indians—little, clean-limbed, red fellows, whose skins glowed like polished bronze in the strong sunlight. A tall, thin white man was standing beside them, his head bowed, his arms folded, his whole attitude expressive of his horror and dejection. There was no mistaking the angular form of Professor Summerlee.

In front of and around this dejected group of prisoners were several ape-men, who watched them closely and made all escape impossible. Then, right out from all the others and close to the edge of the cliff, were two figures, so strange, and under other circumstances so ludicrous, that they absorbed my attention. The one was our comrade, Professor Challenger. The remains of his coat still hung in strips from his shoulders, but his shirt had been all torn out, and his great beard merged itself in the black tangle which covered his mighty chest. He had lost his hat, and his hair, which had grown long in our wanderings, was flying in wild disorder. A single day seemed to have changed him from the highest product of modern civilization to the most desperate savage in South America. Beside him stood his master, the king of the ape-men. In all things he was, as Lord John had said, the very image of our Professor, save that his coloring was red instead of black. The same short, broad figure, the same heavy shoulders, the same forward hang of the arms, the same bristling beard merging itself in the hairy chest. Only above the eyebrows, where the sloping forehead and low, curved skull of the ape-man were in sharp contrast to the broad brow and magnificent cranium of the European, could one see any marked difference. At every other point the king was an absurd parody of the Professor.

All this, which takes me so long to describe, impressed itself upon me in a few seconds. Then we had very different things to think of, for an active drama was in progress. Two of the ape-men had seized one of the Indians out of the group and dragged him forward to the edge of the cliff. The king raised his hand as a signal. They caught the man by his leg and arm, and swung him three times backwards and forwards with tremendous violence. Then, with a frightful heave they shot the poor wretch over the precipice. With such force did they throw him that he curved high in the air before beginning to drop. As he vanished from sight, the whole assembly, except the guards, rushed forward to the edge of the precipice, and there was a long pause of absolute silence, broken by a mad yell of delight. They sprang about, tossing their long, hairy arms in the air and howling with exultation. Then they fell back from the edge, formed themselves again into line, and waited for the next victim.

This time it was Summerlee. Two of his guards caught him by the wrists and pulled him brutally to the front. His thin figure and long limbs struggled and fluttered like a chicken being dragged from a coop. Challenger had turned to the king and waved his hands frantically before him. He was begging, pleading, imploring for his comrade's life. The ape-man pushed him roughly aside and shook his head. It was the last conscious movement he was to make upon earth. Lord John's rifle cracked, and the king sank down, a tangled red sprawling thing, upon the ground.

"Shoot into the thick of them! Shoot! Sonny, shoot!" cried my companion.

There are strange red depths in the soul of the most commonplace man. I am tenderhearted by nature, and have found my eyes moist many a time over the scream of a wounded hare. Yet the blood lust was on me now. I found myself on my feet emptying one magazine, then the other, clicking open the breech to re-load, snapping it to again, while cheering and yelling with pure ferocity and joy of slaughter as I did so. With our four guns the two of us made a horrible havoc. Both the guards who held Summerlee were down, and he was staggering about like a drunken man in his amazement, unable to realize that he was a free man. The dense mob of ape-men ran about in bewilderment, marveling whence this storm of death was coming or what it might mean. They waved, gesticulated, screamed, and tripped up over those who had fallen. Then, with a sudden impulse, they all rushed in a howling crowd to the trees for shelter, leaving the ground behind them spotted with their stricken comrades. The prisoners were left for the moment standing alone in the middle of the clearing.

Challenger's quick brain had grasped the situation. He seized the bewildered Summerlee by the arm, and they both ran towards us. Two of their guards bounded after them and fell to two bullets from Lord John. We ran forward into the open to meet our friends, and pressed a loaded rifle into the hands of each. But Summerlee was at the end of his strength. He could hardly totter. Already the ape-men were recovering from their panic. They were coming through the brushwood and threatening to cut us off. Challenger and I ran Summerlee along, one at each of his elbows, while Lord John covered our retreat, firing again and again as savage heads snarled at us out of the bushes. For a mile or more the chattering brutes were at our very heels. Then the pursuit slackened, for they learned our power and would no longer face that unerring rifle. When we had at last reached the camp, we looked back and found ourselves alone.

So it seemed to us; and yet we were mistaken. We had hardly closed the thornbush door of our zareba, clasped each other's hands, and thrown ourselves panting upon the ground beside our spring, when we heard a patter of feet and then a gentle, plaintive crying from outside our entrance. Lord Roxton rushed forward, rifle in hand, and threw it open. There, prostrate upon their faces, lay the little red figures of the four surviving Indians, trembling with fear of us and yet imploring our protection. With an expressive sweep of his hands one of them pointed to the woods around them, and indicated that they were full of danger. Then, darting forward, he threw his arms round Lord John's legs, and rested his face upon them.

"By George!" cried our peer, pulling at his moustache in great perplexity, "I say—what the deuce are we to do with these people? Get up, little chappie, and take your face off my boots."

Summerlee was sitting up and stuffing some tobacco into his old briar.

"We've got to see them safe," said he. "You've pulled us all out of the jaws of death. My word! it was a good bit of work!"

"Admirable!" cried Challenger. "Admirable! Not only we as individuals, but European science collectively, owe you a deep debt of gratitude for what you have done. I do not hesitate to say that the disappearance of Professor

Summerlee and myself would have left an appreciable gap in modern zoological history. Our young friend here and you have done most excellently well."

He beamed at us with the old paternal smile, but European science would have been somewhat amazed could they have seen their chosen child, the hope of the future, with his tangled, unkempt head, his bare chest, and his tattered clothes. He had one of the meat-tins between his knees, and sat with a large piece of cold Australian mutton between his fingers. The Indian looked up at him, and then, with a little yelp, cringed to the ground and clung to Lord John's leg.

"Don't you be scared, my bonnie boy," said Lord John, patting the matted head in front of him. "He can't stick your appearance, Challenger; and, by George! I don't wonder. All right, little chap, he's only a human, just the same as the rest of us."

"Really, sir!" cried the Professor.

"Well, it's lucky for you, Challenger, that you are a little out of the ordinary. If you hadn't been so like the king—"

"Upon my word, Lord John, you allow yourself great latitude."

"Well, it's a fact."

"I beg, sir, that you will change the subject. Your remarks are irrelevant and unintelligible. The question before us is what are we to do with these Indians? The obvious thing is to escort them home, if we knew where their home was."

"There is no difficulty about that," said I. "They live in the caves on the other side of the central lake."

"Our young friend here knows where they live. I gather that it is some distance."

"A good twenty miles," said I.

Summerlee gave a groan.

"I, for one, could never get there. Surely I hear those brutes still howling upon our track."

As he spoke, from the dark recesses of the woods we heard far away the jabbering cry of the ape-men. The Indians once more set up a feeble wail of fear.

"We must move, and move quick!" said Lord John. "You help Summerlee, young fellah. These Indians will carry stores. Now, then, come along before they can see us."

In less than half-an-hour we had reached our brushwood retreat and concealed ourselves. All day we heard the excited calling of the ape-men in the direction of our old camp, but none of them came our way, and the tired fugitives, red and white, had a long, deep sleep. I was dozing myself in the evening when someone plucked my sleeve, and I found Challenger kneeling beside me.

"You keep a diary of these events, and you expect eventually to publish it, Mr. Malone," said he, with solemnity.

"I am only here as a Press reporter," I answered.

"Exactly. You may have heard some rather fatuous remarks of Lord John Roxton's which seemed to imply that there was some—some resemblance—"

"Yes, I heard them."

"I need not say that any publicity given to such an idea—any levity in your narrative of what occurred—would be exceedingly offensive to me."

"I will keep well within the truth."

"Lord John's observations are frequently exceedingly fanciful, and he is capable of attributing the most absurd reasons to the respect which is always shown by the most undeveloped races to dignity and character. You follow my meaning?"

"Entirely."

"I leave the matter to your discretion." Then, after a long pause, he added: "The king of the ape-men was really a creature of great distinction—a most remarkably handsome and intelligent personality. Did it not strike you?"

"A most remarkable creature," said I.

And the Professor, much eased in his mind, settled down to his slumber once more.

XIV

"THOSE WERE THE REAL CONQUESTS"

We had imagined that our pursuers, the ape-men, knew nothing of our brushwood hiding-place, but we were soon to find out our mistake. There was no sound in the woods—not a leaf moved upon the trees, and all was peace around us—but we should have been warned by our first experience how cunningly and how patiently these creatures can watch and wait until their chance comes. Whatever fate may be mine through life, I am very sure that I shall never be nearer death than I was that morning. But I will tell you the thing in its due order.

We all awoke exhausted after the terrific emotions and scanty food of yesterday. Summerlee was still so weak that it was an effort for him to stand; but the old man was full of a sort of surly courage which would never admit defeat. A council was held, and it was agreed that we should wait quietly for an hour or two where we were, have our much-needed breakfast, and then make our way across the plateau and round the central lake to the caves where my observations had shown that the Indians lived. We relied upon the fact that we could count upon the good word of those whom we had rescued to ensure a warm welcome from their fellows. Then, with our mission accomplished and possessing a fuller knowledge of the secrets of Maple White Land, we should turn our whole thoughts to the vital problem of our escape and return. Even Challenger was ready to admit that we should then have done all for which we had come, and that our first duty from that time onwards was to carry back to civilization the amazing discoveries we had made.

We were able now to take a more leisurely view of the Indians whom we had rescued. They were small men, wiry, active, and well-built, with lank black hair tied up in a bunch behind their heads with a leathern thong, and leathern also were their loin-cloths. Their faces were hairless, well formed, and good-humored. The lobes of their ears, hanging ragged and bloody, showed that they had been pierced for some ornaments which their captors had torn out. Their speech, though unintelligible to us, was fluent among themselves, and as they pointed to each other and uttered the word "Accala" many times over, we gathered that this was the name of the nation. Occasionally, with faces which were convulsed with fear and hatred, they shook their clenched hands at the woods round and cried: "Doda! Doda!" which was surely their term for their enemies.

"What do you make of them, Challenger?" asked Lord John. "One thing is very clear to me, and that is that the little chap with the front of his head shaved is a chief among them."

It was indeed evident that this man stood apart from the others, and that they never ventured to address him without every sign of deep respect. He seemed to be the youngest of them all, and yet, so proud and high was his spirit that, upon Challenger laying his great hand upon his head, he started like a spurred horse and, with a quick flash of his dark eyes, moved further away from the Professor. Then, placing his hand upon his breast and holding himself with great dignity, he uttered the word "Maretas" several times. The Professor, unabashed, seized the nearest Indian by the shoulder and proceeded to lecture upon him as if he were a potted specimen in a classroom.

"The type of these people," said he in his sonorous fashion, "whether judged by cranial capacity, facial angle, or any other test, cannot be regarded as a low one; on the contrary, we must place it as considerably higher in the scale than many South American tribes which I can mention. On no possible supposition can we explain the evolution of such a race in this place. For that matter, so great a gap separates these ape-men from the primitive animals which have survived upon this plateau, that it is inadmissible to think that they could have developed where we find them."

"Then where the dooce did they drop from?" asked Lord John.

"A question which will, no doubt, be eagerly discussed in every scientific society in Europe and America," the Professor answered. "My own reading of the situation for what it is worth"—he inflated his chest enormously and looked insolently around him at the words—"is that evolution has advanced under the peculiar conditions of this country up to the vertebrate stage, the old types surviving and living on in company with the newer ones. Thus we find such modern creatures as the tapir—an animal with quite a respectable length of pedigree—the great deer, and the ant-eater in the companionship of reptilian forms of Jurassic type. So much is clear. And now come the ape-men and the Indian. What is the scientific mind to think of their presence? I can only account for it by an invasion from outside. It is probable that there existed an anthropoid ape in South America, who in past ages found his way to this place, and that he developed into the creatures we have seen, some of which"—here he looked hard at me—"were of an appearance and shape which, if it had been accompanied by corresponding intelligence, would, I do not hesitate to say, have reflected credit upon any living race. As to the Indians I cannot doubt that they are more recent immigrants from below. Under the stress of famine or of conquest they have made their way up here. Faced by ferocious creatures which they had never before seen, they took refuge in the caves which our young friend has described, but they have no doubt had a bitter fight to hold their own against wild beasts, and especially against the ape-men who would regard them as intruders, and wage a merciless war upon them with a cunning which the larger beasts would lack. Hence the fact that their numbers appear to be limited. Well, gentlemen, have I read you the riddle aright, or is there any point which you would query?"

Professor Summerlee for once was too depressed to argue, though he shook his head violently as a token of general disagreement. Lord John merely scratched his scanty locks with the remark that he couldn't put up a fight as he wasn't in the same weight or class. For my own part I performed my usual role of bringing things down to a strictly prosaic and practical level by the remark that one of the Indians was missing.

"He has gone to fetch some water," said Lord Roxton. "We fitted him up with an empty beef tin and he is off."

"To the old camp?" I asked.

"No, to the brook. It's among the trees there. It can't be more than a couple of hundred yards. But the beggar is certainly taking his time."

"I'll go and look after him," said I. I picked up my rifle and strolled in the direction of the brook, leaving my friends to lay out the scanty breakfast. It may seem to you rash that even for so short a distance I should quit the shelter of our friendly thicket, but you will remember that we were many miles from

Ape-town, that so far as we knew the creatures had not discovered our retreat, and that in any case with a rifle in my hands I had no fear of them. I had not yet learned their cunning or their strength.

I could hear the murmur of our brook somewhere ahead of me, but there was a tangle of trees and brushwood between me and it. I was making my way through this at a point which was just out of sight of my companions, when, under one of the trees, I noticed something red huddled among the bushes. As I approached it, I was shocked to see that it was the dead body of the missing Indian. He lay upon his side, his limbs drawn up, and his head screwed round at a most unnatural angle, so that he seemed to be looking straight over his own shoulder. I gave a cry to warn my friends that something was amiss, and running forwards I stooped over the body. Surely my guardian angel was very near me then, for some instinct of fear, or it may have been some faint rustle of leaves, made me glance upwards. Out of the thick green foliage which hung low over my head, two long muscular arms covered with reddish hair were slowly descending. Another instant and the great stealthy hands would have been round my throat. I sprang backwards, but quick as I was, those hands were quicker still. Through my sudden spring they missed a fatal grip, but one of them caught the back of my neck and the other one my face. I threw my hands up to protect my throat, and the next moment the huge paw had slid down my face and closed over them. I was lifted lightly from the ground, and I felt an intolerable pressure forcing my head back and back until the strain upon the cervical spine was more than I could bear. My senses swam, but I still tore at the hand and forced it out from my chin. Looking up I saw a frightful face with cold inexorable light blue eyes looking down into mine. There was something hypnotic in those terrible eyes. I could struggle no longer. As the creature felt me grow limp in his grasp, two white canines gleamed for a moment at each side of the vile mouth, and the grip tightened still more upon my chin, forcing it always upwards and back. A thin, oval-tinted mist formed before my eyes and little silvery bells tinkled in my ears. Dully and far off I heard the crack of a rifle and was feebly aware of the shock as I was dropped to the earth, where I lay without sense or motion.

I awoke to find myself on my back upon the grass in our lair within the thicket. Someone had brought the water from the brook, and Lord John was sprinkling my head with it, while Challenger and Summerlee were propping me up, with concern in their faces. For a moment I had a glimpse of the human spirits behind their scientific masks. It was really shock, rather than any injury, which had prostrated me, and in half-an-hour, in spite of aching head and stiff neck, I was sitting up and ready for anything.

"But you've had the escape of your life, young fellah my lad," said Lord

Roxton. "When I heard your cry and ran forward, and saw your head twisted half-off and your stohwassers kickin' in the air, I thought we were one short. I missed the beast in my flurry, but he dropped you all right and was off like a streak. By George! I wish I had fifty men with rifles. I'd clear out the whole infernal gang of them and leave this country a bit cleaner than we found it."

It was clear now that the ape-men had in some way marked us down, and that we were watched on every side. We had not so much to fear from them during the day, but they would be very likely to rush us by night; so the sooner we got away from their neighborhood the better. On three sides of us was absolute forest, and there we might find ourselves in an ambush. But on the fourth side—that which sloped down in the direction of the lake—there was only low scrub, with scattered trees and occasional open glades. It was, in fact, the route which I had myself taken in my solitary journey, and it led us straight for the Indian caves. This then must for every reason be our road.

One great regret we had, and that was to leave our old camp behind us, not only for the sake of the stores which remained there, but even more because we were losing touch with Zambo, our link with the outside world. However, we had a fair supply of cartridges and all our guns, so, for a time at least, we could look after ourselves, and we hoped soon to have a chance of returning and restoring our communications with our negro. He had faithfully promised to stay where he was, and we had not a doubt that he would be as good as his word.

It was in the early afternoon that we started upon our journey. The young chief walked at our head as our guide, but refused indignantly to carry any burden. Behind him came the two surviving Indians with our scanty possessions upon their backs. We four white men walked in the rear with rifles loaded and ready. As we started there broke from the thick silent woods behind us a sudden great ululation of the ape-men, which may have been a cheer of triumph at our departure or a jeer of contempt at our flight. Looking back we saw only the dense screen of trees, but that long-drawn yell told us how many of our enemies lurked among them. We saw no sign of pursuit, however, and soon we had got into more open country and beyond their power.

As I tramped along, the rearmost of the four, I could not help smiling at the appearance of my three companions in front. Was this the luxurious Lord John Roxton who had sat that evening in the Albany amidst his Persian rugs and his pictures in the pink radiance of the tinted lights? And was this the imposing Professor who had swelled behind the great desk in his massive study at Enmore Park? And, finally, could this be the austere and prim figure which had risen before the meeting at the Zoological Institute? No three tramps that one could have met in a Surrey lane could have looked more hopeless and bedraggled. We had, it is true, been only a week or so upon the top of the plateau, but all our spare clothing was in our camp below, and the one week had been a severe one upon us all, though least to me who had not to endure the handling of the ape-men. My three friends had all lost their hats, and had now bound handkerchiefs round their heads, their clothes hung in ribbons about them, and their unshaven grimy faces were hardly to be recognized. Both Summerlee and Challenger were limping heavily, while I still dragged my feet from weakness after the shock of the morning, and my neck was as stiff as a board from the murderous grip that held it. We were indeed a sorry crew, and I did not wonder to see our Indian companions glance back at us occasionally with horror and amazement on their faces.

In the late afternoon we reached the margin of the lake, and as we emerged from the bush and saw the sheet of water stretching before us our native friends set up a shrill cry of joy and pointed eagerly in front of them. It was indeed a wonderful sight which lay before us. Sweeping over the glassy surface was a great flotilla of canoes coming straight for the shore upon which we stood. They were some miles out when we first saw them, but they shot forward with great swiftness, and were soon so near that the rowers could distinguish our persons. Instantly a thunderous shout of delight burst from them, and we saw them rise from their seats, waving their paddles and spears madly in the air. Then bending to their work once more, they flew across the intervening water, beached their boats upon the sloping sand, and rushed up to us, prostrating themselves with loud cries of greeting before the young chief. Finally one of them, an elderly man, with a necklace and bracelet of great lustrous glass beads and the skin of some beautiful mottled amber-colored animal slung over his shoulders, ran forward and embraced most tenderly the youth whom we had saved. He then looked at us and asked some questions, after which he stepped up with much dignity and embraced us also each in turn. Then, at his order, the whole tribe lay down upon the ground before us in homage. Personally I felt shy and uncomfortable at this obsequious adoration, and I read the same feeling in the faces of Roxton and Summerlee, but Challenger expanded like a flower in the sun.

"They may be undeveloped types," said he, stroking his beard and looking round at them, "but their deportment in the presence of their superiors might be a lesson to some of our more advanced Europeans. Strange how correct are the instincts of the natural man!"

It was clear that the natives had come out upon the war-path, for every man carried his spear—a long bamboo tipped with bone—his bow and arrows, and some sort of club or stone battle-axe slung at his side. Their dark, angry glances at the woods from which we had come, and the frequent repetition of the word "Doda," made it clear enough that this was a rescue party who had set forth to save or revenge the old chief's son, for such we gathered that the youth must be. A council was now held by the whole tribe squatting in a circle, whilst we sat near on a slab of basalt and watched their proceedings. Two or three warriors spoke, and finally our young friend made a spirited harangue with such eloquent features and gestures that we could understand it all as clearly as if we had known his language.

"What is the use of returning?" he said. "Sooner or later the thing must be done. Your comrades have been murdered. What if I have returned safe? These others have been done to death. There is no safety for any of us. We are assembled now and ready." Then he pointed to us. "These strange men are our friends. They are great fighters, and they hate the ape-men even as we do. They command," here he pointed up to heaven, "the thunder and the lightning. When shall we have such a chance again? Let us go forward, and either die now or live for the future in safety. How else shall we go back unashamed to our women?"

The little red warriors hung upon the words of the speaker, and when he had finished they burst into a roar of applause, waving their rude weapons in the air. The old chief stepped forward to us, and asked us some questions, pointing at the same time to the woods. Lord John made a sign to him that he should wait for an answer and then he turned to us.

"Well, it's up to you to say what you will do," said he; "for my part I have a score to settle with these monkey-folk, and if it ends by wiping them off the face of the earth I don't see that the earth need fret about it. I'm goin' with our little red pals and I mean to see them through the scrap. What do you say, young fellah?"

"Of course I will come."

"And you, Challenger?"

"I will assuredly cooperate."

"And you, Summerlee?"

"We seem to be drifting very far from the object of this expedition, Lord John. I assure you that I little thought when I left my professional chair in London that it was for the purpose of heading a raid of savages upon a colony of anthropoid apes."

"To such base uses do we come," said Lord John, smiling. "But we are up against it, so what's the decision?"

"It seems a most questionable step," said Summerlee, argumentative to the last, "but if you are all going, I hardly see how I can remain behind."

"Then it is settled," said Lord John, and turning to the chief he nodded and slapped his rifle.

* * * * *

The old fellow clasped our hands, each in turn, while his men cheered louder than ever. It was too late to advance that night, so the Indians settled down into a rude bivouac. On all sides their fires began to glimmer and smoke. Some of them who had disappeared into the jungle came back presently driving a young iguanodon before them. Like the others, it had a daub of asphalt upon its shoulder, and it was only when we saw one of the natives step forward with the air of an owner and give his consent to the beast's slaughter that we understood at last that these great creatures were as much private property as a herd of cattle, and that these symbols which had so perplexed us were nothing more than the marks of the owner. Helpless, torpid, and vegetarian, with great limbs but a minute brain, they could be rounded up and driven by a child. In a few minutes the huge beast had been cut up and slabs of him were hanging over a dozen campfires, together with great scaly ganoid fish which had been speared in the lake.

Summerlee had lain down and slept upon the sand, but we others roamed round the edge of the water, seeking to learn something more of this strange country. Twice we found pits of blue clay, such as we had already seen in the swamp of the pterodactyls. These were old volcanic vents, and for some reason excited the greatest interest in Lord John. What attracted Challenger, on the other hand, was a bubbling, gurgling mud geyser, where some strange gas formed great bursting bubbles upon the surface. He thrust a hollow reed into it and cried out with delight like a schoolboy then he was able, on touching it with a lighted match, to cause a sharp explosion and a blue flame at the far end of the tube. Still more pleased was he when, inverting a leathern pouch over the end of the reed, and so filling it with the gas, he was able to send it soaring up into the air.

"An inflammable gas, and one markedly lighter than the atmosphere. I should say beyond doubt that it contained a considerable proportion of free hydrogen. The resources of G. E. C. are not yet exhausted, my young friend. I may yet show you how a great mind molds all Nature to its use." He swelled with some secret purpose, but would say no more.

There was nothing which we could see upon the shore which seemed to me so wonderful as the great sheet of water before us. Our numbers and our noise had frightened all living creatures away, and save for a few pterodactyls, which soared round high above our heads while they waited for the carrion, all was still around the camp. But it was different out upon the rose-tinted waters of the central lake. It boiled and heaved with strange life. Great slate-colored backs and high serrated dorsal fins shot up with a fringe of silver, and then rolled down into the depths again. The sand-banks far out were spotted with uncouth crawling forms, huge turtles, strange saurians, and one great flat creature like a writhing, palpitating mat of black greasy leather, which flopped its way slowly to the lake. Here and there high serpent heads projected out of the water, cutting swiftly through it with a little collar of foam in front, and a long swirling wake behind, rising and falling in graceful, swan-like undulations as they went. It was not until one of these creatures wriggled on to a sand-bank within a few hundred yards of us, and exposed a barrel-shaped body and huge flippers behind the long serpent neck, that Challenger, and Summerlee, who had joined us, broke out into their duet of wonder and admiration.

"Plesiosaurus! A fresh-water plesiosaurus!" cried Summerlee. "That I should have lived to see such a sight! We are blessed, my dear Challenger, above all zoologists since the world began!"

It was not until the night had fallen, and the fires of our savage allies glowed red in the shadows, that our two men of science could be dragged away from the fascinations of that primeval lake. Even in the darkness as we lay upon the strand, we heard from time to time the snort and plunge of the huge creatures who lived therein.

At earliest dawn our camp was astir and an hour later we had started upon our memorable expedition. Often in my dreams have I thought that I might live to be a war correspondent. In what wildest one could I have conceived the nature of the campaign which it should be my lot to report! Here then is my first dispatch from a field of battle:

Our numbers had been reinforced during the night by a fresh batch of natives from the caves, and we may have been four or five hundred strong when we made our advance. A fringe of scouts was thrown out in front, and behind them the whole force in a solid column made their way up the long slope of the bush country until we were near the edge of the forest. Here they spread out into a long straggling line of spearmen and bowmen. Roxton and Summerlee took their position upon the right flank, while Challenger and I were on the left. It was a host of the stone age that we were accompanying to battle—we with the last word of the gunsmith's art from St. James' Street and the Strand.

We had not long to wait for our enemy. A wild shrill clamor rose from the edge of the wood and suddenly a body of ape-men rushed out with clubs and stones, and made for the center of the Indian line. It was a valiant move but a foolish one, for the great bandy-legged creatures were slow of foot, while their opponents were as active as cats. It was horrible to see the fierce brutes with foaming mouths and glaring eyes, rushing and grasping, but forever missing their elusive enemies, while arrow after arrow buried itself in their hides. One great fellow ran past me roaring with pain, with a dozen darts sticking from his chest and ribs. In mercy I put a bullet through his skull, and he fell sprawling among the aloes. But this was the only shot fired, for the attack had been on the center of the line, and the Indians there had needed no help of ours in repulsing it. Of all the ape-men who had rushed out into the open, I do not think that one got back to cover.

But the matter was more deadly when we came among the trees. For an hour or more after we entered the wood, there was a desperate struggle in which for a time we hardly held our own. Springing out from among the scrub the ape-men with huge clubs broke in upon the Indians and often felled three or four of them before they could be speared. Their frightful blows shattered everything upon which they fell. One of them knocked Summerlee's rifle to matchwood and the next would have crushed his skull had an Indian not stabbed the beast to the heart. Other ape-men in the trees above us hurled down stones and logs of wood, occasionally dropping bodily on to our ranks and fighting furiously until they were felled. Once our allies broke under the pressure, and had it not been for the execution done by our rifles they would certainly have taken to their heels. But they were gallantly rallied by their old chief and came on with such a rush that the ape-men began in turn to give way. Summerlee was weaponless, but I was emptying my magazine as quick as I could fire, and on the further flank we heard the continuous cracking of our companion's rifles.

Then in a moment came the panic and the collapse. Screaming and howling, the great creatures rushed away in all directions through the brushwood, while our allies yelled in their savage delight, following swiftly after their flying enemies. All the feuds of countless generations, all the hatreds and cruelties of their narrow history, all the memories of ill-usage and persecution were to be purged that day. At last man was to be supreme and the man-beast to find forever his allotted place. Fly as they would the fugitives were too slow to escape from the active savages, and from every side in the tangled woods we heard the exultant yells, the twanging of bows, and the crash and thud as ape-men were brought down from their hiding-places in the trees.

I was following the others, when I found that Lord John and Challenger had come across to join us.

"It's over," said Lord John. "I think we can leave the tidying up to them. Perhaps the less we see of it the better we shall sleep."

Challenger's eyes were shining with the lust of slaughter.

"We have been privileged," he cried, strutting about like a gamecock, "to be present at one of the typical decisive battles of history—the battles which have determined the fate of the world. What, my friends, is the conquest of one nation by another? It is meaningless. Each produces the same result. But those fierce fights, when in the dawn of the ages the cave-dwellers held their own against the tiger folk, or the elephants first found that they had a master, those were the real conquests—the victories that count. By this strange turn of fate we have seen and helped to decide even such a contest. Now upon this plateau the future must ever be for man."

It needed a robust faith in the end to justify such tragic means. As we advanced together through the woods we found the ape-men lying thick, transfixed with spears or arrows. Here and there a little group of shattered Indians marked where one of the anthropoids had turned to bay, and sold his life dearly. Always in front of us we heard the yelling and roaring which showed the direction of the pursuit. The ape-men had been driven back to their city, they had made a last stand there, once again they had been broken, and now we were in time to see the final fearful scene of all. Some eighty or a hundred males, the last survivors, had been driven across that same little clearing which led to the edge of the cliff, the scene of our own exploit two days before. As we arrived the Indians, a semicircle of spearmen, had closed in on them, and in a minute it was over, Thirty or forty died where they stood. The others, screaming and clawing, were thrust over the precipice, and went hurtling down, as their prisoners had of old, on to the sharp bamboos six hundred feet below. It was as Challenger had said, and the reign of man was assured forever in Maple White Land. The males were exterminated, Ape Town was destroyed, the females and young were driven away to live in bondage, and the long rivalry of untold centuries had reached its bloody end.

For us the victory brought much advantage. Once again we were able to visit our camp and get at our stores. Once more also we were able to communicate with Zambo, who had been terrified by the spectacle from afar of an avalanche of apes falling from the edge of the cliff.

"Come away, Massas, come away!" he cried, his eyes starting from his head. "The debbil get you sure if you stay up there."

"It is the voice of sanity!" said Summerlee with conviction. "We have had adventures enough and they are neither suitable to our character or our position. I hold you to your word, Challenger. From now onwards you devote your energies to getting us out of this horrible country and back once more to civilization."

XV

"OUR EYES HAVE SEEN GREAT WONDERS"

I write this from day to day, but I trust that before I come to the end of it, I may be able to say that the light shines, at last, through our clouds. We are held here with no clear means of making our escape, and bitterly we chafe against it. Yet, I can well imagine that the day may come when we may be glad that we were kept, against our will, to see something more of the wonders of this singular place, and of the creatures who inhabit it.

The victory of the Indians and the annihilation of the ape-men, marked the turning point of our fortunes. From then onwards, we were in truth masters of the plateau, for the natives looked upon us with a mixture of fear and gratitude, since by our strange powers we had aided them to destroy their hereditary foe. For their own sakes they would, perhaps, be glad to see the departure of such formidable and incalculable people, but they have not themselves suggested any way by which we may reach the plains below. There had been, so far as we could follow their signs, a tunnel by which the place could be approached, the lower exit of which we had seen from below. By this, no doubt, both ape-men and Indians had at different epochs reached the top, and Maple White with his companion had taken the same way. Only the year before, however, there had been a terrific earthquake, and the upper end of the tunnel had fallen in and completely disappeared. The Indians now could only shake their heads and shrug their shoulders when we expressed by signs our desire to descend. It may be that they cannot, but it may also be that they will not, help us to get away.

At the end of the victorious campaign the surviving ape-folk were driven across the plateau (their wailings were horrible) and established in the neighborhood of the Indian caves, where they would, from now onwards, be a servile race under the eyes of their masters. It was a rude, raw, primeval version of the Jews in Babylon or the Israelites in Egypt. At night we could hear from amid the trees the long-drawn cry, as some primitive Ezekiel mourned for fallen greatness and recalled the departed glories of Ape Town. Hewers of wood and drawers of water, such were they from now onwards.

We had returned across the plateau with our allies two days after the battle, and made our camp at the foot of their cliffs. They would have had us share their caves with them, but Lord John would by no means consent to it considering that to do so would put us in their power if they were treacherously disposed. We kept our independence, therefore, and had our weapons ready for any emergency, while preserving the most friendly relations. We also continually visited their caves, which were most remarkable places, though whether made by man or by Nature we have never been able to determine. They were all on the one stratum, hollowed out of some soft rock which lay between the volcanic basalt forming the ruddy cliffs above them, and the hard granite which formed their base.

The openings were about eighty feet above the ground, and were led up to by long stone stairs, so narrow and steep that no large animal could mount them. Inside they were warm and dry, running in straight passages of varying length into the side of the hill, with smooth gray walls decorated with many excellent pictures done with charred sticks and representing the various animals of the plateau. If every living thing were swept from the country the future explorer would find upon the walls of these caves ample evidence of the strange fauna—the dinosaurs, iguanodons, and fish lizards—which had lived so recently upon earth.

Since we had learned that the huge iguanodons were kept as tame herds by their owners, and were simply walking meat-stores, we had conceived that man, even with his primitive weapons, had established his ascendancy upon the plateau. We were soon to discover that it was not so, and that he was still there upon tolerance.

It was on the third day after our forming our camp near the Indian caves that the tragedy occurred. Challenger and Summerlee had gone off together that day to the lake where some of the natives, under their direction, were engaged in harpooning specimens of the great lizards. Lord John and I had remained in our camp, while a number of the Indians were scattered about upon the grassy slope in front of the caves engaged in different ways. Suddenly there was a shrill cry of alarm, with the word "Stoa" resounding from a hundred tongues. From every side men, women, and children were rushing wildly for shelter, swarming up the staircases and into the caves in a mad stampede.

Looking up, we could see them waving their arms from the rocks above and beckoning to us to join them in their refuge. We had both seized our magazine rifles and ran out to see what the danger could be. Suddenly from the near belt of trees there broke forth a group of twelve or fifteen Indians, running for their lives, and at their very heels two of those frightful monsters which had disturbed our camp and pursued me upon my solitary journey. In shape they were like horrible toads, and moved in a succession of springs, but in size they were of an incredible bulk, larger than the largest elephant. We had never before seen them save at night, and indeed they are nocturnal animals save when disturbed in their lairs, as these had been. We now stood amazed at the sight, for their blotched and warty skins were of a curious fish-like iridescence, and the sunlight struck them with an ever-varying rainbow bloom as they moved.

We had little time to watch them, however, for in an instant they had overtaken the fugitives and were making a dire slaughter among them. Their method was to fall forward with their full weight upon each in turn, leaving him crushed and mangled, to bound on after the others. The wretched Indians screamed with terror, but were helpless, run as they would, before the relentless purpose and horrible activity of these monstrous creatures. One after another they went down, and there were not half-a-dozen surviving by the time my companion and I could come to their help. But our aid was of little avail and only involved us in the same peril. At the range of a couple of hundred yards we emptied our magazines, firing bullet after bullet into the beasts, but with no more effect than if we were pelting them with pellets of paper. Their slow reptilian natures cared nothing for wounds, and the springs of their lives, with no special brain center but scattered throughout their spinal cords, could not be tapped by any modern weapons. The most that we could do was to check their progress by distracting their attention with the flash and roar of our guns, and so to give both the natives and ourselves time to reach the steps which led to safety. But where the conical explosive bullets of the twentieth century were of no avail, the poisoned arrows of the natives, dipped in the juice of strophanthus and steeped afterwards in decayed carrion, could succeed. Such arrows were of little avail to the hunter who attacked the beast, because their action in that torpid circulation was slow, and before its powers failed it could certainly overtake and slay its assailant. But now, as the two monsters hounded us to the very foot of the stairs, a drift of darts came whistling from every chink in the cliff above them. In a minute they were feathered with them, and yet with no sign of pain they clawed and slobbered with impotent rage at the steps which would lead them to their victims, mounting clumsily up for a few yards and then sliding down again to the ground. But at last the poison worked. One of them gave a deep rumbling groan and dropped his huge squat head on to the earth. The other bounded round in an eccentric circle with shrill, wailing cries, and then lying down writhed in agony for some minutes before it also stiffened and lay still. With yells of triumph the Indians came flocking down from their caves and danced a frenzied dance of victory round the dead bodies, in mad joy that two more of the most dangerous of all their enemies had been slain. That night they cut up and removed the bodies, not to eat—for the poison was still active—but lest they should breed a pestilence. The great reptilian hearts, however, each as large as a cushion, still lay there, beating slowly and steadily, with a gentle rise and fall, in horrible independent life. It was only upon the third day that the ganglia ran down and the dreadful things were still.

Some day, when I have a better desk than a meat-tin and more helpful tools than a worn stub of pencil and a last, tattered notebook, I will write some fuller account of the Accala Indians—of our life amongst them, and of the glimpses which we had of the strange conditions of wondrous Maple White Land. Memory, at least, will never fail me, for so long as the breath of life is in me, every hour and every action of that period will stand out as hard and clear as do the first strange happenings of our childhood. No new impressions could efface those which are so deeply cut. When the time comes I will describe that wondrous moonlit night upon the great lake when a young ichthyosaurus—a strange creature, half seal, half fish, to look at, with bone-covered eyes on each side of his snout, and a third eye fixed upon the top of his head—was entangled in an Indian net, and nearly upset our canoe before we towed it ashore; the same night that a green water-snake shot out from the rushes and carried off in its coils the steersman of Challenger's canoe. I will tell, too, of the great nocturnal white thing—to this day we do not know whether it was beast or reptile—which lived in a vile swamp to the east of the lake, and flitted about with a faint phosphorescent glimmer in the darkness. The Indians were so terrified at it that they would not go near the place, and, though we twice made expeditions and saw it each time, we could not make our way through the deep marsh in which it lived. I can only say that it seemed to be larger than a cow and had the strangest musky odor. I will tell also of the huge bird which chased Challenger to the shelter of the rocks one day—a great running bird, far taller than an ostrich, with a vulture-like neck and cruel head which made it a walking death. As Challenger climbed to safety one dart of that savage curving beak shore off the heel of his boot as if it had been cut with a chisel. This time at least modern weapons prevailed and the great creature, twelve feet from head to foot—phororachus its name, according to our panting but exultant Professor—went down before Lord Roxton's rifle in a flurry of waving feathers and kicking limbs, with two remorseless yellow eyes glaring up from the midst of it. May I live to see that flattened vicious skull in its own niche amid the trophies of the Albany. Finally, I will assuredly give some account of the toxodon, the giant ten-foot guinea pig, with projecting chisel teeth, which we killed as it drank in the gray of the morning by the side of the lake.

All this I shall some day write at fuller length, and amidst these more stirring days I would tenderly sketch in these lovely summer evenings, when with the deep blue sky above us we lay in good comradeship among the long grasses by the wood and marveled at the strange fowl that swept over us and the quaint new creatures which crept from their burrows to watch us, while above us the boughs of the bushes were heavy with luscious fruit, and below us strange and lovely flowers peeped at us from among the herbage; or those long moonlit nights when we lay out upon the shimmering surface of the great lake and watched with wonder and awe the huge circles rippling out from the sudden splash of some fantastic monster; or the greenish gleam, far down in the deep water, of some strange creature upon the confines of darkness. These are the scenes which my mind and my pen will dwell upon in every detail at some future day.

* * * * *

But, you will ask, why these experiences and why this delay, when you and your comrades should have been occupied day and night in the devising of some means by which you could return to the outer world? My answer is, that there was not one of us who was not working for this end, but that our work had been in vain. One fact we had very speedily discovered: The Indians would do nothing to help us. In every other way they were our friends—one might almost say our devoted slaves—but when it was suggested that they should help us to make and carry a plank which would bridge the chasm, or when we wished to get from them thongs of leather or liana to weave ropes which might help us, we were met by a good-humored, but an invincible, refusal. They would smile, twinkle their eyes, shake their heads, and there was the end of it. Even the old chief met us with the same obstinate denial, and it was only Maretas, the youngster whom we had saved, who looked wistfully at us and told us by his gestures that he was grieved for our thwarted wishes. Ever since their crowning triumph with the ape-men they looked upon us as supermen, who bore victory in the tubes of strange weapons, and they believed that so long as we remained with them good fortune would be theirs. A little red-skinned wife and a cave of our own were freely offered to each of us if we would but forget our own people and dwell forever upon the plateau. So far all had been kindly, however far apart our desires might be; but we felt well assured that our actual plans of a descent must be kept secret, for we had reason to fear that at the last they might try to hold us by force.

In spite of the danger from dinosaurs (which is not great save at night, for, as I may have said before, they are mostly nocturnal in their habits) I have twice in the last three weeks been over to our old camp in order to see our negro who still kept watch and ward below the cliff. My eyes strained eagerly across the great plain in the hope of seeing afar off the help for which we had prayed. But the long cactus-strewn levels still stretched away, empty and bare, to the distant line of the cane-brake.

"They will soon come now, Massa Malone. Before another week pass Indian come back and bring rope and fetch you down." Such was the cheery cry of our excellent Zambo.

I had one strange experience as I came from this second visit which had involved my being away for a night from my companions. I was returning along the well-remembered route, and had reached a spot within a mile or so of the marsh of the pterodactyls, when I saw an extraordinary object approaching me. It was a man who walked inside a framework made of bent canes so that he was enclosed on all sides in a bell-shaped cage. As I drew nearer I was more amazed still to see that it was Lord John Roxton. When he saw me he slipped from under his curious protection and came towards me laughing, and yet, as I thought, with some confusion in his manner.

"Well, young fellah," said he, "who would have thought of meetin' you up here?"

"What in the world are you doing?" I asked.

"Visitin' my friends, the pterodactyls," said he.

"But why?"

"Interestin' beasts, don't you think? But unsociable! Nasty rude ways with strangers, as you may remember. So I rigged this framework which keeps them from bein' too pressin' in their attentions."

"But what do you want in the swamp?"

He looked at me with a very questioning eye, and I read hesitation in his face.

"Don't you think other people besides Professors can want to know things?" he said at last. "I'm studyin' the pretty dears. That's enough for you."

"No offense," said I.

His good-humor returned and he laughed.

"No offense, young fellah. I'm goin' to get a young devil chick for Challenger. That's one of my jobs. No, I don't want your company. I'm safe in this cage, and you are not. So long, and I'll be back in camp by night-fall."

He turned away and I left him wandering on through the wood with his extraordinary cage around him.

If Lord John's behavior at this time was strange, that of Challenger was more so. I may say that he seemed to possess an extraordinary fascination for the Indian women, and that he always carried a large spreading palm branch with which he beat them off as if they were flies, when their attentions became too pressing. To see him walking like a comic opera Sultan, with this badge of authority in his hand, his black beard bristling in front of him, his toes pointing at each step, and a train of wide-eyed Indian girls behind him, clad in their slender drapery of bark cloth, is one of the most grotesque of all the pictures which I will carry back with me. As to Summerlee, he was absorbed in the insect and bird life of the plateau, and spent his whole time (save that considerable portion which was devoted to abusing Challenger for not getting us out of our difficulties) in cleaning and mounting his specimens.

Challenger had been in the habit of walking off by himself every morning and returning from time to time with looks of portentous solemnity, as one who bears the full weight of a great enterprise upon his shoulders. One day, palm branch in hand, and his crowd of adoring devotees behind him, he led us down to his hidden workshop and took us into the secret of his plans.

The place was a small clearing in the center of a palm grove. In this was one of those boiling mud geysers which I have already described. Around its edge were scattered a number of leathern thongs cut from iguanodon hide, and a large collapsed membrane which proved to be the dried and scraped stomach of one of the great fish lizards from the lake. This huge sack had been sewn up at one end and only a small orifice left at the other. Into this opening several bamboo canes had been inserted and the other ends of these canes were in contact with conical clay funnels which collected the gas bubbling up through the mud of the geyser. Soon the flaccid organ began to slowly expand and show such a tendency to upward movements that Challenger fastened the cords which held it to the trunks of the surrounding trees. In half an hour a good-sized gas-bag had been formed, and the jerking and straining upon the thongs showed that it was capable of considerable lift. Challenger, like a glad father in the presence of his first-born, stood smiling and stroking his beard, in silent, self-satisfied content as he gazed at the creation of his brain. It was Summerlee who first broke the silence.

"You don't mean us to go up in that thing, Challenger?" said he, in an acid voice.

"I mean, my dear Summerlee, to give you such a demonstration of its powers that after seeing it you will, I am sure, have no hesitation in trusting yourself to it."

"You can put it right out of your head now, at once," said Summerlee with decision, "nothing on earth would induce me to commit such a folly. Lord John, I trust that you will not countenance such madness?"

"Dooced ingenious, I call it," said our peer. "I'd like to see how it works."

"So you shall," said Challenger. "For some days I have exerted my whole brain force upon the problem of how we shall descend from these cliffs. We have satisfied ourselves that we cannot climb down and that there is no tunnel. We are also unable to construct any kind of bridge which may take us back to the pinnacle from which we came. How then shall I find a means to convey us? Some little time ago I had remarked to our young friend here that free hydrogen was evolved from the geyser. The idea of a balloon naturally followed. I was, I will admit, somewhat baffled by the difficulty of discovering an envelope to contain the gas, but the contemplation of the immense entrails of these reptiles supplied me with a solution to the problem. Behold the result!"

He put one hand in the front of his ragged jacket and pointed proudly with the other.

By this time the gas-bag had swollen to a goodly rotundity and was jerking strongly upon its lashings.

"Midsummer madness!" snorted Summerlee.

Lord John was delighted with the whole idea. "Clever old dear, ain't he?" he whispered to me, and then louder to Challenger. "What about a car?"

"The car will be my next care. I have already planned how it is to be made and attached. Meanwhile I will simply show you how capable my apparatus is of supporting the weight of each of us."

"All of us, surely?"

"No, it is part of my plan that each in turn shall descend as in a parachute, and the balloon be drawn back by means which I shall have no difficulty in perfecting. If it will support the weight of one and let him gently down, it will have done all that is required of it. I will now show you its capacity in that direction."

He brought out a lump of basalt of a considerable size, constructed in the middle so that a cord could be easily attached to it. This cord was the one which we had brought with us on to the plateau after we had used it for climbing the pinnacle. It was over a hundred feet long, and though it was thin it was very strong. He had prepared a sort of collar of leather with many straps depending from it. This collar was placed over the dome of the balloon, and the hanging thongs were gathered together below, so that the pressure of any weight would be diffused over a considerable surface. Then the lump of basalt was fastened to the thongs, and the rope was allowed to hang from the end of it, being passed three times round the Professor's arm.

"I will now," said Challenger, with a smile of pleased anticipation, "demonstrate the carrying power of my balloon." As he said so he cut with a knife the various lashings that held it.

Never was our expedition in more imminent danger of complete annihilation. The inflated membrane shot up with frightful velocity into the air. In an instant Challenger was pulled off his feet and dragged after it. I had just time to throw my arms round his ascending waist when I was myself whipped up into the air. Lord John had me with a rat-trap grip round the legs, but I felt that he also was coming off the ground. For a moment I had a vision of four adventurers floating like a string of sausages over the land that they had explored. But, happily, there were limits to the strain which the rope would stand, though none apparently to the lifting powers of this infernal machine. There was a sharp crack, and we were in a heap upon the ground with coils of rope all over us. When we were able to stagger to our feet we saw far off in the deep blue sky one dark spot where the lump of basalt was speeding upon its way.

"Splendid!" cried the undaunted Challenger, rubbing his injured arm. "A most thorough and satisfactory demonstration! I could not have anticipated such a success. Within a week, gentlemen, I promise that a second balloon will be prepared, and that you can count upon taking in safety and comfort the first stage of our homeward journey." So far I have written each of the foregoing events as it occurred. Now I am rounding off my narrative from the old camp, where Zambo has waited so long, with all our difficulties and dangers left like a dream behind us upon the summit of those vast ruddy crags which tower above our heads. We have descended in safety, though in a most unexpected fashion, and all is well with us. In six weeks or two months we shall be in London, and it is possible that this letter may not reach you much earlier than we do ourselves. Already our hearts yearn and our spirits fly towards the great mother city which holds so much that is dear to us.

It was on the very evening of our perilous adventure with Challenger's homemade balloon that the change came in our fortunes. I have said that the one person from whom we had had some sign of sympathy in our attempts to get away was the young chief whom we had rescued. He alone had no desire to hold us against our will in a strange land. He had told us as much by his expressive language of signs. That evening, after dusk, he came down to our little camp, handed me (for some reason he had always shown his attentions to me, perhaps because I was the one who was nearest his age) a small roll of the bark of a tree, and then pointing solemnly up at the row of caves above him, he had put his finger to his lips as a sign of secrecy and had stolen back again to his people.

I took the slip of bark to the firelight and we examined it together. It was about a foot square, and on the inner side there was a singular arrangement of lines, which I here reproduce:

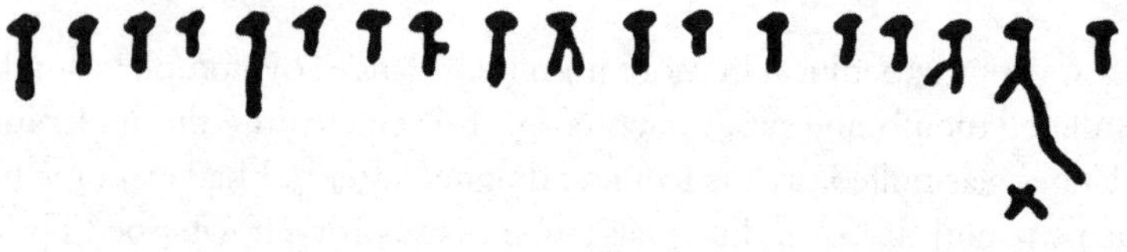

They were neatly done in charcoal upon the white surface, and looked to me at first sight like some sort of rough musical score.

"Whatever it is, I can swear that it is of importance to us," said I. "I could read that on his face as he gave it."

"Unless we have come upon a primitive practical joker," Summerlee suggested, "which I should think would be one of the most elementary developments of man."

"It is clearly some sort of script," said Challenger.

"Looks like a guinea puzzle competition," remarked Lord John, craning his neck to have a look at it. Then suddenly he stretched out his hand and seized the puzzle.

"By George!" he cried, "I believe I've got it. The boy guessed right the very first time. See here! How many marks are on that paper? Eighteen. Well, if you come to think of it there are eighteen cave openings on the hill-side above us."

"He pointed up to the caves when he gave it to me," said I.

"Well, that settles it. This is a chart of the caves. What! Eighteen of them all in a row, some short, some deep, some branching, same as we saw them. It's a map, and here's a cross on it. What's the cross for? It is placed to mark one that is much deeper than the others."

"One that goes through," I cried.

"I believe our young friend has read the riddle," said Challenger. "If the cave does not go through I do not understand why this person, who has every reason to mean us well, should have drawn our attention to it. But if it does go through and comes out at the corresponding point on the other side, we should not have more than a hundred feet to descend."

"A hundred feet!" grumbled Summerlee.

"Well, our rope is still more than a hundred feet long," I cried. "Surely we could get down."

"How about the Indians in the cave?" Summerlee objected.

"There are no Indians in any of the caves above our heads," said I. "They are all used as barns and store-houses. Why should we not go up now at once and spy out the land?"

There is a dry bituminous wood upon the plateau—a species of araucaria, according to our botanist—which is always used by the Indians for torches. Each of us picked up a faggot of this, and we made our way up weed-covered steps to the particular cave which was marked in the drawing. It was, as I had said, empty, save for a great number of enormous bats, which flapped round our heads as we advanced into it. As we had no desire to draw the attention of the Indians to our proceedings, we stumbled along in the dark until we had gone round several curves and penetrated a considerable distance into the cavern. Then, at last, we lit our torches. It was a beautiful dry tunnel with smooth gray walls covered with native symbols, a curved roof which arched over our heads, and white glistening sand beneath our feet. We hurried eagerly along it until, with a deep groan of bitter disappointment, we were brought to a halt. A sheer wall of rock had appeared before us, with no chink through which a mouse could have slipped. There was no escape for us there.

We stood with bitter hearts staring at this unexpected obstacle. It was not the result of any convulsion, as in the case of the ascending tunnel. The end wall was exactly like the side ones. It was, and had always been, a cul-de-sac.

"Never mind, my friends," said the indomitable Challenger. "You have still my firm promise of a balloon."

Summerlee groaned.

"Can we be in the wrong cave?" I suggested.

"No use, young fellah," said Lord John, with his finger on the chart. "Seventeen from the right and second from the left. This is the cave sure enough."

I looked at the mark to which his finger pointed, and I gave a sudden cry of joy.

"I believe I have it! Follow me! Follow me!"

I hurried back along the way we had come, my torch in my hand. "Here," said I, pointing to some matches upon the ground, "is where we lit up."

"Exactly."

"Well, it is marked as a forked cave, and in the darkness we passed the fork before the torches were lit. On the right side as we go out we should find the longer arm."

It was as I had said. We had not gone thirty yards before a great black opening loomed in the wall. We turned into it to find that we were in a much larger passage than before. Along it we hurried in breathless impatience for many hundreds of yards. Then, suddenly, in the black darkness of the arch in front of us we saw a gleam of dark red light. We stared in amazement. A sheet of steady flame seemed to cross the passage and to bar our way. We hastened towards it. No sound, no heat, no movement came from it, but still the great luminous curtain glowed before us, silvering all the cave and turning the sand to powdered jewels, until as we drew closer it discovered a circular edge.

"The moon, by George!" cried Lord John. "We are through, boys! We are through!"

It was indeed the full moon which shone straight down the aperture which opened upon the cliffs. It was a small rift, not larger than a window, but it was enough for all our purposes. As we craned our necks through it we could see that the descent was not a very difficult one, and that the level ground was no very great way below us. It was no wonder that from below we had not observed the place, as the cliffs curved overhead and an ascent at the spot would have seemed so impossible as to discourage close inspection. We satisfied ourselves that with the help of our rope we could find our way down, and then returned, rejoicing, to our camp to make our preparations for the next evening.

What we did we had to do quickly and secretly, since even at this last hour the Indians might hold us back. Our stores we would leave behind us, save only our guns and cartridges. But Challenger had some unwieldy stuff which he ardently desired to take with him, and one particular package, of which I may not speak, which gave us more labor than any. Slowly the day passed, but when the darkness fell we were ready for our departure. With much labor we got our things up the steps, and then, looking back, took one last long survey of that strange land, soon I fear to be vulgarized, the prey of hunter and prospector, but to each of us a dreamland of glamour and romance, a land where we had dared much, suffered much, and learned much—our land, as we shall ever fondly call it. Along upon our left the neighboring caves each threw out its ruddy cheery firelight into the gloom. From the slope below us rose the voices of the Indians as they laughed and sang. Beyond was the long sweep of the woods, and in the center, shimmering vaguely through the gloom, was the great lake, the mother of strange monsters. Even as we looked a high whickering cry, the call of some weird animal, rang clear out of the darkness. It was the very voice of Maple White Land bidding us good-bye. We turned and plunged into the cave which led to home.

Two hours later, we, our packages, and all we owned, were at the foot of the cliff. Save for Challenger's luggage we had never a difficulty. Leaving it all where we descended, we started at once for Zambo's camp. In the early morning we approached it, but only to find, to our amazement, not one fire but a dozen upon the plain. The rescue party had arrived. There were twenty Indians from the river, with stakes, ropes, and all that could be useful for bridging the chasm. At least we shall have no difficulty now in carrying our packages, when tomorrow we begin to make our way back to the Amazon.

And so, in humble and thankful mood, I close this account. Our eyes have seen great wonders and our souls are chastened by what we have endured. Each is in his own way a better and deeper man. It may be that when we reach Para we shall stop to refit. If we do, this letter will be a mail ahead. If not, it will reach London on the very day that I do. In either case, my dear Mr. McArdle, I hope very soon to shake you by the hand.

XVI

"A PROCESSION! A PROCESSION!"

I should wish to place upon record here our gratitude to all our friends upon the Amazon for the very great kindness and hospitality which was shown to us upon our return journey. Very particularly would I thank Senhor Penalosa and other officials of the Brazilian Government for the special arrangements by which we were helped upon our way, and Senhor Pereira of Para, to whose forethought we owe the complete outfit for a decent appearance in the civilized world which we found ready for us at that town. It seemed a poor return for all the courtesy which we encountered that we should deceive our hosts and benefactors, but under the circumstances we had really no alternative, and I hereby tell them that they will only waste their time and their money if they attempt to follow upon our traces. Even the names have been altered in our accounts, and I am very sure that no one, from the most careful study of them, could come within a thousand miles of our unknown land.

The excitement which had been caused through those parts of South America which we had to traverse was imagined by us to be purely local, and I can assure our friends in England that we had no notion of the uproar which the mere rumor of our experiences had caused through Europe. It was not until the Ivernia was within five hundred miles of Southampton that the wireless messages from paper after paper and agency after agency, offering huge prices for a short return message as to our actual results, showed us how strained was the attention not only of the scientific world but of the general public. It was agreed among us, however, that no definite statement should be given to the Press until we had met the members of the Zoological Institute, since as delegates it was our clear duty to give our first report to the body from which we had received our commission of investigation. Thus, although we found Southampton full of Pressmen, we absolutely refused to give any information, which had the natural effect of focusing public attention upon the meeting which was advertised for the evening of November 7th. For this gathering, the Zoological Hall which had been the scene of the inception of our task was found to be far too small, and it was only in the Queen's Hall in Regent Street that accommodation could be found. It is now common knowledge the promoters might have ventured upon the Albert Hall and still found their space too scanty.

It was for the second evening after our arrival that the great meeting had been fixed. For the first, we had each, no doubt, our own pressing personal affairs to absorb us. Of mine I cannot yet speak. It may be that as it stands further from me I may think of it, and even speak of it, with less emotion. I have shown the reader in the beginning of this narrative where lay the springs of my action. It is but right, perhaps, that I should carry on the tale and show also the results. And yet the day may come when I would not have it otherwise. At least I have been driven forth to take part in a wondrous adventure, and I cannot but be thankful to the force that drove me.

And now I turn to the last supreme eventful moment of our adventure. As I was racking my brain as to how I should best describe it, my eyes fell upon the issue of my own Journal for the morning of the 8th of November with the full and excellent account of my friend and fellow-reporter Macdona. What can I do better than transcribe his narrative—headlines and all? I admit that the paper was exuberant in the matter, out of compliment to its own enterprise in sending a correspondent, but the other great dailies were hardly less full in their account. Thus, then, friend Mac in his report:

THE NEW WORLD
GREAT MEETING AT THE QUEEN'S HALL
SCENES OF UPROAR
EXTRAORDINARY INCIDENT
WHAT WAS IT?
NOCTURNAL RIOT IN REGENT STREET
(SPECIAL)

"The much-discussed meeting of the Zoological Institute, convened to hear the report of the Committee of Investigation sent out last year to South America to test the assertions made by Professor Challenger as to the continued existence of prehistoric life upon that Continent, was held last night in the greater Queen's Hall, and it is safe to say that it is likely to be a red letter date in the history of Science, for the proceedings were of so remarkable and sensational a character that no one present is ever likely to forget them." (Oh, brother scribe Macdona, what a monstrous opening sentence!) "The tickets were theoretically confined to members and their friends, but the latter is an elastic term, and long before eight o'clock, the hour fixed for the commencement of the proceedings, all parts of the Great Hall were tightly packed. The general public, however, which most unreasonably entertained a grievance at having been excluded, stormed the doors at a quarter to eight, after a prolonged melee in which several people were injured, including Inspector Scoble of H. Division, whose leg was unfortunately broken. After this unwarrantable invasion, which not only filled every passage, but even intruded upon the space set apart for the Press, it is estimated that nearly five thousand people awaited the arrival of the travelers. When they eventually appeared, they took their places in the front of a platform which already contained all the leading scientific men, not only of this country, but of France and of Germany. Sweden was also represented, in the person of Professor Sergius, the famous Zoologist of the University of Upsala. The entrance of the four heroes of the occasion was the signal for a remarkable demonstration of welcome, the whole audience rising and cheering for some minutes. An acute observer might, however, have detected some signs of dissent amid the applause, and gathered that the proceedings were likely to become more lively than harmonious. It may safely be prophesied, however, that no one could have foreseen the extraordinary turn which they were actually to take.

"Of the appearance of the four wanderers little need be said, since their photographs have for some time been appearing in all the papers. They bear few traces of the hardships which they are said to have undergone. Professor Challenger's beard may be more shaggy, Professor Summerlee's features more ascetic, Lord John Roxton's figure more gaunt, and all three may be burned to a darker tint than when they left our shores, but each appeared to be in most excellent health. As to our own representative, the well-known athlete and international Rugby football player, E. D. Malone, he looks trained to a hair, and as he surveyed the crowd a smile of good-humored contentment pervaded his honest but homely face." (All right, Mac, wait till I get you alone!)

"When quiet had been restored and the audience resumed their seats after the ovation which they had given to the travelers, the chairman, the Duke of Durham, addressed the meeting. 'He would not,' he said, 'stand for more than a moment between that vast assembly and the treat which lay before them. It was not for him to anticipate what Professor Summerlee, who was the spokesman of the committee, had to say to them, but it was common rumor that their expedition had been crowned by extraordinary success.' (Applause.) 'Apparently the age of romance was not dead, and there was common ground upon which the wildest imaginings of the novelist could meet the actual scientific investigations of the searcher for truth. He would only add, before he sat down, that he rejoiced—and all of them would rejoice—that these gentlemen had returned safe and sound from their difficult and dangerous task, for it cannot be denied that any disaster to such an expedition would have inflicted a well-nigh irreparable loss to the cause of Zoological science.' (Great applause, in which Professor Challenger was observed to join.)

"Professor Summerlee's rising was the signal for another extraordinary outbreak of enthusiasm, which broke out again at intervals throughout his address. That address will not be given in extenso in these columns, for the reason that a full account of the whole adventures of the expedition is being published as a supplement from the pen of our own special correspondent. Some general indications will therefore suffice. Having described the genesis of their journey, and paid a handsome tribute to his friend Professor Challenger, coupled with an apology for the incredulity with which his assertions, now fully vindicated, had been received, he gave the actual course of their journey, carefully withholding such information as would aid the public in any attempt to locate this remarkable plateau. Having described, in general terms, their course from the main river up to the time that they actually reached the base of the cliffs, he enthralled his hearers by his account of the difficulties encountered by the expedition in their repeated attempts to mount them, and finally described how they succeeded in their desperate endeavors, which cost the lives of their two devoted half-breed servants." (This amazing reading of the affair was the result of Summerlee's endeavors to avoid raising any questionable matter at the meeting.)

"Having conducted his audience in fancy to the summit, and marooned them there by reason of the fall of their bridge, the Professor proceeded to describe both the horrors and the attractions of that remarkable land. Of personal adventures he said little, but laid stress upon the rich harvest reaped by Science in the observations of the wonderful beast, bird, insect, and plant life of the plateau. Peculiarly rich in the coleoptera and in the lepidoptera, forty-six new species of the one and ninety-four of the other had been secured in the course of a few weeks. It was, however, in the larger animals, and especially in the larger animals supposed to have been long extinct, that the interest of the public was naturally centered. Of these he was able to give a goodly list, but had little doubt that it would be largely extended when the place had been more thoroughly investigated. He and his companions had seen at least a dozen creatures, most of them at a distance, which corresponded with nothing at present known to Science. These would in time be duly classified and examined. He instanced a snake, the cast skin of which, deep purple in color, was fifty-one feet in length, and mentioned a white creature, supposed to be mammalian, which gave forth well-marked phosphorescence in the darkness; also a large black moth, the bite of which was supposed by the Indians to be highly poisonous. Setting aside these entirely new forms of life, the plateau was very rich in known prehistoric forms, dating back in some cases to early Jurassic times. Among these he mentioned the gigantic and grotesque stegosaurus, seen once by Mr. Malone at a drinking-place by the lake, and drawn in the sketchbook of that adventurous American who had first penetrated this unknown world. He described also the iguanodon and the pterodactyl—two of the first of the wonders which they had encountered. He then thrilled the assembly by some account of the terrible carnivorous dinosaurs, which had on more than one occasion pursued members of the party, and which were the most formidable of all the creatures which they had encountered. Thence he passed to the huge and ferocious bird, the phororachus, and to the great elk which still roams upon this upland. It was not, however, until he sketched the mysteries of the central lake that the full interest and enthusiasm of the audience were aroused. One had to pinch oneself to be sure that one was awake as one heard this sane and practical Professor in cold measured tones describing the monstrous three-eyed fish-lizards and the huge water-snakes which inhabit this enchanted sheet of water. Next he touched upon the Indians, and upon the extraordinary colony of anthropoid apes, which might be looked upon as an advance upon the pithecanthropus of Java, and as coming therefore nearer than any known form to that hypothetical creation, the missing link. Finally he described, amongst some merriment, the ingenious but highly dangerous aeronautic invention of Professor Challenger, and wound up a most memorable address by an account of the methods by which the committee did at last find their way back to civilization.

"It had been hoped that the proceedings would end there, and that a vote of thanks and congratulation, moved by Professor Sergius, of Upsala University, would be duly seconded and carried; but it was soon evident that the course of events was not destined to flow so smoothly. Symptoms of opposition had been evident from time to time during the evening, and now Dr. James Illingworth, of Edinburgh, rose in the center of the hall. Dr. Illingworth asked whether an amendment should not be taken before a resolution.

"The Chairman: 'Yes, sir, if there must be an amendment.'

"Dr. Illingworth: 'Your Grace, there must be an amendment.'

"The Chairman: 'Then let us take it at once.'

"Professor Summerlee (springing to his feet): 'Might I explain, your Grace, that this man is my personal enemy ever since our controversy in the Quarterly Journal of Science as to the true nature of Bathybius?'

"The Chairman: 'I fear I cannot go into personal matters. Proceed.'

"Dr. Illingworth was imperfectly heard in part of his remarks on account of the strenuous opposition of the friends of the explorers. Some attempts were also made to pull him down. Being a man of enormous physique, however, and possessed of a very powerful voice, he dominated the tumult and succeeded in finishing his speech. It was clear, from the moment of his rising, that he had a number of friends and sympathizers in the hall, though they formed a minority in the audience. The attitude of the greater part of the public might be described as one of attentive neutrality.

"Dr. Illingworth began his remarks by expressing his high appreciation of the scientific work both of Professor Challenger and of Professor Summerlee. He much regretted that any personal bias should have been read into his remarks, which were entirely dictated by his desire for scientific truth. His position, in fact, was substantially the same as that taken up by Professor Summerlee at the last meeting. At that last meeting Professor Challenger had made certain assertions which had been queried by his colleague. Now this colleague came forward himself with the same assertions and expected them to remain unquestioned. Was this reasonable? ('Yes,' 'No,' and prolonged interruption, during which Professor Challenger was heard from the Press box to ask leave from the chairman to put Dr. Illingworth into the street.) A year ago one man said certain things. Now four men said other and more startling ones. Was this to constitute a final proof where the matters in question were of the most revolutionary and incredible character? There had been recent examples of travelers arriving from the unknown with certain tales which had been too readily accepted. Was the London Zoological Institute to place itself in this position? He admitted that the members of the committee were men of character. But human nature was very complex. Even Professors might be misled by the desire for notoriety. Like moths, we all love best to flutter in the light. Heavy-game shots liked to be in a position to cap the tales of their rivals, and journalists were not averse from sensational coups, even when imagination had to aid fact in the process. Each member of the committee had his own motive for making the most of his results. ('Shame! shame!') He had no desire to be offensive. ('You are!' and interruption.) The corroboration of these wondrous tales was really of the most slender description. What did it amount to? Some photographs. {Was it possible that in this age of ingenious manipulation photographs could be accepted as evidence?} What more? We have a story of a flight and a descent by ropes which precluded the production of larger specimens. It was ingenious, but not convincing. It was understood that Lord John Roxton claimed to have the skull of a phororachus. He could only say that he would like to see that skull.

"Lord John Roxton: 'Is this fellow calling me a liar?' (Uproar.)

"The Chairman: 'Order! Order! Dr. Illingworth, I must direct you to bring your remarks to a conclusion and to move your amendment.'

"Dr. Illingworth: 'Your Grace, I have more to say, but I bow to your ruling. I move, then, that, while Professor Summerlee be thanked for his interesting address, the whole matter shall be regarded as 'non-proven,' and shall be referred back to a larger, and possibly more reliable Committee of Investigation.'

"It is difficult to describe the confusion caused by this amendment. A large section of the audience expressed their indignation at such a slur upon the travelers by noisy shouts of dissent and cries of, 'Don't put it!' 'Withdraw!' 'Turn him out!' On the other hand, the malcontents—and it cannot be denied that they were fairly numerous—cheered for the amendment, with cries of 'Order!' 'Chair!' and 'Fair play!' A scuffle broke out in the back benches, and blows were freely exchanged among the medical students who crowded that part of the hall. It was only the moderating influence of the presence of large numbers of ladies which prevented an absolute riot. Suddenly, however, there was a pause, a hush, and then complete silence. Professor Challenger was on his feet. His appearance and manner are peculiarly arresting, and as he raised his hand for order the whole audience settled down expectantly to give him a hearing.

"'It will be within the recollection of many present,' said Professor Challenger, 'that similar foolish and unmannerly scenes marked the last meeting at which I have been able to address them. On that occasion Professor Summerlee was the chief offender, and though he is now chastened and contrite, the matter could not be entirely forgotten. I have heard tonight similar, but even more offensive, sentiments from the person who has just sat down, and though it is a conscious effort of self-effacement to come down to that person's mental level, I will endeavor to do so, in order to allay any reasonable doubt which could possibly exist in the minds of anyone.' (Laughter and interruption.) 'I need not remind this audience that, though Professor Summerlee, as the head of the Committee of Investigation, has been put up to speak tonight, still it is I who am the real prime mover in this business, and that it is mainly to me that any successful result must be ascribed. I have safely conducted these three gentlemen to the spot mentioned, and I have, as you have heard, convinced them of the accuracy of my previous account. We had hoped that we should find upon our return that no one was so dense as to dispute our joint conclusions. Warned, however, by my previous experience, I have not come without such proofs as may convince a reasonable man. As explained by Professor Summerlee, our cameras have been tampered with by the ape-men when they ransacked our camp, and most of our negatives ruined.' (Jeers, laughter, and 'Tell us another!' from the back.) 'I have mentioned the ape-men, and I cannot forbear from saying that some of the sounds which now meet my ears bring back most vividly to my recollection my experiences with those interesting creatures.' (Laughter.) 'In spite of the destruction of so many invaluable negatives, there still remains in our collection a certain number of corroborative photographs showing the conditions of life upon the plateau. Did they accuse them of having forged these photographs?' (A voice, 'Yes,' and considerable interruption which ended in several men being put out of the hall.) 'The negatives were open to the inspection of experts. But what other evidence had they? Under the conditions of their escape it was naturally impossible to bring a large amount of baggage, but they had rescued Professor Summerlee's collections of butterflies and beetles, containing many new species. Was this not evidence?' (Several voices, 'No.') 'Who said no?'

"DR. ILLINGWORTH (rising): 'Our point is that such a collection might have been made in other places than a prehistoric plateau.' (Applause.)

"PROFESSOR CHALLENGER: 'No doubt, sir, we have to bow to your scientific authority, although I must admit that the name is unfamiliar. Passing, then, both the photographs and the entomological collection, I come to the varied and accurate information which we bring with us upon points which have never before been elucidated. For example, upon the domestic habits of the pterodactyl—'(A voice: 'Bosh,' and uproar)—'I say, that upon the domestic habits of the pterodactyl we can throw a flood of light. I can exhibit to you from my portfolio a picture of that creature taken from life which would convince you—'

"DR. ILLINGWORTH: 'No picture could convince us of anything.'

"PROFESSOR CHALLENGER: 'You would require to see the thing itself?'

"Dr. Illingworth: 'Undoubtedly.'

"Professor Challenger: 'And you would accept that?'

"Dr. Illingworth (laughing): 'Beyond a doubt.'

"It was at this point that the sensation of the evening arose—a sensation so dramatic that it can never have been paralleled in the history of scientific gatherings. Professor Challenger raised his hand in the air as a signal, and at once our colleague, Mr. E. D. Malone, was observed to rise and to make his way to the back of the platform. An instant later he reappeared in company of a gigantic negro, the two of them bearing between them a large square packing-case. It was evidently of great weight, and was slowly carried forward and placed in front of the Professor's chair. All sound had hushed in the audience and everyone was absorbed in the spectacle before them. Professor Challenger drew off the top of the case, which formed a sliding lid. Peering down into the box he snapped his fingers several times and was heard from the Press seat to say, 'Come, then, pretty, pretty!' in a coaxing voice. An instant later, with a scratching, rattling sound, a most horrible and loathsome creature appeared from below and perched itself upon the side of the case. Even the unexpected fall of the Duke of Durham into the orchestra, which occurred at this moment, could not distract the petrified attention of the vast audience. The face of the creature was like the wildest gargoyle that the imagination of a mad medieval builder could have conceived. It was malicious, horrible, with two small red eyes as bright as points of burning coal. Its long, savage mouth, which was held half-open, was full of a double row of shark-like teeth. Its shoulders were humped, and round them were draped what appeared to be a faded gray shawl. It was the devil of our childhood in person. There was a turmoil in the audience—someone screamed, two ladies in the front row fell senseless from their chairs, and there was a general movement upon the platform to follow their chairman into the orchestra. For a moment there was danger of a general panic. Professor Challenger threw up his hands to still the commotion, but the movement alarmed the creature beside him. Its strange shawl suddenly unfurled, spread, and fluttered as a pair of leathery wings. Its owner grabbed at its legs, but too late to hold it. It had sprung from the perch and was circling slowly round the Queen's Hall with a dry, leathery flapping of its ten-foot wings, while a putrid and insidious odor pervaded the room. The cries of the people in the galleries, who were alarmed at the near approach of those glowing eyes and that murderous beak, excited the creature to a frenzy. Faster and faster it flew, beating against walls and chandeliers in a blind frenzy of alarm. 'The window! For heaven's sake shut that window!' roared the Professor from the platform, dancing and wringing his hands in an agony of apprehension. Alas, his warning was too late! In a moment the creature, beating and bumping along the wall like a huge moth within a gas-shade, came upon the opening, squeezed its hideous bulk through it, and was gone. Professor Challenger fell back into his chair with his face buried in his hands, while the audience gave one long, deep sigh of relief as they realized that the incident was over.

"Then—oh! How shall one describe what took place then—when the full exuberance of the majority and the full reaction of the minority united to make one great wave of enthusiasm, which rolled from the back of the hall, gathering volume as it came, swept over the orchestra, submerged the platform, and carried the four heroes away upon its crest?" (Good for you, Mac!) "If the audience had done less than justice, surely it made ample amends. Every one was on his feet. Every one was moving, shouting, gesticulating. A dense crowd of cheering men were round the four travelers. 'Up with them! up with them!' cried a hundred voices. In a moment four figures shot up above the crowd. In vain they strove to break loose. They were held in their lofty places of honor. It would have been hard to let them down if it had been wished, so dense was the crowd around them. 'Regent Street! Regent Street!' sounded the voices. There was a swirl in the packed multitude, and a slow current, bearing the four upon their shoulders, made for the door. Out in the street the scene was extraordinary. An assemblage of not less than a hundred thousand people was waiting. The close-packed throng extended from the other side of the Langham Hotel to Oxford Circus. A roar of acclamation greeted the four adventurers as they appeared, high above the heads of the people, under the vivid electric lamps outside the hall. 'A procession! A procession!' was the cry. In a dense phalanx, blocking the streets from side to side, the crowd set forth, taking the route of Regent Street, Pall Mall, St. James's Street, and Piccadilly. The whole central traffic of London was held up, and many collisions were reported between the demonstrators upon the one side and the police and taxi-cabmen upon the other. Finally, it was not until after midnight that the four travelers were released at the entrance to Lord John Roxton's chambers in the Albany, and that the exuberant crowd, having sung 'They are Jolly Good Fellows' in chorus, concluded their program with 'God Save the King.' So ended one of the most remarkable evenings that London has seen for a considerable time."

So far my friend Macdona; and it may be taken as a fairly accurate, if florid, account of the proceedings. As to the main incident, it was a bewildering surprise to the audience, but not, I need hardly say, to us. The reader will remember how I met Lord John Roxton upon the very occasion when, in his protective crinoline, he had gone to bring the "Devil's chick" as he called it, for Professor Challenger. I have hinted also at the trouble which the Professor's baggage gave us when we left the plateau, and had I described our voyage I might have said a good deal of the worry we had to coax with putrid fish the appetite of our filthy companion. If I have not said much about it before, it was, of course, that the Professor's earnest desire was that no possible rumor of the unanswerable argument which we carried should be allowed to leak out until the moment came when his enemies were to be confuted.

One word as to the fate of the London pterodactyl. Nothing can be said to be certain upon this point. There is the evidence of two frightened women that it perched upon the roof of the Queen's Hall and remained there like a diabolical statue for some hours. The next day it came out in the evening papers that Private Miles, of the Coldstream Guards, on duty outside Marlborough House, had deserted his post without leave, and was therefore court-martialed. Private Miles's account, that he dropped his rifle and took to his heels down the Mall because on looking up he had suddenly seen the devil between him and the moon, was not accepted by the Court, and yet it may have a direct bearing upon the point at issue. The only other evidence which I can adduce is from the log of the SS. Friesland, a Dutch-American liner, which asserts that at nine next morning, Start Point being at the time ten miles upon their starboard quarter, they were passed by something between a flying goat and a monstrous bat, which was heading at a prodigious pace south and west. If its homing instinct led it upon the right line, there can be no doubt that somewhere out in the wastes of the Atlantic the last European pterodactyl found its end.

And Gladys—oh, my Gladys!—Gladys of the mystic lake, now to be renamed the Central, for never shall she have immortality through me. Did I not always see some hard fiber in her nature? Did I not, even at the time when I was proud to obey her behest, feel that it was surely a poor love which could drive a lover to his death or the danger of it? Did I not, in my truest thoughts, always recurring and always dismissed, see past the beauty of the face, and, peering into the soul, discern the twin shadows of selfishness and of fickleness glooming at the back of it? Did she love the heroic and the spectacular for its own noble sake, or was it for the glory which might, without effort or sacrifice, be reflected upon herself? Or are these thoughts the vain wisdom which comes after the event? It was the shock of my life. For a moment it had turned me to a cynic. But already, as I write, a week has passed, and we have had our momentous interview with Lord John Roxton and—well, perhaps things might be worse.

Let me tell it in a few words. No letter or telegram had come to me at Southampton, and I reached the little villa at Streatham about ten o'clock that night in a fever of alarm. Was she dead or alive? Where were all my nightly dreams of the open arms, the smiling face, the words of praise for her man who had risked his life to humor her whim? Already I was down from the high peaks and standing flat-footed upon earth. Yet some good reasons given might still lift me to the clouds once more. I rushed down the garden path, hammered at the door, heard the voice of Gladys within, pushed past the staring maid, and strode into the sitting-room. She was seated in a low settee under the shaded standard lamp by the piano. In three steps I was across the room and had both her hands in mine.

"Gladys!" I cried, "Gladys!"

She looked up with amazement in her face. She was altered in some subtle way. The expression of her eyes, the hard upward stare, the set of the lips, was new to me. She drew back her hands.

"What do you mean?" she said.

"Gladys!" I cried. "What is the matter? You are my Gladys, are you not—little Gladys Hungerton?"

"No," said she, "I am Gladys Potts. Let me introduce you to my husband."

How absurd life is! I found myself mechanically bowing and shaking hands with a little ginger-haired man who was coiled up in the deep armchair which had once been sacred to my own use. We bobbed and grinned in front of each other.

"Father lets us stay here. We are getting our house ready," said Gladys.

"Oh, yes," said I.

"You didn't get my letter at Para, then?"

"No, I got no letter."

"Oh, what a pity! It would have made all clear."

"It is quite clear," said I.

"I've told William all about you," said she. "We have no secrets. I am so sorry about it. But it couldn't have been so very deep, could it, if you could go off to the other end of the world and leave me here alone. You're not crabby, are you?"

"No, no, not at all. I think I'll go."

"Have some refreshment," said the little man, and he added, in a confidential way, "It's always like this, ain't it? And must be unless you had polygamy, only the other way round; you understand." He laughed like an idiot, while I made for the door.

I was through it, when a sudden fantastic impulse came upon me, and I went back to my successful rival, who looked nervously at the electric push.

"Will you answer a question?" I asked.

"Well, within reason," said he.

"How did you do it? Have you searched for hidden treasure, or discovered a pole, or done time on a pirate, or flown the Channel, or what? Where is the glamour of romance? How did you get it?"

He stared at me with a hopeless expression upon his vacuous, good-natured, scrubby little face.

"Don't you think all this is a little too personal?" he said.

"Well, just one question," I cried. "What are you? What is your profession?"

"I am a solicitor's clerk," said he. "Second man at Johnson and Merivale's, 41 Chancery Lane."

"Good-night!" said I, and vanished, like all disconsolate and broken-hearted heroes, into the darkness, with grief and rage and laughter all simmering within me like a boiling pot.

One more little scene, and I have done. Last night we all supped at Lord John Roxton's rooms, and sitting together afterwards we smoked in good comradeship and talked our adventures over. It was strange under these altered surroundings to see the old, well-known faces and figures. There was Challenger, with his smile of condescension, his drooping eyelids, his intolerant eyes, his aggressive beard, his huge chest, swelling and puffing as he laid down the law to Summerlee. And Summerlee, too, there he was with his short briar between his thin moustache and his gray goat's-beard, his worn face protruded in eager debate as he queried all Challenger's propositions. Finally, there was our host, with his rugged, eagle face, and his cold, blue, glacier eyes with always a shimmer of devilment and of humor down in the depths of them. Such is the last picture of them that I have carried away.

It was after supper, in his own sanctum—the room of the pink radiance and the innumerable trophies—that Lord John Roxton had something to say to us. From a cupboard he had brought an old cigar-box, and this he laid before him on the table.

"There's one thing," said he, "that maybe I should have spoken about before this, but I wanted to know a little more clearly where I was. No use to raise hopes and let them down again. But it's facts, not hopes, with us now. You may remember that day we found the pterodactyl rookery in the swamp—what? Well, somethin' in the lie of the land took my notice. Perhaps it has escaped you, so I will tell you. It was a volcanic vent full of blue clay." The Professors nodded.

"Well, now, in the whole world I've only had to do with one place that was a volcanic vent of blue clay. That was the great De Beers Diamond Mine of Kimberley—what? So you see I got diamonds into my head. I rigged up a contraption to hold off those stinking beasts, and I spent a happy day there with a spud. This is what I got."

He opened his cigar-box, and tilting it over he poured about twenty or thirty rough stones, varying from the size of beans to that of chestnuts, on the table.

"Perhaps you think I should have told you then. Well, so I should, only I know there are a lot of traps for the unwary, and that stones may be of any size and yet of little value where color and consistency are clean off.

Therefore, I brought them back, and on the first day at home I took one round to Spink's, and asked him to have it roughly cut and valued."

He took a pill-box from his pocket, and spilled out of it a beautiful glittering diamond, one of the finest stones that I have ever seen.

"There's the result," said he. "He prices the lot at a minimum of two hundred thousand pounds. Of course it is fair shares between us. I won't hear of anythin' else. Well, Challenger, what will you do with your fifty thousand?"

"If you really persist in your generous view," said the Professor, "I should found a private museum, which has long been one of my dreams."

"And you, Summerlee?"

"I would retire from teaching, and so find time for my final classification of the chalk fossils."

"I'll use my own," said Lord John Roxton, "in fitting a well-formed expedition and having another look at the dear old plateau. As to you, young fellah, you, of course, will spend yours in gettin' married."

"Not just yet," said I, with a rueful smile. "I think, if you will have me, that I would rather go with you."

Lord Roxton said nothing, but a brown hand was stretched out to me across the table.

THE SCARLET PLAGUE

Jack London

I

The way led along upon what had once been the embankment of a railroad. But no train had run upon it for many years. The forest on either side swelled up the slopes of the embankment and crested across it in a green wave of trees and bushes. The trail was as narrow as a man's body, and was no more than a wild-animal runway. Occasionally, a piece of rusty iron, showing through the forest-mold, advertised that the rail and the ties still remained. In one place, a ten-inch tree, bursting through at a connection, had lifted the end of a rail clearly into view. The tie had evidently followed the rail, held to it by the spike long enough for its bed to be filled with gravel and rotten leaves, so that now the crumbling, rotten timber thrust itself up at a curious slant. Old as the road was, it was manifest that it had been of the monorail type.

An old man and a boy travelled along this runway. They moved slowly, for the old man was very old, a touch of palsy made his movements tremulous, and he leaned heavily upon his staff. A rude skull-cap of goat-skin protected his head from the sun. From beneath this fell a scant fringe of stained and dirty-white hair. A visor, ingeniously made from a large leaf, shielded his eyes, and from under this he peered at the way of his feet on the trail. His beard, which should have been snow-white but which showed the same weather-wear and camp-stain as his hair, fell nearly to his waist in a great tangled mass. About his chest and shoulders hung a single, mangy garment of goat-skin. His arms and legs, withered and skinny, betokened extreme age, as well as did their sunburn and scars and scratches betoken long years of exposure to the elements.

The boy, who led the way, checking the eagerness of his muscles to the slow progress of the elder, likewise wore a single garment—a ragged-edged piece of bear-skin, with a hole in the middle through which he had thrust his head. He could not have been more than twelve years old. Tucked coquettishly over one ear was the freshly severed tail of a pig. In one hand he carried a medium-sized bow and an arrow.

On his back was a quiverful of arrows. From a sheath hanging about his neck on a thong, projected the battered handle of a hunting knife. He was as brown as a berry, and walked softly, with almost a catlike tread. In marked contrast with his sunburned skin were his eyes—blue, deep blue, but keen and sharp as a pair of gimlets. They seemed to bore into aft about him in a way that was habitual. As he went along he smelled things, as well, his distended, quivering nostrils carrying to his brain an endless series of messages from the outside world. Also, his hearing was acute, and had been so trained that it operated automatically. Without conscious effort, he heard all the slight sounds in the apparent quiet—heard, and differentiated, and classified these sounds—whether they were of the wind rustling the leaves, of the humming of bees and gnats, of the distant rumble of the sea that drifted to him only in lulls, or of the gopher, just under his foot, shoving a pouchful of earth into the entrance of his hole.

Suddenly he became alertly tense. Sound, sight, and odor had given him a simultaneous warning. His hand went back to the old man, touching him, and the pair stood still. Ahead, at one side of the top of the embankment, arose a crackling sound, and the boy's gaze was fixed on the tops of the agitated bushes. Then a large bear, a grizzly, crashed into view, and likewise stopped abruptly, at sight of the humans. He did not like them, and growled querulously. Slowly the boy fitted the arrow to the bow, and slowly he pulled the bowstring taut. But he never removed his eyes from the bear.

The old man peered from under his green leaf at the danger, and stood as quietly as the boy. For a few seconds this mutual scrutinizing went on; then, the bear betraying a growing irritability, the boy, with a movement of his head, indicated that the old man must step aside from the trail and go down the embankment. The boy followed, going backward, still holding the bow taut and ready. They waited till a crashing among the bushes from the opposite side of the embankment told them the bear had gone on. The boy grinned as he led back to the trail.

"A big un, Granser," he chuckled.

The old man shook his head.

"They get thicker every day," he complained in a thin, undependable falsetto. "Who'd have thought I'd live to see the time when a man would be afraid of his life on the way to the Cliff House. When I was a boy, Edwin, men and women and little babies used to come out here from San Francisco by tens of thousands on a nice day. And there weren't any bears then. No, sir. They used to pay money to look at them in cages, they were that rare."

"What is money, Granser?"

Before the old man could answer, the boy recollected and triumphantly shoved his hand into a pouch under his bear-skin and pulled forth a battered and tarnished silver dollar. The old man's eyes glistened, as he held the coin close to them.

"I can't see," he muttered. "You look and see if you can make out the date, Edwin."

The boy laughed.

"You're a great Granser," he cried delightedly, "always making believe them little marks mean something."

The old man manifested an accustomed chagrin as he brought the coin back again close to his own eyes.

"2012," he shrilled, and then fell to cackling grotesquely. "That was the year Morgan the Fifth was appointed President of the United States by the Board of Magnates. It must have been one of the last coins minted, for the Scarlet Death came in 2013. Lord! Lord! Think of it! Sixty years ago, and I am the only person alive today that lived in those times. Where did you find it, Edwin?"

The boy, who had been regarding him with the tolerant curiousness one accords to the prattlings of the feeble-minded, answered promptly.

"I got it off of Hoo-Hoo. He found it when we was herdin' goats down near San José last spring. Hoo-Hoo said it was money. Ain't you hungry, Granser?"

The ancient caught his staff in a tighter grip and urged along the trail, his old eyes shining greedily.

"I hope Hare-Lip's found a crab . . . or two," he mumbled. "They're good eating, crabs, mighty good eating when you've no more teeth and you've got grandsons that love their old grandsire and make a point of catching crabs for him. When I was a boy—"

But Edwin, suddenly stopped by what he saw, was drawing the bowstring on a fitted arrow. He had paused on the brink of a crevasse in the embankment. An ancient culvert had here washed out, and the stream, no longer confined, had cut a passage through the fill. On the opposite side, the end of a rail projected and overhung. It showed rustily through the creeping vines which overran it. Beyond, crouching by a bush, a rabbit looked across at him in trembling hesitancy. Fully fifty feet was the distance, but the arrow flashed true; and the transfixed rabbit, crying out in sudden fright and hurt, struggled painfully away into the brush. The boy himself was a flash of brown skin and flying fur as he bounded down the steep wall of the gap and up the other side. His lean muscles were springs of steel that released into graceful and efficient action. A hundred feet beyond, in a tangle of bushes, he overtook the wounded creature, knocked its head on a convenient tree-trunk, and turned it over to Granser to carry.

"Rabbit is good, very good," the ancient quavered, "but when it comes to a toothsome delicacy I prefer crab. When I was a boy—"

"Why do you say so much that ain't got no sense?" Edwin impatiently interrupted the other's threatened garrulousness.

The boy did not exactly utter these words, but something that remotely resembled them and that was more guttural and explosive and economical of qualifying phrases. His speech showed distant kinship with that of the old man, and the latter's speech was approximately an English that had gone through a bath of corrupt usage.

"What I want to know," Edwin continued, "is why you call crab 'toothsome delicacy'? Crab is crab, ain't it? No one I never heard calls it such funny things."

The old man sighed but did not answer, and they moved on in silence. The surf grew suddenly louder, as they emerged from the forest upon a stretch of sand dunes bordering the sea. A few goats were browsing among the sandy hillocks, and a skin-clad boy, aided by a wolfish-looking dog that was only faintly reminiscent of a collie, was watching them. Mingled with the roar of the surf was a continuous, deep-throated barking or bellowing, which came from a cluster of jagged rocks a hundred yards out from shore. Here huge sea-lions hauled themselves up to lie in the sun or battle with one another. In the immediate foreground arose the smoke of a fire, tended by a third savage-looking boy. Crouched near him were several wolfish dogs similar to the one that guarded the goats.

The old man accelerated his pace, sniffing eagerly as he neared the fire. "Mussels!" he muttered ecstatically. "Mussels! And ain't that a crab, Hoo-Hoo? Ain't that a crab? My, my, you boys are good to your old grandsire."

Hoo-Hoo, who was apparently of the same age as Edwin, grinned.

"All you want, Granser. I got four."

The old man's palsied eagerness was pitiful. Sitting down in the sand as quickly as his stiff limbs would let him, he poked a large rock-mussel from out of the coals. The heat had forced its shells apart, and the meat, salmon-colored, was thoroughly cooked. Between thumb and forefinger, in trembling haste, he caught the morsel and carried it to his mouth. But it was too hot, and the next moment was violently ejected. The old man spluttered with the pain, and tears ran out of his eyes and down his cheeks.

The boys were true savages, possessing only the cruel humor of the savage. To them the incident was excruciatingly funny, and they burst into loud laughter. Hoo-Hoo danced up and down, while Edwin rolled gleefully on the ground. The boy with the goats came running to join in the fun.

"Set 'em to cool, Edwin, set 'em to cool," the old man besought, in the midst of his grief, making no attempt to wipe away the tears that still flowed from his eyes. "And cool a crab, Edwin, too. You know your grandsire likes crabs."

From the coals arose a great sizzling, which proceeded from the many mussels bursting open their shells and exuding their moisture. They were large shellfish, running from three to six inches in length. The boys raked them out with sticks and placed them on a large piece of driftwood to cool.

"When I was a boy, we did not laugh at our elders; we respected them."

The boys took no notice, and Granser continued to babble an incoherent flow of complaint and censure. But this time he was more careful, and did not burn his mouth. All began to eat, using nothing but their hands and making loud mouth-noises and lip-smackings. The third boy, who was called Hare-Lip, slyly deposited a pinch of sand on a mussel the ancient was carrying to his mouth; and when the grit of it bit into the old fellow's mucous membrane and gums, the laughter was again uproarious. He was unaware that a joke had been played on him, and spluttered and spat until Edwin, relenting, gave him a gourd of fresh water with which to wash out his mouth.

"Where's them crabs, Hoo-Hoo?" Edwin demanded. "Granser's set upon having a snack."

Again Granser's eyes burned with greediness as a large crab was handed to him. It was a shell with legs and all complete, but the meat had long since departed. With shaky fingers and babblings of anticipation, the old man broke off a leg and found it filled with emptiness.

"The crabs, Hoo-Hoo?" he wailed. "The crabs?"

"I was fooling Granser. They ain't no crabs! I never found one."

The boys were overwhelmed with delight at sight of the tears of senile disappointment that dribbled down the old man's cheeks. Then, unnoticed, Hoo-Hoo replaced the empty shell with a fresh-cooked crab. Already dismembered, from the cracked legs the white meat sent forth a small cloud of savory steam. This attracted the old man's nostrils, and he looked down in amazement.

The change of his mood to one of joy was immediate. He snuffled and muttered and mumbled, making almost a croon of delight, as he began to eat. Of this the boys took little notice, for it was an accustomed spectacle. Nor did they notice his occasional exclamations and utterances of phrases which meant nothing to them, as, for instance, when he smacked his lips and champed his gums while muttering: "Mayonnaise! Just think—mayonnaise! And it's sixty years since the last was ever made! Two generations and never a smell of it! Why, in those days it was served in every restaurant with crab."

When he could eat no more, the old man sighed, wiped his hands on his naked legs, and gazed out over the sea. With the content of a full stomach, he waxed reminiscent.

"To think of it! I've seen this beach alive with men, women, and children on a pleasant Sunday. And there weren't any bears to eat them up, either. And right up there on the cliff was a big restaurant where you could get anything you wanted to eat. Four million people lived in San Francisco then. And now, in the whole city and county there aren't forty all told. And out there on the sea were ships and ships always to be seen, going in for the Golden Gate or coming out. And airships in the air—dirigibles and flying machines. They could travel two hundred miles an hour. The mail contracts with the New York and San Francisco Limited demanded that for the minimum. There was a chap, a Frenchman, I forget his name, who succeeded in making three hundred; but the thing was risky, too risky for conservative persons. But he was on the right clue, and he would have managed it if it hadn't been for the Great Plague. When I was a boy, there were men alive who remembered the coming of the first aeroplanes, and now I have lived to see the last of them, and that sixty years ago."

The old man babbled on, unheeded by the boys, who were long accustomed to his garrulousness, and whose vocabularies, besides, lacked the greater portion of the words he used. It was noticeable that in these rambling soliloquies his English seemed to recrudesce into better construction and phraseology. But when he talked directly with the boys it lapsed, largely, into their own uncouth and simpler forms.

"But there weren't many crabs in those days," the old man wandered on. "They were fished out, and they were great delicacies. The open season was only a month long, too. And now crabs are accessible the whole year around. Think of it—catching all the crabs you want, any time you want, in the surf of the Cliff House beach!"

A sudden commotion among the goats brought the boys to their feet. The dogs about the fire rushed to join their snarling fellow who guarded the goats, while the goats themselves stampeded in the direction of their human protectors. A half dozen forms, lean and gray, glided about on the sand hillocks and faced the bristling dogs. Edwin arched an arrow that fell short. But Hare-Lip, with a sling such as David carried into battle against Goliath, hurled a stone through the air that whistled from the speed of its flight. It fell squarely among the wolves and caused them to slink away toward the dark depths of the eucalyptus forest.

The boys laughed and lay down again in the sand, while Granser sighed ponderously. He had eaten too much, and, with hands clasped on his paunch, the fingers interlaced, he resumed his maunderings.

"'The fleeting systems lapse like foam,'" he mumbled what was evidently a quotation. "That's it—foam, and fleeting. All man's toil upon the planet was just so much foam. He domesticated the serviceable animals, destroyed the hostile ones, and cleared the land of its wild vegetation. And then he passed, and the flood of primordial life rolled back again, sweeping his handiwork away—the weeds and the forest inundated his fields, the beasts of prey swept over his flocks, and now there are wolves on the Cliff House beach." He was appalled by the thought. "Where four million people disported themselves, the wild wolves roam today, and the savage progeny of our loins, with prehistoric weapons, defend themselves against the fanged despoilers. Think of it! And all because of the Scarlet Death—"

The adjective had caught Hare-Lip's ear.

"He's always saying that," he said to Edwin. "What is *scarlet?*"

" 'The scarlet of the maples can shake me like the cry of bugles going by,'" the old man quoted.

"It's red," Edwin answered the question. "And you don't know it because you come from the Chauffeur Tribe. They never did know nothing, none of them. *Scarlet* is red—I know that."

"Red is red, ain't it?" Hare-Lip grumbled. "Then what's the good of gettin' cocky and calling it scarlet?"

"Granser, what for do you always say so much what nobody knows?" he asked. "Scarlet ain't anything, but red is red. Why don't you say red, then?"

"Red is not the right word," was the reply. "The plague was scarlet. The whole face and body turned scarlet in an hour's time. Don't I know? Didn't I see enough of it? And I am telling you it was scarlet because—well, because it *was* scarlet. There is no other word for it."

"Red is good enough for me," Hare-Lip muttered obstinately. "My dad calls red red, and he ought to know. He says everybody died of the Red Death."

"Your dad is a common fellow, descended from a common fellow," Granser retorted heatedly. "Don't I know the beginnings of the Chauffeurs? Your grandsire was a chauffeur, a servant, and without education. He worked for other persons. But your grandmother was of good stock, only the children did not take after her. Don't I remember when I first met them, catching fish at Lake Temescal?"

"What is *education?*" Edwin asked.

"Calling red scarlet," Hare-Lip sneered, then returned to the attack on Granser. "My dad told me, an' he got it from his dad afore he croaked, that your wife was a Santa Rosan, an' that she was sure no account. He said she was a *hash-slinger* before the Red Death, though I don't know what a *hash-slinger* is. You can tell me, Edwin."

But Edwin shook his head in token of ignorance.

"It is true, she was a waitress," Granser acknowledged. "But she was a good woman, and your mother was her daughter. Women were very scarce in the days after the Plague. She was the only wife I could find, even if she was a *hash-slinger,* as your father calls it. But it is not nice to talk about our progenitors that way."

"Dad says that the wife of the first Chauffeur was a lady—"

"What's a *lady?*" Hoo-Hoo demanded.

"A *lady*'s a Chauffeur squaw," was the quick reply of Hare-Lip.

"The first Chauffeur was Bill, a common fellow, as I said before," the old man expounded; "but his wife was a lady, a great lady. Before the Scarlet Death she was the wife of Van Warden. He was President of the Board of Industrial Magnates, and was one of the dozen men who ruled America. He was worth one billion, eight hundred millions of dollars—coins like you have there in your pouch, Edwin. And then came the Scarlet Death, and his wife became the wife of Bill, the first Chauffeur. He used to beat her, too. I have seen it myself."

Hoo-Hoo, lying on his stomach and idly digging his toes in the sand, cried out and investigated, first, his toe-nail, and next, the small hole he had dug. The other two boys joined him, excavating the sand rapidly with their hands till there lay three skeletons exposed. Two were of adults, the third being that of a part-grown child. The old man hudged along on the ground and peered at the find.

"Plague victims," he announced. "That's the way they died everywhere in the last days. This must have been a family, running away from the contagion and perishing here on the Cliff House beach. They—what are you doing, Edwin?"

This question was asked in sudden dismay, as Edwin, using the back of his hunting knife, began to knock out the teeth from the jaws of one of the skulls.

"Going to string 'em," was the response.

The three boys were now hard at it; and quite a knocking and hammering arose, in which Granser babbled on unnoticed.

"You are true savages. Already has begun the custom of wearing human teeth. In another generation you will be perforating your noses and ears and wearing ornaments of bone and shell. I know. The human race is doomed to sink back farther and farther into the primitive night ere again it begins its bloody climb upward to civilization. When we increase and feel the lack of room, we will proceed to kill one another. And then I suppose you will wear human scalp-locks at your waist, as well—as you, Edwin, who are the gentlest of my grandsons, have already begun with that vile pigtail. Throw it away, Edwin, boy; throw it away."

"What a gabble the old geezer makes," Hare-Lip remarked, when, the teeth all extracted, they began an attempt at equal division.

They were very quick and abrupt in their actions, and their speech, in moments of hot discussion over the allotment of the choicer teeth, was truly a gabble. They spoke in monosyllables and short jerky sentences that was more a gibberish than a language. And yet, through it ran hints of grammatical construction, and appeared vestiges of the conjugation of some superior culture. Even the speech of Granser was so corrupt that were it put down literally it would be almost so much nonsense to the reader. This, however, was when he talked with the boys.

When he got into the full swing of babbling to himself, it slowly purged itself into pure English. The sentences grew longer and were enunciated with a rhythm and ease that was reminiscent of the lecture platform.

"Tell us about the Red Death, Granser," Hare-Lip demanded, when the teeth affair had been satisfactorily concluded.

"The Scarlet Death," Edwin corrected.

"An' don't work all that funny lingo on us," Hare-Lip went on. "Talk sensible, Granser, like a Santa Rosan ought to talk. Other Santa Rosans don't talk like you."

II

The old man showed pleasure in being thus called upon. He cleared his throat and began.

"Twenty or thirty years ago my story was in great demand. But in these days nobody seems interested—"

"There you go!" Hare-Lip cried hotly. "Cut out the funny stuff and talk sensible. What's *interested?* You talk like a baby that don't know how."

"Let him alone," Edwin urged, "or he'll get mad and won't talk at all. Skip the funny places. We'll catch on to some of what he tells us."

"Let her go, Granser," Hoo-Hoo encouraged; for the old man was already maundering about the disrespect for elders and the reversion to cruelty of all humans that fell from high culture to primitive conditions.

The tale began.

"There were very many people in the world in those days. San Francisco alone held four millions—"

"What is millions?" Edwin interrupted.

Granser looked at him kindly.

"I know you cannot count beyond ten, so I will tell you. Hold up your two hands. On both of them you have altogether ten fingers and thumbs. Very well. I now take this grain of sand—you hold it, Hoo-Hoo." He dropped the grain of sand into the lad's palm and went on. "Now that grain of sand stands for the ten fingers of Edwin. I add another grain. That's ten more fingers. And I add another, and another, and another, until I have added as many grains as Edwin has fingers and thumbs. That makes what I call one hundred. Remember that word—one hundred. Now I put this pebble in Hare-Lip's hand. It stands for ten grains of sand, or ten tens of fingers, or one hundred fingers. I put in ten pebbles. They stand for a thousand fingers. I take a mussel-shell, and it stands for ten pebbles, or one hundred grains of sand, or one thousand fingers . . ." And so on, laboriously, and with much reiteration, he strove to build up in their minds a crude conception of numbers. As the quantities increased, he had the boys holding different magnitudes in each of their hands. For still higher sums, he laid the symbols on the log of driftwood; and for symbols he was hard put, being compelled to use the teeth from the skulls for millions, and the crab-shells for billions. It was here that he stopped, for the boys were showing signs of becoming tired.

"There were four million people in San Francisco—four teeth."

The boys' eyes ranged along from the teeth and from hand to hand, down through the pebbles and sand-grains to Edwin's fingers. And back again they ranged along the ascending series in the effort to grasp such inconceivable numbers.

"That was a lot of folks, Granser," Edwin at last hazarded.

"Like sand on the beach here, like sand on the beach, each grain of sand a man, or woman, or child. Yes, my boy, all those people lived right here in San Francisco. And at one time or another all those people came out on this very beach—more people than there are grains of sand. More—more—more. And San Francisco was a noble city. And across the bay—where we camped last year, even more people lived, clear from Point Richmond, on the level ground and on the hills, all the way around to San Leandro—one great city of seven million people. Seven teeth . . . there, that's it, seven millions."

Again the boys' eyes ranged up and down from Edwin's fingers to the teeth on the log.

"The world was full of people. The census of 2010 gave eight billions for the whole world—eight crab-shells, yes, eight billions. It was not like today. Mankind knew a great deal more about getting food. And the more food there was, the more people there were. In the year 1800, there were one hundred and seventy millions in Europe alone. One hundred years later—a grain of sand, Hoo-Hoo—one hundred years later, at 1900, there were five hundred millions in Europe—five grains of sand, Hoo-Hoo, and this one tooth. This shows how easy was the getting of food, and how men increased. And in the year 2000 there were fifteen hundred millions in Europe. And it was the same all over the rest of the world. Eight crab-shells there, yes, eight billion people were alive on the earth when the Scarlet Death began.

"I was a young man when the Plague came—twenty-seven years old; and I lived on the other side of San Francisco Bay, in Berkeley. You remember those great stone houses, Edwin, when we came down the hills from Contra Costa? That was where I lived, in those stone houses. I was a professor of English literature."

Much of this was over the heads of the boys, but they strove to comprehend dimly this tale of the past.

"What was them stone houses for?" Hare-Lip queried.

"You remember when your dad taught you to swim?" The boy nodded. "Well, in the University of California—that is the name we had for the houses—we taught young men and women how to think, just as I have taught you now, by sand and pebbles and shells, to know how many people lived in those days. There was very much to teach. The young men and women we taught were called students. We had large rooms in which we taught. I talked to them, forty or fifty at a time, just as I am talking to you now. I told them about the books other men had written before their time, and even, sometimes, in their time—"

"Was that all you did? Just talk, talk, talk?" Hoo-Hoo demanded. "Who hunted your meat for you? And milked the goats? And caught the fish?"

"A sensible question, Hoo-Hoo, a sensible question. As I have told you, in those days food-getting was easy. We were very wise. A few men got the food for many men. The other men did other things. As you say, I talked. I talked all the time, and for this food was given me—much food, fine food, beautiful food, food that I have not tasted in sixty years and shall never taste again. I sometimes think the most wonderful achievement of our tremendous civilization was food—its inconceivable abundance, its infinite variety, its marvelous delicacy. O my grandsons, life was life in those days, when we had such wonderful things to eat."

This was beyond the boys, and they let it slip by, words and thoughts, as a mere senile wandering in the narrative.

"Our food-getters were called *freemen.* This was a joke. We of the ruling classes owned all the land, all the machines, everything. These food-getters were our slaves. We took almost all the food they got, and left them a little so that they might eat, and work, and get us more food—"

"I'd have gone into the forest and got food for myself," Hare-Lip announced; "and if any man tried to take it away from me, I'd have killed him."

The old man laughed.

"Did I not tell you that we of the ruling class owned all the land, all the forest, everything? Any food-getter who would not get food for us, him we punished or compelled to starve to death. And very few did that. They preferred to get food for us, and make clothes for us, and prepare and administer to us a thousand—a mussel-shell, Hoo-Hoo—a thousand satisfactions and delights. And I was Professor Smith in those days—Professor James Howard Smith. And my lecture courses were very popular—that is, very many of the young men and women liked to hear me talk about the books other men had written.

"And I was very happy, and I had beautiful things to eat. And my hands were soft, because I did no work with them, and my body was clean all over and dressed in the softest garments—"

He surveyed his mangy goat-skin with disgust.

"We did not wear such things in those days. Even the slaves had better garments. And we were most clean. We washed our faces and hands often every day. You boys never wash unless you fall into the water or go swimming."

"Neither do you Granser," Hoo-Hoo retorted.

"I know, I know, I am a filthy old man, but times have changed. Nobody washes these days, there are no conveniences. It is sixty years since I have seen a piece of soap.

"You do not know what soap is, and I shall not tell you, for I am telling the story of the Scarlet Death. You know what sickness is. We called it a disease. Very many of the diseases came from what we called germs. Remember that word—germs. A germ is a very small thing. It is like a woodtick, such as you find on the dogs in the spring of the year when they run in the forest. Only the germ is very small. It is so small that you cannot see it—"

Hoo-Hoo began to laugh.

"You're a queer un, Granser, talking about things you can't see. If you can't see 'em, how do you know they are? That's what I want to know. How do you know anything you can't see?"

"A good question, a very good question, Hoo-Hoo. But we did see—some of them. We had what we called microscopes and ultramicroscopes, and we put them to our eyes and looked through them, so that we saw things larger than they really were, and many things we could not see without the microscopes at all. Our best ultramicroscopes could make a germ look forty thousand times larger. A mussel-shell is a thousand fingers like Edwin's. Take forty mussel-shells, and by as many times larger was the germ when we looked at it through a microscope. And after that, we had other ways, by using what we called moving pictures, of making the forty-thousand-times germ many, many thousand times larger still. And thus we saw all these things which our eyes of themselves could not see. Take a grain of sand. Break it into ten pieces. Take one piece and break it into ten. Break one of those pieces into ten, and one of those into ten, and one of those into ten, and one of those into ten, and do it all day, and maybe, by sunset, you will have a piece as small as one of the germs." The boys were openly incredulous. Hare-Lip sniffed and sneered and Hoo-Hoo snickered, until Edwin nudged them to be silent.

"The woodtick sucks the blood of the dog, but the germ, being so very small, goes right into the blood of the body, and there it has many children. In those days there would be as many as a billion—a crab-shell, please—as many as that crab-shell in one man's body. We called germs microorganisms. When a few million, or a billion, of them were in a man, in all the blood of a man, he was sick. These germs were a disease. There were many different kinds of them—more different kinds than there are grains of sand on this beach. We knew only a few of the kinds. The micro-organic world was an invisible world, a world we could not see, and we knew very little about it. Yet we did know something. There was the *bacillus anthracis;* there was the *micrococcus;* there was the *Bacterium termo*, and the *Bacterium lactis*—that's what turns the goat milk sour even to this day, Hare-Lip; and there were *Schizomycetes* without end. And there were many others . . ."

Here the old man launched into a disquisition on germs and their natures, using words and phrases of such extraordinary length and meaninglessness, that the boys grinned at one another and looked out over the deserted ocean till they forgot the old man was babbling on.

"But the Scarlet Death, Granser," Edwin at last suggested.

Granser recollected himself, and with a start tore himself away from the rostrum of the lecture-hall, where, to another world audience, he had been expounding the latest theory, sixty years gone, of germs and germ-diseases.

"Yes, yes, Edwin; I had forgotten. Sometimes the memory of the past is very strong upon me, and I forget that I am a dirty old man, clad in goat-skin, wandering with my savage grandsons who are goatherds in the primeval wilderness. 'The fleeting systems lapse like foam,' and so lapsed our glorious, colossal civilization. I am Granser, a tired old man. I belong to the tribe of Santa Rosans. I married into that tribe. My sons and daughters married into the Chauffeurs, the Sacramentos, and the Palo-Altos. You, Hare-Lip, are of the Chauffeurs. You, Edwin, are of the Sacramentos. And you, Hoo-Hoo, are of the Palo-Altos. Your tribe takes its name from a town that was near the seat of another great institution of learning. It was called Stanford University. Yes, I remember now. It is perfectly clear. I was telling you of the Scarlet Death. Where was I in my story?"

"You was telling about germs, the things you can't see but which make men sick," Edwin prompted.

"Yes, that's where I was. A man did not notice at first when only a few of these germs got into his body. But each germ broke in half and became two germs, and they kept doing this very rapidly so that in a short time there were many millions of them in the body. Then the man was sick. He had a disease, and the disease was named after the kind of a germ that was in him. It might be measles, it might be influenza, it might be yellow fever; it might be any of thousands and thousands of kinds of diseases.

"Now this is the strange thing about these germs. There were always new ones coming to live in men's bodies. Long and long and long ago, when there were only a few men in the world, there were few diseases. But as men increased and lived closely together in great cities and civilizations, new diseases arose, new kinds of germs entered their bodies. Thus were countless millions and billions of human beings killed. And the more thickly men packed together, the more terrible were the new diseases that came to be. Long before my time, in the middle ages, there was the Black Plague that swept across Europe. It swept across Europe many times. There was tuberculosis, that entered into men wherever they were thickly packed. A hundred years before my time there was the bubonic plague. And in Africa was the sleeping sickness. The bacteriologists fought all these sicknesses and destroyed them, just as you boys fight the wolves away from your goats, or squash the mosquitoes that light on you. The bacteriologists—"

"But, Granser, what is a what-you-call-it?" Edwin interrupted.

"You, Edwin, are a goatherd. Your task is to watch the goats. You know a great deal about goats. A bacteriologist watches germs. That's his task, and he knows a great deal about them. So, as I was saying, the bacteriologists fought with the germs and destroyed them—sometimes. There was leprosy, a horrible disease. A hundred years before I was born, the bacteriologists discovered the germ of leprosy. They knew all about it. They made pictures of it. I have seen those pictures. But they never found a way to kill it. But in 1984, there was the Pantoblast Plague, a disease that broke out in a country called Brazil and that killed millions of people. But the bacteriologists found it out, and found the way to kill it, so that the Pantoblast Plague went no farther. They made what they called a serum, which they put into a man's body and which killed the pantoblast germs without killing the man. And in 1910, there was Pellagra, and also the hookworm. These were easily killed by the bacteriologists. But in 1947 there arose a new disease that had never been seen before. It got into the bodies of babies of only ten months old or less, and it made them unable to move their hands and feet, or to eat, or anything; and the bacteriologists were eleven years in discovering how to kill that particular germ and save the babies.

"In spite of all these diseases, and of all the new ones that continued to arise, there were more and more men in the world. This was because it was easy to get food. The easier it was to get food, the more men there were; the more men there were, the more thickly were they packed together on the earth; and the more thickly they were packed, the more new kinds of germs became diseases. There were warnings. Soldervetzsky, as early as 1929, told the bacteriologists that they had no guaranty against some new disease, a thousand times more deadly than any they knew, arising and killing by the hundreds of millions and even by the billion. You see, the micro-organic world remained a mystery to the end. They knew there was such a world, and that from time to time armies of new germs emerged from it to kill men.

"And that was all they knew about it. For all they knew, in that invisible microorganic world there might be as many different kinds of germs as there are grains of sand on this beach. And also, in that same invisible world it might well be that new kinds of germs came to be. It might be there that life originated—the 'abysmal fecundity,' Soldervetzsky called it, applying the words of other men who had written before him . . ."

It was at this point that Hare-Lip rose to his feet, an expression of huge contempt on his face.

"Granser," he announced, "you make me sick with your gabble. Why don't you tell about the Red Death? If you ain't going to, say so, an' we'll start back for camp."

The old man looked at him and silently began to cry. The weak tears of age rolled down his cheeks and all the feebleness of his eighty-seven years showed in his grief-stricken countenance.

"Sit down," Edwin counselled soothingly. "Granser's all right. He's just gettin' to the Scarlet Death, ain't you, Granser? He's just goin' to tell us about it right now. Sit down, Hare-Lip. Go ahead, Granser."

III

The old man wiped the tears away on his grimy knuckles and took up the tale in a tremulous, piping voice that soon strengthened as he got the swing of the narrative.

"It was in the summer of 2013 that the Plague came. I was twenty-seven years old, and well do I remember it. Wireless dispatches—"

Hare-Lip spat loudly his disgust, and Granser hastened to make amends.

"We talked through the air in those days, thousands and thousands of miles. And the word came of a strange disease that had broken out in New York. There were seventeen millions of people living then in that noblest city of America. Nobody thought anything about the news. It was only a small thing. There had been only a few deaths. It seemed, though, that they had died very quickly, and that one of the first signs of the disease was the turning red of the face and all the body. Within twenty-four hours came the report of the first case in Chicago. And on the same day, it was made public that London, the greatest city in the world, next to Chicago, had been secretly fighting the plague for two weeks and censoring the news dispatches—that is, not permitting the word to go forth to the rest of the world that London had the plague.

"It looked serious, but we in California, like everywhere else, were not alarmed. We were sure that the bacteriologists would find a way to overcome this new germ, just as they had overcome other germs in the past. But the trouble was the astonishing quickness with which this germ destroyed human beings, and the fact that it inevitably killed any human body it entered. No one ever recovered. There was the old Asiatic cholera, when you might eat dinner with a well man in the evening, and the next morning, if you got up early enough, you would see him being hauled by your window in the death-cart. But this new plague was quicker than that—much quicker.

"From the moment of the first signs of it, a man would be dead in an hour. Some lasted for several hours. Many died within ten or fifteen minutes of the appearance of the first signs.

"The heart began to beat faster and the heat of the body to increase. Then came the scarlet rash, spreading like wildfire over the face and body. Most persons never noticed the increase in heat and heartbeat, and the first they knew was when the scarlet rash came out. Usually, they had convulsions at the time of the appearance of the rash. But these convulsions did not last long and were not very severe. If one lived through them, he became perfectly quiet, and only did he feel a numbness swiftly creeping up his body from the feet. The heels became numb first, then the legs, and hips, and when the numbness reached as high as his heart he died. They did not rave or sleep. Their minds always remained cool and calm up to the moment their heart numbed and stopped. And another strange thing was the rapidity of decomposition. No sooner was a person dead than the body seemed to fall to pieces, to fly apart, to melt away even as you looked at it. That was one of the reasons the plague spread so rapidly. All the billions of germs in a corpse were so immediately released.

"And it was because of all this that the bacteriologists had so little chance in fighting the germs. They were killed in their laboratories even as they studied the germ of the Scarlet Death. They were heroes. As fast as they perished, others stepped forth and took their places. It was in London that they first isolated it. The news was telegraphed everywhere. Trask was the name of the man who succeeded in this, but within thirty hours he was dead. Then came the struggle in all the laboratories to find something that would kill the plague germs. All drugs failed. You see, the problem was to get a drug, or serum, that would kill the germs in the body and not kill the body. They tried to fight it with other germs, to put into the body of a sick man germs that were the enemies of the plague germs—"

"And you can't see these germ-things, Granser," Hare-Lip objected, "and here you gabble, gabble, gabble about them as if they was anything, when they're nothing at all. Anything you can't see, ain't, that's what. Fighting things that ain't with things that ain't! They must have been all fools in them days. That's why they croaked. I ain't goin' to believe in such rot, I tell you that."

Granser promptly began to weep, while Edwin hotly took up his defense.

"Look here, Hare-Lip, you believe in lots of things you can't see."

Hare-Lip shook his head.

"You believe in dead men walking about. You never seen one dead man walk about."

"I tell you I seen 'em, last winter, when I was wolf-hunting with dad."

"Well, you always spit when you cross running water," Edwin challenged.

"That's to keep off bad luck," was Hare-Lip's defense.

"You believe in bad luck?"

"Sure."

"An' you ain't never seen bad luck," Edwin concluded triumphantly. "You're just as bad as Granser and his germs. You believe in what you don't see. Go on, Granser."

Hare-Lip, crushed by this metaphysical defeat, remained silent, and the old man went on. Often and often, though this narrative must not be clogged by the details, was Granser's tale interrupted while the boys squabbled among themselves. Also, among themselves they kept up a constant, low-voiced exchange of explanation and conjecture, as they strove to follow the old man into his unknown and vanished world.

"The Scarlet Death broke out in San Francisco. The first death came on a Monday morning. By Thursday they were dying like flies in Oakland and San Francisco. They died everywhere—in their beds, at their work, walking along the street. It was on Tuesday that I saw my first death—Miss Collbran, one of my students, sitting right there before my eyes, in my lecture-room. I noticed her face while I was talking. It had suddenly turned scarlet. I ceased speaking and could only look at her, for the first fear of the plague was already on all of us and we knew that it had come. The young women screamed and ran out of the room. So did the young men run out, all but two. Miss Collbran's convulsions were very mild and lasted less than a minute. One of the young men fetched her a glass of water. She drank only a little of it, and cried out:

" 'My feet! All sensation has left them.'

"After a minute she said, 'I have no feet. I am unaware that I have any feet. And my knees are cold. I can scarcely feel that I have knees.'

"She lay on the floor, a bundle of notebooks under her head. And we could do nothing. The coldness and the numbness crept up past her hips to her heart, and when it reached her heart she was dead. In fifteen minutes, by the clock—I timed it—she was dead, there, in my own classroom, dead. And she was a very beautiful, strong, healthy young woman. And from the first sign of the plague to her death only fifteen minutes elapsed. That will show you how swift was the Scarlet Death.

"Yet in those few minutes I remained with the dying woman in my classroom, the alarm had spread over the university; and the students, by thousands, all of them, had deserted the lecture-room and laboratories. When I emerged, on my way to make report to the President of the Faculty, I found the university deserted. Across the campus were several stragglers hurrying for their homes. Two of them were running.

"President Hoag, I found in his office, all alone, looking very old and very gray, with a multitude of wrinkles in his face that I had never seen before. At the sight of me, he pulled himself to his feet and tottered away to the inner office, banging the door after him and locking it. You see, he knew I had been exposed, and he was afraid. He shouted to me through the door to go away. I shall never forget my feelings as I walked down the silent corridors and out across that deserted campus. I was not afraid. I had been exposed, and I looked upon myself as already dead. It was not that, but a feeling of awful depression that impressed me. Everything had stopped. It was like the end of the world to me—my world. I had been born within sight and sound of the university. It had been my predestined career. My father had been a professor there before me, and his father before him. For a century and a half had this university, like a splendid machine, been running steadily on. And now, in an instant, it had stopped. It was like seeing the sacred flame die down on some thrice-sacred altar. I was shocked, unutterably shocked.

"When I arrived home, my housekeeper screamed as I entered, and fled away. And when I rang, I found the housemaid had likewise fled. I investigated. In the kitchen I found the cook on the point of departure. But she screamed, too, and in her haste dropped a suitcase of her personal belongings and ran out of the house and across the grounds, still screaming. I can hear her scream to this day. You see, we did not act in this way when ordinary diseases smote us. We were always calm over such things, and sent for the doctors and nurses who knew just what to do. But this was different. It struck so suddenly, and killed so swiftly, and never missed a stroke. When the scarlet rash appeared on a person's face, that person was marked by death. There was never a known case of a recovery.

"I was alone in my big house. As I have told you often before, in those days we could talk with one another over wires or through the air. The telephone bell rang, and I found my brother talking to me. He told me that he was not coming home for fear of catching the plague from me, and that he had taken our two sisters to stop at Professor Bacon's home. He advised me to remain where I was, and wait to find out whether or not I had caught the plague.

"To all of this I agreed, staying in my house and for the first time in my life attempting to cook. And the plague did not come out on me. By means of the telephone I could talk with whomsoever I pleased and get the news. Also, there were the newspapers, and I ordered all of them to be thrown up to my door so that I could know what was happening with the rest of the world.

"New York City and Chicago were in chaos. And what happened with them was happening in all the large cities. A third of the New York police were dead. Their chief was also dead, likewise the mayor. All law and order had ceased. The bodies were lying in the streets unburied. All railroads and vessels carrying food and such things into the great city had ceased running and mobs of the hungry poor were pillaging the stores and warehouses. Murder and robbery and drunkenness were everywhere. Already the people had fled from the city by millions—at first the rich, in their private motor cars and dirigibles, and then the great mass of the population, on foot, carrying the plague with them, themselves starving and pillaging the farmers and all the towns and villages on the way.

"The man who sent this news, the wireless operator, was alone with his instrument on the top of a lofty building. The people remaining in the city—he estimated them at several hundred thousand—had gone mad from fear and drink, and on all sides of him great fires were raging. He was a hero, that man who staid by his post—an obscure newspaperman, most likely.

"For twenty-four hours, he said, no transatlantic airships had arrived, and no more messages were coming from England. He did state, though, that a message from Berlin—that's in Germany—announced that Hoffmeyer, a bacteriologist of the Metchnikoff School, had discovered the serum for the plague. That was the last word, to this day, that we of America ever received from Europe. If Hoffmeyer discovered the serum, it was too late, or otherwise, long ere this, explorers from Europe would have come looking for us. We can only conclude that what happened in America happened in Europe, and that, at the best, some several score may have survived the Scarlet Death on that whole continent.

"For one day longer the dispatches continued to come from New York. Then they, too, ceased. The man who had sent them, perched in his lofty building, had either died of the plague or been consumed in the great conflagrations he had described as raging around him. And what had occurred in New York had been duplicated in all the other cities. It was the same in San Francisco, and Oakland, and Berkeley. By Thursday the people were dying so rapidly that their corpses could not be handled, and dead bodies lay everywhere. Thursday night the panic outrush for the country began. Imagine, my grandsons, people, thicker than the salmon-run you have seen on the Sacramento river, pouring out of the cities by millions, madly over the country, in vain attempt to escape the ubiquitous death. You see, they carried the germs with them. Even the airships of the rich, fleeing for mountain and desert fastnesses, carried the germs.

"Hundreds of these airships escaped to Hawaii, and not only did they bring the plague with them, but they found the plague already there before them. This we learned, by the dispatches, until all order in San Francisco vanished, and there were no operators left at their posts to receive or send. It was amazing, astounding, this loss of communication with the world. It was exactly as if the world had ceased, been blotted out. For sixty years that world has no longer existed for me. I know there must be such places as New York, Europe, Asia, and Africa; but not one word has been heard of them—not in sixty years. With the coming of the Scarlet Death the world fell apart, absolutely, irretrievably. Ten thousand years of culture and civilization passed in the twinkling of an eye, 'lapsed like foam.'

"I was telling about the airships of the rich. They carried the plague with them and no matter where they fled, they died. I never encountered but one survivor of any of them—Mungerson. He was afterwards a Santa Rosan, and he married my eldest daughter. He came into the tribe eight years after the plague. He was then nineteen years old, and he was compelled to wait twelve years more before he could marry. You see, there were no unmarried women, and some of the older daughters of the Santa Rosans were already bespoken. So he was forced to wait until my Mary had grown to sixteen years. It was his son, Gimp-Leg, who was killed last year by the mountain lion.

"Mungerson was eleven years old at the time of the plague. His father was one of the Industrial Magnates, a very wealthy, powerful man. It was on his airship, the Condor, that they were fleeing, with all the family, for the wilds of British Columbia, which is far to the north of here. But there was some accident, and they were wrecked near Mount Shasta. You have heard of that mountain. It is far to the north. The plague broke out amongst them, and this boy of eleven was the only survivor. For eight years he was alone, wandering over a deserted land and looking vainly for his own kind. And at last, travelling south, he picked up with us, the Santa Rosans.

"But I am ahead of my story. When the great exodus from the cities around San Francisco Bay began, and while the telephones were still working, I talked with my brother. I told him this flight from the cities was insanity, that there were no symptoms of the plague in me, and that the thing for us to do was to isolate ourselves and our relatives in some safe place. We decided on the Chemistry Building, at the university, and we planned to lay in a supply of provisions, and by force of arms to prevent any other persons from forcing their presence upon us after we had retired to our refuge.

"All this being arranged, my brother begged me to stay in my own house for at least twenty-four hours more, on the chance of the plague developing in me. To this I agreed, and he promised to come for me next day. We talked on over the details of the provisioning and the defending of the Chemistry Building until the telephone died. It died in the midst of our conversation. That evening there were no electric lights, and I was alone in my house in the darkness. No more newspapers were being printed, so I had no knowledge of what was taking place outside.

"I heard sounds of rioting and of pistol shots, and from my windows I could see the glare of the sky of some conflagration in the direction of

Oakland. It was a night of terror. I did not sleep a wink. A man—why and how I do not know—was killed on the sidewalk in front of the house. I heard the rapid reports of an automatic pistol, and a few minutes later the wounded wretch crawled up to my door, moaning and crying out for help. Arming myself with two automatics, I went to him. By the light of a match I ascertained that while he was dying of the bullet wounds, at the same time the plague was on him. I fled indoors, whence I heard him moan and cry out for half an hour longer.

"In the morning, my brother came to me. I had gathered into a handbag what things of value I purposed taking, but when I saw his face I knew that he would never accompany me to the Chemistry Building. The plague was on him. He intended shaking my hand, but I went back hurriedly before him.

" 'Look at yourself in the mirror,' I commanded.

"He did so, and at sight of his scarlet face, the color deepening as he looked at it, he sank down nervelessly in a chair.

" 'My God!' he said. 'I've got it. Don't come near me. I am a dead man.'

"Then the convulsions seized him. He was two hours in dying, and he was conscious to the last, complaining about the coldness and loss of sensation in his feet, his calves, his thighs, until at last it was his heart and he was dead.

"That was the way the Scarlet Death slew. I caught up my handbag and fled. The sights in the streets were terrible. One stumbled on bodies everywhere. Some were not yet dead. And even as you looked, you saw men sink down with the death fastened upon them. There were numerous fires burning in Berkeley, while Oakland and San Francisco were apparently being swept by vast conflagrations. The smoke of the burning filled the heavens, so that the midday was as a gloomy twilight, and, in the shifts of wind, sometimes the sun shone through dimly, a dull red orb. Truly, my grandsons, it was like the last days of the end of the world.

"There were numerous stalled motor cars, showing that the gasoline and the engine supplies of the garages had given out. I remember one such car. A man and a woman lay back dead in the seats, and on the pavement near it were two more women and a child. Strange and terrible sights there were on every hand. People slipped by silently, furtively, like ghosts—white-faced women carrying infants in their arms; fathers leading children by the hand; singly, and in couples, and in families—all fleeing out of the city of death. Some carried supplies of food, others blankets and valuables, and there were many who carried nothing.

"There was a grocery store—a place where food was sold. The man to whom it belonged—I knew him well—a quiet, sober, but stupid and obstinate fellow, was defending it. The windows and doors had been broken in, but he, inside, hiding behind a counter, was discharging his pistol at a number of men on the sidewalk who were breaking in. In the entrance were several bodies—of men, I decided, whom he had killed earlier in the day. Even as I looked on from a distance, I saw one of the robbers break the windows of the adjoining store, a place where shoes were sold, and deliberately set fire to it. I did not go to the groceryman's assistance. The time for such acts had already passed. Civilization was crumbling, and it was each for himself."

IV

I went away hastily, down a cross-street, and at the first corner I saw another tragedy. Two men of the working class had caught a man and a woman with two children, and were robbing them. I knew the man by sight, though I had never been introduced to him. He was a poet whose verses I had long admired. Yet I did not go to his help, for at the moment I came upon the scene there was a pistol shot, and I saw him sinking to the ground. The woman screamed, and she was felled with a fist-blow by one of the brutes. I cried out threateningly, whereupon they discharged their pistols at me and I ran away around the corner. Here I was blocked by an advancing conflagration. The buildings on both sides were burning, and the street was filled with smoke and flame. From somewhere in that murk came a woman's voice calling shrilly for help. But I did not go to her. A man's heart turned to iron amid such scenes, and one heard all too many appeals for help.

"Returning to the corner, I found the two robbers were gone. The poet and his wife lay dead on the pavement. It was a shocking sight. The two children had vanished—whither I could not tell. And I knew, now, why it was that the fleeing persons I encountered slipped along so furtively and with such white faces. In the midst of our civilization, down in our slums and labor-ghettos, we had bred a race of barbarians, of savages; and now, in the time of our calamity, they turned upon us like the wild beasts they were and destroyed us. And they destroyed themselves as well.

"They inflamed themselves with strong drink and committed a thousand atrocities, quarreling and killing one another in the general madness. One group of workingmen I saw, of the better sort, who had banded together, and, with their women and children in their midst, the sick and aged in litters and being carried, and with a number of horses pulling a truck-load of provisions, they were fighting their way out of the city. They made a fine spectacle as they came down the street through the drifting smoke, though they nearly shot me when I first appeared in their path. As they went by, one of their leaders shouted out to me in apologetic explanation. He said they were killing the robbers and looters on sight, and that they had thus banded together as the only means by which to escape the prowlers.

"It was here that I saw for the first time what I was soon to see so often. One of the marching men had suddenly shown the unmistakable mark of the plague. Immediately those about him drew away, and he, without a remonstrance, stepped out of his place to let them pass on. A woman, most probably his wife, attempted to follow him. She was leading a little boy by the hand. But the husband commanded her sternly to go on, while others laid hands on her and restrained her from following him. This I saw, and I saw the man also, with his scarlet blaze of face, step into a doorway on the opposite side of the street. I heard the report of his pistol, and saw him sink lifeless to the ground.

"After being turned aside twice again by advancing fires, I succeeded in getting through to the university. On the edge of the campus I came upon a party of university folk who were going in the direction of the Chemistry Building. They were all family men, and their families were with them, including the nurses and the servants. Professor Badminton greeted me, I had difficulty in recognizing him. Somewhere he had gone through flames, and his beard was singed off. About his head was a bloody bandage, and his clothes were filthy.

"He told me he had prowlers, and that his brother had been killed the previous night, in the defense of their dwelling.

"Midway across the campus, he pointed suddenly to Mrs. Swinton's face. The unmistakable scarlet was there. Immediately all the other women set up a screaming and began to run away from her. Her two children were with a nurse, and these also ran with the women. But her husband, Doctor Swinton, remained with her.

"'Go on, Smith,' he told me. 'Keep an eye on the children. As for me, I shall stay with my wife. I know she is as already dead, but I can't leave her. Afterwards, if I escape, I shall come to the Chemistry Building, and do you watch for me and let me in.'

"I left him bending over his wife and soothing her last moments, while I ran to overtake the party. We were the last to be admitted to the Chemistry Building. After that, with our automatic rifles we maintained our isolation. By our plans, we had arranged for a company of sixty to be in this refuge. Instead, every one of the number originally planned had added relatives and friends and whole families until there were over four hundred souls. But the Chemistry Building was large, and, standing by itself, was in no danger of being burned by the great fires that raged everywhere in the city.

"A large quantity of provisions had been gathered, and a food committee took charge of it, issuing rations daily to the various families and groups that arranged themselves into messes. A number of committees were appointed, and we developed a very efficient organization. I was on the committee of defense, though for the first day no prowlers came near. We could see them in the distance, however, and by the smoke of their fires knew that several camps of them were occupying the far edge of the campus. Drunkenness was rife, and often we heard them singing ribald songs or insanely shouting. While the world crashed to ruin about them and all the air was filled with the smoke of its burning, these low creatures gave rein to their bestiality and fought and drank and died. And after all, what did it matter? Everybody died anyway, the good and the bad, the efficients and the weaklings, those that loved to live and those that scorned to live. They passed. Everything passed.

"When twenty-four hours had gone by and no signs of the plague were apparent, we congratulated ourselves and set about digging a well. You have seen the great iron pipes which in those days carried water to all the city-dwellers. We feared that the fires in the city would burst the pipes and empty the reservoirs. So we tore up the cement floor of the central court of the Chemistry Building and dug a well. There were many young men, undergraduates, with us, and we worked night and day on the well. And our fears were confirmed. Three hours before we reached water, the pipes went dry.

"A second twenty-four hours passed, and still the plague did not appear among us. We thought we were saved. But we did not know what I afterwards decided to be true, namely, that the period of the incubation of the plague germs in a human's body was a matter of a number of days. It slew so swiftly when once it manifested itself, that we were led to believe that the period of incubation was equally swift. So, when two days had left us unscathed, we were elated with the idea that we were free of the contagion.

"But the third day disillusioned us. I can never forget the night preceding it. I had charge of the night guards from eight to twelve, and from the roof of the building I watched the passing of all man's glorious works. So terrible were the local conflagrations that all the sky was lighted up. One could read the finest print in the red glare. All the world seemed wrapped in flames. San Francisco spouted smoke and fire from a score of vast conflagrations that were like so many active volcanoes. Oakland, San Leandro, Haywards—all were burning; and to the northward, clear to Point Richmond, other fires were at work. It was an awe-inspiring spectacle. Civilization, my grandsons, civilization was passing in a sheet of flame and a breath of death. At ten o'clock that night, the great powder magazines at Point Pinole exploded in rapid succession. So terrific were the concussions that the strong building rocked as in an earthquake, while every pane of glass was broken. It was then that I left the roof and went down the long corridors, from room to room, quieting the alarmed women and telling them what had happened.

"An hour later, at a window on the ground floor, I heard pandemonium break out in the camps of the prowlers. There were cries and screams, and shots from many pistols. As we afterward conjectured, this fight had been precipitated by an attempt on the part of those that were well to drive out those that were sick. At any rate, a number of the plague-stricken prowlers escaped across the campus and drifted against our doors. We warned them back, but they cursed us and discharged a fusillade from their pistols. Professor Merryweather, at one of the windows, was instantly killed, the bullet striking him squarely between the eyes. We opened fire in turn, and all the prowlers fled away with the exception of three. One was a woman. The plague was on them and they were reckless. Like foul fiends, there in the red glare from the skies, with faces blazing, they continued to curse us and fire at us. One of the men I shot with my own hand. After that the other man and the woman, still cursing us, lay down under our windows, where we were compelled to watch them die of the plague.

"The situation was critical. The explosions of the powder magazines had broken all the windows of the Chemistry Building, so that we were exposed to the germs from the corpses. The sanitary committee was called upon to act, and it responded nobly. Two men were required to go out and remove the corpses, and this meant the probable sacrifice of their own lives, for, having performed the task, they were not to be permitted to reenter the building. One of the professors, who was a bachelor, and one of the undergraduates volunteered. They bade good-bye to us and went forth. They were heroes. They gave up their lives that four hundred others might live. After they had performed their work, they stood for a moment, at a distance, looking at us wistfully. Then they waved their hands in farewell and went away slowly across the campus toward the burning city.

"And yet it was all useless. The next morning the first one of us was smitten with the plague—a little nurse-girl in the family of Professor Stout. It was no time for weak-kneed, sentimental policies. On the chance that she might be the only one, we thrust her forth from the building and commanded her to be gone.

"She went away slowly across the campus, wringing her hands and crying pitifully. We felt like brutes, but what were we to do? There were four hundred of us, and individuals had to be sacrificed.

"In one of the laboratories three families had domiciled themselves, and that afternoon we found among them no less than four corpses and seven cases of the plague in all its different stages.

"Then it was that the horror began. Leaving the dead lie, we forced the living ones to segregate themselves in another room. The plague began to break out among the rest of us, and as fast as the symptoms appeared, we sent the stricken ones to these segregated rooms. We compelled them to walk there by themselves, so as to avoid laying hands on them. It was heartrending.

But still the plague raged among us, and room after room was filled with the dead and dying. And so we who were yet clean retreated to the next floor and to the next, before this sea of the dead, that, room by room and floor by floor, inundated the building.

"The place became a charnel house, and in the middle of the night the survivors fled forth, taking nothing with them except arms and ammunition and a heavy store of tinned foods. We camped on the opposite side of the campus from the prowlers, and, while some stood guard, others of us volunteered to scout into the city in quest of horses, motor cars, carts, and wagons, or anything that would carry our provisions and enable us to emulate the banded workingmen I had seen fighting their way out to the open country.

"I was one of these scouts; and Doctor Hoyle, remembering that his motor car had been left behind in his home garage, told me to look for it. We scouted in pairs, and Dombey, a young undergraduate, accompanied me. We had to cross half a mile of the residence portion of the city to get to Doctor Hoyle's home. Here the buildings stood apart, in the midst of trees and grassy lawns, and here the fires had played freaks, burning whole blocks, skipping blocks and often skipping a single house in a block. And here, too, the prowlers were still at their work. We carried our automatic pistols openly in our hands, and looked desperate enough, forsooth, to keep them from attacking us. But at Doctor Hoyle's house the thing happened. Untouched by fire, even as we came to it the smoke of flames burst forth.

"The miscreant who had set fire to it staggered down the steps and out along the driveway. Sticking out of his coat pockets were bottles of whiskey, and he was very drunk. My first impulse was to shoot him, and I have never ceased regretting that I did not. Staggering and maundering to himself, with bloodshot eyes, and a raw and bleeding slash down one side of his bewhiskered face, he was altogether the most nauseating specimen of degradation and filth I had ever encountered. I did not shoot him, and he leaned against a tree on the lawn to let us go by. It was the most absolute, wanton act. Just as we were opposite him, he suddenly drew a pistol and shot Dombey through the head. The next instant I shot him. But it was too late. Dombey expired without a groan, immediately. I doubt if he even knew what had happened to him.

"Leaving the two corpses, I hurried on past the burning house to the garage, and there found Doctor Hoyle's motor car. The tanks were filled with gasoline, and it was ready for use. And it was in this car that I threaded the streets of the ruined city and came back to the survivors on the campus. The other scouts returned, but none had been so fortunate. Professor Fairmead had found a Shetland pony, but the poor creature, tied in a stable and abandoned for days, was so weak from want of food and water that it could carry no burden at all. Some of the men were for turning it loose, but I insisted that we should lead it along with us, so that, if we got out of food, we would have it to eat.

"There were forty-seven of us when we started, many being women and children. The President of the Faculty, an old man to begin with, and now hopelessly broken by the awful happenings of the past week, rode in the motor car with several young children and the aged mother of Professor Fairmead. Wathope, a young professor of English, who had a grievous bullet-wound in his leg, drove the car. The rest of us walked, Professor Fairmead leading the pony.

"It was what should have been a bright summer day, but the smoke from the burning world filled the sky, through which the sun shone murkily, a dull and lifeless orb, blood-red and ominous. But we had grown accustomed to that blood-red sun. With the smoke it was different. It bit into our nostrils and eyes, and there was not one of us whose eyes were not bloodshot. We directed our course to the southeast through the endless miles of suburban residences, travelling along where the first swells of low hills rose from the flat of the central city. It was by this way, only, that we could expect to gain the country.

"Our progress was painfully slow. The women and children could not walk fast. They did not dream of walking, my grandsons, in the way all people walk today. In truth, none of us knew how to walk. It was not until after the plague that I learned really to walk. So it was that the pace of the slowest was the pace of all, for we dared not separate on account of the prowlers. There were not so many now of these human beasts of prey. The plague had already well diminished their numbers, but enough still lived to be a constant menace to us. Many of the beautiful residences were untouched by fire, yet smoking ruins were everywhere. The prowlers, too, seemed to have got over their insensate desire to burn, and it was more rarely that we saw houses freshly on fire.

"Several of us scouted among the private garages in search of motor cars and gasoline. But in this we were unsuccessful. The first great flights from the cities had swept all such utilities away. Calgan, a fine young man, was lost in this work. He was shot by prowlers while crossing a lawn. Yet this was our only casualty, though, once, a drunken brute deliberately opened fire on all of us. Luckily, he fired wildly, and we shot him before he had done any hurt.

"At Fruitvale, still in the heart of the magnificent residence section of the city, the plague again smote us. Professor Fairmead was the victim. Making signs to us that his mother was not to know, he turned aside into the grounds of a beautiful mansion. He sat down forlornly on the steps of the front veranda, and I, having lingered, waved him a last farewell. That night, several miles beyond Fruitvale and still in the city, we made camp. And that night we shifted camp twice to get away from our dead. In the morning there were thirty of us. I shall never forget the President of the Faculty. During the morning's march his wife, who was walking, betrayed the fatal symptoms, and when she drew aside to let us go on, he insisted on leaving the motor car and remaining with her. There was quite a discussion about this, but in the end we gave in. It was just as well, for we knew not which ones of us, if any, might ultimately escape.

"That night, the second of our march, we camped beyond Haywards in the first stretches of country. And in the morning there were eleven of us that lived. Also, during the night, Wathope, the professor with the wounded leg, deserted us in the motor car. He took with him his sister and his mother and most of our tinned provisions. It was that day, in the afternoon, while resting by the wayside, that I saw the last airship I shall ever see. The smoke was much thinner here in the country, and I first sighted the ship drifting and veering helplessly at an elevation of two thousand feet. What had happened I could not conjecture, but even as we looked we saw her bow dip down lower and lower. Then the bulkheads of the various gas-chambers must have burst, for, quite perpendicular, she fell like a plummet to the earth.

"And from that day to this I have not seen another airship. Often and often, during the next few years, I scanned the sky for them, hoping against hope that somewhere in the world civilization had survived. But it was not to be. What happened with us in California must have happened with everybody everywhere.

"Another day, and at Niles there were three of us. Beyond Niles, in the middle of the highway, we found Wathope. The motor car had broken down, and there, on the rugs which they had spread on the ground, lay the bodies of his sister, his mother, and himself.

"Wearied by the unusual exercise of continual walking, that night I slept heavily. In the morning I was alone in the world. Canfield and Parsons, my last companions, were dead of the plague. Of the four hundred that sought shelter in the Chemistry Building, and of the forty-seven that began the march, I alone remained—I and the Shetland pony. Why this should be so there is no explaining. I did not catch the plague, that is all. I was immune. I was merely the one lucky man in a million—just as every survivor was one in a million, or, rather, in several millions, for the proportion was at least that."

V

"For two days I sheltered in a pleasant grove where there had been no deaths. In those two days, while badly depressed and believing that my turn would come at any moment, nevertheless I rested and recuperated. So did the pony. And on the third day, putting what small store of tinned provisions I possessed on the pony's back, I started on across a very lonely land. Not a live man, woman, or child, did I encounter, though the dead were everywhere. Food, however, was abundant. The land then was not as it is now. It was all cleared of trees and brush, and it was cultivated. The food for millions of mouths was growing, ripening, and going to waste. From the fields and orchards I gathered vegetables, fruits, and berries. Around the deserted farmhouses I got eggs and caught chickens. And frequently I found supplies of tinned provisions in the store-rooms.

"A strange thing was what was taking place with all the domestic animals. Everywhere they were going wild and preying on one another. The chickens and ducks were the first to be destroyed, while the pigs were the first to go wild, followed by the cats. Nor were the dogs long in adapting themselves to the changed conditions. There was a veritable plague of dogs. They devoured the corpses, barked and howled during the nights, and in the daytime slunk about in the distance. As the time went by, I noticed a change in their behavior. At first they were apart from one another, very suspicious and very prone to fight. But after a not very long while they began to come together and run in packs. The dog, you see, always was a social animal, and this was true before ever he came to be domesticated by man. In the last days of the world before the plague, there were many many very different kinds of dogs—dogs without hair and dogs with warm fur, dogs so small that they would make scarcely a mouthful for other dogs that were as large as mountain lions. Well, all the small dogs, and the weak types, were killed by their fellows. Also, the very large ones were not adapted for the wild life and bred out. As a result, the many different kinds of dogs disappeared, and there remained, running in packs, the medium-sized wolfish dogs that you know today."

"But the cats don't run in packs, Granser," Hoo-Hoo objected.

"The cat was never a social animal. As one writer in the nineteenth century said, the cat walks by himself. He always walked by himself, from before the time he was tamed by man, down through the long ages of domestication, to today when once more he is wild.

"The horses also went wild, and all the fine breeds we had degenerated into the small mustang horse you know today. The cows likewise went wild, as did the pigeons and the sheep. And that a few of the chickens survived you know yourself. But the wild chicken of today is quite a different thing from the chickens we had in those days.

"But I must go on with my story. I travelled through a deserted land. As the time went by I began to yearn more and more for human beings. But I never found one, and I grew lonelier and lonelier. I crossed Livermore

Valley and the mountains between it and the great valley of the San Joaquin. You have never seen that valley, but it is very large and it is the home of the wild horse. There are great droves there, thousands and tens of thousands. I revisited it thirty years after, so I know. You think there are lots of wild horses down here in the coast valleys, but they are as nothing compared with those of the San Joaquin. Strange to say, the cows, when they went wild, went back into the lower mountains. Evidently they were better able to protect themselves there.

"In the country districts the ghouls and prowlers had been less in evidence, for I found many villages and towns untouched by fire. But they were filled by the pestilential dead, and I passed by without exploring them. It was near Lathrop that, out of my loneliness, I picked up a pair of collie dogs that were so newly free that they were urgently willing to return to their allegiance to man. These collies accompanied me for many years, and the strains of them are in those very dogs there that you boys have today. But in sixty years the collie strain has worked out. These brutes are more like domesticated wolves than anything else."

Hare-Lip rose to his feet, glanced to see that the goats were safe, and looked at the sun's position in the afternoon sky, advertising impatience at the prolixity of the old man's tale. Urged to hurry by Edwin, Granser went on.

"There is little more to tell. With my two dogs and my pony, and riding a horse I had managed to capture, I crossed the San Joaquin and went on to a wonderful valley in the Sierras called Yosemite. In the great hotel there I found a prodigious supply of tinned provisions. The pasture was abundant, as was the game, and the river that ran through the valley was full of trout. I remained there three years in an utter loneliness that none but a man who has once been highly civilized can understand. Then I could stand it no more. I felt that I was going crazy. Like the dog, I was a social animal and I needed my kind. I reasoned that since I had survived the plague, there was a possibility that others had survived. Also, I reasoned that after three years the plague germs must all be gone and the land be clean again.

"With my horse and dogs and pony, I set out. Again I crossed the San Joaquin Valley, the mountains beyond, and came down into Livermore Valley. The change in those three years was amazing. All the land had been splendidly tilled, and now I could scarcely recognize it, 'such was the sea of rank vegetation that had overrun the agricultural handiwork of man. You see, the wheat, the vegetables, and orchard trees had always been cared for and nursed by man, so that they were soft and tender. The weeds and wild bushes and such things, on the contrary, had always been fought by man, so that they were tough and resistant. As a result, when the hand of man was removed, the wild vegetation smothered and destroyed practically all the domesticated vegetation. The coyotes were greatly increased, and it was at this time that I first encountered wolves, straying in twos and threes and small packs down from the regions where they had always persisted.

"It was at Lake Temescal, not far from the one-time city of Oakland, that I came upon the first live human beings. Oh, my grandsons, how can I describe to you my emotion, when, astride my horse and dropping down the hillside to the lake, I saw the smoke of a campfire rising through the trees. Almost did my heart stop beating. I felt that I was going crazy. Then I heard the cry of a babe—a human babe. And dogs barked, and my dogs answered. I did not know but what I was the one human alive in the whole world. It could not be true that here were others—smoke, and the cry of a babe.

"Emerging on the lake, there, before my eyes, not a hundred yards away, I saw a man, a large man. He was standing on an outjutting rock and fishing. I was overcome. I stopped my horse. I tried to call out but could not. I waved my hand. It seemed to me that the man looked at me, but he did not appear to wave. Then I laid my head on my arms there in the saddle. I was afraid to look again, for I knew it was an hallucination, and I knew that if I looked the man would be gone. And so precious was the hallucination, that I wanted it to persist yet a little while. I knew, too, that as long as I did not look it would persist.

"Thus I remained, until I heard my dogs snarling, and a man's voice. What do you think the voice said? I will tell you. It said: 'Where in hell did you come from?'

"Those were the words, the exact words. That was what your other grandfather said to me, Hare-Lip, when he greeted me there on the shore of Lake Temescal fifty-seven years ago. And they were the most ineffable words I have ever heard. I opened my eyes, and there he stood before me, a large, dark, hairy man, heavy-jawed, slant-browed, fierce-eyed. How I got off my horse I do not know. But it seemed that the next I knew I was clasping his hand with both of mine and crying. I would have embraced him, but he was ever a narrow-minded, suspicious man, and he drew away from me. Yet did I cling to his hand and cry."

Granser's voice faltered and broke at the recollection, and the weak tears streamed down his cheeks while the boys looked on and giggled.

"Yet did I cry," he continued, "and desire to embrace him, though the Chauffeur was a brute, a perfect brute—the most abhorrent man I have ever known. His name was . . . strange, how I have forgotten his name. Everybody called him Chauffeur—it was the name of his occupation, and it stuck. That is how, to this day, the tribe he founded is called the Chauffeur Tribe.

"He was a violent, unjust man. Why the plague germs spared him I can never understand. It would seem, in spite of our old metaphysical notions about absolute justice, that there is no justice in the universe. Why did he live? An iniquitous, moral monster, a blot on the face of nature, a cruel, relentless, bestial cheat as well. All he could talk about was motor cars, machinery, gasoline, and garages—and especially, and with huge delight, of his mean pilferings and sordid swindlings of the persons who had employed him in the days before the coming of the plague. And yet he was spared, while hundreds of millions, yea, billions, of better men were destroyed.

"I went on with him to his camp, and there I saw her, Vesta, the one woman. It was glorious and . . . pitiful. There she was, Vesta Van Warden, the young wife of John Van Warden, clad in rags, with marred and scarred and toil-calloused hands, bending over the campfire and doing scullion work—she, Vesta, who had been born to the purple of the greatest baronage of wealth the world had ever known. John Van Warden, her husband, worth one billion, eight hundred millions and President of the Board of Industrial Magnates, had been the ruler of America. Also, sitting on the International Board of Control, he had been one of the seven men who ruled the world. And she herself had come of equally noble stock. Her father, Philip Saxon, had been President of the Board of Industrial Magnates up to the time of his death. This office was in process of becoming hereditary, and had Philip Saxon had a son that son would have succeeded him. But his only child was Vesta, the perfect flower of generations of the highest culture this planet has ever produced. It was not until the engagement between Vesta and Van Warden took place, that Saxon indicated the latter as his successor. It was, I am sure, a political marriage. I have reason to believe that Vesta never really loved her husband in the mad passionate way of which the poets used to sing. It was more like the marriages that obtained among crowned heads in the days before they were displaced by the Magnates.

"And there she was, boiling fish-chowder in a soot-covered pot, her glorious eyes inflamed by the acrid smoke of the open fire. Hers was a sad story. She was the one survivor in a million, as I had been, as the Chauffeur had been. On a crowning eminence of the Alameda Hills, overlooking San Francisco Bay, Van Warden had built a vast summer palace. It was surrounded by a park of a thousand acres. When the plague broke out, Van Warden sent her there. Armed guards patrolled the boundaries of the park, and nothing entered in the way of provisions or even mail matter that was not first fumigated. And yet did the plague enter, killing the guards at their posts, the servants at their tasks, sweeping away the whole army of retainers—or, at least, all of them who did not flee to die elsewhere. So it was that Vesta found herself the sole living person in the palace that had become a charnel house.

"Now the Chauffeur had been one of the servants that ran away. Returning, two months afterward, he discovered Vesta in a little summer pavilion where there had been no deaths and where she had established herself. He was a brute. She was afraid, and she ran away and hid among the trees. That night, on foot, she fled into the mountains—she, whose tender feet and delicate body had never known the bruise of stones nor the scratch of briars. He followed, and that night he caught her. He struck her. Do you understand? He beat her with those terrible fists of his and made her his slave. It was she who had to gather the firewood, build the fires, cook, and do all the degrading camp-labor—she, who had never performed a menial act in her life. These things he compelled her to do, while he, a proper savage, elected to lie around camp and look on. He did nothing, absolutely nothing, except on occasion to hunt meat or catch fish."

"Good for Chauffeur," Hare-Lip commented in an undertone to the other boys. "I remember him before he died. He was a corker. But he did things, and he made things go. You know, Dad married his daughter, an' you ought to see the way he knocked the spots outa Dad. The Chauffeur was a son-of-a-gun. He made us kids stand around. Even when he was croaking he reached out for me, once, an' laid my head open with that long stick he kept always beside him."

Hare-Lip rubbed his bullet head reminiscently, and the boys returned to the old man, who was maundering ecstatically about Vesta, the squaw of the founder of the Chauffeur Tribe.

"And so I say to you that you cannot understand the awfulness of the situation. The Chauffeur was a servant, understand, a servant. And he cringed, with bowed head, to such as she. She was a lord of life, both by birth and by marriage. The destinies of millions, such as he, she carried in the hollow of her pink-white hand. And, in the days before the plague, the slightest contact with such as he would have been pollution. Oh, I have seen it. Once, I remember, there was Mrs. Goldwin, wife of one of the great magnates. It was on a landing stage, just as she was embarking in her private dirigible, that she dropped her parasol. A servant picked it up and made the mistake of handing it to her—to her, one of the greatest royal ladies of the land! She shrank back, as though he were a leper, and indicated her secretary to receive it. Also, she ordered her secretary to ascertain the creature's name and to see that he was immediately discharged from service. And such a woman was Vesta Van Warden. And her the Chauffeur beat and made his slave.

"—Bill—that was it; Bill, the Chauffeur. That was his name. He was a wretched, primitive man, wholly devoid of the finer instincts and chivalrous promptings of a cultured soul. No, there is no absolute justice, for to him fell that wonder of womanhood, Vesta Van Warden. The grievousness of this you will never understand, my grandsons; for you are yourselves primitive little savages, unaware of aught else but savagery. Why should Vesta not have been mine? I was a man of culture and refinement, a professor in a great university. Even so, in the time before the plague, such was her exalted position, she would not have deigned to know that I existed. Mark, then, the abysmal degradation to which she fell at the hands of the Chauffeur. Nothing less than the destruction of all mankind had made it possible that I should know her, look in her eyes, converse with her, touch her hand—ay, and love her and know that her feelings toward me were very kindly. I have reason to believe that she, even she, would have loved me, there being no other man in the world except the Chauffeur. Why, when it destroyed eight billions of souls, did not the plague destroy just one more man, and that man the Chauffeur?

"Once, when the Chauffeur was away fishing, she begged me to kill him. With tears in her eyes she begged me to kill him. But he was a strong and violent man, and I was afraid. Afterwards, I talked with him. I offered him my horse, my pony, my dogs, all that I possessed, if he would give Vesta to me. And he grinned in my face and shook his head. He was very insulting. He said that in the old days he had been a servant, had been dirt under the feet of men like me and of women like Vesta, and that now he had the greatest lady in the land to be servant to him and cook his food and nurse his brats. 'You had your day before the plague,' he said; 'but this is my day, and a damned good day it is. I wouldn't trade back to the old times for anything.' Such words he spoke, but they are not his words. He was a vulgar, low-minded man, and vile oaths fell continually from his lips.

"Also, he told me that if he caught me making eyes at his woman he'd wring my neck and give her a beating as well. What was I to do? I was afraid. He was a brute. That first night, when I discovered the camp, Vesta and I had great talk about the things of our vanished world. We talked of art, and books, and poetry; and the Chauffeur listened and grinned and sneered. He was bored and angered by our way of speech which he did not comprehend, and finally he spoke up and said: 'And this is Vesta Van Warden, one-time wife of Van Warden the Magnate—a high and stuck-up beauty, who is now my squaw. Eh, Professor Smith, times is changed, times is changed. Here, you, woman, take off my moccasins, and lively about it. I want Professor Smith to see how well I have you trained.'

"I saw her clench her teeth, and the flame of revolt rise in her face. He drew back his gnarled fist to strike, and I was afraid, and sick at heart. I could do nothing to prevail against him. So I got up to go, and not be witness to such indignity. But the Chauffeur laughed and threatened me with a beating if I did not stay and behold. And I sat there, perforce, by the campfire on the shore of Lake Temescal, and saw Vesta, Vesta Van Warden, kneel and remove the moccasins of that grinning, hairy, apelike human brute.

"—Oh, you do not understand, my grandsons. You have never known anything else, and you do not understand.

" 'Halter-broke and bridle-wise,' the Chauffeur gloated, while she performed that dreadful, menial task. 'A trifle balky at times, Professor, a trifle balky; but a clout alongside the jaw makes her as meek and gentle as a lamb.'

"And another time he said: 'We've got to start all over and replenish the earth and multiply. You're handicapped, Professor. You ain't got no wife, and we're up against a regular Garden-of-Eden proposition. But I ain't proud. I'll tell you what, Professor.' He pointed at their little infant, barely a year old. 'There's your wife, though you'll have to wait till she grows up. It's rich, ain't it? We're all equals here, and I'm the biggest toad in the splash. But I ain't stuck up—not I. I do you the honor, Professor Smith, the very great honor of betrothing to you my and Vesta Van Warden's daughter. Ain't it cussed bad that Van Warden ain't here to see?' "

VI

"I lived three weeks of infinite torment there in the Chauffeur's camp. And then, one day, tiring of me, or of what to him was my bad effect on Vesta, he told me that the year before, wandering through the Contra Costa Hills to the Straits of Carquinez, across the Straits he had seen a smoke. This meant that there were still other human beings, and that for three weeks he had kept this inestimably precious information from me. I departed at once, with my dogs and horses, and journeyed across the Contra Costa Hills to the Straits. I saw no smoke on the other side, but at Port Costa discovered a small steel barge on which I was able to embark my animals. Old canvas which I found served me for a sail, and a southerly breeze fanned me across the Straits and up to the ruins of Vallejo. Here, on the outskirts of the city, I found evidences of a recently occupied camp.

"Many clam-shells showed me why these humans had come to the shores of the Bay. This was the Santa Rosa Tribe, and I followed its track along the old railroad right of way across the salt marshes to Sonoma Valley. Here, at the old brickyard at Glen Ellen, I came upon the camp. There were eighteen souls all told. Two were old men, one of whom was Jones, a banker. The other was Harrison, a retired pawnbroker, who had taken for wife the matron of the State Hospital for the Insane at Napa. Of all the persons of the city of Napa, and of all the other towns and villages in that rich and populous valley, she had been the only-survivor. Next, there were the three young men—Cardiff and Hale, who had been farmers, and Wainwright, a common day-laborer. All three had found wives. To Hale, a crude, illiterate farmer, had fallen Isadore, the greatest prize, next to Vesta, of the women who came through the plague. She was one of the world's most noted singers, and the plague had caught her at San Francisco. She has talked with me for hours at a time, telling me of her adventures, until, at last, rescued by Hale in the Mendocino Forest Reserve, there had remained nothing for her to do but become his wife. But Hale was a good fellow, in spite of his illiteracy. He had a keen sense of justice and right-dealing, and she was far happier with him than was Vesta with the Chauffeur.

"The wives of Cardiff and Wainwright were ordinary women, accustomed to toil with strong constitutions—just the type for the wild new life which they were compelled to live. In addition were two adult idiots from the feeble-minded home at Eldredge, and five or six young children and infants born after the formation of the Santa Rosa Tribe. Also, there was Bertha. She was a good woman, Hare-Lip, in spite of the sneers of your father. Her I took for wife. She was the mother of your father, Edwin, and of yours, Hoo-Hoo. And it was our daughter, Vera, who married your father, Hare-Lip—your father, Sandow, who was the oldest son of Vesta Van Warden and the Chauffeur.

"And so it was that I became the nineteenth member of the Santa Rosa Tribe. There were only two outsiders added after me. One was Mungerson, descended from the Magnates, who wandered alone in the wilds of Northern California for eight years before he came south and joined us. He it was who waited twelve years more before he married my daughter, Mary. The other was Johnson, the man who founded the Utah Tribe. That was where he came from, Utah, a country that lies very far away from here, across the great deserts, to the east. It was not until twenty-seven years after the plague that Johnson reached California. In all that Utah region he reported but three survivors, himself one, and all men. For many years these three men lived and hunted together, until, at last, desperate, fearing that with them the human race would perish utterly from the planet, they headed westward on the possibility of finding women survivors in California. Johnson alone came through the great desert, where his two companions died. He was forty-six years old when he joined us, and he married the fourth daughter of Isadore and Hale, and his eldest son married your aunt, Hare-Lip, who was the third daughter of Vesta and the Chauffeur. Johnson was a strong man, with a will of his own. And it was because of this that he seceded from the Santa Rosans and formed the Utah Tribe at San José. It is a small tribe—there are only nine in it; but, though he is dead, such was his influence and the strength of his breed, that it will grow into a strong tribe and play a leading part in the recivilization of the planet.

"There are only two other tribes that we know of—the Los Angelitos and the Carmelitos. The latter started from one man and woman. He was called Lopez, and he was descended from the ancient Mexicans and was very black. He was a cowherd in the ranges beyond Carmel, and his wife was a maidservant in the great Del Monte Hotel. It was seven years before we first got in touch with the Los Angelitos. They have a good country down there, but it is too warm. I estimate the present population of the world at between three hundred and fifty and four hundred—provided, of course, that there are no scattered little tribes elsewhere in the world. If there be such, we have not heard from them. Since Johnson crossed the desert from Utah, no word nor sign has come from the East or anywhere else. The great world which I knew in my boyhood and early manhood is gone. It has ceased to be. I am the last man who was alive in the days of the plague and who knows the wonders of that far-off time. We, who mastered the planet—its earth, and sea, and sky—and who were as very gods, now live in primitive savagery along the water courses of this California country.

"But we are increasing rapidly—your sister, Hare-Lip, already has four children. We are increasing rapidly and making ready for a new climb toward civilization. In time, pressure of population will compel us to spread out, and a hundred generations from now we may expect our descendants to start across the Sierras, oozing slowly along, generation by generation, over the great continent to the colonization of the East—a new Aryan drift around the world.

"But it will be slow, very slow; we have so far to climb. We fell so hopelessly far. If only one physicist or one chemist had survived! But it was not to be, and we have forgotten everything. The Chauffeur started working in iron. He made the forge which we use to this day. But he was a lazy man, and when he died he took with him all he knew of metals and machinery. What was I to know of such things? I was a classical scholar, not a chemist. The other men who survived were not educated. Only two things did the Chauffeur accomplish—the brewing of strong drink and the growing of tobacco. It was while he was drunk, once, that he killed Vesta. I firmly believe that he killed Vesta in a fit of drunken cruelty though he always maintained that she fell into the lake and was drowned.

"And, my grandsons, let me warn you against the medicine-men. They call themselves *doctors*, travestying what was once a noble profession, but in reality they are medicine-men, devil-devil men, and they make for superstition and darkness. They are cheats and liars. But so debased and degraded are we, that we believe their lies. They, too, will increase in numbers as we increase, and they will strive to rule us. Yet are they liars and charlatans. Look at young Cross-Eyes, posing as a doctor, selling charms against sickness, giving good hunting, exchanging promises of fair weather for good meat and skins, sending the death-stick, performing a thousand abominations. Yet I say to you, that when he says he can do these things, he lies. I, Professor Smith, Professor James Howard Smith, say that he lies. I have told him so to his teeth. Why has he not sent me the death-stick? Because he knows that with me it is without avail. But you, Hare-Lip, so deeply are you sunk in black superstition that did you awake this night and find the death-stick beside you, you would surely die. And you would die, not because of any virtues in the stick, but because you are a savage with the dark and clouded mind of a savage.

"The doctors must be destroyed, and all that was lost must be discovered over again. Wherefore, earnestly, I repeat unto you certain things which you must remember and tell to your children after you. You must tell them that when water is made hot by fire, there resides in it a wonderful thing called steam, which is stronger than ten thousand men and which can do all man's work for him. There are other very useful things. In the lightning flash resides a similarly strong servant of man, which was of old his slave and which some day will be his slave again.

"Quite a different thing is the alphabet. It is what enables me to know the meaning of fine markings, whereas you boys know only rude picture-writing. In that dry cave on Telegraph Hill, where you see me often go when the tribe is down by the sea, I have stored many books. In them is great wisdom. Also, with them, I have placed a key to the alphabet, so that one who knows picture-writing may also know print. Some day men will read again; and then, if no accident has befallen my cave, they will know that Professor James Howard Smith once lived and saved for them the knowledge of the ancients.

"There is another little device that men inevitably will rediscover. It is called gunpowder. It was what enabled us to kill surely and at long distances. Certain things which are found in the ground, when combined in the right proportions, will make this gunpowder. What these things are, I have forgotten, or else I never knew. But I wish I did know. Then would I make powder, and then would I certainly kill Cross-Eyes and rid the land of superstition—"

"After I am man-grown I am going to give Cross-Eyes all the goats, and meat, and skins I can get, so that he'll teach me to be a doctor," Hoo-Hoo asserted. "And when I know, I'll make everybody else sit up and take notice. They'll get down in the dirt to me, you bet."

The old man nodded his head solemnly, and murmured:

"Strange it is to hear the vestiges and remnants of the complicated Aryan speech falling from the lips of a filthy little skin-clad savage. All the world is topsy-turvy. And it has been topsy-turvy ever since the plague."

"You won't make me sit up," Hare-Lip boasted to the would-be medicine-man. "If I paid you for a sending of the death-stick and it didn't work, I'd bust in your head—understand, you Hoo-Hoo, you?"

"I'm going to get Granser to remember this here gunpowder stuff," Edwin said softly, "and then I'll have you all on the run. You, Hare-Lip, will do my fighting for me and get my meat for me, and you, Hoo-Hoo, will send the death-stick for me and make everybody afraid. And if I catch Hare-Lip trying to bust your head, Hoo-Hoo, I'll fix him with that same gunpowder. Granser ain't such a fool as you think, and I'm going to listen to him and some day I'll be boss over the whole bunch of you."

The old man shook his head sadly, and said:

"The gunpowder will come. Nothing can stop it—the same old story over and over. Man will increase, and men will fight. The gunpowder will enable men to kill millions of men, and in this way only, by fire and blood, will a new civilization, in some remote day, be evolved. And of what profit will it be? Just as the old civilization passed, so will the new. It may take fifty thousand years to build, but it will pass. All things pass. Only remain cosmic force and matter, ever in flux, ever acting and reacting and realizing the eternal types—the priest, the soldier, and the king. Out of the mouths of babes comes the wisdom of all the ages. Some will fight, some will rule, some will pray; and all the rest will toil and suffer sore while on their bleeding carcasses is reared again, and yet again, without end, the amazing beauty and surpassing wonder of the civilized state. It were just as well that I destroyed those cave-stored books—whether they remain or perish, all their old truths will be discovered, their old lies lived and handed down. What is the profit—"

Hare-Lip leaped to his feet, giving a quick glance at the pasturing goats and the afternoon sun.

"Gee!" he muttered to Edwin, "The old geezer gets more long-winded every day. Let's pull for camp."

While the other two, aided by the dogs, assembled the goats and started them for the trail through the forest, Edwin stayed by the old man and guided him in the same direction. When they reached the old right of way, Edwin stopped suddenly and looked back. Hare-Lip and Hoo-Hoo and the dogs and the goats passed on. Edwin was looking at a small herd of wild horses which had come down on the hard sand. There were at least twenty of them, young colts and yearlings and mares, led by a beautiful stallion which stood in the foam at the edge of the surf, with arched neck and bright wild eyes, sniffing the salt air from off the sea.

"What is it?" Granser queried.

"Horses," was the answer. "First time I ever seen 'em on the beach. It's the mountain lions getting thicker and thicker and driving 'em down."

The low sun shot red shafts of light, fan-shaped, up from a cloud-tumbled horizon. And close at hand, in the white waste of shore-lashed waters, the sea-lions, bellowing their old primeval chant, hauled up out of the sea on the black rocks and fought and loved.

"Come on, Granser," Edwin prompted. And old man and boy, skin-clad and barbaric, turned and went along the right of way into the forest in the wake of the goats.

HERLAND

Charlotte Perkins Gilman

I

A NOT UNNATURAL ENTERPRISE

This is written from memory, unfortunately. If I could have brought with me the material I so carefully prepared, this would be a very different story. Whole books full of notes, carefully copied records, firsthand descriptions, and the pictures—that's the worst loss. We had some bird's-eyes of the cities and parks; a lot of lovely views of streets, of buildings, outside and in, and some of those gorgeous gardens, and, most important of all, of the women themselves.

Nobody will ever believe how they looked. Descriptions aren't any good when it comes to women, and I never was good at descriptions anyhow. But it's got to be done somehow; the rest of the world needs to know about that country.

I haven't said where it was for fear some self-appointed missionaries, or traders, or land-greedy expansionists, will take it upon themselves to push in. They will not be wanted, I can tell them that, and will fare worse than we did if they do find it.

It began this way. There were three of us, classmates and friends—Terry O. Nicholson (we used to call him the Old Nick, with good reason), Jeff Margrave, and I, Vandyck Jennings.

We had known each other years and years, and in spite of our differences we had a good deal in common. All of us were interested in science.

Terry was rich enough to do as he pleased. His great aim was exploration. He used to make all kinds of a row because there was nothing left to explore now, only patchwork and filling in, he said. He filled in well enough—he had a lot of talents—great on mechanics and electricity. Had all kinds of boats and motorcars, and was one of the best of our airmen.

We never could have done the thing at all without Terry.

Jeff Margrave was born to be a poet, a botanist—or both—but his folks persuaded him to be a doctor instead. He was a good one, for his age, but his real interest was in what he loved to call "the wonders of science."

As for me, sociology's my major. You have to back that up with a lot of other sciences, of course. I'm interested in them all.

Terry was strong on facts—geography and meteorology and those; Jeff could beat him any time on biology, and I didn't care what it was they talked about, so long as it connected with human life, somehow. There are few things that don't.

We three had a chance to join a big scientific expedition. They needed a doctor, and that gave Jeff an excuse for dropping his just opening practice; they needed Terry's experience, his machine, and his money; and as for me, I got in through Terry's influence.

The expedition was up among the thousand tributaries and enormous hinterland of a great river, up where the maps had to be made, savage dialects studied, and all manner of strange flora and fauna expected.

But this story is not about that expedition. That was only the merest starter for ours.

My interest was first roused by talk among our guides. I'm quick at languages, know a good many, and pick them up readily. What with that and a really good interpreter we took with us, I made out quite a few legends and folk myths of these scattered tribes.

And as we got farther and farther upstream, in a dark tangle of rivers, lakes, morasses, and dense forests, with here and there an unexpected long spur running out from the big mountains beyond, I noticed that more and more of these savages had a story about a strange and terrible Woman Land in the high distance.

"Up yonder," "Over there," "Way up"—was all the direction they could offer, but their legends all agreed on the main point—that there was this strange country where no men lived—only women and girl children.

None of them had ever seen it. It was dangerous, deadly, they said, for any man to go there. But there were tales of long ago, when some brave investigator had seen it—a Big Country, Big Houses, Plenty People—All Women.

Had no one else gone? Yes—a good many—but they never came back. It was no place for men—of that they seemed sure.

I told the boys about these stories, and they laughed at them. Naturally I did myself. I knew the stuff that savage dreams are made of.

But when we had reached our farthest point, just the day before we all had to turn around and start for home again, as the best of expeditions must in time, we three made a discovery.

The main encampment was on a spit of land running out into the main stream, or what we thought was the main stream. It had the same muddy color we had been seeing for weeks past, the same taste.

I happened to speak of that river to our last guide, a rather superior fellow with quick, bright eyes.

He told me that there was another river—"over there, short river, sweet water, red and blue."

I was interested in this and anxious to see if I had understood, so I showed him a red and blue pencil I carried, and asked again.

Yes, he pointed to the river, and then to the southwestward. "River—good water—red and blue."

Terry was close by and interested in the fellow's pointing.

"What does he say, Van?"

I told him.

Terry blazed up at once.

"Ask him how far it is."

The man indicated a short journey; I judged about two hours, maybe three.

"Let's go," urged Terry. "Just us three. Maybe we can really find something. May be cinnabar in it."

"May be indigo," Jeff suggested, with his lazy smile.

It was early yet; we had just breakfasted; and leaving word that we'd be back before night, we got away quietly, not wishing to be thought too gullible if we failed, and secretly hoping to have some nice little discovery all to ourselves.

It was a long two hours, nearer three. I fancy the savage could have done it alone much quicker. There was a desperate tangle of wood and water and a swampy patch we never should have found our way across alone. But there was one, and I could see Terry, with compass and notebook, marking directions and trying to place landmarks.

We came after a while to a sort of marshy lake, very big, so that the circling forest looked quite low and dim across it. Our guide told us that boats could go from there to our camp—but "long way—all day."

This water was somewhat clearer than that we had left, but we could not judge well from the margin. We skirted it for another half hour or so, the ground growing firmer as we advanced, and presently we turned the corner of a wooded promontory and saw a quite different country—a sudden view of mountains, steep and bare.

"One of those long easterly spurs," Terry said appraisingly. "May be hundreds of miles from the range. They crop out like that."

Suddenly we left the lake and struck directly toward the cliffs. We heard running water before we reached it, and the guide pointed proudly to his river.

It was short. We could see where it poured down a narrow vertical cataract from an opening in the face of the cliff. It was sweet water. The guide drank eagerly and so did we.

"That's snow water," Terry announced. "Must come from way back in the hills."

But as to being red and blue—it was greenish in tint. The guide seemed not at all surprised. He hunted about a little and showed us a quiet marginal pool where there were smears of red along the border; yes, and of blue.

Terry got out his magnifying glass and squatted down to investigate.

"Chemicals of some sort—I can't tell on the spot. Look to me like dyestuffs. Let's get nearer," he urged, "up there by the fall."

We scrambled along the steep banks and got close to the pool that foamed and boiled beneath the falling water. Here we searched the border and found traces of color beyond dispute. More—Jeff suddenly held up an unlooked-for trophy.

It was only a rag, a long, raveled fragment of cloth. But it was a well-woven fabric, with a pattern, and of a clear scarlet that the water had not faded. No savage tribe that we had heard of made such fabrics.

The guide stood serenely on the bank, well pleased with our excitement.

"One day blue—one day red—one day green," he told us, and pulled from his pouch another strip of bright-hued cloth.

"Come down," he said, pointing to the cataract. "Woman Country—up there."

Then we were interested. We had our rest and lunch right there and pumped the man for further information. He could tell us only what the others had—a land of women—no men—babies, but all girls. No place for men—dangerous. Some had gone to see—none had come back.

I could see Terry's jaw set at that. No place for men? Dangerous? He looked as if he might shin up the waterfall on the spot. But the guide would not hear of going up, even if there had been any possible method of scaling that sheer cliff, and we had to get back to our party before night.

"They might stay if we told them," I suggested.

But Terry stopped in his tracks. "Look here, fellows," he said. "This is our find. Let's not tell those cocky old professors. Let's go on home with 'em, and then come back—just us—have a little expedition of our own."

We looked at him, much impressed. There was something attractive to a bunch of unattached young men in finding an undiscovered country of a strictly Amazonian nature.

Of course we didn't believe the story—but yet!

"There is no such cloth made by any of these local tribes," I announced, examining those rags with great care. "Somewhere up yonder they spin and weave and dye—as well as we do."

"That would mean a considerable civilization, Van. There couldn't be such a place—and not known about."

"Oh, well, I don't know. What's that old republic up in the Pyrenees somewhere—Andorra? Precious few people know anything about that, and it's been minding its own business for a thousand years. Then there's Montenegro—splendid little state—you could lose a dozen Montenegroes up and down these great ranges."

We discussed it hotly all the way back to camp. We discussed it with care and privacy on the voyage home. We discussed it after that, still only among ourselves, while Terry was making his arrangements.

He was hot about it. Lucky he had so much money—we might have had to beg and advertise for years to start the thing, and then it would have been a matter of public amusement—just sport for the papers.

But T. O. Nicholson could fix up his big steam yacht, load his specially made big motorboat aboard, and tuck in a "dissembled" biplane without any more notice than a snip in the society column.

We had provisions and preventives and all manner of supplies. His previous experience stood him in good stead there. It was a very complete little outfit.

We were to leave the yacht at the nearest safe port and go up that endless river in our motorboat, just the three of us and a pilot; then drop the pilot when we got to that last stopping place of the previous party, and hunt up that clear water stream ourselves.

The motorboat we were going to leave at anchor in that wide shallow lake. It had a special covering of fitted armor, thin but strong, shut up like a clamshell.

"Those natives can't get into it, or hurt it, or move it," Terry explained proudly. "We'll start our flier from the lake and leave the boat as a base to come back to."

"If we come back," I suggested cheerfully.

" 'Fraid the ladies will eat you?" he scoffed.

"We're not so sure about those ladies, you know," drawled Jeff. "There may be a contingent of gentlemen with poisoned arrows or something."

"You don't need to go if you don't want to," Terry remarked drily.

"Go? You'll have to get an injunction to stop me!" Both Jeff and I were sure about that.

But we did have differences of opinion, all the long way.

An ocean voyage is an excellent time for discussion. Now we had no eavesdroppers, we could loll and loaf in our deck chairs and talk and talk—there was nothing else to do. Our absolute lack of facts only made the field of discussion wider.

"We'll leave papers with our consul where the yacht stays," Terry planned. "If we don't come back in—say a month—they can send a relief party after us."

"A punitive expedition," I urged. "If the ladies do eat us we must make reprisals."

"They can locate that last stopping place easy enough, and I've made a sort of chart of that lake and cliff and waterfall."

"Yes, but how will they get up?" asked Jeff.

"Same way we do, of course. If three valuable American citizens are lost up there, they will follow somehow—to say nothing of the glittering attractions of that fair land—let's call it 'Feminisia,' " he broke off.

"You're right, Terry. Once the story gets out, the river will crawl with expeditions and the airships rise like a swarm of mosquitoes." I laughed as I thought of it. "We've made a great mistake not to let Mr. Yellow Press in on this. Save us! What headlines!"

"Not much!" said Terry grimly. "This is our party. We're going to find that place alone."

"What are you going to do with it when you do find it—if you do?" Jeff asked mildly.

Jeff was a tender soul. I think he thought that country—if there was one—was just blossoming with roses and babies and canaries and tidies, and all that sort of thing.

And Terry, in his secret heart, had visions of a sort of sublimated summer resort—just Girls and Girls and Girls—and that he was going to be—well, Terry was popular among women even when there were other men around, and it's not to be wondered at that he had pleasant dreams of what might happen. I could see it in his eyes as he lay there, looking at the long blue rollers slipping by, and fingering that impressive mustache of his.

But I thought—then—that I could form a far clearer idea of what was before us than either of them.

"You're all off, boys," I insisted. "If there is such a place—and there does seem some foundation for believing it—you'll find it's built on a sort of matriarchal principle, that's all. The men have a separate cult of their own, less socially developed than the women, and make them an annual visit—a sort of wedding call. This is a condition known to have existed—here's just a survival. They've got some peculiarly isolated valley or tableland up there, and their primeval customs have survived. That's all there is to it."

"How about the boys?" Jeff asked.

"Oh, the men take them away as soon as they are five or six, you see."

"And how about this danger theory all our guides were so sure of?"

"Danger enough, Terry, and we'll have to be mighty careful. Women of that stage of culture are quite able to defend themselves and have no welcome for unseasonable visitors."

We talked and talked.

And with all my airs of sociological superiority I was no nearer than any of them.

It was funny though, in the light of what we did find, those extremely clear ideas of ours as to what a country of women would be like. It was no use to tell ourselves and one another that all this was idle speculation. We were idle and we did speculate, on the ocean voyage and the river voyage, too.

"Admitting the improbability," we'd begin solemnly, and then launch out again.

"They would fight among themselves," Terry insisted. "Women always do. We mustn't look to find any sort of order and organization."

"You're dead wrong," Jeff told him. "It will be like a nunnery under an abbess—a peaceful, harmonious sisterhood."

I snorted derision at this idea.

"Nuns, indeed! Your peaceful sisterhoods were all celibate, Jeff, and under vows of obedience. These are just women, and mothers, and where there's motherhood you don't find sisterhood—not much."

"No, sir—they'll scrap," agreed Terry. "Also we mustn't look for inventions and progress; it'll be awfully primitive."

"How about that cloth mill?" Jeff suggested.

"Oh, cloth! Women have always been spinsters. But there they stop—you'll see."

We joked Terry about his modest impression that he would be warmly received, but he held his ground.

"You'll see," he insisted. "I'll get solid with them all—and play one bunch against another. I'll get myself elected king in no time—whew! Solomon will have to take a back seat!"

"Where do we come in on that deal?" I demanded. "Aren't we Viziers or anything?"

"Couldn't risk it," he asserted solemnly. "You might start a revolution—probably would. No, you'll have to be beheaded, or bowstrung—or whatever the popular method of execution is."

"You'd have to do it yourself, remember," grinned Jeff. "No husky black slaves and mamelukes! And there'd be two of us and only one of you—eh, Van?"

Jeff's ideas and Terry's were so far apart that sometimes it was all I could do to keep the peace between them. Jeff idealized women in the best Southern style. He was full of chivalry and sentiment, and all that. And he was a good boy; he lived up to his ideals.

You might say Terry did, too, if you can call his views about women anything so polite as ideals. I always liked Terry. He was a man's man, very much so, generous and brave and clever; but I don't think any of us in college days was quite pleased to have him with our sisters. We weren't very stringent, heavens no! But Terry was "the limit." Later on—why, of course a man's life is his own, we held, and asked no questions.

But barring a possible exception in favor of a not impossible wife, or of his mother, or, of course, the fair relatives of his friends, Terry's idea seemed to be that pretty women were just so much game and homely ones not worth considering.

It was really unpleasant sometimes to see the notions he had.

But I got out of patience with Jeff, too. He had such rose-colored halos on his womenfolks. I held a middle ground, highly scientific, of course, and used to argue learnedly about the physiological limitations of the sex.

We were not in the least "advanced" on the woman question, any of us, then.

So we joked and disputed and speculated, and after an interminable journey, we got to our old camping place at last.

It was not hard to find the river, just poking along that side till we came to it, and it was navigable as far as the lake.

When we reached that and slid out on its broad glistening bosom, with that high gray promontory running out toward us, and the straight white fall clearly visible, it began to be really exciting.

There was some talk, even then, of skirting the rock wall and seeking a possible footway up, but the marshy jungle made that method look not only difficult but dangerous.

Terry dismissed the plan sharply.

"Nonsense, fellows! We've decided that. It might take months—we haven't got the provisions. No, sir—we've got to take our chances. If we get back safe—all right. If we don't, why, we're not the first explorers to get lost in the shuffle. There are plenty to come after us."

So we got the big biplane together and loaded it with our scientifically compressed baggage: the camera, of course; the glasses; a supply of concentrated food. Our pockets were magazines of small necessities, and we had our guns, of course—there was no knowing what might happen.

Up and up and up we sailed, way up at first, to get "the lay of the land" and make note of it.

Out of that dark green sea of crowding forest this high-standing spur rose steeply. It ran back on either side, apparently, to the far-off white-crowned peaks in the distance, themselves probably inaccessible.

"Let's make the first trip geographical," I suggested. "Spy out the land, and drop back here for more gasoline. With your tremendous speed we can reach that range and back all right. Then we can leave a sort of map on board—for that relief expedition."

"There's sense in that," Terry agreed. "I'll put off being king of Ladyland for one more day."

So we made a long skirting voyage, turned the point of the cape which was close by, ran up one side of the triangle at our best speed, crossed over the base where it left the higher mountains, and so back to our lake by moonlight.

"That's not a bad little kingdom," we agreed when it was roughly drawn and measured. We could tell the size fairly by our speed. And from what we could see of the sides—and that icy ridge at the back end—"It's a pretty enterprising savage who would manage to get into it," Jeff said.

Of course we had looked at the land itself—eagerly, but we were too high and going too fast to see much. It appeared to be well forested about the edges, but in the interior there were wide plains, and everywhere parklike meadows and open places.

There were cities, too; that I insisted. It looked—well, it looked like any other country—a civilized one, I mean.

We had to sleep after that long sweep through the air, but we turned out early enough next day, and again we rose softly up the height till we could top the crowning trees and see the broad fair land at our pleasure.

"Semitropical. Looks like a first-rate climate. It's wonderful what a little height will do for temperature." Terry was studying the forest growth.

"Little height! Is that what you call little?" I asked. Our instruments measured it clearly. We had not realized the long gentle rise from the coast perhaps.

"Mighty lucky piece of land, I call it," Terry pursued. "Now for the folks—I've had enough scenery."

So we sailed low, crossing back and forth, quartering the country as we went, and studying it. We saw—I can't remember now how much of this we noted then and how much was supplemented by our later knowledge, but we could not help seeing this much, even on that excited day—a land in a state of perfect cultivation, where even the forests looked as if they were cared for; a land that looked like an enormous park, only it was even more evidently an enormous garden.

"I don't see any cattle," I suggested, but Terry was silent. We were approaching a village.

I confess that we paid small attention to the clean, well-built roads, to the attractive architecture, to the ordered beauty of the little town. We had our glasses out; even Terry, setting his machine for a spiral glide, clapped the binoculars to his eyes.

They heard our whirring screw. They ran out of the houses—they gathered in from the fields, swift-running light figures, crowds of them. We stared and stared until it was almost too late to catch the levers, sweep off and rise again; and then we held our peace for a long run upward.

"Gosh!" said Terry, after a while.

"Only women there—and children," Jeff urged excitedly.

"But they look—why, this is a civilized country!" I protested. "There must be men."

"Of course there are men," said Terry. "Come on, let's find 'em."

He refused to listen to Jeff's suggestion that we examine the country further before we risked leaving our machine.

"There's a fine landing place right there where we came over," he insisted, and it was an excellent one—a wide, flat-topped rock, overlooking the lake, and quite out of sight from the interior.

"They won't find this in a hurry," he asserted, as we scrambled with the utmost difficulty down to safer footing. "Come on, boys—there were some good lookers in that bunch."

Of course it was unwise of us.

It was quite easy to see afterward that our best plan was to have studied the country more fully before we left our swooping airship and trusted ourselves to mere foot service. But we were three young men. We had been talking about this country for over a year, hardly believing that there was such a place, and now—we were in it.

It looked safe and civilized enough, and among those upturned, crowding faces, though some were terrified enough, there was great beauty—on that we all agreed.

"Come on!" cried Terry, pushing forward. "Oh, come on! Here goes for Herland!"

II

RASH ADVANCES

Not more than ten or fifteen miles we judged it from our landing rock to that last village. For all our eagerness we thought it wise to keep to the woods and go carefully.

Even Terry's ardor was held in check by his firm conviction that there were men to be met, and we saw to it that each of us had a good stock of cartridges.

"They may be scarce, and they may be hidden away somewhere—some kind of a matriarchate, as Jeff tells us; for that matter, they may live up in the mountains yonder and keep the women in this part of the country—sort of a national harem! But there are men somewhere—didn't you see the babies?"

We had all seen babies, children big and little, everywhere that we had come near enough to distinguish the people. And though by dress we could not be sure of all the grown persons, still there had not been one man that we were certain of.

"I always liked that Arab saying, 'First tie your camel and then trust in the Lord,'" Jeff murmured; so we all had our weapons in hand, and stole cautiously through the forest. Terry studied it as we progressed.

"Talk of civilization," he cried softly in restrained enthusiasm. "I never saw a forest so petted, even in Germany. Look, there's not a dead bough—the vines are trained—actually! And see here"—he stopped and looked about him, calling Jeff's attention to the kinds of trees.

They left me for a landmark and made a limited excursion on either side.

"Food-bearing, practically all of them," they announced returning. "The rest, splendid hardwood. Call this a forest? It's a truck farm!"

"Good thing to have a botanist on hand," I agreed. "Sure there are no medicinal ones? Or any for pure ornament?"

As a matter of fact they were quite right. These towering trees were under as careful cultivation as so many cabbages. In other conditions we should have found those woods full of fair foresters and fruit gatherers; but an airship is a conspicuous object, and by no means quiet—and women are cautious.

All we found moving in those woods, as we started through them, were birds, some gorgeous, some musical, all so tame that it seemed almost to contradict our theory of cultivation—at least until we came upon occasional little glades, where carved stone seats and tables stood in the shade beside clear fountains, with shallow bird baths always added.

"They don't kill birds, and apparently they do kill cats," Terry declared. "*Must* be men here. Hark!"

We had heard something: something not in the least like a birdsong, and very much like a suppressed whisper of laughter—a little happy sound, instantly smothered. We stood like so many pointers, and then used our glasses, swiftly, carefully.

"It couldn't have been far off," said Terry excitedly. "How about this big tree?"

There was a very large and beautiful tree in the glade we had just entered, with thick wide-spreading branches that sloped out in lapping fans like a beech or pine. It was trimmed underneath some twenty feet up, and stood there like a huge umbrella, with circling seats beneath.

"Look," he pursued. "There are short stumps of branches left to climb on. There's someone up that tree, I believe."

We stole near, cautiously.

"Look out for a poisoned arrow in your eye," I suggested, but Terry pressed forward, sprang up on the seat-back, and grasped the trunk. "In my heart, more likely," he answered. "Gee! Look, boys!"

We rushed close in and looked up. There among the boughs overhead was something—more than one something—that clung motionless, close to the great trunk at first, and then, as one and all we started up the tree, separated into three swift-moving figures and fled upward. As we climbed we could catch glimpses of them scattering above us. By the time we had reached about as far as three men together dared push, they had left the main trunk and moved outward, each one balanced on a long branch that dipped and swayed beneath the weight.

We paused uncertain. If we pursued further, the boughs would break under the double burden. We might shake them off, perhaps, but none of us was so inclined. In the soft dappled light of these high regions, breathless with our rapid climb, we rested awhile, eagerly studying our objects of pursuit; while they in turn, with no more terror than a set of frolicsome children in a game of tag, sat as lightly as so many big bright birds on their precarious perches and frankly, curiously, stared at us.

"Girls!" whispered Jeff, under his breath, as if they might fly if he spoke aloud.

"Peaches!" added Terry, scarcely louder. "Peacherinos—apricot-nectarines! Whew!"

They were girls, of course, no boys could ever have shown that sparkling beauty, and yet none of us was certain at first.

We saw short hair, hatless, loose, and shining; a suit of some light firm stuff, the closest of tunics and kneebreeches, met by trim gaiters. As bright and smooth as parrots and as unaware of danger, they swung there before us, wholly at ease, staring as we stared, till first one, and then all of them burst into peals of delighted laughter.

Then there was a torrent of soft talk tossed back and forth; no savage sing-song, but clear musical fluent speech.

We met their laughter cordially, and doffed our hats to them, at which they laughed again, delightedly.

Then Terry, wholly in his element, made a polite speech, with explanatory gestures, and proceeded to introduce us, with pointing finger. "Mr. Jeff Margrave," he said clearly; Jeff bowed as gracefully as a man could in the fork of a great limb. "Mr. Vandyck Jennings"—I also tried to make an effective salute and nearly lost my balance.

Then Terry laid his hand upon his chest—a fine chest he had, too, and introduced himself; he was braced carefully for the occasion and achieved an excellent obeisance.

Again they laughed delightedly, and the one nearest me followed his tactics.

"Celis," she said distinctly, pointing to the one in blue; "Alima"—the one in rose; then, with a vivid imitation of Terry's impressive manner, she laid a firm delicate hand on her gold-green jerkin—"Ellador." This was pleasant, but we got no nearer.

"We can't sit here and learn the language," Terry protested. He beckoned to them to come nearer, most winningly—but they gaily shook their heads.

He suggested, by signs, that we all go down together; but again they shook their heads, still merrily. Then Ellador clearly indicated that we should go down, pointing to each and all of us, with unmistakable firmness; and further seeming to imply by the sweep of a lithe arm that we not only go downward, but go away altogether—at which we shook our heads in turn.

"Have to use bait," grinned Terry. "I don't know about you fellows, but I came prepared." He produced from an inner pocket a little box of purple velvet, that opened with a snap—and out of it he drew a long sparkling thing, a necklace of big varicolored stones that would have been worth a million if real ones. He held it up, swung it, glittering in the sun, offered it first to one, then to another, holding it out as far as he could reach toward the girl nearest him. He stood braced in the fork, held firmly by one hand—the other, swinging his bright temptation, reached far out along the bough, but not quite to his full stretch.

She was visibly moved, I noted, hesitated, spoke to her companions. They chattered softly together, one evidently warning her, the other encouraging. Then, softly and slowly, she drew nearer. This was Alima, a tall long-limbed lass, well-knit and evidently both strong and agile. Her eyes were splendid, wide, fearless, as free from suspicion as a child's who has never been rebuked. Her interest was more that of an intent boy playing a fascinating game than of a girl lured by an ornament.

The others moved a bit farther out, holding firmly, watching. Terry's smile was irreproachable, but I did not like the look in his eyes—it was like a creature about to spring. I could already see it happen—the dropped necklace, the sudden clutching hand, the girl's sharp cry as he seized her and drew her in. But it didn't happen. She made a timid reach with her right hand for the gay swinging thing—he held it a little nearer—then, swift as light, she seized it from him with her left, and dropped on the instant to the bough below.

He made his snatch, quite vainly, almost losing his position as his hand clutched only air; and then, with inconceivable rapidity, the three bright creatures were gone. They dropped from the ends of the big boughs to those below, fairly pouring themselves off the tree, while we climbed downward as swiftly as we could. We heard their vanishing gay laughter, we saw them fleeting away in the wide open reaches of the forest, and gave chase, but we might as well have chased wild antelopes; so we stopped at length somewhat breathless.

"No use," gasped Terry. "They got away with it. My word! The men of this country must be good sprinters!"

"Inhabitants evidently arboreal," I grimly suggested. "Civilized and still arboreal—peculiar people."

"You shouldn't have tried that way," Jeff protested. "They were perfectly friendly; now we've scared them."

But it was no use grumbling, and Terry refused to admit any mistake. "Nonsense," he said. "They expected it. Women like to be run after. Come on, let's get to that town; maybe we'll find them there. Let's see, it was in this direction and not far from the woods, as I remember."

When we reached the edge of the open country we reconnoitered with our field glasses. There it was, about four miles off, the same town, we concluded, unless, as Jeff ventured, they all had pink houses. The broad green fields and closely cultivated gardens sloped away at our feet, a long easy slant, with good roads winding pleasantly here and there, and narrower paths besides.

"Look at that!" cried Jeff suddenly. "There they go!"

Sure enough, close to the town, across a wide meadow, three bright-hued figures were running swiftly.

"How could they have got that far in this time? It can't be the same ones," I urged. But through the glasses we could identify our pretty tree-climbers quite plainly, at least by costume.

Terry watched them, we all did for that matter, till they disappeared among the houses. Then he put down his glass and turned to us, drawing a long breath. "Mother of Mike, boys—what Gorgeous Girls! To climb like that! to run like that! and afraid of nothing. This country suits me all right. Let's get ahead."

"Nothing venture, nothing have," I suggested, but Terry preferred "Faint heart ne'er won fair lady."

We set forth in the open, walking briskly. "If there are any men, we'd better keep an eye out," I suggested, but Jeff seemed lost in heavenly dreams, and Terry in highly practical plans.

"What a perfect road! What a heavenly country! See the flowers, will you?"

This was Jeff, always an enthusiast; but we could agree with him fully.

The road was some sort of hard manufactured stuff, sloped slightly to shed rain, with every curve and grade and gutter as perfect as if it were Europe's best. "No men, eh?" sneered Terry. On either side a double row of trees shaded the footpaths; between the trees bushes or vines, all fruit-bearing, now and then seats and little wayside fountains; everywhere flowers.

"We'd better import some of these ladies and set 'em to parking the United States," I suggested. "Mighty nice place they've got here." We rested a few moments by one of the fountains, tested the fruit that looked ripe, and went on, impressed, for all our gay bravado by the sense of quiet potency which lay about us.

Here was evidently a people highly skilled, efficient, caring for their country as a florist cares for his costliest orchids. Under the soft brilliant blue of that clear sky, in the pleasant shade of those endless rows of trees, we walked unharmed, the placid silence broken only by the birds.

Presently there lay before us at the foot of a long hill the town or village we were aiming for. We stopped and studied it.

Jeff drew a long breath. "I wouldn't have believed a collection of houses could look so lovely," he said.

"They've got architects and landscape gardeners in plenty, that's sure," agreed Terry.

I was astonished myself. You see, I come from California, and there's no country lovelier, but when it comes to towns—! I have often groaned at home to see the offensive mess man made in the face of nature, even though I'm no art sharp, like Jeff. But this place! It was built mostly of a sort of dull rose-colored stone, with here and there some clear white houses; and it lay abroad among the green groves and gardens like a broken rosary of pink coral.

"Those big white ones are public buildings evidently," Terry declared. "This is no savage country, my friend. But no men? Boys, it behooves us to go forward most politely."

The place had an odd look, more impressive as we approached. "It's like an exposition." "It's too pretty to be true." "Plenty of palaces, but where are the homes?" "Oh there are little ones enough—but—." It certainly was different from any towns we had ever seen.

"There's no dirt," said Jeff suddenly. "There's no smoke," he added after a little.

"There's no noise," I offered; but Terry snubbed me—"That's because they are laying low for us; we'd better be careful how we go in there."

Nothing could induce him to stay out, however, so we walked on.

Everything was beauty, order, perfect cleanness, and the pleasantest sense of home over it all. As we neared the center of the town the houses stood thicker, ran together as it were, grew into rambling palaces grouped among parks and open squares, something as college buildings stand in their quiet greens.

And then, turning a corner, we came into a broad paved space and saw before us a band of women standing close together in even order, evidently waiting for us.

We stopped a moment and looked back. The street behind was closed by another band, marching steadily, shoulder to shoulder. We went on—there seemed no other way to go—and presently found ourselves quite surrounded by this close-massed multitude, women, all of them, but—

They were not young. They were not old. They were not, in the girl sense, beautiful. They were not in the least ferocious. And yet, as I looked from face to face, calm, grave, wise, wholly unafraid, evidently assured and determined, I had the funniest feeling—a very early feeling—a feeling that I traced back and back in memory until I caught up with it at last. It was that sense of being hopelessly in the wrong that I had so often felt in early youth when my short legs' utmost effort failed to overcome the fact that I was late to school.

Jeff felt it too; I could see he did. We felt like small boys, very small boys, caught doing mischief in some gracious lady's house. But Terry showed no such consciousness. I saw his quick eyes darting here and there, estimating numbers, measuring distances, judging chances of escape. He examined the close ranks about us, reaching back far on every side, and murmured softly to me, "Every one of 'em over forty as I'm a sinner."

Yet they were not old women. Each was in the full bloom of rosy health, erect, serene, standing sure-footed and light as any pugilist. They had no weapons, and we had, but we had no wish to shoot.

"I'd as soon shoot my aunts," muttered Terry again. "What do they want with us anyhow? They seem to mean business." But in spite of that businesslike aspect, he determined to try his favorite tactics. Terry had come armed with a theory.

He stepped forward, with his brilliant ingratiating smile, and made low obeisance to the women before him. Then he produced another tribute, a broad soft scarf of filmy texture, rich in color and pattern, a lovely thing, even to my eye, and offered it with a deep bow to the tall unsmiling woman who seemed to head the ranks before him. She took it with a gracious nod of acknowledgment, and passed it on to those behind her.

He tried again, this time bringing out a circlet of rhinestones, a glittering crown that should have pleased any woman on earth. He made a brief address, including Jeff and me as partners in his enterprise, and with another bow presented this. Again his gift was accepted and, as before, passed out of sight.

"If they were only younger," he muttered between his teeth. "What on earth is a fellow to say to a regiment of old Colonels like this?"

In all our discussions and speculations we had always unconsciously assumed that the women, whatever else they might be, would be young. Most men do think that way, I fancy.

"Woman" in the abstract is young, and, we assume, charming. As they get older they pass off the stage, somehow, into private ownership mostly, or out of it altogether. But these good ladies were very much on the stage, and yet any one of them might have been a grandmother.

We looked for nervousness—there was none.

For terror, perhaps—there was none.

For uneasiness, for curiosity, for excitement—and all we saw was what might have been a vigilance committee of women doctors, as cool as cucumbers, and evidently meaning to take us to task for being there.

Six of them stepped forward now, one on either side of each of us, and indicated that we were to go with them. We thought it best to accede, at first anyway, and marched along, one of these close at each elbow, and the others in close masses before, behind, on both sides.

A large building opened before us, a very heavy thick-walled impressive place, big, and old-looking; of gray stone, not like the rest of the town.

"This won't do!" said Terry to us, quickly. "We mustn't let them get us in this, boys. All together, now—"

We stopped in our tracks. We began to explain, to make signs pointing away toward the big forest—indicating that we would go back to it—at once.

It makes me laugh, knowing all I do now, to think of us three boys—nothing else; three audacious impertinent boys—butting into an unknown country without any sort of a guard or defense. We seemed to think that if there were men we could fight them, and if there were only women—why, they would be no obstacles at all.

Jeff, with his gentle romantic old-fashioned notions of women as clinging vines. Terry, with his clear decided practical theories that there were two kinds of women—those he wanted and those he didn't; Desirable and Undesirable was his demarcation. The latter as a large class, but negligible—he had never thought about them at all.

And now here they were, in great numbers, evidently indifferent to what he might think, evidently determined on some purpose of their own regarding him, and apparently well able to enforce their purpose.

We all thought hard just then. It had not seemed wise to object to going with them, even if we could have; our one chance was friendliness—a civilized attitude on both sides.

But once inside that building, there was no knowing what these determined ladies might do to us. Even a peaceful detention was not to our minds, and when we named it imprisonment it looked even worse.

So we made a stand, trying to make clear that we preferred the open country. One of them came forward with a sketch of our flier, asking by signs if we were the aerial visitors they had seen.

This we admitted.

They pointed to it again, and to the outlying country, in different directions—but we pretended we did not know where it was, and in truth we were not quite sure and gave a rather wild indication of its whereabouts.

Again they motioned us to advance, standing so packed about the door that there remained but the one straight path open. All around us and behind they were massed solidly—there was simply nothing to do but go forward—or fight.

We held a consultation.

"I never fought with women in my life," said Terry, greatly perturbed, "but I'm not going in there. I'm not going to be—herded in—as if we were in a cattle chute."

"We can't fight them, of course," Jeff urged. "They're all women, in spite of their nondescript clothes; nice women, too; good strong sensible faces. I guess we'll have to go in."

"We may never get out, if we do," I told them. "Strong and sensible, yes; but I'm not so sure about the good. Look at those faces!"

They had stood at ease, waiting while we conferred together, but never relaxing their close attention.

Their attitude was not the rigid discipline of soldiers; there was no sense of compulsion about them. Terry's term of a "vigilance committee" was highly descriptive. They had just the aspect of sturdy burghers, gathered hastily to meet some common need or peril, all moved by precisely the same feelings, to the same end.

Never, anywhere before, had I seen women of precisely this quality. Fishwives and market women might show similar strength, but it was coarse and heavy. These were merely athletic—light and powerful. College professors, teachers, writers—many women showed similar intelligence but often wore a strained nervous look, while these were as calm as cows, for all their evident intellect.

We observed pretty closely just then, for all of us felt that it was a crucial moment.

The leader gave some word of command and beckoned us on, and the surrounding mass moved a step nearer.

"We've got to decide quick," said Terry.

"I vote to go in," Jeff urged. But we were two to one against him and he loyally stood by us. We made one more effort to be let go, urgent, but not imploring. In vain.

"Now for a rush, boys!" Terry said. "And if we can't break 'em, I'll shoot in the air."

Then we found ourselves much in the position of the suffragette trying to get to the Parliament buildings through a triple cordon of London police.

The solidity of those women was something amazing. Terry soon found that it was useless, tore himself loose for a moment, pulled his revolver, and fired upward. As they caught at it, he fired again—we heard a cry—

Instantly each of us was seized by five women, each holding arm or leg or head; we were lifted like children, straddling helpless children, and borne onward, wriggling indeed, but most ineffectually.

We were borne inside, struggling manfully, but held secure most womanfully, in spite of our best endeavors.

So carried and so held, we came into a high inner hall, gray and bare, and were brought before a majestic gray-haired woman who seemed to hold a judicial position.

There was some talk, not much, among them, and then suddenly there fell upon each of us at once a firm hand holding a wetted cloth before mouth and nose—an order of swimming sweetness—anesthesia.

III

A PECULIAR IMPRISONMENT

From a slumber as deep as death, as refreshing as that of a healthy child, I slowly awakened.

It was like rising up, up, up through a deep warm ocean, nearer and nearer to full light and stirring air. Or like the return to consciousness after concussion of the brain. I was once thrown from a horse while on a visit to a wild mountainous country quite new to me, and I can clearly remember the mental experience of coming back to life, through lifting veils of dream. When I first dimly heard the voices of those about me, and saw the shining snowpeaks of that mighty range, I assumed that this too would pass, and I should presently find myself in my own home.

That was precisely the experience of this awakening: receding waves of half-caught swirling vision, memories of home, the steamer, the boat, the airship, the forest—at last all sinking away one after another, till my eyes were wide open, my brain clear, and I realized what had happened.

The most prominent sensation was of absolute physical comfort. I was lying in a perfect bed: long, broad, smooth; firmly soft and level; with the finest linen, some warm light quilt of blanket, and a counterpane that was a joy to the eye. The sheet turned down some fifteen inches, yet I could stretch my feet at the foot of the bed free but warmly covered.

I felt as light and clean as a white feather. It took me some time to conscientiously locate my arms and legs, to feel the vivid sense of life radiate from the wakening center to the extremities.

A big room, high and wide, with many lofty windows whose closed blinds let through soft green-lit air; a beautiful room, in proportion, in color, in smooth simplicity; a scent of blossoming gardens outside.

I lay perfectly still, quite happy, quite conscious, and yet not actively realizing what had happened till I heard Terry.

"Gosh!" was what he said.

I turned my head. There were three beds in this chamber, and plenty of room for them.

Terry was sitting up, looking about him, alert as ever. His remark, though not loud, roused Jeff also. We all sat up.

Terry swung his legs out of bed, stood up, stretched himself mightily.

He was in a long nightrobe, a sort of seamless garment, undoubtedly comfortable—we all found ourselves so covered. Shoes were beside each bed, also quite comfortable and good-looking though by no means like our own.

We looked for our clothes—they were not there, nor anything of all the varied contents of our pockets.

A door stood somewhat ajar; it opened into a most attractive bathroom, copiously provided with towels, soap, mirrors, and all such convenient comforts, with indeed our toothbrushes and combs, our notebooks, and thank goodness, our watches—but no clothes.

Then we made a search of the big room again and found a large airy closet, holding plenty of clothing, but not ours.

"A council of war!" demanded Terry. "Come on back to bed—the bed's all right anyhow. Now then, my scientific friend, let us consider our case dispassionately."

He meant me, but Jeff seemed most impressed.

"They haven't hurt us in the least!" he said. "They could have killed us—or—or anything—and I never felt better in my life."

"That argues that they are all women," I suggested, "and highly civilized. You know you hit one in the last scrimmage—I heard her sing out—and we kicked awfully."

Terry was grinning at us. "So you realize what these ladies have done to us?" he pleasantly inquired. "They have taken away all our possessions, all our clothes—every stitch. We have been stripped and washed and put to bed like so many yearling babies—by these highly civilized women."

Jeff actually blushed. He had a poetic imagination. Terry had imagination enough, of a different kind. So had I, also different. I always flattered myself I had the scientific imagination, which, incidentally, I considered the highest sort. One has a right to a certain amount of egotism if founded on fact—and kept to one's self—I think.

"No use kicking, boys," I said. "They've got us, and apparently they're perfectly harmless. It remains for us to cook up some plan of escape like any other bottled heroes. Meanwhile we've got to put on these clothes—Hobson's choice."

The garments were simple in the extreme, and absolutely comfortable, physically, though of course we all felt like supes in the theater. There was a one-piece cotton undergarment, thin and soft, that reached over the knees and shoulders, something like the one-piece pajamas some fellows wear, and a kind of half-hose, that came up to just under the knee and stayed there—had elastic tops of their own, and covered the edges of the first.

Then there was a thicker variety of union suit, a lot of them in the closet, of varying weights and somewhat sturdier material—evidently they would do at a pinch with nothing further. Then there were tunics, knee-length, and some long robes. Needless to say, we took tunics.

We bathed and dressed quite cheerfully.

"Not half bad," said Terry, surveying himself in a long mirror. His hair was somewhat longer than when we left the last barber, and the hats provided were much like those seen on the prince in the fairy tale, lacking the plume.

The costume was similar to that which we had seen on all the women, though some of them, those working in the fields, glimpsed by our glasses when we first flew over, wore only the first two.

I settled my shoulders and stretched my arms, remarking: "They have worked out a mighty sensible dress, I'll say that for them." With which we all agreed.

"Now then," Terry proclaimed, "we've had a fine long sleep—we've had a good bath—we're clothed and in our right minds, though feeling like a lot of neuters. Do you think these highly civilized ladies are going to give us any breakfast?"

"Of course they will," Jeff asserted confidently. "If they had meant to kill us, they would have done it before. I believe we are going to be treated as guests."

"Hailed as deliverers, I think," said Terry.

"Studied as curiosities," I told them. "But anyhow, we want food. So now for a sortie!"

A sortie was not so easy.

The bathroom only opened into our chamber, and that had but one outlet, a big heavy door, which was fastened.

We listened.

"There's someone outside," Jeff suggested. "Let's knock."

So we knocked, whereupon the door opened.

Outside was another large room, furnished with a great table at one end, long benches or couches against the wall, some smaller tables and chairs. All these were solid, strong, simple in structure, and comfortable in use—also, incidentally, beautiful.

This room was occupied by a number of women, eighteen to be exact, some of whom we distinctly recalled.

Terry heaved a disappointed sigh. "The Colonels!" I heard him whisper to Jeff.

Jeff, however, advanced and bowed in his best manner; so did we all, and we were saluted civilly by the tall-standing women.

We had no need to make pathetic pantomime of hunger; the smaller tables were already laid with food, and we were gravely invited to be seated. The tables were set for two; each of us found ourselves placed vis-à-vis with one of our hosts, and each table had five other stalwarts nearby, unobtrusively watching. We had plenty of time to get tired of those women!

The breakfast was not profuse, but sufficient in amount and excellent in quality. We were all too good travelers to object to novelty, and this repast with its new but delicious fruit, its dish of large rich-flavored nuts, and its highly satisfactory little cakes was most agreeable. There was water to drink, and a hot beverage of a most pleasing quality, some preparation like cocoa.

And then and there, willy-nilly, before we had satisfied our appetites, our education began.

By each of our plates lay a little book, a real printed book, though different from ours both in paper and binding, as well, of course, as in type. We examined them curiously.

"Shades of Sauveur!" muttered Terry. "We're to learn the language!"

We were indeed to learn the language, and not only that, but to teach our own. There were blank books with parallel columns, neatly ruled, evidently prepared for the occasion, and in these, as fast as we learned and wrote down the name of anything, we were urged to write our own name for it by its side.

The book we had to study was evidently a schoolbook, one in which children learned to read, and we judged from this, and from their frequent consultation as to methods, that they had had no previous experience in the art of teaching foreigners their language, or of learning any other.

On the other hand, what they lacked in experience, they made up for in genius. Such subtle understanding, such instant recognition of our difficulties, and readiness to meet them, were a constant surprise to us.

Of course, we were willing to meet them halfway. It was wholly to our advantage to be able to understand and speak with them, and as to refusing to teach them—why should we? Later on we did try open rebellion, but only once.

That first meal was pleasant enough, each of us quietly studying his companion, Jeff with sincere admiration, Terry with that highly technical look of his, as of a past master—like a lion tamer, a serpent charmer, or some such professional. I myself was intensely interested.

It was evident that those sets of five were there to check any outbreak on our part. We had no weapons, and if we did try to do any damage, with a chair, say, why five to one was too many for us, even if they were women; that we had found out to our sorrow. It was not pleasant, having them always around, but we soon got used to it.

"It's better than being physically restrained ourselves," Jeff philosophically suggested when we were alone. "They've given us a room—with no great possibility of escape—and personal liberty—heavily chaperoned. It's better than we'd have been likely to get in a man-country."

"Man-Country! Do you really believe there are no men here, you innocent? Don't you know there must be?" demanded Terry.

"Ye—es," Jeff agreed. "Of course—and yet—"

"And yet—what! Come, you obdurate sentimentalist—what are you thinking about?"

"They may have some peculiar division of labor we've never heard of," I suggested. "The men may live in separate towns, or they may have subdued them—somehow—and keep them shut up. But there must be some."

"That last suggestion of yours is a nice one, Van," Terry protested. "Same as they've got us subdued and shut up! You make me shiver."

"Well, figure it out for yourself, anyway you please. We saw plenty of kids, the first day, and we've seen those girls—"

"Real girls!" Terry agreed, in immense relief. "Glad you mentioned 'em. I declare, if I thought there was nothing in the country but those grenadiers I'd jump out the window."

"Speaking of windows," I suggested, "let's examine ours."

We looked out of all the windows. The blinds opened easily enough, and there were no bars, but the prospect was not reassuring.

This was not the pink-walled town we had so rashly entered the day before. Our chamber was high up, in a projecting wing of a sort of castle, built out on a steep spur of rock. Immediately below us were gardens, fruitful and fragrant, but their high walls followed the edge of the cliff which dropped sheer down, we could not see how far. The distant sound of water suggested a river at the foot.

We could look out east, west, and south. To the southeastward stretched the open country, lying bright and fair in the morning light, but on either side, and evidently behind, rose great mountains.

"This thing is a regular fortress—and no women built it, I can tell you that," said Terry. We nodded agreeingly. "It's right up among the hills—they must have brought us a long way."

"We saw some kind of swift-moving vehicles the first day," Jeff reminded us. "If they've got motors, they *are* civilized."

"Civilized or not, we've got our work cut out for us to get away from here. I don't propose to make a rope of bedclothes and try those walls till I'm sure there is no better way."

We all concurred on this point, and returned to our discussion as to the women.

Jeff continued thoughtful. "All the same, there's something funny about it," he urged. "It isn't just that we don't see any men—but we don't see any signs of them. The—the—reaction of these women is different from any that I've ever met."

"There is something in what you say, Jeff," I agreed. "There is a different—atmosphere."

"They don't seem to notice our being men," he went on. "They treat us—well—just as they do one another. It's as if our being men was a minor incident."

I nodded. I'd noticed it myself. But Terry broke in rudely.

"Fiddlesticks!" he said. "It's because of their advanced age. They're all grandmas, I tell you—or ought to be. Great aunts, anyhow. Those girls were girls all right, weren't they?"

"Yes—" Jeff agreed, still slowly. "But they weren't afraid—they flew up that tree and hid, like schoolboys caught out of bounds—not like shy girls."

"And they ran like marathon winners—you'll admit that, Terry," he added.

Terry was moody as the days passed. He seemed to mind our confinement more than Jeff or I did; and he harped on Alima, and how near he'd come to catching her. "If I had—" he would say, rather savagely, "we'd have had a hostage and could have made terms."

But Jeff was getting on excellent terms with his tutor, and even his guards, and so was I. It interested me profoundly to note and study the subtle difference between these women and other women, and try to account for them. In the matter of personal appearance, there was a great difference. They all wore short hair, some few inches at most; some curly, some not; all light and clean and fresh-looking.

"If their hair was only long," Jeff would complain, "they would look so much more feminine."

I rather liked it myself, after I got used to it. Why we should so admire "a woman's crown of hair" and not admire a Chinaman's queue is hard to explain, except that we are so convinced that the long hair "belongs" to a woman. Whereas the "mane" in horses is on both, and in lions, buffalos, and such creatures only on the male. But I did miss it—at first.

Our time was quite pleasantly filled. We were free of the garden below our windows, quite long in its irregular rambling shape, bordering the cliff. The walls were perfectly smooth and high, ending in the masonry of the building; and as I studied the great stones I became convinced that the whole structure was extremely old. It was built like the pre-Incan architecture in Peru, of enormous monoliths, fitted as closely as mosaics.

"These folks have a history, that's sure," I told the others. "And *some* time they were fighters—else why a fortress?"

I said we were free of the garden, but not wholly alone in it. There was always a string of those uncomfortably strong women sitting about, always one of them watching us even if the others were reading, playing games, or busy at some kind of handiwork.

"When I see them knit," Terry said, "I can almost call them feminine."

"That doesn't prove anything," Jeff promptly replied. "Scotch shepherds knit—always knitting."

"When we get out—" Terry stretched himself and looked at the far peaks, "when we get out of this and get to where the real women are—the mothers, and the girls—"

"Well, what'll we do then?" I asked, rather gloomily. "How do you know we'll ever get out?"

This was an unpleasant idea, which we unanimously considered, returning with earnestness to our studies.

"If we are good boys and learn our lessons well," I suggested. "If we are quiet and respectful and polite and they are not afraid of us—then perhaps they will let us out. And anyway—when we do escape, it is of immense importance that we know the language."

Personally, I was tremendously interested in that language, and seeing they had books, was eager to get at them, to dig into their history, if they had one.

It was not hard to speak, smooth and pleasant to the ear, and so easy to read and write that I marveled at it. They had an absolutely phonetic system, the whole thing was as scientific as Esparanto yet bore all the marks of an old and rich civilization.

We were free to study as much as we wished, and were not left merely to wander in the garden for recreation but introduced to a great gymnasium, partly on the roof and partly in the story below. Here we learned real respect for our tall guards. No change of costume was needed for this work, save to lay off outer clothing. The first one was as perfect a garment for exercise as need be devised, absolutely free to move in, and, I had to admit, much better-looking than our usual one.

"Forty—over forty—some of 'em fifty, I bet—and look at 'em!" grumbled Terry in reluctant admiration.

There were no spectacular acrobatics, such as only the young can perform, but for all-around development they had a most excellent system. A good deal of music went with it, with posture dancing and, sometimes, gravely beautiful processional performances.

Jeff was much impressed by it. We did not know then how small a part of their physical culture methods this really was, but found it agreeable to watch, and to take part in.

Oh yes, we took part all right! It wasn't absolutely compulsory, but we thought it better to please.

Terry was the strongest of us, though I was wiry and had good staying power, and Jeff was a great sprinter and hurdler, but I can tell you those old ladies gave us cards and spades. They ran like deer, by which I mean that they ran not as if it was a performance, but as if it was their natural gait. We remembered those fleeting girls of our first bright adventure, and concluded that it was.

They leaped like deer, too, with a quick folding motion of the legs, drawn up and turned to one side with a sidelong twist of the body. I remembered the sprawling spread-eagle way in which some of the fellows used to come over the line—and tried to learn the trick. We did not easily catch up with these experts, however.

"Never thought I'd live to be bossed by a lot of elderly lady acrobats," Terry protested.

They had games, too, a good many of them, but we found them rather uninteresting at first. It was like two people playing solitaire to see who would get it first; more like a race or a—a competitive examination, than a real game with some fight in it.

I philosophized a bit over this and told Terry it argued against their having any men about. "There isn't a man-size game in the lot," I said.

"But they are interesting—I like them," Jeff objected, "and I'm sure they are educational."

"I'm sick and tired of being educated," Terry protested. "Fancy going to a dame school—at our age. I want to Get Out!"

But we could not get out, and we were being educated swiftly. Our special tutors rose rapidly in our esteem. They seemed of rather finer quality than the guards, though all were on terms of easy friendliness. Mine was named Somel, Jeff's Zava, and Terry's Moadine. We tried to generalize from the names, those of the guards, and of our three girls, but got nowhere.

"They sound well enough, and they're mostly short, but there's no similarity of termination—and no two alike. However, our acquaintance is limited as yet."

There were many things we meant to ask—as soon as we could talk well enough. Better teaching I never saw. From morning to night there was Somel, always on call except between two and four; always pleasant with a steady friendly kindness that I grew to enjoy very much. Jeff said Miss Zava—he would put on a title, though they apparently had none—was a darling, that she reminded him of his Aunt Esther at home; but Terry refused to be won, and rather jeered at his own companion, when we were alone.

"I'm sick of it!" he protested. "Sick of the whole thing. Here we are cooped up as helpless as a bunch of three-year-old orphans, and being taught what they think is necessary—whether we like it or not. Confound their old-maid impudence!"

Nevertheless we were taught. They brought in a raised map of their country, beautifully made, and increased our knowledge of geographical terms; but when we inquired for information as to the country outside, they smilingly shook their heads.

They brought pictures, not only the engravings in the books but colored studies of plants and trees and flowers and birds. They brought tools and various small objects—we had plenty of "material" in our school.

If it had not been for Terry we would have been much more contented, but as the weeks ran into months he grew more and more irritable.

"Don't act like a bear with a sore head," I begged him. "We're getting on finely. Every day we can understand them better, and pretty soon we can make a reasonable plea to be let out—"

"*Let* out!" he stormed. "*Let* out—like children kept after school. I want to Get Out, and I'm going to. I want to find the men of this place and fight!—or the girls—"

"Guess it's the girls you're most interested in," Jeff commented. "What are you going to fight *with*—your fists?"

"Yes—or sticks and stones—I'd just like to!" And Terry squared off and tapped Jeff softly on the jaw. "Just for instance," he said.

"Anyhow," he went on, "we could get back to our machine and clear out."

"If it's there," I cautiously suggested.

"Oh, don't croak, Van! If it isn't there, we'll find our way down somehow—the boat's there, I guess."

It was hard on Terry, so hard that he finally persuaded us to consider a plan of escape. It was difficult, it was highly dangerous, but he declared that he'd go alone if we wouldn't go with him, and of course we couldn't think of that.

It appeared he had made a pretty careful study of the environment. From our end window that faced the point of the promontory we could get a fair idea of the stretch of wall, and the drop below. Also from the roof we could make out more, and even, in one place, glimpse a sort of path below the wall.

"It's a question of three things," he said. "Ropes, agility, and not being seen."

"That's the hardest part," I urged, still hoping to dissuade him. "One or another pair of eyes is on us every minute except at night."

"Therefore we must do it at night," he answered. "That's easy."

"We've got to think that if they catch us we may not be so well treated afterward," said Jeff.

"That's the business risk we must take. I'm going—if I break my neck." There was no changing him.

The rope problem was not easy. Something strong enough to hold a man and long enough to let us down into the garden, and then down over the wall. There were plenty of strong ropes in the gymnasium—they seemed to love to swing and climb on them—but we were never there by ourselves.

We should have to piece it out from our bedding, rugs, and garments, and moreover, we should have to do it after we were shut in for the night, for every day the place was cleaned to perfection by two of our guardians.

We had no shears, no knives, but Terry was resourceful. "These Jennies have glass and china, you see. We'll break a glass from the bathroom and use that. 'Love will find out a way,'" he hummed. "When we're all out of the window, we'll stand three-man high and cut the rope as far up as we can reach, so as to have more for the wall. I know just where I saw that bit of path below, and there's a big tree there, too, or a vine or something—I saw the leaves."

It seemed a crazy risk to take, but this was, in a way, Terry's expedition, and we were all tired of our imprisonment.

So we waited for full moon, retired early, and spent an anxious hour or two in the unskilled manufacture of man-strong ropes.

To retire into the depths of the closet, muffle a glass in thick cloth, and break it without noise was not difficult, and broken glass will cut, though not as deftly as a pair of scissors.

The broad moonlight streamed in through four of our windows—we had not dared leave our lights on too long—and we worked hard and fast at our task of destruction.

Hangings, rugs, robes, towels, as well as bed-furniture—even the mattress covers—we left not one stitch upon another, as Jeff put it.

Then at an end window, as less liable to observation, we fastened one end of our cable, strongly, to the firm-set hinge of the inner blind, and dropped our coiled bundle of rope softly over.

"This part's easy enough—I'll come last, so as to cut the rope," said Terry.

So I slipped down first, and stood, well braced against the wall; then Jeff on my shoulders, then Terry, who shook us a little as he sawed through the cord above his head. Then I slowly dropped to the ground, Jeff following, and at last we all three stood safe in the garden, with most of our rope with us.

"Good-bye, Grandma!" whispered Terry, under his breath, and we crept softly toward the wall, taking advantage of the shadow of every bush and tree. He had been foresighted enough to mark the very spot, only a scratch of stone on stone, but we could see to read in that light. For anchorage there was a tough, fair-sized shrub close to the wall.

"Now I'll climb up on you two again and go over first," said Terry. "That'll hold the rope firm till you both get up on top. Then I'll go down to the end. If I can get off safely, you can see me and follow—or, say, I'll twitch it three times. If I find there's absolutely no footing—why I'll climb up again, that's all. I don't think they'll kill us."

From the top he reconnoitered carefully, waved his hand, and whispered, "OK," then slipped over. Jeff climbed up and I followed, and we rather shivered to see how far down that swaying, wavering figure dropped, hand under hand, till it disappeared in a mass of foliage far below.

Then there were three quick pulls, and Jeff and I, not without a joyous sense of recovered freedom, successfully followed our leader.

IV

OUR VENTURE

We were standing on a narrow, irregular, all too slanting little ledge, and should doubtless have ignominiously slipped off and broken our rash necks but for the vine. This was a thick-leaved, wide-spreading thing, a little like Amphelopsis.

"It's not quite vertical here, you see," said Terry, full of pride and enthusiasm. "This thing never would hold our direct weight, but I think if we sort of slide down on it, one at a time, sticking in with hands and feet, we'll reach that next ledge alive."

"As we do not wish to get up our rope again—and can't comfortably stay here—I approve," said Jeff solemnly.

Terry slid down first—said he'd show us how a Christian meets his death. Luck was with us. We had put on the thickest of those intermediate suits, leaving our tunics behind, and made this scramble quite successfully, though I got a pretty heavy fall just at the end, and was only kept on the second ledge by main force. The next stage was down a sort of "chimney"—a long irregular fissure; and so with scratches many and painful and bruises not a few, we finally reached the stream.

It was darker there, but we felt it highly necessary to put as much distance as possible behind us; so we waded, jumped, and clambered down that rocky riverbed, in the flickering black and white moonlight and leaf shadow, till growing daylight forced a halt.

We found a friendly nut-tree, those large, satisfying, soft-shelled nuts we already knew so well, and filled our pockets.

I see that I have not remarked that these women had pockets in surprising number and variety. They were in all their garments, and the middle one in particular was shingled with them. So we stocked up with nuts till we bulged like Prussian privates in marching order, drank all we could hold, and retired for the day.

It was not a very comfortable place, not at all easy to get at, just a sort of crevice high up along the steep bank, but it was well veiled with foliage and dry. After our exhaustive three- or four-hour scramble and the good breakfast food, we all lay down along that crack—heads and tails, as it were—and slept till the afternoon sun almost toasted our faces.

Terry poked a tentative foot against my head.

"How are you, Van? Alive yet?"

"Very much so," I told him. And Jeff was equally cheerful.

We had room to stretch, if not to turn around; but we could very carefully roll over, one at a time, behind the sheltering foliage.

It was no use to leave there by daylight. We could not see much of the country, but enough to know that we were now at the beginning of the cultivated area, and no doubt there would be an alarm sent out far and wide.

Terry chuckled softly to himself, lying there on that hot narrow little rim of rock. He dilated on the discomfiture of our guards and tutors, making many discourteous remarks.

I reminded him that we had still a long way to go before getting to the place where we'd left our machine, and no probability of finding it there; but he only kicked me, mildly, for a croaker.

"If you can't boost, don't knock," he protested. "I never said 'twould be a picnic. But I'd run away in the Antarctic ice fields rather than be a prisoner."

We soon dozed off again.

The long rest and penetrating dry heat were good for us, and that night we covered a considerable distance, keeping always in the rough forested belt of land which we knew bordered the whole country. Sometimes we were near the outer edge, and caught sudden glimpses of the tremendous depths beyond.

"This piece of geography stands up like a basalt column," Jeff said. "Nice time we'll have getting down if they have confiscated our machine!" For which suggestion he received summary chastisement.

What we could see inland was peaceable enough, but only moonlit glimpses; by daylight we lay very close. As Terry said, we did not wish to kill the old ladies—even if we could; and short of that they were perfectly competent to pick us up bodily and carry us back, if discovered. There was nothing for it but to lie low, and sneak out unseen if we could do it.

There wasn't much talking done. At night we had our marathon-obstacle race; we "stayed not for brake and we stopped not for stone," and swam whatever water was too deep to wade and could not be got around; but that was only necessary twice. By day, sleep, sound and sweet. Mighty lucky it was that we could live off the country as we did. Even that margin of forest seemed rich in foodstuffs.

But Jeff thoughtfully suggested that that very thing showed how careful we should have to be, as we might run into some stalwart group of gardeners or foresters or nut-gatherers at any minute. Careful we were, feeling pretty sure that if we did not make good this time we were not likely to have another opportunity; and at last we reached a point from which we could see, far below, the broad stretch of that still lake from which we had made our ascent.

"That looks pretty good to me!" said Terry, gazing down at it. "Now, if we can't find the 'plane, we know where to aim if we have to drop over this wall some other way."

The wall at that point was singularly uninviting. It rose so straight that we had to put our heads over to see the base, and the country below seemed to be a far-off marshy tangle of rank vegetation. We did not have to risk our necks to that extent, however, for at last, stealing along among the rocks and trees like so many creeping savages, we came to that flat space where we had landed; and there, in unbelievable good fortune, we found our machine.

"Covered, too, by jingo! Would you think they had that much sense?" cried Terry.

"If they had that much, they're likely to have more," I warned him, softly. "Bet you the thing's watched."

We reconnoitered as widely as we could in the failing moonlight—moons are of a painfully unreliable nature; but the growing dawn showed us the familiar shape, shrouded in some heavy cloth like canvas, and no slightest sign of any watchman near. We decided to make a quick dash as soon as the light was strong enough for accurate work.

"I don't care if the old thing'll go or not," Terry declared. "We can run her to the edge, get aboard, and just plane down—plop!—beside our boat there. Look there—see the boat!"

Sure enough—there was our motor, lying like a gray cocoon on the flat pale sheet of water.

Quietly but swiftly we rushed forward and began to tug at the fastenings of that cover.

"Confound the thing!" Terry cried in desperate impatience. "They've got it sewed up in a bag! And we've not a knife among us!"

Then, as we tugged and pulled at that tough cloth we heard a sound that made Terry lift his head like a war horse—the sound of an unmistakable giggle, yes—three giggles.

There they were—Celis, Alima, Ellador—looking just as they had when we first saw them, standing a little way off from us, as interested, as mischievous as three schoolboys.

"Hold on, Terry—hold on!" I warned. "That's too easy. Look out for a trap."

"Let us appeal to their kind hearts," Jeff urged. "I think they will help us. Perhaps they've got knives."

"It's no use rushing them, anyhow," I was absolutely holding on to Terry. "We know they can out-run and out-climb us."

He reluctantly admitted this; and after a brief parley among ourselves, we all advanced slowly toward them, holding out our hands in token of friendliness.

They stood their ground till we had come fairly near, and then indicated that we should stop. To make sure, we advanced a step or two and they promptly and swiftly withdrew. So we stopped at the distance specified. Then we used their language, as far as we were able, to explain our plight, telling how we were imprisoned, how we had escaped—a good deal of pantomime here and vivid interest on their part—how we had traveled by night and hidden by day, living on nuts—and here Terry pretended great hunger.

I know he could not have been hungry; we had found plenty to eat and had not been sparing in helping ourselves. But they seemed somewhat impressed; and after a murmured consultation they produced from their pockets certain little packages, and with the utmost ease and accuracy tossed them into our hands.

Jeff was most appreciative of this; and Terry made extravagant gestures of admiration, which seemed to set them off, boy-fashion, to show their skill. While we ate the excellent biscuits they had thrown us, and while Ellador kept a watchful eye on our movements, Celis ran off to some distance, and set up a sort of "duck-on-a-rock" arrangement, a big yellow nut on top of three balanced sticks; Alima, meanwhile, gathering stones.

They urged us to throw at it, and we did, but the thing was a long way off, and it was only after a number of failures, at which those elvish damsels laughed delightedly, that Jeff succeeded in bringing the whole structure to the ground. It took me still longer, and Terry, to his intense annoyance, came third.

Then Celis set up the little tripod again, and looked back at us, knocking it down, pointing at it, and shaking her short curls severely. "No," she said. "Bad—wrong!" We were quite able to follow her.

Then she set it up once more, put the fat nut on top, and returned to the others; and there those aggravating girls sat and took turns throwing little stones at that thing, while one stayed by as a setter-up; and they just popped that nut off, two times out of three, without upsetting the sticks. Pleased as Punch they were, too, and we pretended to be, but weren't.

We got very friendly over this game, but I told Terry we'd be sorry if we didn't get off while we could, and then we begged for knives. It was easy to show what we wanted to do, and they each proudly produced a sort of strong clasp-knife from their pockets.

"Yes," we said eagerly, "that's it! Please—" We had learned quite a bit of their language, you see. And we just begged for those knives, but they would not give them to us. If we came a step too near they backed off, standing light and eager for flight.

"It's no sort of use," I said. "Come on—let's get a sharp stone or something—we must get this thing off."

So we hunted about and found what edged fragments we could, and hacked away, but it was like trying to cut sailcloth with a clamshell.

Terry hacked and dug, but said to us under his breath. "Boys, we're in pretty good condition—let's make a life and death dash and get hold of those girls—we've got to."

They had drawn rather nearer to watch our efforts, and we did take them rather by surprise; also, as Terry said, our recent training had strengthened us in wind and limb, and for a few desperate moments those girls were scared and we almost triumphant.

But just as we stretched out our hands, the distance between us widened; they had got their pace apparently, and then, though we ran at our utmost speed, and much farther than I thought wise, they kept just out of reach all the time.

We stopped breathless, at last, at my repeated admonitions.

"This is stark foolishness," I urged. "They are doing it on purpose—come back or you'll be sorry."

We went back, much slower than we came, and in truth we were sorry.

As we reached our swaddled machine, and sought again to tear loose its covering, there rose up from all around the sturdy forms, the quiet determined faces we knew so well.

"Oh Lord!" groaned Terry. "The Colonels! It's all up—they're forty to one."

It was no use to fight. These women evidently relied on numbers, not so much as a drilled force but as a multitude actuated by a common impulse. They showed no sign of fear, and since we had no weapons whatever and there were at least a hundred of them, standing ten deep about us, we gave in as gracefully as we might.

Of course we looked for punishment—a closer imprisonment, solitary confinement maybe—but nothing of the kind happened. They treated us as truants only, and as if they quite understood our truancy.

Back we went, not under an anesthetic this time but skimming along in electric motors enough like ours to be quite recognizable, each of us in a separate vehicle with one able-bodied lady on either side and three facing him.

They were all pleasant enough, and talked to us as much as was possible with our limited powers. And though Terry was keenly mortified, and at first we all rather dreaded harsh treatment, I for one soon began to feel a sort of pleasant confidence and to enjoy the trip.

Here were my five familiar companions, all good-natured as could be, seeming to have no worse feeling than a mild triumph as of winning some simple game; and even that they politely suppressed.

This was a good opportunity to see the country, too, and the more I saw of it, the better I liked it. We went too swiftly for close observation, but I could appreciate perfect roads, as dustless as a swept floor; the shade of endless lines of trees; the ribbon of flowers that unrolled beneath them; and the rich comfortable country that stretched off and away, full of varied charm.

We rolled through many villages and towns, and I soon saw that the parklike beauty of our first-seen city was no exception. Our swift high-sweeping view from the 'plane had been most attractive, but lacked detail; and in that first day of struggle and capture, we noticed little. But now we were swept along at an easy rate of some thirty miles an hour and covered quite a good deal of ground.

We stopped for lunch in quite a sizable town, and here, rolling slowly through the streets, we saw more of the population. They had come out to look at us everywhere we had passed, but here were more; and when we went in to eat, in a big garden place with little shaded tables among the trees and flowers, many eyes were upon us. And everywhere, open country, village, or city—only women. Old women and young women and a great majority who seemed neither young nor old, but just women; young girls, also, though these, and the children, seeming to be in groups by themselves generally, were less in evidence. We caught many glimpses of girls and children in what seemed to be schools or in playgrounds, and so far as we could judge there were no boys. We all looked, carefully. Everyone gazed at us politely, kindly, and with eager interest. No one was impertinent. We could catch quite a bit of the talk now, and all they said seemed pleasant enough.

Well—before nightfall we were all safely back in our big room. The damage we had done was quite ignored; the beds as smooth and comfortable as before, new clothing and towels supplied. The only thing those women did was to illuminate the gardens at night, and to set an extra watch. But they called us to account next day. Our three tutors, who had not joined in the recapturing expedition, had been quite busy in preparing for us, and now made explanation.

They knew well we would make for our machine, and also that there was no other way of getting down—alive. So our flight had troubled no one; all they did was to call the inhabitants to keep an eye on our movements all along the edge of the forest between the two points. It appeared that many of those nights we had been seen, by careful ladies sitting snugly in big trees by the riverbed, or up among the rocks.

Terry looked immensely disgusted, but it struck me as extremely funny.

Here we had been risking our lives, hiding and prowling like outlaws, living on nuts and fruit, getting wet and cold at night, and dry and hot by day, and all the while these estimable women had just been waiting for us to come out.

Now they began to explain, carefully using such words as we could understand. It appeared that we were considered as guests of the country—sort of public wards. Our first violence had made it necessary to keep us safeguarded for a while, but as soon as we learned the language—and would agree to do no harm—they would show us all about the land.

Jeff was eager to reassure them. Of course he did not tell on Terry, but he made it clear that he was ashamed of himself, and that he would now conform. As to the language—we all fell upon it with redoubled energy. They brought us books, in greater numbers, and I began to study them seriously.

"Pretty punk literature," Terry burst forth one day, when we were in the privacy of our own room. "Of course one expects to begin on child-stories, but I would like something more interesting now."

"Can't expect stirring romance and wild adventure without men, can you?" I asked. Nothing irritated Terry more than to have us assume that there were no men; but there were no signs of them in the books they gave us, or the pictures.

"Shut up!" he growled. "What infernal nonsense you talk! I'm going to ask 'em outright—we know enough now."

In truth we had been using our best efforts to master the language, and were able to read fluently and to discuss what we read with considerable ease.

That afternoon we were all sitting together on the roof—we three and the tutors gathered about a table, no guards about. We had been made to understand some time earlier that if we would agree to do no violence they would withdraw their constant attendance, and we promised most willingly.

So there we sat, at ease; all in similar dress; our hair, by now, as long as theirs, only our beards to distinguish us. We did not want those beards, but had so far been unable to induce them to give us any cutting instruments.

"Ladies," Terry began, out of a clear sky, as it were, "are there no men in this country?"

"Men?" Somel answered. "Like you?"

"Yes, men," Terry indicated his beard, and threw back his broad shoulders. "Men, real men."

"No," she answered quietly. "There are no men in this country. There has not been a man among us for two thousand years."

Her look was clear and truthful and she did not advance this astonishing statement as if it was astonishing, but quite as a matter of fact.

"But—the people—the children," he protested, not believing her in the least, but not wishing to say so.

"Oh yes," she smiled. "I do not wonder you are puzzled. We are mothers—all of us—but there are no fathers. We thought you would ask about that long ago—why have you not?" Her look was as frankly kind as always, her tone quite simple.

Terry explained that we had not felt sufficiently used to the language, making rather a mess of it, I thought, but Jeff was franker.

"Will you excuse us all," he said, "if we admit that we find it hard to believe? There is no such—possibility—in the rest of the world."

"Have you no kind of life where it is possible?" asked Zava.

"Why, yes—some low forms, of course."

"How low—or how high, rather?"

"Well—there are some rather high forms of insect life in which it occurs. Parthenogenesis, we call it—that means virgin birth."

She could not follow him.

"*Birth*, we know, of course; but what is *virgin?*"

Terry looked uncomfortable, but Jeff met the question quite calmly. "Among mating animals, the term *virgin* is applied to the female who has not mated," he answered.

"Oh, I see. And does it apply to the male also? Or is there a different term for him?"

He passed this over rather hurriedly, saying that the same term would apply, but was seldom used.

"No?" she said. "But one cannot mate without the other surely. Is not each then—virgin—before mating? And, tell me, have you any forms of life in which there is birth from a father only?"

"I know of none," he answered, and I inquired seriously.

"You ask us to believe that for two thousand years there have been only women here, and only girl babies born?"

"Exactly," answered Somel, nodding gravely. "Of course we know that among other animals it is not so, that there are fathers as well as mothers; and we see that you are fathers, that you come from a people who are of both kinds. We have been waiting, you see, for you to be able to speak freely with us, and teach us about your country and the rest of the world. You know so much, you see, and we know only our own land."

In the course of our previous studies we had been at some pains to tell them about the big world outside, to draw sketches, maps, to make a globe, even, out of a spherical fruit, and show the size and relation of the countries, and to tell of the numbers of their people. All this had been scant and in outline, but they quite understood.

I find I succeed very poorly in conveying the impression I would like to of these women. So far from being ignorant, they were deeply wise—that we realized more and more; and for clear reasoning, for real brain scope and power they were A No. 1, but there were a lot of things they did not know.

They had the evenest tempers, the most perfect patience and good nature—one of the things most impressive about them all was the absence of irritability. So far we had only this group to study, but afterward I found it a common trait.

We had gradually come to feel that we were in the hands of friends, and very capable ones at that—but we couldn't form any opinion yet of the general level of these women.

"We want you to teach us all you can," Somel went on, her firm shapely hands clasped on the table before her, her clear quiet eyes meeting ours frankly. "And we want to teach you what we have that is novel and useful. You can well imagine that it is a wonderful event to us, to have men among us—after two thousand years. And we want to know about your women."

What she said about our importance gave instant pleasure to Terry. I could see by the way he lifted his head that it pleased him. But when she spoke of our women—someway I had a queer little indescribable feeling, not like any feeling I ever had before when "women" were mentioned.

"Will you tell us how it came about?" Jeff pursued. "You said 'for two thousand years'—did you have men here before that?"

"Yes," answered Zava.

They were all quiet for a little.

"You should have our full history to read—do not be alarmed—it has been made clear and short. It took us a long time to learn how to write history. Oh, how I should love to read yours!"

She turned with flashing eager eyes, looking from one to the other of us.

"It would be so wonderful—would it not? To compare the history of two thousand years, to see what the differences are—between us, who are only mothers, and you, who are mothers and fathers, too. Of course we see, with our birds, that the father is as useful as the mother, almost. But among insects we find him of less importance, sometimes very little. Is it not so with you?"

"Oh, yes, birds and bugs," Terry said, "but not among animals—have you *no* animals?"

"We have cats," she said. "The father is not very useful."

"Have you no cattle—sheep—horses?" I drew some rough outlines of these beasts and showed them to her.

"We had, in the very old days, these," said Somel, and sketched with swift sure touches a sort of sheep or llama, "and these"—dogs, of two or three kinds, "that that"—pointing to my absurd but recognizable horse.

"What became of them?" asked Jeff.

"We do not want them anymore. They took up too much room—we need all our land to feed our people. It is such a little country, you know."

"Whatever do you do without milk?" Terry demanded incredulously.

"*Milk*? We have milk in abundance—our own."

"But—but—I mean for cooking—for grown people," Terry blundered, while they looked amazed and a shade displeased.

Jeff came to the rescue. "We keep cattle for their milk, as well as for their meat," he explained. "Cow's milk is a staple article of diet. There is a great milk industry—to collect and distribute it."

Still they looked puzzled. I pointed to my outline of a cow. "The farmer milks the cow," I said, and sketched a milk pail, the stool, and in pantomime showed the man milking. "Then it is carried to the city and distributed by milkmen—everybody has it at the door in the morning."

"Has the cow no child?" asked Somel earnestly.

"Oh, yes, of course, a calf, that is."

"Is there milk for the calf and you, too?"

It took some time to make clear to those three sweet-faced women the process which robs the cow of her calf, and the calf of its true food; and the talk led us into a further discussion of the meat business. They heard it out, looking very white, and presently begged to be excused.

V

A UNIQUE HISTORY

It is no use for me to try to piece out this account with adventures. If the people who read it are not interested in these amazing women and their history, they will not be interested at all.

As for us—three young men to a whole landful of women—what could we do? We did get away, as described, and were peacefully brought back again without, as Terry complained, even the satisfaction of hitting anybody.

There were no adventures because there was nothing to fight. There were no wild beasts in the country and very few tame ones. Of these I might as well stop to describe the one common pet of the country. Cats, of course. But such cats!

What do you suppose these Lady Burbanks had done with their cats? By the most prolonged and careful selection and exclusion they had developed a race of cats that did not sing! That's a fact. The most those poor dumb brutes could do was to make a kind of squeak when they were hungry or wanted the door open, and, of course, to purr, and make the various mother-noises to their kittens.

Moreover, they had ceased to kill birds. They were rigorously bred to destroy mice and moles and all such enemies of the food supply; but the birds were numerous and safe.

While we were discussing birds, Terry asked them if they used feathers for their hats, and they seemed amused at the idea. He made a few sketches of our women's hats, with plumes and quills and those various tickling things that stick out so far; and they were eagerly interested, as at everything about our women.

As for them, they said they only wore hats for shade when working in the sun; and those were big light straw hats, something like those used in China and Japan. In cold weather they wore caps or hoods.

"But for decorative purposes—don't you think they would be becoming?" pursued Terry, making as pretty a picture as he could of a lady with a plumed hat.

They by no means agreed to that, asking quite simply if the men wore the same kind. We hastened to assure her that they did not—drew for them our kind of headgear.

"And do no men wear feathers in their hats?"

"Only Indians," Jeff explained. "Savages, you know." And he sketched a war bonnet to show them.

"And soldiers," I added, drawing a military hat with plumes.

They never expressed horror or disapproval, nor indeed much surprise—just a keen interest. And the notes they made!—miles of them!

But to return to our pussycats. We were a good deal impressed by this achievement in breeding, and when they questioned us—I can tell you we were well pumped for information—we told of what had been done for dogs and horses and cattle, but that there was no effort applied to cats, except for show purposes.

I wish I could represent the kind, quiet, steady, ingenious way they questioned us. It was not just curiosity—they weren't a bit more curious about us than we were about them, if as much. But they were bent on understanding our kind of civilization, and their lines of interrogation would gradually surround us and drive us in till we found ourselves up against some admissions we did not want to make.

"Are all these breeds of dogs you have made useful?" they asked.

"Oh—useful! Why, the hunting dogs and watchdogs and sheepdogs are useful—and sleddogs of course!—and ratters, I suppose, but we don't keep dogs for their *usefulness*. The dog is 'the friend of man,' we say—we love them."

That they understood. "We love our cats that way. They surely are our friends, and helpers, too. You can see how intelligent and affectionate they are."

It was a fact. I'd never seen such cats, except in a few rare instances. Big, handsome silky things, friendly with everyone and devotedly attached to their special owners.

"You must have a heartbreaking time drowning kittens," we suggested. But they said, "Oh, no! You see we care for them as you do for your valuable cattle. The fathers are few compared to the mothers, just a few very fine ones in each town; they live quite happily in walled gardens and the houses of their friends. But they only have a mating season once a year."

"Rather hard on Thomas, isn't it?" suggested Terry.

"Oh, no—truly! You see, it is many centuries that we have been breeding the kind of cats we wanted. They are healthy and happy and friendly, as you see. How do you manage with your dogs? Do you keep them in pairs, or segregate the fathers, or what?"

Then we explained that—well, that it wasn't a question of fathers exactly; that nobody wanted a—a mother dog; that, well, that practically all our dogs were males—there was only a very small percentage of females allowed to live.

Then Zava, observing Terry with her grave sweet smile, quoted back at him: "Rather hard on Thomas, isn't it? Do they enjoy it—living without mates? Are your dogs as uniformly healthy and sweet-tempered as our cats?"

Jeff laughed, eyeing Terry mischievously. As a matter of fact we began to feel Jeff something of a traitor—he so often flopped over and took their side of things; also his medical knowledge gave him a different point of view somehow.

"I'm sorry to admit," he told them, "that the dog, with us, is the most diseased of any animal—next to man. And as to temper—there are always some dogs who bite people—especially children."

That was pure malice. You see, children were the—the raison d'etre in this country. All our interlocutors sat up straight at once. They were still gentle, still restrained, but there was a note of deep amazement in their voices.

"Do we understand that you keep an animal—an unmated male animal—that bites children? About how many are there of them, please?"

"Thousands—in a large city," said Jeff, "and nearly every family has one in the country."

Terry broke in at this. "You must not imagine they are all dangerous—it's not one in a hundred that ever bites anybody. Why, they are the best friends of the children—a boy doesn't have half a chance that hasn't a dog to play with!"

"And the girls?" asked Somel.

"Oh—girls—why they like them too," he said, but his voice flatted a little. They always noticed little things like that, we found later.

Little by little they wrung from us the fact that the friend of man, in the city, was a prisoner; was taken out for his meager exercise on a leash; was liable not only to many diseases but to the one destroying horror of rabies; and, in many cases, for the safety of the citizens, had to go muzzled. Jeff maliciously added vivid instances he had known or read of injury and death from mad dogs.

They did not scold or fuss about it. Calm as judges, those women were. But they made notes; Moadine read them to us.

"Please tell me if I have the facts correct," she said. "In your country—and in others too?"

"Yes," we admitted, "in most civilized countries."

"In most civilized countries a kind of animal is kept which is no longer useful—"

"They are a protection," Terry insisted. "They bark if burglars try to get in."

Then she made notes of "burglars" and went on: "because of the love which people bear to this animal."

Zava interrupted here. "Is it the men or the women who love this animal so much?"

"Both!" insisted Terry.

"Equally?" she inquired.

And Jeff said, "Nonsense, Terry—you know men like dogs better than women do—as a whole."

"Because they love it so much—especially men. This animal is kept shut up, or chained."

"Why?" suddenly asked Somel. "We keep our father cats shut up because we do not want too much fathering; but they are not chained—they have large grounds to run in."

"A valuable dog would be stolen if he was let loose," I said. "We put collars on them, with the owner's name, in case they do stray. Besides, they get into fights—a valuable dog might easily be killed by a bigger one."

"I see," she said. "They fight when they meet—is that common?" We admitted that it was.

"They are kept shut up, or chained." She paused again, and asked, "Is not a dog fond of running? Are they not built for speed?" That we admitted, too, and Jeff, still malicious, enlightened them further.

"I've always thought it was a pathetic sight, both ways—to see a man or a woman taking a dog to walk—at the end of a string."

"Have you bred them to be as neat in their habits as cats are?" was the next question. And when Jeff told them of the effect of dogs on sidewalk merchandise and the streets generally, they found it hard to believe.

You see, their country was as neat as a Dutch kitchen, and as to sanitation—

but I might as well start in now with as much as I can remember of the history of this amazing country before further description.

And I'll summarize here a bit as to our opportunities for learning it. I will not try to repeat the careful, detailed account I lost; I'll just say that we were kept in that fortress a good six months all told, and after that, three in a pleasant enough city where—to Terry's infinite disgust—there were only "Colonels" and little children—no young women whatever. Then we were under surveillance for three more—always with a tutor or a guard or both. But those months were pleasant because we were really getting acquainted with the girls. That was a chapter!—or will be—I will try to do justice to it.

We learned their language pretty thoroughly—had to; and they learned ours much more quickly and used it to hasten our own studies.

Jeff, who was never without reading matter of some sort, had two little books with him, a novel and a little anthology of verse; and I had one of those pocket encyclopedias—a fat little thing, bursting with facts. These were used in our education—and theirs. Then as soon as we were up to it, they furnished us with plenty of their own books, and I went in for the history part—I wanted to understand the genesis of this miracle of theirs.

And this is what happened, according to their records.

As to geography—at about the time of the Christian era this land had a free passage to the sea. I'm not saying where, for good reasons. But there was a fairly easy pass through that wall of mountains behind us, and there is no doubt in my mind that these people were of Aryan stock, and were once in contact with the best civilization of the old world. They were "white," but somewhat darker than our northern races because of their constant exposure to sun and air.

The country was far larger then, including much land beyond the pass, and a strip of coast. They had ships, commerce, an army, a king—for at that time they were what they so calmly called us—a bi-sexual race.

What happened to them first was merely a succession of historic misfortunes such as have befallen other nations often enough. They were decimated by war, driven up from their coastline till finally the reduced population, with many of the men killed in battle, occupied this hinterland, and defended it for years, in the mountain passes. Where it was open to any possible attack from below they strengthened the natural defenses so that it became unscalably secure, as we found it.

They were a polygamous people, and a slave-holding people, like all of their time; and during the generation or two of this struggle to defend their mountain home they built the fortresses, such as the one we were held in, and other of their oldest buildings, some still in use. Nothing but earthquakes could destroy such architecture—huge solid blocks, holding by their own weight. They must have had efficient workmen and enough of them in those days.

They made a brave fight for their existence, but no nation can stand up against what the steamship companies call "an act of God." While the whole fighting force was doing its best to defend their mountain pathway, there occurred a volcanic outburst, with some local tremors, and the result was the complete filling up of the pass—their only outlet. Instead of a passage, a new ridge, sheer and high, stood between them and the sea; they were walled in, and beneath that wall lay their whole little army. Very few men were left alive, save the slaves; and these now seized their opportunity, rose in revolt, killed their remaining masters even to the youngest boy, killed the old women too, and the mothers, intending to take possession of the country with the remaining young women and girls.

But this succession of misfortunes was too much for those infuriated virgins. There were many of them, and but few of these would-be masters, so the young women, instead of submitting, rose in sheer desperation and slew their brutal conquerors.

This sounds like Titus Andronicus, I know, but that is their account. I suppose they were about crazy—can you blame them?

There was literally no one left on this beautiful high garden land but a bunch of hysterical girls and some older slave women.

That was about two thousand years ago.

At first there was a period of sheer despair. The mountains towered between them and their old enemies, but also between them and escape. There was no way up or down or out—they simply had to stay there. Some were for suicide, but not the majority. They must have been a plucky lot, as a whole, and they decided to live—as long as they did live. Of course they had hope, as youth must, that something would happen to change their fate.

So they set to work, to bury the dead, to plow and sow, to care for one another.

Speaking of burying the dead, I will set down while I think of it, that they had adopted cremation in about the thirteenth century, for the same reason that they had left off raising cattle—they could not spare the room. They were much surprised to learn that we were still burying—asked our reasons for it, and were much dissatisfied with what we gave. We told them of the belief in the resurrection of the body, and they asked if our God was not as well able to resurrect from ashes as from long corruption. We told them of how people thought it repugnant to have their loved ones burn, and they asked if it was less repugnant to have them decay. They were inconveniently reasonable, those women.

Well—that original bunch of girls set to work to clean up the place and make their living as best they could. Some of the remaining slave women rendered invaluable service, teaching such trades as they knew. They had such records as were then kept, all the tools and implements of the time, and a most fertile land to work in.

There were a handful of the younger matrons who had escaped slaughter, and a few babies were born after the cataclysm—but only two boys, and they both died.

For five or ten years they worked together, growing stronger and wiser and more and more mutually attached, and then the miracle happened—one of these young women bore a child. Of course they all thought there must be a man somewhere, but none was found. Then they decided it must be a direct gift from the gods, and placed the proud mother in the Temple of Maaia—their Goddess of Motherhood—under strict watch. And there, as years passed, this wonder-woman bore child after child, five of them—all girls.

I did my best, keenly interested as I have always been in sociology and social psychology, to reconstruct in my mind the real position of these ancient women. There were some five or six hundred of them, and they were harem-bred; yet for the few preceding generations they had been reared in the atmosphere of such heroic struggle that the stock must have been toughened somewhat. Left alone in that terrific orphanhood, they had clung together, supporting one another and their little sisters, and developing unknown powers in the stress of new necessity. To this pain-hardened and work-strengthened group, who had lost not only the love and care of parents, but the hope of ever having children of their own, there now dawned the new hope.

Here at last was Motherhood, and though it was not for all of them personally, it might—if the power was inherited—found here a new race.

It may be imagined how those five Daughters of Maaia, Children of the Temple, Mothers of the Future—they had all the titles that love and hope and reverence could give—were reared. The whole little nation of women surrounded them with loving service, and waited, between a boundless hope and an equally boundless despair, to see if they, too, would be mothers.

And they were! As fast as they reached the age of twenty-five they began bearing. Each of them, like her mother, bore five daughters. Presently there were twenty-five New Women, Mothers in their own right, and the whole spirit of the country changed from mourning and mere courageous resignation to proud joy. The older women, those who remembered men, died off; the youngest of all the first lot of course died too, after a while, and by that time there were left one hundred and fifty-five parthenogenetic women, founding a new race.

They inherited all that the devoted care of that declining band of original ones could leave them. Their little country was quite safe. Their farms and gardens were all in full production. Such industries as they had were in careful order. The records of their past were all preserved, and for years the older women had spent their time in the best teaching they were capable of, that they might leave to the little group of sisters and mothers all they possessed of skill and knowledge.

There you have the start of Herland! One family, all descended from one mother! She lived to a hundred years old; lived to see her hundred and twenty-five great-granddaughters born; lived as Queen-Priestess-Mother of them all; and died with a nobler pride and a fuller joy than perhaps any human soul has ever known—she alone had founded a new race!

The first five daughters had grown up in an atmosphere of holy calm, of awed watchful waiting, of breathless prayer. To them the longed-for motherhood was not only a personal joy, but a nation's hope. Their twenty-five daughters in turn, with a stronger hope, a richer, wider outlook, with the devoted love and care of all the surviving population, grew up as a holy sisterhood, their whole ardent youth looking forward to their great office. And at last they were left alone; the white-haired First Mother was gone, and this one family, five sisters, twenty-five first cousins, and a hundred and twenty-five second cousins, began a new race.

Here you have human beings, unquestionably, but what we were slow in understanding was how these ultra-women, inheriting only from women, had eliminated not only certain masculine characteristics, which of course we did not look for, but so much of what we had always thought essentially feminine.

The tradition of men as guardians and protectors had quite died out. These stalwart virgins had no men to fear and therefore no need of protection. As to wild beasts—there were none in their sheltered land.

The power of mother-love, that maternal instinct we so highly laud, was theirs of course, raised to its highest power; and a sister-love which, even while recognizing the actual relationship, we found it hard to credit.

Terry, incredulous, even contemptuous, when we were alone, refused to believe the story. "A lot of traditions as old as Herodotus—and about as trustworthy!" he said. "It's likely women—just a pack of women—would have hung together like that! We all know women can't organize—that they scrap like anything—are frightfully jealous."

"But these New Ladies didn't have anyone to be jealous of, remember," drawled Jeff.

"That's a likely story," Terry sneered.

"Why don't you invent a likelier one?" I asked him. "Here *are* the women—

nothing but women, and you yourself admit there's no trace of a man in the country." This was after we had been about a good deal.

"I'll admit that," he growled. "And it's a big miss, too. There's not only no fun without 'em—no real sport—no competition; but these women aren't *womanly*. You know they aren't."

That kind of talk always set Jeff going; and I gradually grew to side with him. "Then you don't call a breed of women whose one concern is motherhood—womanly?" he asked.

"Indeed I don't," snapped Terry. "What does a man care for motherhood—when he hasn't a ghost of a chance at fatherhood? And besides—what's the good of talking sentiment when we are just men together? What a man wants of women is a good deal more than all this 'motherhood'!"

We were as patient as possible with Terry. He had lived about nine months among the "Colonels" when he made that outburst; and with no chance at any more strenuous excitement than our gymnastics gave us—save for our escape fiasco. I don't suppose Terry had ever lived so long with neither Love, Combat, nor Danger to employ his superabundant energies, and he was irritable. Neither Jeff nor I found it so wearing. I was so much interested intellectually that our confinement did not wear on me; and as for Jeff, bless his heart!—he enjoyed the society of that tutor of his almost as much as if she had been a girl—I don't know but more.

As to Terry's criticism, it was true. These women, whose essential distinction of motherhood was the dominant note of their whole culture, were strikingly deficient in what we call "femininity." This led me very promptly to the conviction that those "feminine charms" we are so fond of are not feminine at all, but mere reflected masculinity—developed to please us because they had to please us, and in no way essential to the real fulfillment of their great process. But Terry came to no such conclusion.

"Just you wait till I get out!" he muttered.

Then we both cautioned him. "Look here, Terry, my boy! You be careful! They've been mighty good to us—but do you remember the anesthesia? If you do any mischief in this virgin land, beware of the vengeance of the Maiden Aunts! Come, be a man! It won't be forever."

To return to the history:

They began at once to plan and built for their children, all the strength and intelligence of the whole of them devoted to that one thing. Each girl, of course, was reared in full knowledge of her Crowning Office, and they had, even then, very high ideas of the molding powers of the mother, as well as those of education.

Such high ideals as they had! Beauty, Health, Strength, Intellect, Goodness—for those they prayed and worked.

They had no enemies; they themselves were all sisters and friends. The land was fair before them, and a great future began to form itself in their minds.

The religion they had to begin with was much like that of old Greece—a number of gods and goddesses; but they lost all interest in deities of war and plunder, and gradually centered on their Mother Goddess altogether. Then, as they grew more intelligent, this had turned into a sort of Maternal Pantheism.

Here was Mother Earth, bearing fruit. All that they ate was fruit of motherhood, from seed or egg or their product. By motherhood they were born and by motherhood they lived—life was, to them, just the long cycle of motherhood.

But very early they recognized the need of improvement as well as of mere repetition, and devoted their combined intelligence to that problem—how to make the best kind of people. First this was merely the hope of bearing better ones, and then they recognized that however the children differed at birth, the real growth lay later—through education.

Then things began to hum.

As I learned more and more to appreciate what these women had accomplished, the less proud I was of what we, with all our manhood, had done.

You see, they had had no wars. They had had no kings, and no priests, and no aristocracies. They were sisters, and as they grew, they grew together—not by competition, but by united action.

We tried to put in a good word for competition, and they were keenly interested. Indeed, we soon found from their earnest questions of us that they were prepared to believe our world must be better than theirs. They were not sure; they wanted to know; but there was no such arrogance about them as might have been expected.

We rather spread ourselves, telling of the advantages of competition: how it developed fine qualities; that without it there would be "no stimulus to industry." Terry was very strong on that point.

"No stimulus to industry," they repeated, with that puzzled look we had learned to know so well. "*Stimulus? To industry?* But don't you *like* to work?"

"No man would work unless he had to," Terry declared.

"Oh, no *man!* You mean that is one of your sex distinctions?"

"No, indeed!" he said hastily. "No one, I mean, man or woman, would work without incentive. Competition is the—the motor power, you see."

"It is not with us," they explained gently, "so it is hard for us to understand. Do you mean, for instance, that with you no mother would work for her children without the stimulus of competition?"

No, he admitted that he did not mean that. Mothers, he supposed, would of course work for their children in the home; but the world's work was different—that had to be done by men, and required the competitive element.

All our teachers were eagerly interested.

"We want so much to know—you have the whole world to tell us of, and we have only our little land! And there are two of you—the two sexes—to love and help one another. It must be a rich and wonderful world. Tell us—what is the work of the world, that men do—which we have not here?"

"Oh, everything," Terry said grandly. "The men do everything, with us." He squared his broad shoulders and lifted his chest. "We do not allow our women to work. Women are loved—idolized—honored—kept in the home to care for the children."

"What is 'the home'?" asked Somel a little wistfully.

But Zava begged: "Tell me first, do *no* women work, really?"

"Why, yes," Terry admitted. "Some have to, of the poorer sort."

"About how many—in your country?"

"About seven or eight million," said Jeff, as mischievous as ever.

VI

COMPARISONS ARE ODIOUS

I had always been proud of my country, of course. Everyone is. Compared with the other lands and other races I knew, the United States of America had always seemed to me, speaking modestly, as good as the best of them.

But just as a clear-eyed, intelligent, perfectly honest, and well-meaning child will frequently jar one's self-esteem by innocent questions, so did these women, without the slightest appearance of malice or satire, continually bring up points of discussion which we spent our best efforts in evading.

Now that we were fairly proficient in their language, had read a lot about their history, and had given them the general outlines of ours, they were able to press their questions closer.

So when Jeff admitted the number of "women wage earners" we had, they instantly asked for the total population, for the proportion of adult women, and found that there were but twenty million or so at the outside.

"Then at least a third of your women are—what is it you call them—wage earners? And they are all *poor*. What is *poor*, exactly?"

"Ours is the best country in the world as to poverty," Terry told them. "We do not have the wretched paupers and beggars of the older countries, I assure you. Why, European visitors tell us, we don't know what poverty is."

"Neither do we," answered Zava. "Won't you tell us?"

Terry put it up to me, saying I was the sociologist, and I explained that the laws of nature require a struggle for existence, and that in the struggle the fittest survive, and the unfit perish. In our economic struggle, I continued, there was always plenty of opportunity for the fittest to reach the top, which they did, in great numbers, particularly in our country; that where there was severe economic pressure the lowest classes of course felt it the worst, and that among the poorest of all the women were driven into the labor market by necessity.

They listened closely, with the usual note-taking.

"About one-third, then, belong to the poorest class," observed Moadine gravely. "And two-thirds are the ones who are—how was it you so beautifully put it?—'loved, honored, kept in the home to care for the children.' This inferior one-third have no children, I suppose?"

Jeff—he was getting as bad as they were—solemnly replied that, on the contrary, the poorer they were, the more children they had. That too, he explained, was a law of nature: "Reproduction is in inverse proportion to individuation."

"These 'laws of nature,'" Zava gently asked, "are they all the laws you have?"

"I should say not!" protested Terry. "We have systems of law that go back thousands and thousands of years—just as you do, no doubt," he finished politely.

"Oh no," Moadine told him. "We have no laws over a hundred years old, and most of them are under twenty. In a few weeks more," she continued, "we are going to have the pleasure of showing you over our little land and explaining everything you care to know about. We want you to see our people."

"And I assure you," Somel added, "that our people want to see you."

Terry brightened up immensely at this news, and reconciled himself to the renewed demands upon our capacity as teachers. It was lucky that we knew so little, really, and had no books to refer to, else, I fancy we might all be there yet, teaching those eager-minded women about the rest of the world.

As to geography, they had the tradition of the Great Sea, beyond the mountains; and they could see for themselves the endless thick-forested plains below them—that was all. But from the few records of their ancient condition—not "before the flood" with them, but before that mighty quake which had cut them off so completely—they were aware that there were other peoples and other countries.

In geology they were quite ignorant.

As to anthropology, they had those same remnants of information about other peoples, and the knowledge of the savagery of the occupants of those dim forests below. Nevertheless, they had inferred (marvelously keen on inference and deduction their minds were!) the existence and development of civilization in other places, much as we infer it on other planets.

When our biplane came whirring over their heads in that first scouting flight of ours, they had instantly accepted it as proof of the high development of Some Where Else, and had prepared to receive us as cautiously and eagerly as we might prepare to welcome visitors who came "by meteor" from Mars.

Of history—outside their own—they knew nothing, of course, save for their ancient traditions.

Of astronomy they had a fair working knowledge—that is a very old science; and with it, a surprising range and facility in mathematics.

Physiology they were quite familiar with. Indeed, when it came to the simpler and more concrete sciences, wherein the subject matter was at hand and they had but to exercise their minds upon it, the results were surprising. They had worked out a chemistry, a botany, a physics, with all the blends where a science touches an art, or merges into an industry, to such fullness of knowledge as made us feel like schoolchildren.

Also we found this out—as soon as we were free of the country, and by further study and question—that what one knew, all knew, to a very considerable extent.

I talked later with little mountain girls from the fir-dark valleys away up at their highest part, and with sunburned plains-women and agile foresters, all over the country, as well as those in the towns, and everywhere there was the same high level of intelligence. Some knew far more than others about one thing—they were specialized, of course; but all of them knew more about everything—that is, about everything the country was acquainted with—than is the case with us.

We boast a good deal of our "high level of general intelligence" and our "compulsory public education," but in proportion to their opportunities they were far better educated than our people.

With what we told them, from what sketches and models we were able to prepare, they constructed a sort of working outline to fill in as they learned more.

A big globe was made, and our uncertain maps, helped out by those in that precious yearbook thing I had, were tentatively indicated upon it.

They sat in eager groups, masses of them who came for the purpose, and listened while Jeff roughly ran over the geologic history of the earth, and showed them their own land in relation to the others. Out of that same pocket reference book of mine came facts and figures which were seized upon and placed in right relation with unerring acumen.

Even Terry grew interested in this work. "If we can keep this up, they'll be having us lecture to all the girls' schools and colleges—how about that?" he suggested to us. "Don't know as I'd object to being an Authority to such audiences."

They did, in fact, urge us to give public lectures later, but not to the hearers or with the purpose we expected.

What they were doing with us was like—like—well, say like Napoleon extracting military information from a few illiterate peasants. They knew just what to ask, and just what use to make of it; they had mechanical appliances for disseminating information almost equal to ours at home; and by the time we were led forth to lecture, our audiences had thoroughly mastered a well-arranged digest of all we had previously given to our teachers, and were prepared with such notes and questions as might have intimidated a university professor.

They were not audiences of girls, either. It was some time before we were allowed to meet the young women.

"Do you mind telling what you intend to do with us?" Terry burst forth one day, facing the calm and friendly Moadine with that funny half-blustering air of his. At first he used to storm and flourish quite a good deal, but nothing seemed to amuse them more; they would gather around and watch him as if it was an exhibition, politely, but with evident interest. So he learned to check himself, and was almost reasonable in his bearing—but not quite.

She announced smoothly and evenly: "Not in the least. I thought it was quite plain. We are trying to learn of you all we can, and to teach you what you are willing to learn of our country."

"Is that all?" he insisted.

She smiled a quiet enigmatic smile. "That depends."

"Depends on what?"

"Mainly on yourselves," she replied.

"Why do you keep us shut up so closely?"

"Because we do not feel quite safe in allowing you at large where there are so many young women."

Terry was really pleased at that. He had thought as much, inwardly; but he pushed the question. "Why should you be afraid? We are gentlemen."

She smiled that little smile again, and asked: "Are 'gentlemen' always safe?"

"You surely do not think that any of us," he said it with a good deal of emphasis on the "us," "would hurt your young girls?"

"Oh no," she said quickly, in real surprise. "The danger is quite the other way. They might hurt you. If, by any accident, you did harm any one of us, you would have to face a million mothers."

He looked so amazed and outraged that Jeff and I laughed outright, but she went on gently.

"I do not think you quite understand yet. You are but men, three men, in a country where the whole population are mothers—or are going to be. Motherhood means to us something which I cannot yet discover in any of the countries of which you tell us. You have spoken"—she turned to Jeff, "of Human Brotherhood as a great idea among you, but even that I judge is far from a practical expression?"

Jeff nodded rather sadly. "Very far—" he said.

"Here we have Human Motherhood—in full working use," she went on. "Nothing else except the literal sisterhood of our origin, and the far higher and deeper union of our social growth.

"The children in this country are the one center and focus of all our thoughts. Every step of our advance is always considered in its effect on them—on the race. You see, we are *Mothers*," she repeated, as if in that she had said it all.

"I don't see how that fact—which is shared by all women—constitutes any risk to us," Terry persisted. "You mean they would defend their children from attack. Of course. Any mothers would. But we are not savages, my dear lady; we are not going to hurt any mother's child."

They looked at one another and shook their heads a little, but Zava turned to Jeff and urged him to make us see—said he seemed to understand more fully than we did. And he tried.

I can see it now, or at least much more of it, but it has taken me a long time, and a good deal of honest intellectual effort.

What they call Motherhood was like this:

They began with a really high degree of social development, something like that of Ancient Egypt or Greece. Then they suffered the loss of everything masculine, and supposed at first that all human power and safety had gone too. Then they developed this virgin birth capacity. Then, since the prosperity of their children depended on it, the fullest and subtlest coordination began to be practiced.

I remember how long Terry balked at the evident unanimity of these women—the most conspicuous feature of their whole culture. "It's impossible!" he would insist. "Women cannot cooperate—it's against nature."

When we urged the obvious facts he would say: "Fiddlesticks!" or "Hang your facts—I tell you it can't be done!" And we never succeeded in shutting him up till Jeff dragged in the hymenoptera.

"'Go to the ant, thou sluggard'—and learn something," he said triumphantly. "Don't they cooperate pretty well? You can't beat it. This place is just like an enormous anthill—you know an anthill is nothing but a nursery. And how about bees? Don't they manage to cooperate and love one another? as that precious Constable had it. Just show me a combination of male creatures, bird, bug, or beast, that works as well, will you? Or one of our masculine countries where the people work together as well as they do here! I tell you, women are the natural cooperators, not men!"

Terry had to learn a good many things he did not want to. To go back to my little analysis of what happened:

They developed all this close inter-service in the interests of their children. To do the best work they had to specialize, of course; the children needed spinners and weavers, farmers and gardeners, carpenters and masons, as well as mothers.

Then came the filling up of the place. When a population multiplies by five every thirty years it soon reaches the limits of a country, especially a small one like this. They very soon eliminated all the grazing cattle—sheep were the last to go, I believe. Also, they worked out a system of intensive agriculture surpassing anything I ever heard of, with the very forests all reset with fruit- or nut-bearing trees.

Do what they would, however, there soon came a time when they were confronted with the problem of "the pressure of population" in an acute form. There was really crowding, and with it, unavoidably, a decline in standards.

And how did those women meet it?

Not by a "struggle for existence" which would result in an everlasting writhing mass of underbred people trying to get ahead of one another—some few on top, temporarily, many constantly crushed out underneath, a hopeless substratum of paupers and degenerates, and no serenity or peace for anyone, no possibility for really noble qualities among the people at large.

Neither did they start off on predatory excursions to get more land from somebody else, or to get more food from somebody else, to maintain their struggling mass.

Not at all. They sat down in council together and thought it out. Very clear, strong thinkers they were. They said: "With our best endeavors this country will support about so many people, with the standard of peace, comfort, health, beauty, and progress we demand. Very well. That is all the people we will make."

There you have it. You see, they were Mothers, not in our sense of helpless involuntary fecundity, forced to fill and overfill the land, every land, and then see their children suffer, sin, and die, fighting horribly with one another; but in the sense of Conscious Makers of People. Mother-love with them was not a brute passion, a mere "instinct," a wholly personal feeling; it was—a religion.

It included that limitless feeling of sisterhood, that wide unity in service, which was so difficult for us to grasp. And it was National, Racial, Human—oh, I don't know how to say it.

We are used to seeing what we call "a mother" completely wrapped up in her own pink bundle of fascinating babyhood, and taking but the faintest theoretic interest in anybody else's bundle, to say nothing of the common needs of *all* the bundles. But these women were working all together at the grandest of tasks—they were Making People—and they made them well.

There followed a period of "negative eugenics" which must have been an appalling sacrifice. We are commonly willing to "lay down our lives" for our country, but they had to forego motherhood for their country—and it was precisely the hardest thing for them to do.

When I got this far in my reading I went to Somel for more light. We were as friendly by that time as I had ever been in my life with any woman. A mighty comfortable soul she was, giving one the nice smooth mother-feeling a man likes in a woman, and yet giving also the clear intelligence and dependableness I used to assume to be masculine qualities. We had talked volumes already.

"See here," said I. "Here was this dreadful period when they got far too thick, and decided to limit the population. We have a lot of talk about that among us, but your position is so different that I'd like to know a little more about it.

"I understand that you make Motherhood the highest social service—a sacrament, really; that it is only undertaken once, by the majority of the population; that those held unfit are not allowed even that; and that to be encouraged to bear more than one child is the very highest reward and honor in the power of the state."

(She interpolated here that the nearest approach to an aristocracy they had was to come of a line of "Over Mothers"—those who had been so honored.)

"But what I do not understand, naturally, is how you prevent it. I gathered that each woman had five. You have no tyrannical husbands to hold in check—and you surely do not destroy the unborn—"

The look of ghastly horror she gave me I shall never forget. She started from her chair, pale, her eyes blazing.

"Destroy the unborn—!" she said in a hard whisper. "Do men do that in your country?"

"Men!" I began to answer, rather hotly, and then saw the gulf before me. None of us wanted these women to think that our women, of whom we boasted so proudly, were in any way inferior to them. I am ashamed to say that I equivocated. I told her of certain criminal types of women—perverts, or crazy, who had been known to commit infanticide. I told her, truly enough, that there was much in our land which was open to criticism, but that I hated to dwell on our defects until they understood us and our conditions better.

And, making a wide detour, I scrambled back to my question of how they limited the population.

As for Somel, she seemed sorry, a little ashamed even, of her too clearly expressed amazement. As I look back now, knowing them better, I am more and more and more amazed as I appreciate the exquisite courtesy with which they had received over and over again statements and admissions on our part which must have revolted them to the soul.

She explained to me, with sweet seriousness, that as I had supposed, at first each woman bore five children; and that, in their eager desire to build up a nation, they had gone on in that way for a few centuries, till they were confronted with the absolute need of a limit. This fact was equally plain to all—all were equally interested.

They were now as anxious to check their wonderful power as they had been to develop it; and for some generations gave the matter their most earnest thought and study.

"We were living on rations before we worked it out," she said. "But we did work it out. You see, before a child comes to one of us there is a period of utter exaltation—the whole being is uplifted and filled with a concentrated desire for that child. We learned to look forward to that period with the greatest caution. Often our young women, those to whom motherhood had not yet come, would voluntarily defer it. When that deep inner demand for a child began to be felt she would deliberately engage in the most active work, physical and mental; and even more important, would solace her longing by the direct care and service of the babies we already had."

She paused. Her wise sweet face grew deeply, reverently tender.

"We soon grew to see that mother-love has more than one channel of expression. I think the reason our children are so—so fully loved, by all of us, is that we never—any of us—have enough of our own."

This seemed to me infinitely pathetic, and I said so. "We have much that is bitter and hard in our life at home," I told her, "but this seems to me piteous beyond words—a whole nation of starving mothers!"

But she smiled her deep contented smile, and said I quite misunderstood.

"We each go without a certain range of personal joy," she said, "but remember—we each have a million children to love and serve—our children."

It was beyond me. To hear a lot of women talk about "our children"! But I suppose that is the way the ants and bees would talk—do talk, maybe.

That was what they did, anyhow.

When a woman chose to be a mother, she allowed the child-longing to grow within her till it worked its natural miracle. When she did not so choose she put the whole thing out of her mind, and fed her heart with the other babies.

Let me see—with us, children—minors, that is—constitute about three-fifths of the population; with them only about one-third, or less. And precious—! No sole heir to an empire's throne, no solitary millionaire baby, no only child of middle-aged parents, could compare as an idol with these Herland children.

But before I start on that subject I must finish up that little analysis I was trying to make.

They did effectually and permanently limit the population in numbers, so that the country furnished plenty for the fullest, richest life for all of them: plenty of everything, including room, air, solitude even.

And then they set to work to improve that population in quality—since they were restricted in quantity. This they had been at work on, uninterruptedly, for some fifteen hundred years. Do you wonder they were nice people?

Physiology, hygiene, sanitation, physical culture—all that line of work had been perfected long since. Sickness was almost wholly unknown among them, so much so that a previously high development in what we call the "science of medicine" had become practically a lost art. They were a clean-bred, vigorous lot, having the best of care, the most perfect living conditions always.

When it came to psychology—there was no one thing which left us so dumbfounded, so really awed, as the everyday working knowledge—and practice—they had in this line. As we learned more and more of it, we learned to appreciate the exquisite mastery with which we ourselves, strangers of alien race, of unknown opposite sex, had been understood and provided for from the first.

With this wide, deep, thorough knowledge, they had met and solved the problems of education in ways some of which I hope to make clear later. Those nation-loved children of theirs compared with the average in our country as the most perfectly cultivated, richly developed roses compare with—tumbleweeds. Yet they did not seem "cultivated" at all—it had all become a natural condition.

And this people, steadily developing in mental capacity, in will power, in social devotion, had been playing with the arts and sciences—as far as they knew them—for a good many centuries now with inevitable success.

Into this quiet lovely land, among these wise, sweet, strong women, we, in our easy assumption of superiority, had suddenly arrived; and now, tamed and trained to a degree they considered safe, we were at last brought out to see the country, to know the people.

VII

OUR GROWING MODESTY

Being at last considered sufficiently tamed and trained to be trusted with scissors, we barbered ourselves as best we could. A close-trimmed beard is certainly more comfortable than a full one. Razors, naturally, they could not supply.

"With so many old women you'd think there'd be some razors," sneered Terry. Whereat Jeff pointed out that he never before had seen such complete absence of facial hair on women.

"Looks to me as if the absence of men made them more feminine in that regard, anyhow," he suggested.

"Well, it's the only one then," Terry reluctantly agreed. "A less feminine lot I never saw. A child apiece doesn't seem to be enough to develop what I call motherliness."

Terry's idea of motherliness was the usual one, involving a baby in arms, or "a little flock about her knees," and the complete absorption of the mother in said baby or flock. A motherliness which dominated society, which influenced every art and industry, which absolutely protected all childhood, and gave to it the most perfect care and training, did not seem motherly—to Terry.

We had become well used to the clothes. They were quite as comfortable as our own—in some ways more so—and undeniably better looking. As to pockets, they left nothing to be desired. That second garment was fairly quilted with pockets. They were most ingeniously arranged, so as to be convenient to the hand and not inconvenient to the body, and were so placed as at once to strengthen the garment and add decorative lines of stitching.

In this, as in so many other points we had now to observe, there was shown the action of a practical intelligence, coupled with fine artistic feeling, and, apparently, untrammeled by any injurious influences.

Our first step of comparative freedom was a personally conducted tour of the country. No pentagonal bodyguard now! Only our special tutors, and we got on famously with them. Jeff said he loved Zava like an aunt—"only jollier than any aunt I ever saw"; Somel and I were as chummy as could be—the best of friends; but it was funny to watch Terry and Moadine. She was patient with him, and courteous, but it was like the patience and courtesy of some great man, say a skilled, experienced diplomat, with a schoolgirl. Her grave acquiescence with his most preposterous expression of feeling; her genial laughter, not only with, but, I often felt, at him—though impeccably polite; her innocent questions, which almost invariably led him to say more than he intended—Jeff and I found it all amusing to watch.

He never seemed to recognize that quiet background of superiority. When she dropped an argument he always thought he had silenced her; when she laughed he thought it tribute to his wit.

I hated to admit to myself how much Terry had sunk in my esteem. Jeff felt it too, I am sure; but neither of us admitted it to the other. At home we had measured him with other men, and, though we knew his failings, he was by no means an unusual type. We knew his virtues too, and they had always seemed more prominent than the faults. Measured among women—

our women at home, I mean—he had always stood high. He was visibly popular. Even where his habits were known, there was no discrimination against him; in some cases his reputation for what was felicitously termed "gaiety" seemed a special charm.

But here, against the calm wisdom and quiet restrained humor of these women, with only that blessed Jeff and my inconspicuous self to compare with, Terry did stand out rather strong.

As "a man among men," he didn't; as a man among—I shall have to say, "females," he didn't; his intense masculinity seemed only fit complement to their intense femininity. But here he was all out of drawing.

Moadine was a big woman, with a balanced strength that seldom showed. Her eye was as quietly watchful as a fencer's. She maintained a pleasant relation with her charge, but I doubt if many, even in that country, could have done as well.

He called her "Maud," amongst ourselves, and said she was "a good old soul, but a little slow"; wherein he was quite wrong. Needless to say, he called Jeff's teacher "Java," and sometimes "Mocha," or plain "Coffee"; when specially mischievous, "Chicory," and even "Postum." But Somel rather escaped this form of humor, save for a rather forced "Some 'ell."

"Don't you people have but one name?" he asked one day, after we had been introduced to a whole group of them, all with pleasant, few-syllabled strange names, like the ones we knew.

"Oh yes," Moadine told him. "A good many of us have another, as we get on in life—a descriptive one. That is the name we earn. Sometimes even that is changed, or added to, in an unusually rich life. Such as our present Land Mother—what you call president or king, I believe. She was called Mera, even as a child; that means 'thinker.' Later there was added Du—Du-Mera—the wise thinker, and now we all know her as O-du-mera—great and wise thinker. You shall meet her."

"No surnames at all then?" pursued Terry, with his somewhat patronizing air. "No family name?"

"Why no," she said. "Why should we? We are all descended from a common source—all one 'family' in reality. You see, our comparatively brief and limited history gives us that advantage at least."

"But does not each mother want her own child to bear her name?" I asked.

"No—why should she? The child has its own."

"Why for—for identification—so people will know whose child she is."

"We keep the most careful records," said Somel. "Each one of us has our exact line of descent all the way back to our dear First Mother. There are many reasons for doing that. But as to everyone knowing which child belongs to which mother—why should she?"

Here, as in so many other instances, we were led to feel the difference between the purely maternal and the paternal attitude of mind. The element of personal pride seemed strangely lacking.

"How about your other works?" asked Jeff. "Don't you sign your names to them—books and statues and so on?"

"Yes, surely, we are all glad and proud to. Not only books and statues, but all kinds of work. You will find little names on the houses, on the furniture, on the dishes sometimes. Because otherwise one is likely to forget, and we want to know to whom to be grateful."

"You speak as if it were done for the convenience of the consumer—not the pride of the producer," I suggested.

"It's both," said Somel. "We have pride enough in our work."

"Then why not in your children?" urged Jeff.

"But we have! We're magnificently proud of them," she insisted.

"Then why not sign 'em?" said Terry triumphantly.

Moadine turned to him with her slightly quizzical smile. "Because the finished product is not a private one. When they are babies, we do speak of them, at times, as 'Essa's Lato,' or 'Novine's Amel'; but that is merely descriptive and conversational. In the records, of course, the child stands in her own line of mothers; but in dealing with it personally it is Lato, or Amel, without dragging in its ancestors."

"But have you names enough to give a new one to each child?"

"Assuredly we have, for each living generation."

Then they asked about our methods, and found first that "we" did so and so, and then that other nations did differently. Upon which they wanted to know which method has been proved best—and we had to admit that so far as we knew there had been no attempt at comparison, each people pursuing its own custom in the fond conviction of superiority, and either despising or quite ignoring the others.

With these women the most salient quality in all their institutions was reasonableness. When I dug into the records to follow out any line of development, that was the most astonishing thing—the conscious effort to make it better.

They had early observed the value of certain improvements, had easily inferred that there was room for more, and took the greatest pains to develop two kinds of minds—the critic and inventor. Those who showed an early tendency to observe, to discriminate, to suggest, were given special training for that function; and some of their highest officials spent their time in the most careful study of one or another branch of work, with a view to its further improvement.

In each generation there was sure to arrive some new mind to detect faults and show need of alterations; and the whole corps of inventors was at hand to apply their special faculty at the point criticized, and offer suggestions.

We had learned by this time not to open a discussion on any of their characteristics without first priming ourselves to answer questions about our own methods; so I kept rather quiet on this matter of conscious improvement. We were not prepared to show our way was better.

There was growing in our minds, at least in Jeff's and mine, a keen appreciation of the advantages of this strange country and its management. Terry remained critical. We laid most of it to his nerves. He certainly was irritable.

The most conspicuous feature of the whole land was the perfection of its food supply. We had begun to notice from that very first walk in the forest, the first partial view from our 'plane. Now we were taken to see this mighty garden, and shown its methods of culture.

The country was about the size of Holland, some ten or twelve thousand square miles. One could lose a good many Hollands along the forest-smothered flanks of those mighty mountains. They had a population of about three million—not a large one, but quality is something. Three million is quite enough to allow for considerable variation, and these people varied more widely than we could at first account for.

Terry had insisted that if they were parthenogenetic they'd be as alike as so many ants or aphids; he urged their visible differences as proof that there must be men—somewhere.

But when we asked them, in our later, more intimate conversations, how they accounted for so much divergence without cross-fertilization, they attributed it partly to the careful education, which followed each slight tendency to differ, and partly to the law of mutation. This they had found in their work with plants, and fully proven in their own case.

Physically they were more alike than we, as they lacked all morbid or excessive types. They were tall, strong, healthy, and beautiful as a race, but differed individually in a wide range of feature, coloring, and expression.

"But surely the most important growth is in mind—and in the things we make," urged Somel. "Do you find your physical variation accompanied by a proportionate variation in ideas, feelings, and products? Or, among people who look more alike, do you find their internal life and their work as similar?"

We were rather doubtful on this point, and inclined to hold that there was more chance of improvement in greater physical variation.

"It certainly should be," Zava admitted. "We have always thought it a grave initial misfortune to have lost half our little world. Perhaps that is one reason why we have so striven for conscious improvement."

"But acquired traits are not transmissible," Terry declared. "Weissman has proved that."

They never disputed our absolute statements, only made notes of them.

"If that is so, then our improvement must be due either to mutation, or solely to education," she gravely pursued. "We certainly have improved. It may be that all these higher qualities were latent in the original mother, that careful education is bringing them out, and that our personal differences depend on slight variations in prenatal condition."

"I think it is more in your accumulated culture," Jeff suggested. "And in the amazing psychic growth you have made. We know very little about methods of real soul culture—and you seem to know a great deal."

Be that as it might, they certainly presented a higher level of active intelligence, and of behavior, than we had so far really grasped. Having known in our lives several people who showed the same delicate courtesy and were equally pleasant to live with, at least when they wore their "company manners," we had assumed that our companions were a carefully chosen few. Later we were more and more impressed that all this gentle breeding was breeding; that they were born to it, reared in it, that it was as natural and universal with them as the gentleness of doves or the alleged wisdom of serpents.

As for the intelligence, I confess that this was the most impressive and, to me, most mortifying, of any single feature of Herland. We soon ceased to comment on this or other matters which to them were such obvious commonplaces as to call forth embarrassing questions about our own conditions.

This was nowhere better shown than in that matter of food supply, which I will now attempt to describe.

Having improved their agriculture to the highest point, and carefully estimated the number of persons who could comfortably live on their square miles; having then limited their population to that number, one would think that was all there was to be done. But they had not thought so. To them the country was a unit—it was theirs. They themselves were a unit, a conscious group; they thought in terms of the community. As such, their time-sense was not limited to the hopes and ambitions of an individual life. Therefore, they habitually considered and carried out plans for improvement which might cover centuries.

I had never seen, had scarcely imagined, human beings undertaking such a work as the deliberate replanting of an entire forest area with different kinds of trees. Yet this seemed to them the simplest common sense, like a man's plowing up an inferior lawn and reseeding it. Now every tree bore fruit—edible fruit, that is. In the case of one tree, in which they took especial pride, it had originally no fruit at all—that is, none humanly edible—yet was so beautiful that they wished to keep it. For nine hundred years they had experimented, and now showed us this particularly lovely graceful tree, with a profuse crop of nutritious seeds.

They had early decided that trees were the best food plants, requiring far less labor in tilling the soil, and bearing a larger amount of food for the same ground space; also doing much to preserve and enrich the soil.

Due regard had been paid to seasonable crops, and their fruit and nuts, grains and berries, kept on almost the year through.

On the higher part of the country, near the backing wall of mountains, they had a real winter with snow. Toward the south-eastern point, where there was a large valley with a lake whose outlet was subterranean, the climate was like that of California, and citrus fruits, figs, and olives grew abundantly.

What impressed me particularly was their scheme of fertilization. Here was this little shut-in piece of land where one would have thought an ordinary people would have been starved out long ago or reduced to an annual struggle for life. These careful culturists had worked out a perfect scheme of refeeding the soil with all that came out of it. All the scraps and leavings of their food, plant waste from lumber work or textile industry, all the solid matter from the sewage, properly treated and combined—everything which came from the earth went back to it.

The practical result was like that in any healthy forest; an increasingly valuable soil was being built, instead of the progressive impoverishment so often seen in the rest of the world.

When this first burst upon us we made such approving comments that they were surprised that such obvious common sense should be praised; asked what our methods were; and we had some difficulty in—well, in diverting them, by referring to the extent of our own land, and the—admitted—carelessness with which we had skimmed the cream of it.

At least we thought we had diverted them. Later I found that besides keeping a careful and accurate account of all we told them, they had a sort of skeleton chart, on which the things we said and the things we palpably avoided saying were all set down and studied. It really was child's play for those profound educators to work out a painfully accurate estimate of our conditions—in some lines. When a given line of observation seemed to lead to some very dreadful inference they always gave us the benefit of the doubt, leaving it open to further knowledge. Some of the things we had grown to accept as perfectly natural, or as belonging to our human limitations, they literally could not have believed; and, as I have said, we had all of us joined in a tacit endeavor to conceal much of the social status at home.

"Confound their grandmotherly minds!" Terry said. "Of course they can't understand a Man's World! They aren't human—they're just a pack of Fe-Fe-Females!" This was after he had to admit their parthenogenesis.

"I wish our grandfatherly minds had managed as well," said Jeff. "Do you really think it's to our credit that we have muddled along with all our poverty and disease and the like? They have peace and plenty, wealth and beauty, goodness and intellect. Pretty good people, I think!"

"You'll find they have their faults too," Terry insisted; and partly in self-defense, we all three began to look for those faults of theirs. We had been very strong on this subject before we got there—in those baseless speculations of ours.

"Suppose there is a country of women only," Jeff had put it, over and over. "What'll they be like?"

And we had been cocksure as to the inevitable limitations, the faults and vices, of a lot of women. We had expected them to be given over to what we called "feminine vanity"—"frills and furbelows," and we found they had evolved a costume more perfect than the Chinese dress, richly beautiful when so desired, always useful, of unfailing dignity and good taste.

We had expected a dull submissive monotony, and found a daring social inventiveness far beyond our own, and a mechanical and scientific development fully equal to ours.

We had expected pettiness, and found a social consciousness besides which our nations looked like quarreling children—feeble-minded ones at that.

We had expected jealousy, and found a broad sisterly affection, a fair-minded intelligence, to which we could produce no parallel.

We had expected hysteria, and found a standard of health and vigor, a calmness of temper, to which the habit of profanity, for instance, was impossible to explain—we tried it.

All these things even Terry had to admit, but he still insisted that we should find out the other side pretty soon.

"It stands to reason, doesn't it?" he argued. "The whole thing's deuced unnatural—I'd say impossible if we weren't in it. And an unnatural condition's sure to have unnatural results. You'll find some awful characteristics—see if you don't! For instance—we don't know yet what they do with their criminals—their defectives—their aged. You notice we haven't seen any! There's got to be something!"

I was inclined to believe that there had to be something, so I took the bull by the horns—the cow, I should say!—and asked Somel.

"I want to find some flaw in all this perfection," I told her flatly. "It simply isn't possible that three million people have no faults. We are trying our best to understand and learn—would you mind helping us by saying what, to your minds, are the worst qualities of this unique civilization of yours?"

We were sitting together in a shaded arbor, in one of those eating-gardens of theirs. The delicious food had been eaten, a plate of fruit still before us.

We could look out on one side over a stretch of open country, quietly rich and lovely; on the other, the garden, with tables here and there, far apart enough for privacy. Let me say right here that with all their careful "balance of population" there was no crowding in this country. There was room, space, a sunny breezy freedom everywhere.

Somel set her chin upon her hand, her elbow on the low wall beside her, and looked off over the fair land.

"Of course we have faults—all of us," she said. "In one way you might say that we have more than we used to—that is, our standard of perfection seems to get farther and farther away. But we are not discouraged, because our records do show gain—considerable gain.

"When we began—even with the start of one particularly noble mother—we inherited the characteristics of a long race-record behind her. And they cropped out from time to time—alarmingly. But it is—yes, quite six hundred years since we have had what you call a 'criminal.'

"We have, of course, made it our first business to train out, to breed out, when possible, the lowest types."

"Breed out?" I asked. "How could you—with parthenogenesis?"

"If the girl showing the bad qualities had still the power to appreciate social duty, we appealed to her, by that, to renounce motherhood. Some of the few worst types were, fortunately, unable to reproduce. But if the fault was in a disproportionate egotism—then the girl was sure she had the right to have children, even that hers would be better than others."

"I can see that," I said. "And then she would be likely to rear them in the same spirit."

"That we never allowed," answered Somel quietly.

"Allowed?" I queried. "Allowed a mother to rear her own children?"

"Certainly not," said Somel, "unless she was fit for that supreme task."

This was rather a blow to my previous convictions.

"But I thought motherhood was for each of you—"

"Motherhood—yes, that is, maternity, to bear a child. But education is our highest art, only allowed to our highest artists."

"Education?" I was puzzled again. "I don't mean education. I mean by motherhood not only child-bearing, but the care of babies."

"The care of babies involves education, and is entrusted only to the most fit," she repeated.

"Then you separate mother and child!" I cried in cold horror, something of Terry's feeling creeping over me, that there must be something wrong among these many virtues.

"Not usually," she patiently explained. "You see, almost every woman values her maternity above everything else. Each girl holds it close and dear, an exquisite joy, a crowning honor, the most intimate, most personal, most precious thing. That is, the child-rearing has come to be with us a culture so profoundly studied, practiced with such subtlety and skill, that the more we love our children the less we are willing to trust that process to unskilled hands—even our own."

"But a mother's love—" I ventured.

She studied my face, trying to work out a means of clear explanation.

"You told us about your dentists," she said, at length, "those quaintly specialized persons who spend their lives filling little holes in other persons' teeth—even in children's teeth sometimes."

"Yes?" I said, not getting her drift.

"Does mother-love urge mothers—with you—to fill their own children's teeth? Or to wish to?"

"Why no—of course not," I protested. "But that is a highly specialized craft. Surely the care of babies is open to any woman—any mother!"

"We do not think so," she gently replied. "Those of us who are the most highly competent fulfill that office; and a majority of our girls eagerly try for it—I assure you we have the very best."

"But the poor mother—bereaved of her baby—"

"Oh no!" she earnestly assured me. "Not in the least bereaved. It is her baby still—it is with her—she has not lost it. But she is not the only one to care for it. There are others whom she knows to be wiser. She knows it because she has studied as they did, practiced as they did, and honors their real superiority. For the child's sake, she is glad to have for it this highest care."

I was unconvinced. Besides, this was only hearsay; I had yet to see the motherhood of Herland.

VIII

THE GIRLS OF HERLAND

At last Terry's ambition was realized. We were invited, always courteously and with free choice on our part, to address general audiences and classes of girls.

I remember the first time—and how careful we were about our clothes, and our amateur barbering. Terry, in particular, was fussy to a degree about the cut of his beard, and so critical of our combined efforts, that we handed him the shears and told him to please himself. We began to rather prize those beards of ours; they were almost our sole distinction among those tall and sturdy women, with their cropped hair and sexless costume. Being offered a wide selection of garments, we had chosen according to our personal taste, and were surprised to find, on meeting large audiences, that we were the most highly decorated, especially Terry.

He was a very impressive figure, his strong features softened by the somewhat longer hair—though he made me trim it as closely as I knew how; and he wore his richly embroidered tunic with its broad, loose girdle with quite a Henry V air. Jeff looked more like—well, like a Huguenot Lover; and I don't know what I looked like, only that I felt very comfortable. When I got back to our own padded armor and its starched borders I realized with acute regret how comfortable were those Herland clothes.

We scanned that audience, looking for the three bright faces we knew; but they were not to be seen. Just a multitude of girls: quiet, eager, watchful, all eyes and ears to listen and learn.

We had been urged to give, as fully as we cared to, a sort of synopsis of world history, in brief, and to answer questions.

"We are so utterly ignorant, you see," Moadine had explained to us. "We know nothing but such science as we have worked out for ourselves, just the brain work of one small half-country; and you, we gather, have helped one another all over the globe, sharing your discoveries, pooling your progress. How wonderful, how supremely beautiful your civilization must be!"

Somel gave a further suggestion.

"You do not have to begin all over again, as you did with us. We have made a sort of digest of what we have learned from you, and it has been eagerly absorbed, all over the country. Perhaps you would like to see our outline?"

We were eager to see it, and deeply impressed. To us, at first, these women, unavoidably ignorant of what to us was the basic commonplace of knowledge, had seemed on the plane of children, or of savages. What we had been forced to admit, with growing acquaintance, was that they were ignorant as Plato and Aristotle were, but with a highly developed mentality quite comparable to that of Ancient Greece.

Far be it from me to lumber these pages with an account of what we so imperfectly strove to teach them. The memorable fact is what they taught us, or some faint glimpse of it. And at present, our major interest was not at all in the subject matter of our talk, but in the audience.

Girls—hundreds of them—eager, bright-eyed, attentive young faces; crowding questions, and, I regret to say, an increasing inability on our part to answer them effectively.

Our special guides, who were on the platform with us, and sometimes aided in clarifying a question or, oftener, an answer, noticed this effect, and closed the formal lecture part of the evening rather shortly.

"Our young women will be glad to meet you," Somel suggested, "to talk with you more personally, if you are willing?"

Willing! We were impatient and said as much, at which I saw a flickering little smile cross Moadine's face. Even then, with all those eager young things waiting to talk to us, a sudden question crossed my mind: "What was their point of view? What did they think of us?" We learned that later.

Terry plunged in among those young creatures with a sort of rapture, somewhat as a glad swimmer takes to the sea. Jeff, with a rapt look on his high-bred face, approached as to a sacrament. But I was a little chilled by that last thought of mine, and kept my eyes open. I found time to watch Jeff, even while I was surrounded by an eager group of questioners—as we all were—and saw how his worshipping eyes, his grave courtesy, pleased and drew some of them; while others, rather stronger spirits they looked to be, drew away from his group to Terry's or mine.

I watched Terry with special interest, knowing how he had longed for this time, and how irresistible he had always been at home. And I could see, just in snatches, of course, how his suave and masterful approach seemed to irritate them; his too-intimate glances were vaguely resented, his compliments puzzled and annoyed. Sometimes a girl would flush, not with drooped eyelids and inviting timidity, but with anger and a quick lift of the head. Girl after girl turned on her heel and left him, till he had but a small ring of questioners, and they, visibly, were the least "girlish" of the lot.

I saw him looking pleased at first, as if he thought he was making a strong impression; but, finally, casting a look at Jeff, or me, he seemed less pleased—and less.

As for me, I was most agreeably surprised. At home I never was "popular." I had my girl friends, good ones, but they were friends—nothing else. Also they were of somewhat the same clan, not popular in the sense of swarming admirers. But here, to my astonishment, I found my crowd was the largest.

I have to generalize, of course, rather telescoping many impressions; but the first evening was a good sample of the impression we made. Jeff had a following, if I may call it that, of the more sentimental—though that's not the word I want. The less practical, perhaps; the girls who were artists of some sort, ethicists, teachers—that kind.

Terry was reduced to a rather combative group: keen, logical, inquiring minds, not overly sensitive, the very kind he liked least; while, as for me—I became quite cocky over my general popularity.

Terry was furious about it. We could hardly blame him.

"Girls!" he burst forth, when that evening was over and we were by ourselves once more. "Call those girls!"

"Most delightful girls, I call them," said Jeff, his blue eyes dreamily contented.

"What do *you* call them?" I mildly inquired.

"Boys! Nothing but boys, most of 'em. A standoffish, disagreeable lot at that. Critical, impertinent youngsters. No girls at all."

He was angry and severe, not a little jealous, too, I think. Afterward, when he found out just what it was they did not like, he changed his manner somewhat and got on better. He had to. For, in spite of his criticism, they were girls, and, furthermore, all the girls there were! Always excepting our three!—with whom we presently renewed our acquaintance.

When it came to courtship, which it soon did, I can of course best describe my own—and am least inclined to. But of Jeff I heard somewhat; he was inclined to dwell reverently and admiringly, at some length, on the exalted sentiment and measureless perfection of his Celis; and Terry—Terry made so many false starts and met so many rebuffs, that by the time he really settled down to win Alima, he was considerably wiser. At that, it was not smooth sailing. They broke and quarreled, over and over; he would rush off to console himself with some other fair one—the other fair one would have none of him—and he would drift back to Alima, becoming more and more devoted each time.

She never gave an inch. A big, handsome creature, rather exceptionally strong even in that race of strong women, with a proud head and sweeping level brows that lined across above her dark eager eyes like the wide wings of a soaring hawk.

I was good friends with all three of them but best of all with Ellador, long before that feeling changed, for both of us.

From her, and from Somel, who talked very freely with me, I learned at last something of the viewpoint of Herland toward its visitors.

Here they were, isolated, happy, contented, when the booming buzz of our biplane tore the air above them.

Everybody heard it—saw it—for miles and miles, word flashed all over the country, and a council was held in every town and village.

And this was their rapid determination:

"From another country. Probably men. Evidently highly civilized. Doubtless possessed of much valuable knowledge. May be dangerous. Catch them if possible; tame and train them if necessary This may be a chance to re-establish a bi-sexual state for our people."

They were not afraid of us—three million highly intelligent women—or two million, counting only grown-ups—were not likely to be afraid of three young men. We thought of them as "Women," and therefore timid; but it was two thousand years since they had had anything to be afraid of, and certainly more than one thousand since they had outgrown the feeling.

We thought—at least Terry did—that we could have our pick of them. They thought—very cautiously and farsightedly—of picking us, if it seemed wise.

All that time we were in training they studied us, analyzed us, prepared reports about us, and this information was widely disseminated all about the land.

Not a girl in that country had not been learning for months as much as could be gathered about our country, our culture, our personal characters. No wonder their questions were hard to answer. But I am sorry to say, when we were at last brought out and—exhibited (I hate to call it that, but that's what it was), there was no rush of takers. Here was poor old Terry fondly imagining that at last he was free to stray in "a rosebud garden of girls"—and behold! the rosebuds were all with keen appraising eye, studying us.

They were interested, profoundly interested, but it was not the kind of interest we were looking for.

To get an idea of their attitude you have to hold in mind their extremely high sense of solidarity. They were not each choosing a lover; they hadn't the faintest idea of love—sex-love, that is. These girls—to each of whom motherhood was a lodestar, and that motherhood exalted above a mere personal function, looked forward to as the highest social service, as the sacrament of a lifetime—were now confronted with an opportunity to make the great step of changing their whole status, of reverting to their earlier bi-sexual order of nature.

Beside this underlying consideration there was the limitless interest and curiosity in our civilization, purely impersonal, and held by an order of mind beside which we were like—schoolboys.

It was small wonder that our lectures were not a success; and none at all that our, or at least Terry's, advances were so ill received. The reason for my own comparative success was at first far from pleasing to my pride.

"We like you the best," Somel told me, "because you seem more like us."

"More like a lot of women!" I thought to myself disgustedly, and then remembered how little like "women," in our derogatory sense, they were. She was smiling at me, reading my thought.

"We can quite see that we do not seem like—women—to you. Of course, in a bi-sexual race the distinctive feature of each sex must be intensified. But surely there are characteristics enough which belong to People, aren't there? That's what I mean about you being more like us—more like People. We feel at ease with you."

Jeff's difficulty was his exalted gallantry. He idealized women, and was always looking for a chance to "protect" or to "serve" them. These needed neither protection nor service. They were living in peace and power and plenty; we were their guests, their prisoners, absolutely dependent.

Of course we could promise whatsoever we might of advantages, if they would come to our country; but the more we knew of theirs, the less we boasted.

Terry's jewels and trinkets they prized as curios; handed them about, asking questions as to workmanship, not in the least as to value; and discussed not ownership, but which museum to put them in.

When a man has nothing to give a woman, is dependent wholly on his personal attraction, his courtship is under limitations.

They were considering these two things: the advisability of making the Great Change; and the degree of personal adaptability which would best serve that end.

Here we had the advantage of our small personal experience with those three fleet forest girls; and that served to draw us together.

As for Ellador: Suppose you come to a strange land and find it pleasant enough—just a little more than ordinarily pleasant—and then you find rich farmland, and then gardens, gorgeous gardens, and then palaces full of rare and curious treasures—incalculable, inexhaustible, and then—mountains—like the Himalayas, and then the sea.

I liked her that day she balanced on the branch before me and named the trio. I thought of her most. Afterward I turned to her like a friend when we met for the third time, and continued the acquaintance. While Jeff's ultra-devotion rather puzzled Celis, really put off their day of happiness, while Terry and Alima quarreled and parted, re-met and re-parted, Ellador and I grew to be close friends.

We talked and talked. We took long walks together. She showed me things, explained them, interpreted much that I had not understood. Through her sympathetic intelligence I became more and more comprehending of the spirit of the people of Herland, more and more appreciative of its marvelous inner growth as well as outer perfection.

I ceased to feel a stranger, a prisoner. There was a sense of understanding, of identity, of purpose. We discussed—everything. And, as I traveled farther and farther, exploring the rich, sweet soul of her, my sense of pleasant friendship became but a broad foundation for such height, such breadth, such interlocked combination of feeling as left me fairly blinded with the wonder of it.

As I've said, I had never cared very much for women, nor they for me—not Terry-fashion. But this one—

At first I never even thought of her "in that way," as the girls have it. I had not come to the country with any Turkish-harem intentions, and I was no woman-worshipper like Jeff. I just liked that girl "as a friend," as we say. That friendship grew like a tree. She was such a good sport! We did all kinds of things together. She taught me games and I taught her games, and we raced and rowed and had all manner of fun, as well as higher comradeship.

Then, as I got on farther, the palace and treasures and snowy mountain ranges opened up. I had never known there could be such a human being.

So—great. I don't mean talented. She was a forester—one of the best—but it was not that gift I mean. When I say great, I mean great—big, all through. If I had known more of those women, as intimately, I should not have found her so unique; but even among them she was noble. Her mother was an Over Mother—and her grandmother, too, I heard later.

So she told me more and more of her beautiful land; and I told her as much, yes, more than I wanted to, about mine; and we became inseparable. Then this deeper recognition came and grew. I felt my own soul rise and lift its wings, as it were. Life got bigger. It seemed as if I understood—as I never had before—as if I could Do things—as if I too could grow—if she would help me. And then It came—to both of us, all at once.

A still day—on the edge of the world, their world. The two of us, gazing out over the far dim forestland below, talking of heaven and earth and human life, and of my land and other lands and what they needed and what I hoped to do for them—

"If you will help me," I said.

She turned to me, with that high, sweet look of hers, and then, as her eyes rested in mine and her hands too—then suddenly there blazed out between us a farther glory, instant, overwhelming—quite beyond any words of mine to tell.

Celis was a blue-and-gold-and-rose person; Alma, black-and-white-and-red, a blazing beauty. Ellador was brown: hair dark and soft, like a seal coat; clear brown skin with a healthy red in it; brown eyes—all the way from topaz to black velvet they seemed to range—splendid girls, all of them.

They had seen us first of all, far down in the lake below, and flashed the tidings across the land even before our first exploring flight. They had watched our landing, flitted through the forest with us, hidden in that tree and—I shrewdly suspect—giggled on purpose.

They had kept watch over our hooded machine, taking turns at it; and when our escape was announced, had followed along-side for a day or two, and been there at the last, as described. They felt a special claim on us—called us "their men"—and when we were at liberty to study the land and people, and be studied by them, their claim was recognized by the wise leaders.

But I felt, we all did, that we should have chosen them among millions, unerringly.

And yet "the path of true love never did run smooth"; this period of courtship was full of the most unsuspected pitfalls.

Writing this as late as I do, after manifold experiences both in Herland and, later, in my own land, I can now understand and philosophize about what was then a continual astonishment and often a temporary tragedy.

The "long suit" in most courtships is sex attraction, of course. Then gradually develops such comradeship as the two temperaments allow. Then, after marriage, there is either the establishment of a slow-growing, widely based friendship, the deepest, tenderest, sweetest of relations, all lit and warmed by the recurrent flame of love; or else that process is reversed, love cools and fades, no friendship grows, the whole relation turns from beauty to ashes.

Here everything was different. There was no sex-feeling to appeal to, or practically none. Two thousand years' disuse had left very little of the instinct; also we must remember that those who had at times manifested it as atavistic exceptions were often, by that very fact, denied motherhood.

Yet while the mother process remains, the inherent ground for sex-distinction remains also; and who shall say what long-forgotten feeling, vague and nameless, was stirred in some of these mother hearts by our arrival?

What left us even more at sea in our approach was the lack of any sex-tradition. There was no accepted standard of what was "manly" and what was "womanly."

When Jeff said, taking the fruit basket from his adored one, "A woman should not carry anything," Celis said, "Why?" with the frankest amazement. He could not look that fleet-footed, deep-chested young forester in the face and say, "Because she is weaker." She wasn't. One does not call a race horse weak because it is visibly not a cart horse.

He said, rather lamely, that women were not built for heavy work.

She looked out across the fields to where some women were working, building a new bit of wall out of large stones; looked back at the nearest town with its woman-built houses; down at the smooth, hard road we were walking on; and then at the little basket he had taken from her.

"I don't understand," she said quite sweetly. "Are the women in your country so weak that they could not carry such a thing as that?"

"It is a convention," he said. "We assume that motherhood is a sufficient burden—that men should carry all the others."

"What a beautiful feeling!" she said, her blue eyes shining.

"Does it work?" asked Alima, in her keen, swift way. "Do all men in all countries carry everything? Or is it only in yours?"

"Don't be so literal," Terry begged lazily. "Why aren't you willing to be worshipped and waited on? We like to do it."

"You don't like to have us do it to you," she answered.

"That's different," he said, annoyed; and when she said, "Why is it?" he quite sulked, referring her to me, saying, "Van's the philosopher."

Ellador and I talked it all out together, so that we had an easier experience of it when the real miracle time came. Also, between us, we made things clearer to Jeff and Celis. But Terry would not listen to reason.

He was madly in love with Alima. He wanted to take her by storm, and nearly lost her forever.

You see, if a man loves a girl who is in the first place young and inexperienced; who in the second place is educated with a background of caveman tradition, a middle-ground of poetry and romance, and a foreground of unspoken hope and interest all centering upon the one Event; and who has, furthermore, absolutely no other hope or interest worthy of the name—why, it is a comparatively easy matter to sweep her off her feet with a dashing attack. Terry was a past master in this process. He tried it here, and Alima was so affronted, so repelled, that it was weeks before he got near enough to try again.

The more coldly she denied him, the hotter his determination; he was not used to real refusal. The approach of flattery she dismissed with laughter, gifts and such "attentions" we could not bring to bear, pathos and complaint of cruelty stirred only a reasoning inquiry. It took Terry a long time.

I doubt if she ever accepted her strange lover as fully as did Celis and Ellador theirs. He had hurt and offended her too often; there were reservations.

But I think Alima retained some faint vestige of long-descended feeling which made Terry more possible to her than to others; and that she had made up her mind to the experiment and hated to renounce it.

However it came about, we all three at length achieved full understanding, and solemnly faced what was to them a step of measureless importance, a grave question as well as a great happiness; to us a strange, new joy.

Of marriage as a ceremony they knew nothing. Jeff was for bringing them to our country for the religious and the civil ceremony, but neither Celis nor the others would consent.

"We can't expect them to want to go with us—yet," said Terry sagely. "Wait a bit, boys. We've got to take 'em on their own terms—if at all." This, in rueful reminiscence of his repeated failures.

"But our time's coming," he added cheerfully. "These women have never been mastered, you see—" This, as one who had made a discovery.

"You'd better not try to do any mastering if you value your chances," I told him seriously; but he only laughed, and said, "Every man to his trade!"

We couldn't do anything with him. He had to take his own medicine.

If the lack of tradition of courtship left us much at sea in our wooing, we found ourselves still more bewildered by lack of tradition of matrimony.

And here again, I have to draw on later experience, and as deep an acquaintance with their culture as I could achieve, to explain the gulfs of difference between us.

Two thousand years of one continuous culture with no men. Back of that, only traditions of the harem. They had no exact analogue for our word home, any more than they had for our Roman-based family.

They loved one another with a practically universal affection, rising to exquisite and unbroken friendships, and broadening to a devotion to their country and people for which our word patriotism is no definition at all.

Patriotism, red hot, is compatible with the existence of a neglect of national interests, a dishonesty, a cold indifference to the suffering of millions. Patriotism is largely pride, and very largely combativeness. Patriotism generally has a chip on its shoulder.

This country had no other country to measure itself by—save the few poor savages far below, with whom they had no contact.

They loved their country because it was their nursery, playground, and workshop—theirs and their children's. They were proud of it as a workshop, proud of their record of ever-increasing efficiency; they had made a pleasant garden of it, a very practical little heaven; but most of all they valued it—and here it is hard for us to understand them—as a cultural environment for their children.

That, of course, is the keynote of the whole distinction—their children.

From those first breathlessly guarded, half-adored race mothers, all up the ascending line, they had this dominant thought of building up a great race through the children.

All the surrendering devotion our women have put into their private families, these women put into their country and race. All the loyalty and service men expect of wives, they gave, not singly to men, but collectively to one another.

And the mother instinct, with us so painfully intense, so thwarted by conditions, so concentrated in personal devotion to a few, so bitterly hurt by death, disease, or barrenness, and even by the mere growth of the children, leaving the mother alone in her empty nest—all this feeling with them flowed out in a strong, wide current, unbroken through the generations, deepening and widening through the years, including every child in all the land.

With their united power and wisdom, they had studied and overcome the "diseases of childhood"—their children had none.

They had faced the problems of education and so solved them that their children grew up as naturally as young trees; learning through every sense; taught continuously but unconsciously—never knowing they were being educated.

In fact, they did not use the word as we do. Their idea of education was the special training they took, when half grown up, under experts. Then the eager young minds fairly flung themselves on their chosen subjects, and acquired with an ease, a breadth, a grasp, at which I never ceased to wonder.

But the babies and little children never felt the pressure of that "forcible feeding" of the mind that we call "education." Of this, more later.

IX

OUR RELATIONS AND THEIRS

What I'm trying to show here is that with these women the whole relationship of life counted in a glad, eager growing-up to join the ranks of workers in the line best loved; a deep, tender reverence for one's own mother—too deep for them to speak of freely—and beyond that, the whole, free, wide range of sisterhood, the splendid service of the country, and friendships.

To these women we came, filled with the ideas, convictions, traditions, of our culture, and undertook to rouse in them the emotions which—to us—seemed proper.

However much, or little, of true sex-feeling there was between us, it phrased itself in their minds in terms of friendship, the one purely personal love they knew, and of ultimate parentage. Visibly we were not mothers, nor children, nor compatriots; so, if they loved us, we must be friends.

That we should pair off together in our courting days was natural to them; that we three should remain much together, as they did themselves, was also natural. We had as yet no work, so we hung about them in their forest tasks; that was natural, too.

But when we began to talk about each couple having "homes" of our own, they could not understand it.

"Our work takes us all around the country," explained Celis. "We cannot live in one place all the time."

"We are together now," urged Alima, looking proudly at Terry's stalwart nearness. (This was one of the times when they were "on," though presently "off" again.)

"It's not the same thing at all," he insisted. "A man wants a home of his own, with his wife and family in it."

"Staying in it? All the time?" asked Ellador. "Not imprisoned, surely!"

"Of course not! Living there—naturally," he answered.

"What does she do there—all the time?" Alima demanded. "What is her work?"

Then Terry patiently explained again that our women did not work—with reservations.

"But what do they do—if they have no work?" she persisted.

"They take care of the home—and the children."

"At the same time?" asked Ellador.

"Why yes. The children play about, and the mother has charge of it all. There are servants, of course."

It seemed so obvious, so natural to Terry, that he always grew impatient; but the girls were honestly anxious to understand.

"How many children do your women have?" Alima had her notebook out now, and a rather firm set of lip. Terry began to dodge.

"There is no set number, my dear," he explained. "Some have more, some have less."

"Some have none at all," I put in mischievously.

They pounced on this admission and soon wrung from us the general fact that those women who had the most children had the least servants, and those who had the most servants had the least children.

"There!" triumphed Alima. "One or two or no children, and three or four servants. Now what do those women do?"

We explained as best we might. We talked of "social duties," disingenuously banking on their not interpreting the words as we did; we talked of hospitality, entertainment, and various "interests." All the time we knew that to these large-minded women whose whole mental outlook was so collective, the limitations of a wholly personal life were inconceivable.

"We cannot really understand it," Ellador concluded. "We are only half a people. We have our woman-ways and they have their man-ways and their both-ways. We have worked out a system of living which is, of course, limited. They must have a broader, richer, better one. I should like to see it."

"You shall, dearest," I whispered.

"There's nothing to smoke," complained Terry. He was in the midst of a prolonged quarrel with Alima, and needed a sedative. "There's nothing to drink. These blessed women have no pleasant vices. I wish we could get out of here!"

This wish was vain. We were always under a certain degree of watchfulness. When Terry burst forth to tramp the streets at night he always found a "Colonel" here or there; and when, on an occasion of fierce though temporary despair, he had plunged to the cliff edge with some vague view to escape, he found several of them close by. We were free—but there was a string to it.

"They've no unpleasant ones, either," Jeff reminded him.

"Wish they had!" Terry persisted. "They've neither the vices of men, nor the virtues of women—they're neuters!"

"You know better than that. Don't talk nonsense," said I, severely.

I was thinking of Ellador's eyes when they gave me a certain look, a look she did not at all realize.

Jeff was equally incensed. "I don't know what 'virtues of women' you miss. Seems to me they have all of them."

"They've no modesty," snapped Terry. "No patience, no submissiveness, none of that natural yielding which is woman's greatest charm."

I shook my head pityingly. "Go and apologize and make friends again, Terry. You've got a grouch, that's all. These women have the virtue of humanity, with less of its faults than any folks I ever saw. As for patience—they'd have pitched us over the cliffs the first day we lit among 'em, if they hadn't that."

"There are no—distractions," he grumbled. "Nowhere a man can go and cut loose a bit. It's an everlasting parlor and nursery."

"And workshop," I added. "And school, and office, and laboratory, and studio, and theater, and—home."

"Home!" he sneered. "There isn't a home in the whole pitiful place."

"There isn't anything else, and you know it," Jeff retorted hotly. "I never saw, I never dreamed of, such universal peace and good will and mutual affection."

"Oh, well, of course, if you like a perpetual Sunday school, it's all very well. But I like Something Doing. Here it's all done."

There was something to this criticism. The years of pioneering lay far behind them. Theirs was a civilization in which the initial difficulties had long since been overcome. The untroubled peace, the unmeasured plenty, the steady health, the large good will and smooth management which ordered everything, left nothing to overcome. It was like a pleasant family in an old established, perfectly run country place.

I liked it because of my eager and continued interest in the sociological achievements involved. Jeff liked it as he would have liked such a family and such a place anywhere.

Terry did not like it because he found nothing to oppose, to struggle with, to conquer.

"Life is a struggle, has to be," he insisted. "If there is no struggle, there is no life—that's all."

"You're talking nonsense—masculine nonsense," the peaceful Jeff replied. He was certainly a warm defender of Herland. "Ants don't raise their myriads by a struggle, do they? Or the bees?"

"Oh, if you go back to insects—and want to live in an anthill—! I tell you the higher grades of life are reached only through struggle—combat. There's no Drama here. Look at their plays! They make me sick."

He rather had us there. The drama of the country was—to our taste—rather flat. You see, they lacked the sex motive and, with it, jealousy. They had no interplay of warring nations, no aristocracy and its ambitions, no wealth and poverty opposition.

I see I have said little about the economics of the place; it should have come before, but I'll go on about the drama now.

They had their own kind. There was a most impressive array of pageantry, of processions, a sort of grand ritual, with their arts and their religion broadly blended. The very babies joined in it. To see one of their great annual festivals, with the massed and marching stateliness of those great mothers, the young women brave and noble, beautiful and strong; and then the children, taking part as naturally as ours would frolic round a Christmas tree—it was overpowering in the impression of joyous, triumphant life.

They had begun at a period when the drama, the dance, music, religion, and education were all very close together; and instead of developing them in detached lines, they had kept the connection. Let me try again to give, if I can, a faint sense of the difference in the life view—the background and basis on which their culture rested.

Ellador told me a lot about it. She took me to see the children, the growing girls, the special teachers. She picked out books for me to read. She always seemed to understand just what I wanted to know, and how to give it to me.

While Terry and Alima struck sparks and parted—he always madly drawn to her and she to him—she must have been, or she'd never have stood the way he behaved—Ellador and I had already a deep, restful feeling, as if we'd always had one another. Jeff and Celis were happy; there was no question of that; but it didn't seem to me as if they had the good times we did.

Well, here is the Herland child facing life—as Ellador tried to show it to me. From the first memory, they knew Peace, Beauty, Order, Safety, Love, Wisdom, Justice, Patience, and Plenty. By "plenty" I mean that the babies grew up in an environment which met their needs, just as young fawns might grow up in dewy forest glades and brook-fed meadows. And they enjoyed it as frankly and utterly as the fawns would.

They found themselves in a big bright lovely world, full of the most interesting and enchanting things to learn about and to do. The people everywhere were friendly and polite. No Herland child ever met the overbearing rudeness we so commonly show to children. They were People, too, from the first; the most precious part of the nation.

In each step of the rich experience of living, they found the instance they were studying widen out into contact with an endless range of common interests. The things they learned were related, from the first; related to one another, and to the national prosperity.

"It was a butterfly that made me a forester," said Ellador. "I was about eleven years old, and I found a big purple-and-green butterfly on a low flower. I caught it, very carefully, by the closed wings, as I had been told to do, and carried it to the nearest insect teacher"—I made a note there to ask her what on earth an insect teacher was—"to ask her its name. She took it from me with a little cry of delight. 'Oh, you blessed child,' she said. 'Do you like obernuts?' Of course I liked obernuts, and said so. It is our best food-nut, you know. 'This is a female of the obernut moth,' she told me. 'They are almost gone. We have been trying to exterminate them for centuries. If you had not caught this one, it might have laid eggs enough to raise worms enough to destroy thousands of our nut trees—thousands of bushels of nuts—and make years and years of trouble for us.'

"Everybody congratulated me. The children all over the country were told to watch for that moth, if there were any more. I was shown the history of the creature, and an account of the damage it used to do and of how long and hard our foremothers had worked to save that tree for us. I grew a foot, it seemed to me, and determined then and there to be a forester."

This is but an instance; she showed me many. The big difference was that whereas our children grow up in private homes and families, with every effort made to protect and seclude them from a dangerous world, here they grew up in a wide, friendly world, and knew it for theirs, from the first.

Their child-literature was a wonderful thing. I could have spent years following the delicate subtleties, the smooth simplicities with which they had bent that great art to the service of the child mind.

We have two life cycles: the man's and the woman's. To the man there is growth, struggle, conquest, the establishment of his family, and as much further success in gain or ambition as he can achieve.

To the woman, growth, the securing of a husband, the subordinate activities of family life, and afterward such "social" or charitable interests as her position allows.

Here was but one cycle, and that a large one.

The child entered upon a broad open field of life, in which motherhood was the one great personal contribution to the national life, and all the rest the individual share in their common activities. Every girl I talked to, at any age above babyhood, had her cheerful determination as to what she was going to be when she grew up.

What Terry meant by saying they had no "modesty" was that this great life-view had no shady places; they had a high sense of personal decorum, but no shame—no knowledge of anything to be ashamed of.

Even their shortcomings and misdeeds in childhood never were presented to them as sins; merely as errors and misplays—as in a game. Some of them, who were palpably less agreeable than others or who had a real weakness or fault, were treated with cheerful allowance, as a friendly group at whist would treat a poor player.

Their religion, you see, was maternal; and their ethics, based on the full perception of evolution, showed the principle of growth and the beauty of wise culture. They had no theory of the essential opposition of good and evil; life to them was growth; their pleasure was in growing, and their duty also.

With this background, with their sublimated mother-love, expressed in terms of widest social activity, every phase of their work was modified by its effect on the national growth. The language itself they had deliberately clarified, simplified, made easy and beautiful, for the sake of the children.

This seemed to us a wholly incredible thing: first, that any nation should have the foresight, the strength, and the persistence to plan and fulfill such a task; and second, that women should have had so much initiative. We have assumed, as a matter of course, that women had none; that only the man, with his natural energy and impatience of restriction, would ever invent anything.

Here we found that the pressure of life upon the environment develops in the human mind its inventive reactions, regardless of sex; and further, that a fully awakened motherhood plans and works without limit, for the good of the child.

That the children might be most nobly born, and reared in an environment calculated to allow the richest, freest growth, they had deliberately remodeled and improved the whole state.

I do not mean in the least that they stopped at that, any more than a child stops at childhood. The most impressive part of their whole culture beyond this perfect system of child-rearing was the range of interests and associations open to them all, for life. But in the field of literature I was most struck, at first, by the child-motive.

They had the same gradation of simple repetitive verse and story that we are familiar with, and the most exquisite, imaginative tales; but where, with us, these are the dribbled remnants of ancient folk myths and primitive lullabies, theirs were the exquisite work of great artists; not only simple and unfailing in appeal to the child-mind, but true, true to the living world about them.

To sit in one of their nurseries for a day was to change one's views forever as to babyhood. The youngest ones, rosy fatlings in their mothers' arms, or sleeping lightly in the flower-sweet air, seemed natural enough, save that they never cried. I never heard a child cry in Herland, save once or twice at a bad fall; and then people ran to help, as we would at a scream of agony from a grown person.

Each mother had her year of glory; the time to love and learn, living closely with her child, nursing it proudly, often for two years or more. This perhaps was one reason for their wonderful vigor.

But after the baby-year the mother was not so constantly in attendance, unless, indeed, her work was among the little ones. She was never far off, however, and her attitude toward the co-mothers, whose proud child-service was direct and continuous, was lovely to see.

As for the babies—a group of those naked darlings playing on short velvet grass, clean-swept; or rugs as soft; or in shallow pools of bright water; tumbling over with bubbling joyous baby laughter—it was a view of infant happiness such as I had never dreamed.

The babies were reared in the warmer part of the country, and gradually acclimated to the cooler heights as they grew older.

Sturdy children of ten and twelve played in the snow as joyfully as ours do; there were continuous excursions of them, from one part of the land to another, so that to each child the whole country might be home.

It was all theirs, waiting for them to learn, to love, to use, to serve; as our own little boys plan to be "a big soldier," or "a cowboy," or whatever pleases their fancy; and our little girls plan for the kind of home they mean to have, or how many children; these planned, freely and gaily with much happy chattering, of what they would do for the country when they were grown.

It was the eager happiness of the children and young people which first made me see the folly of that common notion of ours—that if life was smooth and happy, people would not enjoy it.

As I studied these youngsters, vigorous, joyous, eager little creatures, and their voracious appetite for life, it shook my previous ideas so thoroughly that they have never been re-established. The steady level of good health gave them all that natural stimulus we used to call "animal spirits"—an odd contradiction in terms. They found themselves in an immediate environment which was agreeable and interesting, and before them stretched the years of learning and discovery, the fascinating, endless process of education.

As I looked into these methods and compared them with our own, my strange uncomfortable sense of race-humility grew apace.

Ellador could not understand my astonishment. She explained things kindly and sweetly, but with some amazement that they needed explaining, and with sudden questions as to how we did it that left me meeker than ever.

I betook myself to Somel one day, carefully not taking Ellador. I did not mind seeming foolish to Somel—she was used to it.

"I want a chapter of explanation," I told her. "You know my stupidities by heart, and I do not want to show them to Ellador—she thinks me so wise!"

She smiled delightedly. "It is beautiful to see," she told me, "this new wonderful love between you. The whole country is interested, you know—how can we help it!"

I had not thought of that. We say: "All the world loves a lover," but to have a couple of million people watching one's courtship—and that a difficult one—was rather embarrassing.

"Tell me about your theory of education," I said. "Make it short and easy. And, to show you what puzzles me, I'll tell you that in our theory great stress is laid on the forced exertion of the child's mind; we think it is good for him to overcome obstacles."

"Of course it is," she unexpectedly agreed. "All our children do that—they love to."

That puzzled me again. If they loved to do it, how could it be educational?

"Our theory is this," she went on carefully. "Here is a young human being. The mind is as natural a thing as the body, a thing that grows, a thing to use and enjoy. We seek to nourish, to stimulate, to exercise the mind of a child as we do the body. There are the two main divisions in education—you have those of course?—the things it is necessary to know, and the things it is necessary to do."

"To do? Mental exercises, you mean?"

"Yes. Our general plan is this: In the matter of feeding the mind, of furnishing information, we use our best powers to meet the natural appetite of a healthy young brain; not to overfeed it, to provide such amount and variety of impressions as seem most welcome to each child. That is the easiest part. The other division is in arranging a properly graduated series of exercises which will best develop each mind; the common faculties we all have, and most carefully, the especial faculties some of us have. You do this also, do you not?"

"In a way," I said rather lamely. "We have not so subtle and highly developed a system as you, not approaching it; but tell me more. As to the information—how do you manage? It appears that all of you know pretty much everything—is that right?"

This she laughingly disclaimed. "By no means. We are, as you soon found out, extremely limited in knowledge. I wish you could realize what a ferment the country is in over the new things you have told us; the passionate eagerness among thousands of us to go to your country and learn—learn—learn! But what we do know is readily divisible into common knowledge and special knowledge. The common knowledge we have long since learned to feed into the minds of our little ones with no waste of time or strength; the special knowledge is open to all, as they desire it. Some of us specialize in one line only. But most take up several—some for their regular work, some to grow with."

"To grow with?"

"Yes. When one settles too close in one kind of work there is a tendency to atrophy in the disused portions of the brain. We like to keep on learning, always."

"What do you study?"

"As much as we know of the different sciences. We have, within our limits, a good deal of knowledge of anatomy, physiology, nutrition—all that pertains to a full and beautiful personal life. We have our botany and chemistry, and so on—very rudimentary, but interesting; our own history, with its accumulating psychology."

"You put psychology with history—not with personal life?"

"Of course. It is ours; it is among and between us, and it changes with the succeeding and improving generations. We are at work, slowly and carefully, developing our whole people along these lines. It is glorious work—splendid! To see the thousands of babies improving, showing stronger clearer minds, sweeter dispositions, higher capacities—don't you find it so in your country?"

This I evaded flatly. I remembered the cheerless claim that the human mind was no better than in its earliest period of savagery, only better informed—a statement I had never believed.

"We try most earnestly for two powers," Somel continued. "The two that seem to us basically necessary for all noble life: a clear, far-reaching judgment, and a strong well-used will. We spend our best efforts, all through childhood and youth, in developing these faculties, individual judgment and will."

"As part of your system of education, you mean?"

"Exactly. As the most valuable part. With the babies, as you may have noticed, we first provide an environment which feeds the mind without tiring it; all manner of simple and interesting things to do, as soon as they are old enough to do them; physical properties, of course, come first. But as early as possible, going very carefully, not to tax the mind, we provide choices, simple choices, with very obvious causes and consequences. You've noticed the games?"

I had. The children seemed always playing something; or else, sometimes, engaged in peaceful researches of their own. I had wondered at first when they went to school, but soon found that they never did—to their knowledge. It was all education but no schooling.

"We have been working for some sixteen hundred years, devising better and better games for children," continued Somel.

I sat aghast. "Devising games?" I protested. "Making up new ones, you mean?"

"Exactly," she answered. "Don't you?"

Then I remembered the kindergarten, and the "material" devised by Signora Montessori, and guardedly replied: "To some extent." But most of our games, I told her, were very old—came down from child to child, along the ages, from the remote past.

"And what is their effect?" she asked. "Do they develop the faculties you wish to encourage?"

Again I remembered the claims made by the advocates of "sports," and again replied guardedly that that was, in part, the theory.

"But do the children *like* it?" I asked. "Having things made up and set before them that way? Don't they want the old games?"

"You can see the children," she answered. "Are yours more contented—more interested—happier?"

Then I thought, as in truth I never had thought before, of the dull, bored children I had seen, whining; "What can I do now?"; of the little groups and gangs hanging about; of the value of some one strong spirit who possessed initiative and would "start something"; of the children's parties and the onerous duties of the older people set to "amuse the children"; also of that troubled ocean of misdirected activity we call "mischief," the foolish, destructive, sometimes evil things done by unoccupied children.

"No," said I grimly. "I don't think they are."

The Herland child was born not only into a world carefully prepared, full of the most fascinating materials and opportunities to learn, but into the society of plentiful numbers of teachers, teachers born and trained, whose business it was to accompany the children along that, to us, impossible thing—the royal road to learning.

There was no mystery in their methods. Being adapted to children it was at least comprehensible to adults. I spent many days with the little ones, sometimes with Ellador, sometimes without, and began to feel a crushing pity for my own childhood, and for all others that I had known.

The houses and gardens planned for babies had in them nothing to hurt—no stairs, no corners, no small loose objects to swallow, no fire—just a babies' paradise. They were taught, as rapidly as feasible, to use and control their own bodies, and never did I see such sure-footed, steady-handed, clear-headed little things. It was a joy to watch a row of toddlers learning to walk, not only on a level floor, but, a little later, on a sort of rubber rail raised an inch or two above the soft turf or heavy rugs, and falling off with shrieks of infant joy, to rush back to the end of the line and try again. Surely we have noticed how children love to get up on something and walk along it! But we have never thought to provide that simple and inexhaustible form of amusement and physical education for the young.

Water they had, of course, and could swim even before they walked. If I feared at first the effects of a too intensive system of culture, that fear was dissipated by seeing the long sunny days of pure physical merriment and natural sleep in which these heavenly babies passed their first years. They never knew they were being educated. They did not dream that in this association of hilarious experiment and achievement they were laying the foundation for that close beautiful group feeling into which they grew so firmly with the years. This was education for citizenship.

X

THEIR RELIGIONS AND OUR MARRIAGES

It took me a long time, as a man, a foreigner, and a species of Christian—I was that as much as anything—to get any clear understanding of the religion of Herland.

Its deification of motherhood was obvious enough; but there was far more to it than that; or, at least, than my first interpretation of that.

I think it was only as I grew to love Ellador more than I believed anyone could love anybody, as I grew faintly to appreciate her inner attitude and state of mind, that I began to get some glimpses of this faith of theirs.

When I asked her about it, she tried at first to tell me, and then, seeing me flounder, asked for more information about ours. She soon found that we had many, that they varied widely, but had some points in common. A clear methodical luminous mind had my Ellador, not only reasonable, but swiftly perceptive.

She made a sort of chart, superimposing the different religions as I described them, with a pin run through them all, as it were; their common basis being a Dominant Power or Powers, and some Special Behavior, mostly taboos, to please or placate. There were some common features in certain groups of religions, but the one always present was this Power, and the things which must be done or not done because of it. It was not hard to trace our human imagery of the Divine Force up through successive stages of bloodthirsty, sensual, proud, and cruel gods of early times to the conception of a Common Father with its corollary of a Common Brotherhood.

This pleased her very much, and when I expatiated on the Omniscience, Omnipotence, Omnipresence, and so on, of our God, and of the loving kindness taught by his Son, she was much impressed.

The story of the Virgin birth naturally did not astonish her, but she was greatly puzzled by the Sacrifice, and still more by the Devil, and the theory of Damnation.

When in an inadvertent moment I said that certain sects had believed in infant damnation—and explained it—she sat very still indeed.

"They believed that God was Love—and Wisdom—and Power?"

"Yes—all of that."

Her eyes grew large, her face ghastly pale.

"And yet that such a God could put little new babies to burn—for eternity?" She fell into a sudden shuddering and left me, running swiftly to the nearest temple.

Every smallest village had its temple, and in those gracious retreats sat wise and noble women, quietly busy at some work of their own until they were wanted, always ready to give comfort, light, or help, to any applicant.

Ellador told me afterward how easily this grief of hers was assuaged, and seemed ashamed of not having helped herself out of it.

"You see, we are not accustomed to horrible ideas," she said, coming back to me rather apologetically. "We haven't any. And when we get a thing like that into our minds it's like—oh, like red pepper in your eyes. So I just ran to her, blinded and almost screaming, and she took it out so quickly—so easily!"

"How?" I asked, very curious.

"'Why, you blessed child,' she said, 'you've got the wrong idea altogether. You do not have to think that there ever was such a God—for there wasn't. Or such a happening—for there wasn't. Nor even that this hideous false idea was believed by anybody. But only this—that people who are utterly ignorant will believe anything—which you certainly knew before.'"

"Anyhow," pursued Ellador, "she turned pale for a minute when I first said it."

This was a lesson to me. No wonder this whole nation of women was peaceful and sweet in expression—they had no horrible ideas.

"Surely you had some when you began," I suggested.

"Oh, yes, no doubt. But as soon as our religion grew to any height at all we left them out, of course."

From this, as from many other things, I grew to see what I finally put in words.

"Have you no respect for the past? For what was thought and believed by your foremothers?"

"Why, no," she said. "Why should we? They are all gone. They knew less than we do. If we are not beyond them, we are unworthy of them—and unworthy of the children who must go beyond us."

This set me thinking in good earnest. I had always imagined—simply from hearing it said, I suppose—that women were by nature conservative. Yet these women, quite unassisted by any masculine spirit of enterprise, had ignored their past and built daringly for the future.

Ellador watched me think. She seemed to know pretty much what was going on in my mind.

"It's because we began in a new way, I suppose. All our folks were swept away at once, and then, after that time of despair, came those wonder children—the first. And then the whole breathless hope of us was for *their* children—if they should have them. And they did! Then there was the period of pride and triumph till we grew too numerous; and after that, when it all came down to one child apiece, we began to really work—to make better ones."

"But how does this account for such a radical difference in your religion?" I persisted.

She said she couldn't talk about the difference very intelligently, not being familiar with other religions, but that theirs seemed simple enough. Their great Mother Spirit was to them what their own motherhood was—only magnified beyond human limits. That meant that they felt beneath and behind them an upholding, unfailing, serviceable love—perhaps it was really the accumulated mother-love of the race they felt—but it was a Power.

"Just what is your theory of worship?" I asked her.

"Worship? What is that?"

I found it singularly difficult to explain. This Divine Love which they felt so strongly did not seem to ask anything of them—"any more than our mothers do," she said.

"But surely your mothers expect honor, reverence, obedience, from you. You have to do things for your mothers, surely?"

"Oh, no," she insisted, smiling, shaking her soft brown hair. "We do things *from* our mothers—not *for* them. We don't have to do things for them—they don't need it, you know. But we have to live on—splendidly—because of them; and that's the way we feel about God."

I meditated again. I thought of that God of Battles of ours, that Jealous God, that Vengeance-is-mine God. I thought of our world-nightmare—Hell.

"You have no theory of eternal punishment then, I take it?"

Ellador laughed. Her eyes were as bright as stars, and there were tears in them, too. She was so sorry for me.

"How could we?" she asked, fairly enough. "We have no punishments in life, you see, so we don't imagine them after death."

"Have you *no* punishments? Neither for children nor criminals—such mild criminals as you have?" I urged.

"Do you punish a person for a broken leg or a fever? We have preventive measures, and cures; sometimes we have to 'send the patient to bed,' as it were; but that's not a punishment—it's only part of the treatment," she explained.

Then studying my point of view more closely, she added: "You see, we recognize, in our human motherhood, a great tender limitless uplifting force—patience and wisdom and all subtlety of delicate method. We credit God—our idea of God—with all that and more. Our mothers are not angry with us—why should God be?"

"Does God mean a person to you?"

This she thought over a little. "Why—in trying to get close to it in our minds we personify the idea, naturally; but we certainly do not assume a Big Woman somewhere, who is God. What we call God is a Pervading Power, you know, an Indwelling Spirit, something inside of us that we want more of. Is your God a Big Man?" she asked innocently.

"Why—yes, to most of us, I think. Of course we call it an Indwelling Spirit just as you do, but we insist that it is Him, a Person, and a Man—with whiskers."

"Whiskers? Oh yes—because you have them! Or do you wear them because He does?"

"On the contrary, we shave them off—because it seems cleaner and more comfortable."

"Does He wear clothes—in your idea, I mean?"

I was thinking over the pictures of God I had seen—rash advances of the devout mind of man, representing his Omnipotent Deity as an old man in a flowing robe, flowing hair, flowing beard, and in the light of her perfectly frank and innocent questions this concept seemed rather unsatisfying.

I explained that the God of the Christian world was really the ancient Hebrew God, and that we had simply taken over the patriarchal idea—that ancient one which quite inevitably clothed its thought of God with the attributes of the patriarchal ruler, the grandfather.

"I see," she said eagerly, after I had explained the genesis and development of our religious ideals. "They lived in separate groups, with a male head, and he was probably a little—domineering?"

"No doubt of that," I agreed.

"And we live together without any 'head,' in that sense—just our chosen leaders—that *does* make a difference."

"Your difference is deeper than that," I assured her. "It is in your common motherhood. Your children grow up in a world where everybody loves them. They find life made rich and happy for them by the diffused love and wisdom of all mothers. So it is easy for you to think of God in the terms of a similar diffused and competent love. I think you are far nearer right than we are."

"What I cannot understand," she pursued carefully, "is your preservation of such a very ancient state of mind. This patriarchal idea you tell me is thousands of years old?"

"Oh yes—four, five, six thousand—every so many."

"And you have made wonderful progress in those years—in other things?"

"We certainly have. But religion is different. You see, our religions come from behind us, and are initiated by some great teacher who is dead. He is supposed to have known the whole thing and taught it, finally. All we have to do is believe—and obey."

"Who was the great Hebrew teacher?"

"Oh—there it was different. The Hebrew religion is an accumulation of extremely ancient traditions, some far older than their people, and grew by accretion down the ages. We consider it inspired—'the Word of God.' "

"How do you know it is?"

"Because it says so."

"Does it say so in as many words? Who wrote that in?"

I began to try to recall some text that did say so, and could not bring it to mind.

"Apart from that," she pursued, "what I cannot understand is why you keep these early religious ideas so long. You have changed all your others, haven't you?"

"Pretty generally," I agreed. "But this we call 'revealed religion,' and think it is final. But tell me more about these little temples of yours," I urged. "And these Temple Mothers you run to."

Then she gave me an extended lesson in applied religion, which I will endeavor to concentrate.

They developed their central theory of a Loving Power, and assumed that its relation to them was motherly—that it desired their welfare and especially their development. Their relation to it, similarly, was filial, a loving appreciation and a glad fulfillment of its high purposes. Then, being nothing if not practical, they set their keen and active minds to discover the kind of conduct expected of them. This worked out in a most admirable system of ethics. The principle of Love was universally recognized—and used.

Patience, gentleness, courtesy, all that we call "good breeding," was part of their code of conduct. But where they went far beyond us was in the special application of religious feeling to every field of life. They had no ritual, no little set of performances called "divine service," save those religious pageants I have spoken of, and those were as much educational as religious, and as much social as either. But they had a clear established connection between everything they did—and God. Their cleanliness, their health, their exquisite order, the rich peaceful beauty of the whole land, the happiness of the children, and above all the constant progress they made—all this was their religion.

They applied their minds to the thought of God, and worked out the theory that such an inner power demanded outward expression. They lived as if God was real and at work within them.

As for those little temples everywhere—some of the women were more skilled, more temperamentally inclined, in this direction, than others. These, whatever their work might be, gave certain hours to the Temple Service, which meant being there with all their love and wisdom and trained thought, to smooth out rough places for anyone who needed it. Sometimes it was a real grief, very rarely a quarrel, most often a perplexity; even in Herland the human soul had its hours of darkness. But all through the country their best and wisest were ready to give help.

If the difficulty was unusually profound, the applicant was directed to someone more specially experienced in that line of thought.

Here was a religion which gave to the searching mind a rational basis in life, the concept of an immense Loving Power working steadily out through them, toward good. It gave to the "soul" that sense of contact with the inmost force, of perception of the uttermost purpose, which we always crave. It gave to the "heart" the blessed feeling of being loved, loved and *understood.* It gave clear, simple, rational directions as to how we should live—and why. And for ritual it gave first those triumphant group demonstrations, when with a union of all the arts, the revivifying combination of great multitudes moved rhythmically with march and dance, song and music, among their own noblest products and the open beauty of their groves and hills. Second, it gave these numerous little centers of wisdom where the least wise could go to the most wise and be helped.

"It is beautiful!" I cried enthusiastically. "It is the most practical, comforting, progressive religion I ever heard of. You *do* love one another—you do bear one another's burdens—you *do* realize that a little child is a type of the kingdom of heaven. You are more Christian than any people I ever saw. But—how about death? And the life everlasting? What does your religion teach about eternity?"

"Nothing," said Ellador. "What is eternity?"

What indeed? I tried, for the first time in my life, to get a real hold on the idea.

"It is—never stopping."

"Never stopping?" She looked puzzled.

"Yes, life, going on forever."

"Oh—we see that, of course. Life does go on forever, all about us."

"But eternal life goes on *without dying.*"

"The same person?"

"Yes, the same person, unending, immortal." I was pleased to think that I had something to teach from our religion, which theirs had never promulgated.

"Here?" asked Ellador. "Never to die—here?" I could see her practical mind heaping up the people, and hurriedly reassured her.

"Oh no, indeed, not here—hereafter. We must die here, of course, but then we 'enter into eternal life.' The soul lives forever."

"How do you know?" she inquired.

"I won't attempt to prove it to you," I hastily continued. "Let us assume it to be so. How does this idea strike you?"

Again she smiled at me, that adorable, dimpling, tender, mischievous, motherly smile of hers. "Shall I be quite, quite honest?"

"You couldn't be anything else," I said, half gladly and half a little sorry. The transparent honesty of these women was a never-ending astonishment to me.

"It seems to me a singularly foolish idea," she said calmly. "And if true, most disagreeable."

Now I had always accepted the doctrine of personal immortality as a thing established. The efforts of inquiring spiritualists, always seeking to woo their beloved ghosts back again, never seemed to me necessary. I don't say I had ever seriously and courageously discussed the subject with myself even; I had simply assumed it to be a fact. And here was the girl I loved, this creature whose character constantly revealed new heights and ranges far beyond my own, this superwoman of a superland, saying she thought immortality foolish! She meant it, too.

"What do you *want* it for?" she asked.

"How can you *not* want it!" I protested. "Do you want to go out like a candle? Don't you want to go on and on—growing and—and—being happy, forever?"

"Why, no," she said. "I don't in the least. I want my child—and my child's child—to go on—and they will. Why should *I* want to?"

"But it means Heaven!" I insisted. "Peace and Beauty and Comfort and Love—with God." I had never been so eloquent on the subject of religion. She could be horrified at Damnation, and question the justice of Salvation, but Immortality—that was surely a noble faith.

"Why, Van," she said, holding out her hands to me. "Why Van—darling! How splendid of you to feel it so keenly. That's what we all want, of course—Peace and Beauty, and Comfort and Love—with God! And Progress too, remember; Growth, always and always. That is what our religion teaches us to want and to work for, and we do!"

"But that is *here*," I said, "only for this life on earth."

"Well? And do not you in your country, with your beautiful religion of love and service have it here, too—for this life—on earth?"

None of us were willing to tell the women of Herland about the evils of our own beloved land. It was all very well for us to assume them to be necessary and essential, and to criticize—strictly among ourselves—their all-too-perfect civilization, but when it came to telling them about the failures and wastes of our own, we never could bring ourselves to do it.

Moreover, we sought to avoid too much discussion, and to press the subject of our approaching marriages.

Jeff was the determined one on this score.

"Of course they haven't any marriage ceremony or service, but we can make it a sort of Quaker wedding, and have it in the temple—it is the least we can do for them."

It was. There was so little, after all, that we could do for them. Here we were, penniless guests and strangers, with no chance even to use our strength and courage—nothing to defend them from or protect them against.

"We can at least give them our names," Jeff insisted.

They were very sweet about it, quite willing to do whatever we asked, to please us. As to the names, Alima, frank soul that she was, asked what good it would do.

Terry, always irritating her, said it was a sign of possession. "You are going to be Mrs. Nicholson," he said. "Mrs. T. O. Nicholson. That shows everyone that you are my wife."

"What is a 'wife' exactly?" she demanded, a dangerous gleam in her eye.

"A wife is the woman who belongs to a man," he began.

But Jeff took it up eagerly: "And a husband is the man who belongs to a woman. It is because we are monogamous, you know. And marriage is the ceremony, civil and religious, that joins the two together—'until death do us part,' " he finished, looking at Celis with unutterable devotion.

"What makes us all feel foolish," I told the girls, "is that here we have nothing to give you—except, of course, our names."

"Do your women have no names before they are married?" Celis suddenly demanded.

"Why, yes," Jeff explained. "They have their maiden names—their father's names, that is."

"And what becomes of them?" asked Alima.

"They change them for their husbands', my dear," Terry answered her.

"Change them? Do the husbands then take the wives' 'maiden names'?"

"Oh, no," he laughed. "The man keeps his own and gives it to her, too."

"Then she just loses hers and takes a new one—how unpleasant! We won't do that!" Alima said decidedly.

Terry was good-humored about it. "I don't care what you do or don't do so long as we have that wedding pretty soon," he said, reaching a strong brown hand after Alima's, quite as brown and nearly as strong.

"As to giving us things—of course we can see that you'd like to, but we are glad you can't," Celis continued. "You see, we love you just for yourselves—we wouldn't want you to—to pay anything. Isn't it enough to know that you are loved personally—and just as men?"

Enough or not, that was the way we were married. We had a great triple wedding in the biggest temple of all, and it looked as if most of the nation was present. It was very solemn and very beautiful. Someone had written a new song for the occasion, nobly beautiful, about the New Hope for their people—the New Tie with other lands—Brotherhood as well as Sisterhood, and, with evident awe, Fatherhood.

Terry was always restive under their talk of fatherhood. "Anybody'd think we were High Priests of—of Philoprogenitiveness!" he protested. "These women think of *nothing* but children, seems to me! We'll teach 'em!"

He was so certain of what he was going to teach, and Alima so uncertain in her moods of reception, that Jeff and I feared the worst. We tried to caution him—much good that did. The big handsome fellow drew himself up to his full height, lifted that great chest of his, and laughed.

"There are three separate marriages," he said. "I won't interfere with yours—nor you with mine."

So the great day came, and the countless crowds of women, and we three bridegrooms without any supporting "best men," or any other men to back us up, felt strangely small as we came forward.

Somel and Zava and Moadine were on hand; we were thankful to have them, too—they seemed almost like relatives.

There was a splendid procession, wreathing dances, the new anthem I spoke of, and the whole great place pulsed with feeling—the deep awe, the sweet hope, the wondering expectation of a new miracle.

"There has been nothing like this in the country since our Motherhood began!" Somel said softly to me, while we watched the symbolic marches. "You see, it is the dawn of a new era. You don't know how much you mean to us. It is not only Fatherhood—that marvelous dual parentage to which we are strangers—the miracle of union in life-giving—but it is Brotherhood. You are the rest of the world. You join us to our kind—to all the strange lands and peoples we have never seen. We hope to know them—to love and help them—and to learn of them. Ah! You cannot know!"

Thousands of voices rose in the soaring climax of that great Hymn of the Coming Life. By the great Altar of Motherhood, with its crown of fruit and flowers, stood a new one, crowned as well. Before the Great Over Mother of the Land and her ring of High Temple Counsellors, before that vast multitude of calm-faced mothers and holy-eyed maidens, came forward our own three chosen ones, and we, three men alone in all that land, joined hands with them and made our marriage vows.

XI

OUR DIFFICULTIES

We say, "Marriage is a lottery"; also "Marriages are made in Heaven"—but this is not so widely accepted as the other.

We have a well-founded theory that it is best to marry "in one's class," and certain well-grounded suspicions of international marriages, which seem to persist in the interests of social progress, rather than in those of the contracting parties.

But no combination of alien races, of color, of caste, or creed, was ever so basically difficult to establish as that between us, three modern American men, and these three women of Herland.

It is all very well to say that we should have been frank about it beforehand. We had been frank. We had discussed—at least Ellador and I had—the conditions of The Great Adventure, and thought the path was clear before us. But there are some things one takes for granted, supposes are mutually understood, and to which both parties may repeatedly refer without ever meaning the same thing.

The differences in the education of the average man and woman are great enough, but the trouble they make is not mostly for the man; he generally carries out his own views of the case. The woman may have imagined the conditions of married life to be different; but what she imagined, was ignorant of, or might have preferred, did not seriously matter.

I can see clearly and speak calmly about this now, writing after a lapse of years, years full of growth and education, but at the time it was rather hard sledding for all of us—especially for Terry. Poor Terry! You see, in any other imaginable marriage among the peoples of the earth, whether the woman were black, red, yellow, brown, or white; whether she were ignorant or educated, submissive or rebellious, she would have behind her the marriage tradition of our general history. This tradition relates the woman to the man. He goes on with his business, and she adapts herself to him and to it. Even in citizenship, by some strange hocus-pocus, that fact of birth and geography was waved aside, and the woman automatically acquired the nationality of her husband.

Well—here were we, three aliens in this land of women. It was small in area, and the external differences were not so great as to astound us. We did not yet appreciate the differences between the race-mind of this people and ours.

In the first place, they were a "pure stock" of two thousand uninterrupted years. Where we have some long connected lines of thought and feeling, together with a wide range of differences, often irreconcilable, these people were smoothly and firmly agreed on most of the basic principles of their life; and not only agreed in principle, but accustomed for these sixty-odd generations to act on those principles.

This is one thing which we did not understand—had made no allowance for. When in our pre-marital discussions one of those dear girls had said: "We understand it thus and thus," or "We hold such and such to be true," we men, in our own deep-seated convictions of the power of love, and our easy views about beliefs and principles, fondly imagined that we could convince them otherwise. What we imagined, before marriage, did not matter any more than what an average innocent young girl imagines. We found the facts to be different.

It was not that they did not love us; they did, deeply and warmly. But there are you again—what they meant by "love" and what we meant by "love" were so different.

Perhaps it seems rather cold-blooded to say "we" and "they," as if we were not separate couples, with our separate joys and sorrows, but our positions as aliens drove us together constantly. The whole strange experience had made our friendship more close and intimate than it would ever have become in a free and easy lifetime among our own people. Also, as men, with our masculine tradition of far more than two thousand years, we were a unit, small but firm, against this far larger unit of feminine tradition.

I think I can make clear the points of difference without a too painful explicitness. The more external disagreement was in the matter of "the home," and the housekeeping duties and pleasures we, by instinct and long education, supposed to be inherently appropriate to women.

I will give two illustrations, one away up, and the other away down, to show how completely disappointed we were in this regard.

For the lower one, try to imagine a male ant, coming from some state of existence where ants live in pairs, endeavoring to set up housekeeping with a female ant from a highly developed anthill. This female ant might regard him with intense personal affection, but her ideas of parentage and economic management would be on a very different scale from his. Now, of course, if she was a stray female in a country of pairing ants, he might have had his way with her; but if he was a stray male in an anthill—!

For the higher one, try to imagine a devoted and impassioned man trying to set up housekeeping with a lady angel, a real wings-and-harp-and-halo angel, accustomed to fulfilling divine missions all over interstellar space. This angel might love the man with an affection quite beyond his power of return or even of appreciation, but her ideas of service and duty would be on a very different scale from his. Of course, if she was a stray angel in a country of men, he might have had his way with her; but if he was a stray man among angels—!

Terry, at his worst, in a black fury for which, as a man, I must have some sympathy, preferred the ant simile. More of Terry and his special troubles later. It was hard on Terry.

Jeff—well, Jeff always had a streak that was too good for this world! He's the kind that would have made a saintly priest in earlier times. He accepted the angel theory, swallowed it whole, tried to force it on us—with varying effect. He so worshipped Celis, and not only Celis, but what she represented; he had become so deeply convinced of the almost supernatural advantages of this country and people, that he took his medicine like a—I cannot say "like a man," but more as if he wasn't one.

Don't misunderstand me for a moment. Dear old Jeff was no milksop or molly-coddle either. He was a strong, brave, efficient man, and an excellent fighter when fighting was necessary. But there was always this angel streak in him. It was rather a wonder, Terry being so different, that he really loved Jeff as he did; but it happens so sometimes, in spite of the difference—perhaps because of it.

As for me, I stood between. I was no such gay Lothario as Terry, and no such Galahad as Jeff. But for all my limitations I think I had the habit of using my brains in regard to behavior rather more frequently than either of them. I had to use brain-power now, I can tell you.

The big point at issue between us and our wives was, as may easily be imagined, in the very nature of the relation.

"Wives! Don't talk to me about wives!" stormed Terry. "They don't know what the word means."

Which is exactly the fact—they didn't. How could they? Back in their prehistoric records of polygamy and slavery there were no ideals of wifehood as we know it, and since then no possibility of forming such.

"The only thing they can think of about a man is *Fatherhood!*" said Terry in high scorn. "*Fatherhood!* As if a man was always wanting to be a *father!*"

This also was correct. They had their long, wide, deep, rich experience of Motherhood, and their only perception of the value of a male creature as such was for Fatherhood.

Aside from that, of course, was the whole range of personal love, love which as Jeff earnestly phrased it "passeth the love of women!" It did, too. I can give no idea—either now, after long and happy experience of it, or as it seemed then, in the first measureless wonder—of the beauty and power of the love they gave us.

Even Alima—who had a more stormy temperament than either of the others, and who, heaven knows, had far more provocation—even Alima was patience and tenderness and wisdom personified to the man she loved, until he—but I haven't got to that yet.

These, as Terry put it, "alleged or so-called wives" of ours, went right on with their profession as foresters. We, having no special learnings, had long since qualified as assistants. We had to do something, if only to pass the time, and it had to be work—we couldn't be playing forever.

This kept us out of doors with those dear girls, and more or less together—too much together sometimes.

These people had, it now became clear to us, the highest, keenest, most delicate sense of personal privacy, but not the faintest idea of that *solitude à deux* we are so fond of. They had, every one of them, the "two rooms and a bath" theory realized. From earliest childhood each had a separate bedroom with toilet conveniences, and one of the marks of coming of age was the addition of an outer room in which to receive friends.

Long since we had been given our own two rooms apiece, and as being of a different sex and race, these were in a separate house. It seemed to be recognized that we should breathe easier if able to free our minds in real seclusion.

For food we either went to any convenient eating-house, ordered a meal brought in, or took it with us to the woods, always and equally good. All this we had become used to and enjoyed—in our courting days.

After marriage there arose in us a somewhat unexpected urge of feeling that called for a separate house; but this feeling found no response in the hearts of those fair ladies.

"We *are* alone, dear," Ellador explained to me with gentle patience. "We are alone in these great forests; we may go and eat in any little summer-house—just we two, or have a separate table anywhere—or even have a separate meal in our own rooms. How could we be aloner?"

This was all very true. We had our pleasant mutual solitude about our work, and our pleasant evening talks in their apartments or ours; we had, as it were, all the pleasures of courtship carried right on; but we had no sense of—perhaps it may be called possession.

"Might as well not be married at all," growled Terry. "They only got up that ceremony to please us—please Jeff, mostly. They've no real idea of being married."

I tried my best to get Ellador's point of view, and naturally I tried to give her mine. Of course, what we, as men, wanted to make them see was that there were other, and as we proudly said "higher," uses in this relation than what Terry called "mere parentage." In the highest terms I knew I tried to explain this to Ellador.

"Anything higher than for mutual love to hope to give life, as we did?" she said. "How is it higher?"

"It develops love," I explained. "All the power of beautiful permanent mated love comes through this higher development."

"Are you sure?" she asked gently. "How do you know that it was so developed? There are some birds who love each other so that they mope and pine if separated, and never pair again if one dies, but they never mate except in the mating season. Among your people do you find high and lasting affection appearing in proportion to this indulgence?"

It is a very awkward thing, sometimes, to have a logical mind.

Of course I knew about those monogamous birds and beasts too, that mate for life and show every sign of mutual affection, without ever having stretched the sex relationship beyond its original range. But what of it?

"Those are lower forms of life!" I protested. "They have no capacity for faithful and affectionate, and apparently happy—but oh, my dear! my dear!—what can they know of such a love as draws us together? Why, to touch you—

to be near you—to come closer and closer—to lose myself in you—surely you feel it too, do you not?"

I came nearer. I seized her hands.

Her eyes were on mine, tender radiant, but steady and strong. There was something so powerful, so large and changeless, in those eyes that I could not sweep her off her feet by my own emotion as I had unconsciously assumed would be the case.

It made me feel as, one might imagine, a man might feel who loved a goddess—not a Venus, though! She did not resent my attitude, did not repel it, did not in the least fear it, evidently. There was not a shade of that timid withdrawal or pretty resistance which are so—provocative.

"You see, dearest," she said, "you have to be patient with us. We are not like the women of your country. We are Mothers, and we are People, but we have not specialized in this line."

"We" and "we" and "we"—it was so hard to get her to be personal. And, as I thought that, I suddenly remembered how we were always criticizing *our* women for *being* so personal.

Then I did my earnest best to picture to her the sweet intense joy of married lovers, and the result in higher stimulus to all creative work.

"Do you mean," she asked quite calmly, as if I was not holding her cool firm hands in my hot and rather quivering ones, "that with you, when people marry, they go right on doing this in season and out of season, with no thought of children at all?"

"They do," I said, with some bitterness. "They are not mere parents. They are men and women, and they love each other."

"How long?" asked Ellador, rather unexpectedly.

"How long?" I repeated, a little dashed. "Why as long as they live."

"There is something very beautiful in the idea," she admitted, still as if she were discussing life on Mars. "This climactic expression, which, in all the other life-forms, has but the one purpose, has with you become specialized to higher, purer, nobler uses. It has—I judge from what you tell me—the most ennobling effect on character. People marry, not only for parentage, but for this exquisite interchange—and, as a result, you have a world full of continuous lovers, ardent, happy, mutually devoted, always living on that high tide of supreme emotion which we had supposed to belong only to one season and one use. And you say it has other results, stimulating all high creative work. That must mean floods, oceans of such work, blossoming from this intense happiness of every married pair! It is a beautiful idea!"

She was silent, thinking.

So was I.

She slipped one hand free, and was stroking my hair with it in a gentle motherly way. I bowed my hot head on her shoulder and felt a dim sense of peace, a restfulness which was very pleasant.

"You must take me there someday, darling," she was saying. "It is not only that I love you so much, I want to see your country—your people—your mother—" she paused reverently. "Oh, how I shall love your mother!"

I had not been in love many times—my experience did not compare with Terry's. But such as I had was so different from this that I was perplexed, and full of mixed feelings: partly a growing sense of common ground between us, a pleasant rested calm feeling, which I had imagined could only be attained in one way; and partly a bewildered resentment because what I found was not what I had looked for.

It was their confounded psychology! Here they were with this profound highly developed system of education so bred into them that even if they were not teachers by profession they all had a general proficiency in it—it was second nature to them.

And no child, stormily demanding a cookie "between meals," was ever more subtly diverted into an interest in house-building than was I when I found an apparently imperative demand had disappeared without my noticing it.

And all the time those tender mother eyes, those keen scientific eyes, noting every condition and circumstance, and learning how to "take time by the forelock" and avoid discussion before occasion arose.

I was amazed at the results. I found that much, very much, of what I had honestly supposed to be a physiological necessity was a psychological necessity—or so believed. I found, after my ideas of what was essential had changed, that my feelings changed also. And more than all, I found this—a factor of enormous weight—these women were not provocative. That made an immense difference.

The thing that Terry had so complained of when we first came—that they weren't "feminine," they lacked "charm," now became a great comfort. Their vigorous beauty was an aesthetic pleasure, not an irritant. Their dress and ornaments had not a touch of the "come-and-find-me" element.

Even with my own Ellador, my wife, who had for a time unveiled a woman's heart and faced the strange new hope and joy of dual parentage, she afterward withdrew again into the same good comrade she had been at first. They were women, plus, and so much plus that when they did not choose to let the womanness appear, you could not find it anywhere.

I don't say it was easy for me; it wasn't. But when I made appeal to her sympathies I came up against another immovable wall. She was sorry, honestly sorry, for my distresses, and made all manner of thoughtful suggestions, often quite useful, as well as the wise foresight I have mentioned above, which often saved all difficulty before it arose; but her sympathy did not alter her convictions.

"If I thought it was really right and necessary, I could perhaps bring myself to it, for your sake, dear; but I do not want to—not at all. You would not have a mere submission, would you? That is not the kind of high romantic love you spoke of, surely? It is a pity, of course, that you should have to adjust your highly specialized faculties to our unspecialized ones."

Confound it! I hadn't married the nation, and I told her so. But she only smiled at her own limitations and explained that she had to "think in we's."

Confound it again! Here I'd have all my energies focused on one wish, and before I knew it she'd have them dissipated in one direction or another, some subject of discussion that began just at the point I was talking about and ended miles away.

It must not be imagined that I was just repelled, ignored, left to cherish a grievance. Not at all. My happiness was in the hands of a larger, sweeter womanhood than I had ever imagined. Before our marriage my own ardor had perhaps blinded me to much of this. I was madly in love with not so much what was there as with what I supposed to be there. Now I found an endlessly beautiful undiscovered country to explore, and in it the sweetest wisdom and understanding. It was as if I had come to some new place and people, with a desire to eat at all hours, and no other interests in particular; and as if my hosts, instead of merely saying, "You shall not eat," had presently aroused in me a lively desire for music, for pictures, for games, for exercise, for playing in the water, for running some ingenious machine; and, in the multitude of my satisfactions, I forgot the one point which was not satisfied, and got along very well until mealtime.

One of the cleverest and most ingenious of these tricks was only clear to me many years after, when we were so wholly at one on this subject that I could laugh at my own predicament then. It was this: You see, with us, women are kept as different as possible and as feminine as possible. We men have our own world, with only men in it; we get tired of our ultra-maleness and turn gladly to the ultra-femaleness. Also, in keeping our women as feminine as possible, we see to it that when we turn to them we find the thing we want always in evidence. Well, the atmosphere of this place was anything but seductive. The very numbers of these human women, always in human relation, made them anything but alluring. When, in spite of this, my hereditary instincts and race-traditions made me long for the feminine response in Ellador, instead of withdrawing so that I should want her more, she deliberately gave me a little too much of her society—always de-feminized, as it were. It was awfully funny, really.

Here was I, with an Ideal in mind, for which I hotly longed, and here was she, deliberately obtruding in the foreground of my consciousness a Fact—a fact which I coolly enjoyed, but which actually interfered with what I wanted.

I see now clearly enough why a certain kind of man, like Sir Almroth Wright, resents the professional development of women. It gets in the way of the sex ideal; it temporarily covers and excludes femininity.

Of course, in this case, I was so fond of Ellador my friend, of Ellador my professional companion, that I necessarily enjoyed her society on any terms. Only—when I had had her with me in her de-feminine capacity for a sixteen-hour day, I could go to my own room and sleep without dreaming about her.

The witch! If ever anybody worked to woo and win and hold a human soul, she did, great superwoman that she was. I couldn't then half comprehend the skill of it, the wonder. But this I soon began to find: that under all our cultivated attitude of mind toward women, there is an older, deeper, more "natural" feeling, the restful reverence which looks up to the Mother sex.

So we grew together in friendship and happiness, Ellador and I, and so did Jeff and Celis.

When it comes to Terry's part of it, and Alima's, I'm sorry—and I'm ashamed. Of course I blame her somewhat. She wasn't as fine a psychologist as Ellador, and what's more, I think she had a far-descended atavistic trace of more marked femaleness, never apparent till Terry called it out. But when all is said, it doesn't excuse him. I hadn't realized to the full Terry's character—I couldn't, being a man.

The position was the same as with us, of course, only with these distinctions. Alima, a shade more alluring, and several shades less able as a practical psychologist; Terry, a hundredfold more demanding—and proportionately less reasonable.

Things grew strained very soon between them. I fancy at first, when they were together, in her great hope of parentage and his keen joy of conquest—that Terry was inconsiderate. In fact, I know it, from things he said.

"You needn't talk to me," he snapped at Jeff one day, just before our weddings. "There never was a woman yet that did not enjoy being *mastered.* All your pretty talk doesn't amount to a hill o' beans—I *know.*" And Terry would hum:

> *I've taken my fun where I found it.*
> *I've rogued and I've ranged in my time, and*
> *The things that I learned from the yellow and black,*
> *They 'ave helped me a 'eap with the white.*

Jeff turned sharply and left him at the time. I was a bit disquieted myself.

Poor old Terry! The things he'd learned didn't help him a heap in Herland. His idea was to take—he thought that was the way. He thought, he honestly believed, that women like it. Not the women of Herland! Not Alima!

I can see her now—one day in the very first week of their marriage, setting forth to her day's work with long determined strides and hard-set mouth, and sticking close to Ellador. She didn't wish to be alone with Terry—you could see that.

But the more she kept away from him, the more he wanted her—naturally.

He made a tremendous row about their separate establishments, tried to keep her in his rooms, tried to stay in hers. But there she drew the line sharply.

He came away one night, and stamped up and down the moonlit road, swearing under his breath. I was taking a walk that night too, but I wasn't in his state of mind. To hear him rage you'd not have believed that he loved Alima at all—you'd have thought that she was some quarry he was pursuing, something to catch and conquer.

I think that, owing to all those differences I spoke of, they soon lost the common ground they had at first, and were unable to meet sanely and dispassionately. I fancy too—this is pure conjecture—that he had succeeded in driving Alima beyond her best judgment, her real conscience, and that after that her own sense of shame, the reaction of the thing, made her bitter perhaps.

They quarreled, really quarreled, and after making it up once or twice, they seemed to come to a real break—she would not be alone with him at all. And perhaps she was a bit nervous, I don't know, but she got Moadine to come and stay next door to her. Also, she had a sturdy assistant detailed to accompany her in her work.

Terry had his own ideas, as I've tried to show. I daresay he thought he had a right to do as he did. Perhaps he even convinced himself that it would be better for her. Anyhow, he hid himself in her bedroom one night . . .

The women of Herland have no fear of men. Why should they have? They are not timid in any sense. They are not weak; and they all have strong trained athletic bodies. Othello could not have extinguished Alima with a pillow, as if she were a mouse.

Terry put in practice his pet conviction that a woman loves to be mastered, and by sheer brute force, in all the pride and passion of his intense masculinity, he tried to master this woman.

It did not work. I got a pretty clear account of it later from Ellador, but what we heard at the time was the noise of a tremendous struggle, and Alima calling to Moadine. Moadine was close by and came at once; one or two more strong grave women followed.

Terry dashed about like a madman; he would cheerfully have killed them—he told me that, himself—but he couldn't. When he swung a chair over his head one sprang in the air and caught it, two threw themselves bodily upon him and forced him to the floor; it was only the work of a few moments to have him tied hand and foot, and then, in sheer pity for his futile rage, to anesthetize him.

Alima was in a cold fury. She wanted him killed—actually.

There was a trial before the local Over Mother, and this woman, who did not enjoy being mastered, stated her case.

In a court in our country he would have been held quite "within his rights," of course. But this was not our country; it was theirs. They seemed to measure the enormity of the offense by its effect upon a possible fatherhood, and he scorned even to reply to this way of putting it.

He did let himself go once, and explained in definite terms that they were incapable of understanding a man's needs, a man's desires, a man's point of view. He called them neuters, epicenes, bloodless, sexless creatures. He said they could of course kill him—as so many insects could—but that he despised them nonetheless.

And all those stern grave mothers did not seem to mind his despising them, not in the least.

It was a long trial, and many interesting points were brought out as to their views of our habits, and after a while Terry had his sentence. He waited, grim and defiant. The sentence was: "You must go home!"

XII

EXPELLED

We had all meant to go home again. Indeed we had not meant—not by any means—to stay as long as we had. But when it came to being turned out, dismissed, sent away for bad conduct, we none of us really liked it.

Terry said he did. He professed great scorn of the penalty and the trial, as well as all the other characteristics of "this miserable half-country." But he knew, and we knew, that in any "whole" country we should never have been as forgivingly treated as we had been here.

"If the people had come after us according to the directions we left, there'd have been quite a different story!" said Terry. We found out later why no reserve party had arrived. All our careful directions had been destroyed in a fire. We might have all died there and no one at home have ever known our whereabouts.

Terry was under guard now, all the time, known as unsafe, convicted of what was to them an unpardonable sin.

He laughed at their chill horror. "Parcel of old maids!" he called them. "They're all old maids—children or not. They don't know the first thing about Sex."

When Terry said *Sex*, sex with a very large *S*, he meant the male sex, naturally; its special values, its profound conviction of being "the life force," its cheerful ignoring of the true life process, and its interpretation of the other sex solely from its own point of view.

I had learned to see these things very differently since living with Ellador; and as for Jeff, he was so thoroughly Herlandized that he wasn't fair to Terry, who fretted sharply in his new restraint.

Moadine, grave and strong, as sadly patient as a mother with a degenerate child, kept steady watch on him, with enough other women close at hand to prevent an outbreak. He had no weapons, and well knew that all his strength was of small avail against those grim, quiet women.

We were allowed to visit him freely, but he had only his room, and a small high-walled garden to walk in, while the preparations for our departure were under way.

Three of us were to go: Terry, because he must; I, because two were safer for our flyer, and the long boat trip to the coast; Ellador, because she would not let me go without her.

If Jeff had elected to return, Celis would have gone too—they were the most absorbed of lovers; but Jeff had no desire that way.

"Why should I want to go back to all our noise and dirt, our vice and crime, our disease and degeneracy?" he demanded of me privately. We never spoke like that before the women. "I wouldn't take Celis there for anything on earth!" he protested. "She'd die! She'd die of horror and shame to see our slums and hospitals. How can you risk it with Ellador? You'd better break it to her gently before she really makes up her mind."

Jeff was right. I ought to have told her more fully than I did, of all the things we had to be ashamed of. But it is very hard to bridge the gulf of as deep a difference as existed between our life and theirs. I tried to.

"Look here, my dear," I said to her. "If you are really going to my country with me, you've got to be prepared for a good many shocks. It's not as beautiful as this—the cities, I mean, the civilized parts—of course the wild country is."

"I shall enjoy it all," she said, her eyes starry with hope. "I understand it's not like ours. I can see how monotonous our quiet life must seem to you, how much more stirring yours must be. It must be like the biological change you told me about when the second sex was introduced—a far greater movement, constant change, with new possibilities of growth."

I had told her of the later biological theories of sex, and she was deeply convinced of the superior advantages of having two, the superiority of a world with men in it.

"We have done what we could alone; perhaps we have some things better in a quiet way, but you have the whole world—all the people of the different nations—all the long rich history behind you—all the wonderful new knowledge. Oh, I just can't wait to see it!"

What could I do? I told her in so many words that we had our unsolved problems, that we had dishonesty and corruption, vice and crime, disease and insanity, prisons and hospitals; and it made no more impression on her than it would to tell a South Sea Islander about the temperature of the Arctic Circle. She could intellectually see that it was bad to have those things; but she could not *feel* it.

We had quite easily come to accept the Herland life as normal, because it was normal—none of us make any outcry over mere health and peace and happy industry. And the abnormal, to which we are all so sadly well acclimated, she had never seen.

The two things she cared most to hear about, and wanted most to see, were these: the beautiful relation of marriage and the lovely women who were mothers and nothing else; beyond these her keen, active mind hungered eagerly for the world life.

"I'm almost as anxious to go as you are yourself," she insisted, "and you must be desperately homesick."

I assured her that no one could be homesick in such a paradise as theirs, but she would have none of it.

"Oh, yes—I know. It's like those little tropical islands you've told me about, shining like jewels in the big blue sea—I can't wait to see the sea! The little island may be as perfect as a garden, but you always want to get back to your own big country, don't you? Even if it is bad in some ways?"

Ellador was more than willing. But the nearer it came to our really going, and to my having to take her back to our "civilization," after the clean peace and beauty of theirs, the more I began to dread it, and the more I tried to explain.

Of course I had been homesick at first, while we were prisoners, before I had Ellador. And of course I had, at first, rather idealized my country and its ways, in describing it. Also, I had always accepted certain evils as integral parts of our civilization and never dwelt on them at all. Even when I tried to tell her the worst, I never remembered some things—which, when she came to see them, impressed her at once, as they had never impressed me. Now, in my efforts at explanation, I began to see both ways more keenly than I had before; to see the painful defects of my own land, the marvelous gains of this.

In missing men we three visitors had naturally missed the larger part of life, and had unconsciously assumed that they must miss it too. It took me a long time to realize—Terry never did realize—how little it meant to them. When we say *men, man, manly, manhood*, and all the other masculine derivatives, we have in the background of our minds a huge vague crowded picture of the world and all its activities. To grow up and "be a man," to "act like a man"—the meaning and connotation is wide indeed. That vast background is full of marching columns of men, of changing lines of men, of long processions of men; of men steering their ships into new seas, exploring unknown mountains, breaking horses, herding cattle, ploughing and sowing and reaping, toiling at the forge and furnace, digging in the mine, building roads and bridges and high cathedrals, managing great businesses, teaching in all the colleges, preaching in all the churches; of men everywhere, doing everything—"the world."

And when we say *women*, we think *female*—the sex.

But to these women, in the unbroken sweep of this two-thousand-year-old feminine civilization, the word *woman* called up all that big background, so far as they had gone in social development; and the word *man* meant to them only male—the sex.

Of course we could *tell* them that in our world men did everything; but that did not alter the background of their minds. That man, "the male," did all these things was to them a statement, making no more change in the point of view than was made in ours when we first faced the astounding fact—to us—that in Herland women were "the world."

We had been living there more than a year. We had learned their limited history, with its straight, smooth, upreaching lines, reaching higher and going faster up to the smooth comfort of their present life. We had learned a little of their psychology, a much wider field than the history, but here we could not follow so readily. We were now well used to seeing women not as females but as people; people of all sorts, doing every kind of work.

This outbreak of Terry's, and the strong reaction against it, gave us a new light on their genuine femininity. This was given me with great clearness by both Ellador and Somel. The feeling was the same—sick revulsion and horror, such as would be felt at some climactic blasphemy.

They had no faintest approach to such a thing in their minds, knowing nothing of the custom of marital indulgence among us. To them the one high purpose of Motherhood had been for so long the governing law of life, and the contribution of the father, though known to them, so distinctly another method to the same end, that they could not, with all their effort, get the point of view of the male creature whose desires quite ignore parentage and seek only for what we euphoniously term "the joys of love."

When I tried to tell Ellador that women too felt so, with us, she drew away from me, and tried hard to grasp intellectually what she could in no way sympathize with.

"You mean—that with you—love between man and woman expresses itself in that way—without regard to motherhood? To parentage, I mean," she added carefully.

"Yes, surely. It is love we think of—the deep sweet love between two. Of course we want children, and children come—but that is not what we think about."

"But—but—it seems so against nature!" she said. "None of the creatures we know do that. Do other animals—in your country?"

"We are not animals!" I replied with some sharpness. "At least we are something more—something higher. This is a far nobler and more beautiful relation, as I have explained before. Your view seems to us rather—shall I say, practical? Prosaic? Merely a means to an end! With us—oh, my dear girl—cannot you see? Cannot you feel? It is the last, sweetest, highest consummation of mutual love."

She was impressed visibly. She trembled in my arms, as I held her close, kissing her hungrily. But there rose in her eyes that look I knew so well, that remote clear look as if she had gone far away even though I held her beautiful body so close, and was now on some snowy mountain regarding me from a distance.

"I feel it quite clearly," she said to me. "It gives me a deep sympathy with what you feel, no doubt more strongly still. But what I feel, even what you feel, dearest, does not convince me that it is right. Until I am sure of that, of course I cannot do as you wish."

Ellador, at times like this, always reminded me of Epictetus. "I will put you in prison!" said his master. "My body, you mean," replied Epictetus calmly. "I will cut your head off," said his master. "Have I said that my head could not be cut off?" A difficult person, Epictetus.

What is this miracle by which a woman, even in your arms, may withdraw herself, utterly disappear till what you hold is as inaccessible as the face of a cliff?

"Be patient with me, dear," she urged sweetly. "I know it is hard for you. And I begin to see—a little—how Terry was so driven to crime."

"Oh, come, that's a pretty hard word for it. After all, Alima was his wife, you know," I urged, feeling at the moment a sudden burst of sympathy for poor Terry. For a man of his temperament—and habits—it must have been an unbearable situation.

But Ellador, for all her wide intellectual grasp, and the broad sympathy in which their religion trained them, could not make allowance for such—to her—sacrilegious brutality.

It was the more difficult to explain to her, because we three, in our constant talks and lectures about the rest of the world, had naturally avoided the seamy side; not so much from a desire to deceive, but from wishing to put the best foot foremost for our civilization, in the face of the beauty and comfort of theirs. Also, we really thought some things were right, or at least unavoidable, which we could readily see would be repugnant to them, and therefore did not discuss. Again there was much of our world's life which we, being used to it, had not noticed as anything worth describing. And still further, there was about these women a colossal innocence upon which many of the things we did say had made no impression whatever.

I am thus explicit about it because it shows how unexpectedly strong was the impression made upon Ellador when she at last entered our civilization.

She urged me to be patient, and I was patient. You see, I loved her so much that even the restrictions she so firmly established left me much happiness. We were lovers, and there is surely delight enough in that.

Do not imagine that these young women utterly refused "the Great New Hope," as they called it, that of dual parentage. For that they had agreed to marry us, though the marrying part of it was a concession to our prejudices rather than theirs. To them the process was the holy thing—and they meant to keep it holy.

But so far only Celis, her blue eyes swimming in happy tears, her heart lifted with that tide of race-motherhood which was their supreme passion, could with ineffable joy and pride announce that she was to be a mother. "The New Motherhood" they called it, and the whole country knew. There was no pleasure, no service, no honor in all the land that Celis might not have had. Almost like the breathless reverence with which, two thousand years ago, that dwindling band of women had watched the miracle of virgin birth, was the deep awe and warm expectancy with which they greeted this new miracle of union.

All mothers in that land were holy. To them, for long ages, the approach to motherhood has been by the most intense and exquisite love and longing, by the Supreme Desire, the overmastering demand for a child. Every thought they held in connection with the processes of maternity was open to the day, simple yet sacred. Every woman of them placed motherhood not only higher than other duties, but so far higher that there were no other duties, one might almost say. All their wide mutual love, all the subtle interplay of mutual friendship and service, the urge of progressive thought and invention, the deepest religious emotion, every feeling and every act was related to this great central Power, to the River of Life pouring through them, which made them the bearers of the very Spirit of God.

Of all this I learned more and more—from their books, from talk, especially from Ellador. She was at first, for a brief moment, envious of her friend—a thought she put away from her at once and forever.

"It is better," she said to me. "It is much better that it has not come to me yet—to us, that is. For if I am to go with you to your country, we may have 'adventures by sea and land,' as you say [and as in truth we did], and it might not be at all safe for a baby. So we won't try again, dear, till it is safe—will we?"

This was a hard saying for a very loving husband.

"Unless," she went on, "if one is coming, you will leave me behind. You can come back, you know—and I shall have the child."

Then that deep ancient chill of male jealousy of even his own progeny touched my heart.

"I'd rather have you, Ellador, than all the children in the world. I'd rather have you with me—on your own terms—than not to have you."

This was a very stupid saying. Of course I would! For if she wasn't there I should want all of her and have none of her. But if she went along as a sort of sublimated sister—only much closer and warmer than that, really—why I should have all of her but that one thing. And I was beginning to find that Ellador's friendship, Ellador's comradeship, Ellador's sisterly affection, Ellador's perfectly sincere love—none the less deep that she held it back on a definite line of reserve—were enough to live on very happily.

I find it quite beyond me to describe what this woman was to me. We talk fine things about women, but in our hearts we know that they are very limited beings—most of them. We honor them for their functional powers, even while we dishonor them by our use of it; we honor them for their carefully enforced virtue, even while we show by our own conduct how little we think of that virtue; we value them, sincerely, for the perverted maternal activities which make our wives the most comfortable of servants, bound to us for life with the wages wholly at our own decision, their whole business, outside of the temporary duties of such motherhood as they may achieve, to meet our needs in every way. Oh, we value them, all right, "in their place," which place is the home, where they perform that mixture of duties so ably described by Mrs. Josephine Dodge Daskam Bacon, in which the services of "a mistress" are carefully specified. She is a very clear writer, Mrs. J. D. D. Bacon, and understands her subject—from her own point of view. But—that combination of industries, while convenient, and in a way economical, does not arouse the kind of emotion commanded by the women of Herland. These were women one had to love "up," very high up, instead of down. They were not pets. They were not servants. They were not timid, inexperienced, weak.

After I got over the jar to my pride (which Jeff, I truly think, never felt—he was a born worshipper, and which Terry never got over—he was quite clear in his ideas of "the position of women"), I found that loving "up" was a very good sensation after all. It gave me a queer feeling, way down deep, as of the stirring of some ancient dim prehistoric consciousness, a feeling that they were right somehow—that this was the way to feel. It was like—coming home to mother. I don't mean the underflannels-and-doughnuts mother, the fussy person that waits on you and spoils you and doesn't really know you. I mean the feeling that a very little child would have, who had been lost—for ever so long. It was a sense of getting home; of being clean and rested; of safety and yet freedom; of love that was always there, warm like sunshine in May, not hot like a stove or a featherbed—a love that didn't irritate and didn't smother.

I looked at Ellador as if I hadn't seen her before. "If you won't go," I said, "I'll get Terry to the coast and come back alone. You can let me down a rope. And if you will go—why you blessed wonder-woman—I would rather live with you all my life—like this—than to have any other woman I ever saw, or any number of them, to do as I like with. Will you come?"

She was keen for coming. So the plans went on. She'd have liked to wait for that Marvel of Celis's, but Terry had no such desire. He was crazy to be out of it all. It made him sick, he said, sick; this everlasting mother-mother-mothering. I don't think Terry had what the phrenologists call "the lump of philoprogenitiveness" at all well developed.

"Morbid one-sided cripples," he called them, even when from his window he could see their splendid vigor and beauty; even while Moadine, as patient and friendly as if she had never helped Alima to hold and bind him, sat there in the room, the picture of wisdom and serene strength. "Sexless, epicene, undeveloped neuters!" he went on bitterly. He sounded like Sir Almwroth Wright.

Well—it was hard. He was madly in love with Alima, really; more so than he had ever been before, and their tempestuous courtship, quarrels, and reconciliations had fanned the flame. And then when he sought by that supreme conquest which seems so natural a thing to that type of man, to force her to love him as her master—to have the sturdy athletic furious woman rise up and master him—she and her friends—it was no wonder he raged.

Come to think of it, I do not recall a similar case in all history or fiction. Women have killed themselves rather than submit to outrage; they have killed the outrager; they have escaped; or they have submitted—sometimes seeming to get on very well with the victor afterward. There was that adventure of "false Sextus," for instance, who "found Lucrese combing the fleece, under the midnight lamp." He threatened, as I remember, that if she did not submit he would slay her, slay a slave and place him beside her and say he found him there. A poor device, it always seemed to me. If Mr. Lucretius had asked him how he came to be in his wife's bedroom overlooking her morals, what could he have said? But the point is Lucrese submitted, and Alima didn't.

"She kicked me," confided the embittered prisoner—he had to talk to someone. "I was doubled up with the pain, of course, and she jumped on me and yelled for this old harpy [Moadine couldn't hear him] and they had me trussed up in no time. I believe Alima could have done it alone," he added with reluctant admiration. "She's as strong as a horse. And of course a man's helpless when you hit him like that. No woman with a shade of decency—"

I had to grin at that, and even Terry did, sourly. He wasn't given to reasoning, but it did strike him that an assault like his rather waived considerations of decency.

"I'd give a year of my life to have her alone again," he said slowly, his hands clenched till the knuckles were white.

But he never did. She left our end of the country entirely, went up into the fir-forest on the highest slopes, and stayed there. Before we left he quite desperately longed to see her, but she would not come and he could not go. They watched him like lynxes. (Do lynxes watch any better than mousing cats, I wonder!)

Well—we had to get the flyer in order, and be sure there was enough fuel left, though Terry said we could glide all right, down to that lake, once we got started. We'd have gone gladly in a week's time, of course, but there was a great to-do all over the country about Ellador's leaving them. She had interviews with some of the leading ethicists—wise women with still eyes, and with the best of the teachers. There was a stir, a thrill, a deep excitement everywhere.

Our teaching about the rest of the world has given them all a sense of isolation, of remoteness, of being a little outlying sample of a country, overlooked and forgotten among the family of nations. We had called it "the family of nations," and they liked the phrase immensely.

They were deeply aroused on the subject of evolution; indeed, the whole field of natural science drew them irresistibly. Any number of them would have risked everything to go to the strange unknown lands and study; but we could take only one, and it had to be Ellador, naturally.

We planned greatly about coming back, about establishing a connecting route by water; about penetrating those vast forests and civilizing—or exterminating—the dangerous savages. That is, we men talked of that last—not with the women. They had a definite aversion to killing things.

But meanwhile there was high council being held among the wisest of them all. The students and thinkers who had been gathering facts from us all this time, collating and relating them, and making inferences, laid the result of their labors before the council.

Little had we thought that our careful efforts at concealment had been so easily seen through, with never a word to show us that they saw. They had followed up words of ours on the science of optics, asked innocent questions about glasses and the like, and were aware of the defective eyesight so common among us.

With the lightest touch, different women asking different questions at different times, and putting all our answers together like a picture puzzle, they had figured out a sort of skeleton chart as to the prevalence of disease among us. Even more subtly with no show of horror or condemnation, they had gathered something—far from the truth, but something pretty clear—about poverty, vice, and crime. They even had a goodly number of our dangers all itemized, from asking us about insurance and innocent things like that.

They were well posted as to the different races, beginning with their poison-arrow natives down below and widening out to the broad racial divisions we had told them about. Never a shocked expression of the face or exclamation of revolt had warned us; they had been extracting the evidence without our knowing it all this time, and now were studying with the most devout earnestness the matter they had prepared.

The result was rather distressing to us. They first explained the matter fully to Ellador, as she was the one who purposed visiting the Rest of the World. To Celis they said nothing. She must not be in any way distressed, while the whole nation waited on her Great Work.

Finally Jeff and I were called in. Somel and Zava were there, and Ellador, with many others that we knew.

They had a great globe, quite fairly mapped out from the small section maps in that compendium of ours. They had the different peoples of the earth roughly outlined, and their status in civilization indicated. They had charts and figures and estimates, based on the facts in that traitorous little book and what they had learned from us.

Somel explained: "We find that in all your historic period, so much longer than ours, that with all the interplay of services, the exchange of inventions and discoveries, and the wonderful progress we so admire, that in this widespread Other World of yours, there is still much disease, often contagious."

We admitted this at once.

"Also there is still, in varying degree, ignorance, with prejudice and unbridled emotion."

This too was admitted.

"We find also that in spite of the advance of democracy and the increase of wealth, that there is still unrest and sometimes combat."

Yes, yes, we admitted it all. We were used to these things and saw no reason for so much seriousness.

"All things considered," they said, and they did not say a hundredth part of the things they were considering, "we are unwilling to expose our country to free communication with the rest of the world—as yet. If Ellador comes back, and we approve her report, it may be done later—but not yet.

"So we have this to ask of you gentlemen [they knew that word was held a title of honor with us], that you promise not in any way to betray the location of this country until permission—after Ellador's return."

Jeff was perfectly satisfied. He thought they were quite right. He always did. I never saw an alien become naturalized more quickly than that man in Herland.

I studied it awhile, thinking of the time they'd have if some of our contagions got loose there, and concluded they were right. So I agreed.

Terry was the obstacle. "Indeed I won't!" he protested. "The first thing I'll do is to get an expedition fixed up to force an entrance into Ma-land."

"Then," they said quite calmly, "he must remain an absolute prisoner, always."

"Anesthesia would be kinder," urged Moadine.

"And safer," added Zava.

"He will promise, I think," said Ellador.

And he did. With which agreement we at last left Herland.

ARMAGEDDON 2419 A.D.

Philip Francis Nowlan

FOREWORD

Elsewhere I have set down, for whatever interest they have in this, the 25th Century, my personal recollections of the 20th Century.

Now it occurs to me that my memoirs of the 25th Century may have an equal interest 500 years from now—particularly in view of that unique perspective from which I have seen the 25th Century, entering it as I did, in one leap across a gap of 492 years.

This statement requires elucidation. There are still many in the world who are not familiar with my unique experience. Five centuries from now there may be many more, especially if civilization is fated to endure any worse convulsions than those which have occurred between 1975 A.D. and the present time.

I should state therefore, that I, Anthony Rogers, am, so far as I know, the only man alive whose normal span of eighty-one years of life has been spread over a period of 573 years. To be precise, I lived the first twenty-nine years of my life between 1898 and 1927; the other fifty-two since 2419. The gap between these two, a period of nearly five hundred years, I spent in a state of suspended animation, free from the ravages of catabolic processes, and without any apparent effect on my physical or mental faculties.

When I began my long sleep, man had just begun his real conquest of the air in a sudden series of transoceanic flights in airplanes driven by internal combustion motors. He had barely begun to speculate on the possibilities of harnessing sub-atomic forces, and had made no further practical penetration into the field of ethereal pulsations than the primitive radio and television of that day. The United States of America was the most powerful nation in the world, its political, financial, industrial and scientific influence being supreme; and in the arts also it was rapidly climbing into leadership.

I awoke to find the America I knew a total wreck—to find Americans a hunted race in their own land, hiding in the dense forests that covered the shattered and leveled ruins of their once magnificent cities, desperately preserving, and struggling to develop in their secret retreats, the remnants of their culture and science—and the undying flame of their sturdy independence.

World domination was in the hands of Mongolians and the center of world power lay in inland China, with Americans one of the few races of mankind unsubdued—and it must be admitted in fairness to the truth, not worth the trouble of subduing in the eyes of the Han Airlords who ruled North America as titular tributaries of the Most Magnificent.

For they needed not the forests in which the Americans lived, nor the resources of the vast territories these forests covered. With the perfection to which they had reduced the synthetic production of necessities and luxuries, their remarkable development of scientific processes and mechanical accomplishment of work, they had no economic need for the forests, and no economic desire for the enslaved labor of an unruly race.

They had all they needed for their magnificently luxurious and degraded scheme of civilization, within the walls of the fifteen cities of sparkling glass they had flung skyward on the sites of ancient American centers, into the bowels of the earth underneath them, and with relatively small surrounding areas of agriculture.

Complete domination of the air rendered communication between these centers a matter of ease and safety. Occasional destructive raids on the waste lands were considered all that was necessary to keep the "wild" Americans on the run within the shelter of their forests, and prevent their becoming a menace to the Han civilization.

But nearly three hundred years of easily maintained security, the last century of which had been nearly sterile in scientific, social and economic progress, had softened and devitalized the Hans.

It had likewise developed, beneath the protecting foliage of the forest, the growth of a vigorous new American civilization, remarkable in the mobility and flexibility of its organization, in its conquest of almost insuperable obstacles, in the development and guarding of its industrial and scientific resources, all in anticipation of that "Day of Hope" to which it had been looking forward for generations, when it would be strong enough to burst from the green chrysalis of the forests, soar into the upper air lanes and destroy the yellow incubus.

At the time I awoke, the "Day of Hope" was almost at hand. I shall not attempt to set forth a detailed history of the Second War of Independence, for that has been recorded already by better historians than I am. Instead I shall confine myself largely to the part I was fortunate enough to play in this struggle and in the events leading up to it.

It all resulted from my interest in radioactive gases. During the latter part of 1927 my company, the American Radioactive Gas Corporation, had been keeping me busy investigating reports of unusual phenomena observed in certain abandoned coal mines near the Wyoming Valley, in Pennsylvania.

With two assistants and a complete equipment of scientific instruments, I began the exploration of a deserted working in a mountainous district, where several weeks before, a number of mining engineers had reported traces of carnotite* and what they believed to be radioactive gases. Their report was not without foundation, it was apparent from the outset, for in our examination of the upper levels of the mine, our instruments indicated a vigorous radioactivity.

On the morning of December 15th, we descended to one of the lowest levels. To our surprise, we found no water there. Obviously it had drained off through some break in the strata. We noticed too that the rock in the side walls of the shaft was soft, evidently due to the radioactivity, and pieces crumbled under foot rather easily. We made our way cautiously down the shaft, when suddenly the rotted timbers above us gave way.

I jumped ahead, barely escaping the avalanche of coal and soft rock, but my companions, who were several paces behind me, were buried under it, and undoubtedly met instant death.

I was trapped. Return was impossible. With my electric torch I explored the shaft to its end, but could find no other way out. The air became increasingly difficult to breathe, probably from the rapid accumulation of the radioactive gas. In a little while my senses reeled and I lost consciousness.

When I awoke, there was a cool and refreshing circulation of air in the shaft. I had no thought that I had been unconscious more than a few hours, although it seems that the radioactive gas had kept me in a state of suspended animation for something like 500 years. My awakening, I figured out later, had been due to some shifting of the strata which reopened the shaft and cleared the atmosphere in the working. This must have been the case, for I was able to struggle back up the shaft over a pile of debris, and stagger up the long incline to the mouth of the mine, where an entirely different world, overgrown with a vast forest and no visible sign of human habitation, met my eyes.

I shall pass over the days of mental agony that followed in my attempt to grasp the meaning of it all. There were times when I felt that I was on the verge of insanity. I roamed the unfamiliar forest like a lost soul. Had it not been for the necessity of improvising traps and crude clubs with which to slay my food, I believe I should have gone mad.

Suffice it to say, however, that I survived this psychic crisis. I shall begin my narrative proper with my first contact with Americans of the year 2419 A.D.

* A hydrovanadate of uranium, and other metals; used as a source of radium compounds.

I

FLOATING MEN

My first glimpse of a human being of the 25th Century was obtained through a portion of woodland where the trees were thinly scattered, with a dense forest beyond.

I had been wandering along aimlessly, and hopelessly, musing over my strange fate, when I noticed a figure that cautiously backed out of the dense growth across the glade. I was about to call out joyfully, but there was something furtive about the figure that prevented me. The boy's attention (for it seemed to be a lad of fifteen or sixteen) was centered tensely on the heavy growth of trees from which he had just emerged.

He was clad in rather tight-fitting garments entirely of green, and wore a helmet-like cap of the same color. High around his waist he wore a broad, thick belt, which bulked up in the back across the shoulders, into something of the proportions of a knapsack.

As I was taking in these details, there came a vivid flash and heavy detonation, like that of a hand grenade, not far to the left of him. He threw up an arm and staggered a bit in a queer, gliding way; then he recovered himself and slipped cautiously away from the place of the explosion, crouching slightly, and still facing the denser part of the forest. Every few steps he would raise his arm, and point into the forest with something he held in his hand. Wherever he pointed there was a terrific explosion, deeper in among the trees. It came to me then that he was shooting with some form of pistol, though there was neither flash nor detonation from the muzzle of the weapon itself.

After firing several times, he seemed to come to a sudden resolution, and turning in my general direction, leaped—to my amazement sailing through the air between the sparsely scattered trees in such a jump as I had never in my life seen before. That leap must have carried him a full fifty feet, although at the height of his arc, he was not more than ten or twelve feet from the ground.

When he alighted, his foot caught in a projecting root, and he sprawled gently forward. I say "gently" for he did not crash down as I expected him to do. The only thing I could compare it with was a slow-motion cinema, although I had never seen one in which horizontal motions were registered at normal speed and only the vertical movements were slowed down.

Due to my surprise, I suppose my brain did not function with its normal quickness, for I gazed at the prone figure for several seconds before I saw the blood that oozed out from under the tight green cap. Regaining my power of action, I dragged him out of sight back of the big tree. For a few moments I busied myself in an attempt to staunch the flow of blood. The wound was not a deep one. My companion was more dazed than hurt. But what of the pursuers?

I took the weapon from his grasp and examined it hurriedly. It was not unlike the automatic pistol to which I was accustomed, except that it apparently fired with a button instead of a trigger. I inserted several fresh rounds of ammunition into its magazine from my companion's belt, as rapidly as I could, for I soon heard, near us, the suppressed conversation of his pursuers.

There followed a series of explosions round about us, but none very close. They evidently had not spotted our hiding place, and were firing at random.

I waited tensely, balancing the gun in my hand, to accustom myself to its weight and probable throw.

Then I saw a movement in the green foliage of a tree not far away, and the head and face of a man appeared. Like my companion, he was clad entirely in green, which made his figure difficult to distinguish. But his face could be seen clearly. It was an evil face, and had murder in it.

That decided me. I raised the gun and fired. My aim was bad, for there was no kick in the gun, as I had expected, and I hit the trunk of the tree several feet below him. It blew him from his perch like a crumpled bit of paper, and he floated down to the ground, like some limp, dead thing, gently lowered by an invisible hand. The tree, its trunk blown apart by the explosion, crashed down.

There followed another series of explosions around us. These guns we were using made no sound in the firing, and my opponents were evidently as much at sea as to my position as I was to theirs. So I made no attempt to reply to their fire, contenting myself with keeping a sharp lookout in their general direction. And patience had its reward.

Very soon I saw a cautious movement in the top of another tree. Exposing myself as little as possible, I aimed carefully at the tree trunk and fired again. A shriek followed the explosion. I heard the tree crash down; then a groan.

There was silence for a while. Then I heard a faint sound of boughs swishing. I shot three times in its direction, pressing the button as rapidly as I could. Branches crashed down where my shells had exploded, but there was no body.

Then I saw one of them. He was starting one of those amazing leaps from the bough of one tree to another, about forty feet away.

I threw up my gun impulsively and fired. By now I had gotten the feel of the weapon, and my aim was good. I hit him. The "bullet" must have penetrated his body and exploded. For one moment I saw him flying through the air. Then the explosion, and he had vanished. He never finished his leap. It was annihilation.

How many more of them there were I don't know, but this must have been too much for them. They used a final round of shells on us, all of which exploded harmlessly, and shortly after I heard them swishing and crashing away from us through the tree tops. Not one of them descended to earth.

Now I had time to give some attention to my companion. She was, I found, a girl, and not a boy. Despite her bulky appearance, due to the peculiar belt strapped around her body high up under the arms, she was very slender, and very pretty.

There was a stream not far away, from which I brought water and bathed her face and wound.

Apparently the mystery of these long leaps, the monkey-like ability to jump from bough to bough, and of the bodies that floated gently down instead of falling, lay in the belt. The thing was some sort of anti-gravity belt that almost balanced the weight of the wearer, thereby tremendously multiplying the propulsive power of the leg muscles, and the lifting power of the arms.

When the girl came to, she regarded me as curiously as I did her, and promptly began to quiz me. Her accent and intonation puzzled me a lot, but nevertheless we were able to understand each other fairly well, except for certain words and phrases. I explained what had happened while she lay unconscious, and she thanked me simply for saving her life.

"You are a strange exchange," she said, eying my clothing quizzically. Evidently she found it mirth provoking by contrast with her own neatly efficient garb. "Don't you understand what I mean by 'exchange'? I mean ah—let me see—a stranger, somebody from some other gang. What gang do you belong to?" (She pronounced it "gan," with only a suspicion of a nasal sound.)

I laughed. "I'm not a gangster," I said. But she evidently did not understand this word. "I don't belong to any gang," I explained, "and never did. Does everybody belong to a gang nowadays?"

"Naturally," she said, frowning. "If you don't belong to a gang, where and how do you live? Why have you not found and joined a gang? How do you eat? Where do you get your clothing?"

"I've been eating wild game for the past two weeks," I explained, "and this clothing I—er—ah—." I paused, wondering how I could explain that it must be many hundred years old.

In the end I saw I would have to tell my story as well as I could, piecing it together with my assumptions as to what had happened. She listened patiently; incredulously at first, but with more confidence as I went on. When I had finished, she sat thinking for a long time.

"That's hard to believe," she said, "but I believe it." She looked me over with frank interest.

"Were you married when you slipped into unconsciousness down in that mine?" she asked me suddenly. I assured her I had never married. "Well, that simplifies matters," she continued. "You see, if you were technically classed as a family man, I could take you back only as an invited exchange and I, being unmarried, and no relation of yours, couldn't do the inviting."

II

THE FOREST GANGS

She gave me a brief outline of the very peculiar social and economic system under which her people lived. At least it seemed very peculiar from my 20th Century viewpoint.

I learned with amazement that exactly 492 years had passed over my head as I lay unconscious in the mine.

Wilma, for that was her name, did not profess to be a historian, and so could give me only a sketchy outline of the wars that had been fought, and the manner in which such radical changes had come about. It seemed that another war had followed the First World War, in which nearly all the European nations had banded together to break the financial and industrial power of America. They succeeded in their purpose, though they were beaten, for the war was a terrific one, and left America, like themselves, gasping, bleeding and disorganized, with only the hollow shell of a victory.

This opportunity had been seized by the Russian Soviets, who had made a coalition with the Chinese, to sweep over all Europe and reduce it to a state of chaos.

America, industrially geared to world production and the world trade, collapsed economically, and there ensued a long period of stagnation and desperate attempts at economic reconstruction. But it was impossible to stave off war with the Mongolians, who by now had subjugated the Russians, and were aiming at a world empire.

In about 2109, it seems, the conflict was finally precipitated. The Mongolians, with overwhelming fleets of great airships, and a science that far outstripped that of crippled America, swept in over the Pacific and Atlantic Coasts, and down from Canada, annihilating American aircraft, armies and cities with their terrific *disintegrator* rays. These rays were projected from a machine not unlike a searchlight in appearance, the reflector of which, however, was not material substance, but a complicated balance of interacting electronic forces. This resulted in a terribly destructive beam. Under its influence, material substance melted into "nothingness"; i.e., into electronic vibrations. It destroyed all then known substances, from air to the most dense metals and stone.

They settled down to the establishment of what became known as the Han dynasty in America, as a sort of province in their World Empire.

Those were terrible days for the Americans. They were hunted like wild beasts. Only those survived who finally found refuge in mountains, canyons and forests. Government was at an end among them. Anarchy prevailed for several generations. Most would have been eager to submit to the Hans, even if it meant slavery. But the Hans did not want them, for they themselves had marvelous machinery and scientific process by which all difficult labor was accomplished.

Ultimately they stopped their active search for, and annihilation of, the widely scattered groups of now savage Americans. So long as they remained hidden in their forests, and did not venture near the great cities the Hans had built, little attention was paid to them.

Then began the building of the new American civilization. Families and individuals gathered together in clans or "gangs" for mutual protection. For nearly a century they lived a nomadic and primitive life, moving from place to place, in desperate fear of the casual and occasional Han air raids, and the terrible disintegrator ray. As the frequency of these raids decreased, they began to stay permanently in given localities, organizing upon lines which in many respects were similar to those of the military households of the Norman feudal barons, except that instead of gathering together in castles, their defense tactics necessitated a certain scattering of living quarters for families and individuals. They lived virtually in the open air, in the forests, in green tents, resorting to camouflage tactics that would conceal their presence from air observers. They dug underground factories and laboratories, that they might better be shielded from the electrical detectors of the Hans. They tapped the radio communication lines of the Hans, with crude instruments at first; better ones later on. They bent every effort toward the redevelopment of science. For many generations they labored as unseen, unknown scholars of the Hans, picking up their knowledge piecemeal, as fast as they were able to.

During the earlier part of this period, there were many deadly wars fought between the various gangs, and occasional courageous but childishly futile attacks upon the Hans, followed by terribly punitive raids.

But as knowledge progressed, the sense of American brotherhood redeveloped. Reciprocal arrangements were made among the gangs over constantly increasing areas. Trade developed to a certain extent, as between one gang and another. But the interchange of knowledge became more important than that of goods, as skill in the handling of synthetic processes developed.

Within the gang, an economy was developed that was a compromise between individual liberty and a military socialism. The right of private property was limited practically to personal possessions, but private privileges were many, and sacredly regarded. Stimulation to achievement lay chiefly in the winning of various kinds of leadership and prerogatives, and only in a very limited degree in the hope of owning anything that might be classified as "wealth," and nothing that might be classified as "resources." Resources of every description, for military safety and efficiency, belonged as a matter of public interest to the community as a whole.

In the meantime, through these many generations, the Hans had developed a luxury economy, and with it the perfection of gilded vice and degradation. The Americans were regarded as "wild men of the woods." And since they neither needed nor wanted the woods or the wild men, they treated them as beasts, and were conscious of no human brotherhood with them. As time went on, and synthetic processes of producing foods and materials were further developed, less and less ground was needed by the Hans for the purposes of agriculture, and finally, even the working of mines was abandoned when it became cheaper to build up metal from electronic vibrations than to dig them out of the ground.

The Han race, devitalized by its vices and luxuries, with machinery and scientific processes to satisfy its every want, with virtually no necessity of labor, began to assume a defensive attitude toward the Americans.

And quite naturally, the Americans regarded the Hans with a deep, grim hatred. Conscious of individual superiority as men, knowing that latterly they were outstripping the Hans in science and civilization, they longed desperately for the day when they should be powerful enough to rise and annihilate the Yellow Blight that lay over the continent.

At the time of my awakening, the gangs were rather loosely organized, but were considering the establishment of a special military force, whose special business it would be to harry the Hans and bring down their air ships whenever possible without causing general alarm among the Mongolians. This force was destined to become the nucleus of the national force, when the Day of Retribution arrived. But that, however, did not happen for ten years, and is another story.

Wilma told me she was a member of the Wyoming Gang, which claimed the entire Wyoming Valley as its territory, under the leadership of Boss Hart. Her mother and father were dead, and she was unmarried, so she was not a "family member." She lived in a little group of tents known as Camp 17, under a woman Camp Boss, with seven other girls.

Her duties alternated between military or police scouting and factory work. For the two-week period which would end the next day, she had been on "air patrol." This did not mean, as I first imagined, that she was flying, but rather that she was on the lookout for Han ships over this outlying section of the Wyoming territory, and had spent most of her time perched in the tree tops scanning the skies. Had she seen one she would have fired a "drop flare" several miles off to one side, which would ignite when it was floating vertically toward the earth, so that the direction or point from which if had been fired might not be guessed by the airship and bring a blasting play of the disintegrator ray in her vicinity. Other members of the air patrol would send up rockets on seeing hers, until finally a scout equipped with an ultrophone, which, unlike the ancient radio, operated on the ultronic ethereal vibrations, would pass the warning simultaneously to the headquarters of the Wyoming Gang and other communities within a radius of several hundred miles, not to mention the few American rocket ships that might be in the air, and which instantly would duck to cover either through forest clearings or by flattening down to earth in green fields where their coloring would probably protect them from observation. The favorite American method of propulsion was known as "rocketing." The rocket is what I would describe, from my 20th Century comprehension of the matter, as an extremely powerful gas blast, atomically produced through the stimulation of chemical action. Scientists of today regard it as a childishly simple reaction, but by that very virtue, most economical and efficient.

But tomorrow, she explained, she would go back to work in the cloth plant, where she would take charge of one of the synthetic processes by which those wonderful substitutes for woven fabrics of wool, cotton and silk are produced. At the end of another two weeks, she would be back on military duty again, perhaps at the same work, or maybe as a "contact guard," on duty where the territory of the Wyomings merged with that of the Delawares, or the "Susquannas" (Susquehannas) or one of the half dozen other "gangs" in that section of the country which I knew as Pennsylvania and New York States.

Wilma cleared up for me the mystery of those flying leaps which she and her assailants had made, and explained in the following manner, how the inertron belt balances weight:

"Jumpers" were in common use at the time I "awoke," though they were costly, for at that time inertron had not been produced in very great quantity. They were very useful in the forest. They were belts, strapped high under the arms, containing an amount of inertron adjusted to the wearer's weight and purposes. In effect they made a man weigh as little as he desired; two pounds if he liked.

"Floaters" are a later development of "jumpers"—rocket motors encased in inertron blocks and strapped to the back in such a way that the wearer floats, when drifting, facing slightly downward. With his motor in operation, he moves like a diver, head-foremost, controlling his direction by twisting his body and by movements of his outstretched arms and hands. Ballast weights locked in the front of the belt adjust weight and lift. Some men prefer a few ounces of weight in floating, using a slight motor thrust to overcome this. Others prefer a buoyance balance of a few ounces. The inadvertent dropping of weight is not a serious matter. The motor thrust always can be used to descend. But as an extra precaution, in case the motor should fail, for any reason, there are built into every belt a number of detachable sections, one or more of which can be discarded to balance off any loss in weight.

"But who were your assailants," I asked, "and why were you attacked?"

Her assailants, she told me, were members of an outlaw gang, referred to as "Bad Bloods," a group which for several generations had been under the domination of conscienceless leaders who tried to advance the interests of their clan by tactics which their neighbors had come to regard as unfair, and who in consequence had been virtually boycotted. Their purpose had been to slay her near the Delaware frontier, making it appear that the crime had been committed by Delaware scouts and thus embroil the Delawares and Wyomings in acts of reprisal against each other, or at least cause suspicions.

Fortunately they had not succeeded in surprising her, and she had been successful in dodging them for some two hours before the shooting began, at the moment when I arrived on the scene.

"But we must not stay here talking," Wilma concluded. "I have to take you in, and besides I must report this attack right away. I think we had better slip over to the other side of the mountain. Whoever is on that post will have a phone, and I can make a direct report. But you'll have to have a belt. Mine alone won't help much against our combined weights, and there's little to be gained by jumping heavy. It's almost as bad as walking."

After a little search, we found one of the men I had killed, who had floated down among the trees some distance away and whose belt was not badly damaged. In detaching it from his body, it nearly got away from me and shot up in the air. Wilma caught it, however, and though it reinforced the lift of her own belt so that she had to hook her knee around a branch to hold herself down, she saved it. I climbed the tree and, with my weight added to hers, we floated down easily.

III

LIFE IN THE 25TH CENTURY

We were delayed in starting for quite a while since I had to acquire a few crude ideas about the technique of using these belts. I had been sitting down, for instance, with the belt strapped about me, enjoying an ease similar to that of a comfortable armchair; when I stood up with a natural exertion of muscular effort, I shot ten feet into the air, with a wild instinctive thrashing of arms and legs that amused Wilma greatly.

But after some practice, I began to get the trick of gauging muscular effort to a minimum of vertical and a maximum of horizontal. The correct form, I found, was in a measure comparable to that of skating. I found, also, that in forest work particularly the arms and hands could be used to great advantage in swinging along from branch to branch, so prolonging leaps almost indefinitely at times.

In going up the side of the mountain, I found that my 20th Century muscles did have an advantage, in spite of lack of skill with the belt, and since the slopes were very sharp, and most of our leaps were upward, I could have distanced Wilma easily. But when we crossed the ridge and descended, she outstripped me with her superior technique. Choosing the steepest slopes, she would crouch in the top of a tree, and propel herself outward, literally diving until, with the loss of horizontal momentum, she would assume a more upright position and float downward. In this manner she would sometimes cover as much as a quarter of a mile in a single leap, while I leaped and scrambled clumsily behind, thoroughly enjoying the novel sensation.

Half way down the mountain, we saw another green-clad figure leap out above the tree tops toward us. The three of us perched on an outcropping of rock from which a view for many miles around could be had, while Wilma hastily explained her adventure and my presence to her fellow guard; whose name was Alan. I learned later that this was the modern form of Helen.

"You want to report by phone then, don't you?" Alan took a compact packet about six inches square from a holster attached to her belt and handed it to Wilma.

So far as I could see, it had no special receiver for the ear. Wilma merely threw back a lid, as though she were opening a book, and began to talk. The voice that came back from the machine was as audible as her own.

She was queried closely as to the attack upon her, and at considerable length as to myself, and I could tell from the tone of that voice that its owner was not prepared to take me at my face value as readily as Wilma had. For that matter, neither was the other girl. I could realize it from the suspicious glances she threw my way, when she thought my attention was elsewhere, and the manner in which her hand hovered constantly near her gun holster.

Wilma was ordered to bring me in at once, and informed that another scout would take her place on the other side of the mountain. So she closed down the lid of the phone and handed it back to Alan, who seemed relieved to see us departing over the tree tops in the direction of the camps.

We had covered perhaps ten miles, in what still seemed to me a surprisingly easy fashion, when Wilma explained, that from here on we would have to keep to the ground. We were nearing the camps, she said, and there was always the possibility that some small Han scoutship, invisible high in the sky, might catch sight of us through a projectoscope and thus find the general location of the camps.

Wilma took me to the Scout office, which proved to be a small building of irregular shape, conforming to the trees around it, and substantially constructed of green sheet-like material.

I was received by the assistant Scout Boss, who reported my arrival at once to the historical office, and to officials he called the Psycho Boss and the History Boss, who came in a few minutes later. The attitude of all three men was at first polite but skeptical, and Wilma's ardent advocacy seemed to amuse them secretly.

For the next two hours I talked, explained and answered questions. I had to explain, in detail, the manner of my life in the 20th Century and my understanding of customs, habits, business, science and the history of that period, and about developments in the centuries that had elapsed. Had I been in a classroom, I would have come through the examination with a very poor mark, for I was unable to give any answer to fully half of their questions. But before long I realized that the majority of these questions were designed as traps. Objects, of whose purpose I knew nothing, were casually handed to me, and I was watched keenly as I handled them.

In the end I could see both amazement and belief begin to show in the faces of my inquisitors, and at last the Historical and Psycho Bosses agreed openly that they could find no flaw in my story or reactions, and that unbelievable as it seemed, my story must be accepted as genuine.

They took me at once to Big Boss Hart. He was a portly man with a "poker face." He would probably have been the successful politician even in the 20th Century.

They gave him a brief outline of my story and a report of their examination of me. He made no comment other than to nod his acceptance of it. Then he turned to me.

"How does it feel?" he asked. "Do we look funny to you?"

"A bit strange," I admitted. "But I'm beginning to lose that dazed feeling, though I can see I have an awful lot to learn."

"Maybe we can learn some things from you, too," he said. "So you fought in the First World War. Do you know, we have very little left in the way of records of the details of that war, that is, the precise conditions under which it was fought, and the tactics employed. We forgot many things during the Han terror, and—well, I think you might have a lot of ideas worth thinking over for our raid masters. By the way, now that you're here, and can't go back to your own century, so to speak, what do you want to do? You're welcome to become one of us. Or perhaps you'd just like to visit with us for a while, and then look around among the other gangs. Maybe you'd like some of the others better. Don't make up your mind now. We'll put you down as an exchange for a while. Let's see. You and Bill Hearn ought to get along well together. He's Camp Boss of Number 34 when he isn't acting as Raid Boss or Scout Boss. There's a vacancy in his camp. Stay with him and think things over as long as you want to. As soon as you make up your mind to anything, let me know."

We all shook hands, for that was one custom that had not died out in five hundred years, and I set out with Bill Hearn.

Bill, like all the others, was clad in green. He was a big man. That is, he was about my own height, five feet eleven. This was considerably above the average now, for the race had lost something in stature, it seemed, through the vicissitudes of five centuries. Most of the women were a bit below five feet, and the men only a trifle above this height.

For a period of two weeks Bill was to confine himself to camp duties, so I had a good chance to familiarize myself with the community life. It was not easy. There were so many marvels to absorb. I never ceased to wonder at the strange combination of rustic social life and feverish industrial activity. At least, it was strange to me. For in my experience, industrial development meant crowded cities, tenements, paved streets, profusion of vehicles, noise, hurrying men and women with strained or dull faces, vast structures and ornate public works.

Here, however, was rustic simplicity, apparently isolated families and groups, living in the heart of the forest, with a quarter of a mile or more between households, a total absence of crowds, no means of conveyance other than the belts called jumpers, almost constantly worn by everybody, and an occasional rocket ship, used only for longer journeys, and underground plants or factories that were to my mind more like laboratories and engine rooms; many of them were excavations as deep as mines, with well finished, lighted and comfortable interiors. These people were adepts at camouflage against air observation. Not only would their activity have been unsuspected by an airship passing over the center of the community, but even by an enemy who might happen to drop through the screen of the upper branches to the floor of the forest. The camps, or household structures, were all irregular in shape and of colors that blended with the great trees among which they were hidden.

There were 724 dwellings or "camps" among the Wyomings, located within an area of about fifteen square miles. The total population was 8,688, every man, woman and child, whether member or "exchange," being listed.

The plants were widely scattered through the territory also. Nowhere was anything like congestion permitted. So far as possible, families and individuals were assigned to living quarters, not too far from the plants or offices in which their work lay.

All able-bodied men and women alternated in two-week periods between military and industrial service, except those who were needed for household work. Since working conditions in the plants and offices were ideal, and everybody thus had plenty of healthy outdoor activity in addition, the population was sturdy and active. Laziness was regarded as nearly the greatest of social offenses. Hard work and general merit were variously rewarded with extra privileges, advancement to positions of authority, and with various items of personal equipment for convenience and luxury.

In leisure moments, I got great enjoyment from sitting outside the dwelling in which I was quartered with Bill Hearn and ten other men, watching the occasional passers-by, as with leisurely, but swift movements, they swung up and down the forest trail, rising from the ground in long almost-horizontal leaps, occasionally swinging from one convenient branch overhead to another before "sliding" back to the ground farther on. Normal traveling pace, where these trails were straight enough, was about twenty miles an hour. Such things as automobiles and railroad trains (the memory of them not more than a month old in my mind) seemed inexpressibly silly and futile compared with such convenience as these belts or jumpers offered.

Bill suggested that I wander around for several days, from plant to plant, to observe and study what I could. The entire community had been apprised of my coming, my rating as an "exchange" reaching every building and post in the community, by means of ultronic broadcast. Everywhere I was welcomed in an interested and helpful spirit.

I visited the plants where ultronic vibrations were isolated from the ether and through slow processes built up into sub-electronic, electronic and atomic forms into the two great synthetic elements, ultron and inertron. I learned something, superficially at least, of the processes of combined chemical and mechanical action through which were produced the various forms of synthetic cloth. I watched the manufacture of the machines which were used at locations of construction to produce the various forms of building materials. But I was particularly interested in the munitions plants and the rocket-ship shops.

Ultron is a solid of great molecular density and moderate elasticity, which has the property of being 100 percent conductive to those pulsations known as light, electricity and heat. Since it is completely permeable to light vibrations, it is therefore absolutely invisible and non-reflective. Its magnetic response is almost, but not quite, 100 percent also. It is therefore very heavy under normal conditions but extremely responsive to the repellor or anti-gravity rays, such as the Hans use as "legs" for their airships.

Inertron is the second great triumph of American research and experimentation with ultronic forces. It was developed just a few years before my awakening in the abandoned mine. It is a synthetic element, built up, through a complicated heterodyning of ultronic pulsations, from "infra-balanced" sub-ionic forms. It is completely inert to both electric and magnetic forces in all the orders above the ultronic; that is to say, the sub-electronic, the electronic, the atomic and the molecular. In consequence it has a number of amazing and valuable properties. One of these is the total lack of weight. Another is a total lack of heat. It has no molecular vibration whatever. It reflects 100 percent of the heat and light impinging upon it. It does not feel cold to the touch, of course, since it will not absorb the heat of the hand. It is a solid, very dense in molecular structure despite its lack of weight, of great strength and considerable elasticity. It is a perfect shield against the disintegrator rays.

Rocket guns are very simple contrivances so far as the mechanism of launching the bullet is concerned. They are simple light tubes, closed at the rear end, with a trigger-actuated pin for piercing the thin skin at the base of the cartridge. This piercing of the skin starts the chemical and atomic reaction. The entire cartridge leaves the tube under its own power, at a very easy initial velocity, just enough to insure accuracy of aim; so the tube does not have to be of heavy construction. The bullet increases in velocity as it goes. It may be solid or explosive. It may explode on contact or on time, or a combination of these two.

Bill and I talked mostly of weapons, military tactics and strategy. Strangely enough he had no idea whatever of the possibilities of the barrage, though the tremendous effect of a "curtain of fire" with such high-explosive projectiles as these modern rocket guns used was obvious to me. But the barrage idea, it seemed, has been lost track of completely in the air wars that followed the First World War, and in the peculiar guerilla tactics developed by Americans in the later period of operations from the ground against Han airships, and in the gang wars which, until a few generations ago I learned, had been almost continuous.

"I wonder," said Bill one day, "if we couldn't work up some form of barrage to spring on the Bad Bloods. The Big Boss told me today that he's been in communication with the other gangs, and all are agreed that the Bad Bloods might as well be wiped out for good. That attempt on Wilma Deering's life and their evident desire to make trouble among the gangs, has stirred up every community east of the Alleghenies. The Boss says that none of the others will object if we go after them. So I imagine that before long we will. Now show me again how you worked that business in the Argonne forest. The conditions ought to be pretty much the same."

I went over it with him in detail, and gradually we worked out a modified plan that would be better adapted to our more powerful weapons, and the use of jumpers.

"It will be easy," Bill exulted. "I'll slide down and talk it over with the Boss tomorrow."

During the first two weeks of my stay with the Wyomings, Wilma Deering and I saw a great deal of each other. I naturally felt a little closer friendship for her, in view of the fact that she was the first human being I saw after waking from my long sleep; her appreciation of my saving her life, though I could not have done otherwise than I did in that matter, and most of all my own appreciation of the fact that she had not found it as difficult as the others to believe my story, operated in the same direction. I could easily imagine my story must have sounded incredible.

It was natural enough too, that she should feel an unusual interest in me. In the first place, I was her personal discovery. In the second, she was a girl of studious and reflective turn of mind. She never got tired of my stories and descriptions of the 20th Century.

The others of the community, however, seemed to find our friendship a bit amusing. It seemed that Wilma had a reputation for being cold toward the opposite sex, and so others, not being able to appreciate some of her fine qualities as I did, misinterpreted her attitude, much to their own delight. Wilma and I, however, ignored this as much as we could.

IV

A HAN AIR RAID

There was a girl in Wilma's camp named Gerdi Mann, with whom Bill Hearn was desperately in love, and the four of us used to go around a lot together. Gerdi was a distinct type. Whereas Wilma had the usual dark brown hair and hazel eyes that marked nearly every member of the community, Gerdi had red hair, blue eyes and very fair skin. She has been dead many years now, but I remember her vividly because she was a throwback in physical appearance to a certain 20th Century type which I have found very rare among modern Americans; also because the four of us were engaged one day in a discussion of this very point, when I obtained my first experience of a Han air raid.

We were sitting high on the side of a hill overlooking the valley that teemed with human activity, invisible beneath its blanket of foliage.

The other three, who knew of the Irish but vaguely and indefinitely, as a race on the other side of the globe, which, like ourselves, had succeeded in maintaining a precarious and fugitive existence in rebellion against the

Mongolian domination of the earth, were listening with interest to my theory that Gerdi's ancestors of several hundred years ago must have been Irish. I explained that Gerdi was an Irish type, evidently a throwback, and that her surname might well have been McMann, or McMahan, and still more anciently "mac Mathghamhain." They were interested too in my surmise that "Gerdi" was the same name as that which had been "Gerty" or "Gertrude" in the 20th Century.

In the middle of our discussion, we were startled by an alarm rocket that burst high in the air, far to the north, spreading a pall of red smoke that drifted like a cloud. It was followed by others at scattered points in the northern sky.

"A Han raid!" Bill exclaimed in amazement. "The first in seven years!"

"Maybe it's just one of their ships off its course," I ventured.

"No," said Wilma in some agitation. "That would be green rockets. Red means only one thing, Tony. They're sweeping the countryside with their dis beams. Can you see anything, Bill?"

"We had better get under cover," Gerdi said nervously. "The four of us are bunched here in the open. For all we know they may be twelve miles up, out of sight, yet looking at us with a projecto'."

Bill had been sweeping the horizon hastily with his glass, but apparently saw nothing.

"We had better scatter, at that," he said finally. "It's orders, you know. See!" He pointed to the valley.

Here and there a tiny human figure shot for a moment above the foliage of the treetops.

"That's bad," Wilma commented, as she counted the jumpers. "No less than fifteen people visible, and all clearly radiating from a central point. Do they want to give away our location?"

The standard orders covering air raids were that the population was to scatter individually. There should be no grouping, or even pairing, in view of the destructiveness of the disintegrator rays. Experience of generations had proved that if this were done, and everybody remained hidden beneath the tree screens, the Hans would have to sweep mile after mile of territory, foot by foot, to catch more than a small percentage of the community.

Gerdi, however, refused to leave Bill, and Wilma developed an equal obstinacy against quitting my side. I was inexperienced at this sort of thing, she explained, quite ignoring the fact that she was too; she was only thirteen or fourteen years old at the time of the last air raid.

However, since I could not argue her out of it, we leaped together about a quarter of a mile to the right, while Bill and Gerdi disappeared down the hillside among the trees.

Wilma and I both wanted a point of vantage from which we might overlook the valley and the sky to the north, and we found it near the top of the ridge, where, protected from visibility by thick branches, we could look out between the tree trunks, and get a good view of the valley.

No more rockets went up. Except for a few of those warning red clouds, drifting lazily in a blue sky, there was no visible indication of man's past or present existence anywhere in the sky or on the ground.

Then Wilma gripped my arm and pointed. I saw it; away off in the distance; looking like a phantom dirigible airship, in its coat of low-visibility paint, a bare spectre.

"Seven thousand feet up," Wilma whispered, crouching close to me. "Watch."

The ship was about the same shape as the great dirigibles of the 20th Century that I had seen, but without the suspended control car, engines, propellors, rudders or elevating planes. As it loomed rapidly nearer, I saw that it was wider and somewhat flatter than I had supposed.

Now I could see the repellor rays that held the ship aloft, like searchlight beams faintly visible in the bright daylight (and still faintly visible to the human eye at night). Actually, I had been informed by my instructors, there were two rays; the visible one generated by the ship's apparatus, and directed toward the ground as a beam of "carrier" impulses; and the true repellor ray, the complement of the other in one sense, induced by the action of the "carrier" and reacting in a concentrating upward direction from the mass of the earth, becoming successively electronic, atomic and finally molecular, in its nature, according to various ratios of distance between earth mass and "carrier" source, until, in the last analysis, the ship itself actually is supported on an upward rushing column of air, much like a ball continuously supported on a fountain jet.

The raider neared with incredible speed. Its rays were both slanted astern at a sharp angle, so that it slid forward with tremendous momentum.

The ship was operating two disintegrator rays, though only in a casual, intermittent fashion. But whenever they flashed downward with blinding brilliancy, forest, rocks and ground melted instantaneously into nothing, where they played upon them.

When later I inspected the scars left by these rays I found them some five feet deep and thirty feet wide, the exposed surfaces being lava-like in texture, but of a pale, iridescent, greenish hue.

No systematic use of the rays was made by the ship, however, until it reached a point over the center of the valley—the center of the community's activities. There it came to a sudden stop by shooting its repellor beams sharply forward and easing them back gradually to the vertical, holding the ship floating and motionless. Then the work of destruction began systematically.

Back and forth traveled the destroying rays, ploughing parallel furrows from hillside to hillside. We gasped in dismay, Wilma and I, as time after time we saw it plough through sections where we knew camps or plants were located.

"This is awful," she moaned, a terrified question in her eyes. "How could they know the location so exactly, Tony? Did you see? They were never in doubt. They stalled at a predetermined spot—and—and it was exactly the right spot."

We did not talk of what might happen if the rays were turned in our direction. We both knew. We would simply disintegrate in a split second into mere scattered electronic vibrations. Strangely enough, it was this self-reliant girl of the 25th Century, who clung to me, a relatively primitive man of the 20th, less familiar than she with the thought of this terrifying possibility, for moral support.

We knew that many of our companions must have been whisked into absolute non-existence before our eyes in these few moments. The whole thing paralyzed us into mental and physical immobility for I do not know how long.

It couldn't have been long, however, for the rays had not ploughed more than thirty of their twenty-foot furrows or so across the valley, when I regained control of myself, and brought Wilma to herself by shaking her roughly.

"How far will this rocket gun shoot, Wilma?" I demanded, drawing my pistol.

"It depends on your rocket, Tony. It will take even the longest range rocket, but you could shoot more accurately from a longer tube. But why? You couldn't penetrate the shell of that ship with rocket force, even if you could reach it."

I fumbled clumsily with my rocket pouch, for I was excited. I had an idea I wanted to try; a "hunch" I called it, forgetting that Wilma could not understand my ancient slang. But finally, with her help, I selected the longest range explosive rocket in my pouch, and fitted it to my pistol.

"It won't carry seven thousand feet, Tony," Wilma objected. But I took aim carefully. It was another thought that I had in my mind. The supporting repellor ray, I had been told, became molecular in character at what was called a logarithmic level of five (below that it was a purely electronic "flow" or pulsation between the source of the "carrier" and the average mass of the earth). Below that level if I could project my explosive bullet into this stream where it began to carry material substance upward, might it not rise with the air column, gathering speed and hitting the ship with enough impact to carry it through the shell? It was worth trying anyhow. Wilma became greatly excited, too, when she grasped the nature of my inspiration.

Feverishly I looked around for some formation of branches against which I could rest the pistol, for I had to aim most carefully. At last I found one. Patiently I sighted on the hulk of the ship far above us, aiming at the far side of it, at such an angle as would, so far as I could estimate, bring my bullet path through the forward repellor beam. At last the sights wavered across the point I sought and I pressed the button gently.

For a moment we gazed breathlessly.

Suddenly the ship swung bow down, as on a pivot, and swayed like a pendulum. Wilma screamed in her excitement.

"Oh, Tony, you hit it! You hit it! Do it again; bring it down!"

We had only one more rocket of extreme range between us, and we dropped it three times in our excitement in inserting it in my gun. Then, forcing myself to be calm by sheer will power, while Wilma stuffed her little fist into her mouth to keep from shrieking, I sighted carefully again and fired. In a flash, Wilma had grasped the hope that this discovery of mine might lead to the end of the Han domination.

The elapsed time of the rocket's invisible flight seemed an age.

Then we saw the ship falling. It seemed to plunge lazily, but actually it fell with terrific acceleration, turning end over end, its disintegrator rays, out of control, describing vast, wild arcs, and once cutting a gash through the forest less than two hundred feet from where we stood.

The crash with which the heavy craft hit the ground reverberated from the hills—the momentum of eighteen or twenty thousand tons, in a sheer drop of seven thousand feet. A mangled mass of metal, it buried itself in the ground, with poetic justice, in the middle of the smoking, semi-molten field of destruction it had been so deliberately ploughing.

The silence, the vacuity of the landscape, was oppressive, as the last echoes died away.

Then far down the hillside, a single figure leaped exultantly above the foliage screen. And in the distance another, and another.

In a moment the sky was punctured by signal rockets. One after another the little red puffs became drifting clouds.

"Scatter! Scatter!" Wilma exclaimed. "In half an hour there'll be an entire Han fleet here from Nu-yok, and another from Bah-flo. They'll get this instantly on their recordographs and location finders. They'll blast the whole valley and the country for miles beyond. Come, Tony. There's no time for the gang to rally. See the signals. We've got to jump. Oh, I'm so proud of you!"

Over the ridge we went, in long leaps toward the east, the country of the Delawares.

From time to time signal rockets puffed in the sky. Most of them were the "red warnings," the "scatter" signals. But from certain of the others, which

Wilma identified as Wyoming rockets, she gathered that whoever was in command (we did not know whether the Boss was alive or not) was ordering an ultimate rally toward the south, and so we changed our course.

It was a great pity, I thought, that the clan had not been equipped throughout its membership with ultrophones, but Wilma explained to me, that not enough of these had been built for distribution as yet, although general distribution had been contemplated within a couple of months.

We traveled far before nightfall overtook us, trying only to put as much distance as possible between ourselves and the valley.

When gathering dusk made jumping too dangerous, we sought a comfortable spot beneath the trees, and consumed part of our emergency rations. It was the first time I had tasted the stuff—a highly nutritive synthetic substance called "concentro," which was, however, a bit bitter and unpalatable. But as only a mouthful or so was needed, it did not matter.

Neither of us had a cloak, but we were both thoroughly tired and happy, so we curled up together for warmth. I remember Wilma making some sleepy remark about our mating, as she cuddled up, as though the matter were all settled, and my surprise at my own instant acceptance of the idea, for I had not consciously thought of her that way before. But we both fell asleep at once.

In the morning we found little time for love making. The practical problem facing us was too great. Wilma felt that the Wyoming plan must be to rally in the Susquanna territory, but she had her doubts about the wisdom of this plan. In my elation at my success in bringing down the Han ship, and my newly found interest in my charming companion, who was, from my viewpoint of another century, at once more highly civilized and yet more primitive than myself, I had forgotten the ominous fact that the Han ship I had destroyed must have known the exact location of the Wyoming Works.

This meant, to Wilma's logical mind, either that the Hans had perfected new instruments as yet unknown to us, or that somewhere, among the Wyomings or some other nearby gang, there were traitors so degraded as to commit that unthinkable act of trafficking in information with the Hans. In either contingency, she argued, other Han raids would follow, and since the Susquannas had a highly developed organization and more than usually productive plants, the next raid might be expected to strike them.

But at any rate it was clearly our business to get in touch with the other fugitives as quickly as possible, so in spite of muscles that were sore from the excessive leaping of the day before, we continued on our way.

We traveled for only a couple of hours when we saw a multi-colored rocket in the sky, some ten miles ahead of us.

"Bear to the left, Tony," Wilma said, "and listen for the whistle."

"Why?" I asked.

"Haven't they given you the rocket code yet?" she replied. "That's what the green, followed by yellow and purple means; to concentrate five miles east of the rocket position. You know the rocket position itself might draw a play of disintegrator beams."

It did not take us long to reach the neighborhood of the indicated rallying, though we were now traveling beneath the trees, with but an occasional leap to a top branch to see if any more rocket smoke was floating above. And soon we heard a distant whistle.

We found about half the Gang already there, in a spot where the trees met high above a little stream. The Big Boss and Raid Bosses were busy reorganizing the remnants.

We reported to Boss Hart at once. He was silent, but interested, when he heard our story.

"You two stick close to me," he said, adding grimly, "I'm going back to the valley at once with a hundred picked men, and I'll need you."

V

SETTING THE TRAP

Inside of fifteen minutes we were on our way. A certain amount of caution was sacrificed for the sake of speed, and the men leaped away either across the forest top, or over open spaces of ground, but concentration was forbidden. The Big Boss named the spot on the hillside as the rallying point.

"We'll have to take a chance on being seen, so long as we don't group," he declared, "at least until within five miles of the rallying spot. From then on I want every man to disappear from sight and to travel under cover. And keep your ultrophones open, and turned on ten-four-seven-six."

Wilma and I had received our battle equipment from the Gear Boss. It consisted of a long-gun, a hand-gun, with a special case of ammunition constructed of inertron, which made the load weigh but a few ounces, and a short sword. This gear we strapped over each other's shoulders, on top of our jumping belts. In addition, we each received an ultrophone, and a light inertron blanket rolled into a cylinder about six inches long by two or three in diameter. This fabric was exceedingly thin and light, but it had considerable warmth, because of the mixture of inertron in its composition.

"This looks like business," Wilma remarked to me with sparkling eyes. (And I might mention a curious thing here. The word "business" had survived from the 20th Century American vocabulary, but not with any meaning of "industry" or "trade," for such things being purely community activities were spoken of as "work" and "clearing." Business simply meant fighting, and that was all.)

"Did you bring all this equipment from the valley?" I asked the Gear Boss.

"No," he said. "There was no time to gather anything. All this stuff we cleared from the Susquannas a few hours ago. I was with the Boss on the way down, and he had me jump on ahead and arrange it. But you two had better be moving. He's beckoning you now."

Hart was about to call us on our phones when we looked up. As soon as we did so, he leaped away, waving us to follow closely.

He was a powerful man, and he darted ahead in long, swift, low leaps up the banks of the stream, which followed a fairly straight course at this point. By extending ourselves, however, Wilma and I were able to catch up to him.

As we gradually synchronized our leaps with his, he outlined to us, between the grunts that accompanied each leap, his plan of action.

"We have to start the big business—*unh*—sooner or later," he said. "And if—*unh*—the Hans have found any way of locating our positions—*unh*—it's time to start now, although the Council of Bosses—*unh*—had intended waiting a few years until enough rocket ships have been—*unh*—built. But no matter what the sacrifice—*unh*—we can't afford to let them get us on the run—*unh*—. We'll set a trap for the yellow devils in the—*unh*—valley if they come back for their wreckage—*unh*—and if they don't, we'll go rocketing for some of their liners—*unh*—on the Nu-yok, Clee-lan, Si-ka-ga course. We can use—*unh*—that idea of yours of shooting up the repellor—*unh*—beams. Want you to give us a demonstration."

With further admonition to follow him closely, he increased his pace, and Wilma and I were taxed to our utmost to keep up with him. It was only in ascending the slopes that my tougher muscles overbalanced his greater skill, and I was able to set the pace for him, as I had for Wilma.

We slept in greater comfort that night, under our inertron blankets, and were off with the dawn, leaping cautiously to the top of the ridge overlooking the valley which Wilma and I had left.

The Boss scanned the sky with his ultroscope, patiently taking some fifteen minutes to the task, and then swung his phone into use, calling the roll and giving the men their instructions.

His first order was for us all to slip our ear and chest discs into permanent position.

These ultrophones were quite different from the one used by Wilma's companion scout the day I saved her from the vicious attack of the bandit Gang. That one was contained entirely in a small pocket case. These, with which we were now equipped, consisted of a pair of ear discs, each a separate and self-contained receiving set. They slipped into little pockets over our ears in the fabric helmets we wore, and shut out virtually all extraneous sounds. The chest discs were likewise self-contained sending sets, strapped to the chest a few inches below the neck and actuated by the vibrations from the vocal cords through the body tissues. The total range of these sets was about eighteen miles. Reception was remarkably clear, quite free from the static that so marked the 20th Century radios, and of a strength in direct proportion to the distance of the speaker.

The Boss' set was triple powered, so that his orders would cut in on any local conversations, which were indulged in, however, with great restraint, and only for the purpose of maintaining contacts.

I marveled at the efficiency of this modern method of battle communication in contrast to the clumsy signaling devices of more ancient times; and also at other military contrasts in which the 20th and 25th Century methods were the reverse of each other in efficiency. These modern Americans, for instance, knew little of hand to hand fighting, and nothing, naturally, of trench warfare. Of barrages they were quite ignorant, although they possessed weapons of terrific power. And until my recent flash of inspiration, no one among them, apparently, had ever thought of the scheme of shooting a rocket into a repellor beam and letting the beam itself hurl it upward into the most vital part of the Han ship.

Hart patiently placed his men, first giving his instructions to the campmasters, and then remaining silent, while they placed the individuals.

In the end, the hundred men were ringed about the valley, on the hillsides and tops, each in a position from which he had a good view of the wreckage of the Han ship. But not a man had come in view, so far as I could see, in the whole process.

The Boss explained to me that it was his idea that he, Wilma and I should investigate the wreck. If Han ships should appear in the sky, we would leap for the hillsides.

I suggested to him to have the men set up their long-guns trained on an imaginary circle surrounding the wreck. He busied himself with this after the three of us leaped down to the Han ship, serving as a target himself, while he called on the men individually to aim their pieces and lock them in position.

In the meantime Wilma and I climbed into the wreckage, but did not find much. Practically all of the instruments and machinery had been twisted out of all recognizable shape, or utterly destroyed by the ship's disintegrator rays which apparently had continued to operate in the midst of its warped remains for some moments after the crash.

It was unpleasant work searching the mangled bodies of the crew. But it had to be done. The Han clothing, I observed, was quite different from that of the Americans, and in many respects more like the garb to which I had been accustomed in the earlier part of my life. It was made of synthetic fabrics like silks, loose and comfortable trousers of knee length, and sleeveless shirts.

No protection, except that against drafts, was needed, Wilma explained to me, for the Han cities were entirely enclosed, with splendid arrangements for ventilation and heating. These arrangements of course were equally adequate in their airships. The Hans, indeed, had quite a distaste for unshaded daylight, since their lighting apparatus diffused a controlled amount of violet rays, making the unmodified sunlight unnecessary for health, and undesirable for comfort. Since the Hans did not have the secret of inertron, none of them wore anti-gravity belts. Yet in spite of the fact that they had to bear their own full weights at all times, they were physically far inferior to the Americans, for they lived lives of degenerative physical inertia, having machinery of every description for the performance of all labor, and convenient conveyances for any movement of more than a few steps.

Even from the twisted wreckage of this ship I could see that seats, chairs and couches played an extremely important part in their scheme of existence.

But none of the bodies were overweight. They seemed to have been the bodies of men in good health, but muscularly much underdeveloped. Wilma explained to me that they had mastered the science of gland control, and of course dietetics, to the point where men and women among them not uncommonly reached the age of a hundred years with arteries and general health in splendid condition.

I did not have time to study the ship and its contents as carefully as I would have liked, however. Time pressed, and it was our business to discover some clue to the deadly accuracy with which the ship had spotted the Wyoming Works.

The Boss had hardly finished his arrangements for the ring barrage, when one of the scouts on an eminence to the north, announced the approach of seven Han ships, spread out in a great semi-circle.

Hart leaped for the hillside, calling to us to do likewise, but Wilma and I had raised the flaps of our helmets and switched off our "speakers" for conversation between ourselves, and by the time we discovered what had happened, the ships were clearly visible, so fast were they approaching.

"Jump!" we heard the Boss order, "Deering to the north. Rogers to the east."

But Wilma looked at me meaningly and pointed to where the twisted plates of the ship, projecting from the ground, offered a shelter.

"Too late, Boss," she said. "They'd see us. Besides I think there's something here we ought to look at. It's probably their magnetic graph."

"You're signing your death warrant," Hart warned.

"We'll risk it," said Wilma and I together.

"Good for you," replied the Boss. "Take command then, Rogers, for the present. Do you all know his voice, boys?"

A chorus of assent rang in our ears, and I began to do some fast thinking as the girl and I ducked into the twisted mass of metal.

"Wilma, hunt for that record," I said, knowing that by the simple process of talking I could keep the entire command continuously informed as to the situation. "On the hillsides, keep your guns trained on the circles and stand by. On the hilltops, how many of you are there? Speak in rotation from Bald Knob around to the east, north, west."

In turn the men called their names. There were twenty of them.

I assigned them by name to cover the various Han ships, numbering the latter from left to right.

"Train your rockets on their repellor rays about three-quarters of the way up, between ships and ground. Aim is more important than elevation. Follow those rays with your aim continuously. Shoot when I tell you, not before. Deering has the record. The Hans probably have not seen us, or at least think there are but two of us in the valley, since they're settling without opening up disintegrators. Any opinions?"

My ear discs remained silent.

"Deering and I remain here until they land and debark. Stand by and keep alert."

Rapidly and easily the largest of the Han ships settled to the earth. Three scouted sharply to the south, rising to a higher level. The others floated motionless about a thousand feet above.

Peeping through a small fissure between two plates, I saw the vast hulk of the ship come to rest full on the line of our prospective ring barrage. A door clanged open a couple of feet from the ground, and one by one the crew emerged.

VI

THE "WYOMING MASSACRE"

"They're coming out of the ship." I spoke quietly, with my hand over my mouth, for fear they might hear me. "One—two—three—four, five—six—seven—eight—nine. That seems to be all. Who knows how many men a ship like that is likely to carry?"

"About ten, if there are no passengers," replied one of my men, probably one of those on the hillside.

"How are they armed?" I asked.

"Just knives," came the reply. "They never permit hand-rays on the ships. Afraid of accidents. Have a ruling against it."

"Leave them to us then," I said, for I had a hastily formed plan in my mind.

"You, on the hillsides, take the ships above. Abandon the ring target. Divide up in training on those repellor rays. You, on the hilltops, all train on the repellors of the ships to the south. Shoot at the word, but not before.

"Wilma, crawl over to your left where you can make a straight leap for the door in that ship. These men are all walking around the wreck in a bunch. When they're on the far side, I'll give the word and you leap through that door in one bound. I'll follow. Maybe we won't be seen. We'll overpower the guard inside, but don't shoot. We may escape being seen by both this crew and ships above. They can't see over this wreck."

It was so easy that it seemed too good to be true. The Hans who had emerged from the ship walked round the wreckage lazily, talking in guttural tones, keenly interested in the wreck, but quite unsuspicious.

At last they were on the far side. In a moment they would be picking their way into the wreck.

"Wilma, leap!" I almost whispered the order.

The distance between Wilma's hiding place and the door in the side of the Han ship was not more than fifteen feet. She was already crouched with her feet braced against a metal beam. Taking the lift of that wonderful inertron belt into her calculation, she dove headforemost, like a green projectile, through the door. I followed in a split second, more clumsily, but no less speedily, bruising my shoulder painfully, as I ricocheted from the edge of the opening and brought up sliding against the unconscious girl; for she evidently had hit her head against the partition within the ship into which she had crashed.

We had made some noise within the ship. Shuffling footsteps were approaching down a well lit gangway.

"Any signs we have been observed?" I asked my men on the hillsides.

"Not yet," I heard the Boss reply. "Ships overhead still standing. No beams have been broken out. Men on ground absorbed in wreck. Most of them have crawled into it out of sight."

"Good," I said quickly. "Deering hit her head. Knocked out. One or more members of the crew approaching. We're not discovered yet. I'll take care of them. Stand a bit longer, but be ready."

I think my last words must have been heard by the man who was approaching, for he stopped suddenly.

I crouched at the far side of the compartment, motionless. I would not draw my sword if there were only one of them. He would be a weakling, I figured, and I should easily overcome him with my bare hands.

Apparently reassured at the absence of any further sound, a man came around a sort of bulkhead—and I leaped.

I swung my legs up in front of me as I did so, catching him full in the stomach and knocked him cold.

I ran forward along the keel gangway, searching for the control room. I found it well up in the nose of the ship. And it was deserted. What could I do to jam the controls of the ships that would not register on the recording instruments of the other ships? I gazed at the mass of controls. Levers and wheels galore. In the center of the compartment, on a massively braced universal joint mounting, was what I took for the repellor generator. A dial on it glowed and a faint hum came from within its shielding metallic case. But I had no time to study it.

Above all else, I was afraid that some automatic telephone apparatus existed in the room, through which I might be heard on the other ships. The risk of trying to jam the controls was too great. I abandoned the idea and withdrew softly. I would have to take a chance that there was no other member of the crew aboard.

I ran back to the entrance compartment. Wilma still lay where she had slumped down. I heard the voices of the Hans approaching. It was time to act. The next few seconds would tell whether the ships in the air would try or be able to melt us into nothingness. I spoke.

"Are you boys all ready?" I asked, creeping to a position opposite the door and drawing my hand-gun.

Again there was a chorus of assent.

"Then on the count of three, shoot up those repellor rays—all of them—and for God's sake, don't miss." And I counted.

I think my "three" was a bit weak. I know it took all the courage I had to utter it.

For an agonizing instant nothing happened, except that the landing party from the ship strolled into my range of vision.

Then startled, they turned their eyes upward. For an instant they stood frozen with horror at whatever they saw.

One hurled his knife at me. It grazed my cheek. Then a couple of them made a break for the doorway. The rest followed. But I fired pointblank with my hand-gun, pressing the button as fast as I could and aiming at their feet to make sure my explosive rockets would make contact and do their work.

The detonations of my rockets were deafening. The spot on which the Hans stood flashed into a blinding glare. Then there was nothing there except their torn and mutilated corpses. They had been fairly bunched, and I got them all.

I ran to the door, expecting any instant to be hurled into infinity by the sweep of a disintegrator ray.

Some eighth of a mile away I saw one of the ships crash to earth. A disintegrator ray came into my line of vision, wavered uncertainly for a moment and then began to sweep directly toward the ship in which I stood.

But it never reached it. Suddenly, like a light switched off, it shot to one side, and a moment later another vast hulk crashed to earth. I looked out, then stepped out on the ground.

The only Han ships in the sky were two of the scouts to the south which were hanging perpendicularly, and sagging slowly down. The others must have crashed down while I was deafened by the sound of the explosion of my own rockets.

Somebody hit the other repellor ray of one of the two remaining ships and it fell out of sight beyond a hilltop. The other, farther away, drifted down diagonally, its disintegrator ray playing viciously over the ground below it.

I shouted with exultation and relief.

"Take back the command, Boss!" I yelled.

His commands, sending out jumpers in pursuit of the descending ship, rang in my ears, but I paid no attention to them. I leaped back into the compartment of the Han ship and knelt beside my Wilma. Her padded helmet had absorbed much of the blow, I thought; otherwise, her skull might have been fractured.

"Oh, my head!" she groaned, coming to as I lifted her gently in my arms and strode out in the open with her. "We must have won, dearest, did we?"

"We most certainly did," I reassured her. "All but one crashed and that one is drifting down toward the south; we've captured this one we're in intact. There was only one member of the crew aboard when we dove in."

Less than an hour afterward the Big Boss ordered the outfit to tune in ultrophones on three-twenty-three to pick up a translated broadcast of the Han intelligence office in Nu-yok from the Susquanna station. It was in the form of a public warning and news item, and read as follows:

"This is Public Intelligence Office, Nu-yok, broadcasting warning to navigators of private ships, and news of public interest. The squadron of seven ships, which left Nu-yok this morning to investigate the recent destruction of the GK-984 in the Wyoming Valley, has been destroyed by a series of mysterious explosions similar to those which wrecked the GK-984.

"The phones, viewplates, and all other signaling devices of five of the seven ships ceased operating suddenly at approximately the same moment, about seven-four-nine." (According to the Han system of reckoning time, seven and forty-nine one hundredths after midnight.) "After violent disturbances the location finders went out of operation. Electroactivity registers applied to the territory of the Wyoming Valley remain dead.

"The Intelligence Office has no indication of the kind of disaster which overtook the squadron except certain evidences of explosive phenomena similar to those in the case of the GK-984, which recently went dead while beaming the valley in a systematic effort to wipe out the works and camps of the tribesmen. The Office considers, as obvious, the deduction that the tribesmen have developed a new, and as yet undetermined, technique of attack on airships, and has recommended to the Heaven-Born that immediate and unlimited authority be given the Navigation Intelligence Division to make an investigation of this technique and develop a defense against it.

"In the meantime it urges that private navigators avoid this territory in particular, and in general hold as closely as possible to the official inter-city routes, which now are being patrolled by the entire force of the Military Office, which is beaming the routes generously to a width of ten miles. The Military Office reports that it is at present considering no retaliatory raids against the tribesmen. With the Navigation Intelligence Division, it holds that unless further evidence of the nature of the disaster is developed in the near future, the public interest will be better served, and at smaller cost of life, by a scientific research than by attempts at retaliation, which may bring destruction on all ships engaging therein. So unless further evidence actually is developed, or the Heaven-Born orders to the contrary, the Military will hold to a defensive policy.

"Unofficial intimations from Lo-Tan are to the effect that the Heaven-Council has the matter under consideration.

"The Navigation Intelligence Office permits the broadcast of the following condensation of its detailed observations:

"The squadron proceeded to a position above the Wyoming Valley where the wreck of the GK-984 was known to be, from the record of its location finder before it went dead recently. There the bottom projectoscope relays of all ships registered the wreck of the GK-984. Teleprojectoscope views of the wreck and the bowl of the valley showed no evidence of the presence of tribesmen. Neither ship registers nor base registers showed any indication of electroactivity except from the squadron itself. On orders from the Base Squadron Commander, the LD-248, LK-745 and LG-25 scouted southward at 3,000 feet. The GK-43, GK-981 and GK-220 stood above at 2,500 feet, and the GK-18 landed to permit personal inspection of the wreck by the science committee. The party debarked, leaving one man on board in the control cabin. He set all projectoscopes at universal focus except RB-3," (this meant the third projectoscope from the bow of the ship, on the right-hand side of the lower deck) "with which he followed the landing group as it walked around the wreck.

"The first abnormal phenomenon recorded by any of the instruments at Base was that relayed automatically from projectoscope RB-4 of the GK-18, which as the party disappeared from view in back of the wreck, recorded two green missiles of roughly cylindrical shape, projected from the wreckage into the landing compartment of the ship. At such close range these were not clearly defined, owing to the universal focus at which the projectoscope was set. The Base Captain of GK-18 at once ordered the man in the control room to investigate, and saw him leave the control room in compliance with this order. An instant later confused sounds reached the control-room electrophone, such as might be made by a man falling heavily, and footsteps reapproached the control room, a figure entering and leaving the control room hurriedly. The Base Captain now believes, and the stills of the photorecord support his belief, that this was not the crew member who had been left in the control room. Before the Base Captain could speak to him he left the room, nor was any response given to the attention signal the Captain flashed throughout the ship.

"At this point projectoscope RB-3 of the ship now out of focus control, dimly showed the landing party walking back toward the ship. RB-4 showed it more clearly. Then on both these instruments, a number of blinding explosives in rapid succession were seen and the electrophone relays registered terrific concussions; the ship's electronic apparatus and projectoscopes apparatus went dead.

"Reports of the other ships' Base Observers and Executives, backed by the photorecords, show the explosions as taking place in the midst of the landing party as it returned, evidently unsuspicious, to the ship. Then in rapid succession they indicate that terrific explosions occurred inside and outside the three ships standing above close to their rep-ray generators, and all signals from these ships thereupon went dead.

"Of the three ships scouting to the south, the LD-248 suffered an identical fate, at the same moment. Its records add little to the knowledge of the disaster. But with the LK-745 and the LG-25 it was different.

"The relay instruments of the LK-745 indicated the destruction by an explosion of the rear rep-ray generator, and that the ship hung stern down for a short space, swinging like a pendulum. The forward viewplates and indicators did not cease functioning, but their records are chaotic, except for one projectoscope still, which shows the bowl of the valley, and the GK-981 falling, but no visible evidence of tribesmen. The control-room viewplate is also a chaotic record of the ship's crew tumbling and falling to the rear wall. Then the forward rep-ray generator exploded, and all signals went dead.

"The fate of the LG-25 was somewhat similar, except that this ship hung nose down, and drifted on the wind southward as it slowly descended out of control.

"As its control room was shattered, verbal report from its Action Captain was precluded. The record of the interior rear viewplate shows members of the crew climbing toward the rear rep-ray generator in an attempt to establish manual control of it, and increase the lift. The projectoscope relays, swinging in wide arcs, recorded little of value except at the ends of their swings. One of these, from a machine which happened to be set in telescopic focus, shows several views of great value in picturing the falls of the other ships, and all of the rear projectoscope records enable the reconstruction in detail of the pendulum and torsional movements of the ship, and its sag toward the earth. But none of the views showing the forest below contain any indication of tribesmen's presence. A final explosion put this ship out of commission at a height of 1,000 feet, and at a point four miles S. by E. of the center of the valley."

The message ended with a repetition of the warning to other airmen to avoid the valley.

VII

INCREDIBLE TREASON

After receiving this report, and reassurances of support from the Big Bosses of the neighboring Gangs, Hart determined to reestablish the Wyoming Valley community.

A careful survey of the territory showed that it was only the northern sections and slopes that had been "beamed" by the first Han ship.

The synthetic-fabrics plant had been partially wiped out, though the lower levels underground had not been reached by the dis ray. The forest screen above it, however, had been annihilated, and it was determined to abandon it, after removing all usable machinery and evidences of the processes that might be of interest to the Han scientists, should they return to the valley in the future.

The ammunition plant, and the rocket-ship plant, which had just been about to start operation at the time of the raid, were intact, as were the other important plants.

Hart brought the Camboss up from the Susquanna Works, and laid out new camp locations, scattering them farther to the south, and avoiding ground which had been seared by the Han beams and the immediate locations of the Han wrecks.

During this period, a sharp check was kept upon Han messages, for the phone plant had been one of the first to be put in operation, and when it became evident that the Hans did not intend any immediate reprisals, the entire membership of the community was summoned back, and normal life was resumed.

Wilma and I had been married the day after the destruction of the ships, and spent this intervening period in a delightful honeymoon, camping high in the mountains. On our return, we had a camp of our own, of course. We were assigned to location 1017. And as might be expected, we had a great deal of banter over which one of us was Camp Boss. The title stood after my name on the Big Boss' records, and those of the Big Camboss, of course, but Wilma airily held that this meant nothing at all—and generally succeeded in making me admit it whenever she chose.

I found myself a full-fledged member of the Gang now, for I had elected to search no farther for a permanent alliance, much as I would have liked to familiarize myself with this 25th Century life in other sections of the country. The Wyomings had a high morale, and had prospered under the rule of Big Boss Hart for many years. But many of the gangs, I found, were badly organized, lacked strong hands in authority, and were rife with intrigue. On the whole, I thought I would be wise to stay with a group which had already proved its friendliness, and in which I seemed to have prospects of advancement. Under these modern social and economic conditions, the kind of individual freedom to which I had been accustomed in the 20th Century was impossible. I would have been as much of a nonentity in every phase of human relationship by attempting to avoid alliances, as any man of the 20th Century would have been politically, who aligned himself with no political party.

This entire modern life, it appeared to me, judging from my ancient viewpoint, was organized along what I called "political" lines. And in this connection, it amused me to notice how universal had become the use of the word "boss." The leader, the person in charge or authority over anything, was a "boss." There was as little formality in his relations with his followers as there was in the case of the 20th Century political boss, and the same high respect paid him by his followers as well as the same high consideration by him of their interests. He was just as much of an autocrat, and just as much dependent upon the general popularity of his actions for the ability to maintain his autocracy.

The sub-boss who could not command the loyalty of his followers was as quickly deposed, either by them or by his superiors, as the ancient ward leader of the 20th Century who lost control of his votes.

As society was organized in the 20th Century, I do not believe the system could have worked in anything but politics. I tremble to think what would have happened, had the attempt been made to handle the A. E. F. this way during the First World War, instead of by that rigid military discipline and complete assumption of the individual as a mere standardized cog in the machine.

But owing to the centuries of desperate suffering the people had endured at the hands of the Hans, there developed a spirit of self-sacrifice and consideration for the common good that made the scheme applicable and efficient in all forms of human co-operation.

I have a little heresy about all this, however. My associates regard the thought with as much horror as many worthy people of the 20th Century felt in regard to any heretical suggestion that the original outline of government as laid down in the First Constitution did not apply as well to 20th Century conditions as to those of the early 19th.

In later years, I felt that there was a certain softening of moral fiber among the people, since the Hans had been finally destroyed with all their works; and Americans have developed a new luxury economy. I have seen signs of the reawakening of greed, of selfishness. The eternal cycle seems to be at work. I fear that slowly, though surely, private wealth is reappearing, codes of inflexibility are developing; they will be followed by corruption, degradation; and in the end some cataclysmic event will end this era and usher in a new one.

All this, however, is wandering afar from my story, which concerns our early battles against the Hans, and not our more modern problems of self-control.

Our victory over the seven Han ships had set the country ablaze. The secret had been carefully communicated to the other gangs, and the country was agog from one end to the other. There was feverish activity in the ammunition plants, and the hunting of stray Han ships became an enthusiastic sport. The results were disastrous to our hereditary enemies.

From the Pacific Coast came the report of a great transpacific liner of 75,000 tons "lift" being brought to earth from a position of invisibility above the clouds. A dozen Sacramentos had caught the hazy outlines of its rep rays approaching them, head-on, in the twilight, like ghostly pillars reaching into the sky. They had fired rockets into it with ease, whereas they would have had difficulty in hitting it if it had been moving at right angles to their position. They got one rep ray. The other was not strong enough to hold it up. It floated to earth, nose down, and since it was unarmed and unarmored, they had no difficulty in shooting it to pieces and massacring its crew and passengers. It seemed barbarous to me. But then I did not have centuries of bitter persecution in my blood.

From the Jersey Beaches we received news of the destruction of a Nu-yok-A-lan-a liner. The Sand-snipers, practically invisible in their sand-colored clothing, and half buried along the beaches, lay in wait for days, risking the play of dis beams along the route, and finally registering four hits within a week. The Hans discontinued their service along this route, and as evidence that they were badly shaken by our success, sent no raiders down the Beaches.

It was a few weeks later that Big Boss Hart sent for me.

"Tony," he said, "There are two things I want to talk to you about. One of them will become public property in a few days, I think. We aren't going to get any more Han ships by shooting up their repellor rays unless we use much larger rockets. They are wise to us now. They're putting armor of great thickness in the hulls of their ships below the rep-ray machines. Near Bah-flo this morning a party of Eries shot one without success. The explosions staggered her, but did not penetrate. As near as we can gather from their reports, their laboratories have developed a new alloy of great tensile strength and elasticity which nevertheless lets the rep rays through like a sieve. Our reports indicate that the Eries' rockets bounced off harmlessly. Most of the party was wiped out as the dis rays went into action on them.

"This is going to mean real business for all of the gangs before long. The Big Bosses have just held a national ultrophone council. It was decided that America must organize on a national basis. The first move is to develop sectional organization by Zones. I have been made Superboss of the Mid-Atlantic Zone.

"We're in for it now. The Hans are sure to launch reprisal expeditions. If we're to save the race we must keep them away from our camps and plants. I'm thinking of developing a permanent field force, along the lines of the regular armies of the 20th Century you told me about. Its business will be twofold: to carry the warfare as much as possible to the Hans, and to serve as a decoy, to beep their attention from our plants. I'm going to need your help in this.

"The other thing I wanted to talk to you about is this: Amazing and impossible as it seems, there is a group, or perhaps an entire gang, somewhere among us, that is betraying us to the Hans. It may be the Bad Bloods, or it may be one of those gangs who live near one of the Han cities. You know, a hundred and fifteen or twenty years ago there were certain of these people's ancestors who actually degraded themselves by mating with the Hans, sometimes even serving them as slaves, in the days before they brought all their service machinery to perfection.

"There is such a gang, called the Nagras, up near Bah-flo, and another in Mid-Jersey that men call the Pineys. But I hardly suspect the Pineys. There is little intelligence among them. They wouldn't have the information to give the Hans, nor would they be capable of imparting it. They're absolute savages."

"Just what evidence is there that anybody has been clearing information to the Hans?" I asked.

"Well," he replied, "first of all there was that raid upon us. That first Han ship knew the location of our plants exactly. You remember it floated directly into position above the valley and began a systematic beaming. Then, the Hans quite obviously have learned that we are picking up their electrophone waves, for they've gone back to their old, but extremely accurate, system of directional control. But we've been getting them for the past week by installing automatic re-broadcast units along the scar paths. This is what the Americans called those strips of country directly under the regular ship routes of the Hans, who as a matter of precaution frequently blasted them with their dis beams to prevent the growth of foliage which might give shelter to the Americans. But they've been beaming those paths so hard, it looks as though they even had information of this strategy. And in addition, they've been using code. Finally, we've picked up three of their messages in which they discuss, with some nervousness, the existence of our 'mysterious' ultrophone."

"But they still have no knowledge of the nature and control of ultronic activity?" I asked.

"No," said the Big Boss thoughtfully, "they don't seem to have a bit of information about it."

"Then it's quite clear," I ventured, "that whoever is 'clearing' us to them is doing it piecemeal. It sounds like a bit of occasional barter, rather than an out-and-out alliance. They're holding back as much information as possible for future bartering, perhaps."

"Yes," Hart said, "and it isn't information the Hans are giving in return, but some form of goods, or privilege. The trick would be to locate the goods. I guess I'll have to make a personal trip around among the Big Bosses."

VIII

THE HAN CITY

This conversation set me thinking. All of the Han electrophone intercommunication had been an open record to the Americans for a good many years, and the Hans were just finding it out. For centuries they had not regarded us as any sort of a menace. Unquestionably it had never occurred to them to secrete their own records. Somewhere in Nu-yok or Bah-flo, or possibly in Lo-Tan itself, the record of this traitorous transaction would be more or less openly filed. If we could only get at it! I wondered if a raid might not be possible.

Bill Hearn and I talked it over with our Han-affairs Boss and his experts. There ensued several days of research, in which the Han records of the entire decade were scanned and analyzed. In the end they picked out a mass of detail, and fitted it together into a very definite picture of the great central filing office of the Hans in Nu-yok, where the entire mass of official records was kept, constantly available for instant projectoscoping to any of the city's offices, and of the system by which the information was filed.

The attempt began to look feasible, though Hart instantly turned the idea down when I first presented it to him. It was unthinkable, he said. Sheer suicide. But in the end I persuaded him.

"I will need," I said, "Blash, who is thoroughly familiar with the Han library system; Bert Gaunt, who for years has specialized on their military offices; Bill Barker, the ray specialist, and the best swooper pilot we have." Swoopers are one-man and two-man ships, developed by the Americans, with skeleton backbones of inertron (during the war painted green for invisibility against the green forests below) and "bellies" of clear ultron.

"That will be Mort Gibbons," said Hart. "We've only got three swoopers left, Tony, but I'll risk one of them if you and the others will voluntarily risk your existences. But mind, I won't urge or order one of you to go. I'll spread the word to every Plant Boss at once to give you anything and everything you need in the way of equipment."

When I told Wilma of the plan, I expected her to raise violent and tearful objections, but she didn't. She was made of far sterner stuff than the women of the 20th Century. Not that she couldn't weep as copiously or be just as whimsical on occasion; but she wouldn't weep for the same reasons.

She just gave me an unfathomable look, in which there seemed to be a bit of pride, and asked eagerly for the details. I confess I was somewhat disappointed that she could so courageously risk my loss, even though I was amazed at her fortitude. But later I was to learn how little I knew her then.

We were ready to slide off at dawn the next morning. I had kissed Wilma good-bye at our camp, and after a final conference over our plans, we boarded our craft and gently glided away over the tree tops on a course, which, after crossing three routes of the Han ships, would take us out over the Atlantic, off the Jersey coast, whence we would come up on Nu-yok from the ocean.

Twice we had to nose down and lie motionless on the ground near a route while Han ships passed. Those were tense moments. Had the green back of our ship been observed, we would have been disintegrated in a second. But it wasn't.

Once over the water, however, we climbed in a great spiral, ten miles in diameter, until our altimeter registered ten miles. Here Gibbons shut off his rocket motor, and we floated, far above the level of the Atlantic liners, whose course was well to the north of us anyhow, and waited for nightfall.

Then Gibbons turned from his control long enough to grin at me.

"I have a surprise for you, Tony," he said, throwing back the lid of what I had supposed was a big supply case. And with a sigh of relief, Wilma stepped out of the case.

"If you 'go into zero' (a common expression of the day for being annihilated by the disintegrator ray), you don't think I'm going to let you go alone, do you, Tony? I couldn't believe my ears last night when you spoke of going without me, until I realized that you are still five hundred years behind the times in lots of ways. Don't you know, dear heart, that you offered me the greatest insult a husband could give a wife? You didn't, of course."

The others, it seemed, had all been in on the secret, and now they would have kidded me unmercifully, except that Wilma's eyes blazed dangerously.

At nightfall, we maneuvered to a position directly above the city. This took some time and calculation on the part of Bill Barker, who explained to me that he had to determine our point by ultronic bearings. The slightest resort to an electronic instrument, he feared, might be detected by our enemies' locators. In fact, we did not dare bring our swooper any lower than five miles for fear that its capacity might be reflected in their instruments.

Finally, however, he succeeded in locating above the central tower of the city.

"If my calculations are as much as ten feet off," he remarked with confidence, "I'll eat the tower. Now the rest is up to you, Mort. See what you can do to hold her steady. No—here, watch this indicator—the red beam, not the green one. See—if you keep it exactly centered on the needle, you're O.K. The width of the beam represents seventeen feet. The tower platform is fifty feet square, so we've got a good margin to work on."

For several moments we watched as Gibbons bent over his levers, constantly adjusting them with deft touches of his fingers. After a bit of wavering, the beam remained centered on the needle.

"Now," I said, "let's drop."

I opened the trap and looked down, but quickly shut it again when I felt the air rushing out of the ship into the rarefied atmosphere in a torrent. Gibbons literally yelled a protest from his instrument board.

"I forgot," I mumbled. "Silly of me. Of course, we'll have to drop out of compartment."

The compartment, to which I referred, was similar to those in some of the 20th Century submarines. We all entered it. There was barely room for us to stand, shoulder to shoulder. With some struggles, we got into our special air helmets and adjusted the pressure. At our signal, Gibbons exhausted the air in the compartment, pumping it into the body of the ship, and as the little signal light flashed, Wilma threw open the hatch.

Setting the ultron-wire reel, I climbed through, and began to slide down gently.

We all had our belts on, of course, adjusted to a weight balance of but a few ounces. And the five-mile reel of ultron wire that was to be our guide, was of gossamer fineness, though, anyway, I believe it would have lifted the full weight of the five of us, so strong and tough was this invisible metal. As an extra precaution, since the wire was of the purest metal, and therefore totally invisible, even in daylight, we all had our belts hooked on small rings that slid down the wire.

I went down with the end of the wire. Wilma followed a few feet above me, then Barker, Gaunt and Blash. Gibbons, of course, stayed behind to hold the ship in position and control the paying out of the line. We all had our ultrophones in place inside our air helmets, and so could converse with one another and with Gibbons. But at Wilma's suggestion, although we would have liked to let the Big Boss listen in, we kept them adjusted to short-range work, for fear that those who had been clearing with the Hans, and against whom we were on a raid for evidence, might also pick up our conversation. We had no fear that the Hans would hear us. In fact, we had the added advantage that, even after we landed, we could converse freely without danger of their hearing our voices through our air helmets.

For a while I could see nothing below but utter darkness. Then I realized, from the feel of the air as much as from anything, that we were sinking through a cloud layer. We passed through two more cloud layers before anything was visible to us.

Then there came under my gaze, about two miles below, one of the most beautiful sights I have ever seen; the soft, yet brilliant, radiance of the great Han city of Nu-yok. Every foot of its structural members seemed to glow with a wonderful incandescence, tower piled up on tower, and all built on the vast base-mass of the city, which, so I had been told, sheered upward from the surface of the rivers to a height of 728 levels.

The city, I noticed with some surprise, did not cover anything like the same area as the New York of the 20th Century. It occupied, as a matter of fact, only the lower half of Manhattan Island, with one section straddling the East River, and spreading out sufficiently over what once had been Brooklyn, to provide berths for the great liners and other air craft.

Straight beneath my feet was a tiny dark patch. It seemed the only spot in the entire city that was not aflame with radiance. This was the central tower, in the top floors of which were housed the vast library of record files and the main projectoscope plant.

"You can shoot the wire now," I ultrophoned Gibbons, and let go the little weighted knob. It dropped like a plummet, and we followed with considerable speed, but braking our descent with gloved hands sufficiently to see whether the knob, on which a faint light glowed as a signal for ourselves, might be observed by any Han guard or night prowler. Apparently it was not, and we again shot down with accelerated speed.

We landed on the roof of the tower without any mishap, and fortunately for our plan, in darkness. Since there was nothing above it on which it would have been worth while to shed illumination, or from which there was any need to observe it, the Hans had neglected to light the tower roof, or indeed to occupy it at all. This was the reason we had selected it as our landing place.

As soon as Gibbons had our word, he extinguished the knob light, and the knob, as well as the wire, became totally invisible. At our ultrophoned word, he would light it again.

"No gun play now," I warned. "Swords only, and then only if absolutely necessary."

Closely bunched, and treading as lightly as only inertron-belted people could, we made our way cautiously through a door and down an inclined plane to the floor below, where Gaunt and Blash assured us the military offices were located.

Twice Barker cautioned us to stop as we were about to pass in front of mirror-like "windows" in the passage wall, and flattening ourselves to the floor, we crawled past them.

"Projectoscopes," he said. "Probably on automatic record only, at this time of night. Still, we don't want to leave any records for them to study after we're gone."

"Were you ever here before?" I asked.

"No," he replied, "but I haven't been studying their electrophone communications for seven years without being able to recognize these machines when I run across them."

IX

THE FIGHT IN THE TOWER

So far we had not laid eyes on a Han. The tower seemed deserted. Blash and Gaunt, however, assured me that there would be at least one man on "duty" in the military offices, though he would probably be asleep, and two or three in the library proper and the projectoscope plant.

"We've got to put them out of commission," I said. "Did you bring the 'dope' cans, Wilma?"

"Yes," she said, "two for each. Here," and she distributed them.

We were now two levels below the roof, and at the point where we were to separate.

I did not want to let Wilma out of my sight, but it was necessary.

According to our plan, Barker was to make his way to the projectoscope plant, Blash and I to the library, and Wilma and Gaunt to the military office.

Blash and I traversed a long corridor, and paused at the great arched doorway of the library. Cautiously we peered in. Seated at three great switchboards were library operatives. Occasionally one of them would reach lazily for a lever, or sleepily push a button, as little numbered lights winked on and off. They were answering calls for electrograph and viewplate records on all sorts of subjects from all sections of the city.

I apprised my companions of the situation.

"Better wait a bit," Blash added. "The calls will lessen shortly."

Wilma reported an officer in the military office sound asleep.

"Give him the can, then," I said.

Barker was to do nothing more than keep watch in the projectoscope plant, and a few moments later he reported himself well concealed, with a splendid view of the floor.

"I think we can take a chance now," Blash said to me, and at my nod, he opened the lid of his dope can. Of course, the fumes did not affect us, through our helmets. They were absolutely without odor or visibility, and in a few seconds the librarians were unconscious. We stepped into the room.

There ensued considerable cautious observation and experiment on the part of Gaunt, working from the military office, and Blash in the library; while Wilma and I, with drawn swords and sharply attuned microphones, stood guard, and occasionally patrolled nearby corridors.

"I hear something approaching," Wilma said after a bit, with excitement in her voice. "It's a soft, gliding sound."

"That's an elevator somewhere," Barker cut in from the projectoscope floor. "Can you locate it? I can't hear it."

"It's to the east of me," she replied.

"And to my west," said I, faintly catching it. "It's between us, Wilma, and nearer you than me. Be careful. Have you got any information yet, Blash and Gaunt?"

"Getting it now," one of them replied. "Give us two minutes more."

"Keep at it then," I said. "We'll guard."

The soft, gliding sound ceased.

"I think it's very close to me," Wilma almost whispered. "Come closer, Tony. I have a feeling something is going to happen. I've never known my nerves to get taut like this without reason."

In some alarm, I launched myself down the corridor in a great leap toward the intersection whence I knew I could see her.

In the middle of my leap my ultrophone registered her gasp of alarm. The next instant I glided to a stop at the intersection to see Wilma backing toward the door of the military office, her sword red with blood, and an inert form on the corridor floor. Two other Hans were circling to either side of her with wicked-looking knives, while a third evidently a high officer, judging by the resplendence of his garb tugged desperately to get an electrophone instrument out of a bulky pocket. If he ever gave the alarm, there was no telling what might happen to us.

I was at least seventy feet away, but I crouched low and sprang with every bit of strength in my legs. It would be more correct to say that I dived, for I reached the fellow head on, with no attempt to draw my legs beneath me.

Some instinct must have warned him, for he turned suddenly as I hurtled close to him. But by this time I had sunk close to the floor, and had stiffened myself rigidly, lest a dragging knee or foot might just prevent my reaching him. I brought my blade upward and over. It was a vicious slash that laid him open, bisecting him from groin to chin, and his dead body toppled down on me, as I slid to a tangled stop.

The other two startled, turned. Wilma leaped at one and struck him down with a side slash. I looked up at this instant, and the dazed fear on his face at the length of her leap registered vividly. The Hans knew nothing of our inertron belts, it seemed, and these leaps and dives of ours filled them with terror.

As I rose to my feet, a gory mess, Wilma, with a poise and speed which I found time to admire even in this crisis, again leaped. This time she dove head first as I had done and, with a beautifully executed thrust, ran the last Han through the throat.

Uncertainly, she scrambled to her feet, staggered queerly, and then sank gently prone on the corridor. She had fainted.

At this juncture, Blash and Gaunt reported with elation that they had the record we wanted.

"Back to the roof, everybody!" I ordered, as I picked Wilma up in my arms. With her inertron belt, she felt as light as a feather.

Gaunt joined me at once from the military office, and at the intersection of the corridor, we came upon Blash waiting for us. Barker, however, was not in evidence.

"Where are you, Barker?" I called.

"Go ahead," he replied. "I'll be with you on the roof at once."

We came out in the open without any further mishap, and I instructed Gibbons in the ship to light the knob on the end of the ultron wire. It flashed dully a few feet away from us. Just how he had maneuvered the ship to keep our end of the line in position, without its swinging in a tremendous arc, I have never been able to understand. Had not the night been an unusually still one, he could not have checked the initial pendulum-like movements. As it was, there was considerable air current at certain of the levels, and in different directions too. But Gibbons was an expert of rare ability and sensitivity in the handling of a rocket ship, and he managed, with the aid of his delicate instruments, to sense the drifts almost before they affected the fine ultron wire, and to neutralize them with little shifts in the position of the ship.

Blash and Gaunt fastened their rings to the wire, and I hooked my own and Wilma's on, too. But on looking around, I found Barker was still missing.

"Barker, come!" I called. "We're waiting."

"Coming!" he replied, and indeed, at that instant, his figure appeared up the ramp. He chuckled as he fastened his ring to the wire, and said something about a little surprise he had left for the Hans.

"Don't reel in the wire more than a few hundred feet," I instructed Gibbons. "It will take too long to wind it in. We'll float up, and when we're aboard, we can drop it."

In order to float up, we had to dispense with a pound or two of weight apiece. We hurled our swords from us, and kicked off our shoes as Gibbons reeled up the line a bit, and then letting go of the wire, began to hum upward on our rings with increasing velocity.

The rush of air brought Wilma to, and I hastily explained to her that we had been successful. Receding far below us now, I could see our dully shining knob swinging to and fro in an ever widening arc, as it crossed and recrossed the black square of the tower roof. As an extra precaution, I ordered Gibbons to shut off the light, and to show one from the belly of the ship, for so great was our speed now, that I began to fear we would have difficulty in checking ourselves. We were literally falling upward, and with terrific acceleration.

Fortunately, we had several minutes in which to solve this difficulty, which none of us, strangely enough, had foreseen. It was Gibbons who found the answer.

"You'll be all right if all of you grab the wire tight when I give the word," he said. "First I'll start reeling it in at full speed. You won't get much of a jar, and then I'll decrease its speed again gradually, and its weight will hold you back. Are you ready? One—two—three!"

We all grabbed tightly with our gloved hands as he gave the word. We must have been rising a good bit faster than he figured, however, for it wrenched our arms considerably, and the maneuver set up a sickening pendulum motion.

For a while all we could do was swing there in an arc that may have been a quarter of a mile across, about three and a half miles above the city, and still more than a mile from our ship.

Gibbons skilfully took up the slack as our momentum pulled up the line. Then at last we had ourselves under control again, and continued our upward journey, checking our speed somewhat with our gloves.

There was not one of us who did not breathe a big sigh of relief when we scrambled through the hatch safely into the ship again, cast off the ultron line and slammed the trap shut.

Little realizing that we had a still more terrible experience to go through, we discussed the information Blash and Gaunt had between them extracted from the Han records, and the advisability of ultrophoning Hart at once.

X

THE WALLS OF HELL

The traitors were, it seemed, a degenerate gang of Americans, located a few miles north of Nu-yok on the wooded banks of the Hudson, the Sinsings. They had exchanged scraps of information to the Hans in return for several old repellor-ray machines, and the privilege of tuning in on the Han electronic power broadcast for their operation, provided their ships agreed to subject themselves to the orders of the Han traffic office, while aloft.

The rest wanted to ultrophone their news at once, since there was always danger that we might never get back to the gang with it.

I objected, however. The Sinsings would be likely to pick up our message. Even if we used the directional projector, they might have scouts out to the west and south in the big inter-gang stretches of country. They would flee to Nu-yok and escape the punishment they merited. It seemed to be vitally important that they should not, for the sake of example to other weak groups among the American gangs, as well as to prevent a crisis in which they might clear more vital information to the enemy.

"Out to sea again," I ordered Gibbons. "They'll be less likely to look for us in that direction."

"Easy, Boss, easy," he replied. "Wait until we get up a mile or two more. They must have discovered evidences of our raid by now, and their dis-ray wall may go in operation any moment."

Even as he spoke, the ship lurched downward and to one side.

"There it is!" he shouted. "Hang on, everybody. We're going to nose straight up!" And he flipped the rocket-motor control wide open.

Looking through one of the rear ports, I could see a nebulous, luminous ring, and on all sides the atmosphere took on a faint iridescence.

We were almost over the destructive range of the disintegrator-ray wall, a hollow cylinder of annihilation shooting upward from a solid ring of generators surrounding the city. It was the main defense system of the Hans, which had never been used except in periodic tests. They may or may not have suspected that an American rocket ship was within the cylinder; probably they had turned on their generators more as a precaution to prevent any reaching a position above the city.

But even at our present great height, we were in great danger. It was a question how much we might have been harmed by the rays themselves, for their effective range was not much more than seven or eight miles. The greater danger lay in the terrific downward rush of air within the cylinder to replace that which was being burned into nothingness by the continual play of the disintegrators. The air fell into the cylinder with the force of a gale. It would be rushing toward the wall from the outside with terrific force also, but, naturally, the effect was intensified on the interior.

Our ship vibrated and trembled. We had only one chance of escape—to fight our way well above the current. To drift down with it meant ultimately, and inevitably, to be sucked into the destruction wall at some lower level.

But very gradually and jerkily our upward movement, as shown on the indicators, began to increase, and after an hour of desperate struggle we were free of the maelstrom and into the rarefied upper levels. The terror beneath us was now invisible through several layers of cloud formations.

Gibbons brought the ship back to an even keel, and drove her eastward into one of the most brilliantly gorgeous sunrises I have ever seen.

We described a great circle to the south and west, in a long easy dive, for he had cut out his rocket motors to save them as much as possible. We had drawn terrifically on their fuel reserves in our battle with the elements. For the moment, the atmosphere below cleared, and we could see the Jersey coast far beneath, like a great map.

"We're not through yet," remarked Gibbons suddenly, pointing at his periscope, and adjusting it to telescopic focus. "A Han ship, and a 'drop ship' at that—and he's seen us. If he whips that beam of his on us, we're done."

I gazed, fascinated, at the viewplate. What I saw was a cigar-shaped ship not dissimilar to our own in design, and from the proportional size of its ports, of about the same size as our swoopers. We learned later that they carried crews, for the most part of not more than three or four men. They had streamline hulls and tails that embodied universal-jointed double fish-tail rudders. In operation they rose to great heights on their powerful repellor rays, then gathered speed either by a straight nose dive, or an inclined dive in which they sometimes used the repellor ray slanted at a sharp angle. He was already above us, though several miles to the north. He could, of course, try to get on our tail and "spear" us with his beam as he dropped at us from a great height.

Suddenly his beam blazed forth in a blinding flash, whipping downward slowly to our right. He went through a peculiar corkscrew-like evolution, evidently maneuvering to bring his beam to bear on us with a spiral motion.

Gibbons instantly sent our ship into a series of evolutions that must have looked like those of a frightened hen. Alternately, he used the forward and the reverse rocket blasts, and in varying degree. We fluttered, we shot suddenly to right and left, and dropped like a plummet in uncertain movements. But all the time the Han scout dropped toward us, determinedly whipping the air around us with his beam. Once it sliced across beneath us, not more than a hundred feet, and we dropped with a jar into the pocket formed by the destruction of the air.

He had dropped to within a mile of us, and was coming with the speed of a projectile, when the end came. Gibbons always swore it was sheer luck. Maybe it was, but I like pilots who are lucky that way.

In the midst of a dizzy, fluttering maneuver of our own, with the Han ship enlarging to our gaze with terrifying rapidity, and its beam slowly slicing toward us in what looked like certain destruction within the second, I saw Gibbons' fingers flick at the lever of his rocket gun and a split second later the Han ship flew apart like a clay pigeon.

We staggered, and fluttered crazily for several moments while Gibbons struggled to bring our ship into balance, and a section of about four square feet in the side of the ship near the stern slowly crumbled like rusted metal. His beam actually had touched us, but our explosive rocket had got him a thousandth of a second sooner.

Part of our rudder had been annihilated, and our motor damaged. But we were able to swoop gently back across Jersey, fortunately crossing the ship lanes without sighting any more Han craft, and finally settling to rest in the little glade beneath the trees, near Hart's camp.

XI

THE NEW BOSS

We had ultrophoned our arrival and the Big Boss himself, surrounded by the Council, was on hand to welcome us and learn our news. In turn we were informed that during the night a band of raiding Bad Bloods, disguised under the insignia of the Altoonas, a gang some distance to the west of us, had destroyed several of our camps before our people had rallied and driven them off. Their purpose, evidently, had been to embroil us with the Altoonas, but fortunately, one of our exchanges recognized the Bad Blood leader, who had been slain.

The Big Boss had mobilized the full raiding force of the Gang, and was on the point of heading an expedition for the extermination of the Bad Bloods.

I looked around the grim circle of the sub-bosses, and realized the fate of America, at this moment, lay in their hands. Their temper demanded the immediate expenditure of our full effort in revenging ourselves for this raid. But the strategic exigencies, to my mind, quite clearly demanded the instant and absolute extermination of the Sinsings. It might be only a matter of hours, for all we knew, before these degraded people would barter clues to the American ultronic secrets to the Hans.

"How large a force have we?" I asked Hart.

"Every man and maid who can be spared," he replied. "That gives us seven hundred married and unmarried men, and three hundred girls, more than the entire Bad Blood Gang. Every one is equipped with belts, ultrophones, rocket guns and swords, and all fighting mad."

I meditated how I might put the matter to these determined men, and was vaguely conscious that they were awaiting my words.

Finally I began to speak. I do not remember to this day just what I said. I talked calmly, with due regard for their passion, but with deep conviction. I went over the information we had collected, point by point, building my case logically, and painting a lurid picture of the danger impending in that half-alliance between the Sinsings and the Hans of Nu-yok. I became impassioned, culminating, I believe, with a vow to proceed single-handed against the hereditary enemies of our race, "if the Wyomings were blindly set on placing a gang feud ahead of honor and duty and the hopes of all America."

As I concluded, a great calm came over me, as of one detached. I had felt much the same way during several crises in the First World War. I gazed from face to face, striving to read their expressions, and in a mood to make good my threat without any further heroics, if the decision was against me.

But it was Hart who sensed the temper of the Council more quickly than I did, and looked beyond it into the future.

He arose from the tree trunk on which he had been sitting.

"That settles it," he said, looking around the ring. "I have felt this thing coming on for some time now. I'm sure the Council agrees with me that there is among us a man more capable than I, to boss the Wyoming Gang, despite his handicap of having had all too short a time in which to familiarize himself with our modern ways and facilities. Whatever I can do to support his effective leadership, at any cost, I pledge myself to do."

As he concluded, he advanced to where I stood, and taking from his head the green-crested helmet that constituted his badge of office, to my surprise he placed it in my mechanically extended hand.

The roar of approval that went up from the Council members left me dazed. Somebody ultrophoned the news to the rest of the Gang, and even though the earflaps of my helmet were turned up, I could hear the cheers with which my invisible followers greeted me, from near and distant hillsides, camps and plants.

My first move was to make sure that the Phone Boss, in communicating this news to the members of the Gang, had not re-broadcast my talk nor mentioned my plan of shifting the attack from the Bad Bloods to the Sinsings. I was relieved by his assurance that he had not, for it would have wrecked the whole plan. Everything depended upon our ability to surprise the Sinsings.

So I pledged the Council and my companions to secrecy, and allowed it to be believed that we were about to take to the air and the trees against the Bad Bloods.

That outfit must have been badly scared, the way they were "burning" the ether with ultrophone alibis and propaganda for the benefit of the more distant gangs. It was their old game, and the only method by which they had avoided extermination long ago from their immediate neighbors—these appeals to the spirit of American brotherhood, addressed to gangs too far away to have had the sort of experience with them that had fallen to our lot.

I chuckled. Here was another good reason for the shift in my plans. Were we actually to undertake the exterminations of the Bad Bloods at once, it would have been a hard job to convince some of the gangs that we had not been precipitate and unjustified. Jealousies and prejudices existed. There were gangs which would give the benefit of the doubt to the Bad Bloods, rather than to ourselves, and the issue was now hopelessly beclouded with the clever lies that were being broadcast in an unceasing stream.

But the extermination of the Sinsings would be another thing. In the first place, there would be no warning of our action until it was all over, I hoped. In the second place, we would have indisputable proof, in the form of their rep-ray ships and other paraphernalia, of their traffic with the Hans; and the state of American prejudice, at the time of which I write held trafficking with the Hans a far more heinous thing than even a vicious gang feud.

I called an executive session of the Council at once. I wanted to inventory our military resources.

I created a new office on the spot, that of "Control Boss," and appointed Ned Garlin to the post, turning over his former responsibility as Plants Boss to his assistant. I needed someone, I felt, to tie in the records of the various functional activities of the campaign, and take over from me the task of keeping the records of them up to the minute.

I received reports from the bosses of the ultrophone unit, and those of food, transportation, fighting gear, chemistry, electronic activity and electrophone intelligence, ultroscopes, air patrol and contact guard.

My ideas for the campaign, of course, were somewhat tinged with my 20th Century experience, and I found myself faced with the task of working out a staff organization that was a composite of the best and most easily applied principles of business and military efficiency, as I knew them from the viewpoint of immediate practicality.

What I wanted was an organization that would be specialized, functionally, not as that indicated above, but from the angles of: intelligence as to the Sinsings' activities; intelligence as to Han activities; perfection of communication with my own units; co-operation of field command; and perfect mobilization of emergency supplies and resources.

It took several hours of hard work with the Council to map out the plan. First we assigned functional experts and equipment to each "Division" in accordance with its needs. Then these in turn were reassigned by the new Division Bosses to the Field Commands as needed, or as Independent or Headquarters Units. The two intelligence divisions were named the White and the Yellow, indicating that one specialized on the American enemy and the other on the Mongolians.

The division in charge of our own communications, the assignment of ultrophone frequencies and strengths, and the maintenance of operators and equipment, I called "Communications."

I named Bill Hearn to the post of Field Boss, in charge of the main or undetached fighting units, and to the Resources Division, I assigned all responsibility for what few aircraft we had; and all transportation and supply problems, I assigned to "Resources." The functional bosses stayed with this division.

We finally completed our organization with the assignment of liaison representatives among the various divisions as needed.

Thus I had a "Headquarters Staff" composed of the Division Bosses who reported directly to Ned Garlin as Control Boss, or to Wilma as my personal assistant. And each of the Division Bosses had a small staff of his own.

In the final summing up of our personnel and resources, I found we had roughly a thousand "troops," of whom some three hundred and fifty were, in what I called the Service Divisions, the rest being in Bill Hearn's Field Division. This latter number, however, was cut down somewhat by the assignment of numerous small units to detached service. Altogether, the actual available fighting force, I figured, would number about five hundred, by the time we actually went into action.

We had only six small swoopers, but I had an ingenious plan in my mind, as the result of our little raid on Nu-yok, that would make this sufficient, since the reserves of inertron blocks were larger than I expected to find them. The Resources Division, by packing its supply cases a bit tight, or by slipping in extra blocks of inertron, was able to reduce each to a weight of a few ounces. These easily could be floated and towed by the swoopers in any quantity. Hitched to ultron lines, it would be a virtual impossibility for them to break loose.

The entire personnel, of course, was supplied with jumpers, and if each man and girl was careful to adjust balances properly, the entire number could also be towed along through the air, grasping wires of ultron, swinging below the swoopers, or stringing out behind them.

There would be nothing tiring about this, because the strain would be no greater than that of carrying a one or two pound weight in the hand, except for air friction at high speeds. But to make doubly sure that we should lose none of our personnel, I gave strict orders that the belts and tow lines should be equipped with rings and hooks.

So great was the efficiency of the fundamental organization and discipline of the Gang, that we got under way at nightfall.

One by one the swoopers eased into the air, each followed by its long train or "kite-tail" of humanity and supply cases hanging lightly from its tow line. For convenience, the tow lines were made of an alloy of ultron which, unlike the metal itself, is visible.

At first these "tails" hung downward, but as the ships swung into formation and headed eastward toward the Bad Blood territory, gathering speed, they began to string out behind. And swinging low from each ship on heavily weighted lines, ultroscope, ultrophone, and straight-vision observers keenly scanned the countryside, while intelligence men in the swoopers above bent over their instrument boards and viewplates.

Leaving Control Boss Ned Garlin temporarily in charge of affairs, Wilma and I dropped a weighted line from our ship, and slid down about half way to the under lookouts, that is to say, about a thousand feet. The sensation of floating swiftly through the air like this, in the absolute security of one's confidence in the inertron belt, was one of never-ending delight to me.

We reascended into the swooper as the expedition approached the territory of the Bad Bloods, and directed the preparations for the bombardment. It was part of my plan to appear to carry out the attack as originally planned.

About fifteen miles from their camps our ships came to a halt and maintained their positions for a while with the idling blasts of their rocket motors, to give the ultroscope operators a chance to make a thorough examination of the territory below us, for it was very important that this next step in our program should be carried out with all secrecy.

At length they reported the ground below us entirely clear of any appearance of human occupation, and a gun unit of long-range specialists was lowered with a dozen rocket guns, equipped with special automatic devices that the Resources Division had developed at my request, a few hours before our departure. These were aiming and timing devices. After calculating the range, elevation and rocket charges carefully, the guns were left, concealed in a ravine, and the men were hauled up into the ship again. At the predetermined hour, those unmanned rocket guns would begin automatically to bombard the Bad Bloods' hillsides, shifting their aim and elevation slightly with each shot, as did many of our artillery pieces in the First World War.

In the meantime, we turned south about twenty miles, and grounded, waiting for the bombardment to begin before we attempted to sneak across the Han ship lane. I was relying for security on the distraction that the bombardment might furnish the Han observers.

It was tense work waiting, but the affair went through as planned, our squadron drifting across the route high enough to enable the ships' tails of troops and supply cases to clear the ground.

In crossing the second ship route, out along the Beaches of Jersey, we were not so successful in escaping observation. A Han ship came speeding along at a very low elevation. We caught it on our electronic location and direction finders, and also located it with our ultroscopes, but it came so fast and so low that I thought it best to remain where we had grounded the second time, and lie quiet, rather than get under way and cross in front of it.

The point was this. While the Hans had no such devices as our ultroscopes, with which we could see in the dark (within certain limitations of course), and their electronic instruments would be virtually useless in uncovering our presence, since all but natural electronic activities were carefully eliminated from our apparatus, except electrophone receivers (which are not easily spotted), the Hans did have some very highly sensitive sound devices which operated with great efficiency in calm weather, so far as sounds emanating from the air were concerned. But the "ground roar" greatly confused their use of these instruments in the location of specific sounds floating up from the surface of the earth.

This ship must have caught some slight noise of ours, however, in its sensitive instruments, for we heard its electronic devices go into play, and picked up the routine report of the noise to its Base Ship Commander. But from the nature of the conversation, I judged they had not identified it, and were, in fact, more curious about the detonations they were picking up now from the Bad Blood lands some sixty miles or so to the west.

Immediately after this ship had shot by, we took the air again, and following much the same route that I had taken the previous night, climbed in a long semi-circle out over the ocean, swung toward the north and finally the west. We set our course, however, for the Sinsings' land north of Nu-yok, instead of for the city itself.

XII

THE FINGER OF DOOM

As we crossed the Hudson River, a few miles north of the city, we dropped several units of the Yellow Intelligence Division, with full instrumental equipment. Their apparatus cases were nicely balanced at only a few ounces weight each, and the men used their chute capes to ease their drops.

We recrossed the river a little distance above and began dropping White Intelligence units and a few long- and short-range gun units. Then we held our position until we began to get reports. Gradually we ringed the territory of the Sinsings, our observation units working busily and patiently at their locators and scopes, both aloft and aground, until Garlin finally turned to me with the remark:

"The map circle is complete now, Boss. We've got clear locations all the way around them."

"Let me see it," I replied, and studied the illuminated viewplate map, with its little overlapping circles of light that indicated spots proved clear of the enemy by ultroscopic observation.

I nodded to Bill Hearn. "Go ahead now, Hearn," I said, "and place your barrage men."

He spoke into his ultrophone, and three of the ships began to glide in a wide ring around the enemy territory. Every few seconds, at the word from his Unit Boss, a gunner would drop off the wire, and slipping the clasp of his chute cape, drift down into the darkness below.

Bill formed two lines, parallel to and facing the river, and enclosing the entire territory of the enemy between them. Above and below, straddling the river, were two defensive lines. These latter were merely to hold their positions. The others were to close in toward each other, pushing a high-explosive barrage five miles ahead of them. When the two barrages met, both lines were to switch to short-vision-range barrage and continue to close in on any of the enemy who might have drifted through the previous curtain of fire.

In the meantime Bill kept his reserves, a picked corps of a hundred men (the same that had accompanied Hart and myself in our fight with the Han squadron) in the air, divided about equally among the "kite-tails" of four ships.

A final roll call, by units, companies, divisions and functions, established the fact that all our forces were in position. No Han activity was reported, and no Han broadcasts indicated any suspicion of our expedition. Nor was there any indication that the Sinsings had any knowledge of the fate in store for them. The idling of rep-ray generators was reported from the center of their camp, obviously those of the ships the Hans had given them—the price of their treason to their race.

Again I gave the word, and Hearn passed on the order to his subordinates.

Far below us, and several miles to the right and left, the two barrage lines made their appearance. From the great height to which we had risen, they appeared like lines of brilliant, winking lights, and the detonations were muffled by the distances into a sort of rumbling, distant thunder. Hearn and his assistants were very busy: measuring, calculating, and snapping out ultrophone orders to unit commanders that resulted in the straightening of lines and the closing of gaps in the barrage.

The White Division Boss reported the utmost confusion in the Sinsing organization. They were, as might be expected, an inefficient, loosely disciplined gang, and repeated broadcasts for help to neighboring gangs. Ignoring the fact that the Mongolians had not used explosives for many generations, they nevertheless jumped at the conclusion that they were being raided by the Hans. Their frantic broadcasts persisted in this thought, despite the nervous electrophonic inquiries of the Hans themselves, to whom the sound of the battle was evidently audible, and who were trying to locate the trouble.

At this point, the swooper I had sent south toward the city went into action as a diversion, to keep the Hans at home. Its "kite-tail" loaded with long-range gunners, using the most highly explosive rockets we had, hung invisible in the darkness of the sky and bombarded the city from a distance of about five miles. With an entire city to shoot at, and the object of creating as much commotion therein as possible, regardless of actual damage, the gunners had no difficulty in hitting the mark. I could see the glow of the city and the stabbing flashes of exploding rockets. In the end, the Hans, uncertain as to what was going on, fell back on a defensive policy, and shot their "hell cylinder," or wall of upturned disintegrator rays into operation. That, of course, ended our bombardment of them. The rays were a perfect defense, disintegrating our rockets as they were reached.

If they had not sent out ships before turning on the rays, and if they had none within sufficient radius already in the air, all would be well.

I queried Garlin on this, but he assured me Yellow Intelligence reported no indications of Han ships nearer than 800 miles. This would probably give us a free hand for a while, since most of their instruments recorded only imperfectly or not at all, through the death wall.

Requisitioning one of the viewplates of the headquarters ship, and the services of an expert operator, I instructed him to focus on our lines below. I wanted a close-up of the men in action.

He began to manipulate his controls and chaotic shadows moved rapidly across the plate, fading in and out of focus, until he reached an adjustment that gave me a picture of the forest floor, apparently 100 feet wide, with the intervening branches and foliage of the trees appearing like shadows that melted into reality a few feet above the ground.

I watched one man setting up his long-gun with skillful speed. His lips pursed slightly as though he were whistling, as he adjusted the tall tripod on which the long tube was balanced. Swiftly he twirled the knobs controlling the aim and elevation of his piece. Then, lifting a belt of ammunition from the big box, which itself looked heavy enough to break down the spindly tripod, he inserted the end of it in the lock of his tube and touched the proper combination of buttons.

Then he stepped aside, and occupied himself with peering carefully through the trees ahead. Not even a tremor shook the tube, but I knew that at intervals of something less than a second, it was discharging small projectiles which, traveling under their own continuously reduced power, were arching into the air, to fall precisely five miles ahead and explode with the force of eight-inch shells, such as we used in the First World War.

Another gunner, fifty feet to the right of him, waved a hand and called out something to him. Then, picking up his own tube and tripod, he gauged the distance between the trees ahead of him, and the height of their lowest branches, and bending forward a bit, flexed his muscles and leaped lightly, some twenty-five feet. Another leap took him another twenty feet or so, where he began to set up his piece.

I ordered my observer then to switch to the barrage itself. He got a close focus on it, but this showed little except a continuous series of blinding flashes, which, from the viewplate, lit up the entire interior of the ship. An eight-hundred-foot focus proved better. I had thought that some of our French and American artillery of the 20th Century had achieved the ultimate in mathematical precision of fire, but I had never seen anything to equal the accuracy of that line of terrific explosions as it moved steadily forward, mowing down trees as a scythe cuts grass (or used to 500 years ago), literally churning up the earth and the splintered, blasted remains of the forest giants, to a depth of from ten to twenty feet.

By now the two curtains of fire were nearing each other, lines of vibrant, shimmering, continuous, brilliant destruction, inevitably squeezing the panic-stricken Sinsings between them.

Even as I watched, a group of them, who had been making a futile effort to get their three rep-ray machines into the air, abandoned their efforts, and rushed forth into the milling mob.

I queried the Control Boss sharply on the futility of this attempt of theirs, and learned that the Hans, apparently in doubt as to what was going on, had continued to "play safe," and broken off their power broadcast, after ordering all their own ships east of the Alleghenies to the ground, for fear these ships they had traded to the Sinsings might be used against them.

Again I turned to my viewplate, which was still focussed on the central section of the Sinsing works. The confusion of the traitors was entirely that of fear, for our barrage had not yet reached them.

Some of them set up their long-guns and fired at random over the barrage line, then gave it up. They realized that they had no target to shoot at, no way of knowing whether our gunners were a few hundred feet or several miles beyond it.

Their ultrophone men, of whom they did not have many, stood around in tense attitudes, their helmet phones strapped around their ears, nervously fingering the tuning controls at their belts. Unquestionably they must have located some of our frequencies, and overheard many of our reports and orders. But they were confused and disorganized. If they had an Ultrophone Boss they evidently were not reporting to him in an organized way.

They were beginning to draw back now before our advancing fire. With intermittent desperation, they began to shoot over our barrage again, and the explosions of their rockets flashed at widely scattered points beyond. A few took distance "pot shots."

Oddly enough it was our own forces that suffered the first casualties in the battle. Some of these distance shots by chance registered hits, while our men were under strict orders not to exceed their barrage distances.

Seen upon the ultroscope viewplate, the battle looked as though it were being fought in daylight, perhaps on a cloudy day, while the explosions of the rockets appeared as flashes of extra brilliance.

The two barrage lines were not more than five hundred feet apart when the Sinsings resorted to tactics we had not foreseen. We noticed first that they began to lighten themselves by throwing away extra equipment. A few of them in their excitement threw away too much, and shot suddenly into the air. Then a scattering few floated up gently, followed by increasing numbers, while still others, preserving a weight balance, jumped toward the closing barrages and leaped high, hoping to clear them. Some succeeded. We saw others blown about like leaves in a windstorm, to crumple and drift slowly down, or else to fall into the barrage, their belts blown from their bodies.

However, it was not part of our plan to allow a single one of them to escape and find his way to the Hans. I quickly passed the word to Bill Hearn to have the alternate men in his line raise their barrages and heard him bark out a mathematical formula to the Unit Bosses.

We backed off our ships as the explosions climbed into the air in stagger formation until they reached a height of three miles. I don't believe any of the Sinsings who tried to float away to freedom succeeded.

But we did know later, that a few who leaped the barrage got away and ultimately reached Nu-yok.

It was those who managed to jump the barrage who gave us the most trouble. With half of our long-guns turned aloft, I foresaw we would not have enough to establish successive ground barrages and so ordered the barrage back two miles, from which positions our "curtains" began to close in again, this time, however, gauged to explode, not on contact, but thirty feet in the air. This left little chance for the Sinsings to leap either over or under it.

Gradually, the two barrages approached each other until they finally met, and in the grey dawn the battle ended.

Our own casualties amounted to forty-seven men in the ground forces, eighteen of whom had been slain in hand to hand fighting with the few of the enemy who managed to reach our lines, and sixty-two in the crew and "kite-tail" force of swooper No. 4, which had been located by one of the enemy's ultroscopes and brought down with long-gun fire.

Since nearly every member of the Sinsing Gang had, so far as we knew, been killed, we considered the raid a great success.

It had, however, a far greater significance than this. To all of us who took part in the expedition, the effectiveness of our barrage tactics definitely established a confidence in our ability to overcome the Hans.

As I pointed out to Wilma:

"It has been my belief all along, dear, that the American explosive rocket is a far more efficient weapon than the disintegrator ray of the Hans, once we can train all our gangs to use it systematically and in co-ordinated fashion. As a weapon in the hands of a single individual, shooting at a mark in direct line of vision, the rocket-gun is inferior in destructive power to the dis ray, except as its range may be a little greater. The trouble is that to date it has been used only as we used our rifles and shot guns in the 20th Century. The possibilities of its use as artillery, in laying barrages that advance along the ground, or climb into the air, are tremendous.

"The dis ray inevitably reveals its source of emanation. The rocket gun does not. The dis ray can reach its target only in a straight line. The rocket may be made to travel in an arc, over intervening obstacles, to an unseen target.

"Nor must we forget that our ultronists now are promising us a perfect shield against the dis ray in inertron."

"I tremble though, Tony dear, when I think of the horrors that are ahead of us. The Hans are clever. They will develop defenses against our new tactics. And they are sure to mass against us not only the full force of their power in America, but the united forces of the World Empire. They are a cowardly race in one sense, but clever as the very Devils in Hell, and inheritors of a calm, ruthless, vicious persistency."

"Nevertheless," I prophesied, "the Finger of Doom points squarely at them today, and unless you and I are killed in the struggle, we shall live to see America blast the Yellow Blight from the face of the Earth."

THE DUNWICH HORROR

H. P. Lovecraft

"Gorgons, and Hydras, and Chimeras—dire stories of Celaeno and the Harpies—may reproduce themselves in the brain of superstition—but they were there before. *They are transcripts, types—the archetypes are in us, and eternal. How else should the recital of that which we know in a waking sense to be false come to affect us at all? Is it that we naturally conceive terror from such objects, considered in their capacity of being able to inflict upon us bodily injury? O, least of all!* These terrors are of older standing. They date beyond body—*or without the body, they would have been the same . . . That the kind of fear here treated is purely spiritual—that it is strong in proportion as it is objectless on earth, that it predominates in the period of our sinless infancy—are difficulties the solution of which might afford some probable insight into our antemundane condition, and a peep at least into the shadowland of pre-existence."*

—Charles Lamb: WITCHES AND OTHER NIGHT-FEARS

I

When a traveler in north central Massachusetts takes the wrong fork at the junction of the Aylesbury pike just beyond Dean's Corners he comes upon a lonely and curious country. The ground gets higher, and the brier-bordered stone walls press closer and closer against the ruts of the dusty, curving road. The trees of the frequent forest belts seem too large, and the wild weeds, brambles, and grasses attain a luxuriance not often found in settled regions. At the same time the planted fields appear singularly few and barren; while the sparsely scattered houses wear a surprising uniform aspect of age, squalor, and dilapidation. Without knowing why, one hesitates to ask directions from the gnarled, solitary figures spied now and then on crumbling doorsteps or in the sloping, rock-strewn meadows. Those figures are so silent and furtive that one feels somehow confronted by forbidden things, with which it would be better to have nothing to do. When a rise in the road brings the mountains in view above the deep woods, the feeling of strange uneasiness is increased. The summits are too rounded and symmetrical to give a sense of comfort and naturalness, and sometimes the sky silhouettes with especial clearness the queer circles of tall stone pillars with which most of them are crowned.

Gorges and ravines of problematical depth intersect the way, and the crude wooden bridges always seem of dubious safety. When the road dips again there are stretches of marshland that one instinctively dislikes, and indeed almost fears at evening when unseen whippoorwills chatter and the fireflies come out in abnormal profusion to dance to the raucous, creepily insistent rhythms of stridently piping bullfrogs. The thin, shining line of the Miskatonic's upper reaches has an oddly serpent-like suggestion as it winds close to the feet of the domed hills among which it rises.

As the hills draw nearer, one heeds their wooded sides more than their stone-crowned tops. Those sides loom up so darkly and precipitously that one wishes they would keep their distance, but there is no road by which to escape them. Across a covered bridge one sees a small village huddled between the stream and the vertical slope of Round Mountain, and wonders at the cluster of rotting gambrel roofs bespeaking an earlier architectural period than that of the neighboring region. It is not reassuring to see, on a closer glance, that most of the houses are deserted and falling to ruin, and that the broken-steepled church now harbors the one slovenly mercantile establishment of the hamlet. One dreads to trust the tenebrous tunnel of the bridge, yet there is no way to avoid it. Once across, it is hard to prevent the impression of a faint, malign odor about the village street, as of the massed mould and decay of centuries. It is always a relief to get clear of the place, and to follow the narrow road around the base of the hills and across the level country beyond till it rejoins the Aylesbury pike. Afterward one sometimes learns that one has been through Dunwich.

Outsiders visit Dunwich as seldom as possible, and since a certain season of horror all the signboards pointing toward it have been taken down. The scenery, judged by any ordinary aesthetic canon, is more than commonly beautiful; yet there is no influx of artists or summer tourists. Two centuries ago, when talk of witch-blood, Satan-worship, and strange forest presences was not laughed at, it was the custom to give reasons for avoiding the locality. In our sensible age—since the Dunwich horror of 1928 was hushed up by those who had the town's and the world's welfare at heart—people shun it without knowing exactly why. Perhaps one reason—though it can not apply to uninformed strangers—is that the natives are now repellently decadent, having gone far along that path of retrogression so common in many New England backwaters. They have come to form a race by themselves, with the well-defined mental and physical stigmata of degeneracy and inbreeding. The average of their intelligence is woefully low, whilst their annals reek of overt viciousness and of half-hidden murders, incests, and deeds of almost unnamable violence and perversity. The old gentry, representing the two or three armigerous families which came from Salem in 1692, have kept somewhat above the general level of decay; though many branches are sunk into the sordid populace so deeply that only their names remain as a key to the origin they disgrace. Some of the Whateleys and Bishops still send their eldest sons to Harvard and Miskatonic, though those sons seldom return to the mouldering gambrel roofs under which they and their ancestors were born.

No one, even those who have the facts concerning the recent horror, can say just what is the matter with Dunwich; though old legends speak of unhallowed rites and conclaves of the Indians, amidst which they called forbidden shapes of shadow out of the great rounded hills, and made wild orgiastic prayers that were answered by loud crackings and rumblings from the ground below. In 1747 the Reverend Abijah Hoadley, newly come to the Congregational Church at Dunwich Village, preached a memorable sermon on the close presence of Satan and his imps, in which he said:

> "It must be allow'd that these Blasphemies of an infernall Train of Daemons are Matters of too common Knowledge to be deny'd; the cursed Voices of *Azazel* and *Buzrael*, of *Beelzebub* and *Belial*, being heard from under Ground by above a Score of credible Witnesses now living. I myself did not more than a Fortnight ago catch a very plain Discourse of evill Powers in the Hill behind my House; wherein there were a Rattling and Rolling, Groaning, Screeching, and Hissing, such as no Things of this Earth cou'd raise up, and which must needs have come from those Caves that only black Magick can discover, and only the Divell unlock."

Mr. Hoadley disappeared soon after delivering this sermon; but the text, printed in Springfield, is still extant. Noises in the hills continued to be reported from year to year, and still form a puzzle to geologists and physiographers.

Other traditions tell of foul odors near the hill-crowning circles of stone pillars, and of rushing airy presences to be heard faintly at certain hours from stated points at the bottom of the great ravines; while still others try to explain the Devil's Hop Yard—a bleak, blasted hillside where no tree, shrub, or grass-blade will grow. Then, too, the natives are mortally afraid of the numerous whippoorwills which grow vocal on warm nights. It is vowed that the birds are psychopomps lying in wait for the souls of the dying, and that they time their eerie cries in unison with the sufferer's struggling breath. If they can catch the fleeing soul when it leaves the body, they instantly flutter away chittering in demoniac laughter; but if they fail, they subside gradually into a disappointed silence.

These tales, of course, are obsolete and ridiculous; because they come down from very old times. Dunwich is indeed ridiculously old—older by far than any of the communities within thirty miles of it. South of the village one may still spy the cellar walls and chimney of the ancient Bishop house, which was built before 1700; whilst the ruins of the mill at the falls, built in 1806, form the most modern piece of architecture to be seen. Industry did not flourish here, and the Nineteenth Century factory movement proved short-lived. Oldest of all are the great rings of rough-hewn stone columns on the hilltops, but these are more generally attributed to the Indians than to the settlers. Deposits of skulls and bones, found within these circles and around the sizable table-like rock on Sentinel Hill, sustain the popular belief that such spots were once the burial-places of the Pocumtucks; even though many ethnologists, disregarding the absurd improbability of such a theory, persist in believing the remains Caucasian.

II

It was in the township of Dunwich, in a large and partly inhabited farmhouse set against a hillside four miles from the village and a mile and a half from any other dwelling, that Wilbur Whateley was born at 5 a.m. on Sunday, the second of February, 1913. This date was recalled because it was Candlemas, which people in Dunwich curiously observe under another name; and because the noises in the hills had sounded, and all the dogs of the countryside had barked persistently, throughout the night before. Less worthy of notice was the fact that the mother was one of the decadent Whateleys, a somewhat deformed, unattractive albino woman of 35, living with an aged and half-insane father about whom the most frightful tales of wizardry had been whispered in his youth. Lavinia Whateley had no known husband, but according to the custom of the region made no attempt to disavow the child; concerning the other side of whose ancestry the country folk might—and did—speculate as widely as they chose. On the contrary, she seemed strangely proud of the dark, goatish-looking infant who formed such a contrast to her own sickly and pink-eyed albinism, and was heard to mutter many curious prophecies about its unusual powers and tremendous future.

Lavinia was one who would be apt to mutter such things, for she was a lone creature given to wandering amidst thunderstorms in the hills and trying to read the great odorous books which her father had inherited through two centuries of Whateleys, and which were fast falling to pieces with age and worm-holes. She had never been to school, but was filled with disjointed scraps of ancient lore that Old Whateley had taught her. The remote farmhouse had always been feared because of Old Whateley's reputation for black magic, and the unexplained death by violence of Mrs. Whateley when Lavinia was twelve years old had not helped to make the place popular.

Isolated among strange influences, Lavinia was fond of wild and grandiose daydreams and singular occupations; nor was her leisure much taken up by household cares in a home from which all standards of order and cleanliness had long since disappeared.

There was a hideous screaming which echoed above even the hill noises and the dogs' barking on the night Wilbur was born, but no known doctor or midwife presided at his coming. Neighbors knew nothing of him till a week afterward, when Old Whateley drove his sleigh through the snow into Dunwich Village and discoursed incoherently to the group of loungers at Osborn's general store. There seemed to be a change in the old man—an added element of furtiveness in the clouded brain which subtly transformed him from an object to a subject of fear—though he was not one to be perturbed by any common family event. Amidst it all he showed some trace of the pride later noticed in his daughter, and what he said of the child's paternity was remembered by many of his hearers years afterward.

"I dun't keer what folks think—ef Lavinny's boy looked like his pa, he wouldn't look like nothin' ye expeck. Ye needn't think the only folks is the folks hereabouts. Lavinny's read some, an' has seed some things the most o' ye only tell abaout. I calc'late her man is as good a husban' as ye kin find this side of Aylesbury; an' ef ye knowed as much abaout the hills as I dew, ye wouldn't ast no better church weddin' nor her'n. Let me tell ye suthin'—*some day yew folks'll hear a child o' Lavinny's a-callin' its father's name on the top o' Sentinel Hill!*"

The only persons who saw Wilbur during the first month of his life were old Zechariah Whateley, of the undecayed Whateleys, and Earl Sawyer's common-law wife, Mamie Bishop. Mamie's visit was frankly one of curiosity, and her subsequent tales did justice to her observations; but Zechariah came to lead a pair of Alderney cows which Old Whateley had bought of his son Curtis. This marked the beginning of a course of cattle-buying on the part of small Wilbur's family which ended only in 1928, when the Dunwich horror came and went; yet at no time did the ramshackle Whateley barn seem over-crowded with livestock. There came a period when people were curious enough to steal up and count the herd that grazed precariously on the steep hillside above the old farmhouse, and they could never find more than ten or twelve anemic, bloodless-looking specimens. Evidently some blight or distemper, perhaps sprung from the unwholesome pasturage or the diseased fungi and timbers of the filthy barn, caused a heavy mortality amongst the Whateley animals. Odd wounds or sores, having something of the aspect of incisions, seemed to afflict the visible cattle; and once or twice during the earlier months certain callers fancied they could discern similar sores about the throats of the gray, unshaven old man and his slatternly, crinkly-haired albino daughter.

In the spring after Wilbur's birth Lavinia resumed her customary rambles in the hills, bearing in her misproportioned arms the swarthy child. Public interest in the Whateleys subsided after most of the country folk had seen the baby, and no one bothered to comment on the swift development which that newcomer seemed every day to exhibit. Wilbur's growth was indeed phenomenal, for within three months of his birth he had attained a size and muscular power not usually found in infants under a full year of age. His motions and even his vocal sounds showed a restraint and deliberateness highly peculiar in an infant, and no one was really unprepared when, at seven months, he began to walk unassisted, with falterings which another month was sufficient to remove.

It was somewhat after this time—on Hallowe'en—that a great blaze was seen at midnight on the top of Sentinel Hill where the old table-like stone stands amidst its tumulus of ancient bones. Considerable talk was started when Silas Bishop—of the undecayed Bishops—mentioned having seen the boy running sturdily up that hill ahead of his mother about an hour before the blaze was remarked. Silas was rounding up a stray heifer, but he nearly forgot his mission when he fleetingly spied the two figures in the dim light of his lantern. They darted almost noiselessly through the underbrush, and the astonished watcher seemed to think they were entirely unclothed. Afterward he could not be sure about the boy, who may have had some kind of a fringed belt and a pair of dark blue trunks or trousers on. Wilbur was never subsequently seen alive and conscious without complete and tightly buttoned attire, the disarrangement or threatened disarrangement of which always seemed to fill him with anger and alarm. His contrast with his squalid mother and grandfather in this respect was thought very notable until the horror of 1928 suggested the most valid of reasons.

The next January gossips were mildly interested in the fact that "Lavinny's black brat" had commenced to talk, and at the age of only eleven months. His speech was somewhat remarkable both because of its difference from the ordinary accents of the region, and because it displayed a freedom from infantile lisping of which many children of three or four might well be proud. The boy was not talkative, yet when he spoke he seemed to reflect some elusive element wholly unpossessed by Dunwich and its denizens. The strangeness did not reside in what he said, or even in the simple idioms he used; but seemed vaguely linked with his intonation or with the internal organs that produced the spoken sounds. His facial aspect, too, was remarkable for its maturity; for though he shared his mother's and grandfather's chinlessness, his firm and precociously shaped nose united with the expression on his large, dark, almost Latin eyes to give him an air of quasi-adulthood and well-nigh preternatural intelligence. He was, however, exceedingly ugly despite his appearance of brilliancy; there being something almost goatish or animalistic about his thick lips, large-pored, yellowish skin, coarse crinkly hair, and oddly elongated ears. He was soon disliked even more decidedly than his mother and grandsire, and all conjectures about him were spiced with references to the bygone magic of Old Whateley, and how the hills once shook when he shrieked the dreadful name of *Yog-Sothoth* in the midst of a circle of stones with a great book open in his arms before him. Dogs abhorred the boy, and he was always obliged to take various defensive measures against their barking menace.

III

Meanwhile Old Whateley continued to buy cattle without measurably increasing the size of his herd. He also cut timber and began to repair the unused parts of his house—a spacious, peaked-roofed affair whose rear end was buried entirely in the rocky hillside, and whose three least-ruined ground-floor rooms had always been sufficient for himself and his daughter. There must have been prodigious reserves of strength in the old man to enable him to accomplish so much hard labor; and though he still babbled dementedly at times, his carpentry seemed to show the effects of sound calculation. It had really begun as soon as Wilbur was born, when one of the many tool-sheds had been put suddenly in order, clapboarded, and fitted with a stout fresh lock. Now, in restoring the abandoned upper story of the house, he was a no less thorough craftsman. His mania showed itself only in his tight boarding-up of all the windows in the reclaimed section—though many declared that it was a crazy thing to bother with the reclamation at all. Less inexplicable was his fitting-up of another downstairs room for his new grandson—a room which several callers saw, though no one was ever admitted to the closely-boarded upper story. This chamber he lined with tall, firm shelving; along which he began gradually to arrange, in apparently careful order, all the rotting ancient books and parts of books which during his own day had been heaped promiscuously in odd corners of the various rooms.

"I made some use of 'em," he would say as he tried to mend a torn black-letter page with paste prepared on the rusty kitchen stove, "but the boy's fitten to make better use of 'em. He'd orter hev 'em as well sot as he kin for they're goin' to be all of his larnin'."

When Wilbur was a year and seven months old—in September of 1914—his size and accomplishments were almost alarming. He had grown as large as a child of four, and was a fluent and incredibly intelligent talker. He ran freely about the fields and hills, and accompanied his mother on all her wanderings. At home he would pore diligently over the queer pictures and charts in his grandfather's books, while Old Whateley would instruct and catechize him through long, hushed afternoons. By this time the restoration of the house was finished, and those who watched it wondered why one of the upper windows had been made into a solid plank door. It was a window in the rear of the east gable end, close against the hill; and no one could imagine why a cleated wooden runway was built up to it from the ground. About the period of this work's completion people noticed that the old tool-house, tightly locked and windowlessly clapboarded since Wilbur's birth, had been abandoned again. The door swung listlessly open, and when Earl Sawyer once stepped within after a cattle-selling call on Old Whateley he was quite discomposed by the singular odor he encountered—such a stench, he averred, as he had never before smelt in all his life except near the Indian circles on the hills, and which could not come from anything sane or of this earth. But then, the homes and sheds of Dunwich folk have never been remarkable for olfactory immaculateness.

The following months were void of visible events, save that everyone swore to a slow but steady increase in the mysterious hill noises. On May Eve of 1915 there were tremors which even the Aylesbury people felt, whilst the following Hallowe'en produced an underground rumbling queerly synchronized with bursts of flame—"them witch Whateleys' doin's"—from the summit of Sentinel Hill. Wilbur was growing up uncannily, so that he looked like a boy of ten as he entered his fourth year. He read avidly by himself now; but talked much less than formerly. A settled taciturnity was absorbing him, and for the first time people began to speak specifically of the dawning look of evil in his goatish face. He would sometimes mutter an unfamiliar jargon, and chant in bizarre rhythms which chilled the listener with a sense of unexplainable terror. The aversion displayed toward him by dogs had now become a matter of wide remark, and he was obliged to carry a pistol in order to traverse the countryside in safety. His occasional use of the weapon did not enhance his popularity amongst the owners of canine guardians.

The few callers at the house would often find Lavinia alone on the ground floor, while odd cries and footsteps resounded in the boarded-up second story. She would never tell what her father and the boy were doing up there, though once she turned pale and displayed an abnormal degree of fear when a jocose fish-peddler tried the locked door leading to the stairway. That peddler told the store loungers at Dunwich Village that he thought he heard a horse stamping on that floor above. The loungers reflected, thinking of the door and runway, and of the cattle that so swiftly disappeared. Then they shuddered as they recalled tales of Old Whateley's youth, and of the strange things that are called out of the earth when a bullock is sacrificed at the proper time to certain heathen gods. It had for some time been noticed that dogs had begun to hate and fear the whole Whateley place as violently as they hated and feared young Wilbur personally.

In 1917 the war came, and Squire Sawyer Whateley, as chairman of the local draft board, had hard work finding a quota of young Dunwich men fit even to be sent to a development camp. The government, alarmed at such signs of wholesale regional decadence, sent several officers and medical experts to investigate; conducting a survey which New England newspaper readers may still recall. It was the publicity attending this investigation which set reporters on the track of the Whateleys, and caused the *Boston Globe* and *Arkham Advertiser* to print flamboyant Sunday stories of young Wilbur's precociousness, Old Whateley's black magic, the shelves of strange books, the sealed second story of the ancient farmhouse, and the weirdness of the whole region and its hill noises. Wilbur was four and a half then, and looked like a lad of fifteen. His lip and cheek were fuzzy with a coarse dark down, and his voice had begun to break. Earl Sawyer went out to the Whateley place with both sets of reporters and camera men, and called their attention to the queer stench which now seemed to trickle down from the sealed upper spaces. It was, he said, exactly like a smell he had found in the tool-shed abandoned when the house was finally repaired, and like the faint odors which he sometimes thought he caught near the stone circles on the mountains. Dunwich folk read the stories when they appeared, and grinned over the obvious mistakes. They wondered, too, why the writers made so much of the fact that Old Whateley always paid for his cattle in gold pieces of extremely ancient date. The Whateleys had received their visitors with ill-concealed distaste, though they did not dare court further publicity by a violent resistance or refusal to talk.

IV

For a decade the annals of the Whateleys sink indistinguishably into the general life of a morbid community used to their queer ways and hardened to their May Eve and All-Hallow orgies. Twice a year they would light fires on the top of Sentinel Hill, at which times the mountain rumblings would recur with greater and greater violence; while at all seasons there were strange and portentous doings at the lonely farmhouse. In the course of time callers professed to hear sounds in the sealed upper story even when all the family were downstairs, and they wondered how swiftly or how lingeringly a cow or bullock was usually sacrificed. There was talk of a complaint to the Society for the Prevention of Cruelty to Animals; but nothing ever came of it, since Dunwich folk are never anxious to call the outside world's attention to themselves.

About 1923, when Wilbur was a boy of ten whose mind, voice, stature, and bearded face gave all the impressions of maturity, a second great siege of carpentry went on at the old house. It was all inside the sealed upper part, and from bits of discarded lumber people concluded that the youth and his grandfather had knocked out all the partitions and even removed the attic floor, leaving only one vast open void between the ground story and the peaked roof. They had torn down the great central chimney, too, and fitted the rusty range with a flimsy outside tin stove-pipe.

In the spring after this event Old Whateley noticed the growing number of whippoorwills that would come out of Cold Spring Glen to chirp under his window at night. He seemed to regard the circumstance as one of great significance, and told the loungers at Osborn's that he thought his time had almost come.

"They whistle jest in tune with my breathin' naow," he said, "an' I guess they're gittin' ready to ketch my soul. They know it's a-goin' aout, an' dun't calc'late to miss it. Yew'll know, boys, arter I'm gone, whether they git me er not. Ef they dew, they'll keep up a-singin' an' laffin' till break o' day. Ef they dun't, they'll kinder quiet daown like. I expeck them an' the souls they hunts fer hev some pretty tough tussles sometimes."

On Lammas Night, 1924, Dr. Houghton of Aylesbury was hastily summoned by Wilbur Whateley, who had lashed his one remaining horse through the darkness and telephoned from Osborn's in the village. He found Old Whateley in a very grave state, with a cardiac action and stertorous breathing that told of an end not far off. The shapeless albino daughter and oddly bearded grandson stood by the bedside, whilst from the vacant abyss overhead there came a disquieting suggestion of rhythmical surging or lapping, as of the waves on some level beach. The doctor, though, was chiefly disturbed by the chattering night birds outside; a seemingly limitless legion of whippoorwills that cried their endless message in repetitions timed diabolically to the wheezing gasps of the dying man. It was uncanny and unnatural—too much, thought Dr. Houghton, like the whole of the region he had entered so reluctantly in response to the urgent call.

Toward 1 o'clock Old Whateley gained consciousness, and interrupted his wheezing to choke out a few words to his grandson.

"More space, Willy, more space soon. Yew grows—an' *that* grows faster. It'll be ready to sarve ye soon, boy. Open up the gates to Yog-Sothoth with the long chant that ye'll find on page 751 *of the complete edition*, an' *then* put a match to the prison. Fire from airth can't burn it nohaow!"

He was obviously quite mad. After a pause, during which the flock of whippoorwills outside adjusted their cries to the altered tempo while some indications of the strange hill noises came from afar off, he added another sentence or two.

"Feed it reg'lar, Willy, an' mind the quantity; but dun't let it grow too fast fer the place, fer ef it busts quarters or gits aout afore ye opens to Yog-Sothoth, it's all over an' no use. Only them from beyont kin make it multiply an' work . . . Only them, the old uns as wants to come back . . ."

But speech gave place to gasps again, and Lavinia screamed at the way the whippoorwills followed the change. It was the same for more than an hour, when the final throaty rattle came. Dr. Houghton drew shrunken lids over the glazing gray eyes as the tumult of birds faded imperceptibly to silence. Lavinia sobbed, but Wilbur only chuckled whilst the hill noises rumbled faintly.

"They didn't git him," he muttered in his heavy bass voice.

Wilbur was by this time a scholar of really tremendous erudition in his one-sided way, and was quietly known by correspondence to many librarians in distant places where rare and forbidden books of old days are kept. He was more and more hated and dreaded around Dunwich because of certain youthful disappearances which suspicion laid vaguely at his door; but was always able to silence inquiry through fear or through use of that fund of old-time gold which still, as in his grandfather's time, went forth regularly and increasingly for cattle-buying. He was now tremendously mature of aspect, and his height, having reached the normal adult limit, seemed inclined to wax beyond that figure. In 1925, when a scholarly correspondent from Miskatonic University called upon him one day and departed pale and puzzled, he was fully six and three-quarters feet tall.

Through all the years Wilbur had treated his half-deformed albino mother with a growing contempt, finally forbidding her to go to the hills with him on May Eve and Hallowmass; and in 1926 the poor creature complained to Mamie Bishop of being afraid of him.

"They's more abaout him as I knows than I kin tell ye, Mamie," she said, "an' naowadays they's more nor what I know myself. I vaow afur Gawd, I dun't know what he wants nor what he's a-tryin' to dew."

That Hallowe'en the hill noises sounded louder than ever, and fire burned on Sentinel Hill as usual, but people paid more attention to the rhythmical screaming of vast flocks of unnaturally belated whippoorwills which seemed to be assembled near the unlighted Whateley farmhouse. After midnight their shrill notes burst into a kind of pandemoniac cachinnation which filled all the countryside, and not until dawn did they finally quiet down. Then they vanished, hurrying southward where they were fully a month overdue. What this meant, no one could quite be certain till later. None of the countryfolk seemed to have died—but poor Lavinia Whateley, the twisted albino, was never seen again.

In the summer of 1927 Wilbur repaired two sheds in the farmyard and began moving his books and effects out to them. Soon afterward Earl Sawyer told the loungers at Osborn's that more carpentry was going on in the Whateley farmhouse. Wilbur was closing all the doors and windows on the ground floor, and seemed to be taking out partitions as he and his grandfather had done upstairs four years before. He was living in one of the sheds, and Sawyer thought he seemed unusually worried and tremulous. People generally suspected him of knowing something about his mother's disappearance, and very few ever approached his neighborhood now. His height had increased to more than seven feet, and showed no signs of ceasing its development.

V

The following winter brought an event no less strange than Wilbur's first trip outside the Dunwich region. Correspondence with the Widener Library at Harvard, the Bibliotheque Nationale in Paris, the British Museum, the University of Buenos Aires, and the Library of Miskatonic University at Arkham had failed to get him the loan of a book he desperately wanted; so at length he set out in person, shabby, dirty, bearded, and uncouth of dialect, to consult the copy at Miskatonic, which was the nearest to him geographically. Almost eight feet tall, and carrying a cheap new valise from Osborn's general store, this dark and goatish gargoyle appeared one day in Arkham in quest of the dreaded volume kept under lock and key at the college library—the hideous Necronomicon of the mad Arab Alhazred in Olaus Wormius' Latin version, as printed in Spain in the Seventeenth Century. He had never seen a city before, but had no thought save to find his way to the university grounds; where, indeed, he passed heedlessly by the great white-fanged watchdog that barked with unnatural fury and enmity, and tugged frantically at its stout chain.

Wilbur had with him the priceless but imperfect copy of Dr. Dee's English version which his grandfather had bequeathed him, and upon receiving access to the Latin copy he at once began to collate the two texts with the aim of discovering a certain passage which would have come on the 751st page of his own defective volume. This much he could not civilly refrain from telling the librarian—the same erudite Henry Armitage (A. M. Miskatonic, Ph. D. Princeton, Litt. D. Johns Hopkins) who had once called at the farm, and who now politely plied him with questions. He was looking, he had to admit, for a kind of formula or incantation containing the frightful name *Yog-Sothoth*, and it puzzled him to find discrepancies, duplications, and ambiguities which made the matter of determination far from easy. As he copied the formula he finally chose, Dr. Armitage looked involuntarily over his shoulder at the open pages; the left-hand one of which, in the Latin version, contained such monstrous threats to the peace and sanity of the world.

"Nor is it to be thought," [ran the text as Armitage mentally translated it] "that man is either the oldest or the last of earth's masters, or that the common bulk of life and substance walks alone. The Old Ones were, the Old Ones are, and the Old Ones shall be. Not in the spaces we know, but between them. They walk serene and primal, undimensioned and to us unseen. *Yog-Sothoth* knows the gate. *Yog-Sothoth* is the gate. *Yog-Sothoth* is the key and guardian of the gate. Past, present, future, all are one in *Yog-Sothoth.* He knows where the Old Ones broke through of old, and where They shall break through again. He knows where They have trod earth's fields, and where They still tread them, and why no one can behold Them as They tread. By Their smell can men sometimes know Them near, but of Their semblance can no man know, *saving only in the features of those They have begotten on mankind;* and of those are there many sorts, differing in likeness from man's truest eidolon to that shape without sight or substance which is *Them.* They walk unseen and foul in lonely places where the Words have been spoken and the Rites howled through at their Seasons. The wind gibbers with Their voices, and the earth mutters with Their consciousness. They bend the forest and crush the city, yet may not forest or city behold the hand that smites. Kadath in the cold waste hath known Them, and what man knows Kadath? The ice desert of the South and the sunken isles of Ocean hold stones whereon Their seal is engraven, but who hath seen the deep frozen city or the sealed tower long garlanded with seaweed and barnacles? Great Cthulhu is Their cousin, yet can he spy Them only dimly. *Iä Shub-Niggurath!* As a foulness shall ye know Them. Their hand is at your throats, yet ye see Them not; and Their habitation is even one with your guarded threshold. *Yog-Sothoth* is the key to the gate, whereby the spheres meet. Man rules now where They ruled once; They shall soon rule where man rules now. After summer is winter, and after winter summer. They wait patient and potent, for here shall They reign again."

Dr. Armitage, associating what he was reading with what he had heard of Dunwich and its brooding presences, and of Wilbur Whateley and his dim, hideous aura that stretched from a dubious birth to a cloud of probable matricide, felt a wave of fright as tangible as a draft of the tomb's cold clamminess. The bent, goatish giant before him seemed like the spawn of another planet or dimension; like something only partly of mankind, and linked to black gulfs of essence and entity that stretch like titan phantasms beyond all spheres of force and matter, space and time.

Presently Wilbur raised his head and began speaking in that strange, resonant fashion which hinted at sound-producing organs unlike the run of mankind's.

"Mr. Armitage," he said, "I calc'late I've got to take that book home. They's things in it I've got to try under sarten conditions that I can't git here, an' it 'ud be a mortal sin to let a red-tape rule hold me up. Let me take it along, sir, an' I'll swar they wun't nobody know the difference. I dun't need to tell ye I'll take good keer of it. It wa'n't me that put this Dee copy in the shape it is . . ."

He stopped as he saw firm denial on the librarian's face, and his own goatish features grew crafty. Armitage, half ready to tell him he might make a copy of what parts he needed, thought suddenly of the possible consequences and checked himself. There was too much responsibility in giving such a being the key to such blasphemous outer spheres. Whateley saw how things stood, and tried to answer lightly.

"Wal, all right, ef ye feel that way abaout it. Maybe Harvard wun't be so fussy as yew be." And without saying more he rose and strode out of the building, stooping at each doorway.

Armitage heard the savage yelping of the great watchdog, and studied Whateley's gorilla-like lope as he crossed the bit of campus visible from the window. He thought of the wild tales he had heard, and recalled the old Sunday stories in the *Advertiser;* these things, and the lore he had picked up from Dunwich rustics and villagers during his one visit there. Unseen things not of earth—or at least not of tri-dimensional earth—rushed fetid and horrible through New England's glens, and brooded obscenely on the mountain tops. Of this he had long felt certain. Now he seemed to sense the close presence of some terrible part of the intruding horror, and to glimpse a hellish advance in the black dominion of the ancient and once passive nightmare. He locked away the *Necronomicon* with a shudder of disgust, but the room still reeked with an unholy and unidentifiable stench. "As a foulness shall ye know them," he quoted. Yes—the odor was the same as that which had sickened him at the Whateley farmhouse less than three years before. He thought of Wilbur, goatish and ominous, once again, and laughed mockingly at the village rumors of his parentage.

"Inbreeding?" Armitage muttered half aloud to himself. "Great God, what simpletons! Show them Arthur Machen's Great God Pan and they'll think it a common Dunwich scandal! But what thing—what cursed shapeless influence on or off this three-dimensioned earth—was Wilbur Whateley's father? Born on Candlemas—nine months after May Eve of 1912, when the talk about the queer earth noises reached clear to Arkham—what walked on the mountains that May Night? What Roodmas horror fastened itself on the world in half-human flesh and blood?"

During the ensuing weeks Dr. Armitage set about to collect all possible data on Wilbur Whateley and the formless presences around Dunwich. He got in communication with Dr. Houghton of Aylesbury, who had attended Old Whateley in his last illness, and found much to ponder over in the grandfather's last words as quoted by the physician. A visit to Dunwich Village failed to bring out much that was new; but a close survey of the *Necronomicon*, in those parts which Wilbur had sought so avidly, seemed to supply new and terrible clues to the nature, methods, and desires of the strange evil so vaguely threatening this planet. Talks with several students of archaic lore in Boston, and letters to many others elsewhere, gave him a growing amazement which passed slowly through varied degrees of alarm to a state of really acute spiritual fear. As the summer drew on he felt dimly that something ought to be done about the lurking terrors of the upper Miskatonic valley, and about the monstrous being known to the human world as Wilbur Whateley.

VI

The Dunwich horror itself came between Lammas and the equinox in 1928, and Dr. Armitage was among those who witnessed its monstrous prologue. He had heard, meanwhile, of Whateley's grotesque trip to Cambridge, and of his frantic efforts to borrow or copy from the *Necronomicon* at the Widener Library. Those efforts had been in vain, since Armitage had issued warnings of the keenest intensity to all librarians having charge of the dreaded volume. Wilbur had been shockingly nervous at Cambridge; anxious for the book, yet almost equally anxious to get home again, as if he feared the results of being away long.

Early in August the half-expected outcome developed, and in the small hours of the third Dr. Armitage was awakened suddenly by the wild, fierce cries of the savage watchdog on the college campus. Deep and terrible, the snarling, half-mad growls and barks continued; always in mounting volume, but with hideously significant pauses. Then there rang out a scream from a wholly different throat—such a scream as roused half the sleepers of Arkham and haunted their dreams ever afterward—such a scream as could come from no being born of earth, or wholly of earth.

Armitage hastened into some clothing and rushed across the street and lawn to the college buildings, saw that others were ahead of him; and heard the echoes of a burglar-alarm still shrilling from the library. An open window showed black and gaping in the moonlight. What had come had indeed completed its entrance; for the barking and the screaming, now fast fading into a mixed low growling and moaning, proceeded unmistakably from within. Some instinct warned Armitage that what was taking place was not a thing for unfortified eyes to see, so he brushed back the crowd with authority as he unlocked the vestibule door. Among the others he saw Professor Warren Rice and Dr. Francis Morgan, men to whom he had told some of his conjectures and misgivings; and these two he motioned to accompany him inside. The inward sounds, except for a watchful, droning whine from the dog, had by this time quite subsided; but Armitage now perceived with a sudden start that a loud chorus of whippoorwills among the shrubbery had commenced a damnably rhythmical piping, as if in unison with the last breath of a dying man.

The building was full of a frightful stench which Dr. Armitage knew too well, and the three men rushed across the hall to the small genealogical reading-room whence the low whining came. For a second nobody dared to turn on the light; then Armitage summoned up his courage and snapped the switch. One of the three—it is not certain which—shrieked aloud at what sprawled before them among disordered tables and overturned chairs. Professor Rice declares that he wholly lost consciousness for an instant, though he did not stumble or fall.

The thing that lay half-bent on its side in a fetid pool of greenish-yellow ichor and tarry stickiness was almost nine feet tall, and the dog had torn off all the clothing and some of the skin. It was not quite dead, but twitched silently and spasmodically while its chest heaved in monstrous unison with the mad piping of the expectant whippoorwills outside. Bits of shoe-leather and fragments of apparel were scattered about the room, and just inside the window an empty canvas sack lay where it had evidently been thrown. Near the central desk a revolver had fallen, a dented but undischarged cartridge later explaining why it had not been fired. The thing itself, however, crowded out all other images at the time. It would be trite and not wholly accurate to say that no human pen could describe it, but one may properly say that it could not be vividly visualized by anyone whose ideas of aspect and contour are too closely bound up with the common life-forms of this planet and of the three known dimensions. It was partly human, beyond a doubt, with very manlike hands and head, and the goatish, chinless face had the stamp of the Whateleys upon it. But the torso and lower parts of the body were teratologically fabulous, so that only generous clothing could ever have enabled it to walk on earth unchallenged or uneradicated.

Above the waist it was semi-anthropomorphic; though its chest, where the dog's rending paws still rested watchfully, had the leathery, reticulated hide of a crocodile or alligator. The back was piebald with yellow and black, and dimly suggested the squamous covering of certain snakes. Below the waist, though, it was the worst; for here all human resemblance left off and sheer fantasy began. The skin was thickly covered with coarse black fur, and from the abdomen a score of long greenish-gray tentacles with red sucking mouths protruded limply. Their arrangement was odd, and seemed to follow the symmetries of some cosmic geometry unknown to earth or the solar system. On each of the hips, deep set in a kind of pinkish, ciliated orbit, was what seemed to be a rudimentary eye; whilst in lieu of a tail there depended a kind of trunk or feeler with purple annular markings, and with many evidences of being an undeveloped mouth or throat. The limbs, save for their black fur, roughly resembled the hind legs of prehistoric earth's giant saurians; and terminated in ridgy-veined pads that were neither hooves nor claws. When the thing breathed, its tail and tentacles rhythmically changed color, as if from some circulatory cause normal to the non-human side of its ancestry. In the tentacles this was observable as a deepening of the greenish tinge, whilst in the tail it was manifest as a yellowish appearance which alternated with a sickly grayish-white in the spaces between the purple rings. Of genuine blood there was none; only the fetid greenish-yellow ichor which trickled along the painted floor beyond the radius of the stickiness, and left a curious discoloration behind it.

As the presence of the three men seemed to rouse the dying thing, it began to mumble without turning or raising its head. Dr. Armitage made no written record of its mouthings, but asserts confidently that nothing in English was uttered. At first the syllables defied all correlation with any speech of earth, but toward the last there came some disjointed fragments evidently taken from the Necronomicon, that monstrous blasphemy in quest of which the thing had perished. Those fragments, as Armitage recalls them, ran something like *"N'gai, n'gha'ghaa, bugg-shoggog, y'hah; Yog-Sothoth, Yog-Sothoth . . ."* They trailed off into nothingness as the whippoorwills shrieked in rhythmical crescendoes of unholy anticipation.

Then came a halt in the gasping, and the dog raised his head in a long, lugubrious howl. A change came over the yellow, goatish face of the prostrate thing, and the great black eyes fell in appallingly. Outside the window the shrilling of the whippoorwills had suddenly ceased, and above the murmurs of the gathering crowd there came the sound of a panic-struck whirring and fluttering. Against the moon vast clouds of feathery watchers rose and raced from sight, frantic at that which they had sought for prey.

All at once the dog started up abruptly, gave a frightened bark, and leaped nervously out the window by which it had entered. A cry rose from the crowd, and Dr. Armitage shouted to the men outside that no one must be admitted till the police or medical examiner came. He was thankful that the windows were just too high to permit of peering in, and drew the dark curtains carefully down over each one. By this time two policemen had arrived; and Dr. Morgan, meeting them in the vestibule, was urging them for their own sakes to postpone entrance to the stench-filled reading-room till the examiner came and the prostrate thing could be covered up.

Meanwhile frightful changes were taking place on the floor. One need not describe the *kind* and *rate* of shrinkage and disintegration that occurred before the eyes of Dr. Armitage and Professor Rice; but it is permissible to say that, aside from the external appearance of face and hands, the really human elements in Wilbur Whateley must have been very small. When the medical examiner came, there was only a sticky whitish mass on the painted boards, and the monstrous odor had nearly disappeared. Apparently Whateley had had no skull or bony skeleton; at least, in any true or stable sense. He had taken somewhat after his unknown father.

VII

Yet all this was only the prologue of the actual Dunwich horror. Formalities were gone through by bewildered officials, abnormal details were duly kept from press and public, and men were sent to Dunwich and Aylesbury to look up property and notify any who might be heirs of the late Wilbur Whateley. They found the countryside in great agitation, both because of the growing rumblings beneath the domed hills, and because of the unwonted stench and the surging, lapping sounds which came increasingly from the great empty shell formed by Whateley's boarded-up farmhouse. Earl Sawyer, who tended the horse and cattle during Wilbur's absence, had developed a woefully acute case of nerves. The officials devised excuses not to enter the noisome boarded place; and were glad to confine their survey of the deceased's living quarters, the newly mended sheds, to a single visit. They filed a ponderous report at the court-house in Aylesbury, and litigations concerning heirship are said to be still in progress amongst the innumerable Whateleys, decayed and undecayed, of the upper Miskatonic valley.

An almost interminable manuscript in strange characters, written in a huge ledger and adjudged a sort of diary because of the spacing and the variations in ink and penmanship, presented a baffling puzzle to those who found it on the old bureau which served as its owner's desk. After a week of debate it was sent to Miskatonic University, together with the deceased's collection of strange books, for study and possible translation; but even the best linguists soon saw that it was not likely to be unriddled with ease. No trace of the ancient gold with which Wilbur and Old Whateley always paid their debts has yet been discovered.

It was in the dark of September ninth that the horror broke loose. The hill noises had been very pronounced during the evening, and dogs barked frantically all night. Early risers on the tenth noticed a peculiar stench in the air. About 7 o'clock Luther Brown, the hired boy at George Corey's, between Cold Spring Glen and the village, rushed frenziedly back from his morning trip to Ten-Acre Meadow with the cows. He was almost convulsed with fright as he stumbled into the kitchen; and in the yard outside the no less frightened herd were pawing and lowing pitifully, having followed the boy back in the panic they shared with him. Between gasps Luther tried to stammer out his tale to Mrs. Corey.

"Up thar in the rud beyont the glen, Mis' Corey—they's suthin' ben thar! It smells like thunder, an' all the bushes an' little trees is pushed back from the rud like they'd a haouse ben moved along of it. An' that ain't the wust, nuther. They's *prints* in the rud, Mis' Corey—great raound prints as big as barrel-heads, all sunk daown deep like a elephant had ben along, only *they's a sight more nor four feet could make!* I looked at one or two afore I run, an' I see every one was covered with lines spreadin' aout from one place, like as if big palm-leaf fans—twict or three times as big as any they is—hed of ben paounded daown into the rud. An' the smell was awful, like what it is araound Wizard Whateley's ol' haouse . . ."

Here he faltered, and seemed to shiver afresh with the fright that had sent him flying home. Mrs. Corey, unable to extract more information, began telephoning the neighbors; thus starting on its rounds the overture of panic that heralded the major terrors. When she got Sally Sawyer, housekeeper at Seth Bishop's, the nearest place to Whateley's, it became her turn to listen instead of transmit; for Sally's boy Chauncey, who slept poorly, had been up on the hill toward Whateley's, and had dashed back in terror after one look at the place, and at the pasturage where Mr. Bishop's cows had been left out all night.

"Yes, Mis' Corey," came Sally's tremulous voice over the party wire, "Cha'ncey he just come back a-post-in', and couldn't haff talk fer bein' scairt! He says Ol' Whateley's haouse is all blowed up, with the timbers scattered raound like they'd ben dynamite inside; only the bottom floor ain't through, but is all covered with a kind o' tarlike stuff that smells awful an' drips daown offen the aidges onto the graoun' whar the side timbers is blowed away. An' they's awful kinder marks in the yard, tew—great raound marks bigger raound than a hogshead, an' all sticky with stuff like is on the blowed-up haouse. Cha'ncey he says they leads off into the medders, whar a great swath wider'n a barn is matted daown, an' all the stun walls tumbled every which way wherever it goes.

"An' he says, says he, Mis' Corey, as haow he sot to look fer Seth's caows, frighted ez he was; an' faound 'em in the upper pasture nigh the Devil's Hop Yard in an awful shape. Haff on 'em's clean gone, an' nigh haff o' them that's left is sucked most dry o' blood, with sores on 'em like they's ben on Whateley's cattle ever senct Lavinny's black brat was born. Seth he's gone aout naow to look at 'em, though I'll vaow he wun't keer ter git very nigh

Wizard Whateley's! Cha'ncey didn't look keerful ter see whar the big matted-daown swath led arter it leff the pasturage, but he says he thinks it p'inted towards the glen rud to the village.

"I tell ye, Mis' Corey, they's suthin' abroad as hadn't orter be abroad, an' I fer one think that black Wilbur Whateley, as come to the bad eend he desarved, is at the bottom of the breedin' of it. He wa'n't all human hisself, I allus says to everybody; an' I think he an' Ol' Whateley must a raised suthin' in that there nailed-up haouse as ain't even so human as he was. They's allus ben unseen things araound Dunwich—livin' things—as ain't human an' ain't good fer human folks.

"The graoun' was a'talkin' lass night, an' towards mornin' Cha'ncey he heerd the whippoorwills so laoud in Col' Spring Glen he couldn't sleep none. Then he thought he heerd another faintlike saound over towards Wizard Whateley's—a kinder rippin' or tearin' o' wood, like some big box or crate was bein' opened fur off. What with this an' that, he didn't git to sleep at all till sunup, an' no sooner was he up this mornin', but he's got to go over to Whateley's an' see what's the matter. He see enough, I tell ye, Mis' Corey! This dun't mean no good, an' I think as all the men-folks ought to git up a party an' do suthin'. I know suthin' awful's abaout, an' feel my time is nigh, though only Gawd knows jest what it is.

"Did your Luther take accaount o' whar them big tracks led tew? No? Wal, Mis' Corey, ef they was on the glen rud this side o' the glen, an' ain't got to your haouse yet, I calc'late they must go into the glen itself. They would do that. I allus says Col' Spring Glen ain't no healthy nor decent place. The whippoorwills an' fireflies there never did act like they was creaters o' Gawd, an' they's them as says ye kin hear strange things a-rushin' an' a-talkin' in the air daown thar ef ye stand in the right place, atween the rock falls an' Bear's Den."

By that noon fully three-quarters of the men and boys of Dunwich were trooping over the roads and meadows between the new-made Whateley ruins and Cold Spring Glen; examining in horror the vast, monstrous prints, the maimed Bishop cattle, the strange, noisome wreck of the farmhouse, and the bruised, matted vegetation of the fields and road-sides. Whatever had burst loose upon the world had assuredly gone down into the great sinister ravine; for all the trees on the banks were bent and broken, and a great avenue had been gouged in the precipice-hanging underbrush. It was as though a house, launched by an avalanche, had slid down through the tangled growths of the almost vertical slope. From below no sound came, but only a distant, undefinable fetor; and it is not to be wondered at that the men preferred to stay on the edge and argue, rather than descend and beard the unknown Cyclopean horror in its lair. Three dogs that were with the party had barked furiously at first, but seemed cowed and reluctant when near the glen. Someone telephoned the news to the *Aylesbury Transcript;* but the editor, accustomed to wild tales from Dunwich, did no more than concoct a humorous paragraph about it; an item soon afterward reproduced by the Associated Press.

That night everyone went home, and every house and barn was barricaded as stoutly as possible. Needless to say, no cattle were allowed to remain in open pasturage. About 2 in the morning a frightful stench and the savage barking of the dogs awakened the household at Elmer Frye's, on the eastern edge of Cold Spring Glen, and all agreed that they could hear a sort of muffled swishing or lapping sound from somewhere outside. Mrs. Frye proposed telephoning the neighbors, and Elmer was about to agree when the noise of splintering wood burst in upon their deliberations. It came, apparently, from the barn; and was quickly followed by a hideous screaming and stamping amongst the cattle. The dogs slavered and crouched close to the feet of the fear-numbed family. Frye lit a lantern through force of habit, but knew it would be death to go out into that black farmyard. The children and the women-folk whimpered, kept from screaming by some obscure, vestigial instinct of defense which told them their lives depended on silence. At last the noise of the cattle subsided to a pitiful moaning, and a great snapping, crashing, and crackling ensued. The Fryes, huddled together in the sitting-room, did not dare to move until the last echoes died away far down in Cold Spring Glen. Then, amidst the dismal moans from the stable and the demoniac piping of late whippoorwills in the glen, Selina Frye tottered to the telephone and spread what news she could of the second phase of the horror.

The next day all the countryside was in a panic; and cowed, uncommunicative groups came and went where the fiendish thing had occurred. Two titan swaths of destruction stretched from the glen to the Frye farmyard, monstrous prints covered the bare patches of ground, and one side of the old red barn had completely caved in. Of the cattle, only about a quarter could be found and identified. Some of these were in curious fragments, and all that survived had to be shot. Earl Sawyer suggested that help be asked from Aylesbury or Arkham, but others maintained it would be of no use. Old Zebulon Whateley, of a branch that hovered about half-way between soundness and decadence, made darkly wild suggestions about rites that ought to be practised on the hilltops. He came of a line where tradition ran strong, and his memories of chantings in the great stone circles were not altogether connected with Wilbur and his grandfather.

Darkness fell upon a stricken countryside too passive to organize for real defense. In a few cases closely related families would band together and watch in the gloom under one roof; but, in general there was only a repetition of the barricading of the night before, and a futile, ineffective gesture of loading muskets and setting pitchforks handily about. Nothing, however, occurred except some hill noises; and when the day came there were many who hoped that the new horror had gone as swiftly as it had come. There were even bold souls who proposed an offensive expedition down in the glen, though they did not venture to set an actual example to the still reluctant majority.

When night came again the barricading was repeated, though there was less huddling together of families. In the morning both the Frye and the Seth Bishop households reported excitement among the dogs and vague sounds and stenches from afar, while early explorers noted with horror a fresh set of the monstrous tracks in the road skirting Sentinel Hill. As before, the sides of the road showed a bruising indicative of the blasphemously stupendous bulk of the horror; whilst the conformation of the tracks seemed to argue a passage in two directions, as if the moving mountain had come from Cold Spring Glen and returned to it along the same path. At the base of the hill a thirty-foot swath of crushed shrubbery and saplings led steeply upward, and the seekers gasped when they saw that even the most perpendicular places did not deflect the inexorable trail. Whatever the horror was, it could scale a sheer stony cliff of almost complete verticality; and as the investigators climbed around to the hill's summit by safer routes they saw that the trail ended—or rather, reversed—there.

It was here that the Whateleys used to build their hellish fires and chant their hellish rituals by the table-like stone on May Eve and Hallowmass. Now that very stone formed the center of a vast space thrashed around by the mountainous horror, whilst upon its slightly concave surface was a thick fetid deposit of the same tarry stickiness observed on the floor of the ruined Whateley farmhouse when the horror escaped. Men looked at one another and muttered. Then they looked down the hill. Apparently the horror had descended by a route much the same as that of its ascent. To speculate was futile. Reason, logic, and normal ideas of motivation stood confounded. Only old Zebulon, who was not with the group, could have done justice to the situation or suggested a plausible explanation.

Thursday night began much like the others, but it ended less happily. The whippoorwills in the glen had screamed with such unusual persistence that many could not sleep, and about 3 a.m. all the party telephones rang tremulously. Those who took down their receivers heard a fright-mad voice shriek out, "Help, oh, my Gawd! . . ." and some thought a crashing sound followed the breaking off of the exclamation. There was nothing more. No one dared do anything, and no one knew till morning whence the call came. Then those who had heard it called everyone on the line, and found that only the Fryes did not reply. The truth appeared an hour later, when a hastily assembled group of armed men trudged out to the Frye place at the head of the glen. It was horrible, yet hardly a surprise. There were more swaths and monstrous prints, but there was no longer any house. It had caved in like an egg-shell, and amongst the ruins nothing living or dead could be discovered—only a stench and a tarry stickiness. The Elmer Fryes had been erased from Dunwich.

VIII

In the meantime a quieter yet even more spiritually poignant phase of the horror had been blackly unwinding itself behind the closed door of a shelf-lined room in Arkham. The curious manuscript record or diary of Wilbur Whateley, delivered to Miskatonic University for translation, had caused much worry and bafflement among the experts in languages both ancient and modern; its very alphabet, notwithstanding a general resemblance to the heavily shaded Arabic used in Mesopotamia, being absolutely unknown to any available authority. The final conclusion of the linguists was that the text represented an artificial alphabet, giving the effect of a cipher; though none of the usual methods of cryptographic solution seemed to furnish any clue, even when applied on the basis of every tongue the writer might conceivably have used. The ancient books taken from Whateley's quarters, while absorbingly interesting and in several cases promising to open up new and terrible lines of research among philosophers and men of science, were of no assistance whatever in this matter. One of them, a heavy tome with an iron clasp, was in another unknown alphabet—this one of a very different cast, and resembling Sanskrit more than anything else. The old ledger was at length given wholly into the charge of Dr. Armitage, both because of his peculiar interest in the Whateley matter, and because of his wide linguistic learning and skill in the mystical formulae of antiquity and the Middle Ages.

Armitage had an idea that the alphabet might be something esoterically used by certain forbidden cults which have come down from old times, and which have inherited many forms and traditions from the wizards of the Saracenic world. That question, however, he did not deem vital; since it would be unnecessary to know the origin of the symbols if, as he suspected, they were used as a cipher in a modern language. It was his belief that, considering the great amount of text involved, the writer would scarcely have wished the trouble of using another speech than his own, save perhaps in certain special formulae and incantations. Accordingly he attacked the manuscript with the preliminary assumption that the bulk of it was in English.

Dr. Armitage knew, from the repeated failures of his colleagues, that the riddle was a deep and complex one, and that no simple mode of solution could merit even a trial. All through late August he fortified himself with the massed lore of cryptography, drawing upon the fullest resources of his own library, and wading night after night amidst the arcana of Trithemius' *Poligraphia*, Giambattista Porta's *De Furtivis Literarum Notis*, De Vigenere's *Traité des Chiffres*, Falconer's *Cryptomenysis Patefacta*, Davys' and Thicknesse's eighteenth-century treatises, and such fairly modern authorities as Blair, von Marten, and Klüber's *Kryptographik*. He interspersed his study of the books with attacks on the manuscript itself, and in time became convinced that he had to deal with one of those subtlest and most ingenious of cryptograms, in which many separate lists of corresponding letters are arranged like the multiplication table, and the message built up with arbitrary key-words known only to the initiated. The older authorities seemed rather more helpful than the newer ones, and Armitage concluded that the code of the manuscript was one of great antiquity, no doubt handed down through a long line of mystical experimenters. Several times he seemed near daylight, only to be set back by some unforeseen obstacle. Then, as September approached, the clouds began to clear. Certain letters, as used in certain parts of the manuscript, emerged definitely and unmistakably; and it became obvious that the text was indeed in English.

On the evening of September second the last major barrier gave way, and Dr. Armitage read for the first time a continuous passage of Wilbur Whateley's annals. It was in truth a diary, as all had thought; and it was couched in a style clearly showing the mixed occult erudition and general illiteracy of the strange being who wrote it. Almost the first long passage that Armitage deciphered, an entry dated November 26, 1916, proved highly startling and disquieting. It was written, he remembered, by a child of three and a half who looked like a lad of twelve or thirteen.

> "Today learned the Aklo for the Sabaoth, [it ran] which did not like, it being answerable from the hill and not from the air. That upstairs more ahead of me than I had thought it would be, and is not like to have much earth brain. Shot Elam Hutchins's collie Jack when he went to bite me, and Elam says he would kill me if he dast. I guess he won't. Grandfather kept me saying the Dho formula last night, and I think I saw the inner city at the two magnetic poles. I shall go to those poles when the earth is cleared off, if I can't break through with the Dho-Hna formula when I commit it. They from the air told me at Sabbat that it will be years before I can clear off the earth, and I guess Grandfather will be dead then, so I shall have to learn all the angles of the planes and all the formulas between the Yr and

> the Nhhngr. They from outside will help, but they can not take body without human blood. That upstairs looks it will have the right cast. I can see it a little when I make the Yoorish sign or blow the power of Ibn Ghazi at it, and it is near like them at May Eve on the Hill. The other face may wear off some. I wonder how I shall look when the earth is cleared and there are no earth beings on it. He that came with the Aklo Sabaoth said I may be transfigured, there being much of outside to work on."

Morning found Dr. Armitage in a cold sweat of terror and a frenzy of wakeful concentration. He had not left the manuscript all night, but sat at his table under the electric light turning page after page with shaking hands as fast as he could decipher the cryptic text. He had nervously telephoned his wife he would not be home, and when she brought him a breakfast from the house he could scarcely dispose of a mouthful. All that day he read on, now and then halted maddeningly as a reapplication of the complex key became necessary. Lunch and dinner were brought him, but he ate only the smallest fraction of either. Toward the middle of the next night he drowsed off in his chair, but soon woke out of a tangle of nightmares almost as hideous as the truths and menaces to man's existence that he had uncovered.

On the morning of September fourth Professor Rice and Dr. Morgan insisted on seeing him for a while, and departed trembling and ashen-gray. That evening he went to bed, but slept only fitfully. Wednesday—the next day—he was back at the manuscript, and began to take copious notes both from the current sections and from those he had already deciphered. In the small hours of that night he slept a little in an easy-chair in his office, but was at the manuscript again before dawn. Some time before noon his physician, Dr. Hartwell, called to see him and insisted that he cease work. He refused, intimating that it was of the most vital importance for him to complete the reading of the diary, and promising an explanation in due course of time.

That evening, just as twilight fell, he finished his terrible perusal and sank back exhausted. His wife, bringing his dinner, found him in a half-comatose state; but he was conscious enough to warn her off with a sharp cry when he saw her eyes wander toward the notes he had taken. Weakly rising, he gathered up the scribbled papers and sealed them all in a great envelope, which he immediately placed in his inside coat pocket. He had sufficient strength to get home, but was so clearly in need of medical aid that Dr. Hartwell was summoned at once. As the doctor put him to bed he could only mutter over and over again, *"But what, in God's name, can we do?"*

Dr. Armitage slept, but was partly delirious the next day. He made no explanations to Hartwell, but in his calmer moments spoke of the imperative need of a long conference with Rice and Morgan. His wilder wanderings were very startling indeed, including frantic appeals that something in a boarded-up farmhouse be destroyed, and fantastic references to some plan for the extirpation of the entire human race and all animal and vegetable life from the earth by some terrible elder race of beings from another dimension. He would shout that the world was in danger, since the Elder Things wished to strip it and drag it away from the solar system and cosmos of matter into some other plane or phase of entity from which it had once fallen, vigintillions of eons ago. At other times he would call for the dreaded *Necronomicon* and the *Daemonolatreia* of Remigius, in which he seemed hopeful of finding some formula to check the peril he conjured up.

"Stop them, stop them!" he would shout. "Those Whateleys meant to let them in, and the worst of all is left! Tell Rice and Morgan we must do something—it's a blind business, but I know how to make the powder . . . It hasn't been fed since the second of August, when Wilbur came here to his death, and at that rate . . ."

But Armitage had a sound physique despite his seventy-three years, and slept off his disorder that night without developing any real fever. He woke late Friday, clear of head, though sober, with a gnawing fear and tremendous sense of responsibility. Saturday afternoon he felt able to go over to the library and summon Rice and Morgan for a conference, and the rest of that day and evening the three men tortured their brains in the wildest speculation and the most desperate debate. Strange and terrible books were drawn voluminously from the stack shelves and from secure places of storage, and diagrams and formulae were copied with feverish haste and in bewildering abundance. Of skepticism there was none. All three had seen the body of Wilbur Whateley as it lay on the floor in a room of that very building, and after that not one of them could feel even slightly inclined to treat the diary as a madman's raving.

Opinions were divided as to notifying the Massachusetts State Police, and the negative finally won. There were things involved which simply could not be believed by those who had not seen a sample, as indeed was made clear during certain subsequent investigations. Late at night the conference disbanded without having developed a definite plan, but all day Sunday Armitage was busy comparing formulae and mixing chemicals obtained from the college laboratory. The more he reflected on the hellish diary, the more he was inclined to doubt the efficacy of any material agent in stamping out the entity which Wilbur Whateley had left behind him—the earth-threatening entity which, unknown to him, was to burst forth in a few hours and become the memorable Dunwich horror.

Monday was a repetition of Sunday with Dr. Armitage, for the task in hand required an infinity of research and experiment. Further consultations of the monstrous diary brought about various changes of plan, and he knew that even in the end a large amount of uncertainty must remain. By Tuesday he had a definite line of action mapped out, and believed he would try a trip to Dunwich within a week. Then, on Wednesday, the great shock came. Tucked obscurely away in a corner of the *Arkham Advertiser* was a facetious little item from the Associated Press, telling what a record-breaking monster the bootleg whisky of Dunwich had raised up. Armitage, half stunned, could only telephone for Rice and Morgan. Far into the night they discussed, and the next day was a whirlwind of preparation on the part of them all. Armitage knew he would be meddling with terrible powers, yet saw that there was no other way to annul the deeper and more malign meddling which others had done before him.

IX

Friday morning Armitage, Rice and Morgan set out by motor for Dunwich, arriving at the village about one in the afternoon. The day was pleasant, but even in the brightest sunlight a kind of quiet dread and portent seemed to hover about the strangely domed hills and the deep, shadowy ravines of the stricken region. Now and then on some mountain top a gaunt circle of stones could be glimpsed against the sky. From the air of hushed fright at Osborn's store they knew something hideous had happened, and soon learned of the annihilation of the Elmer Frye house and family. Throughout that afternoon they rode around Dunwich, questioning the natives concerning all that had occurred, and seeing for themselves with rising pangs of horror the drear Frye ruins with their lingering traces of the tarry stickiness, the blasphemous tracks in the Frye yard, the wounded Seth Bishop cattle, and the enormous swaths of disturbed vegetation in various places. The trail up and down Sentinel Hill seemed to Armitage of almost cataclysmic significance, and he looked long at the sinister altarlike stone on the summit.

At length the visitors, apprised of a party of State Police which had come from Aylesbury that morning in response to the first telephone reports of the Frye tragedy, decided to seek out the officers and compare notes as far as practicable. This, however, they found more easily planned than performed; since no sign of the party could be found in any direction. There had been five of them in a car, but now the car stood empty near the ruins in the Frye yard. The natives, all of whom had talked with the policemen, seemed at first as perplexed as Armitage and his companions. Then old Sam Hutchins thought of something and turned pale, nudging Fred Farr and pointing to the dank, deep hollow that yawned close by.

"Gawd," he gasped, "I telled 'em not ter go daown into the glen, an' I never thought nobody'd dew it with them tracks an' that smell an' the whippoorwills a-screechin' daown thar in the dark o' noonday . . ."

A cold shudder ran through natives and visitors alike, and every ear seemed strained in a kind of instinctive, unconscious listening. Armitage, now that he had actually come upon the horror and its monstrous work, trembled with the responsibility he felt to be his. Night would soon fall, and it was then that the mountainous blasphemy lumbered upon its eldritch course. *Negotium perambulans in tenebris* . . . The old librarian rehearsed the formulae he had memorized, and clutched the paper containing the alternative ones he had not memorized. He saw that his electric flashlight was in working order. Rice, beside him, took from a valise a metal sprayer of the sort used in combating insects; whilst Morgan uncased the big-game rifle on which he relied despite his colleague's warnings that no material weapon would be of help.

Armitage, having read the hideous diary, knew painfully well what kind of a manifestation to expect, but he did not add to the fright of the Dunwich people by giving any hints or clues. He hoped that it might be conquered without any revelation to the world of the monstrous thing it had escaped. As the shadows gathered, the natives commenced to disperse homeward, anxious to bar themselves indoors despite the present evidence that all human locks and bolts were useless before a force that could bend trees and crush houses when it chose. They shook their heads at the visitors' plan to stand guard at the Frye ruins near the glen; and as they left, had little expectancy of ever seeing the watchers again.

There were rumblings under the hills that night, and the whippoorwills piped threateningly. Once in a while a wind, sweeping up out of Cold Spring Glen, would bring a touch of ineffable fetor to the heavy night air; such a fetor as all three of the watchers had smelled once before, when they stood above a dying thing that had passed for fifteen years and a half as a human being. But the looked-for terror did not appear. Whatever was down there in the glen was biding its time, and Armitage told his colleagues it would be suicidal to try to attack it in the dark.

Morning came wanly, and the night-sounds ceased. It was a gray, bleak day, with now and then a drizzle of rain; and heavier and heavier clouds seemed to be piling themselves up beyond the hills to the northwest. The men from Arkham were undecided what to do. Seeking shelter from the increasing rainfall beneath one of the few undestroyed Frye outbuildings, they debated the wisdom of waiting, or of taking the aggressive and going down into the glen in quest of their nameless, monstrous quarry. The downpour waxed in heaviness, and distant peals of thunder sounded from far horizons. Sheet lightning shimmered, and then a forky bolt flashed near at hand, as if descending into the accursed glen itself. The sky grew very dark, and the watchers hoped that the storm would prove a short, sharp one followed by clear weather.

It was still gruesomely dark when, not much over an hour later, a confused babel of voices sounded down the road. Another moment brought to view a frightened group of more than a dozen men, running, shouting, and even whimpering hysterically. Someone in the lead began sobbing out words, and the Arkham men started violently when those words developed a coherent form.

"Oh, my Gawd, my Gawd!" the voice choked out; "it's a-goin' agin, *an' this time by day!* It's aout—it's aout an' a-movin' this very minute, an' only the Lord knows when it'll be on us all!"

The speaker panted into silence, but another took up his message.

"Nigh on a haour ago Zeb Whateley here heerd the 'phone a-ringin', an' it was Mis' Corey, George's wife that lives daown by the junction. She says the hired boy Luther was aout drivin' in the caows from the storm arter the big bolt, when he see all the trees a-bendin' at the maouth o' the glen—opposite side ter this—an' smelt the same awful smell like he smelt when he faound the big tracks las' Monday mornin'. An' she says he says they was a swishin', lappin' saound, more nor what the bendin' trees an' bushes could make, an' all on a suddent the trees along the rud begun ter git pushed one side, an' they was a awful stompin' an' splashin' in the mud. But mind ye, Luther he didn't see nothin' at all, only jest the bendin' trees an' underbrush.

"Then fur ahead where Bishop's Brook goes under the rud he heerd a awful creakin' an' strainin' on the bridge, an' says he could tell the saound o' wood a-startin' to crack an' split. An' all the whiles he never see a thing, only them trees an' bushes a-bendin'. An' when the swishin' saound got very fur off—on the rud towards Wizard Whateley's an' Sentinel Hill—Luther he had the guts ter step up whar he'd heerd it fust an' look at the graound. It was all mud an' water, an' the sky was dark, an' the rain was wipin' aout all tracks abaout as fast as could be; but beginnin' at the glen maouth, whar the trees bed moved, they was still some o' them awful prints big as bar'ls like he seen Monday."

At this point the first excited speaker interrupted.

"But *that* ain't the trouble naow—that was only the start. Zeb here was callin' folks up an' everybody was a-listenin' in when a call from Seth Bishop's cut in. His haousekeeper Sally was carryin' on fit ter kill—she'd jest seed the trees a-bendin' beside the rud, an' says they was a kind o' mushy saound, like a elephant puffin' an' treadin', a-headin' fer the haouse. Then she up an' spoke suddent of a fearful smell, an' says her boy Cha'ncey was a-screamin' as haow it was jest like what he smelt up to the Whateley rewins Monday mornin'. An' the dogs was all barkin' an' whinin' awful.

"An' then she let aout a turrible yell, an' says the shed daown the rud hed jest caved in like the storm hed blowed it over, only the wind wa'n't strong enough to dew that. Everybody was a-listenin', an' ye could hear lots o' folks on the wire a-gaspin'. All to onct Sally she yelled agin, an' says the front yard picket fence hed jest crumpled up, though they wa'n't no sign o' what done it. Then everybody on the line could hear Cha'ncey an' ol' Seth Bishop a-yellin', tew, an' Sally was shriekin' aout that suthin' heavy hed struck the haouse—not lightnin' nor nothin', but suthin' heavy agin' the front, that kep' a-launchin' itself agin an' agin, though ye couldn't see nuthin' aout the front winders. An' then . . . an' then . . ."

Lines of fright deepened on every face; and Armitage, shaken as he was, had barely poise enough to prompt the speaker.

"An' then . . . Sally she yelled aout, 'O help, the haouse is a-cavin' in' . . . an' on the wire we could hoar a turrible crashin', an' a hull flock o' screamin' . . . jest like when Elmer Frye's place was took, only wuss . . ."

The man paused, and another of the crowd spoke.

"That's all—not a saound nor squeak over the 'phone arter that. Jest still-like. We that heerd it got aout Fords an' wagons an' raounded up as many able-bodied men-folks as we could get, at Corey's place, an' come up here ter see what yew thought best ter dew. Not but what I think it's the Lord's judgment fer our iniquities, that no mortal kin ever set aside."

Armitage saw that the time for positive action had come, and spoke decisively to the faltering group of frightened rustics.

"We must follow it, boys." He made his voice as reassuring as possible. "I believe there's a chance of putting it out of business. You men know that those Whateleys were wizards—well, this thing is a thing of wizardry, and must be put down by the same means. I've seen Wilbur Whateley's diary and read some of the strange old books he used to read, and I think I know the right kind of a spell to recite to make the thing fade away. Of course, one can't be sure, but we can always take a chance. It's invisible—I knew it would be—but there's a powder in this long-distance sprayer that might make it show up for a second. Later on we'll try it. It's a frightful thing to have alive, but it isn't as bad as what Wilbur would have let in if he'd lived longer. You'll never know what the world has escaped. Now we've only this one thing to fight, and it can't multiply. It can, though, do a lot of harm; so we mustn't hesitate to rid the community of it.

"We must follow it—and the way to begin is to go to the place that has just been wrecked. Let somebody lead the way—I don't know your roads very well, but I've an idea there might be a shorter cut across lots. How about it?"

The men shuffled about a moment, and then Earl Sawyer spoke softly, pointing with a grimy finger through the steadily lessening rain.

"I guess ye kin git to Seth Bishop's quickest by cuttin' acrost the lower medder here, wadin' the brook at the low place, an' climbin' through Carrier's mowin' an' the timber-lot beyont. That comes aout on the upper rud mighty nigh Seth's—a leetle t'other side."

Armitage, with Rice and Morgan, started to walk in the direction indicated; and most of the natives followed slowly. The sky was growing lighter, and there were signs that the storm had worn itself away. When Armitage inadvertently took a wrong direction, Joe Osborn warned him and walked ahead to show the right one. Courage and confidence were mounting; though the twilight of the almost perpendicular wooded hill which lay toward the end of their short cut, and among whose fantastic ancient trees they had to scramble as if up a ladder, put these qualities to a severe test.

At length they emerged on a muddy road to find the sun coming out. They were a little beyond the Seth Bishop place, but bent trees and hideously unmistakable tracks showed what had passed by. Only a few moments were consumed in surveying the ruins just around the bend. It was the Frye incident all over again, and nothing dead or living was found in either of the collapsed shells which had been the Bishop house and barn. No one cared to remain there amidst the stench and the tarry stickiness, but all turned instinctively to the line of horrible prints leading on toward the wrecked Whateley farmhouse and the altar-crowned slopes of Sentinel Hill.

As the men passed the site of Wilbur Whateley's abode they shuddered visibly, and seemed again to mix hesitancy with their zeal. It was no joke tracking down something as big as a house that one could not see, but that had all the vicious malevolence of a demon. Opposite the base of Sentinel Hill the tracks left the road, and there was a fresh bending and matting visible along the broad swath marking the monster's former route to and from the summit.

Armitage produced a pocket telescope of considerable power and scanned the steep green side of the hill. Then he handed the instrument to Morgan, whose sight was keener. After a moment of gazing Morgan cried out sharply, passing the glass to Earl Sawyer and indicating a certain spot on the slope with his finger. Sawyer, as clumsy as most non-users of optical devices are, fumbled a while; but eventually focused the lenses with Armitage's aid. When he did so his cry was less restrained than Morgan's had been.

"Gawd almighty, the grass an' bushes is a-movin'! It's a-goin' up—slow-like—creepin' up ter the top this minute, heaven only knows what fer!"

Then the germ of panic seemed to spread among the seekers. It was one thing to chase the nameless entity, but quite another to find it. Spells might be all right—but suppose they weren't? Voices began questioning Armitage about what he knew of the thing, and no reply seemed quite to satisfy.

Everyone seemed to feel himself in close proximity to phases of nature and of being utterly forbidden, and wholly outside the sane experience of mankind.

X

In the end the three men from Arkham—old, white-bearded Dr. Armitage, stocky, iron-gray Professor Rice, and lean, youngish Dr. Morgan—ascended the mountain alone. After much patient instruction regarding its focusing and use, they left the telescope with the frightened group that remained in the road; and as they climbed they were watched closely by those among whom the glass was passed around. It was hard going, and Armitage had to be helped more than once. High above the toiling group the great swath trembled as its hellish maker repassed with snail-like deliberateness. Then it was obvious that the pursuers were gaining.

Curtis Whateley—of the undecayed branch—was holding the telescope when the Arkham party detoured radically from the swath. He told the crowd that the men were evidently trying to get to a subordinate peak which overlooked the swath at a point considerably ahead of where the shrubbery was now bending. This, indeed, proved to be true; and the party were seen to gain the minor elevation only a short time after the invisible blasphemy had passed it.

Then Wesley Corey, who had taken the glass, cried out that Armitage was adjusting the sprayer which Rice held, and that something must be about to happen. The crowd stirred uneasily, recalling that this sprayer was expected to give the unseen horror a moment of visibility. Two or three men shut their eyes, but Curtis Whateley snatched back the telescope and strained his vision to the utmost. He saw that Rice, from the party's point of vantage above and behind the entity, had an excellent chance of spreading the potent powder with marvelous effect.

Those without the telescope saw only an instant's flash of gray cloud—a cloud about the size of a moderately large building—near the top of the mountain. Curtis, who had held the instrument, dropped it with a piercing shriek into the ankle-deep mud of the road. He reeled, and would have crumpled to the ground had not two or three others seized and steadied him. All he could do was moan half-inaudibly:

"Oh, oh, great Gawd . . . *that* . . . *that* . . ."

There was a pandemonium of questioning, and only Henry Wheeler thought to rescue the fallen telescope and wipe it clean of mud. Curtis was past all coherence, and even isolated replies were almost too much for him.

"Bigger 'n a barn . . . all made o' squirmin' ropes . . . hull thing sort o' shaped like a hen's egg bigger'n anything, with dozens o' legs like hogsheads that haff shut up when they step . . . nothin' solid abaout it—all like jelly, an' made o' sep'rit wrigglin' ropes pushed clost together . . . great bulgin' eyes all over it . . . ten or twenty maouths or trunks a-stickin' aout all along the sides, big as stovepipes, an' all a-tossin' an' openin' an' shuttin' . . . all gray, with kinder blue or purple rings . . . *an' Gawd in Heaven—that haff face on top!* . . ."

This final memory, whatever it was, proved too much for poor Curtis, and he collapsed completely before he could say more. Fred Farr and Will Hutchins carried him to the roadside and laid him on the damp grass. Henry Wheeler, trembling, turned the rescued telescope on the mountain to see what he might. Through the lenses were discernible three tiny figures, apparently running toward the summit as fast as the steep incline allowed. Only these—nothing more. Then everyone noticed a strangely unseasonable noise in the deep valley behind, and even in the underbrush of Sentinel Hill itself. It was the piping of unnumbered whippoorwills, and in their shrill chorus there seemed to lurk a note of tense and evil expectancy.

Earl Sawyer now took the telescope and reported the three figures as standing on the topmost ridge, virtually level with the altar-stone but at a considerable distance from it. One figure, he said, seemed to be raising its hands above its head at rhythmic intervals; and as Sawyer mentioned the circumstance the crowd seemed to hear a faint, half-musical sound from the distance, as if a loud chant were accompanying the gestures. The weird silhouette on that remote peak must have been a spectacle of infinite grotesqueness and impressiveness, but no observer was in a mood for esthetic appreciation. "I guess he's sayin' the spell," whispered Wheeler as he snatched back the telescope. The whippoorwills were piping wildly, and in a singularly curious irregular rhythm quite unlike that of the visible ritual.

Suddenly the sunshine seemed to lessen without the intervention of any discernible cloud. It was a very peculiar phenomenon, and was plainly marked by all. A rumbling sound seemed brewing beneath the hills, mixed strangely with a concordant rumbling which clearly came from the sky. Lightning flashed aloft, and the wondering crowd looked in vain for the portents of storm. The chanting of the men from Arkham now became unmistakable, and Wheeler saw through the glass that they were all raising their arms in the rhythmic incantation. From some farmhouse far away came the frantic barking of dogs.

The change in the quality of the daylight increased, and the crowd gazed about the horizon in wonder. A purplish darkness, born of nothing more than a spectral deepening of the sky's blue, pressed down upon the rumbling hills. Then the lightning flashed again, somewhat brighter than before, and the crowd fancied that it had showed a certain mistiness around the altar-stone on the distant height. No one, however, had been using the telescope at that instant. The whippoorwills continued their irregular pulsation, and the men of Dunwich braced themselves tensely against some imponderable menace with which the atmosphere seemed surcharged.

Without warning came those deep, cracked, raucous vocal sounds which will never leave the memory of the stricken group who heard them. Not from any human throat were they born, for the organs of man can yield no such acoustic perversions. Rather would one have said they came from the pit itself, had not their source been so unmistakably the altar-stone on the peak. It is almost erroneous to call them *sounds* at all, since so much of their ghastly, infra-bass timbre spoke to dim seats of consciousness and terror far subtler than the ear; yet one must do so, since their form was indisputably though vaguely that of half-articulate *words*. They were loud—loud as the rumblings and the thunder above which they echoed—yet did they come from no visible being. And because imagination might suggest a conjectural source in the world of non-visible beings, the huddled crowd at the mountain's base huddled still closer, and winced as if in expectation of a blow.

"Ygnaiih ygnaiih . . . thflthkh'ngha . . . Yog-Sothoth . . ." rang the hideous croaking out of space. *"Y'bthnk . . . h'ehye . . . n'grkdl'lh . . ."*

The speaking impulse seemed to falter here, as if some frightful psychic struggle were going on. Henry Wheeler strained his eye at the telescope, but saw only the three grotesquely silhouetted human figures on the peak, all moving their arms furiously in strange gestures as their incantation drew near its culmination. From what black wells of Acherontic fear or feeling, from what unplumbed gulfs of extra-cosmic consciousness or obscure, long-latent heredity, were those half-articulate thunder-croakings drawn? Presently they began to gather renewed force and coherence as they grew in stark, utter, ultimate frenzy.

"Eh-ya-ya-ya-yahaah—e'yaya-yayaaaa . . . ngh'aaaa . . . ngh'aaaa . . . h'yuh . . . h'yuh . . . HELP! HELP! . . . *ff—ff—ff*—FATHER! FATHER! YOG-SOTHOTH! . . ."

But that was all. The pallid group in the road, still reeling at the *indisputably English* syllables that had poured thickly and thunderously down from the frantic vacancy beside that shocking altar-stone, were never to hear such syllables again. Instead, they jumped violently at the terrific report which seemed to rend the hills; the deafening, cataclysmic peal whose source, be it inner earth or sky, no hearer was ever able to place. A single lightning bolt shot from the purple zenith to the altar-stone, and a great tidal wave of viewless force and indescribable stench swept down from the hill to all the countryside. Trees, grass, and underbrush were whipped into a fury; and the frightened crowd at the mountain's base, weakened by the lethal fetor that seemed about to asphyxiate them, were almost hurled off their feet.

Dogs howled from the distance, green grass and foliage wilted to a curious, sickly yellow-gray, and over field and forest were scattered the bodies of dead whippoorwills.

The stench left quickly, but the vegetation never came right again. To this day there is something queer and unholy about the growths on and around that fearsome hill. Curtis Whateley was only just regaining consciousness when the Arkham men came slowly down the mountain in the beams of a sunlight once more brilliant and untainted. They were grave and quiet, and seemed shaken by memories and reflections even more terrible than those which had reduced the group of natives to a state of cowed quivering. In reply to a jumble of questions they only shook their heads and reaffirmed one vital fact.

"The thing has gone for ever," Armitage said. "It has been split up into what it was originally made of, and can never exist again. It was an impossibility in a normal world. Only the least fraction was really matter in any sense we know. It was like its father—and most of it has gone back to him in some vague realm or dimension outside our material universe; some vague abyss out of which only the most accursed rites of human blasphemy could ever have called him for a moment on the hills."

There was a brief silence, and in that pause the scattered senses of poor Curtis Whateley began to knit back into a sort of continuity; so that he put his hands to his head with a moan. Memory seemed to pick itself up where it had left off, and the horror of the sight that had prostrated him burst in upon him again.

"Oh, oh, my Gawd, that haff face . . . that haff face on top of it . . . that face with the red eyes an' crinkly albino hair, an' no chin, like the Whateleys . . . It was a octopus, centipede, spider kind o' thing, but they was a haff-shaped man's face on top of it, an' it looked like Wizard Whateley's, only it was yards an' yards acrost . . ."

He paused exhausted, as the whole group of natives stared in a bewilderment not quite crystallized into fresh terror. Only old Zebulon Whateley, who wanderingly remembered ancient things but who had been silent heretofore, spoke aloud.

"Fifteen year' gone," he rambled, "I heerd Ol' Whateley say as haow some day we'd hear a child o' Lavinny's a-callin' its father's name on the top o' Sentinel Hill . . ."

But Joe Osborn interrupted him to question the Arkham men anew.

"What was it, anyhaow, an' haowever did young Wizard Whateley call it aout o' the air it come from?"

Armitage chose his words carefully.

"It was—well, it was mostly a kind of force that doesn't belong in our part of space; a kind of force that acts and grows and shapes itself by other laws than those of our sort of Nature. We have no business calling in such things from outside, and only very wicked people and very wicked cults ever try to. There was some of it in Wilbur Whateley himself—enough to make a devil and a precocious monster of him, and to make his passing out a pretty terrible sight. I'm going to burn his accursed diary, and if you men are wise you'll dynamite that altar-stone up there, and pull down all the rings of standing stones on the other hills. Things like that brought down the beings those Whateleys were so fond of—the beings they were going to let in tangibly to wipe out the human race and drag the earth off to some nameless place for some nameless purpose.

"But as to this thing we've just sent back—the Whateleys raised it for a terrible part in the doings that were to come. It grew fast and big from the same reason that Wilbur grew fast and big—but it beat him because it had a greater share of the *outsideness* in it. You needn't ask how Wilbur called it out of the air. He didn't call it out. *It was his twin brother, but it looked more like the father than he did.*"